Patricia Gaffney gave up her
diagnosed with breast cance
treatment she has written 12 hi
all been bestsellers in the USA
venture into contemporary fiction, followed by *Circle of Three*, then *Flight Lessons*. Patricia Gaffney lives in Pennsylvania with her husband.

job in 1994, when she was
. Following her successful
historical romances, which have
The Saving Graces was her first

The Saving Graces

Circle of Three

Flight Lessons

PATRICIA GAFFNEY

POCKET BOOKS
LONDON • SYDNEY • NEW YORK • TORONTO

This Patricia Gaffney omnibus edition first published
in Great Britain by Pocket Books, 2004
An imprint of Simon & Schuster UK Ltd
A Viacom Company

1 3 5 7 9 10 8 6 4 2

Simon & Schuster UK Ltd
Africa House
64–78 Kingsway
London WC2B 6AH

www.simonsays.co.uk

Simon & Schuster Australia
Sydney

A CIP catalogue record for this book is available from the British Library

ISBN 1 4165 0206 8

Printed and bound in Great Britain by
Cox & Wyman Ltd, Reading, Berks

The Saving Graces

For Jan, Annie, and Marti.
Also for Carolyn, Jeanne, Jamie, Jodie, and Kathleen.
And Molly.
Most of all, in memory of Midge.

1

Emma

If half of all marriages end in divorce, how long does the average marriage last? This isn't a math problem; I'd really like to know. I bet it's less than nine and a half years. That's how long the Saving Graces have been going strong, and we're not even getting restless. We still talk, still notice things about each other, weight loss, haircuts, new boots. As far as I know, nobody's looking around for a younger, firmer member.

Truthfully, I never thought we'd last this long. I only joined because Rudy made me. The other three, Lee, Isabel, and—Joan? Joanne? She didn't last; moved to Detroit with her urologist boyfriend, and we didn't keep up—the other three didn't strike me at that first meeting as bosom buddy material, frankly. I thought Lee was bossy and Isabel was old—thirty-nine. Well, I'll be forty next year, enough said there, and Lee *is* bossy, but she can't help it because she's always right. She really is, and it's a tribute to her exceptional nature that we don't all loathe her for it.

The first meeting went badly. We had it at Isabel's house—this was back when she was still married to Gary. God, these people are straight, I remember thinking. Straight and *rich*, that's what really got me—but I'd just moved into a dank little basement apartment in Georgetown for eleven hundred a month because of the address, so I was a little touchy about money. Lee looked as if she'd just come from spa day at Neiman's. Plus she was single, still in graduate school, and teaching special ed. part-time—you know how much money there is in *that*—and yet she lived around the block from Isabel in snooty Chevy Chase, in a house she wasn't renting but *owned*. Naturally I had it in for these people.

All the way home I explained to Rudy, with much wit and sarcasm and disdain, what was wrong with everybody, and why I couldn't possibly join a women's group whose members owned electric hedge trimmers, wore Ellen Tracy, remembered Eisenhower, dated urologists. "But they're *nice*," Rudy insisted. Which, of course, missed the point. Lots of people are nice, but you don't want to have dinner with them every other Thursday and exchange secrets.

The other thing was jealousy. I was small enough to mind that Rudy had a good friend other than me. One night a week she and Lee volunteered to teach reading to inner-city illiterates, and had gotten to know each other during the training. I never worried, then or now, that they would become *best* friends; I mean, if ever there were two people with nothing in common, it's Lee and Rudy. But I was my old insecure self (then and now), and too neurotic to recognize the potential beauty of the Saving Graces even when it was staring me in the face.

We weren't the Saving Graces yet, of course. Even now, we don't go around calling ourselves that in public. It's corny; it sounds like a TV sitcom. Doesn't it? "The Saving Graces," starring Valerie Bertinelli, Susan Dey, and Cybill Shepherd. Notice these are all attractive, smart, funny women who happen to be a little long in the tooth. Anyway, the genesis of our name is a private matter. Not for any particular reason—it's kind of funny, and it reflects well on us all. But we just don't talk about it. It's personal.

We were driving back from dinner at a restaurant in Great Falls (we eat out when the person whose turn it is doesn't feel like cooking), taking the long way because Rudy missed the Beltway turnoff. We'd been a group for about a year by then; we'd just lost Joan/Joanne but hadn't yet acquired Marsha, transient member number two, so it was just the four of us. I was sitting in the back seat. Rudy turned around to catch my impersonation of the waitress, who we all thought looked and sounded just like Emma Thompson. Isabel yelled, "Look out!" and a split second later we hit the dog.

I can still see the expression on that yellow mutt face in the instant before the fender caught her on the shoulder and flipped her over the hood of Rudy's Saab—quizzical, curious, just mildly concerned. As if she were thinking, "Well, *hm*, isn't this interesting."

Everybody screamed. I kept saying, "It's dead, it's dead, it's got to be dead," while Rudy jerked the car off the pavement. To tell the truth, if I'd been driving by myself, I might've kept going: I was *sure* it was dead, and I didn't want to see. When I was twelve I ran over a frog with my bike, and I'm still not over it. But Rudy killed the engine and everybody piled out, so I had to get out with them.

It wasn't dead. But we didn't know that until Lee suddenly metamorphosed, right there on MacArthur Boulevard, into Cherry Ames, Highway Nurse. Have you ever seen a human being give CPR to a dog? It's funny, but only in retrospect. While it's happening it's sort of thrilling and revolting, like something that's still illegal in most of New England. Rudy whipped off her black cashmere cloak, which I have always coveted, and wrapped it around the dog because Lee said it was going into shock. "A vet, we need a vet," Isabel fretted, but there wasn't a house in sight, no store, no nothing except a darkened church on the other side of the road. Isabel jumped up and waved her arms at a car coming on our side. When it pulled over, she ran up and had a conversation with the driver. I stood there and wrung my hands.

Between them, Rudy and Lee got the dog in the back seat of the Saab. Blood spotted its muzzle, I noticed in my peripheral vision, the only vision I was capable of looking at it in. "Curtis will have a fit," I remember muttering, watching a dark stain seep into the 900 Turbo's honey-colored leather. But Rudy, the one who would pay for it if Curtis had a fit, never batted an eye.

"Okay, there's a vet in Glen Echo," Isabel reported, sliding into the front seat next to Rudy so she could give directions. I had to get in back with Lee and the dog. I'm not good with the bleeding and possibly dying: they make me sick. Literally; once I saw a man, a neighbor of mine, pull an electric lawnmower over his own foot, and I doubled up and vomited on the sidewalk. This is true. So I stared out the window, concentrating on the way the car headlights illuminated the sign in front of the church across the way, OUR LADY OF GRACE—and if you're wondering what the punch line of this story is and if I'll ever get to it, that's pretty much it.

Rudy drove like a stock car racer to the vet's in Glen Echo. He wasn't there—it was eleven o'clock at night—but he came when the sleepy-faced night guy called him. Grace, the dog, had a collapsed lung, a broken leg, and a dislocated shoulder, but she lived, and the bill was only eleven hundred and forty dollars. Nobody claimed her—*quelle surprise!*—but after she got out of the hospital Lee and Isabel had a fight over which one would get to keep her. Ernie, Isabel's old beagle, had just died, so she won, or lost, depending on your point of view, and has Grace to this day. She's old and grizzled, like us, and her highway-running days are over, but she is the *sweetest* dog, and I'm not even that much of a dog person. I've always thought she could hold it against us for hitting her, but instead she adores us for saving her. When we celebrate our group anniversaries, we say it's Grace's birthday, too, and regale her with lots of toys and edible gifts.

So that's it, the story of how we got our name. You've noticed I'm the only one who didn't actually do anything, who performed no semiheroic act whatsoever. The group, like Grace in its benevolence and generosity, chose to overlook this. Nobody's ever pointed it out even for a joke (something I myself couldn't have resisted, at least *once* in nine and a half years). No, I've always been unquestioningly accepted as a Saving Grace, and that alone, even if there were no other instances of support and love, kindness, fidelity, sympathy, comfort, and solidarity, would have guaranteed my loyalty for life.

But there are. A thousand. And since I didn't join an order of nuns, I should mention there have also been instances of jealousy, pettiness, pigheadedness, and let us not forget the occasional nervous breakdown. But they're nothing, and now I find it scary to think that prejudice against the upper middle class almost persuaded me to beg off with a polite excuse after that first meeting at Isabel's.

Good old Rudy, she kept me on the straight and narrow. Which is funny when you think about it. Because of us all, Rudy's by far the one who comes closest to being genuinely certifiable. Lee's the normal one. We even call her that—she takes it as a compliment. Which sort of says it all about Lee.

2

Lee

The women's group held its first meeting on June 14, 1988, at Isabel's house on Meadow Street. She made Thai chicken in peanut sauce with cellophane noodles. There were five of us that first time—Isabel, Rudy, Emma, Joanne Karlewski, and me. At my suggestion, we made the rule about pot luck contributions that night, after four of us showed up with salads. We said that, unless you were making the main dish because the meeting was at your house, the assignments would be: Rudy, hors d'oeuvres; Emma, salad; Joanne, bread; Isabel, fruit; me, dessert. Except for Rudy's, the assignments have stayed the same ever since. (We had to switch her from hors d'oeuvres to desserts because she's never on time.)

Meetings were on the first and third Wednesdays of the month until September of '91, when I went back to school and had a conflict with an evening class. So we switched to Thursdays, and we've pretty much stuck with them ever since. We begin at seven-thirty and break up around ten or ten-fifteen. For the first few years, we would have a semiformal discussion of a topic we'd picked the week before—mothers and daughters, ambition, trust, sex, that sort of thing—beginning immediately after dinner and lasting for an hour or so. However, this practice has fallen by the way, and I for one miss it. From time to time I'll suggest to the group that we reinstate it, but I never get any support. "We've already talked about everything under the sun," Emma argues, "there's nothing left." There's some truth to that, I'll admit, but I think the true problem is laziness. It's so much easier to gossip than it is to organize one's thoughts around a genuine, objective *topic* and stick to it. I like gossip as much as the next person, but I'm quite sure we had better discussions when we were organized.

It was when Susan Geiser was a member (February of '94 to April of '95) that we instituted the fifteen-minute rule, and that one is still in effect, although we don't need it now that Susan is gone. The Saving Graces had been without a fifth member for quite a while when Isabel met Susan and proposed her for membership. She had some lovely qualities, Susan did, and she could be quite interesting and funny. But she had one flaw: she never shut up. I didn't mind it that much, but it drove Emma and Rudy wild. So one night Isabel suggested the fifteen-minute rule—in some wonderfully tactful way, as only Isabel could—and from that time on we've each taken fifteen minutes at dinner to tell how we are, what we've been doing or thinking lately. We're not rigid about it, nobody looks at her watch or anything; it's simply a guideline. I'm usually finished in five minutes, whereas Rudy needs at least twenty, so it works out very well.

Emma and Rudy always say I'm the one who thought up the idea for the group and did the original planning and organizing, but in truth it was Isabel at least as much as me. We'd been friends for about a year and a half, Isabel and I, ever since that Halloween night when Terry, her son, threw up on my new shoes. It was my first Halloween in the Chevy Chase house, and I was having the nicest time giving out popcorn and candy apples I'd made myself to all the little trick-or-treaters. Dozens and dozens of them—I'd moved from a high-rise in College Park, and I couldn't get over how many children lived in my new neighborhood. And they were so dear, so sweet in their little costumes, the tiny princesses and witches and Power Rangers. I'll admit I was having what Emma calls a "kid Jones." By eight-thirty the doorbell had almost stopped ringing, though, and by nine o'clock, Halloween seemed to be over.

I was turning out the porch light, getting ready to go up and take my shower, when something fell against the door. A heavy thud—I thought someone had thrown something, perhaps one of the pumpkins I'd carved and set out on the steps. I looked through the peephole and saw a boy. Two boys. One I recognized, so I opened the door.

"Trick or treat."

That cracked them up; both boys, neither of whom was wearing a costume, bumped against each other and bent over double, convulsed with laughter. Drunken laughter.

"Are you clowns?" I asked.

"No, we're thugs," said the one whose name, I later learned, was Kevin. That sent them into more gales. They were holding pillowcases weighted down with candy, evidence of a long, successful night of trick-or-treating. Which meant no one had taken them in hand. And people wonder why today's youth is in trouble.

These two had finally come to the wrong house. "I know you," I said, pointing my finger in Terry's face. "You live on Meadow Street, the white house on the corner. Does your mother know what you and your friend are up to tonight?"

"Sure," he said. But he stopped laughing. The chilly, drizzly night had spiked his blond hair and reddened his cheeks. Terry was fifteen then, but he looked much younger in his slouchy, cocky, too-big clothes, like a little boy playing dress-up.

I whipped around on Kevin. "Where do you live?"

"Leland Street," he muttered, backing away toward the steps. I have this effect on children: when I'm stern with them, they sober up. (In this case, literally.) But it's not from fear, I assure you; it's a way I have of making them see reality the way I see it: sensibly.

"Which side of Connecticut?"

"This side," said Kevin.

"Good." I didn't want him crossing that busy street drunk. "You go home, right now. And whatever you're drinking, I'll take it." I held out my hand.

Kevin looked like a baby, too, but not a very nice one. He had a buzz cut and a fake tattoo of a skull on his cheek; going for the Nazi look, I supposed. "Fuck you," he said, "and anyway, Terry's got it," while he tottered down the steps and wove a crooked route to the sidewalk. I turned my back on him. "See ya, T! See ya when the bitch is gone!"

"Nice talk."

Terry backed up and hit the screen door with a thump. He was trying to smile carelessly, but it wasn't working. "Kev's an asshole," he slurred. "S'cuse me." The pillowcase slipped out of his slack fingers and thunked on the porch floor.

I picked it up. An almost-empty pint bottle of vodka sagged at the bottom under the candy. I moved a pumpkin and set the bottle on top of the newel post.

"Can you make it home by yourself?"

"Sure." But he didn't move, and all that kept him from sliding to the floor were his locked knees.

I sighed. "All right, let's go."

I took his arm to get him moving. We were about the same height then—now he's over six feet, and burly—but I was stronger, and it was no effort to take half his weight as we staggered and tacked down the empty sidewalk to the corner. He protested at first but said less and less the closer we got to his house. The porch light was out; otherwise I might have noticed Terry getting paler, greener, and the dots of perspiration popping out on his whiskerless upper lip. He hung back at the front door—reluctant to face the music, I thought.

I knocked, and almost immediately Isabel pulled open the door, smiling, holding out a bowl of bite-size Snickers. I recognized her and couldn't help smiling back. She was that pleasant-faced older woman who walked her beagle in the same vacant lot—"the dog park," we call it in our neighborhood—where I walked Lettice, my Brittany spaniel.

"Terry?" She saw her son behind me and frowned in puzzlement.

"Mom?" Well, no, what he actually said was, "Mo—?" If he'd gotten his mouth closed in time, my shoes could have been saved. But up came a disgusting stream of half-digested M&M's, Mounds, Milky Ways, and vodka, and most of it landed on my one-day-old, dove-gray suede Ferragamos.

Isabel rushed outside. Right behind her came Gary. I can't remember what I thought of him that first time. Not much—husband, older, short and stocky, nondescript. He ended up taking care of Terry, and Isabel ended up taking care of me.

I've sat in her kitchen a thousand times since that night. Isabel isn't like any friend I've ever made, and, at first, even though I was drawn to her and liked her a lot, I couldn't imagine us ever being close. She was older, for one thing—only eight years, but it seemed like much more. It's because she's from another generation, Isabel says, but I think it's something else as well. Some people are born knowing things the rest of us spend our lives trying to learn. Then, too, she *looked* so much older, with her streaky gray hair in a bun, of all things, and no fashion sense whatsoever. (I've helped her a lot with her sense of style over the years.) But she was still beautiful. To me, that night, she looked like an aging Madonna—I don't mean the singer. This was in 1987, so her real troubles hadn't even begun, but already there was sadness in Isabel's face, and serenity, and that lit-from-within quality that's so extraordinary to me.

And I . . . well, my life was busy and full with part-time teaching and a full course load, as well as a thesis to write for my M.Ed., but I was still a bit lonely. And maybe . . . in the market for a mother. Not that I haven't got a mother. As my husband says, *Oy*, have I got a mother. What I mean is—I might have been in the market for a little mothering.

Emma says I don't understand irony, but I believe this is the definition of it: except for Isabel, none of the Saving Graces has ever had children, and the only one who wants any is me. And I can't. Plus—this is ironic, too—I think Isabel and I were born to be mothers, and yet we both had rather cold parents. I'm dying to be a mother, to be mothered. And she mothers everybody, but who mothered her? No one.

On second thought, perhaps this isn't ironic. Perhaps it's just pathetic.

She made me take off my pantyhose and put on a pair of clean socks—Terry's—and she gave me a mug of hot mulled cider to sip while she cleaned my shoes in her powder room sink. When she came back, we had the nicest, most comfortable conversation. She asked me all about myself. In particular, I remember telling her about some of the scrapes my two brothers used to get into as teenagers, and how they've both turned into pillars of the community, as the saying goes. I said that so she wouldn't worry too much about Terry being on the road to ruin. I didn't stay long, but as I was leaving, it occurred to me that she'd found out a lot more about me than I had about her.

Terry came over the next day with a very nice apology, and also an invitation to dinner. So that's how it started. Isabel and I became friends. When we weren't visiting in each other's house, we were walking Lettice and Ernie in the dog park, or playing tennis together, or going for drives in the country. I cried with her when Terry decided to go to college at McGill in Montreal. She listened to every detail of my husband's long, shy courtship. After she walked out on Gary, she and Grace lived in my spare room for three weeks, and when she got cancer I felt as if it had happened to me. I can't imagine not knowing Isabel, can barely remember what my life was like before I met her.

A year or so after Terry's Halloween escapade, we were sitting on the linoleum floor, drying our dogs after their last bath of the summer, when Isabel said, "Leah Pavlik, you spend too much time with me in this kitchen. You ought to go out and play with friends your own age." I said, "*You* ought to go out and play with friends my own age." We laughed, and then—I'm not sure who said what, but before we knew it we were talking about starting a women's group.

All my life I've had a lot of girlfriends, and I admit I enjoy organizing them. I founded a girls-only club that met in my basement during sixth and seventh grades, and in high school I was cocaptain of the pompom squad, then president of my sorority in college. But since moving to Washington, I guess because I was so busy, except for Isabel I hadn't made that many women friends. I *loved* the idea of starting a group. It wouldn't be a book club, and not a political group, not a feminist organization. Just women we liked and respected and thought we could learn something from, meeting every so often to talk about issues of interest to us. Quite a modest agenda. Little did we know we were planting the first seeds of a beautiful garden.

Isabel said that, not me, years later. She said we were growing wholesome vegetables for sustenance and gorgeous flowers for joy. I asked her which one I was, certain she'd say a wholesome vegetable, but she said I was both. "We're all both, you dolt," were her exact words.

First impressions. After we'd been a group for about a year, we had a meeting at which the topic (at my suggestion) was what we had all thought of each other—those of us who didn't know each other already—at the first Graces' meeting. I started us off, saying I'd thought Emma looked like someone in the arts, or the fringes of the arts, possibly a rock star. (More of a *fading* rock star, I really meant, because of the sort of blasé, world-weary air Emma likes to project. In reality she's not jaded in the least, and I don't understand why it's so important to her to look "cool" all the time.) Well, she was *thrilled* to hear that she looked like a rock star. She wanted to know which one, and I came up with Bonnie Raitt—thinking they both have pretty, sharp-featured faces and (it must be said) the same slightly snotty expression at times. Also the same hair—long, reddish blond, and, to put it charitably, *self-styled*. (I am dying to introduce Emma to Harold, my hairdresser, but she says she can't be bothered.)

Rudy and Emma both said they had loved Isabel on sight, thought she was wonderful, although maybe a little old-fashioned, just a tad conservative. "Matronly, but in a *good* way," Emma said, and Rudy said, "No, *motherly*." I do remember that during that first meeting Isabel wore a red denim apron over her sweater and slacks—kept it on the whole evening, just forgot to take it off. That's how lacking in vanity she is. But conservative? No, no, no, no, no. Here is obvious proof that first impressions can be wildly inaccurate.

Isabel said she thought Rudy was one of the most beautiful women she'd ever seen in real life, and of course Emma and I agreed. The rest of us are fairly attractive women in a normal, average way, I would say. But Rudy's special. Everybody notices her; we can't go anywhere together and not attract attention. She has skin like an angel, a cover model's body, shiny, perfect, blue-black hair that does anything she wants it to. If she had only a gorgeous face, you could hate her, but behind the classic features there's such a sweetness, so much innocence and vulnerability, she brings out everybody's protective instincts. Everyone wants to save Rudy—men especially, she says. But so far, I'm sorry to say, I don't think anyone has.

As for me, Emma claimed she'd thought *I* looked like a rock star, too. Who? I asked eagerly. (Once an old beau told me I reminded him of Marie Osmond—"the perkiness," he'd said.) But Emma said, "Sinéad O'Connor." *What?* "Oh, not the baldness, although your hair was pretty short, Lee. More that, you know, humorless, self-righteous schtick you do." Oh, thank you very much! I was offended, but Emma added, "No, Sinéad O'Connor's *gorgeous*, haven't you ever noticed her eyes?" No. "She's a beautiful woman, Lee, I meant that as a *compliment*." Oh, really. I doubt that, but in any case, I look *nothing* like Sinéad O'Connor. I look like my mother: small, wiry, dark, and intense. And I am never self-righteous, although it's true that I'm frequently right.

So, again, so much for first impressions.

When I married Henry, it crossed my mind that I might not need the group as much anymore, or that my enthusiasm would slack off, I might not have the same time and energy for it. None of that happened. There was a period of seven or eight months when I was so fixated on sleeping with Henry, very little else registered on my consciousness, but that was an across-the-board phenomenon and didn't reflect on the Saving Graces specifically.

Emma and Rudy got a great deal of amusement out of that time in my life, I must say. I don't know what they thought I was like before I met Henry—a prude, I suppose. Which I am not, and never have been. I don't happen to swear, and I do like to keep certain thoughts to myself, not share them with the world at large. Or if I do share them, apparently I put them in terms that sound old-fashioned, even quaint to certain people. So when I met Henry and suddenly the only thing on my notoriously rational and unimaginative mind was sex, they thought this was hilarious.

I could have put a lid on their fun by simply keeping quiet, but for some reason, I guess the hormone circus going on inside, I couldn't stop talking about it. Could not keep my mouth closed. Nothing like this had ever happened to me before, and I was thirty-seven years old. One Thursday night, I made the mistake of telling the group how Henry looked in his blue cotton uniform, with his name in gold over the front pocket, and PATTERSON & SON HEATING, PLUMBING & AC on the back. And he wore a tool belt. A *tool belt*. Who knew? Rudy and Emma said they knew about tool belts—I'm talking about the ultimate in male allure, that irresistible combination of sexuality and visible evidence of problem-solving capability—and even Isabel allowed that the concept wasn't new to her. I wonder where I've been.

Then I made an even bigger mistake. I told them about the first time he came to my house (which at that point was only to fix a stopped-up toilet; I hadn't hired him yet to replace the old pipes and put in new heating ducts), and he showed me a diagram in a plumbing book so that I could see exactly what was wrong and how he was going to fix it. "It's pawd o' the suhvice," he told me in his low, thrilling, solicitous southern accent. "An infawmed customah is a satisfahed one." He had his sleeves rolled up, and the sun through the bathroom window illuminated every golden hair on his—well, I believe in this case the word really is *sinewy*—forearms. You would have to see the diagram he showed me to understand what I mean, but believe me when I say that the drawing of the "closet auger" angling its long, tubular way into the narrow, back-slanted overflow passage of the toilet looked exactly, *exactly* like a man's penis in a woman's vagina.

You can imagine the "plumbing" jokes I've had to put up with for the last four years.

Here is some more irony. In addition to the clean, liberating lust I've felt for Henry since almost the moment we met, I also knew he would make the world's most wonderful father. My genes called to his genes, I used to say, in a joking way. Together we were going to make beautiful Jewish/Protestant, intellectual/blue-collar babies (the intellectual component coming from my parents, not me; my father teaches quantum physics at Brandeis and my mother is a stockbroker). But things are not looking hopeful in the baby-making department nowadays. Something seems to be wrong with my plumber's plumbing. Or maybe it's me, they're not quite sure.

I try not to think about the worst that could happen to us: childlessness. Such a forlorn word. And alien. I've never associated it with myself before. I feel mocked now by all the years I religiously took the pill or used foam, an IUD, a diaphragm, scrupulously making sure I kept myself barren.

I've managed to hide the worst of my fears from the group better than I hid my oh-so-funny libido, but I probably won't be able to for much longer. And why would I want to? To preserve their image of me as the sober, sensible, coolheaded one, I suppose.

But Isabel knows already. As usual. Once she told me she couldn't have gotten through her divorce and then the cancer and chemo and all that without me—which is very kind, very typical of her, but not true. But it will be in my case. If the worst happens—if Henry and I can't conceive a child—I'm quite sure that, without Isabel, I won't be able to bear it.

3

Rudy

I don't know why my friends bother with me, I'm so high-maintenance. I would run if I saw me coming. But they're always so patient and supportive. They put their arms around me and say, "Oh, Rudy, you are doing so *well*." That's code; it means, since nobody's put me in a straitjacket yet, I must be all right. I agree, but I always feel like knocking on wood after they say that.

What I don't tell anybody, not even Emma, who thinks she knows everything about me, is how large a part norpramin and amitriptyline have been playing in my mental health. And before them, protriptyline and alprazolam. And meprobamate. I could go on.

Nobody knows this about me except Curtis, my husband, and Eric, my therapist. I'm frank about the rest, my family's total dysfunction, the decades I've spent in counseling, my fights with depression and melancholia and mania. Everybody in the world is on Prozac or Zoloft, so there's no shock value there anymore, no shame, as Emma says, in better living through chemistry.

But I keep it to myself. The thing is, I need my friends to believe that what I do, how I behave, is *real*. Because it is real—but if they knew about my secret army of psychopharmaceuticals, anything I did right would be "because of the drugs," and anything wrong—same thing. Nothing about me would be authentic. In their minds, there would be no real Rudy.

Wait till I tell them what I did today. I already know what their reactions are going to be: Emma will laugh, Isabel will sympathize and console, and Lee will disapprove (gently). And all of them will be wondering in private, *Well, what were they thinking of when they hired her in the first place?* But it's not their judgments I'm worried about. It's Curtis's.

What happened was, I got fired from the Call for Help Hotline. I'm ashamed to say I only lasted a week. Mrs. Phillips, my supervisor, said I got too personal with one of the callers, in direct violation of training guidelines. I know I handled it wrong, I *know* there have to be rules, but the truth is, if this girl—Stephanie—if she called again, I know I would do the same thing.

They tell us to be cautious at first, and already I had taken some prank calls from teenagers. But Stephanie's young, thin, strung-out voice gave her away so quickly, I was sure after only a few seconds that this was no game.

"Call for Help Hotline, this is Rudy speaking. Hello? This is Rudy, is somebody there?"

"Hi, yeah. I'm, um, calling for a friend."

"Hi. Okay. What's your friend's name?"

Long pause. "Stephanie."

"Stephanie. Does Stephanie have a problem?"

"Yeah, you could say that. She's got a lotta problems."

"A lot of problems. Okay, which one is the worst? The one that's making her the most unhappy."

"Oh, God, I don't know. She cries a lot. You know. Over, you know, a lot of stuff. Like, her family. Her friends."

"What's wrong with her family?"

Snort. "What isn't?"

I waited.

"Her mother, okay, she's a real mess."

"In what way?"

Silence.

"In what way is she a real mess?"

No answer.

"I bet she drinks too much."

"*What?*"

"Does Stephanie's mother drink too much?"

"Jeez. Yeah. She does. So—did you just, like, *guess* that?"

"Well, my mother drinks too much. So, yeah, I guess I just guessed it." Why did I say that? Why?

"Really? So she's a drunk? My mother's a total drunk, it's so awful, I don't see how I can . . . Oh, man. Oh, shit."

"No, wait, that's okay. Hey, Stephanie? Listen, it's okay, really. About ninety percent of the people I talk to start out telling me they're calling for a friend. But, you know, I think it's good—you probably *would* call for a friend, because you're a nice person." (This is not exactly how I usually talk; I mean, it's not quite my *voice*. But whoever I'm talking to on the Hotline, I find myself—found myself—falling into their idiom. Mrs. Phillips, before she fired me, said it was one of my most effective counseling strategies.)

"Right," Stephanie said skeptically.

"No, you are, I can tell."

"How old are you?"

"Me? Forty-one."

Scoffing sounds. "Yeah, so like, what do you know about teenage angst?"

"Teenage angst." I laughed, and Stephanie started to laugh with me—I thought she was laughing, but then I realized she was crying.

"Oh, man . . ." I heard her fingers slide on the receiver—she was going to hang up.

I said very quickly, "Yeah, my mother was a drunk, she tried to kill herself when I was twelve. When I was eleven, my father *did* kill himself."

Long, long silence. I had plenty of time to ponder what made me blurt that out. I knew it was against the rules, but at the time, I couldn't think of any other way to keep her on the line.

Anyway, it worked. She started talking. "My mother . . . almost every day when I come home from school she's, like, plastered. Or else she's sick. And I have to take care of her. I can't bring anybody over, so I don't have any friends. Well, one, I have one friend, Jill. But she doesn't . . . you know, I can't tell her what's going on, so . . ."

"I know what that's like. I didn't have any friends, either, the whole time I was growing up. But that was a mistake. I made that mistake."

"How do you mean?"

"Well, I mean, I did it all to myself, because I couldn't stop feeling ashamed. Like *I* was the one with the problem. But, Stephanie, listen to me, you didn't do anything, you really didn't. You're innocent. You're a baby. You don't deserve what's happening to you."

She burst into tears then. I did, too. Neither of us could speak for quite some time. I'm not sure, but I think this was when Mrs. Phillips started listening in.

"And, you know, this isn't even the main thing," Stephanie went on when she could talk. "Except it is, it's like *over* everything, you know?"

"I know."

"But right now it's something else, something even . . . "

"What? What, Steph?"

"God." She started to cry again. I just waited. I was crying, too, but silently now. I thought of Eric, my therapist, and how he *never* cries, no matter how badly I go to pieces in his office. And yet I never think he's cold or indifferent—oh, no, just the opposite. But he doesn't cry. Which is good, thank God, because *somebody's* got to stay composed.

So I tried to pull myself together for Stephanie. "What happened?" I finally asked her. "I know it's something bad."

"It's bad. Something I did."

"With a boy?"

Stunned silence. Then, "Well, *shit*."

I had to laugh again. "It's okay, really, just another wild guess. What did you do? You can tell me if you want to."

"Are you married? What was your name, again?"

"Rudy. Am I married? Yes."

"For how long?"

"Four and a half years, almost five."

"So you were, like, thirty-seven?"

"Yes. Old," I said, before she could. I could tell that's what she was thinking.

"So did you ever, like . . . do anything with a guy that . . ."

"That I felt ashamed of afterward?"

"Yeah."

We're not supposed to tell parallel stories. We're trained to listen and ask questions, and refer callers to the appropriate social service agencies. So all I said—and I don't really think this was so bad—was, "Steph, I've done things with men that I haven't even told my therapist about."

She gave a nervous, relieved laugh. "So you mean, like, you go to a shrink?"

"I'll give you his name. Eric Greenburg, he's in Maryland—"

"Hey, wait—"

"No, write it down. Just in case." I gave her the phone number, too. I think she wrote it down. Needless to say, this is something else we're not allowed to do.

"Okay," Stephanie said, clearing her throat, "this guy, he's in my math class. His name is George but everybody calls him Spider, Spider Man, I don't know why. I don't even like him that much, I mean, he's not my boyfriend or anything, but he was in the mall with these other guys last night, and I was with Jill, and we started talking and everything, and pretty soon Spider said why don't we come out to his car because he's got some stuff, you know, and we can smoke it. So Jill goes, no way, we're leaving, and—okay, this was really, really stupid, I know, but I told her to go on, because I was staying."

"Uh-huh."

"So she left, and I went out in the parking lot with Spider and these two other guys and got high."

"Uh-huh."

"I've smoked before, it wasn't the first time or anything. I think it was my mood or something. And, you know . . ."

"Not wanting to go home."

"Yeah."

"Wanting to shake things up a little. Bust out."

"Yeah. Oh God, Rudy."

"I know. So . . ."

"So . . . you know what I did after that."

"I guess so. How was it?"

She giggled—but then she started to cry again. My telephone is on a table with two fiberglass panels on either side that are about chin height. If I don't want anyone to see me, I have to hunch over, practically put my face on the table. I covered the back of my head with my hand and listened to Stephanie cry and cry. "It's okay. It's okay. You're all right," I told her over and over. "You're still yourself. You're still you."

"It was awful, Rudy, it was so awful. Oh, God, and I don't even like him! And he'll tell everybody, all his friends, and then . . ."

"Who cares? You're not like that and *you* know it. Screw them."

"Jill's not even talking to me!"

"Well, she's angry, but—"

"No, she *hates* me, my best friend *hates* me."

"No, she doesn't."

"Yes, she *does*."

"She's confused and she's mad at you, but she doesn't hate you, Steph. Is she really your best friend? For how long?"

"Since sixth grade. *Four years*." She said that like I would say *forty years*. "Oh, what am I going to do?"

"Well, I guess you have to talk to her."

"She won't talk to me! And anyway, I can't tell her all this stuff."

"Well, you can. You told me. It'll just be really hard."

"I can't. She's so straight. And she's good, she's always been good.

Sometimes I think if I had a sister, it wouldn't be so awful. Or even a brother, if I just had someone—"

"Well, not necessarily."

"No, I mean, if I had a sister or something, then at least there would be somebody to share it with, all this *crap*."

"Well, you'd think so."

"No, I think it would be a lot easier. A lot. You know, being lonely and everything . . ."

I did it again. I said, "Well, I'll tell you, I've got siblings, and they just made everything worse. When I was your age."

"I don't get that."

"You know how your mother's drinking makes you feel like a failure?"

"Yeah?"

"Well—think if you had a brother and sister, and you felt as if you were failing them, too. Instead of one person to worry about, you had three. I'm just saying, it doesn't necessarily make anything better."

"I still wish I had someone."

Why couldn't I just leave it at that? "Listen, Stephanie—Claire, my sister, ran away when I was sixteen and she was eighteen and joined a religious cult. She still belongs to it."

"Huh."

"Yeah. This is a cult that believes we should revere *cats* because they're the direct descendants of Yahweh. *Cats*."

"Who? Yahweh?"

"God—Yahweh means God."

Stephanie burst out laughing.

"I'm not kidding. And this is just *one* thing they believe. And my brother, Allen, well, he's just lost, he's gone. *This is my family*, Steph. My father committed suicide and my mother was a lush, my sister joined a cult, my brother's a lost soul—and here I am at this crisis center, acting like a sane person! So—no, listen"—she was still snickering—"I think the first thing you should do is call Dr. Greenburg, and the second thing is, call Jill. Because you really need her right now."

"Yeah, but I don't know . . ."

A little red light on the telephone starts blinking when the supervisor wants to break in. We're supposed to put the caller on hold, hit the button, and see what she wants. My red light had been blinking for about two minutes.

"I'm just saying, I think you should probably go for it with Jill. That's what I'd do if I were you. Do you really love her?"

"Yeah. I guess." She started to cry again. Really cry—she was sobbing. What a nerve I'd touched that time.

"Hey, Stephanie, it's all right. Oh, baby, it's okay, it's okay. Shhh, you're all right." The red light kept flashing, flashing.

"Rudy?"

"What, baby."

"Are you really okay now?"

"I am, I really am."

We're allowed to lie. And if we're not, we should be.

"Well, but . . . what about your mother?" Stephanie asked in a small voice.

"She's around. We both survived. She lives in Rhode Island with my stepfather, and we talk on the phone sometimes." No point in mentioning I haven't seen her in almost five years, not since my wedding. "She says she's sorry. Well, she said that once."

"She did?"

"Yeah. That meant a lot to me."

"God, Rudy." She heaved a sigh. "It sounds like your family's more fucked up than mine is. Oh—I'm sorry—can I say that?"

Oh, sweet Stephanie. "My family. Steph, if I started to tell you about my family, you'd be late for school tomorrow." Tickled laughter. I liked her so much. I had an idea. "Hey, do you live in the District?"

"Yeah, Tenley Circle. I go to Wilson."

"You know, if you wanted to, I could meet you sometime and we could talk some more. Would you like to? It's just an idea—"

"I'd like it. Like some Saturday or something?"

"That would be great. My husband usually works on Saturdays, so we could have lunch—"

"Oh Jeez, I forgot you were married."

"Yeah, I'm married."

"So—is that cool?"

"Being married? Very cool. You know. Usually."

"Yeah, usually." Her voice dropped one whole, cynical octave. It broke my heart.

"So," I said, "how about Saturday? Do you want to meet?"

"Oh, that would—"

Click.

"Hello? Steph? Stephanie? Hello?"

I stared at the dead receiver in my hand. On my console, six or seven green lights flickered, indicating callers talking to volunteers. Had they transferred Stephanie to somebody else? I pushed a button at random.

". . . coming out at this particular time, it's *inconvenient*, and that queen *knew*—"

Click.

"*Mrs. Lloyd.*"

I jolted up straight. Mrs. Phillips never called me "Mrs. Lloyd"—I called her Mrs. Phillips and she called me Rudy. She's a large, beautiful, statuesque black woman, and she scares the hell out of me. She was standing over me, looming, really, her intimidating bosom heaving. I couldn't do anything but stare up at her. I felt like a guilty child.

"Mrs. Lloyd, hang up that phone, get your things, and get the hell out of this office."

"Wait, I know I was—"

"Out." She pivoted sideways and pointed through the window to the street. She had painted, one-inch fingernails and a lot of rings, a lot of clattering bracelets. She reminded me of a goddess, an Amazon.

"Please, Mrs. Phillips, if I could just talk to that girl for two more minutes, I think she—"

"Lady," she said, incredulous, "you are *fired*. What were you thinking of?" She wasn't indignant, she was furious. Until now I'd never even heard her raise her voice.

"Mrs. Phillips, I was wrong, I know that, and I'll never—"

"We serve clients, Mrs. Lloyd. What do you think we're here for, to give *you* therapy?"

"No, I—"

"You're lucky if I don't decide to have charges brought against you."

"Charges!"

It was every nightmare come true. *Access your anger*, Eric tells me—but if I had any now, it was buried too deeply, under too much guilt and remorse and misery and mortification. This was—this was one of the most classic failures of my life.

Poor Stephanie, I agonized all the way home. What would happen to her now? What if she went back to Spider Man? If I could find her somehow—she lived in Tenley Circle, she went to Wilson High, she was fifteen years old . . .

What made me think *I* could help her? All I'd done was tell her about myself, *my* alcoholic mother, *my* screwed-up family. Mrs. Phillips was right about everything. I deserved this disgrace, and much more.

Well, I would get more. The worst punishment hadn't started yet, but it was about to. As soon as I tried to explain all this to Curtis.

4

Isabel

I've been reading a book by a woman who believes that, in her most recent past life, she was a Nazi sympathizer. She collaborated with the SS, she says, spied on her neighbors, and made herself rich (or rather *him*self rich; she's positive she was a man in this life) by shameless war profiteering. She bases this conviction not only on past-life regression therapy, but also on the circumstances of her current life. Poor woman, she's a quadriplegic; she lost the use of all but her facial muscles in a horrific automobile accident when she was sixteen. She says the suffering she endures now is in payment for the sins she committed in Germany in the 1940s.

Karma. What goes around comes around.

I have never been hypnotized or regressed, and if I've lived past lives, I've lost track of them. But I would not rule out the possibility. Skepticism is a luxury I don't indulge anymore—I leave that to the young and immortal. But if it's true that the yin and yang are always counterbalancing each other, I'd like to think they're doing it within me *now*, in *this* life. I even know where I'd place the fulcrum for the most perfect equilibrium: at the center of my forty-sixth year. Before and after that dubious milestone, the halves of my life fall away like wings, like a heart broken in two. I am reborn. Here in the third year of my new life, I try to balance the old one with hope and love, sympathy, warmth and superfluous kindnesses, gratuitous outbursts of delight. There is so much to counterweigh (although nothing so heinous as the erstwhile Nazi's sins); I only hope I have time. It would help if I could live to ninety-two. Forty-six and forty-six.

* * *

Among good friends, ten years isn't much of an age difference, and yet sometimes I feel as if the Saving Graces and I come from different centuries. I'm not quite fifty; technically I'm a boomer. My father was a missionary, though, and I spent half my childhood in Cameroon and Gabon, the other half in Iowa. Then, too, my husband's job kept us stationed in Turkey for the first six years of our marriage; our son was born there, in fact. These are the most obvious explanations for my lifelong uneasiness with the popular culture, but I think something else is also at work. Something in me. Terminal unhipness, Emma would call it. That's as good an explanation as any.

We're all productive, tolerably sane, functioning adults, we Graces, with no more emotional baggage—well, except for Rudy—than you would expect in a random sample of aging yuppie women. And yet our childhoods were disasters. Some more than others, of course. Rudy could write a book; Emma probably *will* write a book. Lee's family and mine have in common an outward appearance of normalcy, a very different reality inside. Occasionally we four play the intriguing "What keeps us together?" game, and the fact that we all survived our childhoods is mentioned early and often.

I wonder if I could have survived my cancer without their loving-kindness. Survived—yes, probably. But only that: barest survival. Nothing, no other experience has ever leveled me to such an extent. I believed I would never recover, that I was forever changed. And I was, but not in the way I expected. I'd read all the pamphlets and books on the disease, as many as I could find. The first-person stories of women who claimed that cancer changed their lives, turned them into different people, *was a blessing in disguise*—oh God, these stories infuriated me. I felt cheated and betrayed, lied to, and deeply, personally offended. And now—now I'm one of those women. It's been two years since I lost my breast, and I hear myself uttering the very same sentiment that used to make me grind my teeth: "Not that

I'd wish it on anyone, but it was *good* that this happened to me. It's turned my life around."

Well, it needed turning around. It had taken a little detour, my life, occasioned by, among other things, the discovery of my husband's chronic unfaithfulness. I don't know why, but I've been thinking about Gary quite a lot these days. I've been wondering if I was right to turn his last act of betrayal into the catalyst for our breakup. If we were still married and it happened today, would I forgive him? I believe I would. I hope so. Because I'm not the same person; I don't have that anger inside me anymore. Thank God. Oh, but what would Lee say if I told her this? Or Emma, or Rudy? It doesn't bear thinking about! The only bright spot in the long horror of my divorce was their friendship, the way they rallied around, united in loathing Gary. In the space of one women's group meeting, they went from being rather fond of him to wishing him dead, and at the time I found that enormously comforting.

To this day, I haven't told the Graces the whole story of his infidelities. Too embarrassed, I guess; it's shameful, Gary's behavior, and some of the shame has stuck to me, as if part of the blame were mine. Perhaps it is—I'm sure it is. But I'll never forget and I'll always be grateful for their savage, righteous fury when I told them how I discovered his *first* peccadillo. It happened on the night of our nineteenth wedding anniversary—which, in retrospect, seems fitting; as long as I've known Gary, he's always had terrible timing.

He took me to a new Turkish restaurant in Bethesda—a little gift of nostalgia for the good old days, when we were first married and lived in Ankara. I was surprised and touched. We drank raki and ate skewered lamb with eggplant, and went home and made love on the couch. Most unlike us, but Terry was in Richmond on a glee club overnight, and for once the house was ours. I fell asleep afterward, and woke up in the dark. Carrying my clothes, I wandered upstairs, feeling cozy and smug because my marriage was nineteen years old and I still had sex on the sofa. Gary's voice, low and confidential, came to me from the half-closed bedroom door, and I paused on the landing, nothing but curious. Who could he be talking to on the telephone at midnight? In that voice?

Betty Cunnilefski—a name that didn't amuse me in the slightest until much, much later. She worked as an administrative assistant in his office. I'd met her once, recalled her vaguely: small, wispy, beige, the sort of woman you see dining alone in restaurants, who's careful to keep the cover of the book she's reading facedown on the table.

Gary confessed everything that night in a rush. He wouldn't see her again, he swore, and he'd have her transferred to another office. Even in the midst of my hurt and anger, I felt a small pang for Betty—who, true to his word, Gary moved to a different department within the week. And presumably never saw again. I believed him at the time, he wept so convincingly, begged my forgiveness so sincerely. He seemed almost as shocked as I was, and unable to explain why he'd done it. Which was just as well, because if he'd claimed he was lonely, misunderstood, sexually deprived, drunk, seduced, in midlife crisis—*any* excuse would have ignited the silent, seething volcano of anger in me. I was barely aware of it, frankly thought myself incapable of it. And Gary would have been flabbergasted if he'd guessed at a fraction of it.

It took three years for the volcano to erupt. Betty may or may not have been his first mistress, but she wasn't his last. How did he get these women? That's all I want to know, now that the fury has burned itself out. Gary is short, jowly, on the stocky side; he has a full beard, and still plenty of salt-and-pepper hair. He's bull-chested, thick-necked, and short-legged. In bed he's ramlike, a batterer. Fine if you like that sort of thing, but over the years I grew to hate it. Behind a friendly smile, he's really quite cool and measuring, predatory. He flirts energetically and ineptly; it's impossible—was impossible—to imagine him scoring with any woman. But he does. What is it about him?

For one thing, he's an earthy, passionate man—that's why I fell in love with him. And for another, he chooses needy, lonely, awkward girls, the pathetic sure things of this world—girls exactly like I used to be. I can't say if it's deliberate on his part, and therefore cruel and calculating, or only blind, unerring instinct. I've never been able to decide. I want to give him the benefit of the doubt. I want to forgive.

This is not altruism, not saintliness. There's no room inside for bitterness anymore—it's that simple. At the risk of sounding fatuous, I'll make an observation that life is full of Bettys. I don't know whom I have to thank for this new, sanguine attitude, and it's amusing to think it may be, in part, my minister father's Lutheran God. But only in part. I'm equally drawn nowadays to what Emma calls woo-woo, meaning crystals and rocks, the Tarot, reincarnation, past lives, astrology, numerology, meditation, hypnotherapy—anything and everything under the rubric of New Age (anything spiritual other than orthodox Protestantism, according to Emma). I believe in them all. My friend's scorn knows no bounds, and yet she teases me so gently, so affectionately. It's a lovely form of play between us. Emma and I are closer than we've ever been.

I could tell her how purely delighted I am to see God in so many new places. The dual burdens of conventionality and rationality fell away when I realized I might die, *I really might die*. Now I'm free. Free and forty-nine, and so grateful to be starting life over again. Yin and yang. I've gone back to school, I've moved from Chevy Chase to Burleith to Adams-Morgan—a progression that speaks volumes all by itself. I color my hair. I might take a lover. Waking up in the morning isn't a tedious and dutiful act, it's the start of a possible adventure. I've recreated myself. No, that's not it. I have *been* recreated, by a new definition of mortality forced on me by circumstances. And it was worth it: all I had to give in return was a breast.

The deal of a lifetime.

5

Emma

Bad news doesn't hurt as much if you hear it in good company. It's like—if somebody pushes you out a fifth-floor window and you bounce off an awning, a car roof, and a pile of plastic garbage bags before you smash onto the pavement, you've got a pretty good chance of surviving.

This analogy is too unwieldy to go on with, plus I can't decide whom to equate with the plastic garbage bags. So I'll just say, the night I found out Mick Draco was married, I thought of my three best friends as fall-breakers extraordinaire.

We were having dinner on a Thursday, our regular meeting night, at La Cuillerée in Adams-Morgan instead of at Isabel's apartment because her stove was broken. "My short story got another rejection," I had just announced to Rudy, Lee, and Isabel, and I was in the process of laughing off their concern and sympathy, even though it felt like balm, so they wouldn't know how wrecked I was—when all of a sudden Lee looked past my shoulder and said, "Mick Draco."

I froze, disoriented—five minutes ago I'd been fantasizing about him. *Lee read my mind,* I marveled, and then, following her gaze, I glanced around and saw him. An X-rated dream come true.

She said his name again and waved, but since Lee's the kind of person who would rather eat a cockroach than raise her voice in a public place, he didn't hear her. But—*Lee knew him?* Flustered, I stood up and shouted, "Hey, Mick!" and he whipped around, grinned, and walked over to our table.

I had been thinking about him for the last four days, ever since our brief, pre-interview meeting in the seedy coffee shop across from his grungy art studio on Eighth Street. He'd told me he lived in nearby Columbia Heights, but still, suddenly seeing him in this middling-trendy French bistro on Columbia Road threw me off.

He still looked good, though. Still straight and lean and not too tall, my favorite body type. And he still had dark, silver-streaked hair, a big, intelligent head, and light brown eyes that warmed when he saw me. "It's that guy I told you about," I had time to whisper to Rudy, before he loomed over us with his hands in his pea jacket pockets, smiling and glad, a little nervous, a little self-conscious. And then I thought, *Shit—he'll take one look at Rudy and forget my name*. That's what men do—I've gotten used to it, I'm philosophical about it. Tonight, though, I wanted to stuff a bag over her head.

Lee said, "Mick, hello, it's nice to see you. I've been meaning to call Sally. Do you and Emma know each other? I had no idea."

Sally, who's Sally, I thought while Lee introduced him to Rudy and Isabel. But then I knew. The little wife. Oh, *perfect*, the story of my life. And it wasn't even going to make for a good joke, no funny routine about the date from hell or the newest hilarious bedroom blunder by one of my famously inept sex partners. No, this just hurt. I was blindsided, totally unprepared for how bad it felt. Do you think this was peculiar of me? Immature or unstable? I mean, to react this strongly to the married status of a man I barely knew? Well, so do I. I can't explain it. It's never happened before.

"Mick's son Jay goes to the Center," Lee was saying, sparkling her black eyes at him, obviously pleased to see him. "That's how I met Sally."

Another jolt: a wife *and* a kid. In Lee's day care center, no less. I put on a big smile and told everybody how *I* knew Mick. "We just met a few days ago. Mick's going to be the star of an article I'm writing about midlife career changes." Rudy and Isabel made interested noises. He didn't pick up on it, so I said, "He used to be a patent attorney, and now he's an artist."

He moved his hands around in his pockets and muttered, "Struggling, would-be artist," with a crooked smile.

Shy—he was shy. Oh, God. That's my other weakness. I have two: men who are shy, and men who are smarter than I am. He hadn't been shy before, though, not when it was just him and me in the coffee shop. And now he wasn't blinded by Rudy, either; in fact, he kept glancing at me while he and Lee made small talk. Isabel sat quietly and watched, not saying anything. Absorbing it all.

Technically we were having a meeting, so nobody asked him to sit down with us. I was glad—why torture myself until I had to? When the conversation got sparse, he told Rudy and Isabel it was nice meeting them, told Lee he'd tell Sally to call her. *Sally*. I've never known one, but I had no trouble picturing her. *Sally* would be a natural blonde with a wholesome, perky outlook. She'd wear an apron when she baked special, complicated but healthful cookies for her men. That's what she'd call them—"my men."

Mick backed up a step, looking directly at me for the first time. "So, Monday," he said.

"Right. Monday."

"Would you like to get some lunch first?"

"No, can't, let's start in the studio like we said." My voice sounded snippy—how stupid. He hadn't done anything wrong. He didn't wear a wedding band, but he hadn't lied, hadn't even done that shuffle-dance men do to *imply* that they're single without saying it. If this was anybody's fault, it was mine, for making an assumption based on nothing but wishful thinking. Rookie mistake. I could've sworn foolishness like that had been bled out of me years ago.

We all said good-bye, and Mick went off to join a stoop-shouldered man with a white ponytail at a window table. I watched them out of the corner of my eye while Lee chattered about *Sally*, how nice she was, how they were thinking of taking ballet lessons together. The moment came and went when I could have blurted out that my heart was broken—in a humorous way, of course. I still have a few secrets I keep from the group, but this kind of thing, man trouble, isn't usually one of them. Why didn't I speak up? Lee knowing the wife made it sticky, that was one thing. The other was Isabel. Her divorce isn't that old, and adultery is still a touchy subject with her.

Not that I was contemplating adultery. God, no, I hate cheating, cheaters, infidelity, the whole sleazy package. But still. Something about Isabel, quietly sitting there with her gentle face and her Buddha smile, something in her that's fine, not judgmental, kept me from making any cynical, self-effacing quips about the crush I had on married Mick Draco.

We'd saved Rudy for last, as usual, because her fifteen-minute allotment has a way of stretching to thirty, forty, forty-five. Nobody minds; it's just better to plan ahead. She told a long, funny story about losing her job at the Help Hotline.

"Well, I knew *you'd* laugh," she said to me. "But I'm telling you, it wasn't that funny."

"You really gave her Greenburg's phone number? Oh, Rudy."

"Why not? He's a family therapist, he counsels adolescents. And if ever a girl needed—"

"Because it's a violation of the rules," Lee said in that tolerant, teacher-to-student voice she uses a lot on Rudy. She doesn't use it on me, because if she does I use it right back. Only I exaggerate, make it sound even more irritating, which is saying something.

"I know," Rudy said, "but—"

"Places like that aren't allowed to recommend individuals, Rudy. Didn't they explain that? Wasn't there any training before they let you start answering phones?"

"Yes, there was training. They told us all about not recommending individual doctors or clinics or hospitals, not even programs. I know it was wrong, but I couldn't help it. If you'd heard her"—deliberately, she turned from Lee and me to Isabel—"you'd have done the same thing."

Isabel smiled. "I hope I would have."

"But you can't *do* that," Lee insisted, "because then the hot line becomes nothing more than an advertising service. Just think of the potential for abuse."

Isabel sat back, fluffing her soft cap of ash-blonde curls—a dye job; she looks *fabulous* these days, not a minute over forty-five. "Rudy," she said mildly, "how many charitable organizations do you volunteer for?"

"Right now?" She counted. "Four."

"Really. What are they?"

"Literacy, Sunday Soup Kitchen, humane society, and story hour."

"Story hour—"

"At Children's Hospital."

"Ah."

Moment of silence while we took that in. There's an old black lady who plays slide guitar on the corner of Fifteenth and G. Sometimes I drop a dollar in her cigar box as I'm rushing past. Except for some Christmas checks, assuming I'm flush, that's the extent of my charity work.

Isabel didn't press the point. She didn't have to. Lee stopped lecturing and I stopped laughing. Rudy, sweet, oblivious Rudy, asked the waiter for more water. She didn't even know Isabel had made a point.

Rudy caught me beaming at her. "What?" she said, smiling back.

"Nothing."

I really love Rudy's squinty-eyed smile. Twelve years ago, on the student side of the reference desk at the Duke University library, she must not have smiled much, because otherwise I'd have noticed. We were only nodding acquaintances then, harried grad students who knew but never really registered on each other. Nowadays we love to marvel about luck, timing, providence—*fate*, if we're drinking—and what a tragedy it would've been if we hadn't moved to D.C. the same year, and then, clearly a miracle, joined the same book club.

"What did you first see in me?" We never get tired of asking each other that question, although we word it more artfully, less baldly. "You laughed at all my jokes," I always say; "nobody else in that group had any sense of humor whatsoever. Plus you've got a terrific laugh."

True, but an even truer reason is because Rudy always said out loud the things I was only thinking. She had *words* for everything, and they fit with my inner life, meshed with my deepest feelings, as if she were me. It was as if I'd met my double. I'm her best friend, but she attracts other people for the same reason. I don't know if it's all the years in therapy, but Rudy has a way of saying the unsayable and making it sound normal and human. Forgivable.

When I ask what she saw in me, she says, "You were so funny." That's nice; I like making people laugh, and I don't need a therapist to tell me why. "And you were honest. And sort of snotty, but in a good way, not really mean. A smart-ass with a heart of gold."

It's the nicest thing anybody's ever said to me.

Over dessert, my mind wandered. Also my eyes. Mick Draco had incredible shoulders. Draco—it's Greek, isn't it? But the bump in his nose looked Roman. I put on my glasses. He had a mole at the flared end of his right eyebrow. And the neatest, tidiest hairline, something so clean about it, even though his straight, streaky hair was too long. (For fashion; not too long for him.) He laughed at something his friend said. I couldn't hear the laugh over the restaurant din, but it made me smile in sympathy.

Lee smiled back at me.

I took off my glasses and pulled myself together. Mick Draco's a dead end. And I'm a bust at the man-woman thing. Half a lifetime of trying and failing to connect with the opposite sex for longer than a year or two can't be discounted or called "finding myself" anymore. I'm never going to find myself, because I'm a loser.

"What would I do without you guys?" I interrupted Rudy to ask, out of the blue, in the middle of the crème brûlée. Everybody smiled at me fondly; Isabel glanced at my wineglass—just checking, a tolerant, motherly gesture. "No, I mean it. If my luck was as rotten with women as it is with men, I'd have to shoot myself."

Rudy gave me a little pat on the shoulder and went back to a story she was telling about her shrink. But, you know, it's true. I might die an old maid, but I'll always have my pals. God knows there are worse things than living alone. Most men are only speed bumps anyway, aggravating distractions scattered along life's otherwise pretty nice highway. You might run into a good one every long once in a while, but even then he's usually got something wrong with him. Good women, on the other hand, are everywhere. You can pick and choose, find the best ones, start a club, and have friends for life.

Walking out of La Cuillerée, Lee turned at the door and waved good-bye to Mick Draco, but I didn't. I sailed on out, didn't even glance his way. I was over him. Thanks to my friends, I had it all in perspective. Saved by the Graces once more.

Then, too, I'd be seeing him again on Monday.

6

Rudy

I had an awful dream last night. I was rushing, late for something, the dream was half over before I realized what—my session with Eric. I was driving Curtis's car instead of mine, and there was no place to park, so I drove right over the curb and parked on the sidewalk in front of Eric's office. *Uh-oh,* I thought, *he won't like that.* Now I'm not sure who I meant, Eric or Curtis. Eric, I think. Anyway, I was wild to see him. I had something important to tell him, something about my father. (What?) I ran into the building, up the stairs, through the waiting room and into his office, I didn't even knock—and—there he was, having sex on the floor with somebody.

I couldn't see the woman's face. They still had their clothes on—funny that the dream censored that—but they were definitely making love. Eric looked up at me and smiled, just the way he always does, and then I saw the woman's red hair and her pale, laughing face. Emma.

Should I tell Eric about this dream? Should I tell Emma? She'll laugh, I can hear her. It wasn't funny when it was happening, though. Not in the least.

I started to cry. My heart was broken. I went behind the door, hiding so they couldn't see me. But they did, and then I felt humiliated. Then—then it changed, and it was Eric and *me* making love, on his velour-upholstered sofa. With our clothes *off.* Emma appeared, hands on her hips. She said, "Well, *this* is just great, wait till Curtis hears about *this,*" and as soon as she said *Curtis,* I woke up and started shaking.

I could see the outline of his shoulder under the quilt, his back turned to me. I stared and stared, watching him breathe in and out, so frightened that somehow he knew what I'd dreamed and he was only pretending to be asleep. *It didn't mean anything,* I wanted to tell him. *Don't be sad, it didn't mean anything, I love only you.*

But, of course, the longer I stared, the more I woke up, and after a little while I slipped my arm around his waist and pressed up against him. And then I was safe.

But—should I tell Eric about this dream? At least he would know what it means. I could never tell Curtis, oh God, never. The sex wasn't even any good. If that makes a difference. In fact, it was better watching it than doing it. It meant something else besides sex, I'm sure, control or domination, maybe even love. Why is it that sex in dreams never seems to really mean sex? Like the death card in the Tarot never means death. Or so they always tell you. But was my dream a dream about what I want or what I fear? Or both?

I don't know, I don't know. But then, I never know anything. Once Eric said, "Rudy, what is the worst that could happen if you had a strong opinion about something and you were wrong?" But I don't think that's it, quite. I don't fear being wrong, I'm wrong all the time, ask Curtis. It's that—if you pick one thing to believe, you eliminate all the others. So it's not fair. Why choose, then? It's better, it's *gentler* not to. And also, it's important to leave yourself room to escape, always make sure there's a way out. Always have a hiding place.

No, I've decided. I'm not telling anyone about this dream.

Eric is fascinated by the Saving Graces. Whenever he gets glassy-eyed because I'm droning on about something that bores him, I can always wake him up by mentioning them. I think there's something sexual going on. He would probably deny it, but if you ask me, my therapist not only likes hearing about the Saving

Graces, he wouldn't mind sleeping with them, too. All of us, all at the same time.

Not that he would, of course, even if he could. Nobody's straighter than Eric. But deep, deep down in that noble unconscious, I'm pretty sure old Eric would like to shag us all.

"What do the Graces look like?" he asked me once. "What does Emma look like?"

"Oh, she's beautiful. I think—she doesn't, she thinks she's fat. She has reddish hair and white, white Irish skin that freckles in the summer and turns pink when she blushes—she can't hide anything. She tries to look cool all the time and she's got this careless air that fools people, but she's really—well, I was going to say as neurotic as I am, but let's not get carried away."

"Ha. And Isabel?"

"She's older, of course, but really pretty. To me. When I first met her she had gray hair, but now it's blonde. She has blue eyes. She's tall, but not as tall as me. She keeps in shape by walking a lot. In fact, she looks better now than before she got cancer." I couldn't really think of anything else to tell him. Isabel is a quiet person, and her looks are quiet, too. You have to be especially observant or else know her for a long time to really see how lovely she is.

"Lee's cute—which she hates, but it's true. She's tiny, she looks like an elf. Kids love her, and I always think it's partly because she's about their size. Dark hair, and for as long as I've known her she's worn it really, really short. She says it's more practical. Which is Lee to a *T*."

"So you're all good-looking," Eric said, rubbing his chin, with that certain light in his eye, innocent but interested, that always makes me laugh. He's so transparent sometimes.

"Why, thank you," I said, acknowledging the compliment to me. "I've never thought about it much, but I guess we are."

Yesterday he asked me, out of the blue, "How does Curtis feel about your women's group these days?"

"Curtis? Oh," I said, "he's ambivalent." A good catchall word that Eric, of all people, appreciates.

"But he was against it at first, wasn't he?"

"Oh . . ." Had I admitted that to him? It seemed disloyal now. "Maybe a little, but only in the beginning. And he never came out and said so, not in words. It's just that he's so busy."

"So . . . ?"

"So, he likes me to be there when he gets home."

Curtis is a legislative aide to Congressman Wingert; his days start at six and go until eight, nine, sometimes ten at night. He says, "I spend all day talking to assholes, Rudy, and when I come home I'd like you to be there." (I don't think this is unreasonable.) "I need to spend time with you," he says, "just the two of us. I *need* it, I don't just want it. You keep me in sync."

Imagine me maintaining anybody's equilibrium.

Eric said, "So . . . he didn't want you to join the group because it would—what? Take you out of the house too much?"

"No, that's not it. Nothing so—I don't know, what would you call it?"

He shrugged, but I knew what he was thinking: passive-aggressive.

Once I made the mistake of telling Eric about how Curtis enjoys warning me that biology is destiny. The biological imperative. Curtis says the strain of psychosis in my family runs so strong, it's probably congenital. Naturally Eric took offense at that. That's the last thing a psychiatrist wants to hear. (It's the last thing I want to hear, too, but I can't escape it. If Curtis isn't reminding me, I'm reminding myself.) The "heredity connection" goes against everything Eric believes in. He even questioned Curtis's motive in suggesting it.

But in the dark times, it makes perfect sense to me, and then Curtis is my comforter and my solace. He folds me in his arms and swears he'll protect me, and as long as he holds me like that I know I'm safe. I'm safe.

Eric says I take care of Curtis too much, but he doesn't understand. If anything, it's the other way around.

"And how do the other three Saving Graces feel about Curtis?" Eric asked after a couple of silent minutes.

"Oh, they don't talk about him much. That's not really what the group is, Eric. I mean, it's not like we sit around talking about men all the time."

He made a patient face. Eric usually knows, although not always, when I'm hedging.

"Okay, we do talk about Curtis some. Obviously. Away from the group, I probably talk most to Isabel about him."

"Really? Not Emma?"

"No, not Emma. No. Actually . . ." This memory is so painful, I try never to think about it. "Emma and I . . . the worst fight we ever had was over Curtis. Years ago. So now we just leave him out. Pretty much. Pleasantries—how's Curtis, fine, tell him I said hi—that's about it."

"You never told me this. A fight with Emma? When did it happen?"

I didn't want to tell him now. "A long time ago. I still think most of it was her fault."

"Why?"

"Because she waited until the eve of my wedding, I mean literally, the night before, to tell me what she really thinks of Curtis. I've forgiven her—well, there's nothing to forgive. But it's hard to forget."

"Well, tell me."

"It's really old news, Eric."

"I know, but I'm interested."

"Why?"

"Because. Come on, tell me."

I sighed, and told him.

It was four years ago, five in December. Curtis and I had been living together for years, forever, but on the night before the wedding he moved out, just for fun, and Emma came over to stay with me. She was maid of honor, and she was taking the job seriously, being very solicitous and practical and take-charge. Which was good, because I needed taking care of. My mother and stepfather had flown down from Rhode Island that day, my brother from L.A. that night, and my sister had a one-day pass from the cult and was due in the next morning. It was going to be the first time we'd all been together, all of us in one place, in about twenty-five years. Since my father's funeral.

So there was that, plus Curtis's parents who had come up from Georgia two days earlier and were staying at the Willard. I can never decide whose family makes me crazier, his or mine. He calls his people "Old South aristocrats," although how you can be aristocratic and stone broke at the same time, I'm not sure. The Lloyds have a kind of slow, brittle southern charm that freezes my New England blood. They smile and smile, but in their hearts I don't think there's anything but contempt. And none of them talk, they all *drawl.* They remind me of fat brown lizards sunning themselves on hot rocks, too lazy to move a muscle. They drink all the time, and publicly, not in secret like my family—gin martinis, three fingers of bourbon, scotch from tarnished sterling flasks, beakers of warm, smoky brandy. They've refined drinking to a delicate, sensual, obscene art. When we go for visits, I watch them like a voyeur; I feel like I'm viewing erotica from behind a hedge of magnolia or honeysuckle, and everything is sweet and cloying, and I can almost hear that character from Tennessee Williams yelling, "Men*da*city!"

Well, I'm exaggerating, but not much. Curtis claims I hyperbolize his family's eccentricities in order to minimize mine. That's true.

The night before the wedding, Emma came home with me after the rehearsal dinner. The plan was for her to spend the night, then get up early and help me dress for the wedding. We were both starving, even though we'd supposedly just eaten, so we made Spanish omelettes and opened a bottle of wine. This was after about two dozen champagne toasts at the rehearsal dinner, but by then I wasn't counting. I know I drink too much, but on this particular night that was only part of the problem.

We couldn't make ourselves go to bed. Midnight came, but we kept drinking and talking, singing along to the stereo. Exchanging final confidences as single women, I guess. But we were careful not to say that. In fact, we were pretending just the opposite—that nothing would change, my marrying Curtis was only a technicality. I remember Emma was sprawled on the floor in the living room—this was in my old D Street house on Capitol Hill, a dark, skinny row house with six rooms on three floors—and I was on the couch, in my oldest, raggediest nightgown, because I'd packed the good ones for the honeymoon.

"Of course I knew she didn't like Curtis," I told Eric. "I'd known that since I introduced them to each other ten years ago, not long after Curtis and I moved to Washington. But until that night she'd never said so. Well, not in words."

"Nice timing," Eric said sympathetically.

"Yeah."

It started out harmlessly. We were talking about Curtis's new job on the Hill, how much money he would make, how soon we could move to a bigger house. Emma said, "Yeah, that's great, but what I still don't get is the marriage part. I mean, why exactly do you have to *tie the knot*?" I was surprised by how riled she sounded, but I just said something about ritual and ceremony and public commitment—that standard answer.

It was June; hot; Emma had on a sleeveless football jersey and her underpants. She stuck her knees inside the jersey and wrapped her arms around her calves, shook her wild red hair out of her eyes. "Yes, but why not just keep living with him? Why bring the *law* into it?" And she made some joke about Mickey Rooney or Liz

Taylor, how much trouble they'd have saved themselves by just shacking up. We laughed, but it wasn't real. I saw anger when she flicked her eyes away from me.

That scared me, of course, but I said, "This might come as a surprise to you, but Curtis makes me happy. The problem is, Em, you've never known me without him. You don't know what I'm like when he's not around." I gave another false laugh. "I mean, if you think *this* is bad—"

"That's not true. Why are you saying that? I see you with him and I see you without him. When he's around, you don't even talk, Rudy. Or—you look at him, you check with him to make sure what you said was okay. That makes me *sick*."

The revulsion in her voice shocked both of us. I said, "That's a lie," without smiling, and we recoiled again. I got up and turned off the stereo.

Not once in all the years we'd been friends had we used that tone with each other. Or said words that blunt. *Lie*—that's such an ugly word; you only say it to a close friend if you're kidding.

Eric said, "You were frightened."

"I was. Scared to death. We'd had our differences, things that irritated us about each other, but we'd always smoothed them over with humor. Emma's good at getting a serious point across by making a joke—that's her style, and it works for her. She doesn't think anybody knows it, but she'll do almost anything to avoid a confrontation. Because she's afraid of anger. Especially mine, I think." I laughed. "If you can believe that."

"You were *both* scared."

"Yes. Scared and mad and drunk."

That night she tried to pacify me by saying, "Is it because you want children? You and Curtis? I could understand getting married for kids."

"No," I said, "of course not. I want kids, but that's not why I'm marrying him. Emma, why are you being so . . ." Awful pause while we both looked at everything except each other. "I love Curtis. Why is that so hard to understand? Curtis is *good* for me."

"No, he's not." She stood up, glass of warm Chardonnay in one hand, lit cigarette in the other, big maroon "28" on her chest—some Redskin's number. Emma doesn't drink that much, and she only smokes when she's with me, so this was really an incongruous pose. And. . . cute. There's no other word for it. I was dying for her to say something funny now, to erase this conversation, get us back where we'd always been. But she said, "I don't know how, but he's made you *think* he's good for you. Can't you see that's just his trick?"

"His trick? Oh, for—"

"Oh, Rudy, you are so much stronger than he lets you believe! Would you have dropped out of school if it weren't for Curtis? No, and you'd have a real job by now, you'd have a profession."

"Oh, now you don't like my job, either. Well, great, this is just wonderful." Oh, that really hurt. I was selling designer jewelry in a Georgetown boutique, and okay, it wasn't my life's work, but it was all right and I was pretty good at it. But it certainly wasn't Curtis's fault. We moved to D.C. after he graduated from law school, and—well, I just never went back to finish my art history master's. I said, "How in the world is Curtis responsible for what my job is? What do you think he did, *force* me to quit school?"

"Yeah, that's exactly what I think. Only he did it so you didn't even know he was doing it."

"Oh, that's funny. You are so full of it, it's—"

"Rudy, he's manipulative and controlling—those words were *invented* for Curtis Lloyd, and I don't know why you can't see it! He makes you think *you're* crazy, and meanwhile he's this creepy southern sociopath, like Bruce Dern when he used to play those psychotic bayou maniacs—"

I threw a CD at her. It hit her on the side of the throat and made a little cut—tiny, but it bled. She went paper white. We gaped at each other, completely horrified, and both wanting the other to apologize first. If we hadn't been drinking since five o'clock in the afternoon, I know we'd have found a way out, some face-saving retreat. Oh, but we were drunk. And we were both just so tired of lying about Curtis.

Eric was staring at me as if I had two heads. "You did that? You really threw a CD?"

"You can't picture it, can you?" I didn't blame him; I'm notoriously nonviolent.

"What happened? How did it end?"

"I told her if she felt that way about Curtis, maybe she ought not to come to my wedding."

Eric has enormous brown eyes, like a figure in a Velázquez painting. When he opens them wide behind his steel-rimmed glasses, I know I've said something amazing.

"And she said, 'All right, if that's what you want,' and I said, 'I think it's what you want.' She said, 'Well, what do *you* want?' and we went around like that for a while. That's another thing Emma's good at—hiding behind questions, throwing up diversions. People who don't know her think she's really frank and open, but she's not. She's one of the most reserved people I know."

"Did she go to the wedding?"

"Oh, sure. But we didn't resolve anything."

"Did she spend the night?"

"Yes, because we just let it go. We chickened out. I started taking plates and glasses out to the kitchen, and when I came back she was standing over her suitcase, pulling on her jeans. I was shaking inside, walking stiff, like a puppet. I said, 'So you're going home?' She said, 'Yeah.' She didn't look at me, but I could tell by her voice she was crying. And that did it, that just killed me. Because she never cries. So we both started crying, and I told her I wanted her to come to my wedding, and she said she wanted to come, and that was sort of the end of it. But we didn't make up, not really, and neither of us ever apologized. We just went to bed. Or passed out, in my case. I took some pills and went to sleep, just—got *out* of there.

"The wedding—God, the wedding was horrible. I woke up with a headache that lasted for three days. I could see the little scratch on her neck above the collar of her maid-of-honor suit, and every time I saw it I'd sink down into this black hole of depression. Lee and Isabel were the bridesmaids, and it only took them about thirty seconds to realize something was wrong between us. Emma and I stayed mad at each other for three months."

"But you reconciled."

"Yes. Finally. I wish I'd known you then," I said, and Eric smiled.

"How did it come about? The reconciliation."

"Oh, well . . . I can't tell you that. It's Emma's story, not mine. Another calamity involving a man, but that's all I can say. But it was her man that time, not mine."

Eric couldn't stop shaking his head. "How did you feel when she told you Curtis was manipulative and—what was it? Manipulative and—"

"She called him a sociopath, Eric, that's what she called him, and how do you think I felt? It was like a stab in my heart. These are the two people in the world I love most, and I can't stand it that they hate each other. But he *doesn't* hate her, and that makes it even worse. He never says *anything* bad about her, he never has."

"Do you think so? Rudy, do you really think Curtis likes Emma?"

I said, "The only good thing about my wedding was, we finally got to meet Lee's boyfriend. Although he wasn't her boyfriend yet, it was their first date. 'Henry the plumber' we'd been calling him. We were dying to meet him, because you know Lee, the original Jewish American princess, and she was absolutely in *lust* with this man who was installing heating ducts and copper wiring in her basement. But we all ended up falling in love with him, and so did she, and nine months later she married him."

And that was the end of our fifty minutes.

7

Emma

What do you do when you look at a piece of modern art and it looks like nothing at all, your mind goes blank, and you can't even think of a joke or something smart-mouthed to say about it if you happen to be viewing it with a pal, and all you can think is, Either I'm crazy or you are, Mr. Big Shot Artist, and since you've got this exhibit in a real building and all these people are standing around contemplating your stuff and saying intelligent things about it, it must be me? Well, what do you do?

What I do is get out as fast as I can without saying much of anything, and I also try to drink as much of the cheap white wine as I can if it's an opening, so at least the night isn't a total loss, and plus I find I have a lot more to say about the artist's oeuvre if I am, how shall I say, slightly oiled.

But these solutions don't apply if you're in his studio with the artiste himself, and it's just you, him, and his work. And say his work mystifies you; it might be priceless, it might be dreck, you don't have a clue. And say you're supposed to be doing a serious, paid, legitimate piece on the artist for the major newspaper that employs you, and, oh yeah, you also have this painful, yearning, lustful attraction to the artist's body, not to mention a helpless and wholly out of character passion for his heart, both of which are married? Then what?

You're fucked.

"So, Mick. Tell me the story of how you went from patent law to fine art. Constitution Avenue to Seventh Street." It's never too early to start thinking in headlines, I always say. "Bourgeois to Bauhaus. Buttoned-down to PoMo."

"Well—"

"And while you're at it, what exactly is postmodernism?"

When I'm nervous, I become insufferable. I can see it happening, but I can't stop it, can't shut up, and the more important the occasion is to me, the more obnoxious I get. Today, boy, I was really outdoing myself.

We were standing in the middle of Mick Draco's chilly, cluttered studio, which was smaller than I'd expected, considering he shares it with two other people. Richard, the photographer from the paper, had just left after taking about two hundred pictures, from every angle you can imagine and some you'd never dream of, of Mick smearing yellow paint on a canvas with a trowel. I got a good, long look at him then, because I didn't have to talk, I could just stare. I lied, I have three weaknesses. I don't like to admit to the third one. It's physical beauty. I know, I'm shallow, and I hate it. Sometimes I go out with unattractive men on purpose so no one can accuse me of superficiality. But in truth, all other things being equal, I'd rather they were good-looking.

Watching him, I decided Mick's beauty came from the way he moved as much as from his great-looking body, and his facial expressions—humor and self-consciousness, patience, rapt concentration, finally impatience—as much as the handsome face itself. He was wearing black slacks, a tweed jacket, a blue work shirt, and a red tie, and I had on jeans and a T-shirt, and I was thinking it was funny, maybe kind of sweet, that he'd dressed up and I'd dressed down. As if we'd been thinking about each other when we put our clothes on this morning.

To his credit, he didn't even try to answer any of my facetious questions. He said, "Would you like to sit down?" He took an oily rag from his work table and swished it around a coating of plaster dust on the only chair in the room.

I gave the dirty chair a look and said, "Uh, no thanks," sort of deadpan.

He has a beautiful smile, truly self-deprecating. He lowers his eyelashes, which are longer than mine, and curves his lips up at the sharp corners, and you imagine he's thinking, *That's a good joke on me*. He sort of mumbled, "Yeah, I guess this isn't the best place to talk. Want to go across the street?"

Yes! Yes! Let's go there again, Murray's, that dump with the rotten food and congealed air, where everybody looks like a corpse and the coffee tastes like antifreeze! Let's sit across from each other in a cracked booth by the smudged window in the livid light, like we did last week, and talk and talk and talk!

"Yeah, okay," I mumbled back. "If you want to."

On the way, huddled in our coats against the November drizzle, he answered the main question, or I guess he thought he did. I was struck again by the idea that he was shy, or at least deeply reserved, because of the way he turned away from me, peering down shiny, wet G Street while he explained what had to be one of the most significant events of his life. I could barely hear him. And he'd picked the least focused, most distracted moment to deal with the subject—us in the middle of traffic—as if he wanted to slip his answer in without anyone noticing. "I got into art when it felt like I could get into it," he said—or I thought he said; he was muttering again. "You were joking about postmodernism—"

"No, I wasn't."

"—but you know it redeemed representation in some ways, made the figure respectable again, I guess you could say. Brought back the concept of meaning in painting. Which wasn't allowed so much during modernism."

He took my arm in the intersection, and we scuttled across. I said, brilliantly, "Come again?"

He cleared his throat. "Abstraction never appealed to me, I

couldn't feel it or understand it. I looked at it and knew I couldn't do it, and I was proud or stupid enough to think that meant I couldn't be an artist. Yeah, stupid. Stupid enough. Years." He muttered something I couldn't hear. I started to say, "What?" but he was holding the door open, so I passed him and went inside.

Murray's has a counter on the right with cracked red leatherette stools, and on the left a row of cracked red leatherette booths. Last week we sat at the counter, but today we took a booth. The decor . . . think of a bus station coffee shop in Trenton. The walls are lined with blurry, sepia-colored mirrors, and you start when you first catch sight of yourself, because in the sick fluorescent glare you don't look nearly as bad as the person you're talking to does; the grease on the mirrors acts like a gauze filter, and you actually look pretty good. The temperature hovers around eighty degrees, which is why artists in the lofts and studios in this neighborhood come here, Mick says: to get warm. "Coffee?" he asked. I nodded, and he went up to the counter to get it. You wait on yourself at Murray's.

"So," I said when he returned, my pencil poised, notebook open. Ready for business. "You're saying you became a painter because the postmodern atmosphere in the art world finally freed you to feel like one."

"No, that sounds ridiculous. Don't write that."

I'd thought it sounded pretty good. "Well, what? This is a piece about people who give up straight jobs that aren't satisfying them for a dream they think will." I'd explained that before, but I was thinking we both needed to hear it again. "What I'm looking for is policy wonks who decide to be forest rangers. Dentists who want to write mystery novels. Washington's perfect for this, people love to read about some guy at the Bureau of Standards who threw it all away to become a horse jockey or a mime, a dog trainer, a Deadhead—"

"I know, I understand what you're after."

"Okay. Well, let's try it this way. What was wrong with patent law? Why did you leave that profession?"

He smiled at me, light eyes twinkling. "I'm impressed."

"How come?"

"You asked me that with a straight face."

I laughed. I felt light and airy inside, buoyant for some reason. Well, he looked so appreciative. As if he was noticing things about me and he liked them. But he wasn't coming on to me, he just liked me. We sat for a minute, not talking, just stirring our coffees and pulling one-ply napkins out of the metal dispenser.

"Well, anyway." My notebook recalled me to my purpose. "Back to postmodernism. Now, you—"

"No, Emma, forget that. I'll tell you the truth." But he looked pained.

I said, "Fine," uncertainly. "But it's not a police interrogation or anything. Don't tell me anything that's going to hurt anybody." The hard-hitting investigative journalist at work. Earlier, he'd asked me not to tape our conversation, and usually I push that a little, try to assure the interviewee that it won't hurt a bit, it's for my convenience but also for his protection, blah blah. But when Mick asked, I gave in without a fight.

He rested his forearms on the table and hunched his shoulders, circling the thick, stained coffee cup with his hands. Nice hands, by the way, bony and smart, long-fingered. "It's . . . well, it's not exactly a secret." He looked up, looked me in the eye.

I stared back without blinking, trying to project professionalism and integrity. But I felt like a doe caught in a flashlight beam. It was so obvious he was sizing me up, trying to decide if he could trust me. I kept quiet—what could I say?—but the phrase that kept coming to my mind was *Oh, Mick, if you only knew*.

He sat back, twisting sideways so he could slouch against the wall, one foot drawn up on the cracked seat. He loosened his tie. "Draco is a Greek name," he said conversationally. I scribbled down "Greek," although I didn't know what to think yet, wasn't sure what he'd decided. "My father is Philip Draco. Do you know the name?" I shook my head. "Percy, Wells, Draco, & Dunn. Pretty well-known law firm, offices in most of the big cities. My name isn't Draco, though."

I looked up. "It's not?"

"I mean it's not my real name, my birth name. I was adopted. Never knew my real parents."

"Oh."

"I was an only child, and I grew up knowing what I was supposed to be—a lawyer like my dad. Who is a good man," he added, "really a great man in some ways. He's brilliant at his work, probably one of the top fifty lawyers in the country."

"Did you grow up in Washington?"

"Chicago."

"How old were you when you found out you were adopted?"

"I always knew."

"Even when you were little?"

"I never remember not knowing it." He hesitated, started to fiddle with the paper place mat, a child's map of D.C.'s major tourist attractions. "Believe me, no one wanted to make me feel as if I were on trial. My parents were terrific. Anything like that, I did it to myself. Because . . ." He held his empty cup up and scrutinized the manufacturer's name on the bottom.

I know better than to prompt someone I'm interviewing. But I said, "Because you didn't want them to be sorry. For choosing you."

"That's it." The surprise and the gratitude in his face were too good—they made me dizzy. I grabbed his coffee cup and mine, got up, and went to the counter for refills. Now all I could think was, *We have to stop having these moments*.

But when I came back and sat down, and stirred and sipped and acted normal, I noticed he was looking at me in a new way. You know how you can tell when you've done or said something, inadvertently or not, that makes the other person go to the next level, so to speak, some alternate way of seeing you? And sometimes that's good, and sometimes you wish you'd been more circumspect? I couldn't decide which it was in this case, but one thing was clear: Mick didn't just interest me anymore. I interested him.

I picked up my pencil. He resumed.

"About four years ago, after giving it a lot of thought, I made up my mind to try to find out who my birth mother was. By then I'd been practicing law for seven years. Not very happily. Miserably," he said with a laugh, glancing up. "I was married, my son was almost two. Sally—that's my wife—she'd quit her job after Jay was born so she could be a full-time mother."

"What was her job?" I sounded businesslike, as if the story would crumble without that vital tidbit.

"She was a paralegal. That's how we met."

Paralegal, I wrote. "And did you find your mother?"

"Eventually. I should tell you something about myself first. I've always painted or sketched or sculpted or built constructions, collages—I've always made things. Even as a kid."

"You've always been an artist."

"Well, but I didn't call it that. It would never have occurred to me. We didn't have any artists in my family, not even remotely. A second cousin who dabbles in photography—that's it. Except for him, nothing."

It hit me. "*Your mother.* You found her—and? Who was she? What was she?"

He smiled; he liked my excitement. "Yeah, I found her. When she gave me up, she was a second-year student at the Art Institute in Chicago."

"My God. Mick, oh, wow, that's amazing."

"I thought you'd like that. It makes a good story for you, doesn't it?"

"Are you kidding?" My CPA-turned-bluegrass fiddler, my UPS man-turned-pentecostal preacher—they were in danger of looking anemic in comparison. "This is terrific, this could be the *whole* story. So do you see her now? What does she do, is she still—"

"I've never met her."

"Oh. No?"

"I wrote her a letter, and I know she got it, but she didn't write back. So I had to let it go. I never tried to see her."

He has a way of compressing his lips in a tight half-smile when he says things that pain him. It discourages sympathy. I took the hint and didn't offer any. But I hurt for him.

"The point is," he said after a moment, "finding that out about my mother was like"—he touched his fingertips to his temple, then flung his hand out—"an explosion. When the smoke cleared, everything fell into place—I knew what I was supposed to do. For the first time, I really understood myself."

"Wow." I felt a definite spark of envy. "Like figuring out you're gay and coming out of the closet or something."

"Exactly. Not that it happened overnight. Don't misunderstand—it took about a year for the smoke to clear."

"Well, that was the lawyer part, I guess. You know, being cautious."

"Partly."

He didn't elaborate on that, and I started thinking how I might phrase a question about his wife, how all this had sat with her. But then—I didn't. In the same situation, I'd have asked it of somebody else. But my motives were impure. I couldn't quite bring myself to ask it of Mick.

Instead I asked him about the early days, and if it had been scary resigning from his job. He said it was terrifying; his paycheck went from—he caught himself. "It dropped about ninety-eight percent," he said, watching me write that down. "I've been a full-time painter for three years now, and I've sold two paintings, both to friends. I may *never* make any money." But I don't think he believed that, because he said it without any anxiety, and he didn't strike me as the kind of man who could indulge himself without guilt indefinitely.

A kindred spirit.

He'd opened the door, though, and I had a responsibility to walk through it. "Your wife—um—"

"Sally."

"Sally." I wrote it down. "So she's okay with all this, she's—"

"She's been great. She's been great." He nodded and nodded, and I scribbled, *S. been great*. I looked at him expectantly. It's amazing how much you can get out of someone by saying nothing, just waiting. Mick rubbed his cheek in a raspy circle—he needed a shave—and finally said, "Jay's in day care—well, you know that, you know Lee Patterson—because Sally's had to go back to work. She's an administrative assistant at the Labor Department."

"Uh-huh."

"She had to do it. Otherwise we'd've starved. And we've moved to Columbia Heights."

"From?"

"Q Street, Dupont Circle. Near the Park."

"Uh-huh."

"We're fixing up an old row house."

"Been there."

"Really?"

"Well, no, I mean, I just bought one. An old town house. Somebody else fixed it up."

"Uh-huh." He smiled, but I think he was mimicking me. "Well, that's a little different."

"I guess." The change of address suggested he'd come down in the world, and his manner said he minded. What wasn't clear was if he minded for himself or for Sally, and I couldn't think of a way to ask. Not that it was any of my business.

I glanced over my notes. "So tell me, what would you call the kind of art you're doing now?"

He put his chin on his knee, frowning. "What would you call it?" I gave a nervous laugh, but he wasn't being hostile or aggressive. He sounded curious.

"Listen, Mick, I have to tell you, I don't know the first thing about art. Honestly, I'm a complete dunce, so if you want this article to sound good and be true, you should talk to me straight. In fact, you should talk down to me. Pretend I'm your kid." He laughed. God, I liked making him laugh. I liked it too much. "Failing that, just talk very, very slowly."

So he did. At length. The gist of it was that he hadn't found his own style yet, or even his true subject, but he was working in a formalist, figural mode because he needed the practice and because abstraction was a dead end for him. He thought postmodernism wasn't a real epoch, just the last gasp of modernism before the next phase started. He wouldn't presume to say what that would be like, but when I pressed, he said he thought it might involve a revival of formal excellence, which contemporary art was incapable of and had therefore cynically dismissed.

I asked him who he admired, and he said Rembrandt, Fantin-Latour, Arshile Gorky, Alice Neel, Eric Fischl. Who did he hate? He said he would tell me, but only off the record, and then he rattled off about five names, all men, none I'd ever heard of. He saw himself moving more and more toward portraiture, he said; in fact, lately he'd noticed a recurring character in his paintings and sketches, a young man, maybe an adolescent, whom he was calling "Joe" and who he thought was probably himself. Color was his strength, drawing his weakness; he took two different drawing classes, four nights a week, and he was beginning to see a little progress. He wished he had the time and money to go for a master of fine arts somewhere, because he was at a point where his lack of formal training was becoming more and more of a handicap.

I got most of it down, but the longer he talked, the more distracted I got. He was so beautifully intense. Art was his passion, obviously, it bordered on his obsession, and I am such a sucker for men who really love their work. I find their single-mindedness incredibly sexy and desirable. And the best part is, they don't depend on *me* to make sense out of their lives.

I ran out of questions. I glanced at my watch.

"Let's eat something, I'm starting to shake." Mick held out his hand; sure enough, his fingers were trembling. "I never drink coffee like this," he admitted and got up to go to the men's room.

We ordered cheeseburgers, french fries, and milkshakes, the kind of food we both swore we never ate, but I noticed we polished it all off without any trouble. While we ate, he asked *me* questions. At first I didn't even notice; it seemed like the usual give-and-take, just normal conversation. But when he said, "Is newspaper work what you've always wanted to do? Or—if you suddenly found out you had a different birth mother, who would you like her to be?"—I realized he was turning the tables and interviewing me.

Okay, I was flattered. In my experience, the majority of people don't care that much about other people's inner lives. They're nice, they're polite, they ask how you're doing—and as soon as you start telling them they click off. Their eyes glaze, they go into wait mode, and what they're waiting for is you to run down or take a breath, so they can jump in and tell you how much more interesting their lives are than yours. This isn't cynicism. I'm telling you, it happens all the time.

The exception, of course, is men who are trying to sleep with you. The better they are at it, the harder they listen; the more they want you, the more entranced they become by your every random utterance. What's funny is that this tried-and-true method really works, at least on me. As one who has, as they say, been around the block a few times, I ought to know better, but I don't. It gets me every time.

So it was with considerably mixed feelings that I stared back into Mick Draco's intelligent brown eyes, currently focused on me with much interest and expectancy, and contemplated his acute question. *Are you trying to seduce me?* I asked him via mental telepathy. *God, I hope so.*

No, I don't, I'd hate that.

"Mary McCarthy."

His eyebrows shot up. "The writer?"

"Yeah, or Iris Murdoch. Katherine Anne Porter. No, not really—I was trying to think of who'd be the right age to give birth to me about forty years ago. Thirty-nine." *Shit*, I told him my age. And he was younger! Only one year, but still.

"Oh, so you'd like to write fiction?"

Now that was the really disconcerting thing, not that I'd told him my age but that I'd told him my secret dream. Not that secret—the Graces know, although Rudy's the only one who knows how *much* I want it; and my mother knows; a couple of ex-boyfriends know, because I was stupid enough to blurt it out to them. But it's *supposed* to be a secret. Why? Because I hate to fail in public. And because the journalist-who-yearns-to-write-the-great-American-novel is such a foolish, humiliating cliché, I don't care to be associated with it.

But I was speaking to a man who had given up lawyering for painting. If anyone would understand the dream, it ought to be Mick. So I didn't back down or try to wriggle out with a joke, I looked straight at him and said, "Yes, I would. Someday. It's what I want to do most. But I'm, you know. Afraid."

"Yeah," he said, as if nothing could be more natural. "Because it's terrifying."

"It is, it's terrifying." Just thinking about it was scaring me.

"So what are you going to do?"

"Hm? Well, I've written some short stories that stink, nobody wants them." Defenses creeping back; arms halfway into full metal jacket. "And I'm playing around with something longer, but it's no good. Really. I'm not being modest."

"Has anybody read it?"

"Are you kidding?" I laughed, ha ha. "Luckily, I've got a very highly developed sense of shame, it keeps me out of all sorts of trouble."

Mick smiled and looked away.

I went cold, realizing he was a little embarrassed. For me. Because what I'd said was so transparent.

"I wonder," he said slowly, "which is more personal, a painting or a poem. I wonder which one is more revealing."

"That's easy. A poem."

"How come?"

"Because it's easier to hide behind a painting."

"Is it? Why?"

I grinned, trying to win him back with candor. "Because I don't understand paintings."

"I don't understand poems."

I laughed, but he didn't. "Okay," I said testily, "I get your point."

"What point?"

"You're braver than I am. You're a hero, I'm a chicken. Look, I'm not arguing with you, you're right. No contest."

"That's not what I meant. Wait a second, that's not what I'm saying, I'm—"

"Okay, my mistake. Forget it, it doesn't matter anyway. I don't even know what we're talking about."

His sigh sounded exasperated. "I'm quite sure I'm not braver than you are, Emma."

"Well, but you don't know me."

"True, but I can tell you're not a chicken."

"How?" Oh, how embarrassing, how childish, how immature, how pathetic, how needy. "Hm? How can you tell?"

He never got to answer. The ear-splitting siren of a police car, then an ambulance, then another police car made it impossible to talk. Mick smiled and shrugged, and turned around to watch them roar by in the bleary, grease-smeared window. "Oh, no. My God, it's ten to three."

I saw the clock over the front door. "So—?"

He started rooting around in his pockets, hunting for his wallet. He looked stunned. "I've got to pick up Jay. I'm sorry, I had no idea it was this late, I've got ten minutes to get to Judiciary Square. But I can make it. But how did this happen? So—did we finish?"

"Yeah, I guess." I couldn't think; my mind had blanked. "I'll get this," I said, shoving dollar bills back at him.

"No—"

"It's on the paper. I've got an expense account."

"Oh. Okay. Look, I'm sorry I have to go, but I have to."

"Sure. Go. Take the subway, it's only one stop."

"No, I think I'll just run." He stood over me, frowning and smiling, smoothing his hair back, harried, uncertain. "Well, so. If you need to ask me any more questions, you know how to get in touch with me, I guess."

"Right. And here's my card, you can call me if, you know, you think of anything else."

"It should be a great article."

"Thanks for a terrific interview."

"I really enjoyed it. Obviously." He made a sheepish gesture back at the clock.

"Yeah, me, too."

"Well. Good luck to you."

"Thanks. I'll be looking for your stuff in *Art World* from now on."

"Ha."

I finally had to stop smiling. Mick's face changed from hectic courtesy to awareness. For the space of about three seconds, we were both naked. I started to say something, but then I couldn't.

He couldn't either. It was over, it was ending. Hello, good-bye. If we shook hands—

But no—he just said my name and bowed his head, and I saw his lips press together in that grimacing smile he makes when things aren't good. And then he walked out of my life without touching me.

Which was just as well. Close call. I might not have let go.

I took the bus home. I've got a car, but I like to take the bus or the subway around the city, it gives me time to think. If I'm in a good mood, I like to look at my fellow passengers and speculate on their lives, measure them on the narrow, unforgiving scale of Emma's Criteria for Normalcy. If I'm in a bad mood, I like to sink deeper and deeper into it while I stare lifelessly out the window of the No. 42 or the Red Line Metro, converting every building, every pedestrian, every telephone pole into a metaphor for corruption, decay, and urban ennui. It cheers me up.

But today I was beyond bad moods or good moods. I was flummoxed. I couldn't understand myself. I'm my best friend, I trust me, I keep a constant conversation going with myself—audible, if I'm alone—and it's important to me that I know myself. Vital. Otherwise, *chaos*.

Why was I devastated? Oh, please. Even the word *devastated* offends me, it's so melodramatic. I drank coffee all afternoon with a man, and we talked. It was a good conversation, and there had been bursts of honesty that thrilled me, little explosions of candor that don't occur that often between me and other people, except for Rudy, and hardly ever between me and the men I've been seeing for, oh, the last five years or so. Especially sober.

Fine, but it still wasn't that extraordinary. If Mick had let me record the interview, I could play it back, and I bet I'd scratch my head and think, *What's the big deal?* On the surface, not that much happened. Why was I in such disarray? And pain. I felt like an accident had happened to me, but I was hurt in a place I couldn't put my finger on. All over.

Sense of proportion needed here. I saw something I wanted and I can't have it, that's all. They call it loss, and the standard reaction is grief. So I'm normal. And how long can it last? Not long—I'm Emma DeWitt, not Emma Bovary.

At four o'clock in the afternoon, my house was as dark as nighttime. I went around turning on lamps, turning up the heat, wondering if I should get a cat. Or a bird, one that would make a lot of noise when I came home. I made a cup of tea—more caffeine, that's the ticket—and leafed through my boring mail. Then I watched the rain glide down the kitchen window in long, slow, monotonous trails.

The phone rang, and my heart flipped right into my throat.

"Hello?"

"Sondra?"

"Who?"

"Oh. Sor—" Click.

Same to you.

Well, that was a revealing little incident. I felt weak in the knees. Elbows on the counter, I held my head in my hands and wallowed in misery for one full minute.

Mick wasn't going to call me. In my heart, I didn't even want him to. And I wasn't going to dream up some specious, last-minute interview question and call him. Both of us were better than that.

There's some comfort in finality, even if it's grim. I hate ambiguity, give me all or nothing. I can take nothing as long as it really is nothing, undiluted by hope or *yes, but maybe if*.

I would take a bath, I decided. I'm a shower person, but there's something healing about submersion in scalding water when you've got the blues. A bath, or a bowl of hot oatmeal with lots of butter—those are the two best depression remedies I know. Well, no, but they're the two wholesomest. And I'd take the phone in the tub with me and call Rudy. Curtis wouldn't be home yet, she'd be able to talk.

Upstairs in my study, the answering machine was blinking a message.

"Hi, Em, it's Lee, it's Monday, it's approximately. . . two-forty-seven in the afternoon. I'm calling to see if you can come to dinner on Friday."

Great! A diversion. And I hadn't seen Henry, who cracks me up, in ages.

"Are you still seeing that Brad, the engineering consultant guy?" Unfortunately, yes. "Well, anyway, bring him if you want to, or anybody else, whoever you'd like. Or come alone if you'd rather, it doesn't matter. Although the table won't be balanced." Gotcha. "So, I really hope you can make it and it's not too short notice." Lee has a wonderfully flattering misconception of my social life. "Very informal, just pot luck, come in anything." Meaning I'd show up in leggings and a sweater, and she'd wear a two-hundred-dollar hostess gown. Do they still call them that, "hostess gowns"?

"I think the only other couple I'm asking is the Dracos. I ran into Sally yesterday, and then I remembered you already know Mick, so I thought it might be fun if we all got together. You'll like Sally, Em, she's smart. And nice, I'm really having fun getting to know her."

Oh Jesus Christ God Almighty.

"Well, okay, call me when you get a chance, I'll be home all evening. Or tomorrow—leave a message if you're out all night gallivanting. Ha ha. B'bye."

As I say, I hate ambiguity. It makes dealing with simultaneous joy and wretchedness a special challenge. I headed back downstairs because it was time for the big guns. A bowl of oatmeal *in* a scalding hot bath.

8

Lee

I'd have enjoyed my dinner party more if Emma and Mick Draco, Sally's husband, had gotten along better. I think it's rude to bring your personal animosities to a social function; it discomfits everybody. Not that they had a fight—far from it; they didn't even speak. They barely *looked* at each other, and I for one think that's discourteous. To each other, certainly, but even more, to the hostess. Me. Clearly their interview last Monday didn't go well, but that's not *my* fault.

I smoothed things over as best I could, and a less perceptive observer probably wouldn't even have noticed anything amiss. Henry didn't, as he told me afterward when we discussed it. But that's a man for you. Women are the discerning ones when it comes to the dynamics of interpersonal relationships.

After dinner, I served dessert (apple mousse with drizzled calvados sauce) in the living room. "How long have you two been married?" Sally asked sociably, sipping coffee.

"Four years," I said. "And you and Mick?"

"Six. Six?" She looked at her husband, who nodded. "Gosh, it doesn't seem that long. How did you meet? I love to hear stories about how happy couples first got together, don't you?" She's such a friendly woman, and I appreciated her effort to keep the conversation fresh and interesting—like me, she must've noticed the strain between Mick and Emma.

I started to answer, but Henry spoke first. "Well, I was driving home from work one day, and I got a call on the car phone from my mom. She was stuck on a job in Alexandria and wanted me to take her last call."

"Oh, your mother's a—?"

"She's a plumber, like me. I'm the son in Patterson and Son."

"Oh, really? I didn't realize that."

"Yeah, so she asked me to take her last job for her, some lady in Maryland with a stopped-up toilet."

Sally laughed. "How romantic! I'm assuming this was Lee."

Henry nodded. "I drove over to Chevy Chase and knocked on the door—this door—and that was that. One look, and I was gone."

"Aww," Emma said. "What were you wearing, Lee?"

"Oh, golly, I don't remember."

"I do." Henry grinned, slanting me a lazy-eyed look that brought back some memories. "A little checked suit, with a vest and a black bowtie. Masculine, you know, which made me want to laugh, 'cause she sure wasn't masculine. And she had on real high heels, red ones, but still she only came up to my chin. She was cute as a basket o' kittens."

Now, I've never owned a pair of red high heels in my life. Burgundy, yes, and a pair of medium-heeled cranberry patent leather pumps, but no red. I don't mention that when Henry recounts this story, however; the memory is so clear to him, and evidently so satisfying, I would never want to correct it.

I, on the other hand, remember perfectly what *he* wore that first day: his blue uniform and his tool belt. With scuffed work boots. And he had that gorgeous southern accent, and even though his eyes said he wanted to eat me up, still he was *so* polite and painstakingly gentle and careful of me in every way, even then, when all we were talking about was toilets. I'm the one who was "gone."

"After I finished the repair, she gave me a cup of tea and a cookie—"

"A scone." I had to correct that.

"A scone, and we sat at the kitchen table and talked for an hour and a half."

"What about?" Sally looked fascinated.

Henry and I glanced at each other and shrugged. "I couldn't tell you," he said, "but by the time I left, she'd hired me to tear out all her old water pipes and put in new copper."

"And after that, all new heating ducts."

"And then whole-house air-conditioning."

"Then we had to get married," I joked, "because I was broke."

Sally got up to pour everybody more coffee. "What about you, Emma? How did you and Brad meet?" She smiled invitingly, trying to disarm Emma, who squirmed and scowled and pretended she wasn't uncomfortable.

"Oh, you know," she mumbled, "the usual. A bar."

"Uh-oh," Sally said humorously, "*this* sounds interesting."

"Not really."

Brad, beside Emma on the sofa, put his hand on her thigh. She looked very pretty tonight, I thought, with proper makeup on for a change and her hair in a French braid. She'd dressed up, too—I couldn't remember the last time I'd seen Emma in a skirt. She must like Brad; she doesn't usually go to so much trouble for her dates. Brad said, "Well, *I* thought it was pretty interesting. She played hard to get, I had to use all my masculine charm."

"You just had to keep buying drinks."

"She's kidding," I assured Sally—Emma's humor can be a little difficult until you know her. And even then.

"I was with a couple of guys from the office, and Emma was with a girlfriend—"

"Who?" I interrupted, curious. I'd never heard this story.

"You don't know her," Emma told me, "a woman from the paper. You know, it really isn't all that—"

"This was at Shannon's on L Street, a weeknight, a Wednesday night," Brad went on, "that time between happy hour and dinner, when you can't decide whether to go home or stay and make a night of it." He's an engineer, and always very precise. Except for being good-looking, he's not really Emma's type, I wouldn't have said. Too normal.

"My table was next to hers. I'd been staring at her all night, of course, and when she got up to go to the ladies' room, I stood up too. I said—well, you tell it."

"No, you," Emma said quickly. She looked completely blank.

"Okay—I said, 'Can I tell you a joke?' and she said, 'Why?' and I said, 'Because you've got a great laugh and I want to hear it again.'"

"Oh, that's a *wonderful* line," Sally said. "Isn't that a good line?" she asked her husband, and he said yes, great.

"So then it took another hour to talk her into having dinner with me—right, Em?—and by then we were both feeling no pain, so—"

"See?" Emma interrupted, crossing her leg to move his hand. "This isn't interesting at all."

"—so then it only took *two* more hours to talk her into letting me take her home. And then we—"

"Story over," Emma snapped. "We lived happily ever after."

"Okay, okay," Brad said, laughing, "fade to black. I'm getting that the rest of this is censored."

Sally laughed knowingly. "And how long have you been together?"

Emma shrugged.

Brad said, "Four, going on five months now. That's right, because it was the night after the Fourth of July, and the subway was still littered with trash. Remember, Em?"

"Right," she said, shaking her head no.

I looked at Emma more closely, to see if she was really blushing. *Yes*—she ducked her head, but I saw her cheeks flush. Well, how interesting. She doesn't make it a habit, as far as I know, to pick up men in bars and take them home with her—but at the same time, she's not the kind of woman who would care that much if anybody *thought* she did; she'd say, "Screw you," and go on about her business. But here she was, turning red from embarrassment because apparently she and Brad had slept with each other on their first date. Very interesting. It had to be because of Sally, who's so fresh and wholesome. Emma must be worried about offending her.

"Well," Sally said, sliding her arm through Mick's, "*we* met when he rescued me. My shining knight. He foiled a mugger who was trying to rip my handbag off my shoulder in McPherson Square."

"Wow, *that's* exciting," I said. Mick leaned over to pet Lettice, who was dozing with her chin on his shoe; I couldn't see his face. He and Sally make a very attractive couple, and such a sharp contrast to each other—he tall and dark and quiet, she fair, petite, and animated. They really look as if they were made for each other.

"Wait, it gets better," she said, sitting forward. "He wouldn't stay and let me thank him, he said he was late, had to run—he just made sure I was okay and then he left. Well, I was bereft! I thought he was *so* good-looking in his three-piece suit. He even wore suspenders! I'm *mad* for a man in suspenders."

I laughed. "I've never thought about it."

"Really? Emma, don't you love a man in suspenders?"

"Sometimes. I guess."

"And *vests*—I love it when they take off their suit coats, and all they have on is a vest and their crisp shirtsleeves. So sexy." Sally wriggled her eyebrows at Mick, who ran a finger over his lips, half smiling.

"I'll have to remember this," Brad said, nudging Emma. "Remind me to take my coat off more often." She sent him one of her famous quelling looks, but he just laughed.

"So then—this was on a Thursday—on *Fri*day, guess who I ran into at the office Christmas party. Yes!"

"No, really?" I marveled. "Mick?"

"It turned out we worked in the same building on Vermont Avenue. Can you believe it? For the same law firm."

"We'd never met before," Mick cleared his throat to say, "because she was new, plus I'd been out of the office a lot on travel."

"Still, quite a coincidence," Brad said.

"I thought it was a miracle," Sally said, leaning back against Mick's shoulder. "Definitely a sign that we were fated to be together. Kismet!"

"Very romantic," I said.

"Yeah, Romeo and Juliet." Emma stood up. We stared at her; she looked a little surprised to find herself on her feet. "I'm sorry, I have to go. I forgot, I have to work tomorrow."

"On Saturday?" Brad looked amazed.

"What can I say. It's a seven-day newspaper."

So then *everybody* decided they had to go, and the evening ended much too early. While I held her coat for her, Emma apologized under her breath. "I'm sorry, Lee, I've broken up your nice party."

"Well, I wish you'd told me."

"I know, I just forgot, I was having too good a time. Really sorry, and it was great, everything was perfect, as usual. You're the *best* hostess."

I whispered, my back to the others, who were busy putting their coats on and talking, "I'm sorry you didn't like him."

"Who?"

"Mick," I mouthed.

Emma kept blinking, jerking her head toward me in small spasms. "*What?*"

"Shh. I'll call you, we'll talk."

"Okay." And then she laughed. She threw her head back and crowed. Everybody stopped talking and looked at her.

"What's funny?" Henry wanted to know.

I said, "Nothing," and turned away to open the door. I thought, *Well, maybe I was mistaken.* But then Sally hugged me and everybody else, Brad shook hands with Henry and Mick, Henry hugged Emma, Mick hugged me—and Mick and Emma didn't even look at each other. I think they might've mumbled, "G'night," but that was it. So I knew. I rarely err when it comes to this sort of thing.

"Good dinner," Henry said later that night, peering at his teeth in the bathroom mirror.

"It was." I'd made *thaazi saag aur narial* (beef with curried spinach and coconut); the recipe said "serves ten," but six of us ate it all. That's my definition of a successful dinner. I said, "Sally's awfully nice, isn't she?" Henry grunted. "And you and Mick really hit it off." But that didn't surprise me; I've yet to meet anyone who doesn't like Henry.

"Yeah, I liked him. Interesting guy. Know what he said? Prob'ly won't come to anything, but he's gonna recommend me and Jenny to his studio landlord for plumbing work. And guess who his landlord is."

"Who?"

"Carney Brothers. If we could get any kind of a foothold downtown in one o' those big ol' buildings—something's always going wrong, they're a gold mine for repairs. Just a couple o' maintenance contracts, and we'd be set. Wouldn't that be something?"

"It would be."

"I'll call Jenny tomorrow—guess it's too late tonight. Prob'ly won't come to anything," he said again, "but it was nice of Mick to offer. Most people wouldn't think of it."

Henry calls his mother Jenny. I used to think it was strange—I can't imagine calling my mother "Irene." But he grew up in a women's commune in North Carolina back in the 1960s, so he had a lot of mothers. No fathers, but a lot of mothers. Rather than call them all "Mom," he called them by their names, including his own mother. I guess it makes sense.

"Yeah, it was a nice party, but something was in the air, I thought," Henry said, moving aside so I could take off my makeup in front of the sink. "I thought maybe Emma didn't like Sally, or maybe she and Brad were fighting. Can't figure out what she sees in that guy anyway."

"Brad? Oh, I think he's nice. No, Emma likes smart people, and Sally's so clever, that's not it. It's Mick she doesn't like."

"Mick! You think?"

"Well, did you ever hear them say two words to each other?"

Henry said, "Huh," thoughtfully.

"They looked at each other, but they never talked. That interview they did together for the paper didn't go well, obviously."

"Huh."

I finished brushing my teeth and yawned. "Tired?" Henry was watching me in the mirror. I was tired, but I shrugged and said, "Oh," in a noncommittal voice. In case he had anything in mind.

But then I spoiled the mood by saying, "You know those fruit-stuffed game hens I make? Do you think they'd be good enough to serve to my parents when they come in December?"

He'd been giving me a little back rub. He took his hands away and said, "Prob'ly not," and walked out. Throwing over his shoulder, "But then, what could be?"

I finished what I had to do and followed him, with Lettice shuffling down the hall in front of me. Henry was already in bed with his reading light out, eyes closed, hands folded over his stomach. *Oh, no, you don't,* I thought. I settled Lettice in her dog bed, then sat down on Henry's side of the mattress so he had to look at me. "Don't you want them to come? It's only for two nights."

"Sure I want 'em to come. They're your parents."

"Really?"

"Sure. But it's not two nights, honey, it's four."

"No, two."

"Two on the way down, two on the way back. Four."

"No, *one* on the way down, one back." My parents were planning to stay at our house on either side of their annual trip to Florida.

"Oh."

He looked so relieved, I laughed. I twisted the ends of his mustache between my fingers, trying to make them curl up. He smiled and closed his eyes again. My husband looks like an aging hippie. You might not think I'd like that look, but on him I do. He wears his hair in a neat, tidy ponytail during the day, but at night he lets it down and it falls across the pillow like a shiny, dark red flag, thick and gorgeous. I can't keep my hands out of it.

"Anyway, it won't be so bad," I told him. "They like you, they really do."

"Sure they do."

"They *do*."

"Lee, give up. You married a blue-collar gentile. A *redneck* blue-collar gentile. As far as your parents are concerned, you couldn't have done worse if you'd married an Arab."

"Oh, boy, *that* really shows what you know." I got up and went over to my own side, flouncing down in bed, yanking the sheet out from under his hip to cover myself. "You married a heterosexual, but your mother doesn't hate *me*."

Good one. Score a point for Lee.

Henry started laughing. I didn't see anything funny, so I just lay there. When he saw I wasn't amused, he turned away, clasping his hands across his forehead and staring up at the ceiling. Brooding.

I hate to say it, but my family intimidates Henry. They honestly like him, but he can't see it. He can't get over it that my father is a physicist, my mother's an economist, one brother is a psychologist, and the other is a cardiologist. And he's a fatherless plumber from the South, in business with his mother. It's true I have more money than Henry has, but it's not because I earned it. My field is early childhood development, a woman's profession, which means no status and no money. I happen to be well off because my mother tells me what stocks to buy, and she's rarely wrong. I'm sorry to say that this is another sore point with Henry. He doesn't blame me, he blames himself, and then he gets quiet and moody. Our troubles conceiving a child aren't helping anything either, believe me.

I touched his ankle with the side of my foot, then held still, pretending it was an accident. Every night he puts on clean shorts and a fresh T-shirt before bed. I love the fragrance of the fabric softener and that fresh, linty, dryer smell. It always puts me in the mood.

But sex between us has gotten so complicated. It's almost not even connected to love anymore, it's all about temperature charts and fertility windows. Getting up early to pee in a cup, and botching a test that only has three steps. Ask me anything about urinary LH—luteinizing hormone. I have three ovulation prediction kits in the bathroom. We thanked God when we found out Henry had a varicocele—a varicose vein in his scrotum; it raises testicular temperature, and it's the most common cause of male infertility. So he had microsurgery to repair it and we started over. Nothing. Now we're back to basal thermometers and fertility periods and little pink sticks that turn blue. You have to make love when they turn blue whether you want to or not.

I moved my foot a little, stroking, fluffing the hair on his calf. This was a good time for me, hormonally speaking. But he knew that—I'd told him so this morning. If I made a suggestion now, he'd think it was because of the timing. And the truth is, it would be. Partly.

Oh, God, what's going to happen? Sometimes Henry can't perform. Not often—only twice. It's because of the stress, obviously, we both know that. The second time, he said, "I've never been impotent in my life!" and I said, "Well, I'm impotent, too, it just doesn't show!" That helped us a little. It hasn't happened since then.

Oh, I want a child so badly. I'm stuck, my life is stalled, I can't get on with it until I solve this problem. I know it's not fair to anybody, especially Henry, but I don't know what to do. I don't know how to get out of this cycle of trying and failing, trying and failing.

I sighed and turned out the light. We always kiss, the last thing before going to sleep. Once in a while it leads to something, but usually it's just a sweet, good-night peck. We groped for each other in the dark, finally found each other's lips.

"Night."

"Night."

I started to roll back to my side, but Henry kept my hand and pulled me over, halfway onto his chest. He has a very deep chest. It's not comfortable to sleep on—I've tried, it's like a too-high pillow. I said, "Honey—"

But he reached down and grabbed me around the hips, hauling the rest of me on top of him. "Hey, I was thinking."

Well, this was better. I stretched out, getting comfortable. "Thinking what?"

He slipped his big hands inside my pajama bottoms. "Thinking you might like to ravish me."

I yawned. "I might, but I'm pretty tired."

He tried to see my face in the dark. I'm not what you would call a big kidder—he didn't know if I was teasing or not. "Really?"

"No, not really." I put my arms around his neck.

So we made love. And it was good, it's always good, but at the critical moment I didn't climax. I don't think Henry knew. I wanted to, but my mind was distracted. All I could think of was, *This time it's going to work. This time. This time for sure.*

9

Isabel

Kirby kissed me last night. I couldn't have been more surprised if he'd drawn a gun and shot me. I thought he was gay.

I've assumed it for months, and now I see the assumption was based on very little, hardly anything at all. I'd never known him to have a date, and he didn't talk about women he used to date—that was one thing. He's a part-time actor—that was another. (I'm deeply embarrassed. Honestly, I deplore stereotypes.) There's something rather monklike about him, a certain contemplative quality. He's a quiet, very kind, extraordinarily gentle man, who would rather listen to me than talk about himself.

On second thought, what else could I think?

We were walking home from a play at the Church Basement Theater on Seventeenth Street, an experimental production by a local playwright in which Kirby had played a mute turnpike tollbooth operator. I hadn't understood a word of it, and he was trying, with much diffidence and tact, to explain it to me. It had just begun to snow, the first fall of the season, and we'd stopped to watch the thick, wet flakes swirl in the halo of a streetlamp. We had never touched before, never so much as held hands. Still, it felt quite natural to turn my head and rest it, just lightly, on his shoulder and say, "Isn't it lovely?" We might have been actors in a movie—because he looked into my eyes and echoed, "Lovely." And he touched my face with his gloved fingertips.

He kissed my cheek. All I could do was stare at him, nonplussed and suddenly shy, fumbling in my mind for an explanation for this confusing turn of events. I thought, *But you're gay!* And then he kissed my mouth, and I knew he wasn't. It was like discovering that someone you thought you knew has been in drag all along. Exactly like that—like finding out your woman friend is really a man.

He drew back to smile at me, but I couldn't smile back, couldn't even speak. I was utterly dumbfounded. Gradually my silence began to embarrass him. "I'm sorry," he said. "Isabel, I'm very sorry."

"It's all right," I said automatically. Meaninglessly. We started to walk again. He went back to explaining the play, but of course now it was terribly awkward. And I couldn't do anything to smooth the situation over—I was too busy trying to rearrange everything I had ever thought about him.

We live in the same building, in the noisy heart of Adams-Morgan. His third-floor apartment is directly over mine. He's a quiet neighbor, and yet the walls and floors are so thin, I can still hear him with rather unsettling clarity; I can tell what room he's in, for example, and more often than not, what he's doing. I daresay he can hear me almost as well—the first time we spoke, he called on the telephone to ask if I would please turn my stereo *up* so that he could hear the "Appassionata" without straining. His deep, cultured voice intrigued me, even though I thought at first he was being sarcastic. Another false assumption.

When we met in person, his looks neither confirmed nor contradicted the mistaken impression which was to grow, slowly but surely, the longer I knew him, that he was a homosexual. He's tall, thin as a stalk, almost completely bald. His eyes would be piercing, because of the intense way he has of staring at people, if they weren't such a benign shade of soft brown. His nose is like a blade, sharp and pointed on the end, but his lips are soft. Surprisingly soft. As I have discovered. He looks malnourished, but he's really quite strong—I know this from all the furniture-moving and household repairs he's done for me over the course of our friendship. What drew us together, a passion for music, is still our strongest bond. We love to go to concerts together, and now we marvel that we never met before or at least noticed each other, for we invariably occupy the cheapest seats at the Kennedy Center, the DAR, the Lisner, the Baird Auditorium.

Last night, after our awkward walk home in the snow, Kirby came to my door, as he always does, to see me in and say good night. But of course it was different this time.

"Would you like to come in?" I asked.

"No, I'll go up. Thanks. It's late."

I almost let him go, but then I couldn't. Something needed to be said. To pretend nothing had happened would be insulting to him, cowardly of me. On the other hand, what if I were making too much of it? What if his kiss had been an impulse, a gesture of friendship, no more? No, it *was* more than that for him, I was sure of it.

"My life is changing, Kirby, *I'm* changing, so quickly these days, I can hardly keep up with myself. I'm completely self-absorbed just now. It's simply the wrong time for me to form a—a romantic attachment. I'm too selfish, too caught up in myself to do justice to anyone else. I love our friendship, I don't want it to change. I'm so fond of you. Please understand."

I said more, I can't remember what, and through it all he listened intently, his body inclined toward me, his head cocked in polite attention. He really is the most wonderful listener.

Finally I stopped. I felt sheepish and dissatisfied, and very much as if I were missing something.

He said in a low, controlled voice, "Isabel, the last thing I wanted to do was upset you. I didn't know it would take you so much by surprise. The truth is, I've wanted to kiss you for a long time."

I may have blushed. I said, "I had no idea."

He frowned, as if that amazed him. Whatever may happen between us, I can never, ever tell him what I thought. Already it's almost inconceivable to me that I believed, as recently as yesterday, that this man was gay.

He put one hand in his coat pocket and looked down at his feet. "You could think about it some more. Let the shock wear off. Then . . ." He made a casual, hopeful gesture, stealing a glance at me through his eyelashes.

"I can truthfully say that tonight I'll think of little else."

"Well, that'll make two of us."

A good exit line. He made a little bow, murmured good night, and walked away. Nice timing, too. Must be the theatrical background. He's the reverse of Gary in that way—Gary had awful timing. But then, he's the reverse of Gary in almost every way.

I kept my word and thought about him at length. It's possible the time has come for me to find someone. I divorced Gary four years ago, and there's been no one at all since Richard Smith. "The aptly named Dick," as Emma always calls him. I try never to think of him; he comes with too many bad memories. A year and a half after the divorce, three months after Richard and I began a relationship—he was an instructor in my graduate school program—I found the lump in my breast. Or rather, Richard found it, fooling around at the movies. "What's this?" he whispered, breaking in on a touching scene in *Sense and Sensibility*.

I knew exactly what it was. In fact, I knew everything in an instant, all that would happen, up to and including my death. Fortunately, I was half wrong. But half was enough for Dick. He stayed around for the surgery, but after that he "couldn't see us going anywhere." I wasn't angry—I left all that to Emma. What would I do without her? My surrogate man hater and grudge holder.

But Richard was over two years ago, and since then there's been no one. I haven't felt the lack; I'm delighted by the pleasures of my solitary life. I love my cramped apartment. I painted it peach, white, and sea green, and I ripped up the rusty carpets and left the scarred wood floors bare. There was too much furniture in my Chevy Chase house, Gary is welcome to all of it. I have my bookshelves, my rocking chair. An old sofa, an assortment of rickety floor lamps, and for my friends, oversize pillows to sit on when they come to see me. I have enough dishes and silver to serve dinner to eight people, the perfect number. I have raucous neighbors, quiet neighbors, eccentric neighbors. My landlady, Mrs. Skazafava, barely speaks English. Lee says I'm living like a hippie, and I suppose I am—I missed that era when I was young. Ramakrishna says our lives move through cycles in no prescribed order. I'm traversing a circle that my contemporaries experienced thirty years ago. No matter; it's only the journey that counts.

I was daydreaming at my desk in the afternoon, petting Grace and staring out the window instead of studying for my families-at-risk exam when, overhead, I heard the door to Kirby's apartment open and close. I hear it all the time and unconsciously, unwillingly, keep tabs on him that way. Soon I heard footsteps in the hall, a knock at my door.

Grace stopped barking the second I opened it and she saw Kirby. He had on his uniform: corduroy trousers and a baggy sweater. And something in his hand. "Look what I bought," he said, and held out a still-wrapped CD. It was Beethoven, the Triple Concerto. "Would you like to hear it?"

So I made a pot of tea, and we sat and listened to the concerto, and it was almost like old times. Except that it wasn't. When the music ended, I decided against small talk and asked him a straight question. No pun intended.

"Have you ever been married?"

"Yes."

"Really." I masked my surprise by fiddling with the tea strainer. "You've never mentioned it."

"I was married for nineteen years. I had a son and a daughter." He stirred sugar into his cup and sipped. "They were killed eleven years ago. All three, in an accident on the Beltway. Julie was twelve, Tyler was eight."

"I'm so sorry." Why do those words always sound feeble, heartbreakingly inadequate? You wish and you search for better ones, but there aren't any. But Kirby said, "Thank you," as if he meant it, and that sad little ritual was over.

"Eleven years," he said after a pause. "It's a long time to be alone. It suited me at first. Not anymore." And he looked at me with frank meaning over the rim of his cup.

I stood up and went to the stereo, took his CD out of the player, put it back in the box. Leaned over and ran a finger across the titles in my music holder, looking for something suitable to accompany what I was going to say to him next. I couldn't find anything.

"Kirby . . ." I leaned back against the windowsill. "You know about my breast cancer." He did—I'd told him months ago. It's not something I keep secret, but then again, I don't go around blurting it out to people, either. But I'd told Kirby. Just the bare fact of it, no details. "I thought that . . . maybe you thought I only had the tumor removed, a lumpectomy. Or that I had had reconstruction. But, no. I just have—nothing. Here." I gestured. "A prosthesis in my bra."

Except for medical professionals, no one has ever seen my naked, asymmetric chest. Of late I had been coming, quite easily, to terms with the idea that no one ever would. And so I had stopped imagining myself having this unbelievably awkward conversation with a prospective lover.

Kirby unwound his long legs and levered himself up from the floor, coming to stand in front of me. I folded my arms across my chest. His narrow face looked stern and ever so slightly impatient. "That doesn't matter to me in the slightest. I don't give a damn. I couldn't care less."

"Well," I said. I believed him.

"Isabel, I'm falling in love with you."

I moved away from him, shocked. That I *didn't* believe. I wasn't interested in falling in love with anyone. I've done that. Now I'm too old, too selfish, I want to concentrate on me, not someone who's *falling in love* with me.

"Oh, Kirby. I wish you hadn't said that."

He turned, and it was a huge relief to see that he didn't look miserable or angry or embarrassed. He looked thoughtful. He smiled. "Then I wish I hadn't said it, too." He took something from his pocket and came toward me, holding it out. A ring—I started back in horror. "I brought down some washers to try," he said mildly.

"You . . . What?"

"The faucet in the kitchen. It's still leaking, isn't it?"

I nodded stupidly.

"I'll see if I can fix it." He went out of the room, into the kitchen, and started puttering.

I sank down on the floor, right where I was. Grace hauled herself up from her place by the radiator, padded over, flopped down beside me. Grace loves Kirby, I mused, stroking her soft gray muzzle. Other than that, there wasn't a coherent thought in my head.

On Tuesday, I would be having my last six-month checkup. After that, assuming all was well, I'd only have to see my surgeon/oncologist once a year. Another breast cancer milestone. Petting Grace, staring into space, it came to me that I'd made a decision. If I was all right, no spread, no lumps or bumps, no fishy X rays—and I was sure there wouldn't be—then I would think, *think* about the possibility of a relationship with Kirby. Just consider it. No pressure, no timetables, no agendas. I'd just give it some thought.

Meanwhile, it was nice to sit here with Grace and listen to the rattles and thumps and clanks of a man doing a chore for me in my kitchen. Mysterious, masculine sounds. Comforting. They made me feel like a woman. Now, that's something I haven't felt in a long time.

10

Rudy

Curtis thinks I shouldn't get a real job because we don't need the money. He says my volunteer work (excluding the Call for Help Hotline) helps others and satisfies me, and any sort of paying, full-time career would make me crazy, I couldn't handle the stress.

I don't know. I'm not sure. I guess he's right.

But I look at Lee, a Ph.D., director of a federal child care center. She always knew what she wanted, and for her it's been a matter of taking step after logical step to get it. I can't even *imagine* being that responsible or that clear-sighted. And Isabel, going back to school at fifty, methodically working on a degree that will get her exactly where she wants to go. How do they *know* what they want? Even Emma knows, although she's careful not to let anybody in on her secret.

Like me, she's afraid. Her fear comes from pride, though, and not wanting to make a fool of herself. Mine comes from understanding my own incompetence.

I tried to explain that to her, driving home from the movies last night, but I couldn't. Curtis is the only one who really understands. Emma and I almost had a fight. I stopped the car in front of her house, wishing we'd gone for drinks instead of ice cream after the movie, because then I'd have been able to argue better.

She glared at me with one hand on the door handle, the other crushing out her cigarette in the ashtray. She wears a black wool beret when the weather's bad; she pulls it low over her forehead, almost past her eyebrows, and her crazy red hair shoots out like fire all around. "Rudy, you're an *artist*. You are incredibly talented, you could be anything you want, but it's like you're frozen or something. You're stuck, and for the life of me I can't figure out what's holding you back."

Cowardice. Inadequacy. Inertia. I felt defensive, but I didn't want to fight, and throwing Emma's own fears back in her face would've hurt her feelings.

"I *am* doing things. I might enter some prints in a photo contest at the Corcoran. Oh, and they want me to teach a pottery class at the Free School next year."

"A pottery class? But you don't even throw pots anymore."

Another sore subject. Emma blamed Curtis when I sold my potting wheel. I kept it in the basement, and it's true his exercise equipment started crowding everything else out, but that's not really why I gave up potting. It took up a lot of time, and Curtis said, and I eventually agreed, that if I wasn't going to do it full-time, actually make a career for myself in ceramics, why do it at all?

"I don't do it actively," I told Emma, "but I could still teach it to beginners. So anyway—I am working on some things, I just don't always tell you."

"Yeah, okay. I know you are." She was backtracking; she knew she'd hurt my feelings by being so blunt. "I'm sorry if I came on like your mother. Well, not *your* mother. Some normal mother."

"Yeah, not my mother." I laughed, to make her laugh, and then we were okay again. But when she asked me to come in, I said I'd better not. In spite of that last-second mollifying, Emma was in a feisty mood, and I was afraid she'd start in again if I stayed.

"Night," she said, and gave me a light slap on the shoulder—she's not much of a hugger. I waited while she ran up to her front porch in the rain. Once inside, she flicked the porch light on and off—our signal that we're safe, no rapists hiding in the shrubbery—and I tooted the horn and pulled away.

The rain turned to sleet as I drove home along Rock Creek, and then I was glad instead of sorry we hadn't ended the evening with a few drinks. And when I got home and saw all the downstairs lights on in my house, I was more than glad.

Thank God I'm sober, I prayed as I circled the block, looking for an empty space. Curtis was back from Atlanta a day early, and I should've been there. He hates to come home to an empty house.

I thought of Eric's advice about pointless guilt—I'm supposed to ask myself exactly what I've done wrong, and the answer, he says, will almost always be nothing. Well, maybe, but I never *feel* innocent. There's always this sense, especially with Curtis, that I could do, should do, more, better, something else.

"Curtis?"

He'd left the lights on, but he wasn't downstairs. I went up, taking my coat off as I went. He wasn't in the bedroom, wasn't in the bathroom. "Curtis?"

I heard a noise from his darkened study. I went in, but he didn't turn around; he stayed slumped in his chair at his desk, staring at his black computer screen. "Curtis?"

He still had on his suit. I touched his shoulder. When he didn't move, I slid my hand to the back of his neck, feeling the tight tendons there bunch and flex. "What are you doing, baby? All by yourself in the dark."

His hair grows to a perfect little V at the back. He hates it; he instructs his expensive Capitol Hill hairstylist to blunt it every two weeks, but it never quite goes away. I used to like to play with it, but he doesn't let me anymore. It annoys him.

"Where've you been?" he asked in his slow, meticulous southern drawl.

"I thought you weren't coming home till tomorrow."

He waited for the real answer.

"I just went to the movies."

"Alone?"

"No, with Emma. She wanted to see this French film, a love story, I've already forgotten the name. She liked it, but I thought it was silly." That wasn't quite the truth. "It had subtitles you could barely see," I added. To make it clearer that I hadn't had a very good time.

I slipped my fingers under the collar of his jacket and started a soft, slow massage. I could smell his cologne, still fresh after his long day, and the musk-scented mousse he puts on his neat, glossy hair. His head bowed slowly, a little at a time, and I felt him begin to relax. "How was Atlanta?" I asked.

A mistake. I shouldn't have asked him that, not yet. All his muscles tensed. "A disaster."

Why did I feel responsible? Whatever happened in Atlanta, it didn't have anything to do with me, but still I heard his words as an accusation.

I waited, but when he didn't explain, I said, "What happened?"

"Morris."

"Oh, no." I made a scornful, sympathetic sound, squeezing his shoulders. Frank Morris is Curtis's enemy. He has much less seniority, but he wants Curtis's job, and he always tries to make him look bad in front of the congressman. "What did he do?"

No answer.

"Hm? What did Morris do?"

"What do you care?"

I could feel that heavy, smothering fog of guilt seep inside, bog me down. From where? Why? "You know I care." But what had I done? Something, I knew it was something. Curtis knew what it was, but I didn't dare ask him.

A long minute passed, and I realized he wasn't going to tell me. That was his worst punishment—not letting me in. But why couldn't he see that it punished him, too?

I put my arms around him, leaning over to rest my cheek against his ear. "Oh, baby," I whispered. If I could just warm him, soften him. "Curtis, it's—"

He stood up. My hands fell away as I stepped back. Without a glance, he passed beside me and walked out of the room.

We have a ritual. This was just part of it, this would pass. He wasn't really shutting me out. No one understands that Curtis needs me as much as I need him. More sometimes. But he's the strong one. I would be lost without him. Eric says no, but I would.

Later, I brought him a glass of cognac in bed. "I don't want this," he said, and he wouldn't take it.

I sipped it, watching him. I'd put on the nightgown he likes best, black and cut low, soft crushed velvet. "Tired?"

He shrugged. He almost smiled at me.

"You have such long days." I set the glass down. He let me take the *Forbes* out of his hand and put it on the night table. A lock of his hair fell across his forehead; he looked so boyish and young, and I thought of the early days, in Durham, when we first moved in together. The happiest, safest time of my life. He really loved me then.

"Morris is such an idiot," I said. "I've never been able to stand him." Curtis grunted. "And he's going bald awfully fast." He sniffed his breath out, a kind of a laugh, and reached for my hand. His smile meant the beginning of forgiveness.

"I'm getting out of there," he said, pulling on the black ribbon bow at the top of my nightgown. "I'm going with Teeter and Jack."

"You're what? You are?" He kept yanking at the ties; I had to cover his hands to make him stop. "You mean you're quitting?"

"I decided tonight."

"But—"

"Assholes, Rudy, I can't deal with it anymore. And I don't have to."

"No—no, you *should* leave, you haven't been happy in ages." What a surprise! I could hardly think. But he *hadn't* been happy in his work; there was too much back stabbing in Congressman Wingert's office, he said, too much hypocrisy. Teeter Reese and

Jack Birmingham were old friends from law school. They'd started a lobbying firm, and they were making tons of money, according to Curtis. Maybe that would be perfect. He couldn't bear authority. But if he could be a partner, his own boss instead of somebody's underling, he might thrive. And the springboard to political office—Curtis's true ambition—was almost as direct, I imagined. It was just a different route.

He was peeling my nightgown over my shoulders, starting to caress me. "Wingert can fuck himself," he said, his eyes shining, white teeth flashing. "He can fuck Morris, too. They can fuck each other." His vulgarity shocked me—he rarely swears. He pulled me down. I let him touch me too roughly, but he needed to, because of the strange mood he was in. But he finally stopped when he realized I wasn't with him, wasn't ready. He gentled his hands, grew tender.

Tenderness—it breaks me down, and he knows me so well. He knows I'll be anything he wants if he's tender with me. He stroked the tears off my face with his fingers, murmuring, "Good, Rudy, that's right," and spreading my legs with his knees. I wanted him to fill me, take up all the empty space inside with himself. Complete me. He never, never lets go of himself, never loses control, but he can make me so hot. I was panting for him, calling him baby, calling out, "God, God," wanting it so much. He buried his face in my hair. Then he stopped.

"Oh, Christ."

I went still, too, appalled by the disgust in his tone. "What's wrong?"

His lips curled, still wet from kissing me. "What's wrong? I'll tell you. You smell like a God damn ashtray." I reached for him. He shrugged off my hand and rolled away.

"I'm sorry." My skin prickled everywhere, I was freezing. "I'm sorry. I thought I had quit, but Emma and I, we just—she had some and I started again, I smoked in the car. I'm sorry—" I made myself stop. It wasn't the smoking, anyway.

"I *hate* when you do this," I whispered to his back. I touched his hip with one finger, but he jerked at the covers angrily, and I snatched my hand away. "Curtis, *please*."

He wouldn't answer, not if I went on my knees and begged him. It's easy for me to hate myself, harder to hate him. But sometimes he even manages that.

I got up and took two Phrenilin for my head, a couple of Nembutals for oblivion. Deep, black sleep is the only analgesic for this particular kind of pain. Too bad it's impossible to come by naturally. I need a guarantee.

The next morning, my mother called.

I hadn't spoken to her in about three months. I suppose that sounds like a long time, but it's not unusual for us. She sounded awful. I shut my eyes and thought, *Shit, shit, she's drinking again*.

"Rudelle? Oh, it's good to hear your voice. How are you, darling?"

"I'm fine, Mother. Is something wrong?"

"August is in the hospital."

"Oh, no. What's wrong with him? Mom?" A sharp noise hurt my ear—I had to pull the telephone away. "Are you there?"

"I dropped it." She started to cry.

I took the phone into the hall outside the bedroom. I lay down on the floor, curled onto my side on the crisp mauve carpet.

"Please don't cry, Mom, don't cry. What's wrong with August?" My stepfather turned eighty in September. He's sixteen years older than my mother.

"His heart. Late last night. I called Allen, but he won't come. Oh, Rudelle, if only you would."

"Mother—"

"I'm not drinking. I haven't been."

Maybe. Maybe not. "Did he have a heart attack?"

"An episode, they called it. I don't know what else they said, I can't listen."

"But—then he's going to be okay?"

"They're making him come home today."

"They're—" I opened my eyes. "Okay, then, he's all right. It was just a warning. It can't be serious, Mom, or they wouldn't let him leave." I lay still, thinking, *She called Allen first,* while she blew her nose. My brother is an alcoholic with two ex-wives, a drug habit, and no job, and my mother called him first for help. I could feel my muscles getting weak, lax, my face going slack. The start of my own "episode."

"Can you come? It's been so long, Rudelle."

"I don't think I can right now."

"You could come for Christmas. It's beautiful here. Remember? How beautiful at the holidays? You and Curtis. It's been so long."

"We can't. Curtis has to work." That probably wasn't a lie. "Mother, I'll have to call you back."

"Rudelle—"

"I've got another call. Have to go, I'll call you." I clicked off and cut the connection.

She used to be beautiful. I wonder if she still is. I haven't seen her in almost five years, not since my wedding. To my friends I call her Felicia, not "Mother" or "my mom," so that's what they call her to me. "How are Felicia and the playboy?" Emma will say. The eighty-year-old playboy. August is Swiss; Mother met him in Geneva the year before my father killed himself. They were lovers, of course. They must have been.

Every once in a while my mother decides she wants to see me. She'll call up and go on about how long it's been, how wonderful it would be, how much she misses me. I can't bring myself to follow through and arrange a visit. Eric thinks I should. He thinks I've got issues with my mother I need to resolve. But I don't do anything. Can't.

I got a mental picture of how I probably looked, curled up in a ball on the hall floor. Eric taught me to do that—see myself, visualize the way I look when I think I'm getting sick. It works sometimes. Shocks me into doing something.

I got up and started toward the bathroom. I made it through the doorway, but as soon as I flicked on the light, I couldn't go any farther. I froze with my foot in midair, inches from the white tile floor. *Stop it,* I thought in a panic, but I couldn't go in. I could make my hand work—I turned out the bathroom light. And then I could go backward, back out into the hall. I kept going and went into the bedroom and sat on the edge of the bed.

I still had the phone in my hand. I hit memory and the number two. The receptionist in Wingert's office said Curtis was in a meeting. Was there a message? "No, thanks." I couldn't recognize my voice. I disconnected quickly and dialed again.

Emma's voice on her answering machine steadied me. I could see her so clearly, trying not to laugh, eyes dancing while she made her witty, tongue-in-cheek recording. When I spoke into the machine, I almost sounded normal.

"Hi, it's me. I was hoping you'd be home. Guess you're at work. It's nothing . . . nothing important." I had to whisper, "Bye," because all of a sudden I was crying.

Rudy, Rudy. Rudelle. How I hate that name. It's German for "famous one." I was born in Germany. My parents liked Europe better than America. I called myself Rudi when I was a child. I was Rudi O'Neill until my mother married August. I had to take his name, Lacretelle. Rudelle Lacretelle. In college I took my mother's name, Surratt, and changed Rudi to Rudy. Rudy Surratt. I liked it. I felt comfortable. But when I married Curtis, he asked me to take his name, so now I'm Rudy Lloyd. Emma loves to say my name. She calls me "Roodie," high and soft like a song, for no reason at all—if we're driving somewhere, for instance. She just starts singing my name.

I got off the bed and dialed again, memory-one. Eric's machine answered, but he picked up in the middle of the message and said hello.

"Can you see me today?"

"Rudy? Has something happened?"

"No, not really. Eric, can I see you? Something—yes—happened, but I don't know what."

"Is four o'clock okay?"

"Thank you. Thanks. Thanks."

"The first two years after my father died were the worst. We were living in Austria for some reason, a ski resort in the mountains. Have I told you this? My brother was living with us because he'd flunked out of his prep school in Rhode Island. Claire and I went to a convent school in the village. August stayed with us most of the time, but he hadn't married my mother yet. We lived in a hotel. I've told you this, haven't I?"

"It doesn't matter."

"You know this part. My mother. That day I found her."

"Tell me again."

"I am, I have—I want to. It was the summer when I was twelve and Claire was fourteen. Allen, my brother, he'd go away every day, we didn't know where. Walking, he said. My mother couldn't make him stay home. But she couldn't do anything. Well, no—she could drink and sleep, and when she took the right pills she could be loving and so very, very sweet. I loved her so much, Eric. I have never felt so much pain. For anyone. Not since that summer. I think . . . I've been sort of numb since then."

I stopped talking and closed my eyes. Eric stayed still and quiet, waiting for me. Behind my eyelids, the scene came on like an old movie, black and white except for the blood.

"My sister and I found her together. Dead, we thought. Naked on the white tiles, the bathtub full of bloody water. *Get help, get a doctor*—I kept screaming at Claire. But I should've known from her face, half smiling, blank, as if she were falling asleep. She just walked out. Some people found her and brought her back the next day. Riding her bike, they said."

"Rudy," Eric said.

"I'm all right. I didn't tell you this before, did I? That I stayed with my mother, just me, for hours? She was almost as white as the tiles. And cold, she felt like rubber. I thought if I let her go, she'd die. A bruise on her face from where she fell, but—the blood, like red coins on the floor—the blood—it was menstrual blood. Because she'd used pills, not a razor. Pills and vodka. Didn't she know? Oh, how could she not know who would find her! Her little girls, her babies. Oh, Mother. I held her and held her, thinking we'd changed places, mother and child, my child was dying and I couldn't stop it, could not keep her."

I was choking, blood pounding in my head—Eric's hands took my hands and squeezed tight, tight, and I stopped sobbing. "I'm all right. I am. I'm fine."

When I was calm, I told him about my mother's phone call this morning. "So—that's why all this came back. It's funny. Years pass and you think it's gone, but it isn't. Does it ever go away?"

"I don't think so."

"No. I knew it," I said.

"It doesn't have to be so painful, though."

"What makes it stop hurting? Not time. It's been thirty years. Thirty years. Eric?"

"Yes?"

I smiled at him so he would think I was teasing. "Am I ever going to get well?"

I didn't expect him to answer, that's the kind of question he usually ignores. But I had frightened him today. His face, when he'd held my hands, hadn't been calm, for once. "I think you are," he said, nodding solemnly. "I wouldn't see you if I didn't believe that."

"You wouldn't see me?" I rubbed my chilled arms.

"I wouldn't keep seeing you. If I didn't think you'll get better."

But I'm worse now than when we started. Couples therapy,

that's what he wants to try next. I've told him that's impossible, but it makes no impression on him, he doesn't understand. Curtis won't come here. If I were dying and it would save my life, Curtis wouldn't come here.

"I'd better go," I said, although we still had ten minutes. "Curtis thought he might come home early tonight, and he likes me to be there."

Eric said nothing. He pressed his lips together and let me go.

11

Emma

"This isn't worth it for women."

I actually said that, out loud and with force. Sure, I had cause: deveining shrimp brings out the worst in anybody, and twenty-five minutes of it hunched over the sink with nothing but *All Things Considered* for company could drive Patricia Ireland, or whoever it is these days, around the p.c. bend. Nevertheless. I'm supposed to be a feminist. It's part of my identity, my persona, it goes with Irish, agnostic, lapsed Democrat. Old maid. I'm supposed to be *above* thinking that excessive shrimp-cleaning, apple-peeling, and snow pea string-pulling are only worth it if men are coming for dinner.

Ach, but I do love my gerruls. I was thinking in a Scottish brogue, because I'd just heard this guy interviewed on NPR, Lonnie McSomething. He wrote a profane Glaswegian coming-of-age novel, big deal, and now they're treating him like the Second Coming. No jealousy here, though, no siree. I flicked off the radio with the side of my wrist and started on another pile of shrimp.

Anyway, I go to at least as much trouble when it's my turn for the women's group as I do for dinner parties with couples. And a hell of a lot more trouble than I go to for individual guys, who are lucky to get a cup of coffee in the morning before I push them out the door. Politely—I'm always polite. And I enjoy cooking for my gerruls. Three of us are in an unspoken competition for second best chef (Isabel has a lock on first), and tonight's curried shrimp with snow peas and apples is a tough contender. Plus I have made a cake. Not from scratch—what am I, June Cleaver?—but I did add red food coloring to the white frosting and write in big letters, over an extremely artistic rendering of an hourglass, "Two Years & Counting—You Go Girl!" That's how long it's been, two years this month, since Isabel found the lump in her breast. They say you can't really start to relax until five years have passed, but this is still an anniversary, and by God, we're celebrating.

Seven-fifteen. Rudy was late. I told her to come at seven so we could talk. Should've known; should've said six-thirty.

I finished the shrimp and squeezed dishwashing soap on my palms, wondering how many other people can't clean the smell of fish from their hands anymore without thinking of Susan Sarandon. Hey—would that make a good piece for something? American film iconography, how it intrudes on our everyday lives. Some pseudosmart mag might go for it if I threw in enough sarcasm. My specialty. But I'd rather write it straight. Sweet. There have to be a hundred examples—indelible psychic connections between, say, whistling and Lauren Bacall. Tricycles and extraterrestrials. Question: Why do you feel sexy when you see an Amish guy in a field? Answer: Harrison Ford, *Witness*. Okay, trite example, but still, there have to be hundreds.

"Stinks," I decided. Too obvious, nothing behind it; once you said it, you'd said it. Which is the trouble with about 90 percent of my story ideas. Still, I scribbled "Sarandon/lemons/cult. assn." on the scratch pad stuck to the refrigerator. Because you never know.

The doorbell rang. I flicked on the porch light to see Rudy through the beveled sidelight, looking tall and glamorous in her long black cloak—the same cloak she wrapped Grace in eight years ago on MacArthur Boulevard. The cloak I still want. Her face looked morose, distracted, before she saw me through the glass; then it brightened in a wide, sparkling, squinty-eyed smile. I pulled open the door, and Rudy swept in on a blast of cold air, cashmere, perfume, and—gasoline?

"I ran out of gas. Can you believe it? In the middle of Sixteenth

Street, and nobody stopped, nobody helped me, I had to schlepp all the way to Euclid and back for one lousy gallon."

"Wow, that's terrible." But what an excellent excuse, and so unexpected. Rudy's chronically late and never thinks a thing of it, never even apologizes. I was thrown off my stride. "I never get that," I said peevishly, "how anybody can run out of gas. Don't you look at the gauge when you start your car?"

She just laughed. "Hey, you look great! You got your hair cut."

I'm not too good at hugging, or so the group is always telling me. I braced for Rudy's strong, one-armed embrace, wondering what we were crushing between us in the grocery bag she had in her other arm. "Yeah," I said, "I had to do something with it. It's not too short, is it? I told him medium. Look at my new coat rack—a Christmas present from me. So, come on in the kitchen, let's get a drink."

I found glasses, opened wine, poured peanuts in a bowl, while Rudy prowled around, looking for new things since she'd been here last. "Oh, you hung it," she exclaimed, pointing to the "kitchen collage" she had made me for Christmas. "That's a good place for it, over the door."

"I absolutely love it." It's truly a masterpiece: an assemblage of 1950s-style aluminum kitchen implements that somehow suggest a face. It's got two measuring spoons for eyes, a cheese grater for the nose and eyebrows, a bent orange jar cap for lips—oh hell, I can't describe it, you'd have to see it to appreciate it. But trust me, you can't look at this piece without laughing. Rudy could make a living doing this stuff.

"I can't get over how much I love home ownership," I told her, handing over a glass of merlot, her favorite. "It fills me with a lot of revolting middle-class satisfaction."

I've lived in classier places—Georgetown, Foggy Bottom, Woodley Park—but I didn't *own* those apartments, so they didn't count. My eighty-year-old Mt. Pleasant town house doesn't look like much, especially from the outside, and the neighborhood is what they call transitional, meaning you're smart not to go out at night without your own personal pit bull. But it's all mine.

"To the Sloans," I said.

"The Sloans."

We drank to the previous owners, who rehabbed my house within an inch of its life, then did a white flight when the wife got pregnant and decided they'd rather bring Junior up in the suburbs. "Their paranoia is my gain. I'm even starting to like the bars on the windows."

"Why not?" Rudy said. "White wrought iron is beautiful. It's just a matter of separating form from function."

"And not getting hysterical."

"Hey. You choose to live in our lovely and historic nation's capital—"

"You takes your chances."

We toasted again.

"So," I said, settling down on the bench at the kitchen table, making room for Rudy. "How did it go with Greenburg?" Sometimes you can tell if she's been talking to her shrink because her eyes look puffy and bloodshot. Not tonight, though. "Wasn't this a Greenburg day?"

"Yes." She shook two Winstons out of a pack and offered me one. "It was good. We talked about my father. Which is always pretty intense. Eric says it's all right to think he might not have killed himself."

"Might not have killed himself? Wait—he did, didn't he? That's what you've always said. You mean he didn't?"

"Well, I'm just saying, it's possible he might not have. No one knows. It's a myth in my family that he did it on purpose, but it could just as easily have been that he got drunk and fell out of the boat."

It wasn't only a family myth, it was a women's group myth, too. I heard the story years ago, and now I have an image of it in my mind that's as vivid as a home movie. It happened on Lake Como about thirty years ago, when Rudy was eleven. I can see the blue sky and the white sailboat, the soft yellow Italian light. It's dusk. Rudy's dad, Allen Aubrey O'Neill, has on baggy white trousers and a white sweater. He's barefooted; he smokes Camels; he looks like Joseph Cotton. He tosses back the last of the vodka in his leather-covered hip flask. He reaches for the stanchion, hauls himself up. Seagulls dip and soar, and he listens to their hungry, heartless cries for a second, takes a last sniff of the sweet, sunny breeze. Then he steps out, into the air and the smooth, cool blue of the lake.

That's the end of the movie—no unseemly splashing or gasping, and I never follow him down or try to imagine his panic or his sick second thoughts. Rudy's handsome, aristocratic father has simply taken himself off.

"Well, I guess," I said slowly. "He drank a lot, didn't he?"

"Oh, God."

"Yeah. So . . ." I started to nod. "Why not? You're right, he could just as easily have fallen overboard. In which case, my God, everything changes. Oh, Rudy—" I leaned forward, beginning to get an idea of what that would mean to her. "So he didn't commit suicide. Maybe. This is great, because if he was just a drunk, not—"

"He was still manic-depressive. It doesn't mean he wasn't crazy, Emma."

"No, I know, but still—"

"It's just something to think about, that's all."

"Yeah."

"It's not that big a deal."

"Right." I backed off with a joke. "I bet Greenburg gets more APA journal articles out of your family than he does from the whole rest of his shrink practice."

She smiled, craned her long neck to blow smoke at the ceiling. "Well," she said, and then she laughed self-consciously. "I thought I was ready to hope for this, but it looks like I'm not. Not out loud, anyway. Not in public."

"Well, I'm not public."

Rudy has fine gray eyes, as they used to say in books about English governesses. I watched them soften and mellow, turn tender. "No, you're not." She set her glass down. "Okay. I hope he got shit-faced and fell in the damn lake and drowned, because then I'll only have to worry about my genetic predisposition to alcohol, depression, drug addiction, and paranoid schizophrenia. But not suicide."

Neither of us mentioned her mother, and we laughed the loud, too-long, healing laugh that's part of our therapeutic repertoire and as vital to us, to our relationship, as kind words or sympathy—no, more so. And after that there was nothing left to say, at least not now, on the subject of Rudy's father's death. We'd covered it all.

We poured more wine, lit up again. I was thinking I ought to get up and start chopping onions or something; Lee and Isabel and the new woman, Sharon, would be here any minute. But this was too nice. Sitting in the kitchen with Rudy, smoking and drinking and talking about life—like the beer commercial said, it doesn't get any better than this.

"Well, I had a rotten day," I said cheerfully, and told her about the piece for the *Washingtonian* I was bogged down in, couldn't seem to finish even though it was due Monday. Rudy sympathized and told me about a landscaping course she really wanted to take. It started in the spring, and it was a two-year program, you got a certificate in residential landscape design, and then you could probably apprentice with a landscaping company or a master gardener and be on your way. She was excited about it, but she backed off at the end, saying it was just a thought, she probably wouldn't do it, it cost a lot, it would take too long.

"Oh, but it sounds terrific, like something you'd really love. And you'd be great at it. Landscaping? You love to garden and you love to design. Oh, Rudy, it's perfect for you."

"I don't know, I don't know. Anyway, I don't think I have time.

This would be full-time, very intensive, so I don't know, I just don't think . . ." She crossed her ankles and slid down on her backbone, sleek as a seal. What Rudy *could've* been is a model. "I probably won't do it. We haven't even talked about it."

"We" meaning Curtis. I've gotten used to biting my tongue in situations like this, it's not even that hard anymore. "How is Curtis?" I said in my best neutral voice. But I was kissing our pleasant conversation good-bye.

"He's fine." She kept her eyes on the glowing tip of her cigarette. "Said to give you his love."

Sure he did. Curtis is brimming over with love for me. "Give him mine," I lied back, and got up to chop the onions.

A long time ago I learned that, on the subject of her husband, the price of Rudy's friendship is smiles, lies, and teeth-gritting silence. I hate this deal, I despise the hypocrisy and the unfairness, but I stick to it like a sacred vow. What choice do I have? It's Rudy. But there's nobody else in the world I'd do it for.

I heard her stand up. "So, Em. Tell me. What's new on the Mick Draco front these days?"

I couldn't believe it—my heart actually missed a beat. Good thing my paring knife is dull or I might've sliced off a digit. I had to duck my head so Rudy wouldn't see me flushing. *Christ, it's worse than I thought.* The other thing I hadn't realized was how badly I wanted to talk about him.

But I was cool. "Oh, not that much. We had coffee again on Friday. Thursday or Friday. Friday. In that dive across from his studio again. We just, you know, talked."

"Talked."

"Yeah, about stuff. His kid, my work. His painting."

"His wife."

"Ha. No."

It's been three months since I met him. Three months. Of torture. I'm used to men torturing me, but not like this. We'll call each other up and say something like, "Guess what, I happen to be in your neighborhood right now, want to have coffee?" if it's me calling him, or "I just learned how to do lithographs, want to see them?" if it's him calling me. Since neither of us likes coffee that much and I don't even know for sure what a lithograph is, it's safe to say these are subterfuges. Innocent ones, though. Excruciatingly innocent. I'm dying here.

Rudy leaned in, elbows on the counter, her Acqua di Gió adding class to the odor of the onions. "Well? What's going on? Come on, give me the lowdown."

"*Nothing.* Nothing's changed, we just, you know, we see each other every once in a while and we talk. We're friends. That's it." I put down the knife and met her eyes. "Oh, Rudy. I'm going insane."

She smiled, and her eyes crinkled with sympathy. "Poor Emma."

"I can't stand it. We've never even touched hands. But I'm falling, I'm really—and it's the same for him, I think, although he would never say. And nothing can change, nothing can ever happen."

"Look at you," Rudy said wonderingly. When she put her arm around my waist, I had the stupidest urge to burst into tears. So I shuffled away, muttering, "Oh, I'm okay," laughing to cover it. I was torn between wanting to blurt out everything—even though there honestly is nothing to tell—and wanting to keep it all to myself. But what I wanted most was to get over him and tell Rudy about it in retrospect—"You wouldn't believe how gone I was on that Mick guy—remember him?"

"If it's making you this miserable," she said, "maybe you ought to stop seeing him."

"I'm not miserable. Not all the time." Misery alternates with euphoria. "But I know I have to stop seeing him. And then Lee has a party and invites Mick and the lovely Sally—she's done it twice now—"

"You have to tell Lee who he is."

"I can't, it's too late, I waited too long. So even if I *try* not to see him, I do see him, and I'm just—I'm losing my mind! And he's—"

The doorbell rang.

"Shit," we said in unison.

"But it's okay, I'm fine, I really am. I'll tell you the rest later. Listen," I blurted, backing toward the hall, "don't say anything, his name or anything, you know—" Rudy's expression, *Don't insult me*, made me laugh nervously and blush again. "I know—I'm just crazy. Oh, God, Rudy!"

Chaos rules for the first twenty minutes or so of every women's group meeting while everybody hugs and kisses, pours wine, tries to find a cutting board, a knife, jockeys for a place at the sink, catches up on everybody else's news—all at the same time, and all, except for Lee's, in kitchens the size of really big bathrooms.

"Are you through with that colander?"

"Em, your hair looks darling."

"This cheese is good—is it Saga?"

"Can I take a shower? I just came from ballet class."

"Isabel, make your rice in the microwave, okay? I need this whole stove. And nobody talk to me while I'm doing this shrimp, I need five minutes of peace and quiet."

"Oh, heck, I'm not taking a shower."

"She is so bossy when she cooks."

I love this. Making a nice meal for my best friends, listening to them joke and laugh and tell how they've been, throwing in a zinger of my own now and then—this is the *best* time. Wine, cheese, gossip, and pals. If you could get sex in there somehow, you'd have it all.

The telephone rang. "Can somebody get that?" I was at the Dijon-and-cream-sauce stage, very tricky. Lee picked up the phone and said, "DeWitt residence. Oh, hi, Sharon. No, this is Lee. Oh, no, really? Oh, I'm sorry."

"I *knew* it," Rudy said in a stage whisper.

"I didn't like her that much anyway," I said. Lee made a face at me and took the phone into the dining room. "I didn't. She plucks her eyebrows and then pencils them back on. What is that?"

"This is a record, though. Usually they last longer than two meetings."

Lee came back in, grim-faced. "Another one bites the dust." She slumped down on a stool. "Is it something we're doing?" She looked so dejected, Rudy and I burst out laughing. "No, I mean it." She turned to Isabel. "This is the third in—what?"

"About two years."

"Well, I knew she wouldn't last."

"Me, too," Rudy agreed with me.

"Did she say why she was quitting?" Isabel asked.

"She doesn't have time."

"Right."

"Oh, right," said Rudy. "What else did she say?"

"Nothing. Well, she did say she thought we'd discuss issues more. Topics."

"Topics? Please." I snorted. "Women in the workplace. Post-feminism in a preliberation era. Authenticating your life. Juggling work and family in a—"

"Didn't you tell her," Isabel interrupted mildly, "that we quit having topics quite a few years ago?"

"Yes, but—"

"Topics," Rudy said, "are what people talk about when they don't know each other well."

"Topics," I said, "are what men talk about."

Lee shook her head at us, disappointed.

"I think it must be hard for someone new to break into this group," Isabel said. Sharon was another one of Lee's finds—Isabel didn't want her to feel bad. "We're established now, a unit. Any newcomer's bound to feel like an outsider, no matter how welcoming we try to be."

"Well, I don't see why." Of course Isabel was right, but I wanted to keep it going. "Aren't we a fun buncha gals?" I turned to Rudy. "Remember the bald one? Sort of a middle-age punk deal going on. What was her name—"

"Moira, and she was nice," Rudy said defensively—she'd proposed her.

"I didn't say she wasn't nice, I said she was bald. Bald as an egg, bald as a cue ball. Bald—"

"How long have we been a group?" Isabel said to divert me.

Somebody asks that question every fourth or fifth meeting. Lee always knows the answer, and everybody always acts surprised and disbelieving. "It'll be ten years in June," Lee said.

"Ten *years*."

"My God."

"Who'd've thought."

Rudy lifted her glass high. "To us."

"To us." Everybody clinked, and we drank. I was thinking two things: *God, we're so lucky*, and *I want this to last forever.*

"So tomorrow," Lee wound up, "Henry has his third and last sperm test. They've been inconsistent up to now, so we're hoping this one finally tells us something."

"His sperm have been inconsistent? I hate when that happens."

"The test results. After the first one, they said his count was low, and after the second they said it was normal. The morphology was okay in the second, but abnormal in the first. And in both tests the motility was Grade II, which means slow and meandering."

"What's morphology?" Rudy asked.

"The shape. If the sperm is too tapered, it could be missing the acrosome, which is the packet of enzymes at the tip that helps it bore through the egg's coating."

"Hey, I'm eating here." I just wanted to lighten the mood. Lee's battles with infertility have been going on for about two years now, half the length of her marriage, and it's really starting to get to her. I'm so used to her being the cheerful, normal, competent one in the group, it's hard to watch her playing in a game she keeps losing. You know how some people are so chronically, outrageously successful, you can't help feeling a little satisfaction when they finally fail at something? Well, I do. But not with Lee. She has a terrific job, plenty of money, a hunk of a husband who adores her. I've known her for almost ten years, and in my opinion she deserves everything she's got. I never want to see her disillusioned or disappointed, never. It *hurts* me. A couple of meetings ago, during her fifteen minutes, she got tears in her eyes talking about how much she wanted a baby. That's all—but I couldn't stand it, I had to get up and go in the kitchen. I couldn't look at her.

"Well, at least after tomorrow you'll know more," Isabel said. "The uncertainty has to be the worst part."

"The worst," Lee agreed. She stuck her fingers in her short brown hair and ruffled it, a body-language change of subject. Lee is five-foot-two, small-boned and delicate-looking, but she's anything but fragile. She plays golf and tennis, swims, dances—upper-class sports—and she's good at all of them. One night I had too many gin and tonics and challenged her to an arm-wrestling contest. She twisted me right under the table.

"Well, I'm done," she said briskly. "Rudy, you go next."

"That's it? Work's fine, your parents drove you crazy over Hanukkah, and Henry's got a sperm test tomorrow?"

"That's it." Lee grinned. "That leaves you twenty minutes, which I'm sure you can use."

Rudy laughed, but it's true.

"Well, okay, I'll go. One thing that's going on with me . . ." She leaned toward Lee and touched her hand. "Curtis and I, we've been thinking a lot about it lately, and . . ."

"What?"

"Well, we've decided it's probably time for *us* to try for a baby."

She kept her eyes on Lee and didn't look at me after she delivered this news. I joined in the surprised exclamations and good wishes, but inside I went numb. As long as they were childless, the inevitable collapse of Rudy and Curtis's marriage could only hurt two people, and I only cared about one of them. *Oh, no, not a baby*. Deeper and deeper. Across the table, Isabel sent me a quick, veiled glance. She was thinking the same thing. Her opinion of Curtis Lloyd is a kinder, gentler version of mine, but when I pin her down we agree on the basics: he's an asshole.

"I thought a lot about whether I should tell you this right now," Rudy was saying to Lee, "but it seemed worse to keep it from you. Like I couldn't trust you to be able to handle it or something—"

"Oh, no, I'm glad you told me. Oh, Rudy, I'm really, *really* happy for you."

"And then I thought, well, what if I do get pregnant? Will I have to hide that from her, too?"

They started laughing, making jokes about giving the baby to a family of gypsies to raise in secret. Lee might or might not be pretending, I couldn't tell. If anyone in her situation would be glad for Rudy, it would be Lee. But Jeez, what timing. Lee's only human. If Rudy gets pregnant, how can it be anything for her but a stake through the heart?

I got up to get more bread, and when I came back Rudy was talking about the landscaping course again. I kept my mouth shut and let Lee and Isabel urge her to do it, enroll in the program. But I bet she doesn't. Last year she was excited about a job that would have involved consulting on corporate art purchases for one of the big associations in town, the home builders or the franchise owners, I can't remember. It would've been a miracle if she'd gotten it, since she threw away her master's in art history with nothing left to do but the thesis. But it was good to see her interested in anything, so we all encouraged her to go for it. In the end she never applied, though, never even sent in a résumé. Oh, Rudy, why not? we asked her. Well, it would've involved a lot of travel. So? Curtis didn't go for that.

I cannot stand that slippery, psychotic little prick.

When it was my turn, I told a pretty funny story about the blind date I had on New Year's Eve—which, believe me, wasn't funny at all while it was happening. Lee laughed so hard, she had to get out a Kleenex and wipe her eyes. "Oh, Emma, that is priceless," she wheezed, "where do you *find* these guys?"

"I'm a rotten date magnet, they stick to me like lead filings. You girls have no idea how lucky you are. Well, that's it, I'm done—Isabel, you go. Nothing else is new with me. I've got this *Washingtonian* deadline on Monday, that's it. Now, Isabel."

Lee said, "Wait a second, not so fast. What about your married guy? Anything happening there?"

A couple of weeks ago, in a really stupid moment, I made the mistake of mentioning Mick to Lee and Isabel. But I didn't say his name or give any details that would've identified him. I just said I was occasionally seeing a man who happened to be married and we didn't do anything but I was incredibly attracted to him and it was driving me out of my mind. Which trivializes what I feel, but I figure the group knows me well enough to decipher my self-protection codes. Anyway, it just spilled out—I couldn't control it. And it didn't even give me any satisfaction, since I couldn't go into any gory specifics. Lee's taking dance lessons with Sally now, and Henry's becoming pals with Mick, and it's all just a big, ugly mess. So I told them he was "somebody from work," which you must admit is technically true.

"Nope," I said, "nothing new on the married guy scene."

"You've stopped seeing him?"

"Oh, I still run into him every once in a while. We just talk."

"So—does that mean you're still interested in him?"

"Oh, you know. It's hopeless, so—" I grinned, shrugged, got really interested in spacing my silverware just so.

Lee got the hint. "Okay, I just wondered, because you haven't mentioned him lately. But you're okay, Em, right?"

"Sure, I'm fine, and the reason I don't talk about him is because there's nothing to talk about."

"Okay."

"Okay," I said, laughing. Rudy sent me a very dry look, which I ignored. "Now, Isabel. Tell us how school's going."

"School is wonderful—I got an A minus on my families-at-risk final." Cheering and table thumping. Isabel's getting a master's in social work at American U. "Other than that . . ." We waited, but she just shook her head and smiled. She was unusually quiet tonight, I realized. I looked at her more closely. Isabel grows younger and prettier to me all the time. Most of her long gray hair fell out while she was having chemotherapy, and when it grew back it came in curly and soft, like a young girl's hair. It suits her, doesn't look incongruous or too youthful, because her calm face is almost unlined. She doesn't look placid, though; that's not what I mean. Serene. Beneficent. She has a quality of repose I associate more with medieval saints than social work grad students. She's not like anyone else. Isabel is unique.

"Nothing at *all* is going on?" Lee pressed.

"Not really. Nothing much."

"What about your neighbor? And didn't you have a doctor's appointment—"

"Well, I *was* thinking about Gary today," she said quickly. Everybody groaned. "Or more precisely, I was thinking about infidelity and forgiveness. Sexual infidelity, how it's different between men and women. For us, it's all but unforgivable. For them, it's nothing."

"Not all men," Lee corrected.

"No." The softness in her voice when she said that one word, the way she touched Lee's arm just for a second—there's so much love between those two, I felt a stab of jealousy. "Definitely not all men." She put her chin on her folded hands. "I'll tell you a story during my fifteen minutes," she said. "Gary's been on my mind lately. I'll tell you about his last girlfriend."

"You mean Betty Cunnilefski?" We snickered—as we always do when Betty's name comes up.

"No, Betty was his first girlfriend. Or at least the first one I knew about. There were others."

"Others? *Plural*, Isabel?" I glanced at Rudy, who looked as surprised as I felt. Lee said nothing—she must already know about this.

Rudy blurted out what I was thinking: "Why didn't you ever tell us?"

"It was—I just—" Isabel gave a helpless shrug. "Because—I didn't want to. Until now."

"Were you embarrassed?" Rudy theorized gently.

"No. Well, yes. Yes, partly. It is hard to admit you've loved a man who was unfaithful for most of the twenty-two years you lived with him."

"Oh, but—"

"But mostly—I think I had to be able to forgive him myself before I could tell you."

"*Forgive* him? Forgive that bastard? Isabel, it was bad enough when it was only the cunnilingus bitch. Now—how the hell many women are we talking about?" I was swearing at Gary, but the truth is I was angry with Isabel, too, for keeping this little detail about her life a secret from us. She knew it, too; she held her hand out toward me along the tablecloth.

"Emma, it was too ugly. If I'd told you, there would only have been more anger, more bitterness."

"You're damn right."

"But don't you see, it wouldn't have helped. It would only have added to the negativity."

"Oh, okay. I get it. Balance, you wanted cosmic balance. Well, say no more."

She made a patient face. "Don't be mad. There's a time for everything, and the time for telling you this about Gary and me wasn't right. Until now."

"It's all right." I smiled—no hard feelings—and didn't mention that the time for telling *Lee* this had been right quite awhile ago, apparently. But that would have been admitting to childish jealousy, a card in my hand of character flaws I like to keep close to the vest.

Rudy broke an uncomfortable pause to ask, "So who was this last floozy, Isabel?"

"Her name was Norma, and she wasn't much of a floozy. She was an accountant, another one of Gary's office conquests. After Betty, I always knew when he was seeing someone, but this—"

I couldn't keep quiet. "Jesus, Isabel, how many were there?" *Gary Kurtz*? I still couldn't picture it. He's this stocky, middle-aged guy with a beard, sort of a Santa Claus type of fellow but without the heartiness. A government drone, probably a GS–14 or so, does something in the Commerce Department that's so dull I can't remember what it is. Back when I used to speak to him, he talked a lot about his grass.

"I don't know how many," Isabel answered, raising an eyebrow at me in a rare show of testiness. "I just know the last one wouldn't go away. So I went to see her."

We gasped.

"Really?"

"You went to *see* her?"

"I looked her up in the phone book, and there she was—Norma Stottlemyer, in an apartment on Colesville Road."

"How did you know her name?"

"Gary told me. He never denied anything, I'll give him that. He never lied to me."

"I just think that makes it worse," Lee said fiercely.

"I picked a Saturday morning when he was home, and told him I was going to the Safeway. I drove over to Silver Spring, one of those brick garden apartments set close to the road on Colesville. Children outside, plastic toys everywhere—I was terrified she was married and I'd end up wrecking *her* home. But I had a story in case a man answered, or a child—I was collecting for leukemia."

"Good one."

"Except you didn't have any I.D.," Lee noted, always practical.

"Anyway, she came to the door herself, wearing a pink corduroy bathrobe. Even before I went in, I knew she lived alone. Just something about her."

"How old?" I asked.

"Late twenties."

"Rat bastard. What did she look like?"

"It was still early, I'd caught her off guard, she hadn't fixed up yet."

Rudy and I shook our heads at each other: *Are you hearing this?* Trust Isabel to make excuses for the slut who was banging her husband. "So she was ugly," I said.

"No, not ugly, just not attractive. Not sexy, not even interesting-looking. Quite ordinary. When I said, 'I'm Isabel Kurtz,' she looked blank. Then I said, 'Gary's wife,' and I thought she was going to faint."

"She didn't *know*?"

"Yes, she knew he was married, but she was shocked, not thinking fast. She backed up, sort of waved me in, and that's when I knew we weren't going to be having any dramatic scene. There was just no fight in her."

"Wimp. Dirtbag wuss."

"Her apartment was all Pier I and Door Store—you'd have written something scathing and funny about it, Emma." I decided to take that as a compliment. "She took me into the kitchen, not the living room. I could hear music from the apartment next door, just the bass thumping. There was half a bowl of soup on the counter, I remember—she'd been eating soup for breakfast. Bean with bacon." She smiled with one side of her mouth, dry and wistful and bitter at the same time.

"She had one of those cheap, six-jar spice racks over the stove. Glass jars with name tags. She bought spices and poured them into the little jars and wrote CINNAMON and BLACK PEPPER and GARLIC POWDER on the labels. Only six." She looked around at us in pity and amazement, but I don't know what she found more pathetic, the fact that Norma labeled her spices or that she only used six. "And—she had kitten magnets on the refrigerator. One played a tune. She backed up against it and it fell on the floor and started to play 'You Are My Sunshine.'"

"Isabel," I said, "you're killing me."

"So what *happened*?" Rudy said.

"I could see she wasn't going to start us off, so I said, 'I just wanted to see what kind of person you are.' I meant it literally; that's exactly why I'd come, to *see* her, try to understand what Gary found so attractive. But she took it as a condemnation and started to cry."

"Oh, Jesus."

"What did you do?"

"I cried with her. I did. We turned our backs on each other and buried our faces—well, I had my handkerchief and she used a paper towel."

Rudy was trying not to laugh. "God, I can see it."

"After that, I just lost interest. She was such a pitiful enemy, I couldn't even hate her. But for the first time, I felt contempt for Gary. Just utter contempt."

"Gary's a pig," I said.

"Norma stopped crying and said she was sorry, so sorry, and she would stop seeing him. I asked her if she was in love with him, and she said yes." She smiled faintly. "But, you know, I don't think she was. And I think she realized it at that moment. I said it didn't matter to me if she kept seeing him or not, because I was leaving him. And I said I thought she could do better."

I clapped my hands. "*Good* one."

"After that, I went home and told Gary it was over. My only mistake—"

"Was leaving him instead of throwing him out," Lee finished for her, and we all nodded grimly. That satisfying gesture had cost Isabel the house in the divorce settlement. Gary the pig is still living there in suburban splendor, still mowing his fucking lawn, while Isabel makes do in a cramped, one-bedroom apartment on a tough street in Adams-Morgan. She got breast cancer less than two years after she left him, and Gary demonstrated what a class act he is by trying to get her cut out of his government health insurance policy. She finally won, but it wasn't a battle she needed to be fighting at that particular time in her life. I think I hate him for that more than anything, even the womanizing.

"Well, I'm not sure why I told that story," Isabel marveled, shaking her head. "I honestly haven't thought about Norma in ages."

"It's a sad story," Rudy said.

"You said you'd been thinking about infidelity," Lee reminded her.

"Yes. But not for any particular reason."

Was it my guilty imagination that Isabel flicked a look at me then? A quick, appraising glance to see if I'd gotten a message? Because infidelity has been on my mind lately, too. I don't know if I could commit adultery. If she was trying to tell me something, she'd done a clever job. It's useful to keep in mind that if I began an affair with Mick Draco, there would be nothing more than her Door Store furniture to distinguish me from the Norma Stottlemyers of the world.

Isabel put her forearms on the table, leaning in. "No, I do know why I told you." She spoke in a low, earnest tone; we bent toward her, catching her intensity. "I wanted you to know that I've forgiven him. No, wait"—I must've made some scornful noise—"listen to me, it's important. Nobody knows why a man does what he does—"

"Isabel, there are *standards*, there's—" She made a violent slicing motion with the side of her hand. I closed my mouth.

"No one knows why someone acts in a certain way, not all the reasons, not the compulsions or inducements that led up to it, what weapons a person has inside himself to fight temptation. We can't know that. Listen, all I want to tell you is—life is so short. It's so short, and I can't waste any more of mine on resentment. Forgiveness isn't weak, it doesn't mean you have no moral center. Buddha said wanting revenge is like spitting in the wind—you only hurt yourself." She spread her hands—honest to God, she looked like an angel in the vanilla-scented glow of the candles. "I believe it's true that we're all one, all . . . one." Her smile was wry and self-conscious, perfectly aware of how daffy this sounded to someone like—say—me. "And separations are an illusion. When I forgive Gary, I forgive myself."

Talk about a conversation stopper.

"Yeah, except you didn't do anything," I threw in, mostly to break the silence. Isabel's sad smile said I'd missed the point, but she loved me anyway. I got up to make coffee.

I dimmed the lights to bring in dessert—Isabel's homemade, candelit cake. It was a big hit. We sang "For she's the jolly good fellow," and she blew out her candles.

"Oh, why didn't I bring my movie camera?" Lee wailed. "I'm so proud of you," she told Isabel, kissing her on both cheeks.

"Me, too," Rudy said, leaning over to hug her. "I love it that you're doing things for *yourself* for a change. And from now on it's just going to get better."

"Right," I said. "The second half of your life is going to be great."

"To the second half of Isabel's life," Lee proposed, and we toasted with our coffee cups and waterglasses and wine dregs.

I didn't think she was going to be able to say anything. I've never seen Isabel so overcome; it almost made *me* cry. Her soft blue eyes were shimmering, but finally she managed to say, "To all of us."

"To all of us," I seconded, and added my all-time favorite toast: "May we live forever."

Rudy stayed after Lee and Isabel left. I put on my coat and we went outside on the porch to smoke cigarettes and look at the moon. My neighborhood is about one-third black, one-third white, one-third other, mostly Hispanic, and I like it that way. It's real. Sometimes it's a little too real, like when you wake up to sirens and cop radios at four in the morning, or read about a mugging in the next block, or stumble into a drug deal in front of the Latino grocery store. Still, I like the mix of colors and classes, most of us law-abiding, all of us just trying to get along, as Rodney said. Tonight it was peaceful, the quiet sweetened by the soft yellow light in the windows of my neighbors, nobody out except the dog walkers.

"Isabel was awfully quiet, wasn't she? Except for the Norma story," Rudy said, and I said I'd noticed that, too. "Emma, do you think Lee really doesn't mind about Curtis and me? Trying for a baby?"

I answered carefully. "I think it's bound to be hard on her. Whether she knows it yet or not. I think she and Henry are in for a pretty rough time." Rudy sighed. I watched my breath condense in the cold, silvery air. "So. A baby. I thought Curtis wasn't interested in having children."

She got that pleasant, determined look we both wear when we talk about him. "He wasn't at first, but he's come around. The new job I was telling you about is almost a cinch now, and when that happens our income will more than double. And that's only to start."

"The lobbying job? So he'll be a lobbyist?" Perfect.

"Yes, so money won't be an issue anymore."

"Money was what was holding him back?" And here I thought it was total self-involvement.

"Mostly. Oh, Emma, I'm so excited. I didn't want to show it because of Lee. But, God, can you imagine me a mother?"

I sidestepped that by asking, "What does Greenburg think about it?"

She took a nervous drag and flicked ashes over the porch rail. "He won't say, he just keeps asking what I think. So . . ." She laughed giddily. "He's probably against it."

"Well, you can't live your life according to what your shrink thinks." Although sometimes it wouldn't be a bad idea. I'm always trying to find out, in clever, oblique ways, what Greenburg thinks about Curtis. Rudy never tells me, which either means she's too smart for me or Greenburg's too smart for her. I'm not even sure I'd *want* Greenburg to disillusion her about Curtis. Sometimes I think he must be in the same conspiracy I'm in, which involves saying nothing bad about Curtis in order to keep Rudy from getting hurt.

"That's right, and you also can't put off having a child until you're in perfect mental health. God, I'll be *dead* by then."

"Well, I hope it's a girl and it looks like you, not Curtis," I said, pretending that was a joke.

She hugged herself, laughing. Her eyes were shiny with wistfulness and hope, and it finally hit me how much she wanted a child. "Oh, think of it, Em. I could be somebody's mother in nine months." She turned her face up to the moon, and when she shivered, it wasn't from the cold.

"I hope so," I said truthfully. "I really hope so, and I think it's great. I hope it happens soon."

"Thank you. Really. That means a lot. Well, hey, it's late, I'd better get going."

She gave me a strong hug, which I returned weakly. She'd forgotten to ask me about Mick. And I'm so screwed up on this subject, I couldn't bring him up first. "Do you really have to go? It's only eleven." Hint, hint. *Stay longer and ask me about the man I'm obsessed with.*

"No, I should go, Curtis doesn't like me driving at night." She started down the steps.

"Want me to call him?" Yuck. "Tell him you're on your way?"

"That's okay, I've got my phone." She patted her purse. "Thanks for dinner, everything was great. Hey, do you want to go to the movies on Monday?"

I brightened. "Sure. I'll call you Sunday night."

"Sunday's good." She blew me a kiss. "Night, Em."

She'd parked half a block up the street. *Rats*, I thought, watching her negotiate the grass strip between sidewalk and curb with the dog shit–avoiding grace of a D.C. veteran. Thoughtlessness, self-absorption, preoccupation, negligence—you expect these from the average run of your acquaintances, but not from your best friend. From her you want perfection. You want her to read your mind.

Parking is a bitch on my street. The car behind Rudy's khaki-colored Wrangler had boxed her in. She inched back and forth, back and forth, about ten times before she finally jerked free of the space. As she started to pull away, a speeding car roared past, practically sideswiping the Jeep, and slid to a long, screeching stop fifty feet down from the front of my walkway. My heart stopped but started again and began to race when I saw what kind of car it was—Volvo station wagon—and who was getting out of it. Lee.

Rudy and I converged on her. "What happened, where's Isabel? What's wrong?"

She grabbed us both and held on. She was crying and couldn't talk, I had to shake her. "I took her home—she told me. I'm not supposed to tell—"

"*What*?"

"The cancer."

"Oh, my God."

She kept swallowing. I had her hand, I felt it shaking. "A recurrence. The doctor's almost sure. She has to have a bone scan." Lee broke down, and Rudy hugged her. I hung my arms around both of them; we stood there in the middle of the street, holding on for our lives.

A car came and honked at us. I gave it the finger. "Let's go." I started for Lee's car, which was still idling. "Rudy, you drive."

"Where? You mean to Isabel's?"

"Well, where the hell else?"

"But I wasn't supposed to tell you," Lee cried, "you're not supposed to know!"

I just stared at her.

"Right," she said, coming out of her trance. "Let's go."

12

Isabel

A lot of my youth is a blur, great chunks of it simply missing, as if I periodically contracted amnesia along with the usual measles and chicken pox of childhood. And yet my recollection of the night I gave up on my parents is as clear and vivid as a piece of clip art. I was eight. I know because I tagged it in my consciousness as if with a book mark, quite aware that something significant had happened. *I'm eight*, I thought, *and this is true. This is something I know about Mother and Daddy*.

It was in Marshalltown, Iowa, early on a winter evening. I remember the lamps burning in the living room, the smell of hot dust from a hissing radiator. The sound of a page turning, and then the dry, unnecessary cough, *uh ehh*, of my mother. Creeping down the staircase, I paused to look at my parents, peering at them over the banister rail. Our small house had no office; my father wrote sermons in the living room seated in his morris chair, using the broad arms for a desk, notebook on one side, Bible on the other. He sat with his foot propped up on the needlepoint stool, his elbow on his knee, forehead on the heel of his hand. Slowly, steadily, and without pausing, he composed the dry, ineffably dull discourse he would deliver in a passionless monologue next Sunday at the Concordia Evangelical Lutheran Church.

Across the blue oval of the braided rug, in the cheap, sixty-watt, old-gold beam of the tole lamp, my mother bowed over a fall of heavy cloth on her lap—curtains, perhaps, or some dark, dreary garment of my father's. Her forehead furrowed slightly at the first prick of each stitch, cleared with every long, smooth pull of the thread. There was no music playing, no television, no radio. Definitely no conversation. My parents faced each other in perfect half-profile, still and silent as coins.

In that moment I understood—without knowing the word, of course—the meaning of stasis. And the futility of hoping that anything could change, not here, not in this room. Silence reigned; silence saturated. There couldn't possibly be any communication between them, or among us. My father spoke more in church on Sunday than at home the rest of the week. And here is the insight that ultimately saved me: *Something is wrong. Other people aren't like this.*

Arrested, I came down the rest of the way and drifted over to my mother, stood beside her chair. She made some gesture, a nod or a shrug of her shoulder, but she didn't look up or speak to me. She wore a tan woolen jumper with a mustard-colored blouse, white kneesocks, and loafers. She was fifty-three years old. I leaned against her tough, stringy shoulder, watching the changes in her face, thinking how gray her dry, wavy hair was. When I pressed my arm against her arm, she looked at me, startled. "What's wrong?" And she covered my forehead with her cool, spidery hand. To see if I was sick.

I considered my answer. "I don't feel good," I could have said. Had said in the past. I was a clever child, not above malingering for attention. Not above hypochondria, either.

But this night was different; this was the night I grew up. I said, "Nothing," and sidled away. My father never looked up or stopped writing. And I gave up on them. In that moment, I ran out of hope.

How lugubrious that sounds. Poor little me. In fact, it wasn't that dire. And much better to give up cleanly then and there, I think, than to yearn and long and nurse false hopes for a closeness that can never come. My parents weren't monsters. I never hated them. Years later, when my father was dying, I kept watch with my mother and sister as he lay in his steel hospital bed, stone-faced and speechless as ever. "I love you, Daddy," I told him once—only once. He was still conscious then. He turned his pale blue eyes on me and blinked. His tongue came out to wet his lips, and I thought he was going to speak. He didn't. But he nodded a little. And I thought—maybe he thinks it's understood. All these years, maybe for him it's been a given, not worth saying out loud. Maybe.

My sister is just like them. I barely know her. Eighteen years older, she's more like an aunt than a sister, some relative I rarely see. I write her spare, jovial thank-you notes when she remembers my birthday with a card. Lately I've been hearing from her more often, though. "Shall we put Mother in an assisted living facility?" she wonders. Oh, I should think so. Mother is ninety-four and losing her mind. Odd: she never gave much of herself to me, my mother, only the bare essentials, no frivolous extras like hugs, silliness, laughter, conversation. And yet now that she's all but gone, I miss her very much. My father, too. It's odd.

Why didn't I grow up remote and cold, or frightened and clinging, pursuing one wrong man after another in search of the elusive embrace of acceptance? Maybe it's only in self-help books or on television talk shows that such a fate lies in store for every lonely child. Real life is much more complicated. Or much simpler. One thing I know: love or the search for it is stronger than neglect, or indifference, or rejection. I looked for it in other places, not in my parents' house, and I found it. Occasionally.

The Graces didn't come to see me after all, that night Lee raced back to Emma's and told her and Rudy what I had just asked her not to tell them. They drove to my street and parked in front of my building for ten minutes, debating what to do. They decided to reconnoiter—drive through the alley to the back, see if my lights were on. If they were, they would park, knock at my door, and demand entrance.

The lights weren't on.

They debated again, and eventually drove back to Emma's. Where they sat in Lee's car for an hour and fifteen minutes, talking about me. This was the best of all possible resolutions, since talking about me that night would have been infinitely more satisfying for everybody than talking to me. "Nobody wanted to get out of the car," Lee reported afterward. "We didn't want to *land*. We didn't want to go in, sit down, drink coffee, look at each other in the light. So we just sat and talked and stared straight out the windshield. Like we were at the drive-in."

Emma's feelings were hurt because I'd told Lee but not her. (She didn't confide that in me, of course; Rudy did. Emma still imagines that if she hides her vulnerabilities, no one will notice she has any.) But there was no help for it, nothing I could have done except what I did. The news was too fresh—I was too raw. I shouldn't have gone to Emma's house at all that night, but at the last minute I couldn't stay away. I knew it would be warm there, and I was freezing cold.

"A metastasis, I'm almost certain," Dr. Glass said. "I'm very sorry." It was hard to listen after that. I heard "stage four," though. And I heard "bone," and thought of the mild ache in my hip I'd thought was a muscle strain. After that, my mind went blank. The oddest thing. I turned icy cold all over, a gelid, numbing horror. I remember leaving Dr. Glass's office, but not getting on the elevator or going out of the building. I remember men digging up the sidewalk on P Street with jackhammers. The noise was so deafening, it jarred me awake and I realized it was raining. The bus stop was blocks away. I thought, Should I take a taxi? But it would only take me home, and what was the point of that? What was the point of anything? I stood on the curb and watched pedestrians come and go in the crosswalk, listened to the Walk/Don't Walk light click on and click off, on and off. A woman bumped me. "Oh, sorry," she said with a quick smile, and I stared at her in dull surprise. *Do you think it matters?* I asked her retreating back. Whether you hit me, or say excuse me, or wear a warm wool coat, or buy an expensive briefcase or read the newspaper—or make an appointment at the optometrist's for new glasses, or have a dinner party, or get enough sleep, or dream about your vacation, or meet a man, or take your vitamins, or buy flowers from the vendor on the corner? Do you think any of that matters? *Nothing* matters. I know it—why don't you?

I had fallen into the rut in my mind from the last time someone told me I had cancer. A habit. Chill rain soaking the shoulders of my trench coat woke me up, like the jackhammers. Mundane reality forced movement on me. I could go home, get warm, get on with it. As long as you're not dead, you're alive. I lifted my hand. Immediately a braking cab splashed water on my shoes. I told the driver my address and he took me home.

Since then, I've survived by getting from one moment to the next moment. I feed the dog, take in the mail, wipe crumbs off the counter. Contrary to how it felt, my life didn't stop in Dr. Glass's office; it keeps moving on, the future as big a mystery as ever. Well, no, that's not quite true. As a matter of fact, the only good thing I've come up with about my situation is: at least the suspense is over. It's looking as if Isabel Thorlefsen Kurtz will die of breast cancer, not in an automobile accident, not peacefully in her sleep of old age, not of AIDS or a heart attack, not in a drive-by shooting. No more wondering; finally knowing. It's something.

I want to be wide awake to the truth, not pretend and not hide, quaking, behind irony or passivity. Acceptance is dead last, though—forgive the pun—on the famous list of five stages. First comes denial, but I seem to have bypassed that one. Because of immediate past experience, I suppose; having had cancer before has inured me, to some small extent. What is the difference between hope and false hope? Who's to say what is "the best way" to die? How am I, how is anyone expected to know that? Oh, I see it's just beginning—I'll be on intimate terms with these and all the other unanswerable questions soon enough.

But I have things to do, decisions to make. I have to keep my head clear, not cloud it with thoughts of loss and dread. Plenty of time for that, too. I'm not ready for the sympathy of people who love me (this is what Emma couldn't understand, and I'll make her understand, but not yet, I can't do it yet), I have to hang on a little longer to my impersonality, my anonymity. That's why I haven't called anyone. I have to put my house in order. It's crucial to keep working, planning, going on with my life just as before, as if it still had meaning. And—I must confess to a little loop in my brain that keeps insisting I still might get out of this. A low, adamant voice saying, *You're only fifty, you won't die. It can't be finished.*

The last two years have been the best ever, and I wouldn't have had them if I hadn't gotten sick in the first place. So, inevitably, I must ask, was it worth it? Is this a fair trade? On the outside, it looked as if the best was just about to happen to me—satisfying work, finally some security and stability, maybe even a man to love. But on the inside, I already had everything. Life is for living, not relishing in retrospect. I've been given two splendid years of rich, tantalizing uncertainty and unexpected contentment. Was it enough?

I'm afraid of the question. I said I wouldn't do this. But everything is conspiring against me, all the things I love. I made a pot of Indian tea and drank it with saffron honey, and I savored the musky, smoky taste as never before. If I had scotch, I would pour a little glass and let it prickle on my tongue, let the hot, masculine fire burn all the way down. An inch of snow fell last night. I opened the window and scooped up a handful, let it melt on my palm. I stuck out my tongue and tasted it, and it was dirty and metallic and delicious. I can't get enough of anything. Music—but I put on the Beethoven piano sonata that always makes me cry, and when the adagio came, I broke down.

Grace suspects something. She watches me. I look up and catch her brown eyes on me, steadfast and worried. Sweet old girl. She's ten, we think, and might outlive me. I never expected that.

Little things. The thought of losing them makes them unbearably dear. It's easy to forget at a time like this that life also features cruelty, indifference, brutality, perversion, bigotry, starvation, greed, venality, madness, corruption. I only think of the sweetness. Simple things. The quarter moon, the taste of an orange. The smell of the pages of a new book. If I pause to listen, I can hear Kirby moving around in his bedroom, right over my bedroom. Would he have been my lover? I listen to the voices of my friends who call and leave me messages—"Isabel, oh God, I don't know what to say," "Isabel, please call me, I love you"—and I know I can't stay away from them much longer. I have to tell my son, my mother, my sister. Oh, the world is hurtling toward me, all the pieces of my heart flying at me at once, I'll be leveled by love if I don't take care.

A bone scan on Tuesday—pro forma; Glass already knows—then his office again on Wednesday. He says he'll tell me everything. I'll take a notebook and write it all down. I have to be smart, stay focused. I'll go with a list of questions. Maybe . . . no.

Yes. I'll ask Lee to go with me.

13

Lee

At first I thought I was the only one who couldn't stand Dr. Glass, but it turned out we all hated him. Except for Emma, though, we managed to be polite.

"I don't understand what you're talking about," she said, leaning forward with her head jutting, as if a leash around her neck was holding her down. "You're the only doctor in the room, notice, so would you mind speaking English?"

I'd never heard her sound so shrill. It would have embarrassed me—in the majority of situations, I think we accomplish very little by being confrontational—but I was angry, too, and in her way Emma was speaking for all of us.

A lot of framed certificates hung on the wall behind Dr. Glass's desk. He had a tasteful office, a large staff, several prestigious hospital associations. What he lacked was a bedside manner, or even one that hinted he cared at all about the people who came to him to hear the worst news. Maybe he did care, but you couldn't tell it from his dead eyes or his thin smile, and not from his virtually inaudible speaking voice. He moved his lips like a ventriloquist—hardly at all. We had to bend over to hear him, me with my notebook pressed to my chest—I was the official note-taker—and strain to catch his low, rapid-fire mumble.

"I'm saying there is no surgical cure for a cancer that's already spread beyond the site of origin. Still, the patient who presents with stage four metastatic breast disease has a number of treatment options, although some or none may be indicated in the individual case. In this case, we have—"

"In *Isabel's* case. She's the 'patient presenting,' and her name is Isabel."

"Emma." Isabel was chalk white but calm, calmer than we were. Even when Glass had enumerated the metastases—"mets" he called them—in her spine and pelvis, both femurs, and her rib cage, she'd sat with her hands folded in her lap and stared straight back at him, not flinching. I could hardly take notes, my fingers were shaking so. It wasn't only the doctor's delivery that made it hard to write down what he said. My mind kept switching on and off, the strangest sensation, as if my fear was shorting out the circuitry in my brain.

At least I wasn't crying. Rudy was crying. To hide it from Isabel, she got up and walked to the window, pretending to look down at the traffic on Reservoir Road. But I saw her sneak her handkerchief out of her pocket and hold it over her mouth and nose. I wanted to shout at her, *Don't you dare break down!* That's all we would need. Emma's rudeness made a distraction, at least—we could focus on it instead of the horrible, devastating things, one after another, Dr. Glass would not stop muttering.

"In *Isabel's* case," he said, narrowing his eyes behind his Ralph Lauren bifocals, "where we have carcinomatosis in a distant site, a patient presently in menopause, with a positive estrogen but negative progesterone receptor status, as well as a prior history of cytotoxin—chemotherapy—I'm saying the treatment modalities available to us have narrowed and are somewhat limited."

"What about a bone marrow transplant?" Emma kept squeezing the arms of her chair with both hands, as if she'd fly out of it if she let go. "That could cure her, couldn't it?"

He bounced his fingertips together and retracted his lips in a slow, annoying rhythm, like a guppy. "There are a number of factors to consider before I would endorse ABMT/BCT. Autologous bone marrow or blood cell transplantation," he said when Emma uncrossed her legs and stomped one boot heel on his carpeted floor. "A number of factors." He turned cold eyes on Isabel. "I wouldn't rule out antiestrogen therapy to begin with, although the fact that you've already tried tamoxifen, with obviously unsuccessful results, makes me less than hopeful on that score. Down the road, there's chemo. At this time there's no way to tell whether you'd respond better to HDC or SDC—"

"High-dose or standard-dose chemotherapy," I interrupted. "I read about it on the Internet."

He actually smiled. "Very good." But the surprise in his voice was insulting, and I sympathized with Emma when she sucked her tongue, *tst*. "Eventually—it's too soon to say yet—you may decide to undergo what we call induction chemotherapy, a prelude for patients considering HDC with ABMT/BCT. It's not a therapy in itself, but it's helpful sometimes in determining whether a cancer will respond to the drugs we use in high-dose chemo. On the other hand, responding to or 'passing' induction therapy doesn't mean HDC with ABMT/BCT will be any more effective than SDC, it simply means the cancer is sensitive to chemotherapy. Also, it doesn't mean you'll live longer or have an equivalent or better quality of life with HDC than SDC."

"So really, it doesn't mean anything."

"It means exactly what I said it means."

We stared back and forth between Glass and Emma, whose eyes were locked. He seemed nettled, but she looked like a witch, a Fury; I could swear her hair was standing on end. Even Rudy turned around, caught by the hostility in the room, thick as a mist.

In the middle of the tense silence, Isabel stood up.

"I'll call you. About hormone therapy, and to set up the test. Tests. What you said, the induction . . ." She waved her hand gently—the real name wasn't important, she meant. All of us, even Glass, especially Emma, looked rueful and embarrassed. Because, for a few minutes, it had been easier to behave as if the problem here were a personality conflict instead of someone's life. Isabel's life.

We rode down in the elevator in a strange, self-conscious silence until Rudy asked where we should go for lunch. Sergei's in Georgetown, we decided, because we could walk there. We couldn't seem to look in one another's faces, and yet we stayed bunched together in the elevator, arms and shoulders touching, like marchers in a demonstration. Isabel had asked *me* to go with her to see Dr. Glass, not Rudy or Emma. Somehow they'd found out, though, and insisted on going with us. That had made me mad; how pushy, I thought, how insensitive. Now . . . oh, God. Now I didn't want to think what I'd have done without them.

We asked for a booth in a corner of the restaurant, and I went to call the office, tell my assistant I'd be a lot later than I'd thought. When I came back, Rudy was ordering drinks.

"Double scotch, rocks," she said—like a man, like my father. Isabel and I asked for iced tea. "Hey, you guys—" Rudy started to protest, but Emma said, "I'll drink with you, Rude. Beer, please, whatever's on tap."

When the drinks came, nobody toasted. That's something we always do, at least for the first one. But this time we just sipped, still not really looking at one another. Everything I thought to say sounded either too light or too dark, so I just sat there. Finally Emma said, "Is it me, or was that guy a flaming asshole?" and we all started talking at once.

Glass had been awful, but I wouldn't have said so in case Isabel still liked him—he'd been her oncologist for the last two years, after all. But she told us, "I went to him because I'd heard he was good, and after that there wasn't any reason to switch—I thought I was cured. But I've always thought he was arrogant."

"*Arrogant*. He's a cartoon," Emma said. "I hated him as soon as I looked at him. Did you see the way he held the door for us? Sarcastic bastard."

He hadn't wanted all of us in his office. "Just one," he'd said with a fake smile. "Don't you think?" Implying it was silly of us, but cute, a girl thing, to want to stay together. But, no, we didn't think. Part of me could even see his point, and yet I'm the one who said, with particular force and composure, "We think it's important that we all hear what you have to say, Doctor. We're acting as Isabel's surrogate family." He chuckled and spread his hands, trying to suggest that that was absurd. We just looked back at him, not budging, and finally there wasn't anything else he could do. Emma was right: he had held the door sarcastically.

We ordered lunch. *We're eating*, I thought. Just like always, just as if something horrible hadn't happened. Isabel got the seafood salad. We could talk about some things but not others. For example, nobody could say, "How do you feel right now? What was it like when he said those things about the cancer in your body? Are you afraid?" All we could do, it seemed, was be together, ourselves, the same as always.

Emma asked the first really personal question. "Have you told Terry or your mother yet?"

"Not yet. I was waiting until I knew for sure." Isabel laid her fork down and sat back. She'd eaten almost nothing. "My mother won't understand—I probably won't tell her at all. There's no point." Her mother just went in a nursing home; she has Alzheimer's disease. "I'll have to tell my sister, though. And Terry. Oh, God," she whispered, and shut her eyes tight.

Rudy's face turned red; she put her hand over her mouth. Emma looked away.

I said, "I'll call Terry. If you want me to."

Isabel reached out and rubbed my arm up and down, hard, smiling with her jaws clenched. "Thanks. I'll call him tonight. It's better." She squeezed my elbow. "Thanks," she mouthed. That was as close as she came to crying all day.

"I can start a Web search," I said, trying to sound brisk. "I've done it before at work. It's amazing how much information is out there, and it's easy to access."

"As a matter of fact, Kirby's already doing that."

"Kirby? Your neighbor?"

Isabel nodded.

"Wait a second. Kirby *knows*?" I couldn't believe it. *Kirby* knew, and Isabel hadn't even told Terry yet?

A little color came into her cheeks. She turned her teaspoon over and over on the tablecloth. "I didn't tell you this yet. I didn't have a chance."

"Tell us what?"

"Kirby . . ." She looked up and laughed. "Kirby's in love with me. He says."

"*What*?"

"But he's gay!"

"You *said* he was gay."

"Yes, well. Apparently I was mistaken."

"Wow." Emma sat back and started to laugh.

"So," Rudy said, grinning, pleased. "Do you like him?"

Isabel shrugged. "Oh," she said, and nothing else.

"Well, are you, you know . . ."

"Lovers? No."

Emma stopped laughing to ask, "Are you going to be?"

Isabel's face had been lively for a minute, but now the animation faded. "I might have. I hadn't decided. Then . . ." She shook her head. "He's a friend, a good friend."

A good friend. It was the first I'd heard. And she'd told him about her illness even before she told her own son. But she'd told me first, and that was . . .

Maybe she hadn't. Maybe she'd told Kirby first. Even before me. I hate jealousy. At least it's its own punishment; it makes me feel like hell.

After a while, we started talking about other things, normal things. I wondered if anyone else was as surprised by that as I was. *This is how it's going to be,* I realized. Whatever happened, Isabel was going to try to make it as easy for us as she could.

Over our coffee, she asked about Henry. "What happened with the sperm test, Lee? Did you get the results yet?"

"Yes," I said, "the nurse called yesterday. They've figured it out."

"They have?"

"What's the story?"

I had been feeling guilty for being happy, for having twinges of gladness in the midst of my closest friend's crisis. But now the Graces' expectant faces and excitement, *Isabel's* excitement, erased all that. "You won't believe it. Henry has *too many* sperm."

Their mouths dropped, then they whooped with laughter—I knew they would.

"He's so relieved. Normal is between twenty million and two hundred million per millimeter, and Henry's got over a billion."

"Get *out*."

"A billion?"

"It's a rare condition."

"Oh, what a manly man," Emma said breathily. "Tell him I'm awed."

"So what happens now?"

"Well, we probably can't get pregnant in the normal way. It's a motility problem—he's got so many sperm, they clump together and can't move. So we'll have to do AI. Artificial insemination."

"With donor sperm?"

"No, they can use Henry's."

"Oh, Lee, that's wonderful!"

"I am so happy for you."

"The nurse said I could be pregnant in six months."

Isabel leaned over and kissed me. This was the news that had kept me going. How could I lose hope for her when this blessing was happening to me?

"This is so great. But you know," Emma said, "fifty years ago you'd've been out of luck. Thank God for the miracle of modern medicine." I saw her start to reach for her glass, then stop.

A sheepish silence fell. Emma had been going to toast the miracle of modern medicine. Then she'd remembered: the one most in need of a miracle here was Isabel.

"All right," I said, pushing my plate away, "what's the plan? How are we going to work this? I'll get on the 'Net again. Kirby, too—that's great, two heads are better than one." I really meant it. "It sounds like you probably need to decide about hormone therapy first, so that's where I'll start. We still have plenty of time to figure out the HDC and SDC or the BMT, if you decide to go that route. My father knows one of the head oncologists at Sloan-Kettering, they used to be golfing buddies, so I can call him and try to get some referrals, preferably local. You'll need at least two second opinions, don't you think? A different one from Glass's, whatever his turns out to be, and a tiebreaker, that would be ideal, but we'll see how it goes. How is your health insurance? Have you checked to see what it considers standard practice versus experimental?" Emma started to laugh. "What?" Isabel joined her—even Rudy looked amused. "What's so funny?"

"Nothing." Isabel put her arm around me.

"Am I being bossy?"

"No."

"No, you're being great," Emma said.

"You are," Rudy said.

"Well, *somebody's* got to get this thing organized. And I'm assuming time is of the essence, right? Am I right?"

They stopped smiling.

"You're right," Isabel said quietly, when no one else answered.

14

Rudy

"She has to be all right, Emma. She looks great, God, she looks beautiful."

"I know. She's never looked better."

"How could this have happened? How can she be so sick?"

"I don't know." Emma shook her head, miserable. It was just us now; Isabel and Lee had left Sergei's together at about three, but Emma and I never even got up. It was understood that we were staying. Like old times.

The waitress came over. "Can I get you ladies some more coffee?"

"No, but I'll have another scotch," I said. "Just a single this time."

Emma lifted her eyebrows at me. "Well, shoot. Guess that means I'll have to have another beer."

So we started drinking. Sometimes alcohol really works for me, really is the answer. Not always. But sometimes, something about the way it goes down, easy and clear and—*bright* or something—well, I can't explain it. But every once in a while, I just know it's going to be perfect.

This time, it gave me the courage to say, "I'm so frightened. It's all I can feel. Oh, Emma, what if she dies?" I could only whisper it. "What if Isabel dies?"

She slid out of her side of the booth and sat down on mine, making me shove over. "I'm scared, too. It's all I can think about."

"I just can't believe it. Still. Last week she was fine, and this week she might be dying. How can that be?"

"She's not dying. People beat it, people have remissions for years, decades. People are *cured*, you read about it all the time."

"That's true."

Emma drew vertical lines through the condensation on her beer glass. "My father died of cancer."

"You were little, though, weren't you? You didn't see it."

"I was eight, and they were already divorced. I don't know anything about it, just that he died of cancer. Of the liver."

"I hate cancer."

"Because it's slow, so you know. God, I'd rather be hit by a bus. Anything."

I stopped tearing my napkin into shreds to stare at my hands. What if I were dying? My skin . . . the shapes of my fingers, the gray-blue veins in my wrists. How could I lose myself? To be something, and then to be nothing. To cease. "She won't die," I said. "She's too young." But I meant, *I'm too young*.

Emma said, "Can I have a cigarette?"

"I quit."

"Oh. Okay, that's cool, we'll both—"

"Let's buy some."

"Okay." She got up and bought us a pack of Winstons.

"Can you believe I've got a date tonight?" she said, blowing a smoke ring at the ceiling. She was back on her side of the booth, and she was changing the subject, changing the mood. For me. She takes care of me.

"Who with?"

"Brad. Same guy."

"I thought you broke up."

"We did, then we sort of reunited. Out of inertia. But tonight I'm telling him it's really over."

"What's wrong with him?"

"Nothing."

We smiled, recognizing that we've had this conversation, about different men, a thousand times. "What's wrong with him?" "Nothing." Emma could write a book and call it that.

She squinted, using her thumbnail to peel the label off the Sam Adams bottle. She was wearing her hair up, to show off the enamel earrings I made her for her birthday. Emma thinks her skin is too pale, she thinks her hips are too big, she thinks her hair is too red or too brassy or something—I've never gotten that one. None of this is true. It used to worry me, how out of touch she is with her own looks, but now I just accept it. It's Emma. Anyway, I have a theory that feelings of inadequacy make people kinder and more tolerant of one another. They help keep us civil.

"Are you in love?"

"Am I in *love*?" She smirked, pretending she thought I was still talking about Brad. She rolled bits of label into balls and dropped them in the ashtray. Finally she quit playing and said, "How could I be? I hardly ever see him."

"Why do you see him at all?"

"Well, for one thing, he's helping me with an article I might do about the D.C. art world."

"*Another* article?"

"This is different, freelance. It wasn't even my idea," she said defensively. "The editor at *Capital* liked the piece I did for the paper and suggested I do something like it for them. The state of art in Washington."

"Do you know anything about the state of art in Washington?"

"No." She laughed. "So Mick said he'd help me."

"But doesn't it hurt, Em? Wouldn't it be better if—"

"We're *friends*, Rudy."

"I know, but—*secret* friends."

I wished I hadn't said that. It made her blanch. She lit a cigarette without looking at me and stopped talking.

I thought of the night we finally patched up our quarrel over Curtis. She called me at two in the morning, and I came. I found her sitting on the sofa in the living room of her old Foggy Bottom apartment, crying bitter tears and cursing Peter Dickenson, whom she had just thrown out. She'd gone with him longer, been more serious about him than any man since I've known her. They were even talking about marriage.

She'd really scared me that night, but in some ways this was worse. It wasn't that violent grief, that brokenhearted anger that I'll never forget—this was quiet and invisible. It was stealing parts of her, eating her up.

We ordered more drinks. Emma cheered up, and that cheered me up. I love the slow, warming sensation of my body going numb when I drink. It starts in strange places, my cheeks, my triceps, my thighs, and eventually it seeps into everything. It's no wonder people sleep with anybody when they're drunk. I feel such loving calm, such understanding, as if I'm everybody and everybody is me. I can control it now, but when I was younger I would screw anybody. I mean anybody. After a few drinks.

Just then, sure enough, a couple of guys came over from the bar and hit on us. One was cute. Sergei's is good for lunch, but later in the day it turns into a singles bar. Emma scowled at the two guys, who looked like lawyers, both younger than us. She reached for my hand across the table. "Hey, do you mind? We're trying to break up here. Jeez, the insensitivity of some peno-Americans."

They said, "Heh, heh," and went back to the bar.

We ordered another round. Emma said, "How did it get to be happy hour?"

"Oh, no. Oh, *no.*"

"What?"

"Curtis is coming home. I'm supposed to pick him up! Oh, my *God.*"

"What time? Take it easy, he can get home by himself. He does it every—"

"The airport. I'm supposed to pick him up at the *airport.*"

"Oh, the airport. That's different." She giggled. "What time?"

"Five-fifty."

"Uh-oh. You're in trouble, Rude. It's six o'clock."

I pressed my hands to my eyes, making everything black. Emma's laughter was catching, but mine sounded hysterical.

"What airline?" she asked.

"Delta."

"Okay, sit tight, I'll call National and leave a message. They'll page him—he'll like that. 'Mr. Curtis Lloyd, Mr. Curtis Lloyd, please come to the white courtesy phone.'"

"What will you say?"

"That you're sloshed and can't drive, what else?" I must have looked terrified, because she squeezed my wrist. "*Kidding*. What do you want me to say?"

"Say . . . I'm with Isabel."

"That's good. It's no big deal, he can take the subway to Eastern Market and walk home, can't he?"

"No, he'll take a cab."

"Of course he will," she said in her bland, ironic, Curtis voice. "Don't worry, Rudy, I'll fix it."

But when she came back, she looked worried and amused and sheepish. "You're screwed."

"Why?"

She sat down on my side again. "I had to leave a message."

"So?"

"They've got a new deal, voice mail. So he'll know it was me who called. I mean, he's going to hear *me*, not some page lady, with a message from you. He'll know I called and not you. I should've hung up."

"What did you say?"

"I said we were all here at Sergei's, comforting Isabel. You wanted to go pick him up, but she was in a bad way and we wouldn't let you leave."

"Oh, Em." One lie was bad enough, but that was about three.

"I know, but I got into it and couldn't stop."

I laughed shakily. I knew I was in trouble, though, even if Curtis believed Emma's lie.

The waitress came over and asked if we wanted another round. We looked at each other. All of a sudden I felt wonderful. "What the hell?" we said together. It really was like old times, when we first moved to D.C., and we'd hang out in bars or restaurants and talk for hours, six hours, eight, start at lunch and talk right through dinner. Before I got married.

"Hey, Rude. You're not really afraid of him, are you?" She must've been drunk. She would never have asked me that question sober.

I must've been drunk, too—I didn't mind it. I didn't lie, either. "Sometimes I am, but it's not his fault."

"Why isn't it?"

"Because I'm afraid of everything."

"How come?"

I shrugged.

She said, "Has he ever hit you?"

"*No.* Jesus, Emma!"

"Okay, I just wondered. I'm sorry. No offense."

"Well, now you know."

"Okay."

"Okay."

He had, though, once. Just one time, and it was so long ago, I never thought of it anymore.

"So what are you afraid of?" Emma asked me again.

"Everything."

"What? Gimme a list."

"Let's see. That he'll stop loving me. That we'll never have a child. That if we do have a child I'll ruin its life." I held my face in my hands and stared into my drink. "That one of these days I'll go crazy, kill myself or something. That Isabel will die. That I'll never make anything of my life. That I'll end up like my mother. That my brother's going to kill himself with drugs."

"Shit, Rudy." Emma put her arm around me. "That's enough for now."

I stopped trying to think of things I was afraid of. "Those are just off the top of my head," I said, and we started laughing. I laughed until my drink tasted salty from the tears trickling down my face. "People are watching us," I noticed, blowing my nose on a napkin.

"Now they really think we're lesbians."

We lounged in our booth, smiling around vacantly. We stared at people. We ate some of the free hors d'oeuvres.

"We should go, probably," Emma said.

"Yeah. Don't forget, you've got a date."

"I *did* forget. Shit. I'd better call and tell him the deal's off." She got up, only a little wobbly.

"You're canceling?"

"God, yes. Shape I'm in, I'd either start a fight or propose to him. And either way, I'd jump him first." She went off to the telephone.

I waited, not thinking of anything much. Feeling pretty good. One of the lawyers came back.

"Hey, did your friend run off and leave you?"

"No," I said, "she had to make a phone call."

"Oh, yeah? What's your name?"

"Rudy."

"Hi, Rudy. I'm Simon."

Simon had a sweet smile and a five o'clock shadow. A yellow tie. Definitely a lawyer.

"You're not really gay, are you?"

He looked friendly, and he didn't sound coy or hostile. So I said, "No, we're not. I'm married, though."

"Ah. What a shame." He sat down on Emma's side and folded his hands in his lap. I liked his unaggressive body language. But then he looked away and nodded, lifting his eyebrows. A signal. His friend got up from the bar, scooping up drinks and cigarettes and change, and started to come over. *Emma's going to kill me*, I thought while Simon said, "So, do you two work around here?"

Three things happened at once. Simon's friend sat down next to me, Emma came back, holding two new drinks and frowning, and I saw Curtis at the same time he saw me.

He must've come straight from the airport—he had his Hartman carry-on over his shoulder. He moved toward me slowly, his eyes huge and dark, gleaming with hurt and calculation. I tried to stand up, but the man, Simon's friend, was big and heavy and he didn't know what was going on, he wouldn't move.

"Curtis," Emma said jovially, putting the drinks down, facing him. Making a shield between him and me. "What a nice surprise! So you got my message, great, great. Have a seat? Too bad you missed Isabel, just missed her. These guys . . ." She bit her lips. Her voice dropped to normal; she quit trying. "Who the hell are you guys?"

"Curtis, please don't—" What? His tight, violent smile was paralyzing me.

"Ready to go home?" Polite. Reasonable. Behind the pain in his face, some kind of resigned excitement showed. *I've got you now*, he was thinking.

Simon's friend finally slid out. I got to my feet in slow motion, fumbling for coat, gloves, purse.

"Don't let her drive," Emma warned.

Curtis whirled around. "Don't tell me what to do with my wife." The naked hate between them shocked but didn't surprise me. *Do you really believe Curtis likes Emma?* Eric asked me that once.

Emma reached past Curtis and touched me. "Are you okay?"

"Yes, sure." I tried to laugh, tried to lessen the awfulness. She looked wound up but indecisive. Sparks were all but shooting off her.

"Hey, why don't we all sit down and cool off," she said unexpectedly, and I realized she was afraid—for me. Curtis stood unmoving, silent. I wanted to tell Emma there was nothing to fear from him, I only feared *for* him.

"We're going. 'Bye." I hugged her. "Call me. Don't *you* drive, hear?"

She nodded. Curtis didn't even look at her when he turned me, just a light hand on my back, and made me walk out ahead of him.

Out on the street, I froze for a minute, my mind a blank. I couldn't remember where I'd parked the car. I started toward Wisconsin, then remembered—the lot on K Street. "Oh, no, this way," I said casually, and Curtis turned around with me without a word. But he knew. I was loaded, and he knew it.

He drove.

"I'm sorry, I'm *so sorry* about the airport," I told him, huddling on the cold car seat, shivering because the Jeep's heater hadn't kicked in yet.

Instead of answering, he turned on the radio.

His handsome face looked sharp and clean against the lights flashing past his window. He'll never look old. He'll die with that boyish mouth, that child's hairline. I tried not loving him—just for a second; an experiment. To my horror, it worked. I jerked my head away and stared past the streetlamps at the icy, empty Mall. The heat came on. Even though I turned the fan up high, I never stopped shivering.

At home, I sat on the bed and watched him unpack. Socks and shorts in the hamper, shirts in the pile to the cleaners, shoes on wooden trees, suit on a padded hanger. He has an electric tie rack. I bought it for him for a joke, but he loves it.

I tried again.

"Listen, I'm sorry. Those men in the bar—you *know* that was nothing."

No answer.

"And I *was* with Isabel before, but she left. Before you came." Four hours before. I caught sight of myself in the mirror over the bureau. Red-rimmed eyes, mascara in blotches like paw prints. A mess. I looked drunk, which I was. The hangover was just starting.

"How did it go in Atlanta?" I asked.

"Badly." He turned away and went into the bathroom. He didn't close the door.

"Oh, no!" I called. "What happened?"

"I was going to tell you about it tonight. I thought we'd go out and talk."

Guilt feels like being smothered under a pile of rocks and mortar and pieces of glass. Buried alive. "We can still go. I'll get dressed, it's only eight o'clock."

"I couldn't eat now." He came out of the bathroom in his pajamas and bathrobe—navy blue with white piping and bright tartan plaid. He looked like a Brooks Brothers model, blond and ruddy-cheeked, healthy and urbane. I was surprised and grateful when he sat beside me on the bed.

"I'm sorry." Sometimes if I say it often enough, he relents. "It was my fault. I had too much to drink and forgot the time. Emma just made that up, that we were still with Isabel. She left much earlier. Oh, Curtis—poor Isabel, it was horrible in the doctor's office, sitting there and listening to him—"

"So Emma lied," he interrupted.

"What? Oh, but that wasn't—she didn't—"

"Rudy. I know how much you like her, but I don't think Emma's the good friend you think she is."

"Oh, no—"

"Listen," he said gently. He touched me, and I leaned into him, limp with relief. He forgave me. The world had stopped when he came into Sergei's and saw me, and now it was starting again.

I turned my head to kiss his clean-smelling neck, sliding my arms around his waist, but he held himself stiffly. I drew back.

"I don't want you to see quite so much of her."

I stared stupidly. "You mean Emma?"

"Look what it's doing to you." He touched my smudged cheek with distaste. Even I could smell the cigarette smoke in my hair, my clothes. "I know you've known her for a long time. I don't expect you to drop her."

"Drop her?"

"But I think it would be better if you didn't see her outside the group." He looked into my eyes, cupping my face in his palms. "For your own good, Rudy. In a way, I'm surprised Greenburg hasn't suggested it already."

My mind was spinning. I took hold of his hands. "Eric likes Emma, he'd never tell me that."

He sighed and pulled away.

I tried to keep his hands. "Don't be angry. Don't—"

He got up and went to the door. Turned. "So you won't do what I'm asking. For your sake."

"Stop seeing Emma? She's my best friend!"

"So you won't?"

"Curtis, don't do this. *Please* don't." I could feel the door shutting, me freezing. He would go away, take his love, take everything. "Please," I begged. "Curtis, please."

"Yes or no."

For my sake, he said, but it was cruel. "No, I can't. I'm sorry, please—Emma is my closest friend. Curtis!"

He'd turned and gone out.

I heard his leather slippers on the stairs. He would go down to the kitchen and make a toasted cheese sandwich in the broiler, with low-fat margarine on one side and nothing on the other. He'd eat it at the kitchen table with a glass of 2 percent milk while he skimmed the latest *Time*, *U.S. News*, and *Money*.

I went in the bathroom and took three sleeping pills. I was afraid to take more after the scotch. Three should do it, though. In bed, I pulled the covers over my head. Blackness, please. I needed a meditation to keep everything out, and I chose, *It's starting*. A time of penitence was coming, and only Curtis could say how long it would last. He held the key.

I slipped into a dream about God. He was sitting in a gilded chair, surrounded by vague-faced, worshipful angels. He looked at his watch, a Rolex like Curtis's. "She's late," he said with terrible sadness. "I'm very sorry, but she's late." He wept just, righteous tears. He reached up over his head and pulled the chain to a big Tiffany lamp, and the world went black.

15

Emma

In March I crossed three onerous tasks off my master To Do list. In increasing order of difficulty, I: broke up with Brad once and for all, drove down to Virginia to see my mother, and turned in my resignation at the paper. Actually the last two tied for degree of difficulty.

Just kidding. My mother's not so bad. After she stopped carping about what an idiot I was to quit my job, she was almost nice to me. I think I've figured out the secret to civility between us: only see each other twice a year.

The scariest part of the visit was realizing how much I'm starting to look like her. Or she's starting to look like me—there's a thought. My mother—Kathleen—looks like me if I stayed up for a week, drinking, smoking, shooting smack, and whoring. And worrying. That's what being sixty-five does to you, I guess, because the only pastime on this list my mother actually indulges in (as far as I know) is the last. But at that, she is truly world-class.

Oh, I'm too hard on her, I know. Force of habit. But I'm getting too old to react to her clumsy manipulations and machinations like the sulky, insufferable teenager I used to be. Anyway, I've won. I won a long time ago. I got out of Danville, Virginia; I didn't get married; I didn't go to state college and become a teacher "for something to fall back on," i.e., in case, like hers, my husband left me. Oh, and I developed this charming wiseass persona on purpose to annoy her.

Quitting my job turned out to be harder than I thought it would be. Because of the money. I'd gotten used to having some. I had started to buy things I saw in shop windows—walk by, stop, look, go in, and *buy*. "I'll have that." "I'll take it." This is what it means to be a grown-up, I'd think, flashing my gold Visa, my platinum MasterCard. I sent my mother a VCR for Christmas. I was planning for a new car in the spring, something sporty, maybe a Miata. The tips I left waitresses had gotten positively philanthropical.

But there was one thing I was even sicker of than poverty, and that was my excuse for not writing a novel, my so-called heart's desire: "I don't have time." Never mind that it was true; working for the paper, freelancing on the side, and writing short stories nobody bought had left me pretty much written out by the end of the day. Something had to go. So I've dumped the nine-to-five, kept the freelancing to pay the mortgage, and hung up the short stories. Now we'll see what I'm made of.

I say that with such gusto, such verve. As if I haven't been procrastinating since birth to avoid this very thing. Could it be? Could I be growing up?

No. Unfortunately. The reason is more craven and doesn't do me nearly as much credit. It's Isabel. Over the years she's taught me many lessons, but this is one I really didn't want to learn, not from her, not like this. It's the one about how short life is, and how foolish we would be to waste it.

I try to understand why this happened to her, why not to Rudy or Lee, or me. Why Isabel? She's the best of us. She has the biggest heart. She believes in everything—I don't believe in anything. It's *chance* that this happened to her, isn't it? She says no, there's no such thing as chance, it happened for a reason. What reason? "Maybe I can stand it and you can't," she said to me. But that's nonsense, isn't it?

She ditched that jerk Glass and got a new oncologist. Searle, this one's name is; he started her on antiestrogen therapy, some drug called Megace that made her gain weight and have hot flashes, but otherwise didn't do anything. Now she's trying two new drugs, Arimidex and something else, I can't remember the name, and we've all got our fingers crossed. Get this: at first Isabel wanted to skip the whole medical model and go for self-healing. *Self*-healing. That's your wheatgrass and coffee enemas, Indian sweat tents and acupuncture and hypnosis. Guided imagery. Bio-fucking-feedback.

But I didn't open my mouth. I bit my tongue and did not say one word. Rudy and Lee finally talked her out of it, and apparently Kirby—gay-guy-turned-hetero-heartthrob—did, too. (I'm sorry; that's snide. I apologize, Kirby. Whom I still haven't met. Isabel says there's nothing between them now except friendship. Maybe, but for some reason I don't like him. So what if the reason is jealousy and possessiveness?)

I can't stand it that this is happening to her. When I call, I never know the right thing to say. I feel awkward and stupid, because this thing between us that neither one of us really wants to talk about anyway has gotten so huge, we can't see around it. So I put off calling her, and then whole days go by when I don't even think about her. That's the worst: that I could forget all about my kindest, truest friend, whose life has turned into an absolute nightmare.

No, that's wrong. *My* life would be a nightmare if I were in Isabel's shoes. Who really knows, but it *seems* as if she's getting through it with the same grace that's seen her through the other rotten deals life's handed her. And speaking of Gary—he hasn't called her, hasn't so much as sent a get-well card. Terry wanted to come, fly down from Montreal for a long weekend, but she told him not to. What a nice kid. I've always liked him. Always wished he were about fifteen years older.

Oh, me, me, me. Nothing like a loved one's crisis to really bring home your own self-absorption. Isabel's illness is all relative: relative to me. How will *my* life change if she gets worse instead of better? How will *I* live without her if she dies? Oh, guilt, guilt, guilt. I thought Jews were the ones plagued for life with guilt, not us ex-Catholic agnostics. Lee's Jewish, and she's the most guilt-free, nonneurotic woman I've ever met. Irritating, but nonneurotic. Isabel's situation is just making Lee more efficient and organized. Bossier.

She's not pregnant yet, by the way, but her spirits are good. Lately, instead of calling, she's been sending me E-mails. I guess it's more efficient.

To: Emma [DeWitt@Dotcom.com]
From: L.P. Patterson [LeePatt@Dotcom.com]
Subject: Healing Circle

Emma:
Just a reminder about Wednesday night, 9:00 to 9:30, EST.
I've mentioned it twice to Rudy, but if you speak to her
between now and then, would you remind her again? You
know how she is. >g<
Cheers,
Lee

On Wednesday we're having our second "healing circle" for Isabel. At a prearranged time, everybody—not just the four Graces but her other friends and family across the country, plus any acquaintances so inclined—stops doing whatever they're doing and meditates on Isabel and her recovery. Some people pray, some imagine bad things happening to her cancer cells, some people "send white light," whatever that means. Rudy stares at a candle flame in a dark room and chants things—she told me this. "What things?" I asked, fascinated. "Just things. It's sort of private." Well, hmpf. I was just looking for some guidance. Because I am such a flop at this. It's never mattered much before, the fact that I'm no good at anything New Age, in fact I'm the poster child for Old Age. But now, when I try to pray or chant or send white light and I end up daydreaming about Mick or hot fudge cake or my car inspection, I worry that I'm personally letting Isabel down.

To: Emma [DeWitt@Dotcom.com]
From: L.P. Patterson [LeePatt@Dotcom.com]
Subject: Anniversary

Emma:
It's all set—we can have the Cape Hatteras cottage the second weekend in June. I wanted the third because, as you know, that's the true 10th anniversary of the S.G.'s, but it was already booked. Henry's planning to drive down Sunday late after everyone else leaves, and we'll stay three more days. Might invite another couple. Care to join us? With or without beau—up to you.
Looking forward to Friday night,
Lee

To: Emma [DeWitt@Dotcom.com]
From: L.P. Patterson [LeePatt@Dotcom.com]
Subject: Friday night

Emma:
You're coming to my cocktail party, aren't you? (I ask because you never RSVP'd.) Assuming you are, I have a tiny emergency. Henry and I have an A.I. appointment tomorrow at 3:30. (Our 4th, and this one is it, I'm positive!) So we'll be rushing and may or may not get home in time to pick up the salmon mousse at Fresh Fields. It's on your way—could you do it? Many thanks. It's paid for; all you have to do is pick it up.
Meanwhile, guess who's coming to the party and BRINGING A FRIEND?
Hurriedly,
Lee

Ha! Must be Jenny, Lee's mother-in-law. And "BRINGING A FRIEND." This should be good. I love to watch Lee's liberal superego fight it out with her conservative id.

And here I thought the only one suffering anxious moments at

Lee's party was going to be me, trying to act natural around Mick and Sally, the Dracos, *en famille*. My, what a fun night this is going to be.

I won't deny that I was watching the door, and yet somehow I missed Mick's entrance. By the time I saw him, he was leaning in the archway to the sunroom, holding a drink. The setting sun poured in through the jalousie windows like fire, backlighting the food-laden buffet table. Backlighting Mick's tall, straight silhouette. Our eyes met. As they say. I started to smile, but bodies came between us, a knot of chatting people shifting to make room for Lee and her tray of crab puffs. When the way cleared, he was bending down, saying something in his wife's ear.

Sally's shy at parties. She needs a drink or two before she ventures away from his side and talks to people on her own.

How do I know that? He told me. I forget in what context. An innocent one, though. All our conversations are innocent, and greasy, sleazy Murray's is still our trysting place. He doesn't help me with my coat, doesn't take my arm when we cross the street. Except for when our knees accidentally bump under the table, we never touch. But I am having the hottest, riskiest, most intense love affair of my life. I think it's the same for him.

Lee glided up. "Thanks for bringing the mousse, Em. It wasn't any trouble, was it?" She looked hostessy in a floor-length skirt and a silk tank; Emanuel Ungaro, she'd told me in an E-mail.

"Oh, no," I said, "it was right on my way. Hey, you look great. So does your house."

"You, too! That's quite a suit."

I guess she meant it, sarcastic understatement being more my style than Lee's. But now that I was here, I was feeling a little unsure of my choice: no blouse under a low-cut cocktail jacket with a matching midthigh skirt. It showed a lot more skin than I'm used to revealing. "Well, it's a cocktail party," I said defensively. "Where else can a girl show off her assets?"

"The beach?" Lee laughed, pleased with her little joke. "Oh, Emma, something I've been meaning to mention—we can't talk about it now, but I just want you to be thinking about it."

"What?"

She glanced over her shoulder and lowered her voice. "How do you feel about asking Sally to join the group? The women's group. The Graces," she specified when all I could do was stare. "Does it sound like a good idea to you?"

I was speechless.

"You've met her a couple of times now. Do you like her? I think she's really nice. And smart, and interesting. And different enough from the rest of us to bring something new to the group." Diversity was important to Lee. Once she vetoed a woman I knew at the paper because we had the same job. "Then we'd have *two* journalists," she'd argued. "It's redundant. Don't we want variety?"

Sally would add variety, I could see that. A young mother, a Southerner, a primary breadwinner: all unique traits. The trouble with Sally, I've thought more than once, is that there's nothing wrong with her.

I fell back on a craven but obvious excuse. "Well, but don't you think it's not the best time to be thinking of a new member? Because of Isabel? Where is she, by the way?"

"She said she might be late. No, I don't think it's—"

"Hey, gorgeous, you look good enough to eat." Henry smothered me in a huge bear hug. Frowning at the interruption, Lee absently took his arm and leaned against him. Mutt and Jeff. He could put her in his pocket. They're so cute together, so . . . unliberated or something. If he *did* put her in his pocket, neither of them would think a thing of it.

"I don't necessarily see that, not at all," Lee said to me. "As soon as they hit on the right drug with Isabel, the worst will be behind her. Then I should think it would be good for her *and* the group to have someone new to get to know. And she's met Sally," she added, dropping her voice again. "I asked her, and she said she likes her."

"You asked her? You asked Isabel about—"

"Not about joining, just if she liked her. And she said yes."

"Oh." But Isabel likes everybody, she's like God that way. "Oh, Lee, I don't know. I don't have anything against Sally, it's just that—I'm still not sure it's a good time for us to be taking on somebody new."

"Well, I don't agree, but if that's your opinion. I'll ask Rudy what she thinks, of course."

You do that. "Sure," I nodded vigorously. Rudy wouldn't let me down. "And Isabel, of course."

"Naturally."

She went off to do hostess duties. Henry hung around, shooting the breeze with me, telling a couple of his cornball dirty jokes. Then he said, "Y'know, Em, I hope I'm wrong, but . . ." He fluffed the carpet with the toe of his shoe.

"What?"

"I'm not sure Lee's being that realistic about Isabel. Her condition. I don't say anything, because I don't want to discourage her. And miracles do happen." He bent his head, rubbing the back of his neck. "What do you think?"

"I think we're all trying hard to handle it in our own ways. Lee's an optimist, she's coping with it optimistically." A more polite way of saying she's in denial. "Rudy's scared to death, but hiding it."

"What about you?"

I looked at him frankly. "I'm a pessimist."

"Yeah." His rugged face softened with sympathy. "I'm just scared Lee might get blindsided. You know, if something bad happens. She's not gonna be prepared."

"I know." Neither am I. If something bad happens. "Well," I said, "good thing she's got you to take care of her." I sidled closer. "So, Mister Horn o' Plenty. Mister hunka burning love. How's it going in the fertility department these days?"

Henry is such a guy, he loves this routine I've been doing since Lee told us about his sperm count. I think he's relieved to be able to talk about the problem, and before, we couldn't. Isn't that ridiculous? It was a taboo subject when it might've been a *low* sperm count, but now it's okay.

After a few more nitwit sperm jokes, he sobered and said, "The timing's perfect for us, considering what all else is goin' on. Lee's counting on it to work this time. Even if it doesn't, we've got two more shots. Being pregnant, you know, it would get her through. If . . ."

"It'll work," I said, not wanting to hear about *if*. "Because you are awesome, Patterson. You are so damn potent, you'll probably have triplets. All sons."

He threw back his head and laughed. And blushed. Oh, I do love Henry. He's like a big, sleepy bear, calm and sturdy, dependable as dawn. He's good to Lee, and he tones down her anal retentiveness like . . . I don't know what. A good sedative. Lee's live-in Seconal prescription.

The party got a little louder, a little sloppier. Not much; Lee's parties never get out of hand. She'd stocked it with all her preschool and early-childhood-development cronies: smart, interesting, good-hearted women whose husbands make more money than they do. I schmoozed with the ones I'd met before, introduced myself to a couple of new ones. Lee's parties are notoriously low on single men, I'm not sure why. My only theory is it's because her friends are so wholesome, they never get divorced.

Tonight I wasn't trolling for single men, of course. Even though I never looked for him, I always knew where Mick was. Radar. We circulated, but always kept the width of a room between us, a clutch of moving bodies. Me, deliberately; him—I couldn't say. But what a painful, addictive game I was playing. It's true that I hurt all over because of the hopelessness of this infatuation, but at the same time I'd never felt so alive.

As usual, Rudy and Curtis arrived late. He may be a schmuck—

no, he's definitely a schmuck—but there's no denying that Curtis Lloyd is a good-looking man. In that Earnest Young Nazi mold, but still. And Rudy, well, besides being beautiful, she's got this effortless model-chic that makes normal people feel gawky and flat-footed and too made-up when they're around her. People like me. I waved to her, hoping she'd extricate herself from Curtis and come over alone. No way. I should've known; he hardly ever lets her out of his sight at parties. Either he doesn't trust her or he's afraid to be by himself. Probably both.

Rudy and I kissed cheeks, while Curtis and I managed to hug without actually touching. "Where's Isabel?" Rudy asked after some small talk.

"Not here yet. Lee said she said she might be late."

"I can't wait to meet this Kirby."

"Me, too."

I can't talk to Rudy when Curtis is around. It's like trying to talk on the phone through glass while the prison guard watches. The only thing worse is talking to Curtis when Rudy's not around.

That's why I could've killed her when she said, "Oh, there's Allison Wilkes, I haven't seen her in ages. I'll be right back," and walked away.

With anyone else I didn't particularly care for, I might've said, "Alone at last," at a time like this, on the theory that getting the worst out of the way early, even if you do it sarcastically, helps dissipate the tension. But I keep my true feelings for Curtis to myself—that time at Sergei's was an exception. Rudy says she's not afraid of him, but I am. Slightly. Because he's creepy. So I'm civil and one-dimensional and deliberately dull with him, practically zombielike in my self-restraint. Pretty admirable, when what I'd really enjoy is punching him out. Anything for Rudy.

Empty-handed—Curtis doesn't drink in public; might lose control—he bounced on his toes a little, surveying the crowd. Checking to see if anybody here could do him any good, I was sure. He's a born politician, except for one thing. He doesn't like people.

"Well, Emma," he roused himself to say. "Rudy tells me you've quit your job."

I said that was true.

"And you're all set to write a book. A novel." He laughed his hard, sharp, machine gun laugh, *Ha ha ha ha*.

"Is that funny? You find that amusing?" I kept smiling, smiling, the hostility only coming out of my eyes. He didn't bother to answer. My anger was out of all proportion, but he's like a marksman, an archer with perfect aim. With one shot, he'd hit me in my tender spot.

"How's *your* new job?" I countered. "Lobbying. That seems so right for you, Curtis. Really a"—I pretended to hunt for the word—"a *noble* profession."

He only smirked. My arrow hadn't even nicked the target. I thought the little game was over, but he said, "So, what is your book about?"

Ah, the question a writer hates most. How do you suppose he knew that? "It's still in the incubation stage," I said, still smiling. Talk about understatement. "I'd really rather not discuss it." Across the room, I could see Mick talking to Henry. Laughing with him, kind of bobbing and weaving the way men do. Their new friendship surprises me a little. They're so different from each other.

"They say you should always write about what you know best," Curtis was telling me.

"Yeah, well. Up to a point."

"So your story would probably be . . ." He frowned and pursed his lips, thinking. "Promiscuous spinster's dark dreams of adultery . . . something like that?" I turned to stare at him. He raised his blond brows innocently, half smiling. His eyes flicked up and down over my body, slowing down contemptuously at the areas of exposed skin.

Guilt and fury are a lethal combination. My neck and throat

flushed with heat. I loathed him, I despised that knowing look on his smug face. I knew if I opened my mouth, I would curse him.

"Well. Think I'll go find my wife. You take care, Em." He sauntered away, hands in his pockets.

On the way to the bathroom, I nodded, smiled, spoke casually to people. But once inside I locked the door and gripped the sides of the sink, staring at myself in the mirror. Curtis saw this stricken face? No wonder he'd looked so satisfied. "Don't fall for it," I warned, fumbling in my bag for mascara and lipstick. This was what he'd wanted: me to feel hurt and betrayed by Rudy.

But how could she tell him my secret? Not that I'd ever told her not to. I didn't think I had to! I thought she treated my confidences the same way I treated hers, sacredly, respectfully. "Promiscuous spinster"—oh, please. To hell with that, that only proves he's as sick as I've always said he was. But, oh, Rudy, how could you tell him about Mick?

Somebody knocked.

Shit. "Just a sec!" Give me a minute, for Pete's sake. I looked as if I'd been crying.

"Sorry, no hurry!"

I recognized the bright, convivial voice of Sally Draco.

Perfect.

I smiled. Grinned. Threw back my head and mimed delighted laughter. My party face. Smoothing down my skirt, I made a decision to confront Rudy later, not tonight, not here, while we were both drinking. We did that once. Never again.

Sally was leaning in the hallway, gazing out across the crowded living room, and she turned when she heard the door open. "Oh, hi! It's you."

The second drink must've kicked in; she really looked glad to see me. In fact, if I hadn't folded my arms, I think she'd have embraced me. Which would've been excessive, considering I'd only met her twice in my life, both times at Lee's dinner parties.

"How've you been, Emma? I keep meaning to call you, but you know how it is—"

"Oh, yeah," I said weakly, "working *and* having a child, that must really keep you busy. Well, so how's the job going?" I asked when it looked like she wanted a real chat, not a hit-and-run.

She rolled her eyes. "Let's just say, it's not my life's work."

"No?" What was she, a paralegal? I can never remember people's jobs. No, she was a paralegal when Mick met her; now she was something in the Labor Department.

"But I guess only one person to a family gets to do his life's work." She laughed with rueful good nature, but I know passive aggression when I hear it. "Oh, that is a *gorgeous* suit, where did you get it?"

So we did girl talk while I checked her out and returned the obligatory compliment on her little white cocktail dress. She was an attractive woman, no question, with straight, sleek yellow hair, cut short and styled in a way women admire more than men. Her wide-spaced eyes and strong cheekbones made her face exotic. The mouth was enormous, but not happy. No, it was worried. But sensual—her whole face was sensual. It eclipsed her body, which seemed oddly asexual in comparison; you hardly noticed it.

"Mick tells me you're almost finished your article. I'm glad he could help you with it."

"Oh, yes, he's been great. I couldn't have done it without him."

"When does it come out?"

"It's hard to say. Maybe June. Whenever they decide to print it."

"I can't wait to read it," she said, eyes big and sincere.

God knows I've tried to be objective. I've asked myself, would I like Sally Draco if Mick didn't exist? If I met her at a party and we just started talking, would I want to be her friend? And the honest answer is no, but not for any good reason; I mean, she's not Satan or anything. She exudes a lot of warmth you're not sure is real, and the longer you talk to her, the less authentic that initial burst of self-confidence seems. She watches carefully, hopefully, waiting for something. Behind the big eyes, I see big need.

Our conversation, such as it was, petered out. She went in the bathroom and I drifted away, thinking about her. Why did she marry Mick? They're total opposites: he's real, she's not. (Not that I'm biased.) He rarely talks about her, and then only in the most politically correct generalities. Which is no more than I would expect of him. It's frustrating, but I like his discretion, his courtliness. But he's no Mr. Rochester; I think he'd have told Jane about the madwoman in the attic on the first date.

I saw Lee in the middle of the living room, holding a plate of miniature lamb kebobs and looking pained. I followed her gaze—she was glaring through the doorway into the kitchen.

Aha. Jenny was here, with A FRIEND. You could tell they were friends because they were holding hands.

"My, what a striking couple." I couldn't resist.

Lee closed her eyes for a second. "Come with me, okay?"

"Sure." I even went first. I like Jenny.

Henry was talking to her and her *friend* while he took little quiches out of the oven and put them on a plate. "Oh, Lee!" Jenny exclaimed when she saw us. "Lee and her friend. Oh, look, Phyllis, it's Lee, my lovely daughter-in-law"—and she scooped Lee up in a terrific embrace, lifting her completely off the floor. I got a similar treatment, although I could see my name escaped her. She can't quite keep the Graces straight, but she loves us, one and all.

"Emma," I said helpfully, offering my hand to small, handsome, fiftyish Phyllis. Jenny was doing a little cradle-robbing. Phyllis sparkled her eyes at me and said how do you do.

The tip-off that Jenny was smitten was that she was wearing a dress—a first in my experience. A nice dress, and technically it fit her, but the sight was so incongruous, she made me think of a guy in drag. Jenny is five-eleven—six feet in her work boots, she loves to say—and what they call big-boned. She dyes her hair dark brown and wears it up in an old-fashioned pompadour. Except for the southern accent, she reminds me of Julia Child.

"Lee, this is Phyllis Orr, my very good friend." Except she said, "Mah verra good *free*-in," in her slow Carolina drawl, like a female Jesse Helms. Henry only has a shadow of it.

"Well, how do you do? It's lovely to meet you, just lovely," Lee burbled, overcompensating. "Welcome to our home. Yes, indeed, any friend of Jenny's . . ." She tapered off, hearing herself. Henry and I gave each other tickled looks. "And how did you two meet? I mean if that's not too—you don't have to—I was just wond—"

"Phyllis manages my apartment building," Jenny said, in a tone of wonder at the unexpectedness of life's gifts. "Somebody tried to break into my place—I told you, Henry, remember?—but all they did was crack the dead bolt. She fixed it." She gave Phyllis a playful but proud jab on the shoulder.

"Well, isn't that something. How about that, and you've been friends ever since," Lee marveled. "I think that's wonderful, I really do."

Phyllis, a slight, wiry, darkly attractive woman who looked as if she'd know her way around a dead bolt, looked at Lee curiously.

"Look who's talking about *friends*," Jenny boomed. "Tell Phyllis about your group, Lee honey, go on. Lee started a club just for women, *years* ago, Phil, and they're still going strong. Emma here is one of her members." *One o' huh membahs*. "How many years have y'all been together now?"

Lee said, "It'll be ten years in June."

"Oh, is that right," Phyllis said.

"We're going to Cape Hatteras to celebrate," I threw in. Lee's family has a cottage they rent out for all but two weeks in June and September. The Saving Graces have celebrated four of their nine anniversaries there so far, so it's a sporadic tradition.

"Well, I'll swan, isn't that marvelous." *Idn that mahvelous*.

Jenny rested an affectionate elbow on top of Henry's shoulder.

Patterson & Son looked great together, both of them so uncharacteristically dressed up this evening. Lee glanced around, rubbing her hands together and smiling anxiously. A couple of her education friends had come in for ice or something, and now they were gathering around, listening in.

"When I was your age—Henry, when was that?" Jenny demanded.

He thought. "Late 70s."

"That's right—twenty years ago when I was your age, I had just about had it up to here with living with women in a group. Did you know I used to live in a commune?" she said to me. "Out in the country near Asheville, *beautiful* place. That's where Henry grew up. I used to worry about him not having a daddy—his was killed in Vietnam, you know—but look how he's turned out." She got his neck in an armlock and squeezed.

"Huh!" I said—as if I hadn't heard these reminiscences from Lee, Henry, and Jenny herself several times already.

"Quiche?" Lee held the plate under her mother-in-law's nose hopefully.

"Women united! There's nothing we can't do when we work together. Right, Emma? Lee honey? Oh, what a bunch we were, though, back then. Free love, and no men allowed. Does y'all's group have a name? We called ourselves the Viragos."

"But you know," Lee pointed out amid the laughter, "we're—ha ha!—not that kind of a group." She lifted her hand to Henry, the one here with the penis, as if to say, Look: living proof I'm heterosexual.

"And radical? Oh, my goodness, we'd demonstrate at the drop of a hat, as long as it was for something militant. I remember one time, we went to an antiwar rally in Raleigh, and named ourselves 'Lesbians for Mao' on the spot. My girlfriend and I took off our shirts and nursed our babies on the Capitol steps. Henry, you've seen that picture."

"Yep. I was eight years old."

"You were *not*," Lee said, aghast.

"Oh, but it didn't last. Couldn't, I guess, and plus we were all so young. We left, one by one, and I hear there's not even a farm there anymore. Out in that pretty place. You remember Sue Ellen Rich?" Jenny asked Henry. "I got a note from her last Christmas—we still keep up—and she says there's a Saturn dealership there now. Mm mmm." She shook her head mournfully; Phyllis patted her arm and said, "Aww."

"We're not very political," Lee said brightly. "We just have dinner."

"But you're still *together*, that's what I envy. Ten years, and you're still a group. Y'all still love each other."

"Oh, we do," I agreed, sliding my arm around Lee's waist. "We still love each other *so much*." At the last second Lee figured out what I was going to do—kiss her on the mouth—and jerked her head away in a panic. All I got was cheek.

"Well, I'd better pass these," she muttered, sidling out of my affectionate grasp. "Before they get cold. Excuse me?" Always polite. But the look she threw me on her way out glittered with homicidal longing.

"I'm so sorry we're late. Kirby dropped me off in front," Isabel said breathlessly. "He's parking the car." Lee started to take her jacket, but she said, "I think I'll keep it." She spied me. "Hi, you," she said, and I gave her a soft, one-armed hug. She felt good, exactly like she always did—not breakable or anything.

Rudy came striding over, beaming with gladness, and wrapped her up in a long, strong Rudy-hug. "I was worried, I thought you'd never get here."

"No, I'm fine, just couldn't get organized."

"How *are* you?" Lee demanded, taking both of Isabel's hands and staring intently into her eyes.

"You *look* wonderful," Rudy said.

That was partly true, partly false. Isabel had on a great dress, the kind that reminds us why basic black is a classic, and she was wearing her hair in a new style that really flattered her. But her complexion was off, too yellow or something, and her eyes looked too big. She claimed she hadn't gained or lost a single pound on the new drugs, but then, why was she slightly puffy-looking around the jaw and throat? Not much; anyone who didn't know her probably wouldn't even notice. But I could hardly see anything else. I monitor her these days like a mother with a sick child. We all do. She hates it.

"How do you *feel*?" Lee persisted, still doing the eye contact thing.

"Fine, great, couldn't be better. Your house looks so pretty." Isabel glanced around, withdrawing her hands. "That's a new mirror, isn't it? I'd give anything to have your taste, Lee. How do you do it?"

O-kay. Even Lee got that message: *We're not talking about my health.* So we four stood in the middle of the living room in a tight, protective circle, laughing and chattering about nothing, Isabel's pretty earrings, my great new shoes, Lee's plans for Passover, was that Obsession Rudy was wearing?—until even I was seduced into forgetting that something dark and menacing had settled over our precious solidarity and changed us forever.

Kirby arrived. Isabel introduced him to Rudy and me—Lee had already met him—with none of the watchful, oh-I-hope-you-like-him anxiety I'd have felt in her situation. And he was kind of an anxiety-inducing guy. He towered over us, although he couldn't have weighed more than 150, 155, soaking wet. Virtually bald; sharp, bony features; stoop-shouldered. Gawky. There was nothing birdlike about him, though; he looked stringy and tough, athletic in spite of the gauntness. His eyes dominated his priest's face, soft brown and sad.

I just said, "Hi, how are you," and kept quiet. We formed a little knot in the sunroom, we four and Kirby, and had a light, semistiff, getting-to-know-you chat. He didn't say much either, although he wasn't aloof or creepily silent. He had to know we were checking him out. Funnily enough, Lee claimed she liked him, and she's more possessive of Isabel than any of us. But she's also famous for her poor judgment of character (witness Sally, not that I'm prejudiced), so her endorsement meant nothing to me. Frankly, I was disposed not to like him, but I was trying to be objective for Isabel's sake.

It wasn't anything he said, and if I hadn't been watching like a cat at a mousehole, I wouldn't even have known it was anything he did. Not that he hovered—it was more like he *guarded* Isabel. A body language thing. And something else—Lee had taken all the chairs out of the room for more space; Kirby vaporized for a few seconds, then reassembled, as it were, holding a kitchen stool, which he placed behind Isabel all but invisibly—the whole transaction had the unobtrusive feel of good magic. In the same way, he brought her a glass of club soda with a lemon slice. Then he made her a plate from the buffet table, and frowned sadly, playfully, until she began to nibble from it. He was like a guardian angel. Inconspicuously benevolent.

It would've been easy to write him off as weird because of his looks, or ghoulish because of the way he'd attached himself to a woman who was, at the least, seriously ill. And I could see why Isabel had thought at first that he was gay; not because he was effeminate, but because he was different, he fit no type. Under the strangeness, though, I came to a realization that he was gentle. I decided to trust him. After half an hour, I felt delighted for Isabel. A man less like Gary Kurtz she couldn't have found without advertising.

He suggested we go sit in the living room, and by now I knew it was because he thought she'd be more comfortable there. As we dispersed, Isabel hung back in the doorway and buttonholed me.

"Well?"

"Well, what?" She made an impatient face, and I laughed. "I like him, I like him."

"Do you? Really, Em?"

I can't tell you how it made me feel, knowing Isabel cared what

I thought of her boyfriend. It was like—the pope clearing his blind date with me first. I was really moved. Isabel is *my* mentor, although neither of us would ever say that out loud, and certainly we'd never use that word. She approves of *me*, not the other way around.

"Of course I like him, who wouldn't? But"—I couldn't resist asking—"what happened to 'just friends'?"

"But we are friends. That's exactly what we are."

"Oh? Have you told him that?"

She smiled slightly, eyes downcast.

"He's in love with you, Is."

"If he ever was, that's over now."

"Why?"

She didn't answer.

"How come? You mean because you got sick again? Well, if he's that—"

"Emma, it's complicated now, that's all. You must admit it's complicated."

"Everything's complicated, Isabel. You're telling me Kirby only likes you when you're glowing with health?"

"No, that's not what I'm saying." She looked shocked. "You really don't understand."

I had a brainstorm. "You're doing it," I realized.

"I'm doing what?"

"*You're* the one who's pulling back—because you're sick. It's not Kirby at all." What a relief, especially since I'd just decided I trusted him.

Isabel stared at me with abstracted eyes, thinking it over. She shook her head, going back to, "No, it's more complicated than that. Really."

"Well, if you say so. But you want to keep a clear head, Is." Amazing how cocky I can get about other people's business after a little encouragement. "It's true I've only met him once, but Kirby doesn't strike me as a guy who can't stand complications. He doesn't look like a deserter, in other words."

Isabel started to say something, but Lee interrupted. "Movies!" she chirped, and she waved the dreaded video camera. "Everybody in the living room, Henry wants to take us all on the couch."

I laughed.

Lee frowned. "What?"

"Nothing." I've never known anybody as oblivious to double entendre.

Henry was such a mensch to put up with this. Candid shutterbuggery was one of Lee's most annoying amusements. It was bad enough when she did it, but when she dragged him into it, too, he proved he's a saint.

We four squeezed onto the damn sofa. I had Isabel on one side, Rudy on the other. Rudy wasn't drunk, but she was feeling no pain. She mugged for the camera, made faces, pretended to stick her tongue in my ear. I didn't want to laugh—I was mad at her—but she made me. I saw Curtis milling among the party guests who were watching us. He didn't laugh with the others; he didn't even smile. That helped me make up my mind.

I'd been stupid and naive to think Rudy would keep my secrets from Curtis. Grow up, Emma. Husbands and wives tell each other things. Marriage supersedes friendship, even marriage to a prick. I wasn't angry with her anymore, I wouldn't make an issue of it, wouldn't even bring up the subject. That's what he wanted me to do. Screw him. I wasn't driving a wedge between Rudy and me to spite myself.

I caught his eye. While he watched, I put my arm around Rudy and gave her a smacking kiss on the temple. Take that, jerkoff.

It wasn't a total victory, though. Because of Curtis, I'd have to watch what I told Rudy about Mick from now on. Thinking of that made me angry all over again.

* * *

"Hi."

"Hello."

All night I'd felt like a bird circling a thicket of prickly bushes, unable to light because of the thorns. Lee's back patio was a wide, soft meadow I'd spied at last with my bird's eye, and Mick was there waiting for me.

Well. I don't know if he was waiting for me. He was just there, smoking a cigarette beside the tastefully faded, Boston ivy–covered stockade fence that separated the Pattersons' house from its neighbor. He wasn't even alone; at the bottom of the yard other guests, three or four men and one woman, laughed and drank and smoked cigars around a rusting swing set as old as the house. It was warm and cloudy, the moon only a smudge in the gray, starless sky. Unlike mine, unlike Mick's, Lee's neighborhood was quiet on Saturday nights.

"Doesn't feel much like home, does it?" I said, and he smiled, moving back a step, inviting me to stand next to him on the last bit of concrete before the grass started. I smiled, too, but I looked down at my feet so he wouldn't see. Euphoria was making my chest tickle. It was alarming, this tension between us. It meant everything was true, everything I had hoped and dreaded.

"I'm surprised that you smoke."

He looked at the burning tip of his cigarette with interest. "Somebody gave it to me. I don't. Once in a blue moon."

"I do, but only with Rudy."

"Want one? I could get you one."

"No." I laughed—euphoria again.

Bugs smacked into the light over the patio. A couple of yards down, somebody's dog barked out of boredom. A plane droned overhead, invisible. Gradually, even though we didn't talk, we began to relax. We were spinning a web around us, making a cocoon. We did this at Murray's, too, so we knew how. But still, I was amazed. How easy.

"My article's almost finished," I said. "Nothing but the final run-through left, and some fact-checking."

He nodded. He didn't say, "Good," I noticed. Finishing the article for *Capital* on the D.C. art world meant I wouldn't have any more excuses to call him at his studio or meet him for coffee and ask questions. There would be no legitimate excuse to stay in touch now. Except friendship. Secret friendship, as Rudy had been good enough to point out. Which more or less negated the legitimacy.

"Thank you for your help," I said formally. "I couldn't have done it without you."

"I didn't do anything."

"That's not true. I wouldn't have known who to talk to and who to keep away from if you hadn't told me. I wouldn't even have known where to start." The *Cap* editor told me to slant the story from the viewpoint of an art know-nothing, a good thing for me, since that's the only way I could have written it.

"You're a reporter," Mick said, "you'd have figured it out."

"Why don't you just say, 'You're welcome'?"

He ducked his head, smiling. "You're welcome."

"Course, they may not like it. No guarantees. They might even turn it down."

"Well, then you can say it was all my fault."

"Oh, don't worry."

This was a little bit of disingenuity on my part. I loved the way the piece had turned out; if they rejected it, I'd be astonished. But I'm nothing if not self-deprecating. It's a form of bet hedging, keeping hope firmly in the middle range so disappointment can't hurt too much. At least not in public.

Through the closed patio doors, we watched the slow-mo shifting of the guests from bar to table, group to group. Their mouths moved, inaudible except for the occasional whoop of laughter. Mick's wife was deep in conversation with Curtis Lloyd, I saw, and my mind spun off in a symmetrical fantasy that they fell deeply in love, left their spouses, and ran off together to Ibiza.

"I spoke to your friend Isabel," Mick said.

"But you've met her before." Here, in fact, at Lee's last dinner party.

He nodded. "But we've never really talked. We did tonight, a little. I like her very much."

"You couldn't not."

He watched me. "It's hard," he said.

Once, at Murray's, I started to tell him how scared I was, and I ended up in tears. Which I *hate*, I would rather eat dirt than let anybody see me cry. So now he was being diplomatic, he thought, showing his sympathy but not saying anything to set me off.

He said, "Lee told Sally about the healing circle, and Sally told me."

"Did you do it?"

"I did," he nodded. "Didn't you?"

"Of course. Sort of. Where were you?" I tried to picture him and Sally hovering around a candle, chanting in harmony.

"On the subway, coming back from a drawing class. I didn't remember until about quarter to ten."

"What did you do?"

"Well, you know. I meditated. What did you do?"

It was so nice to be talking like this. With Rudy and Lee it had seemed too private, and of course with Isabel it was out of the question. "Well," I said, "I *tried* to meditate, but I'm not very good at it. How do you shut your mind off? Mine keeps jumping around."

"I don't know if I really meditated," he said—trying to make me feel better. "I just thought about her. I closed my eyes and . . . wished her well."

"That's what I did, too. I *wished her well*."

A woman I didn't know opened the patio door and peered out into the semidark. Somebody—Lee, undoubtedly—had turned off

Henry's Drifters tape and put on Stephane Grappelli; the jazzy, staccato sound shattered the quiet, like driving by a playground at recess. The woman smiled, decided against coming out, and pulled the door shut. Silence rolled back.

We were quiet, too. Except when I slipped my shoes off and Mick asked if I wanted to go inside and sit. "No," I said, "it's too nice. Unless you do."

"No." He looked at me then. Looked at my body. Something he usually takes pains to avoid, or so it seems to me.

How is it that some men can look at you and make you feel like the sexiest woman in the world, and other men can look at you and make you feel like mashing your spike heel through their instep? With Mick, I was suddenly aware of everything about myself. A fantasy kept intruding on my restless attempts to make small talk, a fantasy that I was holding him. Standing on tiptoes, my arms around his shoulders, leaning into him. It made my mouth dry up, it made me forget what I was saying. My clothes felt too small, or too intimate. Too revealing. I was showing a lot of skin, and I wanted him to have it. I wanted to give myself to him.

I put my drink down on the wrought-iron plant stand. This wasn't like flirting with some cute guy at a party. What I felt was a dangerous lust that could destroy lives. The disaster potential sobered me up like a plunge into cold water.

"What are you working on these days?" I asked, pleased with my assertive, no-nonsense tone.

"Something new. Some watercolor portraits. Come and see them," he invited. "Anytime. Come anytime, Emma."

And there we were, right back where we had been.

I hedged. "That would be nice. I'd like to. Someday."

He never asked me how my writing was going, because a long time ago I had asked him not to. "Nine times out of ten, that's the last thing I want to talk about," I'd told him. "What's to say, anyway? It's going fine, it's going lousy. Either way, it's a conversation stopper." But now I wanted to tell him something, and it was my own fault that I had to bring it up first.

"I'm having trouble with my writing," I said. Yes, that bit of candor amazed me, too. So unwonted. "The thing I'm working on isn't going well. I've been thinking, quitting the paper might have been a mistake."

"No. I don't think it was."

"Well . . . ," I said, so he'd keep going. So far he'd said exactly what I wanted to hear.

"In any case, it's much too soon to tell. How long has it been?"

"A month."

"Not long enough."

"How long will it be before I know it's a mistake?"

"Such an optimist," he said, smiling. "A year. Minimum. Two years would be better."

"How long did it take before you knew you hadn't made a mistake?"

"I still don't know it."

"I wouldn't have done it if you . . . You inspired me," I said with a lopsided smile. "I wouldn't have done it if I hadn't met you. So you get some of the blame when I pancake."

"You won't. You'll be good."

"How do you know?"

"Because. You have a strong voice. For one thing."

"You mean a loud voice."

"And a strong heart. You're alive."

I am with you, I thought.

"You have a—I don't know what to call it. An attitude, and it's going to appeal to people, smart people."

Good thing it was dark, because I actually blushed. "I would give anything if that were true," I admitted, a little breathless. "But I haven't even figured out what I should write *about* yet."

"That'll come. You want everything now."

"I do, I hate to wait. Am I going to make it? Is this going to work? Will I be a success? I want to know it all *now*."

"What if the answer was no, and you knew it? What would you change?"

I shook my head.

"For me," he said, "I knew painting was what I should do when I realized it was the *only* thing I wanted, even if I never succeeded. That was the test. It isn't a question of what other people think, it's—*my* process. Watching myself get better, understanding things that used to be complete mysteries to me. Moving. Changing."

I nodded a lot. Talk like this makes me feel exhilarated and worried and cheered up and inadequate. I take it in and think about it later.

It confirmed one thing, though, something I'd suspected for some time. Mick's more grown up than I am.

I said, "Well, anyway. I wanted to tell you, if I hadn't met you, I probably wouldn't have quit my job. That seemed like taking a big chance to me. What it must've been to you—I didn't appreciate it before. Now I do. I admire you."

He looked down; all I could see was the top of his head. He reached around to his back pocket, and for an awful second I thought he was getting his handkerchief, because he was crying. I felt stupid, but relieved, when he pulled out his wallet and said, "Want to see a picture of Jay?"

His son was beautiful, of course. What else? A towheaded blond with pink cheeks and a goofy, angel smile. "He looks like you," I said. "But I don't know why. None of his features . . ."

"No. People always say he looks like Sally."

"Yeah, but there's something, something . . ." Jay was building a snowman with Dad in the front yard. I recognized the narrow gray town house in the background because, God help me, I once drove past it. On purpose. I wanted to see where Mick lived, I just wanted to fill in that one harmless blank. In the picture, Jay had on so many clothes—blue quilted snowsuit, muffler, a cap with earflaps, soggy wool mittens, clumpy yellow boots—he looked incapable of movement, rooted to the spot with the three snow blobs stacked beside him. My mother's got a picture of me in the same getup, a classic kid pose; I'm holding my sled by a rope, and the little boy who lived two doors down is standing behind me, bigger, older, a tricky look in his eye. But I have no recollection of the event, the day. Will Jay look at this photo one day and not remember anything about it?

"Oh, Mick, he's lovely. Six?"

"Five and a half, he'll be six in December."

"Did you always want children?"

"Not really. Jay was . . . a surprise." I looked up. His face had grown still, inward. He was choosing his words with care. "I never thought anyone else's life could mean more to me than my life. I think Jay's happy. I think he is. His innocence is what scares me the most. I want to protect him, and I know I can't." His low voice dropped lower. "Emma, I couldn't do anything that would hurt Jay. No matter how much I wanted to. No matter . . ."

He let that hang. I handed him his photograph back, with nothing to say. Message received.

It was a relief, really. Like a child, I function better when somebody sets limits. Now that I know the rules, I'll follow them to the letter. *What were you thinking?* I was already asking myself.

The patio door slid open. There was a new innocence in the way we turned at the sound. Sally came toward us, with Lee behind her. Mick appeared to wait until his wife was beside him before he slipped the photo of his son back in his wallet. More blamelessness on display.

We chatted—we women. Mick didn't talk. I felt numb and light, barely there. Lee said Sally wanted to fix me up with a man in her office. Lawyer, late forties, divorced, works for the general counsel. "Now, don't say no without even thinking about it, Em, because he really sounds nice, he—"

"Okay."

Lee blinked. "Hm?"

"Thanks, Sally. Give him my number, tell him to call me."

She looked as surprised as Lee. My reputation preceded me. "I sure will," she said. She took Mick's upper arm in both hands and leaned on him, rested her head on his shoulder. A wifely message: *Let's go soon, honey, I'm tired.*

I made the mistake of looking at him. I wonder how much hurt I could have saved myself if he had turned away then, or if he'd disguised what he was feeling, or even if the light had been bad. But it was bright enough, and Mick's not half as good as I am at dissembling. I saw all his pain, and it was big and raw and humbling. All this time, I had been holding back from loving him. The illusion that I had a choice evaporated.

Two weighty lessons I could have done without: I can't have him, and we are in love with each other.

16

Isabel

Spring is my favorite season, May is my favorite month. I love May's innocence after treacherous April, its artless hope. Sweetness. I can't decide if it's good fortune or another of fate's low blows that the worst experience of my life is unfolding in gentle, good-hearted May.

Antiestrogen therapy didn't work for me. Given my history, Dr. Searle was not hopeful from the beginning, but we'd both wanted, for different reasons, to put off chemotherapy as long as possible. My reason was that I'd had it before and it frightened me. Not only had it failed to stave off a recurrence, it had made me sicker than I'd ever been in my life.

But I didn't know what sick was. Dr. Searle has devised a new cocktail since my last party with chemo. It's called CAF—Cytoxan, Adriamycin, and 5-fluorouracil—and if it doesn't kill me first, I could almost pity my poor cancer cells.

Kirby wanted to go with me for the first treatment, but I dissuaded him; I told him I'd been through it before, I knew what to expect. Anyway—I didn't tell him this—if there were going to be problems, they would begin later, seven to ten hours after the infusions.

My appointment was for one-thirty. At twelve-fifteen, Lee knocked at my door. "I'm taking the afternoon off and going with you," she announced. I knew before I tried that, unlike Kirby, Lee wouldn't be talked out of it, and I was right. But I must confess that under a veneer of exasperation, I felt a prodigious relief.

The doctor had already written my chemo orders, but there was still red tape to go through before the treatment could start: registering, meeting the chemo nurse, getting vitals and blood counts taken, waiting for the drugs to be processed at the pharmacy. I didn't sit down in the comfortable, too-familiar lounge chair in my own private little cubicle until after three. Lee sat on a hard stool beside me and chattered. Who knows what about—I was too wrought up to listen. I doubt that she knew herself because if anything, she was more nervous than I. But, relatively speaking, getting the chemo's nothing, I could have told her. It's *after* when the fun begins.

The staff had changed in two years; I didn't know Dorothy, the petite, pretty, dark-skinned nurse who bustled in, smiling and efficient, with her tray of drugs. "Brought your friend, have you? That's nice," she said in a pleasant English accent while she slapped at the inside of my elbow for a vein. The stick was smooth and quick—thank God, I thought, she's good at it. Some of them are awful.

"What's in that?" Lee asked, eyeing the bright red syringe Nurse Dorothy was attaching to my catheter.

"Adriamycin. That's the one that makes your hair fall out, love." She looked straight into my eyes, her face gentle as a mother's. Her sympathy was real, and it was almost too much. My emotions were ragged, and nothing on earth makes me feel sorrier for myself than chemotherapy. I believe if Lee hadn't been with me, I'd have wept. But I always feel obliged to cheer up anyone who's kind enough to try to cheer me up, and so I made a stupid joke, "Hair today, gone tomorrow," and closed my eyes, while Dorothy monitored the slow, steady pump of red drug in my vein.

Cytoxan came next, via a slow drip. I knew this one; I was prepared for its disconcerting and instantaneous side effect, a feeling as if you've just eaten Chinese mustard and your sinuses are prickly cold and wide open. Five-FU was last, and afterward the nurse removed the catheter and told me to stay where I was, she'd be back in a while to take my vitals and give last-minute instructions on side effects.

I lay with my eyes closed, morbidly alert to every sense, trying to gauge what I felt. Nothing much—too early. Lee had gone very quiet. I thought she would start talking again when I heard her draw her stool up close beside me. Instead, she slipped her hand, which was trembling slightly, into mine. "Let's do an imagery thing," she murmured. "Let's visualize the chemo killing the cancer cells. Want to?"

I don't know what form her visualization took, but mine made me smile. "What's funny?" she asked, but I only shook my head. I didn't think she'd find it as charming as I did—Lee as a gladiator in star-spangled tights and a leotard, smacking hoodlum cancer cells off a platform, one by one, with a giant styrofoam sword.

"Henry and I are fighting," she told me over an early dinner in a Spanish restaurant near my apartment. I was hungry, watching her push pieces of scallop and shrimp around on a plate of saffron rice. But I ordered a cup of lentil soup and a small salad, and worried that even that would prove too much.

"What are you fighting about?"

"Everything. Everything he says or does makes me furious. I just can't help it."

"It's the stress. You're both—"

"I know that. I yelled at him last night that he had to quit drinking, and we haven't talked to each other since."

"Quit drinking? But Henry doesn't drink much, does he?" *Henry?*

"He has a beer sometimes after work. Alcohol affects a man's sperm, Isabel, it's a known fact. I don't think I'm asking that much. *I'm* the one who's doing everything. All he has to do is—is—jerk off in a bottle every few weeks, while I have to—do everything else—" She dropped her fork on her plate and covered her face with her hands.

"Lee, oh, honey—" I was so surprised, all I could do was reach across and pat her arm.

"Sorry." She fumbled in her purse for a tissue. "It's been an awful day." She looked up, red-faced. "I got my period," she whispered, and dissolved into tears.

"Oh, no. Oh, I'm sorry."

"I don't know what's happening to me. I'm sorry to tell you all this now, of all times, but—"

"Doesn't matter."

"—but I can't help it, I'm not *myself* anymore, I can't control my emotions and I just want to cry and cry and *beat* on something. I'm so afraid, oh, Isabel, I'm so scared that we'll never get a baby, and if that happens—" She put her hand on her throat, glancing around in mortification, appalled at the thought that someone might have heard her.

"But there are more things to try, aren't there? If the insemination doesn't work—"

"There are a *million* more things to try. There's in vitro, there's GIFT, there's ZIFT, something called ICSI, there's gestational surrogacy—we're just at the beginning, and everything takes forever and costs a fortune. Henry keeps asking, 'What do *poor* people do?' and I know it's driving him crazy to spend all this money, but it's *my* money, but when I say that, it just makes him angry and hurts his feelings. Oh, God."

I'd never seen her like this. Emma and Rudy joke, fondly, about Lee's self-possession, her rationality, her tendency to see things in black and white and not delve for nuance—but the truth, of course, is that she can be as passionate as any of us. Her private sense of what feelings are fit for public disclosure is strict, though, strict and old-fashioned, and that's exactly what made tonight's outburst so shocking.

She recovered quickly, and then she couldn't stop apologizing. I wanted to pursue the subject, ask her to finish that sentence that had trailed off with "if that happens." But it was the wrong time and the wrong place.

When we finished eating, she insisted on going home with me. "You might feel sick, Isabel, and someone should be with you."

I protested, knowing it was pointless, but once again secretly relieved. I probably would be sick—in fact, I was planning on it—but I told her there was nothing she could do about it. "Anyway, what about Henry? You should go home, Lee, it's Friday night."

"So? He's fine on his own. I'll call and tell him I'll be late, don't worry about him."

Her way of punishing her husband because she was miserable. If only all married couples took their anger out on each other so harmlessly, I thought, remembering Gary and me.

At home, although it was only eight o'clock, I undressed and got in bed. I probably wouldn't sleep, but at least I could relax for a few hours before—or *if*; I was trying to be positive—I began to feel sick.

"How do you feel now?" Lee asked, leaning over me, smoothing the sheet over the top of the blanket. Tucking me in.

"Hard to describe. Warm, and my skin feels a little tight. I just feel odd. A sort of humming."

She sat on the edge of the bed. "No fever," she noted, resting her hand on my forehead. "Don't worry, Isabel, I'll stay with you. We'll get through this."

"Of course we will." I wanted to tell her what a wonderful mother she'd have been—would be—but I was afraid we'd both cry.

"Do you want some water?"

"Yes. Yes, I forgot, I'm supposed to drink lots of water."

"That makes sense. You don't want poison sitting in your bladder and kidneys any longer than necessary," she said practically, and got up. "Want the light out?"

"Yes, please."

"Okay. I'll bring you some water, and then you try to go to sleep."

"What will you do?"

"I'll sit and meditate for a while. Okay if I turn the TV on low?"

"Sure."

"Okay, then. Night, Isabel."

"Good night. Thanks for everything."

She blew me a kiss from the doorway.

A few minutes later, I heard her talking softly on the telephone. To Henry, I guessed. I hoped they made up. I meant to listen, monitor how the reconciliation went by the length of the conversation, but I must have drifted off. I jolted awake when the phone rang.

Lee answered it immediately, before I could get up. "She's fine," I heard her say in a voice, crisp and formal, borderline impolite, that made me certain the caller was Kirby. Seconds later, a wave of sickness rolled over me.

I staggered up. The bathroom was adjacent to the bedroom, across a short, narrow hall. A matter of ten or twelve steps, no more, but I didn't make it.

I vomited on the carpet in the hall and on the pink tile floor and on the round throw rug in front of the sink. An explosion. Everything I'd eaten, dinner, lunch, breakfast, a massive quantity of thick black bile—everything spewed out like a geyser, utterly uncontrollable. I huddled over the toilet, retching and coughing, while Lee put her arm around my waist and said, "There, now, that's much better."

"Hell," I said when I could. "Don't clean up—I will, just—"

"Hush, Isabel. Are you through?"

No. I threw up again, holding my stomach, gagging at the end until there was nothing left. But when I tried to rinse my mouth out at the sink, sickness hit again and I swerved back to the toilet.

Lee finally guided me back to bed, where I lay in a sweaty heap, listening to her scrub the carpet, mop the floor. The smell of Lysol jerked me up. She barely got out of the way before I was heaving again into her spanking clean toilet.

It wouldn't stop. "Where's it coming from? There can't be anything left!" And finally there wasn't anything, but that didn't stop the nausea. "I'm calling the doctor," Lee kept threatening, but I told her there was no point, I'd already taken the antinausea medication. "It's like this, this is how it is, they can't do anything." But this time was worse than before. It had to be the Adriamycin, the new drug in the cocktail. I crawled back to bed and tried to rest, but I couldn't lie still, couldn't find any position that was comfortable for more than a few seconds. The muscles of my stomach felt tender and achy, all my nerves were on fire. Lee wanted me to drink water, but I couldn't—just the thought of it made me gag.

Someone knocked at the door. I looked at the clock: twelve-twenty. Lee went to answer, and presently I heard Kirby's low, solemn voice raised in solicitous questions. I turned my face into the pillow, senselessly mortified. Of course he'd heard me; our bathrooms might as well be connected for all the soundproofing the ceiling provided. I wasn't sorry when Lee sent him away. "All right, I'll *call* you, but there's nothing you can do. But thanks." She closed the door firmly.

I wished we had never had that abortive, semiromantic interlude last December, I wished he had never kissed me, never said those words to me about love. Then the conspicuous absence of a follow-up would not have been so embarrassing to us both. Emma was partly right when she said I was the one who had pulled away from the relationship. But she was partly wrong. Kirby disappeared, didn't call, didn't visit, for six days after I told him about my new diagnosis. A long time for us; we were used to seeing each other daily. When he reappeared, he behaved as if nothing had happened, and since then he'd been helpfulness itself, a model of sympathy and selfless friendship. It was obvious that decency motivated him, not "love," and, of course, I didn't blame him. He'd lost his wife and children to senseless early deaths. He would have to be crazy, he would have to be pathologically self-destructive to choose to be intimate with a woman in my situation. No, no, no, I didn't blame him, but I hated it that here was one more loss to grieve.

When did I become the sort of person who puts *love* in quotation marks?

"Go home," I told Lee at one o'clock. "I think it's getting better." A lie; I was shuddering with sickness, red-skinned and hot, exhausted but unable to lie still.

"I've already called Henry and told him I'm staying. I just wish I could *do* something. Shall I rub your back?"

I shook my head. "Thanks. Don't want anything touching me."

"What about some nice music? To take your mind off it."

"I don't know. I don't think so."

"Well, we could try it. All right?"

I said yes, to humor her. "Terry sent me the Glenn Gould Brahms intermezzos. Put that on."

She did, and minutes later I was stumbling for the bathroom. "Turn it off, oh God, don't ruin it—" I was crying from weakness and frustration, and now fear that this wretched sickness might turn me against something so beautiful, something I loved so much. "Oh, take it off, Lee, stop it, stop—"

She looked scared when I came back into the bedroom and sat down gingerly beside her. "I think we should call the doctor," she said again. "This can't be natural."

"It's not, that's the point. It's poison." I hugged my legs to my aching stomach. "All that gets me through is thinking of it eating the cancer. Like acid."

"But this is too much. Let me call, Isabel, and just ask."

"No point, I'm telling you. This is what it does."

"Let me just *call*."

"Call, then." I was too weak to keep arguing.

She got up and called. I heard her murmuring into the phone, but I didn't listen, didn't care enough.

"I told the answering service it's an emergency," she announced with satisfaction from the doorway. "The doctor's going to call."

I grunted. At least one of us felt better.

A few minutes later the phone rang.

"He's calling in a prescription at the all-night on Columbia," she reported after another low-voiced conversation. "I'm going to pick it up. You'll be okay for about twenty minutes, right? I'll be—"

"You are not driving to the drugstore at one-thirty in the morning." The effort to talk brought on a fresh wave of queasiness.

"Don't be silly. I'll be—"

I sat up. "Don't, Lee, I mean it. I forbid it."

She didn't laugh. To her credit. She stared at me speculatively for a few seconds. "Okay. I'll call Kirby, then, and he can get it."

I said no and started to swear, but she only raised her eyebrows at me and waited until I had to lie down, moaning.

That's how it came about that I was lying under a blanket on my living room sofa at three o'clock in the morning, listening to Lee and Kirby make polite conversation, and beginning to feel just a little bit better. The interludes between episodes of vomiting had lengthened to about thirty minutes, and I no longer felt so feverish. But I still couldn't drink water, and my reaction to Kirby's innocent, never repeated suggestion that I try a few saltines was predictable. Lee made tea; they sipped it quietly, and took surreptitious bites of something, Oreos, I think, when they thought I wasn't looking. As far as feeling awful went, that night was the worst ever, and yet, unexpectedly, I didn't feel like slinking off somewhere to be alone in my sickness, and I had no interest in being noble and not inflicting myself on others. In fact, I craved company.

Kirby sat on the floor like a yogi, legs crossed, wrists rather elegantly draped over his knees. Beside him, in the easy chair, Lee yawned without covering her mouth, a grave lapse for her, and a sure sign of fatigue. "How long have you lived in D.C.? Kirby—is that your first name or your last?"

"Last. Since 1980. My wife and I moved here from Pittsburgh."

"Oh, Pittsburgh, I have friends there. Do you know the Newmans? Mark and Patti?"

Kirby said no.

"So you're *from* Pittsburgh?" Lee asked.

"No, originally from New York. Upstate. And you?"

"My family is from the Boston area."

"Ah."

Pause.

"How did you first meet Isabel?" Kirby asked sociably.

"We used to live two blocks from each other in Chevy Chase. This was back when she was married to Gary. I met her son, Terry, first. On a Halloween night."

I smiled faintly at the memory.

Kirby said, "The first time I saw Isabel, she was talking to the bag lady who used to camp out on the corner by our building. The woman was sitting on the sidewalk, all her possessions piled around her, and Isabel was squatting down beside her so they could be eye-to-eye. Isabel had on a dark green skirt and a light blue blouse and low-heeled shoes. The homeless woman did most of the talking. A couple of times they both laughed. Isabel didn't give her money, but when the visit was over, she squeezed her by her tennis shoe. Gently. I thought the gesture looked very . . . loving."

I turned my head to look at him.

"The second time I saw her," he continued in the same low, matter-of-fact voice, "she sat down beside me on the No. 42 bus. At first I didn't quite recognize her; I thought it might be the same woman who'd spoken so kindly to the homeless lady, but I wasn't positive. This time she wore slacks and a brown sweater. And boots. She was carrying an armload of books, textbooks, I thought, but I couldn't read the titles. Her fingers were ink-stained.

"On F Street, she took a tape player out of her purse and put on a set of headphones. I watched her out of the corner of my eye. Her face smoothed out and she smiled. Just slightly. Her hands in her lap went limp. The music was barely audible; try as I might, I couldn't make it out. I had already decided she was perfect, and yet I was filled with a terrible dread that she was smiling beatifically to Megadeath or the Beastie Boys. Imagine my relief when, at Dupont Circle, she opened the machine to turn the tape over, and I saw that it was a Mozart symphony. The G minor."

"Goodness," Lee said faintly.

"She got off the bus at my stop, and began to walk down Ontario Road toward Euclid. I followed. When she went up the steps to this building and then buzzed herself through the front door, I wondered briefly if I were hallucinating. A wish-fulfillment fantasy. She saw me—for the first time—from the elevator, and held the door for me. We rode up to her floor in silence. Everything I thought to say to her sounded . . . frivolous. Not important enough for the occasion. The door opened, and then I did say something—I don't remember what; I've blocked it—and she ended up telling me her name. I told her mine. The buzzer warned that I'd held the elevator door too long, and she stepped back and said, 'Well,' and waved good-bye."

He stopped talking. The story was over. He didn't look at me, but Lee did, with wide, fascinated eyes.

I sat up. Slowly, I thought. I didn't know what I would say, but something certainly seemed to be called for. But despite my intention, I had moved too quickly. The worst happened—sickness broke over me without warning, and I had time to mutter, "This isn't personal—truly—" before throwing off the blanket and making a mad and extremely undignified dash for the bathroom.

When I returned, Kirby and Lee were talking and laughing with much animation about something else, some completely neutral subject. The loaded moment had passed, and of course that was a relief—and yet, a tender, unused spot in me wanted it back, and didn't care how awkward that would be. I lay on my side and watched Kirby, examined his narrow face, the skin fine and pale over the sharp-boned surfaces, his brown eyes hooded and slightly sunken. I listened while he told a story about his daughter, Julie, whom he'd lost when she was twelve, and as he spoke I saw him patiently, thoroughly, and almost surely unconsciously turning Lee around, from a jealous, suspicious critic to a friend. My eyes blurred, blinked shut, and I finally dozed.

Dawn.

"Both of you, go home."

Kirby had fallen asleep on the floor, Lee in her chair. I huddled inside my blanket, shivering in spasms; I wasn't hot anymore, I was freezing.

"Could you drink some tea now?" Lee asked, staggering up, stretching.

I could. A miracle. We slurped tea and didn't talk. I don't know which of us looked grayer; me, probably, but I wasn't going to look in a mirror.

"What a night." I used both hands to scratch my head. "Scalp itches," I explained—then froze. They looked at me uncomprehendingly. I took my hands away. "Adriamycin," I said, trying to laugh. "Complete hair loss in all takers. No exceptions. I'll be bald in two weeks."

"Oh, Is." Lee came over and sat beside me, put her arm around me and kissed my head. I stiffened, sensing the start of a good cry. I might have enjoyed that if Kirby hadn't been there.

"Why don't you cut it yourself?" he said.

I looked at him. "Pardon?"

"*Yes.*" Lee sat up straight. "Cut it before it can start falling out."

"Cut it myself?" I touched my soft, curly hair with my fingertips. "What—now?"

"Show it who's boss," Lee said, ruthless excitement snapping in her eyes. "Screw it before it can screw you."

"I could shave it for you," Kirby said quietly, watching me. "With my electric razor. We could do it together now, the three of us."

I did cry then, but only a little. I cried for the losses in store for me, and for the love of my friends, and because sometimes kindness is as excruciating as cruelty. And—a little—for my hair.

17

Lee

The Saving Graces have celebrated more anniversaries (four) at Neap Tide, my family's cottage on the Outer Banks, than anyplace else, so deciding where to spend our tenth was simple. We left on Friday morning, later than planned because of some trouble Rudy had getting Curtis's car, and then it took forever to get there because Rudy and Emma had to stop every hour to go to the bathroom. They denied it, but I think it's entirely possible they had a flask and were passing it back and forth in the front seat.

"You two aren't drinking, are you?" I asked after the third pit stop. Emma turned around and looked at me as if she thought I'd lost my mind. So—I don't know. I do know they got louder as the day went on, laughing at nothing and singing along to the tapes she'd brought, old rock and roll songs I didn't care for when they were new, and then country songs that were even worse, sung by Tammy Wynette and Dolly Parton and God knows who else. I finally had to tell them Isabel was trying to sleep, which was the truth. She took a nap every afternoon now that she was on chemo, and even Rudy and Emma weren't immature enough to disrespect that.

Neap Tide is really Neap Tide II, Neap Tide I having suffered so much storm surge damage during Hurricane Emily that it had to be rebuilt. The new cottage is bigger and has a few more amenities, ceiling fans, another roof deck, brand-new appliances, but in the main it's still as homey and unsophisticated as the original. Nothing, in other words, like the half-million-dollar mansions they're building on the ocean side these days. Henry and I come down twice a year; my parents, maybe once every two years; my brothers, never: they prefer Cape Cod. The rest of the season, my family rents Neap Tide out to tourists.

We were exhausted by the time Rudy pulled the car between the stilts under the long, weathered front deck. Emma had to go look at the ocean immediately, while Rudy and I hauled our stuff (and hers) up the two flights of outside stairs and decided on rooms. I suggested Isabel and I each have a room to ourselves, and Rudy and Emma double up in the third bedroom. No one had a problem with that. After Emma came back and everyone unpacked, we met in the kitchen to discuss (again at my suggestion) meals, responsibilities, and other domestic arrangements. That was when we had our first fight.

Not really a fight—I shouldn't say that. Our first emotional moment. I was explaining why it made more sense to eat in tonight and go out tomorrow (we were tired of driving, we had steaks in the cooler ready to grill), and also suggesting certain tasks that seemed more appropriate for some people than others (Emma, for example, is a good cook but horribly messy, whereas Rudy is slightly less creative but just excellent at tidying up as she goes along)—when Emma, who had already opened a beer and drunk half of it, drew herself up straight and saluted. "Sir!" she shouted like a marine.

Well, I'm used to her not-so-veiled sarcasm, so I let that go. But a few minutes later, as I was trying to organize cleanup shifts for the common areas, the living and dining rooms, the kitchen, the outdoor decks—and I don't apologize for this, it was *not* officious of me, *someone* needs to say these things once in the beginning, to prevent misunderstandings later on—Emma made a crack. Under her breath, and supposedly to herself, but we all heard it. It was a reference to my sex life. And who was probably "in charge" of it, me or Henry.

I turned away. Everything went quiet until Isabel said, "Oh,

Emma," very softly. I don't know if it was Emma's crack or the gentle disapproval in Isabel's voice, but for some reason I started to cry.

And then I couldn't stop. I kept trying to turn my back on everybody and Isabel kept trying to turn me around. I sat down at the kitchen table and covered my face.

Emma knelt beside me. "Oh, Lee, I'm sorry," she said, "I'm so sorry," with real fear in her voice, and Isabel hovered behind me, stroking my hair. Rudy brought me a glass of water.

I was mortified. "It's the fertility drugs," I told them, "I'm on Clomid and it causes mood swings. I can't help it."

"No, it's my fault," Emma said. "What an unbelievably stupid thing to say. Lee, come on, don't pay any attention to me."

"No, it's me. It's not working, I can't get pregnant, and I feel like such a fool. I waited too long—I'm forty-one years old! It's my fault, and I can't stand it."

"It's not your fault," Rudy said, "it's Henry's sperm."

"It might not be. The doctor said there might be something else wrong, because it should've happened by now. I think he thinks it's me. And I honestly think Henry is *glad*! Because it's not just him anymore!" I tried to stop crying because I could see I was scaring them, but I couldn't. And I couldn't stop talking.

"What did I do? Is it something I did? Is this happening because I was too promiscuous when I was young? I had a one-night stand!" I said hotly when Emma and Rudy laughed—even Isabel smiled. "I could have gotten an infection and never known it. And I just *had* to have an IUD when I was thirty, to make it *easier* to have sex, and now we know what *they* can do!"

"Lee, this is not—"

"If I just hadn't waited so long, but no, I had to have everything perfect, my career, my house, my husband—why couldn't I have gotten married in my twenties? Oh God, it's just that I've always known what I wanted, I've always planned for it and worked for it, and I've always gotten it. And now everything's failing. It's like I'm paralyzed. I can't do anything, I can't fix it." More tears. This was too embarrassing for words.

Rudy had pulled a chair up close to mine. "And it must be so hard for you at work," she said, "being with all those children. I mean, of all the jobs for you to have."

"*Yes*," I said, sobbing, and so glad somebody had finally acknowledged this out loud. Maybe it was too obvious, but for some reason nobody had ever said it before—that me being in charge of a child care center was a terrible cruelty, a trick life was playing on me for no reason but meanness. "It's *awful*. I don't know if I can keep doing it. It really, really hurts."

"Poor Lee." Emma wrapped her arms around my knees.

"It's too much, it's like constant torture, but what else can I do? I could do consulting, I could write articles, maybe a textbook—but it's still—"

"It's still children," Rudy said. "Constantly."

"Yes, and anyway, what's the difference, even if I was a bank teller I'd still see babies in strollers, babies in car seats, babies being breast-fed in the ladies' room at Nordstrom's. I'd still see mothers buying Pampers at the grocery store, and I'd still read stories about teenagers throwing their newborn babies in the garbage."

Isabel hugged me from behind, laying her cheek on my wet one. "Go on, it's good to cry. Do you tell Henry? I bet he's dying to talk to you."

I pulled away. I felt ashamed, not worthy of her sympathy, but I still had to say—"I'm so *angry* with him. I try not to be, I know it's irrational, but I can't help it. I'm on these awful drugs, I've taken a million tests, peed in a million cups, I've been probed and poked and injected and penetrated, and all he has to do is masturbate." I had to smile when Emma pressed her face to my thigh and snorted. "It's true. Deep down, I'm furious with him, and it doesn't matter that it's not his fault, and I *know* this whole thing is almost as bad for him as it is for me. For Henry, sex is private, and he can't stand this openness, all the questions he has to answer to a lot of nurses and doctors about our personal business. He even said something snotty about the group."

"No. He did?"

"Not about anybody in it, just that he guesses you all know everything about him, every little secret, and he *hates* that. And he hates having to go to the clinic and give his sperm, everybody knowing exactly what he's doing. It makes him feel ridiculous. Plus it's his sperm that are making all this have to be, so—"

"He feels guilty," Rudy said. "He wants to give you everything, and he feels like he's failing at the thing you want the very most."

I nodded. "He won't talk about it, but part of the reason he wants to be a father is to make up for not having one himself. I think a lot of pain from his childhood is coming back. Which makes everything worse."

"God," said Emma. "A double whammy."

"Exactly." It felt wonderful to get all this out and to be understood and sympathized with. But there was even more I *couldn't* say. Like my secret wish that I'd married somebody else, anybody else, just so long as he could give me children. And of course I couldn't tell them how bad sex between Henry and me had gotten. We didn't even do it anymore unless we had to. What was the point? For "passion"? We didn't have any. I felt unattractive and asexual, and Henry felt like a failure. Making love was so mechanical, so self-conscious; the last time we tried, I couldn't climax, and he barely could. I should have pretended, but I didn't care enough. The whole episode embarrassed us so much, we haven't done it since.

"What about counseling?" Rudy said. "What if you both went to somebody and talked about it?"

"Henry won't. And I'm not going by myself."

"It'll work out," Emma said. "Everything could change overnight, you know, Lee. One phone call from the clinic. One blue stick."

"But that's what I've been telling myself for months! Wait and hope, wait and hope—that's what my life has shrunk down to."

"Lee," Isabel said quietly, "you never mention the possibility of adoption."

"No, because Henry doesn't want to, he wants his own. So do I—so do my parents."

"Your parents?"

"Wait, now," Emma said, "Henry doesn't want to adopt? He says that?"

"Jenny says his father was killed in Vietnam, but the truth is—this is a *secret*, now—Henry thinks she doesn't even know who his father was. So he—he really wants his own child. We talked about it a long time ago, and we agreed."

"Well, but maybe now—"

"No. I'm in this, and I'm not giving up. I am going to be pregnant."

"But if it's making you crazy—"

"It's not making me *crazy*, Rudy. I'm determined, that's all. I won't be defeated. There's a difference between being crazy and being determined."

"Of course, I didn't mean really crazy. Not like me, Lee. You're the sanest one here."

"I resent that," Emma said, and we laughed, all of us glad for the levity.

"Oh, enough," I said. I was uncomfortable being the center of attention for so long, plus I didn't want to talk about my parents. I was sorry I'd let that slip—that they want a natural grandchild from me, another little Pavlik to carry on the genius genes. Their attitude embarrasses me; I could already hear what Emma would say about it.

"You're right, it'll work out somehow." I stood up. Everybody fell back, away from me. "It just takes time, and it makes me tired. You guys are great. There, that's my fifteen minutes," I said, laughing, "and I feel a lot better."

They didn't believe me, but they stopped hovering around me and started making drinks to carry out to the front deck. It was as if we'd all realized at once that our anniversary weekend was getting off to a dangerous start, and we'd better shift gears before we spoiled it. They would talk about me as soon as I wasn't around, I knew. "Oh, poor Lee, I had no idea, I've never seen her like that, it was so unlike her." I've never seen me like this, either. I hardly know myself anymore. I want my old life back.

The sunset was blinding; we had to turn our chairs away until it dropped under the haze on the horizon. "This is the life," we took turns saying, lolling on our backbones, bare feet up on the railing. "This is what it's all about." Rudy couldn't remember if this was the third or the fourth time we'd come to Hatteras to celebrate, and everybody started reminiscing. "Why don't we go for a walk on the beach?" I interrupted to suggest. I had a surprise in store for them, but not until tomorrow night; too much nostalgia this early could spoil it.

The tide was running out. We went along the shore two by two, Rudy and Emma in the shallow surf with their pants legs rolled up, Isabel and me higher up on the wet sand. Isabel wore a pretty red and green scarf around her head, and she looked wonderful, you would never suspect anything was wrong with her. She claimed the drugs were making her gain weight, but I couldn't see it.

"How do you feel?" I asked.

"Great."

"It was a long drive—I'm tired myself. Sure you're okay?"

"I'm fine."

"How's Kirby?"

"Great. Sends you his regards."

"I really like him." She smiled. "I wasn't sure about him at first," I admitted. "But after that night. That first chemo night."

She nodded. "What a night, huh?"

Her second treatment was last week, and it had gone a lot better than the first. She wasn't as sick, and the nausea hadn't lasted as long. I didn't stay with her, Emma did, and not all night this time.

"So," I said. "Is he still in love with you?"

She shook her head slightly, not to say no but to shake off the question.

She would never talk about Kirby except to say that his romantic interest came at the wrong time, and that she was grateful she still had his friendship. I can't tell if she's sad about that or not. Isabel's serenity isn't always a blessing. Sometimes it's a wall.

I kept slowing my steps to match hers, until finally she stopped. "You go on, Lee, I think I'll sit for a while and look at the water."

"You *are* tired. I'll sit with you."

"No, go on, catch up with Emma and Rudy. Pick me up on the way back."

These are the little incidents I can't bear. She lulls me into thinking not much is wrong with her, and sometimes I even *forget*—and then she'll tire out much too soon, or I'll catch her sitting down in a chair too carefully, like an old woman with arthritis. Reality closes in, and it's a new shock every time. I suppose it's the same for her, but worse. Oh, much worse.

We ate dinner in the dining room, with candles and soft music and a bowl of the wildflowers Emma stole from the next-door-neighbor's yard. Everything tasted delicious, even the microwave-baked potatoes. We made a lot of toasts, and by the end of the meal we were quite a merry group. I won't say my outburst in the kitchen was forgotten; in fact, I think it overshadowed the whole evening and made us more careful of one another. Emma in particular was on good behavior, speaking gently to me and never being sarcastic; she kept touching me, too, her hand on my hand, a soft nudge on my arm to share a joke. I must've really scared her.

We took our coffee outside and sat in the deck chairs to listen to the surf and watch the clouds slip past the moon. It was a fine night, soft and starry, with a steady breeze blowing in from the ocean. Neap Tide isn't a waterfront cottage, but from the front deck you can easily see the Atlantic on the left and the Pamlico Sound on the right, and at night, after the traffic on Route 12 dies down, you can hear the waves almost as clearly as if you were sitting on the beach.

"Well, I'm not pregnant, either," Rudy said out of the blue, during a lull in our lazy conversation. "In case anybody was wondering." She had her long legs stretched out on the wooden ottoman, long arms bent gracefully behind her head. The rest of us looked vague and shadowy, but the moonlight glinted on Rudy's black hair and glittered in her gray eyes. Even in the dark, she stands out. I started to say something, but she sat up and leaned toward me. "I just didn't want you to think I was hiding it, keeping it a secret not to hurt you. Because I wouldn't do that, it would be . . . "

"Condescending," Emma supplied. "And not necessary." She smiled at me.

"Yes," Rudy said. "So, I just wanted you to know."

To tell the truth, I'd forgotten she and Curtis were trying. I guess I'd put it out of my mind. "Are you worried?" I asked her. "How long has it been?"

"Since January. Yes, I am, a little. Because I was reading somewhere that if nothing's happened in six months, there might be a problem."

"Well, that's what they say." Something I wish I'd known myself two years ago.

Emma peered at Rudy in the dark. "You really think something's wrong? Are you doing it right, taking your temperature and all that?"

"Well, not at first, but for the last two months, yes."

"Oh, two months is nothing," Isabel said.

"I know." Rudy heaved one of her long, heavy, dissatisfied sighs.

"How's Curtis?" I asked. "How is he liking his new job?"

"Curtis . . ." She hesitated for so long, all three of us stopped staring into space and looked at her. "Oh . . ." More silence. Finally she said, "He's okay," in an airy voice, and stood up. "I'm going for a beer, anybody want one?"

How odd. While she was gone, we stared at one another and made soft noises, "Hmm," and "Ha . . ." but we didn't speak. This was too new; we didn't know what to think yet. If there was anything to think. Emma in particular looked bewildered.

"What a beautiful night," Isabel said. "Feel that breeze. Anyone mind if I take off my scarf?"

We scoffed, we disclaimed, Emma even swore—"Jesus, Isabel, how could you even *ask*"—but the truth is, it's always a shock to see Isabel's bare head for the first time. But you get used to it quickly, and then I honestly think she looks cute. I do. She doesn't agree, of course, and even for me it's hard to separate her appearance from the reason for it—hard to appreciate how she looks but not suffer over why she looks that way.

"So how's it going?" Emma said softly. She reached her hand out to the back of Isabel's chair and held on to it. "How's every little thing?"

Isabel looked over and smiled at her. "It's okay. I get tired easily. That's the worst of it."

"What about your hip?" Isabel had been having some pain there lately. She minimized it, but when it was bad it made her limp.

"When it gets worse, the doctor says I can have radiation. That'll take care of it."

"You mean *if* it gets worse," I said.

"Yes."

"Because the chemo should cure you. That's what it's for, I mean, that's it's *job*."

She nodded, smiled. Sometimes I think I have a better attitude than she does.

"Okay, that's the body," Emma said. "How's the spirit?"

"It's fine, too. I'm hopeful."

We listened to the sound of that word. Isabel usually says the simple truth. If she was saying it now, I guess we couldn't ask for more.

Rudy got up and went to stand behind Isabel's chair. "Let's try something. I've been reading about healing touch."

"Think you've got it?" Emma smiled on one side of her mouth.

"I could. So could you, smarty. You don't know till you try."

"I imagine it helps if you believe in it," I said a little coolly. Sometimes Emma's cynicism annoys me. Isabel closed her eyes and smiled.

"Shh," Rudy said. "Think healing thoughts, everybody. I put my hands like this, not touching you but almost, and I feel your aura, Isabel." She moved her long-fingered hands slowly, cupping the air an inch from Isabel's head. She slid them down lower, along her neck and then her shoulders, her arms. "I'm doing your whole body," Rudy murmured, and Isabel nodded slowly. "Do you feel anything?"

"I feel heat where your hands are."

I turned my head to send Emma a victorious glare, but she had her eyes closed. She was concentrating.

"I know I can feel your energy," Rudy said positively. "Which hip hurts?"

"This one," Isabel said, and Rudy did healing touch there.

I shut my eyes and did my favorite healing meditation. I imagine a sort of Mexican firing squad. Isabel's cancer cells are outlaws dressed in black, with gun belts across their chests—not that they have chests; actually they look more like kidney beans, but with sombreros—and they stand in a long line while a knot of good soldiers takes aim with long black rifles and shoots them. They fall over dead, and another line of cancer cells steps up. *Pow*, they're dead, and another line steps up. It's very efficient and it can go on indefinitely.

Rudy finished her healing touch and sat back down. "Want to try?" she said to Emma.

"Hell, no. Isabel's a friend, I might send her into relapse."

They laughed, but I thought the joke was in poor taste.

I got up to go to the bathroom. Even with the door closed, I could plainly hear Emma's voice gradually rising, getting shrill with anger. When I hurried back, she was on her feet, her back to the rail. Ranting.

"I really hate the mind-body connection, if you want to know the truth, and I can't stand that guy Shorter. I think he's done more harm to sick people than anything since leeches."

"Who's Shorter?" I asked Rudy.

"That doctor who wrote the book about—"

"He's a jerk, and he pisses me off. If you believe his spiel, then you believe Isabel gave herself cancer by being an emotional cripple. Well, fuck you, Shorter, Isabel is not guilty of cancer."

"Em, that's not exactly—"

"What gets me is how a *doctor* could be so stupid about *medicine*. And so destructive. Now whenever Isabel gets depressed—which seems like a pretty logical way to feel once in a while, wouldn't you agree? Given the circumstances?—Shorter's telling her she's making her tumors grow! What an idiot!"

Isabel tried again. "I don't think he's really saying—"

"I mean, what a gigantic *crock*. Whatever happened to science? Isabel, he's as good as telling you you made yourself sick. What about germs? Hm? What about heredity? What about smoking and asbestos? Nitrites! Smog!" The sea air made her hair stick out like a witch's broom. She prowled back and forth in front of the railing, and a couple of times she banged her fist on it for emphasis. She wasn't the least bit drunk, she was just mad.

"What's the difference between Shorter blaming your neuroses for your cancer and Jerry Falwell blaming your sins for your HIV? Cancer *happens*. You aren't responsible. Life's not fair—Jesus, do I have to *say* this? What happened, Is, is that you got a raw deal. That's it. God's little joke. Sorry, better luck next time."

"I understand what you're saying—Sit, Emma, would you stop pacing?—and sometimes I feel the same way. But whether we like it or not, there is a connection between our physical and spiritual selves. People with no religious faith die sooner—just for an example. That's been proven."

"Not to me."

Isabel clicked her tongue. "Well, I can't explain it to you, but it has to do with neuropeptides and T cells and endorphins or something. Your brain *communicates* with your body. It does. Take my word for it."

"Okay." Emma flopped down in the chair, sullen.

"I know what you're saying," Rudy said sympathetically. "I don't like it either, the idea that anyone would make herself sick—"

"That *Isabel* would make herself sick," Emma started up again. "It's bullshit. You're going along, living your life the best way you can, trying not to hurt anybody, and *wham*, one day you get cancer. And then this—*twerp* comes along and writes a best-seller about how it's all your fault. Insult to injury!"

"You know you're exaggerating," Isabel chided. "Nowhere do any of these writers, Shorter or anyone else, say it's our *fault*."

"But that's the implication."

Rudy said, "Emma, do you think our healing circles are a crock? Do you think when Isabel meditates, it's pointless?"

"No. No. I don't."

Isabel said, "Well, then, if you believe I can help to heal myself with positive mental energy, why can't you accept the converse—that my own negative energy might've contributed to my disease?"

Emma turned to her fiercely. "Do you believe that?"

"I don't know. I think it's possible."

"Well, I don't. Somebody else, maybe, but not you, Isabel. *Not you.*"

There was a long, charged silence, during which I wasn't sure what might happen, maybe we'd all burst into tears at once.

I'm the one who broke it to say, "I agree with Emma." My voice came out thin and strange; they looked at me curiously. I cleared my throat and said with force, "I think sometimes we can make ourselves sick, and sometimes it just happens. But Isabel isn't toxic to herself. There's nobody"—I searched for the word, and finally came up with—"purer. I mean it. No one gentler." I had to whisper, "And nobody who deserves this less."

Isabel held out her hand. I took it and she pulled me close. Instead of weeping, we four looked at one another with sharp, intense stares. I felt a thrill of fear and excitement. I don't know how much I believe in the mind-body connection, but if everything they say about it is true, I know there was so much psychic energy crackling and snapping among us just in that moment, we four could have cured a hospice full of dying people.

We spent Saturday morning on the beach, listening to Emma warn us about sun exposure. "Don't be fooled because it's overcast," she kept saying, huddled in a beach chair, swathed in terry cloth and smeared with sunscreen and zinc. I don't blame her—she's fair; she freckles first, then burns, then peels. But she sounded like a broken record. "Okay, fine, but when we're old and people come up and ask why a nice-looking young thing like me took a job as nurse-companion to three wrinkled old crones, you'll be—"

"We'll be really sorry," Rudy mumbled into the crook of her arm, facedown on a striped towel. Rudy would never be a wrinkled old crone. Looking at her, lean and long and tan in her bikini bathing suit, I was jealous of her body—well, we all were, who wouldn't be?—and until last night I was jealous of her love life. No, I mean her sex life: definitely not her love life, her marriage, or anything to do with Curtis Lloyd. But I always imagined she and Curtis had an incredibly passionate and satisfying time in bed, although I had no better reason for thinking it than that they're both beautiful. Now to learn that, so far at least, they couldn't conceive—it made me feel shallow and silly, for thoughtlessly mixing up physical attractiveness and fertility. You'd think I'd know better, being married to Henry.

And—something else that's hard to confess. There was a dark, ugly place in me that was secretly glad when she'd told us about their problem. I'm ashamed. But it's true. I want Rudy to have a child, of course I do, *but I want Henry and me to have one first*.

"Going for a walk," Isabel said, shaking sand off her towel and draping it around her shoulders.

"Want company?" I asked.

"No, thanks. I won't be long." She strolled away. We watched her, and when she was out of earshot, we talked about her.

It's what we do when we're together now, we three. At first it felt disloyal, but we've gotten over that. We tell one another everything we know, what we've heard or read lately about cancer, what Isabel said the last time we saw her, how she looked, how she sounded on the telephone.

"She looks good."

"She walks so slowly, though."

"She hasn't been in swimming yet."

"Think she will? She loves to swim."

"She's not very strong. If she goes in, one of us has to go with her."

"I don't think she's eating enough."

"She says the chemo makes her mouth taste bad."

"Her attitude still seems really good, though."

"You don't think she's pretending? Acting more positive for our benefit?"

"Even if she is, it's good for her. Remember that study that showed that smiling makes you feel happier?"

"She's going to get well. She's doing everything right, and the chemo's working."

"If it doesn't kill her first."

"Thank God for Kirby."

"Do you think they'll get together?"

"I do. After she gets her strength back."

"Did you see her collage?"

"No."

"Her collage?

"On the wall in her bedroom. She made a poster of her life. Her past and her future, milestones, major events. She cut out photos of herself when she was little, and her parents, her wedding, pictures of Terry. Us."

"Us?"

"And drawings of herself with cancer, and what she's doing to defeat it."

"Isabel can't draw."

"It's just cartoons, stick figures representing her."

"What did she put for the future?"

"Pictures from travel brochures—places like India and Nepal. A drawing of a diploma. A photograph of her with Terry. Another photo of us. Oh, and the banner from the top of an AARP newsletter. And at the very end, a picture of a baby."

"A baby?"

"She said it's herself. Reincarnated."

"Ah," Rudy said, nodding.

"Whatever," Emma said, smiling. Hopefully.

We went out for dinner, as planned, to a new, almost trendy seafood restaurant in Hatteras. It had been cloudy all day; while we were driving home, it began to rain. "There goes our moonlight walk on the beach," Rudy mourned. "Let's stop at the video store and rent a movie." Nobody but me had any objections. "No, let's not, let's do something else," I kept arguing, and when they said, "Like what?" I had no answer. The conversation got more and more ridiculous. Finally I had to tell them. "Oh, all right, then, ruin the surprise. I've already *got* a video for tonight."

"You do?"

"What is it?"

"I'm not watching any musical cartoons," Emma warned, obviously tired of being nice to me. She was making an ungracious reference to the last time I rented our beach movies. I got *The Hunchback of Notre Dame*, *Pocahontas*, and *Aladdin*. I should've realized she's just the kind of person who would hate Disney.

"It's not cartoons, it's us," I said. "Ten years of the Saving Graces. I had all our old film bits spliced together on one tape for our anniversary. It's twenty-six minutes long."

"Oh, that's wonderful," Isabel exclaimed, and Rudy took her hands off the steering wheel to clap. Even Emma looked pleased, although of course she had to slide down in her seat and say, "Oh, Jeez, home movies," for a joke. But she was glad, they all were, and that was gratifying. Occasionally, not often enough, the thoughtful, competent, organized member of a group gets the appreciation she deserves.

"Lose the bangs, DeWitt." Emma made a face at her image on the screen. "Talk about a bad hair year. How come nobody told me?"

"Shh, I can't hear it."

"I want to know who let me out of the house in that dress," Rudy said. "I'm a summer, I should never wear beige."

"God, remember when we got our colors done?"

"I think you both look beautiful," Isabel said. "We all do."

"Wow, look how skinny I was," Emma marveled, pointing. "What year is this?"

"You're skinny now, you just can't see it," Rudy said.

"Yeah, right."

"I read that women who have positive body images have twice as many orgasms as women who don't."

"Yeah, well, don't worry about me, I'm just fine in that—"

"*Shh*," I repeated. If you kept quiet and listened, sometimes you could actually hear what we were saying on the tape. But usually it was only a crackling din, because we were all overlapping or talking at once. This always surprises me when I look at our old movies, the fact that we never shut up, and what we say rarely sounds important or even particularly coherent. Yet at the time, I always think we're being quite lucid and succinct.

"Fitness camp! Remember that?" Emma pointed at herself on the screen. "I lost seven pounds in six days."

"I lost three."

"Four, and I gained it all back."

"In the first week."

"We ought to go there again," Rudy said. "That was so much fun."

We laughed at the pictures of Emma and Rudy cutting up in the rustic cottage where we stayed for a week, back in 1990. "Fitness camp"—the poor woman's health spa—was just a YWCA camp in the Poconos. We'd gone there instead of someplace nicer because, at the time, Emma didn't have any money.

"You are such a jerk," Rudy said affectionately, ruffling Emma's hair. "Why can't you ever look normal?"

It's true—whenever I point the camera at Emma, she either turns her back or makes a face, or else she makes some subtly obscene gesture, like resting her chin in her hand and extending her middle finger alongside her cheek. All with a sly smile that's funny, I suppose, but childish: I can't tell you how many perfectly nice still photos of the group she's spoiled by putting "horns" behind someone's head at the last second.

I'm rarely in these videos; I'm the cameraperson, a thankless job the others barely tolerate—until it's time to look at the finished product. Then you can't get them away from the TV set.

"Oh, here it comes. I hope," Emma said, rubbing her hands together. "Lee, did you put it in? Did you? I bet you took it out."

I should have. But I didn't, and I hope that squelches for all time anybody's claim that I am not a good sport. And this is why I like being the photographer—because look what happens when someone else (Emma) gets her hands on my camera.

We were having a regular dinner meeting at the house on Capitol Hill Rudy and Curtis had just bought, and I'd brought the video camera to film it, intending to give Rudy the tape afterward so she could send it to her mother or sister or whoever she wanted—her family never visits, and I thought it might be the only way they'd ever see her new home. The other thing was, I had just come from ballet class; I was hot and sweaty and I didn't feel fresh. I asked Rudy if I could take a shower before dinner.

"Oh, here it comes, here it comes," Emma said gleefully. Rudy and Isabel were giggling already. The shaky, inexpertly held camera showed a closed door, and a hand reaching out to turn the knob. Emma's innocent voice on the tape, saying, "Hm, wonder what's in here. What could be behind this door? Shall we see?" Steam poured out when she opened the door. My voice over the sound of running water: "Yes?"

That always cracks them up; I sound too dignified or something.

The camera keeps coming. Through the steam, you can see the blue and white stripes of the shower curtain. "Hello?" I say from behind it. Emma says, "Just getting a—" something inaudible, and I say, still gracious, "Oh, okay."

A hand pulls the curtain back, and there I am. Full frontal nudity. But I'm washing my hair with my eyes closed, and so I am unaware of this indignity for fifteen seconds. (I know, because Henry once timed it.) Fifteen seconds is a long time to be naked on film and not know it. It might have gone on even longer if Emma hadn't finally said, in a breathy, sexy voice, "Hi, there."

I open my eyes, open my mouth, and scream.

Blackout.

Oh, hilarious. My friends fell against one another on the sofa, convulsed with mirth. Even Isabel. I laughed with them, although not quite as heartily. This incident happened over seven years ago, and I am still trying to think of a way to pay Emma back. Nothing nearly good enough has occurred to me yet, but it will. Oh, it will.

The tape skipped ahead to Rudy's wedding.

"Oh God, look at Henry! Look at his *hair*!"

"What a hunk."

This is my favorite part of the video—our first date. Rudy had a formal wedding, and yet Henry had worn a corduroy sportcoat, brown slacks and no tie—and *it didn't matter*. I didn't care! When I realized that, I knew I must be in love. And his hair, oh, it was long and flowing, streaky and gorgeous, prettier than Emma's hair and about the same color.

"Wow, you guys look *hot*," she said, and it was absolutely true. Someone, Isabel, I think, had filmed us dancing at Rudy's reception. The band was playing "Sea of Love," and Henry and I certainly looked lost in it. If I'd had any idea we were moving that way, that that was how we looked, I'd have gone through the floor. Because it's embarrassing. But nice, too. I like looking at it, and frequently run the brief clip back again, because for me it doesn't last long enough. I get caught up in the way Henry's arms are pulling me in around my waist, the way my hands look on the back of his neck, my fingers stiff and flexing, twining in and out of his hair. Our faces are touching; we look as if we're going to kiss, although we never do. It was public foreplay, that dance. A few hours later, we were at home in my bed, making love for the very first time.

Next came a backyard party at Isabel's. Summer 1995. Emma hissed when Gary appeared, but Isabel only looked a little wistful. I think she's really forgiven him. He looked chubby and self-important—the camera never lies, they say—in checked trousers and a sweater with the sleeves rolled up to show off his furry, bulging forearms. He saw the camera and grinned, held his arms out wide—*Look at me, I'm such a teddy bear*. I remember when I used to like him; I thought his flirting was cute, even a little bit flattering. Now, just the sight of him makes my lip curl.

"Lisa Ommert," Rudy exclaimed. "I wonder how she's doing. Anybody ever hear from her? How long did she last, Lee, a year?"

"Nine months," I said, watching Lisa, who was a Saving Grace until she and her husband moved to Switzerland, engaged in a very animated-looking conversation with Gary, Emma, and Emma's boyfriend at the time, Peter Dickenson.

"You have to wonder," Emma said in a strangely grim undertone, "what we could possibly have been talking about."

"It's the tail end of the party," Rudy pointed out. "We were probably all loaded."

"Oh, no question."

I glanced at Emma out of the corner of my eye. She and Peter broke up suddenly—in love one day, bitterly split the next—and we're still not allowed to ask why. Rudy knows, but Isabel and I don't. Well, Isabel might, but only from intuition. My intuition says there was another woman, and that Emma found out in some awful, humiliating way. I don't know what else could have been so hurtful that, this many years later, it's still unmentionable.

"How is it going with Clay?" I asked casually. Clay is the man Sally Draco fixed Emma up with. I couldn't believe it when she agreed, and I was even more surprised when they went out together a second time. The first was supposed to be a double date, but at the last second Sally and Mick canceled; he wasn't feeling well or something.

"Okay," Emma mumbled.

"Just okay?"

She shrugged and kept her eyes on the screen. Her face took on a stubborn set, as it seems to do a lot these days whenever the subject of men comes up. It means, Keep out.

So I wonder why I said, "You haven't mentioned that married fellow in a long time. Is that over now?"

"Well, since it was never *on*, I guess it must be over." She said that through her teeth. "Lee, could we just watch this?"

"Well, excuse me. I didn't realize you were so sensitive."

"Ladies?" Rudy said.

Emma sat hunched forward, forearms on her knees, tense-looking. "Sorry," she said, sitting back abruptly and smiling.

"Sure," I said, meaning *Me, too*. I didn't even know what we were sorry for, but it was nice to make up.

The last few minutes of the video were from exactly a year ago, here at Neap Tide when we'd come to celebrate our ninth anniversary. Watching it, I realized that in some ways it was the perfect ending to a Graces retrospective, because the camera had captured us all being so . . . idiosyncratic, I guess is the word. Ourselves. There was Emma, sitting in a beach chair in the sand, swaddled in towels and a hooded sweatshirt, her nose in a book; Rudy tan and gorgeous beside her, swigging from a thermos of Bloody Marys; Isabel trotting back from a swim, her hair dripping, lips turning blue, laughing at nothing—just gladness. Even the shot Rudy took of me is characteristic, I suppose: I'm in the kitchen, taping to the refrigerator a chart I'd just drafted, "Suggested Chores/Division of Labor, 6/14–6/17." (Emma, I recall, added a new chore category later, "Sleeping," and penciled her name in every block, all the way across.) It was a gay weekend, yes, and yet, watching the images of the four of us in all our silliness and crankiness and sweetness—it made me sad tonight. We looked so innocent. So much was in store for us, but we were too busy being "ourselves," and taking it for granted that we always would be, to give a thought to the future.

The last shot was very artistic, if I say so myself. I took it from behind the dark heads of Isabel, Rudy, and Emma as they stood on the deck and gazed out at a deep red sunset. It's only their heads in silhouette, black against crimson, with the murmur of their voices low and awed-sounding in the background. At the last second,

Isabel heard me and turned. There's just enough light left to see her smile.

Fade-out.

"Do you remember what we talked about that night?" Isabel said after a quiet, appreciative pause.

"I do." Emma reached for the remote and flicked off the staticky screen.

"I do," said Rudy.

"Life goals," I said.

"Yes." Isabel smiled. "I said I wanted to finish my degree, get a job helping old people, and travel."

"I said I wanted a baby."

"I said I couldn't think of anything." Rudy turned to Emma. "*You* said you wanted to live on a dairy farm and see James Brown in concert."

"And spend the night with Harrison Ford," Emma recalled. "By the way, I've changed that to David Duchovny."

I remembered the exercise better now. It had started out as a discussion of life goals but shifted to things we wanted to do before we got too old—things we would regret, on our deathbeds, not having done. I'd wanted to win a PBS auction and dance in *The Nutcracker*. Such a safe topic, it had seemed to us then, only a year ago. Fun. A game.

I couldn't look at Isabel.

She broke the quiet to say, "My goals haven't changed much since that night. That's strange, isn't it? I have more regrets, but exactly the same ambitions."

"What regrets?" Rudy asked shyly.

"Oh . . ." She had on her scarf tonight. She fingered one of the tasseled ends that lay across her shoulder, smiling into space, so sweet-faced and melancholy. "Well, the biggest is still there—that I didn't try harder to make my marriage work. For Terry's sake," she clarified when we all started to interrupt. "Maybe it's a delusion, but if Gary and I had found a way to stay together, Terry might not have gone so far away. Maybe. I don't know."

"No, you don't." Emma pressed her lips together.

"But now I have new regrets, too," she went on. "Ones that never occurred to me before."

"Like?"

"Like . . . I never learned to play the piano. Never watercolored. I never met Carlos Castaneda and asked him if it was all true," she said, laughing. "I never learned the stars, never learned birdsongs—I can't tell a finch from a wren. And wildflowers." Rudy slipped her arm through Isabel's and rested her head on her shoulder. "I never got to be the weather girl on Channel Five," Isabel mused softly. "I never acted or sang or danced, I've never even written a poem. I have no grandchildren."

"Why don't you do them?" Emma said after a forlorn pause. I could have kissed her. "You can do them all. Maybe not weather girl, but that's their loss."

"I think I heard that Carlos Castaneda's dead," Rudy mentioned.

"Okay, but the rest—why can't you, Isabel? I'm serious! You could write a poem right now, nothing to it. I'll help you. Next week, you get some watercolors and an astronomy book and—what was it?" Isabel started laughing. "Birds, you get one of those CDs that plays all the songs while some deep-voiced Audubon guy tells you who's who. Wildflowers, big deal, you get another book and go for a walk in Rock Creek Park. What else? Grandchildren? Well, there you have me, you'll have to take that up with Terry."

"I see." Isabel put her head back against the sofa. Her sadness had disappeared; she looked relaxed and amused and tolerant. Truly, I'm not an envious person, but if I could turn people's moods around the way Emma can (sometimes; when she feels like it), I would be blessed.

"You want to know what I regret?" Emma held up her index

finger. "I've never driven a car at a hundred miles an hour." She added her thumb. "I've never had a long, attitude-adjusting chat with the pope. I've never seen Graceland—"

"Wait," Rudy broke in, "wait a second. I want to say something. To you, Isabel, and—*for* all of us. I know I'm speaking for all of us, I don't even have to ask. I just want to say out loud that we—well, first of all, we know you're going to get well, so that's the bottom line." Emma and I nodded vehemently. "And the second thing is, I think it would be good if we made a commitment right now. I know it's understood, but sometimes it's important to say things in words. So I want to say, for everybody, that no matter what happens, we're here. I mean—we're here for the long haul. You won't be alone. Ever. I'm not saying this right—"

"Yes, you are," Emma said. "It's a good thing to say—that you won't have to face anything by yourself, Isabel. Anything. In fact, you won't be able to get rid of us."

I couldn't chime in and agree, although I knew it was expected of me. I was so afraid of crying, I couldn't say anything. If I did cry, it would be out of anger as much as grief. How dare they speak to her like this, as if she were dying? *She's not.* She is recovering. But they lied, they *don't* believe it, and that felt like a betrayal, not only of Isabel but of me.

She was moved, of course. She hugged them both, blinking so *she* wouldn't weep. I wanted to protect her from their pessimism, but what could I do? When she smiled at me, moist-eyed, and held out her hand, I stood up. "Let's have some ice cream," I said, and walked out. I had my cry in the kitchen.

18

Rudy

"Do you think Lee's going nuts?"

Emma spoke in a low voice, almost a whisper; Lee's room was next door, Isabel's across the hall, and we'd left our door ajar to get a draft of sea breeze from the window.

"You mean about having a child? Well, no," I said, "I think it's good she told us all that. She keeps too much inside, she's—"

"No, I don't mean for letting go a little with us. I agree, that was good for her, that was healthy. I mean the whole baby thing."

"Oh."

"It's like she's gone blind except for that, it's all she can see. And I believe her when she says she'll never give up. Why don't they adopt a child, Rudy? Why? No, she's driven, she's on a course, she's so caught up in the world of baby-making she can't see anything else."

"I know. What was she saying about her parents?"

"I have no idea. Just something else to keep her mind on one track. I wish we could *do* something."

"But what?"

"Nothing. There's nothing to do."

"Just be supportive," I said.

"Yeah." She looked over at me. "Hey, Rude. That was a nice thing you said to Isabel."

"Oh, well. I don't know. I just tried to put myself in her place and figure out what would be the scariest thing. If I thought I might be dying. And it was being alone. So I wanted her to know she never would be."

"Is that the scariest thing?"

"To me. I think."

A candle in a glass hurricane shade burned on the table between our two bunk beds. Between it and the moonlight, I could see Emma clearly, stretched out in her old blue UNC nightshirt, pressing a finger into the top of her white thigh—checking to see if she'd gotten too much sun this afternoon. "To me," she said, "the scariest thing is oblivion. Being, and then not being. Even if everyone you ever knew was with you at the end, everybody holding your hand and telling you it was okay and they loved you and all that, you're still alone at that last second. Wherever you're going, nobody's going with you."

"Wow. That seems so morbid."

"No, it isn't. Why? You can't tell me you don't think about that stuff."

"No, I think about it." But I'd been much better lately. "Could you believe Lee thought we were drinking in the car yesterday?" I guess that sounded like a non sequitur, but after I said it, the connection came to me.

"Well, you know Lee. If you're having that much fun, you must be drunk."

"I haven't been drinking much at all lately," I told her. "Last night was the most I've had in weeks."

"I noticed. Any reason?"

"Well . . . I guess I just feel a little stronger. More comfortable in my real life."

"How come?"

"I don't know. Well, one thing, Eric and I have been doing really good work. Hard work, but it's felt like we're really getting somewhere for a change. He says it's not unusual to go along for a long time without any progress, and then all of a sudden—breakthroughs."

"Like diet plateaus."

"Exactly."

"Oh, like you'd know," Emma scoffed. "Eric—he's very gentle, isn't he? Patient. He doesn't mind going slowly."

I thought I heard a second meaning. "You mean I'm not getting anywhere. He's not doing anything. Really, you think therapy's a waste of time."

Emma rolled her head on the pillow to look at me. "I used to think that," she said—surprising me; I thought she'd deny it. "But now I'm thinking Greenburg may actually be smarter than I am."

"Oh, Emma, the ultimate compliment. He'll be thrilled when I tell him."

We smiled in the dark.

"Hey, Em."

"What."

"You know that landscaping course? Remember the—"

"Sure I remember."

"Well, I've decided I'm going to go ahead and take it."

She sat up. "Oh, *Rudy*."

"It starts in September."

"That's fantastic. What did Curtis say?"

"Um. Well."

She sank back down, but still facing me. "You didn't tell him yet."

"Not yet. I've sort of been waiting for the right time."

"Okay. So, Rudy, what do you think about the fact that you haven't told him because you know he won't like it? I mean, what kind of—"

"I know what you mean. You sounded so much like Eric when you said that, Emma, it's spooky."

"Well, what's the answer?"

"The answer is—I don't like it. I don't like what it says about me *or* Curtis."

"*Or* Curtis. I like that."

"We have to confront some things, I know that. I need to tell him what I'm thinking. It's one thing to tell Eric, or you. I need to tell *him*."

She leaned toward me. "This is new, Rudy, this is good. This is something really different with you."

"I know. About time, don't you think?"

She didn't say anything. Once in a while, Emma's tactful.

"It's not just drugs, either."

"Excuse me?"

I stuck my feet up on the mattress overhead, pushing on it, flexing my knees. "I'm taking this—antidepressant." *New* antidepressant, I might have said. "And it's true I haven't felt depressed, but I don't think that's the only reason. As Eric says, just because the crazy pills are working doesn't mean you're crazy."

That line had never struck me as particularly funny before, but Emma laughed so hard I had to shush her.

Eric also says laughter is cathartic and cleansing, that it's good for the body and the soul, and when it's real it's better than sex. How many hours, I wonder, over the last thirteen years have I shared helpless, snorting, side-aching laughter with Emma? If I'm crazy *now*, what if I'd never met her?

Another thing about shared laughter is that it comes from trust. Which must've been why this popped out of my mouth next: "We didn't have sex for the whole month of December."

"December—last year?"

"Yes."

"You and Curtis?"

"Well, who else?"

"Um . . ." Emma stared at me, feeling her way. "Any particular reason?"

"Well, that's the thing. If there was a reason, I don't know what it was. I hadn't done anything he could've been punishing me for. He never—he just wouldn't—we never did it, that's all. I didn't say anything. I know I should have, but I didn't. I didn't even tell Eric."

"You never said anything at all? To Curtis?"

"No." I winced. How embarrassing. How cowardly of me. "And then on New Year's Day—we did. As if nothing had happened. So afterward I said, 'Well, happy *New* Year,' or something, you know, sort of suggestive, so Curtis could say something if he wanted to. But he—he just looked at me very coldly, so . . . So that was the end of that, and since then we've been fine, normal. Sexually."

"Sexually."

"Yes."

"But not otherwise."

It's funny how it's easier sometimes to talk about your sex life, as intimate a subject as that is, than it is to talk about how the rest of your life is going. "Oh," I said, "it's just a combination of things. Different things adding up over a long time. No one specific thing. Just some thoughts I'm having, and thinking of talking to Curtis about. Soon."

Emma sighed. "Like *what*? Give me an example. So we can say we're having a conversation here."

"Well, for example. Tonight on the videotape. That part when we were all standing around outside my house, getting ready to leave for fitness camp. That shot of Curtis kissing me good-bye."

"Yeah, that was a little weird."

They'd picked me up last, and we were giddy and excited, anxious to get on the road. Each of us had weight-loss goals, but part of the plan was to stop en route for one last glorious, fattening meal at a country inn we'd found listed in a guidebook; that way, we theorized, we'd be at our heaviest for the camp's first-night weigh-in. So we were silly and giggly, already looking ahead, already gone, you might say. I should have known, and in the back of my mind I probably did know, that that kind of inattention or obliviousness on my part hurts Curtis's feelings. Well, more than that, it actually scares him. He needs me to be *aware* of him all the time. He needs to be the center. Otherwise, it's as if he doesn't quite believe he exists.

And so—anyway—when he kissed me, it wasn't that sweet, private peck husbands and wives exchange when they're in front of people who they know are watching. You know the kind I mean—"Bye, honey," "Take care," "Love you," with lips touching briefly, maybe a quick, hard hug. Playful and tender, but pretty impersonal as kisses go. No, this wasn't like that. At all. Without even drawing me away a little from the group, and knowing Lee was filming everything, Curtis put his arms around me and gave me a long, slow, *movie* kiss, very passionate and erotic and forceful—when I tried to stop, he wouldn't let me go. He made every thought in my head revert back to him. He did it on purpose. Kissing me, taking control of me like that, was his way of saying, "Think about *me*," to me, and "She's *mine*," to the Graces. In a way, it was worse watching it on film tonight, years later, than it had been when it happened. Because now it matches up with a lot of other memories. Similar ones, and some of them are even more disturbing.

"I think," I said slowly, "I don't want to be possessed anymore. And I used to."

"Possessed? No, I know what you mean," Emma said, "it's just . . . an odd word."

"I suppose. But I'm afraid, too, of anything changing. I hate change."

"Sure about that? Sure it's not Curtis who hates change, and what you hate is challenging him? Upsetting him?"

"Hm." Food for thought.

"Well, you're going slowly, but that's okay, that's probably good. Like losing weight on a diet—again, not that you would get that analogy. Just as long as there's movement. We have to assume your shrink knows what he's doing."

"I've been smoking in front of him," I said.

"Who? Eric?"

"Curtis."

"Get out."

"Not in the house when he's there, because I think that's rude, but when he's gone. But I don't gargle or spray room freshener on the curtains afterward so he won't know—none of that. And I smoke right in front of him when we're outside or in a restaurant or a bar. Eric says it's great. Well, he says it's *terrible*, he *hates* it that I smoke, but he likes it that I'm not hiding it from Curtis. Much healthier, he says."

"Well, I guess so. Yeah. It's actually very brave of you, Rude, in a perverted sort of way. Rotting your lungs while you stand up for yourself. Personal growth through emphysema."

"Care for a fag?"

"Sure."

We lit up.

"I never did this when I was young," I told her.

"Did what?"

"You know." Propped on our elbows, facing each other in our narrow bunk beds, stretching over occasionally to share the ashtray on the floor, we looked like teenagers on a sleepover. "Had a best girlfriend. Told secrets in the dark. Snuck cigs. I just never had this."

"Because you were too fucked up," Emma said matter-of-factly. "Your family screwed you over, but now you're getting over it. Now you're getting well. Slowly."

"You think?"

"Yes, I do."

She said it so adamantly, I pulled back, out of the candlelight so she couldn't see my face. The fledgling hope on it. I didn't want to look pathetic. "Hope so," I said.

"Oh yeah, I see it happening. Smoking in front of Curtis, my God. Whoa, Rudy, you are a wild woman." She wasn't being sarcastic. "That is fucking fantastic."

And to think that Curtis once asked me to stop being friends with Emma. "For your own good," he'd said. How *despicable*, when you stop to think about it. I couldn't tell Emma about that, it was too embarrassing, I felt ashamed for Curtis. It was proof, I had realized afterward—Eric helped me to see this—that Curtis had been pretending all along about Emma, making me believe he liked her in spite of her antagonism. Not in a good way, either. Not the way Emma bites her tongue and doesn't say what she truly thinks of him. She does that for my sake. She does it out of respect, and tact, and love. Curtis pretends because he's dishonest. It's another way he *possesses* me.

Emma yawned. We put out our cigarettes, blew out the candle.

"We always talk about me," I said sleepily.

"I know." She already had her eyes closed. "It's because you're such an egomaniac."

I snorted. "It's because you make me *ask* everything. You never volunteer, I have to drag it out of you. Oh, I forgot to tell you—Lee asked me what I thought about inviting Sally to join the group."

"Did she? She told me she was going to. What'd you say?"

"I said I was all for it."

"*What?*"

I laughed.

"You jerk," Emma grumbled, settling back down; she'd almost hit her head on the top bunk when she sat up. "Tell me what you really said."

"I said the same thing you did, that I didn't think it was a good time because of Isabel."

Emma got comfortable again. "Think Lee was disappointed?"

"No, not at all. I don't even know why she asked me. Just to be evenhanded, I guess. But that friendship's cooling off, you know." Which reminded me. "How come you told Lee you'd stay down here two more days?" Emma opened one eye. "That doesn't sound safe and sensible to me, Em. In fact, that seems positively out of character."

"You think I'm safe and sensible?"

"Well, compared to me."

"Oh. Compared to you." Even in the dark I could see her smile.

Tonight Lee had begged us—one of us, two, all three, she

didn't care—to stay over until Tuesday and then drive back with her and Henry. Nobody volunteered. We kept asking why, and finally she admitted it: she'd fallen out of her infatuation with Sally Draco. She had invited the Dracos down to the cottage months ago, but now she didn't want to spend two whole days in the exclusive company of Sally, with no one but the husbands to break up the intimacy.

"Why don't you like her anymore?" Emma had asked—trying to sound nonchalant.

"Oh, I don't know, no real reason," Lee had said. "There's nothing wrong with her, I just don't feel quite as comfortable around her as I used to. That's all."

Well, I don't either, but then, I never did. Maybe it takes one to know one, but I think Sally has big problems. And Emma's probably the least of them.

Isabel and I couldn't help Lee out, we both had to be home on Sunday. I could see Emma was thinking it over, but I couldn't have been more surprised when she said, "Okay, I'll stay if you want. I brought some work, I can do it down here as easily as at home."

I'd stared at her; she wouldn't look at me the whole time Lee was thanking her, telling her again it was no big deal, Sally was fine, nothing wrong with her, this would just make things easier. Isabel never said a word.

"So, Em," I said again, "why did you say you'd stay? Don't you think that's dangerous? Don't you think, seeing Mick with Sally for all that time and everything, don't you think it might . . . hurt? Hey, Em," I whispered. "Are you asleep?"

Maybe, maybe not. She didn't answer.

19

Emma

Rudy and Isabel got a late start back on Sunday afternoon. As soon as they left, I went for a walk on the beach. I should've stayed and helped Lee tidy up the cottage—Mick, Sally, and Henry were due within the hour. But I didn't. Why not? It wasn't laziness—I didn't want to be there when they drove up. I couldn't face standing beside Lee at the deck rail, looking down, waving and grinning, "Hey, how are you, you made it!" Also, I wanted Mick to have some warning. He wasn't expecting me, and his face can be so transparent; it would be bad enough if he looked too glad to see me, but worse if he looked . . . what's the word? Speculative.

I guess it was a gorgeous day. Lots of blue sky and white clouds, lacy surf, gulls and sanderlings, shells. Sand. The tide was moving in, not out, I know because I saw people dragging their blankets back and pulling up their umbrellas. But on the whole I was oblivious; I could've been walking along the streets of downtown Poughkeepsie. "Don't you think it might hurt?" Yes, Rudy, I think it might. Why didn't I consider that sooner? I guess because love is not only blind, it's a masochist.

Since Lee's party I'd seen him one time, at his studio. And talked to him once on the telephone. Both were intense, unsatisfying affairs, everything between us unspoken, everything unshown. Believe it or not, I do not thrive on trouble with men, and I'm not one of those women who choose the same dysfunction, whatever it might be, in man after man and obliviously revel in it. No, my pattern is to pick a different dysfunction every time, discover it, and run away as fast as I can. So why am I tormenting myself with Mick, who isn't dysfunctional at all? Why does he keep calling me? We're not reckless people—why are we doing this?

If you cut through the backyards of the three cottages between Lee's and the shore, you can avoid the road entirely, which is convenient if you're barefooted. Lee has forbidden this shortcut because it's "illegal," but when she's not with us we take it anyway. I was one cottage away from Neap Tide II (what is a neap tide, anyway?) when I heard a peal of Sally Draco's loud, high, enthusiastic laughter. That's when I knew I'd made one of the biggest mistakes of my life.

I couldn't see them yet, just hear them, Henry's slow baritone drawl, Lee's voice clear and clipped, Sally's higher, shriller, wound up tighter. I paused, listening for Mick's, and finally heard the low, noncommittal sound of his laughter.

What had I done? I didn't belong here. They did: they belonged to each other. Too late—no escape. A pall of loneliness settled on me, and I shivered under it, wretched and bleak from the knowledge that I deserved everything I was going to get.

Nobody noticed me, even though I stomped up the outside wooden steps to the deck. Too busy talking and laughing. No—somebody noticed me. I started back in surprise, as if a small animal had suddenly darted across my path. A child—Jay, Mick's little boy—I'd forgotten all about him. Had Lee been expecting him? He sat cross-legged on the porch floor, pointy-kneed, yellow-haired. He looked up, not startled at all, from the absorbing task of tying knots in a kite's tail. Blue eyes studied me with serious, shy curiosity for a few seconds. As soon as I smiled, he looked over his shoulder at his parents. *Social help!* you could almost hear him calling.

"There you are," Henry boomed, finally seeing me. Everybody turned around. I went forward, smiling, smiling, "Hi, how are you, how was your trip," kissing Henry, hugging Sally when she made me. Mick, Mick I waved to, a playful little hand salute from six feet away. I barely looked at him, kept him in my peripheral vision only, as if he were the sun. But I saw he'd gotten his hair cut, and it made him look younger, practically callow. It was a bad cut; his white scalp showed through on the sides. And he looked too pale, his face strained, the stubble of his beard blue-black against his white skin. Had he been ill?

"I'm so glad you decided to stay," Sally bubbled. She actually took both of my hands and looked me in the eyes. "How *are* you, how have you *been*?"

The panicky thought occurred that she knew everything and she was torturing me. How *are* you, how have you *been*—I don't give my mother straight answers to those questions. "Fine, *fine*," I said, trying to match her intensity. "Is this your little boy?"

That worked: she dropped my hands and called him. "Jay, come say hi to Emma."

Oh, poor kid. Why do people do that? Just what Jay wanted to do, come over and meet some old lady friend of his parents. He scrambled up and dragged himself over, dutifully mumbling, "Hi," and sticking out his hand to shake while staring at my knees. Mick put his hands on his son's skinny shoulders, and the kid leaned back against him, relaxing. He looked just like his picture, which is to say, angelic. And superficially like his mother because of the fair hair and light eyes, but there was also something dignified and noble about the shape of his head, and that could only have come from Dad. Not that I'm prejudiced.

"Suit up, everybody, we're off to the beach," Henry announced, to Jay's delight.

"Not me," I demurred. "I've had enough sun for one day."

This brought on the usual incredulous laughter and jokes at my expense. Henry was especially inventive, calling me "fish white" and comparing my complexion to that of Casper the friendly ghost.

"That's okay," I told him, "I'm used to the scorn of the ignorant and deluded, who won't be laughing so hard when they drop dead from melanoma."

But the real reason, of course, was because I didn't care to witness all that wholesome family fun, the laughing and splashing and cavorting, just one Kodak moment after another. When everybody finally went away and left me alone, I mixed a gigantic gin and tonic and drank it in the shower. I wouldn't mind drowning, I thought lugubriously. I could slither down the drain with the water and the soap scum and disappear, and nobody would even miss me.

I sobered up in time for dinner. Six of us piled into the Pattersons' station wagon and drove to Brother's, where we pigged out on barbecue and fried fish and potatoes and mountains of mayonnaise-drenched cole slaw. I sat across from Sally, who never stopped talking. Her hair was a new, expensive-looking shade of pewter blond, striking with her high-arched black brows and huge blue eyes. She would be a fascinating woman if she'd just close her mouth. She had an obsessive habit of looking at everyone after she said anything, no matter how commonplace, compulsively checking our facial expressions, monitoring our reactions. A false laugh punctuated almost every utterance, as if she had to announce in advance, *this is going to be funny*. I wondered if she could possibly be high. Probably not, but she was wound up like a spring, trying too hard, shrill.

Maybe they were fighting. Beside her, Mick sat in virtual silence, smiling with strained politeness. But solicitous of her, somehow. I still couldn't look at him directly, but I could see fatigue in the way he held himself, even the tilt of his head. No, they weren't fighting, I didn't think. This was how they lived.

"Mick might get a job," Sally announced. I jerked my head up at that. She gave the nervous laugh and leaned playfully against his stiff arm. I caught his eye for a second and saw dismay. "You know, a real job, one that pays actual money."

Lee shifted with embarrassment. Sally's discontent was uncomfortably transparent. Then, too, public talk about personal finances broke a cardinal rule in Lee's etiquette book. But she stared at Mick expectantly—we all did.

He said lightly, "Yes, I've been thinking of taking a part-time job."

"You wouldn't stop painting," I said.

"No." He flashed me another lightning-quick glance before we both looked away. "No."

"Too bad you don't plumb, you could come and work with me," Henry said in a hearty voice that dissipated the tension. "What kind of a job are you looking for?"

"Night watchman," Jay piped up.

Mick laughed, and Jay grinned up at him in surprise. "That was a joke," father explained to son. "Like working at McDonald's."

"Oh. But you could carry a gun if you was a night watchman."

"Were," Sally said automatically. She laughed the fake laugh again. "Jay wants Mick to work for either the zoo, McDonald's, or the rodeo."

"Or the air force," Jay put in.

"While I," she went on, "would be thrilled if he hired on as a Kelly Girl. Anything for a steady income. Ha!"

I stirred cold french fries around and kept my head down. The stiff-sounding silence stretched to infinity. What galled me was knowing he probably didn't even blame her. She'd convinced him that he'd failed her, but she couldn't come out and say it, she could only snipe.

"They're raising the rent on my studio," Mick explained presently, as if no awkward moment had occurred. "It's still all outgo and no income for me, so I'll probably hook up with my old law firm, do some part-time research for them on patents, claims, that sort of thing." He looked straight at me. "It won't be so bad."

Oh, but his paintings, his beautiful paintings. I felt sick. And scared, and furious at the injustice. And if I hadn't known before that this was love, I knew it now, because the truth is, his paintings still don't make a lick of sense to me.

By the time dinner ended and we drove home, the thought of spending several more hours in Mick and Sally's company was intolerable. Tough luck, Lee, you're on your own. "Are you okay?" she asked when I said I was going to bed early. "Sure, fine. I think I got too much sun." A good distraction; that's always worth several minutes of good-natured ribbing. Good-natured on my part. I said good night and disappeared.

Then I lay in bed and listened to them talking and laughing on the porch above me. Sometimes I could hear the words, usually just the cadences. Rising and falling, opinionated and tentative. I felt like a child, sent to bed at the height of her parents' cocktail party. Jay, speaking of children, was sleeping on a cot at the foot of Mick and Sally's bed. I could have offered to let him sleep with me in Rudy's empty bunk. But I hadn't. Guess why.

Around eleven o'clock, I heard footsteps descending the outside stairs and crunching off down the sandy driveway. I got to the window too late to see which couple it was, but a few minutes later I heard Henry's voice upstairs. So I knew. Mick and Sally. They'd gone for a walk. Full, romantic moon tonight. And they had a child in their bedroom, so . . .

You deserve it is not a solace when you're suffering the scalding agonies of sexual jealousy. Every sixty-second click of my travel clock felt like a bullet in the brain. I struggled against picturing them twined together on the cold sand under the blue moon, but once the image gelled it was indelible. She's lovely, she is, especially when she shuts up, and he's a passionate man, I know that for certain, no matter that he's never touched me.

Eleven-thirty-four, the clock read when Lee and Henry tiptoed down the hall and closed the door to their room. At eleven-forty, I got up and went into the bathroom I was sharing with the Dracos. Ostensibly to swallow a Sominex but really—I amazed myself, what a surprise—to look in Mick's shaving kit. Just look in it. See what he took on trips. A pathetic, embarrassing way to be close to him, but I had lost all shame.

Shaving stuff; he used Mennen soap and a Gillette razor, no aftershave. An ace bandage. Comb, but no brush. Nail clippers. A bottle of generic aspirin, a tube of Chap Stick, a roll of Tums. Sun shades, the kind you clip onto your regular glasses. No condoms. Dental floss. Some Neosporin. Brut stick deodorant. Crest toothpaste and an Oral-B brush. No condoms. Matches and safety pins and a lot of old Band-Aids at the bottom of the bag.

Why no condoms? Three possibilities. One, she took care of the contraception in the family. Two, they were trying to make a baby. Three, they didn't have sex anymore.

Far and away, I liked number three best.

Sally's flowered makeup case sat on top of the toilet, but I didn't touch it. In spite of the condom discovery, I'm telling you it wasn't *information* I was looking for. I just wanted to see his things. Really. Pitiful, I know, but I wanted to run my thumbnail along the teeth of his comb, check out how many aspirins he had left, sniff his shaving soap. See if there was an underarm hair on his deodorant. I don't care—laugh. I tell you, I was *gone*.

At eleven-fifty-six, they returned. They took turns in the bathroom, and by ten after twelve they were in bed with the door closed, the light out. No, I wasn't peeping through the keyhole, I could see it go out in the reflection on the pine tree outside our side-by-side windows.

Silence.

Now I could *really* obsess.

It's not easy to admit that imagining your beloved in the arms of another is not only unmitigated torture, it's also titillating. Sorry, but it is, it's sexy. Why not? Emotional anguish and physical arousal don't always cancel each other out. No, indeed. The anguish only makes the arousal sharper. Darker. And relieving it yourself, if you're reduced to that, only makes you feel worse, even more alone and—superfluous. Expendable. In the gray, nauseating hour before dawn, I thought about packing my things and leaving, but the logistics defeated me. I'd have to steal a car.

When I finally went to sleep, I fell into a coma and slept half the day away. This is a pattern with me, I see; the night after I threw Peter Dickenson out of my apartment—years ago; don't even ask—I went to bed and slept around the clock, a dead woman. Nothing wrong with that; safer than drugs or booze, much cheaper. Call it nature's Nembutal.

I woke up and stumbled upstairs—the common areas in the cottage are on the second floor, bedrooms on the first—to find the house empty. Good, I thought, until the third cup of coffee and the second cheese and tomato sandwich; then my company began to seriously bore me. I put on my bathing suit and headed for the beach.

How quaint—the men were playing Frisbee while the women watched. I endured the inquiries about my health and, after I assured everybody I was fine, the jokes about my shiftlessness. To catch the shade from Lee's umbrella, I spread my towel sideways behind hers. Sally lay next to her. I got all my stuff arranged—book, lotion, sunglasses, hat, rolled-up towel for a pillow—and stretched out on my stomach. And joined the women watching the men.

It was a three-sided game, Henry and Mick at the ends and Jay in the middle. The men flung the disk at each other with muscular, grunting, Olympian hurls, lobbed it softly and gently to the child with scrupulous accuracy. There's something reassuring about watching men play games with children. When they're patient and delicate, when they make allowances, when they compromise and camouflage their own superiority—in other words, when they behave like women—it reinforces our illusion that they're civilized.

Underneath the mindless pleasure of watching this game, though, I was worried about Lee and Henry. I studied their faces, but neither of them was showing anything except bland enjoyment. But how could they not be suffering? Like Rudy, I was glad when Lee had lost it a little, as much as she ever loses it, and opened up to us about her fears and her anger over their childlessness. Because she's the most self-sufficient, Lee uses the group for therapy less than the rest of us. So even though I'd known on some level that she was feeling all the ugly emotions of resentment and jealousy and fury and guilt, it was still a shock to hear her admit it. And now to watch Henry play so prettily, so sweetly with Jay, who's like this golden cherub, this epitome of Perfect Kid, this everyman's dream son—how could it not cut her to the heart?

But they're doing okay, I think. I hope. Deep down. Because these two really were made for each other. From the beginning, Lee's been amazingly frank with the group about her passion for Henry, and when you're with them you can actually *feel* it. Nothing blatant or overt—heavens—but I'm telling you, heat practically vibrates in the air between them. It's partly the way he looks at her, like she's the goddess of sex and he hasn't had any in a hundred years, and partly Lee's prim, buttoned-up manner. Watching them together always starts my imagination moving down a sexy path. Gets me a little hot, if you want to know the truth.

Before I made my early escape last night, I wandered out on the deck for some air, only to find that Lee and Henry were already there, relaxing against the rail in a dark corner. "Oops." I almost mumbled an excuse and backed out. And they weren't even doing anything—he had his arms around her from behind and she was leaning back against him, her hands wrapped around his wrists. They smiled at me, then went back to staring up at the moon. My presence didn't bother them in the least, but *I* felt as if I'd walked in on a love scene. That's how intimate it was, that wall, that blur of tenderness they'd put around each other. When he leaned over and casually rubbed her cheek with his, slow and soft, a purely loving gesture, I had a lump in my throat. I said good night and got out.

Oh, I want what they have. I yearn for it. It's what everybody longs for, isn't it? Sweet, deep intimacy with another? And I know it's a chimera, a dream, it comes in flashes at best, it's hardly ever what it seems—I don't care. The way they blended into each other, the way they turned into one there in the shadows . . . what a well of loneliness that opened in me. Real or not, there are times when I would gladly settle for the dream.

"I'll really miss ballet," Sally said, sitting up to rub sunscreen on her legs. I looked at her blankly. "I was telling Lee," she said in a solicitous tone, anxious to include me. "I've got to drop out of our class. We just can't afford it anymore, too many other things are more important. It's the only activity I do just for myself, so it's hard. But what are you going to do?" Brave, plucky smile.

"Yeah, that's a shame," I said. Lee, I noticed, didn't say anything, barely looked at her. Hm. More of a strain here than I'd expected. And I'd been evading the one task Lee gave me, which was to be the buffer between her and Sally this weekend. I felt bad about that, but God, had she ever tapped the wrong person for the job.

I didn't see the Frisbee until it smacked me in the shoulder—caught the bone and hurt like hell. Henry came trotting over, sweaty and grinning, panting like a dog. "Sorry, Em. You okay?"

"Sure." I handed it up to him with a good-sport smile. His red-white-and-blue-striped suit hung to his knees, baggy and uncharacteristically hip. He heaved the disk in the air, high over Jay's blond head. Mick flexed his knees and executed a stunning vertical leap that made his son shout with approval. Shielding my face from Sally with the side of my hand, I stared at her husband.

He'd definitely lost weight. He was too thin. I shouldn't have blamed her, but I did. Except for his forearms, he was nearly as pale as me. I wanted to touch that tender demarcation line on his biceps, white to golden tan, run my lips along it, my teeth. Everything about him stirred me, everything was exactly right. It felt illicit, practically taboo to look at him like this, stare openly at his thighs and his calves, the ribs in his sides, his chest hair, his collarbone. To see him run and bound, when before I'd only seen him walk or sit.

It was the fact that Mick and his legs and his long back and his hard stomach were *forbidden* to me that made them so unbearably attractive—I knew that—and yet he was beautiful, truly he was, no matter that he was too thin, too pale, his hair too short. "He looks a little bit like Daniel Day-Lewis," Isabel once said, a long time ago. I, of course, said nothing to that, but I remember thinking, *Daniel should be so lucky*.

But why do I keep obsessing about him? What is this doomed, lunatic, self-destructive need to keep him in my mind? Why can't I forget about him—why can't he forget about me?

In my case, it's because I just can't resist. Over and over, I find that my need (not my desire; I'm beyond that) is stronger than my discretion (not my conscience; we still haven't done anything wrong). I rationalize that our infrequent meetings are indiscreet, not immoral. They don't hurt anyone but me. And him.

Oh God, that's the dangerous, seductive part, the chance that he feels what I do. I think it's true. He's not very good at disguise—I'm much better—so he doesn't hide his gladness when we're together, and he isn't cool or suave on the phone. Our conversations get more and more personal. In the last one, I started to tell him about the last time I saw my mother, and ended up describing my childhood. How it felt when my father walked out, how it felt when he died. Now he knows things about me that, before, only Rudy knew.

I know things about him, too. I can picture the earnest overachiever he used to be, winning track medals and getting straight A's for Mom and Dad, dedicating his young life to making his adoptive parents proud of him. Proud and not sorry. He told me it wasn't only Sally he let down when he gave up the law, it was his parents, too. In a way, it was even harder to disappoint them, because their expectations had been even higher. Now they laugh about him to their friends, he thinks—but gently, fondly; philosophically. *What are you going to do?* he imagines them saying. That hurts him so much.

So—we know things about each other. We're intimate in the strangest way, like jail mates who communicate through the plumbing, or bang out a code with our tin cups against the wall. We share secrets, but never touch.

Jay got tired and came slogging through the sand to our umbrella encampment. He collapsed between my towel and his mother's, and asked for a soft drink from the cooler. He drank it noisily, his eyes still on Mick and Henry, whose game had ratcheted up several notches on the macho scale now that it was just the two of them. "Hi," he said to me with a shy, sideways grin.

"Hi, yourself."

"So you slept late," he observed.

"Yep. Guess I was tired."

"How come?"

"Mmm." I thought. "Bad dreams?"

He nodded. "I have them. Nightmares, I have. I wake up, and my dad comes. Or my mother sometimes. Then I go back to sleep."

"Me, too." Except for the mother and father part. "What do you dream about?"

"Monsters. What do you dream about?"

"Well, usually I dream I'm late for something, and I can't find it." Lost and late; I have these dreams incessantly. "I don't know where the train station is, or sometimes it's the bus station, and everybody's giving me different directions. Then the bus comes, or the train, but I don't know where it goes, I can't read the number, and I'm late, I'm so late, and everything keeps repeating and repeating, until finally I wake up out of boredom."

Jay stared at me for a long second, then belched.

"'Scuse me," he muttered, with a glance at Sally. She only smiled and raised her eyebrows at him.

I wish I could say she's a bad mother—No, I don't, no, I don't, that was a figure of speech, even I am not so far gone that I'd wish a lousy parent on a helpless child. In any case, she's *not* a bad mother, she seems like a very good one from what I've seen with my jaundiced eye, very attentive and low-key, very affectionate. And yet—you knew there was an *and yet*—Jay behaves differently with Sally than he does with Mick. He's giggly and loose with Dad, silly and relaxed and happy, a normal, well-adjusted kid. But with Mom, he sobers up fast. His youthful brow furrows and he watches her closely, worriedly. At five and a half, he's already a little caretaker.

Not that I'm an expert on children. Hell no, they scare the daylights out of me. They're so autonomous or something. So unforgivingly straightforward. Irony's not in their vocabulary, so they never get my jokes. As a rule I stay out of their way—but you'll understand that this one fascinated me, so I was paying special attention to him. What I saw was a polite, anxious boy, bashful and very sweet, but wary and much too observant for his age. As if he were compelled to check the temperature, over and over, of whatever emotional atmosphere he found himself in.

Incredibly, Jay has decided he likes me. It happened last night at Brother's, and I could see the change so clearly, see the decision as he was making it in his naked, guileless, child's face. Don't ask me why, I've forgotten the context, but I had launched into a minirant on the perversities of anthropomorphism and the amazing arrogance of us humans toward the so-called lesser creatures—all right, I'd had a couple of beers—and for examples, I was mentioning names like "panfish," "box turtle," "pocket mouse," "fur seal," humble creatures whose very existence we've limited and defined by naming them according to how they relate exclusively to *us*. For some reason the word "panfish" struck Jay as the funniest thing he'd ever heard, and he went off.

He couldn't stop laughing, and he's got this lovely, low, gurgling giggle, just the essence of delight. It's irresistible, and pretty soon we were all snickering along with him. Then Henry and I started naming the silliest-sounding fish we could think of, to try to get him going again—scrod, kipper, fluke, smelt, croaker, you get the idea. I said "crappie," and Jay lost it—he almost slid off his chair. What fun; I think I've found my best audience ever. And when he finally recovered, he kept beaming at me with the goofiest, the most charming, sweet-faced appreciation.

Question: Am I that vain, or is this really the nicest, brightest kid I've ever met?

The day drew to a lazy close that seemed early to me—I'd gotten up so late. We had dinner at home, burgers and hot dogs on the grill. Afterward, Lee got me alone and demanded to know what was wrong.

"Wrong? Nothing. Wrong? What do you mean?" I tried to look astonished, but panic flickered in my chest. Did she know?

"It's Mick, isn't it?"

"No," I denied, horrified.

"What I can't understand is *why* you don't like him."

"But I *do*—"

"I shouldn't have asked you to stay. I'm sorry, Em." She'd been cleaning the stove within an inch of its life. She sat down at the kitchen table, damp dish towel in one hand, a glass of ice water in the other. She looked hot and irritable. She pressed the glass to her forehead, and for the first time I noticed she also looked tired.

"No," I insisted, "I was happy to stay. Really, I'm having a great time."

She dismissed that with a wave. "I don't blame you for hiding out. I would if I could, too. To tell you the truth, it's Sally's company I don't enjoy that much anymore," she all but whispered. A needless precaution, since no one was in the house but us: Henry, Mick, Sally, and Jay had gone for a moonlight walk on the beach. Lee ran her fingers through her short brown hair, sighing. "I just wish she'd stop telling me things I don't want to know."

"Personal things?"

She nodded. "When we were first getting to be friends, I told her a few things about me—us, Henry and me. Nothing really intimate," she said quickly, "not like I would tell the group—"

"No, no."

"But somewhat personal, you know—".

"Sure."

"But I've quit, but she *keeps* telling me things."

"Like . . ." I waited hopefully. Shamelessly.

"Like—they've been in couples counseling for five of the six years of their marriage."

"Wow." Mick had never even hinted at such a thing. How discreet. In the same situation, most men would have, don't you think? What a rationale: *My marriage is a wreck, let's go to bed*.

"And I hate the way she talks about her husband," Lee went on, leaning close. "Henry's crazy about Mick, and I like him, too. We feel more loyal to him now than her."

"What does she say about him?"

"Oh, you know, how she resents his job change and what it's done to their lifestyle, how it's changed everything. She's from Delaware—apparently her family has money. She actually said to me, 'I didn't buy into this.' She laughed afterward, pretending it was a joke, but it wasn't."

"No."

"It's so—it just makes me angry. I married a plumber, but I've never been ashamed of Henry, never. It's part of who he is, which makes it part of what I love about him." She sat back, blowing her bangs out of her eyes. "Then again, what if he decided all of a sudden to give up plumbing and take up—I don't know. Winemaking. How would I like that?"

"Well, how would you?"

She shook her head. "I wouldn't care."

"No, you wouldn't. Because he'd still be Henry."

"And that's who I love."

I thought about Sally and who she loved. Presumably she used to love Mick the lawyer. Michael Draco, Esquire, was worth loving, especially in his three-piece suit and suspenders. But Mick the penniless painter wasn't. She hadn't bought into that.

Oh, she was a piece of work, all right. Her insecurities made you pity her, and her insincerity made you dislike her. But she was a good mother; somehow with Jay she transcended all her neuroses.

Poor Mick. Even I could see that he was trapped.

Around ten o'clock that night, Jay woke up screaming. I didn't even hear him at first; we five were upstairs with the TV on, although only Henry was watching it—some basketball game. Mick jumped up first, but Sally said, "I'll go," and hurried out of the room.

Lee had been reading. She laid her magazine aside and asked, "Does he have nightmares a lot, Mick?"

"Just lately, yes. They're coming almost every night." The crying stopped all at once. He relaxed slightly; some of the tension went out of his face.

"It's not that unusual at his age," Lee assured him. "In fact it's probably more common than otherwise. You shouldn't worry too much. Really."

He thanked her with a smile. "I know it's normal, but still—"

"It's upsetting."

He stood up again. "I just want to go see. Check. You know, make sure," he muttered apologetically, and disappeared.

He came back a few minutes later, looking relieved. "He's asleep and everything's fine," he reported, and we all said, "Good, good." "Sally's going to bed, by the way. She said to say good night."

So then it was just the four of us, spending a quiet last night reading and watching television. Henry had the whole couch to himself; he had a warm beer on his chest, and occasionally he would mutter things like, "*What* loose ball foul?" and "Shoot, *shoot*, what the hell are you waiting for?" Lee sat at the dining room table, absorbed in the July *Vogue*. Mick divided his attention between the game and his book, a library hardcover called *Murder at the Hard Rock*. Me? I was doing an impression of someone reading the latest Louise Erdrich, which I'd brought along on purpose to impress people, but in fact I was watching Mick. And sometimes, he was watching me.

Lee yawned, stretched. "Well, I'm going to bed. Henry?"

"Yep. In a minute."

"Night, you guys," Lee said to Mick and me. We said it back.

Henry's minute stretched to fifteen as his team kept calling time-outs. *I should leave before he does*, I kept advising myself. It was going to be just Mick and me, and it was going to be awkward. But I reread the same paragraph over and over and didn't move.

Henry vaulted off the couch, energized by his side's win at the buzzer. "Great game. Lee go to bed?"

We chuckled and said she had.

"So, early or late start back tomorrow?"

"Early for us, I'm afraid," Mick said. "Sally's folks are driving down for dinner." From Delaware, I assumed. The folks with the money.

"What about you, Em? Any rush?"

"No, not really. Whenever you and Lee want to go."

"Great. Morning on the beach, then." I've never known anybody who likes the ocean as much as Henry, not even Isabel. He's like a kid. "Course," he had to add, "you might've maxed out by now. How many minutes have you spent in the full, undiluted sun this weekend? Ten? Fifteen? Ha ha!"

"Ha ha."

Still laughing, he tossed his beer can in the trash—"Three points!"—and went downstairs.

He'd left the TV on. Mick and I glanced at each other, then turned as one to stare at two sports announcers, a black guy and a white guy, recapping the game. We did that for a while. A new announcer's voice came on to tell us that if we stayed tuned, we could hear all the sports news and scores from around the country. I stood up.

I don't know why the tension was so tight. We'd been alone together before. We were *friends*. But when I looked at Mick, my muscles gave out. I stood there with rubber knees, taking shallow breaths and feeling as if my skin didn't fit me anymore, it had gotten too thin and sensitive, too tight.

He stood up, too. One look at his face, and it was all over. I honestly don't know who moved, who put out a hand first. Even up to the last second, it could've been innocent—just a touch, a goodnight brush of fingers. But we gripped hands hard, and in the next second we were holding each other.

We broke away quickly. Fatalistic, I clutched at the phantom memory of his hard shoulders, the cottony smell of his T-shirt, thinking that was all I could have. He said something. I couldn't understand him, my senses were dazed. "What?" He snatched at my hand and pulled me outside, out onto the deck.

Too bright—too open. We went down the outer stairs as quietly as we could, me barefooted, Mick in his unlaced sneakers. Under the house, in the shadowy space between his car and a padlocked storage shed, we stopped. One last second of sanity while we faced each other, hands off. We could go back up, we could just talk—

We kissed. It was painful, not joyful, but I couldn't stop—like drinking seawater if I were dying of thirst, it would kill me in the end but I had to have it. I clutched at his arms, covered his whole mouth with mine, grinding my body against him. He turned us, pressed me back against the side of the shed. My head struck something—the metal fuse box. "Ow." Mick started to take his hands off me, but I grabbed him back, urgent.

"Kiss me," I said, even though he already was. I kept saying it, like some exciting obscenity, because it felt good to say the *truth* for a change, tell him for once what I really wanted. He wasn't as articulate—he murmured curse words in between kisses, but to me they sounded like love poetry. He put his hands in my hair. "So pretty," he said, and my heart just sang. He'd never given me a compliment before. It meant so much. I kissed him tenderly, not like a madwoman, and we both started shaking. He slid his hands up from behind, inside my blouse. Skin on skin.

Shuddering, hissing in my breath, I gasped out the fatal question. "Mick, Mick, where can we go?"

Glare from the outside spotlight glittered in his eyes when he turned his head, looking around. I saw the same outlaw indifference to consequence that I was feeling. He took my hand. We picked our way past the pilings and stepped off the concrete pad onto the grass, along a narrow, half-beaten path to a row of scrub pines separating Neap Tide from the beach house behind it. From there the path turned toward the sea. Where was he taking me? Would we drop between the pines and kiss some more in the dark? Would we keep going till we reached the water and make love in the cold sand in the moonlight? I followed him blind, thoughtless, loving the feeling of being tugged along, and so glad the choice was his and not mine.

I stepped on a burr.

Mick caught my elbow when I started hopping on one foot and swearing. I stuck my foot out behind me and tore at the stinging thistle, but I only got part of it; as soon as I took one step, I was hobbling again. "Sit," he said, and we sank down together in the sand.

Wasn't this just like my life? A living analogy? Accidental performance art? He made me straighten my leg out and put my foot in his lap. He tried to be gentle, but by the time he plucked out the last of the spiky, prickly nettles in the soft part of my arch, we were different people. We had turned back into our old selves. Our thinking selves. I mourned the loss so sharply, I wanted to weep.

The wind blew the feathery fronds of sea oats and stirred the beach grass, carrying the heavy smell of the sea. So many stars, more stars than black sky, and a moon one night past full. We stayed where we were, enclosed in the steady roar of the surf, watching each other. Mick studied the look of his hand around my ankle, pale on paler, and I measured the weight of my calf on his thigh. He had on gray sweatpants and a black T-shirt. Moonlight picked out the silver in his too-short hair, and I leaned closer to touch him, overcome by a stabbing, irresistible tenderness. We started to speak at the same time. I gestured—*you first.*

"When we got here and I heard you were staying," he said, and stopped. I scooted closer. "I thought I'd just see—remnants of you. I was looking forward to finding an old book you'd read and discarded, a—" He laughed with no sound. "A wet towel."

"I looked in your shaving kit," I blurted. "Just to see. I touched your things." He put his hand on the side of my face, and I closed my eyes. "I shouldn't have stayed. Oh, Mick. I knew it as soon as I saw you."

"But I'm glad you stayed."

"I'm glad, too, but it's crazy."

"I know."

"What are we going to do?"

"I don't know."

So much for having my will taken away from me. That had been my secret hope, that Mick would take charge, make all the decisions, tell me what to do, *make* me do it if I put up any resistance. Kind of like a father and his little girl.

I embarrassed myself.

"Emma—I don't think I can leave my family. I can't leave Jay."

"I know, I know that, I'm not asking you to," I said quickly, stumbling over the words in my haste. That he should think for a second that I wanted to wreck his marriage—and yet he broke my heart with his finality, his lack of equivocation. I didn't want games, but I needed something, some slender thread of made-up hope to hold on to.

I covered his hand on my cheek with my hand. "I have so many things to tell you." He bent his head, leaning closer. "But also, I have nothing to tell you. If you can't leave her."

He swallowed, his face bleak with pain.

I was in pain, too. "Do you still make love to her? Have you had other women besides me? I don't know anything about you. How can I be in love with you, we've never even gone to the movies. I *hate* this. I want—I just want—I want to hold hands with you, Mick, call you up on the telephone—"

This was torture. He didn't say anything, didn't answer. Even now, he couldn't talk to me about his marriage, couldn't bring himself to betray Sally to me. And now would have been the perfect time to say, "Emma, I'm miserable, she doesn't understand me, let's be lovers." But Mick had no rap, no married-guy patter, he couldn't excuse himself by enumerating his wife's failings. Most especially, he couldn't walk out on his little boy, who already worried about Mommy, and woke up screaming in the night from bad dreams.

"This is it, isn't it? This is all we're going to get." I touched Mick's mouth, his raspy cheek. I put my fingers in his hair. "Darling, who gave you this godawful haircut?" I said, choked on tenderness, feeling tears sting behind my eyes.

He said, "I didn't want this to happen. The last thing I wanted to do was hurt you."

"I know that. Anyway, it's too late."

"Emma . . ."

Then we were kissing again, eyes shut tight as if we could stay blind to the truth that this was hopeless, this was just putting off the inevitable. But, God, it felt right to hold him, it felt like the most honest thing I'd done since we met.

It had to stop. We backed off shakily, breathing hard, like teenagers in the backseat at the drive-in. "God," I said, and he said, "Emma, Christ," and we sat back on our haunches and stared at each other.

"Okay. Okay," I said, "it's over. No more. Because this is killing me."

He helped me to stand. That sounds silly, but I needed help. He glanced over my head, back at the cottage, and I looked back, too—a reflex. There was nothing to see, no lights on upstairs, no suspicious wife on the side porch, hands on her hips, surveying the dunes. But his anxiety infected me. It made me feel sick.

"Do you want me to go back first?"

He looked at me sharply. "No."

"You see how we would be at this?" I said a little wildly. "We wouldn't even have any fun. We can't see each other anymore, Mick, not at all. Don't call me, don't do anything."

He nodded once. He put the palms of his hands on his forehead and pressed. "Lee and Henry are bound to have something."

"I know. If I hear you've been invited, I won't go."

"No, you go, I'll stay away."

"No, you're friends with Henry, and I can see Lee anytime. You go."

I turned and started back toward the cottage, keeping my eyes on the path, wary of rogue nettles. Another metaphor for my life. Mick and I had never even made it to the beach, never made glorious, swept-away love beside the crashing waves. Because of a burr, we'd hunkered down in the chilly sand and made do with a few furtive kisses.

I never cry in front of people. It's a matter of pride, or maybe it's a phobia. Anyway, I don't do it. Imagine my chagrin when we got to the bottom of the wooden steps at the side of the house and I realized I couldn't stop. I could have waved good-bye and run up alone—he'd never have known then. But I didn't want to leave him yet.

"Shit," I whispered when he put his arms around me. Were we safe here? What if someone came out—Henry, to smoke a cigar? Jay, sleepwalking? Lee overcome by a sudden compulsion to sweep the porch? "I hate this, I hate it."

"I hate it, too, and it's my fault. I swear I never wanted this."

"Stop saying that, it's nobody's fault. Anyway, we haven't done anything."

"I've made you miserable."

"That's true. I forgive you."

We kissed, smiling. But then I spoiled it by starting up again. "I'm not like this," I assured him, using his T-shirt to dry my face. "I'm really not, this is a first."

He pretended to believe me. He stroked the tears from my cheeks with his fingers, and then he leaned in and pressed his face to mine. "Sorry to hurt you. Not sorry this happened. I've been lying since the beginning."

"I've been lying, too."

"At least . . ."

"Yeah." At least we weren't lying anymore. There was some chilly comfort in that.

"I'll miss you," he whispered.

"Oh, don't." But I didn't break away, I wanted every futile, agonizing second.

A last kiss, very soft. No passion, just—good-bye. I don't like the feel of my heart breaking. It's very romantic, but it stings like acid.

"Bye. I'm sleeping in tomorrow, Mick—I don't want to see you."

Those were the last words. Car lights swung off the highway onto our cul-de-sac, a stranger's car, but it scared us. We backed away from each other. I turned and ran up the steps, tiptoed inside, slunk down the hall past the closed door to Sally's room, and ducked into mine.

Closed the door. Sat on the bed in the dark and waited until I heard Mick in the hall. His door opened and closed softly. I listened like an animal, like a wolf, but there was no sound, no murmur of voices. Nothing.

I had a long time, all night, to suffer for my disappointment. I'd wanted her to catch him. I'd wanted the jig to be up.

He's wrong—he should leave her for me. I could make him happy, and I could fall in love with Jay. In fact, I already have.

But.

But what I love about my lover is that he's true. Damn him. He's killed me.

20

Isabel

I've discovered purgatory. Not hell—it's too boring. Purgatory is low-lit and industrial-carpeted, mauve-walled, library-quiet except for a wall-mounted television permanently tuned to CNN. It's called the Diagnostic Imaging Department.

My heart rate invariably drops in the waiting room. I sit on one of the thinly upholstered, pine-and-tweed chairs and feel my facial muscles go limp. I don't see well; the air is blurred, grainy. My nerves, my energy, everything drains into the pastel walls and the soft-tiled ceiling, the flaccid Renoir reproductions. *Someone take care of me, please*, I'm reduced to pleading. *Be tender. Don't hurt me*. It's a giving over, a relinquishment, the medical version of "Into Thy hands." Utter passivity. Nothing I can do. It's a relief to let go, stop trying to be in charge of my life, if only for this little bit of time.

Today I'm here for a chest X ray. Before, it was days and days of radiation therapy for my hip. Whatever they did, it fixed me up—I have very little pain now, and I walk without a limp. Given that, you might think I'd like this place better. But no. I remind myself of Grace: they've never really hurt her at the vet's, but she begins to shake in terror as soon as she sniffs the parking lot.

But no one looks frightened here, not even the children. I make a covert study of my radiology comrades, hunting for signs of despair, panic, devastation. I'm never successful. No one weeps silently, huddled into herself; no one ever breaks down. Do I look like these people? They could be waiting for their insurance agent, the dentist. Is my face that flat and accepting? That empty of drama?

"Mrs. Kurtz?"

A thin young woman with freckles and wispy hair smiles at me from the double doors. I follow her down two short corridors to the changing area. "Hi, how are you today?" she asks as we walk. She zips a curtain back from one of the tiny booths. "Everything off from the waist up, and put on one of these robes. I'll be back to get you in a minute. Okay?"

I strip out of my sweater, blouse, prosthetic bra, and put on the blue cotton robe. It makes me look hippy, cinched in at the waist over my slacks. My face is ghastly in the fluorescent glare, and yet I feel a rush of love for myself, a painful tenderness. Oh, poor Isabel.

The technician comes back. The tag on her uniform says she's Ms. Willett. Inside the spacious X-ray room, I start to undo my robe, but she says, "That's okay," and stands me up in front of a white square of wood or plastic, like a basketball backboard, my arms at my sides. She disappears. I hear her voice from across the room; she's gone behind the protective shield. "Okay, very still. Deep breath. Hold it, hold it. And relax."

Another picture from the side, and then one more from the back. "Okay, that should do it. Wait here for a minute, okay? I'll be right back."

It's never a minute, it's always longer, five, frequently ten. She's finding the radiologist, who will check to see if she got the pictures right. Sometimes they have to take them over again. This is the worst part, waiting for the technician to return. When she does, she never tells you anything, so the tension is pointless, but I feel it anyway. My fear and fatalism and self-pity reach their peak at this stage. I always go to the magazine stand and pull out *People* or *Woman's Day*, anything. I stand with my face to the wall and flip the pages of slimming chicken recipes, articles on the miracle of antioxidants, fashion ads, "pants that slink and shimmer are the sexiest option for after dark."

"All right," Ms. Willett says brightly, coming back into the room empty-handed. "You can get dressed." I search her face. Was that sympathy in her voice? She knows what the X-rays showed. Did the doctor point to a spot on the film and shake his head with her? No, it couldn't be. Her smile is too chipper. I couldn't have a lung metastasis—she wouldn't look like that.

Right or wrong, I feel better by the minute. Getting dressed in the booth is the precise reverse, emotionally, mentally, of getting undressed. Riding up in the elevator to the first floor, striding through the automatic doors to the sidewalk, breathing in the clean, nonmedicinal air—I'm a new woman. Out here, I'm one of the normal ones, not defined by my illness anymore, indistinguishable from the rushing, bustling, oblivious, healthy people. Just like them, I could be immortal.

I walked across Pennsylvania Avenue and started up K Street, taking my time. On my way to the hospital, I hadn't much noticed what kind of day it was. If I had, I might have resented it. Because it was perfect, one of those golden days when summer is ending but autumn hasn't begun. The air smelled sweet and the sun slanted in the tired, aging, still-green leaves of the trees as if through a sympathetic photographer's gauze filter. Rush hour had just begun, but passersby looked relaxed, not harried, as seduced by the softness of the afternoon as I was.

But I was tired by the time I reached Farragut Square, too tired to stand on Connecticut and wait for the bus. I bought a cup of coffee from a street vendor—the only vice I have left is caffeine; otherwise my diet is strictly macrobiotic—and sat down on a bench in the park.

And fell into a morbid game I catch myself playing at odd times. Wrinkled old ladies, children, young men, pretty girls, mothers with toddlers, surly teenagers, old men—to each of them as they strode or hobbled or ambled past me, I thought, *You're dying. You're dying, and you're dying, and you're dying, and you're dying, and you're dying, and you're dying, and you're dying.* I didn't do this for comfort, certainly. Perhaps it was a way to persuade myself of the unthinkable, the outlandish—that no one gets out alive. The truth is, I still have trouble believing in death. Yes, even now.

Perhaps it's not important anyway. Maybe it's enough to be alive and know it. In this never-to-be-repeated instant in the vastness of time, I, Isabel, have the miraculous privilege to exist. Sipping hot coffee softened with a delicious nondairy powdered creamer. It's really tasty. Starlings are tuning up in the oak trees. The air smells like perfume, then auto exhaust, then perfume again. I love the worn feel of this bench under my fingers, smoothed to velvet softness by a million behinds. Here I am in the world, right now, this minute. I never was before, never will be again. I simply exist, and it's glorious. An honor and a privilege. A marvel beyond belief.

"Mind?"

I looked up to see a man bending toward me at the side of the bench, smiling widely. I was perplexed until he made a stiff-armed gesture toward the empty space beside me. "Yes—no, I don't, go ahead." I moved over a few inches, pulling my purse closer to my hip.

He came around with a series of short, dragging steps and slowly, creakily, lowered his backside to the seat. His breath came out in a long *ahhh* of relief, and he sat back by degrees, settling himself on the bench the way an old dog settles itself on a front porch floor. From the corner of my eye I saw him take a handkerchief out of one pocket of a heavy maroon cardigan, much too warm for the mild September afternoon, and dab under his nose daintily with a horny, discolored hand. He turned to me, full-faced, and pulled his thin lips into the widest smile I've ever seen, practically ear to ear, and said, "Pretty day, isn't it?"

"Beautiful," I nodded.

"I don't like that humidity."

"No, I don't either. None today, though."

"*Pretty* day today."

"It's lovely."

He pushed his mottled cheeks out, froglike, and turned his affable, pale-eyed gaze from me to the branches overhead. He shoved his hands under one knee and hauled it up, crossing it over the other with a huff of breath. His feet bulged out of beige socks and worn brown sandals, as if he had bunions and corns and who knew what else. "Where'd you get that coffee?" he asked.

"Across the street." I pointed.

He smiled and said, "Huh," nodding his head. "Smells good."

"Do you want some? I could get you a cup."

"No, no! Thank you very much!" He grinned, showing bright white false teeth. "I've given it up, it was getting on my nerves. Still like the smell, though. Not like cigarettes. Gave them up, and they smell horrible now, smell like hell. You smoke?"

"No, I never did."

"Very wise. My wife didn't smoke, either." He broke off to cough into his handkerchief, a rough, wet, old man's cough. He turned away to spit discreetly into the handkerchief, then stuffed it back into his pocket. He reached inside his sweater and brought out, presumably from his shirt pocket, a photograph. No, two photographs. "Here's Anna, my wife. We met over in Italy during the war. She was Italian."

He wanted me to take the pictures, not just look at them in his hand. I did, and saw two versions of Anna, slim and pretty in the first, plump and pretty in the second, smiling the same mysterious smile in both. Mysterious to me—it's hard to know what a stranger's smile means.

"I lost her in 1979." He pushed his cheeks in and out, in and out.

"How did she die?" A too-personal question I couldn't stop myself from asking.

"She had cancer of the cervix."

"I'm sorry. Do you have children?"

He shook his head. "A baby," he said, "but we lost her very quickly, very quickly. After that, we couldn't have any more."

"I'm so very sorry." I barely stopped myself from touching him. And I'd said that too fervently; it was so long ago, my sympathy must sound extreme.

He spread his fingers wide over the knees of his shiny brown trousers, a kind of digital shrug. "Thank you," he said with much dignity. "Are you married, if I can ask?"

"No." For some reason I added, "I have a son."

"Is he married?"

"No. But he lives with someone." A woman I've only heard about, never met. Susan; she's an elementary school teacher. When did I lose Terry? He went away to school in Montreal and never came back. I tried for a long time not to call it an escape, but after so many years, that's no longer possible. Terry ran away from his father and me. I don't blame him, and I don't believe in lifelong regrets, but that failure is the singular tragedy of my life.

"They do that nowadays, don't they," the old man said. "Nobody thinks a thing of it."

I nodded. "Shacking up, we used to call it."

"That's right. Shacking up." He laughed merrily. "My name's Sheldon Herman. I won't shake because I've got a cold."

"I'm Isabel."

"Pleased to meet you. Look here." He took out another picture. "That's Moxie." A floppy-eared mongrel, mostly German shepherd, red-eyed from the flashbulb. "Man's best friend," Sheldon Herman said, rough-voiced. "She was quite a girl. Lotta heart. Kept me good company after I lost my wife. She passed on in '88, age of thirteen."

I made a sympathetic sound.

"I buried her in the backyard. Gave her a little funeral, you know, flowers on top, and her tennis ball down there with her. Near her paws."

"Yes."

"After that I had to move. You know how it is when you get old, they make you move. So now I live in a home for old fellers. It's okay. Could be worse." He turned his slack, shapeless body toward me. Crevasses that probably used to be dimples scored his white-whiskered cheeks. It was hard to say what his coloring might have been, fair or dark or in between. He was washed out now. He was almost gone.

"What I missed most," he said, "was having something to take care of. Where I live we're all on our own, pretty much. They got me in a private room. It's all men." He looked me over, smiling the nice, wide-faced smile. "You a squeamish kind of girl, Isabel?"

"Pardon?"

"You the kind of a lady who's scared of spiders and whatnot?"

"No," I said slowly, "I wouldn't say I'm squeamish in that way. Why, Mr. Herman?"

"Now, don't go swooning on me," he said, looking down, reaching into the far pocket of his bulky sweater. I stiffened a bit, not really alarmed but definitely on guard. He brought out—something, I couldn't see what until he opened his spotty, veiny hand. A mouse.

"Found 'er in a trap they set in the kitchen. Her paw's smashed, see? She limps. I could show you, but you might faint dead away. I call her Brownie. She's my little pal now."

"Cute." She was. Bright-eyed and pink-toed, with a smooth, russet coat. Perched on his hand, she looked around nervously, twitching her whiskers.

"I feed her cheese and bread and whatnot. Salad. I don't know if they know I've got her, but nobody bothers me about her. Pet her?" His faded eyes twinkled, daring me.

I stroked my finger along the mouse's satiny back. "She's company for you," I said.

"That's it. You got to have something. Anything, as long as it's alive. Can't be a thing, it has to breathe, but that's the only requirement. I've always thought that. More than ever these days. Part of getting old, I guess."

"I guess."

"You know, I cared for my wife more than anything, more than my own life, but when I look back it doesn't feel like even that was enough. I wish I had her again, so I could do it better. I would, too."

He lifted the mouse and kissed the top of its head with his thin lips. Then he put it back in the pocket of his sweater with great care, like a mother laying her baby down. "Pretty day," he said with a sigh, leaning back to stare up at the tree branches over our heads. "Summer's about up, hm? Not too many more days like this, I'll bet."

"No," I agreed. "Not too many more."

A few minutes later, I saw my bus coming down K Street. I said good-bye to Mr. Herman and left him on the bench, smiling after me while the waning sun threw shadows over his slope-shouldered figure.

When I got home, I didn't go inside immediately. I wandered around to the back of the building to look at my garden. Kirby's garden, really; he did the heavy work of digging and tilling for me last spring, when I was reeling from my first chemo sessions. He did plenty of weeding and watering in the summer, too, when I'd drag home from a late class, too exhausted for anything but bed. Without Kirby, I wouldn't have bothered with a garden this year, although it's by far the nicest perk that comes with my lease. Mrs. Skazafava, my landlady, used to cultivate all the grounds behind the building herself, an area of two thousand square feet or so. Now she's too old, and a few years ago she divided it into four plots for the use of the tenants. Surprisingly, not all the plots get taken every year, even though the building has twelve units. I've taken one every summer since I moved—this is my third year. I love to garden. It's a passion.

Kirby found a wooden spool in the alley last spring and rolled it in to use for a garden seat. My legs had begun to ache; I sat down on the spool. Most of the tenants grow vegetables, but I prefer flowers. This late in the year I had more foliage than flora, but the pink and white cleome were still blooming, and the asters and nicotiana, my transplanted boltonia, the hardy *Chelone obliqua* with their pink turtle heads. Twilight closed in. A bee buzzed in the coleus, then flew up and headed home. The birds were tuning up for one last fling before dark. Across the alley, my neighbor Helen put her head out the back door and sang the hopeful, two-note croon mothers use to call in their children.

I heard a step, and turned to see Kirby coming down the concrete walk that bisects the garden plots, two on a side. He had on his summer uniform—cut-off army fatigue pants, dun-colored T-shirt, and old Birkenstock sandals, no socks. The sandals made me think of Mr. Herman and his bulging, pained-looking feet. A soft drift of melancholy settled over me.

Kirby stopped beside me, hands in his flap pockets. "Hi," we said in unison, smiling and nodding. But his hooded eyes looked sharp. "It's almost time to plant chrysanthemums," I said. "Look how well the anemone's doing, and the cimicifuga. You put them in the perfect spot."

He squatted down beside me, resting his forearms on his bony knees, clasping his hands. "How did it go?"

I didn't know what he meant for a second. "Oh, the X ray? Fine, it went fine."

"Did they say anything?"

"No. But they never do—the doctor calls you if there's anything."

"I see." He frowned, but said no more. He's lovely that way. I know he cares, but he confines his sympathy for me to deeds, not words. And he's one of those rare men who don't feel bound to have an opinion on everything. Or worse, a solution.

He bent his head to gaze at the ground. His slender neck

looked naked and tender, like a young boy's. I had an urge to touch the tight tendons, the soft hair that came to a point in the center. I put out my hand. He turned, and my fingers just grazed his cheek. Instead of withdrawing, I let my hand fall open and press lightly against the side of his face. I caressed him.

"Isabel," he said, quietly astounded.

"I might die," I said. "I might get out of it, there's a chance, but I might not. Probably not. You know that, don't you?"

"Yes."

"No, but do you really? Do you know it, do you really understand?"

"Yes. I know all about it." He moved the palm of my hand to his mouth. I started to pull away, but he held on. We hadn't touched, not like this, since the night he'd kissed me under the streetlight.

I brushed my fingers across his gaunt cheekbone. His lashes swept down, hiding his eyes. "I'm sick, Kirby, and I'm bald, I'm not the real Isabel in my body. I don't know how you could want that, but if . . . "

"But if . . ."

"If you do . . ." I was struck dumb by the most idiotic shyness. And a superstitious dread of putting into words the thing I'd just realized I wanted most.

He stood up, still holding my hand, and carefully raised me. "I haven't changed. Not at all. I've just been waiting." He looked so thankful. He put his arms around my shoulders and held me.

It felt too good, I could hardly trust it. "Only if you want me," I mumbled against his shirt, "not for sympathy. Please, please don't lie."

He pulled back, gripping me hard. "What's happened?"

"Nothing—"

"You're not worse?"

"No!"

"You swear?"

"I'm fine, nothing's happened. Truly." Nothing I could explain to him yet, anyway. A change of my heart. It had to do with regrets, and trying to eliminate as many as I could, while I could. And realizing it doesn't matter where love comes from, or when, or what it looks like. I don't want to end wishing I could do everything over again, better, differently, fuller. This is it. My life. Here, now.

"All right, then," Kirby said. "Stop saying stupid things, Isabel, and let's go inside."

I dreamed I was locked in a tall black closet. I kept flailing with my hands, my fingertips, at the thin, faint strip of light at the bottom of the locked door, crying out, "Help, someone help me, let me out," until the light dimmed and disappeared, and I was alone in absolute darkness. I screamed and screamed, but I had no voice, and when I woke up my face was streaming with tears.

Kirby slept on his side, facing away. He never stirred when I eased the fingers of my right hand under him, between the mattress and his warm-skinned waist. I waited while the soft throbbing of a pulse, his or mine, calmed me down.

Anyway, it was an old dream. I knew what it meant, and I'd dreamt it so often it had lost the power to squeeze me in an icy vise until dawn. I concentrated on the rhythm of Kirby's breathing, soothing as a heartbeat, and drifted back to sleep.

When I awoke, it wasn't to that moment of vague anxiety that suddenly bursts into cold, bright panic. It stops my heart, makes me flush with heat. *Cancer is in my body again, and this time it's going to kill me*. I waited, but for a change the act of waking was safe, not treacherous.

Turning my head, I saw Kirby's sharp-nosed profile in the chalky dawn light. He was either meditating or sleeping. Sleeping, I supposed, although the lines of his austere face weren't lax, and the breath coming and going through his fine white nostrils was inaudible. I thought of Gary, and tried not to make comparisons.

Making love with someone for the first time is always awkward—I assume; until last night, I'd only had the experience once before. Making love with a one-breasted bald woman for the first time—that ought to outdo awkwardness. For me, after Gary, the novelty of lying with a man *shaped* like Kirby was enough to smother passion and fill me with skittishness and misgiving. And sometimes the anticipation of disaster is a self-fulfilling prophesy.

Kirby saved us—I take no credit. I almost ruined it. When we took our clothes off and got in my bed, I lay there and marveled at the toughness of his body, and thought about Gary, and wondered if Kirby were thinking of his wife, and worried that he might feel only pity now that he had me, pity and regret—and all he did was touch me. He had such caring in his hands. Another first, for me.

In the end, I was so easily seduced. "Don't think," he said, pressing hard inside, giving me his fierce, romantic kisses. Easier said than done, I thought, and yet I did forget. He made me forget the strangeness, my clumsiness, the freakishness—some would say—of our joining. For a second I even forgot the worst thing, the deep fear that never leaves. Light burst in and dazzled me. But immediately I thought, *This letting go is a rehearsal*—spoiling it. A morbid fancy; I rather shocked myself.

But the long night was only beginning. Before we fell asleep in each other's arms, Kirby had managed to cure me of morbidity, at least for a while. He's a man of many varied and surprising talents.

I do not believe sex, the act of love, transforms people. Emma would argue, but the fact is, I am not a romantic. Having said that, I have to admit I felt different this morning. I lay very still, and presently it came to me what was missing.

Dread.

The colorless sunrise seeped in around the edges of the curtain, and by its grainy light I studied the lines on my palm. According to this one, which all but winds around the base of my thumb, I will live to be about a hundred and ten. I don't take that lightly, and yet it occurs to me that it doesn't really matter. Yesterday's revelations continue. Ultimately, in the very grand scheme of things, it's irrelevant whether my life lasts fifty more years, or five. Or two. The point is to live it, not wait through it. And I'm alive now—I can pick flowers, pet the dog, eat cinnamon toast. How foolish I would be to let my mortality, which has been there all along, since the second of my birth, spoil my love of these things. So I won't. I'll have to remind myself constantly, but starting now, I intend to live until I die.

I woke Kirby up to tell him so. He went from sleep to full wakefulness in two blinks of his eyes. His smile was blinding. "Thank you," I said, instead of telling him about my epiphany.

"For?"

"The gift you gave me."

"Gift." I could tell he was thinking I meant the sex. It's actually rather refreshing when Kirby acts like a typical man. "You're under a delusion," he said gruffly, running his tongue over his teeth. His hairy forearm lay dark and startling across the virginal pink of the blanket. "I didn't give you anything, Isabel, I took. For me."

"You ruthless cad."

His lips curved. "Just don't turn it around. Don't make it me being selfless and giving," he advised, growing serious. He reached for me, cupping my face in his hands and stroking his thumb along the skimpy hair at my temple. He's very romantic. To me, everything he does is just right.

"How lucky I am," I realized all at once, kissing him all over his surprised face. Starting now, I remembered. No more waiting, nothing but living from here on. "Take advantage of me again," I suggested. A fine beginning.

21

Lee

I was dozing when Henry answered the phone in the hall on the third ring. I heard him say, "Hey, Em," in a glad voice, and start clumping up the stairs. "Yeah, she's still in bed. Well, she's still sore. Yeah. A day or two, they say. Yesterday. No, everything went just fine."

He stopped in the bedroom doorway. "Hold on, I'll see." He put his hand over the receiver. "You awake? Want to talk to Emma?"

I stared at him coldly. "Everything went fine?"

His face closed up; he didn't look so damned happy anymore. "Here she is," he said into the phone. "She'll tell you all about it."

I took the telephone from him and covered up the mouthpiece. "Why did you tell her everything went fine?"

"I meant," he said, "there weren't any complications." He had the nerve to sound exasperated.

"You're glad, aren't you? Why don't you admit it?"

"*What?*"

"It's not your fault anymore."

"Lee, you're—" He took a deep breath, made a big deal of reining in his temper. "You're nuts," he said quietly, and went out of the room.

I blotted my eyes with a new tissue and said hello into the phone.

"Hi! How was it, how are you feeling?"

Oh, knock it off, I thought. What was she trying to sound like, a nurse? "I feel okay. Tired."

"Yeah? Not in any pain?"

"Not anymore."

"What did they do to you?"

"They did an HSG, a hysterosalpingogram, and later they did a laparoscopy."

"Wow. Were you asleep?"

"For the laparoscopy. Not the HSG."

"Did it hurt?"

"Yes."

"Oh, Lee. Was Henry with you?"

"He had to work. He picked me up afterward and brought me home."

Pause. My flat voice finally got through to her. She said hesitantly, "Is it bad news? What did they find?"

"I've got SIN. That's pretty funny, isn't it? I thought you'd appreciate it. Salpingitis isthmica nodosa."

"What does it mean?"

"It means a tubal blockage. It means that little things like eggs and sperm and embryos can't get through."

"Oh, no. Oh, Lee. Can they fix it?"

"Sometimes. Not in my case, though. Because I've got bipolar disease—damage to the tube at both ends, not just one."

"Shit."

"Yes."

"But there must be something they can do. Nowadays—"

"All that's left is in vitro."

"That's like a test tube—"

"They take an egg from the ovary, fertilize it with sperm in a lab environment, an embryo forms, and they put it in the uterus."

"I see. So—that'll work?"

"Possibly. The chances increase if they use donor sperm."

"Donor sperm. You mean—not Henry's?"

"Correct."

"Do you—would that be—"

"At this point, I really couldn't care less."

"Aha. And Henry's okay with that, too?"

I was tired of answering questions. "This is getting a little personal," I said.

She took a quick breath. "Hey, sorry, excuse me, I just—I shouldn't have asked, it's just that we've usually—Well, anyway, sorry."

"Okay."

"So. In vitro next. Well, I'm sure that'll work. In fact, they probably should've started with it, but hindsight's twenty-twenty and all that."

I waited.

"Well, um, you sound tired, so I guess I'll let you go. I'll tell Rudy how you're doing. She'll probably call you."

"Fine."

"Can you believe she's started that landscaping course? I can't believe it. I was sure Curtis would stop her, or else she'd chicken out. I just think it's great. Our Rudy, flexing her muscles."

"Yes, it's great."

"Have you talked to Isabel?"

"Last night. Briefly."

"How did she sound?"

"Fine. She was sorry about what they found. The tubal blockage."

"But how was she? Did she sound okay?"

"She sounded fine, she sounded peachy. I have to get off the phone."

"Lee? Honey, I'm sorry, I know this is rough, but—"

"No, you don't, you don't know anything about it. And I just hope it never happens to you, Emma, because then you won't think it's so damned trivial."

"I don't think it's trivial! What do you mean? Where did that come from?"

"I have to get off the phone."

"Well, get off, then."

"All right."

"Oh, Lee—"

I hung up. I'd told her I had to get off, so I wasn't hanging up on her. Technically.

I got up and got dressed.

Henry was stirring a big pot on the stove. He turned around when he heard me. "You're up." He looked surprised, although not particularly pleased. "You sure you should be out of bed? They said—"

"A day or two, and it's been a day. I feel fine. I'm going over to Isabel's."

"Isabel's? But I'm making dinner—it's seven o'clock."

"I know what time it is. I'm not hungry. Especially for chili." It's all he knows how to make, but still, how thoughtless. Wouldn't you think *anyone* would know that chili isn't the dish you offer someone who's convalescing from surgery?

But everything about him annoyed me, his flannel shirt, the wooden spoon he was dripping sauce on the floor with, his new haircut that made him look like a girl. That's what we'd fought about last week. "You're too old for long hair," I'd told him—so he'd gone out and gotten it cut without consulting me. He didn't like it when I said, "Now you look like Prince Valiant. If you're going to get your hair cut, do it right, try to look like a normal man for a change." We didn't speak again for two days.

"All right," I said to him now, "I'm going."

"When will you be back?"

I put on my jacket gingerly; if I stretched too quickly, something pulled in my abdomen. "I don't know."

"Well, call before you leave," he said, going back to stirring.

"Why?"

"So I'll know."

"Know what?"

He looked around in irritation. "That you're leaving."

"What difference does it make?"

He turned away, angry. Good.

"If I get carjacked, what are you going to do about it? If somebody mugs me in Adams-Morgan, how does my calling you before I leave—"

"Don't, then." He banged the spoon on the stove. "Don't call, who cares?" He walked out of the kitchen into the TV room.

My stomach hurt. I followed him, seething.

"You're glad, aren't you?"

"Shit." He slammed the remote control on the coffee table.

"It's not your precious sperm anymore, it's me."

"You're losing your mind."

"No, I'm not. Tell me you're not secretly relieved—you can't!"

"Lee, it's *both* of us."

"Yes, and you're glad. Somebody to share the blame with."

"The blame?" He swore, which he knows I hate. "Why does anybody have to be to blame? It just happened, it's nobody's fault—"

"Oh, you'd like that."

He stuck his fingers in his hair, messing up his pageboy cut. "What the hell does that mean!"

I had no idea. "It doesn't mean anything." I started to cry.

He didn't move, didn't come over to comfort me. We stood on opposite sides of the room and stared at each other.

"I'm going to Isabel's," I told him, and left.

Kirby answered the door. He carried a napkin in his hand, and he had to swallow before he said, "Come in."

"Oh, no. You're eating—I'm sorry, I thought you'd be—"

"Lee?" Isabel called. Kirby widened the door, and I saw her in the little nook off the kitchen she calls the dining room. "Come on in, we were just finishing."

"Come," Kirby seconded, gesturing. Even Grace plodded over to greet me.

I went in.

The apartment looked like a bower—a church. Every table, every shelf on the bookcase held a vase or a bowl of flowers, dahlias, petunias, cosmos, asters. Classical music played softly on the stereo, and the air smelled exotic, a combination of incense and something gingery. Chinese food? The last rays of the sun were streaming through a stained glass plaque of an angel in the living room window, and the only other light came from candles—they were everywhere, like the flowers.

"What is it?" I asked stupidly. Kirby was trying to get me to take off my jacket. "What's happening?"

"What do you mean? Just dinner, and we're done." Gripping the edge of the table for support, Isabel pushed back her chair and stood up. She reached behind for something, standing at an awkward, half-bent angle, opening and closing her hand until she found it. A cane.

"I've interrupted something. Don't get up, you're having a special evening, I can—"

"No, no." She kept coming, taking slow but normal steps. She reached the natural light in the living room, and I saw how pale she was. Her unlined face was beautifully gaunt, her dark-circled eyes too big, her cheekbones too sharp. The new drug—it had to be that. Making her sick again. The doctor took her off the old drugs and put her on Taxol. She smiled at me, trying to put me at ease. Kirby was still hovering. I burst into tears.

I felt two pairs of hands on me, patting, soothing. I looked up to see Isabel send Kirby a message with her eyes. He said, "Well, I think I'll just," and then he headed for the bedroom, mumbling the rest.

"Oh, no," I wailed, "now look, I've banished him, he's—"

"Shh, shush. He lives here, he's just going to his room, you didn't banish him. Have you eaten?"

"He lives here?"

"Well, virtually." She was leading me back to the dining area, one hand through my arm, the other on her cane. A wooden cane with a brass handle. "Sit. Look at all this food we have left."

"I'm not hungry. Good Lord, Isabel, what is that?"

"This? Miso soup. And tofu and brown rice. Would you like some plum juice?"

"No, thank you."

"We were trying out a new cookbook. I'll bet you didn't know that macrobiotic food likes to be stirred counterclockwise in the northern hemisphere, but clockwise in the southern."

"It likes to be?"

"I can't wait to tell Emma. Are we sitting down, or would you rather talk in the living room?"

"Living room." And by the time we were settled on the sofa, Isabel with a glass of plum juice and me with Grace grinning at my feet, I had pulled myself together, no more snuffling and weeping. "Sorry," I said, blowing my nose for the last time. "This is all you need. I should've called first, but I just—"

"It's all right."

"I sort of escaped. From myself as much as the house. Emma called tonight and I hung up on her."

"You what?"

"I know, it's crazy. I'll call her tomorrow, try to apologize. She didn't do anything, it's me, I'm not myself anymore. And Henry—oh God, we're fighting about the stupidest things. Isabel," I interrupted myself, "is this how you live all the time?" I gestured to the flowers, the candles. "It's *beautiful.*" The sudden question came to me—How could Isabel die? She had that pretty rug she loved, she had these pillows, those wildflower lithographs on the wall. The poignancy of all her things, her belongings, somehow struck me as proof that she couldn't leave, she had to stay. Otherwise, it would be too cruel.

She smiled. "Yes, it's deliberate. Kirby's idea. A place for healing, he says. Now, tell me about the surgery."

"It was awful. You have to lie under this huge X-ray machine with your feet in stirrups. They thread a catheter through your cervix into your uterus. They gave me Advil and told me it wouldn't hurt, but it was absolutely excruciating. My muscles went into spasm."

"Oh, my Lord." She squeezed my hand, wincing.

"They send a dye in through the catheter. If there's no obstruction, it goes to the end of the fallopian tubes, but if there's a block it stops. Mine stopped, so they knew I had to have the laparoscopy. To see how bad it was."

"And?"

"Bad. It can't be fixed, surgery's not possible. I can't have a child except by in vitro fertilization, and the chances of that working at my age are about twelve percent, even with donor sperm. Plus, every time you do it, it costs a fortune."

"How much?"

"About eleven thousand dollars." Isabel's mouth dropped open. "Henry's—he can't even talk about it. So we're barely speaking."

She shook her head in sympathy. "What do you think you'll do?"

"In vitro."

Isabel sat back. She started to say something, then didn't.

"Well, it's *my* money, not his."

"Yes, but it seems like so *much* money."

"What difference does it make? If I had a terrible disease—"

"If you had a terrible disease, what?" she said when I stopped. I wasn't saying *anything* right tonight.

"I just mean, if I needed an operation or something to save my life, he wouldn't mind spending the money for that."

"No."

"Well, it's the same thing."

"Is it?"

"It is for me."

Isabel made a loose fist and pressed it to her lips thoughtfully. Her soft eyes regarded me for so long, I leaned over to pet the dog. "What about adoption, Lee?"

"No, I've told you."

"I know, but—"

"We're not considering it."

"I see."

I sat up and faced her. "The in vitro can work, Isabel," I said, letting my excitement show. "Twelve percent—that's not very good, but each time you do it it's twelve percent, so it adds up. That's how I'm looking at it. I feel hopeful, I really do. I just wish we'd *started* with this, I wish we hadn't wasted so much time."

"Lee . . ."

"What?"

She smiled, and I realized I had snapped at her. "I don't have any advice," she assured me, "don't worry."

"I don't mind advice," I said contritely.

"It's just that I'd hate to see you hurt again. That's all."

"I know. I do know, and you're right—I can feel it happening again, the hope revving up. Every time—every month—" I pressed my hands over my eyes. "I'm so afraid it won't work, and then I think it will—a miracle. Then it doesn't, and I'm scared again. I'm so tired, if I could just have some rest—"

"Why don't you—"

"There's no *time*, I've already let too many years slip away. That's what kills me, or one thing. I've always, always been in control of my life, every part of it, and now the most important part is out of my control, and I'm stuck, I can't move, and I can't stand this uncertainty anymore."

Isabel sighed. She sat back slowly, pulling a pillow against the small of her back. Her fragility disturbed me, but it was the Taxol, I was sure. So much of chemotherapy is worse than the disease it's supposed to cure.

"Lee," she said wearily. "No advice, just a question. Something for you to think about. Okay?"

"Of course. Go ahead." I leaned over again to pet Grace.

"Is having a child the most important thing in your life? More important than Henry?"

My throat closed; I couldn't answer.

"Ask yourself if the need to have your own genetic, biological child outweighs every other need in your life, including your marriage. I know you love Henry, there's no question of that. But if your answer is yes, you may lose him. Why did you marry him?" she asked kindly. "There's no right or wrong—if it was to have a child of your very own, no one else's, well, that's the answer. But you may not be able to keep your husband. Are you crying?"

"I can't help it."

I felt her move closer. She put her arm around me. "I know. All that pain—most of it comes from trying to avoid it. The tyranny of wanting things. Poor Lee, you want this so badly."

"What is that, Buddhism?"

She hugged me. "Yes, as a matter of fact. Sorry."

"I don't mind it. Don't mix me up with Emma." She laughed. I blew my nose. "I know I'm . . . what's the word? Not *obsessed*."

Isabel raised her eyebrows.

"I'm *not*. I'm . . . *consumed*, that's it. I know I'm consumed by our infertility, and that's not fair to Henry. We must've had problems before now, but I can't even remember what they were. He says I blame everything that's wrong between us, everything that's wrong with my whole *life*, on the fact that we can't have children. It's true. I know—I know I'm driving him away, but—"

Isabel leaned against me while I cried some more. What finally made me stop, once and for all, was realizing how badly I wanted to lay my head down in her lap and let her hold me. In fact, I almost did it. My only excuse is that it was the lowest point on one of the most miserable nights of my life, and that Isabel had always been there for me, as caring and tenderhearted as a mother.

But now it was different. She was going to recover eventually, I was sure of that, but for the time being her problems made mine look embarrassingly small. I sat up straight. "I feel much better. Thanks for listening to all that. Let's go in the kitchen, I'll do the dishes while you tell me how *you're* doing." She protested, but I won by ignoring her. "That's new," I said casually as we stood up.

"This? Kirby got it for me." She smiled, running her fingers over the curved brass head of the cane, which was shaped like—something; a horse? "The dragon," she said. "It's a symbol of hope."

"Oh." Did that mean she didn't need it? Or she needed it for luck, but not to walk? I was afraid to ask.

She never did tell me how she was doing, not really. She said the new drug didn't have as many side effects as the old ones, which surprised me. Because she didn't look well. Beautiful, but not well. "I'm just tired," she said, sponging crumbs off the counter into the sink. "I feel like I could sleep for a week."

"How's school going?"

"All right," she answered after a pause. She sounded vague.

"Really? Still taking a full course load?"

She found a spot on the counter that needed scouring and didn't answer.

"Isabel?"

She can't lie. She can evade, but she can't lie. "I've had to drop a few credits. It was a little too much. I'll make them up next summer."

"But you're still enrolled, you haven't—"

"Oh, yes," she said positively. "I'm working hard and really enjoying this semester. Some great courses. I've got a paper due tomorrow, in fact, in Society and Aging."

"Oh, *no*. Is it finished?"

"Just about. I've still—"

"Why didn't you tell me? Oh, Isabel!"

"What? Oh, don't be silly." She followed me into the living room, laughing. "What are you doing, running away?"

"First I drive Kirby out before he's finished eating his dinner—where's my coat, did he hang it up?"

"Lee, you don't have to go."

"Then I go on for half an hour about my problems and you don't get a word in, and then—"

"I got a few words in."

"The only good thing I did was the dishes."

"Don't go, you don't have to. All I have left to do is the footnotes."

I kissed her. She felt different, brittle or something, I was afraid to hug her very hard. "Tell Kirby I'm sorry." She made a face. "I'll call you tomorrow. Thanks for everything. I mean it."

"Be careful driving."

"Bye."

"Good night, Lee."

I was all the way to the elevator, in fact I'd already pressed the button, when I remembered. I hurried back to Isabel's apartment.

She opened the door. "Hi, long time no see," I joked. "Can I do one more thing?"

"Sure." She stood back to let me in. "What?"

"Call Henry. Tell him I'm coming home."

22

Rudy

Eric's office is on Carolina Avenue in Capitol Hill, catty-corner to Eastern Market. I can walk there from my house, and usually I do, but today I was driving. And late. I know—as usual. I found a parking place that might or might not have been legal, and raced through the cold rain, not even stopping to open my umbrella. The building is an old red brick town house converted to offices, and Eric's is on the top floor. I dashed right in, didn't stop in the waiting room to take off my coat, which was dripping wet.

"Sorry, sorry, the traffic, you wouldn't believe, plus no place to park, plus I was late anyway. Can I put this here?" Eric said yes, and I slung my coat over the radiator. "So, I'm here. At last."

I flopped down in the big black lounge chair across from his identical big black lounge chair. Our vantages were the same, except that my chair sat next to the little table holding the always-full box of Kleenex. "How are you?"

"I'm great. And you?"

He always says that. With a searching smile that makes you think he means it, he's really great, but he'd rather talk about you than himself. An excellent quality in a psychotherapist. I know amazingly little about Eric, considering I've been seeing him once a week, more during emergencies, for the last seven years. He's forty-six, and he lives with a slightly older woman, that much I know. Lately it's been tense around his house. He let that slip a couple of weeks ago, and it fascinated me. Out of all proportion. It was as if I'd finally located the whereabouts of my birth parent or something—it felt like I'd found out an important fact I'd never expected to, or I'd given up on.

"Well, I'm great, too," I said, "and how often do you hear me say *that*? I've just come from Emma's, and that was pretty grim, but I *still* feel great."

Eric shook his head wonderingly. "Something in the water?"

"Must be."

"So what's wrong with Emma?"

"Well, that's the other reason I'm late. She sort of let her hair down, something she hasn't done in a long time. With me, anyway."

Eric made his *Go on* face.

"Remember I told you she was in love with a married man?" That was all I'd said, though; I don't tell Emma's secrets. Well—once, to Curtis, just the bare fact that she liked Mick, but no details. And even that was an accident. Alcohol-related. "Well," I said to Eric, "nothing came of it, and I thought she was over him. Which was really deaf and blind of me, I see in retrospect."

"She's not?"

"No, she's just miserable. She isn't seeing anybody, and that's unusual in itself—there's always a man around somewhere with Emma. She's not writing. All she does is stay home. I told her she was in mourning, and she said of course, she knew that. She was so open about it, not hiding anything, which is also unusual. I think her only strategy is waiting, you know, lying low until she gets better. She's gone to ground, and that's definitely not her usual coping mechanism with men, not at all. She says men are like dogs, as soon as one dies, you should go out and buy a puppy."

"Ha."

"So while I was driving over here I was thinking how much safer Emma's way is—staying home and grieving by herself—than, well, say, some of the ways I've used to get out of depressions."

"Maybe her depressions aren't like yours."

"I know, but . . ." Well, that was obvious—mine are chronic, Emma's are acute. Mine are clinical, hers are—whatever. But that cheered me up, what Eric had said. I told him so.

"How come?" he asked.

"Well, because . . . I beat myself up a lot about making the wrong choices, doing crazy things. But everybody starts in a different place, and if you consider where I started . . ."

"What? Go ahead and say it."

"Okay." I took a breath. "I'm doing pretty well."

He beamed. "Very good, Rudy. Very, very good."

He looked so pleased, I thought of something else good to tell him. "Guess who got an A-minus on her planning midterm."

"Hey!"

"We had to design an urban backyard, only fifteen hundred square feet, with all the plantings and pavings, privacy screens, seating, terracing. I even designed a little fountain for mine. Anyway, I aced it."

"That's terrific."

"It was hard, too, I'm finding all the courses hard. But I love it, and I'm so happy I'm doing it. Thank you, Eric."

"For what?"

"Helping me get up the nerve." He opened his mouth to deny it—he always does—so I kept talking. "You did help me, and so did Emma, by nagging. Isabel, too, but in a different way. She never said anything, but I knew she thought I could do it. Not should do it, but could. She had faith. I didn't want to disappoint her—not that I would, not that she'd ever be disappointed in me, exactly, but—I just wanted to make her glad for me. I wanted to make her happy."

Eric nodded in understanding. "How is she?"

"Oh . . ." I sighed. "It's hard to say. She's evasive. She always says she's feeling better, but she doesn't look well. I've heard that you can gain weight on chemotherapy, but she's losing. I think she might even be on some steroid, but she keeps getting thinner. It's alarming. She says it's her new diet, but I don't know, no one knows. Kirby might, but we don't. We Graces."

"Does that bother you?"

"What?"

"That she tells Kirby more than she tells you?"

"No, not me. It probably bothers Emma a little. Lee, definitely, but she's closer to Isabel than Emma and I are."

Eric raised his eyebrows.

"In a way. Not in all ways. It's kind of complicated. Anyway—" There's a clock on the wall over Eric's head; he keeps it there so clients can see it and pace themselves. It said I was over halfway through my session and I hadn't even told him the main thing.

"Anyway—here's what I really wanted to tell you. I think, I'm pretty sure, I'm going to confront Curtis and make him talk about our relationship." I laughed, I even clapped my hands at his expression. "I know, it's amazing, I'm amazed, too! Where's all this gumption coming from? Is it the drugs?"

"What drugs?"

"I mean the new antidepressant. That's the only drug I'm taking."

"I should hope so. But you said drugs."

"Force of habit."

We laughed.

"Well, Rudy," he said, "this is very interesting. What do you think you'll say? Do you want to do some role-playing?"

"Umm . . . No, I don't think so." I could never tell him, but whenever we role-play and Eric tries to be Curtis, it's all I can do not to laugh. "I'm going to start by telling him I love him, which I do. You know, basically. But that I think some things haven't always been so healthy between us. And that there are some patterns I'd like to see us start working to break out of."

Eric waited.

"Such as my needing his approval so much. His controlling me with his approval. Or disapproval. His possessiveness. My allowing him to be possessive—liking it, even."

Eric stroked his chin; he looked mesmerized.

"I'm going to tell him there are some things we do together that I don't think are good for us. Mutual arrangements. A symbiotic relationship, you could say." Emma says that's not as clichéd as codependent. "And . . ."

"And?"

"I'm going to tell him I want joint counseling. With anyone he wants, which probably means not you."

He nodded readily.

"I wish it could be you. But Curtis won't, I can tell you right now—in fact, he won't want anybody, but I'm going to insist."

I stopped, so we could both listen to the sound of that. *Insist*.

"Well?" I said. "What do you think?"

"I'm very pleased," he said, and I squeezed my hands together between my knees, so glad. "This is an excellent, excellent step."

"I know. I'm very hopeful. He's been so good about the landscaping. Well, in the sense that he didn't forbid it or anything. He's not happy about it, of course. I think—" I sat back, deflated. "I think he thinks I'll bomb out, so why bother making a big deal of it. Oh, God, Eric, am I making a mistake?"

"Rudy."

"I know, but what if it makes things worse? What if I tell him all this and he . . ."

"What? What's the worst that can happen? That he'll get angry with you?"

"No. I'm used to that."

"What, then?"

"That he won't love me?" I said fearfully. "Is that the worst?"

"You tell me."

"I don't know! Oh, God." I scrubbed my face, sat up straight.

"But I'm doing it, I'm doing it anyway. Tonight. Maybe." A little thrill of fear made my scalp prickle, but it wasn't debilitating; if anything, it was invigorating. "I'm doing it," I repeated. Talking myself into it.

"Good," Eric said. "It's the right decision. Call me tomorrow, if you like. I'll be thinking about you."

I wanted to make Curtis his favorite dinner, but we were out of veal. Instead I made lamb chops with a peppercorn crust, which he likes almost as well. I felt like the mother on *Father Knows Best*, buttering up the patriarch before she asks him if they can buy a new living room suite or something. I suppose I demean myself with these tricks, but we all do what we have to do. If fixing Curtis lamb chops made me look foolish, I could live with the embarrassment.

I don't know if it was the dinner, but by the time we ate he was in a fairly good mood. A little quiet, but that's not unusual. We ate in the kitchen—he likes to keep half an eye on C-SPAN (with the sound off) while he eats, and I don't mind much anymore. I've gotten used to it.

I was bursting to tell him about the grade I got on my midterm, but I kept it to myself. The method I'm using to make the landscaping course palatable to him involves keeping it out of his sight and hearing as much as possible. I'm always here when he gets home, I never study in front of him, never talk about the course or my teachers, my grades, the people I'm meeting in class. I especially never talk about where it all might be leading, what sort of job I might get when I've earned my certificate.

It's not easy living in two completely separate worlds. But so far it's working, and you can't argue with success.

After dinner, Curtis got his briefcase and carried it into the living room. A good sign. He'd work there while I did the dishes. Some evenings he works upstairs in his office, and then he's off limits, not to be disturbed. Working in the living room meant he was available; he was still in my world.

I came close to pouring myself another glass of wine. It was so tempting—but, no. It was normal to be nervous at a time like this. I would be much better off with a clear head than a glib tongue.

I brought him coffee in a special cup, one I made a few years ago as part of a tea service. I'd used a pale celadon glaze, trying to match with color the airiness and delicacy of the pieces. Really, I was getting pretty good at potting before I gave it up. I still keep my best pieces in the living room, in a little display that both cheers me up and makes me sad when I look at it. It reminds me that I had talent, and that I can't seem to stick to anything.

Maybe, I thought, handing Curtis his pretty cup, I'd take up potting again one of these days. Maybe, if he knew what it meant to me because I *told* him, he wouldn't mind the night classes, or complain about my wheel crowding out his exercise equipment in the basement. Maybe this conversation we were about to have would mark the beginning of a lot of new things.

Curtis said, "Is this decaf?" without even looking at his cup.

I sat down beside him. "Of course."

He took a sip and smiled at me. "How was your day?"

"Fine. Curtis?"

"Hm?"

Deep breath. "We have to talk."

"Oh, no. The four most dreaded words in English," he teased. "What about?"

"Us."

He turned away to set the cup down, and when he turned back, his face was set and cold. "As you can see, I'm a little busy right now."

"I know, but this is important."

"So is this."

"Curtis." I got up and moved to the chair on the other side of the fireplace. Distance and objectivity. I'd forgotten my speech, though. Already this was going badly.

"First of all, you know I love you. That's the main thing—that we love each other. But we have some habits, don't you think, some ways of behaving toward each other that aren't always so—helpful. I just feel we've let ourselves fall into some patterns that don't always work well."

He stood up. He'd taken off his jacket; he looked so tall and handsome in his vest and shirtsleeves, his polka-dotted tie loose. But he rubbed his forehead with both hands in an odd way, as if he were confused or in pain. "Rudy. Please."

"What?"

"I'm not feeling very well."

"You aren't? You were fine about two seconds ago."

I was afraid that would make him mad. He didn't say anything, though. He went a few steps to the mantel and leaned his folded arms against it, keeping his face turned away from me.

I started again. "I just feel we need to discuss some things about our relationship. Any marriage can get—any couple can—just because it's easier, pretty soon you don't even think about what you're doing, and years go by and you realize—" I closed my eyes and did a breathing exercise. "I feel—I want—I'd like us to make some changes. Maybe. Or talk about it, at least. Curtis, are you listening?"

"Rudy, not now." Even his voice sounded strange.

"What's wrong?"

"Nothing."

"Are you really sick?"

"No, I just can't . . ."

I got up and went closer to him. Now or never. "I was thinking about couples counseling," I said in a rush. "It might be just the thing for us. Get us talking, you know? I really think it might be good for us."

I touched his back. He felt hot, damp. "Curtis?" I tried to see his face, but he kept turning. Finally I caught sight of him in the mirror over the mantel. "What's wrong?" To my horror, his knees buckled before he caught himself. I threw my arms around his waist.

"I'm all right." He stood up straight, pulling away. "I'm fine." He made his way to the couch and sat down carefully, turning off the lamp on the side table.

I sank down beside him, tried to take his hand. What was this? He still wouldn't let me look at him.

I saw a tear on his cheek before he could dash it away—it stopped my heart.

"What is it?" I whispered, terrified. "What's happening?"

"I don't want to tell you." His voice was choked, as if his throat hurt. "Don't want you to know."

"Is it something terrible?" He nodded. "Don't tell me." I put my hands over my ears. My skin felt like it was shriveling and puckering, pulling in like a leaf in a freeze.

He didn't move, he sat with his shoulders hunched, his profile pale and frightened.

"All right," I said. "Tell me."

"I might be dying."

I laughed.

"I've known it since Tuesday."

"Stop it. What? Stop it, I don't like that. What are you saying?" He looked me full in the face. "Curtis!" I screamed it, and he folded me up in his arms.

He shook and trembled, holding me tight. "My last checkup. I told Dr. Slater I was tired, that's all. A little dizziness sometimes, some pain in my stomach."

"No, no—you didn't say anything—this didn't happen." My teeth began to chatter.

"I didn't think it was anything. Flu—I thought it was flu. I almost didn't even tell him. But—he ordered tests, and the blood test came back with too many leukocytes. Rudy—I've got CLL. Leukemia."

"No, it's a mistake. Who told you? This is not true."

"It's not a mistake." His eyes were swimming. "They're good doctors, Rudy, they're the best."

"Where?"

"Georgetown."

"Oh, God."

"Don't cry. I'm sorry. This is why I didn't tell you. You've already got Isabel to worry about, I didn't want to add this."

Through a glaze of tears, I saw his strained, anxious face—worried for *me*, solicitous of *me*. I was crushing handfuls of his shirt, kneading his shoulders, unable to reconcile the thing he was telling me with the tough, alive feel of him.

"I don't have any other symptoms yet," he said steadily, keeping my gaze, not letting go of me. "That's a good thing—it means it might be progressing slowly. I could live for years and years and not even need treatment. Or—not. They can't say yet. It's too early to tell how it'll go in my case."

"No, no, no, no, no—"

He pulled me close and rubbed my back, told me it was all right. It wasn't all right, it was an avalanche, the ceiling falling on me, rubble and dust and chunks of plaster cutting off the air, covering me, heavy blows to my head, my back. I could hardly understand what he was saying, he sounded so muffled and far away.

"We can't tell anyone yet, Rudy. If they found out at work, I could lose my job. We can't afford that, not until it's unavoidable."

"Not tell anyone?" I tried to concentrate on that. Not tell anyone? "That's crazy. Isn't it?"

"I know, but that's how it works. And anyway, I couldn't function if anyone knew. Anyone but you—not my family, not yours, not your friends. Greenburg."

"Oh, but—"

"Promise me you won't tell them."

"What?"

"Please, Rudy. I just—I couldn't take it yet. Can't you understand? I couldn't possibly talk about this with anyone but you. Promise. It's important to me."

"All right." Oh my God, oh my God.

He held me again. "We'll fight together, darling. We'll be strong together."

"Yes."

"Us against the world, Rudy. The way it used to be."

I didn't know what he meant. When? When we first fell in love? Those days in Durham when we didn't care about anything but each other, no one else existed. It's true that was the best, the safest time. We've been trying to get back to it ever since. And now we have.

He wanted to make love. I wanted to die. I let him do everything he wanted, and he wanted it right there, in front of the cold hearth with our clothes half on, half off—he likes it that way sometimes, he thinks it's wanton. I couldn't feel anything except fear and cold, as if a ghost was penetrating me. Nothing was real. Curtis could not be dying. What is leukemia, how does it kill you? *Not real, not real*, I thought all the while he moved over me, not minding my passivity, accepting it without a question.

We lay on the prickly rug afterward, and I pretended it was a dream, I'd wake up soon and say, "Curtis, I dreamed you were dying—oh, it was awful, what a nightmare!" I turned to look at his peaceful face, his eyes closed, mouth relaxed. He looked different to me—less defined, insubstantial. Where was his solidity? His skin, his fingernails, the hair on his forearm, everything looked vulnerable and impermanent and tender. But he was smiling slightly, eyelashes fluttering. I had helped to put that smile there, I thought. That would be my job from now on. I wouldn't think about anything but that.

We went upstairs together. While he showered, I thought of calling Emma. I almost did—I had the phone in my hand. Did my promise count? How could I not tell her? How could I not tell Eric!

But I hung up and didn't call anyone. It's hard to explain why. In a way, I've betrayed Curtis for the whole of our marriage. He's a private man, intensely private, and at one time or another I've told secrets of his to everybody I love.

I won't now. This is happening to him, not me. If keeping it a secret makes it easier for him to bear, then how could I not be his accomplice?

"We'll get through this," he told me in bed, holding my hand under the covers. "You can't know how much better I feel now that I've told you. The last few days have been the hardest of my life."

"Darling," was all I could say.

"Maybe I shouldn't have told you. Maybe it was selfish."

"Oh, no."

"But I couldn't help it. I started to feel dizzy, I was even afraid I might faint. So then there was nothing else I could do but tell you. It's nothing to worry about, the faintness, by the way. They told me there might be episodes like that from time to time. Night sweats, too. Fever."

I pressed my face against his shoulder.

"And, Rudy?"

"Yes."

He switched off the bedside lamp. "I just want you to know. I asked them about secondhand smoke, and they said no, probably not."

"What do you mean?"

"I couldn't understand why this had happened to me. I tried to think of anyone in my family—but there's no one. So—no genetic predisposition."

"Secondhand smoke?"

"It's all I could think of. But they said the chances that that had caused it were very slim. Almost nothing, in fact. So that's one thing you don't have to worry about."

He settled the covers over us, making me turn away from him.

He put his heavy arm across my waist, his hand on my breast. "I'll sleep well tonight," he said against my hair. "Thank you, Rudy. I love you, darling."

"I love you, Curtis."

He fell asleep in no time.

I lay still, waiting until he began to snore before I crept out of bed and tiptoed into the bathroom. I had a nearly full bottle of Noludar, because I hadn't taken any in months. I shook out four and swallowed them with tap water. Four was safe, since I wasn't drinking. Yet. All sorts of bad habits were smiling at me, though, waving, dying to get reacquainted. It was hard to know where to begin.

23

Isabel

In late November, Terry came to see me. It was a short visit, only Friday to Sunday, and I had to share him a bit with his father. Gary picked him up at the airport and brought him straight to my apartment on Friday afternoon. My nerves were in knots. I'd been cleaning my three rooms and bath for days, planning meals, vacillating over what to wear. I hadn't seen Terry in nearly two years.

Father and son hid identical expressions of dismay when I opened the door. Terry embraced me stiffly, as if afraid I would break. Gary couldn't stay, had to go, good to see you, you're looking fine, Isabel, he lied. I barely glanced at him; he'd put on weight and lost some hair—that's all I noticed. It was Terry, twenty-seven years old and a man now, not a boy, that I couldn't stop touching, looking at, marveling over.

"You've gotten better-looking," I said, mixing tuna salad for a sandwich while he prowled around the kitchen, making the room seem even smaller in a way Kirby never did. He was nervous, too, I realized; he had the same apprehensions about this visit that I did. "No, it's true," I insisted when he made a face. "Your hair's darker. You've gotten taller."

"Mom, I couldn't have."

"You did. Your eyes look more like Gary's, too. Your father has beautiful eyes." But I could see my father's sternness in Terry's straight, narrow-lipped mouth, and that worried me. I wanted to tell him to bend more, flex more, life doesn't have to be such a struggle.

I sat across from him and watched him eat. "Didn't they feed you on the airplane?"

"Sure. What time's dinner?"

We laughed as we settled into the agreeable fiction that we were still mother and son, that we knew each other intimately enough to joke and mock and hector one another at the kitchen table. But in truth, a scrupulous kind of courtesy had sprung up between Terry and me years ago. Time and distance have only nurtured it, and now we behave like cordial, respectful strangers—like the mother in the host family and the polite foreign exchange student.

But maybe we could foil it this time, break out of our pattern. If ever there were a time, certainly this would be it.

"How's school, Mom?"

"Oh, it's wonderful, I love it. I've been taking a little time off just lately, but I plan to start back in January."

"Time off?"

I hadn't wanted to get into this so soon. "The chemo blindsided me a little bit," I said, shrugging. "I had to miss some assignments. So I decided it was better to back off for a while than risk bad grades."

I couldn't tell him what a blow it had been when I'd realized I couldn't take my finals. School meant everything to me, and not just because it held the key to my working future. It represented normalcy, wellness. The routine of classes, the hard hours of studying, the process of going and coming, adhering to a schedule—all that had given my days shape and structure when cancer was working so hard to turn them into chaos.

"What kind of drugs have they got you on now?"

Oh hell. But maybe it was better to get it all out of the way now and not have to talk about it again. My illness is like a noxious, uninvited guest, too unpleasant to ignore. But Terry always wanted to discuss strategies, protocols, percentages, and I had so many other things to say to him.

"I'm not taking anything at the moment."

"What do you mean? Nothing at all?"

"We're on a break."

"But, Mom—"

"It's all right, the doctor doesn't disapprove. I've been taking chemotherapy for the last eleven months, Terry. We thought my body could use a rest."

"Yes, but . . ." He stopped protesting, suddenly diffident. Becoming my medical advisor at this late date probably struck him as out of line.

"I know it doesn't sit well with you. You're a scientist, why should it?" His specialty is enzyme molecules and substrates, but he understands the significance of a breast cancer metastasis to bone. "You'll be even sorrier to hear that I'm about ready to renounce the medical model altogether."

"In favor of what, crystals?" He laughed—I laughed with him. It was better if he thought I was joking.

"I think I'll try to heal myself. You know, *heal* and *cure* aren't quite the same thing," I said, and he smiled, thinking he was humoring me.

Kirby arrived in time for dinner, according to plan. One of my many worries was what Terry would think of him. Well—and what he would think of the fact that his very ill mother had a lover. I watched them all night like a spy. Kirby has an odd way of behaving in company as if he's alone. At first it's off-putting, then appealing. To most people. But I fretted that Terry would find him aloof instead of self-contained, might take his reticent silences for coldness, even arrogance. I shouldn't have worried. Kirby worked his low-key spell slowly but surely, and by the end of the evening Terry even got his jokes, which are dryer than chalk dust, dryer than hot desert sand.

Sleeping arrangements were something else I'd stewed over at length. My couch is comfortable but short, and it doesn't fold out. Terry's over six feet tall. How sensible to offer him Kirby's room upstairs, a whole apartment to himself, while Kirby slept where he always does: with me.

How sensible—but I couldn't manage it. It would have violated a principle that's as old-fashioned as it is deep-rooted, a code I won't defend and don't even particularly approve of, yet I'm stuck with it. Call it a product of my upbringing. And don't think I'm blind to the charge of hypocrisy in this. In self-defense, I could say that that was part of my upbringing, too. In any event, Terry slept on the couch and Kirby slept upstairs in his own bed.

On Saturday Terry and I went for a ride in Kirby's car. He wanted to see the old neighborhood, the high school, his favorite hangouts. "The Hot Shoppe is *gone*?" He couldn't believe it. "Where's People's? Where's the Bank of Bethesda? When did everything get so swanky?" A long time ago, I could have told him. He'd been away for almost ten years, but his clearest memories were much older. "No wonder you moved out, Mom. You'd have to be stinking rich to live here now."

He pointed out landmarks to me. "That's where you taught me to drive"—the parking lot of the Catholic church on East-West Highway. "Dad tried it one time. One time only. Remember?"

"Vividly. He came home looking like a zombie. I thought he was having a coronary."

"How come you were so calm?"

"Drugs. Rudy used to give me Quaaludes."

"Really?"

"No." I laughed. "Anyway, you were a good driver."

"Dad didn't think so. There's the Domsetts' house. Do they still live there?"

"I don't know, I guess so."

"I used to mow their lawn. I'd always try to collect from her, not him, because she tipped better. Remember when I used to run away from home? You'd pack Fig Newtons for me."

"You wanted them in a bandanna tied to a stick—you'd seen that in a comic book."

"You said it was okay to run away as long as I didn't cross any streets. You'd kiss me good-bye, and I'd walk around and around the block till I got tired, and then I'd come home."

He told me a new, horrifying story about getting drunk on prom night and drag racing with his friend Kevin on Old Georgetown Road. "I could have lived the rest of my life without knowing that," I said. He told me about Sharon Waxman, a girl in his high school home room who committed suicide last year. He asked me if I'd liked being a stay-at-home mom.

I looked at him curiously. He looked like a man, not a boy, maneuvering Kirby's old sedan through the Saturday traffic with care and competence. "Yes, I liked it," I said. "Usually. Did you think it was old-fashioned of me not to have a job?"

"No," he said, sounding surprised. "Anyway, you were always doing something. It's not like you were eating bonbons and watching the soaps. You made the home," he said seriously. "You were the home maker."

I felt ridiculously flattered.

"I guess you weren't that fulfilled, though. Going back to school for your master's now. I guess you wish you'd done that sooner."

This was a new kind of conversation we were having. It happens to most of us eventually, the moment when our parents become real people, with motives and hopes as authentic as our own—but I couldn't help ruing the fact that it was the nature of my situation that had accelerated this adult revelation in Terry. "Yes, in some ways," I answered him truthfully. "It would've been nice to feel more independent. Less reliant on your father. As I'm sure he would agree."

The unspoken subject of Gary hung between us. If Terry had asked me about the divorce then, I would have told him anything he wanted to know. But it had to start with him. When it didn't, the moment passed, and I wasn't sorry.

In the afternoon, Terry visited with his father, then played basketball with old friends from high school. They went to a bar afterward, and he came home late for dinner in high spirits.

"You haven't said a word about Susan," I mentioned over coffee in the living room.

"Nothing to talk about." He lifted his arms over his head, stretching sore muscles. "We've broken up."

"Oh, Terry, no."

"It's okay, Mom. It was mutual."

Mutual, maybe, but obviously it wasn't okay. I still knew all my son's diversionary tactics, the body stretches, the fake yawn, the casual-looking avoidance of my eyes.

"What happened? If I may ask."

"Nothing happened, it just wasn't working out. We had different expectations."

"What were hers?" I asked.

"Oh, the usual. You know, marriage, children."

"Aha. Do you still love her?"

"I don't know, Mom. I guess." He looked surprised by my audacious question. How forthright I am these days. It saves a lot of time, and time doesn't tick past for me in the same rhythm it used to. "It's complicated," he said. "We're still friends."

I waited, but that was all he wanted to say. And somewhere along the way in the last ten years, I've lost the right to pry. But I didn't care for that cynical note in his voice when he said, "Oh, the usual." Most parents feel guilty for every inch their children fall short of perfection, and I'm no exception. Terry's disinterest in the conventional family ("marriage, children") was a failing I feared he could lay directly at my door, mine and Gary's. The subject I'd ducked in the car this afternoon hovered again. But Terry yawned, lay down on the floor, and promptly fell asleep.

I woke him at ten o'clock and helped him make his bed on the sofa. I kissed him good night in a muted panic, and lay awake while the clock marked off the hours of our dwindling time together. I can't bear to acknowledge the most likely result of my situation to the people I love. It's too hurtful; I don't have the courage or the will to inflict such pain. But on Terry's last day, with so much left unsaid between us, I couldn't avoid it any longer.

Kirby and I were to drive him to the airport. I sat on the edge of the couch while Terry crammed dirty clothes into his canvas duffle. He knelt on the floor in his faded jeans, the sleeves of his yellow sweater pushed up to the elbows. Unthinkingly, I reached out and brushed the hair back from his forehead. He grinned at me and went back to his work, but in that second, with his head cocked, eyes merry, he looked so much like himself as a baby and then a boy—the Terry I remember best—my heart twisted.

"I wish you had a brother or a sister, Terry. Sometimes," I added dryly, "I wish I did, too."

"What do you mean? You've got Aunt Patty."

"As I say."

"Oh," he said, grinning. "Yeah, I guess you two aren't that close."

"No, we're not. There's the age difference, of course, but that's not all. I wasn't close to my parents, either. Our house was so cold. Strict. Because of my father, mostly, but my mother was a very closed-up person, too. I never wanted that for my own family. One reason I married your father was because of his passion." Terry looked up, interested. "He's an emotional man. Especially when we were younger. Lots of fire and warmth."

"I guess," he said uncertainly, thinking it over.

"But things didn't work out the way they were supposed to. I blamed everything on Gary when we separated, but it wasn't all his fault. Not by any means." I leaned toward him, intent on getting this right. "If we drove you away, Terry, it was the last thing I wanted. Nothing was ever your fault—do you know that? You were the best thing in my life. I'm sorry if I didn't show you how much I loved you. I did love you. I do. As much as I've ever loved anyone, as much as I can. It feels like a lot—it takes up my whole heart. But if it doesn't feel that way to you, I'm so sorry."

I hadn't seen my son cry since he was twelve. He put his head in my lap to hide his face. His shoulders shook; I could feel his tears through the knees of my jeans. "Oh, it's all right," I told him, stroking his hair, stealing a kiss. I hoped he wasn't ashamed. "It's good to cry, I've found out. Definitely not something to be avoided at all costs. It shows you feel something, that's all."

I brushed Terry's tears away and smiled at him. It was easier to talk now, as easy as talking to my little boy.

"I've never told you what broke up your father and me. You haven't really told me what separated you and Susan. The details don't matter. But, Terry, be sure you have good reasons. Not having perfect happiness—that might not be good enough. Do you love her? Life is so short. It looks endless when you're twenty-seven, I know, but . . ."

I hated to preach, but I'd waited too long and now I had things to tell him.

"Never throw love away, never neglect it. Never assume you'll find better love somewhere else. Take it wherever you're lucky enough to find it, and always try to return it in kind." I pressed my lips to his forehead. "Don't take so much for granted," I whispered. "That's my final bit of wisdom, and it's the most important."

Kirby, as I've said before, has wonderful timing. He chose that moment to give one knock at the front door and walk in. Terry didn't start guiltily or turn away in embarrassment; he dug a handkerchief out of his pocket and blotted his face, blew his nose manfully.

"Ready?" Kirby asked with suitable blandness. "It's just about time to go."

We stood up. Terry shrugged into his jacket, hefted his duffel onto his strong shoulder. "You know," I said, "I've decided not to go with you two after all. I think I'll just say good-bye here."

Terry looked stricken, but he didn't argue. "I'll call you when I get home tonight," he promised, holding me tight. "And I'll come back, Mom, as soon as I can. Or you could come see me—how would that be? Maybe for Christmas."

"That's an idea," I said, entering into the conspiracy gladly. "Take care of yourself in the meantime."

"You, too. You take good care of her, Kirby."

"I will."

"I love you," I whispered, kissing his damp cheek.

"I love you. I love you, Mom." He couldn't break the thread.

I swallowed hard and gave a little sniff that pulled my tears back inside. "Better hurry, you don't want to miss your plane."

"I'll call you," he said again, following Kirby to the elevator. It came almost immediately. "And I'll write more often! I will, Mom."

I smiled and blew kisses until the doors closed.

And then I was so tired, I couldn't make it to the bedroom. I collapsed on the sofa and covered myself with the afghan. Old, smelly-fragrant, holey afghan I knitted myself, years and years ago when I was unashamedly a housewife. Homemaker, as Terry said. There had been many, many happy times in those days that, for no good reason, I had fallen into the habit of dismissing. Nostalgia drifted over me like a pleasant fog, numbing a little the exquisite pain of Terry's leaving. Gary used to take a nap on Sunday afternoons under this blanket. I'd sit with him, reading or knitting with the radio on low, looking up to see his paunchy stomach rise and fall under the then-bright squares of wool. I used to wrap it around my nightgown and run outside for the newspaper. Terry liked to drape it over two dining room chairs and pretend he was a soldier in a fort.

Was Gary home now? I could call him. Just to talk. "Hi, how are you? What do you think of our son? After all, we didn't do so badly, did we?" But the phone was too far away, I was too tired to get up. I closed my eyes and drifted into a dream. A sweet, bright dream about a family. I gave it the happiest ending.

24

Emma

My birthday is three days after Christmas, which makes me a Capricorn. The goat. How unamusingly apt, but never more so than this year.

I often go away for Christmas, drive down to Danville to see my mother, and sometimes I keep going, drive on to Durham and Chapel Hill to visit old friends from grad school, spend New Year's with them. This year, even the thought of packing made me nauseated, never mind leaving, arriving, greeting, smiling, and talking. Especially smiling and talking; those were by far the most retch-inducing. So I stayed home.

It wasn't a pity party, though. No, no. I got fully dressed, called all my loved ones, I even roused myself to go out and take Isabel her present. No, I was saving myself, bathos-wise, for the twenty-eighth, when I could turn forty all by myself. Now we're talking heroic, orgiastic self-pity on the grand scale.

My solitude was by choice—my friends didn't desert me. In good conscience I couldn't inflict myself on them, and so I asked them to stay away. (Rudy was out of town anyway.) The day started out normally, i.e., full of frustration and self-loathing. That novel I started last spring? I threw it out in August. A mercy killing, believe me. It was what they call a coming-of-age novel. Preternaturally articulate adolescent learns about love, life, sex, and redemption among colorful characters in the New South/urban ghetto/Jewish upper-class/soul-stifling Midwest. I set mine in a nasty little town in southern Virginia named Tomstown. As I say, a mercy killing. So much for writing what you know.

Now I'm working on something entirely different (although "working on" may be a tiny euphemism). It's a mystery, a thriller, lots of intrigue and suspense, a woman-in-jeopardy deal, bodies piling up. I think it's got excellent best-seller and movie potential. Too bad it bites. One thing writing this story has taught me, though, is that I really enjoy killing people. I mean I really get off on it. So I keep doing it. The danger here is that all my characters could be dead before the book ends. It might turn out that God was the narrator.

The other thing this book is teaching me, it and its precious, hackneyed predecessor, is that I might be a fraud. All my life I wanted to write fiction, or at least so I've been saying for most of it. Nonfiction didn't satisfy; I wanted the story to go another way, the truth never got to what was really true, et cetera, blah blah. Well, guess what. Turns out I was a much better journalist than I am a novelist. So now I have to wonder if I was only drawn to the image of what it means to write fiction. I wanted to *look* like a novelist. I wanted to answer the "What do you do?" question at cocktail parties with "I write books."

If that's true, I don't know what I'll do. It feels like smashing into a glass door. I thought there was a vista, a future, but maybe there's just shock and embarrassment and bloody lacerations.

Happy birthday, Emma.

What I needed was a cake. An ice cream cake, one of those Viennetta or Violetta things they advertise on TV around the holidays. They always make my mouth water. I almost bought one once, then I read the fat/calorie blurb on the back. Well, fuck it, I'm forty years old, I can have any damn thing I want. Like wine. Wine and ice cream cake. A really good wine, too, not that eight-dollar Mondavi in the refrigerator.

Going outside and getting in my car felt like setting foot on a new planet. How long since I'd been out of the house? Almost four days. God. There's something to be said for a real job. Not much, but something. The low, late-afternoon December sky was that old-diaper shade of gray, heavy with either rain or snow, it couldn't decide. Until I parked on Columbia Road and started to walk the block and a half to the liquor store—then it decided. Sleet.

On Christmas Eve morning I put on some old black sweatpants, a black blouse, and my most comfortable sweater, a snarly, dung-colored cardigan with big pockets and one remaining leather button. I liked this outfit so well, I put it on the next day, too. And the next. And today. I hadn't washed my hair in a week—why bother?—and it goes without saying I hadn't put on any makeup. I'd left the house in a trenchcoat and my beaded bedroom moccasins, no socks. Got the picture?

Mick got it when he opened the door to the liquor store and we almost smacked into each other. He said, "Excuse me," and stood back—for two seconds he actually didn't recognize me. Later I couldn't decide if that was an insult or deeply flattering. Then he did a double take, probably humorous to an impartial observer, and stopped dead.

Me, too. "Mick, hi," I think I said, very casual. Inside, it felt like cardiac arrest. I think I went white, but his cheeks turned red, two streaks of bright color like slap marks. "How are you," I said, "how've you been." I was pressed back against the door frame, clutching a bagful of clanking wine bottles, and he was squeezed back on the other side, holding the glass door wide open with his outstretched arm.

"Emma." He couldn't even smile, he just looked at me with his burning eyes. His shock helped me get over mine. I was ready to say something bright, maybe even true—"I've missed you," something like that—when he jerked his head toward the street. "I've got my family."

Ah, yes, so he did. In the car; I recognized the small white Celica at the curb half a block away. Couldn't see the occupants, though, just their hazy outlines through the sleet and the streaky windshield.

"Well. Tell them I said hi. Really good to see you."

Neither of us moved.

"How are you, Emma?"

"Fine, I've been all right. You?"

I'm not that great a liar, but at least I try. Mick doesn't even try. "I'm terrible," he said.

I felt my face get hot. "Not fair," I whispered. "Damn you, that is no fair."

One customer and then another one, both wanting to use the door, put an end to the torture. We had to separate; I walked out and Mick walked in. We never said good-bye, but we waved to each other through the door. How inane. I thanked God my car was in the opposite direction from his, and I didn't wave to Sally. I slogged through the freezing rain with my wine bottles and went home.

That night when the phone rang, I knew it was Mick. You know how sometimes you can just tell who it is by the sound of the ring? I'd been sitting in front of the fire for so long, it had burned out. To my credit, I wasn't drunk; I'd had a glass or two of a very expensive Cabernet, and given up. Lack of interest.

I picked up the phone in the kitchen on the third ring and said, "Hello?" in a firm, deceptively healthy, clearheaded tone.

"Happy birthday."

"Thanks." It was Lee. I collapsed on a stool and waited for my heart rate to subside. "How are you?"

"Okay." Not that long ago she used to answer that question with, "I'm not pregnant," but she's stopped. Nobody's amused anymore, especially Lee. So far, in vitro isn't working. "How's your birthday going?" she asked.

"Lousy."

"Oh, no. Would you like to come over?"

"No, thanks."

"We're not doing anything. We're not even fighting. Come on, we'll cheer you up."

"No, but thank you, that's nice. Really. How're you doing?"

"Okay," she repeated. "Rudy's back from the Bahamas."

"Oh, yeah? Since when?"

"Today."

"Did she call you?"

"Yes."

Well, shit. Rudy won't say boo to me on my birthday, but she can call Lee to say she's back from her "second honeymoon"—honest to God, that's what she called it. "How did she sound?" I asked.

"The same as before."

"Which is to say . . ."

"Not very good. I think the only reason she called was to say she's not coming to dinner tomorrow. So it'll just be you, Isabel, and me."

Christ, we were falling apart, all four of us. "Did she say why?"

"Something about something she has to go to with Curtis."

I said some really vulgar swear words that made Lee hiss in her breath like a mongoose. I had to ask, "Does she talk to you? Lately? Is she telling you anything about what's going on with her?"

"No. So . . . she's not telling you, either?"

"No, and I know she's not talking to Isabel because I asked her."

We heaved simultaneous sighs.

"Well," Lee said dispiritedly. "See you tomorrow night, I guess. Don't forget to bring salad."

"When did I ever forget?"

"And you'll pick Isabel up?"

"Of course."

"Happy birthday, Em."

"Night, Lee."

We hung up.

Before I could get off my stool, the phone rang again.

"Hello?"

"Emma? It's Mick."

Everything receded, nothing left but my hand on the receiver and his voice in my ear. And I felt sick with wanting, with knowing it was him and this was real. I had come so close to convincing myself that this wasn't true—that he's the only one and I'll never be over him.

"May I see you?"

"Are you all right?"

"I'm fine." He laughed, a huff of breath. "Except that . . ."

I imagined I could hear, in his silences and his deep, frustrated breathing, everything he couldn't say. I pictured him in his house, probably in the kitchen, with Sally upstairs putting Jay to bed. "Are you at home?"

"No, I'm in my car. Sally's cell phone."

"Oh." So much for my intuition. "It's very clear."

Another exhalation of humorless laughter. "That's probably because I'm around the corner from your house."

"Oh, God."

He was quiet for a few awful seconds, then he said thickly, "It's okay, don't worry, I was driving and I just ended up here. I won't—"

"Give me five minutes."

"What's that?"

"I need five minutes. I have to—I'm not quite dressed. But then come."

"Are you sure?"

"Yes. Okay, I'm hanging up now."

He laughed, and it was a real laugh, not sad or forced. I waited until it was completely over, just reveled in it, and then I hung up.

Five minutes. I should've said ten. I raced upstairs to the bathroom and looked at myself in the mirror. I should've said an hour and a half.

Too late to shower or change clothes. Clean my house, buy a

new wardrobe. I took off my ratty sweater and brushed my wine-stained teeth. I tried to comb my hair, but that was impossible, so I piled it up in a bun. I put on mascara, a little lipstick. God, God. I'd keep the lights low.

Downstairs, there wasn't even time to rebuild the fire. I scooped up the newspapers strewn all over, straightened the sofa cushions, blew crumbs off the end tables. I put on music, then turned it off. Would he like my house? It wasn't very artistic. I had some pictures, some prints I liked a lot, but they were probably gauche. Oh God, now he'd find out, he'd see that I was cheap and fraudulent and shallow. What a stupid idea this was. I liked it better when we were a neat, clean tragedy. No potential, no messy reality. Then we were perfect.

The doorbell rang. My heart gave a dangerous leap—if this kept up I'd be dead by morning. Deep, cleansing breath. I put on a normal face and opened the door.

"Hi," we said. He brought in the cold and damp on his wool overcoat. His face was pinched, his ears livid. "Take off your coat," I said. When he gave it to me, I felt his icy hands. "You're freezing. Were you walking?"

"For a while." He moved into the living room, drawn to the hearth, but he stopped when he saw the fire was out.

"It burned down," I said idiotically. "Shall we sit here?"

He took the chair, I sat on the edge of the sofa. A mistake. How could we talk like this? Too weird—Mick and me in the living room, facing each other across my tony sisal carpet. We weren't ourselves, we were actors in a play.

"Would you like a drink? I happen to have a lot of wine."

"No, thank you."

"Coffee?"

"That would be great."

I jumped up. "Come with me."

Much better in the kitchen. He leaned against the counter,

watching me while I filled the kettle, measured the coffee, poured hot water over the grounds a little at a time. Very labor-intensive, the Chemex coffee system, very good for keeping the hands busy. "It's Jay's birthday today," he mentioned, to fill the industrious silence.

I looked up. "Is it really?" What a coincidence.

"He's six. I took the afternoon off for a little party he had at the zoo this afternoon. Only eight friends—that didn't seem like so many when we were planning it." He rubbed his forehead as if his head hurt. "Jesus."

"Oh, you're just trying to make excuses for being in the liquor store."

We laughed. It loosened the tension a little.

He began to pace in front of the black squares of the windows. I watched him out of the corner of my eye. He looked different—again. He had on gray slacks and a good sport coat, a loosened blue tie. He must dress like this, like a businessman, for his part-time job at his old law firm. If he still had it. The fact that I didn't even know, that there could be a hundred new things about his life I had no idea of, struck me as the saddest thing in the world.

"How is Isabel?" he asked, picking up and setting down the red rooster salt shaker. "And Rudy. Sally tells me about Lee sometimes, but I don't hear about the others anymore."

It's no wonder I love him. He wasn't filling silence, he really cared how my friends were doing, and not just because of me.

I poured coffee into mugs, added a lot of milk to his. "Isabel's very sick. I don't know what's going to happen."

"I'm sorry, Emma."

"Yeah." His sympathy almost did me in. I was really on some kind of an edge. I gave him his mug and reached for the cookie jar. "Want a tea biscuit? Rudy's no good, either. She's dropped out of school. Did you know she was studying landscape design?" He shook his head. "Well, she quit. God knows what she's doing now, I sure don't." I sounded so cold and careless.

He just said, "I'm sorry," again.

"Yeah, life sucks." I was on the verge of making an ass of myself by crying or something. "Why did you come here, Mick? Just to chat? Do you want to have an affair with me? But we already know exactly how that will turn out." I hated the tone of my voice. This was crazy—why was I being hateful to him?

"I can go—"

"No, don't, I'm sorry, don't go. I'm—you should know, it's only fair to tell you—I can be an awful bitch, Mick, when I'm—miserable."

"I don't want you to be miserable."

"Too late. Nothing you can do about it." Was there? Why *had* he come?

He set his cup down carefully. "I kept thinking I'd see you. I couldn't believe it when we never ran into each other. Months."

"I know. I *did* see you. On the street, or in a car passing by, on line at the movies. But it was never you." Just some fraud, a Mick look-alike. Sometimes they didn't even look like him; I'd only conjured him up out of some good-looking schlub's generic eyes, hair, mouth. A mirage.

"Then, today," he said.

"Yeah. A vision of loveliness." Oh, shut up, Emma.

"A vision of loveliness." He smiled, but he wasn't kidding, and my fatuous phrase didn't sound stupid when he said it. "It was like taking one drink," he said. "Smoking one cigarette. Readdicted."

Oh, God help me. I'm falling.

"I had to see you. Don't laugh at this. I thought—I had some idea that if we were together, just once, we could leave each other in peace afterward."

"Really." I nodded seriously, not disagreeing. It sounded specious in the extreme to me, if he was talking about what I thought he was talking about. But I wanted it too badly to point out the flaws.

"Just never seeing you again—" He touched the side of my

hand, which was gripping the edge of the counter. "It's worse than being together. It seems that way to me. Unnatural, Emma. More of a—sin."

"A sin." As an ex-Catholic, the word arrested me. "Is that what it would be to you? Sleeping with me would be a sin?"

He shook his head, smiling, helpless.

"Well, I don't care anymore. I don't care about your guilty conscience or your immortal soul, what do you think of that? And I don't care about your wife or your happy home or your—" I choked up, couldn't get it out. It snuck up on me from behind and pounced, all the reasons why this was the same bad idea it's always been. "Your son," I finished, trying to sound bold while I was losing my nerve.

He did the best thing—he put his arms around me and held me. I closed my eyes to block out the pain and doubt in his face. Words had never gotten us anywhere—they never do when the situation is untenable to begin with. I kissed him for a distraction, and it worked: everything melted in a slow dissolve, all but Mick's hot mouth and the whisker stubble on his cheeks and the feel of his hand on the back of my neck. We kissed until we were out of breath and groping, until it was stark sex, not for comfort, not to show we cared. I made a choice to let go, stop thinking, just do it. Maybe something would change if we let it happen, something we couldn't foresee. And it felt so natural, opening my legs so Mick could move between them and press me back, back, the sharp edge of the counter hard and bruising against my spine. I didn't care that it hurt, I wanted sensation, I wanted his hands all over me. "Upstairs," I muttered—I could have more of him if we were horizontal.

We took hands and went blindly down the hall, up the stairs, into the bedroom. I almost didn't turn on the light—afraid of his face again—but the blue, bitter moonlight chilled me. Craving warmth, I closed the curtain and turned on the bedside lamp.

We stood on opposite sides of my handsome, unmade sleigh

bed, watching each other. I was right to be wary of his face—he looked tragic. "What?" I said, and started to unbutton my blouse. Not terribly romantic, but one of us had to go first. Mick turned around and sat on the edge of the bed. But then—he didn't move, he didn't undo his belt or start to take off his shoes. I knew exactly what was going to happen.

I thought of screaming at him, making a scene, letting hot, humiliated fury take over from here—see how that went. I discarded the idea, but I was angry and hurt enough to want to hurt him. I didn't fasten my blouse when I came around the bed and stood in front of him. I have great breasts, twenty men have told me so, they're my best feature. So it was consoling to show them to Mick, gratifying to watch his eyes drop and darken. *See what you missed*, I thought spitefully, sticking them out a little.

He smiled. He looked at me with such tenderness and understanding, I started to cry.

"I'm such an ass," he said, taking my hand and tugging me down next to him. "I know it. You couldn't feel any more contempt for me right now than I do."

"I don't. I don't." But I had to whisper, "What happened?" Between the kitchen and the bedroom, what went wrong? Should we have done it on the counter?

"You know what happened. I've been telling lies."

"What did you tell me that was a lie?" I asked fearfully.

"That we could do this once."

"Oh. That lie. Did you think I believed you?"

He smiled, and we started at the same moment to kiss each other's hand. A little tug-of-war. I rested my head on his shoulder.

"So basically," I said dully, "nothing's changed. You just came here to torture me. Again. I was almost over you. No, I wasn't."

"I came because I . . ." His shoulder lifted and fell when he sighed. "Everything sounds stupid. I can say I couldn't resist. I can say I was sick of needing you, that I had to see you. I don't know if nothing's changed, Emma—something must have. I've been suffering enough for something to have changed."

"Me, too."

He faced me. "There haven't been any other women. You asked me that on the beach. There's only you."

"I asked you something else."

By the downward flick of his lashes, I could tell he remembered. He was quiet for a long time. "I sleep with my wife. Yes. Not often. She needs—the illusion, and I try to provide it when there's nothing else I can do."

"The illusion?"

"That we have a marriage."

"Ah. And you think that's a gift?"

He shifted, almost flinched. "I have no hope of making you understand this."

"Try."

"Emma—I'm all she has. Even though I think she hates me most of the time. I'm afraid to give Jay to her and I'm afraid to take him away." It was as if he had glass in his throat, it was so hard for him to talk. He still hated betraying Sally to me, even this much. And that hurt, too.

"Mick, why did you marry her?"

"Because she was pregnant."

"Oh."

Bleak silence.

He resumed wearily. "She's the opposite of you. She's not strong. She's always defined herself by what other people think, her family, friends."

"You."

"Especially me."

"Did you ever love her?"

"I love you."

"Oh, God." I dropped my head in my hands. "Why did you

come here?" I asked him again. Some strange exhaustion was making me almost ill.

"I think—I must've come to ask you to wait."

"Wait. Because you still can't leave her? You still think staying with her is better for Jay than splitting up?"

He pulled at his hair. "I don't know."

I was pretty sure that meant yes. "Go away, Mick," I said, standing up.

"Emma—"

"I'm not your therapist. Don't come to my house and spill your troubles to me. This is—this is the first selfish thing you've done, and I don't appreciate it. I had a scab over you, and you ripped it off. And you won't even sleep with me. Go away, please, disappear for six more months. I'm no masochist, I'll be over you by then, and that's a promise."

He stood up. He never gets angry—I didn't like that about him now. "I'm sorry," he said, "I'm sorry," and then something that sounded like, "I was freezing." And he walked out.

I caught him in the hall, snaked my arms around him from behind, pressing my cheek against his tweedy coat. A symbolic position—no face-to-face contact; me holding on to the man who keeps leaving me.

He tried to turn around, but I held still and wouldn't let him. Better to say it like this. "Listen to me. I want to marry you, Mick. Have babies. Be a starving artist with you. What I don't want is to be a forty-year-old spinster who's having an affair. Or *not* having an affair, that's even worse." I could feel his heart pounding under the smooth cotton of his shirt. "I can't wait for you," I said, and my stupid voice quavered. "You shouldn't have asked. I have to get on with my life. Don't call me or come over anymore, it just makes it worse."

"I know. I won't." He bowed his head. "I love you. That's not so you'll change your mind. It's just so you'll know." He squeezed my arms around him once, just for a second, and then he left me.

* * *

Late that night, much later, I called Rudy.

"Oh, Christ, you were sleeping."

"Emma?"

"I'm sorry."

"What's wrong? Wait a sec—" She put her hand over the phone. Muffled silence for about half a minute. Her bedroom phone is cordless; I imagined her telling Curtis to go back to sleep, then slipping out of bed and going out in the hall or the bathroom.

"Emma?"

"I didn't even think about the time, Rudy. I'm really sorry."

"It's okay."

"I guess Curtis is pissed."

"No, of course not."

I shouldn't have said that, I could tell by her tone. She was always prickly about him, which was why I kept my rapier Curtis wit sheathed around her, but lately she'd gone beyond touchy. Something really bad was happening, but for the life of me I couldn't figure out what.

"So, Rudy, how was your vacation?"

"Great."

"Was it?"

"Yeah."

"You don't sound like it was great. Are you okay?"

"I just woke up."

"Oh, right."

Silence while she waited for me to come to the point. This was such an unnatural conversation for us, I started to get lost in the weirdness. I could hardly remember why I'd called her.

It came back to me. "I saw Mick today."

"Oh."

Oh? "Yeah, at the liquor store on Columbia Road. You should've seen me, I looked like the wrath of God. As my mother would say.

We didn't—we just looked at each other, couldn't really talk much. It was such a shock, you know? Plus he had his family waiting for him, so . . ."

"Yikes."

"Yeah. Then tonight, he called me. He was in his car. I told him he could come over."

"Oh, Em."

"I know, but there was no way, I mean, I couldn't not see him, you know? Wait, how many negatives is that?"

"Did you sleep with him?"

"No. Almost."

She sighed. It sounded sympathetic.

"It was pretty much a repeat of the beach scene, except this time we really . . . we finally talked about his situation, which is hopeless. So, that's that. It's over, and I'm . . ." I'm bleeding. Help me.

"I'm sorry, Em. Really sorry. Maybe it's for the best."

"Possibly." I waited, but that was it. No more comfort and sympathy coming from Rudy tonight. I should've called Dial-a-Shoulder.

"Well," I said, "it's pretty late."

"It is. I should go. I'll call you."

"Will you? That'll be a novelty."

Oh, I shouldn't have said that, either. That mild reproof should not have passed my lips. I'd hurt her, I could hear it in the hush between us.

"Night, Rudy," I said gently. "Sorry I woke you."

"Night, Em. I really love you."

"Well, hey, that's—"

Click.

I replaced the receiver slowly, frowning and smiling, feeling a little breathless. "I love you, too," I said.

But I was worried sick. I couldn't get angry with her for not being the rock of support and understanding she'd always been. My broken heart hurt like hell, but it would heal. Someday.

Whatever was wrong with Rudy might not. If she would just *talk* to me. What is it, what could be happening to her? It's something to do with Curtis, that's a given, but what?

While we were talking on the phone, I kept thinking about a time, years ago, when she helped get me through another crisis involving a man. This one was Peter Dickenson. Peter the Prick. I was mad for this guy, totally nuts, I was ready to marry him. You think I'm cynical about men? You should've known me six years ago, P.P. Pre-Peter. I was like Gidget, I was like a goddamn puppy. This guy—he looked like Alec Baldwin's brother, the skinny one with the slicked-back hair, the one you can never trust. I was living alone in a great apartment in Foggy Bottom and really enjoying my solitude. But—this is the Gidget Goes to Washington part—I was so gone on Peter the Prick, I invited him to move in with me. We lived together in common-law bliss for almost four months.

Then one night—don't get ahead of me, now—I came home early from a Graces meeting, and guess what. Oh, shoot, you guessed. But you know, it doesn't matter how clichéd this story is, how many times you've heard it bleated about in a country-western song or overacted on some soap opera. When it happens to you, it's not funny. I walked in on it in classic in flagrante style, and it was going on in my own bed.

I exited swiftly, but the image was cauterized on my retinas. The lovers had seen me, too, so I went in the living room and sat on the sofa to wait. It didn't take long. Peter came out first, in his underwear. He knelt at my feet. Talk, talk. He was at the "She means *nothing* to me" stage when the girl came out. At least I didn't know her. She looked like an undergraduate, very leggy, lots of flowy blonde hair. She blanched when she heard she meant nothing to him—I actually felt a little sympathy for her. Then she left, and Peter kept talking. This I remember with crystal clarity: putting my foot in the center of his naked chest and kicking him over backward on his butt. *Get out*, I told him, but he wouldn't, so

I called the police. The first and only time I've ever dialed 911. Peter saw the light and left before the cops came.

So then—here's the point I'm making—I called Rudy. At this time we weren't really speaking. Long story; it was right after she married Curtis, and we'd had a fight about that, the worst in our history, and even though we were pretending all was well for the sake of the Graces, it wasn't. But I called her, and just about all I had to say was, "Oh God, Rudy," and she said, "I'll be right over."

She stayed with me all night. I cried a lot. We drank gin and smoked a thousand cigarettes, and at about 6 A.M. we went to the Howard Johnson's on Virginia Avenue and ate bacon and pancakes. I was a mess, but Rudy got me through it—this is the thing. Who knows how long I'd have pined for Peter without her? And who knows what kind of shit Curtis gave her when she went home at nine o'clock in the morning? That's the point. That's why the fact that she couldn't replicate that daring rescue mission tonight means nothing whatsoever to me as far as our friendship is concerned. Rudy and I are true-blue.

Not long ago I'd have said the problem is men. "Men ruin everything" is a saying of my mother's; I grew up with it, and after a while it's hard to argue with.

But now I'm in love with a man, and as the song says, he's a credit to his gender. I'm miserable, but I can't lay the blame at the usual place. I can't lay blame anywhere, and that ticks me off. Is this called growing up? If so, I'm against it. Middle age—I hit it today and already I despise it. I don't see anything in the future but loneliness and being mature and not having fun and taking hormone replacement therapy.

Happy birthday, Emma. Welcome to the rest of your life.

25

Lee

Dr. Jergens's office always calls late in the day. Good news or bad, 4 to 5 P.M. is the nurses' time to give patients their latest blood tests and lab results. So I knew who was probably calling me at home at four-forty-five on a cold, darkening Monday in the second week of January. I'd had a lifeless feeling all day. A premonition? I let the phone ring three and a half times, almost let the answering machine pick up.

"Mrs. Patterson?"

It was Patti. One of the nice ones. She always sympathizes when the news isn't good. Some of them don't; they could be reading off stock market quotations for all the warmth in their flat, rushed, telephone voices.

"Yes?"

"Hi, how are you?"

"Fine. And you?"

"Fine, thanks, and I'm calling with the results from your last IVF."

"Yes."

"Oh, I'm really sorry. No luck this time."

No luck this time. And Henry spelled *cheese* wrong on the grocery list. *Cheeze* he wrote. I have so many refrigerator magnets. Too many. They look messy. One says, "My karma ran over my dogma"—a present from Emma. It's stuck over a photograph of the Graces, all of us on Rudy's front porch steps last summer. We look leggy and tan in our shorts and sleeveless tops.

"Mrs. Patterson?"

Henry put another magnet, this one shaped like a turkey drumstick, over his Wizards' basketball schedule. Tonight they're playing against the Charlotte Hornets. An away game.

"Mrs. Patterson? You there?"

"Yes. Thank you for calling."

"Okay. Well, I was saying you'll want to make your next appointment before the end of the week, don't forget. You can do that now if you want to. Or, um, you can wait."

I have a magnet that tells how many fluid ounces are in three-quarters of a cup, how many milliliters in a tablespoon, how many tablespoons in a third of a cup. I thought it would come in so handy, but I rarely use it.

"Hello?"

I put the phone back in its cradle very quietly.

I didn't want to take my hand off the receiver. And then I didn't want to go outside. But I made myself open the back door and follow the sound of Henry's ax, sharp thunks of noise, *crack, crack*, that split the cold twilight like ice breaking. He uses an old elm stump behind the garage for a chopping block. I like to watch him heave the heavy, impenetrable-looking chunks of oak or hickory onto the block, haul back, and smash them in half with one clean blow.

He didn't hear me. He turned, reaching down for a slab of wood that had flown sideways. He saw me and straightened, started to smile. Then he stood motionless, the long-handled ax hanging limp from his fist.

"They called."

He came toward me, dropping the ax, crunching over wood scraps and bark in his ashy work boots. "Where's your coat? You'll freeze out here."

Everything got very clear again. Muddy dust on the black windowpanes of the garage, dark places between the bricks where the mortar's gone, a tear-shaped coffee stain on the breast of Henry's plaid jacket. "I'm not pregnant. It didn't work."

"Lee. Honey." He reached out to touch me, just my elbow with his fingertips. I flinched. He drew back.

"It's over."

"What?"

"Four times. That's enough. I'm not doing it anymore."

I waited for him to nod in sad understanding and then hold me, tell me it was the right decision. "It's over," he echoed, but more to himself. Perspiration was drying on the smooth skin of his forehead. He looked into my eyes—making sure I was all right. I felt very little; almost nothing. Fatigue, mostly. "Okay." Henry swallowed. "You're sure?"

"Yes."

He turned and went back to his chopping block, began to throw chunks of wood into the wheelbarrow. I waited while he bent and twisted, snagging pieces in both hands, lobbing them underhand, never missing. I caught a glimpse of his face. By accident—he was trying to keep it turned from me. He was crying.

Shock kept me from moving. I started to feel something. Heat, like a burn widening in the center of my chest. "Henry?" I grabbed for his arm—got the sleeve of his coat. I kept pulling and pulling until he had to face me. Tears streaked down his cold, ruddy cheeks. "Is it wrong? I'll keep doing it. Darling, I'll go back, we can try again."

"*No*. I don't want you to do it anymore, Lee, I want you to stop. I'm—it's—"

"Sad."

He undid the leather buttons of his jacket and pulled me inside, wrapped me up in it, and in a minute his body heat began to ease the burning in my chest. I put my hands on the wet sides of his face and held him. I had never seen Henry cry, never, never. It melted me. It thawed me from the inside.

"I'm so sorry."

"Don't say that—"

"So sorry. Oh, Henry, I'm so sorry."

"It's all right." He held me harder. "Lee, I love you."

"I know. Oh, I'm so sorry." I gave in and wept.

And it didn't hurt. It didn't sting like acid in the backs of my eyes, didn't make me feel afraid and desperate. Henry cried, too, and I thought maybe the mixing of our tears was helping to take the pain away. I know it was a beginning. Hopelessness is a blessing sometimes, Isabel told me once, and now I see it's true.

"Come inside with me. We can warm each other," I said, and that's how it started. Henry and I began to heal.

In early February, Isabel finally had the Graces' meeting at her house. She'd canceled at the last minute for the last two weeks in a row—once she was too tired, once she had a late doctor's appointment—but when I called to confirm on the Thursday afternoon, she said, "Yes, come, come, I can't wait to see you."

On the way to her apartment, I drove down Connecticut Avenue behind a Subaru station wagon. At every red light between Van Ness and the zoo, two little girls in the back waved to me. I waved back the first few times, even blew a kiss; but they grew wilder and sillier at each stop, and soon I put on a calm, adult face to settle them down. They were about six or seven, not sisters but best friends, I decided, one dark, one fair. They pressed their noses flat to the glass, stuck out their tongues, ducked below the window and then jumped up, "scaring" me with grotesque faces. The laughing and shrieking must have gotten too loud: they faced forward abruptly, mirth fading, while the woman in the driver's seat apparently laid down the law. After that the little girls only gave me a couple of backward glances and a grin or two—conspiratorial, I imagined. But I was quickly forgotten, and at Woodley Street the Subaru turned off.

I drove for a few more blocks before it hit me: I hadn't cried. In the past, and not so long ago, I would have. I believe I may be growing a shell around my heart. Henry and I are childless. Childless. I say it out loud sometimes, because I believe in calling a spade a spade.

This is a secret: I've thought of calling Dr. Greenburg, Rudy's therapist, and making an appointment. Wouldn't that amaze the Graces? Lee, the normal one, needing a shrink? I probably won't, though. These days it's old-fashioned, but I also believe in the ideal of self-sufficiency, the individual's responsibility for her own happiness. It's not that I disapprove of psychological counseling for others—I wouldn't last long in my profession with that attitude—but I don't think it's for me. It's not part of my heritage, if you will. Pavliks don't go to psychiatrists. Besides, how would I explain it to my mother?

At Isabel's, Emma answered the door. "Where is she?" I asked in a low voice. "Is she okay?"

"Sure, she's in the kitchen. Come on in."

Isabel was sitting at the table. She didn't get up, but she held her arms out to me. I gave her a long, soft hug. "How are you? How do you feel? You look beautiful." Yes, but also frail and tired. Her sweater and slacks dwarfed her body, just as her wig had gotten too big for her bony face. I wished she wouldn't wear it anymore; I liked her own short, patchy, brittle hair better.

She said what she always says—"I'm just *fine*," patting my back and beaming at me with so much gladness, I got a lump in my throat. "What have you got in your bag?" she asked.

"Dinner. Did you make the rice?" Even though she'd insisted on having the meeting at her house, we wouldn't let her do anything except make brown rice. That's the new staple in her diet nowadays.

"Kirby did," she said. "He's not here, he's acting in a play tonight. Said to give everyone his love."

"What a guy." Emma looked up from chopping vegetables for the salad. "Not many men send their love. They think it's not manly or something."

"That's true," I said. "Henry just sent his 'best.' Emma, what is that? Is that spinach?"

"Yeah?"

"Isabel can't eat that."

"Oh, shit. Isabel?"

She shrugged, smiled. "That's the theory."

"Well, I've also got chicory," Emma said defensively. "You can eat that, it's very yang. Rhubarb, though, is almost completely yin, did you know that? So don't eat it."

"Show-off," Isabel said. We've all bought macrobiotic cookbooks, and now we take turns bringing meals over to Isabel's a few nights a week. It gives Kirby a break.

"Rudy's late," Emma noted. "What else is new. Maybe she won't show up at all."

"Has anybody talked to her?"

"Not really," Isabel said. "She comes by to see me once in a while, but she never stays. She's in and out, and she won't talk about herself."

"A troubling anomaly in itself," Emma muttered.

I caught Isabel's eye. Whatever was wrong with Rudy, it was hurting Emma the most. Until now, as far as I knew, they had never kept a secret from each other. For myself, I couldn't help feeling Rudy had let the whole group down, not only Emma. Yes, she had problems—so what? Who didn't? Whatever was bothering her, and I had no idea what it was, it couldn't possibly be worse than Isabel's situation. If ever there was one, this was a time for rallying round, not wallowing in one's own private neuroses.

I didn't say that out loud, of course. It would have broken a rule—one I didn't make up, by the way; in fact, we've never even put this rule into words, never discussed it. If one person says something negative about another person in the group (Emma's "troubling anomaly" remark, for example), nobody else is allowed to chime in with another negative comment. Because that would throw off the balance; it would be ganging up. It's never happened, but I can imagine the rule relaxing slightly during those times when we have five members instead of four. But as I say, it's never happened. If anything, now that I think of it, we become even more homogeneous when we're five. We core four do, I mean. As if we're closing ranks, sending a message to the poor fifth person, the transient, that she'd better *not* criticize one of us to the others.

"At least she's not drinking," Emma said, as if she wanted to make up for being snotty before. "As far as we know. Then again, how the hell *would* we know?"

"She's unhappy, Emma," Isabel said.

"I know that." She was rhythmically pulverizing a broccoli floret. "But who isn't? You know?"

"How's your writing going these days?" When she glared at me, I realized I might not have timed that question perfectly.

"I threw it out," she snarled.

"Oh, no! Your mystery?"

"Is that what it was? Thanks for telling me, I never knew for sure."

"What will you try next?" Isabel asked.

"Well . . . I was thinking maybe a romance."

I laughed. "You?" But she wasn't kidding. "Sorry," I said when I realized it. "I just thought, you know, it's possible you're too . . ."

"What? I'm too what?"

"Cynical. Maybe. For romance. But what do I know."

"Yeah, what do you know."

"I don't think you're too cynical," Isabel said thoughtfully. "In fact, I don't think you're cynical at all."

Emma blushed.

After a moment, she surprised me by bumping my hip with

hers as we stood at our side-by-side cutting boards. "Your turn, Lee-Lee. How are you doing?"

That's a term of endearment Emma uses only on very rare occasions, mostly when she's had too much wine. Or when she's afraid she's hurt my feelings. "Oh," I said, "I'm all right."

"Really?"

"Really." I told them about the two little girls in the car, and how I hadn't cried. "Mostly, I think I feel relief."

"And still sure you did the right thing? *I* think you did the right thing," Emma said quickly, "I mean, for what that's worth, but I'd hate it if you had regrets."

"Well." There are regrets, and there are regrets. "We did everything, there was nothing left to try."

"Right. You did it all, so you can't look back and—"

"Although we could've gotten on an egg donor list."

"But enough's enough."

"We thought so. We both felt it was the right time to stop."

"How is Henry?"

"He's better, too. We're better together." I laughed. "We're starting to remember why we used to like each other."

"Oh, I'm glad." Emma gave me a shove with her shoulder—another uncommon gesture of affection. "Tell the big lug I send him my *best*."

"Should we wait for Rudy or should I start cooking?" I was making a stir-fry with winter squash, turnips, lotus root, and chickpeas. I'd made it before—it's not as bad as it sounds.

Isabel said, "Wait," at the same moment Emma said, "Cook."

"I'll wait a few more minutes," I decided. I joined Emma and Isabel at the table, bringing a glass of wine for me and a fresh cup of bancha tea for Isabel. Kirby makes about a gallon of it for her every morning. She swears it's doing her good.

"How's your love life?" I asked Emma. I felt a little self-conscious, introducing such a frivolous topic. Shouldn't we have been discussing important things, like the meaning of life? We never did, though. We talked about the same old things we'd always talked about. Isabel didn't seem to mind; these days she didn't say much herself, but she would smile her soft smile, letting her eyes rest calmly, peacefully on whoever was speaking. Sometimes I wasn't sure she was even paying attention to the words; she looked so dreamy, she might've just been listening to our voices.

"My love life?" Emma slid down in the chair on her spine. "It's an oxymoron." She had on all black tonight, black jeans, black sweater, black boots. Let's hope it's a phase, because it's not her color.

"I thought you were dating that real estate guy."

"Stuart. Not anymore."

"Well, what about the lawyer from EPA, Bill, Will—"

"Phil. That didn't work out."

I sighed. "Well, I don't know what to do. I ran out of people to fix you up with about a year ago."

"The lone firm spot in the quagmire of my life."

"Ingrate."

"Pimp."

"So there's no one?" Isabel's voice has changed, I can't imagine why. It's higher, lighter, a little breathy. She ran her index finger back and forth across the top of Emma's hand, a way of saying, *Let's be serious for a second.* I didn't like to look at her wrist bone poking out of the sleeve of her sweatshirt; it was too white and sharp, the skin stretched too tight. "Are you sure, Em? Nobody at all?"

Emma looked at her in alarm—as if she was afraid Isabel might know something she didn't want her to know. Then she ducked her head and stared down at the wineglass balanced on her stomach. When she didn't answer, I thought of something.

"Whatever happened to that man who was married?"

"The one I'd rather not talk about?" she snapped.

"Well, *excuse*—"

"Oh, Lee, I'm sorry." She smiled, trying to make me smile. "I'm sorry, I keep doing that. It's just that this guy . . ." She shook her head.

"But that was months ago, that was last *spring*. You're still not over him yet? Em, I'm sorry, I just didn't know. You should've said something." She'd never even told us his name.

She glanced at Isabel. "Maybe I should have. But the thing is, the man is married. So I haven't felt that comfortable talking about him."

"But you didn't *do* anything," I pointed out. "Or—" Hm.

"We *didn't*. As it happens." But she didn't look very happy about it.

"So—do you really love him?"

She scowled. "Yeah, but let's not talk about it. Nothing's going to change, so what's the point. What?" she demanded of Isabel, who was only watching her. "No words of wisdom from you?" She said it snidely, but I was sure I saw hope in her eyes.

Isabel gave Emma's hand a squeeze. "What a mess," she said softly. "The real thing at last."

"Yeah." She tried to smile. "My luck."

"It still might work out."

"I don't think so, Is. I think it's safe to say I lost this one."

We sat in a sad circle, not speaking until I couldn't help asking, "Why is everything bad happening to all of us at once?" I turned toward Isabel, and so did Emma—as if she might know the answer. "Is it karma? Some group sin we committed a long time ago and can't remember?"

"I know—it's because of that time we lied to what's-her-name, that awful recruit of yours, Lee, about the Graces breaking up, just so we could get rid of her."

Isabel laughed. "I don't think we've committed a sin. Karma—if there is such a thing," she said for Emma's benefit, "—isn't a punishment, it's a lesson. We have to learn them all sometime. If not in this life . . ." She smiled and let that hang.

"The karmic curriculum." Emma grinned.

"Exactly."

"Well, I don't like it," I said. "These are *horrible* lessons, I *never* want to learn them."

Isabel just smiled, but Emma said grimly, "I'm with you," and in that moment I felt closer to her. Closer, in fact, than I felt to Isabel.

We decided to start dinner without Rudy. I was sautéing the bok choy when the doorbell rang. "About damn time," Emma grumbled, but she was relieved, I could tell. "I'll get it."

Over the sound of popping oil, I heard her say, "Jesus! What's wrong?" I turned. Isabel crouched, half in and half out of her chair, staring into the living room with shock on her face. Rudy appeared in the kitchen doorway, ahead of Emma. I turned off the stove and ran to her.

"Rudy, what happened? Did you have an accident?"

"What?" She looked at me through a blur of tears. Her streaming face went bright red, and she made a strangled sound, like a sob. "Did I what?" Emma clutched at her coat sleeve, which was dotted with melted snow. When Isabel struggled to her feet and started toward her, Rudy finally said, "I'm okay, nobody died, nobody's hurt," and Isabel wobbled with relief—we all did.

"Sit," Emma ordered, taking her arms out of her coat and pushing her down in a chair. "Tell us what happened. You didn't have an accident, that's one—"

"No, I did. Just now, in front of your house."

"My house?" Emma stared.

"I forgot we were meeting. I've been driving and driving, and then I went to your house, and I hit a fireplug trying to park. But it doesn't matter, it was Curtis's BMW." She reached out for Emma's wineglass and drank two large swallows, gasping afterward.

We darted glances over her head. Was she drunk? I brought a box of tissues from the windowsill and set it in front of her. She plucked out three at once and buried her face in the pile. She looked awful, her hair sticking out in wet spikes, her eyes bloodshot and frantic. She balled the tissues in her fist and swallowed. "Okay. This is what happened. Curtis said he has cancer and he might be dying."

"No!" I cried. Emma hissed in her breath. Isabel said, "Oh, my God, my God," and collapsed in her chair.

"No!" Rudy grabbed her hand. "No, it's okay," she said, gray eyes swimming again, her hand squeezing Isabel's much too hard. "He doesn't, he's fine, it's all right!"

"What? Oh, thank God," Isabel breathed, staring, bewildered.

Rudy laughed and let go of her hand. Such a strange laugh; it made me shiver. "I've left him. Can I stay with you?"

Emma nodded stupidly. "You've what?"

"Rudy, for the Lord's sake," Isabel said, "tell us what happened."

Emma and I dropped down on either side of Rudy, and the three of us leaned in toward her, riveted. She gave a little hiccup of laughter, this one much more natural. "You guys—thank God—" She blew her nose again, and then she told us the story.

"Okay. Last November, Curtis told me he'd just been diagnosed with chronic lymphocytic leukemia—CLL. There's no cure, but it isn't always fatal. He said his kind was slow, he might not die for five or ten years, and they might even have a cure by then. He was very hopeful."

"Wait—but you're saying he doesn't have leukemia," I said to clarify. "He does not have it."

"He does not have it."

"Jesus fucking Christ." Emma stared, pressing her forehead up with her fingertips, making her eyes go even wider.

"I thought it was strange that he had so few doctor appointments, and when he did he'd never let me go with him. He didn't want me to be upset, he said. He took pills every morning, but that was all." Rudy looked around at us helplessly. "I think they were vitamins."

"Holy God."

"He seemed fine most of the time, and he was in really good spirits. I thought they'd put him on Prozac or even speed or something, to keep him from being depressed. Once in a while he'd say he was weak or dizzy because his white count was off, and I remember one time at the movies when he had double vision."

"Double vision? Caused by *leukemia*?" Emma's disbelief made us laugh, but the story wasn't funny yet. I didn't see how it ever could be.

"He said the doctors had told him his symptoms were normal, that he'd have episodes from time to time, I shouldn't worry. Now I can see that the *episodes* only happened when we were fighting. Not even really fighting, just arguing, or when he wasn't getting his way. Or when I begged him to at least let me tell Eric. And you guys," she said, but she was looking at Emma. "He wouldn't let me tell you. He made me pro—prom—" She broke down in fresh tears.

"Oh, Rudy." Emma put her arms around her. "It's all right, it's okay. Rudy," she said, rocking her, "it's okay, I forgive you."

Isabel and I both got misty-eyed. It sounded funny when Emma said, "I forgive you," and yet it was so clear to me that that's what Rudy wanted. Forgiveness.

"So I went to see Dr. Slater—he's our family doctor. I had a feeling Curtis wasn't telling me everything, and I wanted to know the worst. I thought it must be even worse than he was saying, and that's why he was being so secretive about it—to *protect* me. My God." She pressed her shaking hands to her cheeks. "Can you believe this?"

"No. Here," said Emma, pouring more wine and pushing the glass toward her.

But she ignored it and kept talking. "So I went to see Dr. Slater. Today, this afternoon—God, it feels like *weeks* ago. It might be funny when I think back someday and remember the look on his face when I asked him how much longer Curtis had to live."

Emma gasped, then laughed. Even Rudy laughed, horrified.

"He said he didn't know what I was talking about. I *argued* with him." She covered her face. "I was so *slow*."

"No—" Isabel started to say, but Rudy grabbed her hand.

"Wait," she said, "it's worse." Her eyes glittered. She pulled her lips back in a terrible smile. "Are you ready? I told Dr. Slater I'd stopped trying to get pregnant after Curtis told me about the leukemia, and he said—he said—"

"*What?*"

"He said Curtis had a vasectomy."

"No!"

"Last year. Remember I told you we didn't have sex for the whole month of December?" Emma nodded. "That's why! He was healing! And right after that, he told me he wanted us to have a child!"

She sat back, dazed. She wasn't crying anymore. She looked like she'd been knocked unconscious and she was just starting to come around.

Isabel and I were too shocked to speak, but Emma did enough cursing for everybody. "What the hell was the motherfucker thinking he'd do when his five years were up? That's what I want to know. And how the hell did he think he could keep a vasectomy secret from his own wife? Who went to the same family doctor? Didn't it ever occur to him that someday you might ask Slater why you weren't getting pregnant? I mean, what kind of arrogance is that?"

"What did he say when you told him you knew?" Isabel interrupted. "How did he defend himself?"

Rudy focused on her gradually. "Oh, well, I didn't talk to him yet. I just wrote a note and left. I should've packed a bag, but I wasn't thinking. I took his BMW," she added with a broken-off laugh.

"That'll get him," Emma gloated.

But we were disappointed. But nobody said so. We went over it again, all the gory, unbelievable details of Curtis's lie and Rudy's credulity, the misery she'd been in for the last three months. After a while she stopped shaking. I made her eat some bread, not just drink wine, and soon her color looked more natural, too, not as ghostly. But her eyes were still too dark and glittery.

Isabel, who hadn't said anything for a long time, announced, "Rudy, I think you should go home."

Stunned silence, then we all talked at once. "Never! Leaving Curtis is the healthiest thing she's done in years—Are you crazy?—She *can't*, how *could* she—"

"What are you going to do?" Isabel cut in to ask. "Stay with Emma for a while, I know, but then what?"

"I'll find a place."

"With what?"

She said, "Curtis . . ." and trailed off.

"I've got money," Emma said belligerently.

"I do, too," I said. But I started to think.

We were quiet.

"It's not just the money," Isabel began again in a patient tone.

"Which he'll keep," Emma figured out. "He could get the house, the credit cards, all your assets. Your health insurance."

Everything, we realized.

"At the very least he'll get first crack at it," I said, furious. "He's a fucking *lawyer*."

Their mouths dropped; I thought their jaws would hit the table. It's not that I'm incapable of profanity, for heaven's sake. Unlike most, I save it up for when it's warranted.

"Well, shit," Rudy said, waking up.

"And *you* abandoned *him*," Emma reminded her.

"It's not just the money," Isabel repeated into the dismal silence.

"What do you mean, Is?"

She ran two fingers around the lip of her empty teacup in a slow circle. "I've always regretted walking out on Gary. Not divorcing him," she said over our protests, "*leaving* him. I was the wounded party, and it gave me some small satisfaction to march out and leave him on his own. But he betrayed me, and he's never faced that, never even admitted it. Not to this day. It's beside the point that I've forgiven him."

"He cut a class in the karmic lesson plan."

"It's true," I said when Isabel only sent Emma a bland look. "He wronged you, Isabel, and he never paid for it."

"Yeah," Emma said. "Motherfucking bastard lied and cheated and screwed other women, and he never suffered."

"Like Curtis," I said.

"Oh," Rudy said, "but there's no comparison."

"Yes, there is."

"What Curtis did was *worse*," Emma declared, glancing at Isabel. "I mean, in a way. Don't you think? Sure, he's sick, but no amount of psychosis can forgive what he's done to Rudy. Gary thought with his dick and then lied about it. I hope he rots in hell for that, but it's not really *evil*."

"But Curtis—" Rudy closed her mouth. "No, I'm not saying anything, I'm not defending him."

"Better not," Emma warned darkly.

"Well," said Isabel, and we all looked at her. "The point I was trying to make is, Gary broke faith with me. I don't want to say he 'sinned'—"

"He didn't live up to his human potential? He wasn't sufficiently self-actualized?"

"Thank you," Isabel said. "Whatever you want to call it, he

never had to confront it, and he should have had to pay something. A recompense. And so should Curtis."

"You're damn right."

"Not for revenge," Isabel cautioned, catching the gleam in Emma's eyes. "For balance."

"Whatever."

"She's right, Rudy," I said. "For whatever reason, you owe it to yourself to get him out of there. Is he home now?"

"No, he's on a trip. He'll be back tonight."

"When?"

"Late."

We thought.

"I'm a little afraid of him," Rudy said in a small voice.

The temperature in the room dropped; Isabel and I exchanged a sick glance. "Why?" I asked casually.

"He's never really hit me or anything. Well, one time, but that was so long ago. It's more—it's probably just me, but—" We shifted in our chairs, made impatient noises. Rudy closed her eyes. "God, listen to me. I don't know what he does, how he gets me to do what he wants. It's not by violence. But I'm afraid of him anyway. He scares me, and I'm so ashamed to say that to you."

I put my hand on her arm. "Tell the truth, Rudy. Do you still love him?"

"I don't know, Lee. How could I?" Her nose turned pink. "I think it's dying. Right now. I can feel it. It's like a miscarriage."

Emma broke the bleak silence to say, "I'll go home with you if you want. Because the sonofabitch doesn't scare me."

"Me, either," I said. But I'd call Henry first.

"We'll all go." Isabel leaned on her cane and struggled up. "We'd better take two cars." We looked at her quizzically. "Since Rudy won't be going back to Emma's afterward. She'll be staying home."

26

Rudy

I went wild in graduate school. Not college—for some reason all the poison I ingested in childhood didn't hit my bloodstream until I was twenty-six or twenty-seven. It's a wonder I'm alive. No one who knows me now (except Curtis) knows what I was like then—I hadn't met Emma yet, and I've never told her, not all of it. I had to laugh that night Lee blurted out, "I had a one-night stand!" She looked so cute to me, all defiant and ashamed of herself. If I had a nickel for every one-night stand, every one-*hour* stand . . .

It's funny nobody thought of me as a tramp in those days—at least I don't think they did. For some reason I never got a reputation, as we used to call it. It might be because of the way I look (respectable), but I think it's also a knack I inherited from my mother, a way of projecting a sort of New England propriety in the midst of complete emotional chaos and breakdown. My mother—try to imagine if they'd cast Katharine Hepburn instead of Olivia de Havilland in *The Snake Pit*. You can't, I know, that's the point.

It wasn't just sex I O.D.'d on either, although that excess was the showiest one. I had sex with abusive men, wild men, married men, crazy men. I used it as an analgesic—and I even knew it, knew that word, understood the therapeutic context, got it all. Did it anyway. It helped that men really wanted me and I could have anyone I liked. It never occurred to me to stay to myself, not give it away. And as I said, it wasn't only sex; don't forget drugs and alcohol. I was in therapy—I've been in therapy since I was thirteen—

but the shrink I had in those days in Durham was especially incompetent. He was always good for psycho drugs, though, so I took a lot of legal stuff along with the illegal.

What I was doing was running as fast as I could, using prescriptions for white noise, sex for distraction, alcohol for oblivion, all to escape a growing terror that I either was or soon would be schizophrenic or full-blown manic-depressive. That was no paranoid delusion—both illnesses run in my family. But what a crazy way I chose to avoid craziness, you're thinking. I think so, too, but do you know, I haven't really changed that much. Eric says I have, but I don't believe him. My biggest fear—no, I don't even want to say it. But it's the same, it's always the same. Nothing's really changed.

Here's how I met Curtis. I was going out with a man named Jean-Etienne Leutze, a Swiss national supposedly studying drama at Duke, but what he was really doing was drinking himself to death. Naturally I was drawn to him. We made quite a couple. "Fiery," our smattering of friends in common called us, but they didn't know the half. One night we had a row in Jean-Etienne's cramped, filthy, one-bedroom apartment in a colorfully run-down student neighborhood nowhere near campus. Until that night we'd thrived on our fights, been really creative, I thought, with the insults we traded and the heavy objects we threw at each other. I had an exhilarating sense of breaking out, of opening windows and breathing in fresh, dangerous air. Jean-Etienne was the perfect man for me, I thought, at least in that place, that time.

It couldn't last. Violence always escalates. One night he beat me up and threw me out of his apartment—literally, out the door in a rush, *smash*, up against the wall in the stair landing. I wasn't hurt, no broken bones or anything, but I was very drunk and—this is embarrassing—naked except for my underpants.

Curtis lived next door. I'd seen him once or twice, briefly and only in passing, but long enough to think, *You don't look like you belong here*. Too clean-cut and wholesome. Blond, blue-eyed, and serious, always carrying a stack of books or a briefcase. He'd noticed me, too, but I assumed it was because he'd heard the racket through the wall, always either sex or yelling, and was curious about Jean-Etienne's partner in decadence.

He came out of his apartment and found me huddled on the staircase, half nude, hurting, very confused. It was late, well after midnight, but Curtis was fully dressed in chinos, polo shirt, and loafers—he'd been studying. All the time he looked at me, touched me, helped me to stand and stagger into his apartment, he never seemed to regard me in any sexual way whatsoever. This was novel in my experience. And seductive. It's a power he possesses that he's fully aware of and has put to good use any number of times since then. But it was new to me that night, and I fell under its spell without a thought.

He gave me his bathrobe to put on and coffee to sober me up. He wanted to call the police, I remember, and that moved me, made me feel so grateful, as if I had a knight looking after me. We talked for hours—I talked, rather, and he listened with complete absorption: again, very seductive. He was thinner in those days, and more callow, less all-knowing, but already he had a fine quality of self-restraint that attracted me powerfully. I had so little of it myself.

When it was time to go to bed, I assumed we would sleep together. But he surprised me by bringing sheets, blanket, and a pillow, and tucking me up all nice and neat on his sofa. He didn't even kiss me.

In the morning, I woke up first. I took a shower in his pristine bathroom—quite a contrast to Jean-Etienne's sty—and then I went into Curtis's room and slipped into bed beside him. This was my idea of a thank-you gift. A small favor for a small favor.

He rejected me. He wanted me—he slept naked, so that was obvious—but he wouldn't take me, and the way he put me away from him—no words, just a small, scrupulous smile, his hands kind but firm and somehow practical—made me feel ashamed of myself. And in his power.

A pattern began—I see it so clearly now—of me offending and Curtis forgiving. Me being outré, he disapproving, then relenting. We didn't become lovers for weeks. He made me wild with wanting him first, and even while it was happening I knew he was doing it on purpose. I liked it. I entered the game willingly, denying and disciplining myself because it pleased him, and getting addicted fast to his control over me. He wasn't like any man I'd ever known; he had single-mindedness and focus, and unlike me, he knew exactly what he wanted: a political career. The law he was studying was only to be a stepping-stone.

Our relationship never went smoothly, not even at the start. It looked one-sided to outsiders, Curtis in charge, me in thrall. But things aren't always what they seem, and they're never simple.

Just before we left Durham, I told him I didn't want to live with him anymore, that when we moved to D.C. I wanted to find a place of my own. I wasn't breaking up, I just needed some space, as we used to say. I wanted to slow things down. In a rare moment of self-knowledge, I understood that his possessiveness was hurtful, and that my complicity was borderline pathological.

Then, too, I simply wasn't prepared for total commitment. I still needed a lot of room to act out, a lot of freedom to self-destruct, and I didn't want all that stability Curtis's good side represented—well, I wanted it, but I was afraid of reverting to type and blowing it in some huge, spectacular way.

I couldn't believe what happened next. He tried to talk me out of it, of course, being very reasonable and methodical as only Curtis can be, but for once I stood firm. Then he mocked me and ridiculed me, and that was harder to take, but somehow I did. I wouldn't give in.

So he started drinking.

It's the Lloyd family vice. It's a bad one, no question, but what a luxury, I've always thought, to come from a family with only one serious flaw. But Curtis *didn't* drink, or hardly at all, maybe a beer on Saturday afternoon or one glass of wine in a restaurant, and I'd end up finishing it for him. He was supposed to take the D.C. bar exam in three weeks, and he'd been studying for it like a monk for months. The day after our big blowup over living together, I came home from school (I was still doing an art history master's then) and found him passed out on the couch. I thought he was sick—it just didn't register, not even when I saw the whiskey bottle sticking up between the cushions. When I figured it out, I thought, Oh, this is just an aberration, and I scoffed at him, gave him a stern, disapproving lecture while I poured coffee down his throat and pushed him into the shower. He never said anything, not one word: blind drunk, he could still control himself.

When he sobered up enough to function, he put on clean clothes and went out, still not speaking. (What a potent weapon silence is.) He came back with four fifths of vodka, and for the next six days proceeded to drink them behind the locked bedroom door.

I was frantic. As I've said, we had very few mutual friends, and no one I felt comfortable calling. I called his parents in Savannah. It was futile, the conversation surreal, like trying to interest a fish in the fact that its offspring is drowning. Once when Curtis was in the bathroom, I ran in the bedroom and tried to steal his booze stash. I thought he might die—I thought he was poisoning himself. He *was*—he looked like death, smelly and foul and unkempt, doubly shocking in a man who's usually so fastidious. He caught me before I could escape with the bottles, and for the first and only time in our lives, he struck me. Not a hard blow, he was too drunk, but I lost my balance and cut my forehead on the doorpost.

Curtis saw the blood and started to weep. He went back in the bathroom and vomited. I thought it was over, that that would end it, but he staggered back to his room and started drinking again.

I gave up.

"I won't leave you," I told him, both of us crying like children. "We'll find a place in Washington, a wonderful apartment on the Hill, and we'll be rich and happy and you'll be famous, you'll be president and I'll be first lady, and we'll always be together." He had the shakes, he couldn't stop sobbing, dry, racking barks of pain that I'll never forget, although nothing like that, nothing close to that, ever happened again. His life, once he recovered, went back to normal, and he was completely his old serious, sober, focused self.

That terrified me and thrilled me, the unimaginable notion that *I* might have power over *him*—that I could ruin his life by simply taking myself out of it. An awesome responsibility, I thought. I would have to be so careful and loving, so delicate with him.

It took years to see—and then I only saw it in blurred flashes, never clearly, never for long—that it was just another game, that he was still the one with the power, not me. Like a child holding his breath to get his way.

Well, that analogy is even truer now, isn't it—Curtis threatening his own *death* to get his way. But this time he's gone too far. His true colors are visible at last even to me, the blind woman. It's over. I think it's over. How could I stay with a man that much crazier than I am?

"I think you should throw all his clothes out in the street."

I glanced at Lee as she floored the BMW and merged into two lanes of speeding traffic on Rock Creek Parkway. Maybe letting her drive hadn't been such a good idea. She'd suggested it, Isabel had seconded it, and at the time it had seemed sensible—I was so upset, I had the hiccups. But I'd never seen Lee this angry before, and she was taking chances that had me holding on to the door handle and wishing Curtis's car had a passenger-side airbag. I should've gone with Emma, who was right behind us, trying to keep up in her little red Mazda.

"And definitely call a locksmith," Lee added. "You ought to

call one right now, in fact. You need to get every lock in your house changed, Rudy. I've got my phone, can you get it out of my bag?"

I got the phone out, but calling a locksmith was beyond me. I turned around to see what Isabel thought.

"It might not be a bad idea," she said from the backseat. "But you can probably wait till you get there."

"Okay," said Lee, in a don't-say-I-didn't-warn-you voice, "but they might not be able to come until tomorrow. Time is of the essence. Another thing—as soon as you get home, you have to start calling your credit card companies. If he gets vindictive, he'll try to cut you off, so you have to make a preemptive strike. You've got the edge right now because you know something he doesn't know, but as soon as he catches up, things could get very dicey. Do you know any good lawyers? I'll call my mother, she knows everybody. Isabel, would you recommend the one you used for Gary? To be frank, I think Rudy needs someone tougher. A piranha, that's what we want." She bared her teeth. *Fucking lawyer* still echoed in my head. Before tonight I'd never heard Lee say anything stronger than *damn*. She scared me. I was glad she was on my side.

"Give me the phone," she said, "I have to call Henry."

"I'll dial." She was taking corners at fifty miles an hour; I wanted both her hands on the wheel.

"Don't call the house, he's not home, he's at his mother's." She gave me the number. My fingers were shaking, I had to dial twice. I couldn't tell what I felt more of, fear or excitement, dread or anticipation. And underneath it all lay a streak of sickness, nausea almost, over the thing my husband had done to me. My best friend. The person in the world I had trusted most.

"It's busy," I told Lee. "Let me call Eric." I dialed, and listened in dismay to his answering machine message. "Eric? This is Rudy." I hiccuped, then laughed. "I've got the hiccups. I'm in a speeding car with Lee and Isabel, Emma's behind us, we're going to my house so we can lock Curtis out. *Hic*." Lee and Isabel snickered—

we all sounded hysterical. "This you won't believe. Curtis told me he has leukemia—this is what I haven't been able to tell you—and today I found out it's a lie!"

"Tell him about the vasectomy," Lee said, swerving onto Independence Avenue.

"And he had a vasectomy over a year ago. I'm not drunk, I'm not on anything, this really happened! So I'm leaving him. Or I was leaving him, but now I'm throwing him out. I've got all the Saving Graces with me. I wish you were there. If you get home soon, call me at my house. If you get home ever. Anytime tonight. Call me, please, I really, really want to talk to you."

"Hang up," Lee said, "I have to call Henry."

"Okay," I said into the phone, "signing off. Wish me luck." I dropped the phone on the floor. "Oh God, I'm a mess! How can I do this? Can I do this?"

"Yes." Isabel leaned over the seat and took the phone out of my hand. "Lee, what's your mother-in-law's number, again?"

It turned out Henry wasn't there anyway, he'd gotten an emergency call at Jenny's house and taken it himself instead of her. Lee told Jenny the problem in a few simple sentences, and Jenny said she'd try to get the message to Henry. "Yes, do," Lee said, "because it's really important. Where was his emergency? Oh, shit." Isabel and I stared goggle-eyed at each other. Lee was setting all kinds of records tonight. "He's all the way out in Burke," she relayed to us. "Well, tell him, as soon as he possibly can, to go over to Rudy's. Yes, he knows where it is. Yes. Capitol Hill. He knows. Okay, Jenny, thanks. Yeah. Well, we don't know, anything's possible. We will be. Bye." She clicked off. "She says to be careful. Hah. I hope he *does* try something. No, I don't," she said hastily, getting hold of herself. She turned onto my street. "Should I hide the car?"

"Should you hide the car?"

"If he sees it, he'll take it. Which do you want him to have, the car or the Jeep?"

"Yikes." I couldn't think. "This *is* his car. I think they're *both* his."

"Both of your cars are in Curtis's name?"

"I think so. I don't know. Maybe the Jeep is in both."

Lee mumbled more curse words. "Well, then, the hell with it." She found a place in front of the house and parallel parked. "I hope you like riding Metro."

We got out of the car, and that's when I noticed the porch light.

"Oh, no, oh, no, oh, no."

Isabel took my arm. "He's here?"

I nodded. He was home, so he'd read my note. *I saw Dr. Slater*, it said. *I know everything. I'm leaving you.*

Emma hurried over; she'd parked on the other side of the street. "Rudy, did you leave the lights on?"

"No."

"Uh-oh."

"He's here," Lee confirmed, and by the gleam from the streetlight, I saw anticipation in her eyes.

Emma took me by both hands. "You're freezing cold and your hands are clammy." She started chafing them, trying to warm me up. "Now, listen to me, Rudy. If you want, we'll stay outside." Lee said, "What?" but Emma ignored her. "It's up to you. If you want to talk to him alone, that's your business. Either way, we're with you."

"No, I want you to come in with me."

They all looked relieved.

"You can do this, you're strong," Emma declared, looking into my eyes. "And think, in a few minutes the hardest part will be over."

"And we're with you," Isabel said. "It won't be so bad if it's all of us."

"That's right," Lee said, "it'll only be one-fourth as hard, because we're together."

"Okay?" Emma said, and for a minute I thought she'd make us

do a secret handshake or something, a four-way high five. "Let's go, then. Okay? Let's *do* it."

We marched up the sidewalk arm in arm, a phalanx of slow-moving soldiers. Slow-moving because of Isabel's cane, plus we had to separate at the steps, which were too narrow for four abreast. But we didn't lose our militant spirit, and it *was* like marching into battle, four of us facing one clever, dangerous enemy, whose reactions were unpredictable and with whom, even now, part of me might still be in love.

I got out my key and unlocked the front door. The light in the foyer was on—Curtis was coming down the staircase. He stopped in the middle when he saw me. His face, pale and set before, broke into a glad, astonished smile.

I softened, started to melt like snow in the sun. Then I widened the door, and he saw who was behind me. Raw hostility replaced the relief on his face, and I got my resolve back. But that was a close one.

"What's this, a slumber party?"

That's right, I thought, be obnoxious, help me out. Lee, the last one in, closed the door. Somewhere between the car and the house, I'd stopped having hiccups.

"Curtis?" I said, my voice high and flutey. "Curtis, I want you to leave this house." I actually sounded composed. An act, of course; inside I was veering back and forth between panic and a kind of weird, out-of-body detachment. Seeing him looking exactly like himself but also knowing what I knew about him was disorienting, like trying to match the man with his dark shadow, line the two up perfectly to get the true picture.

"Rudy," Curtis said, as if I hadn't said anything at all, "we have to talk."

"Oh, no, I'm not talking to you. I want you to go. Stay in a hotel or something, stay with your friend Teeter."

"Rudy," he said through his clenched teeth. "Please tell your friends to go. I have a lot to say to you, but I'm not doing it in front of an audience." He put his hand out to me—a subtle capitulation. And he'd said "please."

The others looked at me. They'd hate it, but they would go if I asked them to. Well, Lee and Isabel; I wasn't so sure of Emma. But I said, "No," very firmly, "they're not leaving"—and I could tell in the clearing of their faces, the straightening of their postures, that my friends were proud of me. I felt bold. "Nobody's leaving but you."

A muscle bulged under his left eye. "You're mistaken. We'll talk later," he said, turned, and marched back up the stairs.

Emma, Lee, and Isabel were all looking at me. "Curtis!" I called. "I want you to go!"

No answer. He disappeared around the landing.

Whatever made me think this would be easy? "Now what?" I looked around in despair.

"You were great," Emma said, shaking my shoulder.

"You were," Isabel agreed.

"I was," I said weakly. "I didn't cave."

"But," said Lee, "you still have to get him out of the house."

"*How?*"

"You'll have to talk to him." *Oh, Isabel*, I thought, *I didn't expect naïveté from you*. "And," she added, "we'll go with you."

"You will? You mean—all of us?"

They nodded.

How bizarre. But I didn't want to think about it for long. "Okay, let's go."

Curtis's face when he saw us was—indescribable. He was bending over in front of his open closet; he'd taken off his tie and was starting on his shoes. "What the hell is this?" He tried a laugh, but his face was stiff with outrage.

I pointed a shaky finger to his overnighter, which he'd thrown on the bed. "It's good you haven't unpacked yet, you can take that with you when you go."

He looked at me as if he couldn't recognize me. Then he heaved a heavy, patient sigh; he got that forgiving air that's worked so well for so long. "Rudy, this isn't the time to discuss this."

"I agree. I'm not discussing it. I want you out of this house. I know what you did, and you won't even deny it. I shouldn't have to go, *you* should."

Isabel stood on my right, Lee on my left. Emma had taken a seat on the bed—an escalation of the offense, usurping more enemy territory. Possession is nine-tenths of the law.

Curtis tried a humorous look, a sensible man up against irrational females. "Isabel, can't you talk some sense into your friends?"

She took two steps toward him, away from us. She had her cane in one hand, purse in the other; she still had her coat on—we all did. "Rudy's only asking for fairness. A little generosity from you now. Do you think you might owe her that? To begin righting the balance a little?"

I loved her so much then. She was the best champion, the kindest friend. Surely her simple decency would get through to Curtis, help him to see his deviousness for what it was.

He smiled. Sniffed his breath out through his nose. Didn't even bother to answer her.

Lee cleared her throat. "You don't really think you can get out of this, do you? After what you did, you don't think Rudy's going to forgive you and you can just go back to normal. Do you?"

Curtis snarled, "Butt out."

She only got more dignified. "No one is butting out. You've brought this on yourself. Rudy wouldn't need us here if you weren't such a bully."

"A bully?"

"Yes. An emotional bully."

"Curtis," I said. He looked at me hopefully—he'd given up on my friends. "There's nothing to be said, no possible explanation you can give. I know what you did, I even know why you did it, so there's nothing to talk about. I'm just asking you to go. That's all I'm asking."

He brushed past Isabel and loomed in front of me, so close I had to will myself not to back up. "Then we'll talk later," he said softly but firmly, just to me. "I'll go if that's what you want, but I'll come back after your bodyguards leave and we'll discuss this. Rudy, you *know* we have to talk."

Was he asking so much? After five years of living together and six years of marriage? We *did* have to talk, didn't we? The tight, indecisive silence stretched out. In the mirror on the closet door, I saw Emma look down, her shoulders slump. She knew I was going to give in. And if he got me alone, she knew he'd win.

"No." All around me, I heard a soft gasp. "I'm sorry, Curtis. The next time we talk, it'll be in a lawyer's office."

He kept shaking his head. "You don't mean that. You'll see reason once you've thought about it. On your own. I know you, Rudy—"

"I'm seeing reason now. It's very"—I inhaled—"refreshing. Curtis, will you please, please *go*?"

"Listen to me," he said very fast, "I was going to tell you tonight. I couldn't live with myself anymore. I only did it to keep you—I knew it wasn't fair, wasn't right. Tonight I was going to tell you the truth, I honestly was, and suggest we get counseling. With Greenburg if you wanted."

"Oh, Curtis." I couldn't help it: I laughed. It started Emma and Lee off, and even Isabel smiled sadly. If he had just left Eric out, I might've believed him.

"*Fuck* you, then, just *fuck* you," he said, the malice finally revealed in his bared teeth and his hate-filled eyes. "Get out of my way." He blundered out of the room, smacking into Lee as he went, and pounded downstairs.

But we listened, and the front door didn't open or close.

Lee said, "Well?"

"It's up to you," Emma said. "I can keep this up all night."

Isabel nodded. "Room to room to room."

I couldn't figure out what I was feeling. "Is this funny?" I asked Emma, squeezing my hands together.

"Not yet, but it will be."

"Are you sure?"

"Yes."

"Okay, then." We trooped out. Emma snatched up Curtis's overnight case on the way.

We found him in the kitchen trying to make coffee. We squeezed in, three around the sides with their backs to the counters, me in the middle. The yellow light sallowed our tense faces. Four hunters and one hunted. Curtis had his self-control back, though, and that's a much deadlier weapon than his anger.

"It's hopeless. Curtis"—I felt the need to remind both of us—"*you told me you had leukemia*."

He finished measuring decaffeinated coffee into the maker and flicked the switch. He turned around. He cupped his hands around the sides of his face, like blinders, trying to cut out of his sight everybody but me. "Don't shame me," he said, and for the very first time, he sounded sincere. "If you would just give me a chance to explain why I did it."

Deep down, I felt another treacherous softening.

Thank God for Isabel. She said, "But that's not the only lie you told."

How could I have forgotten? It was good to feel the disbelief and the indignation come roaring back, so loud they made my ears ring. And Curtis had the decency, finally, to drop his eyes.

"That alone sounds like grounds for divorce to me," Lee said. "Telling your wife you want a baby right after you have a secret vasectomy." Her face got a baffled, incredulous look. "Did you *want* to get caught? For God's sake—you and Rudy go to the same *doctor*."

He opened his mouth, closed it. He was changing slowly, before my eyes, into a man I not only didn't love, I didn't even like. At last he thought of something to say to Lee. "This is none of your business."

How pathetic. He made me feel like such a fool. "What in the world have I done?" I said. "Why did I love you for so long?"

"Because he's good at what he does," Lee answered. "Which is to control and manipulate people. I think," she said to Curtis politely, "you're despicable."

"Why don't you go fuck yourself," he repeated. Pitiful! He had two dots of saliva in the corners of his mouth. "Rudy, would you get them *out of here*?"

"No. *You* leave."

He lunged, pushing me back by my shoulders. Not a hard blow, but Emma yelled, "Hey!" and she, Lee, and Isabel crowded up, surrounding us.

The doorbell rang.

It kept ringing, *ding-dong, ding-dong, ding-dong, ding-dong, ding-dong,* whoever it was was leaning on the button. The knot in the middle of the kitchen began to loosen. Curtis started for the door, but Lee made a quick move and beat him to it. I remembered—she'd called Henry.

Emma gave me a searching look as we moved into the living room—*You okay?* I was shaking all over, my whole body, uncontrollable. But the longer this went on, the better I felt. Curtis shoving me—it was like a jolt of amphetamine. I felt almost giddy from it. An unnatural high, but who cared, the danger excited me.

It wasn't Henry at the door, it was his mother.

I'd never seen Jenny in her work clothes. Lee's descriptions didn't do her justice. She had on denim overalls and a red flannel shirt. A leather tool belt around her hips, and muddy black rubber boots to the knees. A billed cap over her pompadour that said PATTERSON & SON and across the breast of her coveralls, *Jenny* in bright yellow script.

She broke off a low-voiced conversation with Lee when she saw us. "Hear y'all havin' some trouble out chere tonight," she said in her slow-as-syrup Carolina drawl.

"Ha ha ha ha," Curtis tried to laugh, but the sound was so phony I felt sorry for him. "This is great! Now the circus begins! Now we get dykes to the rescue."

"Watch your mouth, pretty boy," Jenny warned with a flash of good, clean temper. She was like fresh air in a sickroom.

Curtis felt it, too. Under a thinning, cracking veneer of contempt, he looked hounded. I knew what he was going to do the second before he did it.

"Don't!" I had time to say, and then he grabbed two sides of the tall, heavy, bronze-and-glass étagère beside the window. "Curtis, don't!"

He couldn't lift it, so he shoved it. *Smash*—six feet of glass shelves and ceramics shattered on the parquet. All my pots, my pretty vases and jugs, my bowls, all broken, nothing but clay rubble and shards in a sparkling snow of slivered glass. Gone.

Nobody moved. Curtis breathed hard through his mouth, winded, watching us, daring somebody to react. Emma made a strangled, furious sound. Isabel, I saw from the corner of my eye, had her by the arm and was trying to hold her back.

That sound and Emma's rage—they energized me. I left the protective circle of the Graces and moved toward Curtis, into his space, closer and closer until we were nose to nose. I wasn't afraid at all, and I was glad he'd broken my pots. Like the shove, it had cleared my head.

Still, my voice didn't sound like me in the least; it came out breathy and high, each word standing alone. "Get. Out. Or I'll call the police."

He laughed.

"And. I'll tell Teeter. Tell him what you did."

He froze. Paled. At last, at last I'd found it—the stake through his heart.

"If you ever try to hurt me. You won't get elected. To anything. Dogcatcher."

He shook his head, couldn't believe his ears.

To make it clearer, I enunciated. "Ratcatcher."

Somebody laughed. Jenny, I think.

Curtis whirled. We five closed ranks. I think he still might have done something, committed some violence on us, or me, the house, but we cowed him with our numbers. Also, one of us had a cane and one of us had a twenty-inch Stillson wrench.

"Go," I said.

He went.

Jenny built a fire in the fireplace. Lee poured the coffee Curtis had started. Emma kept saying, "Could I please get some credit for not saying anything?" I had stopped shaking enough to call Eric, but he still wasn't home. I left an incoherent message that ended, "I'm glad you're gone, I am, because this way you couldn't help me, I had to do it myself."

Which wasn't true—I couldn't have done it without the women.

"Here's one that's not broken." Isabel held up a small, purple-glazed vase, eggplant-shaped. An early effort and not very good, but I'd always liked it; it must've survived because it was so heavy. "And I think one or two can be glued, Rudy, I really do."

"You watch out for that glass," Lee warned her from the sofa. "Come over here by the fire, Isabel."

"I knew if I said one word, I'd set him off, so I just kept my mouth shut."

"Emma," Lee said dutifully, "you were wonderful."

"No, but, it wasn't like when you guys rescued Grace and I didn't do anything. This time I didn't do anything on *purpose*. Honestly, it was a real act of will."

I hugged her, and she finally grinned and looked mollified. "You were great. You were. And I knew what you were doing."

"No, *you* were the one," she said. "Oh, Rudy, what a moment. You were awesome."

"Ratcatcher," Lee recalled. "I *loved* that."

"How'd you get mixed up with a crazy ol' boy like that anyway?" Jenny wondered, leaning back on the ottoman. She'd taken off her boots and her tool belt, pushed her cap around backward. She looked like that woman in the old Ma and Pa Kettle movies—Marjorie Main?

"I keep thinking of his face when we all went in the bedroom," Lee said, rubbing her hands together. "Was that priceless?"

"You were great, too," Emma told her. "'I think you're despicable,'" she said in Lee's voice.

"I do. And he couldn't say *anything*, he had absolutely no excuse. Rudy, don't you feel good? You shouldn't have any guilt at all, you should just be proud of yourself."

"I do, I am." But once in a while my teeth chattered and I had a fit of shuddering. The fire, the coffee, the blanket Emma had tucked around me, nothing seemed to be able to touch the cold, shaky center of me. Maybe a drink?

"He won't do anything now," Emma said. "I mean, he'll never stalk you or anything. You really got him where he lives with the dogcatcher thing."

"Yeah," Lee agreed, "threatening to tell his partners, that was brilliant. You can call the shots now, get anything you want out of him."

"I don't want anything."

"You say that now."

"No, I really don't. Enough to get by till I figure out what I'm doing." I hugged myself under the blanket, shivering again.

"Rudy, if you don't take that son of a bitch to the cleaners, I'm never speaking to you again," Emma said, and she was only half joking.

They started to talk about changing the locks and calling the banks, the insurance companies, getting names of good lawyers. Lee was full of advice; you'd have thought she'd been divorced six times. But that's Lee, she always knows everything. Slowly, slowly, I began to unwind, untangle inside. Could this really work? It was looking as if it might. But even that scared me, just the prospect of success. Early days yet, I consoled myself; still a million chances for everything to blow up in my face. And I had the strangest, strongest urge to call my mother. Where did *that* come from? I got up to call Eric again.

"I have to go," Lee said, forestalling me. "Who's driving us back—Emma? Jenny, it's too far out of your way." Henry had called from his car an hour ago, heard we didn't need him, and gone home. "Isabel, are you ready?"

No answer.

"She's asleep," Emma said. "She fell asleep on the floor."

Lee moved quietly to where Isabel lay on her side, half on the rug, half on the hardwood floor. "Is, are you awake? We're getting ready to leave." She knelt down. "Isabel?"

Emma and I froze. We went closer, drawn by something in Lee's tone. Then Isabel opened her eyes and smiled—and I let go of a dark fear that had gripped me so fast, I didn't have time to name it.

"Get up, sleepyhead," Lee murmured.

Isabel put her thin white hand on Lee's knee. "Don't think I can."

"Why? Are you sick? What's wrong?" She craned her neck around. "Rudy, call an ambulance!"

"No, no." Isabel wet her lips. "Call Kirby," she said slowly and carefully. "Lee? Just call Kirby."

27

Isabel

February—

Going through some old letters and papers, I found my last address book, the one I used for about fifteen years before the current update. I read the names I'd written in so carefully, some with reminders to myself of the spouse's first name, the children's birth dates. I don't know what to make of the fact that a fair number of these people, closer to a third than a quarter, didn't even make it into the new book. Natural attrition? Cold words for one of life's little tragedies. People move away, drift away, drop by the way. When Gary and I separated, a lot of acquaintances simply disappeared into the blue. But the loss of others is more mysterious.

This woman—Fay Kemper—lived on Thornapple Street; we met at the dog park, the same place where I met Lee. We both loved gardening; we went on a house tour together; she had a daughter Terry's age, we talked on the telephone for hours about our children. And yet, she slipped away. Didn't make the cut. Our husbands never quite got along, that was one obstacle, but it doesn't explain everything. I was fond of Fay, but I didn't fight to keep her. She didn't fight for me. We simply let each other go. There are a dozen more like her, and I know these near-friends come and go in everyone's life, it's a ruthless necessity occasioned by circumstance, taste, chance, apathy—and yet it makes me sad.

All my life I've wanted to tell people I loved them. Fear usually held me back, that they wouldn't care, or they wouldn't hear, or they would take too much from me once they knew.

It's different now. The years pile up like snow against the windowsill. I don't have a moment to lose.

This time of the day frightens me. I don't want to die in winter. Don't want my last glimpse to be of that blighted sunset through the bedroom window, the sway of bare branches against the twilight sky. The wind is so cold and heartless; I imagine it calling me under its harsh breath.

I want to go when it's warm and the air is blue. I'd like to hear a fly buzzing against the screen, an airplane droning in the cloudless sky. A conversation in another room. Laughter. Smell of grass.

I can't forgive my body for betraying me. I am my best friend, and I've let me down. Who's left to trust? That's silly, I know. But the myth of my immortality is still with me, although necessarily fraying at the edges. It gives way to attacks of panic. *I'm dying,* I'll suddenly recall after a period of inexplicable forgetfulness, and my veins light up like Christmas tree lights in terror. My stomach contracts. I cry quick, hurtful tears. Then the deep breaths, the squaring of the shoulders. The weighty, unshareable sadness. For myself, for everyone in the world. What a burden we carry under the shadow of dying. The dark bird's wing.

Why is death such a mystery? It's taboo, like sex to a virgin, a secret locked carefully away. I lived my whole life believing everyone would die but me.

It's the only way we can live, I suppose. It comes from believing we are our bodies. It's not natural to regard flesh, blood, and bone as temporary housing from which we'll soon be evicted. But lately I'm moving closer to learning the secret, I think, the lesson: that death isn't a bizarre, detestable, unspeakable catastrophe. Life's a circle, not a straight line, the longer the better. The circle never ends, it only widens.

* * *

March—

Emma comes to see me nearly every day. She always makes me laugh. "Oh, God," are a Christian's last words, she tells me; an atheist's: "Oh, shit!"

She has never mentioned Mick Draco's name. So the last time she visited, I brought him up myself. (Waiting for "the right time" is a luxury I don't indulge anymore.) She looked impressed and relieved, but not particularly surprised that I knew who he was. "I thought you might've guessed," she said. "So many times I've wanted to tell you."

"But you thought I'd disapprove. Because he has a wife."

"No, I don't think you would *disapprove* of anything, Isabel. That I did, I mean. Or anyone else you love."

"Not be pleased, then."

"Okay. Not be pleased."

"It's true," I said, "that adultery in the abstract is something I dislike. Abhor, even."

"Well, that makes two of us."

"But in the particular, it's a bit more complex, isn't it?"

"But we still didn't do anything, Mick and I."

"And now it's over?"

"Yeah. I broke it off. He asked me to wait for him. He's trying to get out of his marriage without hurting his wife." She made her dry, sardonic face. "Which doesn't seem too likely to me. Especially since Lee says they've been in couples therapy for the last five years. Put it this way—I'm not sitting around waiting for a breakthrough."

"And are you happy now?"

"No. I'm miserable."

"Maybe you should've told him you'd wait." I have no trouble at all offering advice these days. I'm a fountain of it.

"But waiting is suffering, Isabel. I don't have room for any more."

She meant me—she's suffering because of me. I find myself

comforting the people I love more than I grieve for myself. I'm constantly consoling. It's exhausting. But a good thing, too. Because in the process of convincing them what's happening to me is not a tragedy, I almost convince myself.

Lee is not easy to console, and impossible to convince. She's so very unhappy. The solution to one of her problems seems simple to me, but even I, in extremis, don't quite have the presumption to solve it for her.

She took me out for a ride in her car. I hadn't been out of the apartment in weeks except to see the doctor, the acupuncturist, or the massage therapist. To them I take taxis; Kirby goes with me. But I was feeling unusually strong, and this was a pleasure trip for Lee and me. Pure pleasure. We took Grace with us. Winter is finally over—I thanked all my gods for that: one nuisance worry about dying out of the way. It felt wonderful to speed along with the windows down, the wind in our faces. We drove out to Virginia, those pretty little roads around Purcellville and Philomont. Grace put her gray muzzle out and let her ears blow back—she looked like a flying dog.

"Will you take her for me?"

Lee pretended not to hear me.

"Kirby would take her if I asked him. But I'd rather it was you."

I thought she would let it go, just not answer. But a little time passed, and she said, "Yes, I'll take her." Then we both pretended it was the wind making our eyes water.

Sweet old Grace. These days *grace* means something else to me, too. I've been given a grace to see—well, our connectedness. It's almost primitive, it's so easy. Literally, we're all in this together, and my anger has almost completely dissipated into a feeling of oneness with everything. Everyone.

A gift.

Still. How much easier it would be if we could go with somebody. A partner, a companion. Oh, if only we could take a friend with us. How much less lonely it would be.

* * *

I have help two days a week now. A lady from social services came and interviewed me, and then a nurse began to visit on Tuesday and Thursday afternoons. Roxanne Kilmer is her name; she's young, only twenty-seven, and I worry she's gotten into the wrong line of work, or gotten into it too early. A woman should have more experience, more of life before she has to see the things Roxanne sees.

I like her, though, and I'm selfish enough to want to keep her. She helps me bathe, changes the bed, plans my meals, manages my medications. I like her competence and briskness, the way she's kind to me but not sorry for me. I'm so lucky—I have Roxanne, I have Mrs. Skazafava who happily walks the dog every day at four o'clock, I have the Saving Graces. One of the hardest things to bear by people in my situation—the worry that when the bad time comes there won't be enough caregivers—has been mooted. It's simply not on my list of anxieties anymore.

Then there's Kirby. The social services woman wrote down that he's my "primary caregiver," an obvious, self-evident fact that for some reason I hadn't quite realized or accepted. Because of his capacity for self-effacement, I suppose. And because he slipped into my life so quietly. Like a fast-growing sapling you plant one spring, and seemingly the next it's a strapping maple tree, perfect in its setting, you can't remember that spot in the yard without it. I only worry that he's taking too much time from his job to be with me, but he won't discuss that or let me nag him about it. It's off limits.

These days it tires me to talk for too long anyway, so the balance between us has had to shift: for once, Kirby talks more than I do. He was rusty at it at first, and even now he's not exactly voluble. But he perseveres, because he knows I love to listen. He tells me about his father, one of the highest ranking army officers to die in the Vietnam War, and about his mother, who once danced in musical comedies on the New York stage. I can see both of these contradictory influences on the son, who camouflages his creative, unconventional side with a deceptively quiet, gray-looking conformity.

I've asked him why he stays with me. "Because I love you," he said gravely. "It's simple." But is it? Does it matter? Should I, should anyone, be concerned if he stays with me because it's a way to say good-bye? A proper, humane, dignified way he couldn't have with his wife and his babies because it was stolen from him? Either way, the motive is love. So what does it matter?

He's helping me write a letter to the Graces. I dictate and he types on his laptop computer. In the evenings he reads to me. I lie on the sofa under the afghan with Grace on the floor at my side, and Kirby sits under the lamp in the easy chair, long legs crossed, head tilted back so he can peer down through his half-glasses. His theatrical voice is wonderfully expressive; I can listen to it for hours. He reads classic plays to me, Shakespeare's comedies and Ibsen, Molière, Oscar Wilde. And novels I loved as a child that he finds for me in the library—*Girl of the Limberlost, The Secret Garden, Little Women*. And the Bible, the Koran. Poetry. They're a great comfort to me, these other voices, these other people's worlds. I'm thankful for how completely they take me out of mine.

He helps me with my mail, too. So many get-well cards, so many kind, nervous, graceful, inept, tactless, elegant notes, some from people I haven't communicated with or even thought of in years. Just as interesting to me is the number of people who *don't* write, don't call, don't acknowledge my illness in any way. I forgive them absolutely, and lately I've been scrawling little messages to them to say so—not in those words. I understand that, for some, what's happening to me is unspeakable, literally. They can't help it. I don't take it personally. I did once, but no more. No time.

Gary is one of those who can't speak. I called him on the telephone, hoping for something, closure, acknowledgment, maybe my own forgiveness. It was awkward. No, it was impossible. So: Gary and I are going to die separately and far from each other. I know that for certain now, and it makes me sad. To think that, after all, our vows came to nothing.

April—

Kirby and I don't have sex anymore; it's simply not possible. But we make love. There's an Indian healing ceremony that involves foot-washing and the application to the body of scented oils. He does that for me, chanting the low, slow meditation that goes with it. He makes me feel as if my weakening, withering body is a shrine.

At night we lie together and talk about what our lives have been. We used to plan trips, but not anymore—just lately we've given up that fantasy. That conceit. I'm not greedy the way I once was, I don't ask God to let me live for five more years, or three, or two. My ambitions have dwindled. I don't want to die in winter, and not in a hospital—that's all. How diffident. God, do you see how modest I am?

I think about writing down a word, an allusion to something we've shared—I don't know what it is yet—and Kirby opening it after I'm gone, and remembering. It would be a little way of staying alive.

A surprise—there is something left when there's no more hope. Something you make up. Acceptance—believe me—has a kind of joy in it. Yes, and from there, it's not that far to celebration. I'm longing to be with my dearest friends. I'm having a very good day today—maybe tomorrow will be the same. I want to call Lee and Emma and Rudy and tell them to have the women's group meeting here tomorrow night. It's been so long. And I have a lot to say. Ha. The hardest word is good-bye, and yet I almost think I could say it. I believe I could.

What is the best I can say for myself? That I loved, and I was loved. All the rest drops away at the end. I'm content.

28

Emma

Isabel died in her sleep sometime after midnight on the tenth of April. She had an embolus—a blood clot; it blocked an artery to her lung and killed her instantly. I hope. Kirby wasn't with her, he was sleeping on the sofa in the living room because she'd been restless earlier and he thought she might fall asleep more easily alone.

He found her in the morning, lying on her side with her eyes closed. I like that—I think it proves she was sleeping when she passed away. He said the covers were neat and tidy, not thrown off. She looked peaceful, he said. I believe she was dreaming. A sweet dream, with all of her friends in it, all of us who loved her. And then—I believe she just drifted away.

She didn't want a funeral, she didn't want to be buried. She specified in her will that after her body was cremated she wanted her son, Terry, to have the ashes, to dispose of as he saw fit.

Nobody liked this plan, especially Terry, who had no idea what was best to do with his mother's remains. We particularly hated it that there was no wake, no ceremony, no nothing. And so about three weeks after she died, I invited as many of Isabel's friends, family, and acquaintances as I could track down, and we had a memorial service for her at my house.

The place was packed. Standing room only. People spilled out into the dining room and the hall, the foyer, they sat behind the banister rails halfway up the stairs. We didn't have a minister—Isabel had belonged to most of the major religions and all the minor ones; how could we have chosen?—but we did have Kirby, and that was even better. There's something so gloomy and clerical about him, a priest-like quality that served him well as the master of ceremonies, so to speak, at Isabel's last service. I always thought there was something mysterious about Kirby, too, especially in the beginning, before I knew him. But the mystery turned out to be nothing more than that he loved Isabel with his whole heart, and that's no mystery at all.

I wish now I'd tried harder to know him while she was alive. I wish I'd been nicer to him. Not that I was ever mean, but—oh, I guess I was jealous of him. He was a stranger, an interloper. A man. We Graces don't always cotton to newcomers. But Isabel loved him very much, and I know, I really do know that that took nothing away from the love she had for the rest of us. For me. Isabel had enough love for everybody.

She had so many friends, a lot of them had to sit on the living room floor because there weren't enough chairs. I'd made coffee and put out sweet things, cookies and brownies, a bakery cake. When the crowd thinned, I planned to break out the booze and get into more of a wake mode for the closest mourners. I thought Isabel would appreciate that.

Kirby had brought some of her favorite CDs, and when people weren't eulogizing her we listened to New Age pinging and ponging, Mozart, and Emmylou Harris. New people kept arriving and departing, as if it were an open house, which I guess it was—people from her old neighborhood, classmates and professors from school, women from her old bridge club, cancer support group people, healing circle people, meditation group friends, miscellaneous Adams-Morgan neighbors. It astonished me how many of them stood up, cleared their throats, and spoke movingly and unselfconsciously about what Isabel had meant to them.

I had a small heart stoppage when Mick walked in. Without Sally. He maneuvered through the crowd to where I was standing, in the archway between the living and dining rooms, and he hesitated for what seemed like an hour but was really a split second before he leaned down and kissed me on the cheek. He was approximately the fiftieth person to murmur to me, "I'm so sorry," but *his* words I heard, his sympathy I took to my heart. I parroted, "Thank you so much for coming," and then he left me and found a place to sit on the floor across the room.

By chance, I caught Rudy's eye. She lifted one eyebrow a millimeter. It said everything.

Then she went back to listening to Mrs. Skazafava tell about Isabel's amazing green thumb, and how her little garden plot behind the building put everybody else's to shame. Grace, Isabel's dog, lay at Rudy's feet, her white muzzle draped over her instep. She's Rudy's dog now. She was supposed to be Lee's, but her arrival sent the overly refined Lettice into a decline. Meanwhile Rudy moved out of her house (I know, after all that) and into an apartment that allowed pets, so the solution was obvious. It's a good fit, too, Rudy and Grace. For now, each gives the other exactly what she needs.

Lee cried through the whole service, beginning to end. Henry held her hand, gave her his big red handkerchief, put his arms around her, and let her sob on his shoulder.

Someone read a poem. A woman from the healing circle stood up and sang a song she'd written especially for Isabel. A cappella. And she made everybody join in and sing it with her after teaching us the treacly chorus. I accidentally made eye contact with Rudy again. Big mistake. I had to turn my back to the room and bury my face in my hands, as if overcome with emotion. My good laugh dissolved into a good cry, and then I blew my nose and pulled myself together.

Terry had flown down from Montreal the day after Isabel died, and he hadn't gone back yet. His girlfriend, a beautiful black woman named Susan, had joined him a few days ago, and he'd brought her with him to the memorial service. I thought he might stand up and say something about his mother, but he didn't. I think he was afraid he would cry. (That's why *I* wasn't talking.) He'd brought an oblong mother-of-pearl box with Isabel's ashes in it, and set it on my mantel. Which sounds like it might be weird, but it wasn't. Not in the least. I'd put some lilies around the pretty box, made a little arrangement. Everybody's eyes went to it, over and over, and it looked dignified and peaceful and sweet. Like Isabel.

Gary didn't come. He sent flowers, though, and wrote a short and very nice note, which Kirby read out loud. I had no desire to see or speak to Gary ever again, but I did wonder how he was feeling about losing Isabel. I hoped he hurt. A lot. I hoped he hurt one-tenth as much as I did.

The impromptu speeches began to wind down. Kirby stood up. I'd never seen him in a suit before; he had on a dark gray one with a vest, a white shirt, no tie, and he looked good. Wasted, but good. Isabel's beauty, her facial purity, if you will, had grown more pronounced the sicker she got—and in a strange way, the same thing had happened to Kirby. Isabel's illness seared away everything in their faces except the character.

"I don't have much more to say," he said, hands behind his back in an at-ease military posture. "Isabel never despaired, even though I think she knew everything that was going to happen, right from the beginning. There was a Walt Whitman poem she liked, especially the part that went—'All goes onward and outward,/Nothing collapses/And to die is different from/What anyone supposes/And luckier.' She tried to believe that, and it gave her some comfort, I know. She was very brave. Always. She hid her anguish and sadness, although I know she felt them. Because she wasn't losing only one person she loved—as we have. She was losing all of them."

Kirby got his handkerchief out of his pocket and unashamedly blew his nose.

"Isabel believed death is a process, not an end. She said it was her job to hold on to life for as long and as well as she could—her karmic duty, she called it. But she also had faith that something comes after, something better. Not that she was anxious to get there," he said with a grim attempt at a smile. "She talked very openly about her fears, her grief. But her absolute faith that death isn't the end always kept her from despair. She just wished—she just wished she didn't have to go alone."

He looked helpless, gazing around the room at us with watery eyes, as if he wished he hadn't ended on that note.

"Well, I want to thank you all for coming. Isabel would've been moved by all your kind wishes and your—your eloquent words. Thank you. Thank you all very much."

Nobody from the Saving Graces had talked. Kirby was calling an end to the formal part of the service, and none of us had said anything about Isabel.

Lee had her mouth covered with Henry's kerchief, her head slumped on his chest. She was a hopeless mess. I sent Rudy an urgent look—*Get up! Get up and say something*. But she only smiled tragically and shook her head. I wanted to kill her.

"I would like to say something." My voice came out embarrassingly nasal, as if I had the world's worst cold. People who had started to get up sat back down. All the austere, expectant faces staring at me started my heart pounding.

"I just want to say—thank you, also, for coming, and thanks to Kirby for everything. And I also want to say . . ." How much I'll miss my friend, how much I love her, what she meant to me. How to start? My mind kept skipping back, back, looking for the beginning of what I should tell them about her.

"I should thank Lee, too—Lee Patterson—because about eleven years ago she had the idea for our women's group. The Saving Graces." On the floor at Rudy's feet, Grace heard her name and lifted her head to look at me. "That's how I first met Isabel. In fact, we had our first meeting at her house. I met you that night, too, Terry. Do you remember?" He smiled and shook his head. "You were sixteen and very surly."

Laughter.

"There were five of us in the group then, but over the years we've boiled down to four. Basically. Isabel and Lee, Rudy Lloyd—Rudy Surratt now, sorry—and me. I—if I could—for me—" I stumbled again. "If I tried to tell you what the Saving Graces have meant to me, we'd be here all day and I still wouldn't get it right. Isabel was older than the rest of us, and she was different. I don't mean *because* she was older, but just because she was—unique. I always felt we didn't deserve her. Me, anyway. She was the gentlest person I ever knew. Very quiet. She was a wonderful listener. She watched people, but not to judge them. She never judged anyone. I always knew she loved me. Very much."

Oh, shit. I was going to screw this up by bawling.

"I think," I soldiered on, "our friendships teach us a lot, make us grow and change. The Graces taught each other so many things, like how to tolerate our differences. How a good marriage works. How to understand another person's spiritual . . . longings. A sillier sense of humor, maybe a—sharper sense of irony. Hugging. A hundred other things. And Isabel, she wasn't our leader exactly, but I think she was our spirit. She was behind everything good or unselfish we did. I don't know how to explain this very well, but in the very best way, Isabel was our mother. And—I'm lost without her. I feel like an orphan."

I kept talking, not looking at Lee or Rudy. I knew if I did, we'd all break down.

"I just can't believe she's gone. A thousand times since she died, I've wanted to call her up and tell her something, something only she would get, or care about, or react to just right. I've even picked up the phone and started to dial. Then I remember. Lee does it, too—she's told me. We've lost the dearest friend, the most loving, unselfish friend. I try to think of something good, anything to make this bearable, but I can't. She died before she was in excruciating pain—that's all I can think of. Well, okay. Thank God for that.

"Toward the end it was hard to come and visit her. I never knew what to say. Good-bye was impossible. Because—then there's no more hope. Before you say good-bye, you can always say more, you can still fix things. Get it right. One more try. I think we live our lives like that—putting off getting it right, saying to ourselves, Maybe next time. And then, when there isn't going to be a next time, we can't bear it.

"So I couldn't tell Isabel good-bye. I don't know if she wanted me to or not. She was so kind—she took her cues from us. I think she was dying the way she thought would be easiest for the people who loved her. That was so typical of her.

"And—she was so easy to please. At the last, after I finally accepted the fact that there was nothing I could do to change things, nothing I could do to heal her or make it go away or get better or disappear—after I really knew I was going to lose her—everything got much, much simpler. Since there was no future, everything had to be in the moment. So I could make her face light up when she first saw me. I could make her laugh at a joke. I could say, 'I love you, Isabel,' and she would smile. That's all I could do, but it seemed like enough. And really, it's all we can *ever* do for each other, but we live with the illusion that time is infinite, that we're all immortal and there's no need to get anything exactly right, not now, not yet. Isabel taught me a lot of lessons, but I think that one was the most important.

"Well—I'm sorry, I didn't mean this to be so therapeutic. I wanted to talk about her, not myself. But I think she's smiling right now. She's thinking, *Jeez, she's not even drinking.* She used to say I talked a lot when I had more than one glass of wine. Which is true. So I'll stop. And just say—I love you, Isabel, and I'll miss you so much. Rudy's taking good care of your dog, and we're all going to watch out for Terry. And Kirby—we'll take care of him, too, because he'll be lonely. And we hope you're in some wonderful place now, someplace that deserves you. And that you're at peace. And—we'll never forget you." I hung my head and whispered, "Bye, Isabel." And because that was unbearable, I added to myself, "Talk to you later."

Rudy and Lee got up and hugged me. We made a sniffling, swaying tripod in the middle of the living room, and I guess that was the signal people were waiting for that the service was over.

Many of them left, but a lot stayed to eat and drink and party. That always gets me, how we can do that at wakes and such. I do it, too—I'm not saying it's wrong, just amazing. I've gone to funeral homes where the dead person is lying there in his or her coffin, and except for the immediate family—but sometimes them, too—everybody's carrying on like it's a class reunion. Well, it's just what we do, I suppose. Our primitive, cowardly way of dealing with too much grief or too close a call with death. If anybody would understand that and forgive it, it would be Isabel.

So I turned into a hostess, making drinks and passing food, thanking and thanking and thanking all the people who said it was brave of me to speak, it was good of me to host this service, it was just what Isabel would have liked. Meanwhile, I was constantly aware of Mick. He talked to Lee and Rudy, then to Henry for a long time. Whenever I let myself look at him, he was already looking at me. It was four months since the night we broke up in my bedroom, and I hadn't seen him since, not once. Lee didn't hang out with Sally much anymore, so that source of intelligence had dried up. He looked the same. Which is to say, beautiful. Healthier than he had last winter, not so white. The godawful haircut had grown out, and it had more silver in it than before. Very attractive. I could look at him and feel weak in the knees. So—had *nothing* changed? Maybe it was habit. Pavlovian mouth-watering based on nothing but conditioning. What a stupid affair we'd had anyway, pathetic, hopeless from the beginning. *Quit looking at me with your brown eyes, damn you.*

He must've heard. He turned his back.

Terry took me outside in the backyard for a private word. He's all grown up, very tall and handsome; he's got Gary's blue eyes, but something of Isabel's softness in them. We don't really flirt, but he likes it when I joke about wishing he were fifteen years older.

"Thanks again for having this," he said. "It's really meant a lot to me."

"I'm glad, but I didn't do anything."

"I wish she'd had a regular funeral."

"Well." I did, too, sort of. "But that's not what she wanted."

"I know. Listen, Emma." He squeezed his nose between his fingers, a manly gesture of indecision. I just can't get over how he's grown up.

"What?"

He looked away to say, "I don't know what the hell to do with the ashes."

"Oh."

"I just have no idea. Should I bury them? They have places where you can do that, memorial gardens. But would Mom have liked that?"

We shook our heads in agreement: no.

"Do you know if she had a favorite place? I asked my father, but he didn't know. What do you think I should do? I thought of giving them to Kirby, but . . . I just don't know."

"Hm." It was a problem. Terry would go back to Montreal, probably marry Susan, probably fly home once in a blue moon to see his father. What business did Isabel's ashes have in Canada?

"I was wondering," he said, looking at me hopefully. "I was thinking maybe the Saving Graces would, you know, like to have the responsibility."

I was thinking the same thing. But I said, "I don't know, Terry. She gave them to you. She must've had a reason."

"Well, she said I was supposed to do with them *as I saw fit*."

"Hm." He'd given this some thought. "Did you say anything about this to Lee?" I was more used to her making the big group decisions.

He shook his head. "She's kind of wrecked. I thought I'd ask you."

"Oh." I actually felt a little flattered. Imagine me being the grown-up. "Well, um. Okay, I think I can say for all of us, Rudy and Lee and me, that we'd be honored. So I'm saying yes, but I'll call you or write you and let you know what we're going to do before we do anything."

"That would be great." He grinned with relief, and I got a hint of what a burden this had been to him. How funny. I guess it's understandable. But the thought struck that it was possible we Graces knew Isabel better than her own son did, and that he was mature enough to realize it. And he was handing over her remains to the ones she'd trusted most to do right by them. Was that sad? Or was it a comfort? Something to think about later.

Terry and I hugged, and cried a little, and I told him again how much Isabel had adored him, how proud she was of him. He said he regretted more than anything that she'd never met Susan. I said she'd have loved her, too, and we cried some more.

Back inside, the crowd was thinning out, mostly the hard core of friends left now. People thanked me some more, I thanked them for coming. Out of habit, I looked around for Mick—and found him right behind me. "Emma," he said, "I have to go."

I walked out with him on the front porch. The sun was dying, sinking down orange and gold behind the houses on Nineteenth Street. It was late April, high spring, but still the cruelest month; the spent azaleas along my walk shivered in a frigid breeze, and my front lawn was still more mud than grass. I hugged my arms and thanked Mick for coming.

"I wanted to," he said. The absence of Sally curled around us like smoke. *Where's your wife?* I wanted to ask. *Does she know you're here?* Mick had liked Isabel, of course, but he hadn't known her very well. He'd come because of me.

"I liked what you said," he said.

"I talked too much."

"No."

"Yes. I embarrassed myself. I'm a writer, not a talker."

That reminded him. "How is your—"

"Don't ask."

He smiled, and oh, my idiotic heart turned inside out.

A man and his wife, Stan or Sam and Hilda something, came outside. The husband had been in Isabel's cancer support group. He looked healthy enough now, I noticed with some resentment. "Do you have to go? Well, thanks so much for coming," "Yes, it's late, thank you for inviting us," "Good luck to you," "God bless you"—and so on while Mick stood aside, awkward, waiting until we could be by ourselves again. It seemed to me we did a lot of that.

Stan and Hilda finally went away. Mick and I stood side by side at the porch rail and looked out at nothing, the car-lined street, the row house opposite mine. "You'll miss her," he said.

"I thought I was prepared, but I'm not. I miss her so much."

"At least you have your friends."

"Yeah." I sighed.

"I've always envied you for that."

"What? The Graces?"

"There's a fellow I go trout fishing with every spring, up in the Catoctins. The rest of the year I see him maybe three, four times. I call him my best friend."

"Oh, well, that's because you're a guy. Guys don't have friends the way we do. You have your—wives or your girlfriends for your best friends. We have each other." Oh, just keep talking, Emma, cram your foot all the way in. But it was mortifying to think he might think I was hinting around at the Sally question, when really I'd just been blithering, saying the first thing that came into my head.

"Emma," he said presently. I'd really missed hearing him say my name. "Can I call you?"

"What for?"

He laughed, looking down at his hands gripping the white wood railing. He had on a brown corduroy jacket and a blue shirt. While he kept his head turned, I looked at the line of his profile, the curve of dark stubble his beard made on his hard cheek. I didn't feel elated by his question. All I felt was weary.

"Has anything changed?" I hated having to ask. Anyway, I could see the answer in his face. "No, please don't call me, I don't want to see you. Oh, Mick. I hurt so much. If I added you—"

"Okay. It's okay, Emma."

I have never wanted anyone to hold me so much. But we didn't touch, not even our hands, and after a while it felt right, having absolutely nothing. Isabel was gone, and there was a hole in the world, and I had no hope of filling it.

Mick's bowed head moved me, though. His hair was disturbingly beautiful. I drew away from him abruptly—he looked up. Now his eyelashes, the curl of his nostrils, the shape of his mouth, everything about him was like a heavy weight pulling me under. I had to snap the line before he drowned me.

Luckily some more people came out on the porch, people I had to deal with. "Good-bye," I told him, and I meant it. He knew it—we both knew this was it. I turned away and said all the obligatory things to the departing couple, nice people, one of Isabel's instructors and her husband. When I looked again, Mick was gone.

So then I went inside and said everything that was expected of me, including good-bye, to about twenty more people. You'd think I'd have gotten better at it, smoother, more facile, you'd think the word would be tripping off my tongue. Good-bye, good-bye. Good-bye. By the end, though, it stuck in my throat.

Rudy noticed. Oh God, Rudy, help me, I thought, but she knew already. She got rid of the last of them, and she stayed with me that night. "Maybe I should get a cat," I said, watching her with Grace, their easy, admirable, human-dog relationship.

"That's it," she said gently. She lit a cigarette and handed it over to me. "That's what we'll do next, Emma. We'll get you a cat."

29

Rudy

Nobody thought about the logistics of ash strewing until the time came to do it. "We'll sprinkle them out at sea," we said, not considering past those six words, which sound perfectly feasible, even romantic. Isabel would like it, we agreed; she loved the ocean, particularly the Outer Banks and Cape Hatteras, which was our place, the Saving Graces' special spot. Also she was a water sign (Aquarius), and she believed in things like that, astrology and such. Strewing her ashes at sea would be just right.

But you can't do it, there's no such thing, at least not from the land. The wind blows the ashes straight back, *inland*, not at all what you intended. Luckily we—I should say Lee—discerned this before we opened the mother-of-pearl box, thereby saving Isabel's ashes from being blown back onto the Carolina dunes. Which wouldn't have been so terrible, I didn't think, but we really wanted them *at sea*.

Lee suggested we charter a boat and sail out a ways before strewing the ashes—she'd seen that in a movie, she recalled, and it had worked out quite well. Emma said maybe we could walk out to the end of the fishing pier in Frisco and strew them from there. But eventually both of these suggestions were rejected for the same reason: they involved the presence of other people. We wanted privacy when we said good-bye to Isabel for the last time.

The solution we hit on was another one that's a lot better in theory than practice. We put on our bathing suits and simply swam out as far as we could. The tacit plan was, we'd each say a few words, Lee would open the box, and the wind would take the ashes and blow them gently out to sea. Which it did, finally, but we didn't have time to say much of anything because Emma almost drowned. We'd swum out too far, and we'd forgotten what a poor swimmer she is. Those were our two mistakes.

"Have to go back!" she sputtered, dog-paddling, swallowing saltwater. "I can't go any farther. Do it now, Lee, do it now!"

Lee swims like a dolphin—she'd gotten all that way out with her arms over her head, careful to keep the box out of the water. "Okay," she said, "well, wait, we'll do it here, then, this is far—"

"Now, hurry! I have to go back!"

"Okay. Okay—we commit these ashes of our dear friend to the ocean she loved so much when she was with us. Isabel, we—"

"Help!"

I caught Emma by the hair just before she went under. "Hurry it up, Lee, just do it," I yelled, trying to pull Emma on top of me. "Hold still, I've got you, I've got you. *Say something.*"

"What?" Emma coughed up water and spat.

"Say something about Isabel."

"Bye, Isabel!"

Lee glared at her, treading water strongly. "We commit these ashes to the sea. Okay, I'm opening it. Rudy?"

"I'll miss you, Isabel. I love you. Rest in peace." I had something better planned, but Emma was going to swamp both of us. Lee opened the box—the wind caught the chunky ashes in a blinding, smoky billow, *whoosh*. They lay on the water for an instant, then melted like snowflakes. When the next wave came, they vanished.

"I'm throwing the box, too."

"Oh, no," I said. "Well, okay. But I don't know. Emma, should she—"

"Jesus Christ!"

Lee threw the box, and I started back toward the beach with

my arm around Emma's chest, towing her along like a lifeguard. I didn't even know I could do that. Lee stayed for a minute or two longer, then struck out for shore behind us.

You can laugh later at farces like that, and we did try to even then, but the truth is, we were upset. Maybe if we'd waited longer, a year instead of only two months after Isabel's passing, the perspective of time might have lessened our sense of failure. But we sat in the sand while the sun went down behind us, silent and miserable and, in Lee's case, mad. It wasn't our finest hour. What was supposed to have been moving and important and even cathartic had turned into an undignified fiasco that didn't do Isabel credit. We felt we'd let her down.

It was the first of our two nights at Neap Tide. We hadn't had time to shop for groceries, so we went out to dinner that night at Brother's, our old standby. But not even good, greasy, North Carolina barbecue could cheer us up. Too many memories. And I hadn't been drinking for the last three months, so I couldn't even synthesize a good time.

We moped back to the cottage, where things didn't look up. Nobody said it, but I knew we were all thinking, *Why was this ever fun?* What's special about sitting around playing gin rummy or watching silly television shows you wouldn't be caught dead watching at home, eating too much, reading books you can't concentrate on because somebody's always interrupting? With trivia and nonsense, not anything you'd really want to talk about, because you've already said everything you had to say on the interminable ride down and nothing's left but mindless chatter?

It didn't used to seem like mindless chatter. Maybe it hadn't been profound, but it wasn't mindless when Isabel was here. Maybe we were no good without her. Maybe the group was finished.

Maybe we'd keep meeting for a while, then gradually, imperceptibly, taper off, everyone pretending all was well, until one day we stopped meeting at all.

I always thought it was bossy, officious Lee who kept the Graces in line, kept us going. Had it been Isabel? But she'd been so quiet. Emma said she was our "spirit." What if we were lost without her?

"I think I'll go to bed," I said at ten o'clock. Emma and Lee looked up at me, hollow-eyed as owls, and then quickly away. Neither of them said, "So early?" "Night," we told one another dispiritedly, and I wandered downstairs.

I had a room to myself this time, the one with the bunk beds Emma and I had shared last summer. It was lonely by myself. I missed Grace. I'd wanted to bring her, but I'd asked Kirby to keep her over the weekend. Her back legs are too crippled with arthritis, she couldn't have made it up and down the wooden steps.

Lying in bed, I took it as a good sign that I felt homesick, considering I don't even have a home. I gave it to Curtis—yes, I know, after all that—and now I live in a big, sunny, one-bedroom apartment on the western edge of Georgetown. Curtis isn't fighting the divorce at all. But then, I'm not asking him for much. A cash settlement, that's all I want, enough to keep me on my feet until I start earning a living wage. (At what?) After that, we're done. Dissolved.

This doesn't sit well with Lee and Emma, all this magnanimity from me. Even Eric thinks I'm being hasty. It's worth it, though; anything to make this go smoothly. I'm terrified it's going to backfire. It's working too well, I don't trust my good fortune. I'm walking through a minefield carefully, carefully, panicky at the thought of a bomb exploding under my feet. I used up so much psychic energy leaving Curtis, I'm depleted. But slowly restocking. These things take time.

For instance, I haven't gone back to landscaping class yet. But I will, fall term for sure. So what do I do with myself? I've been throwing pots again, and that's such a pleasure, I can't believe I ever gave it up. I've been keeping a journal. Seeing Eric. Not drinking. Taking long, slow walks with Grace. Doing some volunteer work.

Almost every day I uncover some new way in which Curtis . . . "exploited me" isn't right. Tricked me? Whatever—here's a miniature example. We liked different TV programs. All Curtis ever wanted to watch were CNN, CNBC, and C-SPAN. Period, nothing else. Me, I liked stories—plays, movies, hospital dramas, sitcoms, *Masterpiece Theater*—anything with a story in it. He knew this about me but he ignored it, never acknowledged it. Intelligent people watched the interior secretary address the Senate or the Ways and Means Committee chair give a press conference. And when those were over, intelligent people turned the television off.

The way Curtis got my passive complicity was to make fun of the kinds of shows I liked: they were trite, sentimental, melodramatic, banal, badly acted, phony, meretricious, sleazy—and he always pretended I agreed with him, that we were both above that kind of trash. I know I was a coward, but his scorn was so cutting and dismissive, I *did* agree with him. I lied. I don't know how to explain how he did this to me, all I can say is I was helpless. He made up look down. When I was under his spell, I'd have sworn black was blue if he'd wanted me to.

Now he's gone, and I watch *E.R.* and old movies and *Seinfeld* reruns. I'm a couch potato! It's not so much the programs that perk me up, it's the guiltlessness I feel when I watch them. I feel like a delinquent let out of reform school. I'm on probation, so I still have to watch it, no acting out, no having *too* much fun. But I have something now I can't remember having for ages, maybe ever. Hope.

"Night, Em."

"Night, Lee."

They were whispering; they closed their doors softly, trying not to disturb me. Would they lie awake now like me, fretting and frustrated, mulling over their troubles and wondering why we three couldn't seem to connect? We don't trust ourselves as a group anymore. It's like—if you had four legs and one was amputated, you'd be in a lot of distress while you learned to walk on three, if you ever did. And you probably wouldn't like yourself very much, because you'd be so awkward, so . . . graceless.

I remember the last time I lay in this bunk bed, and Emma lay on that one, and we stayed up late and talked about our lives. Things were just beginning to change for me, I was just starting to feel stronger. Emma said, "Whoa, Rudy, you are a wild woman," when I told her about smoking in front of Curtis. That's when he must have begun to feel the change in me, right around then. So that means he had six months to be afraid of losing me—the old me, the dependent one whose whole life revolved around his—before he took the fatal step of telling me he was dying.

My God, what a desperate act. I still can't get over it. Pathological, Eric calls it. He says Curtis needs therapy a lot more than I do.

Yes, well, I think I've always known that. We were coconspirators in neediness, and it was only an illusion that he was in charge. We held each other up. You can call our relationship sick, but people do all sorts of things to survive, and at least we never hurt anyone but each other. I don't hate him. Eric and I are still working on what I feel, but it's not hate, it's not even anger anymore. I understand Curtis too well, I'm too much like him, I can't honestly keep vilifying what he did to me.

But I can't go back to him, and that proves there really is such a thing as change. For so long I thought there wasn't—well, all my life. I think it's the heart of despair, not being able to believe in change.

Now I've not only seen it, I've *provoked* it. I *am* a wild woman. I alternate between euphoria and stark terror, but it's not like manic depression, you know, it's more like—*normal* insanity. Garden variety neurosis, you could call it. How refreshing and delightful, theoretically.

But I'm frightened, and I need a lot of help, and it scares me to think the Graces might not be able to give it to me. Could that really happen? We're all in mourning, locked away in our private griefs. Isabel is our shared grief, but we have personal ones, too. Mine is Curtis, Emma's is Mick. Lee's is a baby.

Maybe we just need time to adjust to our three-leggedness. But I'm afraid. Not all change is good change. Oh, I wish you were here, Isabel! You wouldn't tell us what to do. But somehow, if you were here, we'd know.

30

Lee

The Graces always make clam chowder at the beach. Well, we did for two out of our four years here. This was the fifth year, and if ever we needed a tradition, now was the time. So I insisted.

"You two start peeling the potatoes," I told Rudy and Emma—I'd brought five pounds down with us; why buy new ones when I had so many at home?—"and I'll go buy fresh clams. Back in twenty minutes."

It turned out to be forty minutes, but they were still peeling when I returned. They sat at the kitchen table, their heads nearly touching, dropping potato peelings into a paper sack on the floor between them. How many dinners have we made in one another's kitchens in the last eleven years? How many glasses of wine have we drunk, how many secrets have we told? They glanced up and smiled at me, then went back to work. The stillness between them was easy and comfortable, they were like an old married couple. I envied them—each still had her best friend. Rudy's thinner these days, though. And Emma's quieter. What am I? Sadder.

Rudy looked up at me curiously. "Did you get the clams?" I hadn't moved from the doorway.

"Yes." I put the bag on the counter. "I went to the post office, too. Sometimes there's a bill in the mailbox, or a tax form or something. I forward it to my mother."

"And?" Emma frowned at me. "What's that?"

I turned the envelope over in my hand. "A letter. It's from Isabel."

They stared. They shoved their chairs back and stood up.

"What do you mean?"

"That's not her handwriting."

"It's her address, though."

"Let me see it. What's the postmark?"

I kept the letter and sat down at the table. "It's Kirby's handwriting. The postmark says May eighth."

"May eighth. But she . . ."

"Kirby mailed it," I said. "Afterward. It's to all of us, and it's to Neap Tide. She must've known we'd come here. She must've wanted us to read it here."

I laid the envelope on the table and we stared at it, our names on separate lines in Kirby's neat script. Isabel's return address in the corner.

"Should we open it?" Rudy stood stiff and straight, gripping her hands under her chin.

"Nah, let's pitch it in the trash. We've got potatoes to peel here."

She stuck her tongue out at Emma. "I mean should we open it *now*? Maybe we should wait until after dinner."

"Why?"

"I don't know. It's more . . ."

"More like a ceremony," I said. "Everything else out of the way. Then we could take it out on the deck and read it."

"It's raining, and it'll be dark," Emma pointed out.

"It could stop by then. We could light candles."

Emma lifted her hands and let them fall, slapping her thighs. *"You want to eat dinner before you read Isabel's letter?"*

So we read it before dinner. But first, Rudy went downstairs and got a fresh pack of cigarettes. Emma opened the best bottle of wine, the Chardonnay we were saving to drink with the chowder, and poured glasses for her and for me. Rudy made herself some iced tea. I went in the bathroom and filled my pockets with Kleenex.

"Who's reading it?"

"I am," I said.

Emma raised her eyebrows, but didn't say anything.

It was still drizzling out, so we sat on the floor in the living room, ashtrays and drinks and tissues placed in strategic spots around us. I slid my thumb under the flap of the envelope, and Rudy said, "Wait," and jumped up. "I have to go to the bathroom."

Emma scowled and sipped her wine while we waited, not looking at me. Steeling herself. She doesn't like to show her emotions in public. Oh, and God forbid she should cry, that would be the end of the world.

Rudy plopped back down and lit up. "Okay," she said, shaking out the match, exhaling a strong stream of smoke. "I'm ready."

Inside the envelope were three typewritten pages, and a fourth page in handwriting on top. "This one's from Kirby."

"Read it."

"'Dear Emma, Lee, and Rudy.'"

"Alphabetical order," Emma noted.

"'In the last few weeks of her life, Isabel began to feel detached from the things she had known and even the people she had loved. She said it was a gift dying bestowed on the still-living, one that, on the whole, she could have done without. She said it was hard to remember who she had been, the "old Isabel," and she found it especially difficult to care or even talk about many of the things that had once been such vital concerns to her.

"'But she wanted to write a letter to the Saving Graces, and so she had to come back. It was a trip she didn't always want to make. A trip back for love, she said, settling on her left side against the sofa cushions, the only position she could be comfortable in at the last, and slowly dictating the words in this letter that I typed on my computer. It took several sessions; as you know, her strength had diminished significantly by then. I know she wanted nothing more than to slip away, and in fact part of her had already gone. She would lie for long periods without speaking, not sleeping but perhaps dreaming, detaching from this life, moving to whatever comes next.

"'I think the speed of her physical deterioration at the end took her by surprise—she thought she had more time. When she realized the truth, she had no choice but to use me to say the things she still wanted to say. I hope you don't mind my part in this. It was unavoidable. That Isabel trusted me to be the intermediary is a point of pride for me, and a deep satisfaction. You had the privilege of knowing her longer, but I don't think it's possible you could have loved her more.

"'With kindest regards, Goodloe Kirby.'"

"Who?"

"Goodloe Kirby."

"Goodloe?"

We smiled. A fitting name.

"Okay," Rudy said softly, and I started to read Isabel's letter.

> My dears. I hope I'm right, and you are all three at Neap Tide. I want to think you're together and hearing this—Lee, you read it—at the same time. Is it a beautiful day? I'm picturing you on the deck in late afternoon, with the sun going down over the sound. Emma's safe from too much exposure now, so she's in her cutoff jeans and her faded red sweatshirt; she's had her nose in a book all day, and she's ready for a drink and some conversation. Rudy, sleek as a long black cat, what have you been doing? Sketching on the beach, I think. And taking walks by yourself. But now you're sipping a Coke or something, ready to be sociable. And Lee, I think you've prepared some clever hors d'oeuvre, or maybe you've mixed up a fancy drink in the blender. You look smashing in something simple and tasteful you just got at Saks; it's the latest color, and it makes you look very beautiful.

"If you're going to cry," Emma warned, "you can't read it."

I thought of writing three separate letters, private letters, but decided against it. We've all kept a secret or two over the years, or shared it with only one other, but most of the time we were a group. So I'm writing to you all at once. Besides, secrets take too much energy.

Rudy—You're my hero. I was never so proud of anyone as I was of you the night you made Curtis move out of the house. So brave! I wish you knew how strong you are. You said you couldn't have done it without us, but I don't believe it. Anyway, even if it were true, isn't that what friends are for? But look at your life—look how gracefully you live it. You don't believe me, I know. Emma, Lee—try to convince her. Rudy, you're so kind, so empty of malice toward anyone. I admire your strength and valor, all your courage in the face of a childhood, a heritage that would've leveled by now anyone less brave than you. I'm sorry to say I don't think you will ever have an easy time of it, not in this life, but I know you'll live well. Never forget your true friends, who will always be there and will always love you.

Now, men. I hope you can learn to trust one again. I know you will, but I hope it's sooner rather than later, because you have so much to give. Share yourself with someone who deserves you the next time. And be careful. Borrow some of Emma's skepticism—just a little. Pray for some of Lee's good luck.

I have one more bit of advice. (I'm allowed that, don't you think, from my exalted position.) If you can, make peace with your mother. Heal that wound. I don't know for certain—Eric would know, ask him—but I don't think you can move on until you try. I can say this to you myself as a daughter and a mother. It may not work, but the trying is everything. You'll never be able to control your family's instabilities, but you won't catch them—they're not contagious anymore, because you've grown immune. You have, Rudy. You're not that little girl anymore, the one who stayed with her mother in the bathroom, lay with her on the bloody tiles until the grown-ups came. You're Rudy Surratt, all grown up, clever and creative, and so lovely with your huge, forgiving heart.

I love you, Rudy. I have so much faith in you. I'll be watching you, because your new life is going to be so interesting. Take good care. Only treat yourself with a little of the gentleness you show others, and you'll thrive.

I paused. "That's all," I said. "The next part is to Emma."

Rudy lay down on her back and folded her hands over her eyes. "Keep going," she said thickly. "What's she say to Emma?"

First I had to blow my nose.

Emma—You know what I'm going to miss most about you? The way you keep it to yourself that you think all my New Age beliefs are bullshit. Such forbearance! I love it when you turn your head and roll your eyes, but never say a word. Tolerance, you know, is the essence of friendship. Your tolerance, thank goodness, came from love, not indifference. Oh, you are so dear to me.

I have advice for you, too, of course. Oh, lots of it. It comes in smug-sounding little epigrams, for some reason:

Fear kills. Protecting yourself backfires eventually. Failure isn't failure, it's a step, and life is nothing but steps. Or failures, with occasional, widely spaced successes. If you don't screw up pretty regularly, you're only running in place. Also, pain isn't all it's cracked up to be. Speaking from experience. And living in fear of pain isn't really living at all.

Got that?

Specifically—How can you not know what to write about? "I haven't found my subject yet," you claim. (And when you tell me about some of your experiments, I must say I can only agree.) I see the problem very clearly: you've been hiding behind stories. They might be good stories, but they're not true, so you hate them. Then you hate yourself. Stop doing this.

Telling the truth is scary, I know, but you have enough courage. You do. Emma, don't you really know what to write about? Us, my darling. Don't you think? Write a book about us.

As for the man you're in love with. This advice may surprise you—you probably think I have no sympathy for the other woman, considering my marital history. I do believe that good behavior is important, and so is honor, and honesty. But if everyone perpetuates a wrong out of the very best of intentions, it's still a wrong. The child you're both protecting can't be protected, not like this, and neither can the woman. It's time to move, Emma, let life go on. It's so short, oh, it's so short. You can take what you want now. I think you really can.

Try not to be so afraid. You told me you didn't have room for any more suffering. Well, I'm gone now; I've freed up a little room for you. Ha. I can't deny that love sometimes requires suffering, but if this man is the one for you, he'll be worth it.

Oh, must I keep calling him 'this man'? For heaven's sake, tell Lee who he is. I promise you, she won't be shocked.

Thank you for the gifts you've given me—so much laughter, your lovable insecurities, your loyalty. There's no one else like you. It's been my privilege to love you. Now, be brave—follow Rudy's example! And all will be well.

I looked up. "That's the end. Okay, who's the guy?" Emma looked close to tears. That was so upsetting to me, I made a joke. "It's Henry, isn't it?"

She gaped—she believed me! It was wonderful—this *never* happens, it's always the other way around. Then she got it, and burst out laughing. "Oh, God," she said, and flopped over on her back next to Rudy. I watched their stomachs bump up and down in time to their teary-faced giggling. Oh, so Rudy knew, too.

"Am I the only one who doesn't know who this man is?"

Emma popped up. "I'm sorry—it was sticky, Lee, I just couldn't tell you."

"Well? So? Tell me now."

She shrugged, trying to look careless, but I could see she was nervous. "Okay. It's Mick."

"Mick! Mick Draco?" I couldn't have been more surprised. "But I thought you didn't even like him!" I wanted details—but first I wanted to read Isabel's letter to me. "Why didn't you tell me? I hardly even see Sally anymore, if that's what you were worried about."

"Well, you know. Yeah. Partly."

"Henry talks to Mick, though," I said. "You know Sally's moved back to Delaware."

Emma's slack-jawed expression said no, she didn't know.

"What's this, now?" Rudy said, sitting up, too.

"They've separated. You didn't know? Mick's probably going to move to Baltimore so he can study art at the Maryland Institute."

"But—Jay—but what about Jay—" Emma couldn't even make her tongue work. First she went white, now she was pink-faced.

"They're working it out. Sally's got him for now, but they're talking about sharing custody. This just happened, according to Henry. Like about a week ago."

"Why didn't you *tell* me?" She went white again. Before I could answer that ridiculous question, she whispered, "Why didn't *he* tell me?" and covered her mouth with her hands. "I told him I wouldn't wait," she mumbled through her fingers. "What if he doesn't care anymore? Oh, but at the service, he was so— But why do you think he didn't tell me? Should I call him? Would that be pushy? What if he's not interested anymore, what if he's moved on? What if he found someone else?"

"In a *week*?"

"It's possible!"

"Well, then you'll suffer," Rudy said.

"Isabel says suffering's worth it," I said.

Emma took her hands away. "Right. Okay. I'll call him." She started to get up.

"Hey!"

"Oh." She dropped back down, laughing, blushing with embarrassment. "Sorry, I'm sorry, go ahead, finish the letter."

"Well, not if it's going to inconvenience you in any way, God knows I wouldn't want to—Stop it, cut it out, would you? That's enough—" But I couldn't help laughing when she put her arms around me and kissed me all over my face. Rudy cracked up. I *hate* when Emma does that, which of course is why she does it.

But it worked—the three of us finally, finally felt normal again, like our old selves with one another. It was the best time for us since Isabel died.

"Okay, I'm reading this now. Do you mind? Get hold of yourselves."

"Right," said Rudy.

"Right. We're serious. Read." Emma drew her knees up and hugged them. Even her face looked different—sharper, as if her skin had tightened or the bones were sticking out more than they had five minutes ago. She was like a stretched wire; if you plucked her she'd make a high, tight, pinging sound.

I turned back to Isabel's letter. I really wanted to read it by myself, but that wouldn't have been fair.

> Lee. Sweetest Lee. What should I say to you? We've talked so much in these last days, there's very little left to say. Except that I'll miss you so much. Have Rudy and Emma thanked you lately for starting our women's group? They should. Once a week at least, I should think.

Watery giggles from Emma and Rudy.

> You're the sane one, we always said. Sometimes, because of that, we forgot to be soft with you, believing you were strong

and didn't need us to be so gentle. You are strong—but also tender in the center. I can't imagine the last dozen years of my life without you. You've been my friend and my daughter. My delight.

Nobody said anything while I stopped for a minute.

A little time has passed since you and Henry gave up trying for your own baby. Mourning time. And I'm gone—you won't mix up those two losses so readily now. You can see more clearly. Lee—good news. Did you know there's a child looking for you? I tried to tell you this before, but I didn't say it right. I've been thinking about it a lot. Emma won't want to hear how I know this, so I won't say—but I do happen to know for certain that there's a child somewhere right now who's looking for you and Henry. You have to try to find him. (Or her; even I don't know this detail, Emma.) And when you do—and you will—you'll have to love him with your whole heart. And you will.

I'm so happy for you. This is a deep, deep comfort to me, knowing this about you. And your baby—ah, what a wonderful mother he'll have. Lucky, lucky baby.

There's so much more I could say. My beloved Graces. Lee, Rudy, Emma, the friends of my heart. Then again, there's really nothing else to say. I feel so close to you. I've thought of something you can do for me. In fact, I insist on it; I'll brook no argument. You have to find a transient member who'll stay. A nontransient; a permanent. Really, you have to try, no halfhearted measures, no false welcomes or disingenuous goodwill. Two new members would be even better. Our group can't be allowed to fade away—you know that. Do this for me. Please. Because it's not really for me, it's for you. I wish it for you.

Thank you for all you've given to me. Lee, Emma, Rudy, I love you. Thank you for staying with me to the end. Do you know what I regret? That I won't be there when what's happening to me happens to each of you. To give back a little of the love and solace and sweetness you've given me.

But then again—Emma, you knew this was coming—maybe I will be. Yes, I think I will. In fact, now that I've thought of it, I'm counting on it. Just not, please God, anytime soon.

All my love,
Isabel

31

Emma

I made Rudy and Lee go outside on the deck when I called Mick. Well, the only phone is in the kitchen, and they'd have been able to hear me. It wasn't raining anymore. Just a little damp. They were fine.

But guess what, the line was busy. Who was he talking to? Any number of loathsome possibilities crossed my mind.

"The line's busy, you can come back."

They returned, and together we set the table and finished making the chowder.

"Okay, go out now, I'm calling him again. Here," I said, sensing mutiny, shoving a bag of pretzels at Rudy. "Eat these if you get hungry."

They left, muttering snide things, and I dialed Mick's number again.

"Hello?"

From now on, I will associate the great emotions, fear, dread, heart-stopping relief, with the smell of cooking clams.

"Mick? This—"

"Emma?"

"Yes. Hi. Um . . . hi. I was just talking to Lee, and she—"

"Are you at home?"

"No, I'm at Hatteras."

"Did you go down today?"

"Yesterday. We got here yesterday."

He laughed, the oddest sound. "That explains it."

"What?"

"I called you all night last night. I was sure you had a date. One of your ubiquitous men."

My legs started to tremble. I slid to the floor slowly, carrying the phone down with me. "One of my ubiquitous men?" Euphoria. I was aware of my jaw, my throat; my lips felt swollen; I didn't sound like myself. "I called you just now," I said, "but the line was busy. I figured it was your new girlfriend."

He laughed again. Giddy. "No, that was Jay."

"Oh." That sobered me up. "Where is he?"

"With his mother. Sally's staying with her parents in Wilmington. While she looks for a place. For her and Jay."

"Oh. So you . . . "

"We've separated. As of about ten days ago. I have a lot to tell you." He paused, then blurted out, "Emma, why the hell are you so far away?"

"I know! Oh, Mick." And then I had to ask, "Why did you wait ten whole days to call me?"

"Well, for one thing, I wasn't sure it would make any difference."

"How could you think that?"

"Because the last time we spoke, you were very clear. About us. Don't you remember?"

"Of course I remember." That excruciating interval on the front porch. "But that's because you didn't give me any hope. You didn't see anything changing."

"I know. It happened all of a sudden. The other reason is because I wasn't sure she'd really go. Stay gone. Now I'm sure, but if she had come back, it would've been bad. For you."

"Why?" I asked fearfully.

"I wouldn't have stayed, that's not what I mean."

"Oh."

"If she'd come back, I'd have left, Emma. Because it's really over."

"Oh."

"But I didn't want you in the middle of that, if it happened. That's why I didn't call you."

"Oh." That was a good reason. It made me grin like a hyena and quietly bang my fist on the floor. "How did it happen? If you want to tell me. I know you've always—"

"I want to tell you. I want to *see* you. What if I drove down there tonight?"

Now I was really coming undone. "Well, you could, but I'll be home tomorrow."

"Tomorrow. I don't know. That's a long time."

"I know."

"I could meet you in Richmond," he said, and we laughed like teenagers. "Or Norfolk."

"I guess that wouldn't make much sense."

"Guess not."

"Fredericksburg, though . . ." More giggling. "Oh, Mick. This is . . ." Just what I've always wanted. To say stupid things to you long-distance.

"What?"

"Good. This is good."

"Yes."

Long, smiling pause.

"What are you doing?" he asked. "Where is everybody?"

"I'm sitting on the kitchen floor. Rudy and Lee are out on the deck—I banished them. They're fine, it stopped raining. Where are you?"

"I'm in the kitchen, too. You've never been in my house before."

"No. Is it nice?"

"Come and see."

"I will." I could not, simply could not, stop grinning. "So are you okay? With the separation? How's Jay?"

"He's much better than I thought he'd be. Unless I'm kidding myself. I miss him—that's the worst of it. Emma, I might move to Baltimore, try to go to the Maryland Institute. If I can get in—it's one of the best private art colleges in the country."

"You'll get in. What would you do, get a master's?"

"Yeah. And I'd like being closer to Jay. Sally surprised me. She's not fighting custody, she wants us both to have him."

"Thank God. That was the main thing."

"So when I see you, you can rub it in about how I should've done this years ago. Except that it couldn't have happened any sooner. I don't think."

"Not one word. I'll be a model of self-restraint."

I could hear him smiling, feel it in the pauses.

"So," he said. "What do you think about Baltimore?"

"I think it's great. It's only an hour's drive. We'll work everything out."

"That's what I was hoping. You know, it's . . ."

"What."

"Hard to switch over from the daydream to reality."

"How do you mean?" I knew, I just wanted to hear him say it.

"The things that seem to be happening now. About to happen. I've been imagining them for a long time, almost since I met you."

"Have you?"

"But I was afraid to hope."

"I know. Me, too."

"But now. Now it seems to be working out."

"It's terrifying. Because it's too good."

"Or else . . ."

He didn't finish, but I knew where that was heading, too. *Or else it won't work.* Always a possibility. Mick didn't have much of a track record for failed relationships—only one that I knew of—but I sure did. And we'd been pining for each other for a year and a half. If that's not a setup for disaster, I don't know what is.

"How come we're not even *more* afraid?" I wondered. "I should be paralyzed. But instead I've got this—ridiculous—*faith*. I feel silly even saying that. But I have it, I do. Because this isn't like anything that's ever happened before. To me. Oh, Mick, I can't say these things to you over the phone."

"I know. Tomorrow."

"Tomorrow. Okay. Oh, *man*. I feel very . . . lustful. All of a sudden."

"Lustful." The way he said it, surprised and glad and in agreement. Mmm.

"Lustful." It was beginning to sound onomatopoeic.

"Call me," he said, "as soon as you get home."

"Don't worry."

"Do you want to come here?"

"I don't know." Ah, the delicious logistics. "No, you come to my house. Is that okay?"

"Yes."

We talked a little longer. But it wasn't very satisfying. Too much to say, and definitely too much lust. And we couldn't even talk dirty because I wasn't really alone. He told me the bare outline of how the split with Sally had come about. She'd asked him point blank, over dinner at the Yenching Palace on Connecticut, if he loved her. He could have said yes and meant it in a charitable, faraway, technical sense; he'd done that often enough before, he said. Instead he told her the barer, harder truth. He said no.

She cried, but she didn't break down and she wasn't destroyed. He thought she might even have been relieved. "Or else I'm kidding myself," he said again. Either way, it was her idea to go back to Delaware. Jay would be with her more than with him at the beginning, and he was almost reconciled to it. "He loves his grandparents, and they're great with him. I think he'll be all right. I'll see him all the time. I'm rationalizing, I know—"

"No, but it's true, you *will* see him."

"But it won't be the same."

"No, it won't. But after a while, maybe it'll be better."

Had I really said that? I wanted to get up and look in a mirror, see if my appearance had changed, too.

"Okay," I said eventually. "I guess I should go. They probably want to eat. Lee and Rudy." I could see their outlines through the screen, lying in the deck chaises, Rudy's cigarette tip a waving red dot in the dark.

"Okay," Mick said. Halfhearted.

Such a juvenile pleasure. It took us ten more minutes to hang up. This is how it's going to be, I thought. Maybe it won't work (but I think it will), but in the meantime we get all this happiness.

"I love you," I whispered. Very brave. *Isabel, are you listening?*

He said it back, and added my name. I can't get enough of that, Mick saying "Emma." Oh, Jeez. Pretty soon I'll be scribbling his name in my geography book.

"See you tomorrow," I said.

"Good night, Emma."

"Night."

"See you tomorrow."

"Yeah. Or you could call me later."

"Okay."

Startled silence, then we laughed at the simplicity of the solution. It made saying good-bye so much easier.

"Well?"

"Well?"

"We talked." I drifted over to the railing and hunched over it, too scattered and dreamy and romantic to sit.

Rudy got up and came to stand beside me. "You talked?"

"We heard that." Lee got up and moved to my other side.

"Right there," I said, leaning over farther. "Well, you can't see from here; farther in."

"What?"

"We kissed for the first time."

Rudy sighed.

Lee gasped. "That *weekend?*"

"Yep."

"I want to hear all about this, every single detail."

"Okay." No problem. I had never felt more generous.

"But first, are you going after him?"

"Am I *going after* him?"

"Isn't that what Isabel said you should do?"

"I guess she did."

"So? Are you?"

I smiled. Wasn't it written all over my face? Lee can be so literal. "Are you going to adopt a child?" I countered.

"Oh, Em." She wrapped her arms around herself and squeezed. "It's looking for me," she whispered, staring up at the sky. The clouds had blown away; the stars were out and winking.

"I take it that's a yes?"

She nodded slowly, dreamy-eyed. "Why did I wait so long?"

Rudy and I exchanged a look. "Well," I said, "why *did* you?"

"It's—I don't know. Now it's obvious, but before—We ruled it out without even really thinking about it. Henry said he wanted his own, but—and I used that, I put it in my ball of reasons, I had this long list of reasons for why it had to be ours, and they didn't even make any sense. Isabel tried to tell me, but I couldn't hear her."

"You were so determined."

"And another thing is, they don't talk about it in fertility clinics. I've spent the last two years in doctors' offices, and not once in all that time was the word *adoption* mentioned. Not once. Isn't that amazing? Not even by a nurse. So I didn't think about it."

"And Henry won't mind?"

"Oh, no. He won't mind."

Now I wished *I'd* had the guts to say something to her sooner, or that Rudy had. But we were too tactful or something, or too intent on being accomplices to her obsession, trying too hard to be "supportive" to bring up an alternative.

"Rudy says we should try for a foreign child because that might be quicker," Lee was saying. "Maybe a Russian orphan, or Romanian. I was thinking a little Ukrainian Jew." She stopped looking at the sky and turned practical. "As soon as we eat, I have to call Henry."

"And if it's a girl, she'll name it Isabel," Rudy said.

"Well, of course," I said. "And if it's a boy, Isadore."

We smiled in the dark.

"Do you think we really have to get a new transient?"

"A permanent," Lee corrected. "She said we did."

We sighed.

"There's this woman at work," Lee said.

We groaned.

"I guess I'll call my mother tonight." Rudy flipped her cigarette over the rail. "Sheesh, I'm surprised she didn't say I had to give up smoking."

I don't know why—I just turned and gave her a strong, hard hug.

"Wow," she said, pleased. "You're getting so much better at that."

"Am I?"

"I've noticed it, too," Lee said.

"Hey, is anybody starving?" I said. But nobody moved. We didn't want to go in quite yet.

"You know what would be nice?" Rudy said. "If we all got old together."

"Why wouldn't we?"

"No, but I mean *together*."

"Yeah," I said, "in an old ladies' home." I'd had this fantasy for years. "We'd sit out in our rocking chairs on the front porch of some neat old house in the country."

"We'd still have all our faculties," Rudy decided, "we'd just be old."

"And you'll still look great. I'll be fat, but Lee'll push me around in my wheelchair, because she'll still be tough and wiry."

"Maybe I will, maybe I won't. If you want me to push you around, you'll have to be a lot nicer to me."

"And we'll still like each other," Rudy said.

"We'll play a lot of canasta."

"Bridge," Lee corrected.

"And whenever one of us dies," I said, "we'll be cremated. But we won't dispose of the remains until the last one goes."

"Okay, but then who'll do it?"

"Isadore. Right out there." I pointed in the direction of Isabel's spot, about fifty yards out in the invisible sea.

"Isadore?"

"Your son. He'll be about sixty by then. I hope he keeps himself in shape for the swim."

"Unlike some people."

The moon loomed over the water. The crickets got louder and louder until they drowned out the sound of the waves. Across the street, two little boys and their father came out to shoot hoops in the driveway.

"Write a book about us," Isabel said. Could that be my subject? I couldn't quite see it. Real life was too damn chaotic; it didn't translate well. Fiction, now, fiction's a lot simpler. I've been thinking a mystery with some romance, some danger, maybe a little amnesia. I always like an amnesia story. It could still be about four women. Who belong to a club, and one gets killed. No, that's too sad. One's *sister* gets killed, and they team up to solve the crime. If this caught on, I could make it a series. The Four Femmes. The Four Yuppie Femmes.

Title needs work.

But she said, "Write a book about us." Oh, Isabel, I don't know.

(I talk to her like this now, as if she's standing next to me, shooting the breeze. I think we all do.) That sounds so adult, so mature. Let me dick around a little while longer, okay? Yes, I know, the time factor; life is short, and you never know how short, I know, I know.

All right, I'll think about it. But if I get stuck, I'm putting in amnesia.

"Dinner?"

We went inside. The table looked pretty. We lit candles, used the cloth napkins. Didn't talk about how much less three is than four. Isabel was absolutely right, we had to get a new transient.

Afterward, everyone wanted to use the phone, Lee to call Henry, Rudy to call her mom, me—I just wanted the line free so Mick could get through.

All this business, all this outreach—we weren't prepared for it. We'd come here for a specific purpose, an *ending*, and here we were making all these new beginnings. Are you liking this, Isabel? Are you smiling and rubbing your hands together, feeling pretty complaisant up there? Over there? Wherever you are. Well, fine, good, I don't begrudge you a thing, not even smugness. I just wish you were here. You know? I just miss you.

Circle of Three

You and me, Jen.
Separated at birth, no question.

1

Nature's Way

It's natural to feel guilty after the death of a loved one. Guilt and grief go together—that's what they say. Because you're still alive, I suppose. Well, lots of things are "natural," including infanticide in some cultures. My teenage daughter's extremely odd friend Raven recently shared with me that the female coot pecks to death all but two of her baby chicks because feeding them just gets to be too big a hassle. It's nature's way.

The presumption behind the guilt-is-natural bromide is that one hasn't actually done anything to precipitate the loved one's death. And there's the rub. I provoked my husband into an argument five minutes before he smashed the car into a tree and killed himself. (That wasn't the only thing I did, but it's the showiest.) An incredibly stupid argument: why couldn't he drive Ruth to her soccer tournament the next day, why did I always have to do it? When was the last time he'd gone to a parent-teacher conference, a science fair, anything? In six years Ruth would be twenty-one and out of his life; did he really want to spend the rest of his only child's adolescence shut up in his office grading papers and writing—yes, I said this—obscure articles on mathematical minutiae that even more obscure journals only published once in a blue moon?

It was eleven o'clock, a Friday night. We were driving home after dinner with my parents, a dinner Stephen hadn't wanted to go to in the first place—but then he never did, so I don't take that so much to heart; I forgive myself for that. He said he was tired, but I thought nothing of it. Ruth, thank God, thank God, wasn't with us;

she'd gone to a birthday sleepover at a girlfriend's. I'd spent the evening keeping a tense peace, smoothing over this, rephrasing that. My mother always liked Stephen, I'm not sure why, but he never liked her, and to this day she doesn't know it. That's my doing. For eighteen years, the length of our marriage, I constantly respun and reinterpreted his rudeness to her, at times his outright contempt. "He's thinking higher thoughts," I'd joke when he couldn't bother to come out of his study when Mama made one of her (admittedly irritating) unannounced drop-ins. And she's so easily intimidated by what she takes for intellectual superiority—except, interestingly, where my father's concerned—so it was never hard to make her believe that Stephen wasn't cold and disdainful, no, he was a genius. Geniuses are eccentric and brusque, they keep to themselves, they don't have time to be ingratiating to their mothers-in-law.

What triggered the argument in the car was fear. I had seen something that night that scared me: a sickening similarity between my husband and my father. Getting angry at Stephen, trying to get a rise out of him, trying to make him yell at me—that would've been ideal—was a way to convince myself I'd seen no such thing.

My father, George Danziger, taught English literature at Remington College for forty years. He recently retired, to write a book with a colleague on some minor eighteenth-century poet whose name I've forgotten. My father is a short, heavyset man, balding, slope-shouldered; he has a paunch; he slouches; pipe ash usually litters his vest or his coat sleeve. He frequently wears a vacant expression, and I suppose he's as close to the cliché of the absentminded professor as a human, as opposed to a cartoon, can be. But there's still a rumpled dignity in his sagging face and his gentle, phlegmatic movements, at least to me. Stephen was his physical opposite. Medium tall with a hard, compact, runner's body, he had handsome, sharp-pointed features—like Ruth's—and a full head of crisp, curling, sandy-gray hair. Quick, economical gestures. And always a restlessness about him, an impatience with his surroundings that could be insulting if you took it personally.

Mama and I did the dishes while the men went outside so Pop could smoke his pipe, a forbidden pleasure in my mother's house. I watched them idly through the kitchen window, standing beside the wrought iron table in the late-August hush, their shoulders hunched, chins pulled into the collars of their short-sleeved shirts. They didn't have much to say to each other, but then, they never did. The college was all they had in common, and Stephen still, after three years, secretly resented Pop for his help, such as it was, in getting him his teaching appointment. They kept a manly distance apart, and even when they spoke they never looked at each other. They shuffled from foot to foot, hands jammed in their pockets, and squinted up at the night sky over the roof as if they were watching a movie.

Just in that moment, as different as they were, they looked the same to me. Identical. I had my hands in hot water, but I remember the coldness that came into me, like the flat of a blade on bare skin. The chill thought crept in that they *were* the same.

Impossible—Stephen had stubbornness in him, a temper, a mean streak, Stephen was *alive*. I thought of my mother's discontent and disappointment, what they've turned her into and who she blames them on, and I thought, What if, by marrying a man as absent and unreachable as Pop, I've made the same mistake she made? Not a similar mistake, *the exact same mistake*.

So I started a fight. Unlike my father, Stephen could give as good as he got—better. His trusty weapon, cold, withering logic, always trounced my teary, incoherent furies, no contest, a sword fight with a balloon. But that night I didn't care, I wanted noise, racket, action. I waited until we were driving home on Clay Boulevard, a straight, well-lit stretch of four-lane highway, no distractions. It didn't matter to me what we fought about, but I was tired, and driving Ruth to her soccer game in Charlottesville on Saturday would mean getting up at six in the morning. So I chose that.

Stephen never said a word. It's been four months, and I can't recall anything he said that night in the car. That makes me inexpressibly sad. I, on the other hand, had quite a lot to say before he rolled down the window—the first indication that something was wrong. It was chilly, I was still fiddling with the heater knobs trying to get warm, I thought he was opening the window to thwart me. "Aren't you going to say anything?"—I can still hear the shrill nastiness in my voice. He made a face, a grimace, but I couldn't see his coloring in the dark, only that his mouth was contorted. "What's wrong?" I still wasn't worried, only puzzled. He said my name, "Carrie," and nothing else. He never clutched at his chest, that cartoon gesture of a man having a heart attack; he clutched his arm, before he slumped over against the door. It happened very fast. One second we were driving in our lane, the next we were careening across the grass median with headlights in our eyes, horns blaring, cars swerving. I grabbed the wheel and we slowed slightly, but Stephen still had his foot on the gas and I couldn't get my legs untangled fast enough to kick it away. Panic swallowed me. Under it, I remember feeling sad because here was the end, the end of me, broken and smashed in high-velocity metal and glass. Ruth wasn't a conscious thought, but she was the weight, the shadow in my brain closing down over everything. *Oh, my baby.*

Steered isn't the right word, somehow I *got* us across two lanes of eastbound traffic without hitting anything. We lurched onto the verge and down a gravel embankment, bumped up a shallow rise. The car's violent motion shoved Stephen back, finally threw his foot off the accelerator. We might've come to a natural stop, but we clipped a line of trees just over the top of the ridge. The car spun around when the bumper caught, and smacked in back against a tree trunk. My head hit something, I think the window on my side before the door snapped open—my seat belt kept me from flying out.

Lights, noise. I was out cold until two boys, Remington students, unbuckled me and pulled me out of the car. They wouldn't let me sit up, made me lie flat on the ground. "Where is my husband? How is he, my husband?" They wouldn't say. Then the police, the ambulance, the rescue squad truck. "Is my husband dead?" I asked a young man in a paramedic's jacket, holding on to his sleeve, not letting go until he told me. "Ma'am," he said, "we're doing everything we can." They were at that moment doing CPR, I discovered later, trying to restart Stephen's heart. But it never beat again.

That's what I did. One can make a little or a lot of it, I'm aware. I've done both, countless times. Either way, I think it's plain that my guilt, alive and well four months after my husband's death, goes beyond the province of "normal." Ruth and my mother say it's time I pulled myself together, started functioning again, found a real job, got on with life. Is that heartless? It's true I'm a mess, no good to anyone, and my daughter needs me now more than she ever has.

What they don't know is that there's more. The argument in the car was only the most conspicuous of my numerous failings and regrets. One in particular pains me. It's a little thing in itself, quite petty. Commonplace. But shabby, you know, distressing to admit. Although nothing truly shameful. Oh, well, it's only this—Stephen and I made love the night before he died. That ought to be a kind memory, a comfort to me—*at least we were intimate that one last time*—a blessing, an incremental notch in favor of life on the big, overbalanced scale. But I ruined even that. I know it's a little thing, but I can't forgive myself. The very last time my husband's body came inside my body, I shut my eyes and dreamed he was someone else.

2

Not Enough Points to Be Anything

I left my mom this really chirpy note on the counter before school. "Yo, yo, I made killer tuna fish salad, eat it for lunch or else! XXOO, Ruth. P.S. Jamie and Caitlin might come over this afternoon to do homework. OK?" I drew two big puffy lips and wrote "smooch" underneath, with an exclamation point.

That was, like, code. It meant, "Eat something healthful for a change, and when I get home could you please have some clothes on so my friends don't have to see you in Dad's old bathrobe."

Well, Jamie and Caitlin didn't come home with me, that was more of a trick anyway, but it didn't work because Mom was nowhere in sight and she'd left her own fake-cheerful note in the exact same spot as mine. "Hi! Drinks and snacks in ref.—don't overdo." She drew a smiley face. "I'm taking a little nap, so could you guys work downstairs? You don't have to be quiet. (Within reason.) Love & kisses, me. P.S. Want to get a pizza tonight?"

Since Dad died, this is so par for the course. She's asleep when I go to school, she's asleep when I get home. I don't know what she does during the day, except that it's not cooking or cleaning. Eating—I know she's doing that, because she's gained about ten pounds in four months. She eats spaghetti with butter on it, mashed potatoes and gravy, Minute rice in a can of mushroom soup with no water—really gross stuff, nothing but carbohydrates. She'll eat right if I'm watching or if I make it, but otherwise it's hot cereal, couscous, popcorn, and pasta. Comfort foods, I guess.

The other thing she does when I'm at school is make flower

arrangements. She has a "job" with a craft shop in town owned by this woman who pays her like two cents per flower arrangement, so you know it's only a matter of time before we're living in a packing crate under the Leap River bridge. *God.* I guess I can't talk, though, because I haven't found a job yet either. I baby-sit for Harry, the next-door neighbor's one-year-old, but the Harmons don't go out that much at night so it's not like I'm getting rich.

I don't know what's going to happen. About a month after the accident Grampa came over without Gram, which was pretty scary in itself, and had a long talk with Mom that I wasn't allowed to hear. After he left, she sat me down and gave me the bad news. Bottom line, we're poor. I thought it was sort of cool at first. "You mean, like, destitute?" No, just poor, which in a way is worse because there's no, like, drama. Apparently my dad didn't teach at Remington long enough to get a pension, so all we have is savings, Social Security, and his tiny little insurance policy.

I don't let Mom know I'm disappointed, but I was supposed to get a car, either a nice used one or a cheap new one, next summer when I turn sixteen. That's out now. Also, I might have to go to Remington. Which is the worst, nobody who lives in Clayborne goes there unless they have to—not because it's terrible or anything, just because it's local. All my life I wanted to go to my dad's alma mater, Georgetown (if I could get in), or else UNC, but they're both impossible now. UVA maybe, but wherever I go it has to be in-state.

I can't stop thinking about what might've happened if I'd been there the night he died. For one thing, I'd probably have been driving, because I've got my learner's and Mom usually lets me drive, even at night, to practice. So even if he'd still had his heart attack, the car wouldn't have crashed, so I could've driven him to the hospital and he'd probably have been saved. Or, I think it's entirely possible he wouldn't have had the attack to begin with, because everything, the atmosphere, the whole night, would've been different if I'd been there. I just have this really strong feeling that if I hadn't gone to Jamie's, he'd still be alive. His fate would've changed. Who's to say the blood in his heart wouldn't have stayed to the correct path or beat in the exact right amounts if he'd been sitting in the car relaxing, looking up at the moon instead of down at the road? I could make him laugh sometimes. What if he'd been listening to me tell some stupid story instead of to Mom or the radio? I just think things would've been different.

I have this picture, I keep it on my bedside table, of Dad, Mom, and me, about three Christmases ago, right before we moved to Clayborne, which is the town my mom grew up in but left when she was like eighteen. The three of us in this picture are lined up outside the old house in Chicago, showing off our new presents. Mom has her coat sleeve pulled up and her arm out, to show the watch Dad gave her. I gave him a green scarf and matching mittens, so he's posing with his hands straight out, with the muffler wound around half his face so only his eyes show. I look even sillier in my new jeans, boots, and down parka, grinning and pointing to my ears to show they're pierced. What a dork.

Sometime around when this picture was taken, maybe the next day but definitely during those same Christmas holidays, my dad and I went ice skating on the lake. Mom was supposed to go with us, but at the last second she said what she'd really like to do was have the house to herself for one whole afternoon. So it was just the two of us. I felt shy around him at first. We hadn't done anything alone since . . . well, I don't even know when. I felt sort of giddy, having him all to myself, almost like a date. I pretended we were a couple, and I watched other people watching us, wondering if they thought he could be my boyfriend. He was forty but he looked pretty young then, it wasn't impossible.

After the skating, we went for hot chocolate in a fancy silver diner on the shore, and I had the feeling, sitting across from him in the red vinyl booth, fingering my sore ears, putting quarters in the jukebox to play fifties songs like "Hound Dog" and "Lipstick on Your Collar," that this was the beginning of our real, true relationship. My dad had just been waiting for me to grow up. I talked a lot, told him about school and my teachers and even this guy I liked in history and how math was my favorite subject by far, a slight exaggeration, and how I'd probably major in math at Georgetown and then go on to teach at some prestigious university.

It was so great. He talked, too, and laughed at my jokes, and told me things I didn't already know. Like one time he and some of his friends from high school cut class to go sledding down Cashbox Hill, which is out in the country in New Jersey where he was from, and he slid into a barbed wire fence and cut his neck in back, under his hairline. He showed me the scar, which for some reason I had never seen before in my life, and just in that moment, everything felt right. Nothing was left out or dangling or mysterious, everything belonged.

The funny thing is, though, nothing ever came of that day. When it was over, we went back to who we'd been before, and it was like nothing had ever happened. He was nice to me, same as always, but he never again suggested we do something together, just the two of us. He went back into his study, you could say, and closed the door.

What I think happened was that I hadn't grown up enough then—I was only twelve—and what's sad is that now I'm probably finally old enough to be his friend and he's gone. We lost our chance. It can never be the way I dreamed it. I thought—maybe this sounds stupid—I thought we'd be partners after I got my degree, my doctorate and everything. I saw us teaming up, having an office in some funky old building in Georgetown and writing books together, solving complicated formulas that have stumped the entire math community for years, for centuries. I could see us with our feet up on either side of his desk when the day was over, drinking coffee, giving each other compliments on our work, planning the next day. VAN ALLEN & ASSOCIATE, it would say on the door. Stephen and Ruth Van Allen, Mathematicians.

No, I can see this is stupid. I don't even know what mathematicians do, not really, except teach, which my dad complained about all the time. He made fun of the other professors in his department, who got ahead by kissing up or playing politics, whereas he just did his job and took care of business. He was sort of a loner.

That's why it would've been so cool to be partners. I feel like, once I was older and had my math degrees and everything, I could've cheered him up, plus he'd've been proud of me. I hate that this is never going to happen.

I have got to do something about my clothes. I took this quiz in a magazine to find out my own personal style. You could be Fun, Preppy, Grunge, Goth, Corporate, I forget what else. Caitlin and Jamie took it, and they were both Fun, but when I added up my scores I didn't have enough points to be anything. God, how pathetic. I can see the same thing going on in my room, which I now hate. I have a Dixie Chicks calendar—yuck! I can't wait till it runs out!—and a picture of Leo D., and a poster of Natalie Imbruglia and some cutouts of Claire Danes and George Clooney and Siouxsie Sioux and the Banshees. I mean, what is that? Exactly what does that mean? So I'm going to take everything down, clear it all out, just have nothing, blank walls, and let my room fill itself back up organically. Then we'll see.

Because Raven came over after dinner tonight, and for the nanosecond Mom let us be alone in my room, his face went into like total disgust and he mumbled, "Happening. Not."

But that wasn't even the worst. I told Mom afterward, if she can't get dressed in regular clothes, daytime clothes, her *own* clothes, not her dead husband's—I almost said, but that sounded mean, and plus we try to avoid the *D* word these days unless there's a good reason—then she can just stay in her room when I have company over. It's funny, I used to worry about what she thought of Raven, and tonight all I could think was what he must be making of *her*. She had on a pair of Dad's old sweatpants, one of his plaid flannel shirts, and his gray wool bathrobe. Oh, and a pair of his running socks. I mean, *God*. No makeup, of course, and I don't know when she last washed her hair. She has goldish brown hair, very long and stick straight, and until now I was always jealous of it. Mine's curly, which I hate, and not as nice a color I don't think, more of an ashy blond like Dad's. Anyway—and her complexion's changed, she used to have very delicate coloring, but now she's like totally gray, probably because of all the junk she eats. She's just washed out. "Um, my mom's still kind of wrecked," I told Raven when he was leaving, and he said, "Obviously." Which I thought was unnecessary.

But he was nice, he came by to lend me a book, some selected stories by Edgar Allan Poe. He likes anything that's creepy. After Poe his favorite authors are Anne Rice and Edward Gorey. I was not feeling that great to begin with, and he wouldn't get off the subject of how everything ends, everything is loss, the only appropriate humor in life is melancholy, which did not exactly cheer me up. But I think it's too cool that his real last name is Black. His first name is Martin, but his last name is Black. Raven Black. It's like a sign.

After he went home, Mom came in my room and sat on my bed, where I was trying to do homework. She's definitely not herself, because she hasn't even been getting on me lately about what a sty my room is.

She didn't say anything, so I kept reading, figuring she'd get to the point eventually. She started picking at the quilt she made me for my thirteenth birthday. It has blue and green stars, and it's about the only thing I still like in my room. "*What?*" I said finally, and she smiled this really shaky smile and said, "Sorry about tonight. Guess I'm not doing so great."

"You're okay," I said.

"I'll be better soon."

"I know."

"How are you, baby?"

"Fine," I said.

"Really?" She touched my cheek with the back of her hand. "Tell me about school."

"It's the same. I got a B on my French test." I didn't tell her about my algebra test, she'd've freaked. That's supposed to be my best subject. "What does it mean when you have a sore in your mouth that won't go away?" I said.

"Let's see."

I showed her the inside of my cheek, which has this tender white spot I keep accidentally biting.

"Oh, that's just a canker sore. It'll go away."

"Canker. That's like cancer."

"It's not like cancer."

I have spots in front of my eyes, too, which could be a warning sign of glaucoma. One of my ankles is bigger than the other.

"So," she said, stretching out on her stomach. "What's with you and Raven."

"God. Nothing, Mom, there's nothing *with* us."

"Does he go to school in that makeup?"

"They won't let him."

"Huh. Do you like him?"

"Jeez, he's not my boyfriend or anything. He's just Raven."

"Oh. Okay. Where does he live?"

"*God*. I don't even *know*."

She punched up one of my pillows and shoved it under her chest and folded her arms around it. "Well, anyway."

"Anyway." I sat up and started giving her a back rub, which she loves. "You're incredibly tense. Your shoulders are like marble. Did you do flowers today?"

"For a while." She groaned into the pillow, and I thought she was enjoying the back rub, but then she said in a pretend-panicky voice, "I have got to get a real job soon."

"You will. I will, too. People are looking for Christmas help, I can get a job in the mall after school."

"Mm. Except you'd need a ride to it."

"You could drive me," I said.

"Not if I'm working, too."

"We could get a job in the same place."

"Hey, that would be neat."

It would be. Well, depending on the place. I could feel her finally starting to relax; the back of her neck wasn't like a block of concrete anymore. When I was little I used to think I was helping to save her life when I'd rub her feet or do some chore for her. Like, if she'd ask me to run upstairs and bring down the aspirin bottle or go down in the basement and get something out of the freezer, I'd grumble and procrastinate, but inside I'd be glad because I had this idea that anything I could do instead of her would save minutes on her life. So if I set the table or got the paper off the front porch or ran and answered the phone before she could get to it—that gave her a couple of extra minutes at the end of her life. It all added up.

"Hey, Mom, did you know that when you pet your dog, it lowers your blood pressure?"

"Mmm."

"But the cool thing is, they found out it also lowers the *dog's* blood pressure. Don't you think that's cool? Can we get a dog?"

"No."

"Why?"

"Oh, honey. We just can't."

We couldn't before, either, because my dad was allergic to anything with hair—dogs, cats, gerbils, whatever. I was just thinking maybe now. . . "Jess has four dogs," I said, "and about fifteen cats.

And a crow that comes up to his back door and lets him feed it. Jess would give us a kitten, I bet. Cats are easy."

"Ruth."

"I know, but he's got all these animals and we don't have any."

"Jess lives on a farm."

"So?"

Jess is great. He's a friend of Mom's from the olden days when she was growing up in Clayborne, and he has a farm right on the Leap River that's over six hundred acres with about two hundred Holstein cows. Last year I had to do a civics paper on a local industry, and I picked Jess's dairy farm and learned all about cows. Then for my science fair project I decided to do a working model of the four stomachs of the cow (the rumen, the reticulum, the omasum, and the abomasum), and he helped me with that, too. I love to go out to his farm and just hang, although I haven't seen him since Dad died—Mom's been too wasted. I miss going there. I miss seeing Jess.

She rolled over, and we stretched out next to each other. "That was great," she said. "Thanks. And by the way, this room is a sty." We smiled up at the ceiling. She made me a mobile that hangs from the light, seven horses galloping or cantering or loping, cut out of thin wood and painted in different colors. It's from my horse phase. I should take it down, but I still like it.

"Mom? Christmas is going to be sad, isn't it?" Thanksgiving was bad enough.

She said, "Yeah," and I was glad she didn't lie. "Because it's the first. But we'll be okay. Some things—we can't go around them. I'm afraid we just have to go through them."

"Do you miss Dad a lot?"

"I do."

"Me, too. Will we still go to Gram's for dinner?"

"Yes, of course."

"And we'll still have presents?"

"Absolutely. Although. . ."

"I know." Not as many.

"The main thing is that we're together. We've still got us."

"Yeah."

Except I don't have her. She's still got me, but she's about half the mother I used to have. When Dad died I lost him and part of her. I'm almost an orphan.

She says she's getting better, but I say not to the naked eye. Well, maybe Christmas will miraculously cheer us up. But I don't think so. I think she's right. Some things we can't go around, we just have to go through them.

3

The Power of Nostalgia

The phone jolted me out of a comatose sleep on the living-room couch. I answered instantly, heart pounding, forgetting to clear my throat first and say hello cheerfully. "Carrie honey, is that you?" my mother's worried voice asked. "What's wrong?"

This happened all the time. Something about my phone voice; if I didn't make an effort to sound bright and clearheaded, people thought something was the matter with me. Are you sick? Were you sleeping? Have you been crying? Today I could've answered yes to all three.

"Oh, hi, Mama. No, I'm fine, how're you? How's Pop?"

"What are you doing?"

"Right now?" The mantel clock said ten after twelve. "I was just getting ready to go out. On my way, in fact. Chores, got things to do, the bank, post office, this and that . . ." I carried the phone into the kitchen and sank down in a chair at the table. Out of steam.

"I was going to run over before the women's club luncheon with one of these casseroles I made. It's Ruth's favorite—scalloped potatoes."

"Mmm. Well, that—"

"I've got enough for an army. You'll be there another half hour, won't you?"

I put my head down on the oak table. God, look at all the crumbs and jelly stains and water marks. How long since I cleaned this table? My nightgown sleeve was stuck to it. "Um, you couldn't just drop it off, could you? Since I'm going out . . ." My mother made wonderful scalloped potatoes. They'd get me through the day. The logistics would be embarrassing, though; I'd have to hide upstairs and wait for her to come in, stick her casserole in the refrigerator, and go away. No, no, it wouldn't work anyway, I realized—she'd see the car.

"Well," she said, "if you're not even going to be there, never mind." Affronted. "Maybe after my luncheon's over, although I can't promise they won't eat everything."

"That might be better. And if you come late enough, you can see Ruth."

That perked her up. "How's my baby? I want you two to come to dinner next Friday night, Carrie. You need to get out of that house."

"Friday. . ."

"Just you and Ruth, a family dinner. It's been ages."

"It's been four months." To the day. Since Stephen died.

She realized it, too. She said too quickly, "Friday night for sure, we'll have a good time, I promise. And now I'll let you get on with your important chores."

"So—you're coming by later?"

"Only if it's not too much *trouble*. If it won't put you out."

I tried to balance the phone on my ear without touching it, so I could drop both arms and go limp. Stay like that all day, lax and drooling, head a complete blank.

"Carrie? I was kidding, I could come over right now if you want. Honey, do you feel like talking?"

I couldn't even make my tongue work. Did I feel like talking? Involuntarily, I snorted into the phone. I turned it into a cough and said, "I'm fine, I'm better today, actually. I should go now, but I'll definitely see you later, okay? 'Bye, Mama."

I would love a vacation from my mother's mind. If she would bump her head—not seriously, nothing fatal or painful or long-lasting, just something to give her amnesia for about six weeks. Lovely, lovely, no calls, no visits, no casseroles, no life advice. No bullying. When I'm in my mother's head, I'm only half myself; she sucks out the other half and swallows it. And I'm so weak these days, I'm lucky if it's only half.

I hung there over the table until my neck hurt. Then I got up slowly, a little dizzy—low blood sugar? pressure? Low something. I put a cup of water and a tea bag in the microwave. Couldn't drink coffee anymore, too harsh; I wanted to *be* awake, not slapped awake. I carried the cup and a handful of Fig Newtons into Stephen's office. Slumped in the doorway, I stared around at the mess I'd made of it.

Six weeks ago I had an idea it might be a comfort to turn his sanctum, his favorite room in the house, into my new flower-arrangement-and-wreath-assembly workroom. A way to stay close to him, I thought, keep his memory vivid, not be so lonely when I was alone. Wrong on all counts, and now I'd ruined his room. He'd kept it neat as a laboratory. I littered his pristine techno-gray carpet with Scotch broom branches and wild grapevine, tansy and goldenrod stalks, crown of thorns, witch hazel. Except for his desk, every surface was covered with pods, nuts, branches, stems, twigs, flowers, containers, driftwood, twist ties, pipe cleaners, wire, silica, sand, salt, borax, clay, vermiculite. And over everything an invisible mist, an allergy sufferer's nightmare fog of dusty dried flower and seed pod detritus. Stephen would've died in here.

But I never touched his desk. Why not? Directly in front of his steel-and-vinyl chair were the notes he'd been taking for a paper on the computation of definite integrals. I hadn't given his clothes away, either, or cleaned out his side of the medicine chest or his bedside table. Ruth said nothing, but she had to think this was bizarre behavior. I thought so, too. I wasn't sure what was behind it, but I didn't believe it was my sad, wistful way of holding on to my husband a little longer. Something more complicated. Less commendable.

I sat down on the floor in my usual place. Even with the blinds open, the light was poor, but I hadn't gotten up the energy yet to drag a floor lamp in from another room. I kept forgetting. Until recently, Margaret Sachs had been paying me eight dollars apiece for dried wreaths and Christmas arrangements, which she sold at a comfortable profit at Clayborne Crafts 'N Candles, her shop on Myrtle Avenue. Last week I began to run low on supplies, so I had to switch to miniatures. I had no choice, it was either downsize or go out into the world and look for more materials, the cattails, teasel, laurel branches, etc., etc., that were the tools of my not-very-lucrative-to-begin-with trade. I couldn't face it. Some kind of agoraphobia; I hoped it was temporary. At any rate, now Margaret was only paying me four dollars per arrangement.

I rationalized the cutback by telling myself I could make twice as many in the same amount of time, so I wasn't really losing money. But that wasn't true—if it were, I'd run out of supplies in half the time, wouldn't I? No, I was just in a miniature frame of mind.

The afternoon dragged by. I could drift into a trance when I made these little arrangements. When I floated up from it because I was out of pinecones or it was too dark to see or my rear end had gone numb, I'd find I had made six or seven tiny floral compositions and they were all identical. Round, fan-shaped, S-curved, pyramid—whatever design I'd chosen for the first, all the rest were exact replicas of it. I found that vaguely appalling. Margaret thought I did it on purpose—"Oh, *these* are cunning, they'll go like hotcakes," she'd say, and ask me to do more of whatever shape I'd unconsciously mass-produced. But I didn't. Not on purpose, anyway.

Hunger nudged me out of my trance today. Stiff-necked, stiff-legged, I hobbled into the kitchen. Almost three; Ruth would be home soon. The cottage cheese had a funny smell, but I scraped off the top and ate in the middle, staring out the window over the sink at my neighbors' house. In our shared driveway, Modean Harmon was unloading her one-year-old from his car seat and carrying him and a bag of groceries inside. I wished I'd thought to ask her to pick up a few things for me while she was out. She was wonderful about that. Wonderful about everything. Modean was shy and quiet, younger than me, very reserved; it was only since Stephen died that we'd become friends. And I wasn't much of one; she did all the initiating. Stephen never cared for Dave, her dentist husband, so we never socialized as couples. But after the accident, Modean was a lifesaver. She didn't say much, and she never tried to draw me out. What she did was leave groceries in the refrigerator, rake the leaves in my yard, drive Ruth to school when she missed the bus. I tried to repay her later by taking care of Harry when Ruth wasn't available, but that was no hardship even for me. He was a big grinning egg of a baby, all he wanted to do was laugh. The hard part was giving Harry back when his mother came home.

The doorbell rang.

Who? I thought, tiptoeing into the foyer. *Who's torturing me now?* It couldn't be my mother, she never knocked, and if the door happened to be locked she had a key. Long stained glass panels bordered the door on both sides—I'd taken a class and made them myself, last year, when screening visitors wasn't a priority. All I could see through the soldered yellow and blue panes was a tall shadow. I opened the door an inch or two. Jess Deeping peered in at me, then took a step back, gray eyes startled. "Hi. Is this a bad time?"

I put him in the living room and excused myself to go make coffee. Wouldn't Ruth revel in this? *I told you*, she'd say, *I told you to get dressed*. I looked ghastly anyway, but more so in Stephen's red Bulls jersey over my oldest, rattiest flannel nightgown. I wasn't vain, but I still had some pride, a shred, a vestige. Measuring coffee into the maker, I watched two fat, humiliated tears spatter on the counter. They weren't remarkable; I cried almost every day about something. *Maybe this is as low as I'll go*, I thought hopefully. *Maybe this is the bottom*.

When I came back in the living room, Jess was bent over with his hands behind his back, studying some small watercolors I did of Ruth when she was a little girl. They weren't very good, but I couldn't part with them; I framed them and put them in a grouping behind the gateleg table, half hidden by the tole lamp. He'd taken off his heavy coat—I'd forgotten to ask him for it. He'd dressed up; he wore pressed slacks and a blue crewneck sweater that looked brand-new. A Christmas present? He had no family, no wife anymore. Who gave Jess presents? His hair was a little thinner now, and darker, a caramel shade, but when we first met, age eleven, he was a towhead blond. In high school it was streaky gold and down to his shoulders. In my illicit dream, the one I can't forgive myself for, it came down around the sides of his face, and my face. It covered us like a tawny curtain.

"These are good," he said, straightening. "Why did you stop painting?"

"How do you know I did?"

"Ruth told me."

"Ah." Should've known. I sat down on the piano bench, crossed my legs, folded my arms. "I have a cold," I said. True, but it didn't explain half of what I wanted it to.

"I've been thinking about you," he said carefully. "How've you been getting along?"

"All right." I nodded a lot, trying to make it sound truer. Something old pulled at me to make him my confidant. How easy to say, *I'm dead inside, Jess. Ruth's all that keeps me going, and I'm failing her.* "I've been all right. Getting by, you know. It's hard," I finally admitted. "But we're okay, Ruth and I. Basically. Tell me about you, what have you been doing?"

He smiled a bit grimly, to let me know he hadn't bought any of that. "Oh, the usual. It's the slow time of the year, so I've been taking it easy. Getting lazy."

"I doubt that. Don't you still have to milk two hundred cows twice a day?"

"Not quite that many."

"Ruth told me that. It's not true?"

"I've got over two hundred head, but not all of them get milked. Maybe a hundred and fifty."

"What happens to the other fifty?"

"Calves, stud cattle, heifers. A few old ladies." He put his hands in his pockets and looked around the room. "I like your house."

"It seems funny that you've never been here before." Because I'd never invited him. Seeing him on his big, busy, wide-open farm, that was all right, and Ruth was always with us. But here in my house, just Jess and me? Not allowed. You didn't have to say the rules out loud to know what they were.

"You did all the remodeling yourself?" He stood stiffly, rocking on his toes a little. Uncomfortable, I realized. Most unusual for Jess. I hadn't seen him since Stephen's funeral. He'd phoned one time. Ruth answered, and they talked for quite a while. I shook my head and waved my hands when she said, "So do you want to talk to my mom?" Then it was awkward, because he said yes and she had to come up with a reason, quick, why he couldn't. "Gosh, she was here a minute ago. Well, I guess she went out. I guess she left while we were talking." He hadn't called again.

"Most of it," I told him. "Ruth helps me paint sometimes. It's not finished. I guess now . . ." I let that hang, weighing how frank I should be. Was it too personal to tell him I might have to sell the house? Ruth loved it, though. Even if we sold it, after only three years of ownership, there wasn't much escrow in our overpriced circa-1880 money sink on the state of Virginia's Historic Register. I smiled at Jess. "Some of my plans have been pushed back, put it that way."

"You need a job."

"God knows I do. Excuse me a sec . . ." I stood up and went to get the coffee.

He followed me into the kitchen. "This is amazing," he said as I filled two mugs with coffee, adding milk to his.

"What?"

"This room. You did all this, Carrie?"

"Yep." I painted the tiles behind the sink and stenciled the wallpaper borders, I even laid the antique bricks I bought cheap at an estate sale. I was quite the craftswoman. "Well, not the counters. I found the slates, but a man cut and installed them for me. And the cabinets were already here, I just refinished them."

It was a great room, my favorite in the house. I could've made it bigger, knocked out a wall and extended into the pantry; that was even allowed under the strict rules of landmark ownership. But it was a 120-year-old house—who had big kitchens in its day? And there were only three of us when I was weighing the decision. And now only two.

Jess scuffed the toe of his shoe across the throw rug he was standing on. "And this?" He looked up and smiled, and raised his eyebrows, and rubbed the flat of his hand against his chest—a combination of gestures I knew very well. In different lights, from different angles, I could still see the boy in his man's face. I felt such tenderness sometimes. It was dangerous, it wasn't even true, but sometimes I felt that I knew Jess better than anyone, that I was the only one who could really see him. But that was only the power of nostalgia. And loneliness. The mind plays tricks.

"I'm afraid so," I said, abashed. SWEET HOME, the rug said, with the date, in green and gray yarn over a replica of my house's façade. "My first and last rug-hooking effort. Months, this took." And it was only four-feet square. Of all the crafts I'd ever taken up out of curiosity, interest, boredom, desperation, whatever—rug hooking was far and away the most tedious. The one that had made me feel the most ridiculous.

"You're an artist."

"No." I laughed. "A frustrated one, maybe. Stephen used to say I took it out on the house." But I was so pleased. It was as if Jess had plucked a hair-thin wire running through me and set it vibrating. I am such a fool.

He set his cup down and came around the kitchen table I'd put between us—we'd been talking across the length of the room. "I have a job for you."

"A what?"

"I could offer you a job."

I saw myself milking cows in his barn. I'd have laughed, but I felt deflated. Stupid, but I thought he might've come for something else. "What job?"

"I'm looking for an artist. To do something. Make something." He looked me over, head to toe. "You're perfect."

I flushed. If he was making fun of me, it was for the first time. "What, you need someone to—to—" I couldn't think of the name of it, the person who used to advertise mattresses in department stores by sleeping, sleeping in a big bed behind a plate glass window while people on the sidewalk stopped and stared. I saw it once in an old movie.

"You wouldn't make a lot of money." I sensed a trick, but the light in his eyes drew me anyway. "But you'd make more than Margaret Sachs is paying you."

"Who told you about that? Ruth," I answered myself. "Well, that's not saying much, believe me. Oh, Jess, I need a *real* job."

"This is a real job."

"What is it?"

"It's kind of a long story. Do you remember Eldon Pletcher?"

"No. Eldon? I remember Landy Pletcher."

"Eldon's Landy's father."

"Landy—you mean from school?" A boy two years ahead of Jess and me at Clayborne High. A shy, backward boy, I remembered; his father had farmed tobacco.

Jess nodded. "Well," he said, and rubbed a long index finger across his sideburn, deciding how to proceed. "Do you know about the Arkists?"

"The what?"

"No, you'd moved away by then. I'm surprised your mother never mentioned them, though. They—they're—" He scratched his head, smiling down at the floor. Such a man, I thought, with his deep voice and his rough hands, the weathered skin around his eyes. Stephen had lived in his head, but Jess lived in his body. I wasn't used to a man like him in my house. "Let's see," he said. "About twenty years ago—about the time you left—Eldon, Landy's father, started a religious group called the Arkists. Also known as the Sons of Noah. Small, mostly local. Well, not that small, they had a couple hundred souls in their heyday. You never heard about this?"

"No. When was their heyday?"

"I use the term loosely. Ten years ago? I'm not sure what they believe in besides the great flood, but probably the usual, what you'd expect. From a southern offshoot of Protestantism."

"They don't handle snakes?"

"No."

"Take multiple wives? Speak in tongues?"

"None of that." He laughed, but he really wanted to reassure me. "They're good people, not well educated but well meaning. Gentle. They don't preach that they're the one true faith."

"That could be why their heyday's over. Like the Shakers. No, wait, they died out because they wouldn't procreate."

"Right. Anyway. . ."

"Anyway. What's the job?"

"When Eldon had his religious conversion, he promised God he'd replicate the ark before he died."

"Replicate the ark?"

"To save the world from a second devastating flood, figuratively speaking. Not to mention his own immortal soul."

"Figuratively speaking?"

"In fact, if he breaks his promise, he believes he'll go straight to hell."

"He's telling you this?"

"Landy told me. He's my neighbor now—he bought the old Price farm next door about twelve, fifteen years ago. We're friends. We help each other out."

"I see."

"Where was I?"

"Eldon Pletcher's going to replicate Noah's Ark. Is he going to sail it?"

I was joking, but Jess said, "Yeah, on the Leap."

"You're kidding. What do I do, skipper it?"

"Ha."

I frowned. He looked so sheepish. "That was a joke," I said. "Right?"

"Right. Right, you don't have to skipper it."

I spread my hands, completely baffled. "Well, *what*?"

"Arks need animals. Figuratively. Eldon thinks God wouldn't mind if he stocked the ark with representations of His creatures somehow, pictures, models—he's not too clear on this, to tell you the truth."

"Who, God?"

"Eldon. But he wants them to look good, you know, he wants realism, and the problem is, there aren't any artists among what's left of the Arkists."

I started to laugh. "And this is where I come in?" Something caught my eye in the window over Jess's shoulder—the fender of my mother's Buick in the driveway. "Oh, no."

"Well, wait, think about it."

"No, I mean—"

"You could do it. You're an artist, Carrie, it's obvious." He waved his arm around my kitchen. "And I know it sounds crazy, it's completely absurd, but that's the beauty of it, isn't it?" Oh, I could never resist that reckless gleam in Jess's eye. "I don't know what he'd pay you. People say he's got money, but nobody knows for—"

"Jess," I said in warning.

The back door flew open and Ruth burst in, red-cheeked from the cold. Everything curves up when she smiles, mouth, eyes, cheeks, eyebrows. Oh, light of my life, apple of my eye. Love for my daughter swamps me at unexpected moments. I flounder in it, flailing for what I can't hold on to much longer. "Hey, Jess," she cried, "I saw your truck! Hi!"

"Ruth—I can't believe it. You *grew*."

Laughing, they stood in front of each other for an awkward few seconds, before finally exchanging a quick, shy hug. Their gladness surprised me—I wasn't sure what I thought of it. Half a dozen times since Stephen died, Ruth had asked me to drive out with her to see Jess, see the cows, his dogs and cats, all the fascinating features of a dairy farm. But I put her off because I was too tired, too weird, too something. I wasn't ready. She'd missed him, it was obvious, and that was my fault. Well, something else to be guilty of.

If Ruth was surprised to see Jess, my mother was floored. She did a double take in her ladies' luncheon finery, fur jacket over a navy wool suit, fur hat, medium-heeled pumps, navy handbag. Oh, Lord, and here came Birdie behind her, Mama's lifelong bridge partner and oldest friend; she'd been a sort of half-dotty aunt to me for as long as I could remember. All of a sudden the kitchen was teeming with women.

"Mama, you remember Jess Deeping," I said in a hostessy voice, thinking, *If she pretends she doesn't know him, I'll kill her.* But she said, "Why, of *course* I do," in her best southern accent, "you came to my son-in-law's funeral, I *so* appreciated that." Such an accomplished liar. Before Stephen's funeral, Mama had been delighted not to lay eyes on Jess Deeping for twenty-five years.

"And Birdie," I said, "Jess, this is Mrs. Costello, my mother's good friend." They said hello, how are you, nice to see you. And then, because the silence was expectant and I was jittery and everybody was staring at me, I blurted out the worst possible thing. "Jess came over to offer me a job."

"A job?" Birdie's faded blue eyes snapped with interest. She rubbed her hands together.

"Wow! What job?" Ruth demanded, crowding in.

My mother said nothing. She stared.

Jess looked hounded, disbelieving. The glance he sent me—*Carrie, what the hell?*—should've cowed me, but it didn't. For some reason it warmed me up. Us against them: just like old times. He closed his eyes for a second. And then with a pained, hopeless smile, he told everybody about Noah's Ark.

4

Good Help

I'll be seventy years old in the spring. I've been sixty-nine for nine months, and hardly enjoyed a minute of it. Sometimes I feel like I'm in a car speeding toward a boulder in the road somebody's chiseled into a giant 7–0. The scenery might be nice, but all I can see is those numbers, high and hard and coming up fast. I've got a one-track mind.

I must be bad off when George notices. "Dana," he said to me the other night, "is anything bothering you?" Well, that got my attention. That was like a blind man saying, "Did somebody turn the lights on?" I tried to remember what I'd just been doing that could've focused George's attention on me instead of his computer screen. Nothing—telling him to move his big feet so I could vacuum under his desk; fighting on the telephone with Birdie, who doesn't think I should run for president of the Clayborne Women's Club; slamming things around in the kitchen for the hell of it, just to make some noise. Calling Carrie twice in an hour with good advice. It must've been the accumulation, all four added up, because by themselves those aren't very remarkable. But imagine George noticing. As I say, it pulled me up.

He was sitting at his desk, working on the book he's been writing with a colleague for the last year and a half. It's about a poet from the 1700s named—well, I forget his name. Alexander Pope called him "Namby Pamby," so that's what I've been calling him. George is sorry he ever told me that. He swears they'll be done with the book by next May, which is about the time I'll be queen of England. When

George retired from the college two years ago, I thought our interesting new lives were about to start. We'd travel, maybe learn a foreign language together, take up some sedentary sport. Talk. Well, surprise, so far that hasn't worked out. He still spends all his time in his study with the door closed, reading, writing, and not talking to me. Carrie called one night about a month ago, teary and upset. "Mama, it's so quiet in this house. It's as if *everybody* died, not just Stephen." I didn't say it, but I thought, oh, honey, it's like that all the time at my house.

I pushed some papers to the side and sat down on the corner of George's desk, next to the computer so he had to look at me. "Is anything bothering me?" Already he looked sorry he'd asked. "My arthritis. My blood pressure medicine. My upcoming senility. Those are off the top of my head."

"Ha ha," he said, humoring me. He had his trifocals on top of his bald, freckled head. He's shrinking; these days when he drives, he needs a pillow to see over the steering wheel. I'm shrinking, too, but not as much as he is. He's two years younger than me, but he looks older. I hope.

"George," I said, "wouldn't you think at our age we'd know something?"

He turned his good ear toward me. "What's that?"

"When you were young, say when you were Ruth's age, didn't you think people as old as us knew something? Knew *something*? I sure did. But don't you feel like the whole thing's still the same mystery it was when you were fifteen?"

He just blinked at me. He's supposed to be the intellectual in the family. I married him partly for his brains, and look where it got me. "What's the trouble?" he said, but his eyes were drifting. He fidgeted when the screen saver came on, a reminder that time was passing.

What's the trouble. If I knew, I could fix it. "Oh, I just haven't felt like myself since the accident, I guess." That's what we call Stephen's death, "the accident."

George nodded solemnly. "We all miss him."

I nodded solemnly, too, but that wasn't it. I'm not sure anyone but Ruth really *misses* Stephen. That sounds terrible, I take it back—Carrie's a mess, sometimes I think she's never going to be her old self again. Well, me, then: as fond as I was of my son-in-law, as much as I approved of him for Carrie, I don't miss him, put it that way. Not that he wasn't a fine, decent, admirable man, good husband and father, all that. He was always standoffish, though, and now it seems to me he's just standing off a little farther.

"Do you remember if heart trouble ran in Stephen's family?" I asked. "Birdie told me I told *her* that's how his father died, but I stood her down and said that wasn't it at all. Do you have any such recollection?"

"Well, now, that rings a bell—"

"No, it was something else, it wasn't heart. Stephen's attack was a fluke, heart does *not* run in that family."

"Maybe so." He shrugged. He doesn't make associations the same way I do—one of our many differences. Stephen's death was Stephen's death; it didn't make George worry more about his prostate, or think about buying a plot at Hill Haven, or look at his old man's face in the mirror and ask it where his life's gone. Supposedly George lives a life of the mind, but it doesn't always seem to me to be his *own* mind.

He started drumming his fingers on the keyboard space bar. "Guess who was at Carrie's this afternoon," I said to keep his attention. "When I got there with Birdie and Ruth."

"Who?"

"Guess."

"I really couldn't say."

"Come on."

"Dana—"

"Okay. Jess Deeping."

He looked blank. Then, "Oh—that fellow, the one who's on the town council?"

"Yes, but—the one who used to be Carrie's boyfriend! In high school." God, men. "You remember, I know you do. You didn't care for him any more than I did."

"That boy? Really?" Hard to believe, but he was just now making the connection between childhood friend and Clayborne city councilman. "Well, he turned out all right, I guess. Did you and Carrie have a nice visit?" he asked politely, eyes drifting toward his computer screen.

"Get this, George." I leaned in closer. He frowned at my hip, which was encroaching on his papers. "Remember the Arkists?"

"The artists?"

"*Arkists*. The religious cult that started up around here years ago, the paper did a story. Those people who called themselves the Arkists? The Sons of Noah?"

"No."

"Oh, you do, too. The ringleader was that tobacco farmer, Pletcher, something Pletcher. Carrie went to school with the son."

"*Oh*, yes, yes, very, very vaguely. But it wasn't a cult, I don't believe, it was a sect. I thought they'd died out by now."

"Cult, sect—no, they didn't die out, and the old man's still alive. And the son not only owns the farm next door to Jess Deeping, he's also his very good *friend*."

"You don't say."

"And—follow me, now—this cult is all set to build an ark—an ark, I'm saying *ark*—and Jess Deeping wants Carrie to build the animals!"

"What?"

"A life-size ark! They want to sail it on the river for the glory of God! Can you believe it?"

No." He joined me in a wonderful laugh, our best in ages, we leaned back and rocked with it. "Why, that makes no sense at all."

"I know! You should've heard Jess Deeping trying to explain it."

"What did Carrie say?"

"She said no, of course." But not forcefully enough, if you ask me; she left room for hope, left the door open a crack. "I don't think so," she told Jess Deeping, and "I just can't imagine it. But I'm flattered you thought of me." Baloney. It wasn't flattering, it was frightening.

"She does need a job, though," I told George. "Soon, because she could lose that house."

"I still say she ought to sell it. Move someplace smaller."

"I know, but Ruth loves it. No, Carrie needs a good paying job, that's what she needs. She has to get out of that house, quit making those damn flower arrangements. Lord, they make me shiver, dried-up little things. They look like nests, they look like dead animals. If she'd gotten an education degree twenty years ago, none of this would be happening. She could've been teaching art at the middle school right now, maybe even the high school. *George*."

"Mm?"

"I've invited Brian Wright to dinner tomorrow night."

He looked up at that. "What for? Brian Wright? I thought Carrie and Ruth were coming tomorrow."

"He's thinking of hiring an assistant."

"Brian is? How do you know?"

"He told me—I ran into him at the bank. This'll be good, wait and see. Brian's on the rise."

George sniffed.

"He is, he's got gumption, he's making something of himself. Carrie could do a lot worse."

He looked alarmed.

"In a *boss*, she could do worse in an *employer*. That's all I'm talking about."

Suspicion narrowed his eyes for a second. But then he lost interest and turned full face to his computer screen. My time was up.

• • •

I served pot roast. I can make smarter, more glamorous meals—the other night I made chicken Monterey for the Becks, and a Peking duck last month for the academic dean and his wife. But Brian Wright is divorced, his wife got the kids, and he lives by himself, and something just told me a nice pot roast would be the thing. Warm and homey.

I thought the evening went well. Brian arrived first, and when Carrie saw him, there was just the tiniest nervous moment, but I don't think anyone noticed it but me. Well, and her. Thank God she looked all right for a change; she had on slacks and a sweater, perfectly nice, and her hair pulled back in a barrette, even a little makeup, hallelujah. Compared to the last time I saw her, she looked like Grace Kelly. She's forty-two, but she never looked it until Stephen died. And Ruth, bless her heart, I swear she gets cuter every day. She's going to be prettier than Carrie, I predict. She needs some poise and some of that nervous energy burned off, but one of these days, look out.

We had drinks in the living room, where it came up that Brian lifts weights. This I didn't know; he's fortyish, and I thought he was stocky, a touch overweight, but no, it's all muscle. Now I can see it—he's got those sloping shoulders bodybuilders have; his neck's as big around as my thigh. He made the room smaller, and not just with his physique. He's so full of energy and enthusiasm, a complete extrovert. He felt like a breath of fresh air on my sad, quiet family. He wears a buzz cut and a neat little goatee, of all things. Now I don't usually care for facial hair on a man, I think it's tacky, and no one should be allowed to wear a crew cut after he's ten. But somehow Brian Wright manages to carry these two fashion mistakes off. Maybe it's his size? You want to give the benefit of the doubt to somebody that big.

And eat? He gobbled up everything in front of him, and I kept the plates moving. No leftovers from this dinner. I know George doesn't like him, but he made an effort to talk and be sociable, and that helped smooth over the times Carrie clicked off. It happens all the time, she'll be pleasant and attentive one minute, lost in space the next. I'm so worried about her. I want to ask, "Honey, are you on drugs?" and I don't mean the kind doctors prescribe.

I was the one who finally brought up business. I waited till we finished eating and were having our second cups of coffee, still at the dining room table. "So, Brian," I said casually, "how are things at the Other School?"

"Great, just great, Mrs. Danziger, this is the best semester we've had. We've got twelve classes up and running right now, and about six more planned for winter term. We'll be going to four quarters starting in the spring."

"Why, that's wonderful, and in such a short time, too."

"Just about three years now." He smiled down, modest but proud, into the bottom of his rice pudding bowl. "I can't complain about growth, that's for sure. The whole thing took off like a rocket."

"Well, the town needed it," I said.

"It did," he agreed, winking at me. "It just didn't know it."

The Other School is one of those alternative, community-based "free" schools that do well in the big cities but aren't very common in towns as small as Clayborne. Except for the college, there's no higher or adult education in our three-county area. Brian saw an opportunity and started the school on a very small scale, practically in his spare time, while he was still working as the registrar at Remington. It grew faster than anybody imagined, and eventually he quit the registrar job to be a full-time entrepreneur. "He's crazy," George said, and plenty of people agreed with him, Carrie's husband included. "It won't fly and he'll lose his shirt," they said, but he didn't, and now the only question they were asking was why somebody hadn't thought of it sooner.

"It must keep you terribly busy," I said. "Tied to the office, no outside life to speak of. Unless, of course, you've got good help."

Carrie set her cup down and looked at me. I thought she'd have figured it out by now, but obviously the plot was just hitting her. She's not usually so slow.

Brian picked up instantly, such a clever boy—of course it helped that I'd already planted the seed in his mind at the bank. "Interesting you should say that, because as it happens I have been looking for some help. Not formally, I haven't advertised yet, just been keeping my eyes open." He looked straight at Carrie. "It's gotten too much for me. I've got a wonderful girl, but she's more clerical, you know, she follows directions. What I need is somebody who can make decisions, somebody *bright* who can talk to the instructors on their own level. Chris—that's my secretary—she's a sweetheart, I'd be lost without her, but now I really need somebody a cut above, you know what I mean." Above his goatee, his cheeks glowed pink with good health. "May I have a little more coffee?"

Carrie cleared her throat. I, her mother, heard amusement, resignation, skepticism, and curiosity, but I expect Brian just heard her clear her throat. "How interesting," she said dryly. "Tell us more."

"Well." He hitched his body around toward her, crossing one muscle-bound thigh over the other. "I'm looking for someone to take some of the load off, and that means dealing with advertisers, the day-to-day troubleshooting, making up the curriculum brochure—that's one of the big things, I want completely out from under that, and it's a big job. Somebody to interface one-on-one with our current instructors, and also help recruit more. I'd like somebody to brainstorm with me over new courses, new angles, trying to keep it fresh and alive. Because you gotta constantly refresh, you can't get stale in this business or you're dead. I subscribe to four newspapers, and I probably read eight more on-line, every day, day in and day out. *Got* to stay fresh. Thanks." He stopped talking to gulp his coffee.

I was getting excited myself—maybe he should give *me* the job. The Other School has courses like "Computers Don't Byte," "Your Backyard Vineyard," "A Closer Look at Van Gogh." They have them on weeknights in places like the Unitarian Church or the Elks Club, anyplace there's an empty room and a proprietor who'll let Brian borrow it. Carrie took a course in tole painting last summer; Birdie and I took one called "The Joys of Grandparenting." (George wouldn't go with me, of course, but it's just as well, because frankly that one was a boondoggle.) The fees are cheap, and the teachers get paid based on how many students enroll in their classes. I imagine overhead's practically nothing. My guess is, in a small, Clayborne-type way, Brian Wright's making a killing.

"It's still a risky business, I won't kid you." He pushed back from the table, wiped his mouth with his napkin, balled it up, and set it beside his plate. *So big*. His shoulders were so broad, I couldn't see the back of his chair. "I couldn't withstand a recession yet, for example. I mean, anything can happen. I'll be honest—anybody I hired would be taking the same chance I'm taking."

Well, I certainly admired his candor. Personally, I would love a job like that, all the riskiness and newness, everything not completely planned out yet. I glanced at Carrie, who was pressing her fingertips together and looking thoughtful.

"May I be excused, please?"

Poor Ruth, she was bored to tears. "Of course," I started to say, "why don't you and your grandfather go watch TV." While I start the dishes, and Carrie and Brian have a little private chat—was my thought. But before I could finish, Brian stood up and said he hated to go but he had an early day tomorrow, dinner was wonderful, thanks so much, etc., etc., good-bye.

People—mostly Birdie; sometimes Carrie—say I have no tact. This is not true. I happen to believe there's a time for tact and a time for action, and here was a perfect example. Tact was what got this business meeting started, and action would see it through to the end.

"'Bye, Brian, I'm so glad you could come, it was lovely seeing you. Carrie, could you get Brian's coat? Ruth honey, you go watch your program. George, can you help me in the kitchen?"

There. Everybody went where they were supposed to go. Except for George, who kept going, out the back door and into the yard to smoke his pipe. I didn't spy on them, but before I closed the kitchen door I saw Carrie and Brian huddled in the foyer, talking in earnest voices. He was leaning forward, she was leaning back.

"Why didn't you just tell me, Mama? It would've been nice to know he was coming, that's all."

"I don't see why, and this way you didn't have to worry. Think of it as a stress-free job interview. Wasn't that a lot nicer than going down to his office and answering questions?"

"But what if he didn't want to interview me? You made it impossible for him *not* to."

"No, no, he did want to, I figured that out in the bank. What you don't understand is that this all started with Brian, not me."

"Oh, sure."

"Well, so? What did he say? Are you going to take it?"

Carrie straightened up from the dishwasher, swatting her hair back over her shoulder. "We both said we'd think it over."

"Oh. But he did offer it to you, the job, formally?"

"Well, I guess. Sort of. He told me more about what I'd do."

"What would you do?"

"Well, write all the copy for the spring semester's course brochure, that sounds like the main thing. Help him recruit new sponsors and advertisers. Write up ads and figure out new places to put them. 'Editorial and administration,' he said."

"My goodness, that sounds exciting."

"You think so?"

"Oh, my, yes. You'll be in charge of everything, sounds like. What will *he* do?"

She smiled, loosening up, getting over her huff. "I guess it might be okay. It doesn't sound too hard, nothing I probably couldn't learn."

"Are you kidding? He's lucky to get you. Did you talk about money?"

"No. Oh—he said he was glad to know I'm good with computers. Mama, what in the world did you tell him?"

"Nothing. Just that the last time you worked, which was in Chicago three years ago, you had a very important administrative position in a busy high-tech office."

"I was a part-time assistant in the math department at Stephen's college."

"Isn't that what I just said?"

Oh, it was good to hear Carrie laugh! Ruth came in while we were still at it. She went to the sink, pushing her mother aside with her hip to get a glass of water. Carrie reached up to push a lock of hair out of her face, but she shrugged away, still drinking. "So are you taking that job, Mom?"

"I don't know, sweetie. We said we'd talk about it some more."

"You and Mr. *Wright*." She set the glass in the sink too hard. She looked disgusted, curling her lip in a very unattractive way.

Carrie frowned. "Don't you want me to take it?"

"God, Mom, I so don't care."

"Well, nothing's formal yet anyway. He may not even offer it to me."

"Oh, he'll offer it to you, don't worry. I bet you a million dollars."

"How do you know?"

"Are you kidding? God, it's so *obvious*. The guy is *hot* for you."

Carrie stared, then laughed. "Oh, that's funny. Boy, are you off base."

"Nuh uhh."

"Ruthie, what am I going to do with you?"

"Jeez, Mom, are you really that dense?"

I didn't care for this conversation. I interrupted it to ask Ruth, hoping to change her mood, "How's that boyfriend of yours? The one I met at the bus stop the other day."

"Mama," Carrie said.

"I don't have any boyfriend, Gram."

"You know," I said, "Gull, Herring—"

"If you're speaking of Raven, he is not my boyfriend."

"Well, that's a relief." I laughed, hoping she'd join me. "I wanted to say to him, 'Honey, where's your calendar, Halloween's *over*.'"

"*Mama*."

"*What*?"

It was a cold, nasty day when I met this person, probably forty degrees and spitting rain, but all "Raven" had on was leather pants and a black fishnet top. *Fishnet*. He had white makeup all over his face, and black lipstick on his mouth, the sides curling up in a creepy smile—it gave me the willies. He'd dyed his hair black, you could tell by the inch-long light-brown roots, and he wore it hacked off short on one side and combed over long on the other, long and stringy and absolutely ridiculous, like Michael Jackson's hair, like Dracula's. I was dying to hear what he had to say for himself, so I smiled at him and held my arm out the car window until he had to come over. Well, it was like shaking hands with the undead. His black lips moved, so he must've said something, but what I could not say. Then he walked backward, into the crowd of kids at the bus stop, and before I knew it he was gone. Like Bela Lugosi turning into a bat.

Ruth said, "I'm watching something on TV," and started to leave.

"But I'm sure he's a lovely boy. Hey, how about some ice cream? Want me to bring you some?"

"No, thanks, Gram."

"We've got chocolate *and* vanilla."

"No, thanks," she called from the dining room.

I could hear football coming from the TV room. "Make Grampa turn on something you like!"

Carrie shook her head at me.

"What? What did I say? I shouldn't have said Halloween. Okay, all right, I shouldn't have—but have you *seen* that boy?"

"He's actually very nice."

"Sure. That's what they said about those two at Columbine."

She turned her back and started drying the glasses.

I let a little time go by. "Now, listen. I hope you know I'd never want to push you into anything, but—" This time her laugh wasn't as pleasant to the ears. A snort, it sounded like. I ignored it. "*But*. I'm thinking you should take Brian Wright up on his offer."

"Oh, God." Her shoulders slumped. "I don't know."

"You should, for a lot of reasons. One, it would save you the trouble of looking for something yourself." Which she's not in any shape to do anyway; she could hardly leave the house to buy groceries. "Two, it sounds like a nice job, very responsible, with plenty of room in the future for growth. Three, it would get you out of your slump, because you'd have to get out and be with people. Four, Brian would make a great boss. And five, you need the money."

"You're right," she said lifelessly, elbows on the counter, staring at her reflection in the black window. "You're right, you're right, you're right."

"And six," I said to lighten the mood, "nobody else has offered you a job except Jess Deeping. To build ark animals!"

"Why do you always call him Jess Deeping?"

"What?"

"You always say his last name. You never call him Jess—you never did."

"Really? I never noticed." Why was everybody mad at me tonight? "Anyway. I still can't get over that ark business. Wasn't that the funniest thing? Even your father had a good laugh. You building ark animals—now I've heard everything. What was he going to pay you for that?"

"I don't know, Mama, we never got that far."

"I guess not."

"Jess wouldn't have paid me anyway. The church would have."

"The *Arkists*. My Lord, it never ceases to amaze me what people will start up a religion over. Next we'll have the Sons of Jonah—the Whalists." Carrie eked out a smile. "I didn't know you and Jess Deeping—excuse me, *Jess*—were friends again. I was surprised to see him at Stephen's funeral, in fact." But not as surprised as I was to see him in Carrie's *kitchen*. What a jolt that was. I hadn't been going to bring this subject up at all, and here I was smack in the middle of it.

"Why wouldn't we be friends again? It's—I thought Ruth might've mentioned him to you."

"Why would Ruth mention Jess Deeping to me?"

"Because they—well, it started when we ran into him at the hardware store last, I don't know, last spring sometime." She finally turned around and leaned back against the counter. "Ruth liked him, and he had a lot of dogs wriggling around in the back of his pickup truck, so of course that cemented the bond. She had to do a paper for school on a local industry, and it was her idea to call Jess up and ask a million questions about dairy farming. And then"—she waved her arm vaguely—"it just, you know—"

"Cow stomachs," I recalled. "The science fair project."

"Right, more research. And so—well, anyway, that's it, end of story. Do these go in here or the dining room?"

"I have to say, I think it's just a little odd that this is the first time I'm hearing about all this."

"All what?"

"You know what I'm talking about."

"No, I don't. I really don't."

"Okay, never mind. The good glasses go in the mahogany cupboard in the dining room, please, top shelf. Thank you."

We stared at each other for a few seconds, but it felt like a lot longer. Were we fighting? We used to, years ago, then we quit—

Carrie put up a wall. I'd give anything for the closeness we used to have. But it's gone, and no matter what I do I can't get it back. I thought when she moved back to Clayborne after twenty years away, the pattern would change and we'd become friends again, the way we were—when? When she was about Ruth's age. That was the best time for us. The only time Carrie ever loved me as much as I love her.

What is it I do, I wonder. What's my fatal flaw? Every mother swears all she wants for her children is happiness, but in my case it's the truth. I love my daughter more than anyone else on this earth, even more than my granddaughter, but she won't let me in. She's like a shadow that moves whenever I move, I can't touch her. She pulls away, turns away, backs away. Did I raise a cold child? Or is it me? We're not even close enough to fight anymore.

"Dining room," Carrie said, and walked out with her hands full of wineglasses.

5

Who Is That American Girl?

I was walking home from school by myself because I missed the bus and Caitlin and Jamie, who I usually walk home with as far as Madison when that happens, had already left without me. I passed a store I've noticed before but never gone in. What caught my eye this time was a sign in the window that said TIRED ALL THE TIME?

I'm not, but my mom is. Also sad all the time—maybe they had something for that, too. Under the TIRED ALL THE TIME sign was a big pyramid of pill bottles, and another sign that said, "Clean, pure Nature's Turn Algae, grown wild in the glacier-fed lakes of Ontario, promotes energy, stamina, and mental clarity." I went inside.

Krystal's Mother Earth Palace and Natural Healing Salon, the store was called. They could also have called it Heat and Incense, which is what rushed out and hit me in the face before I could get the door closed. It was like walking into a furnace burning perfume logs. I unwrapped my muffler and unbuttoned my coat, nodding to the only other person in the store, a lady moving jars around on a shelf. "Need any help?" she asked over the plinking of dulcimer music. "No, thanks," I said, "I'm just looking."

Nature's Turn Algae cost $16.95 a bottle. Tough luck, Mom. Gram and Grampa gave me a big check for Christmas, but I still had to be careful about money. Who knew when I'd get more? I went over to the vitamin shelves, which covered two whole walls, thinking maybe some iron pills. Iron, iron . . . things weren't alphabetical here like they were at the drugstore. Did Mom have chronic fatigue? That would explain a lot. If so, she needed Fibro Malic or Aqua Flora. Or Protykin, a powerful antioxidant to fight the onslaught of free radicals, which wreak havoc by destroying cells and tissues. Okay, but what exactly is a free radical? I pictured it as this, like, boomerang-shaped sickle slicing through the air, invading you through your pores or your nose, maybe your food. Nobody's safe. Fibro Malic or not, something's always going to get you.

Wow, this store had pills for everything. Prostate problems, joint pain, thinning hair, trouble breathing, blotchy skin, hormonal imbalance. I have both of those last two. And I've been having a very slow heartbeat lately, sometimes I can't find my pulse at all. These easy-to-swallow soft gels could help; revolutionary studies revealed the amazing cardio-protectant effect of tocotrienols. Some products had typewritten testimonials taped to the shelf under them. I paused at one for a miraculous intestinal cleaner. Some guy, Clifford C. of Spaulding, VA, wrote, "I used it every day for a month, and I was amazed at how all the poisons and decaying matter just kept coming out." Message to Cliff: *Yuck*.

The incense smell was nice once you got used to it, a sort of lemon and cinnamon combination. It was coming from a pot on top of a woodstove at the back of the store. A bookshelf and a couple of soft, ratty-looking chairs closed the area off and made it look cozy, like somebody's very small living room. The books were what you'd expect, New Age stuff, herbal remedies, spiritual healing, 12-step programs. I ran my finger along the spines and pulled out *Live Well, Live Forever*. Snort. Yeah, right. I carried the book over to one of the chairs and sat down.

Well, whatever ailed you, this book could cure it. Acne, allergies, anemia, anger. Heel spurs, hemorrhoids, hiccups. Jealousy, jet lag. Phobias, poor body image, postnasal drip.

Heart disease, page 253.

Oh, man. All the things, all the tricks he could've tried, the safety measures he could've taken. He could've cut out meat, dairy, and processed foods. He could've taken chromium, magnesium, vitamins C and E, and selenium, he could've done yoga. Or meditated, he could've visualized himself swimming easily through the four clean chambers of his heart and out into the coronary arteries, shining a healing blue light on the artery walls as he swam, letting go of all troubling emotions. "Picture something worrisome to your heart such as anger, sadness, or injustice. Throw it over your left shoulder and let it go."

"That's a good book. On special, forty percent off because it's after Christmas." The woman who had been stocking shelves plopped down in the other chair, and immediately a fluffy white cat that for some reason I hadn't seen before jumped up in her lap. "What are you looking up?" She had a round, smiling face framed by a lot of streaky reddish hair, pleated in cornrows and tied with gold beads. And she had a low, gentle, husky voice that took the edge off her nosy question.

"Heart trouble."

"Have you got heart trouble?"

"No." I closed the book, kept pressing it along the spine, erasing the page I had turned to. "My dad. He had coronary heart disease caused by mild atherosclerosis, hypertension, and elevated blood cholesterol. He died." The woman nodded sadly. "He wasn't a type A, though. He wasn't overweight and he didn't smoke. He jogged every two days."

"What was his dosha?"

"Pardon me?"

"In Ayurveda, you can be either *pitta*, *vata*, or *kapha*. *Pittas* are passionate and fiery and hot-tempered, and interestingly, they often live in New England. *Vatas*, they're creative and romantic, usually have curly hair and dry skin, they can get spacey and very ungrounded when they're nervous. *Kaphas* are more phlegmatic, very calm and forgiving, large-eyed people who tend to gain weight. They're your couch potatoes. We've got all three in us, of course, but usually one predominates."

"Um, well, I guess he'd be mostly . . . What was the first one?"

"*Pitta*. Did he have red hair and freckles?"

"No."

"Blond?"

"Sort of. Light brown."

"There you go. Strong metabolisms and effective digestive systems, that's your *pittas*. It's a shame he didn't take arjuna. That's an herb that strengthens the heart muscle and promotes healing. I'm so sorry." She leaned forward, frowning in sympathy. "I just *know* it could've helped him."

I pressed the book to my chest and looked at the fire in the woodstove, murky orange behind the dirty glass window. I was standing by the stove in the Markuses' kitchen when I heard about my parents' accident. We were making fudge. Jamie, Caitlin, me, and Marianne Werner. It was about eleven-thirty at night, and we were arguing over whether to put in walnuts. The phone rang but stopped ringing before Jamie could answer. "My mom got it," she said, and went back to stirring the pot on the stove. About a minute later Mrs. Markus came in the kitchen with Mr. Markus. He had on his robe and pajamas, but she was still in her clothes. I thought we were making too much noise and she'd brought him with her to lay down the law. But they stood in the doorway and didn't say anything, so then I thought they'd come for some fudge. I kept waiting for Jamie to tell them it wasn't ready yet. Mr. Markus said, "Ruth?" I didn't even think he knew my name. As soon as he said it, I knew something awful had happened.

"Would you like some tea? By the way, I'm Krystal." The lady got up and went behind the counter, coming back with two ceramic mugs. "It's chrysanthemum today."

I said, "Well, um."

"Good for the capillaries."

"Really?"

"No question. Have you had headaches lately? Or insomnia?"

"Yeah. Yes, I have."

"This'll help. You'll find you see better, too."

"Wow. Thanks." I took the mug, which Krystal had filled from a copper pot at the back of the stove. "Mm," I said politely. "It's a little . . ."

"Bitter? Put some honey in. Here. I like it plain now, but it took some getting used to." The white cat jumped back up in her lap. Even over the hiss of the woodstove, I could hear it purring. Krystal had a pretty face, and she was a little overweight; she looked like Tracy Chapman, only white and older. Probably a *kapha*. What I couldn't figure out was how she could wear all those clothes in this hot, hot store. She had on a long brown wool skirt with a yellow turtleneck and a multicolored woven sort of tunic thing over that, plus beaded moccasins and long socks and a bright red and orange scarf around her waist, cinching in the tunic. Wasn't she boiling?

"I'm Ruth," I remembered to say. "Ruth Van Allen."

"Hi." She beamed, her face warm and friendly and bland. "It's quiet today. Not many customers."

"I guess you wouldn't need any help, then."

"Hm?"

I stared into my cup, amazed. "Guess you don't need anybody to work for you. After school for like three hours or something, three to six o'clock, and then weekends." I glanced up. Krystal didn't look embarrassed or disapproving or disgusted, she looked thoughtful. "I've been looking for a job ever since my father died." A little exaggeration; I'd been thinking about getting a job, but this was the first time I'd done anything about it. Mom getting hers pushed me into it.

"I could use somebody, actually." Krystal set her mug on the arm of her chair. She turned the limp-limbed cat over and cradled it like a baby, smiling into its blissed-out face. "I'm getting a certificate in naturopathic doctoring, and I need time to study. You're in high school?"

"A sophomore. I get out at quarter to three and I could be here by five after, every day except Monday and Thursday. Soccer practice."

"That would be good. Know anything about natural healing? Health foods? It's okay," she said when I didn't answer. "Mostly you'd be working with stock anyway, not customers. I could teach you."

As soon as she said "I could teach you," I wanted the job. I had to have it. I could learn everything: Ayurveda, vitamins, aromatherapy. It was all here, the secret was right in this room—and a few minutes ago I didn't even know there was a secret. Here was a way for me right now, I could get in early, not have to wait till I was twenty-one, twenty-five, thirty, to learn it.

"This would be so great," I said, trying not to bounce or yell or do anything stupid. "I'm very responsible. I have a Social Security number. I could work all day on Saturdays and Sundays."

"Well, I'm not open on Sundays."

"Oh." I blushed, hoping I hadn't offended her religious beliefs or something. "Do you want me to fill out a form or anything?"

She shrugged, still cradling the cat. "I don't know what it would be. A form? You could write down your phone number, I guess."

Mom was going to ask me a lot of questions. Like how much this job paid. But I didn't know how to ask without sounding rude. I decided to tell Mom the minimum wage, and if it turned out to be more, that would just be even better.

The bell above the door jingled, somebody came in. Krystal looked over but didn't get up. She was a very laid-back shopkeeper. I already loved that about her. "Well," I said, "I guess I should go home. Thank you for the tea, it was very good. When do you think you would like me to start? I mean . . ." I blushed again. "Is it for sure? Are we doing this?"

"Yeah! I have an excellent feeling about it, don't you?"

"I do! I really do."

"You know, I read auras, among other things. Yours is a sort of slate blue—today, anyway—and my cool greenish silver meshes perfectly. I know we're going to get along great. You're a . . ." She narrowed her eyes, studying me. "Aquarius—am I right?"

"Cancer."

"I knew it, it had to be one or the other. I'm Pisces, which is water, too. Ruth Van Allen, we're going to get along like two koi in a lily pond."

"Oh, wow." I hugged my arms, thrilled.

I woke up from a dream I have a lot these days, that I'm running for a train. It's nighttime and very foggy, rainy, and I hear the train whistle blow and I start running toward the tracks. I have on my black jeans and my army green V-neck sweater—this is very important for some reason, what I'm wearing, because it never changes—and I start running along beside the train, which is going faster and faster. I reach out and grab for the cold metal handle, and *whoosh*, pull myself up, and the train picks up speed. I just hang there, feeling the wet wind in my face—and that's the end. I have this dream *constantly*. Running in my black jeans and green sweater in the fog after a train.

Then I couldn't go back to sleep. I got up to get a drink, and heard the TV on downstairs.

"Mom? You still up? It's three-thirty."

"No, I'm not still up. I fell asleep, I just woke up."

I pretended to believe that. She stays up every night almost all night with the TV or the radio or the CD player on, and in the morning she pretends she's just woken up. Then she sleeps all day. She still hadn't gotten around to taking all the Christmas decorations down. Not that she put that many up this year.

"What are you watching?" I asked.

"Nothing. A movie."

I made her move over so I could sit next to her on the sofa. All the lights were out except for the TV. She was huddled under a chenille throw Gram got her for Christmas, wearing one of Dad's old gray Henley shirts and her nightgown. She looked terrible. "I can see that. What is it?"

"Why are you up? You should be in bed."

"I'll go in a sec."

"It's James Stewart in *Call Northside 777*. I thought it would be a Hitchcock, but it's not."

"Who's this guy?"

"He's in prison, he's been in for eleven years for killing a cop. James Stewart's a reporter who thinks he's innocent and is trying to get him out."

I love watching old movies with Mom. It's one of the best things we do together. That and going shopping and then having lunch in a restaurant. Although we haven't done that in a long time, but we used to. We'd almost always get ice cream instead of food, and she always made that seem exciting and nervy and forbidden. "We won't mention this to your father," she'd say in a low voice, ordering two double hot fudge sundaes, one with nuts and one without, and I'd say, "What he doesn't know won't hurt him." We'd laugh, and eat ice cream until our stomachs hurt.

It was a pretty good movie. James Stewart got Richard Conte out of prison at the last second by enlarging a photograph that showed the date on a newspaper, which proved he was innocent. In the very end, they showed Richard Conte getting out of jail and meeting his wife and son and her new husband. She'd divorced him but she still loved him, and she wasn't going back to him because now she had E. G. Marshall.

"Would you ever get married again?"

We both stared straight ahead at the TV. "I don't know, honey. I don't think so, I doubt it. I can't imagine it."

"What if you fell in love with somebody? You're not that old."

She made a face. "I feel old."

"No, but in ten years you could meet some guy and fall in love all over again. You could. It's possible."

She pulled her knees up under her nightgown, dropped her head, and ran her fingers through her hair, messing it up.

"I'm just saying it's possible," I said, touching her on the foot. She had on a pair of Dad's old woolly socks. She never used to wear his clothes like this when he was alive. "Right? You can't be sad forever. Nobody is, except in books. People start up again, they go on." I had been studying this, noticing. "Sonny Bono's wife started dating like nine months after he died. Remember? And after Diana's wreck, the princes went to parties and stuff, they showed pictures of them laughing and looking happy, and you'd never have thought they could do that from the way they were at the funeral. Remember?"

"Yep." She put her arm around me. I burrowed against her, liking her warmth and her flannel smell, even her dirty hair smell. "Tell me about your day."

"I already did. Oh, we saw a movie in World Cultures. It was on the Scottish Highlands, which are incredibly cold and barren, but really really beautiful, and they have more sheep there than people. I was thinking how cool it would be to live there."

"Why? If it's cold and bleak and nobody lives there."

"Because, it just would be. Nothing could happen to you because nobody would even know you were there. And the rent would be cheap."

In fact, I fell asleep tonight thinking about what it would be like to live in a stone cottage with a thatched roof on a hillside all by myself, just a black and white collie for company. I could be either a writer or a painter. People would talk about me, that

American girl who lives alone and doesn't speak to anyone. They'd observe me walking along the cliffs with my dog and the wind blowing out my hair and my black cape. "How lonely she must be," the natives would say, seeing my solitary figure. I'd have a walking stick. I'd speak with a hint of a brogue. Then a handsome, older man would move into the cottage on the neighboring cliff. He too would be an artist, but a tortured, unsuccessful one. I would become his muse. Because of me he would regain his ability to write haunting poetry. Together we would win the Pulitzer Prize, and in our acceptance speech he'd say that without me he would be nothing. We'd get a lot of money and live on the barren heath forever.

"I can't wait for my new job to start," I said. "When does yours?"

"Next week. Monday morning."

"So you better start getting ready, huh? Going to bed at eleven or so. Right? So you can get up in the morning." I gave her pantyhose and perfume for Christmas, and also a new digital alarm clock, so she's got no excuses.

"Good idea," she said.

"Mine starts tomorrow." It would've started sooner, but I had to get a work permit because I'm not sixteen.

"I know."

"It's so totally cool, Mom, it really is." She nodded and smiled, but she wasn't thrilled about it. But that was because she didn't get it; once she met Krystal and checked out the Mother Earth Palace and all the stuff there, she'd be cool with it. Who wouldn't? Caitlin was like, "Oh, wow, that is so weird," but in a good way, and Raven totally gets it, totally thinks it's an excellent choice. First thing, I have to look up sore throat in one of Krystal's books, because I've had one for two days. Low-grade and not bad enough to stay home, but this is how a lot of things start, including esophageal cancer. But it's probably not that. It's probably, like, a cold.

"So what are you going to wear on your first day?"

Mom laughed. "I have absolutely no idea. You think I'll have to get dressed up?"

"Just show your legs a lot, he'll like that. Mr. *Wright*."

"Ruth, what is this with you? Why don't you like Brian?"

"I just don't."

"But why?"

"He's a jerk. Do you like the way he looks at you?"

"The way he looks at me?"

"The way he does everything."

She shook her head, like I was speaking in some other language besides English. "Honey—Brian's okay, he's just a guy. He'll make a good boss but nothing else, you know? Know what I'm sayin'?" she tried for a joke. I hunched my shoulder and put it between our faces. "Listen," she said. "It's important for you to know that I'm not—playing the field or anything."

"Gee, Mom, you sure know some hip lingo."

"I'm just telling you, I'm not available. Nobody is taking your father's place. Nothing's going to change."

"Right."

"Is that agreement or sarcasm?"

"Did you know him before Dad died?"

"Yes, of course. Not well. We'd run into him at college functions."

"What was he like then?"

"He was fine—what do you mean?"

"Didn't you see his eyes that night at dinner? And before, when you were having drinks, how he swooped down on you?"

"Ruth, really—what are you talking about? Brian's friendly, he's personable, he likes people. He stands close when he talks to you, he—touches you sometimes, just to make contact. It doesn't mean anything. It's probably why he's good at his job, it's just the kind of person he is."

"Right. Like Bill Clinton." She laughed, so I laughed, too. I wanted to get off this subject anyway. "Where is the Other School, anyway?" I said. "If it's near the Mother Earth, we could go home together after work sometimes."

"Well, except I'll probably be finishing up about the time you're just starting."

"Yeah, I guess," I said. "Too bad."

She gave me a hug. I didn't know why until I figured out that she thought it was cool that I wanted to go home from work with her. She's so easy sometimes. "Listen, you," she said. "I am going to take your advice and clean up my act, start going to bed early, getting in shape. But you know that I'm really all right, don't you? You get that?"

"Sure," I said, "I know."

"*Really* all right. So don't worry about me."

"Okay. And you don't worry about me."

"No deal, I'm your mother, I get to do that full-time."

"Seriously, Mom, because I'm fine, too."

"I know you are."

"I *am*."

"I know."

Well, somebody was lying. I wondered if she knew it was both of us, and if she thought I believed her, and if she believed me. It didn't matter that much, though, not while we were huddled up together on the couch, her with her arms wound around my arm, me with my head on her shoulder. Watching Bob Dornan walk down a fancy staircase and explain why *Elephant Walk* was a classic and what Elizabeth Taylor was doing when they made it. Right here under Gram's soft blanket, we were safe. We had each other, we practically *were* each other, and it was like we were full. For tonight.

6

Sensible Meals at Appropriate Hours

At eighteen, I was thrilled to leave Clayborne for the big city—Washington, D.C. I went to school there, met Stephen, married, moved to Chicago, had Ruth. I thought I was through with small towns, and certainly through with the south. I never reckoned on Stephen's pleasant liberal arts college denying him tenure, a turn of fortune that effectively rendered him unemployable for any position his pride would let him accept. Except at Remington College, and there only because my father pulled strings.

When we moved back to Clayborne three years ago, I was filled with misgivings. Dread, make that. The things that drove me wild about my hometown were still there, and most of them could be summed up in the word *small*. But something happened to me during my twenty-year self-exile. Smallness didn't oppress me anymore—now I could even see advantages. Old age, I suppose.

It wasn't as if *nothing* had changed in Clayborne—shopping malls full of the usual chain stores had sprouted up where pretty farms used to be; we had new glass and metal office buildings, a few gentrified, brick-paved, gaslight-lined streets downtown where cars weren't allowed. The Leap River had a new four-lane bridge across it, and a "fitness trail" where the old towpath used to be. But the old college hot spots were in the same wooden two-story buildings on Remington Avenue they'd been in when I was a teenager; only the names had changed. Remington students wore different clothes, different hairstyles, but their faces still looked harried, carefree, snotty, scared, drugged out—same as they did in the sixties and the seventies. And the college still gave Clayborne whatever thin veneer of culture and sophistication it had. Without it, we'd have been just another sleepy Piedmont farm village with tenuous ties to the Confederacy and funky architecture. With it, we were a poor man's Charlottesville. A wannabe Chapel Hill.

My family always disdained the local paper, the *Morning Record*. Pop wouldn't read anything but the *New York Times* or, for slumming, the Richmond *Times-Dispatch*; Stephen didn't even know the *Morning Record* existed. But I liked it. When I was in town, I picked up a copy and read it with as much guilty pleasure as if it were the *National Enquirer*, which it certainly was not. At the *Record*, everything was newsworthy, the school lunch menus, hospital admissions by name—but not ailment, fortunately—minutes of meetings of the zoning board and the PTA, the record of deeds and transfers—they printed how much you paid for your house, how much you got for your farm. Fascinating reading. My favorite section was the police blotter, because there was hardly any crime—teen vandalism, some DUI's, a lot of college drunkenness, the tantalizing "lewd conduct," which usually turned out to be peeing in public. That was about it. "Hit and Run" meant somebody had banged into a mailbox and kept going. The commonest headline for traffic accidents was "No One Hurt."

After Chicago, it was like Oz. When I was a young girl the sleepiness of my town made me crazy, but now I liked it. And it wasn't *altogether* that middle age had turned me into a fossil, as my daughter claimed. It was also Ruth herself. Bad things could still happen—I knew that, I wasn't blind—but they weren't as likely. Simple as that. Here in Clayborne, Virginia, the law of dreadful probabilities was in my child's favor. Proximity to my mother, I often had to remind myself, was a small price to pay for peace of mind.

"Look, there's my first boyfriend," I said to Modean, my neighbor, on a chilly, sunny, Sunday afternoon in the middle of January.

We were sitting on a bench in Monroe Square, Clayborne's town center, and I was stalling, thinking of things to say so she wouldn't get up and make me start jogging again.

"Where?" She squinted her kind, nearsighted eyes, looking out across the concrete and grass at the mothers pushing baby strollers, the jostling students, the old men playing checkers. I pointed. "Oh, *him*. Mm, very handsome."

The Confederate Soldier had been standing in the center of Monroe Square since 1878—the plaque said so. He wasn't famous for anything in particular; Clayborne had sent plenty of sons off to the War between the States but, except for dying, none of them had done anything spectacular. He wasn't even on horseback; he was just a regular soldier, rifle over his left shoulder, right leg jutting out as he strode boldly north, toward trouble. "Such a crush I had on him. I even named him," I confessed to Modean.

"What?"

"Beauregard Rourke. Beau to me." Modean snickered. "I used to coast my bike around and around him and make up dreamy stories."

"Like?"

"Like . . . I was a beautiful spy from Philadelphia and he was my secret contact. And clandestine lover."

"How romantic."

"Already I'd figured out the beauty of a bronze boyfriend is that he has to be anything you want, and he can't change."

Modean said, "Carrie, how was your Christmas?" She'd asked me that question yesterday, when she and Dave got back from three weeks in Atlanta, where his folks live, and I'd said, "Fine! It went well, really, much better than I expected."

But now I told her the truth. "It was sad," I said, leaning over to rub a sore place on my heel through my sneaker. "Ruth was so sweet. She did everything she could think of to cheer me up. I did the same for her, so by one o'clock we were both exhausted and we hadn't even gone to my mother's yet."

"How was that?"

"Okay. Same as always, pretty much. My cousins were there, and Aunt Fan, my father's sister. You know my mother always takes over at things like that, the big family occasions. It's her show. Stephen—well, he tended to recede as much as he could. That was just how he coped."

She nodded. "Yeah, I know he was quiet in groups. Shy."

Shy? That was one way to look at it. "Well, he wasn't much of a participant in family events," I said. "He observed. If anything. I did the work and Stephen . . . attended."

"Oh, well. That's just how men are."

"Oh, I know," I said quickly, "they're all like that."

Modean, who saw nothing but good in everyone, was the last person in the world I could complain to about Stephen. Not that I wanted to complain about him. But I wanted to explain to someone why I hadn't missed him terribly over the holidays. I wanted to tell Modean how he could make himself invisible. He did his duty—strung the lights, wrote checks, bought the booze if we were having a party—then he disappeared. It was the same every year, and eventually I got used to doing everything myself. How could I miss him at my mother's house on Christmas day? His absence was noticeable, but not remarkable. Without him, Mama's show really did go on.

"We had an okay time in Atlanta," Modean was telling me. "Dave's dad has a drinking problem, I think I told you, but he stayed on good behavior because of the baby. But there was always that tension, you know, and not knowing. I worried a lot about Dave because he was worrying a lot about his father. So mostly I guess everybody just worried."

Modean was the most perfect friend I'd ever had. She was kindhearted, happy, simple, direct, and together. I'd given up my cynical search for the crack—the secret drinking, the sudden religious proselytizing, the kleptomania. It wasn't there, and she was a paragon, with the saving grace of a sense of humor. Dave was a tall, reedy guy with bushy gray hair and a perpetually startled look, as if he couldn't believe the amazing turn his luck had taken. He was older, widowed for about fifteen years when he found Modean. And Harry was the perfect baby for these perfect parents. I considered it a point in my favor that I had never, even at my lowest, most miserable, self-pitying point, hated the lot of them.

Forcing me, with Ruth's complicity, to go jogging with her was the first mean thing Modean had ever done to me. "You need to get strong, Carrie, you have to build yourself back up. How do you expect to start working eight-hour days? You'll collapse at that office before lunchtime." All true, but I still hated it. When I was in better shape—before Stephen died—I used to jog with him every once in a while, but it never worked out very well. I only did it for the chance to spend time with him, and he preferred to run alone. Cross-purposes.

"Ready to go?" Modean jumped up and started doing stretching exercises. I mimicked her halfheartedly, stiff as a plank. She was ten years younger than me, but even at her age I was never that fit. She was small but strong, with frizzy blonde hair and fair skin, and blue eyes with blonde lashes. She looked like a baby bird. "Okay?" she said, and took off. I followed creakily. It was only eleven blocks from the square to our street, and she regularly ran ten times that without breaking a sweat. I was panting before we hit Jefferson Street.

"So are you all set for work?" She slowed for me, practically running in place. "What are you going to wear tomorrow?"

"Oh, gosh," I wheezed, "I don't know—there's only one other employee besides Brian—a woman—I think it's pretty casual."

"A pantsuit, maybe."

"That's what I was thinking."

"Heels?"

"For the first day."

"Yeah." She paused, thinking she was letting me catch my breath. "I have a new jacket. Got it in Atlanta. I think it would fit you, and it would be terrific with black slacks. It's just right for now, and it's really office-y. I don't even know why I got it, except that I liked it. You could wear it—you could even have it if you think it looks good. Because I really can't imagine where I'm going to wear it."

The only problem with Modean was that she was too good. I'd never had a friend with no edge or shadow at all, no dark spot, some pettiness, a flair for sarcasm, *something*. I was usually the good one—comparatively speaking—in my relationships with women, the one who gasped, "Oh, that's *terrible*," while stifling guilty laughter over the other's wicked observation or unkind gibe. But with Modean, I was the bad one. I worried that I wasn't up to it, that eventually we'd bore each other to death and drift apart. Well, I hoped not. Because I liked her so much.

The Other School was a two-room storefront on the north side, the rundown side, of Virginia Street. Its neighbor on the left was Dr. Jawaharlal, the chiropractor, and on the right, the Cobra Tae Kwon Do. Across the street the streaky showroom window of Coyle's Appliances was plastered with yellow, peeling, three-year-old GOING OUT OF BUSINESS signs. Clayborne didn't have a real slum or ghetto, at least not one compacted into a single small, identifiable section of town. If it had a disadvantaged commercial district, though, North Virginia Street was its epicenter.

"Well, hi!" Christine Fledergast said after I told her who I was. She jumped up from a desk behind a waist-high Formica counter that stretched the width of the narrow front room of the Other School. Behind her, a dark doorway opened to another office—Brian's, I assumed. Christine came around the counter with one arm stretched out, big smile of welcome on her long, exceptionally plain face. She was at least six feet tall, lanky and rawboned, with coarse blonde hair cut short and spiky; not fashionably spiky, more as if she'd cut it herself. "Hey, how are you, it's great to meet you! Brian's out of town—did he tell you?—he won't be back till tomorrow, so it's just going to be me showing you the ropes today—sorry about that. He'll tell you all the important stuff tomorrow."

Modest self-effacement, I'd find out soon, was typical of Chris Fledergast. By lunchtime I'd figured out who ran the office, and it wasn't Brian. If he needed somebody "bright" who could make decisions, she was right here. The miracle was that she didn't seem to resent me, even though I was going to be, in effect, her supervisor. But how could she not? She'd been Brian's right hand for three years. All my puny work background was in academia, the *fringes* of academia, miles away from a growing, dynamic place like the Other School. What was Brian thinking? What could he see in me that I couldn't see in myself?

"Brian's great to work for," Chris confided over tuna fish sandwiches at Creager's, the nearest lunch spot. "Whenever you need time off, you usually just have to ask. And for a small business he gives super benefits. He pays attention, he's appreciative, and he doesn't make you work any harder than he does."

"That's good to know," I said. Because my salary had been a big disappointment. Brian assured me it was temporary, after a few months he'd be able to pay me a wage "more in keeping with your worth." I wasn't sure what that meant, but it was nice to know I'd enjoy enlightened working conditions in return for the pittance he was paying me in the meantime.

Chris's husband, Oz, was a sales rep for a pharmaceutical company. "He travels a lot. He got back from a trip on Christmas Eve at ten o'clock at night, and he was gone again the day after. I didn't see him for a week! He's got no idea, no conception of what it's like trying to pull Christmas together for two kids by yourself."

She didn't wear a speck of makeup that I could see. She wore flat shoes, hunched her shoulders, and slumped. She was spectacularly unattractive in any conventional way, but I had liked her face the minute I saw it. All of a sudden she clapped her hand to the top of her head. "Oh God, Carrie, I'm sorry."

"Why? What?"

"Listen to me going on about Oz. Me and my big mouth. I always talk before I think."

"Oh, no, it's fine, don't worry."

"No, but it must've been just a *terrible* holiday for you. I can't even imagine it. Brian told me about your husband, how sudden it was. I'm so very, very sorry." Her hazel eyes filled with tears.

Oh, great. And me a sympathetic crier. I snickered wetly and handed over a Kleenex, taking one for myself. We blew our noses in unison.

Chris apologized—"This is all you need, I am so sorry, I cry at Alpo commercials"—and blushed. "Not that this is like an Alpo commercial, I mean, this is *much* more serious."

I had just taken a sip of my drink. When I choked, a fine mist of Pepsi sprayed out over my plate. Chris stared at me for a shocked second, then started to giggle, hesitantly at first, checking to make sure it was okay. Before long we were leaning back in our facing seats, braying at each other. She had a swooping, crazy-woman laugh; the sound of it tickled me so much, I kept on laughing. After a while I lost track of what we were laughing at, but part of it had to be relief over not having to be so damn careful with each other.

Fledergast was Oz's name; hers was really O'Donnell. I told her mine was Danziger. We told each other about our hobbies, my crafts and decorating, her creative writing classes. For some reason I found myself telling her about Jess and the Arkists. I was used to Ruth's and my mother's disdain, and Chris's delight took me by surprise. "What fun," she cried, "what a blast you'd have! You're not doing it?"

"When? When? I can't, I just haven't got time."

"God, I know. If I had time, I know what I'd be doing—writing books for kids."

"Really?"

"I've already written one—well, actually I wrote three when Andy was little. But now he's nine, I don't have the excuse that I'm writing them for him anymore. I miss it."

"Did you ever try to sell them?"

"Oh, no, no. Although they weren't terrible. But they weren't picture books so, you know, I doubt there'd've been much of a market anyway. But honestly, they weren't bad."

"I bet they were great."

"If only we didn't have to make money. You know?"

I laughed.

"Wouldn't it be a happier world? This job's fine, I'm not complaining, but what does it have to do with *us*? For Brian, it's the best job there could ever be, but that's because it's *his*. I'm jealous of him. I think people who have found their life's work are the luckiest people in the world. Join me in the chorus now . . ."

We laughed again, but she was right. It was a disheartening thought for the first day of my new job.

Three weeks later, Brian braced his hands against the edge of my desk, his weight-lifter shoulders hunched, head jutted, eyes intent. "We can go to four quarters by the beginning of next year. We can. Already we have too many classes per term for the amount of space we've got, or we will by next summer. Thanks to you, Carrie."

"Oh, no. That's not true, but thanks." I wasn't being modest. I'd made some contacts, phone calls, had conversations with Brian about new courses, nothing more. Crediting me with pulling off the expansion of the Other School by a full quarter was taking employee boosterism too far. But that was the kind of hype Brian excelled at. The amazing thing was that even when you knew he was doing it, it worked. I glanced past his shoulder at Chris, who winked at me.

"Yep, yep, don't tell me, I know who's making a change around here. New ideas, fresh air, that's what we needed. Got stale, got sleepy, can't let that happen. Like when you get tired driving—you want to get where you're going, you don't pull over and take a nap, no, you open a window, let the cold air blow in your face. That's you, Care, a breath of fresh air."

I laughed, flattered in spite of myself. Oh, he was so full of it.

But my new job wasn't as interesting as he'd made it sound. Or maybe it was me. Chris had been doing the work of two people, so my job was to take over half of her workload. Right now it was challenging, but I couldn't help wondering for how long.

I guessed it was worth it, though, toy salary and all, because I had to get up at seven every day, shower, put on lady clothes, leave the house. Eat sensible meals at appropriate hours. Nobody, not even Margaret Sachs, was sorry to see the end of the assembly line of miniature flower arrangements. As routine and horizonless as I could imagine Brian's job becoming, at least it had accomplished what my mother, guilt over Ruth, and fifty milligrams a day of Zoloft hadn't been able to: my return to the real world. Half of me might still be in the ether, zoned out and inattentive, mired in the old grief and guilt that a death in the family brings—*naturally*—but the other half was coping. It was a start.

Brian leaned in closer. With anyone else, a man especially, I'd have moved back, maintained the conventional distance, but I was getting used to his enthusiastic invasions of my space. "Summer term will tell the tale," he prophesied softly; I could smell the clove-flavored gum he chewed after he smoked a cigarette. "That's the key. If it's big, we'll know. That's the next corner we turn. Right? So are we on schedule? Did you get Lois Burkhart on board again? You have to nail her down, Care—"

"I did."

"—because those finance courses are big in the summer. After April fifteenth everybody wants to reform, turn over a new leaf.

They read the brochure in May, they can't wait to sign up for 'Debt-Free Living' or whatever it is."

"I got her."

"And Albert Meyer, I want him for day trading again, and he didn't reup. Call and get him on the bus. I was thinking we should beef up the touchy-feely stuff for summer, get more girls. I know, but it's *true*, you offer 'Relationships for the Millennium'—that's just off the top of my head—and you've got fifteen, twenty women ready to talk, and not a man among 'em. Am I right?"

"Probably."

"Right, so let's think about it, get somebody from social services or one of the university shrinks. 'Be Your Own Therapist'—how's that? 'Learning to Like Yourself.' Because we've got enough tech stuff, enough computer, Internet, and small business, we need to girly things up a little for summer. I know!" he exclaimed, laughing, throwing up his hands. "But you know what I mean! Okay, I'm a sexist pig, and now I'm getting out of here."

"Where are you going?"

"Got a meeting with Hal Wiley at the paper."

"About an ad?"

"An ad, sure, but I'm talking to him about putting the brochure in the *Record*. The whole summer schedule."

"Printing it? Oh," I said, "that would be great."

"No, not printing it. The whole thing, talking about an insert. Think of the distribution! And hell, it's a community service." He grinned, held his arms out wide. He looked like a fullback. "Heh? Think he'll go for it?"

We women exchanged glances. "I think," Chris said with conviction, "he won't know what hit him."

Part of my job involved editing course copy the instructors sent in, the short, hype-filled paragraph allocated to each class in the brochure. Most of them needed punching up, "sexying," Brian called it, especially the courses that sounded a little dry to begin with—"Amateur Radio Operating," "Problem Solving," "Autumn in the Herb Garden." Any course could be jazzed up to sound more interesting, though, and I was getting pretty good at it. Titles were my forte. Last year's "Basic Waltz, Fox-trot, and Jitterbug," for example, would be "Gotta Dance!" next term; the old "Writing Screenplays for TV and the Movies" would be "Move Over, Quentin Tarantino." And so forth.

Rarely did the course descriptions come to me too sexy already, but Lois Burkhart's were an exception. She was an assistant manager at the Farmers and Merchants Bank on the Square. She sent me her course copy by E-mail:

> *Carrie—Got yr. note re. curric. brochure. Took under advisement and toned down copy. Again. Herewith, 2nd revised blurb:*
>
> LIVE FREE OR DIE!
>
> Wolf at the door? In too deep? Debt and worry ruining your life? Cast off the shackles of forfeiture and dependence! Learn inside secrets of smart money management from a pro NOW, and never fear that ringing phone or doorbell—could it be a CREDITOR?—again. Not a scam, pyramid scheme, or investment trick! Spend less, save more—sounds simple, but is it? Learn how with Lois. Bring a calculator and an open mind, and never lose another night's sleep worrying about filthy lucre. Results guaranteed. Textbook (optional; $45) may be purchased in class from instructor.

"Hello, Lois Burkhart, how can I help you?"

"Lois, it's Carrie Van Allen."

"Carrie! Hey, how are you?" She had a bright, convivial voice, full of warmth and intimacy, like the TV voice-over for a women's hygiene product. "I was just thinking about you. Did you get my last E-mail?"

"Yes—well, I think it's the last. That's why I was calling."

"I nailed it this time, didn't I? You know, I didn't agree at first, frankly, in fact I thought you were being a little—well, ha ha! I'll just say a little *strict*. But I went over it again and now I can see it's better, so all's forgiven. You were right and I was wrong," she declared magnanimously.

Lois claimed we'd met before, that she remembered me perfectly. It was possible; I did have an account at her bank, although nine times out of ten I accessed it from the ATM and never entered the building. Say she was right and we knew each other—did that make it easier or harder to tell her that her copy was still a mess?

"Well, it's much better," I allowed cautiously, "much, much better, no question about that."

"I took out all the exclamation points. It made it more dignified, like you said. You were right about that."

"Well, um, not quite all. Did I say dignified? Also—"

"*Most*. You do want it to have *some* life."

"Definitely, absolutely. It should definitely have some life."

"So what's the problem?"

Why hadn't I done this by return E-mail? "Well, the guarantee." Just for starters. "How does that work, now, I mean, who would pay—"

"Oh, that's nothing, it's irrelevant."

"Well, but who— "

"Carrie, nobody's going to ask for their money back!" A hard, cackling laugh.

"It's just that usually we don't guarantee results, you know, I mean never, we couldn't, and besides—"

"Take it out, then. Go ahead. Just take it out."

"Well, I think maybe we'll have to."

"Do it. Anything else?" The feminine hygiene voice went clipped and businesslike. Still melodic, but now it was selling disaster insurance.

"Well, the, um, textbook sale." So much easier to talk about the little errors, easily expunged, than tackle the larger issue of the blurb's overall inanity. "And the mention of your name in the text, that 'Leave it to Lois.' You know, usually we like to give the impression that somebody else, somebody objective and impartial is actually writing these—"

"Wait a second. What exactly are you suggesting?"

"—is writing these little paragraphs—What?"

"You think I get a cut from the texts? A little kickback? Is that what you're suggesting?"

"No, no. No, of course not."

"Well, I don't. It's a courtesy, a convenience, but you can cut that right out, too. Take out anything you don't like and write it yourself."

"Wait, now. Lois, hold it, that's not what I'm saying. It's just a policy at the school that instructors never sell anything, nothing. It keeps everything—it just looks better, that's all. I'm sorry if that wasn't explained to you."

"Nothing needs to be explained to me. I've taught personal finance for two of the three years the Other School has been in business, long before you were a gleam in Brian Wright's eye. I have a bachelor of science degree in business and two-thirds of a master's in accounting. I am an assistant manager at the fifth largest bank in the Commonwealth of Virginia. I know how to do my job. Overworking perfectly good course descriptions in your little brochure is apparently your job."

"Oh, Lois."

"No one has ever had any trouble with my course copy before, by the way."

"No? Well, first time for—"

"I've improved it, is the only difference. The guarantee, the textbook offer—these are entrepreneurial enhancements. But I wouldn't expect you to appreciate that. You ask Brian to call me, will you do that?"

"Yes, if you—"

"And if I don't hear from him, I'll be calling him myself."

"Fine," I snapped. We hung up simultaneously. With my hand on the receiver, I remembered. "Oh, *no*."

"What?" Chris had stopped typing halfway through the conversation so she could listen. "What happened?"

"I forgot—Brian's got a loan out at that woman's bank."

"So? She's not a loan officer. What happened?"

"No, but—oh, God, I should've been nicer. But she was so rude at the end!"

"You didn't say anything, I heard you."

"I should've given in. Probably. Let her write whatever she wanted. But it's *drivel*."

"No, it is, and we can't let the curriculum go out like that. Brian will support you, you'll see."

"She's calling him."

"Let her."

"Oh, *damn*."

"Carrie, relax, we've had crazy teachers before, plenty of them. And Brian never backs down if something with the school is at stake. Once this gas station guy, he was supposed to teach 'Powder Puff Mechanics,' you know, to girls and women, and he was donating his whole garage on Sundays, when he was closed anyway, and the students were supposed to bring in their cars and get them overhauled or whatever as part of the course. Which was great, we expected a big response, maybe we'd make it year-round instead of just a summer class."

"What happened?

"So this *guy*, he decides he gets a free ad for his service station in the brochure, *plus* he wants to give out discount coupons for oil changes and lube jobs to all the students. And Brian said no, no advertising and no selling, no discounts, no nothing. Guy says screw you and won't teach the course, but Brian held firm and that was that."

"Huh. Is Lois a good teacher?"

She shrugged, made a face.

"She is, isn't she?"

"I don't know, I guess. I've heard she's okay."

"Oh, great."

"But it doesn't *matter*."

"I know, I'm just not used to this."

"What, fighting with people?"

"All of it. The last time I worked, I did research for professors. I looked things up and took notes. I usually communicated by memo."

"Yeah, but you're doing a great job. You're good with people, you are, Carrie. I know Brian's full of it sometimes, but you are just doing an *excellent* job, he's right about that."

I thanked her, really touched. Chris was such a generous person. But it bothered me that I didn't care enough. Deep down, her praise and Brian's didn't mean much to me.

I kept putting off calling Jess. Brian wanted him to teach fly-fishing again, as he had last year. I let the whole week go by, I didn't even know why. On Friday, with the weekend looming, I couldn't keep procrastinating.

I stared out at the cold, gray day through the plate glass window, thinking about a story Chris had told me about her son, Andy. He'd gotten in a fight at school last week. The class bully had called him a girl because he was small and he played the violin and the piano. Andy had gotten the worst of it, and Chris had to go for a parent-teacher conference on Monday.

Jess and I met thirty years ago over a fight on the same school playground. We were just starting sixth grade. He wasn't in my class, but I knew him by sight. In fact, I knew him a little better than the other kids who weren't in my class, because already he'd started to acquire a reputation for wildness. And eccentricity. He was a country rather than a town boy, a big and meaningful distinction in sixth grade; he kissed cows—I knew that for sure because it was major playground gossip. Yes, he *kissed cows*, the ones on his father's dairy farm, and he *admitted* it—unwisely, he must have realized in retrospect, but by then it was too late. (One of my vividest memories of our later, adolescent love affair was the night Jess talked me into kissing one myself. On the nose, between its dewy, wide-spaced, long-lashed eyes. "See, Carrie? She likes it." She had seemed to, she being a two-year-old brown and white Guernsey named Magnesia.) He rode the school bus and got off at the bottom of a muddy lane in the middle of nowhere, and the fact that his house was invisible from the road—sycamore trees and a rise in the lane obscured it—added to the mystery about him. Or the rap against him, the communal school sense that Jess wasn't exactly like everybody else. Which was all it took in Clayborne in those days—probably now, too—to isolate a child and make him Other.

The fight in the school yard wasn't about cow kissing, it was over Jess's mother, who was "crazy." This was news to me. I was on my way home when I happened upon Jess and Mason Beckett beating each other up. Three of Mason's friends stood around in a nasty, excited circle, screaming that Jess Deeping's mother was a loony, a nutcase, a psycho, Mason should kill him, kill him, rip his nuts off. But it was the other way around: Mason was on the bottom and losing, and until his buddies jumped in to save him, I thought Jess might kill *him*.

I was a tomboy, but I was small, and a girl, and there were four of them. All the same, I came close to leaping on top of the pile of flying elbows and fists and just seeing what happened. My instant allegiance to Jess's side wasn't a mystery: he was the outnumbered underdog, and Mason Beckett was a known jerk. Later we romanticized it, but at the time, coming to his aid seemed only natural.

Instead of piling on, I ran in the school building and got the first teacher I saw, elderly Mr. Thayer. He stopped the fight, which had gotten pretty bad—skinny, gangly Jess had blood all over him, and not just from Mason's nose. "He started it!" all the boys swore, and I, Mr. Thayer's only impartial witness, couldn't honestly confirm or deny it. But I knew *why* the fight had started, and even though it was scary to rat on four big, resentful boys, I didn't hesitate. "They were taunting." A new word; I'd learned it that year. It meant teasing, and it was specifically forbidden on the playground. "They called his mother crazy, they said she was in the loony bin, and they said he was crazy, too. They called his mother names."

Jess wouldn't look at me. Mr. Thayer had him by the shirt or he would have turned his back on me. I wanted him to look up, acknowledge me. Well, what I wanted was for him to thank me. But he stood with his head averted, wiping blood out of his yellow hair, and never looked at me once. A disappointment for me—almost a betrayal. I'd thought we were together now, a team. A pair.

Years went by and we never spoke. But I watched and noticed him, and I knew he noticed me. Once, sitting behind him at an assembly, I fixated on the back of his neck. If I cut my hair off, would my neck look that thin and fragile and nervous? Did girls have those two weedy tendons, sensitive cords that appeared and disappeared with the turning of the head? After that day, I paid special attention to the backs of boys' necks—in fact, I still do. Some were flat and uninteresting, some were short and muscular, barely there (like Brian's), some were long and reedy, giraffelike. I was always taken by the kind that had a shallow indentation between the two tendons. That little declivity, that gentle dent, was associated in my mind forever with callowness and pride and skittish bravado.

I found Jess's number in the Rolodex, although I already knew it, and punched in the digits carefully. On the fourth ring, his answering machine picked up.

"Hello. This is Jess Deeping," came his surprisingly stiff, formal voice; for a second I didn't recognize it. "Please leave a message when you hear the tone, and I'll call you back as soon as I can. Thank you."

I hung up.

I pictured him at his desk in his cluttered office, composing his message, reciting it into the machine, maybe trying it again, not satisfied the first time. He'd want it to be right; he'd want to sound cordial and serious. He'd think that was important.

His office was once the living room of his parents' house; the "parlor," his mother called it, he'd told me. We used to do homework on the sprung, Indian-bedspread-covered sofa, me at one end, Jess at the other. And there was a window seat in an alcove you couldn't see from the parlor door because it was in the corner. We'd sit there in the late afternoons, out of sight of sad, slow-moving Mr. Deeping if he happened to pass by. That's where Jess kissed me the first time, in that window seat on a rainy afternoon in the spring, and afterward we wrote each other's names on the fogged-up windowpanes. In those days the view was of a broad, shallow pasture against a blur of maples that obscured the flood plain and the river. Jess bought the long strip of land beyond the pasture a few years ago, cut down the trees, and built a dock on the river. He swam from it, fished for trout, and tied up his little boat, the *Cud*. His house hardly resembled the old stone farmhouse he grew up in, he'd added to and knocked out and renovated so many of the small, dim, low-ceilinged rooms. All that was left of the original was the parlor. His office.

I dialed his number again. Cleared my throat while his message played.

"Jess, this is Carrie, calling from the Other School. I don't know if you knew, but I'm working here now. Um, Brian was wondering if you'll be teaching fishing again next June. Would you call and leave a message, please, one way or the other? Any time over the weekend. Okay, thanks."

I almost hung up.

"And—I also wanted to say, I'm sorry, again, about the, um, ark animals, and how all that—went. My mother—oh, God. Well, you know. Anyway." Yes, I'm great with people. "Ruth misses you, she says hi. Wants to come see you one of these days. She's got an idea that she can drive around on your back roads by herself—I can't imagine who put that in her head. Well, okay. Be seeing you. Don't forget about the course. 'Bye, Jess."

I didn't know if I was hinting around for an invitation or not, I truly didn't. But he called the next day, Saturday, and invited Ruth and me to tea. Yes, tea. Thirty years later, he was still doing the unexpected.

7

Two of Everything

"Mom, this car is such a tool. You know what Connie Rosetta's father gave her for her sixteenth birthday? A brand-new Cabrio. In the school *colors*."

"What's a Cabrio?"

"*God*, Mom. It's a VW convertible."

"Oh."

"This is the dorkiest car in the whole town. Who would buy this car?" A Chevy Cavalier, crud colored, with nothing but a radio, not even a tape deck. Automatic, of course, so you couldn't downshift or rev it in neutral or anything. "Who bought it," I asked her, "you or Dad?"

"I guess we bought it together."

"*God*."

"Be careful on these curves, you're almost speeding. Are you watching your speedometer?"

"Yes, I'm watching. Hey, look, Jess got a new sign."

"Slow down."

"I *am*. Isn't it cool?" DEEPING FARMS, it said in white and gold on a green background, on a wooden plaque just inside the old stone gateposts. I steered the Chevy onto the gravel driveway, slowing to a crawl for Mom's sake. "Why is it 'Farms,' though? Doesn't he just have one farm?"

"He has another place out past Locust Dale, I think. Smaller. A tenant runs it."

"I didn't know that. Hey, whose car is that? It's not Mr. Green's."

"Who's Mr. Green?"

"Jess's hired man. Think he got a new car? Jess, I mean." Not new, I saw; used. A gray Ford Taurus almost as ugly as this one. God, I hoped it wasn't Jess's. But I also hoped there wasn't anybody else here. I wanted it to be just us three.

Except for the house, Jess's farm is really beautiful. Everything matches. All the barns have stone foundations, and they're all painted bright white with red trim. Even the silos are white with red tops. The fences are neat and straight, not falling down or rotting or rickety like you see on a lot of farms, and Jess even keeps the messiest places, like the muddy yard where the cows mill around waiting to be milked, as clean as he can by putting fresh straw down and also sometimes rotating them to an alternate waiting place while the other one dries out. When I first saw the farm, I couldn't get over how perfect it all looked, like a play farm, the kind little kids build with toys for their train set. There's shit and everything, I mean, it's definitely a real farm, but—like, even the cows are clean, they don't clump around with filthy butts from sitting in muck all the time. It must take a lot of extra work to keep your farm looking nice. Think how much easier it would be to let things slide. And tempting, too, because you'd probably get the same amount of milk out of the animals. Jess must have a lot of pride.

"You can turn around in the circle," Mom said. "Stop right here, this is good."

"I know, I am." I stopped, put the car in P, turned the key off, pulled up the hand brake. Before we could get out, we were surrounded by a pack of wild dogs.

Except they weren't really wild and there were only four of them. A stranger would've been scared, which I guess is the point. I got out and clapped my hands and Red, the oldest dog, came right up to me. Then Mouse, the little gray one. I had to get down on my knees to make Tracer come, she's the sheepdog mix, and old

Tough Guy never did—so far I've never even petted Tough Guy, he's too scared. Jess said he bit the UPS man once, but only because he accidentally kicked him.

"Hello!"

"Hi, Jess!" I jumped up, grinning, not sure what to do. He looked good, and really glad to see us. I felt like hugging him, but I didn't for some reason. Something about Mom. Like maybe she'd think it was disloyal to my dad or something.

"Glad you could come," he said, and started walking backward, toward one of the big stone and wood barns instead of his house. He had on brown corduroy pants, a regular blue shirt, and an old leather jacket, unzipped. And sneakers. He'd just combed his hair, you could tell by the comb tracks; he wears it straight back and kind of long, and it's just starting to recede in front. He's tall and on the skinny side, but I know he's strong because I've seen him lift a 120-pound calf like it was my book bag.

"Tracer knows a new trick," he said, still walking backward. "Want to see it?" Tracer's the smartest of the four dogs. When Jess found her she already knew how to shake hands, but he taught her how to turn it into a high five—it's so funny. He called her and she ran over and sat down in front of him. He stuck his hand out and made a gun with his index finger and his thumb and yelled, "Pow!"

Tracer dropped to her stomach, rolled over, and stuck all four feet in the air.

What a riot—Mom laughed almost as hard as I did. Then I tried it, and Tracer did it again, perfectly. "What a great dog! She's so smart."

"She's a genius."

"What else can she do?"

"Well, we're working on milking the cows," he said, not cracking a smile. We looked at him for a second, then burst out laughing. "Let's go in here first," he said, "unless you're starving. Are you?" We said no, not really. "Good, because there's someone I'd like you to meet."

I'd never been in this barn before. It was smaller than the main barns; I figured it was for tractors and machinery and big equipment. The red double doors were as high as garage doors. Jess hauled one open and we went in. Yeah, tractors and combines or whatever, big yellow vehicles sitting up on huge black wheels, blades and paddles and rusty metal teeth behind. It smelled like gas, sawdust, dead grass, and paint, and it was almost as cold inside as outside. Straight back, a light was on in the high, beamed ceiling, and I could see a man with his back to us hunched over a sawhorse, sawing wood.

Damn. I didn't know we had to socialize, I thought it would be just us. We started walking toward the man, and about halfway down the echoey plank floor, it hit me who he was and what he was doing: that Pletcher guy, making ark animals. Jess tricked us.

Sure enough, he said, "Carrie, you remember Landy, don't you?" and to me, "Ruth, this is Mr. Pletcher, my neighbor. Landy—Carrie Van Allen now, and her daughter, Ruth."

Landy, what kind of a name was that? He was short and slight and he smiled without showing his teeth. "Carrie? Well, I declare." He put his saw down and took off his old, stained John Deere cap. He had dull, straw-colored hair, thinning in back. He shook hands with Mom and she said, "Landy, it's been ages. How've you been? You look just the same." He must've always been ugly, then. I had to shake, too, and his hands were rough as sandpaper, with big knobby bumps on the knuckles, it felt like holding an old sock full of stones.

"Why, you do, too," he said, "I'd've known you anywhere," and turned red under his beard stubble. He had on work clothes, denim coveralls under a filthy beige windbreaker, and clunky, mud-caked boots. "How long have you been back home?"

"About three years now. We're living on Leap Street, Ruth and I. We—I lost my husband in August, I don't know if Jess told you."

"He surely did, and I was sorry as I could be." His face got even more crinkled and wrinkly. "I know how it is." How? How could he know how it is?

"Thanks," Mom said quickly. "Well, what's all this?"

As if we didn't know. Jess told us all about it that time he came over and tried to get Mom to take the crazy ark job. This guy's father, Eldon, used to be a tobacco farmer back in the 1970s, and he was fairly rich and also sort of a wild man, he played cards and drank a lot and ran around on his wife. Then he got stricken with lung cancer, which is pretty ironic, and on his deathbed he converted to religion because of a dream. He made God a promise, or more like a deal—if He would spare his life, he'd give up his sinful ways and start a new church based on the story of Noah. And to glorify the Lord he'd build an ark, fill it with animals, and sail it on the Leap River for forty days and forty nights. Well, sure enough, God spared his life, so he had to start a religion called the Arkists. But unfortunately for him, he never did get around to building the ark, and now he's dying again, this time for real because he's like eighty or something. So he got his son to say he'd do it for him because otherwise he'll go straight to hell, and the only problem is that Landy's bitten off more than he can chew because hardly any of the other Arkists are helping and time's running out, which is where Jess was hoping Mom would come in. I think all these people are totally nuts.

Landy started showing Mom his handiwork, which was pretty pitiful. "I've only done four so far," he said, dragging boards or something out from under another sawhorse, these flat wooden shapes painted brown, gray, and yellow. If you looked hard, you could tell the gray one was an elephant and the yellow one was a giraffe, but the two brown ones could've been anything.

"Bears, right?" I guessed.

His shoulders drooped. "This one is. That one's a kangaroo."

"Oh, yeah. Very nice," I said politely. "But don't you have to make two of everything?"

He ducked his head and rubbed the back of his neck and mumbled.

"Pardon?"

"Uh, that's under discussion. Hoping to get around that. Still debating."

"Landy, how's your father?" Mom asked.

"Not too well. Heart trouble. He's weakening every day."

"I'm so sorry. Is your mother still living?"

"Yes, she is. Yes, she is."

A man of few words. I looked around for something to do. This part of the barn was Jess's workshop, cluttered with tools and pieces of machinery and workbenches and different kinds of saws. Power saws, lots of them—so why was Landy using a handsaw? For that matter, why was he using Jess's barn, why not his own? He supposedly lived next door. "Are you also building the ark?" I asked.

"Ha," he said, and did the head ducking thing again. He was either really shy or not all there.

Jess said, "That's still on the drawing board," and he said it so straight and firm, so matter-of-fact or something, it was like, well, at least there's one completely sane person here. "In fact, it's *literally* on the drawing board. Come and look."

We went over to one of the workbenches, where there was a big sheet of drafting paper with a drawing of an ark on it. It had the pointy ends and the flat-roofed box on top like you always see in pictures of arks. I had a lunch box in third grade with an ark and all the animals on it, I don't know why, and it looked like that.

"Cool," I said. "How big is it?" I looked up to see Landy and Jess grinning. "What? What's funny?"

"That's something else that's still under debate," Jess said, and he and Landy started to laugh.

Landy had a big, dark gap between his two front teeth, which must be why he tried to smile with his lips closed. "My father would like it to be three hundred cubits long, fifty cubits wide, and thirty cubits high."

Mom said before I could, "What's a cubit?"

"The distance between the tip of the middle finger and the elbow," Jess said. "Biblically speaking."

"So what does that—"

"It comes out to about four hundred and fifty feet long, seventy-five feet wide, forty-five feet tall."

"Wow!" I said. "That's bigger than a football field!"

"Good heavens," Mom said.

Everybody looked depressed.

"So a cubit is your arm from here to here," I said, measuring mine. "What's that, twenty inches or so. Okay, but everybody's different. What if you took, like, an infant's arm and measured. It'd probably be about a fourth the size of a man's, but it would still be a cubit."

Everybody stared at me.

"Right? So you could still have the ark be three hundred cubits long, but instead of four hundred feet it would only be one hundred. Which is still huge. Does the Bible say whose arm you have to measure?"

You'd've thought I just invented the electric light bulb. Jess and Landy looked stunned and then hopeful. "You think?" "I don't know, what do you think?" Mom said, "Could you do that?" and Landy said, "I think so. I hope. He's very reasonable—when I explain, I think he'll say yes."

Yeah, that's Eldon, all right, Mr. Reasonable.

Landy said he'd like to ask Mom's advice about something if she wouldn't mind, she being an artist and all. That's when I knew he was shy, not mental: he'd hit her right in her weak spot. Oh, no, she said, she wouldn't mind at all, and pretty soon they were having a great time talking about plywood thicknesses and paint finishes.

Boring. "Any new calves?" I asked Jess.

"Twins. Want to see?"

"You bet." And we split.

• • •

Walking through the dirt farmyard toward the real barn, the huge one where most of the cows live in winter, I thought about how much I could say to Jess about this ark project. It looked like he was in on it, though, so I didn't want to hurt his feelings. I started with, "So is that guy going to do all the animals? *All* of them?"

"Probably not."

"Yeah, because wouldn't that be impossible? How many species are there, a thousand? No, more like a million. All the animals you never think of, the wombat, the weasel. The wolverine. Shrike." Jess was grinning, which encouraged me. "Wildebeest. Jackal. Dogs! Hey, if you do dogs, don't you have to do all the different breeds? Because, I mean, after the flood you wouldn't want to be stuck with nothing but, like, Dalmatians."

"True."

"Fish, you have to put in all the fish. All the shrimp and minnows and rockfish, tuna—whales—there's gotta be a million!"

"Don't forget reptiles."

"Yeah, two of all the snakes and lizards and everything. Don't forget the snail darters!" We both started laughing, and it was great, I felt grown up making fun of this adult thing, something adults had dreamed up and it turned out to be crazy. "It's nuts, isn't it?" I asked, just to be sure.

"It is completely nuts."

"I know! So why are you doing it?"

"Hell if I know. Haven't you ever done anything that didn't make any sense? Just because you wanted to?"

"Not that I can think of. Playing and make-believe, okay, but you're supposed to outgrow that, right?"

He just smiled, lifting up one crooked eyebrow at me. It had a scar in the middle, and he'd told me how he got it—when he was twelve a pony he owned named Dylan pulled a barbed-wire fence down on his head. Most of the time Jess looks like he's kidding you, because he smiles a lot and that crooked eyebrow looks funny and playful and in the know. But other times his eyes, which are very light gray, get dreamy and faraway, and then he looks to me like a sad man.

It was much warmer in the cow barn. Jess has about two hundred head of cattle, mostly females—that's what a cow is—and in January and February they live inside. He swears they don't mind it, not even staying in their stalls all day except for the two times, four in the afternoon and five in the morning, when they get milked. He calls them "girls." "Here come the girls," he says when they start plodding out of their barns and crowding around the milking parlor. They scared me the first time I got up close to a whole crowd of them in one place, but I didn't know how gentle they were. They all look the same to me, fat black and white Holsteins with sweet, vacant faces. But Jess actually knows who's who—or so he claims. And this I can hardly believe, but he *says* he knows their *names*. "Okay, who's that?" I'll say, pointing to some cow at random. "Cinnamon," he'll say if it's nearby, or "Can't tell," if it's in the distance. "Might be Tulip, can't see her off side." He could be pulling my leg, but I don't think so. I think he really knows all his cows by name.

"I can see how you could start to like them," I said, leaning beside him against the door to one of the birthing stalls and looking in at two sleeping calf twins. "They're nice. They don't have any . . ." I couldn't think of the word. "They could never plot to do something bad."

"Nope."

"They're simple. They have good souls."

"Except when they break your foot."

"God, that had to hurt. Which one did it?" Last summer Jess got stepped on in the field by a cow that wouldn't move, just stood on his foot until she broke it. He was on crutches for two months.

"That would be Crocus."

"You still have her?"

"'Course."

"Jess, can I pet the calves?"

"Sure."

But I stayed where I was, next to him with my foot braced on the bottom rail, arms folded over the top. The barn smell of cow, urine, manure, and feed is amazing, the first whiff almost knocks you over. Then you get used to it and it's not bad. That surprised me, the fact that all that cow shit and pee doesn't stink to high heaven. It stays in your nostrils for a while after you leave, but you don't really mind it. It's a fresh smell, dark and sweet, like old grass and earth. I almost like it.

"So," Jess said into the peaceful quiet, "how's it been going for you? How's school?" he added—that was in case I didn't want to talk about personal stuff.

"School's okay. I have this pretty cool English teacher, Mrs. Fitzgerald. We're reading some poetry. And she's making us keep journals."

"Who's your best friend?"

"Oh . . . Jamie, I guess. And there's this guy." He made an interested sound. "He's not my boyfriend or anything. His name's Raven. Gram thinks he's bizarre. Mom, too, but she doesn't say it, she's trying to be cool, but it's so obvious."

"What's bizarre about him?"

"You name it. No," I said, laughing, "he's not really, he just wears makeup and dresses like a vampire, it's no big deal." I laughed again, this time at Jess's face. I was *this* close to getting the giggles, which I thought I had finally outgrown. "He's very smart, he's probably the smartest kid in the class, he probably shouldn't even be in school. We just hang together sometimes. He gave me a book of poems. When my dad died. I like him, but it's not like this *grand passion* or anything."

I could see he was thinking it over, figuring out if he should say it or not. Finally he couldn't resist, but he kept his voice really casual. "He dresses like a vampire?"

I put my head down on my arms and snorted. Why was it so funny? Some sort of hysteria felt like it was right around the corner. "Sometimes, yeah. It's nothing, it's just a thing. An expression of his angst and disgust at the hollowness of the culture."

Something rubbed against my leg—I looked down and saw a skinny, dusty black cat. I petted it gingerly until it slunk off. "Which one was that?" I challenged Jess, and he said, "Blackie." I couldn't tell if he was kidding or not. "My dad was allergic to fur or dandruff or something, we could never have pets," I said, "not even a cat. Not that I would want a cat."

"I like cats."

"Yours are okay." He had about a dozen cats or kittens who lived outside, barn cats whose job was to catch mice. "But usually they're sneaky. Once I had a guinea pig for about two days, but Dad said I had to get rid of it. So then I got fish, some goldfish, but all they did was die. It was totally disgusting. I'd wake up in the morning and there would be my new goldfish stuck to the top of my dresser."

He leaned over to rub the pink nose of one of the calves, and I could smell his lemon aftershave. My dad used Old Spice, which is sweeter, more prickly on your nose than Jess's brand. "I was a little older than you," he said seriously, like he was starting a story, "when I lost my father. His name was Wayne. My mother was Ora."

"Wayne and Ora Deeping." They sounded so country.

"He was a small, slight guy, only about five foot five. He started to go bald when he was in his twenties."

"You sure don't take after him."

"Well, not that way. Other ways."

"How did he die?" How people die is the thing I want to know most these days.

"An accident. Threshing machine."

I didn't know what to say.

"I still miss him. It's been nineteen years. I think I stayed here because of him. Wanted to make a go of the place for him, and I guess I did."

"Yeah, sure. You're probably rich."

He laughed, which was a relief, because I didn't hear how rude that sounded until after I said it. "My dad worked harder than any man I ever knew. He taught me that—to love what you do, give everything to it. He was very quiet. He moved like this—" Jess straightened up very deliberately from petting the calf. "Slow as a turtle, so he wouldn't spook his cattle. It worked, too, you never saw such happy cows. His doc told him he had no blood pressure at all."

Death is so weird. Here I am with a dead father, and here's my friend Jess with a dead father and a dead mother. Everybody dies. Millions and millions of people are dead. All the people who ever lived since the beginning of time, since the beginning of the world, are now dead. I picture them as stacked on top of one another, like a gigantic pile of cordwood about a trillion miles high. How could God, if there is one, think this is a good plan? How can it be anything but horrible, the absolute worst?

"My dad's heart gave out," I said. Jess already knew that, but now I was telling him my story. "He was driving home with my mom on a Friday night. They'd just had dinner with my grandparents, but he wasn't drunk or anything. He leaned over against the door, and his heart just stopped. Maybe even before the car crashed. Before that he never had anything wrong with him, he never even got colds. Sometimes." I put my fingers on my lips and whispered. "Sometimes I think it would've been better if it had been her instead of him. And then—I'm glad it was him, because if it was her it would be even worse. And then I feel rotten because I know I'm making it all about me instead of my dad. Mom's still a wreck and there's nothing I can do, I can't fix it. I can't change anything, I can't do anything. I don't even get why he died. Why did he die? Does anybody know? Do priests know? Philosophers? You don't know, do you?"

Jess, of course, said no. The amazing thing was that I said all that, made that whole speech, without ever bursting into tears. That cheered me—a sign of growing up.

I started thinking: if anything ever happened to Mom, say she got a job in another city or something, I bet Jess would let me move in, live on the farm with him. He might think at first that I'd be a pest, but he'd soon change his mind. I could do the cooking and cleaning, I'd help out with the chores. At night we'd keep each other company around the kitchen table or, in the summers, out on the front porch. He's got a swing. Living all by himself, he has to be lonely. I'd be his right hand. Raven could come over sometimes, maybe he'd get a part-time job helping Jess out in the afternoons. I'm sure they'd like each other. They have more in common than meets the eye. Mom would come for visits on the weekends. She'd have her doubts at first, but then she'd see what a good job I was doing holding things together.

I heard a door slam and a car start up. When we went outside, Landy was driving away in his Ford Taurus and Mom was standing in the yard waving good-bye. I guessed they were buddies now. "Now who's starving?" Jess said, and we went in his house and had tea.

The house is not very farmlike, to say the least. It's modern and mostly brick, two stories painted white, and inside there's the living room, dining room, etc., etc., decorated just like some middle-class person's house in the suburbs. It's kind of a disappointment. The best rooms are the kitchen and the office, probably because they look like the only ones he uses. All the others are big, clean, empty, and sort of depressing.

Jess had the kitchen table set for three people, including blue-and-white-checked place mats and matching napkins, plates, cups, saucers, and a teapot. "Have a seat." He started heating a pot of milk on the stove.

"Can I help?" Mom asked. She looked pleased but kind of nervous.

"Nope. Like coffee cake?"

"Is that what that smell is? Oh, *man*." I really was starving all of a sudden. He took a loaf pan out of the oven and set it on the table. "Wow, did you make this yourself? Fantastic. Mom hardly ever bakes anymore."

"Go ahead, cut a piece. Eat. I've got sandwiches, too."

"No, we'll wait for you," Mom said.

"Go ahead."

"Okay," I said, "if you insist."

It was terrific, still warm from the oven, lots of brown sugar and cinnamon on the outside, silky cake on the inside. "Sour cream," Jess said when I asked him the secret. "How come you don't bake anymore?" he asked Mom.

"I know I should, but it's hard with just the two of us. And now that I'm working—"

"It's because she doesn't want to get fat," I explained. "She was moving in that direction, too, but lately the slide has been . . ." I couldn't think of the word.

"Decelerated," Mom said coolly. "Thank you."

"Thank *you*," I said when Jess filled my cup with hot cocoa and dropped a marshmallow on top. "Krystal doesn't eat sugar, but I do. I'll give it up someday, but I'm not ready yet."

"This is delicious, Jess, truly. I didn't know you were such a good cook."

"Thank you. Tea or coffee?"

"Tea, please. Thanks."

They were being sort of formal and stiff with each other. Friendly, but also really . . . alert. I said, "So did you all go to school together, you guys and Landy?"

They started to answer at the same time. She stopped and Jess said, "Landy's older, he was a few years ahead of us. He bought the farm next door about fifteen years ago, not long after his wife died. He's been a good neighbor. We help each other out."

"So the two of you were in the same class? You're the exact same age?" They nodded. "Landy looks a *lot* older than you guys. Maybe he had to stay back?"

"No, I don't think so. He has terrible arthritis in his hands, Jess."

"I know. That's why he can't use any of my power saws—I'm afraid he'll cut his arm off."

"He can't do all that work with a handsaw."

"No."

"What's he doing to do?"

He shook his head. After a minute he said, "I'm going to help him build the ark."

I almost choked on my hot chocolate. "Get out. No. You are, really?"

He smiled. Then he looked at Mom, who wasn't saying anything. "He's only got four months to do everything. He's not completely alone, some of the members of the congregation have been helping him out when they can. But they're old, and a lot of times—today, for example—they don't show up."

"He's not even a member of the congregation," Mom said. "I couldn't believe it when he told me that."

"No, he's a Methodist."

"Whoa," I said, "Landy's not an *Arkist*? Then how come he's doing this?"

"For his father. Because he promised."

"Wow. Wow. So he doesn't even believe in it." This just got stranger and stranger. "How come he only has four months?"

Jess looked funny, embarrassed or something. When he rubbed his cheeks with both hands, the raspy sound of his whiskers reminded me of my dad. "Well, according to Eldon, the Bible says the flood was in the six hundredth year of Noah's life, the second month, the seventeenth day. Apparently that comes out to the seventeenth of May."

"Well," Mom said, wiping her mouth with her napkin. "At least the weather should be nice."

"This is crazy," I reminded them. "Do you know how many animals there are? In the *world*?"

"Eldon had a dream, and in it there were *representations* of the animals," Mom said seriously. "So he doesn't have to make all of them. Luckily."

"Wow, *that's* a convenient dream. But he still has to make two of everything, which automatically doubles the—"

"I had an idea about that," she interrupted me. "I was thinking Landy could paint both sides of his plywood, not just one, each in slightly different colors—or even textures—so one side could represent the male and the other the female. So with his bears, one side could be brown, one side black—or lighter brown, darker brown, something like that. Male and female. You could even do"—she laughed—"different facial expressions on either side, ferocious and friendly, savage and sleepy—I don't know." She made a face. "Okay, I got carried away. But Landy thought it was a great idea."

I had a terrible suspicion. "You're going to start helping him, aren't you?"

"No. No, no. No, I can't, I already have a job."

"Not even on a consulting basis?" Jess said. "In an advisory capacity?" He was grinning, but I didn't think he was joking.

"Hey," I said, "did you know I got a job, too?"

"I did hear that. Who told me? Bonnie, must've been." Bonnie Driver, his former wife. I'm friends with Becky, her daughter; she's in my class. I had a lot of questions about Jess and his ex, but I couldn't see how to ask them. It sounded like they still talked to each other, didn't hate each other or anything. Becky's not Jess's daughter, she's Mr. Driver's, so they had to have gotten divorced at least fifteen years go, which is how old Becky is. Jess would've been about twenty-seven. When did he get married? Why did they split up?

"So do you want to hear about my new job?"

"Absolutely." He pushed his plate away and put his elbows on the table and his chin in his hands. Mom got up and started running water over the dirty dishes and puttering. "What's it called again? I've seen the store but I've never been inside."

"The Mother Earth Palace and Natural Healing Salon. It's far more than a health food store, we provide many other services."

"Such as."

"Well, for instance, we do biological terrain assessments. That's a saliva, blood, and urine test you can get to figure out your terrain, your baseline, biologically. We also do hair analysis, we do iridology, which is studying the eye, the iris, to see if you have a disease. Krystal does that, she's certified as an iridologist and also a reflexologist, and right now she's getting her craniosacral certificate."

"So you're liking this job."

"I love it. I'm learning so much. Krystal's letting me set up this aromatherapy, like, spa in the back of the store, where you can come in and lie down and smell soothing essences, which can change your whole outlook. This way you don't have to buy them all yourself, the different aromas, you can just take a treatment when you need it. You should try it."

"Krystal—she's the boss?"

"She owns it. You don't know her? Krystal Bukowski?"

"I don't think so."

"She's a native, I thought maybe you knew her. She's younger than you, though. She's great. She lives over the store in an apartment. She heats it with a woodstove. She's got three cats, and she has boyfriends who crash there sometimes. She's a vegetarian, but she's trying to be a vegan, which is not eating any animal products at all, not even milk, not even butter. She's teaching me to do transformational breath, because sometimes I can get really, like, hyper and it can calm you down, just breathing correctly. What I like about her is that she cuts through the crap, she goes right to the center of stuff, right to what's important, and it isn't school or studying or taking the college boards."

"No?"

"No, it's living in the moment. Living a gentle life that doesn't hurt anyone. It's moving along a spiritual path like a butterfly, disturbing nothing in creation, leaving no destruction in your wake. And treating God's universe with the utmost respect and love and delicacy."

Jess nodded thoughtfully. "Those are good goals. Can't argue with a single one."

"And of course it all starts with yourself, taking care of the body, which if you think about it is the only thing you have any control over anyway. Say, for example, you can take EDTA, which is a chelate, and it purifies your bloodstream of lead and mercury, which you probably have and don't even know. Oral chelation, this is called. I'm taking it, and I can feel a difference already in one month. So—there's all this stuff we can do, everybody should do. To keep ourselves well."

Wow, I was talking a lot. For some reason Jess touched me on my hand. I smiled, and he said, "It would be nice."

"What would?"

"If we could control things. Take a pill to make our lives work out."

I pulled my hand away. "That's not what I mean. I know we can't do that." Did he think I was stupid? "I'm just saying. There's something for everything if you know what it is. You should just come into the store sometime."

"I will."

"Because we have everything. You don't have to put up with all the stuff that happens to you. Take dry skin—which you have on your hands, I notice, along with damaged nails." He looked down at his hands. "And this is just a for instance, the first thing that comes to my mind. Okay, we have Miracle 2000, made of collagen protein and grape-seed extract, and this can prevent and repair aging skin, hair loss, and damaged nails while increasing strength, endurance, and joint flexibility. Many customers have given written testimonials. I'm not making this stuff up."

"No. No."

"I'm just saying we can take action. We don't have to be so passive."

"Want some more hot chocolate?"

"No, thank you. You can lose weight while you sleep—we've got Night Slim, a blend of chromium, lipotropics, and special amino acids that break down fats while you sleep. Okay, you wouldn't need that, but what about mucus? Did you know death begins in the colon?"

"Ruth," Mom said from the sink, "did you want to take the car for a very short drive?"

"By myself?" I scraped my chair getting up.

"Will this work, Jess? I don't want her on any public roads. Back roads only, and just on your property. And someplace where there aren't any ditches."

So I got to drive by myself! First time, and it was way cool even though the road was windy and bumpy so of course I couldn't speed or anything. But just being by myself made it worth it, nobody watching my every move, telling me to start slowing down, turn on my signal, do this, do that. God, I cannot *wait* to get my license. How can I hold out for seven more months before my real life starts?

But when I got back, something was up. Mom and Jess were on the front porch with their coats on, and before I could even get out of the car she came over and got in on the passenger side. "What's wrong?"

"Nothing. Say thank you to Jess, honey, and let's go. It's getting late, he's got cows to milk."

"Did you have a fight?"

"No, no, everything's fine."

No, it wasn't, she was upset about something. Jess came over and put his hands on the door on my side, leaning in the window. He looked sad, too. *I leave for fifteen minutes,* I thought, *and look what happens.* The dogs were circling the car, looking confused. "Well," I said. " 'Bye, Jess. Thanks, I had a really nice time."

"Me, too. Come back soon." He looked across at Mom.

"Jess—I'm sorry."

"For what, Carrie?"

She waved her fingers in the air, giving this gulping laugh. "Being a mess. All my fault. I'll see you—come on, Ruth."

"Okay, okay." The motor was still running. Jess stood straight and backed up. When he clapped his hands, all the dogs got away from the car and ran to him. I took off the emergency brake, shifted into D, and stepped on the accelerator. The car lurched forward with a screech—I jammed on the brake. Mom grabbed at the glove compartment. Whiplash.

I looked back at Jess, who was trying not to laugh. That made me laugh. Then Mom laughed! All of a sudden I felt giddy and happy, everything was so *great.* I almost gave Jess the finger! Instead I thumbed my nose, and he waved and sent me a big, tickled grin as we zoomed away.

"God, that was great, I had the best time."

"I did, too." Her nose was all stopped up; she sounded like she had a cold.

"So what happened?"

"Nothing happened.

"Come *on.*"

"Nothing, really, I just got sad for some reason."

"Did Jess say something?"

"*No*. Yes—he asked me how I was doing. That's all it took." She laughed again, but I saw her squirrel a tissue out of her coat pocket and wipe her face.

"Shit. Are you crying?"

"No, I'm not, and don't say shit to me."

"Sorry. Mom?"

"I'm fine, I'm fine." She flapped her hand. Then she buried her face in the Kleenex and stayed that way.

The country, the low hills and brown fields and whitish sky that had been pretty before, now they just looked cold and dead. I counted telephone poles, dotted yellow lines, bare trees. Shit, shit, shit, shit. I don't think this is ever going to end. Can grief last for a person's whole life? I thought she was better, I thought the job was helping. "I don't know what to do," I said under my breath, too soft for her to hear.

"Hey, Mom?"

She sat up and started fixing herself, blowing her nose, wiping her eyes. "What?"

I had my Walkman in the nylon duffel I'm using for a purse these days. I found it at the bottom after some one-handed fumbling. "Put the earphones on." Good, the tape was wound right, I saw. "It's the first song. Press 'play' and listen to the first song. Listen to the words."

"What is it?"

"Just listen. It's a song."

Jeez. It took her forever to figure out how the earplugs went in her ears, which button to press, how to work the volume. *It's not brain surgery*, I wanted to say, but smart talk right now would've hurt her feelings.

"Who is this?"

"It's Belle. She used to be with the Storm Sewer Troupers. This is her first solo album."

"Belle?"

"Shh, just listen."

"I can't hear the words."

"Turn it up higher."

More dorky fumbling, then finally I heard the high, tinny crash of music over the car's engine drone. The chorus is the best part.

I am water, I am stone.
Take my heart, I'll take you home.
You're not gone, I've got you here, love,
There's no such thing as good-bye.

And then the ghostly harmonies she does with herself, *Ah-eeeeee, oh don't go, oh-weeeeee, stay in my soul*, over and over in that achy voice that goes straight to your heart, right to the marrow of your bones. It gives me chilly bumps.

"It's about getting over the pain of losing somebody," I explained. "She's saying they're not really gone as long as you can remember them."

Mom nodded slowly. She had her eyes closed again, but now she was smiling. In fact, she looked like she was going to laugh.

Belle is so great. She's better than therapy.

8

The Decency to Feel Bad

Stephen and I met in a bar. Not very romantic, but I was so intrigued by what I took for his tense, brooding aloneness, I freighted our first meeting with the dark romance of a Brontë novel. It was Washington, the summer of 1981. I was twenty-three, living in Logan Circle, beginning to despair that I would ever be an artist—prophetically, as it turned out. He was in graduate school at Georgetown; a math student. If I'd known that when I saw him in Rainy's, a hot, grungy tavern on M Street, I might not have found his melancholy so irresistible. I took him for an artist or a writer, for childish reasons: his intensity, the way he held his cigarette, the fact that he never spoke but wouldn't stop staring at me.

I was with women friends, my housemates in a roach-infested duplex on Fifteenth Street. The hot-eyed stares, eventually mutual, went on until I seized the initiative, something I wasn't accustomed to doing with men, particularly strange ones in bars. I didn't smoke, but I did drink; that night I drank enough chardonnay to make slipping a cigarette from my friend's pack of Winstons, taking it over to Stephen's barstool, and asking for a light seem, if not quite natural, inevitable.

I remember the first thing he said to me. "Can you get away?" Such thrilling directness. I loved the implication under it that we were fated, that we'd both just been waiting. We only went for coffee in a café up the street, but I'd have done more—probably anything he wanted. It was a long time before I understood that his heated concentration on me, his rapt, flattering regard, was as much an illusion as my cigarette.

I wonder if I tolerate Raven, Ruth's friend, because I know so well what attracts her to him. It's that same fascinating otherness, the romantic loner persona, that attracted me to Stephen—and before him, of course, to Jess. How clever women are at self-deception; we swallow whole the stories we've already told ourselves.

Stephen drew me as well because of the otherness of what he *knew*. He read books with titles like *P-Resolutions of Cyclic Quotient Singularities*, and I never understood a single thing he told me about them. I liked to hear him talk, even though he might as well have been explaining a concerto to a deaf woman. I ceded to him most of the power in our relationship because I thought he was a genius. I took his silences and abstraction for depth, evidence of realms of knowledge I could never enter, much less comprehend. And I was so restless in those days, easily sidetracked, unable to apply myself to my various art projects—no doubt because I didn't know what I was doing. I don't think he loved math more than I loved art, but he had intensity and focus and I didn't. I envied him.

He was a formal man, even a little straitlaced, and I found I enjoyed trying to seduce him in inappropriate places. I surprised him one afternoon in his carrel at the university library, and he started telling me about the formula or the problem he was working on. As usual it made no sense—but his attention to it, his absolute passion for it, excited me. Or maybe they made me jealous. I remember squeezing onto the edge of his desk, using his body and the carrel partitions for a shield, and unbuttoning my blouse, undoing my bra. He was angry, shocked, determined not to respond. But I made him. I could take him out of himself, and that made me feel strong—I got some of the power back that way, I thought. We made love standing up behind the stacks that day, and it wasn't the only time. I relished making Stephen lose control. I honestly thought it made us even.

I've been thinking about what sex was like later, after we were married. And what it means that I don't miss it very much now. I know a lot of me has gone dead inside, but it's more than that. Toward the end it was just sex, not much closeness, usually not even kissing. Toward the end? No, that's not true, it started earlier. When Ruth was little. So I don't miss it much. Or—no more than I ever did.

Something funny about Stephen. He always came up from behind to hold me or touch me. He would hardly ever put his arms around me from the front, kiss me on my mouth, my face. It was always from behind, pressing against my back, nuzzling my neck, my cheek. Sex was different—he could and did make love in the face-to-face position—but for everyday, standing-up, fully clothed affection, he literally couldn't face me.

I hadn't been lying to Ruth that afternoon at Jess's; I honestly wasn't sure what had set me off, made me red-eyed and teary again. The usual, I suppose: an excess of emotion and a loose cap on it, combined with too much sensitivity where Jess was concerned. I was like a garden hose shut off at the nozzle, and he was the hot sun: prolonged exposure caused ruptures.

I'd had such a nice time until then, drinking tea in his kitchen, half listening to Ruth's rambling monologues. Meeting shy, shambling Landy after so many years and remembering why I'd always been fond of him. Just being at Jess's farm in the winter quiet, everything fallow, gray, utterly still, smell of woodsmoke in the air. For once, with Jess, I felt relaxed, no forbidden attraction, no push-pull. No guilt.

Then Ruth went for a drive and left us by ourselves. I finished the dishes, and stared out the kitchen window at the white, hilly line of a fence in the distance. "Is it snowing?" I said, and Jess came over to stand beside me. I thought I'd seen snowflakes, but he said no, it was ash; Mr. Green was burning brush today behind one of the barns. We gazed out at the occasional drifting speck, hip to hip, not speaking until he said, "Remember the first time you talked to me, Carrie? A snowy day. Eleventh grade—remember?"

I said yes, I remembered, and it struck me that there was something we had never done together: we'd never reminisced. The circumstances of our separation had cut off the possibility of nostalgia, at least the mutual kind. The truth was, I longed to tell Jess what I remembered best, what had stayed with me all through the years, and to hear him say what had meant the most to him.

"I remember what you had on," he said, standing a little away from me on purpose—to make the conversation seem casual. "A red coat with a hood. Plaid hood. And boots—you made me think of folk songs. Spanish leather."

"I thought you were wild," I said. "I was afraid to speak to you. I'd heard so many stories." He smiled, but it was true; by eleventh grade, Jess was famous for climbing the Cherry Street water tower to impress a girl, for almost drowning trying to swim across the Leap River on a dare. The best story was that he'd read about an Indian healing ceremony for casting out devils, and performed it himself, *nude and in the rain,* for the benefit of his crazy mother. A wild boy.

"But you did speak to me," he said. "I remember what you said."

"Not much. As I recall." I recalled it perfectly. Over the Christmas holidays, his mother had died in a fire at Brookner's, the psychiatric facility in Culpeper where she'd been a resident off and on for years. I'd heard the news in homeroom, along with excited whispers that there were *suspicious circumstances*. Had she set the fire herself? Had she meant to burn the place down or just commit suicide? Overnight, Jess Deeping became an even more interesting character. His mother's sensational death seemed suitable somehow, in hindsight, maybe even predictable. It was so much the sort of thing people had come to expect from him.

The kids who knew him were gentle with him in a shy, awkward way, while the kids who didn't stared at him covertly, fascinated. I was one of the latter. I saw him waiting for his bus outside, by himself on a bench by the concrete walk that led to the school parking lot. Everyone else was either inside, crammed against the fogged-up glass doors in the vestibule, or huddled against the wind under the shallow eaves outside, puffing on forbidden cigarettes. Reserved, standoffish, especially around solitary boys I didn't know, I can't say what made me sidle away from my gaggle of laughing girlfriends and go outside to speak to Jess. His aloneness, I suppose. A sadness that hung around him like a coat. I went to him full of trepidation, breathless from my own daring, but with a vague sense that the inevitable was about to happen. I do remember that—it's not retrospective romanticizing. I really did think, crunching my way across the crusty snow in my new boots, *About time*.

He watched me come with a deepening frown; once he even looked over his shoulder to see what else, besides him, I could possibly be headed for. His hair and his shoulders and his thighs were all white from snow. He must be freezing, I thought, with nothing but a hooded sweatshirt, not even zipped up. I stopped in front of him. "Hi," we both said. He sat up straighter when it was clear I wasn't passing by, I meant to stay and speak to him. His sharp knees poked out under the worn denim of his jeans. In my sixteen years, I had never seen anything as male as Jess Deeping's long legs.

I'm sorry about your mother—that was my only message, the sole purpose for my nerve-stretching trek through the snow, but now I couldn't get the words out. My hand closed around a pack of gum in my coat pocket. I drew it out and offered it to him. Up close, his face wasn't as slick and handsome as I'd thought; I could see flaws, pimples on his chin, a patch of beard he'd missed shaving. One eyebrow arched slightly higher than the other, making him look skeptical or reckless. The nails of his big, dry, cold-reddened hands were chewed down to the quick. *Oh*, I thought, *he's not for me*, and I felt relieved and disappointed. *He's just a boy*. Then his mouth went wide in a sad, surprised smile, and that was it. A click in the brain. Yes.

"Thanks." Delicately, he pulled a silver stick of Wrigley's from the pack. He looked at it a moment, then slipped it in his sweatshirt pocket. These memories are so vivid to me. I feel the wet snow on my cheeks, I can almost smell spearmint.

A gust of wind rocked me. "It's cold," I said.

He looked away, beyond my shoulder. "Here comes your bus."

Damn, I thought, watching it lumber up the narrow lane to the turnaround. Under the dismay, my heart skipped—*he knows my bus number*. "I'm sorry you lost your mother," I said quickly. And Jess's eyes filled with tears. I was covered with embarrassment. I felt feverish, then freezing. I stared at my feet, sick with distress, in over my head.

"She didn't kill herself," he said. He didn't hide his face—crying didn't embarrass him at all. When tears spilled down his cheeks, he swiped them off with the heel of his hand.

"She didn't?"

"No. She didn't, she was better, she was almost ready to come home again. She was smoking a cigarette in bed."

"Oh."

"That's how it happened."

"Oh."

I glanced back at the knot of students queuing up to get on the bus, gauging how many more seconds I could stay before I had to make a run for it. "If my mother died . . ." But I couldn't imagine it. "I don't know, I don't know what I'd do."

He had a two-stage smile. The first was pained and gallant, a hero's grimace; it came an instant before the real, glad, natural smile. It made him look as if he knew the world was a sad and tricky place, but he was in love with it anyway. "You just do what you always do," he said. "Only it's not as good anymore."

"Yeah. God, Jess." Just saying his name made me dizzy. "I have to go now." He kept his face alert, animated, but I thought, as soon as I was gone, it would sink back into that sadness I'd startled him out of. I didn't want to go. The last two kids climbed into the school bus and disappeared. "I can't," I said, although he hadn't asked me anything, and ran.

A coward even then. *Why did you miss your bus?* my mother would have wanted to know, and already I had misgivings about explaining Jess, anything about Jess, to her. That was no shrewd instinct, no flash of clever intuition. More like grasping a simple law of physics or chemistry: oil and water don't mix.

"That was the second time you rescued me, Carrie," Jess said, and I smiled, recalling the first—the sixth grade playground brawl. "No one else would say anything to me about my mother. As if it had never happened, she'd never died. I thought you were brave."

"Me?" What a laugh. Jess was more than I could handle, I knew it in my bones even then. I was young, and I couldn't stop seeing him through my mother's eyes. He scared me. Fear and excitement, fear and wanting, fear and love—I twisted and swiveled and pivoted between them for the next two years. Then I lost my courage completely and ran away.

"Twice you saved me, Carrie, and you didn't even know me."

"Well, but that explains it. It was only *after* I knew you . . ." I swallowed. I'd started out playfully, and walked right into the truth. "That I turned into a chicken," I made myself finish.

I walked to the bench under the opposite window, put my knee on it, looked around his kitchen with ostentatious alertness. "Your house is so different now. You've changed it so much, I'd hardly know it. From the old days."

"I ruined it."

I smiled uncertainly. "That's a funny thing to say."

"It's true. It took a while, but I finally figured out why I did it. I'll tell you, but only if you promise not to laugh."

"What do you mean, Jess?"

"Promise?"

"No—yes. I won't laugh."

"I was trying to make it a house your mother wouldn't hate. I blamed you for giving in to her, but then, in a way, I did the same thing. I think it's turned out that your mother was stronger than both of us."

I could only stare at his pained, amused face. How like him to share the blame for my worst mistake.

"After my father died, and there was no more hope for you and me because we'd both married other people, I started changing my house. I didn't understand why until it was finished. One day I looked around and it hit me. I'd taken all the country out of it and made it a house Mrs. Danziger wouldn't be embarrassed to live in. Shit, Carrie, it's an awful-looking place, isn't it?"

I put my hand over my mouth.

"Don't you laugh," he warned, smiling the saddest smile. "My herd's three times the size of my father's. I lease farmland to tenants in Oakpark and Locust Dale. I'm prosperous and respectable, I'm a gentleman farmer. Hell, I'm on the town council. And I owe it all to your mother."

"Jess."

"I wanted to show her. Show you, too. And all I did was ruin *my* mother's pretty little farmhouse. Don't you think that's funny?" He came closer. "Hey, Carrie. Don't cry. I didn't tell you that to make you sad."

Where was the bitterness, why wasn't he angry? "Sorry—I cry at everything. Ruth's back," I whispered, hearing the car on the hill. "I don't know what to say to you. Give me some time, Jess. To think of something besides 'I'm sorry.' I'm so sick of telling you I'm sorry." I found my coat and went outside to meet Ruth.

What would I do with this new knowledge? He was right, it was funny. And so sad. I wished he hadn't told me—and yet I always knew it. In the car, Ruth thought I was weeping for Stephen. She tried her best to comfort me. The twin absurdities almost did me in: Jess spoiling his house for my mother's sake, me finding consolation in the lyrics of Belle, formerly of the Storm Sewer Troupers. Oh, my heart could melt with tenderness sometimes. Even when I was drowning, going down for the last time, the people I loved saved me from touching bottom. And lately, thin streaks of happiness had been scoring the dark at lengthy intervals, zigzag spurts of hope in the black sky, reminding me that I was getting better. I was.

This is what happened.

Ruth had just turned five, the, sweetest, brightest little girl, the reason for my life. For Stephen and me, the best was ending, if best meant the time for believing your life was a rising line, everything gradually improving, enlarging, like a stock market graphic in good times. My expectations had begun to diminish in the early years after Ruth was born, a time that coincided with Stephen's retreat, the start of his metamorphosis into the subdued, closed-off man he would be until he died. It's ironic that what attracted me in the beginning was what repelled me in the end, and that was no one's fault but mine. I profoundly misunderstood him. So—the best was over, but I didn't *know* it was over because I was living in it, I was in the distraught but hopeful stage, when repairing our married lives still seemed possible, if only because the alternative was unthinkable. Leave my baby fatherless? Not if I could help it. And I still had energy then, a sense of myself as an actor, a doer. A person who could change.

We'd left Washington the same year Ruth was born, moved to Chicago for Stephen's new teaching appointment. That he wasn't going to set the math world on fire, either as a theorist or a teacher, was another dawning downer around that time, and I didn't appreciate until too late how much his professional failures demoralized him. I should have, but I'd made another wrong presumption—

that wife and child were the main ingredients in a happy man's life. Not in Stephen's. But his childhood was awful, one loss after another; how could he not be a sad man, a careful, withholding, brittle man?

We'd been planning for weeks to go home for a long weekend—my home, Clayborne—to see my parents, and to go to my fifteen-year high school reunion. A day or two before, we had an argument. I don't remember what provoked it, just that it was worse than usual because for once Stephen participated in it. Whatever started it, soon enough we were blaming each other for our unhappiness, dredging up old resentments and unveiling new ones, saying hurtful things for no reason except that they were true. When it was over, it seemed that for a change a destination might have been reached, a place where the road might actually fork. We were barely speaking. He refused to go home with me—and that may have been his goal all along, it occurred to me later, since he hated that kind of thing, obligatory social occasions at which, as *husband of*, he was even more peripheral than he wanted to be. In the end Ruth and I went by ourselves, and stayed in my old room in my parents' house (now the guest room, all traces of young Carrie long since swept away during one of my mother's remodeling binges). Stephen had to go to a last-minute math conference, I told Mama, and she believed me.

They had the reunion at the Madison Hotel, downtown Clayborne's finest. What happened seems inevitable now, but at the time, every minute unfolded like a slow surprise, the revelation of a complicated secret. Jess and I hadn't kept in touch, no Christmas cards, no wedding congratulations; when he and Bonnie divorced, I wrote him a very short note saying I was sorry, but then I tore it up. We hadn't seen each other since the year after our high school graduation.

We shook hands cordially in a group of people shaking hands the same way. Chameleons, we were, blending right in. We did it so well, even *I* didn't suspect us. For half the night we did a dance of separating and coming together, parting and finding, until at last we just stayed put—for me, a matter of giving up pretending I wanted to be anywhere else.

It wasn't that we picked up where we'd left off, as if the intervening fifteen years had never happened. For one thing, Jess had changed. Obviously—he was thirty-three, not eighteen—but it was more than that. His house wasn't the only thing he'd toned down, I see now; he'd done it to himself, too—tried to. He'd moderated himself, conventionalized himself—those aren't the right words, I can't describe the new phenomenon of Jess. Anyway, the important thing is that it didn't matter, because it didn't work. I saw through his dark suit and paisley tie then, his side-parted hair and his sober, diffident manner, and I still do.

We talked. I told him everything I could about my life except that I wasn't happy. Which meant I had to leave out a lot. He did the same, scrupulously avoiding all but the most general references to his ex-wife. We never danced, never touched. We stayed to the end, through the toasts and jokes and speeches and prizes. He walked me to my car and we said good-bye. "'Bye, Jess." "Good night, Carrie." We touched hands, and he said, "Or you could come home with me," and I said, "All right," and we got in his car and drove to his house.

It was a soft June night, heat lightning in the distance, I remember, and no moon but a skyful of stars. If that matters. One looks for culprits in retrospect, villains to blame, even inanimate ones, anything to spread the blame around. When it was over, I remember wishing I'd had too much to drink so I could add alcohol to my litany of motivations. But no luck: I was sober and clearheaded, and everything I did was deliberate and on purpose. There. Mea culpa can't be any more ecumenical than that.

I hope I haven't passed any of this sexual guilt down to Ruth. I don't even know where it comes from. Litany, mea culpa, ecumenical—I'm not even a Catholic! And what about this—the only consolation I found in the aftermath of sleeping with Jess came from knowing that at least I hadn't enjoyed it. At least it wasn't a transcendent experience for either of us. The night ended in awkwardness and sorrow, and I suffered for it long after with regret and depression and guilt. My mother didn't teach me this, did she? I'm accustomed to blaming her for most of my flaws, in particular my failures of courage; but if she's in here, it's not as a towering moral figure. Maybe a social one. The goddess of snobbery, observing a tawdry one-nighter.

We never made it upstairs. Looking back, I wondered if Jess had been afraid from the beginning it wouldn't work, and had made love with me on the couch in his living room to give me less time to think. If so, that broke my heart, because it was so unlike him. Neither of us pretended we'd come to his house to talk. We were kissing before we were all the way through the door, deep, passionate kisses that felt like the past and present coming together, as if the years in between didn't exist. We hardly talked at all—how could we? Everything depended on no words being spoken. In the end, though, it was our guilty, unnatural silence that helped break the spell. I disengaged; went cold. It wasn't a return to sanity; more a gathering hopelessness, like a dark, dirty fog blearing a prospect that had been bright and sharp seconds ago. This couldn't work, it hurt too many people. The deeper we went, the more irredeemable it felt. I started to cry before it was over.

Jess stopped, put his clothes on, told me he would drive me back to my car. Before that, I have no idea what it meant to him. Did he like it, did he think we were good together? I don't think so. It was too full of shadows, and too frantic at the end. I remember the kissing more than the sex. I think my brain shut down when he came inside me, I think it was just too much. Too much. Now I can say it happened too soon, that I was still involved in my marriage, that by no means had I severed emotional ties to Stephen, that I wasn't ready for another man, even Jess, especially Jess. But at the time, it only felt like a calamity.

The rest is an embarrassing blur. I kept apologizing—he got quieter and quieter. I promised never to hurt him again—he said that wasn't possible. I cried some more. Understandably, he didn't want to prolong the conversation. He made me get out of his car and into mine, but I kept stalling. I wanted to comfort him and I wanted him to forgive me. Stupid, selfish, impossible.

For years I thought, *What a drip I was*. What a *drip*. I wished Jess had gotten angry, or *shown* it if he was angry, because at least that would've sharpened the squishy, drippy edges, given us something *meaty* to look back on, something to sink our teeth into. Really I wanted it all ways—for it not to have happened, for it to have happened and been wonderful, or for it to have happened and been awful, but with dignity. Instead I got the worst of all the possibilities.

I never told Stephen. He already knew about Jess; my "high school sweetheart," I'd called him, and once I'd gone so far as to say, "I guess I was in love with him." He took my casualness at face value, never questioned it or probed deeper. I would have. If Stephen had loved someone before me, I'd have wanted to know everything. What was she like, why did you like her, how did it end? His disinterest in the details of Jess was typical, though; one might even say emblematic.

On the airplane ride home, I made a decision to rededicate myself to making my marriage work. Something good might still come from the debacle with Jess, I reasoned, and besides, I owed it to Ruth—good as gold, chattering to herself as she turned the pages of a book, her feet sticking straight out in the patent leather Mary Janes her grandmother had bought her. The thought that I might have jeopardized my baby's safe, stable world froze me with horror. Anything, anything I had to do to keep the family together was worth it. No sinner ever embraced her penance more willingly.

I saw a therapist, who told me I was depressed and prescribed pills. I started to feel better. A time came, when Ruth was about eight, when Stephen made the supreme sacrifice and went with me to couples counseling. For four months, after which he declared our marriage "cured" and gave me an emerald ring for our anniversary. And that was the end of that.

Jess is still my one and only . . . what is the word . . . indiscretion. I hated it that I had been unfaithful, that I could never again claim fidelity and truthfulness as virtues of mine. But over the years my harsh judgment faded, as those things do, and I forgave myself, pretty much. Then all that was left was loss.

Deep down, though, I was always glad it was him. I've been drawn to other men from time to time, but I never gave in to the attraction. Self-serving, I know, but I do think, if you're going to cheat on your husband, you should at least have the decency to do it with a man you've loved all your life.

9

What Can You Do But Laugh?

If, God forbid, you had to go in a nursing home, Cedar Hill was probably as good as most. At least it was new; I could stop worrying about sticking George (or him sticking me) in Pacific Acres, the depressing, decaying, god-awful excuse for a rest home out on Route 15, Clayborne's best about forty years ago. Cedar Hill was like a funeral home—it looked a lot nicer than its neighbors. I guess they were trying for a luxurious estate look with all the gray stone and the wood shingles, but it didn't work. The wheelchair ramps gave it away, and the black rubber floor mats and the automatic sliding doors. And all that mulch—my Lord, to have the mulch concession at Cedar Hill. In six months you could retire and move to Florida.

Helen Mintz's room was on the third floor of A wing. Birdie and I signed in at the front desk as usual, where there was a new girl on who didn't recognize us. "Why would a pretty young girl like that want to work in a place like this?" Birdie said as we went down the two-wheelchair-wide, mauve-carpeted corridor.

"Why would anybody." I lowered my voice at the elevator bank, where four or five old ladies in wheelchairs or on walkers waited in silence. Like cows, I thought unkindly, patient and dumb. "Thank God *somebody* wants to," I said close to Birdie's ear. "I couldn't do it, I'm too mean. They're better than we are, Bird, that's all there is to it."

"Oh, yes," she agreed automatically. But come to think of it, Birdie would make a pretty good caretaker of the old and dotty, whose needs couldn't be that complicated—bathing, feeding, changing, medicating. I could see her doing all that with a lot of quick movements, a lot of wasted nervous energy. And all the time she did it, she'd never stop talking.

The elevator finally came. It took forever to get all the old ladies on board, and it was a miracle nobody's wheelchair got stuck on anybody else's, but there were a lot of close calls. I caught Birdie's eye after we finally got wedged in among all the canes and brittle hips and motorized chairs, and we had to look away. It's not the humor, it's the horror. I'm sorry, but what can you do but laugh?

Helen's door was ajar. "Yoo-hoo, anybody home?" No answer, but that didn't mean anything. Birdie pushed open the door to the tiny sitting room, overstuffed with furniture and reeking of air freshener. The TV was on without the sound. "Helen? Yoo-hoo!"

A weak voice from the bedroom, "Hello?"

We went in, and Birdie cried, "Hi! Well, don't you look smart!"

"Hey, Helen, how are you?" I said with a great big smile. "Good, he's not here," I muttered, stripping off my gloves and unbuttoning my coat. Hot, hot, it had to be eighty degrees in the room.

"Lord, yes," Birdie muttered back, and advanced on the bed to give Helen a hug. "Hi, honey, how you doing? You look so pretty! Is that a new peignoir? We always said pink was your color. You look wonderful, I bet you just got your hair done. It's nice, I like that shade of rinse."

I leaned over from the other side of the bed. "Hey, Helen, it's Dana."

"Dana." She blinked her thin-lashed eyes. Impossible to say if she knew me or not.

"Bird and I came to see you. It's been about three weeks since we were here last time, remember?"

"Why, I surely do, I surely do. How have you been?" She was nothing but a china doll, frail and brittle against the fat pillows behind her. The bluish hair was a wig, I saw up close, prissy marcel waves stacked on either side of a low part, freakish-looking above the spotty, deep-grooved, canvas brown that Helen's face has turned into.

She used to have long wavy chestnut hair, and she wore it down and loose until she turned fifty. Then, "I'm too old for long hair," she announced one day at bridge club, and the next week she came back with it all cut off. It looked so cute and young, one by one we all got ours cut off, too. Oh, Helen used to be the style setter at the bridge club. Such a lady. Just last fall, she'd've played hostess from her steel bed, or more likely her wheelchair, seeing to it that we had chairs and mints and cans of Coca-Cola, taking the lead in the gay conversation. Today Birdie and I found seats on our own, and all the talk started with us. All poor Helen could manage was, "Oh, is that right. Well, you don't *mean* it," with a sweet-faced smile.

Birdie plunged in with all her news, then all the news about everybody else she could think of. She forgot about Eunice. "Eunice had a hysterectomy," I mentioned when she paused to take a breath. Helen and Eunice Shavers had been bridge partners for thirty years—same as Birdie and me. "She said it didn't make a damn bit of difference, Henry's *still* not interested."

Birdie cackled. Helen smiled and nodded. "Oh, is that *right*."

"Dana's running for president of the women's club," Birdie informed her next. "Nobody can talk her out of it."

"Most people don't want to talk me out of it."

"Sensible people can't talk her out of it."

"Some people are just jealous."

"Some people choose to go blind and deaf so they can't see the handwriting on the wall. Pride goeth before a fall."

"Oh, dry up."

Helen smiled, eyes peacefully drifting back and forth between Birdie and me. I think she knew us then, just in that second. We had little spitting contests all the time, we were known for them at the bridge club. I think this one helped jog Helen's mind and we finally registered on her: *Oh, it's you two*.

She used to be sharp as a tack. She'd volunteer at the drop of a hat at the hospital, the cancer auction, hospice, the Red Cross. A real dynamo, even if it was just to get out of the house. Years ago the four of us, Helen, Eunice Shavers, Birdie, and I, went to Richmond for a couple of days, stayed at the Jefferson Hotel, went shopping, saw a show, a real ladies' weekend. Saturday night in the hotel bar, we were sitting around yakking, carrying on, enjoying ourselves. Feeling no pain. A man sidled up and started talking to Eunice by herself. Now Eunice is normally a levelheaded woman, but that night she was feeling even less pain than the rest of us. They carried on in private until it got late, time to go. She'll deny it to her dying day, but she was ready to go off with that man. "We're leaving," we kept telling her, but she wouldn't budge.

Helen saved the day. I can still see her herding that man away from Eunice, butting in between them like a sheepdog, chest out, chin up. He was a slick-looking character with silvery hair and a green cashmere sport coat; he sold golf equipment, I remember. He and Helen had words. We never knew what she said to him; afterward, she'd only say, "I called on his better instincts." But it did the trick—Mr. Green Jacket paid the tab for everybody, kissed Eunice on the hand, and said good night. And that was Helen for you, efficient as hell but always a lady. I always wished I had that combination.

Already she was slipping back into her own world. "Carrie's working for Brian Wright now," I told her in a loud voice. "You remember him, he runs that adult education program where we took the cooking class. You and Maxine Stubbs and I, about two years ago?"

"Yes, oh, yes."

"Doesn't pay much, but Brian's such a go-getter, I've got high hopes for Carrie's advancement. That job could take her anywhere. You know she lost her husband," I reminded Helen, who smiled and said, "Oh, is that *right*." "And Ruth's working at a health food store," I went on determinedly, "that Palace of something or other on Remington Avenue. Loves it. She's learning to drive. Worries Carrie to death. It all comes around, doesn't it? I was a nervous wreck when *she* was fifteen and learning. Ruth's fine, though, and at least she doesn't smoke."

"That you know of," Birdie said.

"That I know of."

Birdie's daughter's oldest boy, Jason, took dope and who knows what else before getting thrown out of his fancy prep school in Minneapolis, three or four years ago now. I guess he's straightened out since then, but Birdie was still touchy when it came to other people's grandchildren's wholesome accomplishments. I tried to be sensitive, but every once in a while I couldn't resist bragging about Ruth. The perfect teenager. How she turned out so well considering how permissive Carrie can be—well, that's a mystery. But a good one, so I don't examine it too closely. Wouldn't want to look a gift horse in the mouth.

Birdie said, "What do you hear from Raymond, Helen?"

"Oh, for the Lord's sake." I should've seen that coming, should've followed her train of thought and headed it off.

"What? What did I say? Oh." Birdie saw Helen's eyes fill with tears, and sent me a look of distress. Old fool. Anybody knew the surest way to make Helen cry was to mention her son Raymond's name. He lived in Florida now, Key West or one of those places where gays congregate; he never visited, and as far as I knew he never even called. Or if he did call, his poor mama was in no shape to remember it.

"Helen, honey?" Birdie got up and hovered over her, patting her fluttering hands. "There, now. There, now, sweetheart." The tears kept coming, but by now Helen probably didn't even know what she was crying about, she just knew she was sad. Dear God, I thought, give me the strength to kill myself. Don't let me get this way, I swear I'll blow my brains out first. Not a very Christian prayer, but I didn't mean it anyway. I used to say things like that all the time—"I'll swallow weed killer before I'll end up senile and in a diaper." Funny, though, the older you get, the more you lose interest in disposing of yourself. It ought to work the other way around.

"What the hell's going on here?"

Calvin Mintz filled the doorway with his wide, plaid-shirted bulk. A man that age ought to've started to shrink by now, but if Cal had lost an inch or a pound in the last twenty years, I couldn't see it. Old age hadn't sweetened his temper any, either. He looked mad as a bear.

"Why, hello, Calvin," Birdie chirped. "Helen's fine, she's just fine. Aren't you, honey? Look who's here to see you, it's Calvin."

Helen gave a tired smile, batting her eyes while Birdie wiped her cheeks with a hankie. I got up and gave Cal my side of the bed. He didn't touch or kiss his wife. He stood over her, a hulking man with a fleshy face and invisible lips, small eyes as dark and quick as Birdie's but much more purposeful. A mean face, I always thought. He came to see Helen every day, sat with her from morning to night. Such devotion. Such fidelity. What a shame he hadn't exhibited either one of those fine traits back when she was sharp enough to appreciate them. I despised him, or any man who was so bottled up, so *stunted* he could only be kind to his wife after she'd lost the capacity to recognize him.

"It's time for your arts and crafts class, Helen," he said in a voice that shocked me—so gentle and solicitous, I barely recognized it. "Two o'clock, up and at 'em, that's my girl." He stretched his arm back and snapped his thick fingers. "Oh!" Birdie peeped, realizing he wanted Helen's bathrobe from the foot of the bed. Bastard—that was more like it. She handed the robe to him and moved around to help, but he turned his back on her and fumbled

Helen's bony, listless arms into it by himself. It was like watching a father dress his little girl.

I looked around for the folded wheelchair and opened it without asking. Cal lifted Helen off the bed and set her in it carefully, straightening her robe where the collar had twisted. "Move," he said. I was in the way, I was blocking the path to the door, no question about it. His meanness helped me make a decision.

"We'll come with you," I said brightly, bending over to look Helen in the eyes. "Won't that be fun? Birdie and I'll come with you, honey. We'll *all* play."

"Play," Helen said with happy surprise. She beamed. "Let's all play."

Calvin actually swore. Foul, foul man. Birdie looked confused. I spun around and led the way out of the room.

Arts and crafts was exactly as pathetic and depressing as I'd thought it would be. *Kill me, Lord,* I prayed with new energy. *Put me out of my misery before it comes to this.* Eight old ladies, seven in wheelchairs and one sprightly gal on a walker, sat at card tables and learned how to make valentines out of red construction paper and doilies from an eighteen-year-old cheerleader. Well, she might've been twenty-two, but not a day older. And "learned" was stretching it. Debbie, the cheerleader, went around making all the ladies' valentines for them, leaning over their humped, arthritic shoulders with her strong, slender arms, crooning, "Isn't that pretty? Who's your valentine to? Bet you've got a lot of sweethearts, Margaret, don't you? Bet you're a real heartbreaker, aren't you?" And Margaret would giggle, or Nancy Jo would look vacant, Rebecca would click her dentures.

Calvin wouldn't let Debbie make Helen's valentine, of course, no, he had to do it for her, cutting heart shapes out of white lacy doilies and pasting them on bigger, blood-red paper heart shapes. It would've been touching, all that patience and gentleness, if you didn't know what was what. If you hadn't listened, off and on for the last thirty-five years, to a hundred stories about Calvin Mintz's neglect, coldness, and meanness. If he missed his wife, it was because there was nobody around the house to bully anymore. No sympathy from me. *Wallow in it, you SOB.* Calvin and his like, domineering, abusive men, bring out the worst in me.

It was a stupid idea, coming to arts and crafts. Helen didn't even know we were there. "Let's go, Bird," I said. I'd only wanted to yank Calvin's chain. Mission accomplished, I guessed, although it hadn't been very satisfying. "Bird?"

She looked up from the absorbing task of gluing half a dozen small red hearts on a big white lace heart. Her gray wool coat dwarfed her; she looked like a bag lady. She looked demented. "Thought I'd make one for Kenny." That was her youngest grandson. She winked—and the little chill that had begun to steal into my chest melted away. Just for a second—but no, Birdie was okay, she had her faculties, or as many as she ever had. And she was frequently the world's biggest pain in the you-know-what, but you couldn't not love her. I didn't like how she'd looked at that card table, though, squinting at her hearts, turning them around in her stiff fingers while she snipped them out with a pair of child's scissors. She fit in too well. She looked right at home.

Not me, I thought fiercely. I will *not.* Swear to God, I'll jump off the Leap River bridge first.

A cold February twilight was settling in; the color of the sky through the sliding glass doors to a brick-paved patio made me shiver. I hate winter. I hate the end of daylight savings time. Outside, gray geese were marching around a frozen man-made lake at the bottom of the sloping lawn. This place wouldn't be half bad in the summertime. At least you could get out. I watched a deer gallop across the lawn and skid to a stop not forty feet away. Pretty thing. A doe. It sniffed the air with its delicate snout, shivered, and bolted toward the patio.

That deer's coming right at me, I thought in a frozen part of my mind. *Of course it's not,* my rational side scoffed. *The hell it's not.* I had time to shout, "Look out!" and jerk an amazed Birdie out of her chair by her coat collar before everything went haywire.

Crash! The shock of seeing glass suddenly shatter and fly at you was nothing compared to the sight of an *animal* blundering in right behind. A big, brown, naked *animal* with a lolling tongue and white-rimmed eyes rolling in panic. It made noises—another shock; I thought deer were silent—harsh fluttery neighing sounds through its distended nostrils. It bolted in one direction, butting over a table, another table, crashing its antlerless head against a wall. Nobody was screaming except Birdie and Debbie, the cheerleader; the rest of us were petrified, struck dumb. When it veered toward Helen's chair, Calvin flung himself in front of her, arms spread wide, shielding her with his body.

Nobody was doing anything. I pushed Birdie away. "Baaaah!" I yelled. "Rawwwh!" The terrified deer skidded in front of me and jerked up on its hind legs. I shook my hands over my head. "Wraaah!" I kept shrieking while I went toward it in slow, fearful steps, trying to narrow the escape routes, herding it closer and closer to the broken door. Blood spotted its forehead and chest. It lunged again, overturning a folding chair, and I made a wild run straight at it. It pivoted clumsily—more blood on its dainty front legs—and smashed against the closed door to the hall.

Debbie stopped screaming and crept out of the corner, darting toward a metal floor lamp the deer had knocked over. She picked it up in both hands, like a lance. It had a cheap metal shade, open at the top; she pointed it headfirst at the deer, who was blowing its ribs in and out, panting, looking at—the lamp. I figured it out. Debbie thought she was stunning it by shining a light in its eyes.

Well, that was so stupid, it made me brave. I circled around the now motionless deer, moving toward a walker I could see under one of the still-standing card tables. When I got close enough, I bent over and grabbed it.

"Yah! Go! Go!" I stabbed the air with the walker. "Beat it!" Beside me, Debbie echoed, "Beat it!" and together we took jerky steps toward the deer until the floor lamp went out—she'd pulled the plug out of the socket. The animal looked confused, exhausted, swinging its head from side to side. "Wraaah!" I shouted again, and shook my walker. Suddenly it turned. In one enormous bound, it leapt through the shattered door, over the glass shards and the valentines, and streaked away, white tail flying surrender.

I stood there with my chest heaving and my heart pounding. From her crouch in the corner Birdie called, "Dana?" in a cracked voice. Everybody looked dazed. "Who's hurt?" Debbie said. "Anybody hurt?" A miracle—nobody was. A woman swathed in handmade shawls wept quietly while two other old ladies comforted her. "Okay, if everyone's okay, I'm going to call security," Debbie announced. "Okay? I'll be *right back*."

Calvin huddled over Helen, patting the hands she had gripped to the arms of her wheelchair. "Wasn't that a sight, Helen?" he said in a cheerful tone, as if we'd just witnessed something pleasantly exciting, a balloon launch or a shooting star. "That gave me a turn, I'll say. But we're okay now, aren't we. We're—"

"You made Raymond go hunting." Helen stretched her thin, cordy neck out accusingly, rheumy eyes blazing. "Remember? You made him go up to Bear Lake with you and that redneck friend, what was his name? Bobby Mahr. Ray was eleven years old and you called him a sissy because he didn't want to hunt."

Calvin stared at her stupidly, opening and closing his mouth.

"*Remember*?" she said impatiently.

"Yes."

"And *damn you* if you didn't make him shoot at a doe. He missed—but imagine making a boy like that shoot a deer. *Imagine* it." One balled fist smacked her padded wheelchair arm.

"Helen." Calvin put his hands on his knees and hung his head.

"Oh, my," quavered Birdie, realizing he was crying. I knew I should look away, but I couldn't.

Helen sat back. The piercing look faded; she stretched out a trembly hand and gave his bent, balding head one sad pat. "We lost him," she said. "That's when it started. Our baby. Where is he, Cal, is he dead?"

"No, no. No, he lives in Miami."

"But where is he? Where is he?"

"He's in Miami."

She wilted, just clicked off, a lightbulb going dark. Cal Mintz got a wrinkled handkerchief out of his back pocket and stuck his face in it.

On the drive home, all I wanted to do was brood, but Birdie never met a silence she couldn't fill. "Do anybody's children ever turn out right?" she wanted to know.

A dumb question I had no patience with. "Mine turned out fine," I said.

"Oh, I know ours aren't drug addicts or drunks or thieves or what-have-you. I'm saying, do anybody's children really care about them once they get grown?"

"What are you talking about? Of course they do."

"But not enough, Dana. Don't you feel that? It's not enough. All we do for them, what's it turn out to be for? I would've lain down and died for Mattie and Martha, I'd've done *anything* for them. My babies. And now look, they can't come see their own mother at Christmas. Me a widow, and I haven't seen my grandsons in eighteen months."

I wanted to say soothing, sympathetic things, but I'd seen Birdie with her children. She could not shut up, would not *listen* to them, and her incessant nervous chatter made them roll their eyes. She never stopped talking long enough to hear what their lives were like, so she had no idea in the world what kind of adults her own children had turned into. She exasperated them—they broke her heart.

What is it *I* do? Carrie only came back to Clayborne because she had to—Stephen's job. It's not that I talk too much, I don't think. Something else. The worst is that she wants to be close again, too, but neither of us can punch through the wall. It's sad and it's wrong, two people who ought to be the closest, a mother and her daughter.

I think daughters want too much, though. Carrie wants me to approve of every little thing she does. "Unconditional love," that's called. But what kind of a mother doesn't try to steer her child in the right direction when she sees her veering off the track? I don't even want credit for it—I just want tolerance and understanding and decent treatment.

"I don't even know why we have children," Birdie said. "I think it's because we get pregnant. Did you and George plan for Carrie?"

"No."

"No, most people don't. What do kids *do* for us?"

"Bird, you're just in a mood." I reached over and gave her skinny shoulder a pat.

"You think they'll make your life better," she said, "you think they'll make you happy."

You think they'll give your life meaning, I corrected to myself. And for a while it works, but then they grow up and leave you, and there's nobody left to soften the blow that there isn't any meaning. Not your husband, that's for sure.

"But happy families are only on TV," Birdie was saying. "In real life your kids can't wait to get away from you. It's so unfair." She sniffed and blinked her eyes fast. "Because all you ever wanted was a little love in return. And to try to make their lives happy."

And maybe you can't do both, it occurred to me. In fact, maybe the second one cancels out the first.

10

ARRESTED DEVELOPMENT

Clayborne High School's parent-teacher conference day carried over into the evening, 7 to 9 P.M., for the convenience of the mothers and fathers who worked. A thoughtful accommodation, but I was running late before I started. My plan was to leave the Other School at the usual time, go home and grab a sandwich, change clothes if there was time, pick Ruth up at the health store at six-fifteen, drive her to her grandparents' house, where she was to have dinner, and make it to the school no later than seven—right on time so I could be finished in an hour and a half, pick Ruth up, go home, and collapse.

Nothing worked out. At noon, Brian realized he needed *today*, not tomorrow, the final autumn course offerings list, to include in a small business grant application that had to be postmarked by 6 P.M. We made it, just barely, but by then it was too late to go home. I'd missed lunch, so I stopped at Creager's for a quick bite, where I got the world's slowest, dimmest waitress and a case of indigestion. And a headache. By the time I double-parked in front of the Mother Earth Palace and Natural Healing Salon, where Ruth was supposed to be waiting *outside* but wasn't, it was already quarter to seven.

I'd met Krystal once before, not long after Ruth began to work for her. It was easy to see why Ruth liked her. She was young and hip, undemanding and laid-back; she said "fuck" with great casualness. But she was a kind of throwback, wasn't she? Or were hippies back in style now? Ruth's reaction to my tentative, extremely reluctant question concerning the possibility of dope smoked, or possibly even sold, on the premises was predictable. "*Jeez*, Mom. Like—*no*. God!"

"Hi, Krystal," I called, spying her in the cozy back area, slouched in an easy chair next to the humming woodstove. "Is Ruth here? I'm picking her up."

"Hi, Carrie." She had a low, husky voice, very soothing. She'd have made a good hypnotist. "Ruth? No, she left."

"She left?" I went closer to the stifling heat. "When?"

"Oh . . ." She peered at the fire through the glass door, as if a clock might be in there. "An hour ago? Well, at six, when we close. What time is it?"

"But she was supposed to wait for me. She left at six?"

"Yeah. Bummer. I guess she forgot." She smiled consolingly. She had dry, curly, reddish hair, flat around the front under a leather headband today, bushy and wild in back, an electrified halo.

"Do you know where she went? Did she go home?"

"I don't know. She didn't say, she just left, same as always." She picked up the white cat on her lap, gently set it on the floor, and stood up. "Problem?"

"Can I use your phone?"

"Sure."

Ruth wasn't at home. I got the machine and thought of leaving a sarcastic message, but Krystal was listening; it might embarrass Ruth. I called my mother.

"Hi, Mama. Ruth isn't there, is she?" She could've gotten mixed up, had one of her friends drive her over there.

"Ruth? No. Should she be? I thought you were bringing her. Is she driving? But she can't yet, she doesn't—"

"Long story—we've missed each other. I'll call you back, okay? As soon as I find out where she is."

"Do you think something's happened?"

"No, no, it's just a mix-up. I'll call you back. Don't worry."

Damn.

"Have you got a phone book?" I asked, and Krystal rummaged around and found one under a small counter covered with jars of Aloe-Dent, Astragalus, and Vitamol. What was Caitlin's last name? It was on the tip of my tongue. All Ruth's friends were on speed dial at home; I had no idea what their numbers were. Caitlin, Caitlin . . . I couldn't remember. Jamie, then; Jamie Markus.

She wasn't there. Mrs. Markus thought she might be over at Caitlin's, and gave me the number. Caitlin McReynolds.

Mrs. McReynolds said Caitlin was over at Becky Driver's. Jamie, too, but she wasn't sure about Ruth. I called the Drivers.

"Oh, hi, Mom."

"Why are you not here?"

"Where's here?"

My intense relief at finding her alive and unmolested evaporated very quickly. Underneath lay nothing but irritation. "I'm at Krystal's," I said through my teeth. "Where are you?"

"Oh, wow, I forgot. I'm supposed to go to Gram's, right?"

"Correct."

"Well, I forgot."

"Did you forget to come home, too?"

"No, because I knew you were going out."

"If you knew I was going out, how could you forget you were supposed to go to your grandmother's?"

"I don't know, I just *did*."

I pinched a white trail up and down the bridge of my nose. "I don't have time to pick you up now."

"That's okay, we were just about to eat anyway."

"I don't have time to call your grandmother and apologize, either. You'll have to do that."

"Oh, *man*."

"Ruth? I mean it."

"Okay, okay."

"As soon as we hang up. Now, how were you planning to get home?"

"Jamie'll drive me."

Jamie was sixteen, had been for about a month and a half. "No," I said, "I'll pick you up on my way home. About eight-thirty."

"No, Mom, come *on*. She can drive me, and anyway, eight-*thirty*? We won't even have our homework done by then."

"Oh, you went over to Becky's to do homework."

"Yes. I did! Partly. I *did*."

I was too tired to keep arguing. Stephen always said I gave in too easily, I was too lenient, I had no backbone. All true. I was probably ruining our daughter. The reason I was going to parent-teacher conference day in the first place was because Ruth's grades were sliding, and that was undoubtedly my fault, too. I felt like an invalid, an amputee, I had no control anymore, it was all slipping away.

"Make sure Jamie drives carefully, and I want you home by nine-thirty."

"Nine-thirty? *God*, Mom. Ten, come *on*. Jamie doesn't even have to be home till eleven."

"I very much doubt that."

"Ten, Mom."

"Nine-forty-five, and not a minute later. Hear me?"

"*Okay*."

"What are you going to do when we hang up?"

"Eat dinner?"

"Ruth—"

"Kidding, Mom, it's a joke. Remember jokes? Ha ha?"

"I'll see you at nine-forty-five. I imagine we'll have a lot to talk about."

That sobered her up. She said good-bye without making any more jokes.

"Do you take flaxseed?"

"What?"

"Flaxseed oil," Krystal said, shelving the phone book, "is very good for maintaining a healthy blood pressure. Comes in capsules. You want to take it with sage tea, a nerve tonic."

"Yes, that's—I'm sure that's a good idea. Would you happen to have any aspirin?"

She laughed gently. "No. Headache?"

"It's just starting. Tylenol?"

"Ah, Carrie. Belladonna, gelsemium, feverfew, wintergreen, willow bark, meadowsweet."

"Oh, I see."

"Autogenics, acupressure, aromatherapy, massage, juice therapy. These I can offer you."

"Ha-ha. But no Tylenol?"

"Are you familiar with Ayuveda? You could try a plain warm-water enema if you have a *vata* headache. Or rubbing the scalp and the soles of the feet with sesame oil, followed by a hot shower."

"Oh, thanks. I'll—"

"If it's a shooting, burning *pitta* headache, a sandalwood paste to the forehead and temples works wonders. For a *kapha* headache—does it feel worse when you bend over?—salt water in the nostrils is good."

"That's interesting. I'll certainly remember that. But now I'm so late, and I'm double-parked, I'd better run."

"Well, I wouldn't advise running. What you want to do right now, before it gets a foothold, is to imagine your headache is something else, say a leprechaun. Strike up a conversation with it. Make friends. Try a trade-off—you promise to eat better and get more sleep, your leprechaun promises to back off this time."

All this was said with a straight face and complete confidence. I searched for a twitch of the lip, a self-conscious twinkle in the eye, but in vain. Krystal Bukowski was the real deal.

"I'll do that. I'll try it in the car," I promised, and escaped.

What I tried in the car was speeding. On Cemetery Road, along the half-mile limbo section between residential and rural, where the houses ran out but the cornfields hadn't quite begun—suddenly a blue light flashed in the rearview mirror. Cop.

I slowed but didn't pull over—maybe it would pass, maybe it was after a criminal. I jolted in panic when the siren burst, *Wheep! Wheep!* No, it was me. It wanted *me*. My foot started to shake on the brake pedal and my hands turned clammy on the steering wheel. *Calm down*. I'd been speeding, not robbing a bank. But I was scared, and under the fear was fury, and over everything lay intense, skin-prickling frustration.

"Hello, Officer." I tried a bright, flirty voice. "Is there a problem?"

"Evening, ma'am. In a hurry tonight?" He wouldn't stand next to me, wouldn't come farther than my shoulder, I had to twist my neck to see him. A good tactic; it must deter the armed and hotheaded from shooting him in the face. "See your driver's license and registration, please." I fumbled them out of the glove compartment and handed them over. "Where you headed tonight, ma'am?"

"The high school. It's parent-teacher day." See? How wholesome and innocent?

"Uh-huh. Any reason you were going fifty-three in the thirty-five-mile-an-hour zone?"

I blanked. Should I tell the truth and say I was late? Deny everything? "Fifty-three?" I said wonderingly. "Are you sure?" I still couldn't see his face, but his voice sounded young and unsympathetic. "I never speed, honestly. It was an accident. I'm teaching my daughter to drive, I go *under* the limit usually."

"Ma'am, would you turn on your emergency blinkers, please?" I did, and he sauntered back to his patrol car and got in. I could hear him talking on his radio. I burst into tears.

What in the world was wrong with me? I wanted to sob and sob, not stop for days. It was crazy, I couldn't account for it. I barely had myself pulled together when he came back and handed me a pink ticket through the window.

"I'm going to give you a warning this time, Mrs. Van Allen."

"Oh, thank—" Mortifying tears flooded my face. "Sorry." I found a tissue and blotted my eyes. "Thank you. I'm—I'll—I won't do it again."

He finally leaned in the window, a little late now, but probably to see if I'd been drinking. I saw his face by the dashboard light. Young, yes; he was only a boy. "Better not, because next time, if it's me, I won't be so lenient."

"No, I know. I won't, don't worry."

"You don't want to mess up your good driving record."

"No."

"You want to set a good example for your daughter."

"I know. Yes."

"Okay, ma'am. You take it easy now."

"I will. Thank you, Officer"—I squinted at the badge on his chest—"Sherman."

He followed me all the way to the high school. I drove with exaggerated caution, five or six miles below the limit, careful to stay in the exact center of my lane. I didn't cry again, but I was still on some tricky kind of an edge. What a strange overreaction. Why such childish humiliation and rage? I couldn't remember feeling like this before, not over something so trivial. I looked normal, I wore pantsuits and worked at a computer, I could go for days at a time without crying. "Carrie's finally coming around," my mother was starting to tell her friends, and even Ruth didn't worry about me quite as much. But see how little it took to level me. Officer Sherman hadn't even given me a ticket!

My old school got a face-lift in about 1990, tinted windows and a new pink brick facade, even a tastefully harmonious addition. Now it looked about half its real age—thirty-five. But most of the interior changes were only cosmetic, and when I turned up for open house or one of Ruth's glee club concerts or science fairs, it was very much like stepping back in time. Because of the smell, always the same, always a humid, sweetish mix of chalk dust, mildew, wet wool, and sweat. As soon as I inhaled it, I was seventeen again, and a thousand ripe memories bombarded me. Like fruit falling out of a tree on my head.

No memories tonight, please. I wasn't myself; my poor head ached already, I was so tired, all I wanted to do was go home and pull up the covers. Besides, I was weak and vulnerable, and memories of high school always meant memories of Jess. I needed to focus on who I was, not who I used to be; I was an aging widow, here for her troubled teenage daughter. *Think of Ruth and getting home,* I advised myself, *Ruth and getting home.* That ought to squelch nostalgia.

There were long lines outside the classrooms of the teachers who taught Ruth's new worst subjects—biology, history, and amazingly, math. But that was some consolation, wasn't it, the fact that she wasn't alone? Maybe these teachers were incompetent, maybe lots of kids' grades were slipping.

But, no. Ms. Reedy, the biology teacher, and Mr. Von Bretzel, the history teacher, unfortunately struck me, in ten-minute interviews with each, as entirely capable; they were also sympathetic and understanding, and brought up the subject of Stephen's death even before I could. No scapegoating there. I'd been hoping—I realized it when I saw it wasn't going to work—to put all the blame for Ruth's troubles on the callousness and insensitivity of her teachers.

This must be what it's like waiting for the priest at confession, I thought, queued behind two other mothers outside Mr. Tambor's room. Did my companions feel as guilty as I did, as personally responsible for their children's academic shortcomings? But how could Ruth be failing algebra? There must be a mistake; math had always been her best subject. Now it was English, which made no sense at all. No, this had to be a mistake.

Eventually Mr. Tambor poked his head out the door. "Who's next, please?"

The blackboard across the front of the room was covered with formulas and equations; just the sight gave me a queasy feeling. Unlike Ruth, my worst subject had always been math. Plump, swarthy Mr. Tambor had a fringe of black hair ringing the back of his head and exactly three strands, very long, combed across the dome. How easy, I knew from experience, to make fun of a teacher who looked like that. But Mr. Tambor's brown doe eyes were kind, and when he smiled he looked like an Indian prophet, Meher Baba perhaps. I liked him immediately. Instead of sitting behind his metal desk, he gestured to a student desk in the front row, and took the one across from it only after making sure I was settled.

I introduced myself, and he said, "Ah, Ruth's mother," very sadly. "I am sorry for the loss of your husband."

"Thank you." He had a formal way of speaking, but surely I was imagining the eastern accent; he wasn't really *from* India. "I'm concerned about Ruth's math scores lately, Mr. Tambor. She's always been so good in math—she talks about majoring in it in college. I can't imagine what's happened," I said. Disingenuously. "I mean, to go from A's and A-minuses to a D-plus in three months—it's very worrisome."

"Yes. Yes, it is worrisome." He put his fingertips together thoughtfully, or maybe prayerfully. "Have you asked Ruth what might be the problem?"

"She says the class has gotten harder. She also admits she's not studying quite as hard."

Mr. Tambor pursed his lips. "Mr. Van Allen taught mathematics at the college," he observed.

"That's right, yes."

"Advanced courses, topology, numerical methods, number theory, so on."

"Yes."

"And Ruth was very close to her father?"

I'd seen the question coming, so it didn't surprise me. "Not really. Not as close as she always wanted to be." The fact that I had told this complete stranger the truth—that surprised me.

"Ah?" His lips made a small, fleshy circle. "She spoke of him in class sometimes. Always with great pride."

"Did she?" Oh, why was that so sad?

"But of course Ruth doesn't really have a mathematical mind. I wish it were otherwise—she's so very bright. But she won't study mathematics in college now. Clearly."

"She won't? Why not?"

He smiled and didn't answer.

"Why not? Are you saying she was only good in math to please her father? And now that he's gone—?"

"I believe so, yes. Don't you think?"

"I . . . Well, I have no idea." Yes, of course, it was obvious. Still, I resisted. I hated the thought of Ruth trying so hard to make Stephen notice her, even going against her own *nature* to get his love and attention.

"It's not so sad," Mr. Tambor said, leaning toward me, chubby shoulders straining against the seams of his cheap white shirt. "We'll help her. She'll make C's and B's, as she should. It'll be all right. Yes? Come. Everything will be fine."

I took the immaculate folded handkerchief he handed me, warm from his back pocket. Why be embarrassed? I'd already cried in front of a policeman tonight, why not Ruth's algebra teacher, too?

"Thank you," I told him, handing the handkerchief back after blotting my cheeks but thoughtfully not blowing my nose. "You're very nice. Now I know why Ruth's so fond of you."

He made a little bow of gratitude, palms together.

"Are you from India?" I asked. He'd lulled me into unwonted familiarity. "Or . . . Pakistan?"

Mr. Tambor looked amazed. "No, no. Italy."

"*Really.*"

"Used to be Tamborini. We shortened it to Tambor when Uncle Guido was gunned down in the barbershop."

"No!"

"No." His smile stretched from ear to ear. "I come from Ahmadabad. That was a joke."

I laughed, and blushed, and decided I was in love.

I didn't recognize Bonnie Driver at first, probably because in the back of my mind I'd been thinking she was at home supervising three teenagers, including my daughter. She was walking down the hall ahead of me, and I thought, *That looks like Bonnie Driver's perky little butt*—you notice things like that on your ex-boyfriend's ex-wife. The swingy, chin-length hair looked familiar, too, but I didn't know it was Bonnie until she turned slightly and I saw her in profile. Long, intelligent nose, mild brown eyes, a friendly mouth—she was lovely, and a kind person, and everyone liked her. I liked her myself. Too bad she'd never liked me.

She turned around when I called to her. "Carrie—hi! Ruth said you'd be here. I left Dan at home with the girls, I ran right over as soon as we finished dinner. Don't you hate these nights? How are you?"

"I didn't know she was going to your house—I'm sorry if that was an inconvenience. We had a mix-up—"

"Oh, not at all, Ruth's wonderful, I love having her, so does Becky. So tell me, how is your new job?"

She was so nice. When Stephen died she sent me a sweet, gentle note that made me cry. We didn't even know each other—and yet we did. She was the kind of person who would send a gracious sympathy note to someone she didn't like simply because it was the decent thing to do.

"Oh, the job's all right. Well—not exactly what I was hoping for," I said, truthfully for some reason, "but it's okay. Pays the bills." Barely.

"Maybe it'll get better." She smiled encouragingly. "Sometimes you have to break a new job in."

It was possible she didn't really dislike me. Well, why would she? Certainly not because of jealousy over Jess. She won, after all; she married him, then she divorced him, all long after I was out of the picture. I always felt a certain coolness, though, under the friendliness, as if she were watching me, collecting data, reserving judgment. She *wanted* to like me, but she couldn't quite bring herself to do it. We fascinated each other. God knew we had a lot in common. Well, one thing.

"I hear Jess asked you to help him out with the ark." She smiled less naturally, not as amused as she wanted to appear. "Such a crazy thing, isn't it? Poor old Landy, he's the one I feel sorry for."

I'd forgotten she knew Landy—he'd have moved next door while she and Jess were still married. "Crazy," I agreed. "In a way, I wish I *could* help out."

"Oh, it just seems so strange to me, something you're better off staying away from. It could swallow you up if you weren't careful." The generic *you*, she was using; surely she didn't mean me personally. "And now that the whole thing is public knowledge, it's just going to get bigger. I really wouldn't want any part of it—but that's me."

"What do you mean, it's public knowledge?"

"Didn't you see the paper yesterday?"

"No. The *Record*?"

"Page one—Eldon Pletcher's promised to buy all new playground equipment for Point Park if they'll let him build the ark on the fishing piers, right on the water. And then sail it on the river for forty days. The city council's taking it up at the next meeting. I'm not kidding."

And Jess was on the council. "Wow," was all I could say.

We talked a little longer, about our daughters and their mutual friends, then used the excuse of teacher appointments to separate. "Good to see you," we said, and "Take care," but neither of us was hypocritical enough to say, "Call me," or "Let's get together." I didn't know why her marriage failed—Jess would probably have told me if I'd asked, but I wouldn't. As much as I'd have liked to know. But the fact of their marriage, or rather the fact that it ended, was what kept Bonnie and me at arm's length. Which must've meant—well, I didn't know what it meant. It *seemed* to mean that I was mixed up in it somehow, and I didn't know what to think about that. So I didn't think about it. Much.

Three mothers and a father were waiting in line to see Mrs. Fitzgerald, Ruth's English teacher. My heart sank; if I joined them, it would mean at least a half-hour wait, maybe longer. No, I decided, to hell with it, I was going home. Ruth was doing well in English—that's why I'd wanted to talk to Mrs. Fitzgerald in the first place, to hear some good news for a change. But now I was just too tired.

The way out of the building led past closed double doors to a staircase. *Locked* double doors now, I was sure, but in my day they were always left open. Foolishly—because the stairs went down to the janitor's room, the furnace room, and the infamous Utility Room, No. B–45. Also known as the Make-out Room. This many years later, I could still remember the muffled blast of boilers and water heaters through cinder block walls, the smells of oil and electricity and disinfectant, the dim, grainy light from one flickering fluorescent tube high up in the pipe-lined ceiling. Senior year, the winter months, I had met Jess down there every day at 12:35, for the precious fifteen-minute interval our lunch periods overlapped. We were never alone, other couples trysted in dark corners nearby, but for a public place the utility room had been remarkably intimate.

Since then I'd had a handful of lovers and a longtime husband, and with one or the other of them I imagined I'd done most if not everything that healthy, reasonably inventive people did in the sexual area. But kissing Jess was still my lifetime's most erotic memory, the touchstone, the baseline for all physical passion. Arrested development, I called it after we broke up. I tried to demystify the experience by talking about it to my college friends, describing it, laughing about it. "Up against the wall in this smelly utility closet, kissing and kissing till our mouths hurt! Oh God, it was so funny." A lie. And I even knew I was betraying him. No help for it, though, I'd had to save myself. I was young, stupid, myopic; too much self-knowledge would've been like shining white light in my eyes.

I was aroused, I realized, buttoning my coat, trying to remember what row I'd parked the car in. Ridiculous. But I was; my stomach felt tight and heavy, pulled down by gravity. It was the atmosphere, the circumstances, the power of setting. Well, if you were going to feel like a hormonal schoolgirl, what more logical place than your old high school?

Did Ruth feel like this? Disconcerting thought. Of course she did, she must. We talked about sex occasionally, the wisdom of waiting, the importance of protection, all that sort of thing. What we never talked about was how it was for women, what its place might be in our lives, not with any frankness. We never put sex in context. She was still too young, I told myself, but that was just a cop-out.

My mother was fairly open about sex, even when I was little—open as in willing to speak her mind, that is, not as in liberal or permissive. From the age of about six, the message I received was loud and clear: *don't*. Nice girls wait, cheap girls don't. *Tacky* girls don't—that was the thing. Because in Mama's book being *tacky* was as low as a human being could go. Better to be morally bankrupt, a pervert, better to be a serial killer than *tacky*. It was her strongest prejudice. In a sense, it defined her; it was the motive behind all her life's decisions, large and small.

Well, everybody needed a code, a model for right conduct. Not being tacky: in its way it was a standard, no worse than a lot of others for civilized human behavior. Its limitations—snobbery, intolerance, racism, classism—had driven me crazy for most of my life. It wasn't the philosophy, though, as much as the strength of my mother's belief in it and the power of her personality that had made me a confused, unwilling follower all through my childhood. I think it was the main reason—not the only one—that I never went all the way with Jess. As much as I loved him, as much as I wanted him. Amazing, in retrospect.

Or maybe not. No, probably not. You could only blame your mother for so much. I was the one who was intimidated by his passion for me, his wild, excessive ardor—so it seemed to me. Not giving in to him was the only way I knew to control him. Instinctively, I feared chaos if I gave in, some kind of annihilation.

Another way of saying I chickened out.

So many regrets. I shivered as the car heater blew cold air on my shins, slowing self-consciously at the spot where the policeman had pulled me over. Right . . . there. If I'd left work on time, if Ruth had been where she was supposed to be, if I'd left Krystal's a little later, a little earlier . . .

If only, if only. What if I'd married Jess? He'd asked me. Over Thanksgiving break, my freshman year of college. I almost said yes. He didn't bully me, he said he'd wait till I graduated, but then he wanted me to come back to Clayborne and live with him on the farm.

At first the prospect tantalized me. I loved his house, the land. Live there with Jess? Paradise. But by Christmas I had doubts. College was incredible, everything I'd expected and more, I could *feel* myself turning into the kind of person my childhood, my family—my mother—had been preparing me to be. Men who were going to be lawyers, artists, scientists, wanted to go out with me. I started letting them. Eventually, the idea of spending the rest of my life tending cows on a little farm in Virginia began to seem less and less plausible, until finally it seemed—outlandish.

So I'd told Jess no. We were growing apart, couldn't he see that? We didn't have as much in common anymore, we wanted different things. What pains me now, all this time afterward, is that I honestly didn't think it would hurt him—I thought surely he could see I was right, he must agree, it was so clear. What a shallow, self-involved little twit I was. And when I saw that I *had* hurt him—I offered to sleep with him! At last! What a magnanimous gesture; the perfect farewell present. Oh, that memory can still make me cringe. To Jess's credit and to my everlasting shock and shame, he refused. I didn't see him again for fifteen years.

I unlocked the front door to the dark, chilly house with a shuddery feeling, even a sense of dread. *I'm as empty as this hall. I'm as cold as this living room.* It was only a little after nine, Ruth wouldn't be home for at least half an hour. Sometimes loneliness felt like panic, a low, thudding sensation in the diaphragm. A drink? No, I might end up in tears. Again. But coffee would keep me awake. I hung my coat in the hall closet and went upstairs. Maybe a bath to soak the chill out of my bones. Maybe I was coming down with something.

The answering machine in the bedroom blinked a message. The tape took forever to rewind—that meant it was Mama. I lay down on the bed to listen.

"Hi, it's me," came her bossy, confident voice, booming over the silence. "I thought you'd be home by now. Give me a call when it suits. I've got an idea—I'll tell you about it when we speak." But no, she couldn't wait. "What do you think about a little getaway? Just the three of us, for a weekend someplace interesting." *The three of us*? Me, Mama, and Pop? How bizarre. "I think it would do us all good, I really do. End of the month, maybe, when it's a little warmer. We could go to Richmond, we could go to Washington, Baltimore, wherever we want. I know Ruth works on Saturdays, but surely she could take the day off one time."

Oh, *those* three. An all-girl getaway. Much less bizarre.

"'Course, the sale of colonic cleaning agents may fall through the floor, but homeopathy as we know it will survive." She chortled merrily. "Carrie, erase this tape immediately, hear me? All right, call me when you get in if it's not too late. Oh—Ruth called, by the way. A mix-up tonight, signals crossed. We missed her, but we understood. She is the sweetest child, I could just eat her alive. Let's go to Washington, don't you think she'd have more fun there? Okay, call me. Love you. 'Bye."

I pulled the blanket up over my legs and crossed my hands over my chest. An out-of-town weekend with Ruth and my mother—what a nice idea. Theoretically. Three generations of Danziger women, all at difficult ages and stages, on the loose in the nation's capital. It could be fun. It could be disastrous. It was one of those ideas that were so compelling and irrefutable *in the abstract*, as soon as you thought of them they were virtually inevitable. Destined. If only because all the arguments against them sounded neurotic.

I caught myself dozing. *Get up, get undressed.* I would. In one minute.

I was in the backseat of the family car, the blue Ford we had when I was in junior high. At first I thought Mama was driving, but now I could see it was Ruth. Trees and sky streamed past the open windows, vivid watercolor streaks, blue-green-blue-green-blue-green, and the pine wind blew in my face. "Don't go so fast," I warned, but Ruth paid no attention, didn't even turn her head. Then Stephen was beside me on the seat, his thigh grazing mine. I wanted Ruth to look around and see us, see that we were together. I called to her, but she had her headphones on, keeping time to some cool, silent beat, swaying her shoulders. I couldn't see Stephen's face or his upper body, just the leg of his old green corduroy trousers. I moved my hand on his thigh, studying the contour of my fingers, light on dark, and then it was Jess's leg.

He put his chin on my shoulder—my bare shoulder; all of a sudden I was naked—and kissed me under my chin. "Wait, now," I whispered. Even though my eyes were closed tight, I could see the dazzle of blue-green-blue-green flood past faster, faster. Ruth was driving too fast, something horrible was going to happen. Jess had me pressed down against the seat and our legs were tangled up, his covered with tickly blond hairs, I wanted to stroke along his thigh and ruffle the fine hair, just graze it with my palm. I opened my mouth to tell Ruth to slow down, and Jess slipped his tongue inside, and we made love until the wail of a siren turned my hot blood into icy slush.

Ruth was still speeding, but in slow motion. Jess didn't get it, he wouldn't cover up, wouldn't stop touching me, and I couldn't scream at him because Ruth would hear. Even though the car was still moving, Officer Sherman poked his head in the driver's window and handed Ruth a ticket. *Don't turn around,* I begged, *Oh, don't see us,* frantic, shoving at Jess's slick shoulders. Officer Sherman dissolved, changed into Mr. Tambor. "It's your fault," he said mournfully, wagging his finger in my face. "She is failing all her subjects. You have only yourself to blame."

"Mom?"

"Hey." I struggled up on my elbows, cleared my throat. "You're home. What time is it?" I put on a good-natured smile, in case any of the dream still showed.

"Ten-ish." She waved her hand vaguely. She had an ostentatious stack of books clutched to her chest. I patted the bed and she dropped down beside me, scattering books on the blanket. "Were you asleep? In your *clothes*?"

"No, no. Just thinking with my eyes closed." A joke of Stephen's. We smiled wanly. "Did you have fun at Becky's?"

"It was okay. I heard you saw her mom at school."

"Yes, we had a nice visit. What did she give you for dinner?"

"Some casserole. Then we had cake left over from Becky's little sister's birthday. She's twelve. It was pretty good."

Her arms were bare under her dun-colored short-sleeved sweater. Long, pale, child's arms, the curve of the wrist so tender and defenseless. "Aren't you cold?" I said, pinching the fold of skin at the back of her elbow.

"Yeah, it's freezing in here. So . . . did you just get home?" Casual yawn; bored examination of the line where the wall met the ceiling. My heart squeezed. Helpless love flooded me. *Don't change, don't do anything, don't get older.*

"I had talks with all your teachers except Mrs. Fitzgerald."

"Oh, shoot, Mom. She's the best one."

Shoot. How sweet we could be to each other. I'd been cleaning up my language for Ruth's sake for years, and now she was cleaning hers up for me. "We'll talk about it tomorrow," I said, "it's too late tonight. You look tired, I want you in bed. But I'll just tell you—nobody told me anything tonight I didn't already know."

She bowed her head, relieved.

"We will, however, be making some changes soon. In the studying department."

"Right, okay."

"Right, okay. I'm not kidding."

"I *know*."

I thought about what Mr. Tambor had said, that she probably wouldn't study math in college because Stephen was gone. She didn't have to try to please him anymore. I was different—I'd given up on my father when I was even younger than Ruth, about thirteen. (I could be fairly precise on the date; I uncovered it with the help of a very careful therapist in Chicago nine years ago.) I hadn't stopped loving him, but I gave up expecting fatherliness from him. But Ruth hadn't given up on Stephen yet. I had watched with a sick heart while she persisted, virtually up to the night of his death, in trying to get his attention and his love. That's what scared me the most about her, her puppylike constancy, her hopefulness. At fifteen, a wafer-thin coating of skepticism flavored her language these days, her rotten-teenager attitude, but underneath was a big, sweet smiley face. I counted the days before somebody's thoughtless, random cruelty—please God, don't let it be mine—erased it, killing her innocence.

"Go to bed, sweetie," I said. "Kiss me good night first." The red light on the answering machine reminded me. "Oh, Gram called. She wants us to go away for a weekend sometime. Just the three of us, to Richmond or D.C., someplace like that."

"God. I mean, too weird. So do we have to?"

"Don't you want to? I was thinking it would be fun." She made a face of incredulous revulsion. Did they practice in the mirror? Was there a course they took, "Contemptuous Expressions Sure to Hurt Your Mother's Feelings"? "Well," I said stiffly, "we'll talk about that later, too. Get ready for bed now, you look exhausted."

"I am, I'm really wiped. Can I stay home tomorrow?"

"No, you stayed home today."

"Yeah, but it was a holiday. I am really, really wrecked."

"Then you should've rested today."

"I wasn't tired today, I'm tired *now*."

"Go to bed, then."

"I could have mono for all you know. I could have chronic fatigue. I probably do have a liver dysfunction right now."

"Good night, Ruth."

"*Jeez.*" She snatched her books up, stormy-faced, and flounced out. In the hall she threw back, "Becky gets to stay home tomorrow."

"Oh, really? Now I'm beginning—"

She didn't hear. "Mrs. Driver has a lot more compassion than you," she finished cuttingly, before closing her bedroom door with just enough force to register anger and resentment but not enough to justify the punishment for slamming. She'd perfected the distinction. She had it down to an art.

I slumped against the pillow. Bonnie Driver had a lot more of a lot of things I didn't have. A nice bout of self-pity would've been very comforting right now. With Stephen gone, I ought to have felt *less* underappreciated than I used to. Nothing like a teenage daughter to keep you whittled down to size. No sustained highs allowed. I couldn't remember being hateful to my mother in any long-term, persistent way when I was a girl, although I probably had been. The difference was that Mama was tough and strong and thicker skinned, and when you hurt her, she didn't sulk or get depressed, she got mad.

An out-of-town weekend with Mama and Ruth. Well, maybe so. Maybe it was just what Ruth needed. She might learn important life lessons from her grandmother. Lessons her mother couldn't teach her in a million years.

11

Texas Two-Step

I could've called Landy and asked him about the article in the paper on Noah's Ark. He was the logical one; the ark was his project, after all. But I called Jess. I wanted to hear firsthand about the city council vote, I told myself. Ignoring the obvious fact that, since Landy would undoubtedly have been at the meeting, his account would've been firsthand, too.

Jess was out, as usual. Farmers didn't seem to spend much time in their houses. I left a message. He called back when I was on another line, trying to sign up an instructor in white-water rafting for the summer term. At about three in the afternoon, we finally connected.

"Hi—what's this I hear about playground equipment?" I asked, all business. "Now Pletcher's bribing the city council?"

"He thinks of it as an inducement. How are you, Carrie?"

"Do you think it'll work?"

"Well, the treasurer did some figuring last night, and came up with a little under thirty-nine thousand to replace everything at the park."

"Thirty-nine thousand *dollars*?"

"And that's not even top-of-the-line equipment. There's opposition to the ark on the council, no question, but I think, for that much money, a lot of aesthetic sensibilities are going to roll over."

"It wouldn't surprise me." Wait until my mother heard about this. Launching a fully stocked ark on the Leap even sounded tacky to *me*.

"Meanwhile, Carrie, Landy's animals are getting uglier every day."

"Sorry to hear that."

"The *Morning Record*'s sending a reporter out next week to take pictures. For a feature."

"Uh-oh."

"It's only a matter of time before Eldon and the Arkists all look ridiculous. Landy, too."

"Sorry," I said again. "Nothing I can do about it."

"You could come out and help us."

"Jess—how in the world did you get caught up in this?"

He sighed. "It started out so peacefully. Landy had a woodworking project—that's what he called it—and asked if he could use my band-saw. The next thing I knew, I was cutting out rhinoceroses."

"*You're* doing animals now?"

"Yes, and I don't have time, I've got an ark to build. The original was made out of gopher wood. Any idea where we could get some gopher wood?"

"Eighty-four Lumber?"

"Funny."

"When do you milk your cows?"

"I knew there was something I forgot to do."

I laughed. "This is all your own fault. You could've said no."

"I could've. But I like it. I like the idea."

"But it's so *crazy*."

"That's what I like about it."

I smiled to myself. That was the Jess I knew.

"And you need it, Carrie."

"*I* need it? Oh, I assure you, I don't need it."

"Okay, then, I need you." Quiet for a second. "Come over Saturday, will you? Bring Ruth."

"No, no, I can't. Anyway, Ruth has to work."

"Come by yourself."

"I can't, Jess, really."

"Think about it. Try to come."

"Andy's giving up violin," Chris Fledergast announced, coming to stand in front of my desk while she pulled on her coat and wound a wool scarf around her neck. "Maybe piano, too, but we're putting that decision off till summer."

I turned off my computer. How could it be five o'clock already? "Andy's giving up the violin? Why?"

"Because he hates it."

"Well, sure, but . . ."

"I know. Believe me, if it was up to me, this would not be happening." She jammed a maroon wool cap down so low on her head, it hid her eyebrows. So clumsy and gangly on the outside, so graceful inside, a genuinely gentle person. "It's all Oz's doing," she said, folding the ends of her muffler across her chest and buttoning her quilted coat over them.

"Oz doesn't want Andy to play the violin?"

"It's not that." She smiled at Brian when he came out of his office. "Telling Carrie—Andy's quitting violin, and maybe piano, too."

"How come?" Brian draped one muscular thigh over the corner of my desk and sat down.

"Oh, he hates to practice, he hates the recitals. He's starting to say he hates music."

"It's just a phase," Brian said. "What is he now, ten?"

"Nine. He says he wants to play baseball."

"And Oz is all for that," I guessed. I'd only seen Chris's husband once, when he'd dropped her off at work and come in for a second to meet me. He was nice, I'd liked him, but big and tough, a pretty macho guy—I could imagine him not minding much if his kid gave up piano.

"No, it's not that," Chris said. "It's not a guy thing, you know, not Oz wanting him to get tough or anything."

"Oh." So much for what I knew.

"He says Andy should be allowed to decide for himself." She scowled down, jabbing the side of one gloved hand into the spaces between the fingers of the other. "Oh, I don't know. I just think, how is he supposed to know what's good for him? He's nine, how could he know?"

"Yeah," Brian said, "but if he hates it."

"I know. I don't know. We argued and argued, Oz and me."

"I had to take piano," I said. "Took it for four years, and I can't play a single song." Not strictly true; I could play "Für Elise" and "Country Gardens."

"I always wanted to take piano," Brian said, "but my folks couldn't afford it. I'd've been good, too. Too late now."

"Andy's very musical, his teacher says he's got loads of talent. I say of *course* he wants to play baseball—he'd rather eat ice cream than spinach, too, but we don't let him. But Oz says he's old enough to make his own decisions, so."

"Well, I guess if he's supposed to play the violin—"

"He'll come back to it—that's what Oz says." Chris shook her head, worried. "We'll see."

I tried to think what I'd do if Ruth wanted to give up something she was good at—reading, say. No, bad example, because of course I'd have to discourage that. But—say she wanted to give up both her team sports, soccer and volleyball, and spend her time . . . drawing pictures of fashion models in designer clothes. Just for example. Would I allow that, even though she has no talent for drawing or design but she's excellent at soccer and volleyball?

I wasn't sure. Probably.

I knew who would violently disapprove of that decision, though. Mama. If she thought she knew what was good for you, you didn't have a prayer. She'd wear you down to a nub and you gave in.

"Chris," Brian said, "did you get that payroll spreadsheet printed out before you shut down?"

"In your in box."

"Great. You going home now?"

"Thought I would." She grinned at me, holding out her arms. *What does he think I'm doing in my coat?* We laughed at Brian behind his back sometimes, but in a nice way, tolerant and affectionate, the way women laugh at men they like. Brian took advantage of Chris, though. She was so smart, but she didn't push herself. She did whatever he told her, cleverly and efficiently, because loyalty and hard work were what she thought he'd hired her for. If he'd appreciated her, it would've been different, but he didn't. He took her for granted.

He cracked his knuckles, one of his boyish habits, swinging his leg back and forth against the side of the desk. "I need somebody to brainstorm with," he said, frowning. "You have to get right home?" he said to me.

"Um . . ."

"Because we could do it over dinner. An early one while we talk, if you're free. I need to get back to Carmichael on this Remington thing, and I'm not sure what to tell him."

Remington College recently made an interesting offer: in return for nothing except goodwill and community relations, the college would let Brian hold some Other School courses on campus, in free classrooms, mostly at night, and they'd even spring for on-campus ads to that effect, and include the school in the annual catalog under college-associated community services. I thought it sounded terrific, but Brian was being cautious.

"Well, I could," I realized. "Ruth's going over to a friend's house after work and she won't be home till late, so it's a good night for me."

"Great!" He bounded up from the desk, rattling my computer monitor. "I need ten minutes, then we can go. We'll take my car."

"Hey," Chris said when he had disappeared into his office. "He never invites me to dinner. Guess you have to be good-looking and single."

But she was kidding—I looked to make sure, and she was grinning.

"Too much air?" Brian touched a button discreetly hidden in the leather side panel of his Lincoln Continental, and the window went up without a sound. "I'm just saying it could muddy our image. Is it the Other School or is it Remington College? The distinction won't stay clear in some people's minds."

"Brian, where are we going?" We'd been driving in the country for twenty minutes.

"Great place, you'll see." He threw his right hand across the back of my seat, leaning back to steer with his left. "You're thinking what difference does it make if it's clear in their minds or not. Just as long as it gets us more enrollment."

"No, I'm not."

"I can see your point, too. I'm probably being too proprietary."

"No, I think it's a legitimate concern. One of the school's biggest assets is its independence. It's the *Other* School. Most people have a sense that it's alternative."

"Right, it's out there, it's a little on the edge. You put it on the college campus, it's just another post-secondary program. People think continuing education, adult education, associate degree, Other School. And that's wrong, that's not who we are at all." He smacked his hand against the steering wheel for emphasis. The smell of his cologne was strong at the office; in a closed car it was overwhelming. And the Lincoln was huge, but Brian's bulk made the front seat feel almost cozy.

"On the other hand," I said, "you can't ignore the benefits. The hassle factor—you'd never have to hustle for classroom space again—that's just one thing. Enrollment. I have no idea how much it would go up—"

"Plenty. You got kids sweating through poli sci, trigonometry, the history of the rococo period in Belgium in 1840—and they see a notice that next week there's this cheap night course on how to get laid on the first date and it's *right across the hall*—you got a big jump in enrollment."

"That's a joke, right?" With Brian, you could never be sure.

"I'm talking on that order. We'd definitely gear a lot of courses to attract the students, though, much more than we have been. That's common sense. You'd have to take advantage of what's practically a captive audience."

"But how to get laid on the first date, that's—"

"An example! Of course we wouldn't call it that." He gave my shoulder a playful jab. "I'd count on you to think up something tasteful—'Overcoming Shyness in Your Interpersonal Relationships,' something like that. Huh?" He laughed hard—he always laughed hard at his own jokes. "'Dispensing with Inappropriate Shame'—you like that? Ha ha ha ha!" He'd flicked on the turn signal. He was braking, pulling into the parking lot of a long, shingle-sided, neon-lit restaurant. "We're here," he announced, easing into a space between two shiny pickup trucks. "Ever been here before, Care?"

CACTUS FLATS, read the blinking green-and-yellow sign. Cocktails, beer, steaks and chops. Live entertainment Fri., Sat., Sun. "No," I said. "My first time."

"You'll love it. You like rib eye? Best in the Piedmont. It helps if you can stand country music."

Cactus Flats was an old-fashioned roadhouse, low and dusty, reeking of beer, big enough to maintain separate sections for its three primary activities—drinking, eating, and dancing. Brian wanted to "brainstorm" here? No live music tonight, a Thursday, but the jukebox was as loud as a band, and it never took breaks. After a while the twangy George Jones and George Strait and Vince Gill tunes got into my head. It was true that the older I got the more I could tolerate country music, and it wasn't to embarrass Ruth (as she claimed). I could hear the words and sing the melodies—was that asking too much? Lowbrow, Stephen used to tease me; you can take the girl out of the country, but you can't take Carrie out of Clayborne. He hadn't said it in a very nice way.

We sat in a booth along a knotty pine wall adorned with saddles, spurs, Stetsons, and longhorns. I felt sorry for the waitresses, who all wore tight jeans tucked into high-heeled cowboy boots. "Do you come here a lot?" I asked Brian over a peppy Patty Loveless song, something about only going halfway down. I had to shout my question again, not so much to be heard over the music as to attract Brian's attention. Because he was gone. As soon as he gave the waitress our drink order—a couple of Lone Stars, what else—he went into another world, appeared to get lost in the music and the . . . *ambience* wasn't the right word for Cactus Flats. The experience. He even sang along—I could hear his pitch-perfect falsetto just under Patty's. Sometimes I came upon Ruth in her Walkman headphones, wearing the same intense, absorbed, blissed-out expression and wailing along to the music of bands with names like Hole and Anthrax.

Brian grinned happily and either nodded to my question or continued to keep the beat with his head, I couldn't tell. When the beer came, he clicked his icy stein to mine with so much gusto, I was afraid we'd chip our glasses. "Isn't this great, Carrie? Isn't this the perfect place to unwind?"

I nodded, smiled back. Well, it was. It really was. But I wished I'd had a little notice; I could've unwound more efficiently if I'd known I was supposed to. But how amazing to see this new side of Brian I'd never suspected. He'd taken off his suit jacket and rolled up the sleeves of his shirt, loosened his tie. He looked younger, carefree, not nearly as intense as usual as he slouched against the wall, one foot drawn up on the seat, banging out the beat with his fist on the back of the wooden booth.

The music changed. All of a sudden he shouted, "Two-step!" grabbed my arm, and hauled me up and out of the booth. I tried to resist, but it was ridiculous, Olive Oyl fighting off Bruno. "I can't do this!" I yelled, trotting to keep up as he pulled me along, out onto a huge, nearly empty dance floor. "Brian, wait! I can't do this!"

"'Course you can." He dragged me up in a close clinch, one beefy arm clamped tight around my waist, the other holding my right hand down at my side. "All you do is walk backward. I walk forward, you walk back." He demonstrated by walking into me. When I stumbled he just picked me up, an inch off the floor, and kept walking. It was like dancing with a bear.

A big, sweaty, masculine bear. As the shock wore off and the mysteries of the two-step became clearer, I tried to figure out what I was feeling. How was this? Did I like being held against Brian's strong, hard, weight lifter's body? Yes and no. Impossible to say, the situation was too ambiguous; I couldn't separate the fact from the context. The context was that it was *Brian*'s body, Brian my colleague, Brian who signed my paycheck every two weeks. How could I know what I felt? Was this all good clean fun? Did he just want to get some exercise?

We were panting by the time the dance ended. He held my hand on the way back to the table, swinging it up and down with muscular exuberance. Oh, I thought, this is nothing. The directness, the lack of calculation, the *boisterousness* in the way he touched me—finally I realized he was just being Brian, friendly and bluff and fun loving. And I was an ass for worrying. I always made things too complicated.

The waitress came for our order. Brian was as forceful about rib eye as he was about the two-step, but in this case I didn't mind. "Just don't tell Ruth," I joked. "She's trying to turn me into a vegan."

"How are things going at home?" he asked, leaning in, elbows on the table. "How's Ruth getting along without her dad? It must be really tough on both of you."

"We miss him a lot. Sometimes I think it's getting easier, and then something happens and it's hard again. But we're doing all right. I don't know what I'd do without Ruth—she's my lifesaver."

"I'm sure she feels the same about you."

I made a dubious face. "Hard to say. You know kids."

"Oh, I know kids." His were nine and twelve, both boys. He saw them on weekends, alternating holidays, and a month every summer. "Craig wants to go to computer camp this summer—that's the latest."

"I thought it was basketball camp."

"That was last week. He's the opposite of Gordon, whose goal never changes."

"Uh-oh." Gordon, the twelve-year-old, wanted to play lead guitar in a heavy metal band. "I wonder who's harder to raise," I mused, "boys or girls."

"Boys," Brian said immediately, and told a story about the night Gordon set fire to his mattress by hiding the lit candle he wasn't supposed to be playing with under the bed. That reminded me of the time Ruth put so many newspapers in the fireplace she set the chimney on fire, then the roof. "If the neighbor hadn't seen the flames and called the fire department, we'd have lost the house."

"Oh, that's nothing," Brian said, and told about the time Craig and Gordon decided to "drive" the car by coasting it down the driveway and out into the busy street where, by a miracle, it came to a harmless stop on the grass median between two lanes of traffic. "You don't want to dance, do you?"

"What?"

"You looked funny. Lost in the music."

"Oh, no," I said, laughing, "go on, no, I'm listening."

No, I wasn't. I was listening to Neil Young sing "Helpless." It used to be my favorite song. I'd played it so often, my *Déjà vu* album got warped. Jess borrowed a friend's tape deck and recorded "Helpless" twenty-seven times, one after the other, on both sides of a blank tape, and gave it to me for my eighteenth birthday. To this day, it's the sweetest, funniest gift anyone's ever given me.

Over our steaks, Brian told me his life story. He grew up in eastern North Carolina, oldest of three kids, came to Clayborne to go to Remington, got a B.S. in business administration, married a local girl, and stayed on. For his first job—already an entrepreneur—he started an employment counseling and temp service. But in Clayborne there weren't enough people to counsel or find temporary jobs for, so that failed. Then Norma got pregnant and poor Brian had to settle down and find a real job—registrar at the college. He hated it. "I can't stand working for anybody except myself, is my problem. Don't have the patience. They don't go fast enough, they don't see far enough," he said feelingly, jabbing at a piece of meat with his fork. "When things get screwed up, I don't want to blame anybody but me."

"That's good to know."

"Not that I'm a control freak, at least I don't think so. You think I'm a control freak?"

"No." Yes.

"Yeah, because I don't think so. I pick good employees, tell them what I expect, and then I don't get involved in what's their responsibility. Right?"

"Right, boss."

"Right, because I don't need to. You're good at what you do, Carrie, I'm good at what I do. We make a team."

"And Chris is good at what she does, too."

"Sure." He toasted me with the last of his beer and signaled the waitress for another round.

"Not for me," I said.

"No? Sure? Well, this is my last. Never have more than two drinks when I'm out, not if I'm driving."

The second beer loosened him up enough to talk about his ex-wife. He never had before, not even to joke. I knew, because Chris had told me, that the split had been bitter, that they still only spoke when necessary, and that Brian deeply resented that Norma had gotten custody of the children. Now I got to hear what a bitch Norma was. Not that he ever used the word, but he didn't have to; a woman who was manipulative, shallow, childish, passive-aggressive, unreasonable, withholding, judgmental, and intellectually bankrupt was pretty much, by definition, a bitch.

I listened for as long as I could, then excused myself to go to the ladies' room. On the way, I used a pay phone in the corridor to call Ruth. She was at Jamie's, and this time I had the number with me.

"Mom," she said immediately, "where in the world *are* you?"

I'd gotten used to the noise; it took me a second to realize she could hear the music on the jukebox, currently a bluegrass tune, lots of fiddling and banjo picking. I laughed. "Oh, I'm someplace called Cactus Flats. It's a sort of roadhouse, it's—"

"Out on Route Twenty-nine? *That* place?"

"Have you been here?"

"No, but jeez, I've heard of it. What are you *doing* there?"

"Well, Brian wanted to talk business, and so—and it was time to eat anyway, so—we came here. He likes it, he's been before, I think he comes here regularly, in fact."

"Business?"

Trust Ruth to leap immediately on the only weak point in the explanation. "Yes, actually. We've been brainstorming about a new direction the school might take, or might not." In the car, en route, but that counted. "How are you doing? Get your homework done? I just wanted you to know where I am in case you get home before I do, although—"

"Well, good thing, because I'm just leaving."

"Oh, so early? Well, that is a—"

"It's not that early, Mom, it's eight o'clock. In fact it's *ten after*."

"Is it? Well, that's not so late. Okay, so you're going home now. Got your key? And you know the routine. Lock the doors, don't—"

"I *know*."

"Don't let Jamie drive off until she knows you're safe inside. Blink the porch light so she'll know."

"Mom, I know."

"Okay."

"So when are *you* coming home?"

"Very soon. We're ordering coffee."

"You've been drinking."

"What?"

"Haven't you. I can tell. I can tell by your voice."

"Ruth—" I'd have laughed, but she might think I was drunk. "Honey, I had one beer. About an hour ago."

"Yeah, right. What about *him*?"

"'Him'?"

"Are you on a date?"

"No, I am not on a date. I told you—"

"Right, you're brainstorming, it's a business dinner at Cactus Flats. That's a good one, Mom."

"Listen. I—we're talking about other things, it's true, and we had a drink before dinner, but that's it. We're not—"

"I totally don't care anyway."

"Fine, but this is not a date."

"Okay, fine."

"Ruth."

"But even if it is, I don't care."

"But it's not!"

"Okay."

I banged my forehead lightly against the black metal edge of the phone box. "We'll talk about this when I get home."

"I'll be asleep."

"Tomorrow, then."

"What for? According to you there's nothing to talk about. I gotta go, have a nice evening."

"Ruth—"

She hung up.

In the ladies' room, I leaned over the sink and looked myself in the eye. *Are you on a date?* I honestly didn't know. I touched up my lipstick self-consciously, thinking, I would do this anyway. I'd do this if I were with girlfriends, it doesn't mean anything.

As it turned out, we didn't leave Cactus Flats until after nine. It was open mike night, and Brian said we had to stay at least for the beginning. I worried about Ruth—her suspicions, not her safety—but he wheedled and prodded until I couldn't say no. And then I had to admit, open mike was a hoot. "I told you!" Brian crowed, clapping and whistling for a young man whose cover of a raunchy Hank Williams Jr. song brought down the house. "This is the next best thing to karaoke."

"That was fun," I said truthfully on the drive home. "I'm really glad we did that."

"Good. I thought you could use a night out."

"Thanks, Brian." I smiled at him warmly. It changed things, thinking he'd chosen a place like Cactus Flats for my sake. "That was nice of you."

"Well, sometimes we don't know we're stuck and need a change. We're in a rut."

"It's true."

"You lost Stephen, but you're alive. Gotta keep remembering that. It's not even good for Ruth to see you depressed all the time."

"No. Well . . . I wouldn't say I'm depressed all the time."

"You just need to get out more."

"Probably."

"Definitely. It's been six months."

Six months. That had a ring to it. *She went to a country-western dance hall, and her husband dead only five months*. That sounded callous; that was borderline despicable. But *six* months, now you were veering over into acceptable territory. You could go out to a roadhouse at six months and it sounded respectable. But with a man? Hmm. That muddied the water. But if the man was your boss, that was different, surely.

Who was I imagining the sound of these numbers *for*, though? Not myself, and not for my friends, who couldn't have cared less if I went out to dinner with a man, boss or not. It was for my mother. I was forty-two and I still had conversations in my head, mental dialogues, imaginary debates; in some I played myself and in some I played my mother. A form of self-censorship. Did all daughters do that? Did Ruth? Were we all second-guessing schizophrenics, bound from the start to be both the sound and the distorted echo, the main character in the story of our lives and also the critic? Mother Nature's system of checks and balances. Very efficient, and what it lost in spontaneity it made up for in prudent living. Being a mother and a daughter, I could see the pros as easily as the cons. Mama's emotional hold on me was tiresome and life sapping and unhealthy—mine on Ruth was caring, selfless, sensitive, and benign. That neither of those extremes could possibly be true was just, in my old age, beginning to dawn on me.

We picked up my car at the office, and Brian insisted on following me home. I intended to say good night at the door, or even on the sidewalk by the car, but he parked, got out, and came inside with me. I wasn't sure how that happened; one minute we were on the front porch, me rooting in my purse for the key, the next we were in the foyer and he was helping me take off my coat.

"Well," I said, "thanks again." The living room light was on, but no Ruth. She must be upstairs. "That was really fun. Just what I needed."

"This, too," he said, pulled me into his arms, and kissed me.

Well, that answered that. We *were* on a date.

"Brian . . ." He had a big, soft mouth, furry at the bottom—his goatee. He opened his lips and enveloped me, sucked me in. Behind closed eyes, I had a vision of a dark cave, deep and scary, damp inside. "Brian," I managed to say, "don't."

"Why not?"

Stuck for an answer, I hesitated. He took it as permission to lift me under the arms and pull me up against his chest. The bear maneuver again. He clamped one arm around me and used his other hand to rub the bare skin of my back, under my hiked-up sweater. He kept kissing me, mauling me with his lips, using his tongue. "Stop, stop it," I hissed. I wanted to yell, but I didn't want Ruth to hear. I stuck my chin in the air, out of his range. "Put me down. *Damn it.*" He had me in a vise, pressed back between his body and the front door. The expression on his face looked friendly and interested, excited but in a good way. Anticipatory. "Brian, stop it!" He put his hot mouth on my neck and sucked.

Was this really happening? It could be a joke—he was a kidder, a practical joker, especially with Chris, maybe this was some kind of a—

He wormed his heavy hand between us, got it on my left breast, and squeezed.

I turned into a woman with a lot of joints, especially elbows and knees. None of them did any damage—he was built like a safe—but they finally got his attention. He took his hands off and backed up.

For the first time since it started, my feet touched the floor. My heart was pounding; I felt shaky in the knees. I said, "Jesus, Brian," and wiped my mouth with the side of my hand.

He kept smoothing his palm down one lapel of his jacket, a habit when he wasn't sure of himself. "Bad timing, I see. Sorry, Care. Didn't know you weren't ready."

Weren't ready? To be assaulted? I got a hand on the door knob behind me and jerked the door open. "Good night." I stepped back, letting in the cold.

"No harm done, I hope. Right?" He grinned, friendly and hopeful. Just a big teddy bear. Doubt made me scowl at him. Could I be overreacting? No. But—it was only Brian. Not Jekyll and Hyde, just Brian. My vivid new image of him was already fading, bleeding into the old one, the jovial, easygoing, good-hearted guy, who brought raisin muffins to work because they were Chris's favorite. I just knew something extra about him now. Keep away from him.

"Maybe I gave you the wrong impression," I conceded with reluctance. "I'm not interested in a romantic relationship."

"It's too soon." He nodded understandingly.

"No—ever. I'm just not interested. Sorry." I'd have added more, softened the blow, blamed myself—the art of breaking up was coming back to me fast—but I was still so *angry*. Even "Sorry" came out through my teeth.

Something passed over his face too quickly to read. Anger? Hurt? But he said, "Okay," and grinned some more, buttoning his sport coat, poise regained. "I've got it. You don't have to hit me over the head twice."

I wanted to hit him over the head once. "It's late. Sorry for the misunderstanding."

"Oh, that's all right," he said, forgiving me. "Dating's a tricky business nowadays, huh? You know what we should do? A course on the war between the sexes. Heh?" I froze when he seized my upper arm and gave it a tight, cordial squeeze, passing me in the doorway. On the porch, he turned back. "Well, Care—"

"'Night," I said, and closed the door in his friendly face.

In bed, I went over it again, egged on by insomnia from the two cups of coffee I'd stupidly drunk after dinner. The only good thing about the way the evening ended was that Ruth hadn't witnessed it. I hoped. I'd tiptoed upstairs as soon as Brian left and peeked into her dark, silent room—silent except for soft snoring. Which she could've been faking. But I didn't think so. I prayed not. Literally: *God, please, please let her be really asleep*, bent low over the messy, cluttered bed, scrutinizing the slow rise and fall of the blanket on her shoulder. "Are you awake?" I whispered. Her delicate eyelids may have fluttered, but it was hard to tell in the dark. I put a soft kiss on her cheekbone. "Love you," I murmured, and slipped out.

Anyway, I consoled myself, the very worst that could've happened was that she was feigning sleep and she'd seen everything—why would that be so terrible? Embarrassing and undignified, yucky, all that, yes, but if she had *seen* it, then she'd know once and for all that I wasn't interested in Brian Wright. That should be a relief, not a trauma. In fact, maybe (looking on the brightest possible side) it had all happened for the best. A minor humiliation for Ruth's peace of mind—a good mother would gladly make that trade.

Small consolation at 2 A.M., when I was still tossing and turning. Where exactly had the evening gone wrong? Brian was a jerk, I made no excuses for him, but I must've done something, unconscious or not, to make him think behaving like a jerk might pay off. What, though? I'd never invited him in, so it wasn't that. Some body language maneuver, maybe, around the time he helped me take off my coat. Nothing came to mind, though, no accidental flash of skin or inadvertent intimate contact. No, it had to be that I was just irresistible. I drove men insane.

That moment of hesitation with Brian, that second when I couldn't answer his "Why not?" question—at least I knew what that was about. Curiosity. I'd wanted to experiment, find out what I was like with a man who wasn't Jess and wasn't Stephen. That was why it was so hard to make Brian the villain, even though he deserved to be—because off and on tonight, I'd been comparing him to the other men in my life. My two passions. What if Brian had taken my breath away? It might've changed everything. So my reasoning had gone.

Well, now I had the answer. Imagine making love with Brian—no, no, I didn't want to, it would be like sleeping with a Saint Bernard, a Great Dane, one of those breeds that slobbered on you.

Sleeping with Stephen had been like . . . like sleeping with a computer. A very solicitous, efficient computer, though, one that was programmed to satisfy. Physically. I'd had no legitimate complaints—as he'd often assured me. But somehow our sex life had become detached from our regular life. At the end it wasn't an extension of anything, not an expression of closeness or love, it was just itself. It bored me to tears. Literally.

I got up and took a sleeping pill. I still had a few left—the doctor prescribed them after Stephen died. I'd been hoarding them.

Settling in bed again, I finally thought of something funny. On the drive out to Cactus Flats, I'd come to a decision. Assuming the evening went well, I'd decided to screw up my nerve and do something I'd been putting off for too long. Ask Brian for a raise.

12

Actively Growing Before Your Eyes

"Wanna go somewhere?" Raven slid to the floor with his back against the locker next to mine and crouched there, dangling his hands between his knees. He had on skin-tight black pants, a white poet shirt, and black leather lace-up boots. He looked depressed. What else is new.

"You mean, like, the cafeteria?" It was eleven-thirty, lunchtime. I rummaged around in my locker, exchanging my math book for my English book, getting out a new notebook.

"Someplace that's not here."

"Oh." I looked down at the top of his head. The whole left side was dyed sparkly metallic red today. I liked it better than last week's yellowish green. He had new piercings, too; his left ear looked like the side of a spiral notebook. "Okay," I said, "I guess so. You driving?"

He nodded slowly, staring at his fingers.

"I've got an algebra test fifth period," I felt silly mentioning.

He lifted his head slowly, slowly, until it banged on the locker behind him. Slowly his heavy-lidded eyes met mine. "An . . . algebra . . . test?"

"But it's no big deal, I don't mind cutting. So where do you want to go?"

In the graveyard with Raven. It sounded like a song. Or a Clue game—Raven, in the graveyard, with a joint. We were smoking the joint before we ate lunch because Raven said that was the only way to make the food we'd snuck out of the cafeteria for our picnic edible. But it was Friday, hamburgers and french fries day, my fave before I became a vegetarian, so I didn't really have to smoke to be hungry. I took a few hits to be sociable, though, and so Raven wouldn't have to toke alone. And so I wouldn't look like a dork.

"This is so totally weird."

He took a long time to stop staring at the clouds, roll his head sideways, and look at me. "What's weird?"

"Getting stoned here. Right next to his grave. I mean, what do you think he'd say?"

"He wouldn't say anything. He's dead."

"Yeah." I lay down on my back beside Raven and put my hands behind my head. "Yeah. He's dead."

You could look at the piece of sky in your vision, just that section, and block out everything except your mind and it. Like meditating. So there was nothing in the universe except your eyes and the blank blue and the white clouds. You could even take away the space between, you could be *in* the sky. "Are you being the sky?" I asked Raven, who didn't answer. "Are you, like, up there? I can't even feel the ground under me."

After a long time, he said in a croaky, marijuana voice, "I'm not doing that. I'm doing the clouds. That one." He pointed. "It's a guy with no head. He's been executed. He was a mass murderer, he killed . . . all the algebra teachers."

I snorted. "No, it's a wheelbarrow. And that one's a horse. See the head? See there, the mane?"

"It's not a horse, it's a hatchet. An ax. The one that cut off the murderer's head."

"No, it's a horse. It's coming to save the murderer, who's not dead. He's innocent, it was a frame-up."

"He's got no head."

"No, he's in cahoots with the executioner, it just looks like there's no head, it's a trick."

Raven sighed and shut his eyes. He hardly ever smiles. I used to try to make him, but it was like trying to crack up the guard at Buckingham Palace. "I read this thing in the paper," he said with his eyes closed. "A family, mother, father, two little boys, they were driving home from a trip in an old junky van, the two little boys asleep in the back. They get home, it's late at night, and the parents start carrying the kids into the house. And then they realize the kids aren't asleep, they're dead. They both asphyxiated from carbon monoxide poisoning."

"Oh, God."

"There isn't any God. That proves it."

"Oh, God. I don't know."

"You don't want to see. Nobody does."

I sat up and wrapped my arms around my calves. The dead grass was still damp from yesterday's rain; I could feel it through the coat I was sitting on. It wasn't cold here, the hill behind us blocked the wind. "My mom's never had anyone die on her before, as old as she is. You can get to be forty, even fifty, and if you're lucky no one dies."

"My aunt died."

"But that can never happen to me. For the rest of my life, I'll be a person whose father died when she was young."

Raven lifted his arms and made a square frame with his hands to look at the sky through. The sleeves of his shirt fell back, showing how white and skinny his arms were. "She had one of those aluminum caskets. Like a space capsule. They guaranteed it for twenty years, but who's checking? It's been three years now, the lining's bound to be shot. Dark blue velvet. It's gotta be wet and moldy and rotten. Anyway, nothing's left but her dress, so what's the difference?"

"Bones. She'd still have bones."

"They put her in a red suit, put a lot of makeup on her face. Like she was going to a party." He sat up to relight what was left of the joint. He sucked in a lungful and passed me the roach. "Want the rest?" he said in a strangled voice.

I shook my head. "I put a note in my dad's casket. At the wake. I just slipped it in next to his shoulder."

"What'd it say?"

"Oh, you know. Good-bye and all that." How much I loved him, how much I would miss him. Stuff I couldn't say to him when he was living.

Raven took a few more little puffs on the joint, which was about a millimeter long, and stabbed it out in the grass. "That fence reminds me," he said, lying back down. I glanced over at the spiky wrought iron fence that ran down to the lane separating this high, hilly part of the cemetery from the lower part. "There was this guy who was drunk and slid off a roof and landed on a fence post. It went right through him. Vertically. It went from his groin up through his whole body, it stopped an inch from his heart. He was standing on his feet with a stake inside him."

"Did he die?"

"No, he just stood there, moaning and crying. People thought he was drunk, as usual, so nobody helped him. A couple of hours went by. Then he died."

I rested my cheek on my knees. "Is that really true?"

"Sure."

"How do you hear things like that?"

"How do you not?" He rolled to his side. "So do you want to eat now?"

Everything was cold and greasy and nothing had enough salt. He ate all the french fries and most of my hamburger. I nibbled on an apple while I weeded my father's grave, pulling back the grass from around his bronze plaque. This wasn't the kind of graveyard that had headstones, just plaques, flush to the ground to make it easier to mow the grass, I guessed. In the car, Raven said, "Let's go to the graveyard," but he'd meant the old one, the nice one on

Hickory Street. I said, "Let's go to Hill Haven—that's the one on the way to Culpeper." He hadn't wanted to come here and I didn't blame him, it wasn't spooky or atmospheric or anything, it was more like a golf course, but when I told him it was where my father was buried, he said okay.

"It's not like I care about my algebra test," I said, kneeling on my coat, wiping my hands on my jeans. "I don't care if I flunk algebra."

"Al-ge-bra. What is it for? What does it mean?"

"It's nothing."

"It's nothing." Raven smoked clove cigarettes, which are like ten times worse for you than tobacco. He took one out of his pocket and lit it, blowing smoke rings at the sky. "Everything is nothing."

"So you're really flunking English this semester?"

"Sadly."

"But you're so good at it. You could get A's without doing anything."

He opened one eye to look up at me. "Fuck all," he said softly. "Fuck all, Ruth. Fuck it all."

"Oh, well," I said quickly, trying to erase that. No one knows what happens to you, anything is possible, so it was possible my father could hear us. That's stupid, I know, but still. You shouldn't say "fuck" while you're sitting by your father's grave, maybe sitting right on top of him for all you know, depending on which direction his coffin faced in relation to his plaque. For the same reason, I wasn't telling Raven about Mom's date with Brian Wright. Because if Dad heard that, it would kill him.

"You know how much meaning there is in getting an A in English?" Raven said. He made slow designs in the air with the smoke from his cigarette. His black-painted fingernails were chewed so short, it looked like his fingers were bleeding.

"None?" I guessed.

"There's no meaning in anything. It's all nothing. This is how we end up. I'm lying here now. In a little while I'll be lying here six feet deeper. That's the extent of the significance of our precious lives. For a few years we breathe, then we don't."

"What about reincarnation?" Krystal was heavily into that, channeling and past lives and regression therapy.

He looked at me pityingly. "That's the most obvious example of wishful thinking I know of. Even more than 'God.'"

"But don't you think there's *something*, some being or some outside force that's like a consciousness, like energy or electricity or something?"

"Why?"

"Because."

"Because you want there to be."

"Yeah! But also, how else could the world have been created, I mean, what makes it keep going?"

"Chemistry. Oxygen, hydrogen, carbon di—"

"But don't you just feel there's something that's more than us, a divine something or other, I don't know what, but—"

"There was this woman in New Jersey, she kept her daughter in a cabinet under the sink."

"No, but—"

"From the time she was one year old, this little kid had to live in a cupboard with a padlock on it. When they finally found her, she was like fourteen, and her bones had atrophied and her body was bent over double permanently, her backbone had grown into a curve, she could never stand up."

"Oh, stop."

"Tell me about the divine force who thought that one up. This is the God for me."

"I'm not saying there's not—"

"You know how many people have been slaughtered in the Balkans so far?"

"No, I know, I just—"

"Or Algeria? Or Rwanda, or Ireland, or Cambodia? How many women raped, how many children murdered? Usually in the name of religion?"

I hid my head between my knees and pressed in hard against my temples.

"This is not the Garden of Eden. We're worse than beasts, animals would never do what we do. We're monsters. There was this guy in northern California, he kidnapped a woman and chained her up in his basement. First he cut off one of her arms, and then after that healed, he cut off . . . Ruth? Hey. What's up, what are you doing? Are you crying?"

I couldn't talk.

"Hey, come on, it's okay." He gave my arm a soft, unsure pat. "Don't do that, okay? Everything's all right."

"No, it's not, everything blows, everything's horrible." I dug a wadded-up Kleenex out of my jeans and wiped my nose, keeping my head down. So totally embarrassing.

"Everything's not horrible. Come on, it's almost spring, we'll be out of school in three months. That doesn't blow."

"Everybody just dies, you're right, so what's the point? It's all so stupid." And that wasn't even why I was crying. "My dad, he—he—" I started hiccuping, crying in those short, gaspy inhales like a baby.

Raven put his arm around me. I got my breath back and rested my head on his shoulder. He felt bony and tough through his shirt, like a boy, not a man. The white powder on his face was streaky where I'd wet his cheek with tears. He wore an ankh on a black velvet ribbon around his neck. I touched it with my fingertips, instead of touching him.

"There could be reincarnation," he said after a while. "Nobody knows, I mean, *knows*. Anything is possible."

I nodded gratefully.

"There could even be a God. Shit. There could be a heaven."

He was so sweet, I started crying again—just tears, no sobbing. "No, I don't think there is. But I don't even care. It's not that I want him to be in heaven, I just want him not to be dead. I can't believe I'll never see him again. He was alive—and now he's *dead*?"

Raven held me and rocked me, and then—it was just like in a movie—he kissed me. Except he missed my mouth and got me on the side, mostly cheek. I turned my head, thinking, *Okay, let's do this, I'll freak out later*, and our lips met. His were still black from his lipstick. I opened my eyes to see what he was doing. His eyes were open, too, but when he saw me looking at him he closed them. He had his hands on my shoulders and he was moving them down, pretty soon he would be touching my breasts. I decided to let him. Once Barry Levine touched the side of the right one while we were dancing. I pretended not to notice, and never danced with him again. This would be the first time I really let anybody. That the person was Raven—no, I'd figure that out later, if I thought about it now it would ruin it.

So then we kissed using our tongues, which I'd done once before, but this was better. I worried that I might have bad breath, because Raven did, because of the pot and the clove cigarette, but I didn't mind. At first I didn't even know he was touching me, he did it so lightly. I felt dizzy with my eyes closed; I didn't realize I was slowly falling over backward until my shoulder blades hit the ground. It was scary and exciting, lying on my back with Raven practically on top of me. Except for where he'd sprayed it red, his hair was much softer and cleaner than it looked, and on the other side, where he'd shaved it almost bald, it was nice to run my fingers over the soft, short bristles and hear the whiskery sound. Shouldn't we talk, say something to each other? I couldn't think of anything that wouldn't sound stupid, but the silence, except for our hard breathing, was weird.

He put his hand under my sweater and my blouse, and I stopped thinking. Then I realized I wasn't thinking, then I forgot again. Then I remembered. *I'm making out on my father's grave*. I sat up so quickly, I hit Raven in the nose with my forehead. We both said, "Ow," and leaned over, holding our faces. "Sorry," I said, "I'm really sorry. I can't do this here. I forgot where I was. God! Is that blood?"

I'd given him a bloody nose. He stood up and walked a little ways away, keeping his back to me, hunching his shoulders. He looked just like Raven, slight and tall and gloomy. And to think we'd just been kissing. It was like a dream. I thought about him sometimes, had some fantasies about us being a couple, but more like . . . more like an old married couple that didn't have sex anymore. Or like a nun and a priest who were best friends. One day last fall he wore a skirt to school—just for first period, before they sent him home. He said it was a gesture, we should all challenge gender stereotypes, androgyny was the only sex role that didn't exploit people. But after that some kids thought he was gay or something. I hadn't known what to think. Well, I guess I did now.

"Is it really bleeding?" I scrambled up and went to him. He half turned around to say no, but it was. All I had was my wadded-up Kleenex. I passed it over his shoulder. "I'm really, really sorry. I just, all of a sudden, you know. Remembered."

"We could go over there," he said nasally, pointing to some trees.

"Um, well. I guess I should get back."

"Okay."

"Because I've got that test."

"Whatever."

"But that was . . ." I went blank. I turned away and started gathering up our stuff, pretending I hadn't said anything. How could anyone finish that sentence? Who would be stupid enough to start that sentence? "That was nice"? "That was fun"? "Thanks for feeling me up, let's do it again sometime"? I often think my life would be a lot easier if I were a mute.

Raven's car is an old Plymouth station wagon he spray-painted black to look like a hearse. The vanity license tag says CDVRS RUS, which hardly anyone gets unless they know him. The inside smells like decaying leather, old bananas, and smoke. He always drives slowly and carefully, not like every other kid I know who can drive. I kept sneaking looks at him, trying to figure out how he was feeling. I hoped he wasn't hurt or mad at me. I'd have apologized more, but I didn't necessarily want him to think I wanted to start up again right away or anything—like bloodying his nose was the only thing stopping us from some hot and heavy love affair. But I didn't really think he thought that anyway.

"Hey, you know my friend Jess? The guy I told you about, the ark guy? Jess Deeping? That's his road—if you turn right there, that goes to his farm." Raven nodded but didn't slow down. "Turn! Turn, okay?" The car slowed; we turned in at the gravel drive between the gateposts. "I just—I was thinking we could say hi, is that okay? He's probably not even there. Look, those are his cows, that's all his land, that whole hill. Isn't it pretty? Some of it's on the river, too." Raven kept his eyes on the lane and didn't look around. "We don't have to stay if you don't want to. We can just say hi." We rounded the last corner and the house came into view, then the barns. Raven probably thought farms were hokey or retro or exploitive or something, but I thought Jess's was beautiful. "That's Mr. Green, the hired man," I said, pointing. "Look, he's painting. He's painting that barn red again, and it doesn't even need it. Isn't this place pretty?"

The dogs were swarming the car, barking and growling, pretending they were fierce. "There's Tracer! Hi, girl!" As soon as Raven stopped, I jumped out of the car and dropped to my knees on the gravel. The dogs backed away, still barking, but I called them by their names and gradually they sidled over, all but Tough Guy, and started sniffing my hands, my clothes. "Hey, Mouse, hey, Red. Hi, guys, did you miss me?"

I stood up when I realized Raven wasn't getting out of the car, which was still idling. Mr. Green came over, wiping his hands on a paint-spattered cloth.

"Hey," he said, "how you doing?" He shoved the rag in the pocket of his dirty coveralls and squinted, trying to see who was in the driver's seat of the Plymouth. Mr. Green was an old man, maybe sixty, with a chubby, cracked brown face. He never had much to say, but he smiled a lot, showing two gold front teeth. "Come to see Jess, eh?"

"Yeah," I said, smiling back. "Is he here?"

"Up at the house. Go on in if you want."

"Thanks. How've you been?" I asked politely.

"Good, you?"

"Fine, thank you."

Mr. Green touched his temple with his finger and went back to his painting.

I leaned in the window on my side. Raven was slouched in his seat, lighting a cigarette. His hair hid the side of his face. "So, um . . ."

"Listen, can you get a ride back with this guy?"

I stood back. "Yeah, I guess. You don't want to come in?"

"I've got some things to do."

"Oh." I should go with him. I should go back to school. I was going to get in trouble. Plus I was ditching Raven for no reason, plus Jess probably didn't need company in the middle of the day. "Okay," I said. "Well, see you."

"Yeah."

"Hey."

"What?"

"Are you mad at me?"

"No."

"Sure?"

"Yeah."

"Okay." I didn't move, though, so he had to look at me. He has pretty eyes, light blue with dark, curly lashes. I used my willpower to make him smile. I did—I stared into his eyes with my feminine charm and *made* him smile at me. "See you."

"Yeah. See you."

He waited a second and then very slowly drove away.

Well, that was okay. This day could've been one of the kind that make you squirm at night when you're trying to fall asleep, I mean it could so *easily* have made it onto my Most Embarrassing Moments list, but I fixed it. There at the end I took control somehow, I'm not sure exactly how, and I saved it. So I hope I've got it down in my genetic code or something now for future reference, a DNA memory, because that kind of girl power is definitely going to come in handy again.

Jess's front door was closed but not locked. I went right in. I was about to yell "Yoo hoo" or something when I heard his voice coming from the direction of his office. I went through the living room nobody ever uses, past the kitchen, the dining room. I stuck my head in the door to his study. He was sitting behind his desk, talking on the telephone.

When he saw me, he looked amazed. And glad! He stood up, but he couldn't get off the phone; he waved, gestured to a chair, but he had to keep talking. "So this is an IPO? Sure, I'm interested, but I'd need a prospectus. No. So there's no revenue yet? They're still losing money?" He laughed. "Sounds like my kind of—no, send me the prospectus, I can't tell you until I see it. Okay. Okay. No, I agree with you. That's what I'm saying, I want to look at the internationals. Listen, I'll have to get back to you—" He smiled across at me apologetically. "Good, send it, that's great. Right, and we'll talk next week. So. Yeah. Okay, Bob. Thanks. 'Bye."

He hung up. "Hi," he said, coming around his desk and sitting on the edge in front of me. "Look at you. How'd you get here? Everything okay?" He had on holey jeans and an old green sweater and muddy, ancient-looking work boots, and he looked good, he looked really real. I grinned at him, very glad I'd come, even if I was interrupting his workday.

"Everything's fine," I said, "I just came to say hi—a friend dropped me off. Um . . . can you drive me to work at Krystal's in about an hour and a half?"

He put his head back and looked at me over his nose. "This is a school holiday, is it?"

"Yeah. Teacher training day. In-service."

He lifted one eyebrow. He folded his arms.

"Okay, I'm cutting." I laughed, sparkling my eyes at him. "You won't tell Mom, will you?" I knew he wouldn't, he was too nice. And I was too cute—I could tell I was getting to him.

"Depends. You do this often?" He wasn't smiling back.

"No. Really, I don't, in fact I never do. Really!" It was true, practically. "Just—today it was so nice out, and this friend said let's have a picnic, and so we did." Good; that could sound like a group of kids, not just me and one guy. I smiled winningly, shrugged my shoulders, spread my hands. "Didn't you ever cut class when you were in school?"

"Irrelevant." He shook his head, but I'd made him smile. "I ought to tell Carrie," he said darkly. "If you do it again, I will."

"Never again." I put my hand on my heart.

"You want a soda?"

"Okay."

I followed him out to the kitchen, where he got down a bag of pretzels and opened a Coke. "I've still got some phone calls to make," he said. "Can you take care of yourself for a little while?"

"Sure, go ahead, don't worry about me. You won't even know I'm here."

He looked amused and doubtful, but he didn't say anything. We went back to his office, and I sat on the sofa on the other side of the room from his desk, so he couldn't hear me crunching pretzels while he talked on the phone. He called somebody named Bill to order fish liver oil and TMR, whatever that is, and he called somebody else, I guessed the vet, to talk about some poor cow's inflamed uterus and whether he should give it antibiotics, electrolytes, or dextrose and estrogens. He called two different places for estimates on belts and pumps and vacuum regulators for his milking machines.

I watched him while he talked, thinking how efficient he was but still nice to people. You can learn a lot about somebody by listening to their side of a phone conversation. My mom's formal with strangers, almost too polite sometimes, to the point of sounding cold. Sometimes my dad was rude, especially to salesmen or people asking for charitable contributions. Jess had a soothing voice, even and low; I couldn't imagine him ever yelling at anybody. He was kind of a mystery to me, though. Even though he seemed so peaceful and easygoing, I was sure there was a lot going on inside of him. Would I want a man like him if I were older? A man who felt things a lot, didn't just think things? Jess is quiet, but I think he would tell me anything at all, anything I wanted to know, if I just knew the right questions to ask.

I got up and walked around the room. All the bookshelves were crammed with Holstein journals, Holstein sale catalogs, record books, a million books about dairy farming. On a cork board by the door were photos of cows wearing ribbons. I didn't want to disturb Jess, but I could see that behind his desk were the interesting pictures, ones with people in them, so I sidled around behind his chair, being as quiet as I could, and checked them out.

Wow, he looked exactly like his mother. Ora—I remembered the name. She had a big cloud of shiny light brown hair she wore up in an old-fashioned bun, but otherwise she didn't look old-fashioned at all. She was beautiful, very tall and slender, with big dark eyes and a soft mouth. She was laughing in the picture, standing by a rose trellis in a pretty housedress, and holding out her hand—she had long white arms—as if asking somebody if she could help. Jess, probably; if he'd taken this picture, he'd have been a little boy. I could see his face in the mother's face so clearly, the same long eyelashes and sharp-sided nose, but most of all the same expression in their eyes. Hard to describe—because they *weren't* really sad, were they? But that's how Ora looked, and it was how Jess looked sometimes, like he knew about something painful and heavy, it would make you cry if he told you what it was.

There was a picture of his father, too, a snapshot of him taken in this room, sitting at the same desk where Jess was sitting now. He looked much older than his wife, and smaller; he was a little, serious-looking man with frown lines between his eyes and smile lines around his lips. He looked worried and kind.

The best was a photograph of the whole family, Jess in the middle with his arms around his parents' waists, grinning into the camera. He was so skinny! He couldn't have been more than sixteen, and his long, streaky, rock star hair was much lighter than now. I'd have known it was him anywhere, but he looked so *different*, loose and crazy or something, reckless. I stared and stared, trying to see the man I knew in the boy's features. His mother wasn't laughing in this picture; she was looking at Jess, and her pretty profile was vague and wistful. They weren't at home, they were standing in front of a modern brick building with aluminum windows. Daffodils bloomed between two bushes—maybe it was Easter. Jess's father had on a suit that didn't quite fit him.

Now they were both dead and Jess lived all by himself. Did he get lonely? He had Mr. Green and some other hired men, but they didn't seem like much company. He had all his cows, which he knew by name (he said). He had friends, probably, and an ex-wife but no kids, and he was a member of the city council. Did he have girlfriends? Maybe I'd ask him.

"Going to the bathroom," I mouthed, and he nodded and pointed and kept talking. I went out and down the hall and into the bathroom next to the kitchen.

Jess had left the toilet seat up. Well, why not? Mom used to scold Dad about that all the time, but I could never figure out why it was the man's job any more than the woman's. Jess lived alone, though, so the whole thing wasn't even an issue.

After I peed, I stared at my face in the mirror, especially my lips. How many times would I be kissed in my whole life? So far, about four times, but today was by far the most serious. I'd only done it once with tongues before. Too weird. But I might get used to it. Caitlin did it all the time, or so she claimed. In fact, Caitlin was probably sleeping with Donny Hartman, her boyfriend since ninth grade, but I didn't know for sure. Jamie knew, but she'd sworn not to tell, and I could only get hints out of her.

I stuck out my tongue, examining the little pink bumps on it. It wasn't disgusting because it was mine, but the thought of Raven's tongue, that was different. Tongues. Who'd invented that? Who was the first person to put his tongue in somebody else's mouth and decide that was a good deal? And what did the person whose mouth he'd put it in think the first time? It was like—pesto or something. Who could ever have thought grinding up *leaves* and putting them on *spaghetti* would be a good idea?

Breasts, too—what was the huge deal there? I pulled up my blouse and studied mine in my bra, a 32-A. Caitlin was a 34-A; Jamie didn't even need a bra but she wore one anyway, she wouldn't say what size. My breasts were coming in okay, I guessed; I wasn't obsessed about it like some girls. Leslie Weber, for instance, who stared down at her own chest all the time. She sat across from me in English, and that's all she did, stared at her own breasts, like they were actively growing before her eyes.

"Boys will want to touch you there," Mom said to me once, in the most horrible, the most excruciating conversation we ever had. It wasn't the sex talk—we'd already had that when I was about eight. This was the date talk, brought on by Brad Donnelly asking me out to the movies last summer, just the two of us, not in a group. Big deal. Just because Brad was a junior, Mom decided it was time to talk about date behavior and condoms and AIDS and syphilis and breasts and French-kissing. *Gross*. Like I didn't already know all that. She actually used the word *fondle*. It was like an out-of-body experience, and me thinking, *Is this really happening? Is my mother really saying this?* The horrible part wasn't that she thought what she was saying might actually apply to my life; that was kind of flattering. The horrible part was thinking about how she knew all that stuff—she knew it because she'd done it herself. Which is obvious, but still creepy and revolting and bizarro.

I heard Jess walk by the door, heard water running in the kitchen, and guessed he was finished with his phone calls. It was funny to think of him being a businessman, not just a guy who milked cows and went fishing and taught funny tricks to his dogs. I remember being surprised to see him in a suit and tie and all at my dad's funeral. Like, because he was a farmer all he could ever wear was denim and flannel. Silly. I had a grass stain on the shoulder of my blouse, I saw. I was saving up thinking about Raven for later, though. I combed my hair with my fingers and went to find Jess.

We went outside and walked down to the river, to the dock that went out from the bank along the rough shore, which was half trees, half grass. The dock was high enough so you could sit on the edge with your legs hanging over and not get your feet wet. Except in spring after a hard rain; then the river flooded and the dock disappeared until the water receded. Jess was an expert fly fisherman, but here from the dock he just did what he called coarse fishing, using worms and what-have-you to catch chub and perch and roach fish. Last summer he taught me how to bait a hook with wasp grubs, how to cast a float rod, how to reel in a big fat carp. Maybe someday he'd take me fly-fishing.

We sat on the end of the dock and talked about fish for a while, and how we wished spring would hurry up because we were sick of winter. He must've thought I had something to tell him, that I'd come by for a particular reason, because pretty soon he said, "Everything okay?" and looked out over the water instead of at me, in case I felt shy about talking.

I really hadn't come for a reason, not that I knew of, it had just been a while since I'd seen him and we were driving right by his lane. Spur of the moment. Still, what popped out of my mouth was, "Everything's great, except my mom had a date last night. Can you believe that? My dad's been gone for half a year, and she goes out with this *body*builder."

Jess watched a buzzard flying high up in the sky and didn't say anything.

"Of course she says it wasn't a date, it was business, because the guy's her boss, but since when do you do business at night in a saloon?"

Jess still didn't jump in and sympathize, so I said, "Not that I care who she sees, it's none of my business, for all I care she can go out with every guy in Clayborne. I just don't think she should lie about it. And I don't think it's such a hot idea to date your boss anyway. Especially this guy, who's a total jerk. I mean, he wears a goatee." I bumped Jess with my elbow, trying to get a rise out of him. "A *goatee*. Plus he's got no neck."

Finally he grimaced. "You're talking about Brian Wright."

"Yeah. So do you know him?"

"Slightly. I do a course for the school."

"Oh, yeah. Fishing," I remembered. "So what do you think of him?"

"I don't know him well enough to think anything."

I hadn't expected him to get all discreet on me. Now I wished I hadn't even told him. "It's no big deal, I really don't care what she does."

"Maybe it wasn't a date," he said after a while. "Have you and Carrie talked about it?"

"I don't have to talk about it. She calls me from a nightclub, she's drinking, she's with a guy. I call that a date. Oh, and she gets home after *I* do. I pretended I was asleep—I didn't even *want* to talk to her." Jess started to say something. "Not that I care," I said again quickly, "it's her life, she can do whatever she wants. But I just . . ." I looked away downstream, where the river bent and the sycamore trees leaned over on both sides. From this angle, it almost looked like they touched in the middle. "She told me no one could take Dad's place—that's exactly what she said, 'Nobody's taking his place.' She said she wasn't available."

"Ruth."

"What? You don't have to defend her."

"I'm not."

"I know everything you're going to say. I'm being selfish, she's allowed to have some fun, what she said wasn't really a promise—I know all that. I just don't like it." I leaned out over my knees to stare down at the brownish green current, thinking I always talked too much around Jess and wondering why that was. He couldn't be a father figure because he wasn't anything like my father, and he wasn't exactly a friend because I didn't know that much about him. "Do you have a girlfriend?" I asked him.

"What?" he said, even though he'd heard.

"Are you going out with anybody?"

"No. Not right now."

He looked very uncomfortable, which cheered me up for some reason. "Hey, Jess, did you know Becky Driver's in my class? I met her mother—I had dinner at their house." He nodded pleasantly. "She's nice, Mrs. Driver," I said leadingly. "I mean, she's *really* nice."

"She is nice."

"Becky's not yours, though, right?"

"That's right."

"So . . ." What happened? How come your marriage didn't work out? You couldn't ask questions like that straight out, you had to beat around the bush.

I was trying to think of a subtle approach when Jess said, "Do you have a boyfriend?"

"Ha." Good one. Touché. We grinned at each other. "Well," I said, "there's this one guy. Raven."

"The vampire."

I laughed—he remembered! "Yeah. I'm not sure if he's my *boy*friend," I said, making a face. What a stupid word. "He's the one who dropped me off here."

"Ah. So you were playing hooky together."

"Just today, just this once. Honestly, this is not my practice, I mean, it's not my lifestyle." I decided to tell him. "We went to my dad's grave. We had sort of a picnic. It was nice. I mean, it was respectful and everything." If you didn't count smoking dope and kissing and making out. "I keep thinking, you know, if only he hadn't died. What it would be like. Or if he had to die, if only he'd lived for five more years, say. I think if I'd been, like, twenty, we could've been much closer. Sometimes I think he was waiting for me to grow up to be really friends. Now—he'll never know how I turned out," I managed to say before I started crying. Shit. I turned my head away, put my cheek on my knees, so Jess couldn't see.

He put his arm around me. I thought he would try to cheer me up, tell me my father had loved me very much, blah blah, but he just said, "It's sad," and it went right through me.

"It is," I said gladly, "it's so *sad*. I think trying not to be sad is worse than being sad."

"I do, too."

"So I'm glad I went to his grave." I sat up. "I don't think my mom goes. I don't know, she might. We went together at Christmas and on January ninth, his birthday. If she does go, she doesn't leave flowers, because there weren't any."

"I think she's trying to be strong for you. Trying to do the right thing, be what she thinks you need her to be. I think she's feeling all the things you feel about your father, missing him, and wishing there had been more time. One thing I'm sure of—you're the center of her life."

"Then why'd she go out on a date?" I laughed, to make it sound more like a joke. Less whiny.

He looked pained. "Why did you?" was all he could come up with.

"It's not the same, he was my *father*, not my *husband*. He would've wanted me to have a boyfriend. He wouldn't have wanted her to."

"Maybe you should talk to her about it."

"No. *No*. I don't want to hear her stupid explanations. *God*. She's so *embarrassing*."

"Embarrassing?" Jess gave me a crooked smile. "When I was your age," he said, "fifteen or so." He leaned back on his elbows and stared at his belt buckle. "You saw my mother's picture?"

"In the house? Yeah," I said, "she was really pretty."

"She was schizophrenic."

"Oh." I swallowed.

"It didn't start until I was about ten. Before that, she was fine. But she had a miscarriage, and after that everything changed."

"God. I'm really sorry."

"When she'd get bad, she'd have to go away, go in the hospital. My father and I were close, but we were lost, like orphans when she was gone. Then she'd come home, and I'd drive her crazy by not leaving her alone. I couldn't get enough of her. I was always trying to cure her, with presents and things I'd make for her, food, spells. Tricks." He laughed. "Sometimes it seemed to work, whatever it was—some drink I'd concoct, a special, particular prayer. But not for long. And nothing ever worked twice."

This was bad, but something worse was coming. I already sort of knew what it was.

"She did a lot of crazy things. She'd get lost, wander off and lose herself. We'd have to call the cops. One day we were in Belk's, buying me some clothes for school. It was the end of the summer. She'd been fine for months, her old self, but it was starting again. I could always tell. She was odd in the store, saying things that didn't make sense. She kept complaining that she was hot, burning up, why didn't they turn on the air-conditioning. I was afraid she'd complain to the saleslady, and I didn't want to be around if she did. I wandered off, into a different area of the department. Far enough away so I could pretend nothing was happening."

"Oh, God, Jess."

"I heard a commotion. Raised voices. You could feel it in the air—shock. Somebody called security over the PA. I didn't want to, but I had to go see." He reached out and touched me on the arm with the lightest pat, a reassurance, and he gave me a tickled, helpless smile. "She'd taken off her clothes. Every stitch. She was naked as a jaybird in the men's sweater department at Belk's."

I moved my hand far enough from my mouth to whisper, "What did you do?"

"Ran away."

"No."

"Yeah. But only to the elevator. If it had come immediately, I'd have gotten on and gone down and outside and away—I'd have run away. But it took forever. So."

"You had to go back."

"I've always been ashamed for that, how close I came to leaving her. I had this fierce love for her, I loved her more than anybody else. But she . . ."

"Embarrassed you."

He smiled.

I blushed. But I didn't feel lectured to or guilty or caught in the act in some sin. No question, he'd made his point, but not only was he not rubbing it in, he was helping take the sting out by admitting that once he'd done the same thing, only worse. With better cause, okay, but still.

God! Imagine having a crazy person for a mother. Really crazy, like certifiable, not just weird or irritatingly nuts like Mom. It really put things in perspective.

"That's awful," I said, and I put one finger on the sleeve of Jess's sweater. It was the first time I'd ever comforted *him* for anything. "That's so sad. She looks so beautiful in the picture. I think you look like her. Do you believe in heaven? She could be watching down on you. I'm sure she's very proud of you, you know, how you've turned out and all. *God.*"

"What?"

"That's what people have been saying to me," I realized. "You know, old people, mostly—that my dad's probably still with me, he's proud of me, yadda yadda. Does that comfort you? Because it *never* comforts me. But now I at least get why they say it."

"Why?"

"Well, to be nice. To be kind, to show that you care and you wish the person didn't hurt."

"Yes."

"So that's something. Isn't it? It might be a crock, but the person saying it means well."

"I think it's something. I think it's all we get."

We lay on our backs and watched clouds and sky and birds go by, peaceful as two old, old pals. I almost told him about Raven, that's how comfortable I felt. I might have, but then he sat up and said, "Four o'clock."

"How can you tell?"

"Listen."

"I don't hear anything."

"Listen."

"Oh. Cows." They were mooing way off in the distance. "You have to milk them now?"

"Pretty soon. Mr. Green will start."

I scrambled up from the dock. "I didn't know it was so late," I said, matching Jess's long strides up the hill. "Guess you sort of blew off your afternoon, huh?" He just smiled at me, and I felt fine. "Hey, Jess. Can we take the pickup truck?"

"Sure, if you want."

"And, Jess?"

"Hm?"

"Can I drive?"

"Got your learner's permit with you?"

"Yes."

"Okay, then."

"Yay!" I clapped my hands, did a little dance. Jess's pickup was a stick shift, the most fun of all to drive. "And, Jess?"

"*What*?"

I laughed. "Can we take Tracer? Can we put her in the middle between us? I've always wanted to do that, drive in a pickup truck with a dog and, you know. A guy."

He shook his head. "The cowgirl look."

"I guess."

"Amazing. I thought you were into vampires."

"Well, I am."

"Or health food and vitamins."

"Them, too."

"You're a very versatile person."

"Thanks."

Versatile. I was very versatile. Cool. And here I thought I was just confused.

13

Ballroom Dancer

"Never mind, Dana, you wouldn't have had that much fun anyway. The women's club is full of poops, nothing like our day. You're better off without 'em."

"I'm *not upset*." I'd told Birdie that three times since we got in the car. "It's nothing. I'm not losing one wink of sleep over this, believe you me."

"Well, I should hope not. Because that would be a waste of perfectly good energy. How come your house is so dark?"

"What? Oh, he forgot to turn on the porch light again. I swear, it's like living with a mole."

"You sure he's in there?"

"He's there. He's either working in his office or watching TV in the den. Want to come in?" I invited without much enthusiasm. "Cup of coffee before you go home?"

"Oh, my, no, a cup of coffee would keep me up all night."

"Decaf, I meant."

"Rain check?"

"Sure."

"Unless you want me to. Unless you want to talk."

"I don't want to talk," I said, laughing, "I want to *sleep*. I'm perfectly fine, Bird, this means very little to me."

"Oh, I know that."

"I won't even think about it tomorrow."

"Of course you won't. You're too smart for them, that's the problem. They didn't know a good thing when they saw it."

"Thanks. Thanks for the ride."

"I'll call you tomorrow. Want to go to a movie or something? There's a sale—"

"Can't tomorrow. Maybe next week." Birdie's sympathy was starting to grate on me. Much better if she'd just say, "I told you so," and get it over with.

"'Night, Dana," she called. "Really, don't give it another thought, it's not worth your—"

"Drive carefully," I said, and slammed the door.

The house wasn't just dark, it was cold. More like living with a bear than a mole, some heavy, lumbering animal that hibernates, I thought, going around turning on lights in the living room, the kitchen, turning up the thermostat. Canned laughter sounded from the den. George has two passions, if you can call them that: his book and old TV shows. The older the better; he even buys them on tape from 800 numbers, old episodes of *Lassie*, *Bonanza*, *77 Sunset Strip*, *The Loretta Young Show*. I don't know what to make of that. Was life so much better for him in the 1950s than it is now? Was there some *tone* then, something he responded to, some flavor or style that he's nostalgic for now? I wonder what it is. I would really love to know. But when I ask him, "Why do you like that old stuff?" all he ever says is, "It's amusing."

Tonight it was *I Love Lucy*. I walked into the den just as Lucy was opening her big mouth wide and crying, "*Waaaah*," because Rickie wouldn't take her on a vacation. George looked up at me and smiled with fond, laughing eyes—I smiled back before I realized it wasn't me making him so happy and appreciative. Should I have tried to be more like that? A silly, wacky, zany kind of woman? Was that what he'd wanted?

"You're back," he said, hitching over to make room for me on the couch.

Where did I go?—I almost asked, to test him. But I was blue enough tonight; if he flunked the test, I'd feel even worse. "From the women's club," I said instead, helpfully. "Election night."

A commercial came on, and he muted the sound with the remote control. "How did that go?"

"I lost."

"Oh, dear." He blinked sympathetically through the middle bar of his trifocals. He looked pretty natty in tweed trousers and the blue crew neck sweater Carrie gave him two Christmases ago. He had dandruff on his shoulders, though, and a yellowish stain on his chest, maybe dried orange juice. And he smelled like his pipe. We were a fairly handsome couple in our day, I've got pictures to prove it, but we've turned into the kind of people you don't look at twice. Which one of us will end up at Cedar Hill first? I wonder that too much lately. It's awfully easy to imagine me visiting George in a room like Helen's. Wheeling him down to arts and crafts, bending over his stooped shoulder, showing him how to make pot holders.

"Yep," I said, "the new president of the Clayborne Women's Club is Vera Holland. Who's seventeen years old."

"Really?"

"Or twenty-seven, what's the difference. A younger woman. Her platform was 'diversity.' Translation, let's all go out and recruit more of her tacky friends."

"Tsk." His eyes flicked briefly to the TV. A shampoo commercial.

"I didn't even want the damn job, I just didn't want her to have it." Well now, that wasn't true. "Oh, I sort of wanted it. Shake things up. I wanted to feel, you know . . . active." Alive, rather. "Anybody can belong to a club, that doesn't mean anything. What it was—I think I felt like testing myself before it's too late."

I felt a little breathless from the frankness of that. Showing much of myself to George, revealing my deeper feelings—I quit that years ago, it didn't pay off. A one-sided exercise that usually just left me feeling foolish. Not that *not* telling him things has gotten me anywhere, either. It's pretty much a lose-lose.

"Well," he said.

"Well. Well, what?"

"Well . . . maybe it's for the best. Lot of work you don't need."

"Yeah, maybe." I stood up. "And my life's so rich and full already. I don't know what I was thinking." I scooped up my coat and my purse.

"Dana."

"What?"

"I'm sure you'd have made an excellent president."

"I don't know if I would have or not, but it would've been nice to win. I really did want to win."

He shrugged, shook his head. Pursed his lips, blinked his eyes. Body language attempts at commiseration. *Words, George, I want words*. On TV, Fred and Ethel came into Lucy's apartment. Fred talked out of the side of his mouth, deadpan, and Ethel rolled her eyes.

"Well," I said, "let me get out of your way."

"I'll be up in two seconds," George called. Gales of laughter followed me up the stairs.

It was even colder on the second floor than the first. Undressing in front of my closet, I heard the flick of light switches downstairs, then the clump of George's shoes on the steps, slow and heavy, reluctant sounding. As good as his word, even though it was a little early for him. Did he feel sorry for me? To hell with that. But in the glimpse I got of him passing behind as I bent over to take off my hose, he just looked tired.

Ghastly sight, me in the bathroom mirror. Since 1979, I've been asking George to replace the fluorescent tube over the sink with a regular one, a tungsten bulb. He's never going to do it. I complain to Carrie and she says, "Well, if you can make yourself look halfway human in *that* light, just think how beautiful you must look in the real world." Nice logic, but it doesn't work anymore. Not for the last, oh, twenty years.

I brushed my teeth, brushed my hair. Which is thinning. Took my blood pressure pill. Hunched toward the mirror, I pulled down the collar of my nightgown to study the new lines on my neck. Turkey neck. Turkey jowls. This is a nightly ritual I really ought to discontinue. It's funny, but I'm getting more vain the older I get instead of less. No, *vain* isn't the right word. *Aghast.* That's it.

Would George want to make love with me if I looked prettier? Lost twenty pounds? Doubtful. Truthfully, I can't see him getting excited about sleeping with Sophia Loren. Maybe June Allyson; he's always liked her. Too bad for him he married a woman more like Ethel Merman. Joan Crawford. A coarse brunette, not a perky bone in her body.

He looked up briefly from his newspaper when I slid into bed beside him. "Tired?" he asked.

"Why, do I look tired?"

He shrugged and went back to his paper.

"Well, one thing I accomplished tonight anyway," I said, interrupting him on purpose.

"What's that?"

"I made a motion to start a petition drive to halt this ark-building foolishness, and it passed."

"You mean—the ark on the river?"

"No, the ark on I-95." I really was in a bad mood. "Yes, the ark on the river."

"Why would you do that?"

"Why! That's public property, George, people tie up boats to that dock."

"Oh, but not very many, I don't think."

"Well, what about the stupidity factor?"

"Ah."

"And separation of church and state? I'll tell you what happened—Jess Deeping railroaded that vote through the council before anybody knew what was happening. What if the national news gets a hold of this story? It's like—Charles Kuralt finding some lunatic in Idaho building a shrine to the Blessed Virgin out of bottle caps."

"He did?"

"No, I'm saying—we'll all look ridiculous. It'll be an eyesore, a public nuisance, we just can't have it."

He took off his glasses and started polishing them with the edge of the sheet. "What about Carrie?"

"What about her?"

"Isn't she interested in this? I thought she was—"

"That's just boredom, that's another one of her artsy-craftsy projects. Carrie needs to concentrate on her real job, not ally herself with this fundamentalist religious claptrap. Of all the crazy things! And wouldn't you know Jess Deeping's right in the thick of it? If that isn't typical. Blood tells."

"What are you talking about?"

"His mother. She was insane, don't you remember?"

"No."

"Well, she was, she died in an institution, and he's a chip off the old block."

He shook his head, *not* sympathetically, and rattled the pages of his newspaper. Conversation over.

That's typical, too. Ignore a problem by pretending it doesn't exist. Carrie probably wasn't going to appreciate my petition motion, either. She might even question my motives. Sure as shooting, she'd never *thank* me for it. The petition might not do any good anyway, it might be too late. Talk about an end run. Jess Deeping should be ashamed of himself. Maybe I'll write a letter to the editor.

"You know what Birdie said?"

George sighed. "What?"

"She said I just wanted to be president so I could boss people around."

He looked up at that. I waited for him to scoff, but he just looked at me.

"She said it as a joke, but I didn't appreciate it."

"No . . ."

"You think I'm bossy?"

"Absolutely not, dear." He ducked his bald head, shooting me a glance under his eyebrows. He had a hopeful twinkle in his eye. I laughed. And he laughed, and it was a good few seconds.

He folded his paper and put it away, turned out his bedside lamp. He falls asleep every night on his right side, facing away from me; after about forty minutes, he turns over on his back and snores. He started getting his covers just so, pushing the sheet out at the bottom so his feet weren't constricted—every morning I tuck it back in.

"George?"

"Hm?"

"Nothing. Never mind." A feeling came over me, a squeezing sensation, like a vise, something hopeful pushing up from below, something else old and knowing pushing down from above. "What do you think about taking ballroom dancing?"

He turned his head, craned it over his shoulder. Stared.

"Friday nights, out at the Ramada Inn. Six weeks, and it starts next week. We could have dinner first—a night out for us. Just something to look forward to."

"Well. Hm." He frowned hard. "The only thing is, Friday's the night I've been meeting with Albert on the book. I gather it's the only time he can do it."

"Friday is the only night of the whole week he can meet you? Friday night?"

"Well, that's what he says."

"Fine, never mind."

"Sorry. It would've been fun," he lied. "Maybe next year."

"That's a good idea." I reached for the novel on my table. "Let's wait till we're even older."

"Dana."

"Maybe next year they'll offer ballroom wheelchair dancing." I slapped open the book, found my place from last night. "Quit." I was so mad. I twitched his hand off my hip and turned over. "I'm trying to read."

He sighed like a martyr, rustled the covers, settled on his right side. "Night."

I met George when I was eighteen, working in the customer service department at Willie's Auto Repair. My first job. I did typing and filing and greeting the customers. I don't know where I thought this job would take me—nowhere, I suppose; we just got married in those days, we didn't have careers, not girls from my background anyway. One day George brought in his old rattletrap Plymouth and I waited on him, filling out the little form we had, getting his name and address, writing down what was wrong with his car. He had on an argyle sweater, I remember as if it was yesterday. College boy. I flirted with him because he was sweet and shy, but I'd never have made a play for him. I knew my place. When he asked if he could call me sometime, I almost said no. I thought he didn't know the rules, that, being from Richmond, he must somehow not be aware that Remington boys didn't ask out Clayborne girls. Not with good intentions, anyway.

He took me to an orchestra recital on campus on a Friday night. If he'd been Casanova, if he'd been Don Juan, he couldn't have come up with a more seductive date. I was thrilled out of my mind, and I was absolutely terrified. That very night I set my cap for him. *I want this*, I thought. To be with people who talked softly and said things that were just out of my reach. *Maybe I can learn this*, I thought. Campus—oh, just the word made me dizzy. *Campus*. It meant peace and quiet and safety. Most of all, it meant respectability.

It was easy to make him fall in love with me. I was pretty then, and I just pretended he was the center of the world, I cut out of my mind everything but George, I turned all the wattage on and blinded him. Nowadays I suppose I'd have had to sleep with him, but back then it was enough to make him want me. He's still the only man I've ever been with. He says I'm the only woman, but that's as may be. I don't question that too closely. The only one in many, many years, though, *that* I wouldn't doubt.

I think the reason I wanted to be president of the women's club was to see, before I'm a hundred and it really is too late, if my disguise worked. I come from backward people. My father was a drunk. I carry on like I belong in this house, this town, like faculty parties don't faze me, but I never know for sure if people are on to me. The fact that I lost the election to Vera Holland doesn't prove anything, unfortunately. All it confirms is that I'm over the hill.

I wonder if I shouldn't have married somebody like Calvin Mintz, poor Helen's husband. More in my class. Which one of us is meaner, Cal or me? Which one of us would've won? At least it would've been interesting. If we'd survived.

When I thought I could sleep, I turned out the light and settled on my side, facing away from George. Our rumps bumped. I scooted away an inch, still mad; I didn't want him touching me.

Here's how morbid I am lately—I think about waking up in the middle of the night and finding him stiff and cold in the bed beside me. I'm afraid to touch him. I call either Carrie or 911, I'm not sure which. Carrie, I guess, then *she* can call 911. The paramedics come. They knock at the door, blue and white lights flashing around the yard, the street, and I show them upstairs in my bathrobe and slippers. They do things . . . the fantasy gets less real there. The way a dream can start off hard-edged and then get vague, finally tapering off into nonsense. I never imagine any of the emergency people saying, "He's dead, ma'am." No. It never comes to that.

Time is turning me into somebody I can hardly believe in, I can't seem to make real. *Old lady*. Do other people who are old *feel* old? I always thought they did, they must, but here I am turning seventy any day now and I'm no smarter, no wiser, no happier, no more satisfied or fulfilled or content or enlightened than I was at forty. In fact, less.

I could live to a hundred, I thought, shutting my eyes against the moonlight seeping in around the curtain. Willard Scott could say my name on TV. Who knew, George could live to ninety-eight in the other wing of the nursing home. The *Morning Record* could run a picture in the Lifestyles section of us shriveled up in our wheelchairs, holding each other's knobby hand, cutting a sheet cake.

Foolishness. Why would I want to stretch out marriage to George for thirty more years? Didn't the last fifty teach me anything?

I don't believe in hopelessness, it goes against my raising. But the trouble with hope is it springs eternal. Crazy old ladies think miracles can still happen. George turned over in his sleep and butted his knee up against my rear end. The warmth felt good, so I stayed still, didn't poke him to move. See? He's good for something. That's hopeful.

14

Elephant Day

Alla prima. In painting it meant *at once*, applying all your pigments in one sitting, not layering them on over time. Van Gogh probably painted *Bedroom at Arles alla prima*, they say. The advantage over a more painstaking, considered approach was supposed to be excitement, intensity, fluidity. I must be doing very exciting work these days, that's all I can say. It was good to have an arty foreign word for it, too, *alla prima.* So much nicer than *slapdash.*

Wet otter fur. How did you paint wet otter fur? If I were using oils or acrylics on a good stretched canvas, I would start with a neutral base of ultramarine, Payne's gray, maybe raw umber, some titanium white. If I could afford it I'd use a Richeson no. 10, series 9050 brush, laying in the basic darks and lights first, trying to imagine the otter's body as a landscape, skin, muscle, and bone as hills, valleys, and ridges. I'd compose him in an appropriate setting, maybe climbing onto a log after a dip in a stream. The elements in the composition would provide perspective and proportion; we'd know how big the otter was by the size of the objects around him. He'd be gray, basically, but not drab because I'd put him behind autumn leaves (raw sienna, vermilion, Venetian red, Van Dyck brown) and in front of the wet fallen stump (burnt sienna, ultramarine, lamp black). I'd switch to a Richeson no. 3 brush, series 9000, for the fine work, the detailing and refining of his fur, whiskers, eyes, eyelashes, toenails.

I wasn't doing any of that. I was using a midgrade True Value exterior semigloss ($20.99 a gallon), in a grayish brown shade called "Farewell." I was laying it on with a three-inch nylon and polyester brush over what I hoped was an otter-shaped cutout from a four-by-eight sheet of three-quarter-inch polystyrene foam insulation. It was a handicap.

But not an insurmountable one. And I wasn't working completely *alla prima*, anyway: after the gray latex dried, I'd add white and black highlights with a small red sable round brush, my one indulgence, to enhance the sharp, sideways V shapes I'd decided clumped wet otter fur looked like. The trick was lifting up on the brush quickly when you got to the end of the hair shaft; otherwise the point wasn't fine enough. If I had time, I'd redo his eye with acrylics; I'd have liked to roughen the edge of his pupil, lighten the bottom of his iris with Turner's yellow and some more white. Because I'd decided the light would be coming from directly overhead.

I wouldn't have time, though. God gave Noah 120 years to build the ark, and He threw in the animals for nothing. Eldon Pletcher had given Landy, who gave Jess, who gave me and my "helpers," about three months to stock a three-story ark with, if you included fish, reptiles, and insects, approximately seventy-eight separate animal species.

Landy said pinning the old man down to seventy-eight wasn't easy, and I could believe it. At first some of his choices struck me as arbitrary. He'd insisted on the antelope but not the caribou, for example; wolf but not coyote; moose but not elk; mole but not shrew. Leopard but not puma, dog but not dingo, donkey but not mule—and so on. It made sense when you thought about it: between similar animals, he had consistently chosen the one that was either more immediately recognizable or else more—likable, for lack of a better word. People liked mice, they didn't like rats.

I approved of Eldon's list, on the whole. I was especially looking forward to making a chimpanzee. And an octopus—that would be a mechanical as well as artistic challenge. Landy was going to ask his father if I could have a little discretion with add-ons, because I loved slow, lumbering animals, and his list didn't include possum or manatee. But even if he said yes, I wouldn't have time.

It wasn't altogether a bad thing, the absurd May seventeenth deadline we had no chance of meeting. It allowed no time for second-guessing. My left brain, if there was such a thing, had been all but silenced; by necessity, I was going on uninhibited instinct. I'd never worked that way before. I was like a newspaper reporter who had to finish the story in time for the early edition. It was faster, obviously, but was it any good? I didn't know—I was afraid to hope—I thought it might be. But either way, I was having the time of my life.

The job was seducing me, in spite of all the restrictions and eccentric conditions Eldon had attached to it. It was swallowing me up the way a boa constrictor swallowed a rabbit. (I had been reading up on boa constrictors; Eldon wanted them to represent the snake category—the recognizability factor again.) When I worked, I almost sank into a trance. Not like the miniature flower arrangements trance—that was like sinking into a coma, and this was more like being hypnotized. I was aware of my surroundings, the chilliness of the space, the mooing of a cow outside, the oil, gasoline, and dead grass smells, the hum overhead of the fluorescent lights Jess had hung, along with an inadequate propane heater on the wall, when the barn became the official ark animal assembly area. But nothing distracted me, nothing got between me and what I was working on. It was as if I bled into the paint, and the paint bled into the surface and the surface bled into the object—in this case an otter. Extraordinary! It was the boon, the prize, it was the best part of making art. I used to feel it, but I barely remembered it. I never thought I'd get it back.

Landy broke my concentration, saying, "Sorry I got to go so early today." I jumped. The smooth line of my brush took a hitch upward, like a lie detector printout catching somebody in a whopper. "Oh—'scuse me—I thought you heard me!"

I laughed. We'd been working in Jess's barn since lunchtime, and even though our work areas were fairly close together, I often forgot Landy was there. It wasn't just my own absorption: he was such a quiet man, content to work indefinitely without saying a word.

"Good," he said, leaning over, peering down at my otter. "Looks just like one."

"I haven't finished the fur. Is he too gray? Think he needs more brown?"

"Hmm, could be."

"I'm using these photos and those drawings." I pointed to my otter reference materials, wildlife calendars and a couple of naturalists' journals. "Yes, more brown, I think. Otherwise he looks like a baby seal."

"No, no, he doesn't look anything like a seal."

I believed him, and let that particular worry go. Landy was my trusty, most reliable critic. He was always polite, but he never lied: if my pig cutout looked like an armadillo, he found a nice way to tell me.

"Are you going to see your father?" I asked.

He nodded. "Sorry I got to go so early, and so much still to do, but this is when he likes me to come."

"Don't worry about it." Eldon was in the hospital again, for chest pains and fluid on his lungs. "How's he doing?"

"Better. They say he can probably go home in a coupla days. Tuesday, they're saying."

"I'm so glad. He's a tough old guy." I hadn't met him yet, but that seemed safe to say.

"I got done six sets of wheels, I set 'em right over there. Sorry it's no more." He stretched his hands out and flexed his knobby, arthritic fingers. "Not such a good day today."

"It's the cold." I wore fingerless gloves when I worked, but Landy wouldn't, said they made him clumsy.

He buttoned his plaid jacket to the chin and jammed on his dirty orange hunter's cap. "Did two sets for the elephant, like you said. Front and back." He'd spent the afternoon attaching wheels to heavy wooden bases sawn from four-by-fours, because Eldon wanted to roll the animals onto the ark via a ramp. He could *just see it*, he said.

"Great. Think the brakes will hold?" I asked. We bought wheel sets with little foot-activated brakes; ridiculously expensive, but we got a deal by buying in bulk.

"I reckon. What're you doing after you finish coloring that otter?"

"Oh, I'm going to have some fun," I told him. "Today is elephant day."

His eyes crinkled almost shut when he grinned. "Wish I could stay and see that. You're having a pretty good time, huh?"

"I guess I am."

"Why'd you decide to help out? This sure ain't nothing to do with you, Carrie."

People kept asking me that; I ought to have had a better answer by now. "It crept up on me," was the best I could do. "I didn't think it would get this far. I thought I'd pitch in once or twice, help get things started."

He laughed his shy, wheezing laugh. "That's what happened to me! Hell, same with Jess, too. Pushovers is what we are. Are you sorry?"

"No. But ask me if I'm *tired*."

"Hoo, don't I know it! Say, the Finches told me they can come back one night next week, and then again next Saturday. If that's any help to you."

I hummed, noncommittal. The Finches, two elderly Arkist sisters, both spinsters, sincerely wanted to help me, but they were hopeless—on so many levels, it would've been mean to list them. Color blindness was one, though; another was decrepitude. But the worst was that they had *ideas*; they made *suggestions*. I hadn't known how proprietary I was getting until last week when Miss Sara Finch said the cow should be a Brown Swiss and Miss Edna Finch agreed with her. No, no, no. No. The cow was a black-and-white Holstein. Period. This was not a democracy.

"Just wish I could pay you somehow," Landy mumbled with his head down. "Here it is a Sunday, you could be home spending time with your fam—your daughter. Wish I could pay you back some way, that's all."

It really bothered him, I knew because he said it so often. "Maybe you can, Landy. When things settle down, maybe you can help me with a couple of projects around my house. Things I can't do by myself."

He beamed. "I'd be glad to do that, I'd be pleased. Anything I could do, it would be my pleasure. We'll count on it."

"Good."

No one knew, not even Landy, how much money old Eldon had socked away. He had to have some, or he wouldn't have made his playground equipment offer. (Would he? That was a thought. What if he were pulling one over on the whole town? I wondered if Jess had considered that. I'd ask him.) In any case, Landy wanted the ark effort to be as frugal as possible, because he said it was draining away his mother's inheritance. His, too—but he honestly didn't seem to consider that. He said he didn't want the old man's obsession to impoverish his mother once his father was gone. That was why I was using the cheapest good paint the hardware store sold, and slapping it on polystyrene instead of wood. It was why Landy and Jess, whose combined boatbuilding expertise wouldn't have covered a matchbook, were designing a 119-foot ark in their spare time, with only Arkist help and no professional guidance. I couldn't figure out whether Eldon was crazy like a fox or just crazy.

I said good-bye to Landy and turned my mind to elephants.

Everybody liked them, everybody was soft on them. To my generation they were what dinosaurs had been to Ruth's. But kids outgrew dinosaurs—nobody outgrew elephants. Well, ivory merchants, presumably, but nobody with a soul. There was something about elephants, and I wanted to try to capture it. Their sweetness and shuffling intelligence, their persistence and indefatigability. Honesty.

Like all the animals, I was doing this one life-size—a small elephant, granted, but life-size. The him-her, two-sided idea seemed to be working, although I hadn't succeeded yet at crafting two different *poses* on either side of the cutout silhouettes; I'd only been able to vary the two genders of the same animal with color. But I'd keep trying. I worked with four-by-eight insulation sheets, and until now that had been more than adequate; in fact I often got two small animals, both sides, out of a single sheet. It wouldn't be enough for an elephant, though, so I'd hot glued two sheets together, width-wise, edge-to-edge, then glued two more sheets, one on each side, across the seam to strengthen the joint, and finally glued four two-by-eight half sheets, top and bottom on each side, to fill in the gap. Now I had an eight-foot square of foam two and a half inches thick. Later I'd cut out ears, trunk, and tail, and glue them on separately for added dimension.

It was Chris's brilliant idea to use the polystyrene sheets. In a past life, she designed stage sets for amateur theatrical productions. Plywood, she pointed out, was heavier, more expensive, harder to work with, and buckled when wet. Polystyrene sheets glued together beautifully, cut with a craft knife instead of a band saw, and took latex paint like a dream. Chris only knew Landy from what I'd told her about him, but it tickled her to think how much money her suggestion had already saved him.

I usually drew the basic outline of an animal with the foam sheet flat on the floor, but that wouldn't work with an elephant; too big. Unless I crawled around on my hands and knees, but then I'd probably puncture the foam, which was strong but not indestructible. I stacked my eight-by-eight sheet against the wall, looking around for a box to stand on to reach the top. After dozens of practice drawings, I'd decided on a foreshortened three-quarter profile, so he'd be mostly head, trunk, and massive left flank, facing forward and fixing us with one small, kind, wrinkled eye. I wasn't drawing freehand, I was transposing proportional sections from grid to grid, final drawing to foam sheet.

Feet. Consider the function, I learned a million years ago in art school. The function of an elephant's feet was to hold up several thousand pounds of elephant. Big, round, platform feet at the ends of massive shapeless leathery legs, skin sagging down in bags around what would be ankles on another animal. Great folds of skin at the backs of the shoulders, too, wattlelike, and I hoped that was realistic—would an elephant that small have skin that wrinkled? Well, he was a little old elephant. He was born small. His parents were small and he was a chip off the old block. That's my story and I'm sticking to it.

The trunk was almost five feet long, curving in at the bottom, toward the dainty mouth. He was an Indian elephant, so his back was the highest point, higher than the shoulders, and arched slightly. The ears were big but not gigantic, not the flapping, sail-like ears on an African elephant—who, sadly, wouldn't be boarding the ark. Exclusions like that really gave me pause. I felt sorry about my choice of the grizzly bear, for instance (again, on recognizability grounds), over the black, brown, silver-tip, Kodiak, sloth, sun, Atlas, and spectacled bears. I liked to think old man Pletcher was, too, when he'd picked the walrus but not the seal, and when he'd decided to let the shark represent the entire fish kingdom. *Poor goldfish, poor salmon,* I hoped he thought; *poor speckled trout.*

Well, the rough draft silhouette wasn't bad. Flipping it over, I could see it would transpose well for the female. I'd make her a lighter gray, although it would mean buying another quart of paint; maybe True Value's "Smoky Moss"—the chip looked about right. Head wasn't flat enough on top, I saw. But the muscle in the middle of his forehead, the one that picked up his heavy trunk, I'd gotten that just right. And I liked one ear in and one ear out, but did it look like I'd just made a mistake? I loved the side view of his hip, round and bulging, a mass of moving muscle; clearly he'd just thrown his weight onto his left back leg and was about to pick up his right front. I'd nailed it.

It was when I was shading in the parallel horizontal lines on his trunk, making what amounted to a contour map, trying to show how the light struck the ridges and threw shadow into the hollows, that I had a brainstorm. I could do more than shade and highlight, *I could etch*. I figured it out by accident when I put too much pressure on my drawing pencil and cut into the foam. What if I *inscribed* the deepest wrinkly hollows on his trunk and face, those sad crevasses around his ancient eyes, and then painted dark paint into the etched parts and a second, lighter layer over the top? Texture! It would work, I was almost sure it would. However nicely I painted them, the problem of flatness, of having the animals resemble moving vertical platforms, stage sets on wheels, had plagued me since the beginning. This wasn't the complete answer—already the shortcomings were starting to occur to me—but it was a start. A really good start. I felt lit up inside, full of fresh energy. I'd experiment on scrap foam first, of course. With a pen? Knife? I'd try a craft knife with a new blade. I wanted more than a shallow indentation, I wanted real crags, dramatic black fissures. But without shredding the foam. And how well would gray latex cover black?

Stiff fingers and an ache in the small of my back woke me up from another trance. I'd forgotten my watch, but the edge of an early moon shone through the dusty, high-set barn windows. Late.

I stuffed the mess Landy and I had made, all the foam and wood cuttings, into plastic garbage bags, cleaned up my paints, tidied up the work area. I couldn't leave without looking at what I'd done this afternoon—the finishing touches on a jackrabbit, a nearly complete otter, and a rough drawing of an elephant. Not bad. Not half bad. But, my God, there were *so many more*. Landy needed more help, I could never do all these animals by myself in my spare time. Nobody seemed to be looking that fact squarely in the face.

I'd been hoping Jess would come down by now and talk to me, see what I was up to. I guessed he was still busy with milking. I turned off the heater, turned out the lights, closed the big barn doors. Blinked around in the chilly twilight like a mole. Moles might or might not blink, though; their eyes were approximately the size of pinheads, and since they spent their whole lives underground, probably all they could distinguish was strong light from darkness. I had to do a mole soon; I'd been reading up.

The hum of the milking machine drew me across the bumpy yard to the open, light-filled doors of the milking parlor. Inside, cows stood eight on a side, on two raised platforms over a shallow pit, where Jess and his helpers, Mr. Green and two neighborhood boys, went from cow to cow hooking up milking apparatus. I could never get over how docile cows were, how they plodded into their individual stalls on their own, stopped, and patiently stood until it was their turn to be milked. Why didn't they ever stampede? Jess had laughed when I'd asked him that. "They're peaceable by nature," he'd said, "and anyway, milking's what they like best. After food."

I stood just inside the doorway, enjoying the warmth, watching the mechanical but still earthy process of cow milking. Jess, in rubber boots and rubber gloves, washed the udder of an all-black Holstein with paper towels and disinfectant, then squirted a little milk out of each teat by hand. As he attached the rubber-lined suction cups, the milking machine made four soft, distinct sucking sounds. I glanced at the cow's broad black face, expecting bliss, but it didn't appear to change.

They were almost finished, I could tell from the urine and manure sights and smells. When they first started, it was neat as a pin in the milking parlor; then slowly everything went to hell. When it was over, they hosed it down, every surface, and soon everything was clean and neat again. What a job.

What a life! It wasn't one I'd ever envisioned for my wild, romantic boy, even though it was the only one Jess ever really wanted. At least, that I knew of. He told me something once: he said he hoped he was a mixture of his mother and his father, some of each, but not all of either. It made me wonder if he was afraid of his mother's illness. Maybe the hard physical work, the quiet cycles, the slow, unsurprising routine of Jess's days were a totem for him, a hedge against—craziness. If so, I didn't know what I thought about that. It was working, but was it sad? Was it funny? The problem was, I didn't know if Jess was happy or not. I couldn't tell—he'd turned into a mystery to me. Something else I never expected.

Mr. Green pressed a button in the tile wall of the pit, a metal gate slid open, and a line of milked cows clopped out of the parlor and off to an outdoor pen, where troughs of hay silage waited for them. Another gate opened; a new line of cows plodded in. Jess looked up and saw me. His whole face changed. Gladdened.

He couldn't be a mystery, I knew too much about him. He had a crescent-shaped scar on his right shoulder blade; he got it leaning into a truck engine when the hood slipped and fell on his back. He was thirteen; it was his father's '62 Ford pickup. He taught himself to play the guitar when he was fourteen. His favorite musician had been James Taylor. When we were sixteen, he showed me how to press my forehead into a cow's soft, bulging side and milk her with firm, gentle, rhythmic pulls, squirt, squirt, squirt, squirt. "Don't let your hair tickle her skin, Carrie, she's real sensitive, she can feel everything." The lanky boy with the long, strong fingers gave me my first grown-up lesson in sensuality when he taught me to milk that cow. Yes, he did, and in respectful treatment of the opposite sex. I wanted him to touch me with the same sureness and solicitude as he touched those big bovine ladies, great heavy flaunters of their own femaleness. That milking cows had a sexual component shouldn't have come as any great surprise, but in my adulthood I wrote it off as adolescent hormones in tumult. Now I saw I was wrong. It wasn't a function of age, but of susceptibility.

He stripped off his gloves, calling over something to Mr. Green, who glanced up and waved to me. He was a nice man, Mr. Green, but he was getting old. He wanted to retire and go live with his daughter in North Carolina, and Jess kept talking him out of it. Selfishly—he was the first to admit it. Mr. Green thought building an ark was the funniest thing he'd ever heard of in his life.

"Hey," Jess said. He had an endless stockpile of scruffy clothes. Cow tending was filthy work; why would he dress up? It was always a bit of a shock, though, the first time I saw him in his work clothes. Compared to his city councilman clothes, that is, or his man-about-town clothes. He led a double life. Tonight it was stained khakis torn at the knees, a frayed shirt, a dingy gray cardigan sweater, and a shapeless windbreaker with a broken zipper and both pockets ripped off. "Hey," I said, and we went outside and leaned against the side of the building, gazing off at the livid, streaky sky. "Smells like spring," Jess said, and I inhaled, but all I could smell was cow. "Come in the house," he said, "have some coffee or something—have a drink."

"I can't, have to go home. What time is it?"

"About six."

"I told Ruth I'd be home by six."

"What's she up to today?"

"Studying for a French test at a friend's."

"I thought she might come over with you. Since it's Sunday."

"She didn't want to," I admitted. "She thinks this is so crazy, Jess, she thinks we're all nuts." This morning she'd informed me, with much scorn and derision, "*God,* Mom, you are getting so *weird.*" I said, "Oh, really? You're going to be ten times weirder than I am." "No *way*. How do you figure?" "No one's stopping you," I said, thinking of my mother. "No one's holding you back."

Jess smiled in sympathy. "I know it, we embarrass the hell out of her. How can you blame her?" I loved it that he liked Ruth, and not just because of me. "So what did you do today?" he asked.

"The elephant—the drawing for it. Oh, Jess, I think it's really going to be good."

"Let's see. Show me."

"No, I can't, I have to go." Neither of us moved, though. "What do you think Eldon would say if the tiger was flying through the air? Not standing or walking, but *pouncing*." I had a picture of it I couldn't get out of my head—all four big-pawed legs of the tiger straining forward, the muscular tail flying up and back, toothy mouth wide open, ears flat, and the whole thing at about a seventy-degree angle. A huge, open-air leap.

"How would it stay up?"

"Dowels coming up from the wooden base—from a distance you wouldn't see them. I'm only talking about eight or ten feet off the ground. But do you think it sounds too . . . predatory?"

"I think it sounds terrific. He might not, though."

"Well, he said he wanted realism. He doesn't want cartoons or smiling faces, he doesn't want to anthropomorphize the animals at all—he said that." That's when I said I'd help—when I found out Eldon and I shared the same ark aesthetic.

"True," said Jess, "but he might not want people to think too hard about what the tiger's going to eat on the ark for forty days." He licked his lips. "Tasty chickens, handsome gazelles. Tender, juicy rabbits."

"I never thought of that. Rats—which I don't have to do, luckily. Oh, Jess, you should *see* the elephant."

"Show me."

"I can't. Anyway, you're still working."

"No, we're done."

"You're not, you have all the washing up to do." After the milking came the cleaning, another half hour of washing, rinsing, and scouring until the milking parlor gleamed and the cooling room shone. Then all the record keeping; Jess had to keep track of how many gallons of milk every cow gave at every milking. "I don't see how you can build an ark with all the other work you've got to do," I said. "Oh God."

"What?"

"That sounded like my mother."

"Well, she'd have a point. I'll have to hire another man to help with the milking until this ark's finished." He rubbed his eyes, and I saw how tired he was. "I know it's only a platform, but it still has to float, and I'm not a boatbuilder."

"You'll figure it out. It's basically a raft, right?" He and Landy had explained the latest design they'd come up with. "With a sort of faux hull and two fake stories on top?"

"In theory. It still has to float," he repeated ominously. "And take a man's weight so we can load it with animals."

"I was thinking," I said. "Are you doing portholes?"

"Portholes?"

"You could do fake portholes, just painted circles—but I could paint faces looking out of them. It would be a way to get more animals on board."

"More animals on board."

There weren't many people I could say this to. Maybe only Jess. "Isn't it sad to you that the coyote doesn't get to go? Or the cougar? Or the crow or the penguin—these guys all have to die in the flood. They're going to be extinct. I'm just concerned about the differentiation of species, that's all, the proliferation—whatever it's called."

He kept his head down, but I could see his lips curve when he smiled. It made me smile. I was leaning against the milk parlor, pressing my palms to the wood siding, watching my breath condense in the air. Jess picked up one of my hands. I looked at his face as he stared down at my palm, still smiling, moving his thumb across the soft calluses I was getting at the base of my ring and middle fingers. It felt right to touch him, not shocking at all. Like walking through the snow in new leather boots. *About time.*

But then, just as I thought he would lift my hand and put a kiss on it, I took it away. Took it back. *Mine, you can't have it.*

We shoved our empty hands into our coat pockets and went quiet. What did I want? What the hell did I want? Some things never changed, and my endless capacity to disappoint Jess was one.

"Ruth says you're seeing Brian now."

That took a second to process. "No, I'm not. Ruth told you that? It's not true."

"Okay," he said neutrally.

"We went out to dinner. Believe me, I'm not seeing Brian."

"All right."

"When did she tell you that?"

"Couple of weeks ago."

I'd kill her. As soon as I got home. I'd begun to put that night out of my head. At work, Brian acted as if nothing had happened. I'd tried to copy his obliviousness—it seemed the only way we could work together—but I wasn't as good at it as he was. I wanted to confide in Chris, but I couldn't. She liked him, she'd known him longer, she'd be loyal to him; I couldn't disillusion her to make myself feel better. So, like Brian, I was pretending nothing had happened.

Jess watched me. "I can't come again until Wednesday," I told him. "But then I can get off work early, be here by four or so. Is that okay?"

"Yes."

"Will you be here?"

"Either here or at the Point."

"Okay, then." I hugged my arms, cold all of a sudden. "Well, I better go, let you get back to work. Oh—I can't come next weekend, either. Not at all."

He nodded slowly, as if he'd expected that.

"I want to, I wish I could, but I can't."

"Doesn't matter."

"We're going to Washington. My mother and Ruth and I. For the weekend."

"Ah."

"Yes, it should be interesting." I took a few steps backward, toward my car. But he didn't follow, so I stopped. "Girls together. I just hope we don't kill one another."

"How's your mother's petition going?"

I winced. Sore subject. Mama got her women's club to start a petition drive against the ark on the grounds that public property can't be used for religious purposes. "What do you think Eldon thinks about all the publicity the Arkists are getting?" I asked Jess instead of answering.

"Does your mother know you come here, Carrie?"

"Not—yes—well, no—" I stopped, rueful and defensive. "She knows I want to help."

He smiled.

"I'll tell her tonight," I said recklessly. "I have to call her anyway about the weekend. I'll make a *point* of mentioning it. That I come here as often as I can—which isn't that often anyway."

"Why?"

"Why what?"

"Why tell her?"

I lifted my arms and let them drop. "Why did you ask me?"

"No reason. Curious."

We stared at each other, me anxious, him amused. Maybe; I really couldn't tell what Jess's smile meant, I just knew I didn't like it.

"I'm not afraid of what my mother thinks. I'm not eighteen, you know." Just saying it made me feel like a child.

He said, "That's good"—but now there was nothing he could say that didn't sound like tolerance or sarcasm or condescension. Or baiting. He knew it, too. He kept smiling.

"Oh, good-bye. I'm leaving."

"'Night," he called as I strode away. "I'll be here on Wednesday, Carrie. I'll make a *point* of it."

Oh, now he was mocking me? I got in my car with jerky, frustrated movements, and drove too fast down his rough, stony driveway. Why was it any of his business what I'd told my mother? And why was I angry? I didn't know, but it felt good. Inappropriate, unwarranted, and fine. It felt like just the ticket. I hoped he was mad, too. *About time.*

We'd been through a lot together, but the one thing we'd never been with each other was angry. Why was that? In twelfth grade, when I wouldn't sleep with him, he was understanding and I was guilty. When I wouldn't marry him, he was sad and I was guilty. When we were together after the reunion and I let him down again, he was numb and I was guilty.

I hated this pattern. I'd have enjoyed a good fight, a yelling match, maybe some pushing and shoving. "You hurt me!" he could say, and I could shout back, "I know! How do you think that makes me feel!"

I wasn't myself anymore. I felt as if I were on a drug; a good drug for once, but still a new and unfamiliar one. I couldn't stand confrontation, I'd never liked mixing it up with people—but I would really have enjoyed starting a fight with Jess. I thought that was a good sign. It might mean we'd turned a corner.

Either that or I'd entered the perimenopause.

15

Blah Blah, etc., etc.

Spring's here. Mom let me skip school on Friday, and the three of us, me, her, and Gram, drove up to D.C. for the weekend. I got to drive, but only as far as Gainesville, because after that comes I-66 and then—gasp!—the Beltway, and God knows I'd have killed us all if I'd been the one driving on—faint!—the Beltway. So Mom and I had to switch around in the front seat while Gram ran into the ladies' room at the Exxon and peed for like the fourth time since we left home. I wonder if she's got something wrong with her, but she says no, she's always like this.

It was fun driving up, actually. I've done a lot of stuff with my mom and my grandmother before, but this was the first time I ever felt like I was one of them, not a little girl among the grown-ups. Like we were three women going on an adventure together. Part of it was because Gram said things in the car she usually waits until I'm not around to say, things I don't even necessarily want to hear, like how this trip was the longest time she'd been away from home in two years because Grampa never wants to go anywhere. And how what she thought would be their nice retirement, traveling around and doing things together, etc., etc., was apparently just a dream and is never going to happen. She didn't laugh or make it a joke, either, the way she usually does. Her voice got high and thin, and nobody said anything for a long time, and then I heard her blow her nose, and that was the end of that.

Mom looked miserable. I wonder what she'd have said if I hadn't been there. I mean, it was her own father Gram was dissing.

It's true Grampa can be sort of a drag, and I can see how being married to him would bring you down sometimes, especially if you wanted somebody who'd talk to you. But I never liked it when Mom used to say bad things about Dad. She didn't do it very often (and now she never does, just the opposite, I never even knew she liked him so much), and even then it was only little things, like how he left his beard hairs in the sink or he was too negative or he didn't try hard enough to be sociable to their friends. I hated it, though, and I'd leave the room when she started, I'd never stick around and sympathize, even if I could see her point. I didn't know who I was supposed to be being loyal to, her or him. When they'd fight, I'd get scared and think, what if this argument keeps going and going and doesn't stop, what if it goes on to its natural conclusion and they decide they don't like each other and split up? So I'd always leave, get the hell out, and try to think about something else. When I'd come back things would be okay again, silent but okay. She'd be depressed and he'd be in his office with the door closed, but at least the fight would be over.

So anyway, the trip up was pretty nice, especially when I was driving, and the hotel we checked into was incredible. It was on Massachusetts Avenue, and you could look down and see Dupont Circle from our eighth-floor windows. We had a suite; Mom and I were sleeping in the king-size bed in the bedroom and Gram got the pull-out sofa bed in the parlor. I hoped she didn't snore.

We spent all Friday afternoon looking at artwork. We took the subway to the Mall and went to the National Gallery. First we went to the East Building, which is all modern art, then the West Building, which is old art. I like both, but Mom prefers the modern and Gram only likes classical. My favorite of everything I saw was this special exhibit in the East Building by Monet, who is my favorite painter, who did gorgeous pictures of gardens, wheat fields, seascapes, and of course water lilies. He painted his wife, Camille, too. The info in the brochure said he cheated on her and had a child with some other man's wife two years before Camille died. After you find out something like that, it's hard to know how to feel about the person you used to like. For a while, like ten minutes, I didn't care for Monet's paintings as much as before, but then I got over it. "Artistic license," Gram said. "Men will be men." I wonder if Grampa ever cheated on her. I doubt it, not with a person, anyway. Maybe with a book.

Now that Mom thinks she's an artist again, she's gotten kind of obnoxious. We were looking at this painting by Monet called *The Highway Bridge at Argenteuil*, which is basically a river with a sailboat on the left and a bridge on the right. Well, imagine my surprise when she says to me and Gram, but loud enough for anybody else around to hear, that the dominant link between the four basic forms is the bridge, and isn't it neat the way the sailboat's mast joins the water, the sky, and the far shore, so your eye glides effortlessly—she really said "effortlessly"—across the canvas and into the depth of the picture and back to the surface, a constant interplay of lines and forms. She actually said "interplay."

So I said, "You know, saying 'form' is kind of like having an English accent, it makes people automatically think you're smart. Right, Mom? As soon as you say 'form,' you sound like you know what you're talking about, when really it doesn't mean anything. Thing, it means thing—why don't you just say the *thing* in the picture, why do you have to say *form*?"

She looked surprised. I must've sounded a little hostile. She started to push my bangs out of my face, but I backed out of reach. I *hate* when she does that. She said, "Well, but form is really more like a relationship than a thing. It's what *organizes* things. It dictates the content, like a sonnet or a ballet or—a rock-and-roll song." Oh, thank you for coming down to my level. "Form is really things in relation to other things, and art is the search for form. Which, if you think about it, is another way of saying it's a search for yourself. Art makes form out of chaos—or it finds form *in* chaos. What art is, is making form out of formlessness—"

I walked away.

But then when we were in the West Building looking at these gorgeous Turner seascapes, I couldn't help myself. I said, thinking this would get her—should've known—"I don't get why people paint at all anymore anyway. I mean, what's the point after they invented the camera, you know? Why bother?"

She tried to look really patient and like that wasn't the stupidest thing she'd ever heard. "Well, but think about it. If fifty people painted the same landscape, you'd get fifty different landscapes—or nudes, or vases. You don't paint to make a replica of the thing you're painting—"

"Sure you do."

"No, you don't, you paint it to share the special way you see it with the rest of the world. It's an *expression*."

"Of yourself."

"Yes."

"That sounds pretty egotistical."

"Self-expression? No, it's natural, it's—it's imperative, it's what we—"

"I think it's pretty selfish. Look what *I* painted, look how I made this building so abstract you can't even tell it's a building, stupid you." Meanwhile, I didn't really believe any of this, I just sort of couldn't stop.

"There's nothing selfish about self-expression," she says, starting to get impatient. "If anything, art brings you closer to other people. When you're painting—or whatever, writing a song—there's a feeling you get that you're part of things. You belong, you participate. It's like—it's almost like euphoria. It's the opposite of being alone. Rollo May says creativity brings us relief from our alienation, and I think it's true—I know for me it's—"

"So when you're making a giant squid out of Styrofoam in Jess's barn for the crazy people, you're, like, ecstatic? That's way cool, Mom, it's really great that you're not lonely when you're painting aardvarks, that's just a real relief to me personally.' And I walked off to look at the Courbets by myself. I don't even know why I was so mad, I just was.

After the museum, we went back to the hotel to change clothes, then we had dinner early in a café in Foggy Bottom so we could be near the Kennedy Center when our play started. Gram picked it, and it probably sounded like a nice play for us in the one-sentence review they do every other Sunday in the *Times Dispatch*. It probably said something like, "A mother and her daughter discover the true meaning of family in this heartfelt drama of pain and redemption." They just forgot to mention the heartfelt drama is set in Bosnia and the mother and daughter discover the true meaning of family when the mother shoots the daughter so the evil soldiers can't rape and mutilate her. God! We walked out like zombies! Everybody did! And if there was any redemption, I must've blinked and missed it, because all I saw was the pain.

In the cab on the way home, Mom goes, "Well, *that* was cheerful," and Gram gets huffy, pretending she'd liked it and saying life isn't *The Sound of Music* all the time and once in a while it's good to see how lucky we are compared to people in other lands, blah blah, etc., etc. There was this horrible scene in the play when they were starving and they had to eat a rat, an actual RAT (!!), and so I said to Gram, "Yes, and I myself have a much deeper appreciation for Mom's cooking now." Mom let out this snort, and Gram tried not to laugh, but she couldn't help it, and pretty soon we were snickering in this sort of guilty, embarrassed, but really gleeful way about the very worst things that happened in the play. I was worried the cab driver would think we were fiends or morons or something, but he never looked at us.

Then I couldn't sleep. Mom stayed up late talking to Gram in the parlor. So much for being one of the grown-ups. No, I couldn't stay up and watch Conan O'Brien. No, we couldn't order room service, no, I couldn't eat the macadamia nuts in the honor bar.

No, we couldn't buy a futon, no, I couldn't have a leather jacket, no, we couldn't go to Georgetown tomorrow. That's the only place I really wanted to go, but no, we can't go there. There's no subway stop, plus nowadays it's full of riffraff.

This would've been such a great trip if only I'd gone with anybody besides my mother and my grandmother.

I was wrong—what a day Saturday turned out to be! First thing, Mom got a call from her old college pal who lives in Maryland, finally returning *her* call and saying yes, she could have lunch with her today, how about at the Lord & Taylor in Chevy Chase. So we three spent the morning shopping at Filene's Basement on Connecticut Avenue (I got two pairs of leggings, this really cool sweater, blue with one red stripe across the front, I wore it right out of the store, and some underwear), and then Mom left to go meet her friend. Now it's just me and Gram. The plan was to walk around downtown, have lunch someplace, maybe get in the tour line at the White House, see Lafayette Square, see the Corcoran, etc., etc. Like, boring boring boring, but you do it because you're with your grandmother and everything is her treat.

So we're sitting on a bench on K Street, getting organized, getting our bearings, and Gram goes, "Do you really want to go to Georgetown?" I'm like totally crazed, but I say very coolly, "Oh, I don't know, I guess it's pretty far. I don't even know how we'd get there. You don't want to go, do you?" Gram can be strict and kind of scary sometimes. She scowls, looks me right in the eye, and goes, "Ruth. Do you or do you not want to go to Georgetown with me. Right now." I swallow and say, "Oh, Gram, that would be so great." She stands up, sticks her arm out, a cab screeches over, and off we go to Georgetown!

It is the coolest place! If I can't go to school there, I would very much like to live there. Over a shop or a gallery. I could live on the second or third floor over one of the really funky art galleries and get a job. I'd wear Steve Maddens and a long black skirt and a black sweater. The gallery would have high white or beige walls and be quiet as a library, and I would explain the paintings to good-looking rich people, earn huge commissions, and live in a loft and take lovers. This is a daydream, but it's not impossible.

So, Georgetown. We had to walk pretty slowly because Gram had on the wrong shoes and the brick sidewalks are rough and uneven. She says, before we even get out of the cab, "Put your purse strap around your neck and hold it tight at all times," like every other person we see is definitely a mugger. It's so ridiculous, I am *never* going to be like that when I get old, suspicious and distrustful and always scared, I'd rather get robbed than go through life with that attitude. Mostly we just walked around M Street and Wisconsin Avenue, looking at the people and the stores. The thing about Georgetown is that at first it's almost depressing, you're like, I'll never be this cool, I'll never be this rich, I'll never be rich enough to be this cool. You're embarrassed by yourself. But then that starts to wear off and you get used to it or something and it's not so bad, although still you have this, like, yearning inside, you're wishing so hard you belonged and you know you don't. Sometimes I feel like my head will blow up if I don't grow up soon, if I don't get out of this life soon. This awful life, which is like being in prison or locked in a little dark room and nothing's happening, NOTHING, except that I'm ridiculous and everybody is laughing at me, or they would be if they could see inside my head.

Anyway. We went in a store that sells nothing but kites. We went in a store that sells nothing but maps. Clayborne is so lame. God. We have a few cute shops near the college, like the Book Stop and Pearl's Jewels and the candle store, but compared to Georgetown they're just cheap imitations. I really think I need a leather coat. Black or brown, I can't decide. Black. (Krystal wouldn't like it, though, she won't even wear leather shoes, she won't even drink milk or eat cottage cheese because it comes from a cow.) We went in a store that sells nothing but hats, and Gram said I could get one. So I got a cloche hat! I didn't even know I wanted one until I saw it. It's beige ("granite," according to the saleslady) and made of soft, soft wool and it's really me, everyone agreed. Although how that can be I don't know because it's very sophisticated. It makes me look much older, like nineteen or twenty, especially if I wear my sunglasses. I LOVE IT. No one in Clayborne has a hat like this, but that goes without saying.

We were in a restaurant called the Purple Dog having lunch (grilled pita goat cheese pizza for me, turkey sandwich for Gram) and there was this lady in the booth across from us. By herself. About twenty-eight, I guessed, no older. She had long shiny black hair pulled back in a barrette, down to about her shoulder blades, just straight back, no bangs or anything. She had small silver cluster earrings and a ring, a thin silver band, on the middle finger of her left hand, and no other jewelry. She had on gray slacks, like boot pants, and a black sweater, maybe cashmere. Black two-inch platform shoes, not leather but the stretch fabric kind. She'd already eaten, so she was just having coffee. And she was reading a book, but I couldn't see the title. A paperback with a really tasteful cover, not like a romance or anything. Once she pulled her sweater sleeve up, and I saw her bracelet tattoo. Tiny, just little blue links exactly like a delicate chain bracelet, all the way around her wrist. And when she got up, she put on a cloak, not a coat, with this graceful, floppy hood in back, and she had no purse, she just took money out of her pocket to pay.

She left. Gram said, "What's wrong with you?" and I said, "Nothing," but I don't know, I had this feeling. Worse than just how pathetic my life is, worse than, Here I am in this totally cool restaurant in Georgetown with my grandmother. It was like, Well, I might as well be dead. I'll never have what I want because I don't even know what I want. I look out at the people walking by on the sidewalk and think, Am I like her? Her? Who am I like and when will I know? When will I grow into myself? Ever? I love my new hat, but it's just not enough. If I had everything the black-haired lady has, it wouldn't be enough either. You have to know who you are on the inside before you can start decorating yourself, and in my case, there's nobody home, just ghosts going, "Hello? Anything happening?" Nobody can even see me.

"How's that boy you like? That Raven," Gram said deliberately—trying to make up for the time she called him Herring. "Is he still in the picture?"

"He's just a friend, Gram, I never said I *liked* him." I didn't mention he got suspended for three days last week for bringing his bull snake, Rocky Horror, to school. He said it was to show that the vast pet kingdom is wider than servile and obsequious dogs and cats, but I think it was just to scare girls.

"Oh, I see." She looked like she didn't believe me. Well, I don't know if I was telling the truth or not, because I haven't figured out what I think of Raven. I think if he's ever going to he should've asked me out on a regular date by now. Does he think I go around kissing guys in graveyards all the time? Ever since it happened he's been acting like it didn't. Fine by me, it's not like the earth moved or anything, I mean, big effing deal. I just think it's stupid to pretend something didn't happen when it did. It hurts people's feelings. It makes people feel like they don't exist.

"Want dessert?" Gram said. I hemmed and hawed a while, "Oh, I don't know, do you?" until she called the waitress over and told her we'd have two mousse fudge brownie cakes with vanilla ice cream and one cup of coffee.

I studied Gram, trying to look at her through the eyes of a stranger. Like, did she look like my faculty advisor? I could be a Georgetown student and she could be my art history teacher or my Victorian lit professor. She was trying to get to know me better because I exhibited much promise in one so young. She didn't have lunch on a Saturday with students very often, in fact never, but she was making an exception in my case. She wanted me to cowrite an important scholarly article with her, and she was trying to charm me because she was afraid I might transfer to a superior department at Columbia University.

If it weren't for her clothes, which are always too dressy and colorful and prissy, too Clayborne Women's Club, Gram really could look like a college professor. She wears her gray hair pulled back in a loose bun, no part, no bangs, but it's not as bad as it sounds, in fact it suits her. She's getting saggy in the face, but she's still pretty. Well, "handsome," that's a better word; she reminds me of a picture I saw at the museum by somebody, maybe Picasso, of Gertrude Stein, only Gram is thinner and grayer. But she still has that sort of rock solidness or something, like she can't be moved. And she's still got really good legs. She always says all three of us Danziger women, her, Mom, and me, have the same great legs. It's sort of a family saying.

She signaled the waitress for our check. "Your mother tells me she's been spending a little time over at Jess Deeping's," she said.

"A *little*. She's over there constantly."

"Is that right. How often?"

"At least one night a week, and always one weekend day, half day, I guess, morning or afternoon." It didn't sound like that much when I said it. It felt like much more.

Gram pursed her lips and shook her head. "Ridiculous."

"I know, it's so ridiculous!"

"I don't know what she's thinking."

"I know! It was okay when she was making the stupid flower arrangements, at least she was home, but now she's *never* home."

"It's irresponsible." She blotted her lips with her napkin and said casually, "Has she had any more evenings out with Brian?"

"*No*, Gram." We agreed on everything about the ark, how dumb and embarrassing it was, but we didn't agree on Mr. Wright. When I told her Mom went out on a date with him, she was *glad*. I couldn't believe it!

"Does she talk about him? What does she say?"

"Nothing, Gram, she doesn't say anything. She used to, but not anymore." Not since their date. She's probably in love with him and doesn't want me to know. Nah, but there must be some reason she hardly says his name anymore. "She likes Chris a lot," I said. "They're getting to be pretty good friends."

"Mm," Gram said, not interested.

I switched back to the subject we were together on. "I just don't get these animals, you know? There's so many things Mom could be doing around the house. Like the downstairs powder room, she's been saying forever that that's the next project, and after that, redoing the side porch. Doesn't charity begin at home?"

Gram laughed, as if I'd said something funny—like I was a child and I'd said something inappropriate but almost grown-up. Well, *doesn't* charity begin at home? I don't think it's unreasonable to expect your widowed mother to stay herself for a decent length of time, her same *old* self. That seems like common sense to me, regular human decency. You don't rock the boat, you don't go out and change your whole life, no, you try to provide stability for your loved ones. I.e., me.

So what did Mom do that afternoon while she was out with her old college pal? She got her hair cut! It looked okay, it looked pretty good, actually, after I got over the shock of how short it was, but I couldn't help wondering if she'd done it for Mr. Wright. I'm not saying she has to be single the rest of her life. She's not that old. I don't mind if she gets married again someday, like five or ten years from now or so. Everybody needs companionship, and anyway, by then I'll be long gone.

That night we had dinner in a Vietnamese restaurant near the hotel. I thought it would be a good time to ask Gram what everybody in our family died of. You have to put that down on medical forms when you go to the doctor, for one thing, plus it's just good to know your genetic predispositions. Krystal says heredity is way overrated, and I'm sure that's true. Still, you should know what's behind you so you can be prepared for what might be ahead of you.

Turns out we're riddled with diseases and conditions, especially on the Danziger side. On the Van Allen side, Dad's father had a heart attack, which was news to me, but his mother was killed in a car accident when he was eight, so only one disease there, and afterward he went to live with his grandparents, who were old even then, and they died of old age when he was about twenty. So that side's not too bad. But Mom's side, God, they had everything. Gram's father, my Great Grandfather O'Hara, who I never met, had diabetes and cirrhosis of the liver, Grandmother O'Hara had a stroke, Gram's brother Ralph had phlebitis, glaucoma, gout, and sciatica, and she thinks he died of blood poisoning, and her brother Walter had eczema and an ulcer and died of pneumonia. Meanwhile my grandfather's father had prostate cancer and his mother had lung cancer from smoking since she was thirteen. His brother, my great uncle Edgar, had epilepsy and a stroke, and his sister Fan is still alive but she has anemia and cataracts.

God! I mean, it's a wonder the ones who are left have the nerve to go outside! Right now I myself have a sore knee, for example, plus I have motes in my eyes. (Not always; sometimes.) I'm not saying it's rheumatoid arthritis, and I'm not saying it's macular degeneration. But it could be, it's certainly possible, and I just think it pays to be aware and take precautions. Sometimes my heart beats too slowly, I can hardly feel my pulse, it's like it's disappearing. Do I do nothing? No. Do I do something? Yes, I take arjuna, 500 milligrams two times a day—Krystal gives me a discount—and I do the "thumb walk" every night on the ball of my left foot, which is the reflex point for heart disease. So at least I have some peace of mind. Because you can be going along thinking all's well, that little cough is just a cold, and *whammo,* turns out your immune system's breaking down. You've got AIDS, you've got leukemia, you've got

Lou Gehrig's disease. My dad—he felt fine until all of a sudden. Because he had no idea. He wasn't thinking. We can control a lot of things with our minds, but first we have to *know*. That's the trick. We have to be aware.

So that's what I'm doing, just trying to be aware of everything. Like, sometimes a little muscle under my eye twitches. It could be an early sign of a brain tumor, or it could be Parkinson's. Or it could be nothing. Time will tell. The important thing is that I know about it, it can't sneak up on me. Because I am vigilant.

16

SO MUCH FOR CANDOR

"Your daughter wants a tattoo."

"I know. Is she asleep?"

"Just about." Mama closed the outer of the two doors to the bedroom and padded over in her bedroom slippers. "With her eyes open. What does she write in that journal? I went to kiss her good night, and she covered it up like it was the atom bomb formula."

What was it I said the other day that had gotten such a disgusted rise out of Ruth? I couldn't remember; some outdated expression, though, like "atom bomb formula." Her scorn had known no bounds. I'd felt her hate—there was really no other word. It hurt me, probably too much. I knew, I really did understand that for Ruth right now I was the target, the designated punching bag, if only because there was no one else for her to hit out at. But it still hurt. Had I given my mother pain like that? I must have. Not in the same way, I didn't think, not with such undisguised callousness. I'd hidden my adolescent contempt more cleverly than Ruth did. More charitably? Probably just more fearfully.

Mama groaned under her breath and lowered herself onto the sofa, putting her feet up on the coffee table. "She wants a silver ring and a cloak, too, she's decided. She wants to start drinking coffee. When did you start drinking coffee?"

"I don't remember. College, I think. She loves her new hat—thank you for buying that for her, Mama."

"She looks adorable in it. You're going to have trouble with this tattoo thing, though." She leaned over to massage the toes of her right foot. "She's even trying to get me on her side. Fat chance. Of all the tacky fads!"

"I just want her to get through high school without having anything pierced, burned, or branded."

"Lots of luck. See if there's some juice in the refrigerator, will you? I don't know why, but I feel weakish."

"You shouldn't have let her run you around like that," I said guiltily. I found a bottle of orange juice and poured it in a glass. "Here. Want some peanuts?"

"She didn't run me around, not one bit. She was an absolute angel. Carrie, I can't get over your hair. I guess it suits you, but it's so *different*."

"I know." I leaned over to see myself in the mirror behind the couch. "I don't know why I did it—I wasn't planning on it. Pure impulse."

"And with a complete unknown, that's what gets me. You could've been scalped!"

I could've been. But Mr. Harold had done right by me—I hoped. "I'm too old for long hair," I'd told him, hoping he would disagree. He had, but only politely, then he'd proceeded to whack off my hair—which I'd been wearing in a braid down my back—to about collar length. "Volume," he kept saying, "you need more volume. More spatial extension." Now I couldn't stop looking at myself. I felt naked and fascinating. Voluminous.

"What possessed you? I didn't even know you were thinking about cutting it."

"Do you hate it?"

"No, it's cute. Really. Makes you look young."

That's what Ruth had said, only with a suspicious glint in her eye. "I guess it was seeing Barbara today," I told Mama, sitting down again, putting my feet up next to hers. "She's even older than I am, half a year or something, but she looks terrific. You should see her."

"Have I ever met Barbara?"

"She came home with me in junior year for spring break. Blonde hair, really attractive? She had a boyfriend who called late every night—"

"Oh, I remember. He was a law student at Georgetown. Did she marry him?"

"No."

"Too bad."

"She married a doctor."

"Well, that's good."

"But they split up. *Then* she married a lawyer."

"Oh." Doctors and lawyers were good; divorce was bad. Mama tapped her lips, in a quandary.

"Now she has three kids and a rich husband, a house in Chevy Chase, and a cleaning lady. And a golf habit."

"You envy her."

"Well, not the golf habit. Maybe the cleaning lady." I laughed, but she just looked at me. "Well, sure, Mama, in a way. Her husband's alive. Her youngest child is four and a half, so he still needs her. He even still *likes* her."

She patted me on the hand. "You're still in mourning for Stephen, that's all that's wrong with your life. Things will get better, it just takes time. It does, I can't help it if that's a cliché. And you've got a good job now, interesting work, new friends."

"I know, I'm all right—I didn't mean to sound like I'm miserable. I'm not."

"You still have to go through the process, that's all. You can't skip steps when you're grieving, much as you might like to."

Odd advice coming from Mama, even if she'd just read it in a women's magazine. What was her motive in telling me I wasn't through grieving for Stephen? "Ruth said something that struck me the other day," I said deliberately. "She said that life without her father isn't that different from the way it was before we lost him."

"Oh, I can't believe she meant that. Not that way. What did you say?"

"I don't remember. Maybe I didn't say anything."

"Well, it isn't true, of course."

"It is, though." For once, I wasn't going to let her tell me what my life was like. "It is, in a way. Our family—Stephen was the shadowy one. He was barely there, Mama. The *family* was Ruth and me, we were the—the noisiest or something. We did everything and he . . . observed and critiqued. That's it. He observed and critiqued."

"Oh, but he loved both of you very much."

"Well." Something else it was time to set straight. "He loved us as much as he could."

"Yes. Yes, he did." She set her glass down with a sharp click.

"It's true, I miss him sometimes, I feel forsaken and hurt and lonely, but—the thing is, Mama, I felt that way before I lost him."

She stood up. "Everybody's lonely," she said shortly, and walked out of the room.

Well, well, so much for candor. Press the wrong button and your frank mother-daughter conversation flew out the window. And yet I was *sure* one of the reasons she'd suggested this weekend was so that we could talk, really try to be close again. I wanted it, too, but my expectations were more modest. I knew my mother: she wanted our old, easy friendship back, but only on her terms. She wanted everything to be the way it was twenty-five years ago. When I was her best friend. Before I went away to college and got all those ideas that didn't agree with hers. The good old days.

Barbara had talked a lot about her mother this afternoon. I remembered Mrs. Cavanaugh well, a vivacious, red-haired widow, wild about golf, youthful, full of life. At twenty, I was envious because Barbara's mother was so young and cool. "I've lost my best friend," she told me today, teary-eyed over the second glass of wine. "I miss her every day, Carrie. I could tell her things I couldn't tell anyone else in the world." I could hardly imagine it. "Not that she didn't drive me absolutely crazy," she said, "in fact, nobody did it better. The funny part is, I'm getting more like her every day. Isn't that a good joke? If we live long enough, we turn into the person who gave us the most grief, the one we tried so hard to separate from. I just think that's hilarious."

Oh, yeah, delicious, hilarious irony. While we shuddered in horror, we drew closer and closer to the object of our revulsion, finally fated to understand her. To *be* her. The punishment and the reward all in one.

The toilet flushed; water ran. Mama came out of the bathroom and crossed the room to where her suitcase lay open on the floor beside the sofa. She squatted over it and pulled out her nightgown.

I started to get up. "I didn't think it was so late. You're probably exhau—"

"Stay, sit, sit, I'm not tired. I just want to get out of this dress."

I'd forgotten her trick of taking off or putting on clothes without showing any skin. The dress was unzipped and pulled off the shoulders, bra modestly removed with the back turned, flannel nightgown donned over the head, then dress, half-slip, girdle, and stockings pulled down from underneath. The brief flash of my mother's pale, fleshy back, soft and sagging where it used to be firm, gave me a tender, hollow feeling. Protective. I didn't want life to teach her any more hard lessons. If it meant she was happy, I wanted her to stay exactly as willful, overbearing, and controlling as she was right now. How long would that resolve last, though? Another five minutes?

She sat down beside me, opened a jar of cold cream—Jergens; the flowery scent smelled as old as time—and began to smear it over her cheeks. "I'm not so sure I should've told Ruth about her great-grandfather," she said.

I knew what she meant, but I said, "Told her what about her great-grandfather? Which one?"

"My father."

"Oh—you mean about the cirrhosis?"

"She probably can't make the connection now, but she will eventually. Between liver disease and alcoholism," she explained, a little testily, when I continued to look blank. "You know your grandfather was a drunk."

"Well." I did and I didn't. Mama had never said it like that before: *a drunk*. But I had speculated. I'd known something wasn't right about Grampa O'Hara—whom we never went to see, although he only lived an hour away in Nelson County. On a farm. Some sort of tenant farm, apparently, that she could never mention, and so she rarely did, without a visible tremor of disgust. The fact that she was saying these things now put me on the alert.

"And he wasn't the only one. Ralph drank, too, and Walter was heading that way before he died."

"I didn't know that. Did I ever meet Uncle Ralph?"

"You were too little to remember. We only took you out there to see them once." The way she said *them*—it was the way she always spoke of her family, coldly, unsympathetically. "I couldn't wait to get out of that house."

"You left when you were eighteen." I knew this story. She'd gotten a job at an auto repair shop on Ridge Street in Clayborne. Pop was a student at Remington. They courted for two years, and married each other a week after he got his part-time instructor appointment.

"Seventeen. I've always said eighteen. Doesn't sound as tacky." She took a wad of clean tissues out of her robe pocket and began to wipe cold cream off her face. Softening, wrinkling old face, skin drooping at the strong jaws. She didn't look as sure of everything as she used to. The thing I disliked most about my mother was her bossiness, but if she lost that, who would she be? A diminished woman, not a new one. I didn't want that. I didn't know what I wanted.

"Seventeen?" I laughed. "You never told me that."

"I never told you my father and my brothers were moonshiners, either. And if you ever tell that to another living soul, I'll skin you alive."

"Mama!"

"Hush, you'll wake up Ruth."

I stared. "Moonshiners," I said in a thrilled whisper.

"Not even good ones. They drank up most of the product before they could sell it. We were dirt poor. I hated everything about my life. Nobody abused me—nothing like that, that's not what I mean. But they were nasty, loud, dirty men, wild men, and my mama just took it. She had about as much backbone as a crawfish. I got out. I got out and made something of myself."

I almost smiled, amazing as these revelations were. She didn't look very fierce in the old pink quilted robe, her face stripped of makeup. She didn't look very self-made. What she looked like—I'd have died before telling her—was the woman in old photographs of Grandma O'Hara.

"What do you mean, they were wild men?"

"Not abusive," she said again, "not in a physical way. They yelled all the time, drunk or sober. Everything revolved around them, they were the kings and my mama was their servant. So was I till I got out. I can tell you I never looked back."

"So you came to the big city, and Pop swept you off your feet."

"Swept me off my feet." She snorted. She closed the cold cream jar, wiped her hands with the last tissue, set everything aside on the coffee table. "I wanted a man who couldn't hurt me or change me. I wanted marriage because I thought it would keep me safe, but the last thing I wanted in a husband was gumption."

Gumption? She hadn't said anything I didn't know, but still, I felt defensive on Pop's behalf. "So you never really loved him?" I wanted a hot, stinging denial—I didn't care if it was true or not.

"I admired him. I loved it that he wasn't a country boy. He was a scholar—*that* swept me off my feet. He was probably poorer than

I was in those days, but he always wore a suit and a tie. You could never, ever understand what that meant to me."

"So you never—"

"I *learned* to love him. Your father is a fine man, he has plenty of good qualities, he most certainly does. A solid marriage comes along when both parties know what they want and aren't blinded by—" She waved her hand dismissively. "Extraneous things."

"Like what?"

"Unimportant details. Things that don't last."

Excitement, sex, chemistry, good looks—was that what she meant? What if she meant love? And I had an idea what this conversation was really about. Jess.

"You said you were lonely," she went on, fastening the top button of her robe. "I'm saying I just don't think it's that rare, that remarkable. Everybody's lonely. A man can't make you happy."

"I know that."

"You have to make your own happiness after you've picked as wisely as you can. You have to weigh things like compatibility, good blood, having the same goals—"

"Good blood?"

"Nobody has a perfect marriage, honey. Yours and Stephen's was as good as most."

"How do you know?"

"I observed. And mother knows best," she said, laughing quickly, making it a joke. "Never forget that."

I smiled back grimly. "Did you know I used to see a therapist when we lived in Chicago?" Of course she didn't know, I'd never told her. "One time he said to me, 'All my women clients come to me to talk about Mommy. But do you know, after a while it almost always turns out she's not the problem. It's Daddy.'"

We watched each other.

"About a year ago, Ruth said something. Just a casual remark, but it struck me. Stephen was in his study with the door closed—as usual. She wanted to tell him something, show him something, I don't remember anymore, and she was complaining to me because he wasn't available. She called him 'the Invisible Man.' And I remembered—that's what I used to call Pop when I was a kid. To myself. I'd seen the movie, I guess, and that's what I started to call him. The Invisible Man."

Mama shook her head slowly. "No, no, I don't see that. Stephen was nothing like George, if that's what you're getting at."

It was exactly what I was getting at. "I didn't think so, either." But then I saw them standing outside that night Stephen died, and it was like a puzzle coming together, the last piece in place. *Click*. "It's true, Mama. I married my father." How clever of me. From two different men, I got the identical oblivion and inattention, the same ironic, distanced, fastidious, cerebral frame of mind. A depressing insight, but it wasn't brand-new. Saying it to my mother gave it an unwelcome freshness, though, like a bad smell that hadn't had time to grow stale.

"No," she scoffed. "No, no. I mean, why *would* you?"

"Well, maybe . . . to get it right. That's why they *say* we do these things. You know, repeat the experience that didn't satisfy you in your childhood, try to make it work in adulthood."

"No, I don't think so. They're both academics, that's all. That's as far as it goes. Stephen had opinions, for heaven's sake. He had likes and dislikes, he had *ideas*. George . . ." She heaved a sigh and didn't finish—to my relief. I'd heard enough from her about my father's shortcomings for one night.

"Stephen had a temper," I conceded. "He did like to have his way." So did Pop, but he got his by quiet, passive means that were probably even more infuriating. "You know, we didn't really know each other that well when we married. Ten months. He was a scholar, of course, very smart, dedicated, very ambitious—like Pop." I whispered, "I think it's true, Mama. I think I married my father."

She looked as if she didn't know whether to laugh or cry.

"I think," I said, "I spent the first half of my marriage trying to fix it, and the second half trying to be happy in spite of knowing it was broken. Just trying to make the best of things. Do you remember that time I called you in the middle of the night? From Chicago, when Ruth was little? I started to tell you—oh, a little of what was wrong, and you said—well, I don't remember, but after that—" Yes, I did, I remembered perfectly; she'd basically told me to suck it in, get over myself, welcome to real life. "After that, I pretty much gave up trying to change things between Stephen and me. And now that he's gone, I worry that I was wrong. Maybe I should've done more, maybe I shouldn't have given up so easily. Do you remember that night?" I asked when she kept silent.

"I remember you were drinking." She pressed her lips together tightly. "I don't take drinking talk seriously."

Had I been drinking? It wasn't impossible. But—"I wasn't *drunk*, for heaven's sake. I wasn't!"

She shrugged: *Who's to say?* "Well, Carrie, I did not know you were that unhappy," she said disapprovingly. "I truly did not."

"I wasn't," I said, determined to be honest, although I wasn't sure why anymore. The intimacy we'd both wanted from this frank talk seemed to elude us more the longer it went on. "Or if I was, I didn't know it. I think I spent a lot of time in a daze, frankly, not happy, not unhappy. Sleepwalking."

I looked away, blindsided by longing, a sudden surge of possibility. *I could call Jess. I could dial his number and hear his voice. I could call him right now.*

"Sleepwalking," my mother repeated in a flat tone. "All I can say is, you could've done much worse. If Stephen was a little like George, why is that such a bad thing?"

"It's not—"

"One thing I know, life's too short to sleep through." She stood and started snatching up the tissues she'd thrown on the coffee table.

"I agree with you, I'm—"

"Maybe you'd better wake up and smell the coffee. You had a good husband, you've got a beautiful child—really a very privileged life in many ways. I hope you're not thinking of throwing it away for something that's not worthy of you. Count your blessings, that's what you should do. Get up, Carrie, I need to pull this sofa bed out."

"Mama, what are we talking about?" I said, not moving. "What am I throwing away? What's not worthy of me?"

"You've got a good job now, and you're lucky to have it. You've got a boss who's steady and safe, and he's interested in you. What's funny about that?"

"Nothing."

Oh, I was dying to tell her how steady and safe my boss was. I'd kept it from her for a jumble of lousy reasons—embarrassment, a need to keep her from being disillusioned, uncertainty over her reaction—she might not believe me, or she might find Brian and slug him. Telling her now seemed nasty, though; the timing was just too perfect.

She didn't like my smile, which must've looked more like a smirk. "So Brian Wright is not good enough for you? You're not interested in a man with prospects?"

"A man who wears a suit and tie, you mean."

"*What's wrong with that*?"

"Not a thing. You want to talk about this, Mama?"

She flushed. "What do you mean? We are talking. I'll tell you what I want—you to get up so I can make my bed and go to sleep. I'm tired, I'm an old lady."

"I take it that's a no." I was as angry as she was. I stood up, because I was used to obeying, but I wasn't finished. "I don't like the things you've been saying about the Arkists," I said, pulling the coffee table out of the way. She stopped throwing cushions off the couch and stared at me. "Why are you doing it? You can be opposed to the project, that's up to you, but why do you have to take the lead in it, Mama? You didn't have to start a committee, you didn't have to write a letter to the damn editor."

"Why shouldn't I? I'm a member of the community, I can voice my opinion."

"You know why. Because this *means* something to me."

She clucked her tongue and went back to work. "Foolishness. Your own daughter says you're neglecting her. And for what? *Ark animals*," she said in a harsh, sneering voice; if Ruth hadn't been in the next room, she'd have yelled it. "In a barn, with a farmer. *Two* farmers."

"Well, now we're getting to it. It's got nothing to do with civic duty or church and state or good taste or—what was it?—small-town aesthetics. I should've cut it out of the paper, because you really outdid yourself."

"I didn't write it, the committee did."

"But it's your committee."

"I don't understand your attitude."

"I'm explaining it to you."

"Not now you're not, I'm going to bed. Honestly, Carrie, I'm tired."

I looked at her across the low, beige-blanketed sofa bed, weighing the pros and cons of prolonging the argument. I wasn't used to picking fights with my mother, but I was even less used to her retreating from them. It seemed perverse, upside-down, and I had that impulse again to protect her. Anyway, we had a ritual: she decided what we fought about, I mollified her until I couldn't stand it, we argued, she won or I backed off, and it was over. Comfortable as an old sweater. Look where it had gotten us.

She turned away first, went to the closet to get down extra pillows. "So, tomorrow. Would Ruth hate it if we went to the Botanic Gardens after the National Cathedral? I'd like to go, but not if it's going to bore her to tears."

She was good at this. A timely change of subject, along with a subtle reminder of who was the host on this trip, who were the guests. Gracious guests humored generous hosts; they didn't start family fights at one in the morning.

Message received, Mama. We kissed cheeks, said good night, and retired to our separate camps.

I took a shower to calm down, get the argument out of my head. *In a barn with a farmer* kept ringing in my ears. After a little while the harshness my mother had given the phrase faded, though, and a gentler connotation took its place. I missed my farmer. Missed his barn. I put on my nightgown and stared in the foggy mirror at my new, alarmingly short hair, and wondered if Jess would like it. Men liked long hair on women—I'd always heard that. What if I'd made a terrible mistake?

He touched my hair the last time we were together. Wednesday afternoon, in the ark barn. I took half a day off from work and went to Jess's to paint animals. Landy wasn't there, he'd had to leave early to go see his father.

After he left, Jess didn't talk. He wasn't haughty or cold, he just didn't say anything. On the Sunday before, he'd held my hand, but three days later he wouldn't speak to me. Not that I blamed him—I'd pulled away, spoiling the natural progression. The unspoken natural progression. I think we both knew we were drawing closer—but slowly, slowly, and on my terms, of course. At my pace.

"Come and look at this, tell me if the ears look funny," I said in the dim, drafty barn, standing back from my almost-finished elephant. My masterpiece, I considered it in secret. Jess put down his drill and came to stand next to me. "No, they look fine." "Sure?" "Yes." He started to go back to his wheels.

"I'm sorry about the other day," I said quickly. "Getting defensive about my mother—God, that was stupid." I trusted him to know what I was really apologizing for. "I don't even know why I was mad. I thought I wanted to fight with you. But I don't, that's not what I want."

His eyelashes came down, shuttering his expression. My long, messy braid—gone now—lay on my shoulder, and Jess lifted his hand and stroked it with his fingers. What I felt was the slight weight of his wrist on my collarbone, strong as a burn. Through my jacket, two sweaters, and a T-shirt. "What do you want, Carrie?"

Oh, just everything. I wanted him, mostly, but I was still afraid of him. I wanted to honor my husband's memory. I wanted my mother to approve of me.

"If I told you," I said, making my voice playful, "would you give it to me? Everything I wanted?"

"No." He slid his fingers inside my collar and stroked my skin. "But I'd try."

I had to close my eyes. "I don't know anyone like you," I whispered, "I never have. I need some more time." I looked at him, half afraid I would regret my words, but he nodded. "I'm not running away this time, I swear. But I'm standing still. Please, Jess—you do, too. Wait. Because it would be so easy . . ."

"So easy to . . ."

"Go too fast."

He bent his head and put his face next to mine. "When you make up your mind, let me know it in words." The whisper of his breath on my ear made my skin tingle. "Write it on a big sign, Carrie. Hit me over the head with it. Because I don't want to miss it."

I think he kissed me then, but the quick, warm pressure on my cheek was so fleeting I couldn't be sure. He was smiling when he pulled away. He went back to screwing wheels onto wooden bases, but only for a few more minutes, and then he went off to milk cows. Leaving me in a flutter. I couldn't even finish my elephant.

I could call him now, I thought again. Dial his number and hear his sleepy voice. And say what? "I miss you. Don't give up on me. I'm sorry it's taking so long." He deserved that. But didn't he already know it? If not, I'd been miscalculating for weeks. Months.

"Let me know it in words," he'd said. Well, I would. I would. As soon as the time came.

Ruth had left the lamp on on my side of the king-size bed. She lay fast asleep on her back, one hand in a fist by her head, the other open on her rib cage. Under the thin blanket the slight curve of her breasts, small but definite, rose and fell, rose and fell with her silent breathing. Sometimes I hardly recognized her with her new, stranger's body. She didn't even smell the same. *Who are you?* I went around wanting to ask. If I had the power to stop it right now, stop time this minute, would I? Yes, in a heartbeat. But in a little while, I'd regret it.

Who would she finally choose, I wondered, settling in beside her gingerly, trying not to wake her—neither of us was used to a bedmate these days. Would she choose a man like her father, or a man as unlike him as she could find? Once I'd had that choice. God, God, I hoped for once the whole issue skipped a generation. If only we could go back to arranged marriages, or ban the institution entirely until people turned thirty. Forty. Thank God Ruth didn't have a regular boyfriend yet; she still dated in crowds. The only familiar, recurring face was Raven's, and I couldn't work up much worry about him. Which undoubtedly meant he was the one to worry about.

I leaned over to kiss the air above her cheek. She smacked her lips and turned over, carrying most of the sheet under her arm.

If we could just build cages around them. Big Plexiglas boxes on wheels that they could move about in, really be quite comfortable inside, but never get out of. Involuntary safety. Ruth getting her driver's license next summer was bad enough; the thought of her going away to college in two years was so awful, I couldn't even think about it. I couldn't—I pushed it out of my mind. I had a bit of a knife phobia, couldn't bear thinking about blades, so of course sometimes my nerves played perverse tricks and sent images to the brain of knives, razors, etc., etc.—a minor torture. Same thing with

Ruth and college: my nerves attacked me with random nightmare pictures of dormitories, libraries, caps and gowns. I shook myself and pushed them away. Horrible.

I turned out the lamp, tried to get comfortable. Couldn't sleep in hotels. Twenty years from now, would Ruth and I go away for weekends and tell each other secrets? Would she see me as the kind of mother she could bear to confide things in? But then again, I didn't really want her to have any problems she needed to confide. Mistakes, regrets, defeats, lost opportunities—I wanted her to miss out on them, breeze right by them through some incredible stroke of good fortune. Ruth's life had to be perfect.

I turned over on my side, drawing my knees up and cupping my hands under my chin: my comfort position. And prepared to be terribly disappointed.

17

Party of One

People were leaving and it wasn't even eight o' clock. "Old fuddy-duddies!" I called my friends to their faces, pretending I was kidding, but I wasn't. And it was a perfect night, mellow and almost warm, the prettiest sunset going down over the garage roof, bats starting to flicker in the purple sky. It was the first night of daylight saving time, which in my book is a cause for celebration in itself. "George," I yelled across the patio, "make me another whiskey sour!"

I headed inside to get the portable stereo. Music, that's what this party needed. Where the hell was Carrie? Should've been here two hours ago. Birdie was putting dirty glasses in the dishwasher. "Leave that," I ordered, reaching past her to unplug the boom box on top of the refrigerator. "Quit and come outside, right this minute."

She flapped her hands. "I just want to put these away before they get broken."

"At this party? Not a chance." I slung my arm around Birdie's waist and muscled her out of the kitchen. "I want people to *dance*. I've got a new tape, all songs from the fifties." It hit me. "My God, Bird—fifty years ago today, I was twenty years old."

"I was seventeen," she smirked—she never misses a chance to rub it in that she's younger. "Oh, I don't think anybody's going to dance, Dana. Golly, nobody's still here but the Hoopers and the Dodges."

And the Dodges were leaving. "No!" I cried, sticking my arms out to bar the way across the patio. "You can't leave yet, you *can't*.

Why do you have to go?" I heard the pretend-desperate note in my voice and wondered if I was getting drunk. Well, if not, it wasn't for lack of trying.

"Sorry, I know," Sylvia said, making a heartbroken face. She linked arms with silent, morose Harvey and leaned against him. "Tomorrow's an early day for us. Susie and Earl are coming, bringing their kids." She rolled her eyes, to say it was all too much, children and grandchildren, but what a good sport she was. Sylvia's a faculty wife, like me; the only reason we were friends at all was because our husbands taught in the same department for thirty years. We saw a lot of each other at faculty do's, we were always cordial, we got up to the exact same level of conversational intimacy—and retreated every time. Nothing in common. "Thanks *so* much for having us," she said, kissing me on both cheeks, "and happy *birthday*."

"Happy birthday," old sourpuss Harvey echoed. Hard to believe, but he had even less to say for himself than George. "G'night."

"Hell with 'em," I muttered, flopping down in the Adirondack chair George had put my new drink on. "Make one for Birdie," I called to him across the lawn. "Where do you s'pose Carrie is, Bird?"

"Oh, no, I don't need another thing, I'm—"

"And put some alcohol in it! Swear to God, that man cannot make a drink. Fifty-one years of marriage, and he's yet to make a good one. It's the ice-booze ratio that stumps him. What is so hard about that, would you tell me?"

"Why don't you make your own?"

"Because it's his job. I do everything else, he's not getting out of that one." I took a sip of whiskey sour. "Ek. Too much sour." I set it down to let the ice melt a while. "Nobody drinks anymore anyway, everybody's so goddamn old. We used to have *fun* at parties, didn't we?"

"We surely did. Wild parties."

"They *were* wild. Nobody went home at eight o'clock, that's for sure. My God. 'Course, that was before all the alcoholics died or went on the wagon."

Birdie yawned behind her hand.

I remembered the music. "I'm putting on that tape," I decided, and got up. I'd worn a long red dress, thinking it would be more festive than slacks. I tripped on the hem as I crossed the patio on the way to the electrical plug on the screen porch, had to grab the picnic table to keep my balance. "Damn shoes," I muttered, kicking them off. One flew up and landed on the table, and I left it there. After a little fumbling, I got the boom box plugged in and the right tape in.

Somebody had turned the volume up too high; "Come On-a My House" came out like a police siren. Birdie shrieked; George and the Hoopers turned around with irritable, alarmed faces. Where the hell was the volume knob? I found it, turned it down. Birdie took her hands off her ears.

"Dance with me," I said, pulling her up. She had on slacks, she could be the man. She was so scrawny and brittle, though, it felt more like dancing with a child.

"Oh, Dana, I don't want to dance!"

"You have to, it's my birthday. I'm gonna give you ca-handy," I sang, stumbling through a fox-trot step. Maybe this was a jitterbug. "When was the last time you danced? I can't even remember. Margaret Whiteman's girl's wedding, I think. I mean with a man." I spun Birdie into a turn. "You know what?"

"What?" Her cheeks flushed; she breathed with her mouth open. No stamina.

"It's very possible this is the last time you and I will ever dance. I'm talking about for the rest of our *lives*. Think about that, Bird."

"Honey, you're just drunk." She quit dancing, wouldn't be moved. "Come on and sit down, I'll make you a cup of coffee." Her face crinkled with sympathy, and I pushed her away.

"I'm not drunk, and I'm not feeling sorry for myself. Make me a cup of coffee and I'll pour it down your dress."

"There, you just proved my point." Wounded, she crossed to her chair and sat. "Pour it down my dress. Oh, sure. Somebody I know is going to have a big headache tomorrow."

The most vulgar phrase came into my head, the kind my generation wasn't allowed to say. Carrie's was; Ruth's used it so often it didn't mean anything anymore. Shocking, how much I wanted to say it to Birdie, wipe that prissy look off her face. "Shit," I said instead, but she's heard that from me plenty of times; it only made her squeeze her lips together harder.

The Hoopers had to go, big day tomorrow, something about a chess tournament in Richmond and Edward was in the finals; I tuned out, didn't hear the details. Like the Dodges, Edward was a colleague of George's and Esther was a fake friend of mine. We saw each other at faculty parties but nowhere else, because there just wasn't enough to hang a real friendship on. "Thanks so much for coming," I told Esther as we hugged, thinking it was funny, ha-ha, that the Hoopers were the last to go and the Dodges were second to last, and I didn't give a damn about any of them.

"Where are *my* friends?" I said after the Hoopers were out of earshot. "Are they all dead? Besides you," I added when Birdie looked hurt. "I mean, of course, besides you." I dropped down on the arm of her chair and squeezed her skinny far shoulder. "Don't you think it's funny that George's friends stayed the longest at my birthday party? *His* stuffy old friends?"

"You had friends here, Roberta and Don, Kathryn, Binnie, the Strouds. They just had to go home."

"That's what I mean. How come *my* friends are worse party poopers than *his*?"

Birdie didn't know. George heard, but didn't look up from whatever he was doing to the grill, shaking out the charred briquettes or something. Doris Day began singing, "Once I had a secret love," and I sang along. "What movie is this from? Is it that one with James Cagney? I loved that movie. She wore the most gorgeous clothes."

"I love Doris Day," said Birdie. "She's saving the animals now, you know. She's such a lovely woman."

"She wore a fur stole in that movie. I wanted one just like it in the worst way. George was making nothing in those days, so of course it was out of the question. But *oh,* I wanted me a fur stole."

"I always wanted blonde hair," Birdie said.

"I wanted to be short and petite."

"I wanted to wear it in a ducktail, but Chester said it would look cheap."

I took a swallow of my drink, which was now perfect. "Too bad there's no such thing as reincarnation. Too bad this is it. That is one damn shame."

"Oh, I think there is reincarnation. I believe we come back again and again, until we get it right."

"No, we don't. That's ridiculous. They plant us and we rot, that's it."

"Oh, no, I don't think so." Birdie folded her hands and turned her face away. Old fool. A big rush of affection flooded me, though, rinsing away the irritation. Birdie's like an old song you've heard so many times it annoys you—"Harbor Lights," say, or "Some Enchanted Evening." But it's still a good song, and sometimes, when somebody sings it just right, you remember why it's a standard and you like it all over again.

"Well, you could be right," I said magnanimously. "Nobody knows, that's for sure, not till they're dead anyway, so what's the difference. You want to believe you come back as a cat, honey, be my guest."

The back screen door snapped open. "A cat! Gram, are you coming back as a cat?"

"*There* you are. Finally!" I got up and held my arms out. Ruth came and hugged me. She felt so good, young and squirmy and alive, I didn't want to let go. "Where've you been? This party's over, and it was a bust to begin with. You could've livened it up. Mm *mmm*, you look good enough to eat. Where've you been?"

"We got tied up," Carrie said from behind a gigantic pink azalea plant in her arms. "Where is everybody? Ruth, get this—" But she got the screen door open with her foot and scuttled through sideways before it could slam shut. "Happy birthday." She sounded relieved, a chore off her list, as she plunked the heavy azalea down on the table.

"Oh, how pretty," Birdie said, getting up to give Ruth a shy squeeze. "Dana, isn't it beautiful?"

"I picked it out," Ruth said. "Mom wanted a white one."

"White? No, no," I said, "pink's much better. Why, it's just gorgeous, and I know exactly where I'm going to put it."

"I was thinking for nighttime," Carrie said. "You know how white shows up at night in the garden." She fluffed her hair off the back of her neck. She looked hot, tired, and distracted. I can always tell when her happy face is a mask, because she can't smile naturally, her mouth just won't soften. "Anyway, happy birthday, Mama." Even her arms felt stiff, and her kiss on the cheek didn't have any zip, no energy. "Sorry we missed your party. I thought people would still be here," she said softly, and broke away. "Hey, Pop, I didn't see you." She hugged George, then stood back so Ruth could hug him, too. "How are you? You look mighty spiffy tonight."

George smiled down self-consciously at his sweater and his wrinkled linen trousers. He did look unusually snazzy, but only because Carrie had found the outfit in the Eddie Bauer catalog and given it to him for his birthday. Last year—when she had money. "Thanks." He winked at her.

"Like my dress?" I said, getting Ruth's attention when I couldn't get Carrie's. "Too young for me, I know."

"Oh, no, Gram, it's great, it's really nice."

"Nah, old ladies shouldn't wear red. Makes us look like madams." Ruth giggled. "Sit, everybody sit. George, put that plant on the ground so we can see each other. Are you starving? Carrie, have a drink—I'm having another. There's still plenty of food—" Birdie was already heading for the kitchen to get it. I let her; I was the party girl. "George, get Ruth a Coke or something. What do you want, honey, a Sprite, some ice tea, we've got lemonade all made. Carrie, you want a whiskey sour?"

No, she didn't want anything, and she wasn't hungry—she called out to Birdie not to bring her anything. And they couldn't stay long because Ruth had a soccer game early tomorrow, they'd just come by to give me my present and wish me happy birthday. I couldn't believe it! No way were they getting away like that! I kept after Carrie and kept after her, and finally she broke down and said she'd have a beer. "Well, I should think so," I huffed. "It's my birthday, damn it, I'm seventy years old and you can damn well have a drink to toast me."

That made her lift her eyebrows, but she finally smiled naturally. "How many of those have you had?"

"Not enough." I reached for Ruth's arm and squeezed it. "You do what I say, now, not what I do, you hear?"

"Yes, Gram."

"And I'm saying to you, never drink."

"Yes, Gram." She and her mother exchanged tickled glances, but I didn't care. I'd cheered everybody up. Maybe this was going to be a party after all.

"So," I said. "Why are you so late, what held you up? We grilled salmon, we had vegetable kabobs, Birdie made a cake. What happened?" I repeated when Carrie didn't answer, just looked uncomfortable.

"Oh, we just . . . couldn't get organized, and then something came up, and I didn't think you'd mind, you'd have so many other people here."

Ruth was practically bouncing in her chair. "She got fired," she said quickly, then hunched her shoulders.

"What?"

"You what? You got *fired*?"

Carrie sent Ruth a black stare under the hand she was massaging her forehead with. "Yeah," she said tiredly. "Yes, I got fired."

"*Why*?"

Ruth said, "Because she wouldn't do it with Mr. Wright! Ha—Mr. Jerk Face!" Carrie rolled her head back and shut her eyes.

"Is this true? No, I can't believe it."

"It's true, Mama."

"So we went to her office and got all her stuff, that's why we're late. Chris came down—Mrs. Fledergast—and they had to talk and talk."

George said disbelievingly, "Brian Wright?"

"Yes, Pop, Brian Wright." Carrie opened her eyes and looked at him coldly.

"When they went out on their date," Ruth piped up again, "Mom wouldn't kiss him good night, so he waited a while so it wouldn't look bad and then he fired her!"

"It wasn't a date. I told you, it was not a *date*."

"He did it yesterday afternoon. He said not to come in Monday, but he'll pay her for two weeks. What a dirtbag!"

"My lord," Birdie declared, setting a plate of food in front of Ruth. "I think you should sue him."

"That's what *I* say," Ruth said.

"For sexual harassment," Birdie said.

"I'm not suing anybody," Carrie said, as if she'd been saying it a lot.

"Well, I don't see why not. He shouldn't be able to get away with that."

"I don't understand," I finally got out. "How do you know—why do you think—" I couldn't think of the simplest words.

"*Retaliation.*" That was it. "What makes you think—Well, first of all, what's that about a kiss good night?"

"We can talk about it later," Carrie snapped, eyeing Ruth.

"Oh, for Pete's sake," Ruth exploded, "what do you think I am, Mom, eight? Here's what happened. She wouldn't kiss him good night—"

"Well—it was a little more than that," Carrie said, and we all ogled her. "But less than what you're thinking," she added with a laugh. "Something in between—the details aren't important." That's what she thought. "The point is, I know it's why he fired me." When I shook my head, she glared at me. "I was good at my job, Mama, there was no other reason. You can ask Chris if you don't believe me."

"I believe you." I hated it, but I believed her. I'd had ideas about Brian Wright. I'd discovered him; a diamond in the rough, I thought. I was going to use him to make my daughter happy. I felt like throwing up. "Low-down son of a bitch. If he was here right now I'd kick him in the—crotch."

Carrie clasped her hands together and held them to her chin. "Mama, I love you. You're so predictable." Whatever that meant.

Birdie said, "What are you going to do?"

Carrie shrugged, but she avoided my eyes and I knew the answer. She was going to go to Jess Deeping's and make ark animals. Full-time.

Nothing to do then but have another drink.

"Okay," Carrie said, "that's enough of that, can we please talk about something else?" She looked tired and angry and upset, but not very depressed. For somebody who'd just had her livelihood yanked out from under her, she looked pretty damn chipper. She took the beer her father handed her and lifted it in a toast. "Here's to you, Mama. Many more."

I could hardly even smile. I knew the beginning of the end when I saw it.

Birdie started talking about spring coming and wasn't the weather wonderful and how lucky we were to be outside this early in the season. George never brought me my new drink, so I got up to make it myself. In the process I tipped the table, just a minor jolt, but Carrie had to say, "Are you all right?"

"I'm fine, I'm fine. Don't I look fine?"

And I was in love with Ruth. I perched on the arm of her chair and petted her pretty, curly hair out of her face, stroked the back of her neck, hugged her and pressed the side of her face to my bosom. "I could just eat you up, I could just eat you alive." She even smelled good, sweaty and sweet and real. I buried my nose in her hair and inhaled.

"Dana, for the Lord's sake," Birdie said, "leave that child be."

"Won't. She's too sweet." I gave her a wet, smacking kiss on the temple, and she dropped her eyes, embarrassed. A second later she rubbed her knuckle across her cheekbone.

Across the table, George caught my eye and frowned. He glanced at my drink, glanced at me, back at the drink. Who the hell was he, Carry Nation? "Well, excuse me," I said, "but today I arrived at my eighth decade and I'm entitled to drown my sorrows. What are you, Ruth honey, seventeen?"

"Fifteen, Gram."

"That's right, I knew that. Wait'll you get my age and then see what you've got to look forward to."

"Mama," said Carrie, "you've got plenty to look forward to."

"What? Name something. Life is not such a rosy prospect at seventy, let me tell you. What's something good that can happen to you? Something really good? Nothing, that's what. Your joints hurt a little worse every morning. Bladder control—maybe you'll get to wear a diaper like June Allyson. Then your mind goes, you can't remember diddly-squat. Look at Helen Mintz—she's a vegetable."

"No, she is not," Birdie said, shocked.

"Or maybe you have a stroke. Maybe it's your heart, your arteries, or lung cancer or breast cancer, maybe you get your colon removed."

"Jeez," Ruth said, snickering, "you sound like Raven."

"Ruth's ghoul friend," Carrie explained to Birdie.

"Her what? Girlfriend?"

"I'm telling you, it's not a pretty picture, wait'll you get my age and you'll see. What do you think I'm going to do, take up a new career now? Suddenly start watercoloring? Beekeeping? It's *over*."

"Mama, for heaven's sake."

"Jeez, Gram, you're not a *hundred*."

"Drama queen," Birdie said smugly.

George shoved his chair back and muttered something, patting his pocket.

"Where're you going?"

"Just have a smoke. Right back. 'Scuse . . ." he trailed off vaguely, shuffling away in the direction of the garage.

I sat back. "And there you are, aren't you. There—you—are." I toasted his shadowy retreating back, but my drink tasted bitter. "Don't think you can get old *with* somebody, either," I said, wagging my finger in Ruth's face, "just 'cause you're married to him. Don't make *that* mistake."

"Mama," Carrie said sharply.

"I don't care, needs to be said."

"No, it doesn't."

"Be careful who you pick, Ruth honey. They look good when you're young, they act right, you think you'll never be lonely again, but they fade away. You don't even know it till they're gone, and then it's too late. You married a ghost. Right, Carrie? You're the one who—"

Carrie stood. "All right, we have to go. Kiss your grandmother and come on, Ruth, it's getting late."

I didn't move except to blink fast. I let the shock wear off while I went back over what I'd said. Well, let 'em leave. I meant every word, I didn't take back one. When Carrie touched cheeks with me and said, "Good night, Mama. Happy birthday," I didn't say anything back, just sat there stone-faced and unrepentant. By God, you're allowed to tell the truth on your birthday.

"'Night, Mrs. Costello," Carrie told Birdie.

"'Night, sweetheart. You take care." I didn't look, but I didn't have to—all kinds of secret looks were going on over my head. Carrie said something about going out the back way to say good night to her father. Fine, have a party out there for all I care. Have a love-in.

Then I waited for Birdie to start in. It wouldn't take long; silence is her worst enemy. "Well?" I said when she actually kept her mouth shut. "No words from you for the *drama queen*?"

She stood up slowly, using the table for support. "You've had too many of those whiskey sours, so it's no use talking to you."

"Good."

"But I'll say this."

"Here we go."

"My Chester was no angel, and there were some things about him I've never even told *you*. But I most certainly would never have told them to my children. I didn't try to get sympathy for myself by running down Matt and Martha's father in front of them."

"Well, aren't you just wonderful."

"No, I'm not wonderful. I just know there are rules. And drinking too much and feeling sorry for yourself because you're seventy doesn't give you permission to break them. A child doesn't need to know her father's a failure, no matter how old she is. That's just common decency."

"That's just crap. A mother and child are the closest two people in the world. If you can't tell your own flesh and blood what your life is like, what's the point of anything? I didn't cross any line."

"Yes, you did and you know it. Using Ruth as an excuse, too. 'Be careful who you pick, Ruth honey,'" she mimicked. "You ought to be ashamed of yourself."

"Oh, go home."

"I am."

"When?"

"When I finish my say. You have problems with George, then you should tell them to a therapist or a marriage counselor." I snorted. "Reverend Thomasson, then."

I reached for Carrie's half-finished glass of beer. "Oh, say, that's what I'll do, Bird, I'll go visit the pastor. What a wonderful idea, and so like me, just the kind of thing I'd do. Boy, you sure do know me well." Sarcasm's lost on Birdie unless you hit her over the head with it. "I thought you were leaving."

"Okay, don't, then, just stay home and fester." Leaning forward, she said earnestly, "I'm sorry, but you're getting sourer all the time, and I'm not the only one who's saying so. I just—I just think you could use some help, and not from your own daughter, who's got enough problems of her own."

"Thank you." Warm beer stuck in my throat; I almost spit it back in the glass. "Don't slam the door on your way out."

Birdie sighed. She came around the table, smiling and frowning. "You're the hardest friend I have. I love you, Dana, but you sure are a pain in the neck sometimes. Happy birthday, honey."

I pulled back when she leaned down to kiss me, but she kept coming and got me with a hard one on the cheek. I said, "Hmph," and didn't smile. "Maybe you should write an advice column, get paid for all that wisdom. You could call yourself Miss Buttinsky."

She laughed on her way across the patio. She had on a too-summery print dress, pink on white. The white glowed in the murky twilight—Carrie was right about that. "I take it back, you're not a pain in the neck," she called from the doorway. "You're a pain in the *ass*."

Oh, naughty, naughty, coming from Birdie that was like cursing the Lord. But she'd hissed "ass" in a stage whisper, like a little girl, so the effect was spoiled. She did slam the screen door, though.

I stared around vacantly, listening to the night sounds, trying to figure out what I was feeling. Guilty? Mad? Both. But mostly tired, tired in my mind, too tired to sort out who was right and who was wrong. It just didn't matter. Tomorrow I might wake up sorry and embarrassed for committing a family faux pas and driving my loved ones away, but tonight all I could dredge up was sullenness.

The moon was exactly half full. Chilly, sweet air. Turned earth and fertilizer, a real spring smell. It made me nostalgic for a time I couldn't remember, maybe hadn't even lived. I got up and went to find George.

The streetlight in the alley filtered through the budding branches of the locust tree behind the garage, dappling his bald head as it swayed slightly—he was sitting on one of the swings of the rusty old swing set we put out here years ago, then never called anybody to take away. He had his back to me, his head tilted sideways, resting against the chain. His stooped shoulders looked dreamy; he was watching the smoke from his pipe drift up into the tree branches, musing over something, at peace. I felt keyed up just looking at him, out of sorts, ungainly somehow. He heard me and pivoted, twisting the swing chains over his head. "'Lo," he called, wary.

I strolled over, hands in the pockets of my red dress, watching where I put my feet. Lot of roots around here. If I tripped on one, he'd say I was drunk.

"Hey," I said, and squeezed into the other swing. "I'm leaving all those dishes till morning."

"That's dirty—you're going to get your dress dirty."

"Don't care."

He glanced at me, trying to figure out what mood I was in now. The streetlight reflected off his glasses, dazzling me; I couldn't see his eyes. Presently he said, "Isn't that something now, about Carrie."

"Crazy. Of all things."

"I've known Brian since he was the registrar at Remington. Never liked him, but I never would've guessed at anything like this. Not in a million years." He shook his head, baffled. "Maybe she *should* sue him."

"Suing's tacky. Goddamn sonofabitch." I meant it, but I regretted saying it. He doesn't complain, but George hates it when I swear. But that's how reckless and mad I was feeling. And foolish. Tricked, and old, and hornswoggled. I felt like one of those old ladies you read about who get their life savings swindled away on the telephone by some smooth-talking con artist.

"Carrie will have to find another job now, I guess. She can always help me with my research. I've told her that before. Not forever, but in the interim."

"I don't think she wants to," I said dully.

His pipe went out and he relit it, making the bowl glow. "No, I don't believe so," he said with a wistful, flickering smile. I looked at him curiously. He pulled on his pipe and stared off at nothing.

An owl hooted; not the homey hoo-hoo one, but the one that sounds like somebody gasping or hissing, that eerie, raspy sound that prickles the hair on your arms. I concentrated on the friendlier sound of the traffic in the distance, and the familiar, semihysterical barking of Maisie, the neighbor's dog.

"You think we're like George and Martha?"

"George and Martha?"

"You know, *Who's Afraid of Virginia Woolf*. The old married couple were George and Martha. He was a college professor." She was the college president's daughter, though, so that's where the parallel broke down. I married my George to get out of an old life, but I never learned how to fit into the new one.

George grunted.

"They hated each other," I said. "But they loved each other, too." I let that hang, let the words float in the silence like an invitation. An advance.

George said nothing.

Such a sadness came over me. "Oh, God, what's going to happen?"

He scooted his swing a little closer to mine. Lightly, he patted the side of my thigh.

I picked up his hand and studied it in the meager light. Veiny old hand, wrinkled old hand. Yellow nails that smelled like nicotine. I wanted to lay my cheek against it, but it looked so foreign, like a machine, a device, not quite flesh; the longer I stared at it, the less it even looked like a hand.

I set it on my knee. "Have you been happy?"

"What do you mean?"

"On a scale of one to ten, how would you rate the happiness of your life, George?"

"Oh." He laughed.

"No, I mean it. What would you say? What's your answer?"

He sighed. "Seven."

"Really? Me, too. And here I thought we had nothing in common." We smiled, not looking at each other. We rested our temples against the cool, rusty chains of our side-by-side swings. If we sidled a tiny bit closer, we'd touch.

"Tonight I'm a four, though, George. I'm not doing so hot tonight."

"You had a little too much to drink."

"Maybe. But . . . I wanted something. Some feeling. I don't like this getting old business." I gave a mock shudder. "Hard to believe we used to *celebrate* our birthdays."

He gave my leg a pat and took his hand back to rub the side of his stiff neck. He lit his pipe again.

I didn't even *want* him to talk to me. I outgrew that long ago, the way a child outgrows expecting her stuffed dog to talk back. I just wanted . . . something. Tonight. Some kind of a connection.

"George."

"Hm?"

"You know, you don't have to smoke outside. You can smoke in the house if you want to. I don't mind anymore."

He nodded, looking thoughtful. "I think I'll keep it out here," he said slowly. "It's not so bad. I've gotten used to it."

Down the alley, somebody's garage door groaned before it slammed shut, *crack*, metal on concrete. A nice, final sound. I got up. "Butt hurts. I'm going in."

"I'll be in in a minute."

"Okay."

"Happy birthday," he called.

"Thanks."

I went in the empty house by myself. Something I've done a million times before, but tonight it felt like practicing for the future.

18

Good, Good

"Careful, watch his head. Look out for the door!"

"I got it, I got it. He's fine." The tinge of exasperation in Mr. Green's voice was what clued me in to the possibility that I was being a pain in the ass. Nobody was more even-tempered than Mr. Green.

"I can probably get the rest," I told him, "I just needed you for the big ones. Well—if you could help me with the polar bear, that would be great. Then go, you must have a thousand things to do."

Good humor restored, Mr. Green stood back to admire his placement of the giraffe, eleven and a half feet tall, against the sunny side of the ark barn. We were moving the animals outside so Eldon Pletcher could look at them in natural light. Landy and Jess were taking him to the river this morning to see the almost-finished ark; then he was coming here to check out the animals. He'd be here any minute.

"Looks good," Mr. Green said. High praise—he thought the whole ark project was ridiculous. But he regularly attended a church called the Solemn Brethren of the Bleeding Lamb, so I wasn't sure where he got off. I told him that to his face—we had very lively debates; arguments, really. He liked to play devil's advocate even more than I did.

"Do you think Mr. Pletcher will like them?" I asked, eyeing my colorful animal lineup against the wall.

"Oh, sure." I must've looked dubious, because he added kindly, "I bet he'll be real pleased. You don't have a thing to worry about." He gave me a bracing pat on the back, and I realized I was twisting my hands together. "Which one do you like best?" he asked.

"Me?" I liked them all. I loved them all. Which wasn't to say I wouldn't have loved a chance to do every one of them over again. "I don't know, which one do you?"

He glanced over the double rows of cutout kangaroo, cheetah, porcupine, llama, panda, ferret, goat. "What's that one?" he asked, pointing.

Uh-oh. "Can't you tell?"

He scrunched up his leathery face, peering. "Anteater?"

"Yes!" Relief. "That's your favorite?"

"No, this is. I think. This here donkey."

"Really? How come?"

"'Cause of his face. Looks like one we had when I was a kid, name of Larry. Patient as the day is long. Something about the eyes," he said, going closer. "Just something restful in his eyes. How many more you got to do before D day?"

Mr. Green called our May seventeenth launch D day. "Not too many. I really think we're going to make it. If nothing goes wrong." Like Eldon Pletcher telling me to start over.

"Good thing you got fired, eh?"

He thought he was being funny, but that was something I said to myself about three times a day. Thank you so much, Brian, for turning out to be an ass.

"So you can haul out the rest of the stuff, you think? I'll get on with some chores if you don't need me." He touched his cap.

"Go—thank you. I'm not taking them all out anyway, just some. And Jess can help me put them back. You'll never have to touch another animal again."

He laughed and called back, "You mean until D day!"

We would rent a moving van on the day of the sailing to transport the animals to the river; Mr. Green would help roll them out to the dock, up the ramp, and onto the ark. My job was arranging them around the railings on the first and second decks, for maximum visibility. A simple task, you might think, tall in back, small in front. But a museum curator couldn't have taken her assignment more seriously than I did. After all the work we'd done, I wanted the display to be perfect.

We expected a crowd, but no one could predict how big it might be. The ark story had been picked up in papers as far away as Charlotte and Baltimore. Reporters had called me for interviews. They'd called Jess, too, and of course Landy. I'd gotten Eldon's approval and finally done one, on the Remington College radio station. The only sticky moment came when the interviewer, a perky junior named Marcy, asked me if I considered myself a creationist. I went into an explanation about the purity of self-expression and how the art I was doing was apolitical and not religious in itself—and Marcy interrupted to ask, "So you'd say what you're doing is art?" with an unflattering inflection. I folded and said, well, not fine art, but certainly graphic art, yes, I did believe I was making a kind of illustrative art, and people were free to call it anything they liked.

She must've thought she was getting us back on surer ground when she switched to the topic of how essentially silly it all was, the idea of a modern-day ark. Of course I agreed with her—and yet I heard myself getting defensive on Eldon's behalf, and especially Landy's. I told her about how, just last year, a team of deep-sea explorers found an ancient, undisturbed beach on the floor of the Black Sea, and geologists from Columbia University were pretty sure it was the proof that a sudden, catastrophic flood had occurred about seven thousand years ago. Noah's flood. Marcy said, "Huh," politely but knowingly, and wrapped up.

It felt strange to be so firmly and obviously on the wrong side of a public controversy. Or at any rate, the side I would never have taken under any circumstances except these surpassingly peculiar ones. I wasn't a very effective spokesperson for the religious right. A fact about myself I could truthfully say I'd never expected to regret.

Jess, on the other hand, was relishing all the odd, skewed ambiguities of the situation, the strange-bedfellows syndrome, he called it. Sailing an ark was a phenomenon, he said, a wonder, a spectacle, something you did because you could. I should try harder not to put people into categories, he recommended. "Is Landy a good friend? Is his father dying? Are we hurting anyone?" And the most compelling question: "Is this making you feel better?"

If not for the opposition of my immediate family, I could answer yes to that without misgivings. Ruth's ridicule had hardened to hostility, though, and my mother was still fomenting resistance on the grounds of good taste. In spite of their unhappiness with me, I was, for some reason, happy when I was doing the work. I hadn't had time to ask myself why—I hadn't had time to do anything but make animals! And maybe that was the answer. Maybe it was that simple.

At least my mother couldn't throw irresponsibility in my face. Eldon had come through—he was paying me almost as much as Brian had at the Other School. Ruth pointed out that my hours were twice as long, but that was a gross exaggeration. I said if something excited and consumed and invigorated you, how could it be a bad deal? She didn't see it that way. So I muzzled my enthusiasm and tried to hide my long hours from her, leaving for Jess's after she went to school, getting home just before she did from Krystal's. Come to think of it, that was the same way I used to try to hide from her how much I was sleeping after Stephen died. I could see this wasn't healthy, but I didn't have *time* to fix it. If I'd had *time* I would've insisted on mutual frankness, I would've scheduled long, nonconfrontational truth sessions, tried harder to explain myself, made compromises. In less than three weeks the ark would sail, the flap would die down, and life would go back to normal. Surely Ruth and I could safely misunderstand each other for three more weeks. And I was planning on a big emotional letdown at the end—that ought to cheer her up.

Around noon, Landy drove up in a huge white station wagon I'd never seen before. Barking dogs immediately swarmed it. Jess and Landy got out on opposite sides and opened the two passenger doors. On Landy's side, a tall, round, white-haired woman in a violet sundress climbed out and looked around, shading her eyes from the sun. On his way around, Landy opened the rear door and took out a folding wheelchair. Jess told his dogs to stop barking. I was surprised when he, not Landy, leaned inside the car and lifted an old man out, holding him in his arms like a child, and gently settled him in the opened wheelchair. It was the woman, Mrs. Pletcher—Viola—who pushed him across the stony driveway and the uneven dirt path toward the barn Jess pointed to. Toward me, as well: I waited in the grassy shade of a tree, directly in their path. It seemed more suitable to greet them there for some reason, lower key, simpler—I don't know. Less as if I were Jess's hostess.

Landy made the introductions, calling his father "Reverend." Mrs. Pletcher and I shook hands, hers rough and strong, and I saw where Landy got his bashful smile. "Reverend Pletcher," I said, bending toward the old gentleman. "I've been looking forward to meeting you."

He had a mouth like a turtle's, the thin lips meeting in a point at the center. When he smiled, large, astonishingly white false teeth glittered and gleamed. "Carrie," he said very softly. I was ready to take my hand back, chagrined when he wouldn't shake it, but at last he unclasped his tight-skinned, discolored fingers from one another and slowly reached his right hand toward mine. His was cool and smooth, fragile feeling, thin as a swatch of twigs. We shook very gently.

I'd been expecting someone coarser, an old wreck of a man, making a deal with death years after he'd replaced degeneracy with fanaticism. Not this pale, parchment-skinned, straight-backed gentleman with soft eyes. It seemed his illness had burned away everything nonessential and left just the core of his dignity and his big, obsessed heart. Looking into the pain and patience in his face, I had an idea why Landy was bound to him, and to his last great folly.

I wasn't what he'd expected, either. "Thought you'd be old," he told me. He rolled one hand over weakly, thumb up, indicating Landy. "Like him." Father and son smiled, to my relief. It was a joke.

"Oh, you put 'em outside," Landy said, catching sight of a reindeer's rump sticking out past the side of the barn.

"Some of them," I said, "not all. I was thinking you might like to see them in the light. The way they'll look on the day."

The skin of Eldon's skull shone pinkish, only a fringe of white hair left at the back. Mrs. Pletcher leaned over him. "Ready to go and look?" He nodded, and I realized as she pushed him away what the light in his eyes and the quick clutch of his hands on the armrests meant. Excitement.

At first I couldn't stand near him, I had to wander off a little, like a film director who has to smoke in the lobby while his movie premieres. Jess came and got me. His knowing look did something to me. He took a light hold of my wrists and tugged. "Come on over. Talk to him. You want him mixing up the wombat and the yak?" I made a face, pretending I was insulted. He moved his hands up my arms, put his thumbs in the hollows of my elbows. "Come and get your reward, Carrie."

"How do you know he'll like them? What if he hates them?"

"Find out."

But I just wanted to stay there with Jess's hands on my arms. Over his shoulder, I saw all three Pletchers stop in front of the high, lunging tiger. The reverend looked almost preppy, more like a retired professor than a tobacco farmer in a cardigan sweater, pressed khaki slacks, and huge blue running shoes. I imagined him meeting my father, having a conversation with him. They would probably like each other.

Mrs. Pletcher rolled him on to the next animal. "Okay," I said, and Jess let go of my arms. Nothing to do then but go hear the verdict.

Reverend Pletcher was smiling—I hoped that meant he liked the prairie dog, not that he was laughing at it. It was only visible from the waist up, if a prairie dog had a waist, its head and paws sticking up over the lip of a brown-painted papier-mâché burrow. "Good," he said. And at the kangaroo, he said, "Good," again, and I showed him the baby in the pouch on the mother's side. "I can paint it out if you think three wouldn't be allowed," I said. "Nothing to it, I can fix it in two seconds. I just wasn't sure. You know, biblically speaking."

He pursed his turtle lips. "Mother?" he said after a minute or two of thoughtful gazing.

"She'd smuggle it on," Mrs. Pletcher said immediately. "If the Lord chose her and she had a little baby, she'd hide it. Just like that."

"Yes . . . but . . ."

"The Lord would know, of course. But He'd turn a blind eye."

Eldon smiled, and that was it. Kangaroo was in.

"Good," he said in front of the moose cutout, the skunk. "Good," he said of the lynx and the ferret. For a preacher, he was a man of very few words. I was spoiled now, greedy for more than "Good." He put his hand out to pet the owl. I'd made him out of store-bought turkey feathers hot glued to sculpted urethane foam, with black phone cable taped to L-shaped coat hanger pieces for his legs, a whittled wooden beak, eyes painted on flat oval stones I found in Jess's driveway. "Good," Reverend Pletcher said, his hand lingering. "It's very . . ." His head wobbled on his cordy neck. He closed his eyes. His wife stroked his shoulder soothingly. "Okay?" she said, and he smacked his lips and nodded.

Oh, he was so weak. I hadn't known. Landy sent me a bracing smile behind his father's back, and I shook off the shock, realizing I must've looked stricken. After that I became morbidly conscious of time passing, of the heat, the sun, the fact that Eldon wore no hat. Why didn't he have a hat? I wanted to cup my hands over his unprotected head, shade him. I hated it whenever his wheelchair hit a bump and jostled him. When he'd looked at all the animals outside, I said, "There are more in the barn, but maybe you've seen enough. It's cool in there, though. Whatever you like."

"Oh," he said, "all." I think it was his teeth that made him sound as if he had something, a lozenge, a Life Saver, on his tongue; they were way too big for his mouth.

"Are you thirsty?" it occurred to me to ask.

"Thirsty?" Mrs. Pletcher echoed, leaning over his shoulder. I started to leave, run for the house for a glass of water, but "We have some here," she said, and took a plastic bottle, the kind cyclists carried on their bikes, from a clip holder at the back of the wheelchair. Eldon covered her hands with his while she held the flexible plastic straw to his lips. After every swallow he said, "Ahh," sweetly appreciative, like a baby.

By the time we finished touring the barn, he was pale and perspiring and no longer erect in his chair, his narrow chest caved in, shoulders curving. "I think we better go," said Mrs. Pletcher, who looked tired, too. She didn't protest when Landy took her place and pushed his father's wheelchair back to the car.

Again, Jess was the one who lifted him up and carefully put him in the backseat of the station wagon. I waited to say good-bye, but when Jess straightened up, he said, "He'd like to talk to you, Carrie." I went closer. The old man smiled up at me, patting the seat on his other side. I walked around the car and got in the backseat beside him.

"First," he said, and paused for breath. The skin around his nose and mouth was a pearly blue-white, nearly transparent. "Good job. I'm so happy."

"Thank you. Thank you."

"You have no faith?"

Landy must have told him. It was true, but I answered, "No religion," to save his feelings.

"Why'd you do it?"

"Why did I make the animals?"

"Not for money."

"No. Well—that helped. I'm not sure why I did it. But I wanted to, from the beginning, as soon as Jess told me. It never seemed crazy to me."

He nodded—as if he knew that about me already. "Know what it means?"

"The ark? I think I do."

"Tell me."

I'd rather he'd have told me. "Rebirth," I plunged in. "Starting over from scratch. Being saved—being chosen." I wasn't going to get into the matter of the destruction of the earth for its sin and corruption; that was his department. "I think it's a symbol of rejuvenation. A new beginning, everything pure and clean."

"New life."

"Yes."

He sighed shallowly and relaxed against the seat, hands going limp at his sides. "That's what I thought."

I blinked at him, realizing it hadn't been a test, but a question. And my fumbling answer had reassured him. "How many more?" he asked.

"How many more do I have to do? About six. We'll make it," I said confidently.

"One thing. The cow."

"The cow? It's wrong?" My pretty Holstein?

"If you have time. For me."

"What? Anything."

"I've always . . . liked a Guernsey. But only if there's time."

"You mean—in addition?" He nodded. "I can do it. Okay, a Guernsey, yes, absolutely. Spotted brown, smaller than a Holstein. I like them, too."

"Pretty faces, I always thought. Had one. When I was a boy." I thought of Mr. Green's donkey. Larry.

"I'll start it right away," I said.

He gave a tickled laugh and twinkled his eyes, charming me. "No. Save it for last."

"Okay. But I'll have time, I promise. I'll make time."

He lifted his frail arms and put them around my neck.

I was so surprised, it was a second or two before I could hug him back. He smelled clean and powdery, like an infant, but under the scratchy sweater his body felt as brittle as an armful of sticks. Every time I thought we would let go, we didn't. I kissed his cheek, trying not to cry, and he kissed mine. We drew away. His grip on my hands was amazingly strong. I said, "See you on the seventeenth," and he smiled.

I waited for him to say *God bless you*, I wanted him to say it. Landy opened the driver's door and started to climb in—no more privacy. *I* was the one who whispered "God bless you" in a panic—and I'd never said it before in my life, not to anyone who hadn't just sneezed. The look on his face was surprised, amused, and triumphant. *Gotcha*, it said, but with love.

Jess couldn't stop for lunch. "You go ahead, Carrie, make something for yourself, but I have to get to work."

"I'll make your lunch," I offered, "and bring it to you. Where will you be?"

"In the small barn. Doing nasty things. If you could just leave me a sandwich on the counter, that would be great."

Nasty things? Like what, castrating a bull? One could only speculate. I made him two sandwiches, one turkey and one cheese, and put them in a paper bag with an apple, a banana, and four cookies. I found a Thermos in the cupboard and filled it with ice water. It was radically uncool to bring your lunch to school, according to Ruth, so I hadn't gone through this packing ritual since Chicago. I noticed I hadn't missed it.

Nasty things, indeed. At first I wasn't even sure what Jess was doing. In the smallest barn, he and Mr. Green had a cow, probably a heifer because she was small, in a sort of double yoke, front and back, and they were—I really couldn't tell. Something to do with reproduction or elimination, or quite possibly both.

"Here's your sandwich," I said, putting the bag on the straw-strewn floor. Two cats zipped over to investigate; I picked it up and set it on top of a post. "Mr. Green, I didn't bring you anything."

"Already ate," he said, closing the top of a smoking metal tank at his feet. "Thanks anyway. Liquid nitrogen," he explained—I must've looked curious. "Keeps your bull sperm frozen."

"Oh, I see. So you're doing, um, you're impregnating her?"

"Yup."

"Ah. And yet . . ." I could've sworn Jess had one of his long-gloved arms up the poor cow's *rear end*.

Mr. Green caught his eye and winked, then handed him a long, thin tube with a rubber bulb on the end. "Ready," Mr. Green said, and took hold of the cow's tail so it had to quit swatting Jess in the chest with it. Quickly but carefully, Jess inserted the tube into what I assumed was the cow's vagina, while he did something with his impaled hand; his shoulder moved subtly and his face took on an even more concentrated look. Slowly he squeezed the rubber bulb. Then everything came out, tube, arm, and cow from her bonds. Jess led her into a stall and she went docilely enough, but I couldn't help thinking her heifer face looked indignant.

"I just have one question," I said faintly. "What is the point, um . . . why do you have to use *two* hands?"

Mr. Green, who seemed to be enjoying himself, said, "You got to go in the other way first to get aholt of her cervix. Got to grab it just right through the rectal wall and tip it. Jess here is a expert."

"Is he." How interesting. "So now . . . is she pregnant?"

"We won't know for a few weeks," Jess said, frowning as he wrote something on a clipboard.

"This is her first time," Mr. Green offered, "so she might not settle."

"Did she ever meet the father of her child?" I asked.

"Nope. S'pose to be a sweet little Angus. You want to breed a new girl to a little guy her first time out, so her calf'll be small. We'll just see now, Sophie, won't we? We'll just see what happens." Mr. Green reached over the rail and slapped Sophie affectionately on the behind. "Who's next?"

"Two-forty-one," Jess said. "Carlene."

"Carlene!" He went off to get her. I'd never seen Mr. Green so animated before. Either he really liked artificially inseminating cows or he was having some fun at my expense.

"You look a little green," Jess noted while he thawed a tube of something, presumably bull semen, in a pail of ice water.

"Me? Oh no, I'm fine."

"Going to stick around a while, then?"

"Well, I probably should get to work. Eldon says he wants a Guernsey."

"I heard." We smiled at each other.

"Did he like the ark, Jess?"

"He did. Very, very much."

"He loved the animals, too."

"I know."

Mr. Green came back with Carlene, who was huge, definitely not a new girl. I made a short speech about how much work I had to do in the other barn, and escaped.

But I couldn't concentrate. I leafed through my cow calendars and cow books, looking for just the right Guernsey, then remembered what Eldon had said about waiting till the end. Good idea: I might've had enough of cows for one day. But I couldn't keep my mind on my wild boar cutout, either. I felt restless and keyed up. I caught myself pacing. I wanted to be sad about Eldon and happy about the ark project *with* someone, and there wasn't anyone. Plus I wasn't dressed right, I felt awkward and hampered in the straight skirt I'd worn for the Pletchers' visit. And it was *beautiful* outside, the most perfect spring afternoon. What I really wanted was to be with Jess, and he had his arm up a cow's butt.

Hopeless. Finally I gave up and went outside. If I couldn't work, I should just go home. I could clean the house, which was an absolute wreck; I could make Ruth a real meal for a change, not a slapped-together casserole or last-minute microwaved leftovers. I could go visit my mother. I'd been avoiding her, because she didn't like me much these days. She was mad at me for something I hadn't even done yet.

Yet?

I went for a walk. One of Jess's dogs followed me, Tracer, the smart one. We took the dirt lane that zigzagged uphill for half a mile and deadended in a high, empty meadow. Wild apple trees bloomed in a tangle along the edge; I found one with a smooth trunk and a rockless, rootless base and sat down under it. Below me, a deep-cut creek, blue-brown with the sky's reflection, meandered between Jess's farm and Landy's, forming the boundary in some places. A tributary of the Leap, it came close to drying up in the hot summer, but today it almost overflowed its steep-sided banks. Cows, nearly indistinguishable from boulders at this distance, sprawled under a cover of early willows arched over the creek like chartreuse awnings. Birds chirped, bees buzzed, grasshoppers hopped. Tracer ran off and left me for a more interesting adventure in the meadow. Was I prejudiced or was Jess's farm prettier than Landy's? Landy's stony fields didn't slope as gracefully. His cows didn't look as contented. Even the color of Jess's fields was sweeter, a mellower yellow-green: gold ochre and chrome oxide. Jess had the Italy of farms, I decided. Landy had the Ukraine.

Everything was Jess today, I couldn't get him off my mind. Burgeoning, bursting, swelling, stirring spring didn't help, either. Ruth had taught me a meditation of Krystal's involving the repetition of the phrase "Who am I?" on slow, calming exhales. You were supposed to answer, *I'm a woman,* or *I'm a mother,* then contemplate those responses in a deeply relaxed, nonjudgmental way. When I'd tried it, I'd gotten stuck on *I'm tired,* and *I'm late. I'm wasting valuable time here*. Still, it might be worth a second try, to calm my mind. Get Jess out of it. I slumped lower on my tree trunk, closed my eyes, clasping my hands lightly over my diaphragm. Breathe in, breathe out. *Who am I? Who the hell am I?*

I fell asleep.

Only for a few minutes, but long enough to wake up cranky from a confusing dream about thrashing palm fronds in a rain forest or a jungle. I stood up and brushed the dirt and grass off my skirt, rolled the crick out of my neck. Might as well go home.

I went in Jess's house first for a glass of water. In the kitchen, fresh coffee perked in the machine on the counter. I walked out to the hall and listened, and presently I heard Jess's voice coming from his office. I poured myself half a cup of coffee and drank it while I waited for him, staring out the kitchen window. He needed to pay attention to his flower garden if he wanted his perennials to grow higher than his weeds this year. Me, too; my garden at home looked like the seediest corner of a vacant lot. But at least we would get an ark launched, and that's what counted.

Tired of waiting, I poured another cup of coffee and carried it down the hall to his study. He was sitting on the edge of his desk, talking on the phone to someone about fertilizer—I assumed; I heard "nitrogen content" and "percent potassium." He smiled at me when I handed him his coffee. I stood in front of him. We looked into each other's eyes while he said, "Yes, but I need it now, I can't wait till the end of next week. Well, that would be great. If you can—right. I'd appreciate it." He still had on his barn clothes, but his face and hair were damp, shirtsleeves rolled over his elbows, as if he'd just had a wash. I smelled soap, hay, cow, coffee. What would he do, I wondered, if I put my hand on his jaw, or touched his neck? Pulled on his ear?

I kept my hands to myself. But when I sat down on the arm of the easy chair in front of the desk, I crossed my bare legs slowly to see if he'd look at them. He did.

After he hung up, he sipped coffee for a while without talking. I couldn't decide if it was a comfortable silence or not. "What's up?" he said eventually. "I thought you were working."

"Couldn't seem to make any headway. Restless, I don't know why. What are you doing?"

"Phone calls. Business."

"You have a strange job," I said.

"Do I?"

"Maybe not. Part of it's earthy, part of it's not."

"Most of it is."

"I'm sad, Jess," I said. "I didn't know I'd like Eldon so much."

"I know."

"He's so frail. What if he can't make it to the seventeenth? Poor Landy."

He bowed his head and nodded, rubbing the heel of his hand down the long muscle in his thigh. "They'll sail the ark anyway, Landy says. No matter what happens."

"I'm glad." But what if Eldon thought his salvation depended on sailing it while he was alive? What if he was convinced that, by not fulfilling his promise to God on time, he'd doomed himself? "Good people are too hard on themselves," I said.

Jess smiled. "Sometimes. Landy says his father's got a lot to repent."

I resisted that. I didn't want to imagine Eldon as a great sinner, a man who could do damage to his family out of selfishness or thoughtlessness, or worse. Not that sweet old man.

Jess looked at the clock on his desk.

"How's Sophie?" I asked, to keep him.

"Resting comfortably."

"Do you ever breed them the natural way?"

"Sometimes. Landy's got a bull stud who's sire to about forty of my herd, one way or another."

"He told me he can't stand to ship his cattle." *Ship*; that was a euphemism for sending them to market—which was a euphemism for butchering. "I remember how you used to hate it, too. Do you still?"

"Yes."

"But you do it."

"Sure. Well. Mostly. If you don't count Martha."

"Martha?"

"She's twenty-six."

"No!"

"She quit giving milk about thirteen years ago, but I couldn't ship her. Would've been like killing my elderly aunt."

"So you put her out to pasture. Did I ever meet Martha?"

"I don't remember. She wasn't famous then, she was just a cow."

"How long can they live?"

"Twenty-eight, thirty. That's if you treat 'em like goddesses." He picked up his cup, set it down when he remembered it was empty.

"Want some more coffee? I'll get it."

He crossed his arms, looked at me curiously. "What's behind this urge to take care of me today?"

"Sorry. Didn't mean to hover." I stood up, a little hurt. I wanted him to say, "No, I like it," or something, but he just looked at me. "What time do you have to start milking?" I asked.

"Four. Same as every day."

The clock said 2:20. How did you make a move on a man you'd said *no* to so many times, he'd quit asking? *No* had become our theme song; over the years we'd learned to dance to it with a certain amount of grace. How could I tell Jess now, out of the blue, that I wanted a new song?

I couldn't, of course. You had to lead up to something like that slowly; you dropped girlish hints; you flirted. You changed the temperature gradually, so nobody's system went into shock.

"What if you had an emergency right now," I said. "So you couldn't do your phone calls or your business. Would anything terrible happen?"

"No. Why?"

"I don't know, I just thought—maybe you needed to relax." My God, I sounded like a call girl. This was completely wrong; I pushed the whole idea out of my head and changed tacks. "Sometime when you're not busy, would you like to go out to dinner? With me?"

What was he thinking? The outline of him seemed to get sharper, better defined, more distinct from the desk and the wall behind him, like a bas relief. He steepled his fingers in front of his face, hiding his mouth and nose. "Yes."

"Good. Then sometime we should do that."

I was on my feet, I had delivered my exit line. But instead of leaving I said, "Do you miss being married? Not—I don't mean do you miss Bonnie, but do you miss having someone? To be with?"

"Yes."

"I always wondered what broke you up."

"You know what broke us up."

"I do? No, I don't."

"Carrie, what's going on?"

"Hmm?"

"Why did you bring me lunch? Coffee. Why did you show me your legs?"

I blushed. I considered getting huffy—*I have no idea what you're talking about*—but I said, "I don't know what's going on," truthfully. I was full of wanting him, I was bursting out of my skin with it, and I had no idea how to tell him.

"Are you . . . lonely? Is that what this is about?" He said it *kindly*.

"'Is that what this is about?'" I repeated, laughing. Now I *was* insulted. "Does the widow need a little consoling, you mean? The answer's no." I moved away. "I'm not lonely, not at all. But thanks for asking. As a matter of fact, I can't remember when I've been less lonely. I really don't need a thing."

I stopped at the door to the hall, keeping my back to him. "Oh God, I'm just so bad at this."

"What?"

"No practice, that's the problem."

"Bad at what?" He sounded baffled. But hopeful.

"Telling you I'm ready," I said, turning around. "But I'm not lonely, honestly, not anymore—I don't know why. I don't need you, I just want you. There—you said to say it in words." But now I'd panicked myself. I was afraid he'd touch me, afraid he wouldn't.

He did neither.

"Did you just look at your watch?"

He laughed, a glad, real sound. "Sorry." Still laughing, he came and put his arms around me. Kissed me. Held me, pressed me against the wall, put his hands on me. Happy ending.

Was it like high school, the dark, electric-smelling utility room? Maybe; because I thought of it, I made the association. And there was a familiarity in the feel of him that I wasn't prepared for, I thought everything would be new, strange. Molecularly speaking, doesn't the human body change completely every—so many years? I didn't expect our bodies to recognize each other. "It's the same, isn't it?" I said between long, deepening kisses, but he said, "No, it's completely different." So I don't know.

A little later, I caught him sneaking another glance at his watch, behind my shoulder. "Look, if I'm keeping you from something . . ."

"I have to make a call. Two seconds."

He left me to call and ask if a Mr. Turnbull could come to the farm tomorrow afternoon instead of today, same time. He must've said yes, because Jess thanked him profusely.

"Who was that?"

"A.I. tech."

Artificial insemination technician. "And his name is Turnbull?" Everything was so funny. We laughed our way up the stairs and into Jess's room, and I was so relieved when it wasn't his old bedroom, the one I used to do my homework in. Glad too when it wasn't his parents' big, gloomy room, still cluttered with dark, old-fashioned furniture. Jess's room was the old sleeping porch at the back of the house; he'd enclosed it and added wide, ceiling-high windows. I could see a silver ribbon of the Leap through tree leaves at the bottom of the long, grassy flood plain.

"This room isn't ugly," I said, feigning surprise, glancing around at the plain oak dressers, the sturdy bed—unmade; manly navy sheets in a tangle—both bedside tables covered with magazines and books. "What went wrong?"

"Hmm. Guess I thought your mother would never come up here."

We took off each other's clothes like brand-new lovers, smiling and reverent, practically glowing from gladness. Underneath the excitement, it felt like coming home. I don't know why I wasn't more self-conscious, why I wasn't paralyzed with nerves. The familiarity again, I think. Not a sense that this had happened before; more a feeling that it should have. I did mind that my naked body was twelve years older than the last time Jess had seen it. But he didn't. He told me I was beautiful, so fervently that I believed him. How it was to be with him came back to me quickly, and the best was the way he could make me feel that nothing I did was wrong or clumsy or tentative or silly. With Jess I was lovely, I was a pretty fish gliding through water, all certainty and grace.

He was what I knew he would be, passionate and tender, undisguised. Lost. "I promise not to leave in the middle this time," I whispered to him—in the middle. Questionable timing for a joke, but if we were both remembering our last time together, I thought, we might as well speak of it. Dig it up and disarm it.

It took him a moment to react at all; I could actually see his eyes clear, shift from absent to present, and I remembered that that absorption, that mindless departure into the nothing of sensation was one of the things that had frightened me away from him so long ago. I was a girl then, I couldn't lose myself the way Jess could—that was a goal to spend your life chasing. At least I wasn't afraid of it anymore.

"I wouldn't let you this time," he said, poised above me, his hair backlit, a coppery halo. "That's been the problem, me letting you go." He didn't smile; he wasn't joking. Could that be true, could it really be that simple—the "problem"? I wanted to talk to him almost as much as I wanted to make love to him. And then I wanted to paint him.

In patches of nostalgia, I remembered what it was like to lie in bed with a man, the thrill of someone else's ceiling, a different scent on the pillow, another slant of light from unfamiliar windows. My mind drifted to old lovers—not to Stephen, but men I knew before I knew him. No one in particular; just the sensation of newness, excitement, what it was like to be naked for the first time with a naked man, the lawless, liberating feel of skin on skin, the sense of boundless physical possibility.

It was like that with Jess, and then it was more. Everything between us multiplied, compounded, like mirrors reflecting us in the present, and then an infinite number of diminishing images of our past. We had now, and we had everything that had happened before between us. The most extraordinary combination. Exactly the same and completely different—we were both right.

Afterward, I lay with my head on his chest, listening to his heart beat, feeling his hand in my hair. Our heavy, wordless silence felt right for a time, the only appropriate response to what had just happened. But I was impatient. I wanted answers to all the tantalizing whys—why did he love me, why did he like sleeping with me, why did he pick me and no one else. And how could he want me again after the last time, after *all* the other times I'd disappointed him?

"If it only rains every twelve years, you don't curse it when it finally comes," he said. "You curse the drought."

An analogy. My farmer, my cow herder, my dairyman made a metaphor about *me*. I sank in deeper, seeded in love, planted. "But why did you ever even *like* me?" I was recalling the eighteen-year-old virgin, the overachiever, mama's girl.

He said the nicest things—that I was brave, I had a loving heart, I was kind to him, I liked him even though I didn't understand him. "Caution" ruled me in the end—that was the word he used, *caution*—but by then it was too late, he said, he already loved me.

"It's not wrong to want to please everybody, Carrie. It doesn't work, but it doesn't make you a bad person."

No, just a weak one. But the last thing I wanted to talk to Jess about right now was my mother.

"I always knew you loved me," I said. "It was a secret I tried to hide from myself, but I couldn't, I kept it with me all through the years. I can't imagine my life now without it. Such a gift."

I wanted to know about his wife, but I wouldn't ask. In fact, I wanted to hear about *all* the women in his life, and I wanted him to place me among them. I would've liked a chart, frankly, a detailed graph of the hierarchy of all Jess's women, with me at the tip-top. Not because I was that needy and insecure—I just felt like celebrating. Doing a dance on top of the pyramid.

"Remember when you told me I needed to do the ark animals? And I didn't believe you. You said, 'You *need* this,' and I just laughed. How could you have known that, Jess? Because it's true,"

I felt comfortable telling him, "I did need it, and it *saved* me. All I had before was Ruth to be alive for. The same way . . ." The same way my mother only had me to be alive for. God help her.

"People are like sheepdogs," he said, but his straight face crumpled when I raised up on my elbow to gape at him. "It's true. A sheepdog isn't happy unless he's herding. That's his one and only job, that's his work. You weren't doing your job, but now you are and you feel better. That's why you're here with me right now."

"But what is my job? Making giraffes?"

"Making something. Maybe it doesn't matter what."

"Yeah. No," I realized, "it does matter. It can't be just for me—it has to be more than stenciling wallpaper or refinishing the furniture." Hooking rugs. Shudder. "But I don't know what, and when this is over I don't know what I'll do."

"You'll find out."

"What happened to me? I lost my artist's eye, I forgot how to see. Once—I did a self-portrait out of all the numbers that defined me, my Social Security number, telephone, address, my birth date. For nothing, just for myself. I used to do collages, I did contour drawings, conceptual art, I did rubbings of textures, like—sidewalks and tree bark, bricks. I tried to paint an emotion. I made *connections* between things, I could see sculptures in tree limbs, I could see Renaissance Madonnas in fruit, I could *see*. But then I lost it, I went to sleep. I never thought I'd get it back."

"Your sheep."

"My herd. I got my work back." I moved over him, began to kiss him passionately. "I'm not saying I'm any good—that's a different subject." I wanted him, but I couldn't stop talking. "But I know what I'm supposed to do now. In general, not specifically. Jess, Jess. You are so . . . mmm. Do you have other girlfriends? Do you like my hair short? You've never said."

Well, we'd talk later. Those were reminders; I stuck them in like stick-on notes before Jess shut me up by kissing me back. We made love again, slowly, and so sweetly it made me cry. And it worked this time, and it didn't remind me of anything.

Then it was time to go. "Four o'clock, you have to milk cows." This was going to be a challenging affair, I could see. A daytime affair. "At least it's spring," I said, watching him dress. God, he was good to look at. "Warm. I'm looking forward to a lot of outdoor trysts. Rolls in the hay." I tried a lewd wink, not difficult considering I was flat on my back where he'd left me, naked and uncovered.

"I like your hair," he said, pulling his T-shirt over his head. He looked different to me, more substantial or something. His whole body was real now, not a rumor.

"You never mentioned it. So naturally I assumed you hated it."

"I didn't know what I was allowed to say. I couldn't tell what the new rules were."

"You didn't used to have any rules."

"I changed." He smiled.

"Is that my fault? Do you blame me?"

"I used to. Now I try not to blame anyone for anything about myself."

A model I should try to follow more often. "Anyway," I said, privately defensive, "I don't think you've changed that much. It's more that you've adapted. Really. You're not your house, Jess."

"It doesn't matter. Everybody changes."

But he was sadder, quieter, he'd grown more discreet. I knew some who would say he had room for a little discretion, that curbing his impulsive ways was just part of growing up. I didn't agree with them, now or twenty years ago. Jess had changed because of me—that wasn't ego, it was the truth. But I couldn't despair, even if part of him was lost, because under it all, older, wiser, sadder, gentler, stronger, he really was still Jess. Still mine.

"I might fall asleep," I said, stretching, showing off. What a long time it had been since I'd felt any sexual power at all. You didn't know what you'd missed until you got it back.

"Not for long." His socks had holes in the heels. He pulled on his work boots and tied the laces in knots instead of bows because they were both broken. He needed taking care of! This just got better and better.

"Not for long?"

"Just a catnap."

"Why, are you kicking me out? Got another girl coming at five?"

"Heh heh." He leaned over me. He put his hand on my stomach. His whiskers felt prickly on the skin between my breasts. "Got you coming at five, play your cards right."

"Oh, you're coming back," I said, thrilled. And already the puns were starting, the lovely, corny sex jokes. I could've died from happiness.

"I've got to talk to Mr. Green for a few minutes, get the boys started with the milking. Don't you go away."

"Don't you worry." I sat up when he turned to look at me from the doorway. "Mr. Green's going to know, isn't he?"

"Probably, unless I make something up. Want me to?"

"No, I don't care. Not at all. But . . ."

"Other people."

"Some other people. Ruth. Especially." No need to mention my mother; she was a given.

"Will she hate this?"

"I honestly don't know. Ruth loves you, Jess, but I don't think she's ready for this."

"She's loyal to Stephen."

"Yes. Very. More than that, though. It's a funny age," I tried to explain. "She's using you to grow up. Sometimes you're her father, sometimes you're her friend. And sometimes, more than a friend."

"I know that. I've tried to be careful."

Of course he knew that. I wanted to tell him then that I loved him. The feeling was on me, strong as a flood. What was the barrier? Habit, I decided, listening to the fall of his footsteps on the stairs, the opening and closing of a door. Habit and caution. Jess wasn't the only one who had grown discreet in his old age. But our lives had taken a turn, and by some miracle we were back at the tricky place that had confounded us—me—years ago. Only an idiot would pass up a second chance.

19

Not That I Care

We're supposed to be keeping journals for English. Mrs. Fitzgerald says to write in them every day, preferably first thing in the morning before our censoring brains wake up, so what we say will be freer, like an extension of our dreaming selves, or failing that, right before going to sleep because sometimes the tired mind is as uninhibited as the just-awake one, so it's the same thing.

Yeah, right. I don't have time to eat breakfast in the morning, much less jot down Deep Thoughts, and at night I might get two sentences down before I fall asleep. I think I've got sleeping sickness. It's like the opposite of insomnia. What is that, somnia? I'll ask Krystal. Anyway, I do like writing in my journal, but the only time I can fit it in—and we have to show Mrs. Fitzgerald, she goes down the rows on Fridays to see how our notebooks are filling up; she doesn't read what we've written but she looks to see if there are pages with words on them—so I guess you *could* copy the newspaper or a book or something into your notebook to fool her, but I don't know anybody who's doing that—the only time I can fit it in is when I'm in class. So instead of paying attention in math, say, or biology, I'm writing in my journal, and Mr. Tambor and Ms. Reedy just think I'm taking notes. It's cool.

What's hard about writing in a journal is always having in the back of your mind the thought that somebody besides you is reading it. (Which could happen—Brad Leavitt left his journal on the bus and Linda Morrissy, a sophomore, found it and brought it to Mrs. Fitzgerald the next day, who gave it back to Brad. So that's a minimum of two people who could've read Brad's journal, not to mention potentially Linda Morrissy's entire family and all her friends, plus Mrs. Fitzgerald's friends and her husband and her college student son, and all her son's friends. *Time*, we see, is the only limiting factor.) Anyway, Mrs. Fitzgerald says the only way to get over feeling self-conscious is to write down some embarrassing things about yourself. Don't embellish them, don't let yourself come off as the hero or the innocent victim, just spit it out, something really stupid you did or said, and don't censor it. (But then really make sure you don't leave your notebook on the bus.)

I've been practicing that. The hard part is deciding what to pick among all the humiliating possibilities. So much to choose from. Once I wrote, "I used to stand in front of the bathroom mirror with the door open and pretend the laughter and applause from a program on TV downstairs was for me. I was a famous, beloved performer, and everybody in the audience clapped and laughed uproariously just at my facial expressions, they were so hilarious. I practiced looking surprised and humble during long bursts of applause."

That's the kind of thing that gets you warmed up. You get over being paranoid about confessing something like that, and then you can start writing the real stuff. Like, "I hate my mother. Who's not even my mother anymore, she's turned into some completely different person. It's like the aliens snatched her, implanted a chip in her brain, and sent her back down, and now she's just impersonating herself. She's doing a really shitty job, too."

School sucks. Caitlin is definitely making it with Donny Hartman now, so she and Jamie have, like, circled the wagons and I'm not allowed in, like it's too huge a deal to be a three-way secret. Meanwhile, I am so not interested. I've always known they were better friends with each other than with me. But when I first moved here from Chicago they were having one of their breaks from each other and I got to know Jamie first, then Caitlin after they made up. So I was always the third wheel, which was okay until now, when I'm not much of a wheel at all. I'm getting to be pretty good friends with Becky Driver, but even she has people she's known about a hundred years longer than me.

Raven at least is talking to me again. Except what he's talking to me about is suicide, so that's not too cheerful. Not *his* suicide, just in general, I mean, I'm not worried he'll jump off a bridge or anything. We went to the movies once, but I don't know if it was a date because I just met him at the theater on a Friday after work and we sat with a bunch of other kids from school. We held hands while we watched, but then Mark Terry and Sharon Waxman drove me home because they live nearer. Figure that one out. Not that I care.

So school is a wasteland and even work is sort of boring these days—and *then*, then I get home at six-thirty after a long, hard day and I'm tired and hungry and maybe in the mood for a couple of laughs and some chitchat, a little human contact, not much but some, you know, to keep up the pretense that in my house there still lives an actual family—but what do I get? Nada, because there's nobody home. The house feels shut up, like nobody lives there—I told Mom we should rent it out to crackheads during the day, that way we'd at least get some money from it, and they wouldn't leave it any messier than it already is. All she can say is, "It's temporary." Everything is supposedly going back to normal in one week, when the stupid ark sails.

I wish it was tomorrow. It's getting worse, it's *all* she can talk about—should the horse be a palomino or a regular reddish brown one, wouldn't it be neat if it rained on the seventeenth, should Jess paint the ark white or a color or not at all, and on and on, like I'm somebody who cares. She didn't like it when I told her the first thing Noah did when he landed on land—this is in the Bible—was to get out, build an altar, and sacrifice some animals. Too bad for that species! Instant extinction! She keeps saying she's almost finished, but she gets home later and later every night, and she's so *weird*, either really quiet and off in her own little world or else laughing and talking like she's high, and trying to make *me* happy by telling dumb jokes or tickling me or saying let's go get ice cream—and that's almost worse because it's, like, nothing to do with me, I'm just the one who happens to be there, and whatever mood she's in I'm the one it gets inflicted on.

What if I died? What if the house caught on fire when I was in it and she was out? What if I was asleep and she was the only one who could've saved me, but she was over at Jess's making aardvarks? When she came home she'd turn into our street, wondering what all the fire engines were doing there, why all the flashing lights, who the ambulance was for. The closer she got to our house, the scareder she'd get. And then she'd see it—the stretcher with the body on it in the front yard, the sheet pulled up over the face. The cops would try to hold her back, but she'd break free and throw herself on top of it. "My baby!" I'd have died of smoke inhalation, not burns, so my face would still look nice. In fact I would look very peaceful and beautiful. Mom would completely break down. She'd be ruined.

Sometimes I go over to Modean's after work and play with the baby. It's better than starting my homework or trying to figure out what's for dinner when Mom hasn't left me a clue. Modean always talks to me, asks me about school and work, how my life's going. She bought an aromatherapy kit at Krystal's, and once she let me do an essential oils treatment on her. She said it was great, she wants to do it again sometime. She's a really great mother. Harry's going to grow up without any hang-ups at all, he'll be like the poster child for good parenting. Unlike me, the poster child for neglect.

I call up Gram sometimes and we talk about how stupid the ark is. She's definitely on my side. "Is your mother home yet?" she says, and I'll say, "No," and she goes, "I'm coming over there right now and making your dinner. It's seven o'clock!" But Mom always strolls in around then, so Gram never actually comes over, at least not so far. I wish she would. Wouldn't Mom be embarrassed?

If I just had my driver's license, this wouldn't be happening. It wouldn't feel like solitary confinement around here because I could get out anytime I wanted, like being in prison but with the door open. I told Gram it's like time stopped and I'll *never* get older than fifteen and three-quarters. She said wait till I'm her age and see what I think about time.

What I should do is report Mom. She's starting to get famous, ha-ha, in Clayborne because of the ark; they did a front-page story on her and Jess in the *Morning Record*, and also a feature in the Richmond paper, about how wonderfully zany and nutty it is that they're doing this and what inspired them and blah blah, it was like *gag me*, I could hardly read the articles. So what I should do is call up child welfare and turn her in for neglect. Then you'd have some headlines! "Ark Lady Cruel to Latch-Key Daughter." "Ark Artist Implores Court to Keep Child, But Loses." They'd put me with a kind, loving foster family. She wouldn't even be allowed to visit. No—she could visit, but only an hour a week, and she'd spend the whole time crying. I'd be nice to her, but then it would be time to go back to my foster family. She'd promise to reform and be the best mother ever, but the court would say I had to stay with the foster family until I was eighteen. Then it would be time for college. She'd have missed the best years of my life, and she'd have only herself to blame.

That's better than the house-fire fantasy. It's more grown-up, plus I'm alive at the end. I think I'll put it in my journal.

20

GIVEAWAY INTIMACIES

Chris called while I was baby-sitting for Harry at my house on Saturday afternoon.

"Carrie, hi! How are you?"

"I'm so glad you called," I said, shifting the baby to my other hip and getting a better grip on the phone. "I've been wanting to call you for weeks." I heard relief in her big, braying laugh, and knew I'd said just the right thing. "In fact I was going to call you today or tomorrow, Chris, I really was—"

"Oh, sure."

"No, I was! Because the crunch is finally over and I've got some time to breathe. It's been so crazy, honestly, you can't believe how hectic."

"No, I do believe it. I've been reading about you in the paper."

"Oh, God."

"You're a famous person."

"Famous lunatic. Anyway, it's all over but the sailing, and that's the day after tomorrow."

"Yep, and we'll be there, the whole family."

"You're kidding."

"Absolutely not! We wouldn't miss it for the world."

That was my worst fear and my secret hope, that lots of people would turn out for the launch at Point Park on Monday: an actual crowd. "Well, I'll look for you among the hordes," I joked—sarcastic humor was good for warding off disappointment.

"You sound great, Carrie. You sound a lot better than the last time we talked."

"Do I? Well, I'm feeling pretty good, to tell you the truth."

"I'm glad, that's a relief, because I still feel awful about what happened."

The baby grabbed a fistful of my hair. To distract him, I found his training cup on the counter, still half full of orange juice. "Why should *you* feel bad?"

"I just do. I feel like Betty Currie." We laughed, and it was like old times. "I really miss you," Chris said. "It's dull at work all by myself. I guess it was dull before you came, but I didn't notice."

"I miss you, too."

"God, Carrie. I look at him now. I believe everything you told me, I truly do, and yet—when I look at him, I still can't picture it. I can't believe he'd do such a thing. But I *do* believe it, that's not what I—"

"No, I know exactly what you mean. I couldn't believe it either, the whole time it was happening."

I didn't mean the night Brian mauled me in my front hall, I meant the day he called me into his office and fired me. He did it on a Friday, and he waited till late, after Chris had gone home. I couldn't understand what he was saying at first, I thought it was a joke. I laughed. Then I stopped laughing. "You're serious," I said, staring at him in utter disbelief. "You're firing me." He said, "I don't want to. I *wish* I could keep you," rubbing his hands together with fake boyish nervousness. His forehead was pink and wrinkled with worry, eyes brimming sympathy. *This is the hardest thing I've ever done,* he tried to say with his face, and for half a minute I believed it, actually thought there was some truth in his halting explanation—that I wasn't working out, he really needed somebody with more *personal initiative,* somebody he wouldn't have to give any direction to at all. But when he spread his hands and said, "Almost like a partner, an equal," the truth hit, and I knew he was lying.

"First of all, you don't pay me enough to be a partner," I said—since then I've thought of a dozen much more scathing ways I could've put that. "Brian, why don't you just admit it. This is about that night, isn't it?"

"What night?" The blankness, the absolute incomprehension! I wanted to scream at him, but I knew I'd only feel more humiliated afterward, and he'd still win. All I could do was insult him, inadequately—"You are a complete joke!"—and storm out of his office.

"What *is* it with men?" Chris wailed. "How could he be so stupid, and then be so *mean* about it?"

"But he's never done anything with you, never tried—"

"Never, nothing. Oz asked me that, too, of course, but there's never been anything, not even a hint."

"It's weird."

"It's *weird*. And it's not even so bad that he *tried*, as rotten as that is, it's that he got rid of you afterward! I can't get over that. I'd quit if I could, but I can't."

"No, you can't quit, that wouldn't make any sense."

"That's what Oz says, but I tell you, I feel like it. I'm seeing Brian in a whole new light. I can't trust him anymore, and it changes everything."

"Chris, I'm sorry."

"It's not your fault. If I had something else lined up, you know? Another job to go to. But right now we really need the money, and I feel like I'm stuck."

Harry threw his cup on the floor and shrieked in my ear.

"Modean had to go out, so I've got Harry for a couple of hours. As you can tell, it's lunchtime."

"Oh, okay. Well, see you Monday, then. At the launch."

"You're really coming?"

"Of course!"

"What a pal."

"Listen, now that you're unemployed again, you want to have lunch or something? I could meet you. Away from the office—so you'd never have to see *him*."

"I'd love it. How about next week?"

We made the arrangements, and after we hung up I thought, *There*. One good thing had come out of the Other School—my friendship with Chris. Even Brian couldn't ruin that.

"Where'll it be, big guy, your place or mine? Yours," I decided, eyeing my just-cleaned kitchen floor. If I fed the baby here, I'd have to wash it again afterward. "Want to go home?"

"Mama?"

"No, Mama's not home yet, she'll be home *soon*. Let's go eat lunch!"

"Lunts!"

In Modean's kitchen, I set Harry in his high chair and gave him half a banana to eat while I heated his SpaghettiOs in the microwave. He was a lazy, sweet-natured baby, and so funny, just his facial expressions cracked me up. Spending the afternoon with him was like watching cartoons or the Marx Brothers; you got lost in deep play. "Handsome boy," I cooed, setting his bowl in front of him. I gave him his spoon, too, but only as a courtesy; he ate everything with his fingers. "Want me to feed you?" I offered, waving the spoon. No. His bib was the plastic kind with a food-catcher at the bottom; by meal's end, it was half full of spaghetti, and the other half was on his head. "Did you eat *anything*?" He laughed at me, banging his cup on the table in time with his bouncing legs. He could speak in sentences, long ones, you could even detect the punctuation. You just couldn't get the words. I couldn't; Modean swore she understood everything.

I cleaned him up at the kitchen sink, got a pudding pop from the freezer, and carried him out to the front yard. Should I put sunscreen on him? We'd stay under the maple tree by the porch; surely the dappled shade would be okay for half an hour. I couldn't remember constantly worrying about sunscreen for Ruth when she was an infant, but maybe I did. What different babies they were. There sat Harry on the grass like a Buddha, quietly absorbed in picking apart a dandelion. If I'd turned my back on Ruth at that age, she'd have been three doors down the street by now, staggering along in that cute, drunken, hand-fluttering walk that made you laugh until you realized she was going, she was *gone*.

Harry said, "B-bb-bbbb," which gave me the idea of blowing bubbles—possibly his intent in the first place, you never knew. I carried him inside, found the bottle of bubble liquid in his toy box in the family room, carried him back out to the porch steps. Ruth used to love bubbles. Me, too. Harry let me go first. I blew a perfect stream of airy, iridescent globes, so pretty, gone in seconds, like fireworks. "Bbbbb," the baby said, and I put my cheek next to his soft one and said, "Bbbbb" with a little more air, and we blew a big floating bubble that didn't pop until a grass blade speared it, *poof*.

A car slowed in front of my house and started to park. Not a car, a truck. Jess's pickup. I couldn't see him through the wavy, sun-streaked windshield, but he saw me—he backed up forty feet and parked in front of Modean's house instead of mine. I hadn't seen him in three days.

"Tuck," the baby said. He sat between my legs, leaning back against my chest, pointing. I should get up, but some other kind of weight besides Harry's was keeping me where I was. Jess had on white tennis shoes, maybe running shoes. Was he a jogger? I hadn't known. The jogging farmer. Black jeans and a blue T-shirt, and he was striding toward me, swinging his arms, Jess. Coming up the walk, and Harry stopped pointing and scooted back, amazed. Jess came right up to us and squatted beside my left leg. I could see a place on his jaw where he'd cut himself shaving, and for some reason it made me weak. I rested my chin on the top of Harry's head. Jess smiled his slow, two-stage smile. "Hi," he said. "Who's this?"

"This is Harry. That's Jess," I said softly in the baby's ear. Harry could be skittish with strangers. "Can you say 'hi, Jess'?"

"Tuck," Harry said.

"He likes your truck."

"Tuck!"

So then we had to get up and go over to Jess's truck and look at it and touch it, and Jess let Harry sit in the front seat and play with the steering wheel. I wondered how we looked together. Could people tell we were lovers? I had to remind myself to keep my distance, not lean into him or absentmindedly stick my fingers inside his waistband or in his back pocket—giveaway intimacies I already took for granted. "I missed you," I murmured, surreptitiously brushing his hip with the back of my hand. "I wanted to come see you today, but my neighbor called and asked me to sit for Harry. I couldn't say no." Especially since Modean had been so good about watching out for Ruth while I was up to my eyes in ark animals.

"I haven't been home all day," Jess said. "Missed you, too. Can we go somewhere and kiss?"

I laughed, weak again. "Maybe. What have you been doing?"

"Last-minute things at the river. Guess what I dreamed last night."

"What?"

"The ark sank."

"Oh, no."

"Broke in half and went straight down."

"Like the *Titanic*. Did the animals float?" He laughed at me. "Well, did they?"

"I don't know, I woke up." He took Harry's hand off the gear shift for the third time. "The portholes are perfect."

"Really? Do they show up?" Eldon let me paint extra animal faces on three-foot round plywood shapes Jess cut out for me on his band saw. I hadn't seen them on the ark yet. "Did you put them on all three levels or just around the bottom?"

"All three. The chimpanzees look great hanging off the lower deck. That was a great idea."

"Maybe I'll drive over this afternoon and look. I know, I said I wouldn't, but I can't stand it." The way I made myself stop putting finishing touches on the animals, which were still in Jess's barn, was to take all the paint cans and brushes over to Landy's and store them in his basement. The end. It's over.

"What have you been up to?" Jess asked.

"A million things, all the things I've been putting off since this started. Yesterday I cleaned my house, and it took *all day*. I've been calling people, reminding them I exist. And trying to think about a job, but that's not working—I can't see past Monday. Will you be glad when it's over, or sorry?"

"Both."

"Me, too."

Harry was getting more aggressive; he wanted to take off the hand brake. "It's time for his nap," I told Jess, scooping the baby up. "Come inside with me. You don't have to go right away, do you?" Harry gave a bitter wail. His roly-poly body became all muscle, all of it straining to crawl over my shoulder, fat arms outstretched and beseeching, "Tuck! Tuck!"

Hugs, apple juice, and more bubbles calmed him down. I put him on the floor and let him play with the pots and pans in "his" cabinet (all the others were padlocked) while I heated water for his bottle. "Modean should be home any sec, but I'll put him down first—" Jess turned me around and pulled me into a long, hot kiss. "Oh, I really missed you," I said, holding tight, "I didn't know I would this much."

"You're the only thing in my head. You were before, but that was nothing."

"Can you stay? When Modean comes, we could go to my house."

"Where's Ruth?"

"At Krystal's—she works all day on Saturdays." We kissed again—but it scared Harry for some reason, so we had to stop.

Modean came home. We three chatted in the kitchen for a while. Once she felt comfortable, Modean could talk, and she liked Jess; she'd told me so even before I'd started bringing his name up, so I could talk about him to someone—one of the frustrations of a secret love affair, I'd discovered. Precious minutes ticked by in the kitchen, and eventually Jess said, "Well, Carrie, we should probably go see about that flying squirrel."

Modean didn't even blink. "Oh, okay, see you guys. Thanks again, Carrie," she called, waving to us as we walked across the driveway, trying to look purposeful. That was easy.

Lovemaking was different now. Orgasms with Jess—not at first, but lately—felt as if they were in the exact center of me. As if, before, they all were slightly askew, off middle, but now they were exactly where they were supposed to be. Could that possibly be literally true? Probably not. More likely my body was trying to tell me something. It was making an analogy.

I kept a picture of Stephen on the far bedside table, Jess's side of the bed. He had it propped on his chest when I came back from the bathroom. The photo flattered Stephen, made him look loose and fun loving, shading his eyes from the full sun, his teeth showing in a tight, rare grin. Jess lifted his eyes from the picture to me, and I waited for what he would say. He lay with the sheet twisted between his legs, rumpled and rangy, at ease with everything, and I thought how different they were, the two men in my life. Once Ruth came home from a visit with Jess, talking about who she'd rather marry, a man who felt things or a man who thought things. An oversimplified distinction, but I knew whom she was comparing. Women wanted both, of course, but we were usually drawn toward one more than the other. My mother chose a thinking man because she thought he would be safer. And I guess he was.

I lay down beside Jess. He put the picture back and took my hand without saying anything. I talked more than he did. I had with Stephen, too, but that was different. Jess's silences were safe, intriguing, not indifferent, never dangerous. He was like a—a thermometer, something with mercury in it; my symbol for him in my mind was a tall blue column, upright, running the length of him, and all for me. Jess was true-blue.

"You never ask me about Stephen," I said, draping an arm across his stomach.

"Tell me anything you want."

"Don't you want to know anything?"

He thought. "Me being here—what's it like? I've got my head on his pillow."

"I know. I know, I've been feeling guilty because I don't feel guilty. Enough. I didn't wait long enough, most people would say. In a way, I've been unfaithful to Stephen twice. With you. Once when he was alive, and now."

Jess brushed the back of my hand across his lips, watching me.

"Do you want to know why I married him? One reason?" He nodded, but he didn't have the same compulsion that I had to confess, thrash out, make sense of. "I knew what I'd be getting into. He'd be a college professor, and that was certainly a life I understood, but with Stephen I'd really belong, I'd be his equal." Not like my mother, who had never belonged. "I would be an artist and he'd be a genius. And we'd have perfect children."

"And that's why you loved him?"

"That's why I married him. I fell in love with him because I thought he was someone else. Or maybe he *was* someone else and he changed. Or I changed."

"Who did you think he was?"

"Somebody like you. But safer." This was a hard confession. "I was twenty-three when we met, living in Washington, trying to be an artist. Failing. I'd run completely out of money, and I was down to two choices, get a job or go back to school. The end of my life, I thought. And either one meant caving in to my mother, who always said I should get an education degree and teach art in the public schools. Stephen and I weren't dating anyone but each other, but it wasn't that serious yet. When he finally understood my predicament and what it meant to me, he said—he said, 'Come live with me, and be my love.' In those very words. I guess it sounds silly, but it meant the world to me. His first and his last poetic utterance. He was offering to save me, and he had no motive except generosity. I thought he was like that. I thought . . . I didn't know that this was . . . uncharacteristic. So I fell in love with him."

"And then?"

"Oh . . . we moved in together, but it didn't save me. We fell into marriage, too quickly, and then Ruth was born, and life turned very practical. No more poetry, no more art. Crafts—for money, I started making wreaths and selling them, wreaths for all occasions. Then I made wreath *kits*, and they did pretty well until I got sick of them. Literally. My first depressive period. Is this much, much more than you ever wanted to know?"

"I don't think we can save each other," Jess said.

"No. But—you don't think you saved me?" He smiled. "No, I know," I said, "but it *feels* that way to me."

He began to put his tongue in the spaces between my fingers. "If I didn't exist, if I disappeared, you'd be all right."

"Oh, no." I kept saying no, but it occurred to me that I had changed, and that I would be stronger if I lost Jess than I had been when I lost Stephen. Where was the sense in that? "The sheepdog factor," I realized. "You're saying it's the work. Well, I don't know. I still think it's you." I rubbed against him, pressing kisses on his throat, under his ear. Two months of ark building had made his hands even more rough and jagged, and I liked the feel of them coasting over my skin, pinkening it, arousing me. "Let's not talk about our spouses anymore, not for a while. Let's have a moratorium."

"Okay."

"Don't sound so reluctant." We began to make love again. Slowly this time, not so frantic. At the moment when I began to shudder and spiral up, Jess paused, and I heard it, too—a familiar sound. The squeak of a footstep on the staircase.

I twisted up, fast as a snake, and raced to the closed door, which had no lock. "Hello?" Ruth called from the hall.

"Don't come in." The door knob turned. "Ruth, don't open the door."

"Why? Mom? Who's there?"

My bathrobe lay on the floor at the foot of the bed, but I was afraid to move. Jess rolled off the bed, snatched up the robe, and threw it at me. "I'm coming out," I said, shoving my arms inside the sleeves, yanking at the belt. He'd gone around to the other side of the bed, invisible from the door. I tried to smile—*Sorry—can you believe this?*—but it came out a grimace. He pushed his hair back with his hands, baring his teeth in comical sympathy, and just for a second it calmed me. Just for a second I wasn't sorry. I opened the door.

Ruth looked white and ill. "Are you all right?" In a reflex, I put out my hand, but she flinched away, out of reach.

"Who is it?" she whispered. Fear made her sharp features stiff, like carved wax. Oh, Jesus—she thought it was Stephen. I could see it in the frightened, irrational longing in her eyes.

"Sweetheart," I said, "let's go in your room."

"Who is it?"

"It's Jess."

Incomprehension. Then a split second of relief—oh, *Jess*, well, then—and finally, understanding.

My chest hurt. "Oh, baby." I saw clearly and for the first time that I'd picked the most heartless thing, the worst way to hurt her. She backed up, her mouth open but no words coming out. I followed because I thought she was bolting for the stairs, but she dashed past them and into her room, slamming the door in my face.

Jess, half-dressed, took me by my ice-cold hands and pulled me back into the bedroom. I could hardly feel his arms around me. "Let me stay," he said, but I said no, go, he had to go. He hugged me tighter, even when I tried to push him away. In spite of myself a little warmth began to seep in. I rested my head on his shoulder. "What have I done? I don't mean that, I'm not sorry—but if you'd seen her face—oh God, Jess, I don't think I can fix this. You have to go, please, I can't talk to her, I can't do anything until you leave."

But after he was gone, it was worse. What if this was unmendable? My fingers were shaky when I tried to button my blouse; I put a sweater on over it, I put my shoes on—trying to look *dressed*, I realized. I was afraid to look in the mirror. *Stop*, I thought, but I could feel it coming on, the old contempt for myself. No, a B-movie situation, that's all this was. I'd explain everything to Ruth and—it would break her heart. But she'd recover, and afterward at least there would be no more secrets. But that was a good outcome for *me*: what about this dreadful situation could ever be good for *her*?

I found her doubled up on her bed, arms folded around her stomach. "Are you sick?" When I touched her shoulder she scuttled away, sitting up, pushing back against the headboard. Her eyes looked black in her pale, pinched, merciless face.

"How long has it been going on?"

"I'm so sorry you had to find out that way. I was going—"

"I'll bet. How long have you been screwing him?"

"Stop it. Stop it."

"What, you don't like my language? Hey, I'm really really sorry, I deeply apologize." Her shoulders were jerking in spasms. "How long have you been having sexual intercourse with Jess Deeping?"

"I want to tell you. I would have, but not yet. Because—"

"Because you were ashamed."

"Because I knew it would hurt you."

"Because it's shameful."

"Ruth—I've loved him my whole life—"

I saw how wrong that was as soon as I said it. She recoiled, jumped off the bed. "So did you—did you do it with him while Daddy was still alive?"

"No." But I didn't answer quickly enough.

"You did. God! God!"

"It's not like that—I wasn't having an affair with Jess. I loved your father, you know I did."

"Then how come you're so happy now that he's dead? Anyway, you're lying, I can tell."

"Ruth—"

"You deserve each other. I hate both of you, I can't stand you."

"*Wait*. Hold it!" She hung in the doorway, radiating insolence and loathing, except that her eyes were swimming. "Don't walk out when I'm talking to you. Come back here."

"No. Talk to me from there."

But what could I say? I didn't know any words that could fix this, and I couldn't stop internalizing her disgust. I'd lost sight of my side of the argument, I could only see hers.

"Did you cheat on him or not? Just tell me that, Mom, just say one honest thing. Did you?"

I let too much time go by again. "Once." She winced. "And it was a long time ago."

"A *long time ago*?"

"I don't know how to explain this to you! Anything, anything I say will hurt you. If only you were—"

"That's right! So don't say anything, okay? I don't want to hear a word from you."

I hadn't seen her bottom lip quiver since she was ten years old. It happened when she was trying not to cry. "Darling, please listen to me. If you were older—"

"I'm not too young to know what you are. A slut! Keep away from me, okay? Maybe we'll talk when I'm older. Like five years from now!"

She ran out of the room. My heart stopped—I thought she would fall on the stairs, her loud, banging footsteps sounded so clumsy. I waited for the front door to slam. Instead, a moment later, the kitchen door slammed. Was she going next door? I hoped so—although I hadn't wanted Modean to know about Jess yet. Too bad: exposure was a price we sluts had to pay.

In my room, I stood over the rumpled bed and wrung my hands. The scene of the crime. How could we have been so careless? What kind of a mother did such a thing, took such a risk in her own house? And why was it so easy to feel guilty about my own happiness? Who taught me that, my mother? But she'd been the convenient scapegoat all my life. This time I knew it was me, just me.

I wandered from room to room, unable to settle; in the kitchen, I peeked through the blinds, searching for a sign of Ruth next door. Should I go over there? She might not even be there, she might've gone for a walk.

I took a shower—because I needed one, I told myself, not out of any neurotic Freudian motive. Afterward I went outside and sat on the front porch step. Something felt wrong. The sun was too high—it seemed much later than four o'clock. Milking time; Jess would be thinking of me, worrying about me. I wished I could call him, tell him I was all right. But that I'd blown it with Ruth. But that we'd live.

It took a few more seconds before I figured it out, the thing that wasn't quite right. The piece in the landscape that was missing.

My car.

21

Total Bullshit

Raven wasn't home. His mother looked like an old sitcom mom, like Florence Henderson or somebody, and his house was all wrong, too. He should live in, like, the Addams family mansion, not a long rambler with green aluminum siding and white shutters.

"No, I'm sorry, Martin's not here right now," Mrs. Black said, standing in the front door and drying her hands on a paper towel. "He went to Richmond for the weekend. To visit his father," she added, like she thought I looked sick or lost or something and it would help if she gave a longer explanation.

"Oh," I said. Raven's parents were divorced. He lived with his mother, but he saw his dad pretty often. "Okay, well, thanks."

"Can I tell him who came to see him?"

"Oh, Ruth Van Allen. I just was, um, driving around. It's not anything important. I'll see him Monday." I smiled, walked back down the flagstone walk very casually. Got in the car and started it up like nothing was funny, I drove around by myself all the time. In the rearview mirror I saw my gray, pasty face and the sweat on my forehead. I could almost throw up. I kept the window open as I drove, just in case.

Where should I go? Not Jamie's or Caitlin's. Not Becky Driver's. Krystal's was all that was left. I could park the car in the alley where nobody would see—in case somebody came looking for me. It was only four o'clock; the Palace would be open for two more hours, but Krystal would let me lie down upstairs in her apartment. She might even have Midol or something. No, probably not. Well, some more Menstru-Care, then, but so far its unique combination of B-12, black cohosh, and kava-kava wasn't doing squat.

I parked in back of the store, blocking Krystal's garage, but that was okay. Better than trying to parallel park in the alley. Using the key she gave me, I let myself in the back door.

Krystal was up on the ladder, getting a box down from the top shelf in the storeroom. "Ruth!" She almost lost her balance, she was so surprised. "Wow, you startled me. I thought you were home in bed with a heating pad. It's not that busy, you didn't have to come back." Out in the store, the phone rang. "Oh, shit, can you get that?"

I started to go, then stopped. "Um. That might be my mom."

She gave me a funny look. "Okay," she said, coming down the ladder. "So I'll get it. And I should say—?"

"I'm not here. I went home early with cramps, that's all you know."

She raised her eyebrows and pushed her lips out, fishlike: *Interesting*. Then she made a dash for the phone. I'd never asked her to do anything like this before, lie for me or anything, but I wasn't surprised that she was doing it. Krystal was somebody I could trust.

I couldn't hear what she was saying on the phone, and I didn't want to go any farther into the store. After she hung up, she had to wait on a customer, so I sat on a cardboard box and rocked back and forth, hugging my stomach. Having cramps feels like everything is going wrong inside, like a war happening in your guts. I really could throw up. The more I thought of it, the sicker I felt. The bathroom was only about six long steps away, I could make it. But just then Krystal came back, and I got distracted.

"What happened?"

"It was your mom, all right. She asked if you were here and I said no, you went home early because you were sick." She wrinkled her forehead. "The Menstru-Care didn't work?" I shook my head. "Well, so that was about it, she just asked were you here and I said no. What's up?"

"Can I lie down upstairs for a while?"

"Sure. You running away from home?" she said, grinning. The bell over the front door tinkled. "Go on, I'll bring you some cramp bark tea as soon as I get a break. Fix you right up."

"Cramp bark tea?"

"Absolutely. For muscular support during cyclic changes. Go."

Krystal's apartment was awesome, like in a movie from the 1960s only much cooler, not kitschy at all but, like, retro. She had big orange and brown sculptures on the walls that looked like mud pies, and thick tapestries hanging and sort of finger painting artworks, and the rugs that she'd made herself out of yarn and rope. The furniture was really rough and primitive, twig chairs and splintery cabinets with the nails showing and a couch that was just big upholstered pillows piled on top of one another. And everything in earth tones, and for some reason the shades were drawn, plus she had an electric fountain shaped like a grotto and you could hear water dripping. Being in her apartment was like being in a warm, dim, furnished cave.

I had to pee, plus I needed a new tampon. God—what if Krystal didn't use them? What if she used—leaves, or moss, or recycled cloth made out of—hemp or—

Tampax. There it was behind the toilet, the little blue box. Whew. Then I wanted to check out the medicine cabinet, just *see* if she had Bayer aspirin like everybody else, or Listerine, or Crest toothpaste. It felt a little creepy, being a snoop, so I only opened the mirrored door a crack and peeked inside very quickly. Huh. A mixture. She had some Aspergum and a tube of Ben-Gay, but she also had a bottle of Natrol soy isoflavones and some Earth's Bounty Bladderex with the ancient all-herbal Chinese formula. Cool.

The only thing wrong with the pillow-couch was the cat hair all over it. It was hot in the apartment, which must face west because the sun was baking behind the hand-painted shade over the big window. But the heat felt good; I'd been cold and shivery all day. I pulled a knitted throw over my legs and curled up in the fetal position. Rather than think about Mom and Jess in my father's bed, I went to sleep.

Cramp bark tea tasted like dirt. Krystal made me drink a quarter cup every fifteen minutes, and I told her it was working because if it didn't, the next remedy was two eight-ounce glasses of apple-celery-fennel juice. "For the phytoestrogens," she said. "But what you really need is some reflexology."

Reflexology was a pretty good deal. I got to lie back on the sofa and let Krystal rub my feet. The top of my arch controlled the fallopian tube, and behind my inner and outer ankles were the uterus and ovary, respectively. Sure enough, after about ten minutes of stimulating finger massage, my cramps started to get better.

"Hey, this is working," I told Krystal, who was actually drinking a cup of cramp bark tea, too, and there wasn't even anything the matter with her. I gently shifted the white cat, Charmian, a little lower down on my stomach, closer to my pelvis. I liked the warmth, but after a while the pressure didn't feel so great.

"Sure it is," Krystal said. She had her eyes closed; she might be meditating while she did the reflexology. Right now, she was studying healing touch by mail; in two months she'd have her certificate, then she was going to offer it at the store. Forty dollars an hour, which was a lot, but she planned to *guarantee* results. "Nobody leaves unsatisfied" would be the slogan.

I kept waiting for her to ask questions, like what I was doing there and why I couldn't go home. But she didn't, and that was cool, that was the thing I liked best about Krystal, her live-and-let-live attitude. But on the other hand, if you wanted to talk about anything, you had to bring it up yourself. Which was hard.

"So," I said. "Guess what."

"Hmm," she said dreamily. She was doing the finger walk across the top of my left foot, making little snapping sounds with her index finger joint.

"So. So today I go home early, right? Because I'm sick. And nobody's there. But Jess's truck is in front of the Harmons' house, so I figure he's over there talking to Mom, who had to sit for Harry this afternoon."

"Mm hmm."

"So I get a glass of milk and I—"

"Milk? Oh, Ruth." She scrunched up her face. "The worst, the absolute worst. Almond milk, okay, maybe, but *milk*? Oh, baby, no wonder." She shook her head and began to do the finger walk harder.

"Oh. I didn't know. Well, so anyway. So I was feeling really lousy, but I wanted to see Jess, you know, because he's . . . he was like . . ." A friend. "So I was going up to my room first to comb my hair, try to look less sick, you know, put on some blush or whatever. I get to the top of the steps, and what do I hear in my mom's bedroom? Behind the closed door, which she *never* closes?"

"What?"

"Her voice and some guy's." Except it wasn't voices, because they weren't talking. It was sounds.

"Oh—my—God."

"She goes, 'Don't come in, don't open the door!' So I just stand there. Then she opens up, and she's—she's got on her bathrobe. And her hair all messed up and her face red. It was weird—I barely recognized her, it was like she was her own sister or something. And she looked totally in shock, like somebody just shot her."

"So *who was the guy*?"

"It was Jess. My pal Jess."

Krystal stopped rubbing my foot. Her round eyes got big and wide. She whispered, "Oh, no shit."

"Pretty funny, right?" I laughed, and then I almost started to cry, but I kept swallowing until I got over it. No way, they didn't deserve one tear out of me. "Yeah, it turns out they've been carrying on forever, even before my father died."

"Get *out*. Your mother? No way."

"Way. She told me, she admitted it."

"Oh, Ruth. Oh, man, what a bummer. That is really awful. Are you okay? That is so, so heavy. Jeez, how could she do that? So is the guy really hot or what?"

"I don't know. How should I know?" What a dumb question. "I thought he was our friend, I used to go—over to his house—Ugh." I pretended my stomach hurt and stopped talking until my voice got strong again. I wasn't going to be a baby about this, not in front of Krystal.

"Did you talk to him?"

"No, he left. My mother tried to wriggle out of it—"

"What did she say?"

"Just bullshit, about how she's always loved him. *Always*—get that? Oh, but she loved my dad, too."

"Yeah, right."

"Right—I told you it was bullshit. Basically what she told me was to grow up. So I just left, I walked out and stole the car. Screw it."

"Bitch."

I blinked, thinking she meant me. "Oh, yeah," I said when I realized she meant Mom. "What a total bitch." It sounded ugly and mean, and it felt great.

"I mean, really. That's the lowest, to cheat on your husband."

"I know."

"Even if she loves the other guy, it's still cheating."

"I know."

"You must feel awful."

"I keep thinking about my dad. He would never have done that to her, never. He was so good, and he really loved us. He was the best. One time when I was like eight, she had the flu and he did everything—he cleaned the whole house, he did all the cooking, drove me to school, he did everything." Krystal didn't look impressed enough. "I mean, that's just one thing I remember. He never forgot her birthday or Christmas, and he'd always give me money ahead of time so I could get her something. He was *thoughtful*. And I know he never cheated, I *know* it. How could she? How could she hurt him like that when he never did anything to her?"

"You think he knew?"

"No, I'm—" All of a sudden I was freezing again. "What if he did, what if he saw. Oh, my God. And then he died. His heart broke."

"Well, but you said he had coronary disease."

I pulled my feet out of her lap and curled up over my knees. "What if she did it. What if she made him die." I bit one of my knees until it hurt.

"Wow." Krystal kept shaking her head. "That's too much."

"Maybe he didn't know. Maybe it just happened."

"Yeah. Probably. Still. Kind of a coincidence."

My mouth was making too much water, I couldn't swallow fast enough. I stumbled up and ran, willing the nausea back, not letting it escape until the exact second I got the toilet seat up and my head centered over the bowl.

Then—explosion. Garbage and bile and glue, I made myself sick, I nauseated myself. It didn't stop until all I had left was strings of spit.

Krystal stayed in the doorway, but she wouldn't come in. Mom would've come in. She'd've held my arm or touched me on the back while I threw up, and afterward she'd've talked very calmly so I wouldn't be embarrassed or scared or weirded out. Thinking these things gave me a desperate feeling, a mixture of being mad and feeling hurt, some of it was old and childish and some of it was new and grown-up, and I never wanted to feel that combination again.

• • •

Krystal had a date with Kenny, her current boyfriend. She offered to cancel if I was really sick, but of course I said no, go, it's Saturday night, I'm fine. Before she left, I asked if I could park the Chevy overnight in her garage. "Just in case anybody's looking for me." The police, I was thinking, but I didn't want to say that out loud; it might freak Krystal out. She was being so cool about everything, but I worried that if she thought it through very carefully, she might change her mind. She said sure, put the car in the garage right now, so I went down with her and we switched places.

Kenny came at nine, but I didn't see him. Krystal said she'd go downstairs and meet him in the store so I wouldn't be disturbed. I like him, so I was a little disappointed. Kenny's cute, he always talks to me, he tells funny jokes. He's a lineman for the telephone company. Krystal likes him okay, but she's not in love; once she told me her problem with Kenny is that he smokes too much grass.

After they left, I got hungry. Krystal had said I could help myself to anything I wanted, but when I looked in the refrigerator, except for milk, I couldn't recognize anything as food. Even the vegetables were mysteries, not to mention all the stuff in plastic containers. Everything was beige and looked like oatmeal. I found some granola-looking stuff in Baggies in the bread box and put milk on it in a bowl. Yes—cereal. So then I cut up and added a few pieces of a pinkish yellow fruit I'd seen in the grocery store but never tasted before because it wasn't on Mom's boring shopping list. Delicious. But what was it, a persimmon? Pomegranate? Papaya? The fact that I had no idea just went to show, didn't it? I might as well be living my life in prison. Clayborne—what a joke. If you want to know anything or do anything, if you want to *change* anything, you better make it happen yourself, because nobody around here is going to.

I lay back down on the smelly couch and put Charmian on my chest. "I'm blowing this fleabag," I told her. My stomach bumped the cat up and down when I laughed. "You're the fleabag," I said, rubbing her softly between the eyes. The phone rang.

The machine picked up after the fourth ring. After Krystal's message, Mom said, "Hello, it's Carrie Van Allen. I'm just—I wanted to see, make sure—Krystal, if you're there, pick up, will you?"

I sat straight up. The cat made a hissing noise when she hit the floor. I froze—then remembered: Mom couldn't hear anything on this end.

Her voice sounded thin and high, really strung out. "Ruth's not home yet," she said fast, the words falling on top of each other, "and I can't imagine where she is. I can't find her. If she's been there, if you've heard from her, please, please call me. Right away." And she gave the number. Like Krystal didn't already know it. "If you can't reach me, if the line's busy or—I don't know, just—if you can't get me, call my mother." She gave *that* number. "Okay. Thanks. Call if you hear anything. 'Bye."

I lay back slowly, pressing all my fingers against my teeth. Yikes. Yikes. Sweat prickled in my armpits. It felt like all my nerve endings were electrical circuits shooting out sparks. Oh, yikes.

I could get up and go home right now. "Driving around," I could say when Mom asked where I'd been. She'd be mad, but so what? Eventually this would blow over, the fact that I stole the car, and nothing would come of it.

That's what decided me. Fuck it. I wanted consequences, I wanted trouble. The scarier the better—if it wasn't scary as hell, I wouldn't be doing it right.

Krystal got home at 1:37, I saw by the glow-in-the-dark dial of my watch. I wasn't asleep; I'd just turned the TV off, in fact, after watching a million videos on VH-1. I'd turned it off a couple of times before, but each time I got ready to go to sleep, I'd hear my mother's voice, the way it sounded on the machine—it was like it was haunting me or something. Majorly annoying.

I heard the back door slam shut, some bumping around downstairs, Kenny laughing, Krystal going, "*Shh.*" Would she bring him up? I hoped so, even though I was tired. It would be fun to sit around with them and talk about whatever they'd done this evening. Maybe they were drinking. Maybe they'd give me some.

It got quiet, though. Except for the rain on the window, I couldn't hear anything at all.

I got up from the couch and crept over to the door. They'd better not be coming up now, or Kenny would see me in my underpants. I opened the door to the stairs a crack. Nothing. No—a rustling. Krystal's husky voice saying just one word, but I couldn't make out what it was. The stillness got heavier and heavier, fuller and fuller of meaning. *I bet they are. I bet anything.* I wanted to close the door and hear plain, uncomplicated silence again, but I also wanted to stay put until something definite floated up, a sound clue that proved it. Moaning or something. I hung in the doorway until my neck got sore and the wrist I was leaning on started to tingle and my right foot went to sleep. Now my biggest fear was that they'd hear me close the door and tiptoe back to the sofa, and know I'd been eavesdropping, but it was either that or stand there all night, so I shut the door as softly as I could and took slow, huge steps across the carpeted floor to the couch, and when I got to it I coughed really loudly as I sank down on the sighing pillows and pulled the covers over myself. I lay still, feeling stupid and childish.

Everybody's cool about sex but me. Jamie and Caitlin make jokes about it all the time, and underneath the kidding around there's this feeling that they know everything about it and they aren't even that interested in it except as something to snicker about and make fun of. But how can you make fun of something that's a complete mystery? Were they just lying all the time? Was everybody? I myself am afraid to make sex jokes because I might get something wrong, say something that makes no sense and reveal my total and complete ignorance. Not about the act, I get that, but about the . . . the culture of it, the atmosphere. The history and politics, the do's and don't's, the rules. Well, pretty much everything.

Like, why, really, is it all that great? People build their *lives* around it, and not just guys, either. What exactly is the deal? Sometimes I think the only reason I want to do it is because it's not allowed. If I never did it, if I became a nun or something, would I miss it? How many times do you do it if you live to, say, eighty, and you're so-called normal? And how in the world could you get tired of it—that is really a mystery—just because you're married or middle-aged or whatever? It's still sex, and you're still naked, so how could that ever be boring? And how come everybody but me knows the answers to these questions?

Mom having sex with Jess—I don't have to try to not picture it, because I can't picture it. Even if I wanted to. Which I don't. I can't picture Mom with Dad, either, although once I might've heard them—a long time ago, and I didn't know what I was hearing, just funny noises late one night from behind their closed door. But I must've known more than I thought I knew, because instead of going on to the bathroom, I turned around and quietly went back to my room, without peeing.

Mom and Jess. God. Why? They just couldn't stand it? Like in a movie where the two people get so hot they start ripping each other's clothes off? Gross—I almost pictured it, just for a second it flashed in my mind's eye. I set the scene in Jess's barn, the one where they'd made the ark animals, and I imagined naked Mom and naked Jess twisting around in a pile of sawdust.

"Kitty kitty kitty." I hung my arm down and snapped my fingers to call the cat, distract my mind, because I wasn't going there, no way.

Betrayed was how I felt. By my own mother, who turned out to be two-faced and a lying hypocrite. A cheater. Last summer, Mom rented *Hope Floats* and we watched it together, just the two of us because Dad wasn't interested. Poor Sandra Bullock, we said, cheated on by her horrible, wormy husband. How low could you go? Mom sat there and pontificated on fidelity and faithfulness and the seriousness of the marriage vows, blah blah blah, and it was like we were two grown-up women discussing something really worldly, men's wandering ways, and how women were superior because compared to men they hardly ever cheated. (So who are the men cheating with, is what I never get; if men do it all the time and women hardly ever, who are the men's partners? The same handful of women over and over? Boy, what sluts *they* must be.) But—the *hypocrisy* of that conversation, that's what got me. It showed that somebody you trusted could look you in the eye and lie their head off, and you'd never know it. If I thought about Jess teaching me how to fish, talking to me, listening to me talk about my dad . . . if I thought about that I'd explode, I'd hurt myself. It was like I had gas on my hands and Jess was a fire or a hot stove. If I touched it, I'd blow up and burn everybody around me to a crisp.

So I didn't think of it. When all of a sudden the cat jumped out of nowhere onto my stomach, I let it crawl under the covers, and I talked to it and listened to it purr, and told it a story about mice and cheese and a hole in the wall. And I fell asleep before Krystal came up, so I never knew how long she stayed downstairs making love with Kenny.

22

NO SIN GOES UNPUNISHED

The police didn't care. Unbelievable—I tried to sound calm, but panic was spreading under my skin like a virus. "Can't you put out an APB or something? She's a missing person. And she's not like this, she's not a runaway, *this is not normal.*"

"Yes, ma'am, and you say she's taken your car?" Courteous indifference, that's all I could hear in Officer Springer's voice. It made me clench the phone harder and try not to yell.

"*Yes*. She's gone, it's gone, the keys are gone. It's been more than *five hours.*"

"Well, we've got the make and license and we'll be keeping an eye out, but if I were you I wouldn't worry. I know that's—"

"You don't understand, you don't understand, something's happened. Something's wrong."

"But no note, you say, and you and your daughter had a fight?"

"We had—words, yes. She was upset."

"Well, fifteen, they do this, Mrs. Van Allen, they take off."

"Not Ruth. No. She wouldn't."

"First time for everything, you'd be surprised. My guess is she'll turn up any minute, hoping you didn't notice the car was gone. And when she does—"

"Listen to me—are you saying you're not going to do anything?"

"Ma'am, have you got someone you can call?"

"I've been on the phone calling people for five hours. What do you—"

"I meant a family friend, a relative, somebody to sit with you while you wait. I know it's stressful."

"Yes, it's stressful. Anything could've happened. I think she's alone—I've called everybody, no one's seen her—" Officer Springer, who sounded very young, waited through a polite, embarrassed silence while I pulled myself together. "All right," I said when I could. "You're going to call me when you hear anything."

"Yes, ma'am, we certainly will."

"And I'm going to call you. I'll be calling back."

"That's perfectly okay. If it's any help, we get calls like this every day, every single day, and nine times out of ten the kid turns up fine."

"Okay."

"Just remember to give us a call when she comes home, will you?"

"Yes, I will. Thanks."

My left ear ached from pressing the phone to it. I stood in the doorway, listening to the hum of the refrigerator, the tick of the clock over the stove. Ruth wanted a dog clock; every hour a different breed of dog barked. I told her no, it cost money we needed for a hundred other things. Every day, a dozen times, we butted against each other over something that inconsequential. I want this, you can't have it. Yes, no. Inmate, warden. My purpose on earth was to puncture my daughter's dreams. I probably did it out of habit half the time. The parent-child system worked until adolescence, then it broke down. It was fundamentally flawed from the age of thirteen, when it changed from adults guiding children to people bossing around other people. Everyone hated it, both sides, but nobody had a better idea.

I hated the sound of the clock ticking. The smell of fish was vaguely nauseating—Modean had brought over a plate of tuna casserole for my dinner, but I hadn't been able to touch it. Ruth could have it if she came home hungry. No—she could go to bed starving for all I cared. If nothing was wrong, she hadn't been kidnapped or beaten or molested, if she was all right, if she was safe—I'd grab her by her skinny shoulders and shake her till her teeth rattled. Interesting: the only way she was going to get a warm welcome here was if she could produce evidence of abuse.

I could still think like that, dry, sardonic thoughts, because as frightened as I was, I could not make myself believe anything truly horrible had happened. I had to trust that feeling, I had to think of it as higher intuition, not cowardice or denial. My mind swerved between images of catastrophe and images of safety, innocent, prosaic explanations for Ruth absconding with the car. The catastrophe scenarios made my heart race and my skin flush, but deeper down, I knew Officer Springer was right. Any minute she was going to waltz in with a sullen face and a surly explanation, and I was going to kill her.

The phone rang.

"Carrie?"

I sank down on the sofa. "Oh, Jess."

"Bonnie just told me."

"I called her. To see if Ruth was with Becky, but she's not."

"Why didn't you call me? Bonnie said she's been gone since this afternoon."

"I kept thinking she'd come home. I was sure she'd be here by now. I should've called you, I'm sorry, I wish I had."

"It's all right."

"It's dark out now, and she's not used to driving at night."

"Have you called the police?

"Yes, but they're not worried. They just say to wait."

"What happened after I left?"

"I ruined it. I still don't know what I should've said. She was so angry, and I couldn't comfort her, I couldn't do anything but make it worse."

"I'm sure she's okay."

"Why?" I could tell myself that, but I couldn't stand anyone else humoring me. "It's Saturday night, it's almost ten o'clock. She's got the car, she's out, she's gone, she's driving around somewhere—how can you think she's *okay*?"

"Because she's smart, she wouldn't do anything stupid." He didn't sound calm, though. That scared me more than anything—Jess always sounded calm.

"Taking off was stupid," I told him. "Anyway, it's not her stupidity I'm worried about, it's stupid other people. Oh God," I breathed, covering my face with my hand. "No, I know, you're right, she's probably fine, nothing's happened. But she could be with somebody, and I don't know who."

"You've called all her friends?"

"Everyone I can think of. There's a boy—I even made his mother call his father—they're divorced—to make sure he was there and not with Ruth, that he was in Richmond where he's supposed to be, and he is. And all her friends, nobody knows anything—"

"What about Krystal?"

"No, nothing, Ruth left work early because she didn't feel well, and that's all Krystal knows. The police don't care, they say it happens all the time, not to worry—" I laughed, a garbled sound. "I don't think they're doing anything. They say it's nothing, she'll turn up."

"Are you by yourself?"

"Modean was here before."

"Do you want me to come over?"

"No. Yes, but it wouldn't help, there's nothing you can do."

"Why don't I drive around and look for her, look for the car."

"Jess, would you?"

"I'll leave right now. I'll call you in a little while."

"Thanks. Thanks."

"Try not to worry. I know," he said when I tried to laugh. "Just keep thinking about how smart she is."

"I'll *make* her smart when she gets home." Some joke.

I hung up quickly—we'd talked too long, tied up the line, what if Ruth was trying to call? And about thirty seconds later, the phone rang.

"Any word?" my mother's voice boomed in my ear.

"No." I'd called her earlier, on the slim hope that Ruth had gone over to her house.

"Oh, honey."

I told her about the police, that they didn't care.

"I'm coming over."

"No, Mama."

"Your father's home if she calls or comes over here. I'll come and stay with you."

"No, don't, *honestly*, there's nothing for you to do." We argued a little longer, while I tried to figure out what I really wanted. I'd said no to her without thinking, but would it be better to have someone to wait with? Mama would take over everything, no question about it. Would that be bad or good?

"All right, but call me the *minute* you hear anything, you hear?"

"I will, I promise."

"Doesn't matter what time it is, I won't be asleep anyway."

"Well, you might as well go to bed, there's no point in both of us staying up."

That started it all over again. "Then why don't I just come over and we can stay awake together?"

"Because it's too—I'd just rather not, I'd rather—I just want to—"

"All right, never mind," she said stiffly. Wounded.

Shit. "Mama, I'm no good. You don't want to be around me." She clucked her tongue in disgust. "Anyway, she'll probably drag in here any minute. I'm honestly not that worried. Listen, we should get off the phone in case, you know, she's trying to call. Or the police or something."

"All right, Carrie." Still hurt, but bearing up. "You'll call when you hear?"

"I said I would. 'Night, Mama. Thanks. It really—"

But she'd already hung up. *It really helps that you're there*, I'd been going to say. Not to mollify her, either. It was true.

I couldn't sit still. I called Krystal again, got the machine. I hung up after leaving a message, aware of irrational anger. How could she be out when Ruth was missing? Irresponsible airhead. No, that wasn't fair; Ruth was crazy about Krystal, whose only flaw was flakiness. Plenty of worse qualities she could pass on to an impressionable fifteen-year-old. Still, what if Ruth had gone there, gone to the store looking for guidance or help or friendship? And nobody there, just the empty building. I shivered; a hole opened in the pit of my stomach when I pictured her in the car, driving in the dark, hurt and confused, furious over the injustice I'd done to her.

Upstairs in her room, the familiar locker room smell greeted me, and the exasperating rubble and chaos I hated and loved. Although I tried all the time, I couldn't quite remember myself at fifteen, not with any helpful clarity, not to any purpose. Confused and impatient—I remembered being that, but the details were hazy. My strongest memories were of Jess and my mother. What would Ruth's be? Losing Stephen. Finding me with Jess.

Her notebook journal lay halfway under one rumpled pillow. I put my hand on the edge of it and held it there, not thinking about anything. I made my eyes go blind and pulled the notebook out, ran my thumb along the corner, found the last page she'd written on. Saw the date: yesterday. Blinking, blinking, still half blind, I absorbed the last sentence. "So anything above 75 on the final, which I could do with my eyes closed, and I still get a B for the year, not bad for a Francophobe."

I toppled over, resting my head on the pillow. The ripe, sweet smell of Ruth's hair calmed me. Oh, baby, where are you? If she would just come right now. Right now. Every time I heard a car in the street, I froze, listening like an animal. If the front door would just open right now. I started making promises to God. I wanted to read Ruth's diary so badly, I got up and walked across the room. I should've put it back exactly where I'd found it, but I was afraid if I touched it again I'd open it.

I caught sight of my haggard face in the mirror over the bureau, or the small square in the center of the mirror that wasn't covered with stuck-on photographs, ticket stubs, invitations, funny headlines, magazine cutouts. One of the photos was a close-up of Ruth, Jamie, and Caitlin, taken before Christmas by Jamie's amateur photographer brother. Ruth, the tallest, stood in the middle, and they all had their arms draped across one another's shoulders, smiling for the camera. Happy girls, their sweet friendship on display. But Jamie's brother had also caught a look in Ruth's eyes I knew very well, a half-hidden restlessness, a bafflement that didn't match the cocky, wide-mouthed smile. A look that said, *What am I doing here? I think I might rather be* there.

Stephen had had that same thin-veiled impatience with the here and now. It hadn't made him happy. An unfortunate legacy—but Ruth might outgrow it; already she had more resources than Stephen had ever had. Her inner life was quieter. She was sound—I felt that on a bone level, although the details of her inner life these days were beyond mysterious to me. Had we been as close as we were ever going to be? It was one of my terrors—that the paths of our lives had forked for the last time, and now we would begin to grow progressively wider apart, or at best no nearer, until the day I died.

But maybe not. Glimmers of a new kind of closeness with my mother showed through the murk from time to time. Just glimmers, no shining beacon. Our egos kept butting against each other;

too many things couldn't be said, too much was off-limits. Why wasn't love enough? Why wasn't it ever enough?

I wandered back downstairs. Outside, clouds were piling up around a puny moon behind the locust tree. Heat lightning flickered in the west; the air smelled damp and metallic. I left the door open so I could hear the phone, and sat down on the porch steps in the dark. I should've let Jess come over. No lights on at Modean's house, no lights at the Kilkennys' across the street, only one streetlight burning at the corner. Quiet. No dogs, no night birds, not even a cricket. I should've let Jess come. Or even Mama.

This is the pain I should've felt when Stephen died. No sin went unpunished indefinitely, and I had so many sins. Sleeping with Jess wasn't the worst, it was only the one I was focused on tonight. Stephen always said I was too easy with Ruth, and here was the sickening proof that he was right. If I'd been a better mother, she would never have dreamed of running away. Modean had disagreed violently when I'd told her that tonight—in a weak moment. "You're a terrific mother!" she'd insisted, adamant as a cheerleader. "You're not too lax, what are you talking about? *I'm* too lax. This boy's doomed." She put her lips under Harry's chin and blew, making him shriek. "Carrie, you're not too soft on Ruth, I really don't think."

But I did. My excuse was always that I dreaded being like my own mother, so I backed off, time after time, from imposing my will on my daughter—because that would mean imposing my morals, too, my worldview, my principles, my likes, dislikes—everything Mama had smothered *me* with at Ruth's age and ever after, and see what had come of that—resentment, distance, formality. Yearning for closeness and fearing it at the same time, because it came with the risk of being devoured. "For your own good" excused a multitude of little takeovers. It usurped the will of the one you loved, and caused her to make dreadful, long-lasting mistakes.

To save Ruth from that, I'd gone too far the other way and left her rudderless, maybe valueless. No, that wasn't true—but—I was the most wishy-washy of mothers, a dishrag. Except when I caught myself and overcompensated with some unsuitable, out-of-character act of parental tyranny that accomplished nothing except to piss Ruth off.

My own thoughts antagonized me. *All I want is what's best for her, I only want her to be happy, to be what she wants to be, to live a full life*—every word was true, and yet I knew how loaded each one was because my mother had said them all to me, and believed them just as fiercely. It was love's fault again—love simply wasn't enough. How could you find a balance? How could you let a child go and keep her safe? How could you kill your own ego? Unconditional love—was there any such thing except from a dog? I thought of Modean, bouncing Harry on her hip by the hour, laughing with him, listening intently to his gibberish, rocking him to sleep, worrying about him, doting on him—none of that guaranteed anything. He'd grow up and leave her no matter how well she loved him, and unless she was a saint she'd hate it. She'd spend the rest of her life getting over losing him.

I covered my head with my arms, grinding my eye sockets against the bones of my knees. Misery felt like being filled up with black water and drowning. I didn't always believe in God, but I wished he would kill me if that's what it would take, give him my life for Ruth's. Where was she? *Please, God, please, God, please.* For the first time since he died, I missed Stephen, truly missed him. *I've lost our baby,* I confessed, smothering sobs against my thighs. Inside the house, the phone rang.

I ran. I said "Hello!" and Jess said, "Carrie?" in surprise.

"It's me." I didn't sound like myself. My mouth was gluey, the words sticking to each other. "Did you find her?"

"No. I've been all over, everywhere I could think. I'm at a pay phone on Madison. I'll keep trying."

"Okay." I could hear traffic in the background, like whirring static.

"How are you? Are you alone?"

"Jess?"

"Yes?"

"I wish I could do everything over again. I'm so sorry I ruined it for us. If I had a second chance, I'd change everything. I wouldn't let you go."

"Carrie. Let me come there, let me see you."

"No, I'd rather you kept looking for her. Because no one else is doing anything. The police—"

"I'll call them myself. Right now."

"Okay, that's good."

"Call your mother, call a neighbor. You shouldn't be alone."

"I might. Yeah, I might do that. I love you, Jess," I said, and hung up.

A misty rain started to fall. I stood on the porch step with my face tilted up, letting the cold spray prick my skin. A gust of wind pushed me back on my heels. I turned around and leaned against the screen door; the wet mesh smelled like all the warm, rainy days of my childhood. I put out my tongue and tasted the bitter, salty metal, and a memory drifted back, of my mother holding me, both of us staring out through the screen at a greenish storm. I must've been three or four, small enough to pick up but old enough to remember. I could feel Mama's arms tight around my middle, I could see the dogwood tree sway and bend in the front yard of our old house on Pioneer Avenue. I loved storms. Probably from that afternoon, when we'd watched through the screen together, Mama's cheek on my ear.

Ruth loved storms, too. That was a comfort. I let it seep in, a small reassurance that, after all, I hadn't done everything wrong.

Morning.

Two policemen came early, just after eight o'clock. They didn't look smart, they were too young, one had a whitish stain on his lapel, one kept fingering a shaving cut on his jaw. I didn't like them. But I was excessively nice to them, so they would like me and work harder to find Ruth. All night I'd wanted the police to care, to start taking steps, to get worried and take action. Now that they had, I was petrified.

"I've already called all these people," I said when Officer Fitz, the one with the stained lapel, asked for the names and addresses of Ruth's friends. "But no, you talk to them again, that's good," I added in haste, afraid I might have offended him. After they left, I remembered that neither of them had told me not to worry.

I made a fresh pot of coffee, brought the newspaper in. I was tired enough to collapse in a chair at the kitchen table, but too tense to do anything but slurp coffee and stare around at the walls. About three o'clock last night I'd thought a drink might help. I'd poured a glass of white wine, and got down about half of it before tossing it in the sink. It worked too well, made me feel loose and drowsy, and I couldn't have that. I had to stay vigilant. I could direct Ruth's safety with my mind—I almost believed it. If I let down my guard by relaxing or, God forbid, falling asleep, chaos might win. No, the power of worry was my best, really my only weapon.

When the phone rang, I knew it was my mother.

"Hi. No, not yet. I know. Well, they were just here. They . . . yeah. They didn't really say anything, but they're starting to get serious. I know. About time. Well, you can, but—No, it's just that there's nothing for you to—Sure, I want you to. Okay. Okay. No, don't bring anything, just—okay. 'Bye."

"Fun's over," I said to my reflection in the oven window. No more wallowing alone in misery and desolation, no more holding back chaos single-handed. "Mama's coming."

But before she arrived, a carload of Fledergasts pulled up in front of the house. I was sitting at my usual post on the top porch step, alert to the sound of car engines long before they turned in to Leap Street.

Intent on the sound of my own car, I didn't hear Chris's station wagon until it stopped and she got out on the passenger side. I had never seen her in a dress before, a blue and white seersucker shirtwaist, with white high heels that made her look like a giant. She saw me when she was halfway up the walk. Her frowning face cleared; she waved, smiled. She never dropped by like this. What if—

I jumped up.

"Hey. We're on our way—"

I ran down the steps and dodged past her, trying to peer through the streaky car windows. Oz at the wheel, Andy and the little girl, Karen, in the backseat. No Ruth. Disappointment felt like a surprise slap in the face.

"What is it?" Chris said, staring at me. "You okay? You don't look—"

"Ruth's not with you?"

"Ruth?"

I sagged.

"What's wrong? Where's Ruth?"

"She's missing. I just thought maybe she was with you."

"*Missing.*"

"Since yesterday afternoon." Chris gasped. I turned, but she grabbed me back and gave me a hard, long-armed hug. When it began to feel good, I pulled away. "So," I said. "What's up with you? You guys off to church?"

"Have you called the cops?"

"They're looking, they say they'll find her. She's got the car."

"Oh, my God. Well, she's just out joyriding. We used to do that—didn't you do that?"

"All night?"

She made a quick, frightened face. "She'll come home, Carrie. Any minute, I bet."

"Yeah."

"Who's with you? Shall I stay?"

"No, thanks, my mom's on her way over."

"Are you sure? We're on our way to church, yeah, but they can go without me." She gestured at the car. Oz was drumming his fingers on the steering wheel, but stopped and waved when he saw me glance at him.

"No, you go on. Nothing going on here but waiting."

She looked indecisive. "Well, okay, then, but I'll call you later. Oh—the reason I came by. It seems stupid now, but I'll just tell you. I quit."

"You what? You quit?"

"Brian called me at home last night to tell me the news. He sounded so damn *happy*. He just hired your replacement. Guess who it is."

I could hardly remember my job. "Who?"

"Lois Burkhart."

"Lois—from the bank?"

"Lois from the bank! Can you believe it?"

"No. Well—she's an accountant, isn't she?"

"Brian has an accountant, Carrie, that's not why he hired her."

"Why—"

"They're dating!"

"They are? But isn't she married?"

Chris wriggled her eyebrows. "Oz saw them at the Ramada Inn last week, having breakfast."

"Oh."

"So I quit. I don't need that. We talked about it all night. Oz didn't want me to leave, not right away, but I just couldn't keep it up, not with this on top of what he did to you. I've lost all respect for him, Carrie. I called this morning and told him."

"Oh, Chris."

"He didn't even argue. Three years I've worked for that man. We started that school *together*. I'm not saying he couldn't have done it without me. I'm—"

"Well, he couldn't have!"

"No, but I just thought loyalty counted for more than this," she said, blinking moist eyes. "I guess I'm naive. I guess I was stupid."

"It's Brian who's stupid."

She flapped her hand, taking a step back. "I just wanted to tell you. I don't need cheering up, and anyway, you've got enough to worry about. I'll call you later, when we get home from church. I just know Ruth is fine."

"Chris, I'm so sorry."

"It's not your fault."

It felt as if it was, though. "Do you have any plans, any idea what you'll do?"

"No!" She laughed, a little wildly. "Something will turn up, I'm not worried." Obviously not true. "Andy says we should all pray for a miracle, so that's what we're going to do." She combed nervous fingers through her spiky, dirty-blonde hair. "I don't know where he gets that," she leaned closer to say. "We don't even go to church that often. I'm scared to death he's going to be a priest." She moved in for another hug. "Okay, gotta go, but I'll call you. Try not to worry, okay?"

"Okay."

"Andy'll put Ruth on his prayer list."

"Great."

She walked away, stiff-legged in the clacking white heels. She had nice legs. Standing on the curb, she was twice as tall as her car. She bent over, folded herself into the passenger seat clumsily, knees pressed together. The whole family waved to me as they drove away.

"I can't believe she'd go and do this of her own free will." Mama plumped up a sofa cushion by pushing it against her stomach and pounding it with her fist. "She's not like that, she would not deliberately cause this kind of worry. I just *feel* it."

"I think she did, though."

"No, I don't believe it. The police are not approaching this right. That child did not run away. Something happened. I don't know what," she said, steering away from her worst imaginings again, remembering at the last second that she was supposed to be comforting me, not ratcheting my anxieties up higher. "I'm just saying, if they still think she's out joyriding—for nineteen hours!—they're seriously barking up the wrong tree. When did you talk to them last?"

"I told you, they came by this morning. They—"

"That's the last time? Hell, *I'll* call them. This is a runaround, pure and simple."

I thought, *Good, you call,* because even that little bit of responsibility lifted—as futile as I was sure calling the police again would be—felt like a sack of rocks off my shoulders. And deep down, some childlike faith still lay under the irritation and fatigue and hopelessness that, as awful as everything was, Mama could fix it.

But she plopped down on the couch and didn't reach for the phone. She was vain about her appearance, wouldn't dream of leaving the house without lipstick and mascara; even today she'd taken pains to match her eye shadow to her gray blouse. But I'd never seen her look so old. It wasn't lines or wrinkles as much as the color of her skin, yellow from sleeplessness, and the sag of her flesh from worry and fatigue. Drawn by protectiveness, I started to sit beside her.

"I'm telling you, something's *wrong,*" she roused herself to say, for at least the fourth time since she'd gotten here, and I veered away and sat down in a chair. "How would you know if anything's missing from that room? It's World War Three in there. This is what comes of letting a child have dominion over her own space."

"What?" She must've heard that on a talk show. "Mama, what's her room got to do with anything?"

"Someone could've come in here and stolen her things, her valuables, and you wouldn't even know it."

"She doesn't have any valuables."

"She has a stereo, doesn't she?"

"Yes, but—"

"A camera?"

I shrugged.

"A bank? A telephone, a cashmere sweater, leather boots—"

"She doesn't have a cashmere sweater. *I* don't have a cashmere sweater. Anyway, what's that got—"

"Someone could've robbed her. I'm just saying, I can't see Ruth walking out of this house by herself. Something else happened."

"Mama, nothing else happened."

"How do you know?"

"I know."

"You don't know."

"I do."

"You don't."

I squeezed my eyes shut. "Will you stop? She wasn't kidnapped."

"Don't even say that word!"

"Well, isn't that what you keep hinting at?"

"I'm not hinting at anything."

"You *are*." I stood up, vexed beyond caution. "You're saying somebody came in the house, stole her four-year-old stereo—which is still there, by the way, I saw it—and stole Ruth too while they were at it."

"Carrie, there are weirdos all over the place. I'm not trying to scare you, honey, but that boy she spends too much time with, that vampire person—"

"He's in Richmond with his father, I know that for a fact."

She waved that away. "They're plenty more weirdos where he came from, the high school's crawling with them. They ought to have a dress code, they ought to wear uniforms. But that's not the point—"

"No, it's not."

"The point is, she wouldn't have walked out and stolen the car for no reason. *That's* what the police need to focus on."

"She didn't walk out for nothing. You're right, she didn't."

"There had to be a reason, she wouldn't have just—" She looked at me sharply. "What?"

No going back now. But no going forward, either: when I opened my mouth to finish it, no brilliant explanation came out.

"You had a fight," my mother realized. "Oh, Carrie!" She whacked the flat of her hand against the sofa arm. "For Pete's sake, why didn't you just say so? Lord, Carrie, *damn* it, if you knew what I've been thinking, what I've been through. Well? What happened, what did you fight about?"

Telling her would be as bad as Ruth finding Jess and me in bed. Worse, because she'd zapped me back into my childhood again—as easy as that. I took a deep breath. And jumped when the phone rang.

I hurried around my chair, but Mama was closer and got to it first. "Hello. Yes—no, but this is her mother."

"Mama, give it to me."

"Who?"

"Mama!"

"It's the police," she snapped, shoving the receiver at me.

I turned my back on her. "Hello?"

"Mrs. Van Allen?"

"Yes?"

"It's Officer Springer. Got some news for you this morning."

"You found her." Everything went gray and grainy, little dots of static in front of my eyes. Mama's sharp fingers squeezing the back of my arm kept me upright. "Where is she?"

"Uh, no, ma'am, we haven't exactly found her, but at least we know where she spent the night last night."

"Wait. Mama, *stop*." She was trying to hug me from behind. I twisted away. She saw my face and froze. "Sorry," I said into the phone. "What were you saying?"

"Ma'am, we interviewed your daughter's friends from the list you gave us, and we also talked to Ms. Bukowski there at the, uh, the Mother Earth Palace and Natural Healing Salon, and Ms. Bukowski was suddenly able to recollect that Ruth stayed with her last night."

"Ruth stayed at *Krystal's*?"

"Yes, ma'am, looks like it. Officer Fitz said she was evasive until he reminded her that hiding or harboring a minor's against the law, after which she recalled your daughter sleeping there overnight but leaving the residence early this morning."

"Where did she go?"

"Well, we don't know yet. Officer Fitz said Ms. Bukowski was evasive on that point also."

"*Evasive*?"

"Yes, ma'am. Could be she doesn't know, like she's saying, or could be she's keeping it to herself. Some kind of loyalty."

"Loyalty!" My mother kept dragging at my arm and hissing, "What? What's he saying?" "Can't you make her tell? Can't you *arrest* her?"

"We'll certainly be talking to her again, yes, ma'am. But chances are your daughter will turn up soon, either way. That's how it usually is—they stay out one night just to get your attention, then they go home. You be sure and give us a call when that happens. Some people forget, and that wastes our time because we keep looking."

I said I would, and we hung up.

"Who's evasive?" Mama demanded, finally letting go of me.

"Ruth stayed at Krystal's last night—"

"I got that."

"And she's telling the police she doesn't know where Ruth went, but they think she might be lying."

"Where's the car?"

"I don't know. Not there, I guess, or he'd have said."

"So she took it and she went somewhere. Where?"

"I don't know."

"What's her number?"

"Whose number? Krystal's? I don't know, it's on the—speed dial thing, you press—"

"I know how speed dial works."

She took the phone from me, checked the name printed on the receiver, and dialed. She stood with her feet apart, head up and bust out, the hand not holding the phone clenched in a fist on her hip. Not a trace of fatigue showed on her firm, sturdy body. The Clayborne Women's Club had made a grave error.

"Hello? Krystal Bukowski? This is Dana Danziger, I'm Ruth Van Allen's grandmother. Where is she? What? I think you do. Oh, I doubt that. Listen very carefully, if anything happens to my granddaughter, if she gets a *hangnail* this morning and I find out you know where she is—Pardon? I don't care about that, the police can do whatever they like, I'm telling you what *I'll* do. I'll sue you. No, in *civil* court. For violating my grandchild's civil rights. Yes, I can. Oh, yes, I can. Before I get through with you, you won't have two soybeans to rub together. You think that's funny? I'm perfectly serious—you won't have a vitamin left, you won't have a pinch of wheat germ—"

"Mama—"

"What's that? Call it anything you like, I'm telling you what I am going to do. I'll ask you one more time: *Where did Ruth go*?" Her eyes blazed into mine. Suddenly she grabbed my hand, her knees flexed, and stood up on her toes. Her voice went up an octave. "And you *let her*? You idiot! You silly—fruitcake! Yes, you could've! You could've called her mother, you could've called the police—"

"Where's Ruth? What's she saying?"

"I'm too angry to talk to you, you moronic woman, but this is not the end of it, I promise you. I beg your pardon? What did you say to me?" She took the phone from her ear and stared at it, bug-eyed. Then she slammed it down hard enough to break it.

"What?"

"Do you know what she just said to me?"

"*What*?"

"'Have a nice day.'"

"Mama, where's Ruth?"

"She's gone to Georgetown."

"Georgetown! In Washington? Oh, my God! By herself? Why?"

"So she could get a tattoo." She wilted. She flopped down on the couch, slack jawed, shaking her head from side to side. "A tattoo." She closed her eyes. "My God, how unbelievably tacky."

23

FLASH

The hitchhiker looked like Billy Zane. The girl was no fool; she wouldn't have picked him up if it hadn't been pouring rain. And bitter cold. He had a dangerous look, something wild and careless in his steel blue eyes, but his mouth was kind. Rainwater dripped from his slick black hair into the collar of his Tommy Hilfiger shirt. No, his worn, creased, black leather jacket. They rode for a long time without talking, nothing but the slap of the windshield wipers and the hiss of the tires on the wet pavement breaking the sex-charged silence. Finally, outside Tulsa—no—at the beginning of the Badlands, in the middle of nowhere, he turned to her and said in a low, warm, rough voice, "You're going to help me, I know it." Because he was on the run from the law. But he didn't even have to say it—she knew. And they both knew that she knew.

They kept driving. She played Lauryn Hill on the car stereo, and he knew then how cool she was and how perfect they were for each other. They rented two rooms that night in a sleazy motel, the kind Mulder and Scully stay in. He came in her room when she was in her underwear, cream-colored bikini bottoms and a matching tank top, like Nikita in *La Femme Nikita*. He couldn't take his eyes off her. He told her the truth—he worked for Operations and he was on a job *pretending* to be running from the law, and she had to start working for him. She had stick-straight blonde hair and she always wore black. She could do karate. She was beautiful and feminine, but she could throw men around like stuffed animals.

Her name was Jade. Jada. Her name was Kara. Her name was . . . Ally. Never mess with Ally because she will kill you. Ally has long legs and she slouches in chairs, and when she gets up it's like watching a cat stretch after a nap. She wears tight black leather pants. Wherever she goes, people stare at her. Which makes it harder to work undercover, but . . . she's a master of disguise, so . . .

Three guys in a red Pontiac wouldn't pass, they just drove at exactly the same speed I was going (sixty-five exactly) and stayed next to me in the left lane. I didn't look at them after the first time, because they were scruffy and stupid-looking, probably locals, probably farm boys from Fredericksburg or Stafford. I was driving to D.C. on I-95 instead of the back way because I wanted to go fast, and yet everybody but me was going around ninety. I *would've* gone ninety, but I was keeping a low profile. If I got stopped—disaster.

Out of the corner of my left eye, I could see the Pontiac guys waving or something, gesturing. They had to think I was at least sixteen, probably older, they had to. I had on, from yesterday, my new long-sleeved black and white striped pullover, and I'd pushed my hair behind my left ear so my gold hoop earrings and one silver stud were visible. My watch was dumb, I should put it on my right hand for driving, but my extremely cool silver and onyx ring made up for it. What I couldn't make up my mind about was my baseball cap. There were two ways you could look at ball caps: one, that they were totally out and had always, in retrospect, looked lame, especially when worn backward, and two, they were a fashion basic like T-shirts and would never go out, and wearing them backward if you looked cool in every other respect—that was key—made you cute and sassy, like Cameron Diaz, and sort of like you didn't care. Which was, of course, the ultimate.

A huge truck came up behind the Pontiac and flashed its lights. I let my foot off the gas a little. The Pontiac guys did something I didn't look at, either waved or flipped me off, and roared away. Good riddance. Now everything was perfect. I turned the radio up and tried to find a noncountry station. I stuck my elbow out the window. I rested my temple on my fingertips. A woman with interesting, serious thoughts on her mind. After a while, the mist coming down turned into droplets, I had to close the window. Shit, was it going to rain? Mom's umbrella was in the backseat, but it was so incredibly queer, one of those tiny pastel Totes only old ladies or insane people carried.

Maybe I should stop at a gas station and buy cigarettes. Except I didn't have any I.D. Caitlin got cigarettes sometimes, Marlboros, but she didn't really smoke and neither did Jamie, so I didn't either. So far. But if I was ever going to take up smoking, now was the time, today was the day. I couldn't figure out why I wasn't more worried. I should be, like, a nervous wreck. But it was like I had a shield around me. Mom was the one who'd broken the rules, not me. If I got caught—so what? Nobody could touch me. I was immune.

The radio was full of static, but I could hear "Take It Easy," the old Eagles song. "I'm runnin' down the road," I sang along, and slipped into my second favorite daydream. I was driving by myself in a convertible on a long, straight highway in the midwest with Tracer beside me on the front seat. A girl and her dog. Men fell in love with me, but I never stayed anywhere for long, I was always leaving them, it was just me and my dog. Sometimes I'd take odd jobs for the hell of it, but then I was gone, and the people left behind in the small town said, "Who was she, where did she come from? Do you think she'll ever come back?"

Wow, it was really raining. Stupid car, the windshield wipers only had two speeds, regular and maniac. Maniac went so fast you couldn't see anything but the wiper blades, plus the *whack whack whack* made you nuts after about two minutes. This was going to make it harder to see the turnoff. Especially since I wasn't quite sure where the turnoff was. Maybe I should've gone the back way. I *sort* of knew that way—you hit 66, and then somehow you were in

D.C. But there were bound to be signs, right, when I got close, and if I just stayed in the slow lane, nothing could happen. Theoretically. Driving on a superhighway was much easier than driving in town or on windy two-lane roads, because all you had to do was steer.

There was a gas station exit with fast-food signs, Burger King, McDonald's. I'd left Krystal's at eight and hadn't bothered with breakfast. Should I stop? Nah, I'd wait. I was hungry, but it would be more fun to eat in Georgetown.

There was a lot more traffic all of a sudden. Where were all these people going on a Sunday morning? Not church. Now a lot of signs were preparing me to do something. Backlick Road. Franconia or Old Keene Mill Road. I was still in Virginia, I didn't have to do anything yet. But the Beltway was coming up. Gram hated the Beltway, she wouldn't get on it for anything. "Killers, nuts, they'd rather murder you than slow down." Yikes, here it was! Now what? I was on 95, and 95 turned into the Beltway! Ninety-five turned into 495 if you went to Alexandria, and 495 was the Beltway. Did I want Alexandria? Baltimore? No, but I was in the wrong lane, I had to get one lane over to the left.

God. They wouldn't let me! I put on my turn signal, but a million cars roared past, bumper to bumper, not a single one would let me in. I stepped on the gas, but the exit was coming, coming—I slowed and hit the brakes, and the guy behind honked and almost hit me. "Shit, shit, shit," I yelled, and then I did it—jerked the Chevy into the next lane over, *knowing* there wasn't enough room. But it worked and I got in and the Beltway exit flew by and I was safe.

My hands were sweating and my right foot was jerking on the accelerator because my leg was shaking, but I was in the right lane and I was safe and invisible and *this was how everybody drove*. They just went where they wanted to go, never mind if it was safe or they had enough room or the car behind was going a hundred miles an hour. Drive defensively? Yeah, right! "My ass," I yelled, and my heart was still beating like a drum.

Okay. Okay, settle down. Three ninety-five, I was on 395, and here came Pentagon, no, Arlington Cemetery, no, Memorial Bridge, no. Or maybe. I knew that bridge, it went right to the Lincoln Memorial, which was definitely in D.C. But you had to get off 395 if you went that way, and I didn't want to get off anything. No turns. This went to D.C., too, the sign said so.

Rosslyn, no, Airport, no, Crystal City, no. Jeez, another Memorial Bridge exit. No, I wasn't getting off 395—and look, George Mason Bridge, 395 went right over it. Ha! I was crossing the Potomac, there it was, and there was Washington, dead ahead. And the Jefferson Memorial, my second favorite, right there on the left. So cool. I'd be in Georgetown any minute now. I couldn't wait to park this car and get the hell out. Terra firma.

Nothing looked familiar, though. Did I want Fourteenth Street? Too late, wrong lane, I was going under another bridge. Yikes, the Southeast Freeway. Freeway, I didn't want a freeway. Ninth Street? Too late. My hands were, like, frozen on the steering wheel, I could only go straight. Did I want the Capitol? No. Not South Capitol Street, not the Navy Yard. Where the hell was I? This was wrong, this was completely the wrong part of town.

Okay, Eleventh Street Bridge? What the hell, just get out of here. I was shooting over the river again, but that was okay, even though it was the Anacostia and not even the Potomac. South, okay, that was backward, but now I could start over. *Two*-ninety-five, and the sign said I could hit the Beltway going this way. So if I went south, or west, I should hit 95 again. No panic. Everything was just going to take a little longer.

I got a map at the Exxon in Annandale (exit 6), because the guy at the Mobil on Braddock Road (exit 5) was Indian or something and I couldn't understand his directions, but I was afraid to hurt his feelings, so I just nodded a lot and said, "Uh huh, okay," and drove to the next exit. Maps were better anyway, you were more in control. You never saw Nikita asking anybody for directions.

Okay, now I saw my problem. I should've come in on 66, which went right into town, you got on Memorial Bridge and turned left or something and there you were in Georgetown. Or was that the Roosevelt Bridge? What I needed was a D.C. map, but all they had was Virginia. But this was good enough. Sixty-six, that was the ticket. Also, six was my lucky number.

Okay, the Theodore Roosevelt Bridge, not the Memorial. Now—E Street? That didn't sound right. Stay in the right lane, that was always safest. This was a pretty street, but what was it? Constitution Avenue. Shit, this was wrong! There was the Washington Monument, tourists crawling all over. Didn't people have anything to do? At least I had a Virginia license plate. These people came from Minnesota, North Carolina, Oregon. Hah. They had to be even more lost than I was.

A nice-looking lady in the passenger seat of the car next to me was stopped at the same red light. I rolled down my window. "Excuse me!" The lady heard and rolled down her window. "Do you know how to get to Georgetown?"

The light changed. The lady turned to the guy driving, probably her husband. The car behind them and the car behind me both honked. "Turn here!" the lady said, and she and her husband drove away.

Turn here? Twenty-third Street? O-kay.

Shit! Shit! This was the circle around the Lincoln Memorial, and I couldn't get out of the right lane. Should I keep going around? Start over? But what if the guy in the car knew something, maybe this was—

No! Memorial Bridge, and I had to get on it, they wouldn't let me over. I was going over the river again, back to Virginia.

"Shit, crap, fuck, bastard—" Staying in the right lane blew. Now what? Arlington Cemetery, no. Route 50, no. George Washington Memorial Parkway? No, but I was on it anyway. "God!" Balls, crap, piss. I tried to read the map and stay in my lane and not speed and not go too slow so the giant SUV in the rearview mirror wouldn't crawl into my trunk. "I hate tailgaters!" I yelled, beating my fist on the wheel. I could see Georgetown—right there, right *there*, I recognized the red brick buildings of the university. So close. "And yet so far." I laughed, but it sounded hysterical.

Chain Bridge? Too late, I was in the wrong lane. Nobody was going forty-five, the speed limit, but me, so no wonder. Now a long, long, long, long stretch with nowhere to get off. Well, the CIA, but I wasn't going to get off at the CIA, no way. Finally—495, Maryland. Fine, Maryland. Virginia kept screwing me, why not try Maryland. I couldn't tell if it was hunger or nerves that was making my hands shake. Once I got on the Beltway, I'd take the first exit, find a gas station, and buy a candy bar. And look at the goddamn map.

I'd never parked in an underground lot before. I had a heart attack driving under some low pipes, thinking they'd shear off the top of the car, but they didn't even hit the antenna. On purpose I found a place about three miles from the elevator, so nobody was around and I could forward and reverse, forward and reverse, as long as it took to get the Chevy perfectly straight between two gigantic concrete pillars. When I turned the key and the engine hacked and coughed and finally died, it was like washing up on some island after you've been shipwrecked and swimming in the shark-infested ocean for a week.

At least now I knew how to get to Georgetown: you took the Beltway to River Road and then you got on Wisconsin Avenue and just went straight. It was longer, especially if you got in the left lane for Massachusetts Avenue by accident and had to turn around at the Naval Observatory, which was not allowed, but in theory it was a straight shot, and then you just turned right into Georgetown Park's parking lot and there you were. And it was only four o'clock in the afternoon.

I sort of knew where to go now. Back in March with Gram, we'd walked by the cutest tattoo parlor on one of the side streets off M Street, and I was pretty sure I could find it. At least I was on foot. Sunday afternoon. The rain had stopped, and it was like everybody in the whole city was out for a walk on M Street. God, walking around Georgetown by yourself, not with your grandmother, that's like nine and a half on the scale of coolness, maybe even ten. No, ten would be walking around with your boyfriend.

Maybe I should eat something before getting tattooed. There weren't any cheap restaurants, though. That place, the Purple Dog, where Gram and I ate before—it was gone, if I was remembering right; now it was the Black Cloak Inn, and the prices on the menu outside looked outrageous. Eight dollars for a little salad! On Wisconsin, I stopped at an open-air grocery and bought an apple and an orange, and ate both of them on my way to the tattoo place.

Karma Chameleon—thank God *it* was still there. The outside was painted neon green and yellow, and it looked like a happy place, psychedelic instead of biker. I wanted to look at the pictures and read the signs in the window, soak up the atmosphere, get the lay of the land, but a couple coming out of the door saw me and the guy held the door for me, so I had to go in.

Wow, oh wow, this place was awesome. It was like an art gallery. It even had a bunch of couches and easy chairs around a coffee table littered with tattoo magazines and photo albums. Tasteful gray walls, gray carpet on the floor. That was Georgetown for you. The only way you'd know you were in a tattoo parlor was the clerk behind the counter, and behind him the big framed blowups of the most amazing tattoos I had ever seen. A bunch of Georgetown University kids—you could tell by their sweatshirts—

were sitting in the chairs, talking and laughing, looking at picture albums. I wandered over to the side, to a low table covered with big portfolio books chained to the wall, like the yellow pages in a phone booth. I opened one called *Tattootek* and started leafing through it. Whoa. These weren't like any tattoos I'd ever seen before. Rainbow colors, the truest reds and greens, I didn't even know they could *do* that on skin. Every page was like an explosion of colors in your face, and bold, wild shapes, sometimes you couldn't even tell what the picture was, high-tech designs like in an art museum, like that guy Léger. Well, I didn't want that, I was thinking more along the lines of a flower or something, and smaller, I didn't want anything covering my whole back, not that I could afford it even if I did.

The next book was completely skulls and bones, unbelievable, some of them were absolutely beautiful, just exquisite, until it hit you that you were looking at, basically, death. Why would you want death printed on your arm? Or your butt—here was a guy with a little coffin on his ass, and on the other cheek two skeletons with their arms around each other. Weird.

Lots of medieval stuff, the whole dungeons and dragons thing, and devils, demons, vampires, witches, a lot of fiery swords. Two whole books of religious tattoos, including one of Jesus on somebody's arm that looked like a black-and-white photograph, it was so real.

Nature stuff—some of these tattoos I could go for. I especially liked a beautifully drawn blue jay surrounded by pink and green flowers, and a moon-sun design right above somebody's collarbone. Now that was classy. Yikes—this lady had thick black Chinese writing on both breasts, plus her nipples were pierced with spikes. Not little thin rings, *spikes*, maybe a quarter of an inch thick!

"That's gotta hurt," said a woman standing next to me. She smiled on one side of her mouth, the side that wasn't pierced with a little silver paper clip. "I've done my tongue and my belly button, my septum, this one"—pointing to the paper clip—"but I gotta draw the line at nipples. I *mean*."

"Yeah, really," I said.

"But that's just me."

"Me, too."

"I don't care what anybody else does, pierce your brain for all I care."

"I was actually looking more for a tattoo," I said.

"That's all they do here, no piercings. I got this done." The woman had black hair shaved to a stubble, so it was hard to tell how old she was, she could've been twenty or she could've been thirty. She pulled the sleeve of her T-shirt up over her shoulder to reveal an Egyptian woman, like a goddess, in gorgeous pinks and oranges.

"Wow, fabulous. You got that here?"

"Like it? Ask for Stella if this is the kind of work you want. She's a genius. She did this, too." She pulled up her shirt.

"Oh my God!" It was like a pen-and-ink anatomy drawing over her whole front, all the internal organs drawn to scale in the correct places, labeled in old-fashioned script, LIVER, GALL BLADDER, SPLEEN. "That's awesome," I breathed.

"Isn't it great?"

"Was it expensive?"

"Oh, God. Because they charge by the hour and this is complicated. This is no Sailor Jerry flash, know what I mean?"

"Really."

"So now I'm thinking biceps, and I'm thinking either phoenix or Pegasus, the whole myth thing, or else something zodiacal. Just not sure I want a crab on my arm for all eternity, know what I mean?"

"Ha, right."

"So what are you getting?" She rested her hip on the counter and folded her arms. Her head looked bluish under the whiskery stubble, and fragile somehow, you could see the veins over her ears and the bones in her skull. Maybe she'd get her head done someday, little labeled drawings of the cerebral cortex, the medulla. "This your first tattoo?" she asked, eyeing my naked arms.

"Yeah. I haven't quite decided what to get. So—what happens if you get something and then you don't like it?"

"Laser."

"Oh, right."

"But it's expensive, about a thousand bucks even for a small tat, and your insurance won't even look at it."

"Oh."

"So you have to be really sure."

"Yeah."

"You have to pick something that totally expresses your inner self, your personal spirituality. Your body is a temple and you decorate it according to its unique nature."

"Right."

"Tattooing's an artistic way of declaring who you are, you know? What you believe in. So people can see what you are on the inside from the outside."

"Right, sure." I turned back to the book lying open on the counter. My hand fluttered over the picture of two sea horses, another of a howling coyote, an Indian chief, a unicorn, crawling bumblebees. Did any of them express my inner self? "It's kind of like picking out wallpaper." The woman raised her eyebrows and didn't smile, and I added quickly, "The books, I mean, big and heavy, you know, like at the wallpaper store."

"Yeah. So have you got I.D.?"

"Pardon me?"

"They don't do minors here." She gestured over her shoulder.

"Oh." I saw the small sign right behind the computer on the big counter: MUST BE 18—WE I.D. "Oh, yeah." Shit.

"I think sometimes they'll do it if you have a guardian, though, like your mother or something."

I smiled weakly. "That'll happen."

The woman shrugged, sympathetic. "Let's go ask Tony." And she turned and walked over to the counter.

I followed.

"Hey, Tone."

"Fay, what's happening."

"I'm looking at your Celtic custom, you've got some wicked stuff. Listen, this lady—"

"Ruth," I said politely.

"Ruth might have a little problem with her age."

"If she's not eighteen, she's got a problem." Tony's whole face and neck were pierced, silver rings and spikes and clips stuck through his nostrils, eyebrows, cheeks, lips, ears, jaw, forehead, throat. I didn't want to stare, but how could you not? "So how old are you?" he asked me.

"Um, not quite eighteen. Almost."

"You got a driver's license?"

"I left it at home."

Tony and Fay smiled. After a second, I had to smile, too, to show them I knew they knew I was lying. Well, that was the end of that.

Tony had heavy silver rings through the webbing between his thumbs and forefingers. His left arm had twenty or thirty tiny tassels puncturing the skin in a straight line, wrist to elbow, like a fringed leather jacket, except he had a fringed silver arm. "What are you looking for," he asked, "flash or custom?"

"Um . . ."

"How much money have you got?"

"Oh. About a hundred dollars." All my savings that I hadn't banked, plus an advance from Krystal on my next paycheck.

"Flash," said Tony.

"Yeah." Okay, I was looking for flash.

"She could go to Southeast," Fay suggested.

"Yeah. The Navy Yard, you got scratchers around there, they'd probably do you," Tony said.

"Southeast?"

"Or Anacostia."

"Yeah, more scratchers on Good Hope Road, in that area. I mean, if all you want is flash."

"You could try Tex's," Tony said doubtfully. "Really watch the needles, though, don't let him slide any used by you."

I didn't like the sound of Tex's. Plus I'd have to get back on 295, I'd have to go across the river again. "Isn't there anyplace else in D.C.?"

Tony and Fay narrowed their eyes in thought, then shook their heads. "Nah. Pretty much in D.C., you need I.D."

"Okay. Well, thanks. I'll try Southeast, I guess."

"Just be sure to pick an image that mirrors your inner self," Fay reminded me. "You know, something that's the real you."

"Right," I said. "I will."

The real me, I mulled on the sidewalk. Some of the religious tattoos—tats—were really beautiful, but I wasn't that religious. An animal, maybe; I liked wildlife. Or flowers. Flowers might be dippy though. Karen Angleman got a rose on her shoulder blade in ninth grade, and already it was kind of stale. Hm. The true Ruth . . . How about a giant question mark on my forehead?

"'Scuse me. Say, 'scuse me."

I turned around. A man was hurrying after me along the brick sidewalk. His face looked so friendly, I thought I must know him. He stopped in front of me and we said, "Hi," together.

"Hi," he repeated, "how are you doing?"

"Fine, thank you." No, I didn't know him. I was sure.

"So you'd like to get a nice tattoo, huh?"

He must've been in the store—funny I hadn't noticed him. "Yeah." He looked old, forty at least, and he was dressed like a nerd in a yellow short-sleeved dress shirt tucked into too-small green pants, and a black belt pulled very tight around his waist. "I could help you," he said in a soft voice, smiling. "I know a place you could go that's not too far from here. I'm familiar with them, I'm sure they'd do it."

"Um, well, I was going to go to Good Hope Road."

"Oh, Ruth, you don't want to be going there," he said, pursing his lips, trying to look sad, which wasn't easy, because he had one of those faces that always smile, that can't not smile. He started walking while I was talking, so I had to walk along with him. "Good Hope Road's no place for a young girl. A young white girl," he lowered his voice to say. "It's not a good neighborhood, Ruth. Believe me, you don't want to be going there by yourself. There's a place on Georgia Avenue I could take you to. They know me there. I could help you."

"Um . . ." I was trying to think fast. It was a little creepy that he knew my name.

"Georgia Avenue is near here?"

"Pretty near. A car ride, though."

"Oh, I've got a car."

He looked surprised. When he raised his eyebrows, his whole forehead went up an inch. He had curly, wavy hair the color of tobacco. It didn't look quite natural. "My car's right here." He waved his hand toward the street.

"Um . . ."

"To get a tattoo, if you're underage, you have to have a 'guardian.'" He laughed, making little quotation marks in the air with his fingers. "We could tell them I'm your brother."

My father, more like. He kept smiling, smiling. He looked at my face instead of my body—that reassured me. We'd stopped beside a gray car, some nondescript sedan. I looked at him covertly, noticing how his rosy cheeks stood out in his pale, freckled face. I couldn't see any tattoos on his arms. Pudgy arms; he was really bulging out of his clothes.

"Listen," he said, "this isn't a pickup. To tell you the truth, the guys who run this shop I'm talking about are friends of mine. They'd appreciate the business."

"Oh."

"Yeah, it's really just me trying to do them a favor. And you too while I'm at it."

"Oh, I see." I had to smile back, I had to, you couldn't not respond to a smile that insistent. "Well, and Georgia Avenue, um, where on Georgia Avenue is this place?"

"Hm? Oh, up toward Silver Spring, but not that far. Missouri Avenue, in that area."

I'd have to look at my map. "Well . . ."

"It's not that they don't do good work. This one guy's an artist, a genius—but he's just starting out, not many customers yet. I bet he'd cut you a deal."

"Really?"

"Yeah, sure, a discount on some really fine work, probably as big as you wanted. And you should see the colors these guys work with. Incredible stuff. That place—" He jerked his thumb back at the Karma Chameleon and gave his head a quick shake, grinning.

Wow. Way, way cool. If this guy was being straight, wouldn't that be something? A large, beautiful tattoo, something really special, and at a price I could pay.

He dug a key from his pocket and unlocked the passenger door to the gray car. "So what do you think? Want to try it?" He kept his hand on the door handle but didn't open it. "Huh? No harm in trying, you figure, right?"

I folded my arms, pressing my pocketbook to my stomach. I looked over his shoulder, wishing he would stop smiling. "How about if I follow you? I'll come out of the parking lot where I am and pull up right behind you, then you go and I'll follow. That way I'll have my car and you won't have to bring me back here."

He never stopped smiling, but his eyes got darker, it was almost as if they stopped seeing me. He licked his lips. "Sure. Yeah, okay, that'll work. What're you driving?"

"White LeBaron. Convertible, but the top's up."

He nodded, watching me. "Nice car."

"Yeah, my dad gave it to me. Sweet sixteen." I smiled back, lying through my teeth and liking it. A kind of rush went through me—it was the best I'd felt all day. "Okay," I said, "sit tight. I'll swing right around behind you, shouldn't take more than five minutes. I'll give a toot in case you're asleep." I laughed, and the man stared at me hard before giving a quick, uncertain laugh in reply. "Thanks a lot, hey, this is really nice of you." I started backing up.

"No problem."

"Wow, a cheap tattoo—I can hardly wait. Okay, I'll see you!" I waved, pivoted, and strode off down the sidewalk. I didn't turn around, not even at the crosswalk on Wisconsin, because if I turned around he'd know. The powerful feeling was already gone. I felt breathless, panicky, like that time Lisa Cromarty and I, my best friend in Chicago, thought a creepy guy from the bowling alley was following us home. In the dim underground parking lot, I kept walking fast, trying to look innocent and determined and empty-headed, but at the elevator I finally had to turn around to look behind me. No guy.

Unless he was hiding behind a car, looking at me through the dark windshield. A lady rolled a baby carriage around the corner. The elevator came, and I held the door for her. We rode down in silence; the baby was fast asleep with its mouth open, bare legs curled like commas. For a few seconds I felt safe, until the doors opened and the lady rolled her baby in the opposite direction from my car.

There it was, alone in the middle of nothing except dusty concrete. The last thirty yards felt like walking across a minefield, or like waiting for a sniper to shoot you in the back. I got my key out way ahead of time, but my hand was slick and shaky, it took two tries to get it in the lock. The door wouldn't close, I had to slam it three times, and then I banged the lock down with my thumb so hard I tore the nail. Then the car wouldn't start. On the fourth try it growled to life, and I put my forehead on the steering wheel, my heart pounding. Shifting into reverse, I stepped on the gas and crashed into the pillar beside the right rear bumper.

I couldn't even swear. This was beyond any bad words I knew. Tears stung behind my eyes as I inched forward and backed out again, this time not hitting anything. Still no sign of the guy, anyway, and when I paid the lady in the booth five bucks (!) for parking, there was no gray car lurking in wait on either side of this block of Wisconsin. I turned right, toward the river, then right again on K Street, with no idea where I was going. Just away from him.

So far, I wasn't having any fun.

24

When She Was Me

"Ruth was there all along. She was in the store, and that woman, that *bitch*, lied to my face."

I'd never seen Carrie this angry. She was rigid with fury, her teeth clamped, red in the face. She had her hands in fists, elbows out, she was hitting her knuckles together in time to the beat of her outraged voice.

"She was there, and Krystal lied to me, and now she's let her *go*?"

"She's prob—"

"Mama, Ruth's driving the car by herself to Washington."

"But she's a good driver," I said as calmly as I could, "she'll be all right."

"She's not that good. All alone in D.C.? Anything could happen to her. *She's fifteen years old.*"

"Honey—"

"And she's in a mood. I know her, she's feeling reckless, she might do something—Oh, that *woman!*" She pivoted around, looking at the floor, the door, the couch, something to kick. "If she were here now I'd strangle her, I swear to God I would. How could anybody be so *stupid*?"

"Why was Ruth in a mood?" I took her by the arm and tried to make her sit on the sofa, but she spun away and went to stand with her back to the rainy window. The look on her face made me decide to sit down by myself. "Why was Ruth in a mood?" I repeated, though now I wasn't sure I wanted to hear. "What did you two fight about?"

She had on yesterday's clothes, baggy white shorts and an old T-shirt of Ruth's with a Roadrunner cartoon on the front. She must've slept in those clothes. If she'd slept at all. She looked pale and limp, way beyond exhausted. "I'll tell you," she said, folding her arms across her middle. She opened her eyes wide, like she was getting ready to jump off a cliff. "We fought about Jess."

"Jess *Deeping*?"

I jumped when she jerked one arm down and slammed the wall behind her with her palm. "Yes, Mama, Jess *Deeping*. Ruth came home yesterday afternoon and found us. In my room."

I let that hit, let it come right in like a punch to the stomach. It hurt, and it rearranged things inside, but I can't say it was any big surprise. I'd seen it coming. I got too old to fight, and he won.

"Well," I said. "Well. I'll take a wild guess and say you weren't building llamas up there."

"No."

"What did Ruth see?"

"If you mean—us in bed—"

"That's what I mean."

"She didn't *see* anything."

"Thank God for small favors." A sweaty weakness passed through me, as if I needed something to eat. "Well, well, well. Are you proud of yourself? That's a fine example to set for a young girl. I'd say that's probably the end of Ruth's childhood, wouldn't you?" Carrie turned her face away, and I lost interest in going on in that vein. You don't need to punish somebody who's already taken care of it for you.

"All right, then," I said. "What's done is done, no use picking at it, it's over. Come over here and sit. You don't look right."

"It's worse than that."

"How could it be? My God. You haven't married him, have you?"

She looked at me steadily, a long, searching gaze. Once she almost smiled. But mostly she looked bitter. "Mama, do you remember when I flew home from Chicago for the high school reunion? The fifteenth?"

"Just you and Ruth? I remember."

"Jess and I got together that night. I slept with him."

Funny, that didn't come as much of a shock, either. Somewhere in the back of my mind, I think I might've known that all along.

"It was our first time. That probably surprises you. I imagine you thought we were intimate in high school, but we weren't. No, I was a virgin to the end."

She kept wetting her lips. She looked me straight in the eye, but I had a hunch if I yelled *boo* she'd hit the ceiling. She looked like a girl to me, scared but determined, she looked like herself twenty-five years ago. Then I blinked, and the middle-aged woman came back in focus.

"At least when it finally happened we didn't enjoy it," she said with a sour smile. "That ought to make you happy." She looked down. "Sorry. The point is. Ruth . . ."

"Ruth? Ruth what? She was five years old!"

"I told her."

"Dear God. Why?"

"I could've lied. Maybe I should've, but she asked me straight out." She made her hair stick up running her hands through it. "I told you it was worse."

"You're right."

"Do you think I should've lied?"

"How should *I* know? Oh my Lord, my Lord. Oh, what a mess."

Carrie came and sat down at the other end of the sofa. "It's not a mess, Mama. It's not an unfortunate domestic situation. I love Jess. It's real."

"You don't even know him anymore."

"You don't know what I know. Now or then—you have no idea."

"Then?"

"I loved him then, too, but that didn't mean anything to you."

I sat back. "You know, I just had a feeling this was going to turn out to be my fault."

"No *fault*. I'm just trying to make you understand."

"Oh, I understand, I don't think it's that complicated. You're having a fling with your old high school flame, and you want to say it's love so you won't feel guilty. Fine, but don't drag me into it." She just stared at me. She'd figured out about the same time I did that I was trying to make her mad. Why? So she'd drop the subject and we could forget it? Fat chance.

"You know he was more than a crush, Mama. You knew it then, too."

"*Then, then*. I never told you to break up with that boy, you can't pin that on me. I won't say I wasn't tickled pink when you did, but you did that all by your little self."

Unexpectedly, she smiled. "I catch myself trying that on Ruth, too. Pretending something she's done is her idea, when I know it's because of me. My influence."

"I have no *idea* what you're talking about."

"Yes, you do. Mama." She reached across and touched me on the arm with one finger. "You were always so strong. Too strong for me. In a way, you took advantage of me. Not on purpose, but I wanted your approval more than anybody's, and you knew it. I'm too old to blame you because I married the wrong man—"

"But you do blame me," I snapped, stung.

"No, I don't. I honestly don't. Or—if I do, I know I shouldn't. But—you put your fears into me."

"I what, now?"

"You made me feel afraid of Jess. You did. Because he wasn't . . . controllable. It was more than just his background you couldn't stand, it was him. You thought he was wild, you—"

"He *was* wild."

"But he wasn't *bad*. And you knew we loved each other—"

"You were eighteen years old!"

"Old enough."

"Say that to me when it happens to *your* child!"

Carrie unwound her legs and stood up. "I'm sorry. I said I didn't blame you—"

"But you do, that's obvious."

"Mama, I just wish you could've let go of me. And it's *me* I blame, not you, for making it so easy for you to hold on."

"Oh, I see. I didn't love you perfectly. Well, forgive me, I do apologize, I see you're doing a *wonderful* job of letting go of Ruth."

Unfair. Carrie blanched. "It's not the right time," she said thickly, "for us to be having this conversation."

"I couldn't agree more." She looked awful, like everything bad had hit her again all at once. It took a lot of willpower not to go and put my arms around her. "I'll get those dishes in the kitchen," I said, and abandoned her.

I made coffee, slamming things around, making a lot of noise. I'd put my *fears* into her? What crap. I hadn't approved of Jess Deeping, and for damn good reasons, solid, motherly reasons. She ought to be thanking, not blaming, me. If it weren't for me she'd have married that boy, had eight kids, and be living on a dairy farm. Lord help us. Deeping, what kind of a name was that anyway? I'd always hated it, it sounded backwoods and common and sinister. Van Allen, that was a name you could be proud of.

I remembered the time, years ago, when Jess Deeping first came to our house, a winter day with the trees bare and ice coating the branches. I watched him and Carrie through the kitchen window while they prowled around the backyard in their heavy coats, liking it better out there than in the warm house where I could've heard them. Once, by the old sandbox, he put his arms around her chest from behind, plucked her off the ground, and twirled her around and around, as fast as he could. She yelled and shrieked, hanging on to his arms, laughing so hard she lost her breath. I could hardly look at her face, or his. Especially his, excited and satisfied, full of his gleeful power. *You're mine, I can have you anytime I want.* I'd pressed up close to the window, chilled and revolted. Men like that, men with "passion," hah, passions they didn't even know enough to hide, they frightened the life out of me, always had. I wasn't sorry for anything. If I had saved Carrie from the likes of Jess Deeping, I was nothing but glad.

"Coffee's ready," I yelled.

She came in, sat down. Blew into her cup with her elbows on the table, back hunched. She's got my shoulders; O'Hara women have handsome shoulders. But her streaky, honey-colored hair had more silver strands in it than I'd ever noticed before. Everybody's getting old.

"It stopped raining," she said. "Just drizzling now. It's supposed to start again, though. Supposed to rain all day tomorrow."

"Won't your animals get wet?"

"It doesn't matter, everything's waterproof. Well—I'm not sure about the owl." She rubbed her forehead tiredly.

The ark sails tomorrow. I could let go of being against it now, I supposed, since it had already served its purpose. Done its worst. "You still going to the sailing?"

"I can't think about it now."

"No, I guess not."

We drank coffee in silence.

"I don't blame *my* mother for anything," I mentioned. "And I could if I wanted to. Negative influence, that's what she had on me. She influenced me not to be anything like her."

Carrie just nodded wearily.

"All I ever wanted for you was happiness, and that's the God's truth."

"I know, Mama."

"And I don't know what you're talking about—I *did* let you go. Don't you remember, I'm the one who said yes when you wanted to go away to college? It was your father who wanted you to go to Remington."

"I remember."

And afterward, sure enough, she didn't come back. She moved around with Stephen, she'd probably *never* have come home if he hadn't needed a job so badly. That didn't sound like any unhealthy mama's hold to me. That sounded like an independent woman making her own way in the world, far away from her mother, nowhere near her mother.

As far away from her mother as she could get.

Well, there it was. We danced around it, pretended it wasn't there, that nothing had changed since the olden days when we used to like each other. A pure kind of love—we did have that when I was young and Carrie was a girl, I know we did. I know it's not realistic to think you can keep it, but oh, that's what I want back, that pure love, when Carrie was all mine. When she was me.

No, I don't mean that, not the way it sounds. *You were too strong for me, Mama*—but how can you be too strong? That sounded like I wanted to overpower her. Be her.

"Another thing," I said. "Isn't it good to be strong? Doesn't every mother want to pass along strength to her children? And isn't the best way by example? Yes to all that," I answered myself when Carrie wouldn't. "Anyway, I'm not that strong. I'm just loud. A million things scare the hell out of me."

"Name one."

"No."

She finally smiled.

"All I ever tried to do was save you from danger," I said.

"Danger."

"But I never get any credit for that, oh, no, you had to find out on your *own* what scares you, you couldn't take my common sense word for it."

"Well, that makes no sense at all—"

"So what if I was in favor of you marrying Stephen? Why shouldn't I have been? If you two didn't have perfect happiness together, I don't believe that's my fault—and anyway, you got Ruth out of it, so you can't call it a failure."

"No."

"And if Stephen *was* too much like your father, that's not my fault, either. Right?"

"Right."

Oh, she just didn't want to fight anymore. But she thought I'd used my influence—my *strength*, ha-ha—to get her to marry some kind of a duplicate copy of the man I married. For company, I guess, so I could feel vindicated or something. Exonerated.

I shuddered, and spit back the last sip of cold coffee. I couldn't remember ever feeling so old. Too old to change. If I was a bad mother, I'd have to die a bad mother. I ran my hand over the smooth top of the oak table, stripped, sanded, stained, and varnished by Carrie, and thought, *Where'd she get this craftiness?* Not from me, and definitely not from George. Well, that's a blessing. Kids have gifts, flaws, quirks, streaks, whole sides of themselves that have nothing to do with their parents. That's a big relief, isn't it? At least you don't have to take the blame for every damn thing.

When the doorbell rang, Carrie jolted up like she'd been electrocuted. "I'll get it." Barefooted, she raced out of the kitchen.

I heard a man's voice on the front porch. I got up more slowly and went in the living room. Peering around the corner, expecting a policeman, I recognized Jess Deeping just before Carrie raised up her arms and put them around his neck.

I couldn't take my eyes off them. He didn't see me, he had his eyes closed, his face half buried in her hair. It was like a movie, and they were as far from me and just as untouchable as stars up on a screen. I don't know how long they stood that way, neither one talking or moving, just holding on, as if . . . I don't know what. As if they were getting blood transfusions from each other. Then I couldn't look anymore. I walked backward into the kitchen, one quiet step at a time.

I went to the sink and ran water, squeezed Joy on my hands, rinsed. I yanked a paper towel off the holder, and over the sound of swishing paper I could hear Carrie's urgent voice, high and full, direct, not careful, overlapping Jess Deeping's baritone comfort. She didn't talk to me like that, I didn't know that tone. With me she held back. She protected herself.

The screen door slammed, and I hurried back into the living room. Empty. I pressed my face to the screen door. Jess Deeping drove a pickup truck. What else? You weren't allowed to say "white trash" anymore, but you still knew it when you saw it, and that's what that whole Deeping family had been, the cow farmer husband and his nutty wife and their slouching, long-haired boy. I'd detested them, Carrie was right about that. They came too close to the kind of people I'd been trying my whole adult life to get away from. I had, too.

The two of them stood by the curb next to the truck, oblivious to the misting rain. He had her hand, he was looking down at it while he talked, and she had her head up, looking full in his face. She came up to his cheekbone. He wasn't a bad-looking man. He'd filled out since the days when he used to skulk around her like a starving crow, singed-looking somehow, wounded, always scrawny as a pitchfork. And always with that look in his eye like he wanted to snatch her up in his beak, his claws, and fly her off to his hiding place. That boy had never wanted anything but Carrie. I knew he was the enemy the minute I set eyes on him.

He leaned down and put his cheek on hers. They were saying good-bye. It looked like they'd kiss when they straightened up, but they didn't. He started around the back of his truck—and stopped when a little silver Honda pulled up behind it. George's.

I told him to stay home, I said there was nothing for him to do, and here he was anyway. Was he my knight, or Carrie's? It didn't seem fair that she got two and I didn't get any. He got out of the car like an old man, his tweed pants loose and ash strewn, his eyeglasses bumping against his chest on a chain. Carrie went and hugged him, but she didn't get much back—his worried smile and some pats on the back, as if he were burping her. He kept his hand on her shoulder, though, while the three of them had a serious-looking conversation. To my knowledge George hadn't seen Jess Deeping in twenty-five years, but if he thought anything was funny about him being at Carrie's house, he didn't show it.

I got tired of watching from afar. I punched open the screen door and marched out to join the party.

Carrie watched me come like I was Sherman bearing down on Atlanta. I saw her take a deep breath and lift her chin, girding herself. Lord, was I that formidable a character? If she only knew. That what I wouldn't mind right now was somebody, preferably my husband, to fold me up in his arms and hold me tight and tell me everything was going to be just fine.

I stood next to George and interrupted him. "What's going on?" He didn't touch me, but I wasn't surprised; I even saw it from his side for a change. You don't hug a woman who *punches* and *marches* and *interrupts*. You move back, out of the way.

Jess Deeping bowed his head to me. "Mrs. Danziger," he said in his low, sympathetic voice. You'd've sworn, if you were an outsider, that he didn't despise me. He'd always been that way, I remembered, soft-spoken and respectful. He'd treated me, and George, too, with a funny kind of gentleness, in fact. It always put me on my guard.

"Hello," I said, and I softened to him for a second, something about his size, the way he stayed turned toward Carrie a few protective degrees. Then I thought of poor Ruth finding him and Carrie upstairs in her mama's bed, and I froze up on him again. Predator, I thought. Ravenous crow.

"Mama, Jess and Pop are driving up to D.C. to look for Ruth."

"What?"

"Jess was going by himself, but I said I'd go along with him."

"I'll be glad for the company."

"We can take my car. Smaller."

"That'll be fine."

They had it all figured out. I didn't care for the way George said "Jess," like he'd known him for ten years, like they were old fishing buddies. I thought of saying I'd go, too, just to make trouble. Things were moving too fast, all this action, everybody taking steps but me.

"You be careful driving, Pop," Carrie said, walking Jess over to his side of the car. I saw her give him a quick, surreptitious kiss on the lips before he folded himself up and climbed in the passenger seat of the Honda. It made me smile in spite of myself. It made my heart sink.

"Got plenty of money? Got your gas credit card? Buckle up," I told George, holding the door open while he settled himself and rooted his keys out of his pants pocket. "Watch out for the maniacs on that Beltway. They'll kill you as soon as look at you."

"We'll be careful," he said. "And we'll call when we get there."

"*And* if you find her," I said.

"The D.C. cops know the license number," Carrie said, leaning in the other window. "I don't know how hard they're looking, but they've got it. Oh, I'm so glad you're going. Thank you, Pop." She said something to Jess Deeping I couldn't hear.

"Keep calling," I said, backing up, "in case she shows up here. Which I fully expect her to do any minute."

"Right-o." George started up the car, took the brake off, waved, and crept away.

"Drives like a goddamn turtle," I muttered, waving back. I wished I'd kissed him, though. On his whiskery old cheek. It wouldn't have killed me. I wished I had.

Back to the house with the women. I liked the *idea* of the men going off to put things right, the women keeping the home fires burning. If it worked, it'd be a miracle. I couldn't touch another cup of coffee, but Carrie poured one for herself and sat up straight to drink it. "I'm so glad you're here. You and Pop. And Jess," she added on purpose. "I don't know what I'd do without you guys."

"Them, maybe. I haven't done a thing."

"That's not true—we know where Ruth is only because you got it out of Krystal." She grinned. "What a terror you were, Mama. She never had a prayer."

"Well, what a pinhead."

"Oh, I'm still so angry! I'd like to brain her, I'd like to go over there and beat her up."

"I'll hold her arms."

We leaned against each other for a minute. I got a thick feeling in the throat. I said, "I don't want us to start up again."

"I don't either."

"But I have something to say. I'm not taking any of the blame for your life."

"No. No, and I don't—"

"But you were right about one thing. I picked your father out on purpose. He's a fine, fine man, but I married him because he was soft and dull, and that's the truth."

"Oh, Mama."

"It's okay, nothing's going to change, we'll never split up. What's done is done. Anyway, I'm not interested in going out and finding Ricardo Montalban. I got exactly what I thought I wanted, and that's the end of it."

Carrie looked at me with glittery, worried eyes.

"It's *okay*. I'm not hard up. I've got a good husband, a wonderful daughter, and a perfect grandchild. Usually perfect. I made my bed fifty years ago, and I swear to God this is the last time you'll ever hear me complain about it."

She laid the length of her forearm against mine. "What about Jess?"

"What about him? What kind of a name is that, anyway, *Jess*?" Never mind Deeping. "Is it Jesse or isn't it? What the heck is his name?"

"Jesse Holmes Deeping. Holmes was his mother's maiden name."

"Holmes. That's not too bad."

"Oh, Mama, he'll be so pleased."

I ignored that. "If you choose him . . ."

"What?"

"I always thought if you ended up with that boy . . ."

"What, Mama?"

"I thought it would mean I'd chosen wrong, all those years ago. I thought it would mean my whole life, everything I picked . . . Well, anyway. I think that's how my thinking went." Carrie's face got pink. She put her head down, but I saw a teardrop hit her on the arm. I put my hand on her back and rubbed her softly between her shoulders. "What kills me is having to admit that Mr. Jesse Holmes Deeping turned out to be a goddamn pillar of the community. For what that's worth."

"He makes me happy."

"I noticed. I guess that can't be all bad."

Carrie gave a wet laugh.

"So let's finish this up. You're not me and I'm not you, and here you've got a second chance to pick somebody who might be good for you. So do whatever you want, because you're not me."

"I know I'm not you."

"I'm saying that for my benefit."

"Oh." She looked at me like she'd never seen me before.

"Meanwhile, don't think I'm done with George. Not by a long shot. I've got plans for that guy."

"What will you do?"

"Torture him. Make him take dance lessons, that's number one. We've got a vacation coming up—could be a second honeymoon." Carrie smiled, not looking at me—I'd gone too far with that one. "Maybe I'll take him to Krystal's," I said. "She owes us one. I'm thinking a deal on aromatherapy. Or better yet, a high colonic."

Carrie heaved a great sigh. "You love him, though, don't you?"

A picture of the narrow, dwindling future opened for a second in my mind's eye. "Of course I do," I said, and pushed it out of sight. I felt Carrie relax against me. "'Course I do. And vice versa. In his way." We were both quiet, and I imagined she was thinking that last over, sizing it up against appearances. Weighing it against the evidence. It was true as far as it went.

Now that is a stingy, miserly phrase. *True as far as it went.* I lived seventy years like that, in most ways. I kept it small and quiet, as if there was somebody I was afraid of whose attention I didn't want to attract. But I wasn't meant to be that way—I should've been bigger and louder. When it came down to it, I didn't fit my own life.

"Hey," I said after a while. "How're you holding up?"

"I'm better. I don't know why. I guess because they went up there. Jess and Pop."

"Somebody's doing something."

"I don't feel so crazy."

"They might find her," I said.

"They might."

"I just hope it's them and not the cops."

"Me, too."

Carrie leaned over and kissed me on the cheek. "I love you, Mama."

"I love you, too."

She folded her arms on the table and put her head down, closed her eyes. She fell asleep almost instantly, while I sat still as a statue and hardly breathed. I was sorry when she jolted awake after only about five minutes.

Go on upstairs and take a nap, I told her, I'll answer the phone if it rings. No, she wouldn't. So we moved around the house together all day, dragging from room to room for a change of scene. The humidity had to be 100 percent. Nothing to see from the windows but gray and rain. George called in the afternoon to say they were in Georgetown, starting their search. After that the police called twice—nothing to report. About six o'clock, Carrie was standing at the screen door staring out at the rain when the phone rang again. I answered.

"Hello," George's mild, uncertain voice said. "That you, Dana? Carrie there?"

Carrie hurried over, hissed, "*Who is it?*"

"It's your father. George, what's going on?"

"Well, no luck so far, I'm very sorry to report."

Carrie was poised over me like a cat, eyes wide, every muscle tense. I shook my head, and she went limp. She slumped beside me on the sofa, leaning on me, pressing her ear to the phone.

"We've been driving around, walking around," George went on. "I think we've been in every store in Georgetown."

"What about tattoo parlors? That's where she was going—did you go to all the tattoo places?"

"Oh, yes, we did that first thing, and that was somewhat fruitful, actually, although disturbing as well."

"How do you mean?" I said. Carrie had a death grip on my wrist; I was losing circulation in my hand.

"Well, we talked to a fellow in one place, quite a colorful shop, who remembered a girl who did look a bit like Ruth. At least she seemed to when he described her."

"And?"

"He wouldn't give her a tattoo because she was too young. She had no proof of age, so he sent her on her way."

"And? So?"

"Well, the worrisome thing is, this fellow in the store says when the girl left—and of course she might not have been Ruth—when she left, he thinks perhaps one of his male customers may have followed her. Gone out after her, in any case. It's probably nothing—I just didn't like the sound of it. Don't tell Carrie about this, will you? That might be best."

Too late. She was already curled up in a ball on the sofa with her hands over her ears.

25

Payback

I drove by Rude Boy's Industrial Tattoos and Piercings four times, and never saw creepy guy's gray car. It was getting dark, though, so every car was starting to look gray. But I didn't think he was there. He thought I'd bolted on him. If he was looking for me at all, which he probably wasn't, he was looking in Anacostia or Southeast, not the very place on Georgia Avenue he'd suggested we should go to together. No, I'd pulled a double-blind on him or whatever you call it. I foiled him.

No way would I have ever gotten into creepy guy's car. What was I, crazy? I wouldn't have gotten in any strange man's car, but especially that guy's. First of all, there was something icky about his body. I hated his stomach, the way the tight round curve of it poked out at me, and the long line of his fly. He was probably harmless—people don't get kidnapped in the middle of Georgetown on a Sunday afternoon, not that I ever heard of. But still, something about that guy's shape scared me. Something about his stomach.

On the fifth pass, I spotted a parking place two doors down from Rude Boy's, in front of a boarded-up wig shop. Too bad I couldn't parallel park. I almost always ended up like two yards away from the curb and had to start over, which I preferred not to do with cars backed up and people gawking at me. Especially today, when I was trying to keep a low profile.

It was kind of a scary neighborhood. Georgia Avenue started out okay, but it got rougher and rougher the farther up you went, and this was the roughest part, these blocks around Rude Boy's. People who looked like drug dealers were hanging out in doorways and on the corners, and I saw two women who might be prostitutes. One, who was black but had platinum blonde hair, wore clear plastic boots with high heels and a leopard skin skirt and a purple tank top. Then again, she could be an entertainer, a singer or something in one of the rundown clubs around here. Maybe she sang the blues. Maybe she was just starting out, like Diana Ross in that movie. Probably not, though. She really looked like a prostitute.

Behind Georgia Avenue was a bumpy, smelly alley with parking areas in back of all the stores. Faded signs that looked like they'd been shot said CUSTOMER PARKING ONLY, BINGO'S ARMY SURPLUS, and RAY'S LIQUORS ONLY, TOWING ENFORCED. All the spaces behind Ray's Liquors were taken, although it was Sunday. Rude Boy's lot was filled, too. I found a tiny, possibly illegal crevice by the garbage Dumpster behind Gloria's Wigs and Beauty, which apparently didn't exist anymore, if being boarded-up meant anything, and it only took five minutes to wedge the Chevy into it. It took almost that long for the engine to die after I turned the key off. So embarrassing. Nothing like chronic bronchitis to make your car stand out in a crowd.

Okay. Moment of truth. If I got a tattoo, which Mom was against and had semiforbidden until I was eighteen, it would be to pay her back. Might as well be clear about that. When you looked at it like that, it seemed kind of immature.

So? I'd never felt like this before. This was a little taste of what it was going to be like to be a grown-up. Before, I'd been able to imagine myself being, say, twenty-one or twenty-five, but that was about it; after that it got hazy and not interesting. But now, because of Mom and Jess, my imaginable age had been jacked up to, like, thirty. This was a totally adult deal, and it made me sick, it made me want to throw up. There used to be an order to things, but it got broken, my life cracked. This was the adult part—I had a very strong feeling that I'd crossed over a line and entered a new phase of myself. It turned out the older you got, the less things made sense. And this was what we were all in such a hurry to get to, me and Jamie and Raven and Caitlin and everybody in my whole school! What a crock! It was like that movie where the guy in the cult has this horrible, grotesque near-death experience and he comes back to tell his friends in the cult not to do it, don't commit suicide, there's no white light, it's all bullshit—but they don't believe him and they kill themselves and it's this big disgusting bloodbath and that's the end.

I had to get out of the car on the passenger side because the driver's door was mashed up too close to the Dumpster. Rap music thumped from somewhere—a car, because now it was fading. Clayborne was humid, but this was ridiculous; this air felt muggy and smelled dirty, full of exhaust and garbage and sweat and no trees. At least it wasn't raining right now. I only had three blocks to walk around to Rude Boy's, but two different guys spoke to me, "Hey, baby, how you doin'?" said one, and the other made kissing noises. I tried to ignore them without looking mean. It worked, because neither of them followed me.

Rude Boy's was freezing cold. It felt great, I could feel the perspiration on my skin drying. A bell above the door rang when I opened it, but I stood in the middle of the bright, empty front room for a whole minute and nobody came. No WE I.D. signs, I noticed; only ones that said NO CHECKS, NO CREDIT, and TIPPING IS ENCOURAGED. I could smell chemicals, alcohol and something else, like airplane glue. Well, that was good, maybe, it probably meant they kept the place really clean. It gave me a queasy feeling, though, like being at the doctor's. So did a sound coming from the open door in the back, a sound like the drill at the dentist's office. Tattoo gun.

My stomach turned over. I could still leave, nobody had even seen me yet.

Screw that. I walked over to the right-hand wall, which was covered from top to bottom with pictures of tattoos. Most of them you could rule out right away, naked ladies, skeletons, devils, motorcycles on fire, grim reapers, snakes, sharks, scorpions, worms, Confederate flags. I wasn't that wild about the girly stuff either, the dream catchers and butterflies and pretty hearts and rosebuds. There must be something here that expressed my inner self. Also something I could afford—Rude Boy had helpfully put the prices next to the tattoos. Marvin the Martian cost seventy-five dollars and took fifty minutes. Demon Skull was twice as much, but you could see why, all that detail in the creepy hollowed-out eyes and the evil grin. I was down to about eighty bucks since parking in Georgetown and filling the Chevy with gas.

A man came through the door in back. He stopped and looked at me but didn't say anything.

"Hi," I said.

He nodded. I guessed he was black because of his hair, which was in thick charcoal dreadlocks caught up in a huge woolen cap, but he was very light-skinned and his eyes were silvery blue, not brown. He was about my height but very slender, with a long, thin, braided goatee tied at the bottom with beads.

He didn't say anything, so I couldn't be sure he worked here. "Lotta tattoos," I said, waving at the walls.

He said, "Yeah," very softly, with a sleepy smile. Maybe he was high on ganja.

"I have seventy dollars," I lied. "I was looking for some flash."

He nodded.

"So. That would be . . ."

He lifted his right arm and did a slow, dreamy pivot, indicating the artwork all around us.

"Oh. So—any of these?"

"Mmm. You're eighteen?"

"Oh, yes. Just today. It's my birthday." Stop talking. "A present to myself, I was thinking. Happy birthday to me."

He didn't say anything, but he smiled. And I knew I was in.

Okay. Okay! Now, what to pick? It was really hard to concentrate with the guy watching me. "I guess something simple. And cheap," I added with a laugh, but he didn't laugh back and he didn't suggest anything, didn't wave me over to the simple but cheap section. He just stood and looked at me. Weird. It made me nervous.

I spotted some plain black designs, crucifixes, the man symbol, an ankh. An ankh? Raven wore one around his neck. It was the Egyptian emblem of life. It was certainly simple, and the one in this drawing only cost fifty-five dollars. Life—I believed in life. I was *for* life, very much so. It summed up one of my primary inner beliefs, no question. True, it was kind of a basic belief; not too many people were *against* life. Ha-ha. No, but think of all the people who got skull or coffin or corpse tattoos—they were antilife, or pretending to be. If you looked at it like that, the ankh was a strong positive statement. I would be setting myself apart from the morbid antilifers, the posers who thought it was cool to be macabre and grisly and negative. And this was only my first tattoo, I'd probably get more later on, the ankh was like the foundation symbol the rest would build on. First life, then . . . whatever.

"This one," I said, pointing.

The man drifted over. "No. This?" He sounded like he didn't believe me. His eyes were beautiful when he opened them wide. He looked at me with a new kind of interest, as if this was the last tattoo in the world he thought I'd pick. Doubts and second thoughts hit me. Not this one? This was uncool?

"Okay," he said lightly. "I can fill it in with a color for seventy dollars."

"With a color?"

"One color. If you like." He had an accent; I could hear it now that he was speaking more than one word at a time. His voice was very musical.

"Umm . . . red?"

He shrugged.

"I want it to really show up."

"Where do you want it?" he asked after a long pause.

This I'd given a lot of thought to. I wanted it highly visible, I wanted it *in your face*. So not my ankle or my boob or my shoulder blade, none of those coy places, even my arm would be covered up with clothes most of the time. "Here, I want it right here." I held up the top of my right hand and ran my finger along the joint. "Half on my hand and half on my wrist, like overlapping. Right next to the bone. And as big as you can make it."

He thought about that for a while before nodding slowly. "Okay," he said. "Let's go."

My stomach did another flip. I was doing it! I was following him through the door in back and moving down a corridor past rooms hidden by plastic shower curtains, and the voices and rap music and the humming tattoo machines that had been barely audible in the outer room were loud and busy-sounding and thrilling—this place was jumping! Other people were behind the curtains getting tattooed right now, which was a relief, it made me feel great, more excited and not as scared. The man stopped at the last door on the right, before the fire exit door in the very back, and stood aside so I could go in first, holding the tattered blue plastic shower curtain back for me. "Thank you," I said, and went in.

It was just a room. I was kind of disappointed. "Have a seat," he said, and I sat down in one of the two regular chairs, just plain wooden chairs. I didn't know what I'd expected—maybe like a barbershop chair, a dentist's chair, something that reclined. I looked around, but there wasn't much to see, drawings tacked on the walls of pretty gaudy tattoos, apparently this guy's custom creations. Oh—his name was Julian; I knew because he'd signed some of the tattoos.

He had his back to me, he was doing something at a table in the corner. He wore baggy corduroys and a bulky, no-color sweater, through which I could see his shoulder blades and his hips and the bony curve of his butt. He seemed very nice. I imagined him inviting me to go home with him after he did the tattoo. He'd live right over the shop. He would make me spicy food, curried rice or something, and serve it to me on his lumpy couch. Afterward, we'd become lovers, and it would be earthy and real because he was foreign and older. I'd learn a great deal from him. We would live over the store and take care of each other until it was time for me to move on. Which would be very sad and very sweet, but inevitable.

He turned around, holding a bottle of alcohol and some cotton swabs. All of a sudden I was freezing; no wonder he wore a sweater, it was probably fifty degrees in here. He pulled up the other chair close to mine and lifted my right hand out of my lap. He started cleaning it with the alcohol and swabs, and I stared at the crown of his head, how the hair grew in neat lines, thick and woolly, out of his clean scalp. When we lived together I'd braid it for him. I'd stand behind him while he sat in a kitchen chair with a cat in his lap, sipping the herbal tea I'd made him.

After he cleaned my hand once, he cleaned it all over again, really scrubbed it, and then he sprayed it with something from a can, probably an antiseptic. So that was good, this was a clean place. I thought of what the guy at Karma Chameleon had said about needles, but I didn't know exactly what to say to Julian, how to ask. *Oh, by the way, are your needles clean?* How rude. Anyway, I trusted him, I'd already decided.

He went back over to the table. I wished he would talk to me, try to set me at ease, like Dr. Lane did before he filled my teeth. There was the tattoo gun, I could see it, shiny silver and smaller than I'd expected. Julian was doing something with little wells, putting ink in them, red and black. I turned away, I couldn't look.

Oh, *God*. I couldn't even stand getting a shot, and this was going to be like a million shots. What if I fainted? I wasn't that great with pain. *Chill*, I told myself, people do this all the time. It's like sex, you can't believe so many people could have it, but look at the evidence, the world has six billion people or something so somebody must be doing it. Same with tattoos, look at all those basketball players, look at Dennis Rodman, look at Madonna, look at the Red Hot Chili Peppers. They weren't babies and neither was I, I could do it if they could, and anyway Raven said it was more like vibration than a pain, he said it was practically nothing, you got used to it and then it was almost pleasant, it was like a drug high or—

"I'll start." Julian wheeled over a little padded platform and put my forearm on top of it. He looked up when he saw my hand trembling. "Are you afraid?"

I tried to smile, but my lips were too stiff. "No. Not really. Does it hurt?" I gave a high, childish laugh, and blushed. I could have bolted then, jumped up, grabbed my purse, and run. I had a feeling I might throw up. I was so scared, my whole body was shaking with every heartbeat.

Julian said softly, "It won't be bad," and I tried to believe him. "I'm working here, not over bone." He pointed with his index finger at my wrist bone, but didn't touch it. "Bone is the worst. I won't be there."

"Okay." I inhaled and licked my lips. "Okay, then. Let's go. Hit me."

He started the machine. The whine went right into me, into the back of my mouth where my teeth were clenched. Out of the side of my eye I saw him dip needles into ink. "I'm going to start a line now," he said in his lilting voice. I shut my eyes tight.

Yeeeee-ow. It really really *hurt*. It really hurt! *Owww!* I wasn't going to be able to stand it. "Don't forget to breathe," Julian said, but he didn't stop drilling. I showed him my teeth and turned my face away. Breathe. La la la la la, I sang in my head. Okay, it wasn't as bad. But it was still bad. But I could do this. As soon as I knew I could do it, the pain got better. A little. La la la la la.

I wished Julian would talk. I could talk to him, but I didn't want to distract him, make him go outside the line or something. I glanced down at my arm. Oh wow, he'd done the circle part on my hand, which was bleeding a little, not too much. I got a queasy feeling and had to look away.

"Easy," he said, "not so good here," and I could feel him coming closer to the bone for the crosspiece. I wasn't prepared for this deep, biting pain. Tears got deeper and deeper in my eyes. I blinked fast to get rid of them, squeezing and relaxing my left fist for a diversion. I thought of all the movies where the guy gets shot and somebody has to dig the bullet out while he bites down on a piece of wood or something that always breaks, *crack*, right before the fadeout. If I had a stick in my mouth it would break right . . . about . . . *now*.

"Better now," Julian said, and started down my arm.

It was better. This was doable. I decided to talk. "Are you the actual Rude Boy?" No, it was better not to talk. What a jerk I was whenever I opened my mouth. Julian shook his head without looking up.

I crossed my legs. I wasn't cold anymore. Where he was drilling felt warm, and the warmth was seeping all through me, my whole body. "Have you always been a tattooer?" Okay, that was it. He shook his head again, exactly as before, and I closed my mouth. Two people, a man and a woman, started talking in the hall. Their voices trailed away quickly—they must've gone out in the lobby. I wished I could've seen them. The rap coming from somewhere changed to steel drums and horns, sort of third world music. Julian didn't even have a radio in his room. He liked to work in silence.

It got bad again when he started on the other crosspiece, which was close to the other bone in my wrist. I was expecting it this time, though, so it wasn't as shocking.

"Okay. Just filling in now. Bad part's over."

Yes. This was what Raven must've been talking about, not pain so much as an electrical heat, a buzz. Plus it was a really pretty red

Julian was using, it had pink in it, a definite color but also soft. Strong but feminine. I loved it.

By the time he finished I was in love with him, too. I fantasized that he was doing this to me naked. His hands were so clean and slender. I wanted to touch his braided beard, pull on it. Pull his mouth to mine and kiss him. I was feeling a little drunk. High on endorphins.

"Done." He turned off the machine and stood up, went over to his table. "Do you like it?"

My arm floated up, weightless. "It's lovely. Thank you so much." Little pinpricks of blood seeped out of the veins on the surface of my hand. Nothing hurt. It was a beautiful tattoo. "You're a true artist."

He smiled, not with humility or gratitude, but as if that amused him. I felt a little insulted.

"How much do I owe?" I leaned over to get my purse.

"Seventy."

I got out three twenties, a ten, and five ones. Tipping was encouraged. That left me a five-dollar bill and some change to get home on, but that should be plenty. I had a full tank of gas.

Before I could give him the money, he put my arm on the little platform again and started taping a gauze bandage over the tattoo. "Only leave this on for about two hours," he instructed. "Then wash with cool water and soap. Rinse. Dry. For three days, spray very lightly with Neosporin, every five hours."

"Okay."

"No direct sunlight, not for two weeks."

"Really? How come?"

"Because it will fade. In five minutes in sun it will start to fade."

"No kidding."

"It may itch. Don't scratch it, slap it."

"Slap it?"

"If it becomes infected, put Listerine."

"Listerine?"

"Three times a day."

"Okay."

"That's it."

I stood up. I wasn't dizzy or anything, in fact I felt fantastic. "Thanks a lot. I really like it."

"Good." He held the shower curtain for me, and after I passed through, he came out, too. I was surprised when he walked with me out into the bright front room. At the door, he looked down at his filthy, unlaced sneakers and said softly, "I wouldn't ever have guessed that you were gay."

I laughed.

He looked up, smiling. "Usually I know. But with you." He smiled, shrugged. "I wouldn't have guessed. Anyway, doesn't matter. Take care."

He waited for me to leave. I stood still, staring at him with my mouth open. When I didn't move, he stepped back. "Okay," he said, and went back to the hallway. He ducked into one of the other cubicles, not his. A humming tattoo machine stopped; I heard men's low, casual voices. A laugh.

My skin felt prickly hot on the inside and icy cold on the outside. I got the door open. Warm, humid air smacked against me, tugged everything in me down. My systems started working again. The shock wore off.

If only I could die. Right now. God. Oh God, I really wanted to die.

Nobody hassled me in the three blocks to the car. The last place I wanted to go was home. But maybe I'd get lucky and have an accident on the way and be killed. I could drive off a bridge or a cliff, drive into a stone wall. The car would burst into flames and I'd be incinerated, and no one would ever know about my tattoo except Julian.

The car wouldn't start.

Well, now everything was perfect. A perfect day from beginning to end. How could I commit suicide in Washington, D.C.? I could run out into the middle of Georgia Avenue and get hit by a car. But with my luck, I'd only be maimed. I could wait on a corner to get mugged and hope it was fatal, not just a wounding. I didn't want to be raped, though. I'd always hoped if I was going to get raped it would be after I lost my virginity.

I remembered a White Tower two blocks down on the corner. Unbelievable, but I was hungry. I went in and sat at the counter in the only seat left, between a fat man and a thin man, both black. Practically everybody in here was black. I ordered a toasted cheese sandwich and a small Sprite, thinking I was never, in Clayborne, the only white person. They must be scared around us, always being in the minority. I was scared, but I wasn't showing it, because for one thing it would be rude.

I saw myself in the murky mirror behind the counter. My skin was gray, my hair was dirty, I looked awful. I looked like a raccoon, dark hollows under my eyes. My hand hurt—good, maybe it was infected. I didn't look eighteen. No way, I looked about fourteen. I hoped Rude Boy's got busted and Julian went to jail.

I was such a tool. What a stupid idiot moron. *Retarded* people knew the difference between the ankh and the female symbol. But—Julian had rushed me by staring at me and not talking. He'd made me so nervous. "That one," I'd said, and he'd opened his beautiful eyes in surprise. Oh, if only I could die.

The sandwich just made me hungrier. I asked for the check before I had to watch the fat man eat his dessert, a piece of cherry pie with vanilla ice cream. If I left a 15 percent tip, I'd have exactly two dollars and ninety cents left. Which still should be plenty. I put a quarter and a nickel next to my plate, thanked the waitress, and left.

A girl was hanging up the receiver of the beat-up pay phone on the street just as I passed behind her. So it was like a sign.

Between the cars going by and the kids who should've been in bed by now playing jump rope in the middle of the side street, I had to stick my finger in my ear to hear the operator. "I want to make a collect call," I said, and gave her the number. "From Ruth. To whoever answers."

Mom answered.

"Hello?"

"Hi."

"Ru-uth?" Her voice broke in the middle. Something happened to my throat, too; I couldn't talk for a second. Then Mom said, "Where the hell are you!"

"I'm not telling. Anyway, what do you care?"

"Jess is looking for you, Jess and Grampa, they drove up there togeth—"

"Jess and *Grampa*?" Incredible.

"Tell me where you are!"

"Okay. I'm in D.C."

"I know that."

"How do you know?"

"Your friend finally told us."

"Who, Krystal did?"

"Are you anywhere near a police station? I want you to—"

"No, I'm not near a police station. The car's broken, so I'm sleeping on the street tonight. This is a really crummy neighborhood, Mom. Can you hear it? It's raining again, though—maybe I'll go home with somebody instead of sleeping on the sidewalk."

"Ruth—"

"I could go with some derelict, they're all over the place. A pedophile already tried to pick me up. He wanted me to get in his car, and I almost did. He wanted to take care of me."

"Listen, listen to me."

"I figured out afterward I should've gone with him. I could've been his little girl." Mom gave this high wailing sound. "Maybe I'll share a needle with some of the guys on this street. Maybe have sex with one of them and get AIDS and die." I kept talking even though I was crying. "Why not? I mean, it turns out I'm gay anyway."

"Ruth, please, oh honey, for the love of God—"

"What would you care? If I was dead you could have your lover all to yourself, you and Jess could live happily ever after."

"Ruth—!"

I hung up. I was shaking, I felt hollow inside, I felt like a straw, nothing in me but air. I didn't even know I was that angry. I scared myself.

Stiff-legged, I marched back to the car. It almost started, but then I flooded it and it died.

I crawled over the seat and lay down in the back. I put my good arm over my eyes to block out the glare of the streetlight. The smell from the garbage Dumpster was stronger in the dark. I was sweating from the breathless heat, but I was afraid to roll down a window. My hand hurt. It was almost time to take off the bandage, but I didn't want to look at my tattoo. I wanted my arm to get gangrene and fall off in the night.

I listened to music and the hiss of car tires and the shouts of children and the dangerous, interesting sound of men and women laughing. I thought about how many minutes our phone conversation probably took off Mom's life, and if it was more or less than the number I'd put on with good deeds when I was little. I thought about calling her back and telling her I was okay. A little after midnight, I fell asleep.

26

Floating the Ark

The police left the house a little after ten on Monday morning. They were beginning to look embarrassed, I thought as I ran water over their half-finished coffee cups, but still not worried. What did it take to make them worry? Body parts? Hanging over the sink on my elbows, I let my eyes go out of focus. My brain felt like the rings of water swirling above the drain, aimless, driven by nothing but physics. You couldn't live with the worst fear you'd ever imagined, the one you'd been pushing to the back of your mind since the day your child was born—you couldn't live with that hour by hour and stay clear in the head. I could feel my mind blurring, not from fatigue but for protection.

What was I doing? Oh. This was happening more frequently, amnesiac episodes when I couldn't remember what I had just said, or thought, why I was in a certain room, what a two-way conversation was about. Except for a sick, disorienting hour early this morning, I hadn't slept in over two days. What was that, how many hours? I tried to count, but got lost in the numbers. What did it matter anyway.

My mother came up behind me—I jumped when she put her hands on my shoulders. "Hard as rocks," she said, digging in with her thumbs, Mama's idea of a massage. "Listen, now, today's the day. She'll either come home by herself or they'll find her. This is it, I'm positive."

I nodded; it was easier than speaking. Along with everything else, for some reason I was losing my voice.

"And she's fine. All that bull—that was just stupid, snotty talk, she did *not* sleep on any street last night. Her idea of paying you back."

My throat hurt, or I'd have said, "You didn't hear it, the noise in the background, she was *on* the street." Nightmare sounds; they'd kept me in a state of dread all night. *My baby is in hell and I can't find her.*

"She's all right, Carrie. Come on, you can't get like this."

"I'm all right."

"Tsk. Let me do that."

"I'm finished. Is Jess still here?" He and Pop had been sitting beside each other on the sofa in the sunroom for the last hour, talking quietly, passing sections of the newspaper back and forth. I knew he was still here—I just wanted Mama to talk to me about him.

"He's here." She stopped the sharp-fingered massage abruptly. "I told him to go, but he wouldn't."

I turned around in dismay. "You told him to go?" She'd been civil to him last night, and almost nice to him this morning. She'd brought him coffee, called him Jess, asked him a polite, fairly astute question about the city council's position on the school tax hike proposal—I thought she was making a real effort.

"To the *sailing*. I told him to go see the ark float."

"Oh."

"But he won't."

"No."

"Rather be here." She sniffed, either in approval or disapproval, I couldn't tell. "It's a shame you both had to go and miss it. After all that work you did."

A stunning concession. I wasn't sure I'd heard right. "It'll be there awhile," I said. That was a sore point with Mama, the fact that the town was allowing Eldon to keep the ark tied up on the river until the twenty-sixth of June—forty days and forty nights.

"It'll be there awhile," she agreed gloomily. "Still. I know you wanted to be there when they put the animals on. I'm sorry, but your daughter has a lot to answer for."

"I just want her to come home. I don't care what she's done anymore."

"I know." She put her arm around my shoulder. "You never worried me like this. It never occurred to me to say thanks."

Oh, I didn't want to cry again. "You're welcome," I said, and tried to laugh. "It's never too late to take credit for being the perfect child."

"Don't push your luck," she said, and hugged me.

The phone rang. She stepped out of the way—she'd learned not to try to answer it herself.

"Hello, Carrie?"

"Yes? Is that—Landy?"

"It's me, I'm calling here from the Point. Things are starting to break up now."

"Oh—how are you? Did everything go all right? Jess is here—I'm sorry we couldn't go down there. I don't know if you heard about Ruth, but—"

"Yeah, I did, Jess told me last night. So she's not there yet?"

"No."

"Well, I wondered about that. I didn't want to call you for nothing, but then again, I figured if you knew she was back you'd be down here. It went real well, by the way. Daddy couldn't stay long after the boarding, but he was just as pleased as could be with everything."

"Oh—good. But what were you saying about Ruth—"

"Well, I saw her about halfway through it, about the time we were putting on the medium-size animals."

"What? What?"

"I couldn't stop what I was doing, and after that I lost sight of her—there was a crowd, even the TV people were down here, we were real pleased—"

"Ruth was *there*? Landy, are you sure?"

"It was her all right. It was still raining and she didn't have no umbrella, so she was quite a—"

"Is she still there?"

"That I can't say for sure. I haven't seen her since then, and that was maybe an hour ago, but she could still be. I wished I could've got her, talked to her, but I didn't know if she'd already gone home and come back and you knew it, or just what. Sorry if I messed up—"

"You didn't. Thank you—I'm coming right down."

"Ruth's *there*?" Mama followed me out of the kitchen, into the living room, the sunroom, while I called all the way, "She's back! We found her!"

The men jumped up from the couch. "She's down at Point Park, or she was, Landy just saw her."

Jess shook his head in amazement.

"Who's Landy?" Pop said, beaming, patting Mama on the shoulder.

"Landy Pletcher, Eldon's son," Jess said. "What's she doing down at the Point?"

"I have no idea. Pop, can I have your car? He said the launch went perfectly," I told Jess, "he said TV people were there."

My father dug his keys out of his trouser pocket and tossed them over. "Want me to come with you?"

"I'll go, too," Mama said, looking around for her purse.

"No, Mama, no. Pop—thanks. I'm going by myself."

In the hall, I grabbed an umbrella from the coatrack. I was halfway through the door when I remembered. "Oh—Jess, can you take my parents home?" They'd all followed me into the hall.

"Glad to," he said. We exchanged a secret look. We were enjoying the same mental picture, I knew: of Mama bouncing along between Jess and Pop in the pickup.

• • •

The Leap River was a glorified creek that began at Culpeper and flowed south through Greene County. The deepest part was at the Point and east for a few miles, past Leap River Farm, Jess's farm; after that it turned back into a stream and finally trickled away into the Rapidan. Point Park, Clayborne's main civic recreation area, started at the bridge and ran adjacent to the river for almost half a mile. It had hiking trails, picnic shelters, a children's playground—soon to be refurbished with Eldon Pletcher's money—pretty views, a jogging path, a band pavilion, ball fields. The centerpiece was two wide, side-by-side fishing piers made out of river rock and stretching halfway to the other side of the Leap. Jess, Landy, and the Arkists had constructed the ark between the two piers, which were slightly less than thirty feet apart—a perfect distance for a nineteen-foot-wide ark; if they'd built it at a shipyard they couldn't have found a more convenient staging area.

From the parking lot, I couldn't see it clearly; too far away, too many trees in the way. But what I could see made me laugh, a quick, nervous explosion at the sight of an ark, an *ark*, bobbing on the khaki-colored river. They'd painted it a light charcoal gray to resemble weathered wood, with gay white and black for the doors and portholes and trim. It was a handsome ark, most impressive, you'd never have guessed it was hollow inside, a mere floating stage. What startled the laugh out of me was a glimpse of my lovely giraffe, head jutting up over the flat top of the third deck, so raffish and silly—and as I drove past, his mate on the flip side looking coy, batting her long black pipe cleaner eyelashes. Oh, it worked. Glory be, it really worked. It could've been such a disaster.

The skies were clearing, but raindrops still fell heavily from the trees overhanging the paved lane leading from parking area to parking area. I turned on the wipers and huddled over the steering wheel, my face close to the steamy windshield. Cars and people still clogged the drive; if the crowd had "broken up," as Landy said, it must've been enormous an hour ago. Food and balloon vendors were closing down their concessions. I passed a white van with a satellite dish on top—a TV crew? I slowed to let a mother and her little boy cross in front of me. In red letters across the chest, the boy's T-shirt said I SAW NOAH'S ARK, and the date. What entrepreneurial genius was selling those? Not the Arkists, I was sure. Thank God Mama wasn't here.

I turned around at the dead end without seeing the Chevrolet. Could Ruth have gone home? We'd have passed each other, though, and I'd been watching carefully. Maybe she was on the other side of the river.

I steered slowly out of the park, across the bridge, and turned in at the gravel drive above the tow path. More people, more cars.

There, I saw it. No—that Chevy Cavalier had a huge dent in the fender. I stopped next to it, blocking a car behind me, and rolled down my bleary window. Ha! There was Stephen's expired faculty parking sticker under the rearview mirror. Ruth was nowhere in sight.

A crumbling concrete lane led steeply up the hill behind the river to Ridge Road, where there was another, smaller parking area. Jess and I, a million years ago, used to go there and park. I found a place for the Honda near the overlook. Just as I was getting out, a fresh rain shower started. I opened my umbrella and started back down the slippery road toward the water. Watching my feet, I didn't see Ruth until we almost walked into each other.

"Oh," she said involuntarily. Her surprised face shut down and turned stony. My impulse to reach out for her sank just as fast—but the dark thing, the deep dread inside finally slithered away, out of sight. Gone.

She looked half-drowned. "Are you all right?" She gave a nonchalant nod. "Come on," I said, and turned around. I tried to share the umbrella, but she made a point of slouching up the hill beside me in the downpour. *Drown, then,* I thought. Anger was working hard to overwhelm my relief; the urge to slap my daughter's sullen face had never been stronger. But neither had the urge to grab and hold and never let go.

Inside Pop's car, I fumbled in the glove compartment until I found a clean handkerchief. "Here, dry your hair. At least dry your face." She turned around to comply, surliness in every move, every line of her body. For a second I felt drunk on it, the old familiar sneering meanness, the intimacy, the dearness of it filling my throat like honey, like tears. *We will get through this, and it will be awful, but oh I love you, I love you.*

The rain slacked off again, reduced to trickling streams down the windows. Through the murk and the trees, the little bit of river visible from here was only a muddy, moving blur. "Are you cold?"

She shook her head, staring straight ahead. She looked exhausted, red-eyed and disheveled, the wrinkled knit of her shirt sticking to her childish breasts. She wouldn't look at me. I couldn't stop looking at her.

"Why did you come here? Why didn't you go home?"

"I drove by, saw a million cars. Including the cops."

She must've seen Jess's truck, too. "Are you all right?" I asked again.

She shrugged one shoulder and stared out the window.

"Did you get a tattoo?"

Her nostrils flared. "I don't have to tell you anything."

In spite of everything, I wasn't prepared for more hostility. She leaned forward to wipe the condensation off her side of the window, then switched the wipers on for one swipe and turned them off. The message: anything outside this car is more interesting than anything inside.

"I'm sorry for what happened," I said. "Sorry for the way it happened. I know you're hurt. But if you're waiting for me to apologize for being in love with Jess, that's not going to happen."

"Who cares, Mom, I don't give a damn anyway."

I sighed when she folded her arms across her chest; fortifying the stockade. There was nothing to do but start further back. "You know Jess and I went to school together. When we were in high school, we fell in love. Eleventh grade."

"How come you never told me?" She made her voice sarcastic, as if the answer would be obvious to a child. "How come you kept it a secret?"

"I told your father," I evaded. "It wasn't a secret."

"Oh, yeah, what did he say?"

"Nothing. He—didn't think anything of it."

"Poor bastard."

I blanched, not at *bastard* but at the casual cynicism. I'd never wanted her to be this grown-up.

"Ruth. I know how you feel."

"Bullshit, you don't know anything."

"Then tell me."

"No."

I took hold of the wheel and turned it back and forth until the steering lock clicked. "I'll tell you how I feel, then. I'm sorry I hurt you. I'd rather hurt myself. If you wanted to punish me, you couldn't have picked a better way. And I'm angry about that. Ruth, I am so mad at you."

She scowled straight ahead.

"I *do* know how you feel. You think I dishonored your father. You think the two people you trusted most have been false to you, tricked you. You're furious and you're hurt." Her cheeks turned bright red. She looked out the side window to hide her face. "How was I supposed to tell you?" I said thickly. "Do you think I did any of this on purpose? I didn't want to fall in love with Jess again."

She said through a stuffy nose, "Why didn't you just marry him in the first place?"

"I should have."

She turned on me with burning eyes. "Oh, that's great, Mom, then I wouldn't even exist. Then you and Jess could have everything."

"Oh, stop it. I should've married him because he was right for me. I fell in love with Jess when I was seventeen. No—eleven, the first time we met." I couldn't help smiling, but that only made her flounce around in disgust. "The reason I didn't marry him is because I chickened out. He was . . . a wild boy. Your grandmother couldn't stand him," I said with a careful laugh. Ruth wouldn't look at me, but I could tell she was listening closely. "But he wasn't wild, not like that. I doubt if he ever even broke the law—speeding, maybe. He was just different, he unsettled some people."

"Like Gram."

"Yes."

"Maybe she thought . . ." She stopped, remembering she wasn't talking to me. But then she had to finish. "Maybe she thought it was catching. Jess's mom's disease or whatever."

He'd told Ruth about his mother? I hid my surprise. "I think you're right, I think that was part of it. And I think that's why he changed when he got older. Partly. Became more sedate. Cooler."

"All grown-ups do that."

"I suppose." I gave up; I couldn't explain Jess, it was beyond me. Especially to Ruth, especially now. And what a dangerous job, clarifying for my daughter why I loved someone else and not her father. However I phrased it, how could that do anything but wound?

"Mom?" She fiddled with the radio dials, the heater knobs, hunched forward, giving me her closed profile. "When you, um, whatchacallit. Committed adultery, did Dad know? Was it . . . is that why he crashed the car?"

"No."

"How do you know?"

"Because—it was years before—you were a *baby*." She gawked at me, finally more amazed than angry. "But I'm not—this isn't something I want to talk to you about. I told you, one time, and never after. It was a mistake, and I suffered for it."

"Oh yeah, I'll bet."

"Ruth, listen. People can't always choose who they love, sometimes it just happens. Sometimes we—"

"We can choose who we sleep with!"

Ah, the knife in the heart. She wouldn't look at me, so I let my face crumple, breathing through my mouth, hoping I wouldn't cry. "We can," I said, voice fluttery. "You're right."

"And you were wrong." Implacable.

"That's what I've been trying to tell you."

She wiped the windshield with Pop's handkerchief and turned on the wipers again. Needlessly; the sun was breaking out in patches. A billowy wind chopped the surface of the river, dulling the shine. It was clammy in the car; I rolled my window down a few inches. Finally I had no choice but to find a tissue in my pocket and blow my nose. When I did, Ruth glanced at me.

"*Jeez*, Mom."

I couldn't hear any sympathy. I wiped my face, sniffed in the rest of the tears. Amazing, how prodigiously well I was botching this job. "I was wrong, I admit it. But not only for what happened with Jess. I was guilty of a kind of cowardice, too." But was she old enough for that revelation? No, I decided, backing off; let Stephen stay the innocent, injured party a while longer. Forever, maybe. Yes.

"The important thing is that your father never knew about us."

"How do you know?"

"Because I know. I swear—you can let that go."

She stared at me fixedly for a long minute. "Okay," she said, and we both relaxed slightly. A little light slanted through the murk.

"Here's the thing," I said. "Eventually we have to forgive ourselves. I know you think I'm a hypocrite, a liar, a—a jezebel—"

"What's a jezebel?"

"It's kind of a . . ."

"Slut?" But she blushed when she said it, and smirked, trying to make it sound like a joke.

"The things you think I've done wrong—I did them out of love, and so I forgive myself." Her mouth pulled sideways; I could practically hear her thinking, *How convenient*. "That's not an excuse. Or—it's the *only* excuse. Listen to me. If Stephen had lived, I don't believe we'd have stayed together. Not because of Jess—don't think that. And I know you don't want to hear it, but I *can't* explain this to you until you're older."

"Why not?"

"Because it's not fair to your father. But Ruth—Jess is for me, I can't do anything about it. Do you think it takes anything away from how much I love you? It doesn't. It doesn't. You're the best part of my life, you've always been, that can't ever change. Even if you—tattooed your whole body."

She snorted. And colored again, and stared down at her lap. She almost smiled.

"I know I've been too easy with you sometimes. That's been my biggest failing as a mother, but the reason—"

"No, you haven't."

"The reason—and it's hard for me to tell you, but I'm going to—it's because I've always tried so hard not to be like *my* mother. Who, frankly, wanted to run my life for me—and this I'm telling you in confidence, woman to woman. But she did it out of love—again—so I've forgiven her, too." The reality wasn't as neat and tidy as these linked, symmetrical revelations implied, but I wasn't trying to illuminate a moral lesson, I was just trying to tell the truth. Finally. "But that's beside the point, we're not talking about my mother, we're talking about yours. I've tried—" I sighed, suddenly exhausted. I put my head back. "I've tried to be a good mother. And I know, I can *hear* that that doesn't sound like much. And I'm sorry if I've been permissive or loose or if it's felt to you as if I don't care—"

"Mom—"

"—or I'm uninvolved. Because, believe me, I couldn't *be* more—"

"Mom. You're not lax. I don't even know where you get that."

"I'm not?" I got it from Stephen.

"*No. Jeez.* You're a lot of things that aren't so great, but permissive isn't one of them."

"Oh." That stopped my momentum. "I thought I was. As a reaction."

"Well, you're not. *God.*"

"Okay. Well."

Was she trying to make me feel better? Worse? I was thinking of what to say next when Ruth said, "I didn't mean there's a *lot* of things. You know, that aren't so great. Some, a few things. That's all."

My heart swelled at this overture. "Oh," I said, low-keying it. "Well, that's good. Some; that's better than a lot. There are . . . almost no things about you that aren't so great. To me. Well, one thing. That I'm thinking of right now, but that's it."

Suspenseful pause.

"What? The car, right? That was an accident. I was backing up—"

"No, not the car. Last night. The things you said on the phone. And I didn't know where you were, and I couldn't find you, and I didn't know what to do." The deadliest time of my life. Like being buried alive.

"I know." Her pale face flushed. "That was, like, a really bad time for me."

"I know," I said, anxious to forgive.

"Sorry," she mumbled, playing with the door handle. "I thought about calling back. I knew it was rotten, and I just—did it anyway." She shook her head, looking baffled, as if that instance of adult cruelty didn't fit with her idea of herself.

I reached out to stroke a dark, wet strand of hair behind her ear, something I'd been wanting to do for fifteen minutes. "It's all right. It's okay." I'd have worried I was being too lax, but apparently that wasn't one of my failings after all. On the other hand, Ruth's perspective might not be totally objective.

"God, I'm tired. I'll tell you everything that happened, but not right now, okay?" Her face, bland and accepting as she suffered my increasingly affectionate caress, sharpened all at once. "Oh—I forgot."

"What?"

"The car died. I think. I parked it down there—"

"I saw it."

"And now it won't start. I think this time it's really dead."

Were we finished? For the time being? Ruth had a lot of explaining to do; I had a lot of discipline to mete out. Neither of us was in the mood to get on with either of those. "Let's go see if it starts," I said. "If not, we'll come back for it later."

"Okay. Look, the sun's out."

I started the car and drove down the hill. Double-parked, I waited while Ruth got out and tried to start the Chevy. No luck. "Nope," she reported, getting back in. "All it does is make a clicking sound."

"Could be the battery."

"Or maybe the starter."

We drove out to the highway and across the river bridge.

"Mom, I gotta say, it looks really cool." She meant the ark. I glanced over, suspicious. She didn't *look* sarcastic. "Too bad you missed all the action," she continued, with breathtaking casualness. "Stop here for a sec, okay—look how it looks from here."

I pulled up behind a line of cars parked on the verge, just beyond the bridge, and we gazed down at the floating, bobbing ark, tied with taut, multiple lines between the two long piers. "Let's get out," Ruth said, and so we did, and stood on the grass with our backs against the car, looking down at the ark. "So it's hollow inside? Because guys were walking on it when they put the animals in. Isn't it cool that it rained just for the boarding part? Like, symbolic."

"It's got a solid deck, but no hull, nothing underneath," I said. "It's a raft, basically—"

"But I can see it going down, I can see the sides under water."

"I know, but there's nothing behind, it's just painted sheets of plywood, and they only go down about two feet. It's an illusion."

"Cool."

"It's a raft with two hollow boxes on top. You can stand on the main deck, but the other two are fake. You never saw anybody walking on them, I'll bet."

"No, they went inside with the animals, and then put them out through the windows on the two upper stories. I figured there were stairs in there."

"Nope. A ladder."

"Wow. Everybody really liked it."

"Did they?"

"There were a million people at least, I mean, it was like the Fourth of July almost, you should've . . ." She pulled on her hair, a childish habit, and usually an indication of moral uncertainty.

"I got here about nine-thirty or so," she started again, speaking slowly. A news report. "They were just starting to put the animals on. Some TV cameras were here, and people doing radio interviews, I guess—they just had tape recorders and microphones. I saw Landy, he was with about six guys, I guess Arkists, rolling animals up the gangplank or whatever you call it—which is gone now, they took it away when they were done. Everybody thought the animals were great. For a while I was standing near this family, the parents and these two little girls and one boy. They went nuts over the monkeys especially, Mom, but also that flying cat and the elephant. And the owl. Everybody liked the polar bear. I think the big animals were more, like, crowd pleasers, but that's because most people were far back—anybody on either one of the piers could see the little animals perfectly. I like the prairie dog a lot. And the chicken. The mouse—that was cool how you had it going up the chain.

"I heard this guy near me saying how there was only one of everything, how come there weren't two, so I told him about the different sides. He thought that was neat. I didn't tell him I was related to the person who made everything. I was going to, but then, I don't know, I just didn't.

"I saw Mr. Pletcher. And his wife. He had on a black suit and she had on a navy blue suit and a flowered hat. In fact you could tell all the women who were Arkists because they all wore hats. They had cameras on Mr. Pletcher; I think he gave an interview. He looked pretty, you know, blissed out. Maybe he was on drugs. Landy went and stood with him when they were finished with the animals, and then he gave a speech."

"Landy gave a speech?"

"Yeah, and it wasn't bad. But you could tell he was nervous. He stood right down there, right there, on this raised box thing, right by the water. He just said thanks to everybody for coming out, and he named the people who had helped. He named you. And—Jess. And some others. He read the ark story from the Bible. Then he carried the microphone over to his dad, who was behind him. The P.A. system must've been really cheap, at first all you could hear was squeaks and squeals. Landy held the umbrella over the old guy and he said something, but we couldn't hear him. Everybody got really quiet. His voice was so weak, and it took him forever to say what he said. Which wasn't much, but I can't quote it or anything. Just about how the ark doesn't mean God's wrath, it means forgiveness, and like, starting over from scratch.

Purification. And then something about how kind people were to him, all his dear friends and his family. How much love he felt. Their generosity to him. Because they saved him. Then he said good-bye, and—some people cried, which was weird because, before, it had been like a carnival, almost. The Arkists sang one song, a hymn, and it was really . . . how can I say this . . . terrible. So then the ceremony part was over, and people just crowded around the ark as close as they could get and looked at it. Anybody who had a camera took about a million pictures. They really . . . they really liked it." She paused, thinking. "I guess that's about it," she said, and sat back.

I gazed down, easily imagining, thanks to Ruth, a milling crowd under umbrellas around a makeshift platform in the rain. Landy mumbling into a squawky microphone, screwing up his courage to read the story of Noah to hundreds of strangers. And Eldon, struggling to say his piece in the little bit of time left. Giving thanks for a singular act of love, the expression of which was floating on the river in front of him. An ark.

"Hey, Mom. Wanna see my tattoo?"

"Oh." I tried to sound thrilled. "I definitely do. Is it wonderful?"

She laughed.

"I've been thinking maybe I should get one," popped out of my mouth. "Think I'm too old?"

"No *way*. I think you should get one exactly like mine."

"Really?"

"Absolutely. Mother-daughter tattoos."

There was a glint in her eye that tipped me off. Oh Lord, what had she gotten, a swastika? Coiled snakes? I put a light, very tentative hand, just my fingertips, really, on her spine as we turned away from the river. Immediately her arm came up and circled my waist.

"Want to drive?"

She flashed me a look of surprise. "Sure," she mumbled, pleased, coloring. "Thanks." We separated casually.

"We'll come back for the car tomorrow."

"Good deal."

In the car, Ruth showed me her new tattoo. And then we went home.

27

The Last Straw

School's out, finally. For the very last thing in English, Mrs. Fitzgerald told us to make a list in our journals of the two or three major things most on our minds as we say good-bye to sophomore year and look forward to becoming juniors, and then try to develop strategies for dealing with these issues over the summer vacation. Most kids didn't bother because she was never going to check and see if we did it, but I came up with a big list, a huge list. The first item was—

No. 1. *My tattoo*.

This experience continues to suck and be as putrid and humiliating as ever. First I put a bandage over it for school and told people I had a burn. Then I told Jamie the truth after making her swear never to tell a living soul, not even Caitlin. Surprise, surprise—the whole school knew all about it within one day.

Gram hates my tattoo and said she'd pay to have it lasered off, so she and Mom took me to the dermatologist, Dr. Ewing, who said it would be pretty major to remove the whole thing and how about if he just took off the arms and the top of the circle, and after that healed I could go to a reputable tattoo place and have the arms put in lower and the loop more oval, so like a real ankh tattooed over the old one.

Nobody was in favor of this but me. Luckily the money factor kicked in, so that's probably what we're going to do. I'm pretty stoked, but it won't happen until August, and meanwhile I've got this, like, lollipop on my hand. Not to mention a lot of stupid gay jokes to put up with. Some guy at school called it an "all-day sucker." Which, when you think about it, is pretty much what I was.

Meanwhile, I've been thinking. *Why* is the female symbol a lesbian thing? Men wear stupid macho symbols, swords and guns and flaming motorcycles and what-have-you, and nobody says *they're* gay. Just the opposite. I don't know, I'm torn. Sometimes I think screw it, I'm keeping this, it's a sign of my female power. I'm strong in myself, I know who I am, and to hell with what anyone else thinks. Okay, but then I think—but why does it have to be so hard? And do I really want a tattoo I'll always have to be *living down*? And besides, I really *want* an ankh. Because I'm *for* life.

So I don't know. I still have a few more days to decide.

No. 2. *Raven.*

I guess he's not my boyfriend anymore. Not that he ever was, except once for about five minutes. I'd been noticing he wasn't as friendly as before, and I found out why: The Other Woman. "Cindy." She's this total Goth, a sophomore, honest to God she looks like a corpse, they've sent her home twice that I know of for ghoul makeup. I saw her with him in the library two times and once in his car. They're perfect for each other. I don't miss him. In fact it's a relief not to have to hear his atrocity stories anymore.

I can't believe I used to worry about my name, like it wasn't dark enough or something, I should change it to Hecuba—and now this. *Cindy*??

No. 3. *Krystal.*

Mom made me quit working at the Palace. God, she's still so mad. Much madder at Krystal than me, which doesn't make too much sense. "You're not the adult, she is," is all she'll say. I ran into Krystal in the video store one night—luckily Mom wasn't with me. It was weird at first, but after a few minutes of chatting, it was like old times. She broke up with Kenny. Now she's going out with the UPS man—Walt, I've met him plenty of times. "He's a very gentle meat eater," she says. When we finished catching up and all, Krystal said, "You stay in touch now, and don't be a stranger." I said I wouldn't be, and then I thanked her for helping me out, letting me sleep on her couch and everything. She said, "Anytime," and I was about to go on and thank her for the rest, but when I heard in my head how it would come out—"Thank you for lying to my mom and not telling the cops that I took the car and drove by myself illegally to D.C."—I couldn't say it. Like, it almost sounded sarcastic or something.

I'm not saying Mom's right about Krystal—I definitely think her heart was in the right place and she was a true friend when I needed one. Just saying, there are different ways to be a person's friend, and maybe aiding and abetting them no matter what they do is not the best way every single time. That's all.

No. 4. *Punishment*.

I got grounded for three weeks, including all the end-of-school parties I was invited to, and I have to pay for the dent I made in the car out of my allowance. I guess this puts to rest for all time Mom's theory that she's too lax. Ha ha ha ha ha ha ha ha.

The worst was when the cops were going to push back by one year my eligibility to get my driver's license. Which would've been the end, I might as well have committed suicide. But somebody intervened (guess who? Jess, who's like a big effing deal on the city council), so that went away. Thank God.

No. 5. *My new job*.

Grampa hired me to type on disk all the corrections and revisions to the book he and his colleague are writing. So far there aren't very many, so obviously this was a pity hiring. He gives me the minimum wage, same as Krystal, but it's nowhere near as much fun. I have to work in his office at his house for the first few weeks, until I know what I'm doing. It's more or less part-time.

One thing I'm learning, besides more than I ever wanted to about minor English eighteenth-century poetry, is that Grampa isn't as quiet as I've always thought he was. In fact I can't get him to shut up. What does he talk about? The weather a lot; he's got a weather radio, and he likes to watch the weather channel on TV. Yesterday he talked about this incredible deal he got on four radial tires for his Honda. I mean at length. And other stuff, how his lawn is doing, his tomato crop, how lawyers are ruining the country, why the Atlanta Falcons aren't as good as the Carolina something or others. It's boring. But it's sort of nice, too, because it's easy and relaxing, I can listen or not. I can tell he likes me. We're almost getting to be friends. He's nice. I've figured out the reason he doesn't talk to Gram is because she talks all the time. Which is so funny, because she complains to Mom that she can't get a word out of him and she might as well have married a mute. I feel like sending her an anonymous note—"Shut up for a while, why don't you, put a cork in it!" But I bet she wouldn't even see herself. She'd think it was for somebody else.

No. 6. *The Ark.*

Old Mr. Pletcher died. Late in the afternoon on the day of the ark launch, he had to be rushed to the hospital in an ambulance because of his heart. He stayed there for four days, then he said he wanted to go home to die. And that's exactly what he did, two days later. The Clayborne paper did another long story, and more people than you'd think showed up for his funeral, including Mom, and afterward the ark was even more popular. The Richmond paper did this sort of tongue-in-cheek article that made fun of the whole situation, but not in a mean way, and they said the "animal constructions are imaginative and delightful" and "unexpectedly affecting." Mom was dancing on the ceiling. The only bad part was one night when some kids from out of town (the paper said, but since they never caught them how do they *know*?) threw a burning stick from the pier onto the ark and started a fire that did damage to the owl, the pelican, the panther, and the grizzly bear. Well, that stirred people up and ended up causing even more visitors to come and look at it. It was a genuine tourist attraction.

But then the forty days and forty nights were over, and they dismantled it and sold it for scrap lumber, proceeds going to the Arkists. Up until then, nobody had thought about what would happen to the animals. (I thought they'd just throw them away, but that was before I realized how *imaginative and delightful* they were.) Mrs. Pletcher, who is the actual owner of them, called up one night and told Mom a big petting zoo in Pennsylvania, which happens to be called Noah's Ark, had offered to buy the whole menagerie for three thousand dollars, to put in their welcome building. She wanted to know what she should do—sell them to the zoo and give Mom the three thousand minus expenses for materials, which takes it down to about two thousand, or give them to the new Church of the Sons of Noah she's having built out on Route 634 in her husband's memory. We could really use two thousand dollars. But Mom told her the church should have them—especially since the petting zoo could never have used all of them and would've ended up throwing some away. Plus Mom likes the idea of them decorating the aisles in the Church of the Sons of Noah. Sort of like Stations of the Cross, she says.

No. 7. *Mom's Job.*

She doesn't have a real one yet, but everybody is hopeful. Her friend Chris, who is also unemployed, had an idea that Mom could do illustrations for these kids' books Chris wrote. First it was just an experiment, to see if it would work at all, and Mom only did some pen and ink drawings. But they were good and Chris liked them a lot, so next she tried some watercolors. Well, they were a hit, too, so now they've teamed up. Who knows what will happen, but at least for now they're going to see if they can write and illustrate books for children who are between the ages of four and seven. I read the one they finished and it wasn't bad.

So that's one thing. Another is that some professor's wife in Clayborne wants Mom to paint a mural in her dining room of people sitting at a big table and eating. She wants it to take up two whole walls and be sort of old-fashioned and French, like Renoir or Toulouse-Lautrec or somebody, with lots of French bread and wine bottles and candles on the table and the people dressed like the nineteenth century—EXCEPT—she would like four of the diners to look like herself, her husband, and her two kids! Mom thinks it's a riot! She's probably going to do it. The lady will pay big bucks, even more than the petting zoo would have, so she's going to give it a try.

The third thing is—Mr. Wright asked if she'd teach a course in art next semester at the Other School!! No one could believe the balls on this guy. She said no, of course, especially since he was paying squat, but now she's actually rethinking her decision. She could do it for "practice," she says, because maybe Gram's been right all along and what she should really do is go back to school for a teaching degree and then teach art. Jeez. I'm just glad I'll be out of here by then and there's no way she could ever be my teacher. Who knows if this will happen or not. It's sort of a last resort, as I get it, in case the other gigs don't work out. "Something to fall back on," Gram keeps saying. Mom says she doesn't hate the idea as much as she used to. I guess that's something. But me—whatever I end up doing, I know it won't be the thing I hate the least. It'll be the thing I love the most. Whatever that may be. I said that to Mom the other night, as a matter of fact, but she didn't pick up on it or defend herself or anything. She just said, "Good for you," and let it go. So that made me think. Easy for me to say. I don't have a kid to send to college in two years.

No. 8. *Jess.*

I'm grounded, so naturally I'm in my room last night doing E-mail when Mom comes in and sits on the bed. She's got her serious face, so I know we're going to Talk, and I'm even pretty sure what about, but I say nothing, to make it harder for her to start. This doesn't work, because she says right out, "What are you going to do about Jess?"

I'm not really mad anymore, I'm more like, oblivious. Or trying to be. Just trying to live my life without any of that in my face, and until now she's been okay with it. I mean, maybe she sneaks over to his house all the time, maybe they have hot phone sex every night—I don't know and I don't care to know. (I still can't believe he rode up to D.C. with Grampa. I wish I'd been a fly on that windshield!)

So anyway, I try to cut the conversation short by saying I'm not doing anything about Jess, and if she wants to bring him around and be his girlfriend, hey, be my guest, no skin off my nose. I mean it's not like he needs my permission to come a-courtin', right? This doesn't amuse Mom. We go around for a while, and finally she admits that what she really wants me to do is talk to him.

Long story short, Jess calls today and invites me to go for a ride with him and Tracer in his pickup truck, and I get to drive. Yee-ha, big deal. I outgrew that stupid cowgirl fantasy a long time ago. But I don't point that out or act smart, in fact I am incredibly polite. Butter, as they say, won't melt in my mouth. It's much better to peace out in these situations and act like nothing is going on under the surface, no mental alternative dramas. You've got a lot more clout when you chill than when you act sullen or argue or show your hand. This I have learned over the years and at tremendous personal expense.

Jess freaked me, though. We were going south on back roads, down toward Orange, which is a pretty little town, and I was being extra careful not to speed so he couldn't get anything on me. It was hot, but we didn't turn on the AC, the air smelled so good, even the fertilizer smell when we went by the new fields. Cows everywhere—I used to ask him what the different breeds were and he'd tell me, Hereford, Guernsey, Brown Swiss, Jersey, etc., but today I didn't ask because already I could see how easy it would be to slide back into our old friendship as if nothing had happened. I think it's partly the silences, which are weird with other people unless they're like your parents or your best friend, but they're never weird with Jess. Why is that?

So it's a beautiful day and we're driving along, not talking much because I am being cool, when all of a sudden he goes, "I'll get lost if you want me to." I say something brilliant like, "Huh?" and he says, "It's up to you."

I'm thinking, Shit! I didn't know what to say. Finally I told him I didn't think my mom would agree with him, I seriously didn't think she'd say it was up to me. He said she was taking a lot for granted with me, she was making an assumption that eventually I was going to be okay with them being together, but it was because that's what she wanted to happen. But that he could see clearer. He said, "Ruth, I'll do whatever you want."

Oh, great! I go, "Look, it's none of my business what you do, you're two consenting adults." He smiled when I said that, "two consenting adults," and I just kind of, I don't know, I went mooshy inside. I liked him again, the same as before, and it was so totally annoying, like I was a pushover for anybody who thinks I'm funny or lovable or whatever, which I am. A pushover, I mean.

We drove around Orange for a while, but when he said do you want to get something to eat at the café, I said no thanks. Because this was not a social occasion. I turned around and started driving home on Route 15 because it's faster.

He goes, "I've been thinking." Tracer was sprawled across his lap and halfway out the window, tongue out, ears flying. I didn't want to hear what Jess was thinking, and I almost turned on the radio, but that would've been incredibly rude, plus I didn't have the nerve. He said, "I've been wondering how I'd have felt if my father loved someone after my mother died." (Or before, I thought, but I kept my mouth shut.) He said he thought he'd have pretended to be glad for his father, but inside it wouldn't have made any sense to him, because his mother was the center of their lives, she was what made his family work.

So I said it's not the same. I said my father wasn't like that.

I hated admitting that to him. But he was trying to make some kind of a circle, some parallel story about his life, and it didn't work. These days when I try to think about my dad, it's strange, but I can only picture him in his study in the old place in Chicago, doing his work. I can't see him anywhere else in the house, I can't put him in the kitchen or the bathroom or the yard. I just see him sitting at his desk. He's wearing his light green shirt with his tie undone, and he doesn't look up when anybody comes in. He's busy. He puts his left hand on his forehead to shield his eyes, and keeps writing.

I changed the subject, started talking about Mom and Chris's new book, about a little duck named Schwartz who never cleans up his room so he can't find his winning lottery ticket. I wasn't interested in talking to Jess about my father. That's private. All the way home he kept trying to get back to the point—his point—but I wouldn't help him out. I admit I liked seeing him get more and more frustrated. But he didn't press it, he didn't put the screws on or anything.

When we got home, I turned the motor off and just sat there, didn't jump right out and run off. I knew he wasn't finished, and sure enough, he starts saying how those times when we went fishing or just walking around, the times I came over to see him, he really enjoyed himself and he didn't have any, like, motive going on. He said, "I just liked being with you." I'm thinking, now is the time I'm supposed to say, "I liked being with you, too," and us to make up. I *wanted* to say it. But I didn't. I just couldn't. I sat there and played with the steering wheel.

We got out, and I figured he was going to come in the house with me. I even half wanted him to, so this could finally be over. But he didn't, he climbed back in the truck. I mumbled something like, "It doesn't matter to me if you come in or not. I mean, don't stay away on my account, because I just don't give a damn." That was so bad, I couldn't look at him. Why couldn't I be nice? I think it's because it still feels disloyal—like being nice to Jess is cheating on my dad. It's like giving in and being selfish, doing what I want to instead of what I ought to. Jess goes, How about if we take it really slow, and I go, Yeah, that sounds okay. And he says, "I love your mom. I wasn't waiting for her before, because I never thought it would work out. But now I am, and it doesn't matter how long." I don't know what I said. I was embarrassed. I mean, that was so personal.

So then he said, really quietly, "I love you, too." I looked at him. "I do," he said.

Well, I couldn't talk. But it was kind of the last straw. He put his hand on the side of the truck, and that was like a touch on my hand or my arm. Then he started the engine up and drove away.

So who knows what will happen.

Or else it's obvious.

Mom says we have to forgive each other for the things we do out of love. Oh, I guess. She forgave me for telling her I was sleeping on the street with derelicts. Did I do that out of love? I might have, but you have to go pretty far back to see it. And you'd have to really love the person to bother going back that far. Well, I will work on my forgiveness. Jess is cheating somehow, though; he's making it too easy.

So anyway, I guess that's it for items that are on my mind and strategies to deal with them over the summer. It's been a . . . I don't know what. A some kind of a year. It's been the kind of year I'm not going to understand for a few more years. Like the year when I was twelve and I first got my period and we moved from Chicago to here—I can see now how interesting that year was, but at the time it just felt like one stupid thing after another.

This is the year my father died. I turned into a different person. I am forever changed. The problem here is, I didn't know what kind of a person I was before, so how am I supposed to know who I turned into? Time, I guess. "Time will tell" is a true saying. Nevertheless, one of these days I would very much like to understand things about myself *while they're happening*.

I read somewhere that grief is all about the griever, hardly at all about the person you've lost. Thinking over this past year, I can see how true that is.

Okay. Well, that's it.

EXCEPT! No. 9. *There is this guy.* His name is Robbie Warriner, and he's Chris's next-door neighbor and also a year ahead of me at school, a total computer freak, and a major babe. (I think. Becky says no, he's a tool, but she likes Jason Bellinger, so what does she know.) He's so nice, he comes over to Chris's and helps Andy, her kid, with his new computer and teaches him games and stuff. So of course sometimes when I go over there to see Mom, he's there. He's going to study computers and virtual reality in college, he's already decided. I told him I'd like to learn how to do spreadsheets, since I might take statistics next year, and now he's teaching me! He has red hair, but it's dark red, not orange, and he doesn't have freckles. He's taller than me. He has long, graceful fingers and this really intense face, and when he hunches over the keyboard and stares into the monitor at a pie chart it's like watching Van Cliburn or somebody. He chews Dentyne. Sometimes he sits behind me to show me cell formulas or fields or whatever. I smell that peppery-cinnamon smell and forget what I'm doing. According to Chris he's not going out with anybody. I think the guy being a year and a half older than the girl is exactly right. Mom likes him a lot. Not that that matters.

28

Celtic Circle

Ruth said yes.

I couldn't believe how easy it was. I'd phrased my question very casually: "I was thinking I might drive out to Daddy's grave, clean it up, put some fresh flowers. It's such a beautiful day. But you're probably busy, you wouldn't want to come with me. Only for an hour. I just thought since it's so pretty."

"Sure, Mom. I'll drive."

But just as we were leaving, Mama pulled up in her new car, a sporty red compact with a sunroof. "Where're you going?" she yelled out the window, spotting us on the sidewalk. I told her. "Great, I'll go with you. Get in, this car rides like a dream. Ruth honey, you want to drive?"

And that was that. I seethed all the way to Hill Haven. My mother might be bossy, but she wasn't blind, was she? Surely she could see that this particular mother-daughter foray was tricky enough already, fraught with pitfalls, a minefield of possible disasters. Maybe she thought a third party might ease the way, but honestly, couldn't she see that the whole *point* was the intimacy, the privacy—the mother-daughter part?

No. As it turned out, she *was* blind, but I didn't learn why until later. All I knew then was that she was in a rotten mood and she wanted company.

After a week of stifling heat and humidity, it was a mild, gorgeous day, the sky a puffy cloud-filled azure blue that made my chest ache. Ruth said it felt more like Chicago in spring than

Virginia in July. Along with a clutch of zinnias and rudbeckia, the freshest flowers left in my neglected, baking-hot garden, I'd also brought along a blanket and a Thermos of lemonade. I'd had a hopeful but naive vision of Ruth and me sitting hip-to-hip on the blanket, sharing confidences along with the single cup. The fantasy didn't fit three. Neither did the blanket; Mama plopped down on it heavily, tucking her skirt around her calves, perspiring from the short climb from the paved path, while Ruth stood apart and looked off in the distance, hands on her hips, long legs too tan under her black shorts in spite of my incessant sunscreen carping. With a sigh for lost opportunities, I sat down next to my mother.

Presently Ruth dropped to her knees and began to pull back the dry, dead grass from around Stephen's bronze burial plaque. She'd cut her hair for the summer, shorter than mine, a sun-streaked cap of soft, springy curls. I loved it, loved to touch it, even though it made her jerk away and say, "*Mom*." She'd be sixteen next month. I remembered very well what getting my driver's license had meant to me—freedom, independence, the glorious beginning of my real life. But for a mother it only meant one thing: the beginning of the end.

"Carrie, you look tired." Mama poured half a cup of lemonade from the Thermos and drank it. She sounded peevish. "Ruth honey, doesn't your mother look tired?"

Ruth looked up, narrowed her eyes at me. "No. I think she looks pretty." She shrugged and went back to pulling grass.

"Thanks," I said after a startled second. How long had it been since she'd given me a compliment? Resentments were beginning to crumble, maybe from old age, maybe only to make way for new ones, but I loved our truce and didn't care what motivated it. Ruth liking me, being nice to me again—I hadn't known how much I'd missed that.

"Hey," she said, "look."

"Don't point," Mama said severely. "We see them."

"What?" I exchanged a look with Ruth—*What is with her?*—and glanced over my shoulder. "Oh." A funeral service, above us, forty yards away on top of the hill the cemetery was named for. There weren't many mourners. They stood out in black silhouette against the sky, a very old woman in a long-sleeved dress—she must be stifling—two older men, a young woman, and a boy. A minister was reading from a prayer book, and a word or two drifted down on the shifting breeze, *Almighty Lord . . . beloved . . . we ask . . .*

Ruth put her dirty hands on her thighs and stared. "You never know, do you. It looks like an ordinary funeral, the guy's dead and she's the widow, those are the kids and the grandkids, everybody's sad. But it could be something completely different. It could be anything."

My hand paused on the way to the Thermos. Was that a shot? Ruth's way of implying that my grief at Stephen's funeral had been disingenuous? A lie?

"I mean, the old lady could be the mother instead of the widow, and one of those guys could be the husband of the dead person. Or they could be brothers, the two guys, and they've lost their sister. You know. It could be anything."

"Oh." Relief. "It's true," I said, "we do make assumptions about people based on—"

"Stereotypes," Ruth finished. "Everybody jumps to conclusions about people. It's what causes racism and sexism and religious intolerance. I think it's better to not think *any*thing about people. Just try to keep an open mind at all times."

I nodded thoughtfully. *Native Son*, I recalled, was on her summer reading list. I closed my eyes for a few seconds. I had a sensation of rising, floating, hovering over all the graves in the cemetery, all the graves in the round, blue and green world. Millions and billions of the dead and the living, countless people standing over the stones of their loved ones, praying and wishing, weeping, grieving.

"George lied."

I opened my eyes. "What, Mama?"

"Your father has reneged on his promise." She yanked up a tuft of crabgrass and flung it sideways. "I should've known, I should've seen this coming a mile off."

"What happened?" I looked at Ruth, who kept her head down; she crouched over the plaque, blowing on it, rubbing it with the hem of her T-shirt. *She knows*, I thought. Whatever this is, she already knows about it.

"We're not going on our trip," Mama said flatly.

"Oh, no. Why not? I thought Pop finished his book." He had finished it, Ruth had told me so the night before last. As soon as it was done—the book he'd been collaborating on for the better part of two years—he and Mama were supposed to go away together. Only to the Bahamas, and only for a week, but it would be the first vacation they'd taken together in—fifteen years, she claimed, but that seemed impossible, she had to be exaggerating.

"Oh, he finished it all right. He finished it months ago, if you ask me, and all this so-called *editing* is just dicking around."

Dicking around? Ruth did look up at that, doll-eyed.

"But don't you already have tickets and reservations and everything?" This was bad. I hadn't been paying close attention to the minutiae of my mother's life for the last month or so—too many other things on my mind—but I knew this trip meant more to her than a casual getaway. She'd been seeing it as a transition between past and future, her old and her new life—maybe. The beginning of something different, or at least the possibility of it, between her and Pop. "Oh, Mama, why can't he go?"

"A symposium in Toronto. He gets to read a paper. Very prestigious, he says. They asked him at the last minute," she said with sour triumph. Rolling sideways, she got up using her hands, slapping vigorously at the back of her skirt. "I'm so mad I could spit."

She walked away, keeping her back to us. She was getting old lady feet; one navy blue flat was worn down on the outside, the other on the inside, as if her feet were slowly collapsing on each other. She wore long-sleeved blouses no matter the weather—"My arms are ugly," she claimed, "my elbows look like turkey wattles." I hectored her about taking her calcium, but she was still losing height; after forty-two years, I was finally taller.

Ruth looked up, blank-faced, from the absorbing task of rubbing dirt from her fingernails. These days her loyalties were divided. I loved it when she came home from her sinecure of a summer job and reported snippets of conversations with her grandfather, Grampa said this, Grampa thinks this about that. She was finally getting to know him, even growing close to him, and I envied her for it. But the experience was naturally muddying what had always been clear and uncomplicated, the family line: Gram was fun, lively, and interesting, Grampa was pretty much not there. Grampa was a rumor.

My mother's bowed head worried me. Surely she wasn't crying. I strolled over to where she was running her hands over the pointed stakes of an old iron fence. "Mama?"

"I'm fine."

"I know."

"I'm just mad. I wanted to go. Damn it to hell, I wanted to go on that dumb trip."

"I know you did."

"I feel like going anyway. Not to have fun, just to spite him." She smiled, grim humor returning. "I could ask Calvin Mintz to go with me. Bet he's lonely without Helen to boss around anymore. What a pair we'd make, huh?"

The hard fence spike made a dent in the fleshy pad of the thumb I was pressing into it. For me the summer was passing in a haze, a kind of golden liquid balm, nothing remotely like it had ever happened to me before. I hadn't lost myself in love or lust, I was still me, I could see Jess's flaws—moodiness, self-containment bordering on aloofness—and he could see mine—too numerous to mention. But we fit, we always had, and our time together was filling up places in me that had been empty for so long, years and years. We were still in the chemical dependency stage, addicted to each other. That wouldn't last, but I even looked forward, with curiosity, not dread, to what came next. To leave him now would be like . . . a drought that begins again after one long, healing rain.

"I'll go with you."

"What? Oh, no." Mama laughed self-consciously, dabbing at the perspiration under her nose with the edge of a tissue. In the slant of her downcast eyes, I could see the idea taking root.

"Why not? I haven't been anywhere in ages. Ruth could stay with Pop part of the time, part of the time at Modean's."

"I can stay by myself," Ruth called over. "*Jeez.*"

"You don't need a trip right now," Mama scoffed, striding away a few paces, pivoting, coming back. "You're in the middle of all that business with Chris, you've got"—she flung her hand out—"things going on." Jess, that meant. She'd all but reconciled herself to him. He was like arthritis in a new location, a psoriasis flare-up, one more old age-related affliction she had to accept with grace and dignity.

"Well, nothing's going to collapse in a week. Come on, we'll have fun."

"Oh, shoo." Still playing hard to get. "You don't want to go on a vacation with your old mother."

I did, though. I wanted to give her what she wanted, freely and for nothing. From the heart. For so long Mama had squeezed love out of me like toothpaste from a tube, and see where that had gotten us—at a prickly distance from each other, the hunter and the hunted, her starving, me scared of being eaten. Jess was mixed up in there, too. Loving him, choosing and acknowledging him—that was when I'd finally gotten free, when I was the most bound and committed. Now I could make this not-so-little sacrifice for my mother, give her this gift, for the very reason that she didn't expect it and hadn't asked for it. Hadn't squeezed it out of me.

"I do, Mama. I want to go away for a week in the Bahamas with my old mother. We'll lie on the beach and read all the books we've been saving up."

"Oh . . ."

"We'll eat fish every night, and we'll go shopping, we'll go to the movies, we'll fat-ass. We won't do a damn thing if we don't feel like it. And if we meet two nice-looking guys in the bar, we'll let 'em buy us mai-tais."

She gave a giddy, girlish laugh. "Well, that would serve him right, wouldn't it? Oh, honey." She took my arm and gave it a hard squeeze. "You know what, I'm gonna ask Birdie."

"Birdie? What—to go with you?"

"She needs a trip, she's been down in the dumps."

"*I* need a trip." Now I felt hurt. "You can't ask Birdie, she'll drive you nuts."

"She will, Gram," Ruth agreed, sidling over. "She'll drive you nuts."

"She probably will." She laughed again, a gay sound, and I thought, *I love your face, I love you, Mama*. "I think that's what I'll do, though. Carrie, you are a sweetheart, but you've got enough going on right now. I'll call Bird this afternoon, perk her up. Now, who's doing these flowers? Ruth honey, you know how the little holder in the plaque works? You pull it out of the ground and turn it over and it's a vase. Oh now, aren't those pretty. Carrie, are they from your garden or Modean's?"

So we arranged the flowers on Stephen's grave, and I mused on the interesting fact that my mother could still surprise me, still had tricks up her sleeve. Say what you would, families never got boring. And mothering never got less complicated. All you could do was hope, like a doctor, to do no harm. But it was a futile hope, because harm was inevitable, and then you just hoped someone, someday (Ruth, soon) took into account your good intentions.

My mother shoved up from her knees with a grunt and took a few stiff paces away, pressing both hands to the small of her back, stretching, jutting her chin out. I stayed where I was, barely brushing Ruth's arm with mine. I stroked a finger over the raised letters, STEPHEN EDWARD VAN ALLEN, BELOVED HUSBAND, FATHER, and tried to marshal my thoughts. Now was my chance to say something wise or true or conciliatory about Stephen. Squeezing Ruth's tennis shoe, I said, "Your father—"

"Mom, do you think he can see us? Or hear us? Do you think he's, like, aware of us right now?"

"Hmm. Well, I don't know, but it's possible, it's entirely—"

"Because sometimes I can really feel him near me, but other times . . ." She lowered her voice to a whisper. "I can almost not even remember what he looked like. If I concentrate on that green corduroy shirt, I can still see him." She drew in a deep breath and blew it out. "But for how much longer, you know? What if he becomes invisible?"

"Well, then—"

"Then I guess I'll just carry him around like a feeling. I'll always have that, right, the *sense* of my father."

"You look like him," I said. "Here." I traced my finger along the neat, decisive line of her jaw. "You'll never lose him, because he's in you." She smiled. "That's why I could never not love him. Why I never stopped."

"Yeah, but . . ." A faint pink colored her cheek. Embarrassment? I'd take that over outrage any day. I started to speak, but she said, "Don't talk about that here, Mom, okay? You know." She ran her palm across the brittle grass on top of the grave. "Just in case."

Of course. Just in case. I felt embarrassed by my own indelicacy.

On the hill above us, the service was breaking up. We were ready to go home, but out of respect, we waited for the mourning family to drift down the path to their cars and mill around for a few minutes, getting organized—*you go with him and we'll go with them, see you at the house*—the necessary social business of grief. Then we three strolled down to Mama's car. *We've had our funeral,* I caught myself thinking, *we're safe for a while.* As if loss were apportioned fairly, predictably, at convenient intervals. But hope was a deft deceiver, and I was nothing if not full of hope on this savory, soft, sweet-smelling midsummer day in the Hill Haven Cemetery. The future had vistas, potential, it looked like a pastel sky. The only cloud was that everybody I loved wasn't as full of sappy, sanguine expectation as me. There was something to be said for starting over, for filling your boat with fresh progenitors and sailing off into the downpour. Your new day wouldn't last long, but that was the nature of new days. Grudges resurfaced, bad habits recurred, slights and hurts and meannesses were bound to muddy the floodwaters before they could even start to recede. But then you started over again. As long as you could love and as long as you could forgive, it never had to end. Good thing, because you'd never get it right for long.

"Mama, let me go with you," I said again from the backseat of the car, leaning forward, careful to stay out of Ruth's rearview mirror. "We could have such a good time. Come on. I'd really like to go."

But she wouldn't budge. She was going with Birdie, period, and I wasn't sure why. It wasn't for the pleasure of martyrdom—I knew exactly how that role played out, and today Mama wasn't playing it. Generosity of spirit? A belated demonstration, better late than never, of the art of letting go? I enjoyed not knowing. I liked giving her the benefit of the doubt.

"I've got this great idea," Ruth said, flicking on the turn signal and slowing down smoothly, conscientiously, for the stoplight. She was going to be an excellent driver. Either that or she had her entire family fooled and she was going to be a holy terror. Absently, I reached around for my purse; we were coming into town, and Ruth's great ideas in this vicinity usually had to do with the Dairy Queen or McDonald's. But she said, "Let's *all* get tattoos."

I snorted. Mama rolled her eyes.

"Yeah, no, I mean, wouldn't that be incredible? When I get mine fixed, we could all three get new tattoos. Just a little one for you, Gram, a little bit of flash. It doesn't really hurt, not that much, and if we do it together it would be, like, a distraction. What do you think?" Her eyes danced in the mirror, daring me. "Mom, you could get a sexy one, you could get a butterfly on your ass."

Mama hooted with laughter. "What would I get?" She pushed up her sleeve, holding out her spotty, mottled forearm. "A big bleeding heart with an arrow through it? And underneath, 'George, Forever and Ever.'"

Ruth guffawed, bouncing in her seat. "Cool, or a skull and crossbones, Gram, right on your collarbone or something. Or your boob! Wouldn't that blow them away at the garden club?"

They cackled and snickered, thinking up wilder tattoos and more vulgar places to put them. The idea that my daughter was contemplating, had actually suggested, apparently not in jest, getting group-tattooed with her mother and her grandmother—that hadn't quite sunk in yet. Something to think about later.

Meanwhile, I thought about the tattoo I would get if I ever really did it. Not a butterfly on my ass. What was it called, that symbol of the serpent eating its own tail? It probably signified infinity, endlessness, timelessness. But for me it would mean the effort to love well going on and on, round and round, always imperfect and always forgivable. The best we could ever do for each other.

In the front seat, they'd made decisions. A perfect ankh for Ruth, some kind of flower for Mama—not a rose, though: too common. "Are you in, Mom?" Ruth took her right hand off the steering wheel and lifted it in a fist. Poor hand, still pink and sore from the last laser treatment. Mama clasped it, chuckling. I surrounded it gently with my hand, and the three of us stuck our joined fists through the sunroof and shook them in the air.

I sat back, wistful, feeling a little heavy from all my fond, precarious hopes. Pastel sky or not, the future came too fast sometimes. It flew by in a blur—not unlike the Dairy Queen. But what could you do? Nothing. Hope for the best. Relax, enjoy, and let your daughter, the expert, drive you home.

Flight Lessons

Always for Jon

1

The problem, one of them, was that circumstances had split her life down the middle. She was always of two minds, the hopeful half versus the skeptic, optimist against pessimist. Or maybe it evened out and what she was now was a relativist, a contingency artist. Either way, it didn't help that at this late date a theme was taking shape, a motif or whatever you called it, a *pattern*, consisting of Anna walking in on trusted loved ones in bed with each other.

Then again, two times probably made a soap opera, not a pattern. She tried to lift her situation out of the excessively banal by imagining she had a connection with Sylvia Plath. Not that Anna was suicidal. Over Jay? Please. But it did help to think that she and Sylvia—she called her Sylvia; that's how bonded Anna felt—shared a context, a setting. Really, if anything, her circumstances were *worse*, because that London winter of '63 could not possibly have been any colder than Buffalo after a blizzard in early April—*early April*, for God's sake—and poor Sylvia's flat couldn't have been any icier than the windy, rattling loft Jay had left Anna to huddle in by herself while he cavorted with the voluptuous Nicole, whose apartment had a fireplace *and* central heat.

Jay's idea, the loft. They'd lived in a scruffy corner of it during the first year, the happy time, while he'd used the drafty rest for a studio. Eventually his metal sculptures outgrew it, though, went from enormous to dinosaurian, the ceiling wasn't high enough for the really monstrous ones, they needed a barn of their own. So he'd leased space in an old warehouse on the lake for a studio, and since then, almost another year, they'd had the whole basketball court of an apartment to themselves.

Except for the summer months, they'd spent most of the time in bed. Sleeping, reading, eating, having sex, etc., etc., but mostly trying to keep warm. Had ice crusted on the *insides* of Sylvia's windows? Had she huddled close to a ticking space heater with a blanket over it and her like a hot tent, and worried about setting herself on fire? If so, Anna could see why the kitchen stove had started to call to her, whisper that it was the warm answer. Lay your head flat on the metal rack, like a turkey roaster, close your eyes. Try not to mind the gas smell. Go to sleep.

Again, not that Anna was contemplating suicide. But she'd been betrayed in the cruelest way a woman could be (no, second cruelest; that life-dividing time at age twenty, that was still worse), and at least Ted Hughes had had the decency to conduct his affairs out of Sylvia's direct line of sight, with women she wasn't friends with or employed by. Some decorum had been observed. A little British restraint, missing in her case. Anna had walked in on Jay with Nicole, her boss, tangled up together in her own bed, three hours after she'd woken up from a laparoscopy for an ovarian cyst. A hospital procedure. Outpatient, yes, but still, she could've died from the anesthesia, people did. If Jay had been worried about her, he'd found a stimulating distraction.

Oh, it was such a stale, tired story, but here was another way she was trying to inject a little dignity into it—by casting herself in the role of tragic heroine. In a play by...some Greek, Sophocles, Aeschylus, she was vague on her classical playwrights this many years after freshman English. Her mother had died of ovarian cancer at the age she was now, thirty-six, and Anna had discovered Jay's infidelity on the very afternoon she was fully, fatalistically, expecting a call from the surgeon telling her she had the same disease. She didn't, her cyst was benign, nothing to worry about, would probably go away by itself—but she didn't *know* that then, and wasn't it all just too much, too full of awful significance, as if indifferent gods were playing with her life, making *literature* out of it, throwing in metaphors and parallels and corny portents—

No, it wasn't. It was just soap opera. Her life was like a Greek play only if you imagined a collaboration between Homer and Harold Robbins. And now here she was, trying to keep warm in the big, wide scene of the crime, listening to sleet peck at the frosted-over windows and wind slam them around in their uncaulked sockets, trying not to think about Jay and Nicole.

But it was hard when they'd been here so recently. Enjoyed themselves so thoroughly. They must've enjoyed themselves, otherwise they'd have heard the slow rise of the clanking elevator, at least noticed when the rickety metal doors squealed apart. The loft was wide open and wall-less, but Jay had built a two-sided partition to shield the bed from the view of—well, people like Anna. Intruders. He'd made it from tall, rusting strips of steel, like tree trunks, and painted them with bright birds and winding greenery—ah, a bower, you thought, how romantic. Until you went closer and saw that the birds had human heads with crazed eyes and mad grins, and they were doing lewd things with each other in the greenery. Then, how surreal, you thought, how sardonic and Boschian. How Jay.

She remembered very little, almost nothing of what she'd seen over the partition of the lovers in bed. Situational amnesia, no doubt, the way a car crash survivor can't remember a thing after the light turned red. Jay must've been on the bottom, because she had a vague picture in her mind's eye of his Rasputin hair crosshatching the pillow like an etching, black-on-white. But were he and Nicole visibly naked? Decently hidden under the covers? Blank. Mercifully blank: she had nothing to obsess about—this time—except the *fact* of betrayal, not the look of it.

She jumped when Jay's cat landed on the pillow and began to purr in her ear, kneading the duvet with his claws. He was only nice to her when he was cold. Chip off the old block. She lifted the covers, let him crawl down and curl up at her hip. "Miss your old man, huh?" she said, scratching him softly under the chin. "Tough."

The telephone rang. It couldn't be Jay; he'd already called, and the way they'd left things wouldn't encourage him to call back soon. Not for a couple of years. She grabbed the phone from the night table and pulled her arm back under the covers as fast as possible. On "Hello," she could see her breath.

"Hey, sweetie, me again. How're you feeling today?"

Big, huge mistake to tell Aunt Iris about Jay. But she'd caught her at a bad time last night; Anna had blurted out the truth as soon as her aunt said, "Honey, you sound *terrible*, did something happen?"

Now she forced vitality into her voice and said, "Oh, hi, Aunt I. Much better. Much stronger, really. Much."

"Good, because I've got some great news. Your Aunt Rose needs a manager for the Bella Sorella."

"What? Say that again?"

"Yeah, sweetie, she just told me. The old one quit over the weekend, apparently he wasn't any good anyway, so she's looking. Naturally I told her your situation."

Naturally. Aunt Iris was their go-between, since Anna and Rose didn't speak anymore. Well, not literally; in fact, they were excruciatingly cordial whenever Anna couldn't get out of going home—Maryland's Eastern Shore—for a wedding or a funeral; the last one had been about two years ago. They sent Christmas cards, too—"Have a wonderful holiday! Hope the New Year is your best ever!"—and Rose never forgot a birthday. Aunt Iris was the one who dispensed the lowdown on their *real* lives, though, or as much of them as they cared to share with her. Anna always weighed her words to Iris accordingly, and assumed Rose did the same. It was absurd, really, like a sit-com riff, "Tell your father to pass the salt," "Tell your mother to get it herself." Still, whatever worked.

"My situation," Anna said carefully. "So, what, you're saying Rose thinks *I*... she would like *me*..." She couldn't quite get the natural inference out in words.

"It's not just Rose, honey. Everybody thinks you should come home."

"Who's everybody?"

"The family. Me."

Anna smiled to herself, picturing seventy-year-old Aunt Iris's bony, bossy face, the total conviction in her gestures. She'd have the phone to her ear with her shoulder, because she'd need both hands to make her point. "But what did Rose *say*?" Anna asked. "About the restaurant."

"Well, she thinks the timing's perfect. You need a job, she's got a job, in fact she's in kind of a bind. Plus you've already got a house here to live in. A nice *warm* one," she threw in. "What are they having up there today, a cyclone? Typhoon? Quiet!" she called to the dogs barking in the background, the usual accompaniment to a conversation with Aunt Iris. She bred Labrador retriever–Border collie mixes for a hobby.

"Tell Rose," Anna said, "that managing a full-service restaurant would be a little different from running a forty-seat coffee house." Aunt Iris made scoffing sounds. "But I thank her for the offer. If it was one." A little explosion had gone off in her chest, though. Her skin prickled in the aftermath; she had to work to keep her voice casual. The last thing she wanted was Aunt Iris reporting back to Rose, "She sounded interested!"

"You're not saying no, are you? Come home and think about it, at least. That agent you got, the one that rents your house, he's let it go to the dogs. I'm not kidding, people are talking. You could get a citation. You need to come down here and take charge, some things you can't do by phone, not indefinitely. Now, listen, Anna, you know I would never tell you what to do."

"Never."

"When? When have I ever?"

"I said never."

"Sarcastically. You're a grown woman, far be it from me to give you advice about your life, but I have to say this for your own good. Leave that *sciocco* you live with and come home, where you've got people who love you and a job you could do with one hand tied behind your back. You're a Fiore, it's in your blood."

"Catalano, but—"

"Fiore on your mama's side, and Fiores run restaurants."

"You don't," Anna pointed out.

"I married too young, missed my calling. Honey, just come on home. It's time."

"Oh, God." Part of her wanted to. Part of her wanted to stay and make it up with Jay, part of her wanted to tear out pieces of him with her teeth, part of her wanted to leave him with no words at all, a silent, dignified exit. "I'm torn," she said.

"Be torn at home."

"Home, home—what makes you think I even—" She brought her voice down half an octave. "Okay, I'll take it under advisement, but listen, I have to go, I've got another call on this line." She didn't even try to make that sound true.

"What do you want me to tell Rose?"

"I don't know. Anything."

"I'll tell her you'll think about it."

"You can say that if you want."

Frustrated silence. Aunt Iris would never say so, it might jeopardize her role as intermediary, but Anna knew she was on Rose's side. Deep down, she thought Anna's lingering hostility was childish, she should've outgrown it by now, water under the bridge, her mother had been dead for seven years before her father and Rose had finally found some happiness together. That's what Iris thought.

Too bad it was a closed subject; otherwise Anna could have enlightened her on a couple of things. Chronologies, sequences of events. Iris thought she knew everything, but she didn't.

"Theo's not doing so well," Iris said, instead of hanging up.

"Who's Theo, again?"

She clicked her tongue. "Now, Anna. You know who Theo is."

"Oh, you mean Rose's boyfriend? That guy?" She did know who Theo was, and she wasn't sure why she always pretended she didn't. Except that the whole idea of *Theo* offended her—and that made no sense at all. As if Rose should be faithful to Anna's father's memory, all these years after she'd stolen him away from her own sister. Honor among thieves or something—Anna couldn't even follow her own reasoning.

Iris said, "Theo's still living on that old boat of his, and Rose can't make him move. She's so afraid he'll fall."

Theo had Parkinson's or something. "Sorry to hear that."

"She's spending a lot of time with him these days. It wears her out."

"That's a shame."

"Anna."

"What? You expect me to go home and run the Bella Sorella so Rose can have more time with her boyfriend?"

"Family pulls together in time of need."

"Oh—" Vulgarities piled up in the back of her throat, bitter as vinegar.

"But that's neither here nor there. This is where you should be, baby, not up there in no-man's-land. We love you and we want you to come home."

She got off the phone by swearing she had another call and hanging up.

"I used to be a decisive person," she told the hot, disgruntled cat when it crawled out from under the covers. "I could make decisions. I took chances."

Now it was too much to get out of bed and go to the bathroom. She'd have to put on socks and slippers and her woolly robe, she'd have to sit on the frigid toilet seat, wash her hands in ice water afterward. Too much.

Easier to lie here and wallow in all the grievances against her. Funny, she couldn't picture Jay and Nicole naked together in this bed only two days ago, but somebody else's nude body was as clear in her memory as a photograph: Rose's, scrambling out of bed as twenty-year-old Anna pushed open the door to her father's bedroom. Sixteen years later, she could still see the panicky blur of Rose's long arms and long white calves, her narrow back, the mad snatching up of a shirt from the floor to cover herself. She always wore her dark hair up, always in a bun, a twist, a chignon, she knew a million styles—but on that day it was down and disheveled, and somehow much more shocking than all her bare skin or even her tragic, appalled face.

The angle of her wrist as she'd pressed the collar of the shirt to her heart, that white-skinned clutch, the knuckles protruding like exposed nerves—*I've seen that before*, Anna had thought. And just then, the filmy curtain over a much older memory parted, and everything changed. That was the day disillusionment cut her life in half.

What was it Nicole had said when she'd seen Anna peering over the bower partition? Something, "Oh Christ," "Oh my God." Nothing memorable, definitely nothing mitigating.

Rose had said: "Oh, my dear, I am so sorry. This is—exactly what it looks like. But, Anna, it's never the way I wanted you to find out! We—Paul—" That's all she'd had time to say before the squeak of Anna's father's footstep sounded on the staircase.

What had Jay said when he'd seen her? Nothing at all, she didn't think. Well, he wasn't stupid; he'd understood the futility of words, but even more, the potential for sounding foolish. Jay never wanted to sound foolish. So he'd kept a dignified, actually a slightly *wounded* silence.

Her father had stopped dead in the bedroom doorway. He'd had on maroon sweats and new blue running shoes, a newspaper poking out from under his arm; he'd had an oily paper bag in his hand, coffee and croissants from the deli up the street. Under his morning beard, his face was ashen except for a smear of pink on each cheek. He said: "Annie, hey, what a great surprise! I—I'm just getting in myself, been in Newport News since Thursday. Hi, Rose." Anna said, "Daddy," horrified, but he went right on, "No—Rose stayed here last night, I knew that. How's that bat situation? Can you believe it, your aunt had a bat at her place, maybe more than one, could be a nest—" And then Rose said, "Oh, Paul. Don't," and that was the end of that.

Now Rose wanted her to come home. Just like that, pick up where they'd left off, let bygones be bygones. Why? Because she "loved" her? Anna's cynical half sneered at that, but the reluctant optimist pressed her hands together and speculated. Maybe Aunt Iris was right, maybe it was time. If not for a reconciliation, then a reckoning. How ironic—pattern or not, you had to give it that, at least it was ironic—that the same B-movie situation that had driven her out of town at age twenty was driving her back at thirty-six.

Could she really do this? It went against the grain of everything, every finely sanded principle and prejudice she had. Well, it wouldn't be permanent—that was the key. If she went, that's how she'd get through it. She'd work for Rose while she got her house fixed up and ready to sell, a matter of a couple of months, no more. Then she'd split. As long as everybody understood this was *temporary*, she could do it.

It still felt like giving in, though. She tried to think of a way to glorify going home, something to make it feel less like defeat, but no flattering, humiliation-averting comparisons came to mind. Damn. She might have to go as a grown-up. Not a mortal besieged by capricious gods, not a fierce, romantic, suicidal poet. An adult. If not capable of forgiving old sins, then at least willing to pretend, for the sake of peace, that they'd never been committed.

Clever Rose. Anna hadn't given her credit for so much cunning.

2

Iris called while Rose was drying her hair. "How are you? What are you doing?"

"I feel like I'm going on a date," Rose said. "I've tried on three outfits, and I'm going back to the first one, my old black suit. Do you think"—she laughed self-consciously—"do you think Anna's doing this, too?"

"I don't get why you're so nervous. She knows what you look like."

"Yes, but it's been two years. I just don't want her to think I'm an old lady."

Iris snorted.

"I don't want her to think I'm losing it."

"Baby doll, you haven't lost a thing."

"I don't want her to take the job because she feels sorry for me."

Iris cackled. Then, "I don't think there's too much danger of that."

"Why? What did she say?"

"Nothing, I'm just saying. If Anna takes this job, it'll be because she wants it, not because she's feeling charitable. Anyway, she's here, she didn't move back so she could tell you no."

That's what Rose was hoping, that the decision had already been made. "Iris, I'm rushing, and I still have to pick up Theo's lunch and take it to him."

"Okay, go. But call me tonight and tell me what happened."

"I will—although Vince will probably tell you first."

"I'm his mother, Vincent never tells me anything. You call tonight. And *relax*, will you? Anna's twice as nervous as you are."

"Do you think so?"

"You two, honest to God. This whole thing is ridiculous, it's always been ridiculous."

"*I'm* not the one—"

"I know, it's her, but now she's grown up and ready to act like a mature woman, maybe she'll bury the hatchet."

"It's not her fault."

"Oh, let's not get started on whose fault. I don't know why you always defend her. If you ask me, a person's entitled to one moment of self-righteousness in their life, and then they move on. They grow up and move on."

"You're right, let's not get started," Rose said, and they hung up.

She went back to drying her hair, which looked absurd and childish to her suddenly, much too short. Theo had told her not to cut it, and he'd been right. Anna would think she was a foolish old woman, trying to look young and smart. Maybe some makeup? She never wore anything but mascara and lipstick, but today, maybe some eye shadow? She was always buying it and then not using it. *This is a mistake*, she thought, even as she leaned in and daubed sparkly, taupe-colored powder in the creases of her eyelids. Better? No. Sixty years old and she couldn't put makeup on right.

Well, nobody had ever taught her. Iris was married and long gone by the time Rose turned fifteen and Mama said she could wear a little lipstick. Lily, only two years older, was the one who should've shown her, but already beautiful Lily thought of her little sister as competition. Already? Maybe she always had, even when they were children. Rose didn't know, and Lily took her secrets with her when she died.

What was wrong with this black suit? It didn't flatter her after all, it turned her skin sallow and the skirt was too long. Other than that, she looked like a million bucks. Too late now, and no point in changing anyway: this was one of those days when she wasn't going to like herself. They were coming more frequently than they used to. Inevitable at her age, but it was hard. Life didn't pace itself very gently or conveniently, or even humanely. She was losing too many things all at once.

"Four times I got up to pee last night. You know what I oughta do, Rose?"

"What?"

"Rig up a hose between my dick and the head. Save a lot of time."

"Good idea," she said, swishing Theo's dishes around in the tiny galley sink. If she worked fast, she could usually finish before the hot water ran out. He hated the low-protein, high-carb diet the neurologist had him on, but he'd eaten all the porcini polenta she'd brought him for lunch, and most of his salad. Whatever else he might be losing, he still had his appetite. "Or," she said mildly, "you could move off this boat and in with me."

"How the hell would that help? What the hell would be the point of that? What'll you do when I have to take a piss, drag the damn toilet into the bedroom?"

"No."

"Then how the hell would it help?"

She knew he wanted to yell at her. She wished he could, she'd have loved it if he could scream and shout, bellow out all his frustration. But he couldn't raise his voice above a hushed, breathy undertone anymore, and on the worst days it was only a whisper.

She watched him use both hands to pull his right knee up and brace his foot against the settee behind the cleared table, turning his back on her. His hair needed cutting. She shaved him every other day—his hands shook too much to do it himself—but she hadn't cut his thick, shaggy hair in weeks. Or trimmed the long, droopy mustache he took so much pride in. Used to, rather. Nothing about Theo's body pleased him anymore.

It still pleased her. He hadn't lost weight, so he still looked as solid and planted as he always had on his sturdy legs, his shoulders still thick, chest still wide and furry as a Chincoteague pony's. Short and brawny, he was as far from her old physical ideal—as far from Paul—as a man could be, and yet she'd liked the look of Theo from the beginning. What she regretted was all the trouble she'd given him at the start, when they were first dancing around each other, all that time she'd wasted making him wait. Caution was a virtue the middle-aged couldn't afford.

But he said his body didn't belong to him anymore, it belonged to some old, sick man, not Theophilus Xenophon Pelopidas, waterman, traveler, fisherman, boatbuilder, woodcarver, great lover of beautiful women. She loved it when he talked like that, when he was proud of himself and his old strength and vigor, his old life. But even his memory of himself was fading, and Rose didn't know what was crueler, the slow deterioration of his nerve cells or his ego.

"I brought you panna cotta for dessert," she said, unwrapping the foil around the plate. Calcium and carbohydrates, just what the doctor ordered. "Eat it while it's good and cold. Want some coffee? I'll make you a cup."

"If you'll have one with me."

"I can't, I have to get back. Anna's coming at one o'clock."

He sniffed his breath out to show her what he thought of *that*.

She set his plate on the table in front of him. "Move over," she said, wedging herself onto the narrow settee beside him. His old sailboat was called *Expatriate*. It slept two, just barely, and not with any unnecessary comfort or convenience. It had taken her four years to learn not to hit her head on bulkheads and hanging lockers, but how anyone could live full time in such cramped quarters was still beyond her. Everything on the boat was always fanatically neat and tidy, though, she had to give him that. Shipshape. Her own small apartment wasn't half as organized as Theo's minuscule cabin. And him such a scruffy, unruly man.

"How is it?" she asked, watching him scoop up the creamy dessert with the spoon held tightly in his rigid fist, swallowing with care.

"Who made it, you or Carmen?"

"Me."

"Then it's good. Best I ever ate. Melts in your mouth." He tweaked his lips in a sideways half-smile, all his facial muscles could manage these days. "You look pretty. More than usual." She thanked him by squeezing his thigh. "All dressed up for her highness."

She took her hand back. "You're going to like her, you know. You're going to be surprised."

"That I doubt."

"She's lovely."

"I know what you're trying to do, Rose, but you can't."

"What do you mean?"

"You can't put everything back the way it was."

"I know." She sighed. "But wouldn't it be nice? No, I know, but—Anna wasn't supposed to go away, that was never the plan."

"Whose plan?"

"The family plan. She was going to finish college and then come home and run the restaurant with me. I'd cook, she'd manage." Perfect, their hearts' desires; each of them doing what she did best and loved most.

Theo made a disgusted sound. "You think it's all your fault, every little thing that ever went wrong with that girl's whole life. That's bullshit."

"I know." In her head she knew it. "I love you. You're better than a priest, you know that? What would I do without you?"

"Be a lot better off." He patted her hand with his rough, gnarled one, the one with the missing little finger. She'd heard three or four different stories about how he'd lost the finger, including to a crab the size of a beach ball in the tidal swamps off Tilghman Island. She loved all his defects, all his scars and his weathered skin, his creaky old joints. But what she loved him for most was that he knew all her guilty secrets. No one else did but Anna, but Theo forgave her. No, that wasn't it—he didn't think she'd done anything that needed to be forgiven. He thought she was innocent.

"Am I too dressed up?" she asked him. "It's only a skirt. Too much? I don't want to look like I'm trying too hard."

"You look beautiful, to hell with what she thinks."

That again. "I have to go." She stood up and kept her hands to herself, didn't reach for him when he rocked back once and used the momentum to heave himself up from the bench. And she went first when he waved her toward the companionway steps, even though she'd rather have climbed the four stairs behind him. Just in case. She lived in fear that he would fall—then what? If he got dizzy and tripped, hit his head, hurt himself, and no one here to help him, what would he do? She'd asked him a hundred times to move in with her. So had Mason, his stepson. He wouldn't even discuss it. "Rather go in a nursing home," he'd say, "let strangers wipe the drool off my chin."

"What'll you do this afternoon?" She stood beside him in the cockpit, breathing in the fresh salt smell of the Chesapeake. Cork, Theo's old gray-muzzled mutt, half spaniel, half everything else, thunked his wispy tail in welcome from the patch of sun on the deck where he lay sprawled, stiff-legged. The sound of hammering echoed from a couple of boats away; reggae music drifted over from somebody else's radio. The warm spring weather was bringing out the owners who hadn't checked on their boats since last year. Sun glittered on the water, blinding. Seagulls wheeled and squawked.

"This afternoon? Maybe a round o' golf." Theo held the taffrail with one hand while he scratched Cork behind the ears with the other. "Maybe a pickup basketball game."

She usually laughed when he said things like that, but this time she slipped her arms around his waist and pressed her face against the nubby wool of his sweater. He went stiff. But presently she felt his hand on her back, patting her with a soft, helpless pressure.

Theo's eyes were a pale, bleached-out blue, as if he'd peered for too many years at the sky and the sea, stared at too many horizons. "You believe this spring?" he marveled, using his hand for a sunshade. "Smell the air, Rose. Water's warming up, starts the crabs to crawling. What I wouldn't . . . " He shook his head, trailing off.

What he wouldn't give to be chugging out into the bay on his ancient dead-rise crabber, setting out his lines before the sun came up, checking on his pots, hoping for a good catch of early-season blues. Life on the Chesapeake for all his waterman buddies started in April, and this was the first season since she'd known him that he wouldn't be in the middle of it.

"Shall I come over tonight?" she asked. "It'll have to be late, but we could go for a drive if you feel like it. Want to?"

He shrugged. "Saw a spotted sandpiper this morning. First o' the year. You can tell a spottie by the way she bobs her tail up and down." He caught her smiling at *spottie*. "Yeah, been talking to Mason," he admitted. His stepson knew everything about birds, even more than Theo now; in fact, he photographed them for a living. "They migrate by ones and twos, Mason says, not in packs. The females go around sleeping with—all the males they can find, regular swingers they are." He paused to take a few shallow breaths. "Then when they lay a nest of eggs, they make the *father* sit on 'em till they hatch."

"Smart birds. Is Mason coming over later?" Exercise was the only thing Theo could do anymore for his balance, and Mason took him on walks around the marina.

"Probably. Look." He lifted his right arm very slowly, pointing above the sway of the masts and lines of working boats and pleasure craft moored in the neighboring slips. "Yellowlegs. See 'em?" She saw three or four smallish, grayish birds swooping over the water. "I had one once. Let it go this time o' the year, join the parade."

"You had one?"

"There's greater and lesser. They're little shorebirds. Well, the greater's not so little. I found a lesser yellowlegs in the salt marsh once, had—a busted beak and fishing line tangled around one wing and a leg. Kept him all winter, let him go in the spring. They're moving up the coast now, the flocks. They go up to Canada to breed."

"Did he come back?" Sometimes they did, wouldn't fly away the first time Theo tried to release them, the injured terns and seagulls he had a habit of doctoring. Used to have—he couldn't do it now, his hands shook too much, he said, he couldn't hold them gently anymore. Now Mason was the bird doctor.

"No. Well, he come back by in the fall, like they all do. It's funny, I let 'em go and Mason captures 'em. Tries to."

"On film, you mean."

"Either way, they always come back."

"Or," Rose said, "they always leave."

"Depends on how you look at it."

Mason might look at it a little differently, she considered, having grown up with a stepfather who'd abandoned him about as regularly as some migrating bird. Who would probably still be leaving and coming back, leaving and coming back, if he hadn't gotten too sick to move on.

"I have to go," she said again, looking around for her bag. "Call me after dinner, or I'll call you. Is your phone on? Don't finish those dishes, I'll do them tonight. How did it get to be noon? Tell me the truth, Theo, do I look overdressed? It's just a *skirt*."

"You look fine, and I'll wash the goddamn dishes. I'm not a cripple yet."

She touched his cheek, and immediately the scowl between his thick gray eyebrows relaxed. "Old dog," she called him softly. "My old dog."

"Old lap dog. Got me in the palm of your hand, that's what you think."

"Oh, if only." She leaned in to brush her lips across his dry, chapped ones. "Be good till Mason comes, okay? Try?"

"My other dog walker."

"And don't fall overboard."

He smiled at that, but she didn't: it came too close for comfort. "We might go over to his place later and work on the boat," he mentioned.

"That would be nice. Perfect day for it." He and Mason were rebuilding an old sailboat together—or Mason was; Theo mostly watched. He sat in a chair in Mason's boat shed and gave orders. She kissed him quickly, then let him hold her arm as she stepped up onto the marina dock.

"I like you in a skirt," he strained his voice to say as she started off. "Nice stems for an old broad."

She made an Italian gesture he thought was dirty—a long time ago she'd told him it was obscene, but it wasn't. It always delighted him. Before she passed through the chain-link gate to the parking lot, she glanced back. He was holding on to the rail with both hands, lowering his backside slowly, cautiously, down to the sun-bleached wood of the cockpit seat, next to his old dog.

Theo's marina was about a mile from downtown, on a shallow peninsula whose north shore connected to the city by way of a two-lane drawbridge. Rarely was the bridge up, but today, of course, when Rose was running late, it was, so that an elegant, tall-masted schooner could glide out of the creek and into the river and the bay. She waited impatiently for the light to change, clicking her fingernails on the steering wheel. She tried to look at the water, the docked boats, the bridge, the pedestrians, as if she were new in town and seeing everything for the first time. Like Anna, almost. She'd grown up here, but hadn't been back except for fast dashes, in and out as quickly as possible, in almost two decades. Would she find her hometown drastically changed? It was bigger and more bustling than the city she'd grown up in, and full of tourists year-round now instead of only the summer. Would she like that? Or would she think it was spoiled? Rose could hardly decide herself.

The light changed. She crossed the bridge and drove carefully through the center square, watching for pedestrians holding maps, the ones most likely to stroll blindly into a passing car in their eagerness to ogle the pretty sailboats tied up at Town Dock. The Bella Sorella wasn't on the harbor, had no prospect of the water, not even a peek of blue. But it was on Severn Street, a one-way crescent attached at either end to the city's main tourist thoroughfare. It got foot traffic from both tourists and natives because of its midway location between dock and commercial district. Really, its situation couldn't be better. So why wasn't it thriving?

She slowed as she drove past the restaurant, straining again to see it through Anna's eyes. Carmen liked the maroon awning over the door, said it was classy, but Rose wasn't sure. Suddenly she was positive Anna would hate it. Pretentious, that's what it was, and too big for the narrow brick facade anyway. The yellow pansies in the planter by the door didn't look perky, they looked dusty and bedraggled; Louis had forgotten to water them. He'd shined the brasswork on the door, though, hallelujah, and he'd washed the bronze-tinted window. Had he swept the walk? She couldn't tell.

She turned in at the narrow, hard-to-maneuver access between the antique store and the florist's, right again at the alley, and parked in her little spot behind the garbage stockade. Twelve-twenty; Anna would be here in forty minutes. Luckily it was Wednesday, the slowest day of the week. They'd have a leisurely lunch of three-onion tart, Carmen's best appetizer, and then a lady-like crab salad, and they'd sit at the corner window table, best in the house. Lemon cake for dessert, and cappuccino—if Dwayne had managed to fix the dying machine one more time. They wouldn't talk business until after lunch, when they'd retire to Rose's office. She would make her business proposition, and Anna would...

She had no idea what Anna would do. Iris swore she was interested. She must be, otherwise she wouldn't have come home. Would she? Not just to sell her house—she could've done that long distance. Rose had spoken to her only once since she'd been back, on the telephone, and she'd sounded nice. Pleasant. Not that that meant anything. They'd been pleasant to each other for sixteen years.

She knew what was wrong even before she opened the back door. Nothing smelled like a grease fire as much as a grease fire.

"Grease fire," confirmed Jasper, the pantry cook, lounging against the laundry closet door and smoking a cigarette. She hurried past him, but she took heart from his sleepy-eyed slouch; he'd be a *little* more excited if the kitchen had burned down.

It hadn't, but the massive grill and the stainless steel wall behind it were a scorched black mess under a runny coat of sticky white flame retardant. Marco and Carla looked up from their prep work long enough to say "Hi," with pained, sympathetic faces. Dwayne called over the noise of the dishwasher, "The Sardine did it!" flashing his gold tooth when he grinned.

Carmen quit pounding chicken breasts with a wooden mallet. "It's not as bad as it looks. At least he got it put out before the smoke set off the sprinklers."

"Thank God." What a nightmare that would've been. "How did it start?"

Luca, the grill chef, "Sardine" to his mates because he was short and he came from Sardinia, straightened up from wiping greasy foam off the wall. "*E colpa mia*," he mumbled. "Too much grease, the fire went too high." His ears blazed hot pink; his shoulders slumped. "Sorry, Chef."

"All right," Rose said shortly, "okay, just get it cleaned up. My God, what a mess." Carmen would've beaten him down enough by now, no sense in taking any more whacks at him. And poor Luca was so sensitive, he'd quit over the mildest reproach, thinking he was doing her a favor. He always came back, but she couldn't afford to lose him today. "Get that stuff off the floor first so nobody slips, don't worry about the rest until after lunch. Any grill orders, use the broiler. Or pan sauté—use your imagination."

Luca brightened. Until he heard Carmen's sarcastic snort, then his ears turned pink again. "Okay, Chef." Head down, he went back to mopping up dirty foam.

"Shirl called in sick," Carmen informed her next.

Shirl was the pasta chef. "Can you cover?"

"Me or Luca, yeah. Slow day today."

"Anything else?"

"You're a waiter short. Only Vonnie and Kris, and Tony's busing."

"We should be okay as long as it stays light. Everything else on track? No problems?"

"Nothing to speak of." Heavy, sweating, red-faced Carmen smacked a chicken strip with brute violence, as if it personally offended her. She was the assistant chef, the sous, Rose's right hand in the kitchen. She was also her cousin, and an old maid like her, so they still shared the name Fiore. Luckily for Carmen, her mother hadn't been as enchanted with naming her children after flowers as Rose's had. Luckily—because it was hard to think of a flower that would've suited Carmen and not sounded like an unkind joke. She weighed two hundred pounds. But she carried it well, and she was strong as a man. The cooks were terrified of her, called her "Sarge" behind her back for obvious, unimaginative reasons—and probably much worse things Rose wasn't privy to. She had a short fuse and a surly disposition, and the lowest tolerance for incompetence of anybody Rose had ever known. But no one was more loyal than Carmen, to the restaurant, of course, but especially to Rose. She couldn't imagine the kitchen without her.

"Did Sloan's guy have some nice crabs?" Rose asked her, backing up toward the refrigerator. "I was thinking of having the salad on that sourdough bruschetta if it's—"

"No crabs. I got sole. It'll be fine, I'll roast it with some lemon and bay."

"What? Oh no. Sole? No, I wanted something lighter and, I don't know, local. Sole?" She wrinkled her face, wanting Carmen to talk her into it.

"I can't do the onion tart, either, there aren't any leeks. I can do a zucchini-parmigiana salad, but it'll have to be with pine nuts because nobody ordered walnuts." The grim pursing of Carmen's lips was more satisfied than sorry, which only confirmed what Rose already knew—she was even less thrilled at the prospect of Anna's visit than Theo was. It bothered Rose, but how could she take offense? In their minds, Carmen and Theo were protecting her. They thought Anna was going to break her heart.

"Is the table set, at least?" she asked, resigned.

"I don't know. Ask Vonnie."

"All right—anything you need me for in here?" She wanted to put on fresh lipstick, comb her hair, gather herself for a few minutes in the bathroom. "You're nervous as a girl," Theo had chided her this morning. It was true.

Carmen smirked. "Well, Flaco's behind, you could help him wash greens. Have to cover up your finery with an apron, of course." Her pale, red-lashed eyes flickered over Rose's black suit with amusement, maybe contempt.

"It's just a skirt!" She threw up her hands and stalked out of the kitchen.

Vonnie had set the corner table with the cobalt glasses and the handpainted plates, and pretty saffron-colored napkins folded under the good flatware. They had enough of this service for small parties, not enough for the whole dining room, which seated ninety-seven. There were freesias in the bud vase, not the usual carnation, and the noonday sun cutting across the crisp white tablecloth made a soft, somehow sophisticated diagonal, Rose thought. She caught Vonnie's eye across the room and gave her a smile and a nod—*good job.* Vonnie, her best server, put up her thumb and grinned in agreement.

Not many lunch customers; the restaurant was only about a third full. That was fortunate under the circumstances, and not unusual for midweek, especially before May when the boaters started coming in earnest, but—what would Anna think? She'd think business was slow, and she'd be right. Would it be *too* slow for her? She'd been working in a very modish-sounding bistro sort of place, the Industrial Strength Coffee Shop or some such; she'd be used to trendy people and high prices, European dance music. The Bella Sorella was going to look hopelessly out of date to her. And dowdy. Boring. If she took the job of running it, she'd do it out of pity.

Through the window, Rose saw about half a dozen elderly women, one with a walker, pass slowly in front of the building and stop under the awning. They had a little confab, scanning the menu, checking the name on the door. They decided to come in, and she thought, *Good, Anna will think we do* some *business.* She crossed the room to greet them, and almost immediately another small group of women, much like the first, came in behind them. "Hello, how are you," she said to the first bunch, white-haired and respectable in low-heeled shoes, carrying guidebooks and maps. A tour group.

"Hi," said their leader, the spry one at sixty-ish—Rose's age. "Do we need a reservation?"

"Oh, I don't think so, not today. How many are you?"

"Twenty-six, or we will be when the others get finished at the Nautical Museum."

"Not a problem," Rose said, smiling warmly, confidently, while her mind raced. Vince was coming in early, he could take over from Eddie and Eddie could help wait tables. That would be three servers plus Tony, and Flaco could help bus—

"We were going to call first, but my sister lives here and she said it's usually not crowded."

"Isn't that nice." They were pushing inside, bunches of women, several with canes and one in a wheelchair, and now a couple of old men, backing Rose up against the host's podium. "Have a seat—welcome, hi—sit anywhere, won't you? Your server will be right with you."

"Yo, Chef, I'm taking off now!"

Rose spared half a second to grin at Eddie, bartender and part-time waiter, while she wiped vinaigrette from the side of a plate of mesclun and goat cheese and slid it down the pickup. "Another one, Jasper, and three plain house with Italian. Eddie, when your drink orders slow down, help Vonnie and Kris—we're short and they're swamped. Where's Vince? I thought he'd be here by now."

"Hey, sorry, Chef, I gotta take off."

She looked up. "Take off? What, now? Are you crazy?"

"Hey, sorry, but I got a doctor's appointment and it's really important. I fixed it up with Vince, he'll be here any sec."

Dupes were coming in as fast as Vonnie and Kris could stick them on the board. "Then don't leave until he gets here."

"But if I don't go now I'll be late."

"You can't leave now, don't even think about it."

"C'mon, these old ladies aren't exactly throwing the booze back, you know?"

"Make drinks till Vince comes. I mean it. Here!" she called before he could get out the door. "Take these on your way—table six."

"Who gets what?"

"Read the dupe." She turned away to help Luca, who was already behind and the big hits hadn't even started. Vonnie came in with more orders. "We're out of ravioli," Rose called to her. "Only three more chicken Carmens, and I'm not sure the fettuccini's—" She stopped. Vonnie's sweet, placid face was chalk-white. "What happened? What's wrong?"

"Guy at a four-top with two women and another man."

"Yes?"

"Kris thinks he's the food critic for *City Week*."

"No. No, no, please no. Oh, my God. Carmen?"

"I heard." Pure terror had drained her face, too. The three women looked at each other with wild eyes for a few still, motionless seconds.

"Okay, then," Rose rallied. "Everybody! Listen up—"

Eddie stiff-armed the door open and yelled from the threshold, "Okay, Vince is here, I'm gone. Lady just came in, she's at the bar. Hey, she looks just like you, Chef, it's amazing. Vince says she's his cousin. What's that make her, your niece?"

3

Anna went dead calm the minute she saw Rose. After all the worry and nerves and second thoughts, watching her sweep across the dining room with her long, still-lithe stride, waving, beaming, vivid as a black-and-white photograph except for a flirty streak of red across her mouth—Anna felt the relief of a soldier who finally hears the first mortar shell blow after an all-night wait in a muddy trench. *It's only Rose*, she thought. Rose, not formidable at all with her glad face and her worried eyes. *She's scareder than I am*.

"Anna!" she cried from a distance, arms open wide. "Oh, Anna, finally!"

Maybe her posture was stiff, maybe she had a look in her eye—they ended up shaking hands instead of embracing, and at the moment when Rose would've kissed her, Anna let go and stepped back. Then they both smiled too hard, embarrassed.

"Really good to see you," Anna said, folding her arms, leaning back against the bar. "You haven't changed." Not true; Rose's big dark eyes and her beaky, theatrical nose were the same, and her smile, so sweet and melancholy, hadn't lost the power to cripple and disarm, if you were stupid enough to let down your guard. But she looked tired. The mystery of her, the dark-saint quality that used to fascinate and beguile, had begun to fade, and the smooth beauty of her face couldn't hide it or stop it. She'd grown older, and finally it showed.

"Oh, you're here, I'm so *glad*, and how beautiful you look." Her voice was the same, still rich and earthy, intimate as a touch on the cheek; Anna had forgotten how easily it could charm her. "I just cut my hair, now I wish I hadn't. How *chic* you are, Anna, that suit is fabulous."

"Thanks." They'd dressed alike, she registered dully, although Anna wore her black jacket and cream-colored shirt with pants instead of a skirt. Another thing she'd forgotten was that they had the same taste in clothes. The same weakness for them, too; unless Rose had changed, they were still her biggest vice.

"Has Vince been taking care of you? I'm sorry I wasn't here when you came—but it's a little hectic in the kitchen right now, nothing terrible, just—oh, you know, the usual."

"Don't worry about it. Anything I can do to help?"

"No, oh no, sit here and relax, please. Do you want something to tide you over till lunch, a salad or something—"

"No, I'm fine."

"—because we might be a little bit late with our meal, is that all right? You don't have an appointment, do you, nothing you've got to rush for?"

"No, nothing. Do what you have to do, I'm happy right here."

"You are so nice. I'll be as quick as I can." Her hands fluttered, giving her nerves away. She looked reluctant to leave, as if this first meeting hadn't gone as she'd wanted and if she stayed longer she could fix it. Anna felt the same awkward dissatisfaction, but she didn't want to fix it. She'd come for a job, not to fix things.

Vince returned from delivering drinks to a table. "Hey, Aunt Rose." He leaned across the bar to finish in a lower tone. "Vonnie told Carmen he ordered mussels, and his date wants the veal chop."

Rose's smile froze.

"Who?" said Anna.

"No one, just a customer." She waved for Anna to sit, sit, be comfortable. "I'll be with you shortly. That's our table over there, so stay here or go and sit down, whatever you like. Do you still like a Strega sour? Just tell Vincent what you want—"

"Go," Anna insisted.

Rose sent her a grateful smile and hurried away.

Vince was Anna's favorite cousin. The youngest of Aunt Iris's five children, the thirty-year-old "baby," he'd been a gawky, scrawny adolescent boy when she left home, but she'd liked him best because he was so funny. And happy, such a good-natured little nerd. He'd taught her how to play chess when she was fifteen and he was nine, and she'd taught him how to dance. When she was in college, she'd given him advice over the phone about girls, and it must've been good stuff because these days, at least according to Aunt Iris, women swarmed around him like gnats.

"Look at you," he said as he poured gin, Strega, and sour mix into a shaker. "You look great, Anna. Everybody's so glad you're back." He had a soft brown crewcut and huge soft brown eyes, a bony, priest's face, and a very cool beard, just two thin strips of whisker running along the edge of his jaw, connecting his sideburns. He was still skinny, but he had broad, handsome shoulders. And beautiful hands; she could imagine women sitting here, ordering drink after drink just to watch him work.

"It's great to see you, Vince. I don't know if I'm back, though," she clarified scrupulously. "I'm here, that's . . ." She smiled, made a vague gesture with her hand. "All I can say for now."

"Oh, yeah, I know, but I'm hoping. We're all hoping."

"Thanks. We'll see."

"It's crazy today," he said, pulling down soft drinks from the tap.

"I can see. What's up?" The place was crowded, but she could see only two servers working the floor and they were getting slammed. She recognized that controlled panic under their smiles, the fast walk that wanted to break into a run. "Is it always like this at lunchtime? I mean . . . a lot of old ladies?"

"No, it's a tour group, they're from Baltimore, Leisure City or whatever. They just showed up, no notice, no nothing."

"Yikes." She stole a look in the mirror at Rose, zigzagging gracefully among tables, asking people how they were doing, if they needed anything, if they were having a nice time. She had a way of touching, the lightest brush on the shoulder, a soft pat on the hand, that could hypnotize total strangers, tame or calm them down, whatever she thought they needed. The tactile opposite of a cattle prod, but with the same result: people did what Rose wanted them to do.

She'd stopped at a four-top, two couples, and out of a well of complicated emotions Anna had to admire the solicitous tilt of her head, the casual, interested but never servile incline of her body, her hands clasped at the waist, and now splayed playfully on her hips as she leaned back to laugh, with just the right amount of sincere appreciation, at some guy's jest. She looked fifty from here, no older, still tall, straight, boyishly slim. She'd never colored her hair, and the new style, artless black and silver spikes that complemented her strong face, made her look rakish, practically punk. Anna had been hoping for *something*, but now she couldn't remember what it was—that Rose would've grown bent and slow in the two years since she'd seen her? That she wouldn't have changed at all? In any case, neither was true. She looked tired, but figuring out what other ways Rose might've changed, exactly what she might have lost or gained—that would take some observation and interest, some attention.

Resentment was a sour, unrewarding emotion. It filled Anna up when she realized that she didn't know anybody as interesting as Rose. Anyone she'd rather observe. Sullenly.

"Yeah, first we get hit with the tour group," Vince was telling her, "and then somebody spots a reviewer."

"A reviewer? Oh, my Jesus." In instant sympathy, her blood ran cold. "Who? That guy?" The ginger-haired, heavyset fellow Rose was bending over?

"I think so, gotta be him or the other guy. I know his name is Gerber and he writes a column for the weekly. Meanwhile, we're short-staffed on the floor, and the pasta chef calls in sick at twelve, she's got cramps or something. We are screwed so many ways."

"No veal chops," Anna guessed.

"Fire in the big grill this morning. But that's not the worst." He loaded the drinks onto a round brown server's tray, then started a vodka and tonic. Anna couldn't imagine how things could be any worse. "The pasta cook, this incredible flake named Shirl, wait'll you meet her—she's got really good penmanship, she's like a calligrapher, so she's been writing up the specials for us on the blackboard. You passed it coming in."

She nodded. Linguini al pesto, scallops Parmesan, mussels in garlic tomato sauce. Nothing very exciting, she'd thought. "What's the problem? Oh—oh, shit."

"Right. She didn't do it today because she didn't come in, and nobody remembered to change it. The food critic for *City Week* wants to order mussels, and it's *yesterday's* special, it's *gone*."

"Oh, Vince." Nothing was worse, or potentially better, in the restaurant business than a food critic's surprise visit. She remembered a family story from before she was born, when a food writer from the Baltimore paper had shown up at the Flower Café—the first incarnation of the Bella Sorella on Severn Street, back when it was only a pizza and spaghetti joint and didn't even have a bar. When Liliana, Anna's grandmother, a very tough customer, a no-nonsense woman not known for squeamishness—another family legend had it that she used to wring chickens' necks barehanded for her papa's little *ristorante* in Ventimiglia—when Liliana heard from the waiters that a critic was in the house, she went outside and threw up. But then she came back in and got to work.

"I know," Vince said, shaking his head. "To tell you the truth, we could use a good review right about now. If he'd say one nice thing, we could run it with an ad in the daily. It would really help."

One nice thing. Even if Rose could coax Mr. Gerber out of the veal and mussels without him even knowing it, something entirely within her powers, Anna could still imagine phrases like *caters to an older crowd* showing up in his column. *Uncommonly slow service. Overwhelmed floor staff.*

Rose had last words at the critic's table and headed for the kitchen, conspicuously not hurrying.

Anna stood up, took off her jacket, hung it on the back of her chair, and followed.

The kitchen was all heat, noise, and chaos. Every station was getting hit, plates wouldn't even fit on the pass anymore, dupes were hanging off the slide like Chinese lottery tickets. "Fire number eight!" a woman was screaming. "Pickup eight, goddammit!" She had her broad back turned, but Anna recognized Carmen's ferocious bellow easily; she'd withered and flinched under it often enough as a teenager, when she'd helped out in the kitchen or filled in for somebody on the waitstaff. Rose was over by the walk-in, throwing a chef's apron over her head, tying it twice around her waist, fingers flying. When she saw Anna, her game face cracked. She came toward her with a chagrined look in her dark, dramatic eyes. Anna had never been able to resist them.

"Good thing I wore the uniform," she blurted out before Rose could tell her to go, overwhelm her with gracious no-thanks. "Black pants, white shirt. Look, I even wore flats."

"Anna, no."

"You're getting slammed, so let me help out, okay? Are the table numbers the same? Somebody can spot me. I won't do any harm—what's some broken glass, a little soup in a lap."

Rose ran a frenzied, indecisive hand through her spiky hair. Then she laughed. "Take the first four tables along the banquette, one through four, back to front. Seat one is six o'clock, they go clockwise."

"Got it."

"Do soups and salads first, if any are still up there. And help Tony, he's your busboy—I think some people never even got bread."

"Right." She started to back up, but Rose seized her by the shoulders and hugged her, a fast, shy grab, before she could step away. *Gotcha*. Anna grinned in spite of herself.

"Anna, thank you—*I'm so sorry*."

"Forget it, this'll be fun. I used to be a pretty good waitress, don't you remember?" She turned away quickly, dismayed by Rose's delighted smile. *Shit*, she thought, *I* started it. *Rose* was supposed to be the one who got them going on nostalgic reminiscing. Anna was supposed to quell her with blank, uncomprehending stares. She'd had it all planned.

Rose was right, their first meeting wasn't going at all the way it was supposed to.

4

Stop staring, Rose told herself, but it wasn't easy. The rush was over, and they were finally sitting down, and Anna looked so pretty. Her forehead shone, her cheeks were flushed, her black eyes sparkled. With her heavy hair falling down from two tortoiseshell barrettes, she didn't look sophisticated or remote or cool any longer, she looked like herself. She was even laughing—at Vonnie, who set an Aqua Madonna and lime in front of her and laughed back. In the frantic seventy minutes they'd waited tables together, they'd made friends. Rose listened to their banter with a small smile, keeping her face mild, disguising her giddy gladness. Anna retreated when she detected gladness. And she suffered affection from Rose only on her own terms: stingily.

"Oh, God, it all came back to me, why I could never do what you do," she was saying to Vonnie. "My feet are killing me, and I ran around for what, an hour? How do you stand it?"

"Oh, honey, it was a tough crowd today," Vonnie consoled her, a hand on one full hip, a tray tucked under her arm. "Did you ever hear so many allergy stories? And everybody had to have substitutions. But they were sweet, weren't they? Nice old ladies."

Vonnie was the server Rose always asked to train newcomers—nobody else had the patience for it. Divorced, motherly, endlessly good-natured, Vonnie joked about the Zen of table service, but she definitely did her work in a zone of some kind, a state of natural grace. She was a lifer, not in a holding pattern like the others, waiting for a better job to come along. Vonnie wasn't *waiting* for anything, she was here.

"So, honey, did you make any tips?" she asked Anna.

"Yeah, but only enough to cover what I broke."

They laughed again—music to Rose's ears. Vonnie said, "Bet you two are starving, I'll bring your salads right away," and hurried off.

Rose glanced around the mostly empty dining room, monitoring the cleanup, catching Vince's eye at the bar, but what she really wanted to do was look at Anna for an uninterrupted hour or two. Just feast her eyes on her until the connection between the girl and the woman came back into focus. Until she *recognized* her again.

But that wasn't allowed. The key to success was going to be feigned indifference. *None of this matters much, stay or go, nothing important hinges on what you think of me.* They were like a divorced couple, meeting again long after the bitter breakup, pretending all the messy emotions were in the past. At least Rose was pretending; God only knew what was going on in Anna's head.

Already she'd withdrawn a little, if only by rolling down the sleeves of her blouse and putting back on her handsome suit jacket. Back to business. They looked alike, aunt and niece—everybody said that. Rose could see a superficial something of herself around Anna's eyes, dark and heavy-lidded, and most especially in the deep brackets at the corners of her mouth. From smiling, presumably, although she hadn't done a great deal of that so far in Rose's presence. She searched for a glimpse of Paul somewhere, a hint of his humor and warmth—they were there, she knew it. But they were hiding.

What she could never see, now or twenty years ago, or thirty—was Lily. The fair-haired, angel-faced middle child. Lily was the feminine one, they used to say, with her pale skin and high, round bosom, her restless eyes full of mystery and impatience. A different species from the rest of the Fiore women, who were dark and long-boned and languid, practically masculine in comparison. How that must gall Anna. How she must hate looking more like her faithless aunt than her sainted mother.

"Your aunt tells me the last tenants left your house in terrible shape," Rose opened harmlessly—but what a relief to be speaking *to* Anna, not *through* Iris.

"Yeah, that's an understatement," Anna said, scowling. "Who were those people, gypsies? It's a wreck, I'd sue the rental agent if I could afford it."

"Uh-oh. Any major damage?" Lily and Paul's narrow clapboard colonial on Day Street skirted the historic district, but it wasn't a landmark home, it was just old.

"*Everything*, you name it. Number one, the roof leaks. The furnace makes funny noises, I need a new hot water heater, probably new pipes. Wiring. The appliances are conking out one by one."

Rose shook her head in sympathy. Vonnie brought their salads then, and they ate for a while in silence. "Is it . . ." Rose took a sip of water and cleared her throat. "Are you finding it hard to be back? Being in the old house again? I can imagine it might be sad. A little."

"No, it's not sad, why would it be? It's a stranger's house, everything's been painted or paneled over by now, Rose. The Catalanos got erased a long time ago."

Rose, she called her. Not Aunt Rose, not for a long time. "I should've gone over and checked on it for you. I never even thought. Rental agents, I guess all they care about—"

"Why should you have gone over and checked on my house?" Anna pretended that was a straight question, didn't emphasize *you* or *my.* She didn't have to.

"Oh, I don't know," Rose said lightly. "I guess I could've called someone if I'd seen, you know, bomb-making materials in the front yard."

She finally had to smile. "The carpet in my old bedroom is full of BB's. Every time I vacuum, I get up about a hundred more."

"BB's?"

"It must've been a teenager's room. I'm thinking he spilled a big box of BB's on the shag rug and never told his mom."

"Remember—" Rose coughed, covering up the word. No memories allowed today. But she smiled to herself, remembering the day Anna, six or seven years old, had dumped an entire bottle of olive oil on the floor in the restaurant office. Rose had walked in and found her trying to move the heavy desk to cover it, hide the spreading stain. "I was changing things around," she'd invented, then burst into tears. Rose took her in her arms and uncovered the truth—that she'd been making "a fusion" for her mother, a surprise present, olive oil and basil in a pretty jar she'd already decorated with a ribbon. "Don't tell Mommy I spilled, okay, Aunt Rose?" and Rose promised she wouldn't. They'd cleaned the mess up together, and then Rose had taken Anna in the kitchen and showed her how to make a real oil infusion, pureeing fresh rosemary and marjoram in the big food processor. She couldn't remember if Lily, who was managing the out-front side of the business in those days, had ever found out about the accident. She must have—the office had smelled like basil for days, and the rug was never the same. But if she had, Rose wasn't the one who'd told her.

"So," Anna said, "the roof is the first thing, but it's just number one on a very long list."

Rose had an idea. "I know someone who might be able to help you with that. Maybe other things, too."

"A roofer?"

"No, a friend. Of a friend. I have a friend whose stepson built his own house, so he's handy."

"Well, if he can fix an old slate roof, he's hired. Let me have his number."

"No, you should go see him. It's not far. He's always home, but he doesn't answer his phone. Much."

Anna frowned.

"Because he's in his studio so much. He's a photographer."

"But he fixes roofs?"

"Maybe." Rose smiled, shrugged. "Worth a try. Mason Winograd is his name—I'll give you the address."

"Okay," Anna said doubtfully. "But I'd rather just call him."

"You'd have better luck stopping by."

Carmen had roasted the Dover sole simply, just lemon, oregano, and bay. "Mm," Anna said, "delicious," and seemed to mean it. They talked about neutral subjects in low-key, offhand voices, very polite, very aware. Eventually Rose relaxed enough to take a chance and say, "I was sorry to hear about your friend, Jay. That you'd broken up. The circumstances."

Anna nodded. "I don't miss him."

"You'd been together quite a while."

She reached for her glass, sipped. "Two years. I miss his grandfather more than I miss him."

"His grandfather?"

"Nice old guy. We were friends."

"Two years is a long time, though." Her longest ever with one man, as far as Rose knew; and since leaving home, her longest stay in one city. As she got older, the duration of her romantic relationships had gradually been lengthening, and thank goodness for that. There had been a time in her twenties when she'd been with a different man every—*week*, it seemed. Not that she'd ever shared that information with Rose; they hadn't even been speaking back then. Iris was their interpreter, and she'd had hellish tales to tell. An indirect form of punishment, Rose had always suspected, and very effective, too. But mercifully obsolete these days.

"It must've been hard for you," she ventured, "moving out, leaving Buffalo. Your friends, your job."

"No, not really." Anna looked at her with narrowed eyes, and Rose realized too late the trap she'd walked into. "Leaving's not hard at all when two people you trust stick a knife in your back."

She felt her face grow warm. "Oh, Anna." How stupid to think she might have let some of the bitterness go. "We have to talk, I know—I just didn't think we'd—"

"No, Rose, we don't have to talk. We absolutely don't have to talk. We said it all, don't you remember?"

As if she could forget. After Paul died, in fact on the night of his funeral, they'd said all sorts of hurtful, revelatory things to each other. After that, years had to pass before they'd even gotten back to the stage of politeness.

Now it only took minutes—that was progress, wasn't it? After a short silence, during which the food Rose put in her mouth tasted like chalk, Anna's shoulders lost their combative set. The wine was very good, she mentioned; was it a Sancerre? She still had so much unpacking to do, how did one person acquire so many *things*? What a pretty spring they were having—she didn't miss Buffalo at all—was May still the month when tourist season really started?

Pathetically grateful for these overtures, Rose met her halfway with small talk of her own, and the bad moment passed. *So*, she thought. Was this how they were going to deal with each other? Treat their mutual bad behavior—in her old age, she'd learned to spread the blame around a little, not keep it all to herself—as something in the remote past, something they'd already handled so there was no need to mention it again? That would certainly be easier. Another thing about old age: it heightened one's aversion to risk. But would it be possible? It went against Rose's nature to ignore the obvious and bite her tongue indefinitely. Even with everything at stake. And Anna might hate to hear it, but it was true—in that way she was just like her.

• • •

"You know I've never run a restaurant on my own, right?"

"You've run a café."

"Industrial Coffee was tiny, it served silly sandwiches, wood-roasted artichoke and celery root on poppyseed baguettes—it was more of an art gallery than a restaurant. I mean literally—it had an art gallery in back."

"But you ran it."

"I did." Anna shrugged, giving up that point. They were having coffee in Rose's office, which doubled as a storeroom for anything that didn't fit in the laundry closet, the pantry, or the cellar. Anna sat on the section of sofa that wasn't covered with files, papers, and cardboard boxes, and Rose perched on a cleared edge of her desk to be closer to her. "But why can't you manage this place yourself?" Anna asked her. "I don't understand what you need a manager for anyway. You say Carmen's doing most of the cooking now—why can't you work front *and* back? God knows you've always been good with customers."

"Thanks," Rose said, although Anna hadn't made that sound like much of a compliment. In her mind, Rose *manipulated* people—she'd heard that from Iris years ago, when Anna's sense of injustice had been at its high and mightiest. "But the thing is, I don't have time for both anymore. I'd like to keep doing some cooking, I don't want to give that up completely, ever—if I have to stop doing one, I'd rather it was the business. So I need someone I can trust to take over that side. The last manager I had was a disaster."

"Why do you have to stop doing one or the other?"

Anna looked genuinely puzzled, and Rose decided to be complimented by *that*. "My dear," she said, "I'm sixty years old."

"So?"

She laughed. "Thanks again."

"No, but—are you sick?"

"I'm not. But I have a friend who's ill. I'm spending more time away from the restaurant to be with him. I can't do what I used to do by myself anymore, and it's a situation that's—not going to get any better."

"Oh. This is—I forget the name, Aunt Iris mentioned a guy, somebody you..."

"Theo." Rose doubted very much that Anna had forgotten his name.

"Theo, right. I didn't know it was that serious. I'm sorry."

"It's something we're learning to live with."

Small silence. Anna said, "So. Okay, tell me. How's business? How many covers do you do a day? Roughly. What's your food cost? How many people do you employ, total, full time and part time?"

"About thirty-five—yes, I want you to see everything, I want you to look at the books, understand the complete situation." Rose stood up. "I can show you—"

"I don't want to look at books, not now. You just tell me."

She took a breath. "Well. Things are slow. They started slowing down a year or two ago. No, longer than that, three years. We're still in a good location, in fact it's better than ever, and the city's doing nothing but grow—as you see. A new restaurant opened on the water last fall, Brother's, very big and flashy. Doing great business."

"Taking away yours?"

"No, it's not that—but yes, sure, taking some of ours. The owner has a strip mall in the west end, he has movie theaters, some office buildings downtown. He's telling me he wants to buy this place and call it Brother's Two."

"Oh, great."

"I won't sell—I'm not even considering it. But it feels like the sharks are circling. Every year the lease goes up. If we make any major improvements, the assessed value of the building goes up, which makes the rent go up *more.* I'd need a loan to renovate, and the banks don't want to give money to little independents like us anymore, they only like the big chains."

"You're operating at a loss?"

Rose nodded.

"Why? What do you think went wrong?"

"I don't know, I can't put my finger on it exactly. Except for Waterman's Pub, we're the oldest restaurant downtown. Owned continuously by the same family, I mean." There were older buildings that housed restaurants, but they hadn't been in uninterrupted business for over forty years like the Bella Sorella. "Old age—I think that's what it comes down to. We need new blood. On the management side, because I can't afford a sexy, famous chef."

"And you think *I'd* be new blood?" Anna smiled out of one side of her mouth. "You need a twenty-five-year-old hotshot, Rose, trust me."

"Maybe. But there aren't any of those left in the family." She could see Anna mulling what to say to that. Being called "family" rankled—Rose had used the word deliberately. "The staff wants to change the name," she told her. "They think that'll solve everything."

"Change the name? From Bella Sorella?"

"In fact they've got a contest going. Whoever comes up with a name I like—I'm the judge—gets free drinks from the bar for life."

Anna laughed. "I don't know that changing the name is such a hot idea. But I don't know, I'd have to think about it." She looked at Rose boldly. "Maybe it's time to close up shop. You've had a good run. Why not sell out and move to Florida? Take your friend Theo with you. Lie in the sun and read novels."

Rose laughed.

A second passed. Then Anna laughed with her. At the absurdity.

Rose felt slightly dizzy. It wasn't much, but it was the closest they'd been in sixteen years.

Anna stood. She couldn't pace, not enough room, but she could pivot and scowl and gesture. "Okay. Let's see. You don't have a youth crowd. Not to mention a money crowd. You don't have an identity. Are you couples, family, Italian, seafood, eclectic? Your menu doesn't say anything one way or the other. About anything, frankly. When did you last change it?" Rose opened her mouth, but Anna kept talking. Rose swung her legs to the side of the desk to give her more room. "It was like déjà vu walking in this afternoon, I couldn't believe how many things were the same. I mean *exactly* the same. Even the music—wasn't that the 'O terra, addio' you were playing?"

Rose blushed. "I like *Aida*."

"You've got too many employees, you don't need thirty-five. I know what you're saying about bank money, but you could get *some*, and I think you could do a lot on the cheap. Paint the brick walls white, for a start, because it's too dark, Rose, and not in a good way. Keep the pottery and the paintings if you want to, but lose the maps of Italy's provinces, Jesus, they're cheesy. Get rid of the carpet, and I mean *immediately*, leave the floor bare if you don't want to refinish it. Are those the same yellow signs to the rest rooms, the Signore and Signori? *God*, Rose, I mean—And it's too quiet, the hot restaurants these days are incredibly noisy. Or make it even quieter if you want—but first you have to *decide* what you want to be, then go for it."

They could attract a much more up-market diner in this neighborhood, late-twenties to mid-forties, moneyed Gen X overachievers who were into travel, fashion, the theater. Worry about Gen Y in about five years, Anna advised, but in the meantime don't forget the Boomers. Or the dot-com crowd—they weren't local yet, but they were the ones who moored their brand-new cabin cruisers in the harbor, and they wanted a smart place to eat.

"Consider the possibility that your prices are too low. Most people with money really like paying too much, it makes them feel like they're getting what they deserve."

"But if we raise prices, we'll lose our regulars."

"Sure, some. If you want to keep them you could do bar specials, but then you'd probably be spreading yourself too thin. Bottom line, you can't be all things to all people. You have to decide."

She kept coming back to that, the need to *decide* what the Bella Sorella was and then push it hard, *become* it. "I used to know," Rose said wistfully. "We were a friendly family Italian restaurant. That's what we were."

"I know. That's what we were."

"It started with your grandfather's little crab house on East Island—you never saw that place. He called it Fiore's. He had two other restaurants, each one a little bit more successful, before he bought this place and named it The Flower. Oh, but that wasn't Italian enough, so then it was I Fiori, and then it was Tre Fiori. Finally he settled on Bella Sorella, and of course we little girls used to argue over which *beautiful sister* he'd named it after, Lily or Iris or me. He said it was after all of us, that we were all beautiful." She laughed. "You don't remember him, do you? You were so little when he died."

"No, I don't remember him at all."

Enough of that. Rose couldn't tell what Anna was thinking; she was staring at the floor with her hands stuck in the waistband at the back of her slacks, a drift of hair obscuring her face.

"Maybe I should've left it that way," Rose said ruefully. "A friendly family Italian restaurant. But I guess I muddied up the image, trying to keep up with the times. Adding things like mesclun and arugula"—Anna laughed—"and microbrews, and a wood-burning oven I don't have room for and nobody ever orders anything from anyway."

"Nothing wrong with any of that, Rose. Not if you're consistent."

"And you're right—we've got pasta al pomodoro and a grilled Reuben on the very same lunch menu. It doesn't *say* anything. Except that we can't make up our minds."

Anna tilted her head and looked at her. "You know, it might not work no matter what you do. Restaurants go in cycles—it's possible the Bella Sorella's cycle is over."

"No."

"Or maybe this *version* of it is finished. Maybe you rename it, now it's the—the Piccolo, it specializes in steak and pommes frites."

"No."

"Are you sure?"

"I am very sure."

"Good. Because you're lost if you go that way. It never works, it just drags out the end longer."

"Then why—"

"Because it would be a *faster* end, a mercy killing, and if you decide to do it the hard way you might wish you'd gone that route when things get bad. And you know things are going to get bad."

"But then they'll get better."

"No guarantees."

"I don't expect any. Will you manage it?"

It was what they'd been leading up to, and yet Anna looked surprised and defenseless for a second, as if Rose had caught her off guard. Anna was anything but frail but, standing there in her mannish suit with her sharp elbows out, tall and slight, thick-haired and thin-necked, she looked so much like the coltish girl she used to be, Rose's throat hurt. *What if it beats her?* She didn't care so much for herself, she was old and used to disappointment; a long time ago she'd practically made friends with it. But this had to work. They needed something good to happen to them *together*, it was the only chance they had. She wanted it for the others, too, Carmen and Vonnie, Vince, crazy Dwayne, all the ones who depended on her—but Anna looked so vulnerable to her just then. What if the job Rose was begging her to take defeated her?

"Yes," Anna said.

"Yes? You'll do it?" Rose jumped up. All her second thoughts vanished, all she felt was triumph. "Wonderful, oh, Anna, I'm so glad. I've got something—" She went around and jerked open the bottom drawer of her desk. "Here, and glasses, too. We have to drink a toast."

"Oh no. Whoa! You're not going to make me drink grappa."

"Oh yes, you must, it's a celebration."

"Why don't we just siphon some gas out of my car?"

"Call yourself an Italian. Look at this beautiful bottle, it's exquisite, the hand-blown glass."

"Good idea, let's just look at the bottle."

"Here." She pushed a glass into Anna's hand. "To the Bella Sorella. To success." Oh, she should've left it at that! "To your return. Anna, I'm go glad you've come home."

"Wait, hold it."

Rose paused, even though she wanted more than anything to drink, as if by swallowing the bitter brandy fast she could seal the deal. Her own fault—she'd gone too far.

"Let's be clear about what we're doing here. This is a temporary arrangement, Rose. No matter what happens, I'm not going to be here for the long haul. I'm glad to help you out if I can, but I've got other options. I just want to be clear—if you were thinking this would be a permanent setup, then we're not understanding each other."

"Well." Rose laughed lightly. "I don't suppose anything is permanent." She lifted her glass again.

"No, but I want to make sure we're together. I have a friend, we used to work together at the coffeehouse—she's a chef and she's moved back home, San Diego, her name's Shelly. She's working right now on raising capital to start a restaurant of her own, and as soon as she gets things lined up she wants me to come out and run it for her."

"San Diego."

"But you know how it is, it might not work out, in fact it probably won't. But if it doesn't, I've also got other possibilities, and I'll be sending out some résumés as soon as I get settled."

"I see. What about your house?"

"After it's fixed up, I'll put it on the market. But that could be months."

"Months."

"I'll commit to months—that I can do. This is April. Two months to June, that's still when your high season kicks in, isn't it? June, July, August. One way or the other, we'll know by Labor Day if you can turn this place around. Not if you did, if you *can*. After that, we'll leave it open-ended." Finally she lifted her glass. "To the summer." When Rose didn't move, she reached out and clinked glasses. Drank. "Ack. Oh, my Jesus," she rasped, teary-eyed. "Diesel fuel."

"To the summer," Rose said weakly, and took a sip of the colorless liquor. She felt cheated.

"When do you want me to start? And how much are you going to pay me? I need a living wage, Rose, no gouging because it's family. I could start any time, but it might be better to wait till Monday, I'd like to square things away with my house, line up a couple of repairs. Plus I'm really not unpacked yet. But I could come in on Sunday when it's quiet, check things out. Do you still close on Mondays? You might have to rethink that, you know. When does your dinner crew come in? What is it," she glanced at her watch, "three o'clock now, I could stick around till four or so and meet those guys. Want to introduce me to the lunch shift while I'm waiting?" She was moving toward the door. "I didn't get a chance to say much to Carmen, before. God, it's amazing, she looks exactly the same."

Now she only felt half-cheated. "It's family," Anna had said, probably not even hearing herself. That was a start.

"You're better than a priest," Rose had told Theo in the morning. That night, because neither of them could sleep, she lay in bed with the phone to her ear and whispered a few more of her sins to him in the dark. And thought about how odd it was that the only person she could confide in about the first great love of her life was the last.

"Paul's death was so sudden, out on the road like that. Anna and I weren't prepared, no chance to say good-bye to him. We were sick with grief, but we couldn't comfort each other. Couldn't touch, just hurt. We had an awful fight on the night of his funeral—she reminded me of it today. She thinks we said everything then, we don't need to dig it all up again."

"Finally," Theo said, his voice breathy. "Something I agree with her about."

"But we didn't even speak after that. Years. I'd give anything to erase it, because I said ugly things. I said she had a hard heart. A small heart." *I'm so disappointed in you*, she'd said. *To let your father die without forgiving him. Selfish girl, to punish him with your judgment.*

"I made her so angry, Theo, she finally let go of a secret. She'd been hoarding it, and that night it came bursting out of her."

"What secret?"

"That she knew about Paul and me. She'd known it for years, I mean, long before that day she found me in his bedroom. She knew when she was thirteen years old, before Lily died. Before."

Theo was quiet for a time. She listened to the silence carefully, alert for blame. "How come she never said it before? She kept it to herself for seven years?"

"No, only two—Paul only lived two more years after she found out about us. She didn't *know* what she'd seen when she was a girl, it didn't make sense to her until later. When we hit her in the face with it."

"I don't get it. What happened when she was thirteen?"

"I didn't even know at first, I couldn't remember anything she might've seen. She called me a liar, a cheat." *My mother was upstairs dying, and you were already with him! I saw you—I thought you were comforting him!* "But then I remembered. I'd gone to the house one night late, after the restaurant closed, to bring Paul some dinner. He'd just gotten back from one of his sales trips."

"Like you bring dinner to me. You're the lady who brings food."

"To hungry men I'm in love with." She smiled wanly.

"So what did Anna see?" Theo whispered.

"Nothing, really. Nothing to see. Just a feeling, an atmosphere. Paul and I weren't lovers yet—it was just beginning. But she must've *felt* something, and either she was too young to recognize it or she shut her mind and ignored it for the next seven years. I think probably that was it—the latter."

She'd thought about that night so many times. It had changed the direction of her life, and Paul's, and that seemed fair and natural, orderly. Deserved. Not fair that it had changed Anna's, though. No wonder she hadn't found a man to love for longer than a few years at a time, or a place to live. Did she even have a close woman friend? She'd been made to rearrange what she thought she knew about her parents, her well-loved aunt, half her childhood. Because of Rose and Paul, she'd had to learn a very bad lesson—that what you think is real may not be. And the people you love are probably not what they seem.

That night, late, Rose gave Paul his dinner, then left him in the kitchen while she went up to check on Lily. She was dying of cancer, and everyone but Anna had given up hoping for a miracle. Paul's job took him on the road for days at a time, so the bulk of caring for her had fallen to the women, Mama during the day, Anna after school, Rose at night after work. Paul whenever he could. Lily was in the quiet final days, the stage between the last of the chemo and the start of the heavy narcotics. Most of the time, she slept. At the end she needed the bedside lamp on all the time, she couldn't bear the dark. In the low, gold light that night she'd looked younger than her age—only thirty-six. Wobbly and weak, hairless from the drugs, she looked like a baby bird, all bones and blue-white skin. *This is my sister*, Rose had thought, but it wasn't real. *How can I lose her, how can this be happening?* She'd kissed her on the forehead, and Lily had opened her eyes.

"Hi," they said together, and Lily whispered, "I was just talking about you."

"You mean dreaming? You were dreaming about me?"

"Mmm." She shut her eyes and let Rose stroke her face, smooth away the pain lines between her eyebrows. "We were playing poker. The old house. Remember that white kitchen table? Pauley was your partner. You put your cards down and said, 'I win.' "

Rose ran her hand softly along the soft frizz on Lily's head. "You don't have partners in poker."

Lily opened her eyes. She smiled. "You won," she said distinctly. She turned her face away and drifted back to sleep.

The light had been on in Anna's room, too. She'd been studying and fallen asleep in her white blouse and navy pleated jumper, the uniform at her parochial school. Books and ballpoint pens lay scattered across the bedspread, and her head rested on an open notebook. Everything else in the room was sadly, unnaturally tidy. Anna kept the whole house fanatically neat, much neater than Lily ever had—one way to bring order to the chaos her life had turned into. Her grades were slipping, but no one had intervened, not even Rose. No one had time for anything but Lily. How can I help her? Rose had asked herself all the time. How can I be wise and calm when I feel like a child myself? Her own mother was lost in grief, no help to Rose or Anna or anyone else. Sometimes Rose thought Anna was stronger than all of them. At least she still had faith; she said rosaries for Lily, went to mass every morning, fasted, did secret penances. Mama, Rose, Paul, Iris—they'd all given up on saving her, but not Anna. She still clung to the hope that she could pray her mother back to life.

Rose almost woke her, to tell her to get undressed and under the covers. Instead she found a blanket and floated it over Anna's slack, long-legged body, shoes and all. "Love you," she'd whispered, stroking the hair back from her cheek. Dark, coarse, rippled hair, exactly like hers—their mutual curse. "Love you, baby." Anna had smiled in her sleep.

Downstairs, Paul was in the dark living room, looking out the window. It was raining. The streetlight turned the fine strings of water on the glass blue, and Paul's face ghostly. The house felt leaden, as if the heaviness of Lily's dying were forcing everything down, crushing the air out. Rose crossed the room to turn on a light, but Paul said, "Don't," without looking at her. She didn't have to see his face to know he was crying. In all the time she'd known him, she had never seen him weep.

She'd gone to him hesitantly, touched his sleeve. "They're both asleep. They're fine." Meaningless comfort, all she could give him. He nodded. Because he was exhausted, she could see what his long, mobile face would look like in ten years, twenty.

He rested his temple against the glass and tried to smile. "I wish Lily could've been happy," he said. "I was never able to . . ."

"You made her happy."

"I was never able to make her believe I loved her."

"You did love her. Do love her. She knows that." Nothing had been in her head except the need to comfort him, but words stacked up in her throat like cards, she'd had to press her fingers to her lips to keep her mouth closed.

He took the hand she was resting on the windowsill and examined it in the watery light, holding it with both of his, his eyes downcast. A most intimate gesture; only the naturalness of it had calmed her. "Rose, I never did anything to let her know. She just knows."

"What, Paul?" she'd asked fearfully.

"I never told her or showed her, I never did anything to make her think it. I don't think I did. I tried not to."

Were they going to say these things to each other *now*? At first she was shocked. After all the years of keeping the secret—not from each other, they couldn't, but from Lily—*this* was when they would tell each other the truth, in words? He was right, though—Lily knew. *You won*. She'd dreamed it.

"I've always been faithful to her."

She nodded. "Yes," she said, "of course."

"But, Rose. It was you. You I was being faithful to."

Her eyes swam. She'd been true to him, too, even though there had been men. They laced their fingers together, and she thought of all the years she'd forbidden herself to wish for this. At first it was easy, because she was so angry with him—he'd married the wrong sister—but time had passed and they'd become friends again, and nothing she had ever done was harder than pretending she didn't love Paul. Except knowing he was doing the same thing.

They didn't kiss, although she'd wanted to. She'd wanted to know if it would be the same between them or if everything would be different. They were in a spell, they'd spun a truth-telling web around themselves, a cocoon of feeling, not even words anymore. That's what Anna would interrupt and, seven years later, interpret correctly for exactly what it was. But at the time it was enough to hold hands, the deepest intimacy, she could hardly believe her good fortune. Lily's dark shadow had lifted just for that moment, and they were sad and desperate enough to take advantage. If that was a sin, Rose was too far gone then and too old now to regret it.

"Daddy? Mom's calling you. She wants you to read to her." Anna at the bottom of the stairs.

They sprang apart. So—guilty even then, and they knew it, though they'd done nothing yet except long and yearn. Rose's hand had flown to her heart. Anna saw that. "Oh, you startled me!" she said, and laughed—a good, believable laugh, because even though she was worried about Anna, she was glad, practically euphoric, because the pretense between her and Paul was finally over. She left him in the shadows and walked toward Anna, blocking him from her view. "Hot milk," she said, putting both hands on Anna's shoulders, filling her vision. *Look at my bright eyes. Believe it's because I've been crying for your mother*. "Let's make some hot milk, that'll be good. Then you go straight back to bed."

"I've asked myself," she said to Theo, "if I'd do it again. Be Paul's lover while Lily was still alive, not wait the *decent interval.*"

"What's the answer?"

"I don't know. I think I wouldn't, but that's easy to say now. Everything went to hell when Anna found us together. It was her last year at college—that summer she was going to Europe with a girlfriend, and in August I was supposed to meet them in Italy. Anna and I were going to go to wonderful restaurants and get ideas and recipes for the new, improved Bella Sorella. I'd cook and she'd manage." She closed her eyes. "Oh, Theo. Wasn't that a lovely plan?"

"You can't blame yourself because it didn't work."

"Of course I can."

"She's the one who ran away. Why didn't she say right out as soon as it hit her if she knew about you and Paul? Why wait till he died, why hold it in like that? Like a miser. I don't like her."

She waited till he caught his breath, then said, "I think she kept it inside because it was all she had. Being so angry—it gave her some kind of strength against us. And I think she knew if she told us the truth, she'd have to forgive us. We'd make her. She's soft in the heart, Theo. She is. She felt betrayed. She *was* betrayed."

"Crap. She was a grown woman. She wasn't your mother, she wasn't you. What did she know? You were watching your sister die. People do what they do. Lily never knew, and that's what counts."

"No. Oh, I don't know." She stretched her arms and legs in her empty bed. "Are you sleepy?"

"Yeah."

"Good. We'll hang up, and you go to sleep. Sleep all night, don't get up to pee."

"So she's taking the job and you're all happy."

"She's taking the job, yes. I'm happy."

"I guess you got all kinds of plans in your head, how you're going to make it up, be friends again."

"No plans."

"Just be careful."

"Why? What will happen?"

"You just be careful. No parts of you are as young as they used to be."

"You say the nicest things."

"You know what I mean. Your insides."

Theo had a hard time saying certain things. "My liver?" she guessed. "Pancreas?"

She could almost hear him grinding his teeth. "Heart," he said under his breath.

"Pardon? Did you say *heart*?"

"You just watch your step."

She sighed, flooded with feeling. "I wish you were here. What I wouldn't give. I would love to kiss you right now."

He grunted. "Heart" had taken so much out of him, he couldn't reciprocate in words.

"Do you love me, Theo?"

"You know it."

"I'm so lucky," she said.

5

Jay had told Anna he would call. They couldn't leave it like this, he'd said; they would talk when a little time had passed and she'd had a chance to cool down. She hadn't believed him, she'd thought he just didn't have the guts to say good-bye clean. But when the phone rang and she heard that flat, refined, New England drone he couldn't shake, although he'd tried—once he'd affected a tough New York or New Jersey accent, hoping people would think his sculptures were working class or proletariat or something—when she heard his voice, she thought, *I knew it*, and immediately began to rearrange her mind for all the new possibilities. He wanted her to come back—he wanted to marry her—he was calling from down the street. When none of those proved to be true, she felt silly but not really disappointed.

He asked how she was. Fine. He said he missed her. Really. He said he'd sold *Colossus III* to a bank in Boise. Congratulations. He said, "Mac's had a heart attack."

"What? Oh, Jay! How is he, is he okay?" Mac—Jay's eighty-one-year-old grandfather—Anna adored him.

"Yes, he's stable, they say. Evidently it was minor."

"Thank God! When did it happen?"

"The day before yesterday. They're releasing him tomorrow, although he can't go back to the assisted-living place right away. He'll need nursing care for a short time first." Then she thought he was calling to ask if she'd come back and take care of Mac for him. She'd been as close as a daughter-in-law to the old man—she'd hated leaving him much more than she'd hated leaving Jay. Jay loved him too, of course, but Anna was the one who'd called him every week and gone to see him and invited him to dinner at the loft. The one who'd done things for him.

"Jay, I don't know, I don't think I can—"

"There's a rehab facility quite close to the hospital, so they'll just take him there in an ambulance tomorrow afternoon. Would you like the telephone number of the rehab?"

"Oh. Yes, please. And the address." She wrote them down. "So have you been to see him?"

"Of course I've been to see him."

"How is he? How are his spirits?"

"Fair, I would say. He's still a son of a bitch."

She smiled, knowing he meant that affectionately.

"He still enjoys telling me what an asshole I was."

She wound the curls in the phone line around one finger. "In what particular regard?"

"Spoiling things. Between us."

"He knows?" She couldn't believe it. "You told Mac about Nicole?"

"Not—no, I didn't think that would serve any useful purpose. I simply told him—well, what you told him."

"How do you know what I told him?"

"Because he told me."

"What did he say?"

"He said I was an asshole."

"No, Jay, I never, that's not what—"

"I know, Anna. You said things weren't working out and you needed to get away for a while to think. It's safe to say my grandfather drew his own conclusions."

"Oh. Well, I'm sorry." For what, though? For Mac, she supposed.

There was a long, uncomfortable pause, during which she had the distinct impression that she was expected to say she forgave him.

"Nicole has moved in."

She absorbed that, then came up with, "Oh, has she?"

"It seemed the best thing, under the circumstances."

"More convenient."

He breathed the way he did when she was being difficult. "It was what she wanted. Evidently it enhances her illusion that what you walked in on wasn't a meaningless affair in progress."

Breathtaking. "So you did it for her. *Evidently*."

More put-upon sighing.

"You're really something, aren't you?"

"Anna, I'm trying to tell you that I regret what happened."

"I know. That's what's so amazing." She remembered a story he used to like to tell, because he was proud of it. When he was in college at Columbia, for some kind of performance art project he went around interviewing people on the street in a tough section of the city, a tense, mixed neighborhood, and he took photographs of everyone he interviewed. Later he blew up the photos and posted them around the neighborhood, with the verbatim comments of the people in the pictures printed over them. Some of the comments were racist, all of them were in some way foolish or humiliating. What was the point of it? she'd asked, appalled. To make people hear what they really sound like, he'd said. To make them confront the truth about themselves. Mean, she'd thought. A dirty trick.

"Anna," Jay said, "let's talk later."

"Let's not," she said, and hung up.

How could she ever have loved him? What kind of woman couldn't recognize what a selfish, insensitive, uncaring lout he was? And if she saw it now, why did his betrayal still sting like acid? In self-defense, before the self-loathing could start again, she tried to remember his good points. They all came from the early days—they'd met in Philadelphia—the courtship phase when Jay was all charm and heat and dark, exciting passion. She'd been delighted to move to Buffalo with him when he'd asked; she'd left behind friends, a dull job, and any number of failed relationships without a backward glance. Nicole and Industrial Coffee had seemed like serendipity, good luck on top of good luck, a thrilling new man *and* work that might be fun, might actually mean something to her. Jay's good points: he was smart. He was talented. He was good-looking. Too bad all the good points had corresponding bad points—he was proud and condescending because he was smart, he was insecure about his talent, he was vain about his good looks.

He loved his cat. There—a pure, untainted good quality. And completely unselfish, because the cat never repaid his affection except when it suited him. No wonder they got along so well.

Bitter. Yes, she was bitter. She would never get over him, that's what was so infuriating. He wasn't worth it, he wasn't worth it, but *Jay McGuare* was a name she'd remember on her deathbed if she lived to be a hundred. She resented that more than anything. Last night she dreamed he was making a sculpture out of her hair. Strand by strand, she let him pull it out of her scalp and pretended it didn't hurt, that this was fine with her. She woke up before he could start peeling her skin off.

She wasn't ready to think about how much of what must've been wrong between them for a long time was her fault. Intimations crept in anyway, shades of culpability, complicity. Like most women, she always claimed she wanted intimacy, but she'd kept Jay at arm's length while they went through the motions of domestic togetherness, sex, planning for the future. They'd never combined finances, never had a joint checking account, always split everything down the middle, although he made much more money than she did. Even during their most hopeful and idyllic period, when they were *both* talking about marriage, she'd never stopped using birth control.

The deeper, more interesting question was *why*, yet she was even less inclined to explore that right now. But sometimes she couldn't shut out a truly alarming possibility—that Rose and her father had set her up years ago to prepare for the worst. Forewarned is forearmed. Naturally that attitude would seep into your loved one's consciousness by and by, no matter how self-involved he might be. And how far was it from there to pushing him into someone else's softer, warmer, more trusting arms? From guaranteeing that your dread of betrayal and faithlessness became a self-fulfilling prophesy?

She'd lied to Rose about the house. Nothing looked the same, that was true, but she had X-ray eyes, she could see beneath the paint and the god-awful paneling and the dingy wall-to-wall carpets, the quick disguises thrown up to hide its heart. Its Catalano heart. But she'd been straight when she'd told Rose coming home wasn't sad. Even distorted and denatured, her house was a reminder of something she had the interesting habit of forgetting: she'd had an almost ridiculously happy childhood.

The fireplace didn't work anymore, something about an inadequate chimney liner, but she could sit on the furnished tweed sofa and see her mother shaking an old popcorn popper over the flames while her father smacked the logs with the poker and told her to hold the thing a little higher. "Nuh uh, we like 'em burned," her mother would say, winking at Anna, and her father would groan, pretending he was outnumbered and henpecked. That was one of his favorite games, and so of course it was one of Anna's. She played at bossing him around like a haughty queen from the age of about three. "You have to," she'd say, "you're just the man," mimicking him. "You're just the one who brings home the bacon."

She'd sold the piano a long time ago, but it used to sit in the corner between the bay window and the china cabinet, an old black baby grand her father's parents had given him and Lily for a wedding present. He could play ragtime and boogie-woogie, to Anna's delight, but what she liked even better was when he played "soft songs," late at night after she'd been put to bed. They were for Mommy, the soft songs, and that was fine, but she would fall asleep making believe they were for her.

What was now the den used to be a screened-in back porch. She remembered following her mother out onto the porch one bright, snowy morning, and realizing for the first time in her life what *cold* was. "Brr, it's cold!" her mother had cried, racing back in from whatever chore she'd gone out there for, rubbing her arms, and Anna had copied her and echoed, "Brr, it's cold," and understood. The only interesting thing about that memory was that she *knew* she understood, and now, thirty-some years later, she could still remember knowing it. A consciousness milestone.

The kitchen, still tiny and yellow, was the room that years and tenants had changed the least. Anna had no memories of Mom at the stove, bending into the refrigerator, Mom cutting things up at the counter. Her mother hated to cook; she brought home restaurant food and reheated it in the oven. Daddy used to grumble that he was on the road four or five days a week, and when he got home he couldn't even get a home-cooked meal. But Anna had loved it. They got to eat what Nonna and Aunt Rose fixed the customers at the Bella Sorella, and it was heaven. All her friends thought she was the luckiest kid in the world. She did, too.

Why couldn't she trust that happiness again? Why did what happened later taint it so thoroughly, like a dirty watercolor brush in clear water? Why, in the year and a half she'd wasted in therapy, had she focused on nothing but trivial frustrations and childish disappointments, never the good times—why couldn't she even admit there *were* good times?

Revisionist history. At twenty, she'd rewritten her past to accommodate one enormous act of treachery that happened when she was thirteen. But maybe sooner than thirteen—that was the sticky part. The joker in the deck. Maybe much sooner, maybe it existed from the very beginning, how could she know? Things didn't necessarily start when you first noticed them. And no one could tell her the truth now. Her father was dead, and Rose—well. Her testimony was suspect.

Memories of her father were everywhere in this house, even if she had to look for them under layers of time and cheap rehabs. The window over the kitchen sink still stuck—she vividly recalled both times he'd thrown his back out trying to open it. The dark, earthy, oily smell of the basement brought back every repair or home improvement project he'd ever embarked on and usually never finished. At the bottom of the kitchen door, under who knew how many coats of paint, deep, gouged-out scratch marks were still visible from the time he'd brought home a stray dog. Stinky, they'd named her, and she'd lasted about two days before Anna's mother had taken her to the humane society. Anna remembered sitting on her father's lap in his big chair in the living room, heartbroken, snuffling against his shirt, while he spun a long, detailed story about Stinky's new home and how happy she was there, how kind and loving her new owners were. For his sake, she'd pretended to buy it all and be comforted, but she wasn't. Even at six, she wasn't too young to see that his heart was broken, too.

It wasn't fair, but from the beginning she'd felt more betrayed by Rose than by him. Always felt, as her mother's surrogate, more cheated on by Rose than by him. The thought of her father carrying on behind her mother's innocent, unsuspecting back was too fundamental a violation, too painful. She simply couldn't bear it, and so, a long time ago, she'd laid the lion's share of the blame at Rose's feet. It was Rose's fault. Much worse to betray a sister than a wife. The blood tie—meaner, more basic treachery. Men will be men. Yes, it was sexist, but it was also, in Anna's own unhappy, real-life experience, God's own truth. And so she remembered her father with love and sadness and hardly any anger, and she held Rose accountable for every millimeter she'd strayed from the righteous path of virtue and blamelessness.

It rained that night, not hard but enough to motivate her. The next morning, against Rose's advice, she found Mason Winograd's name in the phone book and called him. Surprise—no answer. She looked at a map and found his street, a cul-de-sac in one of the jagged little river inlets north of town. Must be a new development since her day; she remembered that area across the bridge as woods and wetlands, no houses to speak of.

Mason Winograd's house was something to speak of. He had no close neighbors, no neighbors at all that she could see. A downed chain stretched between two posts at the driveway entrance. She drove over it cautiously, into a dense thicket of budding maples and low-growing mountain laurel on either side of a bumpy lane, morning sunshine dappling the windshield, occasionally blinding her. It was only eleven o'clock, but already warm. Through the open car window the racket of birdsong was even louder than the crunch of tires, and she wondered if that was normal for this time of year, bird-wise, or if Mr. Winograd had more than the usual number on his property. Maybe he lured them there with food and other enticements so he could take their pictures. She didn't know a thing about birds. Imagine choosing birds, nothing else, for your sole artistic subject. Maybe he was eccentric.

No, he was definitely eccentric. She had to laugh when she saw his house, although more from shock than amusement. The long, winding drive had prepared her for something interesting, maybe semi-grand, but never this narrow, blind fortress, three flat stories of weathered shingles, windowless, nothing but a big door in the center to break up the sheer gray blankness. *No windows*? Was that even legal? Maybe Rose was playing a joke on her. A friend of a friend, she'd said, somebody's stepson; he'd built this house, so he was "handy." Well, up to a point. But not if you counted windows.

There was no place for her car unless she blocked a late-model yellow Jeep parked in a gravel clearing by the side of the house. She blocked it, and as she pulled the key from the ignition of her car, a movement behind the house caught her eye. Beyond the grassy backyard, a wooden pier jutted into the pretty river tributary. Water, sparkling like a ribbon of broken mirrors, flowed away from the bay; in front of the pier, its bowsprit poking out from the front of a shed or garage, an unfinished sailboat rested on jack stands. Saws and tools lay scattered on the ground next to a couple of sawhorses covered by a length of raw wood. Sawdust everywhere. The movement she'd seen was a man sprinting away from the shed toward the house. She registered fast legs, shirtless torso, long hair blowing back in an urgent wake, before the figure disappeared around the corner and out of view.

Mr. Winograd, she presumed. She'd have said the phone had rung and he was rushing to answer it, except he didn't answer his phone. It was more as if he'd seen something frightening or alarming—her—and he was running away, trying to escape. She got out of her car with misgivings.

Maybe the windowless exterior was a new style of modern architecture; minimalism gone berserk. She'd have to ask Jay. She followed a flagstone path across the front lawn to a one-step concrete stoop. The wide front door was, what else, windowless. She gave it a few raps with her knuckles, and wasn't surprised when half a minute passed and no one opened it.

She could leave. She was feeling vaguely insulted; definitely shunned. She picked her way back along the path to the driveway and kept going, around the sloping side lawn. Beautiful here with the glinting river for a backdrop, cleared around the dock but overhung elsewhere with budding willow and sycamore trees. A lot of birdhouses and bird feeders on tall poles were clustered around the boat shed. Eureka, a window! Airy and wide open on the first floor of the house, perfectly normal, homey even, maybe a kitchen window, and beyond it, cantilevered out from the back, a long, screened-in porch. Flowering vines climbed up the weathered wood sides, and bees buzzed in the sweet-smelling, trumpet-shaped blooms. Pretty.

The man had left the screen door to the porch half open. "Hello?" she called through it. No answer, so she stepped inside. After the blinding sun, it took a few seconds to make out a glider, flaking white with plaid cushions, against the back wall. She saw a small table with an empty plastic glass on it, a wicker footstool. No other furniture, but a large cardboard box took up space in the shadowy far corner, with a scattering of towels and rags on the floor near it.

Through the door opposite, she could see the kitchen. She crossed the porch and stopped in the threshold, called out again. "Mr. Winograd? It's Anna Catalano—my aunt sent me—Rose Fiore. Hello? Anybody home?"

A soft sound made her glance to the right. Nothing there but the kitchen sink, under the window she'd just walked past. No—there was a stick, a limb, a tree limb, resting at an angle on the windowsill. And now she could see two little somethings on it. Birds. Baby birds sitting side by side, staring back at her very quietly. Not moving. They couldn't possibly be real.

"Something I can do for you?"

She jolted up on her toes, barely suppressing a scream. A man had materialized in the doorway to the next room, living room or whatever. *The* man, she could tell by the bare feet and the jeans, but he'd put on a shirt, and he looked perfectly cool and collected, not like a flying fugitive in the least. He leaned against the door frame with his arms crossed, head at a questioning angle. Insolent angle, actually. A serious-looking camera hung on a strap from his shoulder. Maybe he'd just seen an interesting bird and he'd been rushing inside to get his camera. If she'd spoiled some brilliant, once-in-a-lifetime photo, she could understand why he didn't look very glad to see her.

Her heart slowed, and she said, "Hi," smiling at him, trying to look harmless. "I thought I saw somebody, so I, well, just knocked and came in. I'm Anna."

"Anna." He had to clear the gruffness out of his throat. "Rose's niece."

"Yes."

"You look like her."

"Yeah, that's what they say." She was tired of hearing them say it. "And you're—"

"Mason."

"Nice to meet you."

He didn't echo the sentiment. Or offer to shake hands. She couldn't figure out if he was hostile or shy, dangerous, nuts, or just deeply uninterested. He had beautiful salt-and-pepper hair, but he wore it too long, it fell straight down from a high part and hid half of one side of his face. Even without smiling, he had crow's feet at the corners of light, secretive eyes. A deep cleft cut between his straight black eyebrows, the perfect grim complement to his pained mouth, the lips pressed together, pronouncing the letter M.

"Listen, I'm sorry if I disturbed you, but my aunt said you fix roofs. Rooves," she tried when he looked completely blank. "Mine's leaking around the chimney."

"She said what?"

"Oh." So it was a joke. "Sorry," she repeated, laughing, pretending she was amused, "I think I've made a mistake." Maybe she had the wrong house? "Or I misunderstood, I could've sworn—"

"I fixed Rose's window once. At the restaurant."

"You did?"

"Kids broke it. I put in a new pane of glass."

"Oh." *Because you're so good with windows,* she thought.

He kept one hand on the camera at his hip, smoothing the silver metal with long, nervous fingers either lovingly or compulsively. Except for the sawdust in his hair, he looked like a gunfighter. The gaunt, tortured, over-the-hill kind. Something arrogant about him, the way he looked at her, sort of James Deanish recklessness she found equally attractive and irritating. Then he straightened up from his tough-guy slouch, but, oddly, his shoulders stayed uneven, the left one lower than the right by an inch or so.

The phone rang.

He jumped—it was on the wall about two feet from his ear. They stared at each other during the hour-long interval between the first ring and the second. She folded her arms. He rubbed his chest, the place over his heart, with the flat of his palm. She began to feel torn, part of her daring him not to answer—go ahead, *be* as weird as you possibly can be—but the other part drawn to him for some reason, wanting to throw in her lot with his side in the us-versus-them conspiracy—or whatever was going on around here.

He answered the phone.

"Theo." He breathed it in a low, heartfelt, thankful voice, the very sound of relief. "How are you? No, I'm here—I left it out in the—No, I came in without it, this is fine. How're you doing?"

His phone, he'd come in without his phone, she figured out. Theo had called him on the cell phone he must've left in the sailboat shed, and now he was calling him on the house phone. The one he never answered.

"Well, that's good. That's what I'm doing. Right now, it's no . . . I know, but it's what I'd be doing anyway. I'll pick you up, you can have lunch with me. No, it's not a problem. Not at all. Good, yeah. See you."

He replaced the receiver carefully. "That was Theo," he said, more pleasantly than he'd said anything so far.

She nodded, glad for him. "Who's Theo?" Rose's boyfriend, she knew that. So this guy was Rose's boyfriend's stepson.

"He's my stepfather. I thought Rose might've mentioned him."

"Wait, maybe she did. He lives on a boat, is that right? And he's not well, I think she said, he's sick, or he—"

"He has a condition."

"Yes. I'm sorry, I hope he's better. Well," she said, trying to stay on track, "I don't know why Rose told me you could fix my roof, but honest to God, that's what she said."

"I can fix your roof."

"You can?" She hated to bring it up, but—"She said you built this house."

He nodded.

"It, um, has an interesting facade."

He stroked his upper lip with his fingers, as if he had an invisible mustache. Between his hair and his shielding hand, she could hardly see his face at all. "I'm putting in windows," she thought he said; he mumbled it. "Next project."

"Oh. Because the first time you . . . what." She smiled. "Forgot?"

He blinked rapidly. "Long story."

"Hmm," she said interestedly. But he rubbed his chest with his hand again, and didn't tell it to her.

She glanced around at his kitchen, which was sleek and high-tech, no frills but lots of manly stainless steel and industrial-strength appliances. No dirty dishes, no clutter, and all the surfaces shone. Only one thing looked out of place.

"You have two baby birds on a tree limb over your sink."

"Barn swallows."

"Oh. What happened to the mother?"

"I don't know. Someone found them and gave them to me."

"Won't they fly away? Or fall on the floor, not in a cage or anything?"

"No."

One of the gray-blue babies had come down the limb to take a drink out of a pie tin full of water on the slate counter. Bullet-shaped, it wobbled on its way back up, bow-legged, swinging from side to side. Anna laughed. "He walks like Charlie Chaplin."

Mason smiled, too. The temperature in the room went up about ten degrees.

"I've just moved back to town," she offered in the new warmth. "I grew up on Day Street."

"I know."

He must know lots of things about her, she realized, courtesy of Rose, via *Theo*. All the gory details about Jay, no doubt, all about her being the prodigal daughter come home. "What about you?" she said, jutting her chin at him, aggressive. "Have you lived here all your life?"

"No, I left. Like you."

"But now you're back. From…"

"New York."

"Why did you come home? Better birds down here?"

On cue, something squawked. Not the barn swallows, who still sat docilely on their limb, bobbing their chestnut heads. Mason Winograd moved around her, keeping his distance. She followed him when he went out on the back porch. "I wasn't a photographer in New York," he said in a deliberately calm, quiet voice, crouching beside the cardboard box she'd seen before.

She went closer, trying to see inside. "What were you? If not a photographer." He shifted, making room for her, and she knelt beside him, peering gingerly over his shoulder. "Oh," she breathed. "Oh, the poor thing. What happened to him?" It was a bird, blue-gray, maybe a foot long, but it looked smaller all by itself in the big box. It had a thin strip of white tape around its body, and under and across one of its wings. "Did he break his wing?"

"Lawyer. Yes, a broken wing."

"What kind is he?"

"A kingfisher. I found him on the riverbank, trying to take off."

"And you fixed him?" It was a beautiful bird, all bluish-silver except for a pure white stripe around the neck and a white stomach. It kept opening and closing its long black beak. Mason unscrewed the top of a glass jar and took out a lump of fish, or at least it smelled like fish. He set it on the floor of the cage, but the bird wouldn't move, would only look at it out of its bright black eyes. Short-legged, all head and torso, it had an untidy crest of bluish feathers on the back of its head that gave it a cocky look, like a juvenile delinquent.

"Sometimes..." Mason said, and took up another piece of fish, smaller. Anna jumped, but he didn't move a muscle when all at once the kingfisher stabbed its pointy beak at the fish in his fingers and gobbled it up, throwing its head back to swallow. "Sometimes you have to get him started." After that, the bird hopped down clumsily from its tree-limb perch and devoured the piece of fish on the cage floor. Mason put down more fish, followed by thin strips of something reddish and bloody, probably beef.

"How did you get the tape on him? Didn't he move, didn't he flap around? Or was he unconscious?"

"I put him in the foot of a sock."

"You put him in a sock?"

"I cut the toe out for his head, another hole for the bad wing. It calmed him. I put a Kleenex over his head while I worked so he couldn't see me. Movement is what scares them."

"And then you—taped him up?"

"Under his wing there's a little piece of cardboard—see the edge? That's the splint. He had the simplest kind of break, between the wing tip and the outer joint. No broken skin, no infection. He never went into shock."

"Cardboard for the splint, that's amazing. And he'll be able to fly when he heals?"

"Should be. Know in a week or so."

He was on her right, kneeling. He reached down slowly, smoothly, to retrieve an uneaten piece of food, using his other hand to pull his hair back, out of his eyes. For the space of a second, she saw the left side of his face. Scars. Dear God, scars from his temple to his jaw, burled ridges of crimped, puckered skin, alternating livid and pearl-white, an angry ruching of flesh.

He looked up before she could look away. Whatever was in her face, he saw it. Shock? She hoped not, although she was shocked.

He put a screen on top of the kingfisher's cage and stood up, went back in the kitchen. Was he coming back? She began to think about what she would do if he didn't. Leave, she guessed, what else could—

He came back. With a lighted cigarette in his mouth, and he crossed to the screen door and leaned against the post, dragging on the cigarette and squinting out at the sunshine. She hesitated, then went close to him on purpose. So he wouldn't think she was repelled or afraid or anything stupid like that. She slouched against the other side of the door, leaning back on her crossed hands, mimicking his posture. "So, a lawyer. What kind?"

He glanced at her, glanced away. "Insurance."

"Insurance. That sounds . . . weighty. Did you like it?"

He didn't answer.

She went on as if she hadn't asked. "This job Rose wants me to take, it's not like anything I've done before, so frankly, I don't know where all her confidence is coming from. But I guess I've been circling around the business one way or the other since I got out of school. Once I worked as an assistant to the president of a restaurant supply company, so, you know . . . My last job, I was managing a coffeehouse, but that's the closest I've come to running a real restaurant. Anyway, I guess I've been coming around to it all along. Without knowing it."

At least he was looking at her now, not pretending she wasn't there.

"The earliest memory I have is sitting in the kitchen at the Bella Sorella and playing with paper dolls while women all around me were cooking, my grandmother, Rose, Carmen, even my mother if there was a crunch. So I guess I . . . " She wasn't even sure she believed all this, but it seemed important to keep talking. "I guess you could say I come by the profession naturally. Or you can't escape your destiny. Something like that."

He cleared his throat again. He must not talk much. "So you're going to take the job?"

"Yeah. For a while."

"Then leave." His crooked smile didn't look friendly.

"Yes, then leave. What's wrong with that?"

"Nothing. I'm sure you're good at it."

She straightened. "Wow. Who could you have been talking to?"

He held up his hands.

"Hey, you must think you know a lot about me."

"No."

"Well, you don't. Rose doesn't either, she just thinks she does."

"I'm sorry if I . . . " He paused, frowning, and she waited to hear how he would phrase it. She wasn't clear herself on what he had to apologize for, or why it had made her so angry. "Took something for granted," he said finally.

"That's okay. Forget it."

They stared at each other's feet for a while.

"Do you want to know what I've heard about you?"

She lied and said, "No."

"From Rose, that you haven't found where you want to be yet. That you're not satisfied."

She sniffed. You didn't need a crystal ball to figure that out.

"And from Theo—well, you probably don't want to hear."

"Actually, now I do."

"That you're going to be a troublemaker."

"A 'troublemaker'?" She saw that he was trying not to smile, which made her smile. "I can't wait to meet this guy."

"He thinks he won't like you, but he will. When he sees you." Immediately his face shut down, got grim around the mouth. He was embarrassed. Because what he'd said came close to a compliment? He kept his head turned slightly to the left, she assumed deliberately. But now that she knew they were there, she could see the scars easily, even through the protective curtain of his hair. What had happened to him? Rose would know, but Anna didn't want to give her the satisfaction of asking. Why had she sent her here in the first place, what was the point of disturbing this strange man's solitude? To fix her *roof*? Rose must think it would be therapeutic for him, get him out of the house or something, but to Anna it was just insulting.

"You know, I think Rose was just trying to help me out, just gave me your name because she thought you'd work cheap," she said with a laugh. "Obviously you've got better things to do." She gestured around vaguely; he had a sailboat to build, injured birds to feed. Anything else? "So what I'm going to do is get out of your way—"

"What kind of roof is it?"

"Slate. I'm going to—"

"How many stories?"

"Two and a half, but I don't want you to fix it—but thank you, you're very nice. I'll call a contractor."

He said nothing. He'd gone back to his tough-guy pose, arms folded, dusty feet crossed at the ankles. By now she was fairly sure it was a pose, but what he was trying to camouflage with it was harder to guess.

"Well, so. Nice meeting you. Mason." Some perversity made her stick her hand out. He had to take it, he had no choice, but first he started slightly—she'd surprised him out of his Marlboro Man imitation. "Nice meeting you," he muttered.

She went down the two wooden steps to the yard and started away. She hadn't gone far when she heard a light, metallic *snap*. She spun around. He was lowering his camera—which he'd never taken off his shoulder.

"Did you just take my picture?"

He put his hands on his hips, looked thoughtfully down at the ground, then back up at her. "No." Crooked shoulder, crooked smile.

She laughed, it was such an obvious lie.

"There was an egret over there, up in the tree." He pointed over her shoulder. "I took its picture."

She didn't bother to look around.

"Snowy egret, I think. But maybe a cattle egret, hard to tell from here. Gone now."

"When you get the film developed, you'll have to let me know. Which one it was."

"Well, if you're really interested."

"Vitally." She looked hard into his eyes, trying to make him smile again. No luck. Walking away, she listened carefully, but he didn't take her picture again.

6

"What's this, Rose? A suggestion box? I didn't know we had one."

Rose glanced up from the inventory list she was checking. "There's never much in it. Look inside."

Anna hesitated. "Should I? It's not private?"

"Yes, sometimes, but you're the manager, you get all the complaints now." She stretched her arms over her head with exaggerated contentment. "Not me."

"Where's the key?"

She found it in the desk drawer, and Anna opened the small metal box Rose kept on a shelf in the employees' closet. She took out a crinkled Post-it note and read, " 'Venezia. Vesuvio. Sorrento. Adriatico. Alpi. Padua. Genova. Napoli. Toscana. Billy.' " She looked at Rose blankly. " 'Billy'?"

"Billy Sanchez, the sauté cook. He was only in once this week, he's been sick, you probably—"

"The little guy with the toupee?"

"Oh, he'd hate to hear that. He thinks nobody can tell."

"Okay, but what's Venezia, Vesuvio—"

"Suggestions. I told you, there's a contest going on—name that restaurant."

"Oh, yeah. Do you like any of those?"

"No."

"Good." She picked out another note. " 'Dear Rose. What do you think of The Halfway Café? There must be something the Bella Sorella is halfway between. Love, Vonnie.' " Anna laughed. "Well, that's not too bad. Don't you love Vonnie?"

"I'd be lost without her. Is that it?"

"No, one more." She squinted. " 'I don't think it's fair we have to give Tony 15 percent when he's never around and when you do find him he's hooked up with Suzanne in the linen closet. This I have seen with my own eyes. Also last week Fontaine was late and I saw Luca punch her time card.' "

"Anonymous," Rose guessed. "Let me see." She glanced briefly at the cramped, ungenerous script. "Elise—Tony's her busboy. I keep her on lunches because of her attitude."

"That pale girl, practically white-haired? Goes on about how her true calling is fashion design?"

"That's Elise."

"Okay, she's a malcontent because she's not getting the money shifts—but Rose, what's going on with your pastry cook? Fontaine—is that her name? Really sweet, looks like she's about sixteen?"

"Oh, Fontaine. She has lots of problems." All having to do with men.

"Well, yesterday Vonnie told her some guy said the biscotti were soggy, and she burst into tears. She ran outside and wouldn't come back. She was heartbroken, sobbing, absolutely inconsolable. Finally Luca got her to come back in."

"Poor Fontaine."

"Is she okay? I mean, stable and everything?"

"She's pregnant."

"Oh." Anna sat down on the arm of the sofa in the tiny, cluttered office. "That would explain it. How long?"

"About four months."

"My God, she's a *baby*."

"She's not even twenty."

"Who's the father?"

"She won't say. As far as I know, she hasn't told anyone but me she's pregnant, so . . ."

"So I'll be discreet." Anna folded her arms. "You're sort of the mother confessor around here, aren't you?"

Her expression was amused, not censuring, so Rose smiled back comfortably. "I used to be, but I'm delighted to turn the confessional over to you. My worthy successor."

"Oh, no way, I'm just a novitiate. Nobody trusts me—why should they? I'm an outsider. A foreign devil."

She was kidding, but Rose took the opportunity to say something serious. "Strangely enough, that's not true. I thought it would take longer, but this has been, you must admit, an amazingly smooth transition. Vonnie said to me yesterday, 'It's like she's been here for *months*, instead of a week.' " Anna leaned over to wipe a smudge off the top of her shoe, so Rose couldn't see her face. "Don't you think it's going well? Seriously. Don't you?"

"Some things, yeah," she finally begrudged. "I can't say I'm getting a lot of cooperation out of Carmen."

"I know, but be patient. Sometimes she resists change."

"Ha! Let me jot that down."

Rose had to laugh, too; that was a bit of an understatement. "And what have you done to Dwayne? He's turned into a pussycat."

"Dwayne! My God, he scares me to death. I think he could bench press the walk-in." Anna put her hands on her knees, elbows out, and said in Dwayne's guttural grunt, "Not too fuhckin' *hungry*, were they?" and Rose cracked up. Dwayne had been with her for a year and a half—a record for a dishwasher—but he was temperamental. If a plate came back half full of food he'd had no part in preparing, he took offense. "Not too fuhckin' *hungry*," he'd snarl with real anger, genuine resentment. It was a staff joke; now everyone said it, apropos of anything. Except for Dwayne, nobody had gotten tired of it.

"But he hasn't even threatened to kill anybody since you got here," Rose marveled. "What did you do to him?"

"Me? I did nothing. He hypnotizes me. I just stand there waiting for him to put his hands around my neck and squeeze."

They were only half kidding.

"Sometime we need to get serious about cutting back on staff, Rose. You've got too many people working for you. I keep telling you."

Rose kept sidestepping the issue. If she stayed in the business till she was a hundred, she would never get used to or be any good at firing staff. "But you're going to turn things around any day now," she said, smiling cheerfully. "Then we'll need all our people and *more*." That was the tack she'd been taking with Anna, to jolly her out of the mood and off the subject of firing people.

"Shirl, for example. Right now you don't need a dedicated pasta chef, she's redundant. Luca and Carmen can do what she's doing—"

"*Right now*, maybe, yes, but as soon as things start to pick up—"

"Then you hire her back."

"Oh, I couldn't do without Shirl, she's too entertaining."

"Rose."

"Did you know her son is suing her?"

"Rose, you can't—Her son is suing her?"

"Her and Earl, Shirl's husband. Earl Junior, he's eleven years old—"

"Wait. Earl Junior is suing Shirl and her stalker ex-husband?"

"You didn't know this?"

"I—" Anna shook her head helplessly. "I confess, I did not."

Not surprising. Shirl, Rose's longtime pasta cook, a ditzy, round-bodied woman who dyed her hair a different shade of red every week, talked nonstop about anything and everything, but especially her unbelievably dysfunctional immediate family; it was easy to get lost in the stream of consciousness tidal wave and tune out. "Earl Junior's got a lawyer and he's suing Shirl and Earl for... I forget the legal term—"

"Insanity?"

"Being incompetent parents, in other words."

"I'm on Earl Junior's side," Anna said. "Let me know if he needs a character witness. Okay, if you can't part with Shirl, who's next most expendable? I'm telling you, you're fat and inflated, Rose, you need to get lean and mean."

"How about Eddie?" Speaking of lean and mean.

"No, no, he's too good-looking. He brings in the younger women at lunchtime, you can't get rid of Eddie."

"He brings them in when he's *here*, which is about half as often as I need him. Vince covers for him constantly."

"Yeah, but a really handsome bartender is worth almost anything you have to put up with to keep him. Who else?"

"Nobody." Rose folded her arms.

"Nobody? Come on."

"I need everybody else."

"No, you don't."

"I really think I do."

Their first fight. They watched each other with level, speculative gazes, keeping their polite faces mild. "Okay, well, we'll see," Anna said, and Rose tipped her hat to the vagueness of that. Not a threat, but not a retreat. A postponement.

"Okay, smoking on duty. Servers are leaving lit cigarettes in the ladies' room and coming back every few minutes for a drag. It smells like a wet fireplace in there, Rose, I've got customers complaining. Are we together on this? Are you with me that we're opposed to on-duty waiters stinking up the rest room during dinner shift?"

"I'm with you."

"Excellent!" Anna exaggerated her surprise—a little dig. Rose didn't mind. As battle lines went, the one they'd just drawn seemed pretty spongy.

• • •

Sunday night was staff meal night, "family meal," when the kitchen and floor crews took off their aprons or their chef's tunics and sat down for a late supper in the dining room. Often it turned into a party, especially if the last customer had left and there was no reason to keep the noise down. Barring drugs or obvious drunkenness, Rose tolerated all but the roughest carrying-on, because for her that was the point of family meal—to let hardworking employees act for a few hours as well or as badly as real relations. It boosted morale.

For all her good intentions, though, the long table usually ended up divided in half, kitchen staff at one end, waitstaff at the other. Another function of family meal was to try to blur that line, soften the traditional antagonism between the two sides. But unless there was a hot love affair going on between a cook and a server, and usually there was, the invisible border stayed roughly intact. Business as usual.

Tonight the friction was mostly silent, which made it more dangerous. At both ends, stunned or sullen faces stared down at food no one could do more than pick at. Even Dwayne, whose supply of filthy jokes was normally infinite and unstoppable, wasn't talking. He sat with his massive shoulders slumped and his bulbous shaved head down, cleaning his nails with a chef's knife.

"If you were going to be raped, would you rather be clean and neat, like you just took a shower and washed your hair and everything? Or would you rather be dirty? Which would you rather, or would you care?"

Ah, Shirl. What would Rose do without her? She wished Anna were here so she could tell her, "I rest my case."

"Because last night I heard this noise outside the window of my building? And I'm like, oh shit, it's a rapist, and then I start going, oh no, my hair's dirty, and I'm worrying about how I smell and like that. Is that nuts? But I mean, even if it's rape, you've still got your pride."

Rose said in a bright voice, "I haven't heard any restaurant name suggestions in a while. Anybody have any new ones?"

Silence.

"I think of one," Luca said shyly, from the cooks' half of the table.

"No way," Dwayne protested, "he don't even drink. Sardine can't play."

Luca looked confused. "I can't suggest?"

"If you win you wouldn't get nothing, so what's the point?"

"What's your suggestion, Luca?" Rose asked.

He turned his dark, soulful eyes on her. "Is Italian restaurant, *si*?"

That wasn't as silly as it sounded. Rose had been advised to turn the Bella Sorella into an Indian restaurant so she could name it Curry Favor, and a steak house so she could call it Bone to Pick. "*Si,*" she told Luca.

"And soon it will be better, yes, because of many improvements?"

"That's the idea. That's what we're hoping."

"So—you name it *Adesso Viene il Bello*. Is good, eh?"

Luca had a flatteringly inflated idea of her fluency in Italian. "*Adesso,*" she said slowly, "I know that means 'now.' Now comes the..."

"Is a saying. Now is coming the fine thing, the most, the mostest..."

"Now comes the best part," Carmen said out of the side of her mouth.

"*Si, si.* Is good, yes?"

"It's nice," Vonnie said, and Shirl said, "Yeah, that's not too bad."

Luca beamed.

"It's too long and it's in Italian," said Eddie, the bartender Rose wouldn't mind dismissing; "Ever Eddie," the female bar customers called him. "Nobody could pronounce it."

"Yeah," said Dwayne, "why don't you just call it When the Moon Hits Your Eye Like a Big Pizza Pie?"

Poor Luca. He had the saddest face, droopy eyebrows shadowing tragic, deep-set dark eyes, long-lidded and romantic. Two years ago, just before coming to America, he'd lost his wife and three-year-old son in a car accident. He broke Rose's heart. He smiled at her hopefully, waiting for her verdict.

"It is a little long," she said gently.

"Hah," Dwayne gloated. "I knew she'd hate it. She hates everything." Luca wasn't the only sensitive one—Dwayne was still smarting because Rose hadn't loved his suggestion, Below the Belt.

The table lapsed back into gloomy silence.

Shirl rallied. "Do you think about, like, how you'd clean your teeth if there was a nuclear war? Say everything's gone, all the drugstores and grocery stores and you can't get a toothbrush or toothpaste or anything, forget about dental floss. I think about it when I floss, if this could be, like, the last time. You'd have to find something to get that white stuff off the back of your bottom teeth in front. I have a little pick I got at the drugstore, but if there was a nuclear war, what would you use? And hair, how long would it take before your hair got used to not being washed every day? Nobody would have on makeup, so that would be... except if you were holding your cosmetics case when the bomb went off, then you'd have it. But people would try to steal it off you, so it might turn out to be more trouble than it was worth. Plus it wouldn't last forever. So you'd, like, ration your mascara..."

"Hey, where is everybody?" Anna's voice, in the kitchen. She came around the corner, shedding her wet raincoat. "Hi, guys, looking good. What's for dinner, Dwayne's jockstrap?" Last week, Dwayne had breaded and deep-fried Luca's sneaker and served it to him—Anna's introduction to family meal. "Hey, Rose, hi, Carmen. Vince, my man. Elise, honey, no apron at dinner, it annoys the patrons. They're like, No wonder I can't get a cup of coffee, they're all over there *eating*."

Elise, who might give you the finger if you told her she had lipstick on her teeth, giggled and blushed and took off her waitress's apron.

Rose smiled to herself. Anna thought *she* manipulated people.

"Sit," she said, making room for her between herself and Carmen. "How'd it go? Find anything interesting?" Anna had taken the afternoon off to go to some flea markets and a restaurant supply auction.

"Yes, but I didn't buy anything. Yet." To the table she said, "Hey, I just ate dinner at Brother's, and I'm delighted to report the food was terrible." She frowned when all that got was a few thin smiles. "What's up? Why's everybody so grim?"

"A little bit of a setback," Rose said lightly. "Not the end of the world."

"But close to it," Eddie said from across the table, and reached into his pocket. "We are so screwed. Reviewed and screwed."

Anna looked at Rose sharply. "That thing in *City Week*? It came out?"

She nodded. "I'm afraid it isn't very good."

"It's beyond bad." Eddie unfolded the torn-out newsprint article. "Here's the headline: ALL GOOD THINGS MUST COME TO AN END."

"Here," Anna said, holding out her hand. She looked sick.

Eddie had long, silky black hair he wore in a ponytail, numerous piercings, a diamond-shaped dot on his chin for a beard. Handsome? Rose supposed he was, but he knew it—that spoiled his appeal as far as she was concerned. "No," he said, "I'll read it to you." He cleared his throat theatrically. "It starts out, 'Remember the old Gaiety Theater in the north end? Years ago it was an art movie house, with foreign flicks and independent films you couldn't catch anywhere else between D.C. and New York. Today, alas, the Gaiety is a strip club; naked ladies perform a different kind of act with fire poles, and the closest you can get to *La Dolce Vita* is a lap dance.' "

"Don't read anymore," Vince growled, "just give it to her."

" 'But at least the Gaiety still has some life in it, even if it's the sleazy, pornographic kind. Too bad the same cannot be said for the Bella Sorella, a downtown institution almost as old as I am, and that's saying something. But that's the trouble with institutions: they get older, but they don't always get better.'

"Wow," said Eddie, fanning his face with the article. "And that's just the first paragraph. He goes on. 'Let's start with the service, which veered widely, or rather wildly, on the three occasions I dined at this venerable establishment, between bored and foaming-at-the-mouth frantic.' "

"Three?" Anna said, stiff-lipped. "He came three times?"

"Don't read any more—" Rose said, at the same time Vince leaned over and flicked the paper out of Eddie's hand.

"Hey," he pouted, "just when I was getting to the good part."

Rose already knew the worst by heart, but she leaned against Anna's arm and read it again with her. The menu was "staid and uninteresting, and reads like Basic Italian Cooking 101." The salads were "afterthoughts," the tortellini with sun-dried tomato pesto was "bitter, and if you can get to the bottom of your plate you're rewarded with a pool of oil." The reviewer hated the service, too: "Rarely have I heard so many apologies from the waitstaff," he wrote, "but then, this one had a lot to be sorry for."

Anna moaned and reached out to touch Carmen's arm. She'd gotten to the worst part, Rose saw: "Chicken Carmen comes in a stolid, viscous white sauce, flecked with either red bell peppers or pimientos, it's hard to tell. And what Italian chef ruins lasagne? There's more meat and certainly more flavor in a package of Lean Cuisine than in this runny, pallid, over-noodled excuse for a spinach lasagne."

Carmen hissed, jerking her shoulder to shrug Anna's hand off. It had been a gesture of sympathy, Rose knew, a reflex; but Carmen's pride was scalded, and sympathy would feel like rubbing salt on the burn.

No, the worst part was the end, the last paragraph. "This is a restaurant that's taking up space. With all the talk of preserving our historic downtown from the predations of national chains and franchises, a visit to the Bella Sorella makes one long for nothing so much as a nice plate of rigatoni from the Olive Garden. Or—since the cappuccino machine seems to be permanently on the fritz—a double skim milk latte at Starbucks."

Anna lowered the review to her lap. She kept her eyes on it, even though Rose knew she'd finished reading. She took a soft, shuddery breath and looked up. Into the awkward quiet, she said in a clear, confident voice, "This is bullshit."

The table came back to life.

"Yeah," Vonnie said first, and then others chimed in, "Totally, it's complete bullshit!" and "Who the hell is that guy, anyway?" Anger was better than despair, and Rose was happy to acknowledge a lot of vicious swearing she would ordinarily discourage by pretending not to hear.

"Maybe not *total* bullshit." Anna caught Rose's eye for a second, but the message wasn't clear, Rose didn't know what she was asking for. Permission, she realized, when Anna stood up and said, "You know what this calls for? Champagne. Vince, you and Eddie, would you get us some glasses? And two, no, make that *three* bottles of Schramsburg." She glanced at Rose again, who swallowed and managed to say, "Absolutely," with a carefree smile. What the hell.

Anna stayed on her feet after the glasses were poured. No one drank; they knew she was going to make a toast. "Okay, here's what we're drinking to. Well, wait—first of all, I want to say—this guy is a jerk. There's no question about it," she continued over exclamations of agreement, "we are dealing here with a complete dickhead. The problem is—the problem is, even dickheads get something right once in a while, and this guy Gerber might have ID'd a couple of things we could possibly improve on. Am I right?"

Yeah, maybe, they agreed, yeah, she could be right.

"So now what are we going to do about it? First, let's drink to this moment—because this is the absolute lowest we're going to go. I think that's worth commemorating, don't you? Everybody with me?" She raised her glass. "To the absolute worst it's ever going to get at the Bella Sorella."

Cheers, and everyone drank.

"God, that's good," Anna said in a different voice, an awed aside that got another laugh. "Okay—and now what's the next thing we're going to do?"

Dwayne belched lustily. "Three more bottles."

"Take Tuesday off!"

"No, the next thing, we're going to sit down together, all of us, and figure out how to fix this. I think it's safe to say some changes are going to be made. Not because of this review—this guy can kiss my ass." She touched the newspaper clipping to a lit candle and held on until the flames almost burned her fingers. "Not because of that article," she repeated when the hoots and cheers died down. "It makes a point or two we'll take under advisement—but we want this place to prosper for better reasons than so Mr. Head Up His Ass will like us. For one thing, we want it for Rose."

Heartening applause. Dwayne banged his gigantic fists on the table, upsetting a glass.

"And for Carmen, who doesn't deserve the crap in that pile of ashes. And we want it for *us*, because we have pride in our work and we're good at what we do and we're not taking this lying down. On Tuesday—on Tuesday, we're going to meet, all of us, meet for an hour at four o'clock. Don't worry, you'll get paid. We'll do it in splits, lunch shift can leave at four forty-five, dinner crew comes in half an hour early—that way we overlap and nobody gets screwed. But I want front and back, kitchen and dining room, I want everybody but the part-timers—because this is where we're going to let our hair down, guys, really figure this thing out. I know you've all got good ideas, and Rose and Carmen and I want to hear them."

Rose nodded and said, "Yes, absolutely, yes." At least Carmen didn't snort or roll her eyes.

"This is only a start, and you know I'd be lying if I said it's going to be easy. I see a lot of work ahead. So anybody who's not interested in working hard, now's your chance to go for that job over at the Olive Garden. Last toast." She raised her glass again. "To us. To us, and to the Bella Sorella. And to success."

"That's three," Eddie pointed out.

They drank.

"You can hire all the new line cooks you want, it's not going to make a miracle happen."

"Did I say 'miracle'?" Anna turned her back on Carmen to ask Rose. "Did you ever hear me say 'miracle'?"

"We've got enough cooks," Carmen went on, "too many; if you hire someone new you'll have to fire somebody else to make room. I'm telling you, a new cook is not the answer."

Anna studied her hands.

"No," Rose said calmly, "of course, not the ultimate answer, but maybe it's someplace we could start. I don't like to see you working so hard, and this would help take some of the load off. *If* we found someone you liked and trusted."

Carmen smirked; Rose's try at diplomacy didn't fool or appease her. Anna wanted to hire someone young and fresh in the kitchen, and although she was calling the job "line cook," what she really wanted was an assistant sous-chef. At the least.

"Move on," Carmen grumbled. "You know where I stand, we don't have to keep going over it. I'd like to get to bed sometime tonight."

The staff had gone home; it was just the three of them, still at the big table, sipping coffee instead of champagne. Rose had imagined this scene, Anna, Carmen, and herself at the tired tail end of the day, putting their heads together to think of fun, innovative ways to improve the restaurant. She hadn't thought to include animosity in her daydream.

"All right," Anna said, "we'll move on. I've been looking at some of these online sites that connect restaurants with suppliers. They operate like a co-op, that's how they keep costs down. We could be saving as much as five percent on basic stuff, food as well as equipment, maybe more."

"Rip-off," Carmen said. "Who are they? Strangers. It's taken us years to line up good suppliers we can count on. Local people, so they've got a stake in being fair. And freshness—how're you going to get fresh produce off the Internet?"

"How do you know you're not? How do you know Sloan's Seafood isn't *on* the Internet?"

"Well, that's something to look into," Rose said, "find out more about, because that would be interesting if it worked."

"Speaking of the Internet," Anna resumed after a strained pause. "Our Web site's primitive, it's not linked to much of anything, it's just sitting there. I can fix it, but it would take forever. Don't we employ any computer nerds? And we need to hook up to more sites that make online reservations and also put in a lot of hype for nothing, including your menu."

"Maybe Vonnie's son?" Rose suggested. "He's always playing with one of those game things. How old is he, Carmen, fifteen now?"

Carmen shrugged, not interested. "Food cost, that's all we have to talk about. Ours is too high. End of story."

Anna tapped her fingertips together impatiently. "That's the solution? Lowering costs? Paying less for the food we buy, that's how you see us getting back on our feet?"

"Whose feet? Whose feet is *our* feet?"

"Now," Rose said, "let's—"

Carmen cut her off. "I know a lot of recipes you'd love, honey, they've got all kinds of nifty, trendy ingredients, that asshole in the newspaper would wet his pants telling how great they are. If I made them, we'd go broke in six weeks. The food cost is too high. It's arithmetic, not brain surgery."

Anna made a helpless gesture and slouched back in her chair. "Fine. What's your suggestion?"

"Cut costs."

"And lower prices."

"Not necessarily."

"Oh, I see. So—" Anna closed her mouth, and Rose was glad; she looked ready to boil over. Keeping these two on speaking terms was turning into a full-time job.

"What was that you were saying about dividing up the dining area, Anna?" she tried. "You had a thought—"

"What is the point," Carmen wanted to know, "of cutting the dining room in half? What can you do in one half you can't do in the other?"

"Not in half, I never said divide it down the middle. And the point is *visual interest*," Anna enunciated too clearly. "It *looks* better. The diner thinks he has a choice—I can sit here, or I can sit there. One side's for smoking, too—all you've got separating the sections now is space. Which is wasted."

"What do you want to break it up with," Carmen snarled, "a potted palm?"

"No, something airy, and if possible something *useful*." She turned to Rose again, away from Carmen. "I found a piece of furniture in an antique store today, it's a beautiful old oak and etched glass breakfront or separator or something, it's twelve feet wide, I don't know what it used to be but it would be perfect right—there." She pointed to the area of floor directly behind the U-shaped bar. "You can't see through it, the glass is opaque, but the light coming through is the color of yellow topaz or amethyst. It's really incredible."

"It sounds beautiful."

"How much?" Carmen asked.

Anna drummed her fingers. "We're negotiating."

Carmen shoved up from her chair. "Now I'm really going to bed. I'll sleep like a baby, knowing what good hands all my problems are in."

When she was gone, Anna said a bad word and got up to pour herself a glass of brandy. "Want one?" she asked Rose, who said no thanks. "I don't either. She's driving me to drink."

"Anna, she's hurt. Try to imagine how that review made her feel."

"I know how it made her feel."

"She doesn't show it, but she's embarrassed. It was a blow."

"I know, and I'm sorry, but she's down on *everything*—I could say we ought to change the lightbulbs when they burn out and she'd find a reason why that was stupid."

Rose couldn't deny it.

"She wants to raise the health insurance cutoff from twenty-two to twenty-seven hours a week. *That's* her solution."

"I know."

"You're not doing it, are you? I'm for cutting staff, but I'm not for stabbing in the back the ones you've got. Think what would happen to some of the part-timers, they'd lose—"

"No, I'm not going to do it." Not unless she had to.

"Good. She's just . . . "

"She's just Carmen."

How tempting it would be to go on, sympathize more warmly with Anna's complaints, even add a few of her own. Rose resisted. But it was hard. Nothing brought old antagonists together better than a common enemy, and Carmen was such an easy target. Already Rose felt seduced by the promise of a closeness with Anna she'd tried not even to hope for, not this soon. They'd talked more to each other in the last two weeks than in the last sixteen years. She went around glowing, breathless all the time; Theo wanted to know if she had on "rouge."

"What is her *problem*?" Anna went on. "I mean, has she always been like this? You knew her when she was young—was she an obnoxious little girl, too?"

"No, of course not. Well—no, not obnoxious, but I wouldn't say happy, either. She was always heavy, not what boys considered attractive, so..."

"Were you friends?"

"Well, we were cousins, but the age difference was too big. We weren't really close as kids." Would telling Anna a secret about Carmen be disloyal, another way to set up that us-against-her model she'd just rejected? "Something happened when she was young—or not that young, in her thirties—and it soured her on men. Well, life—she was hurt, and it colored everything. She never really got over it."

Anna came closer, wide-eyed. "Carmen had a tragic love affair? Really? Okay, dish."

Rose smiled. "I don't know all the details. Her mother told my mother, who told Iris, who told Lily and me. A lot of it was hushed up because of the circumstances."

"*What* circumstances?"

"She fell in love with a priest."

"Oh my God." Anna pulled her chair out and sat down again.

"His name was Father Benetta—I only remember him because he was young and handsome, not because I went to church that often. But Carmen was devout, went to mass every morning. She was even on the rectory committee, ladies who volunteered to keep the priests' house clean and that sort of thing."

"Ah ha."

"You know, I don't think there was ever anything between them, not a real affair. Although I don't *know* that. I think it was one-sided, but I also think he used her."

"How?"

"By making her believe they were special friends, and that he could confide in her the same way she confided in him. He did tell her personal things, even that he was thinking of giving up the priesthood. Can you imagine the fantasy she must've built out of that?"

"So what happened?"

"Eventually he did leave the priesthood. With the twenty-five-year-old daughter of a parishioner—they were married within a month. He'd been carrying on with this young woman all along—at least that was the gossip—and using Carmen for a shield."

"Oh, Rose."

"It was very sad. She hid it, but she was crushed. If you asked her today, she'd say it never happened. That's how she played it then, too, so you couldn't comfort her. She pretended none of it mattered because she'd never had any feelings for him. She just denied everything."

"And then got sourer and sourer." Anna turned a water glass in circles on the tablecloth. "That's a sad story. Does she still go to church?"

"Oh yes."

"Wow. But still. None of that makes it any easier for the people who have to try to work with her. Right? I mean, it doesn't really excuse a lifetime of bitchiness, do you think?"

"I wasn't trying to say it did."

"No, I know." She got up, began to prowl the darkened dining room, straightening chairs, lining up ashtrays with bud vases and condiments. "What do you think about tables on the sidewalk after the weather warms up? We used to do that. Do you still?"

"No, not for a while. Carmen thought there was too much upkeep." She stood up, too. "Thank you for tonight, Anna, the things you said. It should've been me trying to cheer everybody up, but I couldn't seem to move. Before you came, we were sitting here like mourners at a wake."

"I should've asked you about the booze first. That was an impulse." She wandered closer, running her hands over the backs of chairs, restless. "Was it too much?"

"Not at all. Under the circumstances, I think it was inspired."

"I didn't know what I was going to say till I said it. And now we have to have a *meeting.*" She laughed a little wildly. "What will that do? I guess I was thinking action, doing something, even just talking about it out loud, letting people think they had a say—maybe it would help take the sting out. A little. Oh, Rose, that review was devastating."

It made her sick to her stomach. "This is more than you bargained for. I'd understand . . ." Then she couldn't bring herself to finish.

"What?"

"It's more than *I* bargained for, frankly."

"What, you think I'd *leave*?"

"It's just that this must be starting much farther back than you ever imagined. More trouble, everything worse—I'm afraid this can't be what you had in mind."

"Oh. Forget that." Rose's guilt seemed to cheer her up. "Yeah, it's worse, but so what? We made a deal."

"I'd let you out of it."

"Oh, you can't get rid of me that easy."

"As if I'd try."

Their smiles slid away, barely brushing, shy as moths.

"I like family meal on Sundays," Anna said. "It's a nice thing. I tried to get Nicole to do it at the café, but she'd never go for it. So every night the dinner crew just grabbed whatever they could find and ate it as fast as they could, sitting on milk crates in back by the laundry. Not even together. And the food was horrible, always overdone penne bolognese, they said it turned them into vegetarians. Anyway—it's nice. A good tradition. I'm glad you still have it."

A compliment. Rose kept her smile within bounds, but inside she basked.

"It's late." Anna found her raincoat and put it on. "Are you leaving? I'll go out with you, I've got my car in the alley."

"I'm going to run upstairs for a minute. Check, just make sure she's all right." Carmen lived by herself in the small apartment Rose sublet to her over the restaurant.

"Oh. Okay, then. Tell her I said... you know, just tell her, not straight out, that nobody thinks Gerber's review is her fault."

Whether it's true or not, Rose could see Anna struggling not to add. "That's nice. I'll be sure to tell her."

"Okay. Night."

"Oh, Anna, I forgot—Iris is coming to town tomorrow."

"Great, I can't wait to see her. I've got those interviews in the afternoon, but we can have lunch."

"No, she can't make it until late, something about the dogs, one isn't weaned or something, and her sitter can't come until the afternoon."

Anna laughed. "Thirty miles away, and I only see my aunt between litters."

"But she's staying the night. At my place," Rose said casually, "so I was thinking you might like to come over for dinner? If you're not busy."

Trapped. She wouldn't want to come to the apartment—too personal, too informal. It would imply all sorts of things that weren't true. "Well, I've got those interviews," she hedged. "They might run late, and I wouldn't want to hold you up."

Flimsy, very flimsy. "Come late, then. If you can't make dinner, come for dessert. Vince will be there."

Anna stared at the floor, hands deep inside the pockets of her oversized raincoat.

"You know Iris will kill you if she comes down and you don't see her."

"Maybe on Tuesday..."

"She's leaving early. The dogs."

She gave up gracefully. "Okay, then. Dessert if I can't make dinner. Your place."

Rose would settle for that.

7

Anna's third interview for the line cook's job didn't look any more promising than the first two. At least she wasn't obviously high, unlike the coked-up second guy with the twitchy chin and the googly eyes. This one's name was Mary Frances O'Malley—Frankie—and the logo on her T-shirt said GLUE SNIFFING WHACK JOB. She had dark red buzz-cut hair, a pierced eyebrow, and huge, haunted eyes in a pale, blue-veined, wren-boned face. As soon as she sat down she pulled out a cigarette, then muttered, "Sorry," and started to shove it back inside her beat-up shoulder bag. "Go ahead," Anna said, "everybody else does," and Frankie fired up a Salem Light with hands that trembled slightly, all the fingernails chewed down to the quick.

She was twenty-nine, her application said, born in Chicago. Moved here from D.C. a year ago. Divorced. Suspicious gap since last full-time job. "Why Italian?" Anna decided to ask first. Not all, but the majority of the chef work this woman had done had been in Italian restaurants, some of them high-end. "Why would Mary Frances O'Malley want to cook Italian?"

"It's Tarantino on my mother's side. My grandmother lived with us when I was little—she was from Lucca, which is in Tuscany."

"Yes, I know. My cooking side is Fiore," Anna mentioned, just trying to set her at ease. "They were all from the north, the Ligurian coast, around in there. So your grandmother taught you how to cook?"

"Yeah, she taught me everything. When she died, I took over all the cooking for the family, because my mother was a—an invalid." Rapid eye blinking when she said *invalid*; either it wasn't true or it was so painful she could barely utter it. "But I know other cuisines, I've worked in French and Spanish restaurants, I love Southwestern, I love California. I love food."

She didn't look like she ate much of it. Fast metabolism, maybe; something was always in motion, a foot bobbing up and down, fingers drumming, quick drags on the cigarette.

"What was your first restaurant job? Your very first."

"I used to work summers in high school at a resort outside Chicago, more of a spa, I guess, for rich women. Healthy food, organic, low fat. I bused tables and washed dishes the first couple of years, but by the end I made it to prep cook, and a couple of times I got to fill in on the hot line. I loved it."

"Why?"

"It was exciting. I liked the pressure. Feeling like I was in the calm place in the middle of a tornado. I ditched college after two years and went to the CIA."

The Culinary Institute, arguably the best cooking school in the country. Anna had made check marks at some of the positives on Frankie's résumé, but around the Culinary she'd drawn a big circle and an exclamation point. She'd hired two CIA grads at Nicole's café; one had been good, the other a screwup. The average kitchen worker harbored a lot of contempt for school-trained chefs, but if nothing else, Anna had always thought, a good school grounded you in basic technique and proper work habits. After that you became whatever you were going to be, but at least you'd learned the fundamentals from experts. It only stood to reason that the better the school, the better the training.

Frankie had worked a succession of jobs in better and better restaurants, her application said, first in New York, then Kansas City, L.A., Washington, D.C., and finally here for the last year. The high point was executive chef in an upscale French bistro in Los Angeles for nine months, just before she moved to D.C. Here she'd worked at À la Notte and Jimmy J's, but only for three months each. She hadn't worked anywhere at all since October.

"What kind of hours were you thinking of putting in?" Anna asked.

"It's up to you. I can work noon to ten, ten to ten, I can work six shifts a week, I can work doubles. Whatever you need."

"Uh-huh. You're divorced?"

"Yes."

"Any kids?"

"I have a little girl. Katie. She's three and a half, almost four."

"Do you have somebody to—"

"My ex-husband's got her. I get to visit." She ground her cigarette in the ashtray on her lap.

"That's tough."

"Yeah." She lit up another one. "What else do you want to know?"

"Tell me what you think your strengths and weaknesses are."

"I'm versatile. I can do specials, I can expedite, I've worked every station except pastry. Anything you need, I can do it. I've got moves, I work fast and clean, and I can improvise. I know technique but I'm not hung up on it, I learned it and went on." She stubbed out the just-lit cigarette and rubbed her palms on the knees of her jeans. "The thing about me, what you want to write down in the space for comments—for me it's all about the food. It's all I care about. I'm a cook."

"Okay. You know this is just a line cook's job, though, right? I'm not hiring a chef today."

"I know. Sure." She blushed.

"Right." But she asked anyway, "What's your theory of good food?" She hadn't bothered to ask the cokehead that question, or the guy before him.

"Freshness," Frankie said, no hesitation. "And simplicity. The best, the smartest place I ever worked was Federico's in K.C. That's where I learned everything that matters. They made everything fresh, every sauce, all the stocks, the pasta, the bread, all of it. That was the best food I ever ate. They even grew their own herbs in the courtyard. Nothing fancy, it was basic stuff, peasant food even, but perfect. It was just . . . sublime." She almost smiled.

Anna cleared her throat. Stupidly, she felt apologetic. "I wouldn't call what we do here sublime."

"Maybe it could be." Again the wisp of a smile. Behind the nerves and the bravado, Anna finally saw awareness. Real intelligence.

"Why here?" she asked. "They're hiring up the street at Figaro—why not try there?"

"I did."

She laughed. "Okay."

"But I like this place better."

"Sure you do. How come?"

"Well, for one thing, I heard you hire women. More than most places."

"That's true." Rose used to talk about an all-woman kitchen being the ideal, like an all-girl band, and she'd only been half kidding.

"And also," Frankie said, "it's not pretentious."

"God knows."

"No, it's neighborhood, but it's still a little nervy. You feel comfortable, but like it's still a cool place. Or it could be," she added, seeing Anna's skeptical face. "It's not rigid, so it's got potential.

Really, it could be anything. Sophisticated but not scary—I think that's just right."

Bullshit, maybe, but at least she knew the right buttons to push. Against her will, Anna felt snowed. "That's what I'd like it to be," she admitted. "I'd like them comfortable, but not so they fall asleep. I want a little edge. They come in and they don't know everything about the place, it could surprise them at any moment. But they're pretty sure it'll be a *good* surprise."

"Yeah, that's it. That's exactly it."

They considered each other.

Anna said, "We're about to go through some changes. To tell you the truth, we've got our backs against the wall. It's going to be hard, it's going to be like labor, and in the end this might be the last restaurant in town you want on your work history."

"I'm not afraid to work hard."

"Your career highpoint was the French place in L.A., where you were executive chef. If you came to work here, you'd practically be starting over. I'd like to know what happened."

"Ups and downs, you know how it is, it's like cycles, first you—"

"Screw that."

Frankie stopped massaging her knees and looked at her.

"Be straight with me. You haven't worked in six months. If I take a chance on you, you have to take a chance on me." Trust, she was talking about, and Frankie knew it, she got it.

"Okay." She stood up. *Popped* up, spring-kneed, propelled by nerves. "What happened was, I had some problems. In the past. There was some drinking."

"I see." Shit.

"But I'm straight now, I've been sober since November. I'm in a program, I'm doing the steps, I've got a sponsor." She came close, came right up to the desk but didn't touch it. "I'm turning it around. I have to, because of my kid. I need this job, but mostly I *want* it, and I know I can do it. I can work sick, I never miss, I never come in late—call anybody on that list, they'll tell you. I've never been fired, even at the worst. I quit my last two jobs, yeah, but they didn't want me to go. And I'm healthy now. You won't be advertising again in three weeks—I swear to God I won't let you down."

Jewel-hard determination blazed in the tough little face. Anna stared back, trying to see the truth behind the intensity, thinking Carmen wasn't going to like this. She hated American cooks; they were all lazy punks demanding *respect*—she always sneered when she said that. She was expecting Anna to hire some speechless, hardworking Ecuadorian or Dominican guy she could terrorize, not this white-faced, high-maintenance, overqualified gringa.

"You don't look very strong," Anna noted. "I need someb—"

"I am, though. Give me something to lift. Your chair—get up, I can lift it with one hand."

"That's okay, I believe you."

The T-shirt and holey jeans, the cheap platform boots, the piercings, the tattoo on her biceps—the longer Anna looked at her, the less Frankie O'Malley fit her clothes. They looked dated on her, not hip or retro. She was too old for the look, she didn't have her heart in it anymore. She was like someone who'd just gotten out of prison, wearing the clothes they'd taken from her when she went in.

"What do you do for fun?"

"Fun?" Frankie stepped back from the desk, frowning. The first question to stump her. "I run. You know, jog. Is that what you mean?"

"I don't know. Is it fun?"

She frowned some more. The question just didn't compute. But now Anna could see it—she weighed about one-ten but she probably was strong, nothing but raw muscle and nerve, no fat anywhere.

"Anything else?" she asked.

"Well . . . I read cookbooks."

"That's good. Anything else?"

"I don't drink." Her smile was a grim tightening of the lips. "That takes up a lot of my time."

Anna tapped her fingertips together, eyeing Frankie O'Malley—and that was another thing Carmen was going to hate. *Irish*, for God's sake. "Do you have a car?"

"Not right now, but the bus is close."

She nodded, thinking she wouldn't care to take the bus home at midnight to the address on Frankie's application.

"You could try me for a week. Trial period. I'll work for nothing for one week."

Anna stood up, embarrassed.

"I can't afford to do it any longer than that."

"Look, it's getting late, my cleaning crew's coming in and I've still got two more guys to interview."

"No problem." Pink-faced, Frankie grabbed her purse from the couch and started to go.

"Hold it, wait—I was going to say—there's no point in me showing you around the kitchen right now, because you haven't even met Carmen yet. You couldn't stick around, could you?"

"Yeah, sure." When her face relaxed, her dark blue eyes got even bigger. With hope. "Carmen's the chef?"

"Pretty much. We call her the sous-chef, though, because technically Rose is the chef. But I can't hire you without Carmen's okay. Naturally."

"No, sure."

"And Rose's," she added, but that wasn't the okay she was worried about. "Hang on a sec, I'll see if Carmen can come down." She picked up the phone, dialed the upstairs number. No answer. "Nope, she's not there." Where could she be? "But listen, now that I think about it, maybe you want to talk to Carmen tomorrow anyway, not today."

"Um, okay. How come?"

It felt like cheating, like giving her the answers to the test, but Anna said, "Because then you can go home and change your shirt. I gotta tell you, Frankie, Carmen's not a big fan of attitude."

She looked down at her chest, looked up. A shy smile spread into a grin. "No problem. I've got another shirt."

"What's it say?"

"Ass-licking boot sucker."

"Oh, much better. Carmen will fall head over heels."

After the last interview, after the cleaning crew left, after finishing her inventory, adding her list to Carmen's and calling in tomorrow's orders for her, Anna pulled her chair closer to Rose's cluttered desk and booted up the computer. "That machine," Carmen called it; Anna should spend more time on the floor and less on that machine if she wanted to improve business, that was Carmen's advice. Anna couldn't wait to tell her about her latest online find—a local computer dating service called "It's Only Lunch." She had some great ideas for attracting couples to the Bella Sorella when they hooked up for that first lunch date. Right now, though, she wasn't cruising the Net for contacts or checking out the competition's Web sites. She was just reading her e-mail.

Aha. A note from Mason. Very short. It made her laugh.

```
Dear Anna,
Your puny threat doesn't scare me. You are invited
to come over and discuss your bill at any time.
                                            M.W.
```

They'd been writing to each other. Did that amaze him as much as it did her? Polite, businesslike notes at first, but lately, real letters. It was fun. Addictive.

She scrolled down and reread their correspondence in order, bottom to top.

Dear Mason Winograd,

I've tried to call, but I can never seem to catch you in. Rose gave me this e-mail address and said you wouldn't mind if I wrote—to thank you for fixing my roof. You left without a trace, I wouldn't even have known you'd been there, but my neighbor saw you on Saturday with your ladder, etc., and said she spoke to you. I particularly wanted to call you on Monday night, after it rained and not a single drop leaked down the wall in the second-floor bathroom. If you haven't already sent a bill, could you please post back and let me know how much I owe you? Thank you again for your excellent work, and for your trouble. I'm sure it was an imposition, and am sorry if, because of Rose, I somehow put you on the spot. In any case, you were very kind to help out a stranger.

Best regards,

Anna Catalano

P.S. How is the kingfisher?

Dear Anna Catalano,

Was lucky and found box of original shingles in your garage, so didn't need to buy any. Hence, no charge. Glad to hear patch is working.

Kingfisher much cheerier after splint and tapes removed yesterday, although not as ready for flight as he thinks. Another week of captivity, I expect. Then freedom.

M. Winograd

Dear Mason,

Don't be ridiculous. Please tell me how much I owe, and make it a fair price or I'll be angry. I've seen but not yet had the courage to go into my garage, so I think it's highly likely you wasted at least half a day in there hunting for shingles. Now tell me what I owe you.

Anna

Dear Anna,

I forgot to tell you, you have a nest of phoebes in the section of gutter over your back door. I counted four white eggs. Your neighbor spoke to me at considerable length about your renovation plans and mentioned, among many other things, that you intended to replace your gutters. If that's true, you might like to postpone until approx. mid-June. But then you'd want to do it fairly quickly, as phoebes sometimes use the same nest for a second brood not long after they've fledged the first. Just a thought.

M.

Dear Mason,

I'm sorry you got waylaid by my neighbor. Mrs. Burdy is a lovely woman, but I remember my mother hissing at me when she'd see her coming up the walk, "Tell her I'm at the store, tell her anything!" just to avoid an hour-long gossip.

Postponing the gutters won't be any hardship. There's quite a lot of flying in and out of that area right now, so I guess the phoebe eggs must've hatched. I can't say I like their song much, but it is thoughtful of them to say their own name, however shrilly and repetitively; so much easier to identify them that way. More birds should do it, imo.

Anna

Dear Anna,

Mrs. Burdy kept me company while I repaired your roof. Standing at the bottom of the ladder, I should say, not actually beside me on the roof. Consequently, you should know that there's hardly anything about your family, infancy, childhood, and young adulthood to which I have not been made privy. Including the time you, age four, rolled the family car down the driveway and into the garage. (In my shingles search, I had already noticed the damage to the back wall; very impressive.) So please don't apologize to me for Mrs. B., who I found to be a most agreeable and informative companion.

Mason

Dear Mason,

I was six, and it wasn't the family car, it was the car my father's company lent him to drive around four states and the District of Columbia in his job as a book and magazine sales rep. And if you think the garage dent is impressive, you should've seen the car. I, as of course Mrs. Burdy will have told you, was unscathed.

Anyway, that's nothing—I found an archived interview of you online at the newspaper's Web site, and now there's nothing about you I don't know. Including that you're a celebrity. The cover of *Audubon*, no less, not to mention a published book. *That's* impressive. Rose didn't tell me you were famous, I had to find out by accident. Frankly, and I hope you won't take this the wrong way, I thought you were a hermit. Which reminds me. About the bill: don't make me come over there and get it.

There, the ultimate threat. I believe that should do it.

Anna

But no, she was invited to come and discuss the bill at any time. Ha! Well, maybe she would, call his bluff, see how he liked it. At least he hadn't minded the hermit crack. She'd worried about that, hoped it wasn't too personal. She'd meant it, though, hadn't really been joking, and she'd been hoping he would respond to it somehow. Explain himself.

The newspaper article about him was fascinating; she'd printed it out so she could reread it. He'd been the subject of "Sunday's Profile," a weekly feature in the arts and entertainment section, about this time last year. The author, a woman, had gone on at length about his "brooding looks" and "laconic manner." There were two reproduced photographs he'd taken of a clapper rail and a pied-billed grebe, but no picture of him. The thrust of the story was that right here in our little town we had a well-known, highly respected bird photographer and conservation writer, whose latest achievements were a published book and a photo and print essay on the decline of migrating waterfowl on the Chesapeake in *Audubon* magazine. Local boy makes good. Only about five hundred people in the world made their living entirely from nature or wildlife photography, and Mason Winograd was one of them. His father had been a Navy test pilot, killed in a plane crash when Mason was five, his mother an elementary school teacher whose second marriage, when Mason was eight, was to "a waterman." Theo, presumably. His mother must be dead or divorced, then, since Theo and Rose were an item. The article went on about how he'd photographed birds all over the world until four years ago, when he'd begun to concentrate and focus exclusively on the Chesapeake. The writer had missed the real story, to Anna's mind, or else Mason had been so *laconic* she couldn't pull it out of him. In one maddeningly short paragraph she referred to "a serious accident" nine years ago that had "left scars" and cut short his law career, "causing Winograd to reevaluate what he wanted to do with his life." Photograph birds, which he'd been doing as an amateur since childhood, she wrote—but what kind of an accident, and how exactly had it shaped his decision, and why didn't he answer his phone, why didn't his house have any front windows. That's what Anna wanted to know. For starters. She could ask Rose, of course. But she didn't want to.

Dear Mason,
Thank you—maybe I'll take you up on your invitation. I don't think you're ever going to send me a bill, though, so here's a compromise. Come to the Bella Sorella and be my guest for dinner. Any night but Monday, when we're closed. The payment won't be equal, but I think we know whose fault that is.

A.

P.S. If you say no, I'll assume it's because you read yesterday's hatchet job in *City Week*. We're still bleeding.

She hit Send, then automatically checked her incoming mail one last time. Oh—another note from Mason! He'd sent it before he got hers.

"P. S.," he wrote. "That fellow Gerber, did you know he's a well-known pedophile, wife beater, and crack addict? Some say—but this can't be confirmed—also a Republican."

Anna put her hands over her mouth and stared at the screen. She snickered through her fingers, but her eyes stung; she could've cried just as easily. She had pushed the awful review to the back of her mind, because thinking about it made her crazy. Hot anxiety came rushing back now, reminding her of just how much trouble they were in. But Mason's silliness was a comfort. What a nice thing to say.

She wanted to send a note back, something clever and grateful, something to make *him* laugh. He might be online right now—they could have a real-time conversation if she hurried. But she looked at her watch and saw it was after eight—she had to log off, lock up, and go, otherwise she'd be late for dessert at Rose's.

8

"Child," Aunt Iris greeted Anna, "oh, look at you. Oh my, oh my." She gathered her into a rough, crushing, long-armed embrace. "I gave up thinking I'd ever see the day."

"Hi, Aunt I," Anna said, misty-eyed in spite of herself.

"Gave up hope. And here you are. Home at last."

"Home for a while," she corrected out of habit. "How are you? You look just the same." Like a frontierswoman, the tough-skinned, bony-butted kind who sat in front of the wagon and drove across the dusty desert, squinting and not complaining. She even wore her ginger-gray hair in braids on top of her head. She was the oldest and plainest Fiore sister, she'd never had Rose's elegance or Lily's feminine prettiness. In Italy, she'd have been the one who worked in the olive groves with the men, brown as a nut and wiry as a vine.

"Oh," she said, "I miss my puppies, but I'm glad to be here, glad to see Rose. And *you*. Oh, *honey*." Another squeeze, even harder. "I know, don't tell me, but it's better than cats."

Anna frowned, thinking about Broadway, Broadway and Aunt Iris—

"If I have to get old and ga-ga, it's better that I raise dogs than cats."

Ah.

"You're late," she went on, drawing Anna into Rose's living room, "so you missed Vince, he had to leave right after we ate. He had a date."

"Vince always has a date."

"He's just like his father. I want that boy to settle down so bad, but I don't see it happening in my lifetime."

"Uncle Tony settled down." Anna assumed; she'd never heard otherwise.

"Yes, and that's the only thing that gives me hope for Vincent. Anna, he's so glad you're back."

"Vince is one of the best things about being back." She put an affectionate hand on her aunt's arm, thinking they'd go out on the balcony together—she could see Rose and somebody else out there in the candlelit dusk, a man; she'd thought it was Vince, but obviously not. But Aunt Iris stayed where she was, leaning toward her, lowering her voice.

"We're having an *incident*," she said, cutting her eyes to the side. "Theo fell down just now, lost his balance and went right over backward. He hurt his head and it's bleeding, but he won't let Rose call the doctor. They're fighting."

Anna looked again at the silhouette of a thick-shouldered, shaggy-haired man, sitting bolt upright with his hands on his chair arms. And Rose, bending over him, in his face, talking to him fast and low. He wasn't talking back.

"She wants him to stay here tonight, but he won't, absolutely refuses, says he's going back to his boat. Rose said she's not taking him, so he called his son, stepson, and he's on his way. You know Rose doesn't get mad that often, but she is fit to be tied. I think she'd like to knock him over again."

"Well," said Anna, nonplused.

"It happened so fast—he was coming back from the bathroom and he just sort of stopped in the middle of the living room like he was stuck. Next thing you know, he's flat on his back on the floor. His head missed the rug and hit on the wood, he got a real *crack*."

"Is he okay?"

"Who knows? I think, I *hope*, it's mostly his pride."

Rose came in from the balcony. Her face was pink, eyes wide and glittery. "Anna," she said, unnaturally gay, "you're here! Come and meet Theo."

"Hi, Rose. Are you sure? We can do this another—"

"No, no, he's fine, he's perfectly all right! What's a little blood, what's a lump on the head the size of a kiwi? Nothing at all, not to a real man!"

Anna came closer, staring, fascinated. "You okay?"

Rose growled instead of answering, opening her eyes even wider and drawing her lips back, showing clenched teeth. She was livid. Anna couldn't help but laugh in sympathy, even though she didn't like being drawn over to Rose's side so quickly.

The bay view from the balcony was still intact, she saw with relief; no one had built a high-rise between it and Rose's three-story apartment building yet. A half moon coming up over the water glittered the blue-black surface in silvery ripples. Candles, flowers, dishes from dinner cluttered the glass-topped table, which was set for four. "Oh, sit down," Rose snapped at the man trying to struggle up from behind it, but he batted her hand away, glowering. Then he almost pulled the table over grabbing onto the edge of it while he rocked himself to his feet.

Anna took the dry, scratchy hand he held out to her. Theo squeezed hers painfully hard, even though his was trembling in spasms. He was stocky and thick-chested, shorter than Rose, with grizzled hair and a long, soft-looking gray walrus mustache. His leathery, beat-up face had a mug-shot quality that more than hinted at hard drinking and hard living, and not in the distant past, either. He had a blood-spotted towel slung over his shoulder, a bloody handkerchief in his other hand. He was a little scary. *This* was

Theo? A man less like the kind she'd always thought Rose liked—a man less like her father—she could barely imagine.

"I heard . . . a lot about you," he said haltingly, and he didn't smile when he said it. The words came out light and breathy—something else she wasn't expecting. He looked like a man whose voice would boom out like gunfire. Breathy or not, the message couldn't have been clearer: what he'd heard about her he didn't like.

Were they going to be enemies? She'd been prepared not to like him since Aunt Iris first mentioned his name. But she could see things were going to be a little more complicated. For her, anyway; apparently not for him. He said next, "Nice of you to come—down and put things right for Rose. Very—charitable of you."

"Theo," Rose warned.

"She'd be helpless without you."

"*Theo.*"

He pulled his lips to the side, only slightly chastened. His nose had been broken a time or two; it went off in two different directions, Z-shaped, from a rough bump in the middle. Prizefighter's face.

Anna said, "I've heard a lot about you, too."

"Yeah?"

"I heard when Rose first met you, you reminded her of Hemingway, only without the stupidity and vanity." Aunt Iris had told her that. Anna watched Theo's pale eyes, faded blue in the twilight, blink in surprise and uncertainty. Rose laughed. He didn't have a retort. "I also heard," Anna went on, "that you think I'm a troublemaker."

His lips were still strong and shapely between the two halves of his mustache. Now they almost smiled. "Who've you been talking to? Mason," he answered himself. "I mighta said that. But now that I meet you—" He paused to take a few breaths. "I can see you're sweet as candy. You wouldn't dream of—treating your Aunt Rose any way—any way but fair and decent. Right?"

"Oh, I've always treated Rose just the way she deserves."

A snarly sound came from the back of his throat. Rose started to say something, but he cut her off. "I always felt bad for meeting up with Rose—so late in my life. Least now I can see what she looked like twenty years ago. I guess . . . that's something I have to say thanks for."

Now Anna wasn't sure how to respond. If that was a peace offering, which she doubted, she didn't want to return it with snottiness. "Twenty-four," she corrected lamely. They stared at each other, wary and interested, and hostile, while Rose cleared her throat and rubbed her hands together.

The doorbell rang.

"I'll get it." Aunt Iris sounded relieved.

"It'll be Mason," Theo mumbled. He put his red-knuckled hands on the table edge and gave a graceless yank, clattering the silver and glassware. He was trying to turn around, but his body wasn't cooperating. A moment passed before Anna caught the signal Rose was sending with her eyes—*Go away. He doesn't want you to see.* She excused herself and went inside.

Aunt Iris was running water in the kitchen sink. Anna looked around at the empty apartment. "Wasn't that Mason?"

"He's outside. He said he'd wait."

"He wouldn't come in?"

Iris shrugged. "Strange family."

Outside, Mason had his back to her, arms braced against the balcony railing, staring down at the parking lot in front of Rose's building. He turned around when he heard the door open, and his guarded face opened up when he saw Anna. He looked amazed—as if he couldn't imagine a less likely spot for her to turn up. When he smiled, she had a sensation of familiarity, as if she knew him much better than she really did. The e-mails? "Hi," they said, and she widened the door so he could come in. But he said, "How's Theo?" and stepped sideways, inviting her to join him on the walkway. "Is he all right?"

So she came outside. "Yeah, I think so. He *seems* okay. Rose is furious, though, because he won't go to the hospital, he won't even let her call his doctor."

"But he's all right? He sounded fine on the phone."

"There was some blood, but I think scalp wounds always bleed a lot. But I'm not a doctor."

"This is how he is," Mason said, sounding resigned. "He won't come home with me, either. He refuses to move in with me or Rose."

"He lives on a boat?"

"By himself. It's not a good situation."

"No." If you had balance problems, a boat would not be a good place to live.

They stood with their arms folded across the cool metal rail, watching two women and a man walk across the parking lot and get into a car. Mason always positioned himself on Anna's left, presumably to keep the scarred side of his face out of her view, and she wished she knew him well enough to say something about that. Like, she couldn't care less.

At least he wasn't hiding behind his hair tonight. He fumbled in his pockets for something, probably cigarettes, but came up empty. Nervous habit. *She* made him nervous. She thought of him slouched in his kitchen doorway that first day, affecting carelessness. In fact, he'd been borderline surly. *Something I can do for you?* Tough guy, she'd thought, but not for long; since then, he'd been letting more and more of that cover-up go. She wondered what was underneath, what the last layer might look like. Not that you ever got to anybody's last layer.

"Theo's always moved around a lot," he was telling her, "job to job, place to place. He can't anymore, so for him the next best thing is to live on his sailboat. It's not moving, but everything around it is."

"Did he move around a lot when you were little?"

"Well, he didn't marry my mother till I was eight."

"That's pretty little."

"They split up because he was never around. It only lasted two years. He'd go away on steamer jobs, or barging, or just move down the coast so he could fish in new water. Always had to keep moving."

So by the time he was ten, Mason had lost two fathers. One every five years. "Is your mother still living?" she asked.

"No."

Stars were popping out in the last blue band of color over the treeline in the distance. In the street, a jogger and a guy on a bike passed each other and waved. Bugs milled in the arc of the floodlights beaming weakly in the shrubbery below. It felt like summer. "Is that a bat?" Anna asked, pointing up at a swooping, flickering shape in the almost-dark.

"Yes."

"I hear it's a myth that they fly into your hair."

"Usually."

She glanced over to see if he was kidding. Yes—she thought.

"Or it could've been two bats," he said.

"I just saw one."

"If it was a female, she could've been carrying a baby. They'll do that for a week or so, take the baby on their nightly hunting trips. Till it gets too heavy to carry."

Anna said, "Huh," an ambiguous sound, more acknowledgment than interest. That *was* interesting, but what if birds and bats were Mason's only topic of conversation, his only subject? Then it wouldn't be wise to encourage him. For some reason she thought of Jay's rusty steel sculpture around the bed in the loft, the pretty painted birds with human heads, grinning, deranged. Mason fed wounded birds by hand, put cardboard splints on their broken wings, let babies roost in his kitchen window.

But she didn't want to compare them. That was too easy, and potentially a trap. She wasn't in the right frame of mind to be fair, and anyway, next to Jay any man would look like a prince.

She moved an inch closer to Mason. "Remember when you said Theo would like me once he met me?"

He leaned closer too, expectant, nodding already, ready to be vindicated.

"Boy, were you wrong. He can't stand me."

"No. No." He shook his head positively. "That's not right." If nothing else, his disbelief was flattering.

"Ask him. Not that it matters," she added, lest he think she cared. "I'm just telling you."

They both glanced back through the open door. They could see Theo in the living room with Rose, saying good night to Aunt Iris.

"The thing about my stepfather," Mason said hurriedly, "is that he's very protective of Rose."

"So?"

"So, he..."

"Wants to save her from me," she finished when he wouldn't. "Yes, I got that. What I can't figure out is what he thinks I'm going to *do* to her. Steal her money? Run the business into the ground?"

"No, of course not. You really don't know?"

She knew, but she shrugged. "What?"

"Leave."

She laughed, feigning incredulity. "He's afraid I'll *leave*?" But Mason didn't laugh with her, wouldn't even put on a sympathetic facial expression. He was in league with them—she'd forgotten that for a second. She liked him and she thought he liked her, so she'd momentarily lost sight of the fact that they weren't on the same side.

Theo and Rose came outside.

"Ready to go?" Mason put his hands in his pockets and moved closer to his stepfather. "Everything okay?"

"Everything's fine," he said, impatience making his whispery voice crack, "nothing the matter with me. Tripped on the goddamn rug, it's got a—rough place. What I oughta do is sue. Got a bump on the head. Doesn't even hurt."

"Because your head's so hard," Mason said, and Theo almost smiled, liking that. They didn't touch; a pocket of air seemed to separate them, an invisible buffer they had to keep between them. Mason hovered, but didn't touch; Theo accepted, but didn't reach out. A man thing, Anna decided—except Rose was doing it too. Apparently nobody was allowed to touch Theo.

Rose hadn't softened to him yet, though. "I'll go down with you," she said brusquely. "Anna, come with us?"

So they all went down the two half-flights of open concrete stairway, Mason first, then Theo, holding on to the banister and moving slowly, one heavy footstep at a time, Rose beside him but not touching. Anna in the rear.

Mason's yellow Jeep was in the visitors' space by the road. Anna said, "I'm glad we met," to Theo, but didn't offer her hand; she didn't feel like getting it crushed again. "I hope I see you again soon."

He said it back, suspiciously, and after he turned away she couldn't resist raising her eyebrows at Mason. *See?*

"Did you get my last e-mail?" she asked him, while Rose went around to the passenger side with Theo.

"Which one?"

"The one inviting you to dinner."

He stared down grimly at his hand on the door handle, thumbing the lock mechanism, making a *click* sound over and over. "You don't have to do that."

She laughed. "I know I don't have to."

"No charge for the roof. I told you, we're even."

"You don't want to have dinner with me?"

He looked up, alarmed. "Sure. Yes."

"Great, name the night."

"It's difficult—my schedule—I'll be out of town, I'm shooting at Assateague and then Blackwater. There's a program, I have to talk, and then on the Pocomoke. It's a very busy season, spring, hard to say a time—but thank you for the invitation, maybe sometime—"

Rose came to his rescue, by slamming Theo's door and coming around the back of the car to join them. Anna looked on in dull surprise when she hugged Mason in the most natural, warmhearted way, as if they did it often. Old friends. A sour feeling spurted through her. Not jealousy, exactly; more like resentment, its ugly cousin.

"I'll get him in bed and settled down," he told Rose in a soft voice. "I'll stay with him for a while before I go, make sure he's okay. Try not to worry."

"Can *you* not worry?" she snapped back, fierce.

He bent his knees to see into her downturned face. "Do you want me to call you later?"

"No, don't. I'm going to bed."

He glanced at Anna, but she just lifted her shoulders. *Don't look at me, I'm not in this.*

She stayed where she was when Mason started the Jeep and backed out of the parking space, thinking she and Rose would wave and watch them out of sight. But Rose deserted her, strode off with her head down and her arms swinging, ankles flashing beneath the kicked-up hem of her long skirt, and marched upstairs by herself.

"You haven't had any dinner? Go outside and I'll bring you a plate," Aunt Iris told Anna.

"No, I couldn't eat. Let's just have coffee—you come out and sit with me. It's getting late, and we haven't had a chance to talk."

"You'll have some dessert, then."

"No, really, I'm not hungry."

"It's Rose's bitter chocolate truffles."

"Oh, my God." She went out on the balcony to wait.

Rose's apartment was aging gracefully. Fancier, taller, more expensive condos and waterfront villas loomed over it now, crowding it in, but it still had its busy view of the water, and inside it was still airy and uncluttered, practically stark. Anna could remember staying here after her mother died, days at a time while her father traveled on his business trips. She'd sleep on the sofa bed in the living room, terribly conscious of what a *sophisticated* place this was, mysterious, the ultimate to her at fifteen or sixteen in grown-up female freedom. Rose would come home tired but revved up from a crazy night at the restaurant, which was thriving in those days, and Anna could usually coax her into letting her stay up even later while Rose told colorful stories about some amazing or funny or bizarre near-catastrophe in the kitchen or out on the floor. In those days they had the same peculiar perspective: that the Bella Sorella was where life at its most intense and real and interesting went on. Did they still? Anna didn't want to get close enough to her to find out.

But back then they could talk about anything, hour after hour. In warm weather they talked on this balcony, slouched at this table or side by side at the railing with their feet up, watching the lights twinkle on the inky water. Anna would tell Rose about school, boys she liked, teachers she hated, girlfriends who hurt her feelings, books that moved her, clothes she wished she could afford. To this day she associated the taste of Campari soda with a feeling of anything goes. Rose wasn't her mother or her best friend, she was a combination, with the bad parts left out—competition, disapproval, possessiveness—and the good parts left in—sympathy, indulgence, fun. Was it right or wrong to look back on that time from the perspective of history and allow what had happened in between to poison it? And if it was wrong, how did you stop it? What was the antidote? After she found out about the affair between her aunt and her father, she couldn't think of this pretty apartment as anything but a *love nest.* She'd reinterpreted Rose's attention to her as self-interest, her kindness as hypocrisy. She'd divided her life between well adjusted but deluded and cynical but clear-eyed. But what did clear-eyed really do for you? Couldn't it just be an excuse for keeping your heart frozen?

Aunt Iris set a tray of coffee and chocolate on the glass-topped table and took the chair next to Anna's, the one Theo had been sitting in. She wore gray slacks and a black sweater with a white check pattern, always trying to minimize the visibility of dog hair. "You don't want a puppy, do you?" she tried, and Anna said no thanks. "Poor Rose," she said, sifting sugar over her coffee cup. "That man's just breaking her heart."

Anna said, "Hmm," and then for some reason defended Theo. "Although it's not his fault he's sick."

"No, but he could take care of himself. It's a kind of selfishness, if you think about it."

"Is it?"

"Your Uncle Tony wasn't any good when he got sick either, but at least he knew when to slow down. Well, he had to. He sure didn't *fight* it like this." Aunt Iris's husband, a pack-a-day man all his life, had succumbed to lung cancer about six years ago. They'd had a wonderful marriage, but she couldn't speak of him now without a certain sharpness to her voice, a small, unsympathetic pull of the lips. She was still mad at him for dying, pretty much by his own hand from Iris's point of view.

"Tony wasn't so proud of his strength, didn't think of himself as a *physical* man as much as some do. Theo, now, you should've seen him when he and Rose were just starting out. He'd pick her up like she didn't weigh anything, like she was a *paddle* when he'd carry her onto that boat of his."

Anna tried to picture that. Couldn't.

"Strong as a horse, and proud of himself for it. It's who he was. Everything about him was big, even his voice, and this great belly laugh. Bit of a drinker, too, though I never knew of him to get drunk. Now, well, now it's just sad, and all Rose can do is watch."

"It is," Anna had to admit. "It's sad."

"I think she was a little afraid of him in the beginning. Which might've been part of what she liked about him," Iris speculated, squinting her eyes and raising her eyebrows. "He had rough manners and he dressed like what he was, a waterman. He certainly wasn't the kind of man you'd've thought she'd go for, and it worried me at first. She kept telling me he was sweet and gentle, but I never particularly believed it till I saw it."

"What?"

"Well, it was just a little thing. She had a party at the restaurant on Christmas Eve for the staff and her best customers, mostly the bar regulars—of course most of those guys were in love with her, which is why they were regulars. Tony had been gone a year; that's why she invited *me*, so I wouldn't be alone on Christmas Eve. She'd been with Theo for about six months by then, and you couldn't fit a match cover between them, they were at *that* stage. So who shows up in the middle of this party?"

"Theo's ex-wife?"

"No, his ex-girlfriend." Aunt Iris scowled, miffed at her for spoiling the story. "A bottle blonde in a fake fur coat, and she was *loaded*. Her name was Clarice, I remember, very hard-looking woman, and she wasn't a happy-go-lucky drunk, I'll tell you, and she was definitely not in the Christmas spirit. I saw the whole thing. She walked right up to Rose and Theo when they were dancing—oh, you should've seen his face, like Scrooge meeting the ghost of Christmas past, and she proceeds to make a *scene*."

"How exciting."

"No, it was horrible."

"That's what I mean, how horrible."

"No, Anna, seriously—she started screaming and yelling, curse words I never heard come out of a woman's mouth except in the movies. Rose had a band, and they actually stopped playing."

"Was Rose embarrassed?"

"Yes, of course, and poor Theo, too. The woman threw a drink in his face"—Anna gasped—"something else I've never seen in real life."

"Wow. I have." At Industrial Coffee, although not a drink, a hot hazelnut latte, and in a lap, not a face.

"As soon as she did that, it was over. She burst into tears and collapsed, that was the end of the fight." Aunt Iris bit into a truffle and washed it down with a gulp of coffee. "Oh Lord, that's good. Eat another one, you don't weigh enough."

"Look who's talking."

"The point is, the reason it's stayed in my mind all these years, is what Theo did after that. He could've hustled her out or ignored her or left himself, but he sat this Clarice down in a chair, right in the middle of everything, and knelt on the floor in front of her and took both her hands and started talking to her. I couldn't hear the words, and believe me I tried, but he just kept on and on, talking to her. She'd get all right for a minute, then break down. Once she got to hitting him with her fists, smacking him in the face and on top of his head—and he didn't do a thing about it, just took it till she gave out. He kept kneeling there, and him a big, heavy man, I can still see him switching from one knee to the other when one would get tired. When she finally got quiet enough, he took her home in her own car. He had to catch a cab back. Christmas Eve, this is."

"Was Rose jealous?"

"No, and there was no need, this poor girl didn't mean a thing to him. And of course who knows what all went on between them *before*—Rose might know, but I do not. But I'll never forget how he was with that Clarice, how kind and patient. I thought, if I ever had a man dump me, I'd want him to do it like that. Just a sweetheart.

"Anyway!" She made a shooing motion with her hand. "How are you? I hear about you—Vince says you're settling in like you never went away."

"Oh well. Not quite."

"Are you loving it? I knew you would." She beamed, smug. "I did, I just knew it. Isn't it everything you wanted? Back in a real restaurant, running it yourself, and it's all in the family, that's the best part."

"It's a job, Aunt I. Sometimes it's satisfying, sometimes it isn't."

"Oh, I know, but I'm just so glad you're here for Rose. This is a horrible time for her, and you being here, it's—"

"I'm not here for Rose. She's here, I'm here. We occupy the same space sometimes, but we're not here *for* anyone."

"I know, but—"

"No, don't make so much of it, okay? I'm working at the restaurant, that's all. It's temporary, and Rose knows that. She needed somebody, and I'm glad to help while I can. The timing is right for both of us, but that's as far as it goes, okay?"

"Okay." Aunt Iris held out her crepey arms and bowed from the waist sarcastically.

Anna pretended to think that was amusing. "Tell me about you. And your dogs. This is the best litter yet, you said. How come? How old are these puppies now?" Oh, she ought to let it go, let Aunt Iris spin her homecoming any way she wanted, quit throwing ice water on her hopes. What difference did it make? But she couldn't, and not just because of the likelihood of this conversation being repeated to Rose. She was bent for some reason on scrupulous accuracy, no shading, no rounding up in the interest of harmony and making nice. She'd come to believe it was her only chance of holding her own.

Anyway, the dog diversion worked. She drank sweet coffee with curls of bitter chocolate and listened to Aunt Iris rhapsodize about the most recent batch of genius puppies she'd gotten out of Hillary, the calm, stately Labrador retriever, and Ray, the sharp-as-tacks Border collie. Why did she mix them? Anna had once been silly enough to ask. Wouldn't she make more money by raising pure versions of one breed or the other? No, because people *loved* this cross, once they knew about it. Hillary was a honey of a dog, steadfast, loyal, and true, but not what you'd call *imaginative*—whereas Ray was so smart, he'd hot-wire your car if you weren't looking. Together, perfection. People paid a thousand bucks a pup, then came back for more.

"You sure you don't need a puppy, honey? In that old house all by yourself? Because for you—eight-fifty."

"That's so generous. Why don't you try Carmen?"

"Carmen? And one of my sweet babies? She'd probably fricassee it." They chortled, back on good terms. "Rose asked her to come over tonight, but she was *busy*." They raised their eyebrows knowingly. Sometimes Anna forgot that Carmen was Aunt Iris's cousin, too. "You two getting along okay?"

"She hasn't thrown any knives at me yet."

They kept looking back, through the sliding doors into the living room. Looking for Rose. Her absence weighed them down, kept their conversational subjects short-term and distracted. They talked about Vince and his succession of girlfriends, his indifference to settling down, and whether or not his true calling was tending bar at the Bella Sorella. He had a B.A. in psychology, and Iris lamented that he'd never used it except on his customers. They talked about her other four kids, Anna's cousins; she barely knew them because they were all older than Vince and mostly scattered. When they circled back around to dogs, Anna said, "Oh, gosh, it's getting late, I hate to go but I'd better. I'll just run in and say good night to Rose."

But the bedroom was empty. Sounds of tooth-brushing came from the closed bathroom door. "Rose?" Anna called. "I'm leaving—thanks for dessert! I'll see you—"

"Wait."

Clouds of fragrant steam billowed out when the door opened. Rose materialized in an old black kimono, open over a short pink nightie. Her hair was damp, her face scrubbed, eyes red-rimmed and bloodshot. Anna recoiled from a mental vision of Rose crying in the shower. The smell of toothpaste and soap and Jean Naté sucked her back to her childhood, mixed memories of Rose and her mother, tangled together so tightly she could no longer separate one from the other. She withdrew physically, took a step back from the siren pull of warmth and comfort, soft as a lap, or a woman's bosom.

"I better get going. Those truffles, Rose, my God." She wanted so much to make her smile. "Are you sure they're legal?"

"Take some with you, I won't eat them. Anna, I'm sorry about tonight. Sorry it was so crazy."

"Don't worry about it."

"He's not usually like that."

"Doesn't matter."

"It's hard for him." She sat down on the closed lid of the toilet, out of energy. Anna had no choice but to come closer, halfway inside the hot, steamy room. Rose leaned her back against the commode and stretched her legs out, contemplating her long-toed feet on the bath mat. "And he's getting worse. So fast. I didn't expect that. Nobody was prepared for it to go this fast."

"Maybe this is a phase. It could plateau right here, like a remission. Or even get better. Is that a possibility?" This was as close as she'd come to asking just what it was Theo had.

Rose smiled fleetingly. The fluorescent light over the sink illuminated every line in her naked, aging nun's face. "I hope. They still haven't told us what it is, not for certain. They said Parkinson's at first, then something called PSP. His brain cells are degenerating, that's as much as we know. It started about three years ago."

"How long have you been together?" But she wanted no part of this, this was Rose's melodrama, it had nothing to do with her.

"Five years."

So, since she was fifty-five and he was sixty, give or take. A December-December romance. Were there other sweethearts between Anna's father and Theo? Of course there must've been; that was a nine-year gap, and men had always liked Rose. Anna wanted to know about them, but she'd never ask. Already she could feel herself being pulled too far into Rose's world, and she hated it. Rose was like a spider, extending her web, reinforcing it in silence and secrecy. Before you knew it you were caught inside the silky, invisible strands. They looked delicate, but they were tough as fishing line.

"He used to carve things—he was a woodcarver. Beautiful things, it's how he courted me." She glanced up and smiled. "First with birds and ducks, they were his specialty, but then with busts of people we knew, friends we had in common. Then, figures of me. They weren't true likenesses, not like his other work. More abstract, just shapes, really. He said he worked with his eyes closed. Toward the end, they were just long, curving forms, very strong, very... graceful. Only vaguely human, you know, more like objects. Objectifications of me." She laughed. "Naturally I fell in love with him."

I don't want to know this. But she said, "What do you mean, toward the end?"

"When the tremors got bad. He can't hold a knife anymore. His hands shake too badly."

"Oh."

Mechanically, shoulders slumped, Rose opened a bottle of moisturizer and began to pat drops of it on her face.

"I think I might've found a cook," Anna said brightly.

She nodded, barely listening. Still remembering.

"Carmen's going to hate her, though. Her name's Frankie. You can meet her tomorrow, see what you think."

She nodded again.

"Well, okay, guess I'll go." Rose looked up, resigned. Anna hung in the doorway. "What happened to Mason?" she said instead of leaving. She hadn't been going to ask Rose that, for complicated reasons she used to understand. Now she couldn't even remember what they were.

"Do you mean how did he get hurt?"

Anna nodded.

"A stupid, senseless accident. Nine or ten years ago, when he was living in New York."

"When he was a lawyer."

"General counsel for an insurance firm, yes. Doing well, making lots of money, I guess. Engaged to another attorney. One day he was jogging in the park—on the sidewalk, the path, not on the road or anything—and a car struck him. It came right over the curb, trying to pass another car on the right. He was thrown up in the air—some horrible number of feet, I don't know, Theo tells the story better than I do. The whole left side of his body was just—broken. His arm, leg, shoulder, his face—he came close to dying, several times. He was in a coma for months. When he finally came to, they told him his mother had died."

"Rose, my *God*."

"His hair turned completely white—he's not going gray now, it's the dark coming back in. It was a year before he could walk, then months and months of rehab. Reconstructive surgery. He moved down here to recover, and afterward, he didn't want to be a lawyer anymore."

"The fiancée?"

"Long gone."

What an awful story. Anna had more questions, but a keen look in Rose's face kept her silent. For some reason, Rose wanted her to know Mason. Well, then. Reason enough to thwart her.

So she should've dropped the subject, but instead she said sharply, "You're not thinking about me and Mason, are you, Rose? Any kind of romantic thing, right? Because that would not work out."

"I wasn't thinking much of anything," she replied softly. Thoughtfully.

"Good, because neither one of us is interested. Oh, and I'm on sabbatical."

"You're still getting over Jay."

"In a way." Funny, though, how infrequently she thought of Jay. In fact, it was slightly alarming. "But mostly, I just don't want the trouble anymore, I'm too old for it."

Rose looked amused. "You're through with men?"

"I'd like to be."

"Because you're so old."

"Don't fix me up, Rose. In any way, I mean it."

"All right. Although I don't think that's what I was doing."

"Just so we're clear."

"You're very big on being *clear*."

"Yes, I am."

"I wish . . ." She sighed. "I wish there were ever some *good* news you wanted to be clear on."

Anna backed away when Rose stood up, afraid she might get hugged or something. "Okay, well," she said again. "See you tomorrow."

"I'm glad you came by. Glad you could meet Theo."

"Yeah. Thanks for dessert—wow, that stuff is incredible. How come it's not on the menu?"

"Too expensive. Carmen says."

Anna made a face, but Rose's answering smile was meager, just a reflex. All her troubles had come back to her now that Anna was leaving. She looked so slight and weary in her worn kimono. She looked like a woman anticipating a long night.

Anna, anxious to get away from her, said, "'Bye," abruptly. But then she reached out and touched her on the arm, the elbow, a swift little pat, embarrassingly stiff.

It startled Rose so much, her mouth dropped open.

Anna's, too. They must be mirrors of each other. For the first time in years, she didn't mind the resemblance.

9

Dear Anna,

I don't think I explained myself very well the other night. Spring is the second busiest time of the year, or else it's tied for first with fall, depending on your point of view, for anybody who photographs birds for a living. Right now any number of activities are going on around the Chesapeake because of IMBD (International Migratory Bird Day, second Sunday in May), and I'm set either to photograph migratory species or give talks and seminars on wildlife photography, conservation, ecological diversity, etc., etc., at Prime Hook, Patuxent Research Refuge, Assateague, and Deal Island. In fact, I'm writing to you on my laptop from the Starlite Motel in Smyrna, Delaware, where I'm staying while I shoot hordes of red knots during their annual horseshoe crab egg feast on Delaware Bay. I'm a busy man. Not a hermit at all. On the contrary, I'm a rolling stone. I could tell you many fascinating things about the red knot, but will refrain because of a certain glazed look I noticed the last time we spoke of birds. I'm sensitive to these things.

Mason

P.S. I apologize for my stepfather if he was rude that night. He repented slightly the following day, allowing that you weren't quite as bad as he'd expected. A handsome admission.

Dear Mason,

Handsome indeed! Tell Theo I thought he'd be much uglier. And that I look forward to a long, cordial friendship between us.

I used to go out with a boy from Smyrna. We dated for a whole semester when I was a junior in college. He was going to be either a microbiologist or a bluegrass fiddler, he couldn't decide. I used to be in a band myself. I played the hip, we used to say, meaning I banged a tambourine against my hipbone in time to the rock and roll classics we did our best to imitate. Our most successful cover was "Satisfaction." We felt the lyrics deeply.

What do you do, then, walk around on the beach all day with a camera? That doesn't sound like a serious occupation. They pay you for this? Seriously, it's good that it consumes you—I'm assuming it does. Most people aren't lucky enough to find their life's work, a job that's so satisfying they'd do it for nothing. How did you get started with birds and cameras? If I may ask. What is the most important quality a good bird photographer should have? And I deny looking glazed. That was my *rapt* look—I wanted you to go on and on about bats. What I'm learning in my new job, which I currently do fourteen hours a day, seven days a week, is that the point isn't to become so successful that I get rich—although that would certainly be a nice side benefit. The point is to find a balance. Someday. I think I'm good at what I do, but I could still fail. I'd like to succeed, but not if success means I can never get out, that the restaurant, this one or the next one, becomes my whole life. In fact, I think finding the balance *is* success. Not the money.

But on a good day I purely love what I do. In fact, it's hard to go home. I'll be bone tired, limp as day-old pasta, but still on some kind of endorphin high after all the close calls and near calamities, not to mention the real ones, the floor and kitchen catastrophes that take years off your life. To survive, to get through another night with no fatal wounds—I get this sort of war rush it can take hours to come down from. I always turn music on as soon as I get home. It's not that I want more stimulation, I just need to crash gradually. No wonder half the people in the restaurant biz are drunks or dopers. The insanity gets to you one way or the other, nobody's immune.

Oh, but I love it. Don't tell Rose. Do you love what you do? She told me what happened to you—I hope you don't mind if I bring it up. If you love what you do now, that's wonderful, but I still think you paid a high price for clarity. Was it worth it? None of my business—don't answer if you don't want to.

Anna

"What *is* that?"

Frankie looked up from adding hot stock to rice in a large sauté pan on the eight-burner. "What?" Her serious face flinched; she looked guilty but baffled, as if she couldn't figure out what crime she'd committed this time. Understandable: Carmen treated her like an ex-con. She was in early this morning, as she was almost every day, trying out recipes for the menu Anna was working on with Rose. And with Carmen, when she could be bothered.

"That smell, that fabulous smell," Anna cried, and Frankie's narrow shoulders relaxed. "It's not the risotto, although that looks great."

"No, it's probably the red peppers and eggplant I've got going in the wood oven. Taste this, though. It's not finished, but what do you think of the broth?"

Anna blew on the liquid in the wooden spoon Frankie held to her lips and took a sip. "Mm, chickeny. Yeah, it's really rich. How'd you get it so strong without being salty?"

"Bones. It's pretty good, isn't it? I'm making a wild mushroom risotto, although we've only got porcini and girolles. If I had chanterelles gris, say, and some trompettes de la mort, this would work better."

But Carmen wouldn't order them, Frankie didn't have to add. She'd consider that extravagant, frou frou, not worth the expense. Frankie was Anna's new ally in the war with Carmen, but her strengthened position had escalated the hostilities on both sides. Rose should've stepped in and made peace, but she was acting like Switzerland, clinging to neutrality at all costs.

Frankie glanced at the big kitchen clock. "Okay, you want to try some wood-roasted vegetables?"

"You bet."

Carmen complained the wood-burning brick oven Rose had installed a couple of years ago was more trouble than it was worth, that everything they made in it was either overdone or underdone, oak and mesquite cost too much, the cooks were always forgetting to add it or else putting in too much, the heat from the oven was too intense, the fire danger raised their insurance premium, and nobody ever ordered anything they made in it except pizza anyway.

Frankie said any restaurant that called itself Italian and aspired to anything more sophisticated than spaghetti and meatballs needed a wood-burning oven. It wasn't to be trendy, it was a matter of being serious about food. Wood-roasted vegetable side dishes were a *necessity*, she said, not a luxury, and in fact what they really needed was *two* brick ovens, one for bread and pizza, one for vegetables, fish, chicken, and meat. She was bristling with new ideas for their underutilized oven, but Carmen was still an obstacle. Anna thought of her as a monster eighteen-wheeler overturned on the highway, lying sideways across all the lanes, backing up traffic for miles in both directions.

"Oh, mama," she said around a steaming bite of stuffed red pepper. "Oh, wow. Okay, olives and anchovies," she guessed; "what else?"

"Capers. Garlic, parsley, lemon juice. I used red wine, but you can use balsamic vinegar if you want. What do you think?"

"I love it."

"You can make it cheaper with California black olives, or you can buy commercial olive paste, some of 'em are pretty good. I used Niçoise olives, but you wouldn't have to."

"Where'd you get Niçoise olives?" Anna couldn't remember seeing them in the pantry.

"I bought them."

"You bought them?"

Frankie turned red. She was skim-milk pale, white as a baby vampire, so when she blushed it was a high-profile event. Even her ears turned pink, as well as the scalp under her bristly red hair. The bones in her face and skull were so delicate, she looked like a hungry baby bird. But Anna had seen her lift a forty-pound stockpot full of water and bones with her skinny, ropy arms, and move a cast iron skillet around a flaming stove burner barehanded. There wasn't anything delicate about Frankie except her feelings.

"Yeah, I bought 'em. It's no big deal, I just wanted you to try this right. You know, the first time."

"Okay," Anna said easily, "fine, but I'll have to cost it out."

"Sure."

"It might be too much."

"I know. Here, try this."

"No, thanks, I hate eggplant."

"Try this. Come on, I guarantee—"

"No, I really hate it. Try it on Carmen."

Frankie laughed—a rare sound; Anna didn't hear it much in the kitchen, not from Frankie. She watched her inhale the steam still rising from a pan of eggplant rounds. She cut off a piece and put it in her mouth. She held it there for a second before she started to chew. It was fun to watch Frankie taste the foods she made; her face got comically concentrated as every other sense went out of focus, including her eyes. "Too much oil," she pronounced after swallowing. "Although it wouldn't be, or it might not be, if only we had—"

"I know, I know. I'm working on it." Frankie thought the olive oil Carmen bought for cooking wasn't good enough. It was extra virgin, but Frankie wanted Lucca oil, the most expensive in the world, and the best. Carmen said no, absolutely not, was she crazy? The usual.

Frankie's ex-husband's name was Mike, Anna knew from asking nosy questions; he was a history professor at the local junior college. They'd lived in D.C. until the split, after which Mike had moved here with two-year-old Katie. Frankie hadn't followed until six months later, and Anna theorized, on no evidence at all, that that's when the drinking must've been at its worst.

Frankie went back to the stove and resumed ladling chicken broth into her sauté pan of rice and stirring, stirring. Anna leaned against the counter and watched her deglaze the pan with stock. The smells were getting more and more irresistible. She stirred porcini into the rice next, then the soaking liquid, careful to keep the sand and sediment out. She worked fast, but she never seemed to hurry. Carmen made fun of her for always wearing a formal white chef's tunic buttoned to the throat, checked pants, clogs, and a cook's toque, no matter how hot it got in the kitchen. For these morning experiments, though, she relaxed her own standards and dispensed with the tunic and the toque. She looked like a kid, one with a lot of tattoos, in jeans and a tank top and a backward-facing baseball cap. She was tireless, a machine; Anna had never known anybody who could work so long without complaints or breaks or encouragement. She was starting to worry about her.

"How's Katie?" she asked her—a sure-fire way to get her to lighten up.

"She's great. She's terrific. Wanna see a picture?"

"Absolutely."

She kept her wallet in her back pocket, like a man. She slipped a couple of photos out of a plastic sleeve and handed them over. "These are from Easter. I took 'em."

"Oh my God." Katie, about three and a half, stood at the bottom of a flight of stairs in a seriously adorable Easter getup, a high-waisted pink dress with puffy sleeves and smocking on the chest, pink Mary Janes and pink socks, a patent leather pink pocketbook clutched in both chubby hands. Pink flowers in her hair, which was an amazing shade of pumpkin orange. "Oh, Frankie," Anna said reverently, "she's beautiful." She was, but her saving grace was that she didn't look as if she knew it. It might've been the freckles, which were everywhere, not just a dainty spray across her nose. Or it might've been the excitement in her eyes, a funny, knowing look, as if she was thinking, "How about this outfit! Am I cute or what?"

"I know." Frankie's tender half-smile was sweet, but also painful to look at. "Hard to believe she's mine, huh?"

"Not at all. I think she looks like you."

Frankie huffed. "No, she's got Mike's eyes and everything. All she got from me is that carrot top—I had the exact same color when I was little. Check out Mike, you'll see."

Mike was in the second picture, sitting beside his daughter on the next-to-last stair step, almost as dressed up as she was in a navy blue suit with a vest, a checked tie. Frankie was right, Katie had Dad's eyes, or at least the good-natured joke in them. He looked much older than the man Anna had been expecting; there was gray in his shaggy professor's hair and deep smile lines around his mouth. She wasn't sure what to say about Mike. "He looks nice," she hazarded, relying on the clue that Frankie had never said anything bad about him.

"He is." She stuck the photos back in the wallet, the wallet back in her pocket. She started beating shredded Parmigiano-Reggiano into the rice, stringy arm muscles bulging. "He put up with a lot of shit. From me. For a long time." She glanced at Anna, gauging her interest. Probably her trustworthiness, too. "I'm the one who screwed it all up," she said with her face turned away, beating, beating, adding more butter, now more cheese, putting her back and shoulders into it. "It was all me."

"I hate when that happens. I hate it when there's nobody to blame but me."

Frankie smiled.

"Maybe, you know, someday..."

"Yeah. That's what I'm working on, getting it back. That's what it's all about." Her pale monkey face looked sharp, almost ruthless with determination. "Okay, this risotto's done."

"Let's try it."

But Frankie wanted more ceremony than standing over the stove and taking turns from the same spoon. She got down two plates and spooned a serving of rice on each, adding a pinch more of the grated cheese on top. They sat on stools by the pantry, plates on their knees, and tasted.

"It's great," Anna said instantly, no hesitation. She hardly had to chew to know she liked it. "God, the mushrooms just explode."

"It's good," Frankie allowed, nodding slowly, more judicious. She took tiny bites and drew in air as she chewed, like a wine taster. "It's not really *doing* anything, but I guess it doesn't have to. It's more the texture I was worried about." She often spoke of flavors *doing* things. Sometimes she talked about food as if it were music: flavors had rhythms, ingredients had tones, high, low, medium, and when you arranged them together just the right way, they made chords.

"No, the texture's great. Really creamy, but the rice grains are still chewy." Anna's was all gone. She considered a second helping.

"It'll be a little different each time, but I guess that's okay."

"Depending on who makes it, you mean?"

"No, even if I make it every time. It's just never exactly the same twice."

"I wish Rose could taste this while it's fresh. Write down everything you used and exactly how much. We call it Wild Mushroom Risotto—right?"

"Well, that's what it is."

"How could Carmen hate this?" Anna wondered out loud. "It's real, it's basic. It's practically comfort food."

"You could call it Tame Mushroom Risotto." Frankie ducked her head, blushing again. It was the first time she'd ever said anything about Carmen that wasn't perfectly respectful. When Anna only laughed, she got bolder. "I know how to get her to go for it." She had a crooked eyetooth that showed only when she grinned, which wasn't often. "Tell her it's gotta be either this or my other risotto specialty. Fennel and vodka."

"Gag. That'll do it," Anna agreed, making a face that made Frankie laugh out loud.

Dear Anna,

I'm in Chincoteague. I just had an incredible morning. I'll tell you about it, and you can glaze over or skim through or ignore it altogether, and I'll never be the wiser. It's all about birds.

It's not crowded here yet, too early in the season, so at five this morning I was the only human at the best spot for shorebirds in this refuge, a spit of sand protruding from the salt marsh into one of the channels of Chincoteague Bay. But the birds were there already. I could just make out their silhouettes in the mist. Most were still asleep, heads tucked into their back feathers, sanderlings, dunlins, sandpipers. A couple of dowitchers already awake, foraging along the edge of the water. The only way you can get close enough is to lie down on your stomach, camera and telephoto in front of your face, and squirm forward about six inches at a time. You can also kneel and creep forward slowly, but I can't last at that for long—bad knee. Or you can sit and shuffle closer on your butt, but then you're not low enough, they can see you. No, lying in the cold wet sand on your stomach, that's the ticket. Eventually, you always get to a place where they notice you, even the calmest birds, and that's the critical time. If one spooks they'll all take off, and nothing's more disheartening than to stalk a flock of birds for an hour or two, only to watch them lift up en masse in a panic, leaving you high and dry. Or in this case, low and wet. I was about thirty feet from my mixed flock when I could tell I was starting to make them nervous. Nothing to do but wait. Not enough light for pictures yet anyway, so I framed the closest birds, playing with compositions and angles. You asked what quality is most important for a bird photographer. Patience. And next, some kind of frame or aura or vibe around yourself that keeps birds from being afraid. Some birders say you have to develop this trait, it takes years of experience, but I think I was born with it. I don't even know what it is. Slow movements, yes, and not staring directly into their eyes—that can terrify some birds, especially hawks. But it's something else, too. Can't describe it. A way to breathe. Be. You erase yourself. You become a piece of the landscape.

Nope, can't describe it.

After 15 or 20 minutes, my flock forgot about me and I started to creep up again. At 15 feet, I stopped. The perfect range with the telephoto I was using, and now all I had to do was wait. This is the best part, and also impossible to describe. All there is is bird, lens, color, light, me. Except I almost disappear, and then it's the pure process.

The sun began to burn off the mist, and I began to shoot. The light was perfect, bright enough for subtle saturation, diffuse enough for magic, one of those golden mornings you dream about. Sometimes you know when it's working, you can already see the photos you're taking, and they're great. Two dunlins shouldering each other out of the way, a laughing gull giving itself a shower, one lone willet, huge among the little spotties. I shot a short-billed dowitcher on one leg in still water, his reflection underneath him. I think it's going to be good, as if he's standing on a mirror, nothing but sky-colored water above and below. For fun, not for sale, just for myself, I take pictures of yawning birds. I've got more than 30 different species, a collection, just birds yawning. (Wake up! No glazing!) Today, on this little sand spit, a double-crested cormorant practically yawned in my face. It was completely unexpected; a bird just waking up will often yawn, but this guy had already fed and was perched on a piece of driftwood with his wings spread out to dry. I can't believe I got him, but I did. I even had to focus by hand, auto would've picked up the tip of his bill and I wanted the back of his red throat, the bright blue roof of his mouth. I think I got it, I'm almost sure, and his green eye and the orange around his mouth. What a picture! I think. Hope. I'll know when I get home.

But that wasn't the end. This amazing day, the kind you only get a couple of times a year if you're lucky, wasn't over. In a few minutes the light was going to get too white, and worse, I could hear a car door slam across the marsh. People coming. A great blue heron skidded into the shallow water from—I don't know where, I wasn't looking, I was shooting a black-bellied plover having a tug of war with a marine worm in the sand. (It's good, too, I think. He looks very serious and determined, and the worm is winning.) Great blues are common here, of course, in all seasons, I have hundreds of pix of blues, and they're terrific birds, big and dramatic, always up to something interesting. You can hardly take a bad picture of a great blue heron, and photo editors love them because they look prehistoric. But me, I've never gotten a really excellent shot, something's always not quite right, I fill the frame too full so there's no room for words—eds. need space in the background of a potential cover shot for text—or else my specimen isn't perfect or the light isn't right or the pose is too static or—whatever it might be. I've got adequate stuff, but nothing classic. Nothing I'm proud of.

Today I got something. Because no sooner did this bird land than his buddy landed next to him. Mate? Brother-in-law? You can't tell a male great blue from a female, so who knows. The point is, now there were two of them, and if you can get two birds together, same species or not, you've automatically got twice as good a picture. Potentially. But especially two great blues, who are usually solitary. Except when they're mating, and it's too early, these two weren't mating. I don't think. Anyway—I know, you're not even reading anymore, and I'm just getting to the good part. I back off with my lens, I've learned my lesson, I don't fill the frame with these birds even though they're standing in three inches of water not six feet from each other. No, I back off and shoot, shoot, going on auto, but not shy about shooting, not waiting for something theatrical to happen and not worrying about conserving film, rookie mistake in a situation like this, and all I'm thinking is this is interesting, two blues hunting together—when all of a sudden, blue on the right spears a frog. I thought it was a fish at first but it's a frog, peeper, little guy, and I snap off half a dozen shots of the heron with the frog in its mouth, waiting for the classic moment when it tosses its S-shaped neck back and goes GULP. It doesn't happen. Here's what happens. Blue on the right extends its neck, black plume on top sticking straight up—these are gorgeous, adult, fully developed great blue herons, flawless, a couple of God's best ideas—blue on right extends frog gift to blue on left, between his two yellow bills. Left-hand blue sidles over and opens her (I know it's a female; by some fluke, these two have jumped mating season) mouth, and right-hand blue deposits delicious mating bribe—and I have this moment on film. I have it, I'll know when it comes back from my slide processor, but I trust my instincts. This is good. They both have their feathers furled, and the light's right, they're as glad as I am, this is an ecstatic moment. It's not just that it's unusual for this time of year, and unusual sells. I don't give a damn about selling, but this will sell. (If I got it. I'm scaring myself by how confident I feel.) If it's as good as I think it is I've got something special. Something you don't see. I don't know what to compare it to—you selling out the restaurant on a Saturday night, every seat taken, 6 p.m. to 10, and every customer had a meal they'll never forget. A home run.

So I got my shot. Somewhere in there is an image you don't see very often, and I took it just right. Everything worked out at the same time. Hello? Still awake? I feel good. I can't stop typing.

Mason

Eddie was supposed to come in early and help, but he never showed up. Anna spent the morning standing on chairs, putting holes in the newly painted walls with a portable drill, hanging gigantic, but luckily lightweight, oil paintings by a local, therefore cheap, artist of fruits and flowers. Not generic, not motel room fruits and flowers, more like—well, not primitive, either, and not really surrealist. Hyper-realist? Expressionist? Jay would know, but then he'd have to deliver a lecture along with the answer. Whatever, the paintings were huge and happy, full of color, and best of all, Vonnie said they made her hungry.

Anna loved the shade of peachy yellow they'd chosen over white for the old brick walls. How much brighter and warmer the dining room looked—but not too feminine, Shirl was quick to agree with her. Shirl, pasta chef and nonstop talker, was her chief decorating consultant, and nobody was more surprised by that than Anna. They agreed on everything, so of course each thought the other had exquisite taste, wonderful judgment. Shirl even hated the faded, path-worn carpet as much as Anna did. "Skanky," she called it, and enjoyed dreaming up ways they could expedite its demise, like "accidentally" setting fire to it. And to think Anna had once thought of letting Shirl go.

Carmen rolled in at about eleven, backing her old white Econoline up to the back door. It was her day to browse the Italian market for produce she could get cheaper than from their everyday suppliers. She stumped up to her apartment and came back down with her apron on, ready to supervise lunch. While Lewis unloaded the van, Anna logged in Carmen's purchases on the master inventory.

Before she was half finished, she was fuming.

She waited until Carmen was alone, busy with opening a carton of canned tomato paste in the pantry. Working on keeping her voice curious and wondering, not irate, Anna asked, "Did you get anything on my list?"

"*Your* list?" She was breathing too hard from the small amount of exertion slitting open a cardboard box required. She straddled the carton to open it, broad-backed, biceps as big as ham shanks, blowing her faded hair out of her face.

"The list I gave you last night. To add to your list. I don't see anything I wanted except the Auricchio cheese."

"Yeah, they had that on sale. We could afford it." She straightened up, sweaty and grinning—not in a nice way. She looked older than her fifty years. She looked cooked. The skin on her arms and neck, even her solid legs, especially her round face, was a bricky, rusty red, like roasted pepper. Well, it made sense—she spent every day in 120-degree heat over fires, grills, stoves, boiling water, steam, frying pans. After thirty years of it, more or less, she'd stewed herself.

Sometimes Anna tried to imagine her as a young woman pining for a priest she knew she shouldn't think about and couldn't have, or reeling from hurt when he callously broke her heart. It was almost impossible to picture, but when she did it softened her antagonism to Carmen a little. And she knew one nice thing about her—every night, late, she sneaked food to a homeless guy in the alley, a stumbly, bad-tempered, usually drunken old bum named Benchester. Everybody knew about it, but nobody was allowed to mention it; if they did, Carmen blew up, went on the attack, and denied it. Nothing made her madder than being confused with a kind person.

"They didn't have fresh sardines or your *particular* brand of passata, sorry to say. And you can forget about San Daniele ham. You know how much they want for that per pound?"

"Okay, I was afraid of that, but how come you didn't get the beef? I know they've got it, and it's *cheaper*. But you got T-bone."

"People like T-bone. They don't want that thin, tough *bistecca* you've got a hard-on for."

"Carmen, we wanted to make it with the new fig-basil sauce. I *told* you." One of Frankie's triumphs, it was a fantastic sauce, ambrosia, one of the best meat accompaniments Anna had ever tasted. Too rich for fish, but it was perfect with chewy, flavorful Italian steak.

"Nobody will order it," Carmen pronounced.

"How do you know? It's leaner, sure, but lots of people *like* leaner cuts of meat."

"Wrong. When they order steak they want a steak, not a piece of shoe leather."

Anna slapped her thighs with her hands. "I wanted fresh peas. Were they out of them, too?"

"You wanted fresh peas for a puree on polenta. Believe me, honey, I just saved you from a *world* of embarrassment." Carmen pushed past her and went back out in the kitchen.

Anna followed. "Linguinette! How come you didn't get that?"

Carmen stopped beside Jasper's station, pretending to take an interest in the baby zucchinis he was prepping for a salad special. Jasper was Carmen's pet, her henchman. "*Linguinette.*" She curled her lips, as only Carmen could, in an expression of amazed contempt. "And this designer pasta would be different from linguine exactly... how?"

"It's smaller!" Anna exploded. "That's why they call it linguinette! It's smaller!"

Carmen burst out laughing. Jasper copied her.

Anna lost all caution. "Have you ever even eaten linguinette? Have you? Do you like capellini, or do you think that's funny, too?"

No—she made herself shut up. Carmen would *not* provoke her into a shouting match. Anyway, she'd lose, because Carmen was a master of scorn. Back when she'd had Frankie doing prep work—before Anna found out and rescued her, moved her back to the line—Frankie had made the mistake of uttering the names of a few simple cooking school terms, mise en place, mirepoix, commonplace phrases to her, but which struck Carmen and her gang, Jasper and a few of the others, as unbearably pretentious. Nothing got punished faster in Carmen's kitchen than hotdogging, or at least her perception of it, and the favored form of punishment was merciless teasing. So now Frankie's nickname was "Concassé," after the tomato dice prep she must regret ever mentioning. Jasper never missed an opportunity to call himself the "garde-manger"—and so on and so on. Routine kitchen hazing, but when Carmen joined in it took on an aspect of harassment, if only because she was so good at it.

Big mistake to have it out with her here, now, with half the staff pretending they weren't straining to hear every word. Anna grabbed her temper back, managed to smile, said, "Actually, capellini is pretty funny," and went outside.

Louis was hosing off the front sidewalk. Anna waved back at Roxanne, who owned the jewelry shop across the street. She waved to the UPS man. She petted Fatso, the alley cat all the storekeepers on the block fed. She and Louis talked about how Rose's flower boxes were doing, and whether she'd been right to plant miniature coxcombs this year instead of old reliable geraniums.

Louis had been Rose's odd-job man for as long as Anna could remember. He never changed. When she was a teenager, he'd looked the same to her as he did now, like an old man, gangly and stoop-shouldered, with freckled, ashy-brown skin and close white hair as matted and compact as cotton balls. "What do you think about putting some tables out here?" she asked him. "Not many, six, say. Think we'd need umbrellas? Or a bigger awning, maybe. Where's the sun around cocktail time in the worst part of the summer, Louis? I can't remember."

He scratched the back of his neck, squinting, pondering. "About there," he decided, pointing west, up the crescent. "Slides behind the Ritz Camera around eight. Hot night, it's a sonofabitch."

"Umbrellas, then. I guess. Lot of upkeep," she said doubtfully. "Carmen's against it." Laminated wood furniture would warp, she warned, and plastic would crack, cloud, peel, or disintegrate. All colors would turn gray. They'd be scraping, painting, and replacing for the rest of their lives.

"Well, then," Louis said decisively. Anna wasn't surprised he was against it; after all, he was the one who'd be stuck with most of the maintenance. But then he winked at her. "Ain't that a good reason to do it?"

Dear Anna,

Forgot to say, in heat of heron moment, I'm glad you love what you do. "Don't tell Rose"? You think she doesn't know? She's my friend, not just Theo's, so I hear things. Sorry that bothers you, the fact that Rose talks about you to her friends. You two had an estrangement, but that's all I know, no details. She protects you.

Theo and I, I'm not sure what we had. He's the one who taught me to love birds. He used to patch up wounded ones, gulls and peeps he'd find when he was out fishing or crabbing. I had him, off and on, for a father, but even before he left for good he wasn't around much. My mother was his second wife; he lost the first one for the same reason—not around. He's only here now because he can't leave. And Rose; he stays for her. Am I supposed to be angry with him because he was a bad father? We're friends now, and we've never talked about the past. Manly men.

Dear Mason,

Things are so crazy here—sorry I didn't have time to write back and say congrats on fabulous heron photos. It sounds like meditation when you write about waiting for the birds to settle and the light to be perfect. The Zen of bird photography. I wish I knew the first thing about birds. I used to go out with a guy who had a cockatiel named Marsha. He bought a record that was supposed to teach her how to talk, but it didn't work, she never said a word. If I were to buy a beginner's book on birds, which one would you recommend?

Re. Theo, Rose, childhood, abandonment, etc., etc.—do you ever feel we're too old for this? How old are you? I'm 36, almost 37, technically a grown-up. I feel very stupid and childish for still having ISSUES with a woman who's not even my mother. When do we grow up? When we have our own children? Somehow I doubt it. I think then we just pretend harder, and show off by dealing with problems of childhood and youth that we really have finally mastered, things like, Don't take dope, Don't have sex yet, knee-jerk "adult" proscriptions that completely hide the fact that we are still stuck in troughs of adolescent angst and indecision and over-all cluelessness.

But that's just me.

I love to read novels, or I used to when I had a life, and my favorite writers seem to be struggling with these questions, but really, my sense is, they understand everything. They write the ILLUSION of confusion, these authors, mostly women, but I doubt any of them are as scattered and hopeless as I am when it comes to being a grown-up. What do you read for pleasure? I like books about women stuck in dire emotional circumstances, abusive husbands, lonely spinsterhood, unappreciative children, etc.,

etc., who triumph in the end because somebody (usually a man, but sometimes, imagine it, the women themselves!) recognizes their worth and rewards them for it. I suppose this has been going on since *Jane Eyre*, but I'm still a sucker for it. I love the happy ending. Cinderella, that's what it is. The prince comes in some form or other, and immediately every rotten thing the evil stepmother ever did is wiped out.

I forget where I was going with this. It wasn't to say that Rose is my evil stepmother, though, or that Theo is your evil stepfather. Although if he is, you've done a lot better job of reconciling with him than I have with Rose. Why do you say she "protects" me? Think about the possibility she's protecting herself.

Your post from yesterday just came today, so you're probably up and out already, shooting albatrosses or something. I guess it's too much to hope for another perfect day, but I hope you have one.

Anna

P.S. How interesting that your father—your real father, birth father—flew airplanes. Am twirling my Freudian mustache over that.

Lunch was light, not what Anna had been hoping for, and on top of that she had to listen to Carmen blame it on the specials. "Too weird," she opined, as if Frankie's monkfish with pureed artichoke had personally scared people away. She spent an hour on the telephone with suppliers, another hour interviewing phone applicants to replace Elise, whom she'd had to let go yesterday for calling Kris a station-stealing bitch. Fine, but not in front of a dining room full of customers. Firing people wasn't any fun, Anna hated it as much as Rose did, but she consoled herself that she'd done Elise a favor by just hurrying along the inevitable.

At three, she grabbed a bite of lunch at the bar. Frankie joined her, looking beat, which was understandable: she'd been on her feet for six hours straight, and she had seven more to go. Vince, who'd switched shifts with no-show Eddie, entertained them with made-up drink names. Vodka, orange juice, and milk of magnesia: a Phillips Screwdriver. Cold Duck and Dr Pepper: a Quack Doctor. It was fun to watch Vince at work, because he was fast, smooth, and obsessively tidy. He made a ceremony out of the simplest drink-mixing; watching him build a martini was like celebrating the Transubstantiation at high mass. He had a lot of regulars, people who came in every day just to see him, get their Vince fix. He could talk on any topic, sports, the stock market, the meaning of life, the movie playing up the street. Aunt Iris said he was good at his job because he was a Fiore, which made him a natural host. It just came out in drink instead of food.

He and Frankie were always arguing. About everything—music in general, but especially what kind they should play during happy hour; whether the TV over the bar was indispensable or an abomination; if they should have a popcorn machine; if the world would end if Rose put in a video game (Vince: no; Frankie: yes). He argued by teasing and bantering, but she was so earnest, she didn't know when he was kidding. Same with flirting: Vince tried out his corny but venerable lines on Frankie, which usually involved exaggerated claims of sexual power, and she responded with blank, uncomprehending stares.

She broke off the current argument—whether happy hour freebies brought in more freeloaders than paying customers—to race into the kitchen and snatch a roasting pan of cherry vine tomatoes out of the brick oven. "Try one," she offered, setting the pan on a folded towel on the bar. The only customers at this hour were a few regulars from the dock and a couple of twentysomethings too wrapped up in each other to notice anybody else. "See what you think," Frankie said. "Careful, they're still hot."

Anna snapped a hot tomato off the bunch and gingerly popped it in her mouth. "Mm, I like." Garlic and thyme burst out when she bit down.

"Yeah, it's great," Vince agreed around a mouthful. "Is this more bar food?"

"Yes," said Anna and Frankie in unison. They were working on a tapas menu, and Vince was their guinea pig.

"I keep telling you," he leaned across the bar to say, "after a few drinks, these guys'll eat their wallets if you put enough salt on. This stuff, the focaccia, the empanadas, they're great, but they'll be wasted on about eighty percent of my customers."

"You sound like Carmen. Where is she," Anna said, "I want her to try these."

"She went to the dentist," Vince told her, picking up the pan and offering some of the roasted tomatoes to the guys on the other side of the bar.

"You're wrong about what people want to eat," Frankie said seriously. "If they're hungry and all you've got is salted wallets, sure, that's what they'll eat, but give them something good and watch what happens."

"Yeah. They'll eat that, too."

"No—okay, yes—but they won't just gobble it, they'll *savor* it."

On cue—"Hey, these are good," one of the regulars, a retired oysterman named Conrad, called over.

Frankie glared at Vince in triumph. "Bar food is an art," she instructed him. "It should be simple but strong, a real hit in your mouth, and you should be able to eat it with your hands. Like chilled oysters. Or like anchovy deviled eggs, like fried potatoes with aioli sauce—"

"Now you're talking."

"Like dates—Anna, here's what I was thinking—dates stuffed with toasted almonds and wrapped in prosciutto."

"Fabulous."

"And also—for happy hour, why couldn't you put out a rapini loaf on the bar? Already sliced, so people just take a piece. You bring it out just once, like at six o'clock, you don't reheat it or anything. There it is, take it or leave it."

"What's rapini?" Vince asked.

Frankie stared, honestly astounded. "What's rapini? It's broccoli rabe."

"Oh."

"You can mix it with garlic and onion and Asiago cheese, and you eat it with bread."

"Ah," Vince said, enlightened. "Like a spinach loaf."

Frankie shook her head, hopeless. "Yes, Vince, like a spinach loaf. Except you hold the mayo. And the water chestnuts," she added, like a punch line. "I've got things to do," she said, slid off her stool, and disappeared.

"Weird chick," Vince said, frowning after her. "She never laughs at my jokes."

"That is weird."

"No, you gotta admit, she's a little intense. I tried to give her a kitten," he said, refilling Anna's coffee cup. "This guy in my building's cat had kittens. You know she lives all by herself, right, out by the warehouse district."

"I know she lives alone."

"A terrible apartment, I mean, not like a tenement but almost. It's depressing. I told her she needed a pet, something to break up the misery."

"How'd that go over?"

"Not well." Anna watched his large round eyes turned mournful. Big waves of affection for Vince came over her at odd times. She wanted to lean over the bar and rub his crewcut head, pat his cheeks, shake him by the shoulders until his head wobbled. She just had an urge to give him an affectionate mauling, like a kid brother or a big friendly dog.

"Oh, good," she said, spying Shirl strolling through from the kitchen. "Here comes somebody who laughs at all your jokes."

"Hi, Anna! Wow, the paintings look incredible." Shirl plumped down heavily on the stool next to hers, dragging a manila folder out of her string bag. "Hey, Vince," she flirted, batting her short, stubby eyelashes. "I love that kind of shirt, that, like, no-collar shirt. It looks rilly good on you."

Vince beamed, he sparkled, back in his element. "How about a lime cola for the lady? No—" He pointed at Shirl with both index fingers. "Ginger ale and bitters. You've got that look in your eye."

Whatever that meant. Vince spouted nonsense to women and they didn't care, probably didn't even hear. Anna interrupted a lot of girlish hair-tossing to ask Shirl if that was the new menu mockup in her folder.

"Yeah. See, look, I did two versions. Earl Junior helped me with the formats. What that kid can't do on a computer you don't even wanna do. So which one do you like better?"

Anna scanned them, pleased with both looks. They weren't the real menu yet, just an experiment with placement and layout. Rose was against changing anything but the logo on the front. "But it's our identity, our signature—the menu is the *face* of the Bella Sorella," she argued. "If you go moving things around too much, you'll disorient people. You know, not *all* change is good change." Well, that was so wrong-headed, Anna had simply ignored it and gone ahead with her plans.

"This one's better," she told Shirl. "Your eye naturally goes here first, top right. So that's where we'll put the specials. And the low-ticket items down here in Siberia, lower right." Eight appetizers, eight entrees, that seemed just right. "And I like the wine list on the back, I like that informality. No separate list. You did a great job,

Shirl. Did it take a long time?" She'd volunteered to do it, but Anna wanted to reimburse her anyway, a little something extra in her pay tonight. Help pay off the lawsuit in case Earl Junior won.

"No," she said happily, twirling a coil of her corkscrew hair, magenta this week, "and I like doing it, it's rilly fun. Which color paper do you like best? The burgundy's for, like, power, but red is sexier."

Vince's ears perked up at that. Anna left them hashing out which was sexier, red or burgundy, and went off to see if Rose was back yet.

She showed up in the middle of dinner service. Anna barely saw her, had time for only a few words before they got steered toward urgent duties in opposite directions. She looked tired but not upset—so she must not have heard any bad news today about Theo. She'd spent the day taking him to therapy sessions and doctors' appointments. Mason usually did that, but he was off in Chincoteague, Anna happened to know, photographing herons.

"I think I'll go home early," Rose told her after the first rush ended. Anna was writing checks at the desk, Rose sitting on a corner of it, scratching her fingers through her hair as if trying to wake herself up. "I wouldn't leave if it was heavy tonight, but it's not." She had on a plain long dress with buttons down the front, brown from the bodice down, dark green above. Fabulous colors on her, Anna registered vaguely. She coveted the dress. "To tell you the truth, I'm running on fumes."

"No, sure," Anna said readily, "no problem. But."

"But. Oh, God." Rose covered her face with her hands, pretending to be overcome. "What?"

"Sometime we have to have a talk. About Carmen."

She slumped lower. "What did she do?"

"Nothing. It's her attitude. Rose—she's grouchy, she's bad-tempered, she's critical. Insensitive. She terrorizes the waitstaff. I've never known anybody so rigid. 'This is the way we've always done it,' she says—like that's a reason not to change anything."

"I know she's difficult." She rubbed her eyes, then scowled down at her fingertips, seeing she'd smudged her mascara. She pulled a tissue out of the box on the desk and wiped her face, and Anna wondered what she thought about her looks, now that she was sixty, if she was vain at all, and what it would feel like, from the standpoint of attractiveness and sex appeal and all that, to be as old as Rose.

"*Difficult*," she said, spoiling for an argument. "She's impossible! I'd like Frankie to be much more involved with planning the new menu, Rose. I want her in charge of it, frankly. She's smart and fast, she has great ideas—and Carmen's got her making marinara!"

"Yes, but it's really *good* marinara. All right," Rose said, sobering when Anna only frowned at that. "I'll talk to her. I will, I promise." She looked as if the prospect excited her about as much as handling snakes. "But not tonight. Please, I have to go home before I fall down."

"Go, I told you, I've got it."

"Shirl had to leave early, did anybody tell you?" Rose got her purse from the file cabinet, then went to stand in the doorway, leaning heavily against the post. "So you're a little short-staffed, but no big deal."

"Yeah, I heard. Cramps again. She was fine this afternoon. I'd say she was trying to get out early on a Friday night, except she looked awful."

"She did."

"Been there," Anna said with a mock shudder. "Not that much anymore, but when I was young. Ugh."

"I remember." She leaned her head back, sent Anna a gentle look down the length of her beaky nose. "Do you remember your first period?"

"Not really. Sort of. Mom taught me how to use a Kotex and all, I remember that."

Rose stayed where she was for a long moment, not moving. Her face seemed to sharpen, then relax; her eyes softened with an emotion that might be sadness or regret—Anna couldn't quite read it.

"What?" Anna said at last, disturbed by the silence.

She smiled. "Nothing. Good night." She pushed away from the door and drifted away.

Anna sat still, staring blankly at the opposite wall and listening to the familiar muffled din from the kitchen, unconsciously separating out the sounds of the cappuccino machine, a tray of glasses clattering out of the dishwasher, Carmen's voice, now Dwayne's, the harsh, intermittent rumble of the garbage disposal. Fontaine, who had finally confided to Anna that she was pregnant, stuck her pretty blond head in the door and asked a question, something about peach puree. Anna answered it. But as much as she wanted to keep it here, her mind was elsewhere. It was back in her house on an afternoon in gray December, the day after her mother's funeral. Or—maybe not the day after, maybe it only seemed that way. Soon after, though, because for years she'd associated the two occasions in her mind: burying her mother and getting her period for the first time. She hadn't lied to Rose about not remembering, at least not in that instant of denial, but now what had really happened came back with a strange immediacy, and she wondered—briefly, not very hard—what other memories she'd mangled or bent or abused in the ongoing effort to write Rose out of her life.

All day—the day after the funeral, or two days, a week—she'd felt heavy and achy, listless, her skin chilly and untouchable, but she'd attributed the symptoms to grief and too much crying, her body's natural reaction to emotional pain. Then, late in the afternoon, she'd found the blood on her underpants, and after a minute of panicky bewilderment she'd realized what it was. She remembered staring at her face in the bathroom mirror, searching for a sign, a clue that she'd turned some corner into womanhood, but all she saw was sickly-pale skin and anxious black eyes. She'd sat on the edge of the bathtub, her arms wrapped around her middle, tense and ill from the first of what was going to be about a hundred, give or take, monthly bouts with cramps and nausea. Eventually her father had knocked on the door. "Annie? You sick? Are you sick, baby?" She wouldn't come out, and she wouldn't tell him why. Was Rose already there or had he called her? Anna couldn't recall—she just remembered letting Rose into the bathroom and quickly closing the door behind her. And a feeling of overwhelming relief, an almost religious unburdening of care, *into thy hands*, except the hands were Rose's.

"Aunt Rose, I got my period."

"Oh, baby—"

"I looked in Mom's closet and under the sink and everything, but I couldn't find anything, you know, any sanitary whatchacallit. I don't think there's anything here." No, there wouldn't have been, she realized now—the chemo would've stopped her mother's menstrual periods.

"That's okay, don't worry about that," Rose had said, "we'll send Paul to the drugstore," and Anna had been glad that Rose was going to tell him. She didn't mind her father knowing, she just didn't want to tell him herself. Rose asked her how she felt, and sympathized with her, and told her how lousy her periods were at first, but then they got better and now she sailed through every month with barely a twinge. "Lily was exactly the same way," she claimed, and Anna believed her, and was finally able to ease into an acceptance of what was happening to her. Stop fighting it or viewing it as an unnatural catastrophe. Move in and occupy it.

Later, Rose had put her to bed with a hot water bottle on her stomach. "Mama used to say put it on your feet, let the heat draw the blood down, but I always liked it better right where it hurts, right there," Rose said, nodding approvingly at the bulge under the blanket over Anna's pelvis. So interesting, she'd thought, intrigued by the notion of her Nonna, a wide, humorless, gray-haired, *sexless* old widow woman, having periods and giving advice about them to her young daughters. Lily, Iris, and Rose. She'd felt connected, not bereft. There were still women in her life, her family, that she could turn to, and she didn't feel so alone.

But she remembered saying to Rose, just as she was about to get up and leave Anna by herself—maybe she'd said it to keep her—"This is the first important thing she'll miss." And Rose hadn't dodged it or pretended she didn't understand or it wasn't that bad, no bromides, no fake remedies. "I've been thinking the same thing," she'd said. "First date, first kiss. Graduation from high school. College. When you fall in love and get married, when you have a baby." Then they'd both started to cry. "Womanly milestones," Rose got out, sniffling.

For some reason that made them laugh. It just sounded funny, like a women's magazine article, "Womanly Milestones"—and yet that's what this *was*, if getting your first period wasn't a womanly milestone, Anna gave up—and so even while they were laughing they'd reached for each other. (*How could she have forgotten this?*) She'd scooted up on her pillow and wrapped her arms around her Aunt Rose, and Rose had put her arms around her, and it was the first time since her mother's death that she had truly felt any warmth or consolation from another person's physical comfort. Even her father couldn't make her feel like this: as if her grief were normal. As if her emotions weren't only natural, they were *next* in a long line of women's natural emotions. Like a totem pole, and her version of her feelings was just the next shape on top, an eagle, a mountain lion, a spear—whatever.

That had been the grace of Rose.

And she'd forgotten it.

Well, but. Still. So what? She'd never said Rose was a monster. She still knew what she knew, that was the point. In fact, Rose and her father might've slept with each other two minutes after Rose kissed Anna's forehead, told her she loved her, and left the room.

She tried to work up some fury over that possibility. Failed.

That wasn't it. She didn't care if they screwed each other's brains out *after her mother died*. That wasn't it.

Before. That's what she cared about, and she couldn't let it go. It was like a lump in her throat, something she couldn't swallow past, a growth. Rose and her father *before*, while her mother—and they loved her, they both loved her!—lay dying. She couldn't swallow past that.

"Hey, Anna?" Eddie called from the doorway, startling her. "You busy?"

"Why?" she asked warily. She was always busy.

"Might have a little situation here."

She looked at him more closely. Ever Eddie was cool at all times, he made a point of it, but he was shifting his weight from one foot to the other and fingering the tiny diamond-spot of beard under his bottom lip. He reminded her of an otter, his black hair so sleek and shiny, slicked back in an elegant, vaguely oriental ponytail. She didn't like Eddie much, but she liked to look at him, the tight clothes and tight body, and always the crotch-accentuating pants. He didn't walk, he strutted, pelvis-first. You just couldn't help yourself.

"What's up?" she asked.

"Got a loud and obnoxious out here."

"Drunk?"

"Definitely. I cut him off and told him to go home, but he ain't moving. I can *throw* him out, no problem there whatsoever." He rolled his shoulders and flexed his fingers, ready for action.

She asked him the obvious question. "How'd the guy get that drunk in the first place?" This was why she wanted Vince on nights, especially weekends, why she frowned on shift-changing. New rules were about to be implemented. If Vince were here, this wouldn't be happening.

Eddie shrugged. "I guess he was hammered when he came in, then all of a sudden he goes off. You can't tell, nobody can tell.

People are still eating, so he's disturbing the peace. A couple of couples at the bar already walked out."

She got up, swearing. "Is he a regular?" she asked, following Eddie out of the office.

"Maybe. Yeah. I think so."

"You think so?"

"I don't know. Somebody called him Bob."

Bob looked like a businessman, fiftyish, well dressed, well built. Red-faced. He sat in the center of the horseshoe-shaped bar, holding forth about something, she caught the emphatic phrase "*and that's not even the half of it,*" to twelve or fourteen drinkers who wouldn't look directly at him. So far, shunning wasn't working. She sat down on one of the two conspicuously vacant stools on either side of him, sat all the way, didn't just perch. She could feel the interested, expectant gazes on her, like little flashlights, of about half the patrons in the restaurant, but she didn't look at anybody but Bob. To show she was on his side. "Hi, how's it going?" she greeted him, very familiar, as if they knew each other from way back.

He cut his sleepy, bloodshot eyes at her, then away. "Who're you?" He had a glass of melting ice in one loose fist, a cigarette in the other.

"I'm Anna."

"Where's Rose?"

"She's not here." So he was a regular.

"She was here."

"Yeah, but she had to go home."

"What're you, her daughter?"

"I'm the manager."

He snorted. "Good, then you can make me another scotch. This a bar or what?"

"Listen, Bob. The reason you can't have another drink is"—she leaned forward and said it in confidence, pal to pal—"some people think you've already had enough."

"Yeah? Fuck some people." He laughed a phlegmy *hah hah*.

She chuckled with him, raising her eyebrows, shaking her head. He wasn't a sloppy drunk, no slurring his words or accidentally jerking his elbow off the edge of the bar. A mean look behind the bleariness in his eyes worried her, though. "Yeah, but," she said with gentle reproach. "You're a *little* drunk, right? You gotta admit."

"Not half as drunk as I'm gonna be."

She shook her head some more, disappointed. "See, the problem is, you're no fun anymore. You need to go home and come back when you're your old self. We like having you here, but not like this."

He looked half-persuaded for a second. But then he snapped back into Sullen Bob. "Fuck that."

They went around like that for a while. She ordered club sodas, one for her, one for him. Every time Eddie came anywhere near him, Bob's belligerence level shot up, a thermometer near a heat source. After he brought the drinks, Anna had to make faces at Eddie to keep him away.

Turned out, Bob wanted to talk. He started telling her about his ex-wife. Cathy. Last Wednesday was their anniversary, they'd have been married thirteen years. "I didn't have one drink all day," he swore, weighting the words with heavy significance. "*Not—one—drink*. Not one. Know why?"

"Why?"

"I wouldn't give her the satisfaction." When he smoothed back the silver hair at his temple, a gold cuff link glinted on his shirtsleeve. Everything he had on was expensive, even his cologne, but she didn't hold that against him. She might have with another loudmouth rich guy, but more misery was coming off Bob than anger. She could feel it, almost see it, like an aura. "You know she's a lesbian," he confided.

"She is? Really?" But she was determined not to get roped into his life story. That wasn't how you handled a drunk, that just wasted time.

"Big time." He nodded slowly and vehemently. He stubbed his cigarette in the ashtray but it didn't go out, just trailed smoke into Anna's left eye. He began to tear his cork coaster into pieces. "Nah," he admitted, sinking his chin down on his chest, hunching his shoulders under his rumpled suitcoat. Getting small. "I'm lying."

"Oh."

"She's a schoolteacher. Eighth-grade social studies. Social studies," he repeated wonderingly. "What the fuck is that?"

"I've never known."

"The kids're crazy about her, she never has any problem with the little motherfuckers." He caught himself again. "They don't know 'er like I do, course."

"Course."

"Bitch on wheels." He sipped his water absentmindedly. "So, Laura. You married?"

...So now not only do I know all about Bob's life, he knows everything about mine. I remember Vince telling me once it's easier for a woman to handle a drunk, providing the drunk is a man, but if it's a woman it's the other way around. I don't think I really "handled" Bob anyway, I just talked to him. After a while, it started to feel like a date. A really bad date. Rose, I'm sure, is better at this than I am; she'd have gotten him out of there a lot faster, but still with no hard feelings. There's an art to it.

He gave me his card at the end. If I ever need legal advice, Bob's my man. (I don't think so.) Tony and I got him in a cab, and I told him good night, come back any time (taking a chance there), have a safe trip home, etc. The last thing he said, talking to me through the half-open back window, was that it was hard to go home. "There's nobody there," he said. He teared up, but he didn't cry. Thank God, because then I would've.

The thing is, I liked him. The even bigger thing is, I like everybody. Almost everybody. Do I sound like an ass? I didn't have this so much when I worked in the coffeehouse, very serious place, the clientele was all artists and wannabes. Homogeneous crowd, no variety, everybody young and cool and not very interesting (to me). Here—I want everybody to have a good time. I'm so *fond* of them, the regulars, the one-timers who might turn out to be regulars. Lonely guys like Bob, and couples on stiff first dates, married couples who never open their mouths, never say one word the whole meal. Girlfriends who get drunk at lunch and talk and laugh until it's time for dinner. I'm starting to think of these people as *property* of the Bella Sorella, people who must be fed and watered and *satisfied*. Stomachs filled, cockles warmed. It's my pleasure. And I think the secret is so easy—just show that you care. Because all anybody wants is to feel important. Oh, they know me here—they want me! That's it, that's all there is to it.

Oh, and really good food.

Exhausted. Don't know why I'm writing this, except I'm keyed up. That weird high I was telling you about. There's a lot of drug and alcohol abuse in the restaurant business—I told you that, right? Makes sense. Luckily I have other ways to cope when the tension gets tight. I talk a lot, and write e-mails if nobody's around to talk to. Play music so loud the neighbors complain. Or my car vibrates, just the thumping bass audible to passersby—yes, I'm one of those.

Okay, I'll stop. Hope you had a successful day in the marshes. Rose took your stepfather to his dr. appts. today, and apparently everything's status quo. So that's good news.

Night,
Anna

10

Theo's hair on top was hot from the sun, cool underneath when Rose slipped her fingers in to pull it, lock by grizzled lock, away from his scalp and snip it with Mason's kitchen scissors. "Don't cut my ear off," he'd growled at the beginning, and so far she'd managed not to, but she had to be careful around his face and the tender back of his neck because of the sudden, unpredictable head jerks he couldn't control—a fairly new symptom in the progression of his ailment. A minor one, comparatively, and it was a glorious June afternoon, it was Monday so the restaurant was closed, and Theo was having a good day. If she could put a glass box around them, here in the bend of Mason's L-shaped dock, sun-warmed, bird-serenaded, with the blinding-bright river chopping along behind for a background, Rose would have to count herself a happy woman. Right here, right now, what more could she want? Two or three things occurred to her in the next thought, but she pushed them away, like distractions during a meditation. Living in the moment wasn't only good advice anymore, it was a way to keep going.

Theo sat in a folding chair on the dock for his haircut. She put her arms around his towel-draped shoulders from behind and pressed her cheek against his cheek. Their heads moved together in a quick twitch, and he croaked, "Watch it, I'll knock you out." She held tighter, the whole warm armful of him, until he patted her wrist with his shaky hand.

"What would you do, Theo, if you could do anything at all today? This beautiful day. Anything in the world."

"This."

She squeezed tight and then straightened up, so he couldn't see her face. "Me, too."

"And then. I'd go to—the Keys on the *Wind Rose*. With you." The rhythm of his speech emphasized the wrong words sometimes; she wasn't always sure of his meaning until she'd processed the whole sentence. "Take as long as we like, all . . . summer if we want."

"You're assuming that boat's ever going to be finished." The blue-tarp-covered bowsprit poked out of the boat shed behind them; occasionally the whine of a power saw broke the sleepy stillness. Mason was doing outside work today, customizing V bunks to fit inside the narrow cabin.

"Cruise 'er down the coast," Theo said dreamily. "Spend a couple months in the Keys. Maybe—coast over to Nassau."

"In that little boat? Just us?"

"We could sail 'er around the world. She's that tough."

"If we sail her around the world, I definitely want an engine."

"Damn right."

Theo and Mason argued endlessly over whether the all-wood sailing cutter they'd been rebuilding for two years needed a motor. Theo said yes, of course, but Mason, the purist, claimed an inboard engine would desecrate it, all they needed was a stout ash sweep for sculling in tight places. For now they were compromising by putting an outboard bracket on the transom. That way they could postpone the decision indefinitely.

When she'd cut as much of his hair as she wanted, she gave Theo a soft head scratch that made him moan. He'd have fallen asleep right there in the chair, but she knelt beside him and began to massage the muscle in his left forearm—he'd had spasms there last night, one in a cluster of unpleasant symptoms called dystonia—and that woke him up.

"C'mere," he said, and pulled her up, onto his lap. She wound her arms around him. She was afraid she was too heavy on his thighs, she kept the toes of one foot on the ground, supporting some of her weight on them. It made for an uncomfortable perch, but she stayed as long as she could. All this touching, massaging, stroking, holding was essential, they couldn't do without it. It calmed them down. Lovemaking had become almost impossible, but touching was still a compulsion.

"Like to take a sail on 'er with Mason, too. One day."

"That would be nice," Rose agreed.

"Father, son. Better late . . ."

He didn't have to finish that. One of his hardest regrets, she knew, was that his second marriage, the one to Mason's mother, hadn't worked out. He'd wanted to walk into that sweet, ready-made family, a beautiful wife, a little boy who loved him, and be "normal," the kind of husband and father he thought they deserved. But he couldn't stay, and now it was hard for him to forgive himself. Mason had, long ago, but Theo was slow to follow.

"Hot," they decided, and got up. Theo folded the chair, and they ambled down the dock to the boat shed, to get out of the sun and see what Mason was up to. Sharp, sour-sweet smells of varnish and paint hovered in the sawdusty air, dim after the glare outside. Mason wasn't there. No—thumping sounds from the hull said he was belowdecks, doing something in the cabin. Theo kicked the keel, and a minute later Mason came up. He clambered over the side and dropped to the paint-spattered concrete, dragging the long cord of a drill after him. No nails or glue on the *Wind Rose*; the mahogany wood was so hard, all the fittings had to be screwed.

It was a beautiful boat, not that Rose knew much about boats, and not that she was prejudiced by this one being named after her. She loved its classic, old-fashioned shape, and the fact that it was all wood, no fiberglass—but that was another bone of contention between the restorers. Theo wanted to fiberglass the hull, Mason wanted to leave it alone. Mason didn't even want electricity! Oil lamps would do for navigating a day sailer, and the radio receiver could run on flashlight batteries. Simplify, he said. Theo said he was out of his mind.

"Got the chocks on the cabin roof," Theo noted approvingly. Mason said yep, he did that yesterday.

"What are they for?" Rose wondered.

"To stow the dinghy," Mason said, "bottom-up, when you're cruising."

"Nice new fiberglass dinghy," Theo said smugly. He'd won that one. Mason had wanted to build the dinghy from scratch, out of mahogany to match the sailboat.

"Haircut?" Rose offered, snapping the scissors in the air invitingly. Mason grinned, shook his head. He wore his hair long because of the scars on his face, but it wasn't down to his shoulders, didn't hang down his back, so somebody must cut it for him sometime. Did he go to a barbershop? A stylist? She couldn't quite picture that. She could picture him cutting it himself, sawing away in the bathroom mirror, guessing at the length in back. "Sure?" she wheedled. "I've even got the barber chair. We can do it out in the wide open-spaces."

"She's not bad," Theo said, showing off his profile. "She works cheap."

"Tempting." Mason poured paint thinner on a rag and rubbed it over his hands and wrists. "Maybe later. Look at this, Theo."

They examined the rudder, newly painted and varnished, clamped between a pair of sawhorses. Should they wrap the handle in tape or doeskin? Or leave it alone? Naturally they couldn't agree. Rose smiled at the picture they made, short and blocky next to tall and rangy, and thought of how different they were. Because of an accident of marriage thirty years ago, they were rebuilding this boat together, and in some ways the *Wind Rose* was all they had in common. But in others, it was only an excuse, the physical bridge they were using to connect, because their attachment went much deeper than similarities or shared experiences. It must, or Mason wouldn't have let Theo back into his life so generously. Theo had a lot to live down, but Mason had never reproached him for any of it. They'd reversed the Bible story: Theo was the prodigal father, Mason the son who welcomed him home with open arms.

"Mason?" Frankie called from the back porch steps. "Hey, Mason! Phone call!"

"Phone call," Rose relayed faintly when he didn't move, kept polishing a rudder hinge with his shirt cuff. He hated the telephone. He gave out his cell phone number to a careful few, and usually let the house phone ring. Now he was trapped.

She watched his shoulders rise and fall in resignation. "Excuse me," he said, and sprinted for the house.

She and Theo followed him much more slowly. "Should I feel guilty?" Rose said. "I never asked him if I could bring Frankie over with me. I wanted to give her a day off, and if I'd left her at the restaurant she'd still be pounding out pork chops." Instead she was pounding out pork chops in Mason's kitchen, but at least she was getting a change of scene on her one day off. Rose had invited Anna, too, but she'd been vague, "Maybe, I don't know, I'll see," and so far she hadn't shown up. "And then Vince heard Frankie and Anna were coming and asked if *he* could come, and now—all of a sudden—"

"Party," Theo finished.

"Party."

"Don't worry about Mason. Do him good. People in the house. High time."

By the time they got to the kitchen, he was hanging up the phone and disappearing around the corner. Escaping? His house wasn't exactly *teeming*; just two people were in the kitchen, Frankie at the sink washing dishes and Vince opening wine bottles, eight different Merlots, for a tasting.

"Who called?" Theo asked nosily.

Frankie and Vince looked at each other and shrugged. "Don't know," Frankie said, "I didn't ask. A man's voice."

On her own time, Frankie always wore black, and today it was cutoffs and a sleeveless T-shirt with a faded Hell's Angels logo. The contrast with her sugar-white skin was stark, like a shrill abstract painting. From the back she looked like a young boy, lithe and quick, small but long-limbed. When she lifted an iron skillet from the sink to the counter, the muscle in her arm bulged like a knot. "Isn't this a great kitchen?" she said to Rose. "Wouldn't it be cool to have this in your own house?"

"I know, it's marvelous. Do you need any help? How's the pork?"

"No, it's done, it's marinating. Takes about an hour."

An experiment. They'd agreed, Frankie, Rose, Carmen, and Anna, that the new, streamlined, eight-entree menu should have only one pork dish, but they kept vacillating over which one. Tonight's chops were in competition with the all-night wood-roasted, fennel-stuffed pork shoulder they'd done last week.

"Good," Rose said, "then you can relax for a while. Go for a walk, why don't you, go look at the river. Have some fun."

"Get some sun," Theo advised from the table.

Frankie flashed a smile and stayed where she was. "I love looking out at these birds," she said, pointing through the window over the sink at the various feeders and birdbaths and watering holes Mason had in his side yard. "I don't know what they are, though. Well, hummingbirds, I know. And that's a catbird, that gray one, but I only know because he told me. But, like, what's that purply one?"

"A finch, I think. House finch." Rose shrugged when Frankie looked impressed. "I only know what he tells me, too. Where's your little girl today?"

"At the beach with Mike. Three-day weekend. I said it'd be okay." She scrubbed harder at the corners of the sink and pressed her lips together. She was allowed to see Katie twice a week, and Monday afternoons had become one of the regular times.

"You miss her," Rose said in sympathy.

She twitched her shoulders, an annoyed, impatient gesture. Rose wanted to put her arm around her, but she'd have squirmed away in embarrassment. Frankie and Theo got along surprisingly well. One reason must be that they'd both rather be disliked than pitied.

Vince came over with a handful of wineglasses. "These are dusty," he said in a low voice, "can you wash 'em?" Frankie said yes. "I think he uses, like, one glass all the time." He'd lined up his wine bottles along the counter, even set out a basket of baguettes for palate-cleansing between tastes. "We're all set except for Anna. How come she's not here? This won't be much of a tasting if only five of us are drinking."

"She was arguing with Carmen about something with inventory when I left," Frankie said.

"Did she say she was coming?"

"No, but she didn't say she wasn't."

Rose had gotten the same reaction when she'd invited her.

"Where'd Mason go?" Theo wanted to know.

"Outside to smoke?" Vince guessed.

Outside to be alone, more likely. "I'll see," Rose said, and went to find him.

He was on the top step of his front stoop. Brooding, not smoking. She felt a pang of remorse to see him staring off at the woods beyond his yard, hands dangling between his knees, his scarred profile bleak. So her homemade therapy hadn't worked on him. She batted open the screen door and came out, and she had to put her hand on top of his shoulder to keep him from getting up. She sat beside him on the step, remembering to sit on his right side—that meant something to him. "Mason," she said before he could speak, "I am so sorry."

He looked at her in alarm. "Why?"

"I thought you wouldn't mind, but I wasn't thinking. All these people—we've just taken over your house. It's my fault."

"No, I don't mind. I like it."

"You do? No, you don't. You're very nice—"

"Rose—"

"But this is a terrible imposition, and I didn't even ask." On purpose; if she'd asked him, he'd probably have said no. She'd done it *for his own good*—how arrogant, really. Presumptuous. "I apologize. I was—"

"Rose, let me tell you something. That was Dr. Eastman on the phone."

"Dr. Eastman?" She repeated the name stupidly. Mason's doctor; he'd seen him through the aftermath of his accident, all the various surgeries and therapies. She put her hand on his knee in concern. Then she gripped it in sudden fright—Eastman was one of Theo's doctors, too. He consulted with the neurological specialists, he translated their opinions into words Theo could understand. Theo indiscriminately hated all doctors, so Eastman had taken to channeling information about him through Rose or Mason.

"Last week's tests came back."

She girded herself. "What is it?"

"It still isn't definite."

"It never is," she said bitterly.

"But that's the good news. Because they're pretty sure, it's looking pretty much now like it's CBD."

She closed her eyes tight. "Oh no. Oh my God." And yet she wasn't surprised. She realized she'd been expecting it. Was Theo, too?

"I wrote it down, I knew I wouldn't remember." Mason took a scrap of paper out of his shirt pocket. "The last CT scan showed asymmetric atrophy of the fronto-parietal region of the cortex. He said that's more like CBD than anything else. Any of the others we were hoping for."

Corticobasal degeneration. Sometimes they called it CBGD, corticobasal ganglionic degeneration, but it was the same thing. It meant Theo's nerve cells were shrinking and atrophying, the ones in the cortex of his brain, and deeper down in the basal ganglia. There was no cure, no way to slow it down. It was worse than Parkinson's, because it went faster. It was the very last diagnosis they'd wanted.

He folded the slip of paper over, again, again, until it was a tiny, unfoldable square, and put it back in his pocket. "At least we know. That's something."

She wanted to lean against him. She wanted to walk by herself into the woods and lie down on the ground. She couldn't think. "I'm not going to cry," she vowed.

"I am."

She laughed, at the same time tears stung the backs of her eyes. "Now, I mean." She did lean against him then, soothed by his solid arm and the sadness in his answering laugh. "Mason, oh, Mason, thank God for you."

"For you."

"I couldn't get through this if you weren't here."

He took her hand. "When should we tell him, Rose? He'll know what it means."

"Yes, he'll know. Not today."

"No," he agreed.

"Who should tell him?"

"I will. If you want me to."

"Which one of us would he hate it less from?"

"Probably Eastman."

She laughed again. "Maybe we shouldn't tell him at all."

Mason pressed his eye socket against the heel of his hand. "Don't you think he'd want to know?"

"Probably. Oh, I don't know. I don't know."

"I want to finish the boat, Rose. I've been stalling, dragging it out, I think to keep him. I think that's why I've been so slow."

That shocked her. "But he could still have years, it all depends—"

"I know, but I want him to sail it. Soon, while he's able. It's important."

They never decided who would tell him, or when. Or how. They heard the sound of tires on gravel, and looked up to see a little white car nose out of the bend in the drive where the woods started. "Anna," they said together. Rose found herself watching Mason from the corner of her eye, trying to read the emotion in his intent face. He and Anna were writing notes to each other, e-mails, but what that meant she had no idea. Courtship? Information exchange? He'd come to the restaurant once that she knew of, to bring Anna a bird book. He hadn't come inside, though, just loitered out in the alley. They'd ended up going for a walk. Anna had accused Rose once of matchmaking, but she hadn't been. She didn't think. If pressed, she'd have said friend-making.

Anna looked sleek and self-possessed in a sleeveless sundress and sandals, and Rose knew they were both admiring her, she and Mason, as she climbed out of her car and crunched her way over the stones, head high, arms swinging, tanned legs flashing. Life, health, vigor—she was the antidote they needed, and Rose was glad she'd interrupted them. Theo would've been, too. Plenty of time for all that. She jumped up, blinking away the last pointless tear, and made her face calm and her voice gay. "Hi, you made it! Just in time for Vince's wine tasting. Everything okay at the restaurant?"

Mason was more subdued, not as comfortable as she was with role-playing. But after forty years in the business, she knew how to make the show go on. "Hello," he said gravely, keeping his hands in his pockets, keeping his distance. Rose could see Anna pull back on her own greeting, following his somber lead. Inaccurate signals were being sent. She wanted to step in the middle, get between them and explain them to each other.

"Here, I brought something for dessert." Anna handed Mason a paper bag. "It's just a ricotta cake."

"Did you make it?" She said yes, and he looked amazed. "You cook?"

"Well, sure. How could I avoid it? For friends, though, not the masses."

He smiled, pleased to be called a friend. "Thank you," he said formally. "Come on in." He seemed a little dazzled, holding the screen door open for the ladies. *Come on in,* just like a regular host. And in the kitchen, he stood aside with his arms folded and let the women bustle around, setting the table, rinsing dust out of cups and glasses he hadn't used in . . . well, probably *never*; he'd probably bought them just to fill up the cabinets. Rose could imagine him washing the same plate and fork meal after meal, since Theo was his only regular visitor. But he looked more interested than dismayed, thank goodness, by this takeover of his house she'd engineered without his permission.

"Okay, people." Vince called them to order, marshaling them around the kitchen table. "This is a formal tasting." He'd poured everybody's first glass of wine. "They're all Merlots, but that's all I'm saying. Okay, four are Italian, two are French, two California, one Chilean, but that's all I'm saying. One's incredibly expensive, so if you like it best, too bad." Why include it, Anna asked, if they couldn't put it on the menu? "Because," Vince said reasonably, "I wanted to try it."

"No, thanks, I'm not in this," Frankie said when he tried to hand her a glass.

"What do you mean? You have to be, I need tasters."

"No, thanks."

"Come on."

"I don't drink."

"You don't drink? You don't drink?" His surprise was comical. But how could he not know that? Rose asked Anna the question with a look, and she signaled back, *I have no idea.*

"Just take a sip," Vince coaxed. "You don't have to swallow if you don't want to. Spit it out in the sink, like a spit bucket. All our taste buds are in the mouth, none in the throat. Did you know that?"

"No." She put her hands behind her back, wouldn't even touch the glass he kept pressing on her. She walked backward until she hit the sink.

"Come on," he said, still disbelieving, "I really need your expertise. Think of it as food. You're a great food taster, so just apply all that sensitivity to wine. Come on, Frankie."

"No."

"Please? It's just wine, everybody drinks wine."

"Vince, leave her be," Anna said, "if she doesn't want any, she doesn't."

He wasn't going to give up. "I know, but just—"

"I'm an alcoholic."

"What?" He laughed.

"I'm a drunk." She said it too loud, and then she blushed, embarrassed by her anger. She looked cornered, holding on to the counter behind her with outspread hands, puffing out her chest to defend herself. "I'm an alcoholic."

No one knew what to say. Rose swirled ruby-colored wine in the bottom of her glass and listened to the silence pile up until the room was full. She should have headed this off somehow, but how?

"Oh," Vince managed eventually. "Okay, no problem. Sorry about that. I didn't know."

"Yeah. Forget it." Frankie pivoted, turned on the faucet, started fiddling with a sponge.

Vince looked at Rose, at Anna. He pretended to tear his hair out by the roots.

Before the lethal silence could start again, Mason said in a wonderfully matter-of-fact voice, "I'd call this one soft. That's a wine term, isn't it? It smells like plums. I'd say it's soft and rounded. It's very good. Are we really grading them?"

Normalcy returned, but what a pointlessly idiotic moment. There were so many better ways that could've been handled, and Rose prided herself on handling awkward moments. She half blamed

Frankie for letting it go so far, but that wasn't fair. How could she know what was impossible for Frankie to say and what wasn't?

They tasted the wines. Vince had devised an overly complicated scoring system based on color, clarity, aroma, body, flavor, etc., and it was impossible not to have fun with it at his expense. "*Be serious*," he kept ordering them, but that got harder to do as the tasting went on, especially for Anna. "This gets an eight and a half for pretension," she declared of a Furlan Venezia Giulia. "But I'm giving it a four over all, because even though its assertive bouquet of ash and tangerine insists its heart is in the right place, there's still that faint aftertaste of, well, hypocrisy. And the finish, I regret, is pure Jimmy Swaggert."

Theo wasn't supposed to drink—another reason he hated doctors. He did anyway, although nothing like in the old days. Rose sat close to him at the table, enjoying his deep rumbling chuckle and the tolerant way he was regarding Anna, who was just getting warmed up. Imagine those two becoming friends. Too much to hope for, and she wasn't pushing it. But wouldn't that be something.

"The ideal restaurant wine list," Vince tried to tell them, "is three things: short, intelligent, and affordable. So if we put only one Merlot on, it has to be the best medium-priced one of these eight. If we put two, then we get more of a range, but we have to make a decision about how long our list is going to be."

"There's more seafood on the menu than there used to be," Frankie pointed out from the counter, where she was slicing pears to go with endive for a salad. "Less meat. If you had, say, eighteen wines, you'd weight it toward the whites, ten and eight, eleven and seven, something like that."

"Eighteen," Vince said worriedly. "That's not very many." He was taking a course in oenology at night, he read wine magazines, he picked the brains of the wine reps and the most knowledgeable customers. Trying to become an expert fast.

"No, but it would fit on the back of the main menu nicely," Anna said, always practical. "Are you including sparkling wines in that? And blush wines? They listed blushes separately at Industrial Coffee, but I don't know why, they were just Zinfandels."

The talk turned technical. Mason and Theo were the only ones taking Vince's scoring system seriously. They liked the Scubla Colli Orientali "Rosso Scuro" best, and were sorry to find out at the end that it retailed for forty-five dollars a bottle. The markup made it much too expensive for the Bella Sorella's cellar. But they were also backslappingly proud of themselves for picking the priciest, so theoretically the best, of the eight wines.

Frankie asked Rose if she'd like to grill the marinated pork chops, or season them, or taste the deglaze. Rose knew a polite offer when she heard one and said no, of course not, this was her day off, Frankie was the chef. All the uncomfortableness from before was gone, smoothed over by wine and Anna's silliness—or so Rose thought. Vince got her alone for two seconds while Frankie was out in the dining room.

"Why didn't you tell me?" he demanded in an angry whisper, pushing his face close to hers.

"What, you mean Frankie's—"

"Sh! Yeah! Did everybody know about that but me?"

"I don't know. Anna told me—I don't know who else knows. What difference does it make?"

"What difference!"

"What do you care?"

"*I'm a bartender*," he said fiercely.

"I remember. I don't see wh—"

"She's an alcoholic and I'm a *bartender*." He glanced over his shoulder, but the coast was still clear. "How is that supposed to work?"

"How is it . . ." The light dawned. "Aha."

"Aha!" he repeated like a curse. "She'll *never* go out with me." He made a bitter smile with his nice lips. "Well, at least now I know why."

"She won't go out with you? You asked her?"

"If I told you how many times, Aunt Rose, you'd laugh."

"Never."

"She thinks I'm just kidding around. I keep it light."

Rose was charmed, unreasonably pleased. Vince and women—it was a joke between Iris and her, how much they loved him. If Frankie wouldn't go out with him, it must be a first. How funny. But she made a sympathetic face for his benefit. "Don't give up," she advised. "Women like persistence."

Vince had given Frankie a turtle, Rose found out at dinner. For a present, because she lived alone in a depressing-sounding apartment building where she wasn't allowed to have pets. "Sebastian," Vince had named this turtle, which he'd found in his yard, because its shell was bashed in. "How's Sebastian?" he asked Frankie, after praising the pork chops to the heavens, not to mention the salad and the herb-buttered tagliatelle. "How does he like his bowl? He might need some toys, like a log or something to sit on."

"What?" Frankie was scowling at a piece of meat on the end of her fork, gauging the pinkness. "Oh, Sebastian. Yeah, thanks. He was delicious."

Vince coughed, sloshing wine on the tablecloth.

Frankie grinned. "Kidding."

It was a very merry dinner, and the unlikeliness of that gave Rose pause more than once. All the wine they'd drunk didn't hurt, but they were simply a congenial group. Theo and Anna were on such good behavior, they forgot they didn't like each other. Frankie told funny stories with a straight face about crazy chefs and homicidal dishwashers she had known; Theo and Mason were sure she was exaggerating, but Rose and Anna knew better. Mason had the least to say, but Rose didn't worry about him. She enjoyed the bemused look on his face, as if he still couldn't believe he was here, in his own dining room, with all these *people*. The only time she wanted to cry was when he came back from fetching something from the kitchen and stood behind her chair for a moment before sitting back down. He put his hands on her shoulders, just held them there while the laughter and conversation flowed around them. She felt comforted and weepy, soft inside. In the midst of this lovely, lighthearted meal there was something sad and frightening—Mason's silent kindness reminded her of that. But also of the reverse: that it was possible to endure sad and frightening things in the company of good friends.

They adjourned after dinner to the windowless living room for coffee and ricotta cake. Anna asked Mason something about heron photos. Heron photos? The words made no sense to Rose until she made Anna repeat them, "*heron* photos, photographs of herons, *great blue* herons," a couple of times. Everyone laughed, even Anna and Mason, when Vince teased them on their way out, "Oh, you're going to show her your *heron* photos. Riiight." Very silly, but by then everything was funny. Frankie and Vince got into their favorite argument, what kind of music people wanted to hear in a good restaurant, what kind made them order another drink, what kind made them get up and leave. "I've never even *heard* of these groups," Rose admitted, and they looked at her with similar expressions of pity and agreement. She was afraid to ask what they thought of the Handel recorder sonata or the Mozart quartet for flute and strings, her two favorite dinner tapes. "Play whatever you like," she told them, giving up. "If you can ever agree on anything." They never could, but she was beginning to hear their arguments as flirtation. Vince was courting Frankie by fighting with her. Did she know? She was all business, rarely smiled, took everything he said seriously. Didn't mind telling him when she thought he was a jerk. "You are such a child," she said, disgusted with his goading insistence on junk food and ESPN in the bar. "Time to grow up, Vincenzo. What do you want on your tombstone?" she asked earnestly, poking her sharp finger into his forearm. " 'He served great nachos during the Super Bowl'?"

"Hey, yeah."

"*No*. 'He knew his people and he gave them what they needed.'

That's what you want. 'He was a brilliant bar man. His Cosmo could make you cry.' "

Vince cracked up.

" 'His wine list consoled you when you felt like dying. Everybody who sat at his bar was satisfied. He was a nice man.' "

That sobered him. "Okay," he said after a thoughtful pause. "But can we have the hockey game on while I make the Cosmos?"

Anna and Mason came back into the room laughing. Now there was a sight. Mason, though, was still a man most at ease with a camera between himself and the world, and Rose wasn't surprised to see him slip the Nikon off his shoulder and begin quietly, unobtrusively to take the pictures of his guests. What did surprise her was Anna's easy compliance with his suggestion that she and Rose sit closer together on the couch for a portrait. They touched shoulders, tilted their heads toward each other, smiling at Mason. "That's good," he said, "that's great," angling the camera sideways for more shots.

"God, you two," said Frankie from across the room. "You look so much like mother and daughter, I can never get over it. You even dress alike."

Rose laughed down at her own sleeveless black dress. She'd dressed it up with a scarf around the neck, red and white; Anna had tied a long yellow scarf around her waist. "Great minds," Rose said, leaning close and giving Anna's shoulder a playful nudge with hers. Anna kept smoothing the hem of her skirt over her bare, crossed knee, pressing and pressing the material with her fingers. She didn't look up or smile back.

"Want to see a picture of Katie?" Frankie rummaged in her beat-up shoulder bag. "She might be starting to look like me a little, I dunno. See what you think."

"Is this the Easter picture?" Rose asked.

"No, it's newer, last week."

"I've seen it," Anna said. She got up abruptly and walked to the other side of the room.

"Oh, what a gorgeous child," Rose said. Mother and daughter were kneeling on the grass in front of a plastic kiddie pool, filling it with a garden hose. Each had a hand on the hose, and they were looking over their shoulders at the camera, grinning, squinting in the sunlight.

"Do you think we look alike?"

"Well..." Not really, but Frankie wanted her to say yes. "Maybe," Rose said, "could be, something... around the eyes?"

"No, she's got Mike's eyes." She took the snapshot back, disappointed.

Rose had always wanted to touch her almost-bald head, see what that quarter-inch of bristly red hair felt like. "Maybe if you let this grow," she said, cupping the back of Frankie's head lightly. A surprise: it was soft, not prickly. She couldn't resist rubbing it lightly with her palm. Such a delicate skull, blue-veined above the ears, and something terribly vulnerable about the slender, soft-skinned neck.

"It's curly." Frankie suffered Rose's touch with downcast eyes and a pleased, self-conscious smile. "If I let it grow, it'd be curly."

"Curly? Really? That would be cute."

"You think? Nah, it's easier this way." She pulled away, recollecting herself. "This is me." She shrugged, pushed out her lips, crossed her ankle over her knee. Feigning masculinity was one of her defenses. Against what, though, Rose wondered. Being nice to herself?

Rose excused herself to go to the bathroom, and when she came back Anna was gone. "She went home," Vince explained. "She said she was tired."

Just like that, without even saying good-bye? "That's funny," Rose said. Mason was taking the spent roll of film out of the back of his camera. He gave a slight shake of his head when she caught his eye. *Beats me.* The others nodded, but nobody had any explanations.

Frankie and Vince did the dishes while she sat on the back steps with Mason and Theo to watch the moon rise and listen to the river. "What a nice day this has been," they took turns saying. Rose couldn't resist pointing out that the bird singing its name over and over in the woods behind them was a whippoorwill. "Right," Mason said, nodding, kindly conveying with his voice that that was quite a spot, not a gimme. "They have whiskers," he told her.

"Whiskers?"

"Not the technical term. Looks like little hairs sprouting out around the beak. Like a seal."

This is my family, Rose thought. If she had married Theo, Mason would be her stepson. Whole stretches of time had gone by tonight when she hadn't thought of Dr. Eastman's news. She'd been distracted by the peacefulness, this seductive illusion of normalcy.

Theo was flagging, though. "Stay here tonight," Mason invited him. "Sleep in the guest room. Go lie down right now. Just go." No, he wouldn't consider it. "Want to wake up in my own place." Rose had given up arguing with him. *Fall, then, break your stubborn neck*, she'd said at the end of their last fight on the subject, and neither of them had the heart to dredge it up again. Just thinking about it made her sigh. She didn't realize she had, though, until Theo, two steps below, wrapped his hand around her bare calf. She leaned over and rubbed his back. "I'll drive you back, then," she said. "Old bear."

"Nope. Mason can take me. Right?"

"Sure," Mason said, surprised.

"Why can't I?"

"I don't like you around... the marina at night. Been too many break-ins. Vandalism."

"There have?"

"You knew that—I told you. Guy two slips down, Charles, you know Charles."

"Charles Bell?"

"Had his cabin door kicked in—radio stolen, battery—charts, everything that wasn't screwed down."

She went cold. That hadn't happened. No, it had happened, but three years ago, and in another marina. Theo had moved *Expatriate* to the new dock because of the burglaries and break-ins at the old one. To Rose's knowledge, he hadn't seen Charles Bell in two years.

Mild to moderate cognitive impairment. Memory loss and difficulty planning. Those were the symptoms that frightened him the most, the prospect of them. They'd joked about it: "Well, at least if you lose your memory, you won't remember." Was this how it started?

"No problem," Mason said after a tense pause, during which she alternated between hoping and dreading Theo would realize his mistake. "I'll be glad to drive you." Mason knew, too: she could tell by his voice, too quiet, and his still, stricken face.

After that, the party broke up quickly. She kissed everyone good-bye, including a startled Frankie, and drove home by herself in the warm, buggy summer night, trying to see some cheer or beauty in the stars and the fireflies, the dark, wild smell of the water when she crossed over the bridge. An hour ago, in spite of everything, the tempting thought that she wasn't alone had been a consolation, but it was gone now. She felt lonely and overwhelmed, too frail for the trouble ahead of her. All by herself.

So her tired, beaten-down heart lifted when she pulled into the parking lot of her building and saw the little white car with New York plates in the space next to hers. It wasn't the answer to a prayer, because she hadn't asked for anything, but she felt gratuitously blessed, and she gave herself a little congratulatory smile in the rearview mirror. *Look what I get*, the smile said. *Lucky me, after all.*

Their doors slammed together. "Hi," Rose said over the roof of Anna's car. Anna was faster, met her between their two cars before she could get hers locked. "Hi," she said again, softer, doubtfully. Anna's eyes were huge, Rose could see the whites around them. And something electrified about her, as if her hair should be standing on end. "What?" she said, feeling her heart skip. "What happened?" She saw Iris dead, Carmen hurt, the restaurant in flames—

"I know. I know who you are."

"What?"

"Don't lie, Rose. Tell me the truth."

"What are you talking about?"

Anna kept her hands stiffly at her sides, forcing them down, as if she didn't trust what she might do with them. Her whole body was stiff, elongated, she was almost standing on her toes, neck extended, as if a string were holding her up from above. "Admit it. Admit you're my mother."

Rose was so surprised, she couldn't speak.

"Just *say* it. You are, aren't you?"

A laugh slipped out—she couldn't help it. Mistake: Anna looked as if she'd slapped her. "Oh, darling, no. No. I'm not."

"I don't believe you." But she did, Rose could see it in her eyes for just a second, a lost look.

"It's the truth," she said gently. "Oh, Anna. You're Lily's child."

"No, I think you gave me to her. She took me. You and my father—and then she took me because you weren't married and she was."

Rose kept shaking her head.

"I think so. You were always there," she accused, "even before she died. You went to—school things, you did homework with me, you're the one who told me about sex! You were always—" She drew in her breath. Her face flushed darkly; she turned around and braced her arms on the side of her car, keeping her head down. The ticking of Rose's car cooling down sounded loud in the sudden hush. Honeysuckle and hot metal mixed their smells in the soft air.

"Lily was your mother. I promise."

"All right," Anna said to the ground.

"I'm sorry."

She straightened up but didn't turn. "What are you sorry for?" She wiped her face, threw her head back, sniffed in deeply.

"I don't know," Rose admitted. "I guess I'm sorry I'm not your mother."

Anna recoiled from that. "*I'm* sorry," she said quickly. "It all—Frankie was like the one millionth person to say we look alike and—something just clicked. It made sense for about two seconds." She tried to laugh. "God, I feel like an idiot."

"Why?" Because she'd exposed too much, Rose guessed when she didn't answer. Given away not only a wrong guess but a false hope?

"*God*, that was stupid. Can we just forget this happened? Don't tell Aunt Iris, okay? Don't tell anybody."

Inexplicably, her embarrassment thrilled Rose. "Your terrible secret is safe," she said gravely, and had to smile when Anna flushed again. She could see her sitting here in her hot car in the dark, waiting, suffering with hope and dread. Rose was dying to put her arms around her. Did she dare to say this? "I always wanted a child, children. But I only loved one man, so I could never have any. Which would've been very sad, except there was you."

Anna backed up rapidly, as if a hole had opened up in front of her feet. "Okay. Good night. Erase this, will you? This whole—Seriously, this never happened."

"Anna, wait."

"Night." She walked around to her car quickly and, somehow, sheepishly. Rose wished she would come back and laugh with her—this would be so wonderfully funny if only Anna could see it that way.

She felt as if she had about half of her now. A very unwilling half, but Anna couldn't help herself. Cracks were showing, z-shaped fissures; the razor wire and pointy stones on top of the wall had blown off a long time ago. Rose just needed patience. Bad times were coming, but she felt light and airy, almost young again as she climbed the stairs to her apartment. Warmed to her bones by Anna's disappointment.

11

Dear Mason,

I tried to call, but then I remembered you're out of town till tomorrow. Hope you check your e-mail so you don't think I've stood you up tomorrow. I can't meet you after all, I have to fly to Buffalo in the morning for a funeral. A friend of mine has died. It was sudden but not unexpected. Or that's what I was told. It was certainly unexpected by me. Sorry I'll miss our appt.—shall I call you when I get back? Which will either be late tomorrow or early Friday, depending on flights and misc. stuff. Anyway—sorry this is so last-minute. Hope this letter makes sense. I'm kind of a mess.

A.

"You still here?"

Anna looked up to see Carmen's red face in the doorway, scowling at her. "Hi. Yeah, some last minute catch-up. Everything okay?"

"Marco cut himself. Again. He'll live. Everybody's gone, kitchen's quiet."

"Good." She smiled briefly, waiting for Carmen to leave.

"There's no reason you have to rush back here tomorrow night, you know. Rose would tell you the same thing."

"I know, but it might be heavy, Thursdays have been picking up a little. And it's the first day of the street fair."

"So? Flying up there and back in one day, it's too much. We can get along without you for one night."

Hard to say if Carmen meant that kindly or not. "I'll see how it goes. And I'll call one way or the other in the afternoon. Let you know."

"Fine." Carmen fingered a bloodstain on her apron, frowning hard at it as if she couldn't imagine how it had gotten there.

"Okay, then," Anna said helpfully. "Good night."

She gave a stolid nod and started to leave, actually disappeared for a second. Then she popped back in. "I'm sorry you lost your friend."

"Oh—thank you. Thanks. That's—"

She was gone again.

Stupid, but that made Anna cry. She'd managed not to when Jay called; he'd been upset, so she'd concentrated on sympathy for him instead of what she was feeling. Which wasn't as admirable as it sounded—mostly she just hadn't wanted to cry in front of him. Now it only took one gentle word from Carmen, and she was off. She put her forehead down on the desk and snuffled.

The phone rang before she could pull herself together. Rose, probably; they kept missing each other. "Hello?"

"Anna?"

"Oh, Mason. Hi. Hang on." She put him on hold while she blew her nose. "Sorry. Hi. I guess you got my e-mail."

"Just now."

"Oh, good. So."

"Are you all right?"

She inhaled shakily. "Yes and no. You know. It's hit me kind of hard. I loved him. I really—" She started up again. "Really sorry, I just need a good cry, then I'll be fine."

"Is there anything I can do?"

"No. Thanks."

"This . . . is this the man you were . . . "

"Oh—no, no, this is his grandfather, Jay's grandfather, Mac. Thomas McGuare. He was old and not in very good health, but I never thought he'd die, I mean not this soon. This has really blindsided me for some reason."

"I'm sorry." It was all there ever was to say. He said it as if he meant it.

She reached for another tissue. "So I'm flying up there for the funeral. He died on Monday, and I'm just finding out. He said—Jay said—he wasn't going to tell me at all, because Nicole doesn't want me to come. His better nature finally won one," she said with weak bitterness. "Nicole—she's the other woman, as I'm sure you already know." She rubbed at the incipient headache behind her left temple. "Oh God, it's going to be awful."

"The funeral?"

"All of it. Going back. Seeing them together—I can hardly wait for that. Wait a second." This time she put the phone down while she wiped her face and got herself together once and for all. "Okay, I'm back."

"Anna."

"Yes?"

"Would you like me to go with you?"

"What?"

"Do you want company? I could go with you."

"No, you can't, you're busy, you're working."

"That doesn't matter. If it would be helpful, I'd go with you. Maybe it would make it worse. Just tell me, would it help?"

"Oh, Mason," she got out before her throat closed. She was about to make a complete fool of herself. "Yes," she said in a pathetic squeak, and muffled grateful sobs into a new Kleenex.

He must've changed his mind.

The announcement came on that Flight 3390 nonstop to Buffalo would be boarding in five minutes, and Mason wasn't here. She wouldn't blame him if he had changed his mind: talk about an impulse offer. What she should've done was thanked him and said no, and she *would* have, under any other circumstances. He'd caught her at a low, pitiful point; she'd been sinking and he'd hauled her out of the deep end. She wasn't responsible.

The phone in her purse rang. Ah, Mason. She forgave him in advance. *Don't give it another thought*, she practiced telling him, *it doesn't matter in the least. I'm so much better this morning.*

"Anna, it's Rose. I just heard the news—Carmen called—I'm still at home. I'm so sorry."

"I tried calling you last night—"

"I was at Theo's. He couldn't sleep, and we went for a drive."

"I figured, and then it got late and I didn't want to wake you up."

"That wouldn't have mattered. Are you all right?"

"Fine. I wasn't so good last night, but now I'm okay. I'm at the airport—we're boarding any second."

"I'm glad I caught you. Everything's fine here, don't worry about anything—Well, Carmen says Fontaine came in this morning with a black eye—"

"Oh, Jeez."

"But other than that we're fine, I just wanted to tell you how sorry I am, and if there's anything I can do, anything at all—"

"Thanks, there's nothing."

"Don't come back tonight, that would be foolish—"

"No, I'm not, I decided. But I'll be in by noon tomorrow."

"Okay, but no rush, we can certainly—"

"Oh, thank God, here comes Mason." She stood up so he could see her. "I thought he wasn't coming." She smiled and waved, watching him lope toward her through the crowded corridor, long-legged, long-haired, unsmiling. He had on khaki slacks and a navy sportcoat, a carry-on backpack over one shoulder and his camera on the other. In the last half hour she'd talked herself out of expecting him. Now that he was here, she felt giddy from relief.

Rose said, "Mason?"

"Yeah, he's coming with me."

"Mason? He's coming with you? On the airplane?"

"Yes. He offered, and I was glad—"

"Wait, Mason doesn't fly."

"What's that?"

"He's terrified of flying. He never flies. He can't fly."

He'd stopped in front of her. He mouthed, "Hi," and she smiled and said, "Hi. You're here. Two secs," and looked down at the floor, cupping her other ear with her hand. "Say that again?"

"Anna, Mason's—he hasn't told you?"

"Told me what?"

"He's—well, he's agoraphobic. Sort of, not exactly, it's more complicated than that, and it's been getting better, but he's not good in places he can't get out of. Especially places with lots of people, like—well, like . . ."

"Airplanes."

Boarding went quickly, no holdups. They had seats together; she'd taken care of that last night, called the airline back and arranged it. "Aisle or window?" he asked her after he'd shoved their carry-ons into the overhead. "Oh," Anna said, "you pick, I don't care, either one, I have no preference, I couldn't care less, whichever one you don't want." He looked at her oddly, then took the window.

She watched him from the corner of her eye while the flight attendant went through the safety drill. What should she do? Say something? Let him know she knew? Or not? What would be best? Only now was it hitting her that what she should've done was send him home. But not tell him why, just say, "I'm fine now, this is silly, thanks for everything, that was so nice of you, I'll call when I get back." Too late. He couldn't escape now because they were moving, they'd joined the queue of planes waiting to take off.

The express to Buffalo was one step up from a puddle jumper as far as she was concerned. Seating capacity about fifty. A prop jet. The pilot came on and said there would be a delay. Not much of one, five minutes, possibly seven. He sounded chipper, too human, like a hardware store clerk or your neighbor on Saturday morning. He didn't speak gravely enough. He made jokes.

Mason had a rubber band around his right wrist, and he was snapping it at intervals. The *ping* sound was almost inaudible over the engine roar; she wouldn't have noticed it if she hadn't had every sense concentrated on him. He took the card out of the seat pocket and studied the diagram of the airplane, a DeHavilland Dash 8. He lifted the shade a couple of inches and glanced out at the runway, but the sight made him pale—she actually saw his scarred cheek drain of color. He snapped the shade down and sat back with his eyes closed.

"Did you . . . what were you doing in, um . . . I forget where you were." His nerves had infected hers; she felt queasy, as if she had stagefright.

"Monie Point."

"Monie Point. Where's that?"

"On the Chesapeake."

"I know, but where?"

He shook his head. She thought he wasn't going to answer. "Somerset County. Near Deal."

"Oh, I know Deal, I used to go out with a guy from Deal."

He turned his head toward her slowly. "You have a lot of boyfriends from the Eastern Shore."

"Do I?" Good, he was talking. "Ex-boyfriends, all I have is exes. Did you get any good shots? In Monie Point? Of birds?"

"No."

"Too bad."

"I wasn't taking pictures."

"What were you doing?"

"Helping to extend the singing grounds of the woodcock."

"Ah. What?"

He started to smile, but his whole body jolted when the pilot's too-loud voice cracked on all at once, telling them they were next in line for takeoff, wouldn't be long now, folks.

"The what, now? The what of the woodcock?"

"Singing grounds. Mating fields. Woodcocks need a very diverse habitat in which to mate and flourish."

"Such as . . . ?"

"Early forest and saplings for the females, tall meadows and grassland for the males."

"So you plant stuff—"

"Plant stuff. Clear stuff. Truck in earthworms. I do it with a group of volunteers. Met on the Internet."

"Is it working? Do we have more woodcocks than we used to?"

"Yes."

"Good." He was getting frozen again. "I don't think I've ever seen a woodcock. What do they do, what do they look like?"

He had his eyes shut, jaws clenched. "They're about the size of a quail. Fat, long-billed, big-eyed. Funny-looking. The male has an interesting mating ritual. I saw it once."

"Tell me about it."

The engines revved higher, deafeningly. They were in that pocket of time just before takeoff, standing still while the raw, screaming gathering of power went on underneath them.

"Tell me how they do it, how the males get the females." Mason looked at her. She nodded. She let him see in her eyes that she knew.

He lifted his arm from the seat divider, she took hers out of her lap, and they gripped hands.

"They roost in the long grass, making a buzzy nasal call, to get themselves ready. They take off, explode in the air, flying up and up in widening spirals, so high you lose them in the dark."

"In the dark? It's nighttime?" Smoothly, the plane began to run forward, roll fast like a car, then faster.

"Dusk. You can see them in moonlight. They disappear in the dark, and then they drop. They fall like paper airplanes, twisting, swooping, gymnastics, all the while singing to the females on the ground. When they land—"

Liftoff forced them back, heads flat to their seats. The weightless interval she usually enjoyed made her sick now, in sympathy. His palm in hers was soaked with sweat. She squeezed it tighter. "When they land?"

"When they land—they take off again. Over and over. You can hear the wind in their feathers, a whistling sound when they fly up. They look like leaves when they fall. It's beautiful. A show."

She swallowed to make her ears pop. "Singing grounds. I like that. I guess—we all do better when people help us with our singing grounds." Babble babble. "You could say running a restaurant is a way to make a nice, comfortable singing ground for people. Some people." Luckily, he wasn't really listening.

They kept climbing, but the pressure slacked off and the engine noise moderated. "Well, that's over," she said with exaggerated finality. "Takeoff's always the worst."

"Sixty percent of crashes occur during takeoff."

"There you go."

"Thirty percent on landing."

"Ten percent . . . ?"

"Cruising."

"Well, ten, that's nothing." He must not agree; his death grip on her hand hadn't loosened. "That's like driving your car to the mall.

Jaywalking. Ten is nothing. And that's what we're doing now," she pointed out. "Cruising."

"I'm sorry about this."

"No. Sorry about what?"

"Rose told you."

Denying it would insult him, she felt obscurely. "Yeah. Oh, Mason. Why in the world did you say you'd come with me?"

"I'm much better than I used to be." Which didn't answer the question, she noticed. He opened one eye, bared his teeth in a sick grin. "I'm in a group, therapy group, people who can't fly. We've gone to the airport, sat around. But never flown. That was coming up."

"You're doing great." He had on a loosely knotted tie; she could see it skitter over his chest with every heartbeat. She let go of his slippery hand—he looked helpless for a second, as if she'd stepped away from him in the middle of a tightrope. She pushed the seat divider up, squeezed over, and put her arm through his arm. They rested their newly clasped hands on top of his thigh. "There," she said. "That's better."

"Thank you."

"Don't mention it." She'd probably embarrassed him, but too bad, this *was* better.

He was tense and hard, the muscle in his arm flexed and slightly trembling. His body felt hot through his clothes. "This isn't how I saw myself impressing you."

She smiled without looking at him. "I didn't know you were trying to impress me."

"Shows what a lousy job I've been doing."

"Doesn't show any such thing." Nothing like flirting to take your mind off crashing. He'd invited her to go to the street fair this afternoon. It would've been their first date, not just meeting by accident or going for a walk. But she hadn't called it a date in the e-mail she'd sent, canceling it; she'd called it "our appt." How could she not have realized by now that he was agoraphobic? Or "sort of" agoraphobic, Rose said, whatever that meant. She'd never seen him inside anywhere except his own house, he was always outside, on the street, in the doorway. As far as she knew, he'd never set foot in the restaurant. And now he was sitting beside her on an airplane.

"Does it help to talk," she asked, "or just make it worse?"

"It helps. You talk."

"What does the rubber band do?"

"Distracts me." He demonstrated. "Throws me out of my thoughts."

"Which are dark and scary."

He shook his head, but he meant yes. As in, *You can't imagine.*

"You could do breathing exercises," she suggested.

"I am."

"Oh. Right now?"

He nodded. "It'll be all right, Anna. I won't do anything crazy—don't worry that I'll embarrass you."

"I'm not worried about that." She imagined *he* was, though. Wasn't that one of the big anxieties with people who got panic attacks, that they were going crazy? And that other people would see?

"Talk to me," he said.

"Do you want some water or anything?"

"No."

"They don't give you any food on this flight. But it's only an hour and a half." Thank God.

"Tell me about your friend who died."

"Mac. Oh, Mac was great. His wife died a long time ago, and he lived on his own until this year, when he had to go into an assisted-living place because of his heart. It made him weak, he couldn't go up and down stairs anymore, couldn't take care of himself." Like Theo, she realized. His days of living by himself on his sailboat were almost over, Rose said.

"Mac is tiny, very dark and spidery, a little monkey of a man. Hardly any hair, and bright blue eyes. False teeth and this crafty grin—you just knew he was a terror when he was young. He used to be a railroad man, and he liked to tell ghoulish stories about people or cars or animals that got hit by locomotives, or stories about bums locked in train cars and discovered frozen solid or starved to death weeks later. He liked to shock you, especially if you were a woman. He thought all women were delicate—I loved that about him. He made fun of Jay's sculptures—but lovingly, he was never mean. He'd say, 'Hey, boy, I got an old tuna fish can you can have,' or, 'The lawnmower broke, you want it?' But he was so proud of him. He kept a scrapbook with all Jay's mentions from the newspapers and magazines.

"He used to come to the café to see me. He made fun of it, too, especially the paintings for sale. 'Look at this, a red circle with a white line under it! And only twelve hundred dollars. Can I get two?' He'd say that as loud as he could while he drank his three-dollar cup of latte. Nicole would cringe when she saw him coming. He wore that kind of running suit that makes a lot of noise when you move, and always in some awful, garish color, purple or chartreuse, and *huge* running shoes, as big as his head. Not that he ever did any actual running. He was such a scamp. But very courtly, too, a ladies' man. He had a lot of buddies from the old days, but they were dying off, dying out. So he was lonely. He loved it when I'd come to see him. He really... he loved me."

And she loved him. Love had to go somewhere. She'd closed off most of the conduits to her own family, so Mac had gotten a big, immoderate share. She had no regrets about that.

"You'll miss him," Mason said.

"I didn't call him enough after I came home—came back. I knew he was sick, and I should've gone up there. I wish I could've seen him one more time. I'd like to have told him good-bye." She indulged in a very short cry. They disengaged arms long enough for her to get a handkerchief out of her purse. The flight attendant rolled the drinks cart past them, and they asked for orange juice.

"Now you talk," Anna said, sipping hers, "I'm dried up. Tell me about your childhood." Safe topic. He looked almost relaxed, wasn't even snapping his rubber band. "You grew up on the Eastern Shore, like me. You're an only child, like me."

"No, I'm not. I've got a sister who's twelve years older. Liz. She lives in San Antonio."

"Wow, the things you learn about people. Were you a happy little kid?"

"Yes. Until my father died."

Shit. Not a safe topic—she was just remembering. His father had died in a plane crash. "I'm sorry," she said miserably. "Is that—did you—no wonder you're—"

"I was fine with planes until about four years ago."

"What happened?" When he hesitated, she realized what a stupid question that was, perhaps the stupidest ever in the history of stupid questions. "Don't answer—we don't have to talk about that *now*. I'm sorry. God, what a great therapist I'd make."

"It's all right." At least she'd made him smile. "But I'll tell you later."

"Right, don't tell me now. Whatever you do." She reached over and snapped his rubber band, and he *laughed*. She felt redeemed, maybe not the worst therapist in the world after all. "Childhood," she reminded him. "But only the good parts. What is your happiest memory?"

His happiest memory—he couldn't remember, but his happiest *feelings*, he said, the times as a child he associated with the strongest sense of well-being, were when his father came back from a trip and, later, when Theo came back from a trip. His fathers coming home.

She said it was the same for her, that her father had traveled constantly and she clearly, vividly remembered throwing her arms around his legs in an absolute ecstasy when he returned—and not coming up much over his knees, so she had to have been tiny, three years old, maybe even two.

Mason said he could remember Theo better than his father, who had died when he was only five. He'd loved Theo immediately, no breaking-in period, no resentment. His best memory...okay, he knew what it was—did she want to hear it, his very best memory from childhood? Yes. "We went out crabbing on his old deadrise, the *Sweet Jean*. That was my mother's name, he rechristened it when they got married. We went down to Crisfield, just Theo and me, and we caught crabs all day on the Annemessex River. That's the way I remember it anyway, me working right alongside him, doing everything he did. We went to a bar for dinner that night, one of his old hangouts, this smoky old joint. We sat at a round wooden table in the back room, and he introduced me to his waterman buddies. 'This is my kid, Mason.' I remember that, and watching him, being proud that I belonged to him. I wanted to be Greek, I wanted to take his last name. He was the best of those men, the biggest and strongest, and he told the best stories. That was a perfect night. I was eight, and it was the first time I ever felt like a man. Just a hint of what it would be like. That brotherhood."

She was about to ask what Theo's last name was when the plane suddenly dropped, lost altitude, not much, and then floated back up to where it had been. Minor turbulence. Mason made a sound, maybe his teeth grinding. She said very quickly, "I had something like that, I know what you mean, not exactly like that but the first time I felt like, you know, one of the women. I think I was eight, same as you. It was my grandmother's birthday and we were having a party for her at our house, outside in the backyard because it was summer. Rose and Aunt Iris did most of the cooking, but my mother helped, too, which was rare—my mother hated to cook—and *I* was given the important job of mashing garlic and salt with a mortar and pestle to make aioli. I took it very seriously, mashing and mashing until my arm was burning, but I wasn't going to stop till it was a perfect, smooth paste. What a smell—mm, God, it made me swoon, I never knew what a powerful food garlic is until that day. *Then*—I'd done such a good job, Rose let me mix the two kinds of olive oil and dribble it in, very slowly at first, a few drops at a time, then a thin stream, while she whisked the egg yolks. 'Is it too thick,' she'd say, 'should we add a little water?' and I got to say yes or no. It was the first time I ever really cooked. Rose and Aunt Iris made poached mussels and squid and tiny clams, I remember, and steamed fennel bulbs with new potatoes and green beans, and Chioggia beets, everything on a big platter in the center of our picnic table. And little bowls of aioli all around to dip the fish and vegetables in. 'Anna made the aioli,' Rose announced at some point, and everybody oohed and ahed and said how delicious it was. Even my grandmother said I'd done well, and she was a hard woman to get a compliment out of." She laughed. "That's the day I arrived at womanhood."

They took turns. Whenever the plane dipped or the engine hum changed from one note to another for no reason, he stopped talking and she started. When things righted themselves, she stopped and he started. He told her he'd spotted a brown pelican on his dock two days ago, and how rare that was, what a good sign because they were still threatened and he'd never seen one that far north on the bay before. She told him she'd had to fire the bartender for only ringing in half the drinks he sold and pocketing the rest. "Vince?" he said, aghast, and she said, "No, no, Eddie, the day guy, a jerk, you don't know him. Turns out he's been ripping Rose off for months. I knew he was giving free drinks away to his friends, but that was okay because it was during the day and otherwise the bar would be empty, which is bad for business. I knew he was running drinks to the kitchen, too, which is frowned on but nobody really cares, even Vince does that. I *didn't* know he was stealing about half the afternoon bar receipts right out of the drawer. So good riddance."

Mason told her what birds' pictures sold the best to magazines and stock agencies: eagles, hawks, owls, falcons, osprey, and kestrels. Birds of prey, in other words. How macho, they agreed, but the next most popular was probably robins pulling worms out of the ground, so there you were. Sports magazines wanted game birds, of course, ducks and grouse and wild turkeys, and shots of big V-shaped geese formations never failed. Woodpeckers pecking, especially if they had red heads or tufts. Any bird feeding its young. Cardinals in snow. And you could never go wrong with penguins, especially in couples or groups; people liked them because they looked like them—like people.

She told him the restaurant finally got a good review. In *Chesapeake* magazine, and the critic had particularly admired the service. "Vonnie and I have been working with the waitstaff, and it's paying off. We've got a new rule, the thirty-second rule—a server has to come over and greet you before you've been sitting down for more than half a minute. Because that's what people hate the most—can you believe it, even more than bad food, people hate to walk into a restaurant and be ignored. So now, even if they can't take your order, the server has to acknowledge you, that's our rule. And smile a lot, which they weren't doing. Someone did a study, and waiters who smile with just their lips make smaller tips than waiters who open their mouths and show their teeth. It's true, it's scientific, I think I do it myself. Tip better, I mean. Meanwhile, I'm starting to learn people's names, customers' names. Rose is so good at this, but she's never there so I'm the one who greets people, and I'm starting to know them. The repeaters, not the old regulars, them I already know, I mean new people. So this is good, a sign that it's starting to turn around. But we're stretched so thin, all we do is worry. We're beginning to see a little light, a little profit—of course it's not really profit, everything goes to the debt, which is huge, but at least we're starting to almost break even. Which is a miracle. This is July, the big month, turnaround month. The menu's set and it's good, it's great, except for the soups. Wouldn't you think we could do a decent minestrone? It's a joke now, except Frankie and Carmen don't think it's funny. They still hate each other, I'm still the referee.

I say quit *trying* to make minestrone, I mean, how retro can you get, but for once they agree with each other, they still want to make the perfect minestrone."

She got gum out of her purse for her raw throat, and handed a piece to Mason. She thought they looked reckless and happy-go-lucky, chewing away together. He said they should try bird's nest soup. There was a bird called the edible nest swiftlet; in breeding season it flew against the four-hundred-foot walls of its cave in Malaysia, clung for a second, and deposited a dab of saliva with its tongue. It did this over and over until it made a little cup. "Out of spit?" Yes, dried spit, that was its nest, and people risked their lives climbing the cave walls to get it because it was a great delicacy in gourmet oriental restaurants. Put it in a bowl with some broth, some vegetables—delicious. "How does it taste?" Anna asked.

"Like chicken."

Things got tense again during the landing. Mason shut up and she wondered if he might actually break her hand, or at least a few fingers, while she kept talking, talking, going on for some reason about Aunt Iris's dogs and did he want a puppy, they were great but they weren't cheap, fabulous dogs, she wished she could have one but she was never home, he could train his not to chase birds—

They landed.

She wanted to cheer. Inside the airport, she almost had to run to keep up with him, but she didn't think he was hurrying to escape. He was striding along out of high spirits, and the silence was his way of keeping a lid on his euphoria. He'd done it! He must be singing that inside. After not flying for four years, what a triumph this must be, a real victory, something to crow about. But he didn't say anything, so she didn't either. At baggage claim, they picked up his suitcase, which was enormous, the kind you took on a two-week vacation. She didn't ask what in the world was in it, though; she was following his lead by keeping quiet. But out on the breezy sidewalk, while they waited in the line for a taxi, she couldn't hold back.

"Well—congratulations! Mason, you were great! Don't you think?"

He did; it was obvious. He shook his hair back and took a deep breath of the exhaust-scented air, as if it were the ocean or a flowery meadow. He smiled with his whole face, and it was the freest she'd ever seen him, the most unguarded. "You don't know," he said. "You can't imagine."

"No, I can't, I know. But I still think you were splendid."

"Thanks to you. If it weren't for you, I'd be dead."

"No, you wouldn't."

"They'd be carrying me off on a stretcher right now. A corpse."

"No, they wouldn't!" She wanted to hug him. She almost did—but then he stopped smiling, and the moment was gone.

"Thanks, Anna," he said seriously.

She sobered, too. "No—thank you. For coming with me."

She shied away from asking him why he'd done it, or even from thinking about it. She hoped it was for selfish reasons, to test himself, to achieve this wonderful personal goal, to put a lot of emotional junk behind him. She hoped it had nothing to do with her. She liked him so much. If it had anything to do with her, she was sure to disappoint him.

Mac hadn't had any religious faith to speak of, so the memorial service was in the funeral home, not a church, where more people than Jay must've been expecting showed up. Anna, who had wanted to arrive at the last possible minute, got there just as the service was beginning. There were no more chairs in the airy, parlor-like room, so she and Mason stood in back against the wall. There was no minister; the only people who spoke were friends. Jay spoke, but too briefly, she thought, and nothing he said got to the heart of it, didn't come close to describing the man his grandfather had been. He called him "hardworking" and "a family man." Maybe he was afraid he'd cry if he went too close to the truth. Jay wasn't afraid of passionate extremes, but they had to make him look good. Weeping over his grandfather in front of his friends—maybe that crossed some uncool line.

Or maybe she was simply incapable of giving him a break. It wasn't hard to see him again, not the shock to her system she'd feared it would be. He looked smaller. Not as if he'd lost weight; as if he'd shrunk. She wanted to correct his version of what Mac was like, but she hadn't prepared anything, and the thought of standing up in front of these people made her heart pound. Some of them would think she'd lost the right—Jay had thrown her away, after all. She was about to do it anyway when an old man she'd never seen before stood up and said, "For a pain in the ass, Mac McGuare was the nicest fella I ever knew." That was about right. *Thank you*, she thought, watching him honk into a big red kerchief before he sat down.

At the end, Jay got up and made another little speech. Thanks for coming, Mac would've been so pleased, etc., etc.—in the middle of it he saw her, and broke off long enough to smile slightly and send her a sort of knowing half-wave. Several people, Nicole among them, turned around to see who he was acknowledging. Anna stared back into her old friend's kittenish face, glad she'd had some warning, glad *she* didn't look as shocked as Nicole did. *Didn't think I was coming, did you?* She hadn't wanted Anna here, had even asked Jay not to tell her Mac was dead until after the funeral. If he'd done that—

But he hadn't, so no point in devising atrocious punishments in her mind for him. He'd done the right thing, leave it at that, and don't speculate on his motives. Such as trying to make Nicole jealous. Trying to get two women to fight over him. No, surely that was unworthy of Jay. If it wasn't, she'd thrown away two years of her life on a man who was even scurvier than she thought.

She left Mason and went to pay her respects to the deceased. Mac lay in a closed metal coffin in an alcove of the parlor, surrounded by enormous floral wreaths and arrangements. She'd sent peonies, which he'd loved—she spotted her little bowl among the giant constructions of gladiolus and carnations, and decided it looked small but powerful. Like him. She put her hand on the cool blue metal of his casket, over the place where his heart would be. *Hey, pal.* Then her mind went blank. He was dead, and she couldn't go any further yet; everything past that was just a dark sadness, too new to penetrate. She said a prayer for him, an old one from her childhood. She didn't have much faith either, but nobody had even mentioned God at his service, and that seemed stupid. She got out her handkerchief and wiped her eyes.

"Anna. I'm very glad you came." Jay held out his arms.

They embraced, and she thought, what a complicated minute this is. She truly wanted to give him her sympathy, only a little more than she wanted to sock him in the eye. "It was a nice service," she said, pulling back. He kept his hands on her shoulders, so she pulled back farther. "He'd have liked it."

"Yes, I believe he would have."

"Will he be buried now?"

"No, cremated."

"Oh. Is that what he wanted?"

"He never said."

Jay wanted to be cremated; he'd told her that a couple of times. So he was cremating his grandfather. Well, what difference did it make? Except now she'd never have a place to visit Mac.

"I've invited some people to come up to the loft this afternoon—I hope you'll come. It's a little reception. Drink a toast to the old man."

This was so uncharacteristic, she could hardly process it. Jay *hated* parties; she'd had to fight for or trick him into every dinner party they'd ever given, and cocktail parties—forget it. She looked around at the quiet crowd, still twenty or thirty people milling, trying not to greet each other too boisterously. Funerals were so weird.

She spotted the man who ran the Monkfish Gallery, and there was Monica Loren, Jay had been courting her for years, trying to get her husband, who was on the city council, to put his sculptures in pocket parks downtown. Ah, it all became clear. A professional opportunity.

"Thanks, Jay, I don't think so."

"Please do come. For Mac."

Right, for Mac. "No, I really—"

"Hello, Anna," Nicole purred, gliding up silently on cork-soled espadrilles, black and beige, Anna had helped her pick them out on a shopping trip, girls' day out, lunch and gossip. Had she already been sleeping with Jay?

"Nicole." She took a step back when it looked like her old friend meant to hug her. Was everybody insane?

"I've asked Anna to join us, after," Jay announced. "At the loft."

"Oh, great." Nicole visibly paled. "Do come."

Oh, yeah. She'd like that. As much as she'd like to chew glass. It made the decision so much easier.

"I'm with a friend." She gestured toward Mason. Jay and Nicole turned to look at him, and she saw for the first time, at least consciously, that he was exactly the sort of man Jay hated. He was tall, for one thing, and uncategorizable, so not easily ridiculed. And mysterious. Oh, and the scar, Jay would loathe the scar. How wonderful. She regretted in passing that her motives for accepting were no better, possibly even worse, than Jay's for inviting her. "Thanks, we'd love to come."

12

"I've always had a strong connection to the crumbling, rusting remnants of the city, call it the wasteland of our industrial past. In my art I reassemble, I reconfigure these found artifacts in new ways, in order to give a voice to what's been left behind, to make you see it again, the economic and social past of the urban landscape."

Anna took Mason's arm and led him away, out of earshot. Listening to Jay explain his *oeuvre* to Monica Loren had the dual effect of embarrassing her and making her feel sick. "Let's go in the kitchen," she muttered. "I happen to know he keeps the good booze in there."

Mason went willingly.

Sure enough, she found Chivas in the cabinet over the refrigerator. "You're drinking, right?" she asked, pouring out a couple of shots.

"Definitely."

They looked each other over. "How are—" they said at the same time. They laughed. "I'm okay," Anna said. "You know, considering."

"Considering this used to be your house."

"Yes, and now I'm the unwanted guest. What about you? Is this excruciating?" She'd interrogated him all the way over in the taxi, trying to make sure she wasn't torturing him, that he was coming of his own free will, and that he wouldn't hyperventilate in the elevator or black out in the loft. He'd said, "I just spent two hours on an airplane. You think your boyfriend's apartment can scare me?" A major piece in the puzzle of Mason Winograd had dropped into her lap this morning, but now it was almost as if she'd known about it from the beginning. It was so obvious in retrospect; she must've been blind not to see it.

"This is excruciating," he said, adding an ice cube to his drink. "But I wouldn't have missed it."

"That's how I feel." They smiled grimly, comrades in arms. "What do you think of Jay?" she asked, casual.

"Don't ask me that."

"Sorry."

"What would be a good answer?"

"You're right. Nothing."

They sipped their drinks, backs to the sink, and watched him talk and gesticulate in front of a ten-foot-high rebar and scrap steel construction called *Convergent Sprocket 3*. So he was working on his sculptures in the loft again. Or—could he have moved this piece into the yawning cavern that used to be their living room just so he could tell Monica, whom he'd lured here under the guise of eulogizing his grandfather, how important it was? Yes, Anna realized on a wave of dismay. It was more than possible.

"He *looks* like an artist," Mason observed.

"I know." It was part of Jay's success, she'd always thought, the fact that he looked so fierce and reckless with his crazy hair and archless eyebrows and his gloomy, petulant mouth. "He looks brooding and intimidating, I know. He actually scares people. But believe me, he's just thinking about what's for dinner."

And she'd gotten some pleasure, especially in the beginning, out of being Jay McGuare's chosen mistress. Living in his showy, gratifying, reflected glory, such as it was. She couldn't deny that. She'd put up with an amazing amount of crap, too, for the privilege. How much, she was only starting to realize. His self-obsession. His unholy ambition. The way he lived in this loft or in his studio as if he were alone, occasionally noticing someone else—she—was with him, mostly when he wanted sex or a meal. He was like a not-very-well-trained animal. And women were mad for him—that had always struck her as funny. It didn't anymore, of course; it had only been funny when she'd thought he was hers.

"You're probably wondering what I saw in him." Leading and disingenuous, but she was feeling the need to explain herself. Apologize for herself.

Mason passed a hand over his face. "Yes and no."

"Oh, well. Never mind, then. No, you're right, anything I could say would just be self-serving. But I'll tell you this: he was better than a lot of men I've hooked up with. In my checkered past." True, but she'd probably exaggerated Jay's good points to herself—he did have some—to encourage the delusion that she was making progress with men.

"Don't expect me to drink to that," Mason said.

"Do you think we get who we deserve? Most of us?"

"Probably."

"I think so, too. Except—there's this girl at the restaurant, a sweetheart, and she falls in love with the worst guys in the world. It's pathological, it never fails. Since I've known her she's had three different boyfriends, and every one of them treated her like crap." And now one was actually *hitting* Fontaine, according to Rose. "No way she deserves *that*."

"No," Mason agreed.

She eyed him curiously. "What about you?"

"What about me?"

"You were engaged once. Rose said. Was she nice?"

He bowed his head and stared down at the floor, arms stretched out behind him along the counter. She wanted to see his face. She slipped a lock of hair behind his ear with her finger, and he turned his crooked smile on her. "I thought she was nice. I could say self-serving things, too, but to tell you the truth I can hardly remember her. Her name was Claire. When I think about her now, mostly I remember her arms."

"Her arms?"

"She did ballet for exercise, and I remember how her arms looked in the air when she danced, jointless, like long white scarves. But that's it. I thought I was in love with her, and she's a blur. Except for her arms."

He didn't speak of Claire with bitterness, but Anna disliked her on principle. She'd abandoned him, hadn't she? She wanted to tie Claire's long white arms around her neck. Maybe it was the drink, but somewhere along the way she'd started to enjoy herself.

"You know what Jay said to me once? Love is like a cup of coffee. It starts out hot, it'll burn you if you're not careful. Then comes the long spell in the middle when it's just right, every sip is warm and stimulating—actually he didn't say it this eloquently, I'm paraphrasing. And then the last stage, when what's left starts to get cold. And the final stage is so bitter, you can't swallow it."

"Profound."

"I know, but what's amazing is that I never saw *us* in that analogy. That's what love is for *everybody else*, I thought, but he wasn't speaking metaphorically at all—he really meant it. Don't you think that's amazing?"

"That he meant it, yes. Not that you believed it wasn't for you."

People interrupted them, separated them; guests she knew well enough to have to speak to, talk about Mac to for a little while, then about herself. They wanted to know how she was doing, naturally, what she was up to, if she was coming back. Mostly they were avid for some revelation, intended or not, even a visual, about her and Jay, her and Nicole, some juicy tidbit to chew over later with their mutual friends. She couldn't blame them. It was fairly delicious, drinking scotch in what used to be her kitchen, watching Nicole pretend she was too sophisticated even to notice that something was wrong with this picture as she passed Industrial Coffee hors d'oeuvres to Jay's friends. He wouldn't help her, either—best she figured that out early. She'd probably like to stay tethered to his arm, hoping for safety in numbers, but counting on support from Jay was always a risky proposition.

"I want to talk to you."

Speak of the devil. He grabbed Anna's hand and led her over to the brick wall he still had nude drawings of her tacked to. Now *that* was nerve. "How are you, Anna?"

"I'm great." She looked around for Mason, saw him by himself, examining the lewd painted figures on the screen around the bed.

"No, how are you *really*."

"How am I really." So many things she could say. "I'm looking forward to the moment when I can get out of here. When are we drinking that toast to Mac, Jay?"

He waved that away, but at least he had the grace to blush. "I'm cut up. That's how *I* am. I didn't expect it to be like this. Stupid, but I didn't think I'd feel this way. Work is all I've got now."

"So, nothing's changed?"

"Everything's changed. It has to be the same for you, too."

"I'm sorry, are we talking about Mac dying or me leaving?"

He cursed. But she'd given him the idea. "That's hit me almost as hard," he said earnestly. "I've just got nothing inside anymore, I can't work."

"I thought—"

"Anna, I think you should come back. We're both in trouble. We could help each other."

Across the room, Nicole sidled around the man she was talking to so she could look over his shoulder at Anna and Jay. Anna could almost feel sorry for her.

"You know, Jay, I just don't see that happening."

"It's not working out with Nicole. If that's the problem."

"If that's the—" Stunning. He'd reduced her to staring.

He had a way of shifting his weight quickly from one foot to the other, as if he were planting himself in the dirt before some physical contest. It meant he knew he was right but he wasn't getting anywhere. "Who's the guy? How long have you known him?"

"Who? Oh, Mason, I told you, I introduced you. Mason Winograd—maybe you've heard of him? He's famous. In a way, you know," she qualified modestly, "in his field." Well, she couldn't resist, and besides, it was true. But mostly it was the surest way to prick Jay, who wanted fame more than anything, certainly more than excellence.

His dark, Celtic face turned blacker. This unlikely jealousy couldn't go on much longer, his ego wouldn't let it, but she could enjoy it while it lasted. "Are you together?" he demanded, jerking his head backward. "You're with him?"

"Well." She smiled. "Obviously." That was true, too, as far as it went.

"Fast work," he sneered. "For you."

"But not for you. You hold the record." When he laughed, she knew he'd given up. "I'm sorry about Mac, Jay. I know you loved him. I came up here for him, and to say that to you. That's all."

"Right." He backed away. He was finished. From now on, he could say he'd tried to make things right but she wouldn't cooperate, she was too bourgeois or conventional or too puritanical or too narrow and hidebound or too anything he liked. From here on in, it wasn't his fault.

"Hi—what's funny?"

Nicole could make her catlike face into a shy, beaming picture of sweetness and caring, really an artwork of kindheartedness, and it wasn't always a disguise. But usually it was. Anna used to admire her for it, wish *she* had such an ingratiating skill, so handy in the restaurant business. But how silly, how pitiful that Nicole thought the sweet face could work here, now, on *her* of all people.

Jay looked ever so slightly disconcerted, not much, to find himself standing between his old lover and his new one, as if he'd caught himself wearing a tie that didn't quite go with his shirt. "Nothing's funny" was his exit line, and he turned his back on both of them and escaped.

"Well, that's for sure," Anna said cheerfully.

Chewing the inside of her lip, Nicole watched him walk away, her eyes narrowed with suspicion. *Here's the payback*, Anna thought. *You'll never trust him*. If she'd tried, she couldn't have devised a fairer comeuppance. "Anna," she said, "I was hoping you and I would get a chance to talk."

"Were you?" She arranged her face into receptive, nonthreatening lines. She was beginning to feel depressed, though, over how little any of this mattered. She disapproved of how easily she'd gotten over Jay, and it appalled her to think that her best woman friend in Buffalo had been this shallow, feckless cheat. She knew everything about Nicole, her social worker ex-husband, her twelve-year-old son with ADD, her icy, inattentive mother, her flirtation with Buddhism, her Pilates phase, how she fudged her corporate income taxes, her fear of cats. They'd belonged to the same book club, gone to the same hairdresser, liked the same movies. And yet, Jay's betrayal had hurt her much worse than Nicole's. In some strange way, she might even have said Nicole's was no shocking surprise. Not that she was expecting it, not that she could have predicted it—just that, unlike Jay's faithlessness, it wasn't a complete bolt from the blue. So what did that mean? Anna was even stupider about women than men?

"I never got a chance to tell you I was sorry about what happened," Nicole said. "The *way* it happened. I mean, what a terrible way for you to find out, and I just feel bad about it."

"Do you?"

"Yes, I really do, because we were friends, and I hate to see a friendship break up."

Anna laughed.

Nicole stiffened and stopped apologizing. "Well, anyway. I just wanted to say that to you." Like Jay, she was now off the hook.

"Jay's vague on how long it was going on," Anna said agreeably. "Can't really get a straight answer out of him. I'm curious—was it weeks? Or months?"

Nicole had thick, tawny hair she wore down her back in a braid. When she was nervous, she stroked it over and over on her shoulder or her breast, like a small animal that needed soothing.

"Days? Years?"

"*No.*"

"Not years. Well, that's something. Oh, forget it, I don't care anyway."

"Anna, I'm so sorry."

"Yeah, we did that. So. How's the café doing?" She was more curious about that than the length of Jay's affair.

"It's doing great! Really great. Marsha and I are both managing now, splitting the job, and that's working out well. We're having a very good summer. *Very* good."

"Marsha's managing?"

"With me, as I said. It's working out fine, better than I hoped." Marsha was the part-time pastry chef; until last year she'd worked out of her own house. She was nice, smart, reliable, but what Marsha knew about restaurant management wouldn't fit inside a profiterole.

"Good," Anna said. "Glad to hear it."

"And how are *you* doing? How's it working out at your aunt's restaurant? Jay said you were having some problems."

"Not anymore. No, we're having the best season ever. It's fantastic. I'm having the time of my life."

"That's wonderful."

Just in that moment, they didn't despise each other. Understanding bloomed in the tacit knowledge that they were both lying about how splendidly things were going, both for the same good reason. When it came to the business, they were in rare agreement: the show must go on.

Like most city residents, or in her case former resident, Anna had no idea where to stay overnight in her own town, what hotels had more than pretty lobbies, which ones were worth the cost. Rather than give it any thought, she'd booked a room, and then another when she'd found out Mason was coming with her, at a chain motel on the outskirts, halfway between the city and the airport, in the middle of a high-tech office park. She regretted it as soon as the taxi pulled into the heavily mulched, Bradford pear tree–lined crescent flanking the sterile brick and black glass exterior. They should've stayed downtown. At least some of the architecture was interesting, and they could've gone for a walk, she could've shown him her former favorite places—the bookstore she liked, the Stetson hat store, the park where old *women* played chess.

"Sorry about this," she said to Mason at the front desk, out of the hearing of the check-in guy. "Pretty boring."

"No, it's fine," he said, but what else could he say.

"What's *in* there?" She pointed to his enormous suitcase on wheels, thinking that was a question, not to mention a tone of voice, she wouldn't have dared to use on him as early as this morning.

"Things." He made a grin or a grimace, hard to tell which, and nervously stroked the long carrying arm of the case with the side of his hand.

"Oh, *things*. Wish I'd thought to bring some of those."

Definitely a grin this time. "Tell you later," he said.

They had second-floor rooms across the hall from each other; her view was of a parking lot and the highway, his was a parking lot and two identical blue glass office buildings. Except for a cracker at Jay's, she hadn't eaten all day. She was starving. She unpacked, which involved putting her toiletries bag in the bathroom and throwing tomorrow's slacks over the back of a chair, and called Mason's room. "Shall we eat here or go out?"

Whichever she liked, he didn't care, he had no preference.

"I just want food," she said. "Okay if we stay here? Try the dining room?"

Fine with him. He'd knock on her door in fifteen minutes.

Fifteen minutes? What was he doing in there? Sometimes she thought she knew all about him and other times, like now, it hit her that she didn't know much of anything. She turned on the all-news channel, and thirteen minutes later he knocked on her door.

The dining room wasn't open—too early. They ended up in the coffee shop, eating grilled cheese sandwiches and french fries. She apologized until he convinced her, through repetition, that he really didn't give a damn where they ate. Or, within reason, what they ate. She clucked over that, told him it was no way to live, food was a gift meant to be enjoyed. How could he not care about food with that gorgeous kitchen of his? Frankie lusted after it, she revealed; she was pretty fond of it herself, and she wasn't even a cook.

He didn't argue or defend himself. He seemed content to agree and let her keep talking. She took to teasing him a little. It made him laugh. She wasn't surprised that he liked it; he struck her as a man who didn't get teased nearly enough.

Over coffee, she talked some more about Mac. It seemed only right, since he'd been cheated out of his tribute at Jay's. It felt good to tell Mason why she'd loved him and what he'd meant to her, how much she was going to miss him. By the time they were ready to get up because they were tired of sitting, she felt as if she'd done Mac justice, as well as she could for today. She was even glad now that she'd gone to the loft and seen Jay and Nicole, put them together there in her mind as a couple. The end. Another phase of her life, call it the Industrial Coffee phase, was over.

They went for a walk. An aimless one since there were no sidewalks, just parking lots and asphalt accesses to office buildings full of companies with the word "Systems" in their names. It was late afternoon; the sun that had baked the acres of parking lot all day was gliding down behind the steel and concrete complexes and the neat plantings of cherry and holly and Japanese maple trees. Men and women in business clothes began to stream out of the buildings, clogging the walkways on the way to the parking lots. The sound of cars starting up became a symphony. To get out of the way of the cars and the pedestrians, they sat on a bench under a flagpole in front of the QualSystems Building. "What are those called?" Anna asked, pointing at low-growing rows of purple and green plants that looked like cabbages. Mason didn't know. She said, "I always wonder if you can eat them. Frankie might know. She's fighting with Carmen over whether we can afford to serve a green called mâche, which grows like a weed but for some reason is ridiculously expens—"

Mason kissed her. Shut her right up by putting his hands on her waist and his mouth on her mouth—for a second she felt like the girl at the piano, that picture of the girl taken unawares by the piano teacher, getting kissed while her startled hands were still on the keys. And then, just as quickly, she stopped being astonished. It was like hearing the first two or three notes of a song and being mystified, then hearing two or three more and recognizing it. Oh, *that* song. I *love* that song.

They got up and started walking again. The parking lots had grown treacherous. A minivan almost backed over them; they had to walk single file on an uneven hillock between rows of cars to escape. Under the concrete pillars holding up the portico of the Systex Building, they stopped to kiss again. "I've forgotten where we live," Anna said, squeezing her fingers around Mason's hard shoulders, the left one a little lower than the right. He'd changed his shirt during the thirteen-minute wait. This one was denim and smelled like clean laundry. "I'm turned around."

He remembered. He led them up and down curbs through the maze of lots and driveways, past bleached mulch slopes of begonia and petunia plantings and waving tufts of ornamental grasses. The lobby of their building was cold and quiet, a relative haven. One of the women behind the registration counter nodded at them in a knowing way as they crossed to the elevator, or at least Anna interpreted the nod as knowing. But she was reinterpreting everything, she was like a computer tax program that comes up with a set of numbers, but then somebody sticks in a new one on line C and *bam*, everything changes. All new total.

"Your place or mine?" You said corny things like that when your mind was jumping ahead, wasn't altogether engaged to begin with.

"Mine." Mason whipped his key card out like a six-gun, and that reminded her of the way he'd slouched in the doorway when they first met, his hand on the camera at his hip, gunfighter style. She'd changed her mind about him a dozen times since then. She'd half concluded he was, among many other things, a tentative man, but there was nothing tentative about him now.

His dim room was a replica of hers. They sat at the foot of the king-size bed that wasn't covered with stuff, mostly clothes, the contents of his gigantic suitcase. He'd left his TV on; they unbuttoned each other's clothes while on the screen an attractive Asian woman in a red suit told about a warm front coming up from the south. "For some reason," Anna said, "I wasn't aware . . . I didn't know we wanted to do this," stroking his hair back, kissing his face. "Now it's just . . . I mean, it seems so obvious."

"I was always aware." He got her undressed and then went in the bathroom and came back nude, with condoms. "Better hope these work," he said, opening one with his teeth. "They're antiques." He smiled to show her he was joking, or maybe that he wasn't but it was still funny—but his smile faded when he saw how she was looking at him. She couldn't help it. "Pretty bad," he said in a terrible voice, such a failed try at carelessness. She grabbed his hand and pulled him down beside her before she ruined everything.

"Look what happened to you." She touched a corner of the garish faultline of raised skin roping his left arm, shoulder to elbow, like twisting strings under the flesh. The left side of his chest was all scar tissue, but the worst wounds were lower, under his ribs and on the side of his belly, and especially devastating over the bone in his hip. She reached across his lap to put her hand there, held it still, didn't caress the maimed flesh—he might not like that. And she didn't embrace him, but that's what she wanted to do most, press her healthy body to his wrecked one, as if that could neutralize the trauma. "Did you break *everything*?" she asked, resting her cheek on his collarbone, rubbing his back.

"Not everything."

"What broke?"

He held himself stiffly, wouldn't touch her with his hands. He began to name bones and body parts. Spleen. Lung. Ilium. Femur, clavicle, sternum. Kidney—

She put her hand over his mouth. "Did anything not break?" Relief flooded through her when he began to smile. Oh, thank God, she hadn't ruined it. "You have the most beautiful mouth," she told him, tracing the shape of it with her fingers. "I'm so glad it didn't get hurt." She could make a sex joke now, she could touch his penis and make a crack about how glad she was that it hadn't been hurt, either. And then they could make love. With Jay, if the circumstances had been the same, she would have. But she wanted this to be real, not easy.

She still wanted to touch him, though. So she did, but without the sex joke. And after that, everything worked out all right.

"It's about this suitcase."

Mason opened his eyes, scrubbed them with the heels of his hands. Stretched. "Whatever could you be talking about?"

"You're not going on another trip right after this one, are you?"

"No."

"Like, around the world?"

"No."

She held up a pair of jeans and a pair of dress slacks. He shrugged. She held up a pair of sneakers and a pair of hiking boots. A raincoat and a collapsible umbrella. A bathrobe. A hat—no, two hats.

"You just never know."

"What's this?" Two boxes of dried soup mix, a package of trail mix, a water-heating coil, a plastic bag full of teabags. A coffee cup. She held it up.

"My lucky mug."

That figured; it had the Nature Conservancy bird on it. "Is this your lucky pillow?" And books, magazines, a lot of camera stuff, films and filters and batteries and such. That made sense, but the rest—"Why do you need all this stuff?"

"Just in case."

"In case what?"

He sat up. He looked like a tall drink of water—that was the phrase that leaped to mind—long and rangy, his scarred skin dark against the white sheet between his legs. Scarred or not, he was all man, as the saying went. "Do you know anything about panic disorder?" he asked.

"You mean like panic attacks?"

"Panic attacks can be part of general anxiety disorder. GAD—isn't that a good acronym? There's something called PDA, panic disorder with agoraphobia. That's mine. For the last five years."

"Five *years*." She put her hands inside his size-twelve loafers and tapped the soles together. "What's it like?"

"It's like normal anxiety times a thousand. You worry about everything, obsess about every possible thing that might go wrong. To keep the panic manageable, you try to control everything around you. Because losing control—that's the ultimate terror, see. That you'll be so scared you do something crazy and people will see. And you'll be humiliated. So you shrink your world down. Farther and farther, until the only place you feel at home is—home."

She walked his shoes along her thighs, up and back. "And so all the things you pack for a trip..."

"I might get hot, I might get cold. I might get hungry." He smiled lopsidedly. "Have to be prepared."

"How did it start? Was it just a gradual thing—"

"No. It happened in the hospital. I'd had some surgery, I was ready to come home." He touched his left cheek. "The last reconstructive surgery I had. I was getting dressed, that's all. Nobody was around. Nothing provoked it, but all of a sudden I couldn't breathe. I thought I was dying, I thought it was a heart attack. I was terrified, sweating, shaking, the walls were closing in, the light blinded me—these are the classic signs of panic attack, but I didn't know it, I just knew I was afraid and there was nothing to be afraid of. You think you're insane, or you will be if you let go, if you let anyone see what's happening to you."

"God. It sounds horrible."

"After the first attack, what you're afraid of most is the next one. That's how you become agoraphobic—you keep narrowing down the places where you feel safe."

"And then you..." She put his shoes aside and looked at him. "You build a house with no windows."

"Just in front." He lay back on the mound of pillows. He crossed his arms over his forehead. "I haven't gotten around to fixing that yet. That was stupid. That's hard to explain."

"You don't have to explain it."

"The funny thing was the timing. The accident was behind me and I was feeling good again, like my old self. Even professionally, I was having good luck, some photo sales that took off, moved me up to the next level. I bought the property on the river and started to build a house. Then I had my last surgery and my first attack. After that... If you think I'm bad now..."

"I don't."

"I'm a standup comedian compared to what I was like then. I could hardly go out at all. I was stuck. I could work on my house if nobody but Theo helped me. He should've stopped me, but he let me do it—I installed the wood siding right over the framed-out windows."

"Because it was safer?"

"I guess."

"Like a fort."

"Yes. Like a fort." He said it to the ceiling, wouldn't look at her.

"I have to say, Mason, that seems a little extreme. I wish I'd known you then. Because I'd've been happy to make you some curtains."

He had his face covered with his folded arms. She started to grin when his stomach bumped up and down. She jumped up and tackled him, and they rolled together.

They went across the hall to her room, mostly for the fun of it but also because she wanted a cold drink and his minibar refrigerator was broken. Somehow they ended up in the shower. Apparently all the talk about his body had given him the idea that it was okay to talk about hers. "Anna, how could your boyfriend keep naked pictures of you on the wall when he's got another girlfriend?"

"Incredible, isn't it?" More incredible was how Mason could tell they were pictures of her. They looked like the sexual fantasies an adolescent boy had created with his Erector Set, nothing but harsh lines and sharp angles and prominent genitalia. But Mason said no, they looked just like her. "Oh, thanks," she said, "thanks so much."

"But they're beautiful. *You're* beautiful."

"Thanks. If you think so. Really."

"You don't think so?"

He was spreading soap over her breasts and her stomach, so it was easy just then to feel beautiful. "I never wanted to look like Rose. Well—later, after I grew up, I mean." As a girl, she'd loved it that she looked like Rose. "I wanted to look like my mother, who was small and curvy, very feminine. She had blue eyes. She was *comparatively* voluptuous. Don't you think that would be better? Tell the truth."

"You can't really feel that way."

"Why not? Jay used to say I had a great shape, but frankly, I don't *want* to look like some elongated Moore sculpture, it's not flattering. I'd rather look like a woman than a modernist mobile."

He shook his head, baffled-looking, and put his arms around her. Obviously he didn't get it. They rubbed their soapy fronts against each other, and the argument began to seem irrelevant. "I love the way Rose looks," he said. "I love the way you look. Modigliani women."

"That's nice." She almost told him about her most embarrassing moment. Right then she could *almost* have admitted to him that she'd thought, for one minute only, that Rose was her mother.

"Don't laugh," he said, "but I envied Theo when he met Rose." He had his hands on her bottom. He dipped his knees a little, abashed. "I almost wished—ha—that I'd met her first."

She pushed him away. "I don't like that." She rinsed off under the warm spray by herself. "I'm sorry, but I don't like that. At all."

"What? What?"

"I'm sorry, but I have trouble with that."

"No—Anna, you don't—"

"No, it's not that, I'm not *jealous*, I don't care if you wanted to *sleep* with Rose. Wanted," she pointed out; "past tense."

"Then—"

"This is my problem, Mason. I understand I'm conflicted. I have lots of, how you say, issues. So let's drop it. I'm getting out, but I'm not mad. Okay?"

She got out. She felt silly, but there was nothing she could do about it. He'd said the exact wrong thing, but she couldn't hold it against him. She didn't understand herself, so she could hardly expect him to.

To make up, she told him he was a better artist than Jay. Lying beside him in her own king-size bed, she said, "You like being successful because it means you're good at what you do—Jay is an artist so he can be successful. It's exactly the opposite. He studies trends and courts people who can help him and gets smothered in the politics. Meanwhile, you take pictures of yawning birds. You should be shooting the eagles, the, what is it, the birds of prey because they sell best, but instead you do studies of herring gulls because you think they're interesting. You have *passion*. Your photos—and I don't even know anything about bird photography, and I know you can't really compare what you do and what Jay does, but your photos are playful, they're not forced, they're honest. Jay's sculptures are all mannered and premeditated and clever and trendy. He's so jealous of you he could spit."

Mason liked that a lot. To repay her, they made love again.

They fell asleep for a while, and when they woke up Anna remembered she'd forgotten to call Rose. "I said I'd call after the funeral. What time is it?" Nine-thirty. They were starving. First she called room service, then she called Rose.

"Hi, it's me. I know, sorry, I meant to—no, everything's fine, I just didn't think about it till—How's it going there? That's great. Terrific. Oh, that's great. Well, you know, it was sad, but... Yeah. Um, he's fine. Yes, no problems. No, it went very well. Is he—no, of course he's not here." She sent Mason an indignant look, to match her tone. "Why would he be here? Well, if so, it's because I'm rushing, I want to get to dinner before the dining room closes. Um, because I fell asleep. I know, now I'll be up half the night. Well, I don't know, Rose, I imagine he found food on his own somehow, he's a grown man. Why don't you call his room and ask?" She pretended to pound her fist on her head wildly—this was getting out of hand. "Yeah, okay. Right, see you tomorrow. No, my flight gets in early, I—yes, I told Carmen, she knows everything. Right. 'Bye. Okay. 'Bye."

She hung up and screamed softly. "She said I sounded funny. Did I? She thought you were *here*."

"You couldn't tell her?"

"Tell her you're here? Oh my God, no, it would give her too much satisfaction. Absolutely not." She laughed, keyed up for some reason. This was so high school. She felt as if she were sixteen and Rose was her mother. Mason didn't laugh with her. "You don't understand, Rose has been wanting this for months. She denies it, but it's true. No, I could never tell her, I'd cut my tongue out first."

The food came. They'd ordered like children, shrimp cocktails, mashed potatoes and gravy, hot fudge sundaes. They ate the sundaes first, in bed, watching a hospital drama. Mason could hardly believe it when she told him she'd never seen it before. When did she have time to watch TV at night? He explained what doctors were in love with each other, which ones had drug problems or trouble with their mothers. They turned it off when she remarked, after the second or third emergency operation, that maybe it wasn't the best show to watch while you ate your dinner.

Later, they argued about Rose again. Mason started it. She said something true but semi-snide about Rose's ingratiating manner, what a born schmoozer she was, how perfect for her profession, how she could hypnotize you if you weren't careful—she sort of got on a roll and couldn't stop. Mason watched her in silence for a while, then said, "You know what feels really good?"

She grinned at him and stood up from the table, where she'd gone to scavenge the last piece of shrimp. He was stretched out on the bed in his khaki slacks, nothing else, and she was drawn by the sight of his long, bony feet—maybe she had a foot fetish; first his shoes, now his feet. Sleeping with him wasn't what she'd expected. Not that she'd been expecting anything. But if she'd been expecting something, it wouldn't have been what Mason was like. Very passionate. Appreciative. He had a way of moving, smooth and quiet, unobtrusive, feline. It mesmerized her, especially after she put it together that he'd probably *learned* to move that way after years of bird stalking. She liked to watch him, say, reach for something. He put his arm out just a little more slowly than other people, a subtle, fluid gesture. Effortless but aware. He made love that way, too.

"What feels really good?" she asked, strolling over.

"Letting people off the hook. Forgiveness."

She halted. "What's that supposed to mean?"

"I want to ask you something. It's personal."

She wasn't going to like it, she could tell. "So ask."

He patted his fingertips together over his chest and looked up at her through his lashes, trying to disarm her. "Did you ever make it up with your father? Before he died, I mean."

"Look, Mason."

He held up his hand.

"Maybe you don't know everything. You know? Maybe you don't know everything you think you know. About me *or* Rose."

"Come over here."

She thought about it, then shrugged and sat down on the edge of the bed. She folded her hands in her lap when he'd have reached for one. "My father. Yes, since you ask, we were okay when he died."

"Good." He curled his wrist around her knees.

"We were speaking and everything. If that's what you mean."

She resented him for making her think of the last time she'd seen her father. He'd come to see her in Baltimore, where she'd moved to get away from him and Rose. She wasn't proud of herself for that now, but at the time she'd been glad to hurt them that way, the only way she could think of—that and withholding what she *really* knew about them: that they'd been lovers forever. She'd hoarded that bit of information for a long time, a way to torture them, she'd thought. Her anger had kept them baffled and worried, but they couldn't call her on it because they *were* guilty. It was the opposite of a healthy situation, but she'd seen it as a way to get back a little bit of the power. Mean-spirited, yes, but it had felt good.

One night her father came to take her out to dinner. He wanted to really put things right, he said, once and for all, get back to the way things used to be. They went to a Spanish restaurant downtown. She remembered his long, craggy face in candlelight, creased with earnestness, full of worry and affection. She'd loved him so much. She'd been easier on him than Rose—she still wasn't even speaking to Rose. Rose must've seduced him, she'd decided, hypnotized him and then sunk her claws into him. But it was time to forgive her father completely, and that night she was ready to do it. Until he lied to her. He'd looked her right in the eye and told her that day she'd caught Rose in his bed was their first time together. "Isn't that something? Talk about irony." He shook his head at the wonder of it. "It was as big a surprise to me as it was to you, honey, to find out Rose and I had feelings like that for each other."

For a salesman, he was a lousy liar. She'd felt embarrassed for him, and contemptuous, and brokenhearted all over again. She pretended to forgive him—"Ancient history, Pop, forget it"—but she was brittle and cool, and they both knew that nothing had changed.

A few weeks later, he was dead.

Afterward, when she tried to comfort herself, she'd focused on his sunny nature. Unlike her, her father was altogether an optimist. She had to believe he'd known she would come around eventually.

To Mason she said, "Listen. I know what you're saying, and forgiveness is fine, but there's not just one way to—I mean, you and Theo, I'm very glad for you. I think he treated you like shit when you were little, and it's great that you've let bygones be bygones, more power to you. But possibly these situations aren't exactly the same, you know?"

"Yes."

"Maybe abandonment is one thing, betrayal is another."

"Maybe they feel the same."

"Okay." She laughed angrily. "I give up, you're a saint, I'm a bitch. I'll stipulate to that if it'll make you happy." She stood up, went to the window, pulled back the curtain, glared out across the parking lot.

Mason came over. This room was too small. Why couldn't they have gone to the movies on their first date? He put his hand on her waist, using the other to draw her hair back so he could put his mouth on the back of her neck. "Are we through arguing?" she said in a querulous voice. He touched her through the thin material of her robe; carefully he undid the sash. Rather than flash the parking lot, she dropped the curtain back into place, then leaned back into the slide of his fingers on her warming skin. She pressed her hands to his over her breasts. "Are you angry with me?" she asked, beginning to lose her breath.

"No."

"Is this just a way to shut me up?"

"Yes."

She turned. His kind, serious, currently preoccupied face was becoming very dear. He kissed her on the throat. He kissed her mouth without using his tongue, but it was a deep, slow, delicious kiss, it broke her down. He had extraordinary hands, they could make her come apart, they and the excruciating slowness of all the things he did. She was always a move or two ahead, at least in the wanting, and it was agonizing to have to be patient. He did it deliberately; he'd found her pace, before, studied her like a boxer, so his countermoves were always good but always late. She knew what she wanted quite a while before he gave it to her.

They moved to the bed. She thought to get a little of her own back by seducing him now, being the aggressor, but he kept confounding her by making it mean something. Or feel like it meant something. Sex wasn't romance unless you pretended; she had a personal history to prove that. Sex was nerve endings and synapses and lucky timing. She didn't even *want* romance, just decent treatment, a little cheerful reciprocity between the sheets. Mason was doing things, in the heat of the moment she couldn't say what, doing things to make it feel... significant. Of a purpose. What was he doing? Saying things in her ear, pretty things, not to turn her on, just to say them to her. She forgot what they were as soon as she heard them; their intimacy unnerved her. And he was touching her, but not in that premeditated, sure-fire, cause-and-effect way she was used to, could predict in advance and found subtly depressing. Nothing he did was *in order*.

He came inside her, finally, and she thought, *Got you now*. My game, my turf. Finesse-wise, men folded after penetration, all but the cold-blooded, and Mason wasn't cold-blooded. No, and he lost control but he didn't stop, he didn't come, he was waiting for her. They kissed sweatily, and Anna said, "Mason—God, this is—God, you know this is only for tonight—"

He paused, and she bucked under him, not interested in another stop-action tease now. She didn't like the quality of the silence all at once. "What," she said when he raised up over her. He bent his head to kiss her, and she didn't like that either, it felt like rue, not passion.

"If you wanted to repay me," he said against her lips, "you could've just said thanks."

"*Hey*."

He pulled away and began to hunt for his clothes.

"Wait. Mason. I didn't mean 'tonight,' that was—I was speaking figuratively, not *tonight*, literally, I mean—ha—what kind of girl do you think I am?"

He found his pants first and put them on, then he found his shorts. He stuffed them in his pocket.

"Mason, wait. I meant *temporary*, that's all. This is temporary. But *everything's* temporary, right?"

"Right."

She got up, scrambled her arms into her robe. "Look, I'm sorry, but what do you want? Really, what do you want from me?" She laughed again. "You don't want to *marry* me, do you?"

He had everything now, shirt, shoes, pocket contents. He headed for the door.

"Well, this is rude," she hurled after him, disbelieving. "You're crazy. You won't even talk to me!"

He turned around. "Sorry. I'd stay and fight it out, but I'm not in shape right now. You'd wipe the floor with me."

"I don't want to fight. I want to have an affair! Can't we have an affair?"

He went out. She stood in the middle of the room and listened to the door open across the hall, then close with a definite-sounding *click.*

Ha! She walked around in a circle. She wanted to be furious, aggrieved, the injured party. "Prick," she said out loud a couple of times. "Insane bastard." What was his *problem*? How—how *womanish* of him. Wasn't that what *she* was supposed to do, leave in a huff when the guy accidentally revealed his one-night-stand intentions?

"Just for tonight"—she had no idea why she'd said that anyway. A figure of speech. She'd just meant it wasn't *permanent*, but why say anything at all, especially at that moment? So that was stupid, but he was even stupider. "You could've just said thank you," something like that—how insulting, as if she'd sleep with him to pay him back for being nice to her. He couldn't possibly really think that. What a jerk.

She studied herself in the bathroom mirror while she brushed her teeth. She'd done the same thing about an hour ago, when she'd come in to pee. She'd made funny faces at herself then, amused because she'd looked so—goofy, like she'd just won a car in a raffle. She didn't look so damn chipper now. She looked like she'd been sucker-punched.

She threw the rumpled spread over the old bed and got in the new one, the untouched bed. She could still smell sex, though, all over herself. She debated taking another shower. She hated the feel of her anger draining away, like a reverse blood transfusion. She wanted it back, but a low, sorry voice was starting to say something in the shadowy back of her mind. She closed her mental ears, but presently she heard it anyway. *I fucked up*.

She called Mason's room.

"What did I do?" she asked him. "Whatever it is, I'm sorry. Write me an e-mail. Tell me in a letter what I did wrong."

"It's all right. You didn't do anything." He sounded exhausted.

"Obviously that's not true."

"It is true. Try to understand, Anna. It's not your fault that you're my worst nightmare." He hung up the receiver very gently.

She threw the [illegible] spread over the old bed [illegible] at the [illegible], the unmatched bed. She could still smell [illegible] over herself. She [illegible] the [illegible] of her upper [illegible] like a [illegible] blood [illegible]. She wanted it back, but [illegible] something in the shadowy back of her mind. She closed her mental [illegible] she heard [illegible].

[illegible]

"What did I do?" [illegible]. "Whatever it is, I'm sorry. [illegible] what I'm sorry."

"It's all right. You didn't do anything." [illegible]

[illegible]

"It is [illegible]. It's not [illegible] that [illegible] nightmare." [illegible]

13

"I thought that was your car."

Anna jumped up and whirled around in one fast move. "Rose." She'd left her thirty minutes ago at the Bella Sorella. "I've got some errands to run," Anna had called across the kitchen, and Rose had waved and called back, "Fine, me too—see you later." And now here they both were.

"I didn't follow you," Rose said with an anxious laugh, watching her feet as she came across the lumpy, just-mown grass in her flat-heeled shoes.

"I know." Although, for a second, the thought had crossed her mind. But it really wasn't much of a coincidence that they would both show up today at her mother's grave. It was Lily's birthday.

"Oh, those are pretty." Rose gestured toward Anna's salmon-colored roses. "She loved roses. I brought these," she said deprecatingly. "Lilies. Not very imaginative, but it's what I always bring." She knelt down in the grass and placed her orange and yellow bouquet by the greening bronze marker, near Anna's roses but not touching them; a respectful distance away.

"Rose, put them in the vase. They'll die there."

"No, I don't want to crowd your roses, they're so pretty."

"No, put them together—"

"This is fine. This is fine. I should've brought a vase, but I always use the one in the marker, and I just wasn't expecting—anyway, this is fine." She stood up, slapping wet grass blades from her hands. "Looks pretty this way. More of a show."

They stood beside each other, looking down at the flowers on Lily Fiore Catalano's grave, admiring the bright pastels against the dark green lawn. "One thing I've always wished she'd lived long enough for me to thank her for," Anna said.

"What, honey?" Rose turned to her consolingly.

"Not naming me Daisy."

Rose let out a bark of laughter that sounded loud, almost raucous in the quiet cemetery, no other sound but birdsong and the faint whiz of cars on the highway beyond the hill. It had rained this morning, but the clouds were sliding away on a fresh-smelling breeze, throwing speeding shadows on the ground between blasts of blinding sunshine. One of those days when you had to keep taking your sunglasses off and putting them back on.

"Iris called this morning. She can't make it down—sometimes she does, and we come here together on Lily's birthday. Either way, we always call each other."

Anna tried to imagine those phone calls. It was odd to think of Rose and Iris mourning her mother together, this long after she'd been gone. Twenty-three years. "Another thing I've always wished," she said, "is that I had a sister."

Rose nodded. "Sisters are a blessing." Anna glanced at her, looking for irony or awareness. "They keep us from feeling like we're alone. More than men do."

Anna pondered that. "Are those for him?" she said too curtly. Speaking of men. She pointed at a clutch of red and white petunias, the stems wrapped in a wet paper towel, that Rose had left on the ground after putting her lilies on her sister's grave. Hoping Anna wouldn't see them?

Rose bent to pick them up. "I stole them out of Louis's planter in the front window." She eyed them critically, plucking away the tan, tissue-thin dead petals and blowing them off her fingers. She went across to the other grave, the one on the far side of Lily's. BELOVED HUSBAND, the marker read; Lily's said BELOVED WIFE. Squatting, she placed her damp, straggly bouquet beside the bronze plaque. She paused, resting her palms on the grass; the side of her face Anna could see looked serene and fond, peaceful. She'd done this often enough to be soothed by the sameness. A ritual. Then she straightened, pushing up with her hands on her knees with a little sigh of breath. Getting old, Anna thought with an unfamiliar pang. Rose said, "Shall we go sit by the water for a minute? Do you have time?"

Anna shrugged. "Sure."

They went down the path to a small, man-made pond that lay between two tiers of graves on the long, sloping lawn. Concrete benches at discreet distances surrounded the pond, but they were all empty today, probably because of the rain. Anna spread her raincoat out on one and sat down. "What a dreary place. Why would they plant weeping willows here?"

"It does seem a little obvious." Rose sat down on the piece of raincoat beside her.

Lily pads floated on the black water in the shady end, but Anna had never seen them bloom. Two little ducks, speckle-breasted, gray-headed, were all that kept the place from being unbearably melancholy, and they weren't doing that good a job. What kind were they? One of the most monogamous birds in the whole bird kingdom was the American black duck, she happened to know, courtesy of Mason. It had come out in some context or other that night. Their one and only night. Oh, she remembered the context—she'd asked him how birds had sex. They did it the same way people did, pretty much, except their equipment was more rudimentary.

"Your mother would've been sixty-three today," Rose said.

"Yes."

"I wonder what she'd look like. If she'd still be beautiful."

"Was she beautiful?"

"Oh, she was. You've seen pictures. You remember."

Anna nodded. She'd just wanted Rose to say it. "What was she like? As a person, not a mother. What sort of a grown-up woman was she?" And why were these questions possible now when they never had been before? Something about the coincidence, or the flowers, the sad black water.

Rose didn't look at her, but there was care and thoughtfulness in the quality of the pause before she answered. "Lily. Oh, Lily was like air and light. Always changing and moving, you couldn't catch her."

Yes, Anna thought; *Look at me, Mommy*—the refrain of her childhood.

"Your grandmother used to say she had a short attention span, but that wasn't it. She was moody and quick, flighty, hard to pin down. Elusive, I guess is the word."

"Was she happy?"

"Sometimes. She had such highs and lows."

And as soon as she got sick, that was the end of the highs. What Anna remembered most about the eighteen months between her mother's diagnosis and death was her closed door and her darkened room, and the necessity to be quiet. She had longed to be with her, make tea, rub her feet, read to her, but her mother had hardly ever felt well enough to let her come close. So Anna had cleaned the house.

"But everyone loved her. In her good moods, Lily was wonderful fun, everybody loved to be around her."

Light and air, present and absent. Interested, indifferent.

"How did she meet my father?" And how strange, that no one had ever told her the story.

"How did Lily meet Paul?" Rose crossed her legs and clasped her hands around her knee. She wore slim black pants and black ballet slippers; the white stretch of ankle between them was bare and trim, blue-veined. "Oh, they met at the restaurant."

"Really? He was a customer?"

"He was living in Baltimore, just starting out selling books and magazines. He had several accounts in town, and one day he came in for lunch."

"And they talked?"

"Yes," she said after a slight pause. "Lily was hostessing that day, so, yes, they talked." Her face softened; she smiled. "Your father had on a plaid shirt and a corduroy sport coat. And he had that New Jersey accent, but it was even worse then. He looked like Tony Perkins—Lily thought. We both thought that."

"You saw him, too?" Rose should've been in the kitchen; that's where Anna had put her in her mind for this story.

"I saw him. It was so funny—he got up to pay and he couldn't find his wallet. You should've seen him blush and stammer—before that he'd been flirting. We ended up lending him five dollars for gas to get home."

"That's funny."

"He left, but then five minutes later he came back, triumphant and vindicated—he'd found his wallet on the floor of his car."

"And so then . . . what? He called her and they just started dating?"

Rose turned to look at her. She smiled, but her eyes had a shuttered look. "Yes, that's right. To make a long story short."

If that was painful, Anna was sorry for her. If she'd fallen in love with Paul that day but he'd fallen in love with Lily, Anna was sad. But in light of the way things had turned out, her sympathy had boundaries.

She changed the subject, began to talk about the restaurant. They'd had another good week last week, and the best weekend yet. "It's fantastic," Rose said, her face lighting up, "I can't believe we're doing so well in such a short time."

"Yeah, it's pretty good. But it's the busiest time of the year anyway, you have to keep that in perspective."

"But everything's working, everything all at once. I haven't had that feeling in so long."

"But don't forget, we've had perfect weather and the economy's good—that means *everybody's* business is up."

"You're right," Rose said. "It's important to guard against too much optimism."

Anna started to agree, then realized she was teasing her. "What did you decide about the floor? Have you thought about it? You can't keep putting it off, we have to *do* something."

"Do we? I'm just not sure what. I'm not convinced a bare floor is that much better."

Bare floor; she always made it sound like a prison cell, like solitary confinement. "We'd refinish. You've got pretty pine boards under that carpet, Rose, it could be beautiful."

"But that would cost so much. And we'd have to close for days, and we can't afford to right now. The timing's not good."

"It'll never be good. You could do it in mid-week, Monday, Tuesday, probably be open for business Wednesday night."

Rose sighed. "But then think how noisy it would be. My old customers, the ones who've been coming for ten or fifteen years, my *friends*, Anna—they'd hate it."

"It's a tradeoff. Yes, you lose a few of the old-timers, but you get more families and young people. *Young* people, Rose, the ones with the cash."

She sighed some more. "Oh, I don't know, I just don't know."

"Well, think of it this way—those old folks are going to have to leave anyway if you keep things exactly the same and then fold."

"I'd hardly say we're keeping things exactly the same."

"Not everything. I exaggerated." They weren't moving nearly fast enough for her, though. Rose wasn't like Carmen, thank God, backward and reactionary for the hell of it. Still, when you cleared away the camouflage and looked past the personal styles, you saw that, deep down, they were pretty much on the same team.

"Yes," Rose said, "you exaggerated. Those paintings!" She laughed too cheerfully, like a mother pretending her teenager's new tattoo was charming. "They've changed the whole look of the dining room."

"Well, wasn't that the idea? I thought you liked them."

"I do. I do. I never *hated* the maps, though. I know you did—"

"The maps? You're kidding."

"—but I thought they were kind of homey."

"They were *yellow*. Look, it all goes back to what you want, what style of restaurant, and I thought we'd agreed on that a long time ago."

"We did agree."

"We must not have, because I want clean, warm, and upscale—you want dingy, friendly, and family."

"I do *not*."

"You do, Rose. If not, why is it like pulling teeth to get you to change anything?"

"Now that is *really* an exaggeration."

Was it? Maybe arguing with Rose about the restaurant was a safe way to fight about something else. Maybe the restaurant was a scapegoat. That wasn't an altogether brand-new thought. This one was new: maybe Anna wanted to change everything about the Bella Sorella, make it *her* restaurant, not Rose's, to pay her back. Steal it from her, the way she'd stolen Paul from Lily.

No, that couldn't be. She wouldn't be staying around long enough, even assuming such a devious plot had seeped into her subconscious. That reminded her.

"Listen, Rose, you know my friend Shelly?"

"Who?"

"The woman I told you about, we used to work together at the café, she moved to San Diego. The one who's starting a restaurant? She wants me to come and manage it?"

"Yes, I remember."

"Well, that's not looking very hopeful all of a sudden. It looks like the people she was counting on for backing aren't coming through after all."

"Oh, dear." Rose's try at a commiserating look was a failure.

"So that option may not be viable anymore, but there's this guy. His name is Joel and he's an old friend, I've known him since I lived in Hudson." Where she had moved for a few years, back in her late twenties, with a man named Tyler. Tyler had wanted to go back to the land, but his main crop on their rented farm in upstate New York had turned out to be marijuana. "Anyway, he's still there, and he's got a vegetarian restaurant he wants to redo, bring it upscale, try to turn it into gourmet vegetarian."

Rose gaped at her. "Is this that—dope grower, that man you—"

"No, no, that was Tyler, this is Joel. Completely different guy. Anyway, he wants me to come up there and help him make the change. I haven't said I'll do it, but it's a fallback if Shelly's thing definitely fizzles. It's a contingency, that's all, and I wanted you to know about it." What could be fairer?

"Thanks," Rose said faintly. "Contingencies, options, and fallbacks. I do appreciate your keeping me up to date on all of them."

Anna tried to read her stiff, half-smiling profile as she looked out over the black pond and the grave-dotted hill behind it. The two little ducks were dabbling at the very edge of the water, so close she could see the yellowish-orange of their feet under them, steadily paddling as they poked their black bills among the weeds.

"I'm just telling you," she said reasonably. "We had an arrangement, and it seems to be working out for both of us. That's great—right? But it was never supposed to be any kind of a lifetime commitment, Rose, it was always open-ended."

Rose kept her eyes on the distance. She let her knee go and uncrossed her legs, rubbing the tops of her thighs as if the circulation had gone out of them. She clasped the gritty sides of the concrete bench and rocked back, looking up at the high coasting clouds. "Theo's worse. Mason's staying with him on the boat now, or I am, since he refuses to move in with either of us. It can't go on this way. We haven't told him. He has a disease called corticobasal degeneration."

"Oh, Rose."

"It means he only has another year or so before he's completely immobile. Then maybe two more years after that. That's all."

"I'm so sorry."

Rose looked at her. "*I'm* sorry," she said, blinking fast. "I should not have told you that. I did it for the wrong reason." She gave Anna's forearm a quick, hard squeeze and stood up.

Anna stayed where she was, watching her move across the lawn toward the pond bank. The ducks paddled backward, then turned in unpanicked half-circles and glided away with soft, irritable quacks. From ten feet, they turned again to look at Rose, who was bent toward them in a graceful L, rubbing her fingers together as if she had food in her hand. They wouldn't come any closer, though. They didn't trust her.

Confession wasn't the same as exoneration. And manipulation, even if you went all guileless and owned up to it, was still manipulation. Admitting you'd done something for the "wrong reason"—was that supposed to cure it? Anna hugged her arms, avoiding the sight of Rose by getting up and walking back to her parents' graves. She began to tear the crabgrass away from the plaques, making neat earthen borders around them.

Mason had never written that letter telling her what she'd done wrong. The morning after their one-night stand in Buffalo she'd called his room, but he'd already checked out. She still didn't know how he'd gotten home, if he'd taken another flight, the train, a rented car. In a few days her anger, which was complicated anyway, mixed up with too many other emotions to give her any satisfaction, died away altogether, and then all she felt was sheepish. The rest of July had been the month of sheepishness.

But it flared up again, her anger, when he hadn't invited her to the launch of the *Wind Rose.* They'd had a little party outside on his dock to celebrate, Rose and Theo and a few of their friends, even Frankie and Vince. But not Anna. And then, insult to injury, he hadn't responded to her casual e-mail, which had simply said, "M: Want to go to the movies or something? A." No answer at all, not even "No," just silence. When Rose mentioned he'd gone to some island in Maine to photograph puffins, Anna had thought, *Aha, no wonder!* and waited for him to come home. But then, again, nothing. After that she didn't feel anger, just disappointment. A hole.

She'd done a stupid thing in Buffalo, and in the aftermath she'd decided it was Jay's fault. Seeing him again had stirred up the poison in her, which had been lying harmless at the bottom, covered up with normal, wholesome emotions. Proximity to Jay soured everything in the glass, and she'd reacted by pulling away from Mason. Who hadn't done anything wrong, hadn't slept with anyone she loved behind her back, didn't deserve to be lumped in with all the ones who had. But that was like reaching a "breakthrough" in therapy—Aha, my little brother hit me when we were on top of the Empire State Building, that's why I'm afraid of heights! Just *knowing* why you did stupid things didn't cure you of stupidity.

At least Mason had never tried to manipulate her. She almost wished he had. And he'd certainly known when to quit—Rose kept trying. She was standing with one hand on her hip, shading her eyes with the other; the sun had broken through again, dazzling on the water. While Anna watched, she turned and came striding toward her, long-legged, arms swinging. Her face was clear again, determinedly cheerful. "It's clearing up. Good, we can eat outside."

"Eat outside?"

"Did you forget? It's somebody else's birthday, too."

"Oh, that's right." She stood up, slapping the dirt from her hands on the seat of her jeans. "Katie. I almost did forget." Frankie's little girl was coming to the restaurant for a little party this afternoon—Rose's idea.

"Well, I'll get going. You stay if you like, there's still plenty of time. I interrupted you."

Anna looked at the pretty roses and lilies on her mother's grave, the wilting hank of petunias on her father's. "That's okay." She'd paid her respects, finished her business. "I'll go back with you."

They walked up the winding asphalt path together, toward the parking lot. Halfway, they had to move aside so an elderly gentleman coming down could pass. Rose put her hand on Anna's back, guiding her, and the old man moved past. They resumed their way, but Rose didn't take her hand away. Anna didn't move over or shrug it off. It felt nice, that light pressure on the back of her waist. Companionable. Warm. *Fine*, she thought, *but I'm still leaving.*

She'd seen pictures of Kate, but for some reason she was expecting the reality to be a sort of miniature Frankie. But no. Frankie's almost bald head and flat chest, and especially the long, baggy shorts and sleeveless jersey she had on today made her look like the world's smallest professional basketball player. Freckle-faced Katie hardly even looked related to her in a yellow pinafore and a starched white blouse, yellow patent leather shoes and matching yellow pocketbook on a shoulder strap. Inside the pocketbook, she was proud to show you, were all the things a young lady might need, comb, mirror, pretend lipstick, a tiny bottle of cologne, a tissue-thin hankie. Marbles. And she had ringlets today, beautiful long, curling trails of carrot-colored hair down to her collarbones. Side by side, Katie and her mother looked a lot like Shirley Temple and Eminem.

They had the party at three o'clock, the slowest time of the day, around one of the new umbrella tables on the sidewalk. It was one of those clear, perfect afternoons, rare in early August; it wasn't hot and the air smelled clean and the sky looked just washed. Rose had bought party favors and hats, in spite of Carmen's prediction that passersby would mistake the Bella Sorella for Chuck E. Cheese, and Frankie had made Katie's three favorite foods, hot dogs, spaghetti with meatballs, and corn on the cob. The guests at the table kept changing as cooks and servers came and went, popping up to do something in the kitchen or on the floor and then coming back, but Katie was too excited to notice. She was at Mommy's restaurant.

"My mommy's a cook," she told everybody she met. "I *know*," they'd exclaim, captivated. She delighted them all, even Carmen, who just this morning had tried to sabotage Frankie's dinner special by "borrowing" the key ingredient—even scary Dwayne, who carved Katie a dolly out of a bar of soap with a boning knife at the table. Dwayne had a lot of extremely vulgar tattoos on his thick, wrestler's arms, but luckily all the bristly black hair growing on them obscured the details. Luckily, too, Katie couldn't read. She got many hastily purchased dime-store gifts and she loved them all, puzzles and games and stuffed animals, a harmonica, a deck of cards. Rose accidentally hit a home run, though, with the best present of all: Ballet Star Barbie.

Frankie sat beside Katie and didn't say much, helping her open packages and exclaiming over them, occasionally coaxing softly, "What do you say?" She was quietly radiant, her small, foxy face lit up with pride and love, madonna with a nose ring. She and Fontaine had collaborated on a three-layer chocolate cake for dessert. They lit Katie's four candles and everybody sang and ate cake and vanilla gelato.

Luca fell in love with Katie. He'd lost his own family, Rose had told Anna, in an accident a few years ago in his native Sardinia. Whenever a child had a birthday at the restaurant, he'd always come out of the kitchen and sing "Happy Birthday" in Italian. "*Tanti auguri a te,*" he sang to a giggling Kate, "*tanti auguri a te. Tanti auguri, carissima* Katie, *tanti auguri a te.*"

"Rose, what do you think of this?" Fontaine said when the singing was over. "Cake and Eat It."

The staff couldn't sit down to a meal anymore without bombarding Rose with new restaurant name suggestions. It was getting a little silly, since she never liked any of them. "Cake and Eat It," she said slowly. "Hmm." If nothing else, she was always polite. "Well, if all we did was desserts . . ."

"Oh, yeah, I guess." Fontaine gave a good-natured shrug. She was about seven months gone, Anna gauged. She had corn-silk blond hair and a sweet, blue-eyed, baby face that suited less and less her expanding waistline. Rose didn't need a full-time pastry chef, but she was letting Fontaine work eight-hour shifts anyway so she could make some money before she had to quit and raise a baby. She wasn't coming to work with any more bruises these days, but that was the only good thing going on in her life. She'd finally confided in Rose who the baby's father was. "Guess," Rose said to Anna. "Think of the worst possible person." "Someone we know?" "Someone we used to know." Then it was easy. "Eddie!" Yes, Ever Eddie, the crooked schmuck of a bartender Anna had fired last month. He couldn't be the black eye–giver, though, because he was long gone by then—to California, somebody said, and somebody else said Las Vegas. Either way, he was out of the picture. Why would a girl as sweet and harmless as Fontaine consistently let one rotten boyfriend after another abuse her? What sort of satisfaction did it give her? "Happens all the time," Carmen had pronounced—like she would know.

Rose listened patiently to more restaurant name suggestions. Vonnie said, "How about the Open Arms? Doesn't that sound warm and welcoming? Or Heart's Content. I thought of Creature Comforts, too."

Rose pursed her lips and looked thoughtful.

"Sweet Home," Vince piped up. "Like that? 'Let's have dinner at the Sweet Home.' "

"Sounds like soul food," Frankie objected.

Luca said he thought Fontaine's suggestion was very good, then bashfully offered one of his own. "*Il Caffe delle Tre Forti Donne.* Eh? Is too long?"

"The Three Strong Women Café," Anna translated over the laughter. "Who would these three strong women be, Luca?" As if she didn't know.

"You, of course," he answered gallantly, "and Carmen, and Chef Rose."

Rose sent Anna an arch look, veiled and playful. "Why, that's not bad," she said in encouraging tones, "not bad at all." But then, when Luca looked stunned by his good fortune, she had to tell him, "It is a little long, though."

"She hates everything," Dwayne muttered, a litany with him now.

"It's true, Rose," Anna said, to pay her back for teasing. "Nobody's come up with anything you'll even consider. Is this a real contest or not?"

"No, no, these are all wonderful suggestions," she denied, laughing, "it's just that—if we really changed the name, the new one would have to be *perfect*, and I know it can't be. Whatever we choose, it'll leave something out, something important. Essential."

"But that's true for anything."

"I know, but—if we call it Open Arms or Heart's Content, it says we're a warm, cozy place, but nothing about the *food*. And if we call it Pasta Pasta"—Shirl's suggestion—"it's the same thing but the other way around. If we call it Con Brio, which is a lovely name, it says we're gay and lively, but also that it's *noisy* here, maybe it's not dark and romantic enough. You see? The Chesapeake Room—I love that, but doesn't it sound like a men's club? I see fishing prints on the walls, and no women eating. Same with Capriccio and

A Capella and Raincheck, Chin-Chin, New Leaf—these are all nice, but they all leave something *out*." She held her palms up in a helpless gesture. "Sorry. Keep trying. Really, I love them all!"

Anna said, "Okay, how about the Love and Happiness Restaurant. Or the Love and Happiness Café. Come on, what does that leave out? Let's call it Love and Happiness."

Rose just laughed.

"You don't like that, either? Not inclusive enough?"

"Not inclusive enough."

"Also," Frankie said, "it sounds Chinese."

"Okay, the Love, Despair, Happiness, and Death Restaurant. How's that?" Anna loved making Rose laugh. "Too long? Luca says it's too long. Then just pick the best two. Come on, Rose, you're the boss, you can pick the two you like best."

But Rose flapped her hand and rolled her eyes, and that was the end of that.

Katie's party ended at four, time for everyone to go off shift or back to work. Mike, Frankie's ex, was due to pick Katie up at four-fifteen, and some of the staff who usually went home at four hung around to get a look at him. Frankie had some prep work in the kitchen that couldn't wait, so Vince put Katie on top of two phone books on a bar stool and did magic tricks while she waited for Dad. He was wonderful with her, and that was a bit of a revelation to Anna—Vince the ladies' man was absolutely charming with children, or at least this child. He had big, round, beautiful eyes, a mobile, expressive face. A clown face, it turned out, and it could send Katie into gales of giddy, skittering laughter.

"Daddy!" Katie cried when she saw Mike. Vince came around and helped her off the stool. There was a funny moment when he could have handed her directly to her father, who was smiling, arms out, ready for her, or set her on the floor. He set her on the floor.

"Hi, I'm Anna. Obviously you're Mike."

"It's good to meet you."

"Sorry you've just missed Rose, she had to leave early."

Mike said he was sorry, too, he'd heard a lot about Rose. He had a nice smile. He looked like an assistant professor, which was what he was, in wrinkled khakis and a blue work shirt, a tweed jacket over his shoulder.

Vince introduced himself, and the two men shook hands. Anna said she'd go get Frankie.

"Mike's here."

"Oh, okay." Frankie was making ribollita, a sort of pureed Tuscan stew. She called it an acquired taste; Carmen called it mush. "Listen, this is finished, all except for the spices that go in last. Luca knows, I told him the whole deal."

"Okay, no problem. Go have fun." Frankie was taking a rare night off. She, Katie, and Mike were going back-to-school shopping, then out to dinner for one last little birthday fling. She'd been talking about it all morning, as thrilled as if they were taking the Concorde to Paris.

She took off her dirty tunic and threw it across the room in the laundry pile. She got a gauzy red shirt out of the employees' closet and put it on over her tank top and baggy shorts. "What do you think?" She stopped at the mirror by the door, the one the waitstaff used to check their lipstick or their hair just before going out on the floor. What was Frankie checking?

"Looks great," Anna said after a startled moment.

"Yeah? I don't know if he's taking us someplace nice or not, after. Could just be Mickey D's. So I look okay?"

"You look fine."

In the mirror, she lifted her chin and opened her eyes wider. Then she scowled. "Oh, fuck it," she said with a nervous shrug, and went out.

Vonnie and Kris had come over, ostensibly to say good-bye to Kate but really to get a gander at Mike. Dwayne, Jasper, and Shirl wandered out of the kitchen for the same reason.

"Hi," Frankie said.

"Hi," Mike said. "How'd it go?"

"Terrific." She was *shy*, Anna saw; she looked at Mike when she thought he wasn't looking at her. "A great time was had by all."

Mike put his hand on top of Katie's head. "Hope she didn't eat too much."

"Forget that, she ate everything in the kitchen. I don't know what Carmen's gonna serve for dinner tonight. Didn't you?"

"I ate everything," Katie confirmed. "It's okay," she told Vince, "I got Mommy's meta-blisa."

"Mommy's metabolism," Mike said. Everybody laughed.

"Okay, we ready to go? Daddy'll have to carry that bag of loot, kiddo, it's too big for me."

Mike put his hand on Frankie's arm. "Uh, slight change of plans. I wanted to call and tell you, but I didn't find out till late."

"You have to work? No problem, we—"

"No, um..." He gave a weak, embarrassed grin at the audience, and everyone started backing up. "Talk to you a sec," he muttered to Frankie, pulling her the other way. Katie followed him. "Hold it," he said when he saw her. He leaned down. "This is a birthday secret, okay? I need two seconds—"

"Birthday secret!"

"Two seconds to talk to Mommy. You go over there for two seconds." He pointed to the bar.

"Secret!"

"Go, go." He turned her around and gave her a little push, and Katie ran straight for Vince.

Anna didn't have to hear what Mike told Frankie to know it was bad. Frankie's stiff posture said it all. The conversation lasted about two minutes, not two seconds, and it probably would've gone on longer if Katie hadn't run out of patience and crashed it. She ran to her dad and wrapped her arms around his legs, demanding to know the birthday secret *now*.

Anna tried not to listen, not because she wasn't curious but because Frankie's flushed, unconvincingly gay face broke her heart. "The surprise is at Colleen's," she told Katie, "so you and I are going shopping *next* week. Next Monday, just the two of us, and we'll have a great time. I promise."

"It's at Colleen's?"

"Yep, the surprise is at Colleen's."

"Are you coming, too?"

Frankie went down on one knee to straighten the crooked collar of Katie's blouse and fluff her hair. They talked in soft voices, low and calm, high and childish, while Mike shifted from foot to foot and jiggled the change in his pants pocket. Anna couldn't help liking him, before. Now she couldn't stand him. Colleen was the woman he'd been seeing off and on—she'd heard all about her from Frankie. She taught art at Mike's college; she lived on a small farm; she had a pony; Katie liked her a lot.

Frankie hugged Katie for the last time, waved to her and Mike at the door, and rushed back into the kitchen without looking at anybody.

"Great," Vince said, "this is just great."

"Sucks," Anna agreed.

"Do something."

"Like what?"

"I don't know, talk to her."

"Oh, she'd love that. Nothing Frankie likes better than a girl-to-girl chat about her love life."

Vince blushed. Anna rubbed the back of his neck for comfort. "I gotta go work," he told her. They didn't talk again until after dinner.

Dinner service was busy but not crazy, no emergencies, no heart stoppers like running out of all the specials by seven-thirty. It was the kind of night when restaurant management didn't seem like an insane career choice. All the elements in the big machine were humming along in harmony, food preparers, food servers, food consumers, and food, and all a conscientious overseer had to do was oversee. That left plenty of time for the fun part, and for Anna that meant schmoozing with the bar regulars and making nice with the customers. She was a host. That was her job and she was good at it, and it had only taken about twenty years to figure that out. Slow learner.

Rose had left her to-do list on the desk. It never seemed to get any shorter. Glancing at it, Anna couldn't help noticing that she was the one doing most of the crossing off. "Order straws, sip-sticks, p. towels for bathrooms, aspirin, masking tape"—she'd done that. "Louis: Sharpen knives, clean capp. machine, wash front window"—Anna had passed that message on. "Run off new schedule & time sheets, call dishwasher man, tell Dwayne—vacuum dust in refrig. compressor units, clean grease trap"—Anna had taken care of those. That left "Reschedule grill fire inspection guy, call workman's comp rep, rewrite phone book ad, trash pickup Tues.?" Not to mention paying a stack of aging bills from the phone company, the laundry service, the water softener service, the building landlord, and eight or nine separate food and beverage suppliers.

Anna didn't begrudge the time Rose was spending away from the restaurant to be with Theo. Not at all—how could she? He was sick and Rose loved him. By the same token, though, didn't it make sense, wasn't it only fair that the one doing most of the work got to make most of the decisions?

She was totaling up receipts when Vince slumped into the office and flopped down on the couch, arms and legs sprawled as if he'd dropped from a height. "I thought you left," Anna said. "I thought you had a date."

"Called it off." He watched her punch numbers on the adding machine for a while. "I asked Frankie if she wanted to go to a movie."

"Yeah?"

"She said no. So then I asked her if she wanted to go for a walk. It's hard to come up with things that don't involve booze."

"I guess."

"She said no. I asked her if she wanted to come over to my place and watch TV, get a video or something. No. I asked her if I could go over to her place and watch TV. No."

"By now you're probably starting to get the idea..."

"She hates me."

"No, she wants to be by herself."

"I don't want her to be, not tonight. You know what I'm scared of, Anna, don't pretend you don't."

"Okay, I won't, but Rose says there's nothing we can do. If she's going to fall off, she'll fall off. We can't stop her."

"Half of all recovering alcoholics relapse in the first six months. Ninety percent do at least once in the first four years."

Anna had nothing to say to that. Frankie got a DUI last year; it's what had finally made her stop drinking, the shock of it. "That was low as I could go," she'd told Anna in a rare confidence. "The bottom. I couldn't get any worse than that." Did Vince know? Frankie was stingy with personal information.

"She ever tell you about her family?" he asked.

"A little. Not much."

"Her father took off when she was seven because her mother was a drunk. Frankie took care of her till she died. That guy Mike." He jabbed his thumb into a hole in the sofa arm, enlarging it with unconscious violence. "How could he toss her out like that?"

"Oh, Vince. You of all people..." But now didn't seem like a charitable time to remind him of what drunks were like.

"I know, but she's *okay* now, she's sober. But he's got *Colleen*." His lips twisted with distaste. "Guess what I did. I bought her a case of nonalcoholic beer. You know, for a present."

"That didn't go over?"

"It's got alcohol in it. Just a fraction. I didn't know, plus she says the smell of it triggers cravings." He hammered the top of his head with his fists. "Smart present, huh?"

"Oh, Vince."

"I just wanted to hang with her tonight, that's all. No moves, just company."

"She'll be all right. She's tough."

"Wrong. She's not tough at all."

After he left, Anna thought about calling Frankie. But what good would it do? None, probably, and it would definitely annoy her.

She picked up the phone.

The low, toneless "Hello?" sounded terrible, but it sounded sober.

"Uh-oh. Sorry—it's me—were you asleep?"

"No. What's wrong?"

"Nothing, I was just calling to say hi." She laughed nervously. "Kate's incredible."

"Yeah, thanks again, you and Rose," Frankie rallied to say, "you made it really nice today."

"Our pleasure. So. How are you?"

"I'm fine. I just can't talk right now, I gotta go."

"Wait. Could I come over?"

"What?" Incredulous. "No."

"Okay, but—do you want to talk or anything?"

"No, I don't. I just said that. Look, I'll see you tomorrow."

"Okay, for sure. See you tomorrow. I might come in a little early myself, get a head start on the inventory. Maybe—maybe you could help me?" Silence. "Or not, I was just—"

"You want me to come in early and help you with *inventory*?"

It even sounded ridiculous. She couldn't tell if Frankie was amused or insulted. "Yeah."

"And that would be why, so I'll lay off the sauce now, get a good night's sleep, and have a real clear head tomorrow for inventory?"

Okay, insulted. "Sorry," she said, miserable. She deserved that. The problem was, she didn't know what she was allowed to say and what was off limits. They were friends, but Frankie's drinking had never been open for discussion. "I'm sorry. I just—"

"I'll see you tomorrow, Anna," she said shortly. "At the usual time, if that's okay with you."

"That's okay with me."

They hung up.

Anna listened to the stillness, nothing but the low hum of machines that heated or cooled food or washed dishes. Rose always said she liked this time of the day best, when the restaurant was empty and quiet. "Like a problem child who's finally gone to sleep. And I'm like the mama who hangs over his crib and thinks, 'Oh, what an *angel*, I forgot how much I love you.'" For Anna, it was the opposite. She preferred the craziness of a full house, when the joint was jumping and chaos ruled. It felt like a family when everybody was here, the whole staff on a good night, a big, noisy, unruly, semi-functional family. Sometimes everybody hated everybody and homicide seemed like the next logical step, but most of the time they got along, and once in a while there was so much love—no other word for it—it was as if they were all drunk on it.

This was new. She could just barely remember it being that way in the old days, after her grandmother died and Rose took over the Bella Sorella. Certainly it had never been like that at Nicole's, where kitchen help lasted about three months and floor help about five. Employee loyalty? No such thing. Nobody's identity was tied up in Industrial Coffee except Nicole's, no sharing, no community, no *us*. At Rose's, the lowest-paid prep cook actually gave a damn. Billy and Shirl and Vonnie kept stuffing the suggestion box with new restaurant names, and not only because they wanted free drinks for life. They wanted to see the Bella Sorella flourish. They really did.

So they were a motley, crossbred kind of a family, scrambling along more or less together to get through the frantic day. But then the last customer paid up, the waiters settled with Vince, the cleaners finished in the kitchen, Anna totaled up receipts, Rose locked the safe—and everybody went home. They scattered, they split off like spokes from the hub of a wheel. Vince lived alone, Frankie lived alone. Carmen, alone upstairs. Vonnie was divorced, her last kid almost gone. Louis, Luca, Fontaine, they all lived alone. The women Dwayne and Jasper and Flaco slept with were mostly in their heads; after work they went drinking, together sometimes, then they went home by themselves.

Before she started feeling sorry for herself, Anna shut off the computer and gathered up her stuff. She was turning off the desk lamp when the phone rang.

"Anna?"

Mason's voice. She left the light out so she could listen to it in the dark. "Hi," she said.

"I called your house. I thought you'd be home by now. Late night for you."

"Yes, I'm the last one here."

"How are you?"

"I'm great, I'm good. You?"

"I'm . . ." A pause, as if he was checking his pulse or taking his temperature. "Fair," he decided. "I'd say I'm fair."

She had so many conflicting feelings, it made it hard to take an approach. How was she supposed to be with him? She'd done one dumb thing, but he'd overreacted—that was still her version. And then he'd ignored her, which made it two to one, her side. Not that she was keeping score. And over all that was this asinine tingling in her chest because of his voice in her ear. She hadn't felt it since she used to get his e-mails. His screen name was SnapShot; she'd see it in her In Box and get that fleshy thrill, miss a heartbeat or two.

"I hear you went to Maine," she said. "Rose mentioned it."

"Macias Island. Somebody canceled at the last minute and I took his spot."

"There's a waiting list?"

"Yes. To photograph puffins."

"Puffins. Puffins. Aren't they sort of like parrots?"

He laughed, an infectious huff of his breath. "Sort of. Maybe if you crossed a parrot with a penguin."

"Did you get any good shots?" Funny how giant emotional upheavals could just drift away, seem like trivia after a few minutes of chitchat. If you were inclined that way to begin with.

"I got a few. Anna. Listen." Silence.

"I'm here," she reminded him.

"I'm sorry I've been . . . invisible."

"Yes, well." She had a sense of giving in too easily, but why? The him-me lines were blurring so quickly; the longer Mason talked, the harder it was to remember, really keep in mind what the problem was.

"You even asked me to the movies."

"Yeah, and you didn't even write back. How rude." She was smiling when she wasn't talking, trying to keep her voice straight so he wouldn't know. She wasn't a connoisseur of making up; she could foresee regretting the speed with which they seemed to be reconciling. She should drag it out for fun, but it wasn't in her. "Luckily," she said, "I'm willing to overlook that."

"Good, because I'm calling to ask if you'd like to go to the movies."

"It doesn't have to be the drive-in, does it?" How reckless: she'd jumped several steps ahead by teasing. She waited for his reaction on a nervous edge.

He laughed.

It came rushing back, why they were good together, everything she liked about him, why keeping away from each other hadn't made any sense. A little taste of anger came back, too, though, like indigestion; she remembered exactly how *cheated* she'd felt when he'd walked out on her. Look at what he'd deprived them of. Who knew how soon she'd be gone, but soon, and look at the time he'd wasted. But she set that aside—bygones—in the interest of expediting a truce. How magnanimous. She felt expansive.

"What are you doing right now?" she asked.

"Um . . ." He was startled into confusion. "Sitting on the dock, looking at the boat, Theo's boat—"

"Which I've never even been on board," she pointed out.

"What are you doing?" he countered.

"Nothing. Thinking about going home." To an empty house that was too big for her. Her aging clapboard reminder that she was literally back where she'd started.

"Come over here," Mason said.

"Give me twenty minutes."

14

Too many people. Too many helpers. Rose had almost finished packing everything Theo would take to Bayside Gardens before Anna and Mason even got there, so there wasn't much for them to do. It all fit in a couple of moldy duffels, meager-looking on the *Expatriate*'s cockpit deck. "It's temporary," Theo insisted. "I'll be back as soon as this heals"—his wrist.

He'd broken it exactly the way Rose had dreaded and feared that he would, by falling down the companionway steps. He'd frozen on the second-to-last one and lost his balance, and when he'd tried to break his fall, he'd snapped his wrist. He kept saying, "Coulda been my neck," as if that was supposed to comfort her. After the shock and fear wore off, she was *glad* he'd fallen, glad the cumbersome cast was on his right hand because it crippled him so effectively. Nothing else could have gotten him off this damn boat and into a place where at least he'd be safe. Miserable, but safe.

And *still* he wouldn't move in with her, or with Mason. As much as he hated the idea of a nursing home, he'd rather be taken care of by strangers than by people who loved him—"people who aren't getting paid to wipe my butt," was how he put it. It was probably too late now anyway; his disease had progressed to the point where he needed the kind of skilled care she or Mason couldn't give. And he was never going to get any better.

"Theo, what about these?" Mason called up the steps, unrolling the soft cloth containing Theo's carving tools, each one in its neat felt pocket.

"What is it? I can't see, what you got there—"

"Chisels, files, awls—"

"That's my woodworking tools. Leave 'em be."

"Okay."

"Take them with you if you like," Rose said quietly, so Theo wouldn't hear. Mason was helping her down in the cabin while Anna tried to keep Theo occupied above. What those two were talking about Rose couldn't imagine, and she was dying to know. Their voices were too faint to hear.

"Take them?" Mason said.

"If you think you could use them. His fishing gear, too."

Mason didn't pretend to misunderstand. He ran his fingertips over the exposed handles of the tools, worn smooth from all the years of use. "I remember when he'd carve things for me. Airplanes, horses, things like that. I wish I'd saved them, but they're gone now, lost or thrown out." He looked up. "I'll leave his tools here, I think."

"All right."

"Anyway, he's already given me the dog to look after. That's enough for the time being."

"And then some," she said, smiling back. "But Cork is so sedentary, I'd be surprised if he gave you any trouble." She could see the old mutt from here, sprawled on the seat next to Anna on deck, his chin on Theo's thigh. "It's nice of you to take him."

"I hate this," Mason said with sudden heat. "All of it. What it comes down to. His whole life in two bags."

She put her hand on his wrist, afraid Theo would hear.

"Rose, is this the right thing? I hate it that he thinks he's coming back."

"But why, if it makes him happy?"

"We're tricking him. What if we're wrong, what if he'd want to know?"

She moved her knees so he could sit beside her on the narrow bunk. If he stood for long in the cramped cabin, he got a stiff neck from keeping his head bent so it wouldn't hit the ceiling. Theo, six inches shorter, had never had that problem. "You're the kind of man who would want to know the truth. You'd *have* to know it, and no one would think of keeping it from you. But Theo's different. It won't always be this way, but right now, Mason, I don't believe he could stand knowing what's going to happen."

"Okay."

"It's too soon."

"All right."

"But we have to be together on this." They'd talked about it for hours. "If you still have doubts—"

"No, I don't, I'm with you. I just don't like it."

"I don't, either. Thank God for you." She told him that all the time.

"For you," he always said back.

She ran her hand along Theo's pillow, the scratchy wool of his blanket. Her mind shied away from the thought that neither of them would sleep on this hard, narrow bunk again, together or apart. "Look at those two," she said, nodding up at Theo and Anna. "I never thought I'd see the day, did you? What do you suppose they're talking about?"

She watched Mason's face as he followed her gaze, and she knew it wasn't the sight of his stepfather making him look intent and fascinated. "Dogs, probably."

"Theo's halfway decided Anna's all right," she said. Because she made Mason happy. Rose didn't say that, though; she left the implication blank, so Mason could fill it in himself. Maybe even elaborate.

He said nothing.

She sighed. Which one was more annoyingly discreet, him or Anna? "Because you seem to like having her around," she tried, conscious of the lameness of that, not to mention the obviousness. But if she was going to get information out of either of them, her chances were better with Mason; nothing sent Anna into clamlike uncommunicativeness faster than a reference to her and him as any sort of item whatsoever. The maddening part was that there was no *reason* for her reticence except spite—she just didn't want to give Rose the satisfaction.

Well, too bad, she was satisfied anyway. Two people she loved dearly, one more than anyone else, two people she had *put together,* don't forget, wittingly or not, were finding each other. They talked on the phone, e-mailed, went on dates, actual dates, walks, picnics, late suppers at Mason's house. That by itself was something of a miracle, Mason walking around in the world, out and about, big as life—"Like he owns the place," Theo said. He was flying again, going on trips up north and out west to photograph birds he never had before, the marbled godwit, the prairie falcon. What a change! Flying with Anna to Buffalo had started it, but Rose wasn't allowed to ask about that. They'd come back changed, both of them, and she'd have said not in a good way, but now everything was fine, so what did she know?

Nothing. That's what was so irritating.

Mason smiled, and roused himself to say, "Yes, I like having her around."

"Good, good," she said encouragingly. "Good."

Nothing.

She gave up. No, one last try. "I take credit for that, you know. I'm the one who told Anna you could fix her roof."

His eyes twinkled. He knew what she was up to. She wasn't going to get any juicy information out of him, that was clear. Anna's doing; he was keeping her secrets, not his own. Did he know what he was getting into? Too late now, but the old *Be careful what you wish for* adage flashed across Rose's mind. Matchmaker, beware.

They went up on deck.

Anna was telling Theo a story about the old man who had died, Mac, her old boyfriend's grandfather. Theo's facial paralysis hid his laughter these days; you had to look for it in his eyes. Anna's story made them light up and the breath wheeze softly through his parted lips. Rose hadn't thought anything could make Theo laugh today. "I'd'a liked that fella," he sighed to Anna, and she smiled at him and said, "He'd've liked you, too."

"All set, I guess." Rose straightened from setting down a cardboard box full of Theo's chess set, some of his books, his favorite coffee mug, next to the duffel bags on deck. "Can you think of anything we've forgotten?"

"A file."

She bent toward him, not sure she'd heard. "A what?"

"So I can saw my way out."

"Oh." She ruffled his hair and helped him to stand up. The cast on his wrist had a side benefit: it was on his shakier arm, and the added weight helped keep it steady. "Are we ready to go?" Mason came around on his other side. Supporting him, they got him safely over the gunwale and onto the dock. Mason went back for the duffels, Anna took the box, Rose took Theo. Slowly, carefully, Cork leading, they made their way down the marina pier, passing the sail and working boats and cruisers of Theo's neighbors. The farther they got from the water, the closer to land, the better Rose liked it, even knowing it was the opposite for him. For almost a year she'd lived with the nightmare fear that he would fall off his boat and drown. Now at least he was safe from that.

At the chain-link gate, he stopped short. Taking shuffling steps, he turned himself around. It was a heavy, cloudy late afternoon, with a wind coming up from the water to cool down the mugginess. The bay, inky black glass an hour ago, rippled like corduroy with a shallow, monotonous chop. Theo lifted his left arm and slowly pointed.

"The clouds?" Rose guessed. He shook his head.

"Osprey nest," Mason said, and Theo nodded. Rose saw it, a messy construction of sticks and moss on top of a buoy about sixty feet out in the water. She thought she could see a head poking out, but it could've been a stick.

"Wanted to be here. Chicks about to fly. There's two. Any day now."

Mason squinted across the sparkle of the water. "I could photograph them for you." Theo snorted a laugh. "I could. You're right, it's any day now. The parents will keep bringing them food while the fledglings learn to fish. That's a sight. Want me to?"

But Theo flapped his good hand and turned himself back around. Didn't answer.

When they got to their cars, Rose's and Mason's parked side by side, Theo said he wanted to go with Rose and he didn't want Mason and Anna to follow. Rose could get him settled at Bayside Jail—he never missed a chance to call it that—and Mason and anybody else who cared to—she guessed that meant Anna—could come and visit if and when it suited them.

Mason looked surprised. "You sure? I thought I'd come with you—all of us. Show of force, let 'em know who they're dealing with."

Theo gave his wheezing laugh again, but shook his head. He looked so weary. Rose tried to guess what was in his mind now. Did he think the nursing home was a humiliation? An end for him that he wanted as few witnesses to as possible? Mason helped him into the front seat of her car and got him buckled in. As soon as he stepped back, Cork jumped up on Theo's lap. They all laughed, and exclaimed over his spryness, and how they hadn't thought the old boy had it in him. Theo laughed, too, but he bent his head and pressed his face against the wiry fur on Cork's neck. When he didn't move, Anna took a few steps back and turned away. Mason hung on the door, staring at the ground. Rose rubbed Theo's shoulder. "He can visit," she said thickly. "I'll bring him, Mason will bring him. We'll both—"

Theo lifted his head. "I don't want to go," he whispered. His pale eyes swam. Rose nodded, unable to talk. "I don't want to go, Rose."

"I know."

"I know I gotta." He lifted Cork's grizzled head. "You miss me?" He kissed his dog between the eyes. "Here, take 'im." Mason reached in and lifted the dog gently from his lap. And held him while Rose closed the door, went around to her side, and started the car.

"I'll call you tonight," Mason leaned in the window to say. "See how you settled in. And I'll come out tomorrow. First thing in the morning." Theo nodded, looking straight ahead. "Next weekend maybe we'll take the sailboat out, cruise down to Deal or Crisfield for the day. Sound good?" He nodded again. "Take it easy," Mason said softly. "Okay?"

"Yeah."

"Give 'em hell."

He grimaced for a smile.

Bayside Gardens wasn't beside the bay, but it did have a garden and Theo's second-floor room looked out on it, neat beds of white daisies, black-eyed Susans, and heat-weary coneflowers. He hated it.

"But why? It's pretty. It's south-facing, you'll have the sun all day. You can look out at the people taking walks on the path."

He said a bad word.

Rose sat down on the edge of his bed. "Now, look."

"Don't," he whispered. "Lecture me. I know."

"You know, but I'm lecturing you anyway. You're off to a bad start, mister. You can't hate everything. Not after..." She looked at her watch. "Four and a half hours." He hated dinner in the perfectly nice dining room downstairs. Hated the announcements for meals and activities that came over the intercom in his room. Hated his neighbors, hated his nurses, hated his bed, his room, the air conditioner, the wheelchair he was supposed to use when he wasn't using the walker.

"Can," he said. "Do."

"Theo." She picked up his twitchy old hand and held it to her cheek. "I've asked you to come and live with me—how many times? A hundred? Mason, too. But you won't."

"Nope."

"This place is no good, I know, because there's no water under it. But what can we do?" She scuffed her cheek with his knuckles. "Try to make the best of it, I guess. I don't know what else to do. If I could think of anything—"

"I know. It's okay."

She nodded against his hand. "It will be. It'll be okay. Tough at first, but then better. You'll get used to things."

"Yeah."

"If not, we'll move. This isn't the only place in town." It was supposed to be one of the best, though. "At least you don't have a roommate," she pointed out.

"That'd be hell," he agreed.

"And hard on you, too."

He shoved at her shoulder, telling her he got that joke.

She bent over and laid her head on his chest. The slow, steady thump of his heart was as precious to her as her own heartbeat. It was getting late. Outside, voices echoed faintly; occasional footsteps passed by the closed door. "Don't want you to go," Theo said. "Wish you could stay."

"Love me, Theo?" she murmured.

"You know it."

She kissed him on the mouth. He wasn't much of a kisser anymore, and she missed it. Nowadays she had to do all the work. She sat up and went to the little desk under the window. She got the matching chair, carried it over to the door, and set it at an angle under the doorknob. Just like in the movies.

Theo blinked at her.

"They really ought to have a lock. Guess they're afraid you'll lock them out." In the middle of the room, she smiled at him and began to unbutton her shirt.

"Hey, now," Theo said, sitting up higher. "What're you doing, Rosie? Aw, now."

She stripped for him slowly, letting the shirt fall to the floor, coming closer to take off her bra. Black bra today, how fortuitous. She dangled it toward him, then flipped it over her shoulder, thinking, if your body was sixty years old, you'd better have an appreciative man to show it off to. Luckily for her, Theo had always been that man. She swayed a little, as if there was music, unzipping her slacks. Theo shook his head, amazed, almost smiling, his eyes full of love and fun. Like old times.

She kicked off her shoes and shimmied out of her slacks. Nothing left now but panties and knee-high stockings. She laughed as she got rid of them.

She ran her hands through her hair, as if it was long and black again, as if she were young again. "See anything you like, sailor?"

"I like it all. Always liked it all," he said, wiping his cheek. He was weeping.

She had to help him with his pants. His erection was a precarious thing, flushed with hope. She stoked it tenderly, the small spark, trying for a flame. "This ain't going to work," he warned her.

"Yes, it is." She kissed him again and again and moved over him, onto him, cradling his face with her arms. "If anybody comes," she whispered, "this is a therapeutic massage."

"I can't do it, Rosie."

"You don't have to do anything. You get to just lie there."

And for a little while it did work, she had him like her old Theo, lusty and sure, everything she needed. She pressed his rigid hand to her breast, calling him by the old names, telling him how much she liked it, loved him, how good he was. Then he groaned and she felt him slip, diminish inside her. They moaned together, and she wanted him to laugh but he couldn't. He turned his face away, wouldn't let her kiss him.

"Christ, Rosie. I told you. Oh, Jesus Christ." He started to curse. He was ashamed of his tears, so she pretended she didn't see them. She slid down beside him, fumbling for the rumpled sheet.

"It doesn't matter." And she wasn't sorry she'd tried. She hugged their hips together with her outflung arm, pulling him hard against her.

He swore some more. "I hate when a woman says that."

She raised up over him. "You mean this has happened *before*?" But he wouldn't smile. "Oh, Theo, I know, but it really doesn't, it just doesn't matter."

"Matters the hell to me."

She stroked his stomach under his T-shirt, fluffing the soft hair under his navel. "Are you sorry? I'm not. Anyway, I don't have to make love with you to love you."

"Wouldn't hurt, though."

She wanted to cry, too, but she never did in front of him. She could cry for months. She went around like a woman at the end of a pregnancy, full, tight, but with sadness inside instead of a new life.

"When I get outta here." Theo tapped the fingers poking out of his cast against her arm. "It'll be better. We'll take that trip."

"On the *Wind Rose*."

"I need to get outta here. This is no place. For me. We'll take that trip."

"We will."

"Not ready. Not done yet."

"Absolutely not. We are not done yet."

She held him until he drifted off to sleep—a blessing; insomnia was one of his plagues. Then she slipped away like a ghost.

15

Hot. Anna's and Mason's sweaty hands stuck together, so they strolled back to the restaurant from the town dock without touching. Not much would have gotten Anna out in the broiling August sun at the hottest time of day on the hottest day of the year. Sex might have, but they hadn't so much as kissed. Too hot.

With her own two hands she'd made crostini with red peppers and goat cheese for a picnic, and they'd taken it out to a sweltering bench by the blinding water in the middle of a swarm of sweating tourists ogling the sailboats in the harbor. They'd stopped in the bookstore afterward, just for some shade and air conditioning, but she didn't have time to dawdle, too much work to do this afternoon.

Just the same, in front of the Bella Sorella, where a few wilted diners were still picking at lunch under the umbrellas, and it was time to say good-bye and part ways, Mason said, "Let's go around to the alley," and she said, "Okay."

If anything it was hotter here, and God knew it smelled worse, especially in the little nook behind the Dumpster. Their special place. It wasn't even private; kitchen staff came out in the alley to cool off, and Frankie came out to smoke. Everyone else smoked in the kitchen, which was expressly forbidden but ignored, but

Frankie wouldn't dream of it. It went against her code of conduct for the serious cook.

Leaning against the gritty brick wall in the aromatic shade of the garbage stockade, they started out with kissing, mouths touching and nothing else because it was so hot, but that didn't last. "Yuck," Anna mumbled, encircling her damp arms around Mason's damp neck and pressing against him.

"Yuck?"

"It's an endearment."

She thought about how close she'd come to missing out on this. "You are," she said between kisses, "the nicest man I know. I like everything about you. I like your nose. I like the way your fingers smell like photographic fixer." The scars on his face barely registered anymore; they were like someone else's mole or port-wine birthmark, there but irrelevant.

Sometimes this public petting they did in the alley got out of hand. They took it too far, and then they either had to cool off or do something about it. Once they did something about it in the office with the door locked, but too many people wanted in, and once in Mason's car, which was a Jeep with no backseat. That was an experience she wasn't anxious to repeat.

He smiled, but he didn't reply to her compliment, didn't say, "I like everything about you, too." She was used to that and didn't mind. She was the one who put things in words in this relationship. Their unspoken deal.

"I have to go away," he said. "On Monday, for four days."

"Where to?"

"Montana."

"*Montana*. What for?"

"Spruce grouse, blue grouse, wild turkey. It's for a magazine story about the Bitterroot Mountains."

"Wow, aren't you the gadabout these days. Will you fly?"

"Yes."

"Who'll hold your hand?"

"Whoever's in 12D."

"Will you take your gigantic suitcase?"

He had a way of dipping his knees and ducking his head when she teased him, like a boy, abashed and delighted. Consequently, she loved teasing him. "I've already got it packed."

"You're not even kidding. Did you pack your lucky bird?" She'd given him a stuffed toy vulture for a present, three feet high, hunched and menacing, cartoonishly fierce.

"I bought it a seat."

"Twelve F. You'll be surrounded." He could fly now, although it was still an ordeal, but he wasn't over being afraid of having another panic attack. Fear of fear, he called it, the core symptom of his disorder. And he still preferred to be either outside or in his own house, but he made himself go places, especially her house or the Bella Sorella. So far, so good.

"I'd better go in," she said. "Stuff to do."

"Me, too."

"We've got a full house tonight. First time this summer."

Their good-bye kiss turned into a prolonged grope. She was addicted to the way the shapes of their bodies fit together, just the right meeting of curves and flats. She loved it that he kissed with his mouth closed until *she* was ready for tongues. She hummed in his ear, not wanting to let go. "Dee-lish," she said in a sibilant whisper, making him shiver.

Another thing they never talked about was how they'd gotten back together. She didn't know why he wouldn't, but the reason she never did was because it seemed unkind and in poor taste to point out that she'd won. For the first time ever, she was carrying on a relationship completely on her terms. Fun, physical, and fleeting, she called it to herself. It was more than that, of course, but she liked the careless sound of the alliteration. Even though it was deceptive. They were living in the moment, and it was just what she wanted. Even Mason had to be feeling grateful to her by now for holding out for this. She was most men's dream lover. Clues that he wasn't as committed to the idyllic temporariness of things turned up from time to time, not in words but intangibles, looks, touching, that sort of thing, but she wisely ignored them. Not to acknowledge the thin line between dream lover and worst nightmare was one way to maintain the satisfying status quo.

"'Bye," she said definitely, stepping back.

"'Bye."

"See you tonight? I'll come over. It'll be late, though."

"I'll be home."

She blew him a kiss. Walking away, she heard a click, and knew it was his camera. A little habit of his she'd almost gotten used to. Strange, strange man. She couldn't wait for tonight.

"Where's Frankie?"

Carmen looked up from the red wine fish broth she was deglazing at the stove. "Outside. In front, talking to her ex."

"Really? Talking to Mike?"

"She left those duck breasts half done. Look at that. They're drying out," she complained, pointing her big spoon at the finely scored yellow breasts on the counter. "While she takes care of her personal business."

Anna walked out without answering.

She found Vince by the front window, peering out from the side in the shadow. "We're spying," she mentioned at his elbow.

"Something's wrong. Look at her."

"I can't see her face."

"You don't have to."

Mike was doing the talking. No jacket today; he had his sleeves rolled up, tie at half mast. Sweat made dark arcs under his arms and stuck his shirt to his back. He rubbed his neck, combed his beard, gestured. Talked and talked. Frankie kept her hands in the pockets of her enormous carpenter pants and her eyes on the sidewalk. The bill of her ball cap shaded her profile, but Vince was right. Something bad was happening.

She straightened up suddenly. She either cursed or said a very short word, and when she pushed past Mike her shoulder struck his, tilting him sideways. She came into the restaurant so fast, Anna and Vince didn't have time to pretend they were doing something else. It didn't matter: she marched back to the kitchen without looking in their direction. Mike stared at the front door for a while longer, a pained look around his mouth, eyes crinkled in distress behind his glasses. Then he clasped his hands behind his neck and walked away.

After a quick, hot debate, Anna convinced Vince their best course was to say and do nothing. None of their business, and if Frankie wanted to talk—not likely—she would. If she didn't, they'd only alienate her by pestering her.

"My prep's done, everything's set," Frankie announced an hour later in the office doorway.

Anna looked up from the computer. "Oh. Great. Well—"

"So I'm going home. I'm sorry, I can't work tonight, I'm sick."

"You are?" She stood up.

Frankie stepped back. She took a cigarette out of her T-shirt pocket and lit it one-handed, with a folded-over match in a matchbook. She waved it out in the air, the whole matchbook, and blew a hard stream of smoke at the ceiling. "Yeah, I've got something, don't come near me. Contagious."

"I heard Mike came by, Carmen mentioned it. I hope you're not upset—"

"Yeah, he came by, we talked. So, nothing. I need to go home. Can I? Carmen says she can live without me."

"Sure, of course, if you're not feeling well." Frankie had never taken a day off before, never so much as come in late.

"Thanks." She pivoted.

"Frankie?"

"Yo."

"Um, are you okay? I mean—"

"No, I'm *sick*. Didn't I just say that?" Her eyes blazed and her pale, tense face flushed. "Jesus Christ!"

"Okay—sorry—"

"Okay!" She disappeared.

She didn't come in the next day, either. Anna got the message from Carmen, who had trouble disguising her satisfaction. "Says she's got a bug, she doesn't want to spread it around." She had her thick arms folded across her middle, her chef's toque jammed low on her forehead. The singed-looking reddish hair sticking out around the sides gave her a sinister-clown look, especially when she scowled and smiled at the same time. "She didn't sound good."

"Well, if she's sick—"

"Sick, yeah, right."

Anna turned her back, unable to stomach the sneer. Carmen infuriated her. "At least she called."

"Before she couldn't dial."

"You'd like that, wouldn't you?" Fighting with Carmen was a no-win, but she felt goaded into it. "You'd love it if she fell off the wagon and ruined her life. *And* her kid's life."

"What?" Carmen looked genuinely shocked. "That's crap."

"Whatever." She left her in the kitchen and went to find Vince.

He was dropping glasses in the bar, he was so distracted. "She's never sick, never. That guy did something to her. I'm calling her up." The chef's knife he was supposed to be slicing lemons with was making a fine dice instead. Soon it would be zest. "Did you talk to her?"

"No, she called Carmen."

"How'd she sound?"

"Carmen says not good, but—"

"I'm calling her." He picked up the bar phone and punched the number. With his back turned, he reminded her of Frankie the last time she'd seen her: same cocked-gun stiffness in the shoulders, same brittle, balls-of-the-feet nervous tension. They both wanted a target, and there was nothing to shoot.

"No answer." He slammed down the phone. "No machine, even—and she's got a machine."

"She could be trying to sleep. If she's really sick, she—"

"She's not sick, you know it. Anyway, if she was sleeping, she wouldn't take the machine off so the phone could ring a hundred times."

"Okay. So—"

"She's in trouble. She's drinking. I'm going over there."

"Vince, I don't think that's a good idea."

"Why?"

"Well—probably she doesn't want to see you."

"You go, then."

"Me?"

"You're her friend. She likes you, she'd talk to you."

"She likes you, too. She's your friend, too."

They went around like that for a while. Then they both went to see Frankie.

They didn't tell anyone, meaning Carmen, where they were going. They said "an errand," and anyone who overheard assumed it was something to do with wine or liquor, Vince's department, an emergency pickup or a meeting with a wholesaler. "Back in an hour," they said.

Vince drove his car as if he knew where he was going. Frankie's neighborhood was south of town, a mean, dreary collection of run-down apartment buildings and beat-up duplexes on a four-lane boulevard famous for late-night drag races and drug busts. She could do better than this. She'd gotten three raises in four months, she could afford something respectable or at least quiet. She talked about moving out as soon as she got joint custody of Katie—as soon as having a nice place mattered. Until then, she was saving every cent. She'd bought a used car, but that was it; everything else went into a savings account for Katie, even though Mike didn't particularly need the money and that wasn't part of the divorce arrangement. She was building up credit for the custody judge, she said, proving she could be a responsible parent.

The parking lot beside her yellow-brick building was crowded with cars for midafternoon on a weekday. All the first-floor windows had bars. The front door was dark green metal, scratched and graffitied, with a deep dent down around car bumper–height. It wasn't locked and there was no buzzer.

The foyer smelled like cooking oil, dog shit, and pot. O'Malley, 3F, one of the tinny mailboxes said. They walked past the out-of-order sign on the elevator and took the stairs. On the first landing, a nursing mother, just a girl herself, sent Vince a sleepy smile. On the second, three boys, all about twelve, casually turned their backs to hide whatever deal they were negotiating, a joint, a gun, a dirty magazine. The third-floor hallway was empty, but behind the thin doors came canned television voices and the high, complaining squeals of children.

Vince knocked at 3F and stood back, flexing his shoulders, smoothing the line of beard on his chin with his knuckle, trying to look casual when he was jumping out of his skin. No answer. He knocked again. They cocked their heads, listening like dogs to the silence behind the door, weighing its sincerity. "She's in there," Vince decided. "Frankie?" He knocked harder, using his fist instead of his knuckles. "Hey, Frankie, it's me and Anna! Open up."

"In the interest of total harrassment," Anna said, rooting her cell phone out of her purse. She dialed Frankie's number. Faint ringing inside the apartment and in her ear: stereo. But no answer. "Hey, hold it," she said, alarmed when Vince started using his foot on the door.

"I don't care, she's in there."

"Okay, but still, we can't break the door down."

"Why not?"

"Vince."

They were staring at each other hopelessly when the clump of fast footsteps on the stairway made them turn. Frankie walked around the corner, hands on her hips, head down, panting; she didn't see them until she was midway down the hall. She stopped. She had on tight black running shorts and a sweat-soaked tank, a terry headband around her egg-white skull. "Hey," she said, more accusation than greeting. She approached looking stoical but disbelieving. "What's up?"

"We . . . we wanted to see how you were feeling," Anna came up with. "Guess you're better. That's good."

Frankie bent over and scrounged a key out of the side of her sock. Unlocked the door, went in. She didn't invite them in, but she left the door open behind her. They looked at each other. Anna felt sheepish, but Vince looked nothing but glad. They went inside.

The apartment was one room and a kitchen. Frankie slept on a sofa-bed, currently out and unmade. She flipped it closed with one hand, rumpled sheets and all, then tossed cushions on it. Her body language broadcast carelessness and disdain and resentment. She dripped perspiration from every pore, like a prizefighter after a tough ten-rounder, flyweight division.

"Want anything?" She had a waist-high refrigerator in the postage stamp kitchen. "All I got is water."

"Oh no, thanks," they said in unison.

She took out a bottle and drank half of it without stopping. Still not looking at them, she put her hands on the wall and began to do leg stretches, extending her ropy calves behind her, flexing slowly, athletically.

Except for the unmade bed, the place was depressingly tidy. More mess would've disguised the grimness. The smell of stale cigarette smoke hung in the under-air-conditioned air, but even the ashtrays were clean. The decor was Early Katie, with pictures either of or by Katie taped to the walls and various constructions of clay or papier mâché on the horizontal surfaces. No TV, but a cheap boombox on the radiator, surrounded by stacks of CDs by rap and hip-hop singers Anna had never heard of. Cookbooks littered the back of the couch, and one paperback novel with a clinch cover—a romance. Anna turned her eyes away from it quickly. She'd seen something she wasn't supposed to see. It moved her in a funny, painful way.

"Hey, look here, you got him a bigger bowl."

Anna went over to see what Vince was crouched over on the deep windowsill. A turtle, brown with yellow spots on his dented shell. Sebastian, she assumed. Vince picked it up, and it retracted its sleepy head halfway and waved its scaly, sharp-toed feet in the air. "And toys," he said wonderingly. "You got him a water slide."

Frankie snorted. "It's not a water slide. It's just—I found a rock when I was out running. It slants, that's all."

"Does he like it?"

"Jesus, Vince. How the fuck do I know?"

He set the turtle back on its slanted rock carefully and stared out the window.

"Sorry we disturbed you," Anna said stiffly. "Vince and I, we didn't know if you were okay or not and we came over to check. We didn't mean to intrude on your privacy."

Already flushed from her run, Frankie's cheeks bloomed redder. "Yeah, it's fine. It's—nice to see you."

"We were afraid you might be upset."

She looked between them, worry-eyed, clenching her hands indecisively. "Mike's getting married." She let her shoulders sag. Just like that, she gave up being tough.

"Oh, Frankie, no."

Vince didn't say anything.

"Yeah, and it kinda hit me, that's all. I'd been thinking something else might happen, so this one blindsided me, that's all. I didn't drink. If that's what you were worried about." She sneered that, but the defiance died out as fast as it flared. "Not that I didn't want to. Last night... well, anyway. Bad night, but I take 'em one at a time, so. So that's it."

"I'm really sorry. I know you were hoping..." It was hard to sympathize with Vince here. Talking about how cut up Frankie was over Mike couldn't be any fun for him. She wished she'd come alone.

He finally said something. "The guy's an asshole."

Frankie frowned, puzzled and disapproving. Then she gave a crooked grin. "Hey, but here's some good news—Luca wants to marry me." She laughed when all Anna and Vince could do was stare. "Yeah, instant family. Whaddaya think? A girl could do worse."

"Um," Anna said, feeling her way. "Well, um—"

"*Are you out of your mind?*"

"Relax," she told Vince, who was all but standing on his toes, "I said no. Anyway, it's Katie he wants, not me. Luca just wants a kid, and I happen to have one."

Anna didn't think it was quite that simple, but she approved of Frankie's decision. Poor Luca.

"So, okay," Frankie said, "I'll be in to work tomorrow. I'd come in tonight, but I got a meeting. I can't miss it."

"That's okay, forget about tonight. But tomorrow, that would be great."

"Okay."

Nothing to do then but leave. Anna said, "Maybe we could do something after work tomorrow night. You know, if you feel like it." Not since Nicole had she suggested such a thing to another woman, she realized. A girlfriend invitation.

Frankie said, "Yeah, maybe."

At the door, Anna looked questioningly at Vince, who hadn't moved.

"Be down in a sec," he said.

"Oh. Sure. See you," she said to Frankie, and hurried out.

Vince had the key to his locked car. She didn't have to wait long in the hot parking lot, just long enough to consider how easy it would be to fall back on old bad habits if you lived in a place like this. How strong you'd have to be in yourself to stay clean and straight here. It wasn't a real slum, not even a project, but it was depressing as hell. No wonder Frankie didn't mind long hours in the kitchen. There was chaos there, too, but she could control it, master it. The one place her toughness worked.

Vince stalked out. He wore a black scowl and he didn't talk. He ground the gears and left rubber in the parking lot peeling out.

"What happened? Are you all right? Would you mind slowing down?"

They came to a red light, so he had to. "She's driving me crazy."

"What's going on?"

He glanced at Anna, then back at the road. "I hate where she lives, so I asked her if she wanted to move in with me."

"You did?"

"Like a roommate, share expenses, that's all. Pool resources."

"She said no," Anna guessed.

"She said"—he mimicked Frankie's nastiest voice—" 'Hey, yeah, Vince, that's how I'll get my kid back, I'll shack up with a bartender.' "

Anna made a disgusted sound, for sympathy. "She didn't mean that. Frankie says stuff."

"Then it was like she felt sorry for me, or she was just sick of dealing with me. She said, 'Look, you want to hook up? Okay, let's do it, let's just get it over with.' "

"Oh, Vince."

"She says, 'Gimme five minutes, I'll take a shower.' " His voice was raw; he sounded close to tears.

"What did you say?"

"Nothing. I left."

"Good."

"I can't help it, I can't let it go. She's got me. I think I'm in love with her." He tried to laugh. "It's not even physical, you know? If we ever made it, it would be bad, it would be terrible. I mean, it's not like she's even sexy."

"Love stinks," Anna said. "I don't see how anybody makes it last."

He drove in silence for a while, at a reasonable speed. "My folks did. They were nuts for each other till Pop died."

She thought of Aunt Iris and Uncle Tony, how they'd seemed younger to her than her own parents when she was little. They'd had a flirty way of fighting, and nicknames for each other, "Sugar Babe," "Pretty Boy," exaggerated endearments they used for laughs. Seeing them hold hands or put their arms around each other had fascinated her as a child, because that sort of thing rarely happened between her parents. Aunt Iris and Uncle Tony had been a little shocking.

"I'm not giving up," Vince said, rallying, confirming Anna's suspicion that between them, she was more cynical in the love department. "Frankie doesn't know me, that's her problem. She doesn't take me seriously. Now Mike's out of the picture, maybe she'll look around. I've got nothing but time." He sat back, drove the car with his wrist over the wheel.

"That's the spirit. Frankie won't know what hit her."

You wanted what you were used to, she supposed. The play your parents performed for you in your childhood. She thought of Mason, and what she wanted from him. Not much. That seemed about right.

16

"You have got to do something about Carmen. No, Rose, I'm serious, you have to do something."

"What is it this time?" The headache she'd been fighting all morning began to throb again behind her right eyebrow. Migraine? She hadn't had one of those since menopause.

"It's—she's—" Anna came into the office in a burst of jerky negative energy. She probably didn't mean to slam the door, but the sharp bang jolted through Rose's system like jagged electricity. "It's the kitchen. She won't listen."

"Ah. Be more specific."

"Frankie's got great ideas for redoing the layout to make things flow, you know, keep people from banging into each other, cut down on the steps you have to take to get from one—"

"Right, yes." Frankie wanted to do things like move the plate elevator, which was directly behind the big range, closer to the dishwasher so Dwayne or his daytime counterpart didn't body-slam servers on their way to and from the line.

"Carmen won't cooperate! Every suggestion, she shoots it down like it's the stupidest thing she's ever heard. And everything's personal—it's like Frankie wants to rearrange the furniture in Carmen's bedroom. I'm sick of dealing with her. She's stubborn, she's shortsighted, she's impossible."

I'm sick of dealing with both of you, Rose thought but didn't say. Sometimes, when she was feeling especially empty and wrung out, she suspected Anna enjoyed making things up to fight about. Otherwise, they would be getting along too well, and she couldn't have that.

"So will you talk to her?"

"Yes, all right," Rose said, although she had no energy for it. She felt . . . finite, her brain only able to hold so much, and all the available space was currently taken by Theo. It was hard to care about all this kitchen sniping, hard not to resent strong, healthy Anna striding around, venting her petty frustrations over Carmen, when Theo could barely swallow solid food anymore.

"It's more than that," Anna said. She braced her hands on the desk and leaned in close.

Rose leaned back. Guilt was all that kept her from snapping, "I don't have *time* for this." Anna spent more time in this chair than she did these days; she felt as if she should get up and switch places.

"Rose," Anna said earnestly, "most chefs would rather work alone, that's just how they are, but a good chef has to fight that impulse and work with a *team*. Don't you agree?"

"Yes," she said cautiously.

"It's not even enough to be creative and motivated and imaginative and innovative—none of which Carmen is, if you ask me, all she is is a hard worker. A real chef has to know how to get the best out of people, *inspire* people. Whatever the chef's like, the kitchen's going to be like, because the chef sets the tone."

"All right."

"Fun, grim, nightmare, paradise—the chef is the one who—who—puts on the music everybody else dances to. Am I—"

"Yes, Anna, I—"

"Okay—but not only that, she has to really care about *people*. Right? She has to *like* them. She has to be a generous person inside herself, or else what's the point of making food? Where's the passion going to come from year after year, hardship after hardship, if you don't give a flick about the people you're supposed to be trying to serve?"

"What are you saying, you want Carmen—what? Out?"

"I want her not to be the chef." Anna straightened up, turning stern and righteous. Getting to the point brought out a militaristic streak in her. "Frankie should be the chef. If you can't fire Carmen—"

"Fire Carmen!"

"—then give her a new title, I don't know what. Not executive chef, something meaningless, and tell her you're worried about her health or something, you want her to consult."

"Consult?"

"Kick her upstairs." She jerked her head toward the ceiling—a pun, and another sore point with Anna, the fact that Carmen sublet from Rose the apartment upstairs for almost nothing. A sinecure, she called it, disapproving because Rose hadn't raised Carmen's rent in about fifteen years. With money so tight, Rose should either make her pay what it was worth or lease it to someone who would. That's what Anna thought.

"Slow down," Rose said, "let's take this a piece at a time. First of all, let me talk to her, maybe I can smooth it over, this kitchen design thing."

"You probably can, and then something else will pop up tomorrow."

"Then we'll—"

"Rose, she's not a nice person. She's bitter, she's an old maid, she's not happy."

"She's family."

"The Bella Sorella is family! Billy Sanchez is family, Vonnie's family. The people who love it and want it to work, they're family. Carmen—she knows food and she works hard, okay, and she's not a bad cook, but she stopped learning anything new about twenty years ago!"

"She *can* change. I'll speak to her. Anna—Anna, put yourself in her place. Of course she resents Frankie, she's everything Carmen isn't, young, strong, excited about the business—"

"Exactly! She's excited about the business. That's what you want for your chef!"

Rose shook her head. "I said I'd speak to her, but my dear, Carmen is the chef. We'll have to solve this some other way."

"Right." She marched to the door.

"Wait—don't be angry."

"I'm not." But obviously that wasn't true. This time when she slammed the door, she meant to.

Rose pressed the heel of her hand against her throbbing right temple. That used to work in the old days. For a minute or two. Migraine at her age? Ridiculous; stress, more likely. Her fault. How had she gotten herself into a relationship with Anna where only one of them was allowed to get mad?

Iris called on Rose's cell phone when she was sitting with Theo, reading the newspaper to him while he half listened, half dozed on the bed, propped up on his pillows. They chatted for a few minutes, then Rose carried the phone out into the hall so she wouldn't disturb him. And so she could tell Iris how he really was.

"He's not mad anymore—that's what scares me the most. He just lies there."

"What do you mean, he's not mad anymore?"

"He used to say this was temporary, as soon as his wrist healed he was moving back to his boat. He *hated* this place. He still hates it, but he doesn't care anymore."

There was a pause, and Rose knew Iris was trying to think of a way to turn that into a positive. Iris the realist, the blunt, plainspoken, some would say the tactless sister, had turned into a Pollyana where Theo was concerned. Rose found it an unexpected comfort to be the pessimistic one for a change, the deliverer of unadorned bad news, at least with one other person. With Iris she could sound as hopeless as she felt.

"Well," Iris said staunchly, "acceptance is a good thing, isn't it? And what a relief for you, not to have to keep the secret from him anymore. You hated that, not telling him what was going on."

"But we've never talked about that."

"Oh. You haven't?"

"Mason and I decided to let it go for now, so I don't know what he thinks. About the future. He still talks about us taking a trip someday on the sailboat."

"Well, that's good. I guess, something to look forward to."

"It's a new kind of lethargy. The aides get him up a couple of times a day, and I make him walk with me when I come, just up and down the hall. Mason takes him outside. But if we didn't make him get up, he'd lie in that bed all day, staring out the window."

"Oh, honey."

The night nurse on the wing, a stout, platinum-haired woman named Shirley, walked by. With raised eyebrows and a pleasant smile, she tapped on the face of her watch.

"I've got to go, Iris, they're shooing me out."

"They're not too strict about closing at ten o'clock, are they?"

"No, they're wonderful. I stay till eleven almost every time I come." It was quarter to eleven now.

"Give Theo a hug for me."

"I will."

"Night, Rose. You try not to worry."

Theo had turned off his bedside table lamp. Did he think she'd gone home? The night light he hated—because he couldn't turn it off—glowed palely in the corner, bluing the room and casting faint shadows. She padded to the bed on tiptoes; if he was asleep, she didn't want to wake him just to say good-bye.

No, his eyes were open. He blinked at her, the only way he could smile these days. "Hey, babe," she whispered. "I'm going to go on now. It's pretty late."

He moved his lips, preparing to say something. His speech became more halting as the day wore on; by nighttime, he was often too tired to talk at all. "Jean," he said. His rigid hand fluttered on the sheet over his chest. "Wondered if you'd come."

She kept her face soft. This had happened twice before, so it didn't sting quite so much this time. "It's Rose." She took his hand between both of hers. "It's Rose, Theo."

"Rose." He nodded, agreeing. "Better—get going. Late."

"Yes, I'd better." She kissed him, letting her lips linger on his for a moment, and when she straightened, his eyes were alive with tenderness and appreciation.

"Love you," he got out. Without prompting, for once. "Love you, Rose."

Sometimes he couldn't let go once he'd grasped something; she had to pry his fingers, one at a time, from their stiff grip around her hand. She'd make a joke, "Just can't bear to let me go, eh?" Tonight she didn't have the heart.

Driving home, she let herself cry for a minute, really just a few seconds. She started at a red light, and by the time it turned green she was all right, herself again. Theo calling her by his long-dead ex-wife's name, Jean—Mason's mother—that's what had set her off, but not because of jealousy. She'd never been jealous of Jean, a woman Theo had loved but should never have married. He could have called Rose any name—*that's* what upset her, the fact that, three times now, he hadn't known her. There were other examples, little things, losing his way coming back from dinner, forgetting what she'd just told him, or not understanding it, making her explain the simplest thing over and over. The doctor had said, "Yes, in part," when she'd asked if it was because of the medications he took for his muscle spasms. She didn't like *in part*.

Summer was almost over. This morning she'd seen yellow poplar leaves falling on the dry wind like fireflies. At night the cicadas were deafening, drowning out everything with that raucous, panicked drone they made at the end of their cycle, end of their lives. The days were still hot, but there was a tiredness in the air that said fall was coming, no mistaking it. All the trees looked weary, burdened. Too heavy to last much longer.

The phone in her purse rang. She hated talking on the phone in the car. She almost let it ring, but what if it was Theo, some emergency at the nursing home—

"Hello?"

"Carmen fired Frankie."

"What? Anna?"

"I just heard. I wasn't there, I'm at home."

"What happened?"

"I'll tell you what happened. After dinner service, Carmen told Frankie she had to clean out the grease trap."

"No. No, I'm sure that was a misunderstanding."

"No misunderstanding. She did it on purpose, because she knew Frankie would refuse because it's not her job, it's ten o'clock at night, and it's—it's punitive, an *insult*. She did it so she'd quit." Anna's voice sounded metallic with anger, vibrating with it.

"Well, we'll straighten it out tomorrow," Rose said, taking her hand off the wheel to put on her turn signal. "I'm sure it's—"

"I already hired her back."

"Ah. You—"

"They can't work together, Rose, one of them has to go."

"Well, that may be true. That may be true."

"I want you to fire Carmen."

She turned her face upward, not wanting Anna to hear her tired sigh through the mouthpiece. "We went through this before."

"I want you to make Frankie head chef."

"Yes, I know. But I can't do that."

"Then Frankie's going to quit."

"I hope we can avoid that. I know I haven't given enough attention to this problem, I've been—"

"And if Frankie goes, I go."

Rose braked hard for a light she didn't see until she was almost through it.

"It would just be sooner rather than later. I was going anyway, you knew that. So—it's nothing new. Just sooner instead of later. Rose?"

"This is the excuse—this is what you're going to use? This business with Carmen?"

"It's not an excuse. What do you mean?"

"But why now? That's what I don't understand. Was it getting too good?"

"Pardon me?"

"Did you catch yourself—not even remembering why you were so angry? What it was about me you hated? That must've been scary for you."

"Look. That's—I don't even—Could we stick to the point here? Are you going to fire Carmen or aren't you?"

"No, of course not."

"Fine. Here's my two weeks' notice. I'm not mad, Rose. This is one of those things, an honest difference of opinion. As I said, it's just happening sooner instead of—"

"*I'm* mad," Rose said, and clicked off.

What has my life been? Losing Theo slowly, one day at a time, had a side effect of exposing dusty corners, dark places Rose normally kept covered up; not buried or hidden, just decently out of sight, if only because they weren't useful or profitable. *What has my life been?* She had had two lovers, innumerable friends, the community of her restaurant. She had a sister. But it was Anna she had loved the most, Anna, the one who had given her the most pain. She'd lost her father, her sister, her mother, Paul, now Theo, but

Anna's ill-will and her disappointment were the chronic wound, the one that would not heal. Rose had never been able to revile her for cruelty—her own guilty conscience would've called that hypocrisy. But this was too much. She hadn't done enough to deserve this.

At Harvard Street she turned left instead of right, back toward town. Heat lightning flared in the pink haze of sky over the black treeline. Anna's neighborhood, oak-shaded Cape Cods and modest colonials, hadn't changed much over the years. Rose would drive past the house, Paul's house, once in a blue moon, pulled by nostalgia or homesickness, but she hadn't been inside since his funeral. Not since she and Anna had had their last fight, as it happened. A fitting setting, then.

She parked on the street near the tiny driveway, sending the neighbor's dog into a bored frenzy. Lights were on downstairs, not upstairs. Good, she was still up. Not that Rose cared.

She wouldn't get sidetracked by memories. She knocked smartly on the freshly painted red door, and when Anna opened up she greeted her with, "Don't you know not to open your door at night until you know who it is?"

"Rose. What a . . ."

"Unexpected pleasure." She moved inside when Anna couldn't seem to form the words "Come in." The house had a neglected, unlived-in look. Anna talked about refurbishing it to sell, but then she never did anything. It looked different and the same, the small foyer, the living room on the left, dining room—still with packed cardboard boxes in stacks on the table—on the right. Maybe Anna had never unpacked them; maybe they traveled with her from town to town, year to year, bulky tributes to impermanence.

"I was making some tea," she said, staring hard at Rose, searching for a clue to tell her what was going on. She was barefoot, but still in the same clothes she'd worn all day: wrinkled straight skirt and tight white blouse. Her face was shiny with fatigue and tense with watchfulness. "Have a cup with me?"

"I didn't really come here for tea." But Anna either didn't hear or pretended not to, and Rose shrugged to herself and followed her into the kitchen.

Same and different again. The table was chipped enamel instead of scarred oak, but still in the only place it could be in such a small room, on the back wall by the door that led to the den. She'd helped Anna with her homework at that table. Talked and listened to her, cried with her over Lily. Cried with Paul, too, and served him meals he ate at midnight, tired from his long drives home. Had she stolen Lily's family, then? Was that what Anna thought?

She was fiddling with cups and saucers, teabags and sugar. Pointedly, Rose took the steaming cup she handed her and set it on the sink counter without tasting it. "I think it's time we had a talk."

"What about?"

"Your mother and father."

"Oh, I don't."

"I do. You'll be leaving soon, and I want you to know something before you go."

"You won't change my mind."

"Of course not. That might prove you've grown up."

Hot fury flashed between them. Anna's head snapped up and her nostrils flared. Just as quickly, she caught her temper and beat it back under control. Rose followed her lead; it would feel good, but they'd get nowhere shouting bitter things.

She leaned back on her hands against the counter. "You asked me how Lily and Paul met."

"In the restaurant. That's what you said. Was that a lie?"

Rose stared at her until Anna had to drop her eyes, stirring and stirring her dark red tea.

"He thought I was his waitress," she said slowly. "He asked me for some ketchup. I told him I was a cook, that I was just taking a break. He liked that, that I was a chef. He started talking about Italian food, and what a terrible cook his mother was. He was sitting at a front window table, the one in the corner. He talked a lot, but he was shy. Very handsome. I told him I liked his accent—he said he didn't have an accent. He was so embarrassed when he couldn't find his wallet. I teased him to set him at ease. Comped him his three-dollar lunch and lent him gas money to get home. He promised to come in and pay me back the next time he was in town."

"Where was my—"

"Lily was hostessing. When he came back with his wallet—remember, he found it in his car—I introduced them."

"Yes? And then?"

"He asked me to have dinner with him."

"You?"

"Not Lily."

Anna's eyes were unreadable, her lips a tight, skeptical line.

"Mama let me out of dinner service, and he took me to a band concert on the water. He talked through the whole thing. He was an amateur inventor, he played the trombone and the banjo, he was a reader of great books, a correspondence course taker. He wanted to have his own bookstore, he wanted to sail down the Mississippi on a houseboat, he wanted to live in San Francisco, see Europe, raise collies. When he brought me home, we sat on the front steps and talked for two more hours. Oh, how he could talk. Mama liked him. She said he reminded her of Papa."

"Well. Go on," Anna said when Rose paused. "This is fascinating."

She ignored the implication that it was a story, something she was making up. Let Anna keep her defenses as long as she could if it made her feel better.

"We fell in love," she said bluntly. "First time, for me—I was only twenty-one. Young, I know, but it felt like love. It was love. Lily claimed not even to like him. She made fun of how skinny he was, how he talked too much, how he could never do all the things he said he wanted to do if he lived six lifetimes. I was used to that, though. Lily never liked it when I had something she didn't."

"My mother was jealous of *you*?"

"Hard to believe. She was the pretty, vivacious one, everyone said so. But she could still be jealous. And selfish, and possessive. She was insecure. Do you really not know this? She couldn't be happy for long. I loved her because she was funny and sweet and generous—if it was just us, nothing outside the two of us for her to crave or to covet, she was a wonderful sister. But she couldn't stand it that Paul loved me, and she took him away from me."

"I don't believe you."

"I know. It happened when we went to the beach for a long weekend. Six of us rented a cottage at Bethany—Iris and Tony and little Theresa—she was four, their only child then—and Paul and me. And Lily. Iris and Tony were the chaperones. There were three rooms—"

"I don't want to hear this."

"I don't want to talk about it."

"Bullshit. You're *dying* to tell me."

Was she? She wasn't dying to tell her that Lily had played and flirted with Paul all weekend in a strange, confusing way, touching him as she passed by, a hand trailing across his back or his shoulders, or pinching him teasingly, leaning against him to laugh at something he said. Rose had watched Paul watch Lily—who was so lovely, fair and feminine and shapely, not straight and tall and dark like her. Lily was a natural flirt, sexually powerful, and unlike Rose, not a virgin. But Rose had only been angry, not worried. And only angry at Lily, not Paul.

"She seduced him. On the last night."

"I can ask Aunt Iris if any of this is true, you know."

"Please do."

Anna's eyes burned with a look that could only be called loathing. "Why tell me this now?"

"Because I'm sick of keeping it from you."

"I know why—for the same reason you told me Theo's worse, Theo's dying. So I'll feel sorry for you. So I'll stay." She came closer, enunciated clearly. "Fat chance." She set her teacup down with a clatter and walked out.

Rose followed. "Lily and I had a room together. She waited until I was asleep and then she went to him. He had no excuse, none. He wouldn't vilify her, afterward, but she overpowered him—that's what happened."

Anna laughed. "*Overpowered him*?" She prowled around the dusty living room, unable to sit, picking things up and putting them down.

"The next day, she told me what she'd done. She couldn't wait to tell me. She said they loved each other. She was so sorry they'd hurt me, but it was too strong, they couldn't help themselves. Paul—Paul—"

"Yes? Don't stop now."

"Paul couldn't explain what he didn't understand himself. I broke it off. I wouldn't listen to his apologies, which—" she laughed thinly—"were not very sympathetic. And so Lily got him. Six weeks later, they married." She might've left it at that, but Anna had a sour, triumphant look on her face that was galling, as if Lily's victory were *her* victory. Rose was sick of protecting her. "They married because she was pregnant. With you."

Anna went paper-white. She sat down hard on the arm of the sofa.

"Mama wasn't even angry. That felt like another betrayal to me. But she loved Paul by then. Lily *should* get married before me, she said, because she was older."

"Why don't you just cut to the chase." Anna's wavery voice sounded high and childish. "When did you start cheating on her?"

"You know when."

"No, I don't."

"That night you saw us. Here. Right in this room, right by that window."

"That's what you say."

"Do you think I'm lying?"

"For thirteen years you just—*pined* for each other?"

"Yes."

She snorted. "Why should I believe you? For all I know, you were sneaking around behind her back for years! Maybe from the beginning—your own sister—maybe you made her whole marriage a lie."

"No. You can believe what you like, but we never touched each other until that night. At first, it was easy. I was so *angry*—I didn't *want* him. And we all pretended so well, all three of us, a conspiracy of silence for the sake of peace. Years went by before I knew that nothing had changed between Paul and me—no, that's not true, everything was much worse because we were older. I was a woman, not a girl, and I was afraid he was the only man I could love. Lily had a husband and a child, but she wasn't happy because she couldn't believe she could keep them.

"Once when you were very little, only a baby, she—wouldn't let me hold you. We couldn't talk about it, we *never* talked about it, but that time, just that once, I said, 'Lily, you've got Paul, can't you let me love this little girl?' After that, she let us be whatever we were going to be—you and me. It was the kindest thing she ever did. I always thought of it as—a recompense."

Tears kept welling in Anna's eyes and spilling down her cheeks, uncontrollable. She backhanded them away angrily. "Say anything you like, put any spin on it you can. She was *dying*. The cruelest time, the ugliest time—why couldn't you wait?" She stood up, shaking. "Was my mother taking too long?"

"Did you know—the world doesn't revolve around you? That what happened between your father and me had *nothing to do with you*? Can you *ever* realize that?"

"Why couldn't you wait for her to die?"

"Who are you? You're not me, you're not my mother. You can't know what it was like to be losing a sister, to be grieving—"

"Grieving, ha—"

"To have lost Paul to her and to see him beaten down by the lie his life had turned into—"

"Why couldn't you wait! Why!"

"Because I didn't want to! I wanted him back. *While* she was alive—yes!"

"To even the score."

"Yes! She stole him from me—I stole him back!"

"People don't *steal* people. You betrayed your own sister, that's what you did."

"All right—that's what I did."

"And I'm not getting over it. It hurts." Anna's face collapsed like a child's.

"*Life* hurts. And you're right, people don't steal people. That woman you hate, that Nicole—she didn't steal Jay from you, either."

Anna blanched. *Low blow*, her dark, naked eyes said, but Rose didn't agree. "I don't forgive you. I never will." She spun around. Her purse was on the gateleg table in the hall; she fumbled in it for something. Keys: they fell on the floor with a clatter.

"If I needed anyone's forgiveness, it wouldn't be yours, it would be Lily's."

"That's not true. You need mine, but I don't forgive you."

"Are you *leaving*? How perfect. How perfect."

The straps on Anna's purse were tangled; she kept pulling, tugging, trying to get them to go over her shoulder.

"You could tell *me* to leave. But I guess that wouldn't be as satisfying."

She gave up on the purse and strode to the door.

"To think I actually considered firing Carmen for you."

Anna sent her a bitter look and yanked open the door.

Rose went after and called out into the dark yard. "Talk about 'family'! Carmen knows about loyalty—she'd never leave like this—for nothing, for another job that doesn't even exist yet, for strangers—for nothing!"

She'd set the neighbor's dog off again. Anna had trouble unlocking her car door. When she got in, she slammed it repeatedly before it closed right, the last time with such force, it shut the dog up for a second. She backed up without looking, and screeched off down sleepy Day Street as if monsters were chasing her.

"That went well," Rose said out loud. It didn't work, though, didn't save the day with a little bravehearted levity.

The truth, whatever that was, had never seemed so insignificant to her. It didn't change anything, not if the damage had already been done. She'd thought she had nothing to lose by telling it, everything to gain if the gamble paid off. But she'd bet wrong, and now she had less than before. As soon as this high wore off, this righteous, anger-fueled elation, the poverty of what she had left was going to sink her.

17

She felt set upon, besieged. Victimized, but not like Sylvia Plath. More like St. Stephen, shot through with arrows. Why the shock, though, why be surprised? Rose had always been able to hurt her, this was nothing new. But she felt blindsided, caught off guard. Lulled by Rose into a false sense of security, then *whack*, cut off at the knees. She turned the radio up for a distraction, but the staticky rock station only stretched her nerves tighter. She felt endangered. She needed a safe haven.

In high school she used to go to a cove on the Severn and neck with a boy named Scottie McGrady. Baldwin's Cove, it was called, nothing but a spit of sand between pine wood tracks, a little bit of beach and some boulders. She'd even gone by herself once in a while, to hang out and think, sit on a rock and throw pebbles in the water. Plan her life.

But they'd killed it. Now it was Trelawny Landing, a gated community of million-dollar wooded estates hugging the river. She backed out in the turnaround beside the guard's kiosk and drove north. Another high school habit was circling the Baltimore Beltway, but in those days driving was the end, you went around and around in your parents' car for the pure pleasure of being on the road and on your own. Anna got as far as the Pikesville exit, turned around, and came back.

She couldn't stand it, she hated how she felt, half-born, as if she was in labor but she was the child instead of the mother. She couldn't go home. She didn't know what to do with herself.

She'd go see Mason. That had been her first impulse, but she felt prickly and sharp, cactus woman, no one could fit next to her, not even him. Or was it some intimation that he wouldn't be as sympathetic as she needed him to be? But she loved his generosity, the way he would let her use him if he knew she needed to. She took him for granted already, and that was odd—it wasn't as if she'd known a lot of men like him before. Something in her must think she deserved him.

His house was dark. What time was it? Christ, midnight already. He kept healthy hours, in bed by eleven-thirty, up at seven. When she stayed over, she disrupted his schedule, but he didn't mind. He said she made it worth his while.

Her car tires on the gravel made a loud crunch, and her slamming door exploded in the silence, startling the crickets. From inside the house, Theo's old dog didn't make a sound, though: he was deaf. "Ow, ow, ow," Anna muttered, hopping and limping across the sharp stones. Stupid to leave home with no shoes, but she'd been in a hurry.

She used the knocker on the front door, and presently she heard sounds inside. Mason should get a peephole. The problem with no front windows was that he never knew who was at the door until he opened it.

"Hi."

"Hi." His sleepy grin was the nicest thing she'd seen all day. He had on cutoff sweatpants and nothing else, and that looked pretty nice, too. Cork sidled around his legs, saw who it was, and wagged his tail.

"Sorry it's so late. Guess I woke you up. Can I come in?"

"Sure." He looked at her more closely. "What's wrong?"

"Oh . . . I just need somebody to tell me I'm not a selfish, heartless bitch." Was she going to cry again?

"I can do that."

"Preferably with their arms around me."

He put his arms around her, and she relaxed into his drowsy warmth, liking his skin and his shaggy hair, the friendly prickle of his whiskers. *Now I'm okay*, she thought, and wondered if she was in love with him. She wanted to go to bed with him, no question about that. She wanted the sweaty ritual of sex, and especially the obliteration at the end. She wanted to use him.

"What's wrong?" he asked again. "What happened?"

"It's Rose."

He pushed her away to see her face. "Is she all right?"

"Yeah." She shrugged his hands off her arms. "She's fine."

She went past him, through the dark living room to the kitchen. She turned on the bright overhead light and got a glass from the cabinet, filled it at the sink. Mason, leaning in the doorway, watched her drink tepid tap water.

"No shoes," he noticed.

"I had to move fast." She prowled around the neat, shiny room. "No wounded birds today." They were doing a replay of the first time they'd met. Except she'd been in a better mood that day. "What's this?" On the kitchen table, wide folds of nylon cloth in camouflage colors, sewed onto big plastic circles—hula hoops, they looked like.

"Something I'm making."

"What is it?"

"A hoop blind."

"What's it do?"

He came over, took the voluminous contraption out of her hands. "Well, you get inside. It covers you up completely. This is for a telephoto lens, this hole. It's for taking pictures from the water—the hoops collapse the farther in you wade. You can go in up to your chin."

"You must look pretty silly."

"Yes, but that's the idea. The birds relax because they're laughing so hard."

"Rose and I had a fight. It's been coming on for a while, I guess. Although *I* didn't know it—I thought we were doing pretty well."

"What did you fight about?"

"My mother. My father."

Mason sat on the edge of the table, crossed his feet, crossed his arms. Waiting for the story. The possibility that he might not automatically take her side occurred to her again. It gave her a queasy feeling.

"I don't want to get into it," she decided, "all the gory details. Too boring for you. Suffice it to say, she tried to rewrite history, but it didn't work on me. I still like my mother."

She had a cache of memories, a collection of the good times, sweet times. Her mother with her hands over her face, shoulders shaking, trying not to laugh in church—her mother letting Anna miss school the next day so they could stay up late and watch the Academy Awards—her mother yelling delicious obscenities at the neighbor woman whose obnoxious son had pulled Anna off a seesaw and bloodied her nose. At the Bella Sorella, she'd worn straight skirts and crisp, tailored blouses, and her high heels had made a smart, decisive clacking sound, so businesslike and irrefutable. She'd had a gay, controlled laugh, slightly theatrical; Anna had delighted in it and tried to provoke it, but it hadn't come often enough.

She had other memories, not such nice ones, and it rankled that Rose's so-called *revelations* had opened the door to them as well. She remembered when her mother had been inaccessible to her, literally not there because she was in her bedroom with the door locked, usually in the wake of a fight with her father. "She's just tired," he would explain to Anna, the two of them at the kitchen table eating his improvised supper of canned chili or scrambled eggs, furtively listening for a sound overhead. They would treat each other with strained care and extra politeness, and her father would minimize the last shouting match by calling her mother "high strung" or "not quite herself." Her mother wasn't so reticent. "Stupid *sciocco*, I can't live like this, I'll go mad!" and then the inevitable slammed door. Anna would skulk around the house as if one false step might blow it up, but she never knew what was best to do, make noise, be quiet, act natural, act like a mourner at a wake. Nothing worked twice anyway; her mother had her own agenda, and her sudden recoveries were as unpredictable as her declines.

Mason made his voice irritatingly reasonable. "Do you really think Rose was trying to discredit your mother? Blacken her memory for you—"

"Yes, Mason. Yes, I do."

"Because it doesn't sound to me like something she'd—"

"I told you, we were fighting. Gloves off. She told me"—this would wipe that *patient* look off his face—"she told me my father fell in love with her first, and my mother took him away from her. *Seduced* him, she claims."

"You don't think it's true?"

"What if it is true? What if it is? What if every fucking thing she said is true, what difference does it make? What does she think I'll do now, Mason, say, 'Oh, *that's* what happened—oh, no wonder, poor Rose, all's forgiven'? Nothing's changed! She still did what she did."

He glanced away from her. To hide his disappointment, she assumed. "Anna." He tugged gently on the cuff of her shirt. "Haven't you ever made a mistake?"

She pulled her arm away. "Yeah. Moving back here."

"You don't mean that."

"I gave Rose two weeks' notice. There's a job in New York I can have any time I want. So I've decided to take it."

He stood up and backed away. His shocked face looked too naked in the stark light, she wanted to glance away from it, out of modesty. "Why?"

"Why? Lots of reasons, not just this business with Rose. Carmen fired Frankie and Rose won't do anything about it, that's the main thing. But mostly, because it's time. I told Rose in the beginning that I'd give her the summer. I've done that. The restaurant's turning a corner, it'll either make it now or it won't, me sticking around won't change that."

Mason didn't speak.

"I'll be sorry to go. I'll miss—you. I don't want to leave you. I don't feel like Rose has left me any choice. But you're the one I'll miss." The way he was looking at her made it impossible to expand on that, not now—but how inadequate it sounded. It didn't represent the whole truth. "And a few other things, but... this isn't my home anymore. I've found that out."

The red streak of scar stood out from the pallid flesh of his cheek like a smear of warpaint. "So you're leaving."

"It's just a matter of sooner rather—"

"The geographic solution."

"Oh." She stiffened. "Is that how you see it? I'm sorry."

"What did you come here for?"

"Don't be angry. Oh, Mason—"

He picked up her half-full water glass and hurled it across the room. She shrieked, throwing her arm up to cover her eyes, jolting backward against the kitchen table. Glass shattered in the sink, too far away to do any damage.

"Don't go." He said that in a quiet voice, but he was in a cold fury.

"I have to. I can't stay. Rose has made it impossible."

"I doubt that. Don't go."

"You doubt that? I'm lying?" Her anger wasn't cold at all, it was burning hot. "Rose can do no wrong, I forgot—I always forget whose side you're on."

"You sound like a child."

She wished *she* had something to throw. She swept his stupid hoop blind off the table with one arm and started away, making a berth around the glinting glass shards on the floor in front of the sink. In the living room, she tossed back, "You know what, I'm really tired of people telling me I sound like—"

He snatched her from behind, one hard arm around her waist and the other across her chest. She gasped in shock—he wasn't playing. She strained away, plucking at his fingers to loosen his grip. They pivoted, grappling, fumbling, neither one speaking a word. She used her feet to kick back at him, savage stabs that never landed, and then finally one heel connected with his shin. They went staggering against the coffee table, scattering the chess set. The dog, startled out of a nap, got to his feet arthritically and began to bark, wagging his tail with excitement. Anna's leg tangled with one of Mason's and she went down hard, taking him with her. They hit, half on the floor, half on the carpet. Her elbow struck something sharp and she squeaked in pain.

He let go.

She got one knee underneath her and started to spring up, but Mason yanked her back with his hand around her bare foot. She shouted a curse and kicked at him, kicked away, hopping backward, out of his reach. She made a mad dash for the door, batted the screen open, slammed outside. When she looked back, he was getting slowly to his feet.

They stared at each other through the screen, baleful-eyed, breathing hard. But he stayed where he was, didn't come any closer. It was over.

The ripped shoulder of her blouse hung down around her elbow. She felt battered and bruised and stupidly exhilarated. On the brink of something. She was shivering all over. She took a couple of steps toward him. "Okay. I hurt you and I didn't mean to. I never saw this coming. I hate it. But I can't be Theo's—replacement, for you or for Rose. Look, Mason, people leave, and you can't change it. Do you think you're not worth staying with? Because of all the ones who've left you? You can't believe that." She wanted to touch him, but she was still wary of him. "You're a good man—please, don't let this *mean* anything. Anything more than what it is."

She stopped talking when he came toward her, scared of him again, but he stopped on the other side of the screen. "Don't let this mean anything." He braced his hands on either side of the door. Backlit, he looked like Christ on the cross, his head down, his lean, scarred body tilted. "Okay," he said. "I'll try that." Careful not to slam it, he shut the door in her face.

Mason finally called, but not for a week.

In the meantime, Anna told Joel she would definitely take him up on his job offer. She needed about a month to square things away at home, but she looked forward to being in New York well before the end of September. He seemed glumly pleased. She liked Joel because he was levelheaded and smart, but she'd never met anyone as gloomy. He was on his third wife; the other two had to get away from his dark life philosophy, in which everything that possibly might go wrong was bound to. That had advantages in the restaurant business, but it also made Joel a lot more effective in the kitchen than the dining room. That was where Anna was supposed to come in. Maybe they would be a good match, but not if he was expecting her to be the hopeful one. Between them, they made up about one quarter of an optimist.

"Come with me," she told Frankie. "Joel's no prima donna, he'll make you the sous as soon as he finds out how good you are. I could probably talk him into it right now, in fact. Vegetarian gourmet. Think about it. Come on, it'll be fun."

But Frankie wouldn't leave Katie, and Anna hadn't really expected her to. Rose had hired her back, and the situation was status quo, no better or worse than before with Carmen. Anna warned her to start looking for another place. "As soon as I'm gone, Carmen's going to find a way to get rid of you, you know she is, and this time for good." Frankie agreed; she was keeping her eyes open for something in town.

So everything was winding down. Besides a lot of pain and confusion, Anna felt smothered by anticlimax. She'd never worked so hard as she had in the last four months. It was as if she'd entered a contest, the decathlon, say, and just before the finish line of the final event she'd been yanked out of the race by—something stupid, a broken shoelace, a cramp. She was exhausted, but she had nothing to show for it. She hadn't won or lost, she'd just—stopped.

She dragged in to work every morning, tired before the day started, ready to collapse by dinnertime. She ought to have *more* energy, not less, with the prospect of a brand-new job, new opportunity around the corner. But a blanketing sense of incompleteness smothered any enthusiasm she could work up.

It didn't help that everyone was angry with her. Not openly—well, except for Vince. And "angry," no, that was too strong. Probably paranoid, too. It was just that she wasn't one of them anymore. Dwayne didn't include her in his vulgar practical jokes on Flaco—a silly example, but it meant something to her. Louis's face didn't light up when he saw her, and he didn't saunter over to smoke a cigarette and shoot the breeze in the morning shade under the awning. Shirl consulted Rose instead of Anna about the new logo for the sign out front. When Luca got his feelings hurt, he confided in Fontaine, and lately even Vonnie wanted to go home after her shift instead of hanging out with Anna and a bottle of Peroni and talking about how the night had gone. Family meal wasn't the same. Nobody shunned her, nobody was rude; they just didn't think to include her anymore. She was a lame duck.

Vince simply couldn't believe she was leaving. "What are you trying for, a raise?" When she convinced him she was really going, he was openly hostile. "Upstate New York? Are you out of your mind?"

"It's a nice town. I thought you'd be glad—there's a winery not far away, I thought you'd like to come up—"

"Why don't you just move to Canada? Or Japan? They like tofu there, you'd fit right in. What the hell is the matter with you? So you had a fight with Rose, so what?"

It was no use explaining to him that she'd never been going to stay forever, that the plan all along was to see how things went, with the option to leave if she liked after giving Rose the summer. "You should stay," he declared flatly. "Leaving's a cop-out. It's stupid." And the final dig: "It's not like you're getting any younger."

Just because she was miserable didn't mean she was wrong—she was down to telling herself that by the end of the exhausting days. Nothing worse than being misunderstood by people who used to like you. Oddly, or maybe not, the one who was nicest to her was Rose. Anna didn't trust her gentleness at first—*it's a trick*, she'd think, *she's trying to kill me with kindness*. Neither of them ever referred to the night she'd stormed out of her own house, never revisited any of that evening's painful disclosures. No need; they hadn't forgotten anything, and what was there to add? They got through what was left of Anna's tenure by treating each other with a rueful, impersonal warmth that was more demoralizing than ire or blame or rancor could ever be.

She tried not to think of that night, but it haunted her. She hated the phrase "geographical solution," hated it with a visceral repugnance verging on nausea. When she felt strong, she lumped Rose and Mason together and made them the common enemy, in cahoots with each other to make her feel guilty for being who she was and not who they selfishly wanted her to be. When she felt weak, they just defeated her.

When Mason called, she was on the phone with the fish supplier. She put him on hold and told the fish guy she'd call back.

She sat up straight behind the desk, as if Mason could see her. She lined up the papers and invoices and moved the stapler over so it was centered in front of the lamp. She brushed a smear of flour off the bosom of her shirt. Neat and tidy. In her mind, everything was chaos, like waves in a storm, everything dark blue-black and whirling. But order was coming, it was a button-push away. Whatever Mason would say, it was going to stop all this suffering and second-guessing and confusion. Thank God, because she had really needed rescuing.

"Mason? Sorry, I can talk now. I had to get rid of—"

"Is Rose there?"

"No. I mean yes, she's in the kitchen, so it's okay, we can—"

"Can I speak to her?"

She took the phone away for a second, as if it had burned her ear. "You want to talk to Rose?"

"Yes, fast. It's important."

"All right. Just a minute, please."

She put the receiver on the desk and stared at it. It flashed through her mind, a picture of herself smashing the phone against the edge of the desk, beating it against the edge until the desk was splintered and the receiver was just wires in her hands, everything else shards of mauve plastic scattered on the floor.

Rose was in the pantry, laughing with Carmen. Frankie hadn't come in yet; she worked normal dinner hours now, she didn't bother coming in in the morning to test specials or start an early prep. Lunch service would begin in half an hour, so the kitchen was already hot, loud, and crazy.

Rose saw her and came over.

"Phone call," Anna said. "Mason."

"Thanks." She took it on the wall phone by the ice maker. "Hello?"

Anna, sullen as a jealous child, felt torn between walking out and staying to listen. She compromised by pretending to care about the dough Shirl was pinching into farfalle on the floury counter. Rose said, "Oh, my God," in a low, panicky voice.

"What happened?" Anna said, coming closer.

"I'll meet you. I'm leaving now." She hung up. She swept past Anna and headed for the office.

"Rose, what's wrong?" she said, following.

Rose jerked open the bottom desk drawer and got out her purse. "Theo. He's gone."

"Gone?"

"They were outside—Mason went in to talk to the floor nurse about his meds, and when he came back out he was gone. And Cork—and Mason's car." She was ash-pale, barely moving her lips. When she passed Anna in the doorway, their shoulders bumped awkwardly. "Sorry—"

She left.

Anna stood with her mouth open, staring. When her wits came back, she bolted after her. "I'll go with you!" Rose didn't hear—she had to run to catch up with her.

18

Rose saw Mason leaning against the decorative split-rail fence edging Bayside Gardens' parking lot when she drove in. The sight of him moving toward her with his slouchy, long-legged stride calmed her a little. His expression was concerned but not desperate, not panicked. He slid into the backseat over Anna's protests—"No, sit up here, Mason, I'll get in back"—and reached his hand over the seat to squeeze Rose's shoulder.

He said, "I've called the police, given them the license number and all that. Told them what he looks like."

"What did they say?" She started to drive out of the parking lot, even though she didn't know where she was going. But idling, not moving, not doing anything was intolerable. Mason might be calm, but she wasn't; her foot shook on the accelerator, her hands on the wheel were damp with sweat. She should've let Anna drive. "What did the police say?"

"Not much. They wanted to know if he had a valid driver's license. They kept asking me if he'd stolen my car."

"You should've said yes!"

"I did, finally." He caught her eye in the rearview mirror and they laughed, a little wildly. "I could see it was the only way they were going to do anything. So now they're looking for him. They say."

"Can he even drive your car? It's a standard shift, isn't it?" Nightmare visions of Theo plowing into something or somebody had plagued her all the way over. He could barely walk, barely feed himself—how could he drive a four-wheel-drive Jeep with a stick shift?

Mason shook his head and didn't answer.

"Where am I going?" she asked, stalled at the stop sign in the first intersection. It was starting to rain. She turned on the wipers, smearing the windshield. "I don't know where I'm going."

"Could he have gone to the marina?" Anna offered. "Where he used to live? Maybe he's just gone back—"

"Wait," Mason said, "listen. Theo kept talking about the *Wind Rose* today. More than usual. About taking a day trip, sailing to Tangier Island, going someplace with you, with me, maybe with some of his old buddies."

"Yes—my God, the *Wind Rose*, it's all he talks about. Mason, you don't think he's taken it!"

"I don't see how he could have, but he might've gone there. He might've gone just to look at it."

"Or he could've gone to the restaurant," Anna said. "To see you, Rose."

Rose drummed her fingers on the steering wheel, fluttery inside from indecision.

"I'll call the restaurant," Anna said, fumbling in her purse, "while you drive to Mason's."

Good. People telling her what to do, that's what she needed. She turned left and drove through the increasing rain to Mason's house.

His Jeep sat in the driveway at a skewed angle, twin ruts of gravel gouged out behind the back tires. The driver's door hanging open chilled her; something alarming in the jaunty haphazardness of it. And when she got out of her car and went close, the sound of the warning buzzer—because Theo had left the key in the ignition—sawed through her like a dentist's drill. She started to run.

Her shoes slid on the wet slates in the grass in Mason's sloping side yard. She'd outdistanced him, but he came up from behind and took hold of her arm, steadying her, trotting beside her. "It's gone," she panted, but she kept on running. The sailboat should've been tied at the end of the dock, but it could've drifted in its moorings, it could be behind the boat shed, invisible from here—

"It's gone."

They halted together, halfway down the slippery wooden pier, hovering in the angle of the turn. The rain came faster, thudding on the dock, hissing on the green-gray river. She strained her eyes, trying to conjure the *Wind Rose* out of empty air, but the lines dangling from the wooden cleats at the side of the dock dropped off into nothing. Nothing, no clue left, not a gas can, not a stray work glove, no bait bucket, no weather-beaten cap. None of the benign, commonplace objects that went with the *Wind Rose* in her mind. Nothing, just rain, washing away the evidence, obscuring the view.

"Come inside," Mason said. "I'll call the cops again. And the Coast Guard."

"Yes, go. I'll stay here."

"Come with me. You'll get soaked out here."

"No, I'll stay."

He hesitated, then sprinted for the house.

Anna took his place beside her. As she had in the car earlier, driving to the nursing home, she tried to encourage Rose by thinking up hopeful scenarios. This time it was that Theo was just out joyriding on the river, taking the sailboat out for a spin, using the engine—he couldn't put the sails up, could he?—and cruising around because he knew Rose and Mason and everybody else would never let him go out by himself. "He's escaped, Rose, he's on a lark, he'll be back as soon as he gets tired."

Rose patted her on the hand absently, not listening.

Mason came back. He made Rose put on his heavy gray slicker. He opened a wide black umbrella over her head, but the wind made it hard to hold. She wrapped her hand over his around the handle and pulled him up close beside her.

"Anna," she said, "would you mind—"

"What, Rose? What?"

"Would you go inside and listen for the phone?"

Her face fell. "Yes. Sure."

Wind gusts blew the rain in Rose's face. Mason put her behind him, to shield her from the worst of it. She watched the silver lines blow sideways from behind his left shoulder, holding on to his waist with one hand, the umbrella with the other. Summer was gone; the smell of fall had settled in the brackish tang of the river. What was Theo wearing? Was he cold? No, he was never cold. And he was still strong, but what would this unkind wind do to his little sailboat?

"We should go in," she told Mason, and he nodded, but neither of them could leave the scent, the trail, the last place they knew he'd been. It would seem too much like giving up. Like leaving him out there by himself.

"Mason, why did he do this?"

"I don't know."

"Is it good or bad that he took Cork with him?"

"I don't know."

"You know how he's been. Not always himself—in his mind."

"Yes."

"What was he like today? How was he when you saw him?"

"He was fine, in a good mood. But quiet. Calm. We mostly talked about the boat."

"Did he say anything, anything at all . . ."

"He said you'd come to see him last night. You'd brought him some pudding."

Ricotta pudding. His favorite. But he'd had trouble swallowing it.

"When he talks about you, you know, his face always relaxes. You're like medicine for him, Rose."

She rested her cheek on his shoulder.

The rain dwindled to a misty drizzle; the wind fell. A bird flew up from one of the tiny marsh islands across the way in the river. A coot, Mason said. It flapped an awkward arc against the low gray sky before it dropped down and disappeared from sight.

"It's wrong," Rose murmured, "it's too soon. I'm not ready to lose him. I've been preparing, trying . . ."

"Yes."

"But this is too soon. I still have things to tell him. I thought there was time."

The rain stopped. Mason closed the umbrella, and immediately she missed its dark, safe cover. They were too open out here, no protection from the dangerous, lightening sky. Something was going to happen and they weren't going to be able to stop it.

Even before she saw Anna's face, she knew. It was in her stiff shoulders and the careful way she walked, her arms out a little from her body, as if she were balancing on an edge. She came up on the dock, her light footsteps shaking the planks, eyes still on the ground. Behind her, Rose felt Mason's chest expand in a deep, defensive breath.

"The police just called." Her voice was clear and steady, but her face had a helpless, pleading look Rose could barely tolerate. "Some boaters, a family, they came on the *Wind Rose* out in the bay. They were heading back in because of the storm warning, a squall—" She waved her hand at the river, the sky. "They thought it looked funny—they came alongside to see why it was still, why there was nobody on deck. Just a dog barking." Her eyes filled.

Mason said, "Is he dead?"

"They found him. He was in the water, next to the boat. His leg, his foot was caught in a line. Yes, he's gone."

"He drowned?"

"Yes."

Rose pushed her face against the front of Mason's shirt, taking handfuls of the damp cloth. She could taste it, cotton and salt, bitter on her lips, indistinguishable from her own tears. Gone. Dead. Drowned. It didn't mean anything. It was sad, but she didn't know why yet, it wasn't real. She wasn't surprised, but she didn't believe it.

"Where is he?" Mason said.

"They brought him on board. They're coming in, towing the sailboat. The police said they were making for someplace called Dutchman Point. They said it's—"

"I know where it is," he said.

"I want to see him."

"Oh, Rose, no." Anna put her hand out.

"I'll take you," Mason said.

They'd thrown a blue tarpaulin over his body. Mason spoke to the two policemen on the deck of the cruiser, and then he came and got Rose and helped her on board. One of the policemen pulled the tarp away. Rose went down on her knees.

Nobody had closed his eyes. She was afraid to touch him at first. And then, as soon as she did, it was all right. It was only Theo. She brushed her fingers over his scruffy mustache, caressing his parted lips. His cheek was icy; she put her cheek next to it to warm him. What made her cry was his green wool sweater, sodden and twisted at his waist; she'd given it to him for Christmas. One of his shoes was gone, the sock half off. He looked disheveled and reckless, his grizzled hair a wet tangle on the deck.

"He looks like himself," she said to Mason. She meant, he looked more like himself than he had in a long time. Dying had loosened the stiffness in his face and let the old familiar lines, the sweetness and heart come back. Now it was real. Theo was gone, this Theo, the one she knew best. She threaded her fingers through his and pressed his big, blocky hand to her heart. *Did you do it on purpose?* She hoped so—she hoped not. Either way, she couldn't bear it. Mason touched her shoulder, and she thought, *Whatever you say, I'll believe. You decide. I can't.*

"Love me, Theo?" she whispered. She put her ear to his lips and listened for his answer.

19

Anna broke down at Theo's funeral. She was mortified, stunned, she couldn't believe it was happening. One minute she was sitting quietly in her pew behind Rose and Mason, half listening to irritating, generic organ music and wondering what Mason would do if she pulled on the little thread sticking out of the back of the collar of his dark blue suitcoat. In the next she was doubled over her knees, desperate to muffle hoarse, croaky sobs, feeling crushed under some kind of racking sorrow. *What was this?* She had no idea, but she couldn't control it. Aunt Iris's patting hand on her spine only made it worse. She hadn't felt like this when *Mac* died. It was as if Theo's funeral was all the funerals of her life, and she was mourning him and every other person she'd ever lost. When the service ended and it was time to go to the gravesite, she asked Rose if she could be excused.

"Do you need me?" she said, eyeing the cars lining up for the procession to the cemetery. "I'll go if it'll help." She was too far gone to phrase that any better. "Really, truly, I'll go if you need me."

Rose put her hand on Anna's hot, swollen, blotchy cheek and said, "No, I don't need you." At least she softened it with a smile.

No, she didn't need her, she had Mason, who'd hardly left her side since Theo died. They had each other.

To Anna's knowledge, Rose had only wept in public once, last night at the funeral home. She'd seen her sway and start to fold in on herself as she stood at the head of Theo's open coffin—Anna had risen from her chair and started to go to her, to catch her if she fell—but Mason got to her first, and supported her in his arms until she recovered. Otherwise, Rose had been calm and steady, practically serene. Or else she was simply shutting Anna out of her grief. That was probably it. Either way, her composure made Anna's highly visible collapse at the funeral feel even more inappropriate and excessive.

Mason stood at Rose's side on the church steps and regarded Anna with a penetrating expression she couldn't decode. *Hysterical female*, he was probably thinking. Maybe he resented her distress—maybe he didn't even believe in it. She wanted to speak to him, but she had nothing to say. She'd already told him how sorry she was, asked if there was anything she could do, said all the things you could say to someone to show you cared and felt sympathy and wished you could console.

But they were reduced to the most excruciating kind of politeness, like strangers but worse, and no matter what she did she couldn't break through. "Thank you," he answered to everything she said. It was almost funny. And he said it *kindly*. Rose was taking the same tone with her, an at-a-distance gentleness that had felt good at first, then frustrating, then intolerable. It was the most infuriating passive-aggressive punishment—although she wasn't so far gone as to think they meant it to be. But she would take a wrestling match with Mason any day over this horrible, aggravating kindness.

Last night, late, determined to have a real, true conversation, she'd waited in the parking lot of the funeral home for Mason to come out. She'd forgotten that he and Rose were joined at the hip; they came out together and saw her at the same time. What did she want? They'd looked at her curiously, possibly with dread, certainly with suspicion, as she crossed the empty lot to where they stood next to their side-by-side cars. She hadn't known what she was going to say to Mason anyway, but she had no idea what to say to *both* of them. Especially since she'd just told them good night.

"I just wanted to say again how sorry I am."

They'd nodded tiredly. They were exhausted, and they'd heard that sentence a hundred times in the last couple of hours.

"And if there's anything I can do . . ."

They murmured, waiting for her to finish and go away.

"I really liked him," came out of her mouth next.

Rose had tipped her head, resting it tiredly on Mason's shoulder.

"He didn't much like me, I know. He was afraid I'd . . ." Had she really blundered into this? At least it was *real*. "Afraid I'd do something to hurt you," she said, looking at Rose. "He was very protective. He loved you so much." Did that sound patronizing? Presumptuous? As if Rose needed Anna to tell her Theo had loved her. She blushed.

"Anyway," she plowed on. "I think he might've started to like me a little, toward the end. That day on the boat, when we moved his stuff to the nursing home—he said to me, he said something like—we were talking about Cork, and he said, 'You seem like a dog person.' I knew he meant it as a compliment. So—that was something. We had a good talk that day." She ran down.

"Anna," Rose said. *Kindly*. "Theo didn't dislike you at all."

She flushed again. Oh, this was dreadful. She'd wanted to make some kind of a connection with Mason, but instead she'd made a little speech that turned Theo's death into a misfortune that was all about *her*. They must think she was such an ass.

"Good night," she'd said, on the brink of tears. "See you tomorrow." She'd worked up the nerve to touch Mason on the sleeve of his jacket.

"Thanks," he'd said. "Good night."

Now she watched them go off, arm in arm, to the town car Rose had hired to follow the hearse to the cemetery. She wanted to run after them and tell them she'd changed her mind, she wanted to go with them after all. She *was* an ass—she couldn't stand herself any more than they could. She liked it better when they were yelling at her. Or tackling her. *Stay, stay*. She'd succeeded so well at self-extrication, nobody gave a damn now whether she stayed or not. She didn't feel free, as a consequence, not like a woman keeping her options open and her horizons refreshingly clear. She felt dismissed.

After the funeral, Rose took some time off from the restaurant. Labor Day was coming up, the end of the season; business would drop off afterward and the summer hires would go back to part-time or back to school, back to something. Anna told Rose she'd be happy to stay on for a while, to help with the transition. "For a while": that's how she'd phrased it. Afterward she'd asked herself why, where time was concerned, she seemed to be congenitally incapable of definiteness. But Rose had said, "That's fine, if you think you can manage it with your friend in New York. Don't jeopardize anything there on our account." She was being earnest, not sarcastic. "We'll get along."

"How is she doing?" Anna called Aunt Iris to ask. "Is she okay? She seems fine, but I don't see that much of her."

"Oh, I expect she'll be all right."

"I know, but does she talk to you? How is she? She *looks* all right. She's only been coming in for a couple of hours a day."

"It's a slow process."

The last thing Anna had expected was her trusty source of intelligence on Rose to dry up. "Yes, but is she depressed? Does she cry? How would you say she *is*, Aunt Iris?"

"I'd say she's doing as well as can be expected under the circumstances. So, dear, have you put your house up for sale yet?"

And that was that. After years of being the go-between, Aunt Iris had chosen sides. It was hard not to feel betrayed, and even harder not to feel sorry for herself. In fact, that was impossible.

Why don't they just book my flight for me, Anna took to wondering, *start packing my bags?*

At the Bella Sorella, she became not so much obsolete as unnecessary. She was used to organizing the family meal, making it a little more special than it had been under Rose's regime by introducing wine and olive oil and ice cream and anchovy tastings for servers and kitchen staff alike, and by letting the cooks take turns preparing the meal, which could be as experimental, as ethnic, as bizarre as they liked; in fact, she'd encouraged weirdness for the fun of it, and some of the dishes they'd eaten together late on Sunday nights had been exceedingly strange, definitely unpredictable. Staff morale had never been higher, Vonnie had told her weeks ago, before Anna gave notice. She'd suspected that was true, but it had meant a lot to hear Vonnie say it—even more so than if Rose had, because of course Rose's motives weren't pure.

But now—now it was *Frankie* who was organizing the last family meal before the Labor Day layoff. *Anna's* job. All the plans were made before she even knew about it. She felt superfluous when she found herself sitting at the big back table between Dwayne and Flaco, sipping an Australian chardonnay with Luca's Sardinian mother's Welsh rarebit with smoked cod in caper sauce and sautéed mustard greens, and toasting the sad, imminent departure of four part-time servers and two cooks.

Shirl announced that she was getting back together with Earl, her stalker ex-husband. He wasn't really her ex, it turned out, because the divorce had never gone through, so instead of remarrying they were just having a simple vows renewal in Atlantic City. Nothing Shirl said shocked anyone anymore, so when she told the table, "Earl Junior's so excited about being ring bearer, he's dropped the lawsuit," people just nodded and hummed and went on eating.

"Luca, this is fantastic," Frankie said, waving her fork over her plate. "How'd you get the cheese sauce so smooth?"

Luca, whose feelings had been hurt when Jasper said he wished there was a dog under the table to feed his mustard greens to, smiled beatifically. "Secret recipe," he answered, and everyone groaned. "You, I tell later," he said in a softer voice to Frankie, who winked at him.

Vince was still in love. Anna watched him watch Frankie, cast sidelong glances down the table whenever she said anything, cock his ears to catch the softest syllable. She wasn't really mean to him, or no meaner than usual; the one time Anna had made a casual reference to his devotion, Frankie had said, "Yeah, well, too bad I'm not interested in being anybody's girlfriend. I'm a mom and a cook, that's all I've got room for."

Rose stood up, interrupting the hilarity of watching Dwayne discover Fontaine had made his piece of tiramisu with spackling compound instead of mascarpone. The table quieted down instantly. Since Theo's death, even the rowdiest of the kitchen crew treated Rose with the most extraordinary gentleness, clumsy and almost embarrassing to watch, but touching, too, because the only explanation for it was that they loved her.

"Let's have a toast. To Kelli and Marco, Popper, Diego, Lorraine, and Bobbie. We're really going to miss you guys. Thank you for all your hard work—and here's to great success wherever the future takes you. And happiness."

They drank, then Jasper brought in a new dessert, Carmen's *torta delizia*—delight cake—because it was a special occasion. More toasts, lots of jokes and jests. In the middle of an unexpectedly tearful farewell speech from one of the departing waitresses, Anna saw Rose get up and slip out. She would go home, not come in again till late on Tuesday. What did she do with herself? In Anna's dark imaginings, she stayed in her small apartment, sitting alone or hanging over the terrace rail at night, staring out at the dark bay. Always by herself, always grieving in solitude. It wasn't right. Iris said it was natural, it would just take time, but to Anna it felt as if they'd abandoned her.

After dinner, Frankie waited till Carmen was out of earshot to corner Anna in the kitchen. "Hey, listen," she said, fingering a buckle on the old army knapsack she used for a purse. "I wanted to tell you first, even before Rose."

Uh-oh, Anna thought, even though she'd been urging Frankie to go for weeks. "You're leaving."

"I got this offer from the Rio Grande, it's kind of an upscale café in the 'burbs—"

"I know it."

"Yeah. And sure, it's basically Tex-Mex, but they want me for chef, so... And the pay's a little better, not much but I have to think about stuff like that."

"Of course."

"I figure it'll help round me out a little, and after a year or so I'll move on to something more interesting. But meanwhile I get a different experience, and it looks eclectic on the old résumé..." She gave *résumé* two syllables, a joke, but she didn't look happy. She had a worried face at the best of times; now it looked dissatisfied, too.

"No, it'll be great." Anna tried to sound cheerful. "It's local, it's something completely different, and you'll be the boss. I'm not seeing a downside."

"Yeah, except I'd stay if I could. If it weren't for Carmen. And you leaving."

Two big obstacles. "How are things otherwise?" Anna asked. "In your actual life."

"In my actual life." Frankie grinned and looked down at her feet. "Not too bad, believe it or not."

"No kidding?"

"Me and Mike, we sorta came to an understanding. We're not getting back together," she said quickly when Anna's face lit up. "This was more like... Hah, more like an intervention, only I was sober."

Anna folded her arms and leaned against the pantry shelf, signaling she had all the time in the world. It was tough to get Frankie to open up; you had to be cool about it, and the last thing you could show was sympathy.

"We had a long talk, that's all. He said he knew how I was, you know, hurting about Colleen and all. He wants me to have partial custody of Kate."

"Oh, Frankie. Oh, that's fantastic, I'm so glad."

"Yeah. It's everything." She lifted her face, and it was glowing. "What happened was, he forgave me. Katie did, too. I didn't know how that would feel until it happened. You're Catholic, right?"

Anna looked at her in alarm. "I used to be."

"Yeah, same here. I always hated confession, that was like the worst, humiliating or something, I never felt better because some guy mumbled a prayer through a screen. But..." She stuck her hands in the back pockets of her camouflage pants and contemplated the floor again. "I pulled so much shit when I was drinking. You don't know. Stuff I thought I'd feel dirty about for the rest of my life. And Mike said it was all okay. And it was like... I don't know." Her ears turned pink. "Extreme unction or something."

Anna wanted to curve her hand around the back of Frankie's skinny white neck and just hold it there. She refrained.

"All along I've been working through the steps, you know, trying to make it up with the people I've let down, and it was like—Mike skipped ahead or traded places or something. He made it right with *me*."

"What a guy," Anna said softly.

"What a guy. I get credit for picking him at least." Her laugh had a hitch in it. "And Katie's so sweet, she doesn't hold anything against me. And she could, too. But she just loves me." She swiped at her eyes. "So anyway, that's the long answer to your question. How I am in my actual life."

"Sounds pretty good."

"Yeah, well. It's a start."

Anna was too familiar with her own tricks and devices for guarding against that dangerous enemy, optimism, to tell Frankie it was a lot more than a start.

The evening wound down. The waitstaff closed out with Vince, the cooks went home, the cleaners finished in the kitchen. Another week over. Anna couldn't decide whether to come in tomorrow or not. They were closed, but she'd hardly missed a Monday yet, there had always been so much work to do. Her own house needed attention—the realtor didn't want to list it until she got new carpeting and painted the outside trim, minimum. But she kept putting it off.

"Rose! My God, you scared me to death, I thought you'd gone home. You *did* go home."

"Then I came back. I'd forgotten these."

Anna moved into the dim office tentatively, careful of Rose's mood. She was sitting behind the desk with the lamp on low, a messy spread of papers fanned out in front of her, a glass of something by her hand. "What's all that?"

"Papers of Theo's, insurance, things like that. I'm the executor of his estate."

"You are? I didn't know that. Is it hard?"

"No. Because *estate* is a bit of an exaggeration." She gave a wan smile. She looked slight and bony, her jaw unnaturally sharp, an aging woman in a black dress in a large black chair. She sat back, folding her hands in her lap. "He had just enough money left in his bank account to pay for his funeral. He'd have liked that. If he knew it. I wonder if he did."

Anna waited in suspense, wondering if she would say something now about the way Theo died. They'd ruled his death an accidental drowning, but Anna had doubts, and she would be amazed if Rose didn't, too.

"Luckily there aren't many other bills. He didn't own a credit card. He never wanted things; if it didn't fit on his little *Expatriate*, he had no use for it."

Anna went closer. She sat on the very edge of the desk, careful not to touch Theo's papers. "How are you doing?" She felt shy asking.

The melancholy smile came and went again. "I'm all right."

"Maybe you should get away for a while. Go someplace exotic, take a vacation." Even while she was saying it, it sounded like a silly idea.

"I'm better off here. With family. The restaurant is family."

"But it must be so sad."

She leaned her head back and let her heavy-lidded eyes close. "I miss him the most at night. If we weren't together, we always talked on the phone. Last thing, both of us in our beds with the lights out. I miss the sound of his voice in my ear. In the dark. That closeness. Sometimes the telephone ringing interrupts a dream, and I'll think it's him." She opened her eyes. "But it's Carmen. Or you, or someone wanting me to change my phone service."

"Oh, Rose."

"It'll be hard getting used to being on my own again. I did it once before, when Paul died, but it seems harder now. I guess because I'm older."

"You're not on your own."

"No."

"You're *not*."

"I know. Just feeling sorry for myself."

That wasn't true, either. Anna was the one in this family who specialized in feeling sorry for herself.

"Well." Rose finished what was left in her glass and stood up, began shoving Theo's papers into a folder. "Do you need to get in here? I'm going, I'll be out of your way. You should go home, too, it's late."

"Rose?"

"Yes?"

"What can I do?" Anna was embarrassed when tears started. "How can I help you?" she said in a thick voice. "I'd do anything."

"Sweet," Rose murmured. "There's nothing."

"I mean it. Just ask me. I'd do anything."

Rose came around from behind the desk. Now her smile looked indulgent. "That's very kind of you—and I mean *that*. Oh, Anna. There's nothing I'd like better than to stop time, but my life is going on. Your life is going on. We came together for a while, and I'll always be thankful for that. But don't be afraid that I'll ask you to stay." She put her hand on Anna's shoulder, leaned over and touched her lips to her cheek. "Go home soon." She whispered, "I love you."

Anna listened to her footsteps fade, then the back door close, a car start in the alley. She listened to the silence flow back for as long as she could stand it, then she got to work, going through the last of the receipts, getting the bank deposit ready for Tuesday morning, stashing everything in the safe.

She finished too soon. *Go home*, Rose said, but she didn't want to. She told herself it was because she'd painted the second-floor bathroom last night, and it would still smell. It would keep her awake, that paint smell. Rose had left the computer on. Despite a dull premonition of defeat, she checked her e-mail. Right the first time—nothing from Mason.

She kept an electronic folder of all his letters. The last ones he'd sent were from Montana, where he'd gone to do a piece on the Bitterroot Mountains. She clicked on the second one, her favorite. He'd written it in a bar on his laptop.

Dear Anna,

Here I am at Bender's Tavern in the town of Stevensville, about 20 miles south of Missoula, waiting for the rain to stop. Can't take pictures in the rain. There's only one thing to do in Stephensville when it's raining—drink beer at Bender's. There aren't so many photographers here that we trip over each other's tripods, not like Macias last month. I got some good pictures, I think, yesterday and this morning, before the sky opened up. As usual I overshot, but if you wait for the perfect photo you end up not shooting a single frame. Shoot fast and shoot often, that's my motto.

Birds I have spotted so far at Lee Metcalf Wildlife Refuge: wild turkey, blue grouse, pileated woodpecker, spruce grouse, red-breasted nuthatch, rufous-crowned sparrow, osprey, long-eared owl, misc. ducks, geese, herons, swans. No surprises here; that's what you expect to see this time of year in the Bitterroots. Most exciting for me—and I know this will delight and amaze you, have you hopping a plane ASAP to see for yourself—a flammulated owl. Yes. My first sighting. You see this tiny, elusive creature, only about 6 inches high, in pictures but rarely in life because he looks exactly like a slab of bark. I shot fast, but if I got anything at all, it's dark and blurry and useless for selling. Too bad, but at least I can add him to my life list. Cause for great joy and excitement.

Speaking of lists, you know we're mental about listmaking, we birders. Some of us—not I—enjoy the lists more than the birds. "Listers," we call these people. It's all in the competition for them, they might as well be counting traffic lights or telephone poles. They have lists for all occasions, birds seen on TV, birds seen from the window of the bus, first bird seen today, dead birds. I know a guy who keeps a list of birds seen from his bathroom window while he sits on the john. Birds spotted while brushing his teeth or showering don't count, he has to be sitting on the actual toilet. He says it's a short list; he keeps sighting the same finches and house sparrows year after year. He's thinking of planting trumpet vine under the window, try to get some hummingbirds.

How are you? I called Theo this morning, didn't talk for long. I miss you. I think about you whenever I'm in a restaurant. Other times too, but definitely in restaurants, where I observe everything much more keenly than I used to. The waiters probably think I'm a food critic. Something I've always wanted to know—how do you keep all the ingredients you'll ever need for every dish on the menu at all times? Especially the ones nobody ever orders. I'm looking at the menu here at Bender's, which is a very good name for a bar, and here's a tongue sandwich. Who would order a tongue sandwich? For all I know it's the most popular sandwich in Stevensville, but for the sake of argument let's say that the vast majority of people here feel about a tongue sandwich as I do, i.e., aghast. But here it is on the menu, so they must have it on hand at all times. Months go by, staff changes, one day somebody orders the tongue sandwich but by now no one currently employed at Bender's remembers how to make one or even where it is. I had no appreciation of the difficulties of restaurant ownership until I met you.

Still raining. Another beer? I'm not much of a drinker. Makes me think I have a lot to say.

I've been watching two men at the bar. Locals, not birders or hunters—you can tell because they don't look out the window every five minutes to see if the rain's stopped. One's fiftyish, going bald, starting to spread, has on a plaid flannel jacket. The other one is late twenties, taller and straighter, has a sandy, receding crewcut. They've got the same nose, almost the same rough-edged profile. They both smoke Camels and drink Pabst. They don't say much to each other, and when they do they keep their eyes on the auto race on TV. The older guy put his hand on the other one's shoulder, and I heard him say to the bartender, "Larry here . . ." I missed the rest. The old one looked smug and proud, the younger one looked shy and pleased.

I thought about my father, something I don't do often because I don't remember him very well. After he died, I used to dream about him coming back. I fantasized that it was somebody else's charred body, not his, in the wrecked F-14 Tomcat. He was a secret agent—that's why the government had to fake his death. I'd pretend he was watching me in my yard or out on the playground at school, always in disguise, not allowed to approach me. As much as he wanted to. Even after Theo came, I kept him in the back of my mind, the way a devout Catholic kid probably keeps God in the back of his mind. Exactly like that—my dad was everywhere, and he could read my thoughts.

Right now I'm thinking what it would be like to sit in a bar with him, drinking beer and watching the stock car races.

Write back if you have time. I miss you. I think this day is shot. I think I'll have to order the tongue sandwich and sober up. Should I call you tonight? No, I'll be asleep. You call me, doesn't matter how late. Wish you were here. I picture you in camouflage and hip waders, a pair of two-pound binoculars around your neck. Then I picture you without them.

Mason

Oh, Mason. What if she wrote him now? She felt caught up in something she used to have control over, but now it was out of hand. She didn't believe in fate, but lately her life had taken some sort of Calvinist turn. Everything was ordained, as if she was acting out a plan that somebody else had devised a long time ago—except it wasn't somebody else, it was her. And the plan used to seem vital, but now it was just painful.

Dear Mason,
Do you think it would be possible for us to stay together even if I didn't live here? A long-distance relationship? I am trying so hard to think of a way not to lose you.

She hit Delete.

Dear Mason,
You're like collateral damage, you were never the one I wanted to hurt. I did anyway. I did that stupid thing they do in the movies, I lumped you in with all the rotten men because of one rotten man who screwed me. Once I looked at you—we were sitting out on your dock, remember that night we

saw the two shooting stars—and I thought, he could be like Jay. He could do that to me, they all could. I caught myself, but the thought was there, it was like a pebble in my shoe. I'm sorry, I apologize. I was gun-shy, that's all I can say. I was like a war veteran who jumps, years later, when a car backfires. So you were like a car backfiring and I thought you were a bomb. I wish we could—

She deleted that, too.

Dear Mason,
It goes back much farther than Jay—he's not the one who's making me crazy. But it's all tangled up now, Jay and Nicole, Rose and my father, you and me. I think I have to go away, but I don't want to leave you. I'm so sorry I'm your worst nightmare. I'm so sorry your mother died while you were sleeping. I think the way she left you was worse than anything, worse than your father's plane crash or even Theo dying. I wish I could be the one who stays. Oh, Mason—

She turned off the computer.

Selfish. Mason was fine. The poison had finally settled to the bottom, and she had the nerve and the ego to try to stir it up again. How irresponsible and mean. She disliked herself intensely.

She moved a case of tomato paste cans and lay down on the sofa in the dark. Lousy couch for sleeping, lumpy and not long enough. It had the shallow, ghost indentation of Rose's body, though, S-shaped, from a thousand little naps and rests, and Anna's fit the same outline precisely. Her eyes went to the square of grainy light around the curtained window from the streetlight in the alley. A siren wail grew louder, peaked, died away.

She fell asleep and dreamed about a little girl in an open railroad car, flying through the Old West, craggy mountains in the distance, dots of cactus in the desert foreground, prickly balls of sagebrush blowing by. The ground was bright yellow, and the railroad car sent up billowy plumes of choking dust in its wake. "It won't stop," the little girl said. Her hands were stuck to the handles of the push-pull thing—it wasn't a railroad car anymore, it was a handcar, and the little girl's back kept bending, straightening, bending, straightening, as she pumped the car through the Old West. One of the craggy mountains loomed up. The tracks ran into a hole in the side, a black, inverted U, like a cartoon mouse hole. "It won't stop," the little girl, who was Anna, said, and the handcar flew straight into the hole and disappeared.

She woke up with the smell of dust in her nostrils. So real. No, not dust, paint. But—she was *here*, she was in the office, not at home. She sat up, groggy.

Smoke.

She leaped off the couch and lunged for the light switch. Was it smoky in this *room*? Where were her shoes? Under the desk. She kicked into them and ran out in the corridor. Slow-moving smoke from the door to the kitchen coiled thick around the ceiling. She raced inside, saw orange flames licking up the front wall. Under the smoke was an electric smell, like burning wire. The ice maker was invisible behind hissing, spitting flicks of fire.

Her mind went blank; she couldn't remember where the fire extinguisher was. They had two. *Where?* The main light switch was behind the worst of the fire; she could only see by the dim glow from the glass-doored refrigerator. There—the extinguisher, on the wall beside the big range. Of course; where else? She grabbed it, fumbled for a minute with the red pin thing, then aimed it at the highest flames, below and behind the ice maker.

It worked for a few seconds; the foam stifled the fire at the bottom. But as soon as she aimed at the flames crawling up the wall behind the machine, new ones bloomed under it. She continued to spray, but she had to keep stepping back, back, as the heat and the smoke increased.

The smoke detector in the dining room went off, then the sprinklers in the ceiling. She hadn't been scared before. As soon as the smoke detector went off, an ear-piercing shriek that felt like a blade slicing through her brain, she was afraid. Not panicked, just frightened, heart racing, blood pounding. *What'll I do? What'll I do?*

Wake up Carmen.

She ran for the back door, then stopped, skidding, almost falling, as it hit her it would be faster to call. Racing back into the smoky kitchen, she grabbed the phone—it was *hot*—off the wall beside the linen closet. She only had to push one button. Good thing, because she'd never have remembered the number.

"Hello?" Carmen's sleepy, groggy voice still managed to sound irritated.

"Can't you hear the smoke alarm? There's a fire in the kitchen. Get up and get out, because I don't know what it's going to do!"

"Did you call the fire department?"

Ice water replaced the blood in her veins. It thawed and she came back to life when she remembered, "No—it dials automatically. As soon as the sprinklers go off in the dining room, it calls the fire department."

"Okay." Carmen hung up.

Anna turned in a circle in the middle of the kitchen, coughing, watching fire flicker above the door and hesitate, as if it couldn't decide if it wanted to eat the big clock or go around it. It was raining in the dining room, not very hard, though, fifteen or twenty delta-shaped deluges pouring out of the smoke-veiled ceiling, drenching tables, chairs, floor. The wet room looked pretty in the blue glow from the reach-in behind the bar; exotic or something. Tropical. Night in the rainforest.

Shit, shit, shit. The smoke and water were going to do more damage than the fire. But just in case, she dashed back to the office and opened the floor safe, grabbed the canvas bag of cash and receipts she'd put in it an hour ago. She took her purse, too. Papers, documents? No, and this was silly, the fire wasn't even that bad. But on the way out, she plucked a framed photograph off the wall—Rose and Theo, hand-in-hand on the deck of the *Wind Rose*—and stuck it under her arm.

The whole front wall of the kitchen was on fire! She couldn't see the dishwasher or the pantry through the flames, and they were moving toward the linen closet. "Jesus!" she shouted. All the clean and dirty laundry would go up like paper.

Carmen burst in from the back door. "Holy Mother of God." She had on flip-flops and a billowy sleeveless yellow nightgown, knee-length. "What are you standing there for? Get out." She went to the maintenance cabinet over the steam table, jerked it open, rummaged around, and pulled out a power screwdriver.

"What are you doing?"

The brand-new meat grinder, Carmen's favorite piece of equipment, was attached to a stainless steel counter in the prep corner. She went down on her knees, her burnt-orange hair sticking out like a rooster's comb, and started unscrewing screws.

"Carmen, what are you doing?"

"Go out in the alley, wait for the firemen."

Anna stared at her for speechless seconds. Then she looked around. "I'll get the microwave."

"No!"

She unplugged it, then took a closer look. She could barely get her arms around it. A cart—Dwayne had one at his station. She tipped a mountain of clean plates and silverware onto the floor and rolled the cart back over, loaded the microwave on it with a lot of graceless shoving. She only ran into walls six or seven times on her way to the back door.

What else was portable? Pasta maker next. Knives. Knife sharpener? "The cappuccino machine! Carmen, help me."

"No, it's gone, it's too close to the fire." She was still working on the meat grinder. "Anna, get the hell *out*."

The enormous range-grill stood next in the fire's path. Besides lights and fans, its exhaust hood had built-in fire prevention equipment. Heat detectors set it off—all at once wet, slimy foam whooshed from the bottom of the hood, soaking the grilltop and dripping down the sides, puddling on the floor.

Carmen yelled at her over the increasing noise and smoke, "Are you sure the sprinklers called the fire department?"

The fire on the front wall had turned the corner and gone into the dining room. The phone was gone, melted. Anna dashed through what was left of the door and stood under one of the inadequate sprinklers, turning her hot face up. Swallowing water, she gasped a chestful of smoky air and fought a dizzy feeling. What if all of Vince's wines got destroyed? He'd picked each bottle so carefully. They should have a cellar, storing them up here was stupid. She couldn't stop coughing. What if the walk-in caught fire? Somebody should save the expensive meats, at least, and that new shipment of she-crabs—

The breakfront! The firemen would never save it. If Carmen was unscrewing the meat grinder, she was rolling the antique oak and beveled glass breakfront out the front door.

She got one shoulder against the wet, slippery side and shoved. It moved a few feet, then caught on a floorboard. The constant shriek of the smoke detector made her deaf. She pushed again, got a few more feet. The smoke was sinking; it didn't hug the ceiling anymore, it had sunk to head level. Nose level. She bent her knees, but she couldn't get enough leverage, couldn't budge the damn breakfront. Sharp popping behind her—bottles breaking. Her muscles weren't working right. This was stupid. Where was her purse, where was her picture of Rose and Theo? She would just get them and get out.

"Carmen!" she tried to scream through the door. She thought it was the door. It looked like the entrance to hell. The stench of her own nose hairs stung in her nostrils.

"Anna!"

They yelled something to each other at the same time. Anna stopped to listen.

"Get out!"

Good idea. She tried to scream it back, but she couldn't get enough air. Her lungs felt scalded. She was wheezing instead of breathing. As soon as she turned around, something exploded behind her. The concussion hit between her shoulder blades and blew her forward; she plowed chest-first into a table. The last thing she heard was glass breaking. She hoped it was men with axes smashing in the plate-glass window.

20

Doctors were impossible to find. They'd either just left or would be there any second, then never materialized. In the afternoon, Rose finally tracked down a nurse with a minute to speak to her, in the hallway outside Carmen's room.

"It's a pretty straightforward SI case, smoke inhalation. They checked her blood gases and now she's getting Albuterol. That's just a bronchodilator, it relaxes the muscles so she can get more air in her airways. We're giving her humidified oxygen and keeping her quiet. Luckily there weren't any serious burns. We'll keep her overnight, make sure there's no infection or anything, no complications, then she can go home, rest there instead of here. The main thing she's going to be is exhausted."

Carmen opened her eyes when the chair Rose pulled closer to the bed scraped the tile floor. No burns, but her eyebrows and eyelashes had singed brown tips, spiky-looking, more like wires than hairs. She wasn't allowed to talk. A clear plastic mask covered her mouth and nose; through the condensation Rose saw her sardonic, one-sided smile. That was progress. In the ER, she'd only been able to grimace.

She took Carmen's big, fleshy hand, inert on the coverlet, and was rewarded with a strong squeeze. They'd cleaned her up since Rose's last quick visit. She'd been ashy-gray all over from soot and smoke, especially around her mouth and nose. The medicine had stopped the convulsive coughing; she looked relaxed, almost comfortable.

"How are you feeling? You don't look bad. Everything considered, you look pretty damn good."

Carmen rolled her watery eyes.

"They say you can go home tomorrow. There's some smoke damage on the second floor, so you'll come to my house while we clean it up. You're just supposed to stay quiet, and you can do that at my place as easily as yours. The main thing is not to worry. Just get well."

Carmen nodded tiredly. It hurt to see her like this, weak, helpless, taking orders from others. It wasn't natural. Behind the mask, she said something Rose couldn't understand.

"How's the restaurant?" she guessed. "Well, the good news is that the wall that burned wasn't weight-bearing, so there's no real structural damage. Thank God. We had some losses," she said airily, evasively, "equipment and so forth, but almost everything in the dining room can be saved. I just talked to the insurance man, and he's being a little cagey but I guess that's his job. It could've been so much worse," she said, and Carmen nodded her head on the pillow, blinking her eyes in thanks. "And," Rose added, "thank *God* we've got our meat grinder, because without that—" She gave a dramatic shrug and raised her eyes to the ceiling. Carmen, whose cheeks were already flushed, turned a little redder. She stuck her tongue out, and that made Rose laugh. A first in the long, hellish day.

"Iris sends her love. I told her not to call because you can't talk, so she says to tell you she's thinking about you."

Carmen smiled and nodded.

She leaned closer. "Okay, I'm going to go now, leave you to sleep. Remember not to worry, because there's nothing to worry about. Anything I can do before I leave? Anything I can bring you? Okay, then." She kissed her very lightly on the cheek, awkward, careful not to dislodge the oxygen mask. She whispered, "Crazy lady. I don't know what I'd do without you. You know that?"

Carmen whispered.

"What? No, don't talk—"

She whispered it again, and Rose heard it through the plastic mask. "Same here."

Unlike Carmen, Anna was a lousy patient.

"Why can't I go home now?" She wasn't supposed to talk, either. She didn't have a mask, she had a cannula—prongs in the nostrils—so there was nothing to shut her up. "They're not even giving me any medicine, so why can't I leave?" What was left of her voice was just a scratchy croak, like a crow with a sore throat.

"I think they have to monitor your blood to make sure it's got enough oxygen in it."

"They already did that. It hurt like hell. Look at this bruise." She held out her arm. "I want to go home."

"Also, you're supposed to shut up."

She swallowed, making a face when it hurt. "The worst is my chest," she complained.

"Your lungs? I can imag—"

"No, my chest. Look what I did." She pulled her washed-out seersucker hospital gown down in front, showing off a wide, alarming, blue-black bruise across her breastbone.

"Oh, honey, that looks terrible. Does it hurt?"

"Yes, it hurts. A lot." She winced to prove it when she tried to sit up straighter. Rose hurried over to help with her pillows. "I went headfirst into a table right after something blew up in the kitchen."

"The gas line to the range. Thank God Carmen was out by then. *Would you stop talking?*"

"Bluh. I feel like I'm going to throw up."

"That's from swallowing smoke. Carmen's sucking ice chips for the nausea."

"I finished mine. Could you get me some more?"

This was a side of Anna Rose had forgotten about, but it was coming back to her quickly: the whiny, querulous, self-pitying sick person. She sighed. "I'll be right back." She went for more ice chips.

When she returned, Anna was trying to get out of bed. "But I have to pee," she sulked when Rose made her get back in.

"Wait for the nurse, you'll pull out your IV."

"It's just saline anyway. You could help me. The nurse is incompetent. If she sticks me one more time, I won't be responsible."

"I'd forgotten how bad you are at this."

"What?"

"Being sick."

She actually pushed her bottom lip out. They hadn't done as thorough a cleaning job on her as they had on Carmen; she still had smoky black smudges around her eyes. The pouting lip reminded Rose—"Remember when you had measles? We took turns staying with you, Lily, Mama, and me." Anna shook her head. "You don't remember? Oh my God, you were awful. It was like baby-sitting a fox terrier puppy. The only thing that would keep you quiet—"

"*The Hobbit*."

"Yes, *The Hobbit*. You loved it."

"I still do. I read it about every ten years. You read it to me first—I'd forgotten that."

She'd forgotten a lot of things. Rose was almost used to it, the memories Anna had either lost or mixed up, confusing her with Lily, sometimes the other way around. Rose, after all, often confused Anna with a daughter. A real mother couldn't have gone through more hell than she had last night, beginning with a 2 A.M. phone call from the police. Fire in the restaurant; significant damage; two women ambulanced from the scene, conditions unknown. She hadn't lost her faith—that seemed like a miracle now. Speeding in her car through mercifully empty streets to the hospital, taking corners at desperate, death-defying angles, she'd kept asking God,

What now, what now, what now? Aghast at the possibility of another loss, a worse loss, surely this would kill her—but not *angry*, thank God. Yet. She'd never berated Him. She had an old Catholic God, not like Anna's good-natured relativist God. Hers would not have been amused if she'd berated Him.

"Here's some good news," she remembered to tell Anna. "Fontaine had her baby this morning. It's a little girl, and they're both doing fine."

"That's great. But, Rose, how in the world..."

"I have no idea." With no help from her family, how Fontaine was going to make it on her part-time pastry chef's salary with a brand-new baby, Rose couldn't imagine. "By the way," she said, "you and Carmen are heroes at the restaurant. Staff's been coming in all day to look at the damage, Louis and Billy, Dwayne, Shirl. Vince and Frankie."

"We weren't heroes, we were idiots."

"Well, now, there I couldn't agree with you more." She put her hands over her cheeks. "What in the name of God were you thinking? Both of you? No—don't tell me, don't talk."

"Is the breakfront okay?"

Rose took her hands away.

"Well, is it?"

"Yes. It's pristine."

Anna gave a satisfied nod. Around an ice chip, she said in a garbled voice, "So what's the damage?"

"The bar is fine, the sprinklers saved it. Vince is so disappointed—he wanted a new one with a zinc top."

"I heard bottles breaking."

"Just the wines in the display rack. They're gone, but the bar wines and liquors are all right. Filthy, but all right."

"What else?"

"Well, the kitchen is bad. The rubber mat melted and now it's stuck to the floor, so that'll be a fun job. About half the major appliances are gone, either destroyed by the fire or damaged so much by smoke and water that they're useless—the dishwasher, the salamander, the smaller range, the smaller refrigerator, all total losses. But the big range and grill are okay, which is a miracle, and the walk-in freezer will probably be all right after it's cleaned up. So that's two big, expensive items we can save. They're still figuring out what happened with the air ducts to the second floor, and that could be a huge expense if it's bad."

"Carmen's apartment?"

"No fire damage, but it's a mess. There's a sticky film from the smoke over everything. She doesn't know that yet, so don't mention it when you talk to her."

"What about the insurance? Are we covered for everything?"

This was the other thing she hadn't told Carmen. "We may not be. I don't understand it, but the agent wasn't all that reassuring. Everybody thinks the fire started with an electrical short, probably in the ice-making machine."

"Right. It did."

"Well, meanwhile, the fire prevention equipment in the grill exhaust hood has to be serviced every six months, and we missed it in August. Technically, it wasn't in compliance."

"You missed it?" She said that too loud; she winced and put her hand on her throat.

"It's my fault. We skipped the last inspection because I didn't want to pay the fire security company that does the cleaning—simple as that. Cash flow. We weren't having a code inspector visit till the end of this month, so I thought we had plenty of time."

"But if the cause was electrical anyway—"

"Yes, that's the point. It's a technicality, it has nothing to do with anything. It even *worked*—the foam stuff, the flame retardant or whatever you call it *came out*—that's what saved the grill. But Mason says they'll do anything to try to lessen their liability. The other thing the insurance man said is the O rings in the sprinkler heads were corroded, so maybe they're not liable for all the smoke damage in the dining room."

"My God."

"I know."

"What if they won't pay?" Anna's teary, bloodshot eyes went wide. "What will you do?"

Rose shook her head. "I can't even think about it."

Anna's roommate was a frail, elderly woman, in for overnight observation after falling and breaking her arm in the bathtub. They listened to her light snoring through the yellow curtain that separated the two beds.

"I was numb at first," Rose said, speaking softly in the confessional silence. "I couldn't make it sink in, not even when I walked around and made myself look at everything." The grim, boarded-up front, every storeowner's nightmare, the stench inside, the vicious damage, everything charred, blackened, stinking, wet, distorted, the rape of the business she had loved and hated and nursed and cursed for two-thirds of her life. "I couldn't make it real. It was like watching myself in a movie."

"Shock," Anna said.

"Iris said I should retire. That's when I woke up. She said I should cut my losses and get out. Because I'm old and tired—she didn't say that, but that's what she meant. I should sell out and move to Florida. For a little while, I have to say, the idea appealed to me."

"No." Anna's outraged face was gratifying.

"Yes. Like falling asleep when you're freezing to death. Just let go. How much easier it would be. I *am* old and tired."

"Bullsh—" She broke off to cough.

Rose laughed. She got her purse from the floor, her sweater from the back of the chair. "But now, do you know how I feel? I'm not numb anymore, that's for sure. My heart's broken. It's as if I'm grieving for a sick person, some injured loved one—and I can't wait to nurse it back to health. They'll have to drag me out of there now with chains and pulleys. Because here's a tragedy I can finally do something about."

Anna grinned. She looked at Rose expectantly.

She leaned over to brush a dirty lock of hair back from Anna's forehead. "I'm going now. Sorry I stayed so long. Do you need anything?"

"Oh, you don't have to go."

"You're exhausted. I am, too. I'll call in the morning, see when they're springing you and Carmen. Vince will probably pick you up and take you home."

"Rose?" Anna croaked.

She turned back at the door. "Hm?"

But then she didn't say anything, just stared across the room at her with her red-rimmed raccoon eyes.

"What?" Rose said.

"Nothing. Thanks for coming." She sank back down on her pillows with a rattling, dissatisfied sigh.

Much later, close to midnight, Anna called.

Rose wasn't asleep. She'd been sleeping badly for weeks, even before Theo died. Every night she told herself to get up and do something, clean a closet, write a letter, at least make insomnia productive. But she was too tired and spiritless to do anything except lie in the dark and drift from memory to memory, worry to worry. Tonight the worries crowded out the memories, and the phone's ring made her cringe. A call this late—what else could it be but more bad news?

"Hi, it's me," Anna said, as if the raven's croak wasn't a giveaway. "Sorry if you were asleep."

"No, I wasn't. Are you all right?"

"Yes, I'm fine. I just, um . . ."

Rose glanced at the clock and sat up, scratching her head to clear it. "Couldn't sleep?"

"Yeah, I mean, it's bright as a bus terminal in here, plus the nurses think nothing of gabbing all night in the hall right outside your door." She went on in that vein for a while, complaining about everything, until Rose remembered—

"Hey, you're not supposed to talk. Why are you calling? You shouldn't even have a phone."

"Oh hell, I can talk, all it does is hurt my throat. Carmen can't talk—she won't even answer the phone in her room. The roommate answers, very unpleasant woman, she sounds very unhappy."

Rose sank back down, burrowing into her pillows. Were they going to have a chat? Fine with her.

"Aunt Iris called after you left. You know, just wanting to know how I'm doing and all."

"She's coming down tomorrow."

"Yeah, she said. She couldn't come today because of some dog's hernia or something. I told her there wasn't anything for her to do anyway."

"She's worried about you. And Carmen."

"I know."

Pause.

"And, um, Mason stopped by," Anna said casually.

"Mason came to the hospital?"

"Mm hm. Just for a minute."

"Really? He hates hospitals. I don't think he's been in one in five years." The doctors wanted to do more surgeries on his face, but he wouldn't cooperate.

"Wow," Anna said. "Well, he was uncomfortable, that's for sure, but I just figured it was because of, you know, the situation and everything. And what he wanted to say to me."

"What did he want to say to you?" She wouldn't have asked, but Anna was in such a forthcoming mood.

"Oh, you know. Not to go, stuff like that."

"I see." She smiled to herself. "He hasn't said that before?"

"He has, but not in a long time. Not lately."

She stifled a yawn. "And what did you say?"

"Nothing," Anna said, sounding dejected. "I told him I couldn't talk. Which was true—my throat really hurt."

"I expect you'll tell him something eventually."

There was another long pause.

"I have to get up early tomorrow," Rose hinted. "I've got another meeting with the insurance agent."

"Oh. Okay, sorry. I'll let you get some sleep."

"You get some sleep, too."

"Rose?"

"Yes?"

"How come..."

"How come what?"

She either laughed or coughed. "You know, everybody asks me to stay. Except you. So I was just wondering—maybe you don't even want me to, and that's why you don't ask."

Rose closed her eyes. "You want to know why I haven't asked you to stay?"

"Well... yeah."

"Because it wouldn't have done any good. You'd only have gotten angry."

"No, I wouldn't."

"Anna—"

"*Before*, I might've, okay. But why didn't you ask me again? Tonight when you were talking about rebuilding, starting over—you could've asked me then."

"I guess I could have."

"How come you didn't?"

"Because it's a foregone conclusion. Frankly, I'm surprised Mason didn't know that. He's usually good at that sort of thing."

"What do you mean? What's a foregone conclusion?"

"That you're staying."

"How do you know?"

"Oh, Anna, you're not going anywhere. You almost died last night."

"So? Anyway, no, I didn't, it was never—"

"You almost died because of a thousand-dollar piece of furniture."

"It was fourteen hundred, and I never—"

"You risked your life to save as much as you could of the Bella Sorella. So did Carmen. It was an incredibly foolish thing to do, and I know you weren't thinking straight, but that's what you did." Silence. No need, but Rose connected the line between the last two dots. "Does that strike you as normal behavior for a person who's just passing through?" Anna mumbled something. Rose said, "I didn't hear you."

"I don't know." More rusty mumbling.

"What?"

"You still could've asked me."

Rose laughed helplessly. "Would that make you feel better?"

"Yes."

She sighed. "Will you stay and help me put my poor, burned-out, under-insured restaurant back on its feet? Again?"

"Okay."

"Even though it may not work? Even though this time we'll probably fail and go down in the ashes and get—bitter and hopelessly broke and in debt and old before our time?"

"You bet. Can't wait."

They snickered together. "You're just my kind of partner."

"Crazy, you mean. Runs in the family."

Rose smiled in the dark. "Good night, Anna."

"You could've said that sooner, you know."

"Good night?"

"No, the other. I could've been fast asleep by now."

"Me, too," Rose realized.

21

Anna hadn't spent so much uninterrupted time in bed, at least alone, since last winter, when staying under the covers had been the simplest way to keep warm in Jay's loft. She was sick of sleeping, sick of being horizontal. At three in the afternoon, she threw off the covers and padded downstairs. Aunt Iris had left a pot of soup this morning when she'd stopped by to see how she was doing. Chicken soup? Vegetable? Hard to say; cooking wasn't Aunt Iris's strong suit. Anna heated a cup in the microwave and ate it leaning against the counter, staring out the window at the bird feeder. It was supposed to be squirrel-resistant, but there was a big bushy one right now, hanging upside-down from the wire, stuffing its face. She rapped on the glass, but it just looked at her with its liquid eyes and kept on chewing a sunflower seed. She knocked harder and waved her hands. "Beat it!" Finally it did, but first it twitched its tail at her in a rude, suggestive way. "Up yours, too." She used to like squirrels, but now they were pests, scarfing up bird-specific food she'd gone to no small trouble and expense to select, like millet for song sparrows and raisins and peanut butter for mockingbirds. The most interesting bird she'd attracted so far was a scarlet tanager, lured with a banana. She'd seen it during the period she and Mason weren't talking to each other, though, so she couldn't call him up and brag about it.

Tiredness was the only symptom she still had, no more coughing or nausea from breathing smoke. Before she finished her soup, she felt too lethargic to stand up. She got as far as the couch in the living room and collapsed.

Poor Carmen had to stay in the hospital another night—she had bronchitis. Anna was dying to talk to her, but Rose and Iris said not to call, she needed her rest. It was hard. Anna was dying to hear her grouchy voice, ask her if she didn't think it was pretty damn funny that they were still alive. Considering what idiots they had been. That was their new bond, she guessed; they had both behaved like complete lunatics. She could still see Carmen in her blowsy yellow nightgown, a human fire hazard, hunkered down under the metal counter while she tried to unscrew the meat grinder. She had, too—Rose said she'd saved it, not to mention a thousand dollars' worth of chef's knives and specialty pots and pans. Really, on the craziness scale, Carmen ranked much higher than Anna, who'd merely tried to save a room divider. She wanted to call her up and tell her so.

She wondered if Carmen was getting as philosophical as she was. Forty straight hours in bed—you couldn't sleep all of them away, so that left plenty of time for thinking. Time enough to figure out that the thing about righteous indignation was that it didn't go anywhere. It just sat there. It had nothing to feed on but itself, so it got fatter and fatter. Its diet consisted of nothing except outrage, reproach, and helplessness, and she could hardly think of three less appetizing ingredients. But she'd dined on it like the world's most unimaginative gourmet since she was twenty—a long time to spend chewing and swallowing an emotion that was indigestible to begin with.

The hardest thing to admit was that she was responsible, not Rose, for just about everything that had ever gone wrong with her adult life. That included the disconnectedness and isolation, the fact that she'd never sustained a relationship with a man beyond a couple of years, she had no best friend, and no home. Not only had she blamed Rose for all those deficiencies, she'd pretended they weren't failures at all, but choices. She'd held a grudge for almost half a lifetime over a perceived wrong that was never any of her business anyway. Four-year-old Katie forgave her mother for *real* sins, but twenty-year-old Anna had gotten on her very high horse and stayed there for almost twenty more. What a jerk.

She cast around for something to occupy her mind besides her inadequacies. In addition to soup, Aunt Iris had dropped off an armload of amusements, magazines and paperback novels, crossword puzzle books, a box of chocolates, a photograph album. She must expect Anna to be laid up for days. She chose the least mentally challenging, the chocolates and the photo album, and hauled them both onto her stomach, settling on the couch under the knitted throw. It was an old family album with puffy white pasteboard covers, yellowed from age, an embossed "Memories" in gilded script on the front. She turned the rusty pages curiously. Why would Iris leave her this? She'd seen most of these old snapshots before in her own family's photo albums.

She could never get over how skinny, about a hundred years ago, her Grandmother Fiore had been. She remembered Nonna as a wide, florid, unsmiling woman, always cooking, as muscular as Carmen and only a little sweeter-tempered—but here she was in a scoop-necked sundress and wedge-heeled sandals, graceful as a dancer. And Nonno—he looked like a gigolo! On their wedding day they'd posed in front of an old rattletrap car, not quite a Model T but almost, proud and excited in their black and white finery. But mysterious too, like silent film stars. Next came the baby pictures, Iris first, already cuddling the family dog, who was bigger than she was. Here she was at three or four, holding her parents' hands in front of their first restaurant, the tiny crab house on East Island, Fiore's Crabs & Beer, the hand-lettered sign in the window said. Then came Lily, then Rose, and here they were together in a sandbox, two cute little girls in corduroy jumpers and sandals with ankle socks. Time went by in photographs of Fiore birthday parties, First Communions and Confirmations, picnics and family reunions. And two more restaurants, a pizza parlor called Luigi's—named after nobody; Nonno, whose Christian name was David, had just wanted something that sounded Italian—and a spaghetti place called Banchetto that also sold homemade gelati to passersby from a sliding window beside the door.

Now pictures of Aunt Iris's wedding to Uncle Tony, with Lily and Rose as the pretty teenage bridesmaids. They'd had their reception at, where else, the Flower Café, Nonno and Nonna's brand-new restaurant on Severn Street—the first incarnation of the Bella Sorella. Anna kept turning the pages, waiting for the point, the punch line, but the album gave out in the late 'fifties with a color photo of Uncle Tony holding Anna's cousin Theresa in his arms, Aunt Iris's first child, on the steps of St. Luke's Church.

She turned the last page and found a few loose photos between it and the back cover. Color shots, more family pictures. Fiores at the beach. She looked at them more closely.

Theresa was about four now, building a sand castle with a red plastic bucket in the surf while thirtyish Aunt Iris hovered over her, grinning hugely, thin and shapeless in an electric-blue one-piece bathing suit. Next, a picture of Lily, lying on her side on a striped towel, one hand resting on the high curve of her hip, gazing into the camera with a sleepy, enigmatic smile. How sophisticated she looked, and much older than her age—twenty-two, according to the date on the back. Had she bleached her hair, Anna wondered, or was it sun-streaked? She thought of old photos of Julie Christie—her mother had that look, sexy but smart, not just a pinup.

Beefcake: Uncle Tony and her very young father faced the camera with their hands on their hips, legs spread, rather shockingly naked-looking in their skintight nylon suits. He-men. Tony was bigger, hairier, actually quite a hunk if you liked that sort of thing, and obviously Aunt Iris did. But Anna thought her lean, black-haired father was much handsomer. She stared at his tan, grinning face and marveled that he'd ever been so young. Either he hadn't shaved in a few days or he was going for a little hippie beard. He looked beautiful to her with his wire-rimmed glasses and shaggy hair, a careless cigarette clamped in his teeth.

The first of the two remaining pictures confirmed what Anna had already deduced—this was the long weekend in Bethany that had changed three people's lives. Possibly the weekend she'd been conceived. Her father and Rose, unaware of the camera, sat beside each other on a white blanket, Paul cross-legged, Rose with her long brown legs folded modestly to the side. She had on a black tank suit, the kind racers wore, not especially flattering but she'd loved to swim—she still did. Her long hair was streaming wet, and stuck to her forehead in lanky waves, styleless and therefore timeless. Everyone else looked right at home in the mid-sixties, but Rose could've come from any era. She rested her hand on Paul's bare knee, her head turned toward him, listening carefully, paying attention—there was so much tenderness in her faint smile and her downcast eyes. He was telling her something earnest and serious, his eyes full on her face. He could be talking about world peace, he could be talking about what kind of beer they should buy tonight for the clambake—either way, it was impossible to look at this photograph and not know they were in love. Solid, delighted love, no doubts, no games. They trusted each other. They thought this was going to last forever.

In the last photo, Paul posed with Rose and Lily in bright, shadowless sunlight, the blue and white Atlantic swirling around their calves. He stood between the two sisters with his arm around Rose's waist, but Lily had his other arm. She was pressing it to her side, her breast. His grin didn't look hip or cool in this one, it looked sheepish. Punchy.

Anna looked again at the photograph of her mother, alone on the striped towel. She studied it, the way she lay with one hand on her hip, the other pulling a pair of sunglasses down her nose so she could stare, languid-eyed, at the photographer. She had pale golden skin, flawless; the bust of her turquoise two-piece pushed her breasts up and out in a showy, generous display. Anna wasn't sure what her smile meant, whether it was flirtatious or bored, or both. Or was there a good-natured joke behind it? She looked and looked.

She wondered again what Iris's motive could've been for leaving her these pictures. Surely it wasn't to nail down Rose's visible, indisputable first claim on Paul; surely it wasn't to unmask her mother as some jealous, man-stealing femme fatale. Iris could not possibly think that would provoke in Anna any kind of epiphany. Besides, she had to know by now that there was no point: Anna and Rose had reconciled, the fight was over, it was ancient history.

Maybe it was simply to show her a picture of the past. These photos had been withheld from her until now. Maybe Iris only wanted her to *see* Rose and Paul in love, to look into their faces and let the years fall away. To believe in it and be glad for it, give up her last confusion about it. Accept the painful, grown-up truth that the mother she'd loved had not been chosen by the father she'd loved.

Fine, she'd done that. Mission accomplished.

She had a nagging sense, though, that there was more. One last lesson to learn. For a long time she'd been avoiding the tiresome, unappealing possibility that her highest, most enlightened life task was to forgive Rose. Now she had to look into the eye of another unpalatable possibility: that she wouldn't really be free until she forgave her mother.

Late in the afternoon, she went to see Mason.

Technically, she wasn't supposed to get out of bed until tomorrow, but she felt well enough after sleeping most of the day away. The thought of calling him on the telephone or, worse, sending him an e-mail left her cold. Literally; a slight but definite chill was coming from Mason's direction. He might be better at e-mails than talking, but she wasn't. She didn't think her own disembodied words would be the medium to thaw the ice.

She pulled in next to an unfamiliar car in his driveway. Sports car; a hunter green convertible with the top down. Who the hell was here, and how dare they? She felt unreasonably aggrieved. Cork lay fast asleep on the shady side of the porch, ineptly guarding the wide-open front door. He didn't see or hear Anna until she touched him on the head; then he jerked up as if he'd been shot. She jumped too, not in fear, just reaction—Cork didn't have a violent bone in his arthritic body. They soothed each other's nerves, she by petting him, he by wagging his tail, while she listened to the faint rise and fall of voices from the back of the house, Mason's and a woman's. Fatigue washed over her unexpectedly; she had to sit down on the top step. She stroked the dog and listened to the voices come closer.

The screen door opened. She turned around but didn't get up when an attractive blonde, fortyish, expensively dressed, stepped outside, followed by Mason. Neither one looked particularly surprised to see her; in fact, the woman smiled briefly but didn't stop talking. Mason pretended to listen to her, but Anna could tell she didn't have his attention anymore. When she paused—they were talking business, making some kind of a deal—Mason looked at Anna and said hi. "Hi," she said back. He said, "This is Cathy Doran—Anna Catalano," and the women said hi to each other.

"I know it's exactly right, I mean it's just what he wants, I absolutely know it." Cathy sounded excited. She was leaving; she said this as she walked across the flagstone path toward the driveway. Mason followed, but she stopped halfway to finish the conversation. "I honestly don't have any qualms about doing this on my own."

"But just in case—" Mason said.

She interrupted, as if they'd been through this already, "No, I have a guy—I told you, I know someone who'll take it down to St. Michael's on the weekend. All I have to do is arrange it. Oh, this is perfect—Frank's birthday is Sunday, it'll be the most incredible surprise." She laughed gaily. "We have a sort of contest going. He'll *never* top this."

Whatever the deal was, they shook hands on it; Cathy said she'd call Mason in the morning, then walked off to her car. He stayed put while she got in. She pulled on a Ravens ball cap at a jaunty angle, started the burbling, low-throated engine, backed out, and pulled away.

"Who was that?" Nosy and none of Anna's business, which was why she asked. She meant to insinuate herself back into Mason's life, and one way would be to take it for granted that she belonged there.

But what she really wanted to say was, "Boy, you sure are a sight for sore eyes." He sauntered over and put one foot on the step beside her, stuck his hands in his back pockets. Last night in the hospital he'd looked a little green around the gills, but today he looked good. Healthy and ruddy-skinned in the slanting sunset, streaky-haired, as if he'd been working outside. Which she guessed he had; according to Rose he'd just gotten back from a trip to Cape May to photograph birds heading south on the flyway. She had a potent urge to touch him, reach inside the bottom of his pants leg and massage his calf. Press her fingers up and down the hard bone in front.

"She wants to buy the *Wind Rose*," he answered her question. "For her husband."

Anna absorbed that with a shock. "You're selling it? I thought—I didn't even know—" She hadn't even known the sailboat was *his*; for some reason she'd assumed it was Rose's.

"Theo and I owned it together, and he left me his half in his will," he said, reading her mind. "But I doubt if that's what he really wanted. He'd have given it to Rose if he could."

"Why couldn't he?"

"Fairness, his notion of it. He couldn't work on the boat much for the last year or so, less and less the sicker he got. I think he meant to pay me back by leaving it to me."

"But you don't want it anymore?" Considering how Theo had died, she couldn't blame him.

"I've got a better use for the money."

And she knew what it was. It came to her in a flash— "You're going to give it to Rose."

He tried to look simultaneously noncommittal and slightly offended. He took his foot off the step and moved back.

"You are, aren't you? You're giving it to Rose because the fire insurance money might not come through—or it might get delayed while the lawyers fight about it. That's all right," she said hastily, "you don't have to tell me, none of my business. But do you think she'll take it? Maybe if it's a loan. Well, anyway. Wow, that's... Okay, we don't have to talk about it."

He scowled at her, foiled and confounded. "Do you want to come inside?"

Good way to change the subject. She noticed she wasn't tired anymore as she got up and followed him into the house. He hesitated in the living room, as if debating where to put her, then proceeded on to the kitchen. "Do you want a cup of coffee or something? A drink? How are you feeling?"

"Have you got any fruit juice? I'm okay. I can still smell smoke in my nose, but that's about it. Thanks," she said when he handed her a glass of orange juice.

He folded his arms and leaned back against the refrigerator. "Sorry about last night," he said, watching her drink.

"Why? I thought it was very nice of you to come." Especially since he was phobic about hospitals.

"I wasn't very nice when I got there."

"You weren't?" Truthfully, she couldn't remember much about his visit. *Was that really Mason who came to see me?* she'd halfway wondered, especially after the nurse gave her a sleeping pill. The standout moment was after he left, when she'd gone into the bathroom and finally gotten a good look at herself in the mirror. She'd let out a croaky obscenity, startling her roommate. Mason had seen her looking like *this*? Dirty eyes, sooty nose, filthy, ashy hair?

"I shouldn't have said you were stupid."

That's right—he'd called her *stupid*. It was all coming back to her. "No," she agreed, "you sure shouldn't have. Very bad sick person etiquette."

He'd said she was stupid to think she was leaving, was what he'd said. Not angrily or hatefully; quite nicely, in fact, but how gentle could you be when you were calling someone stupid? She'd wanted sweetness and sympathy from him, and he'd never even touched her. Clearly he'd noticed the same incongruity Rose had, that she was sucking oxygen in a hospital bed after risking her life to save a place she kept insisting had no emotional hold on her. He and Rose had certainly twigged to the contradiction there a lot faster than she had.

"Why'd you come to see me if you were just going to yell at me?"

He shook his head at her, as if he considered the question disingenuous but he'd be a good sport and answer it anyway. "To make sure Rose wasn't humoring me. I wanted to see for myself that you were all right."

She melted.

Something squawked, a raspy, wooden-sounding quack from the direction of the back porch. "What's that?" she asked. "A new patient? The bird hospital is open again?"

He smiled. "Come and see."

Out on the porch, a white and black bird, medium-size, sat on the bottom of a big metal cage, a real cage, not a cardboard box this time. She followed Mason's lead as best she could and approached it with slow, nonjerky movements. "What is it?" she whispered, squatting down beside him. "What happened to him? Poor thing. Is it a tern?"

He looked at her with unflattering amazement. "What kind?"

"What kind? I don't get credit for knowing it's a *tern*?" It sat quietly, apparently unafraid, blinking its beady eyes and bobbing its long, forked tail. It had a light gauze bandage on its bright white breast, and a splint, an actual splint, on its foot—a tiny cardboard platform taped between each of its clawed orange toes. "What happened to him?"

"Forster's tern," Mason said. "Wait a sec." He went in the kitchen and came back with a plastic container, the contents of which became obvious as soon as he took the lid off. Stinky fish. "Herring," he explained, transferring pieces from the container to a shallow dish inside the cage. "He likes canned clams, too."

"What got hold of him, a cat?"

"More likely an owl or a raccoon. Cork and I found him on the riverbank. They breed out on that marsh island you can see from the dock. Something nocturnal got him."

"Wow, he looks like you were just in time. Did he break his foot?"

"Just a toe. That's why he can't perch. His beak was cracked, too, but that's already healed. Although he'll always have a slight overbite."

She looked at his straight face and decided that wasn't a joke. "Did you give him stitches?"

"Yes."

She'd been joking. "You did? No, you didn't. Really?"

"I was out of silk thread, so I had to use dental floss. Want to see?"

"That's okay." If he was showing off, it was working. She decided to show off, too. "Terns" she said, "are neotropical migratory birds. Which means they spend the summer here and then fly to South America for the winter. This guy should be leaving in a couple of weeks. Think he'll be up for the trip?"

Mason sent her a sly, appreciative look. She followed him back to the kitchen and watched him wash his hands at the sink.

"The distances some birds migrate are truly incredible," she mentioned. "Take the blackpoll warbler. It can go nonstop from Canada to South America in seventy-two hours. That's about thirteen hundred miles. That's like a human being running four-minute miles for eighty consecutive hours."

"Amazing."

"It's a very hazardous journey. Lots of birds don't make it, they get blown out to sea in storms, or they land and find out the place they've been stopping over to rest and eat in for years has turned into a shopping mall. Or they fly into office buildings at night, thousands and thousands of songbirds especially, they fly into the lights of tall office buildings and die. Cities should pass laws making these buildings turn their lights out at night, it's ridiculous."

Mason dried his hands on a paper towel and threw it in the garbage. He watched her.

"I'm against migration," she said.

"You're against migration?"

"It's too perilous. Much safer to stay where you are. Just stay home once you get there."

He went to the refrigerator and took out a bottle of water, opened it, downed a few swallows. Stared at her some more.

He wasn't getting her migration analogy. She decided to stop beating around the bush.

"I've been behaving badly. In particular, I haven't been fair to you. In fact, I've been a real ass. I didn't come here to ask if we can still be friends. You keep doing things that make me think you must care for me, otherwise I can't figure out why you'd do them. That's what gives me the guts to say this to you now. Because, as you know, I'm not very gutsy. In this area."

He wasn't jumping in to disagree with anything. He had his hands on the counter behind him, elbows jacked out, head down, contemplating his tennis shoes.

"I'm suggesting another try. If it doesn't work out, I won't be leaving, after. And if it does work out, no matter how terrifying that is, I won't be leaving, either. I've landed. I'm like the great blue heron," she said recklessly, "I live here now. All year."

"In fact," he said, "the great blue heron is rare around here in the late summer. In winter, we might get New England's great blues, while South Carolina gets ours. Range overlap, that's called. So it's true we have them year-round, but they're not necessarily the same—"

"Oh, for Pete's sake, I'm trying to make up here." She grabbed hold of him. "I'm sorry I was a lousy girlfriend. I can do a lot better." She stood on her toes and kissed him.

He said, "I don't see how."

This was what she needed. Active forgiveness; somebody's arms around her. Making up with Rose on the phone was satisfying, but not in the same way as making up with Mason in bed. She felt like she'd been without him for years, not weeks. Even when she'd had him, she'd kept him at a distance, thinking she was freer that way. A woman who traveled light.

"I have to ask a stupid question," she said while she rooted around in his closet, hunting for his flannel bathrobe. She found it and tied it around her naked self, burying her nose in the shoulder. She'd missed that smell. "Well, not so much stupid as annoying. For you."

She flopped down on the bed and sat cross-legged, facing him. "Mason, what do you see in me? Why do you want to be with me? But wait—first I'll tell you what I see in you, because I don't want this to be all one-way and self-centered. But then back to me, because I'd really like to know. Why you care about me at all when I've been such a jerk."

"But you haven't been."

"See, that's one of the things I love about you. You're so nice." She traced the long scar that went from his rib cage to his hipbone, stroking it very lightly with her fingertips. "You're just . . . nice. And for another thing, I've never known anybody like you. You're mysterious—but that's not too important," she backtracked, "that's like being good-looking, it doesn't mean anything, because eventually all the mysteries get solved. That's just infatuation. What else? I like it that you know things I don't know anything about. I find that sexy. And I trust you. Even when you tackled me, I wasn't truly frightened, not deep down."

"That was a little crazy," he conceded.

"Yes, it was. You don't talk much—I don't know if I like that or not. But you're a man of action, and I know I like that. But the thing I admire most is how brave you are." She knew that would embarrass him, and sure enough, he crossed his arms and legs and made a scoffing face. "No, you are, you do things you're scared to death of doing. And sure, they're irrational, I mean, they're intrinsically nonscary things, but they absolutely terrify you and you do them anyway. I love that." All this "liking" and "loving" of "that" or "that in you" was getting a little silly. How hard would it be just to say, "I love you"? Really, how hard?

"Okay, now you tell me what you see in me. Not that that's the end of the list for you—I've got more, I'm just taking a break."

He sighed. Oh, she'd missed seeing him smile. She loved thinking she could make Mason happy, that she could change his moods and be good for him. She'd forgotten to tell him that she loved the shape of his head, and his snobby, aristocratic feet, and his skinny butt. Later.

"You," he said. "What do I see in Anna. I won't say Rose—that never gets me anywhere."

"You can say it if you want. I'm not as weird about that as I used to be." She lay down beside him, sharing the pillow.

"I never meant you *are* alike. Only that you look alike."

"Why do men always put looks at the top of the list?" she butted in. "We never do, but you guys always say, the very first thing, 'she's pretty,' or 'she's attractive,' when you're describing a woman. Always. Why is that?"

"We're shallow."

"Anyway." She snuggled closer, not wanting to be disagreeable just when he was getting to the good part. "Do go on."

He took her hand and frowned, absently moving his thumb between her fingers, web to web, pressing down. He did that with his own hands when he was thinking hard, and now he was doing it with hers.

"Well?" He was either choosing his words carefully or he was having to dig down awfully deep to come up with reasons he liked her. Or loved her. Whatever.

"Before I met you, my favorite way of looking at things was through my camera. Framed." He held his hands in the air, making a box with his fingers, sighting through it. "I could be right there, between the black sides of the lens, inside the dark box with whatever I was photographing. Safe, like being in an empty movie theater. I kept order by framing a thing exactly the way I wanted, and then I reproduced it. Took its picture. Whatever I wanted, whatever I thought was beautiful, it was mine, and it couldn't fly away, I captured it. Not just birds—landscapes stood still for me, too. They were caught. And people."

She thought of the photographs he used to take of her, Anna leaving, Anna walking away. From the first, he'd been trying to make her stay.

"But people can't be caught," she told him urgently. "They leave. I was trying to say that to you when we were fighting, but I didn't get it right. People leave and it's not your fault, it's nothing you've done." She put her hand on his chest, over his heart, wishing she could fix him. "If I had left, it wouldn't have had anything to do with you. It would've been my failing, not yours."

He said, "You made me want to come out of the black box. I didn't know if I could, I'd gotten so comfortable in there. I have very kind friends, and they put up with a lot from me and didn't challenge it, they just took me for what I was. Rose is one of them."

"Whereas I..." Maybe she didn't like where this was going after all.

"You didn't know. What you were dealing with. I didn't have a history with you. I wanted one."

They had something in common. She was realizing it for the first time, and that was pretty amazing. Also pretty blind, pretty stupid. He called the thing they had in common—which, when you cleared everything away and got down to it, was fear—a form of psychopathology, whereas she'd always called it Anna. Just her way.

"I have to feed the bird," he said. "Every two or three hours—"

"I know, but first—"

"Right, you want to know *why*. And I can't say. It's a mystery. Maybe I thought you could use someone like me. The first day we met, you were so..."

"Bitchy?"

"Prickly. Covering up a hurt. Maybe I recognized you. Or maybe it was just time for me to come around," he theorized, "maybe—"

"Maybe I had nothing at all to do with it. Right place, right time. I could've been anybody. I could've been Cathy Doran." But she had to laugh: it was so obvious that she was saying these things so he would disagree with her.

He cleared his throat. "Things I love about Anna." He held up one finger. "Hair."

She swatted him.

"These aren't in order. Really nice hair."

"I hate my hair. It's like a bird's nest—that's probably why you like it, you see it as habitat."

He put his hands in her hair, and of course then she didn't hate it so much, and he never got around to finishing his list. Or feeding his

Forster's tern, not for quite a while. For a recent victim of smoke inhalation, she had a lot of stamina.

Much later, they went outside with Cork for a walk, and wound up sitting at the end of the dock in the crisp moonshine, listening to the sounds of water and cicadas and rustling leaves. The *Wind Rose* bobbed in the gentle river current, silver light from the moon gleaming on its white-painted spars. In its metaphorical shadow, it was impossible, at last, for Mason not to talk about Theo. Anna had been wanting that intimacy with him for a long time, even when they were barely speaking and she had the smallest right to it. What an openhearted gesture, to share your unglamorous grief with another person, to let someone see all your pain and anguish because of a grievous loss. She didn't take the honor lightly. And not that she was any kind of a substitute, no human quid pro quo, but at least she had something besides sympathy to give him back now, something more substantial than words. Mason, ever generous, seemed grateful for the gift.

22

Warm chocolate and hazelnut, oh, what a luscious smell. Rose stuck a toothpick in the center of the first of her four soufflés. Perfect, still a little runny in the center, and shallow fissures were snaking across the top as the rich cake began its classic fall. Sometimes everything went right. People would marvel over these, and she would smile with modest pride. To those who didn't already know—not too many in this crowd—she wouldn't confide that one of the easiest things in the world to make was a soufflé.

These had cooled enough to refrigerate. "Billy, I'm leaving the whipped cream garnish to you. Use a hot knife when you cut them, and don't forget, more chopped hazelnuts on top of each serving. Ten servings to a soufflé, I'm thinking."

"Okay, Chef." Billy Sanchez stopped slicing blanched asparagus spears long enough to grin at her. "Feels good to be back at work, doesn't it?"

"It feels wonderful." Automatically she checked his neat piles of shaved Parmesan and chopped mint, his bowl of beaten eggs. Billy was making asparagus frittatas for an appetizer. "Easy on the pepper," she cautioned. A joke—Billy had once served pureed jalapeños to Dwayne at family meal and told him it was olive paste.

Billy's station was near the new half-door to the dining room. Beside it, Rose saw that Anna had tacked on the wall a new list of rules for servers, the last thing they'd see before going out on the floor.

1. Never leave the dining room empty-handed.
2. Never say no to a customer. Say, "If we've got the ingredients, you can have anything you want."
3. Compliments to the chef should be delivered immediately. Complaints—handle on your own.
4. Don't run, people think there's a fire.
5. Don't laugh, people think you're laughing at them.
6. Whoever asks for the check first gets it.
7. If business is slow and you want it to pick up,
   a. Sit down to eat.
   b. Light up a cigarette.
8. Smile! Smile! Smile!

Somebody had added a ninth rule in ballpoint pen at the bottom. It couldn't be anyone but Vonnie.

9. Don't bother counting your tips. It all evens out in the end.

The argument at the big stove was rising in volume and getting harder to ignore. Rose wanted to stay far, far away, but she also wanted to check on the polenta she was serving with braised pork and olive sauce in approximately—she checked the brand-new clock on the wall—ten minutes. The last thing she had to do was stir in the cheese and herbs, and timing was critical.

"Rose, come here and taste this," Carmen called over.

Trapped.

Billy kept his head down but he made a low, snorting sound, *skkkk*, in the back of his throat. Rose pretended stepping on his foot was an accident.

Hard to believe, but Carmen and Frankie were still fighting over minestrone. Cannellini or kidney beans, macaroni or ditalini, cabbage versus string beans versus peas. Passionate bickering over stock only or stock with water had gone on for days, *weeks*. What could they still have to disagree about?

"Taste," Carmen commanded, thrusting out a steaming spoon. Close beside her, Frankie stood with her fists on her hips, tense as a spring trap. They'd look wonderful together in a photograph, Rose thought, a splashy profile in a food magazine—big, round, and florid next to milk-pale and minute. *The Chefs of the Bella Sorella*.

Well, this was a no-win. She took a careful slurp of the thick soup and hummed, "Mmm," simultaneously equivocal and appreciative—years, it had taken her to perfect that tone. The soup was really delicious. But whose side would it behoove her to be on this time? She was getting too old for this.

"It's good, right?"

She regarded Carmen's stuck-out chin with caution and said yes.

"Doesn't need anything, right?"

"Need," she echoed thoughtfully. "Well, *need*, you know, that's so..."

"It doesn't need any basil pesto to finish it off," Carmen declared, laying her cards down all at once.

"Ah. What do you think?" Rose asked Frankie straight out—which she was allowed to do; Carmen was the chef and Frankie was the sous-chef, although Rose, who had conferred these titles herself, took every opportunity to avoid them.

"The pancetta wasn't my idea," Carmen got in before Frankie could answer. That was true; Carmen had been violently against the addition of Italian bacon on the grounds that real minestrone was meatless. Nonsense, Frankie argued, Lombardy minestrones always had pancetta, and besides, the whole point of minestrone was to put in whatever you liked, whatever was fresh and on hand, including meat. "Now she wants to add *pesto*," Carmen said, rolling her lips back in revulsion—as if to say, "Now she wants to add *maggots*." "But then it'll be too salty. *Troppo salato!*"

"No, it won't."

"Yes, it will."

"No, it won't. I don't *make* salty pesto."

"You can't *help* making salty pesto."

"Did you taste it?"

"Did you put parmigiana in it?"

"Yes."

"Well, then." Carmen folded her beefy arms. Case closed.

Frankie glared. She'd been moving a little closer with each heated exchange; if they were the same height, they'd be nose to nose now. As it was, they were nose to enormous bosom. Abruptly, she stepped back. "Okay."

Carmen blinked, then stalled out in confusion. "Okay?"

"You're right, it would be a little salty. I think it would give it some depth, some heft, but for some people's tastes it would be too salty."

Carmen set the spoon down distractedly. She looked at Rose. So did Frankie. She was as surprised as they were; she was used to refereeing disagreements, not blessing unions. "How about some lemon juice?" she tried. "At the very end."

"Lemon juice," they repeated. They looked at each other with suspicion.

"Okay with me," Carmen conceded.

"Freshness," Frankie said. "A little acidic goose."

"Finish it off."

"Kick it up a note."

"Give it some bite."

The rehab of the burned-out kitchen included bright white walls and more intense lighting, a handsome wood slat floor, gleaming new stainless steel appliances and equipment. In addition, a lot of things weren't where they used to be. Changes to floor patterns and the placement of work stations made moving around easier, faster, and more logical. For example, the reach-in refrigerator wasn't below the chef's station anymore, it was *beside* it. Result: Carmen and Frankie didn't have to bend their knees and lean over three or four hundred times a day to prepare or finish off plates of food. Rose liked to think their new spirit of cooperation and compromise sprang from the fundamental nobility of their natures, but if it came from aesthetics or ergonomics, that was fine, too, or feng shui for all she cared. Dwayne had a new three-tub pot sink, and it had turned him into a new man.

"Time to start plating," she decided after another glance at the clock. The menu was simple—luckily, because there weren't many of them to serve it. Vince was working drinks and Anna was passing hors d'oeuvres; everybody else was having a good time, and that was as it should be. They were on schedule, though. Billy's frittatas were done, the polenta was perfect. Grilled fennel gratin would be an experiment; same with Carmen's rosemary grissini. Rose was spooning olive sauce over plates of pork and polenta as fast as Frankie could pass them to her when Anna slammed in through the door, carrying a couple of empty trays. She looked harassed but beautiful, Rose thought—not that she was prejudiced. She thought of Anna's phone call last night, to ask what she was wearing. Her dark red dress, Rose had answered; "I don't know if you've seen it or not, it's got—" "Hah," Anna interrupted, "I knew it! I wanted to wear *my* dark red dress." Rose had laughed and told her to go ahead and wear it—but no, she'd chosen a long, heather-gray skirt and a low-cut red sweater, and high-heeled boots she planned to take off later for dancing. *I must have looked like that in my thirties*, Rose thought, with a mellow rue. *I wish I'd known it. I'd have had a better time.*

"The crostini and mussels went like hotcakes," Anna announced to the kitchen at large. "They will absolutely work great for tapas."

"What about the eggplant fritters?" Frankie asked, slicing pork into serving pieces at the speed of light.

"Good, but not as good. But they know we've got a feast coming, so they're saving themselves. How are we doing here?"

"We're good," Rose said, drying her hands at the sink. "Unless you think we should put everything on the bar..."

A chorus of *No*'s—they'd been through this, and she always lost. Majority had ruled that the guests should come into the kitchen to pick up their own plates.

"Okay, then," Anna said, "are we ready?"

"No!" Carmen, Frankie, and Billy finished what they were doing and began to strip out of aprons and tunics and shuck off their clogs, out of their work clothes and into their finery. Frankie finished last. She blushed when Anna and Billy whistled. "Oh, Jeez, cut it out, it's just a skirt. Would you get lives?"

"*Now* are we ready?"

"Ready!"

Anna held the door for Rose and clapped her hands to quiet the revelers in the dining room so Rose could announce, "Dinner is served."

They'd made a big U of the dining room, the long banquette on one side, connecting tables on the other two. The space in the middle would be for dancing, later. This dinner was special, like a formal family meal, except mixed in with the kitchen and waitstaff were some of the Bella Sorella's oldest and best customers, favored guests invited to celebrate the imminent reopening. "Good PR," Anna called it, a clever way to grab the loyalty and goodwill of the old-timers, get them invested in the new place early on. Maybe so, but Rose thought of it more as a gathering of old friends. After the meal and before dessert, she stood up to say so.

"I'll keep this short," she began after the tinkling of silverware on glasses stopped and the room quieted. "Thank you—thank you all for coming—it's wonderful to look out and see the faces of so many of my friends, those of you it's been my pleasure to employ, and those it's been my pleasure to serve for—well, too many years to say, and if I did it would make us all feel ancient. Thank you for coming, thank you for helping us celebrate the fact that we survived. It could never have happened without you, and I have to say thanks in particular to those of you who put in so many long hours, long, *unpaid* hours, helping with the hard, dirty work of cleanup, which we thought would never end. But it did, and now, thanks to you, we're not only going to make it, we're going to come back better than ever. Yes! Look around, just look at our beautiful new restaurant. And smell—did you ever think that smoke smell would go away? And if this fabulous dinner Carmen and Frankie and Billy made for us tonight as a run-through, a sort of dress rehearsal for Tuesday—to make sure everything in our brand new kitchen actually works—if this meal is any indication of things to come, doesn't it make you even *more* confident that we're going to be a fine success? Yes. So let's say thanks to our chefs by toasting them—and I drink to you, all my friends, my family. I love you all. *Salute*."

Other people got up to say grateful, flattering things—Anna, Vonnie, Roxanne, who owned the jewelry store across the street, old Mr. Kern, a retired florist who hadn't missed a Friday night at the Bella Sorella in twenty years. Rose was the recipient of so many toasts, she began to feel like the bride at a wedding reception. Her chocolate hazelnut soufflés were a gratifying triumph. Over coffee—from the brand-new cappuccino machine, a complicated miracle of gleaming copper and stainless steel, big as a pipe organ and almost as expensive—the old game of renaming the restaurant started up again. It didn't seem to faze anybody that the time for a new name had obviously passed—they were opening in four days as the Bella Sorella. But Rose listened to Bella Rosa, Casa Rosa, Mama Rosa, Zia Rosa—Il Giardiniere, Giardiniere di Fiori, Giardiniere di Rosas—and she gave them all her thoughtful, considering look even though nobody believed in it anymore. "She hates everything," Dwayne sulked. Frankie said, "Why don't you just call it

Rose and Anna's Restaurant?" Anna laughed, but Rose patted her chin with her fingers, thoughtful.

Vince and Frankie had argued for days over what kind of music to play after dinner. He'd wanted a classic oldies band, she'd wanted a hip-hop group. The Honey Lickers played rhythm and blues, and were supposed to be a compromise. If that was a compromise, Frankie said, she was Dr. Dre. Beyond the fact that Frankie didn't care for the band, Rose had no idea what that meant.

"Check that out," Carmen said, pointing with a glass of wine at Vince and Frankie on the dance floor. "Look how stiff she is. Like she's never slow-danced in her life."

Rose had to agree. It was easier to see Frankie jumping up and down in a mosh pit than plodding around in Vince's arms to a dreamy Anita Baker love song. "Doesn't she look pretty, though?" She had on a billowy white poet blouse tucked into a tiered skirt of bright, flouncy colors, feminine and bohemian, not Frankie's usual style at all. She wore hoop earrings, too, and a gay fuschia scarf tied around her bald head. She was barefooted. She looked like a gypsy.

But when the dance ended, she looked relieved. She dropped Vince's arms as if she couldn't get away fast enough and padded over to Rose's and Carmen's table for a drink. "Hey," she greeted them, pouring ice water into a glass and drinking it down without stopping. It was hot and she was sweating—before Vince, she'd danced with everybody else—but she kept her pretty scarf on. She had a *little* bit of vanity, Rose was glad to see. "Hey, Carmen," she said, "you wanna dance?"

"Yeah, right." Under the snort and the sarcasm, though, she looked tickled. "So what's the deal with you and Vince?"

"Me and who?" She fanned herself by pulling her blouse away from her chest and fluttering it.

"Come on. You guys an item or what?"

"Jeez, Carmen. No. Shit, no, we're not an *item*. For one thing, one of like a hundred things, he's too young for me. I like an older guy."

"How's that been working out for you?"

Frankie's hard eyes bored into Carmen, gauging if that was a shot. No, she decided, and shrugged. "Hey, Vince is okay. In fact, I just said I'd go out with him, you want the latest. One time, like an experiment, a one-time shot, very unlikely it'll work out."

"Oh, Frankie," Rose said, patting her heart. "You big romantic fool."

The party got louder, crazier. Vince opened another case of Rubesco di Torgiano. "Told you we should've had a cash bar," he whispered to Rose, half serious. It was a good thing they had no neighbors to complain about noise, good thing Carmen wasn't upstairs trying to sleep. In fact, she was out on the dance floor, two-stepping with Dwayne. Check *that* out, Rose thought, spellbound.

The band took a break, and during the interlude of relative quiet Luca approached the microphone on the makeshift stage and asked for silence. He looked small but handsome, Rose thought, more dressed up than anyone else tonight in a black suit, spit-shined black shoes, and matching matinee idol hair. "*Scusi, scusi. Prego*, my friends. *Scusi*. Attention, please. Hey! *Zitto!*"

Quiet.

"*Grazie*. I have announcement, very special to say. Tonight, is even more for celebration than our grand reopening—tonight is *miracolo*, miracle, because—guess what—Fontaine, who you love so much, is consent to be married to me! *Si*, a miracle—Fontaine, *cara*, come, be with me here—"

Oh no. Rose forced a smile and began to clap with the others, but Anna caught her eye and the message passed between them: *Oh no*.

Blonde and radiant, and tiny again in a sheer blue slip dress, Fontaine walked across the floor to the surprised applause, holding her new baby in her arms. Behind the shy smile, Rose thought she looked stunned, as if Luca's announcement still shocked her, too. Gracie, she'd named the baby; she had Fontaine's silky fair hair and delicate features, and nothing of Eddie, everyone had been glad to see, at least not at four weeks.

Luca put his arm around Fontaine's waist and drew her close, beaming down at the sleeping infant. "I am so lucky," he said into the microphone. "Now I have not only Bella Sorella, which I love so much, but also sweet new *bella famiglia*, my wife, my own little baby." He drew an enormous white handkerchief out of the pocket of his black coat and wiped his face. No one laughed or teased him, not even Jasper, not even Dwayne. "Today is best day of all days. Today I'm in love with my life again. Thank you, everybody, *grazie di tutta la sua gentilezza*. I am so happy. So happy."

Maybe it would work. *Un miracolo*. Only half of all marriages lasted anyway, under the best of circumstances—wasn't that the statistic? Oh, but poor Luca, Rose thought, watching him shake hands with his pals from the kitchen, suffer their pounding fists on his slight shoulders, blush under their coarse ribbing. By his lights he was saving Fontaine, and he got a beautiful *bambina* in the bargain. Ready-made family. Fontaine would feel lucky at first, as if she'd been rescued, but what then? She was a child herself—Luca was almost twice her age. Not to mention that she'd never shown any interest in a man like him before, a gentle, nurturing, sweet-tempered mensch of a man. How could this possibly work? And what damage would it do when it unraveled?

She ought to dance, wake herself up from the blue mood she'd fallen into. But Rose stayed where she was, feeling like a duenna, turning down partners with a laugh or a joke. Anna winked at her over Mason's shoulder, and she admired how neatly they danced together, how passionate and controlled, caught up tight in each other's arms. Theo had loved to dance. He'd loved to hold her close and twirl her around, pluck her off her feet like a girl. He was graceful, too, for such a bear of a man. She missed him beyond speaking.

Oh, she didn't want to sink into melancholy, she didn't want to think about Paul or Theo or the inevitability of loss while the band played "Let's Stay Together." But she thought, *Maybe this isn't my world any longer*. Maybe it was time to relinquish it to the young. She'd had her turn. Maybe the best she would ever have was memories. She felt brittle, as if her bones were drying out.

"Rose, could you hold her for a minute? Just for this one song? Luca says we have to dance." Very gently, Fontaine laid the baby on Rose's knees.

Gracie's steel-blue eyes were wide open. They locked on Rose's when she leaned over and murmured, "Hello, baby," stroking the thin, see-through pink of her delicate ear. "Hello, beautiful girl." Gracie blinked back an intent greeting. Who could be sad or distant or ironical with a month-old baby in her arms? Life was for being alive, being with people you loved already or might love someday. Eat, dance, laugh. Warm, squirmy life was right here, Gracie's little bow mouth still pursing on her mama's phantom breast. Rose put her lips on the baby's satiny temple and let herself be comforted.

The Honey Lickers played their last song, the guests began to trickle away. Rose quashed a halfhearted staff movement to clean up the mess in the kitchen tonight. "No, no, tomorrow's soon enough," she insisted, although it broke her cardinal rule against leaving cleanup for the morning. "But that's an open invitation to vermin," Vonnie reminded her—"that's what you always say, Rose, you know you do." Yes, but this was a special occasion, and besides, a hostess couldn't very well ask her honored, dressed-up guests to stay late, put on their aprons, and clean up after themselves.

She said good night to her friends, her employees, one by one. Carmen had gone up already, complaining her feet were killing her. Rose intended to be the last out and lock up after herself, so she was surprised, after a final trip back from the kitchen, to find Anna sitting by herself at the bar, waving good night to the last guests, a wobbly Tony and Suzanne.

"I called them a cab," she told Rose. She turned in her stool and patted the one next to it invitingly. "Sit for a minute?"

She sat, and couldn't help admiring the new floor in the soft light over the bar. It was faux tiles, bright squares of clay, yellow, and pale blue, painted over the old pine boards. Water damage from the fire had ruined the old carpet, to Anna's delight; she'd wanted to strip the floors bare throughout the restaurant, no rugs at all, and Rose had wanted pretty new carpet everywhere. This was their compromise: cheerful, painted floor around the bar and at the host's podium, beautiful new peach-colored carpet in the dining room. They both won.

"Where's Mason?" Rose asked.

"Oh, he went home, he has to get up early tomorrow. He's going to Canada."

"*Canada*."

"Yeah, didn't he tell you? Some place in Saskatchewan called Last Mountain Lake. He's taking pictures of cranes."

"Heavens."

"I know. It's like he's making up for lost time."

"All those hours he missed flying on airplanes," Rose joked, although it wasn't really a laughing matter. Mason had had a setback a couple of weeks ago—out of the blue, he couldn't walk into a lecture hall for a long-planned talk and slide show on marsh birds of the Chesapeake. It wasn't public speaking, it was *being inside* that had panicked him, simply being in a place he couldn't legitimately get out of for an indefinite length of time. Strangely enough, though, the next day he'd breezed through a scheduled appearance for the local Audubon chapter, and that had also involved being inside, being captured—the same circumstance as the night before, but this time without incident. It was the unpredictability of his attacks, he said, that gave them their power.

"Do you think he'll be all right?" Rose wasn't sure if she meant in Canada or in general.

"Yes," Anna said, "I do. Eventually. Because he's getting more and more philosophical about it, which means less and less ashamed. He says when the embarrassment dies, so does the fear. He wanted me to go with him," she added, smiling. "Not to save him or anything, just for fun."

"You *should* go. Why don't you?"

"Oh, too much to do, plus I'd miss the reopening—he's not coming back till Wednesday." That reminded her of something. She got up and went behind the bar, began poking around in the back-lit pyramid of liquors and liqueurs, searching for something.

"But you'd have gone with him if the timing had been better? To Last Mountain Lake? You wouldn't have been bored?"

"I know, it's pathetic. If I wanted to see him at all, I'd have to stand in a wet, cold blind all day, handing him telephoto lenses."

"But you'd've gone anyway?"

"What can I tell you." She made a face. "We're at that stage."

Rose felt a stab of pleasure for her; sympathetic excitement. She might be getting old, but thank God she could still enjoy her loved ones' romantic prosperity. "Do you think it will work?" And she could ask questions like that now, and Anna would answer, shyly—still getting used to telling secrets again—but without the slightest sign that she thought they were too personal or none of Rose's business. A sea change.

"Well, I guess that depends on what you mean by work."

"I guess I mean *last*."

"Oh, Rose. I don't know. I want it to—but I always want it to, and it never has before. I'm afraid to hope."

"But where does that get you? You should never be afraid to hope. I say that at the risk of sounding pompous."

"That's nice, but tell me, does that optimism spread as far as Fontaine and Luca?"

Rose groaned. "I don't know why I didn't see that coming." She put her elbow on the bar and her cheek on her hand.

"What, you don't think they'll live happily ever after?"

"Oh, dear lord. I hope they live happily through the honeymoon."

"Really. Now, see, I think they've got a shot. She's young, he's sensible. She's sweet, he's adorable. And the baby's an angel. What's not to work?"

Rose smiled. Anna was only disagreeing with her, she suspected, because she liked the novelty of reversing their optimist-pessimist roles. "I hope and pray," Rose said fervently, "that you're right and I'm wrong."

"Ah, here it is. Look what I got. I hid it so Vince couldn't find it."

"Why?" It was a bottle of Jacopo Poli, beautiful, the frosted miniature globe a work of art.

"Because it's just for us. To toast." She slipped two brandy snifters from the new overhead brass rack—the old wooden one was too smoke-blackened to save. "Want an ice cube? I'm having an ice cube, I don't care. How can you drink this stuff at room temperature?"

"I thought you hated grappa."

"I'm coming around. It's an acquired taste and I'm acquiring it." She filled two glasses and handed one to Rose. "Okay, well." She was self-conscious all of a sudden. "To the new Bella Sorella. Better than ever. To the grand reopening. And—to us."

"To us."

They sipped the crisp, intense brandy, hummed over it, held their glasses to the light, talked about wholesale prices, and what Vince had said about ice-cold grappas replacing neat vodkas as a new, fashionable drink with young people. Then Rose said, "Speaking of being afraid to hope. I used to be. For this."

"What?"

"You and me, sitting here together, toasting an enterprise. Not only without antagonism, but with . . ." She paused, searching for a word that wouldn't scare Anna to death.

"Yeah," she said, before she could find it. She came around to the front again, pushing her stool aside with her stockinged foot and leaning against the polished wood bar. Their forearms touched. "Me, too. I never pictured this, to tell you the truth. I might've wanted it, but I'd never have hoped for it. I'd've thought the odds were bad, and I hate losing." She leaned over to put her nose close to a bowl of scentless chrysanthemums, a leftover party decoration. "Rose?" She swirled the ice cube in her glass and took another small sip of grappa. "Thanks."

"For what?"

"For letting me come home."

She laughed. "*Letting* you."

"Thank you for not giving up a long time ago. Even though I gave you plenty of good reasons."

"Oh no."

"You could've written me off a hundred times. Nobody around here would've blamed you."

That was sweet, but Rose didn't want apologies. "Don't be so hard on yourself."

"Don't be so nice to me. I haven't forgotten anything you said. That night at my house. You said a lot of true things."

It seemed so long ago. "All I regret," Rose said, sighing, "is the time we wasted. I'm getting very miserly about time." She liked the look of their side-by-side images in the mirror. Without her glasses, she could only see two dark-haired, narrow-faced women with big black eyes. One young, one old. "I've thought of the new name for the restaurant," she said.

"You what?" Anna stopped staring back in the mirror and faced her. "No, you haven't. This close to the reopening? Rose, we don't have time! Oh, you're kidding. Aren't you?"

"I know, it's absurd, the timing couldn't possibly be worse. But I can't help it, it just came to me tonight. What it has to be, what it absolutely has to be."

"*What?*"

"But," she said hastily, "if you don't like it, that's fine—just because I thought of it doesn't mean we have to use it."

"Right, okay—*what*?"

Then she didn't want to say it out loud. Superstitious or something. She reached for a pencil on the bar and wrote it on a cocktail napkin. ROSEANNA.

What did Anna do? She laughed. With surprise at first, surprise and delight, but then her laughter went low and knowing, as if at an old joke she knew well but still loved. A laugh of recognition.

Funny, Rose thought, that's just how she'd felt when the name came to her—as though it wasn't new at all. As though it had been there all the time.

"Well?" she said when Anna's laughter finally sighed to a stop. The suspense was gone, but she still wanted to hear the verdict.

Anna used the napkin to blot her eyes. "It's perfect. And it's so obvious."

"It's so obvious. But I couldn't have thought of it any sooner."

"It wouldn't have been perfect any sooner."

It had to grow into itself. *They'd* had to grow into it. Germinate, ripen, and flower, Rose thought. She was feeling a little drunk.

"Roseanna. Roseanna," Anna said, experimenting. "Wow, it's sexy. It's Italian, it's very womanly. It's sophisticated, but it's also sort of...homey. Isn't it? Warm. Roseanna will take care of you."

"It doesn't leave anything out." That was the thing.

"And just think, Rose, you'll get free drinks for life. Is it the Roseanna Restaurant? Café?"

"It's just Roseanna."

"Yes. It's just Roseanna. Let's toast."

They touched glasses again. "Roseanna," they said, and drank to themselves.